THE WORKS OF
MR. FRANCIS RABELAIS

MANY ARE AT THIS DAY DUKES ON THE EARTH WHOSE EXTRACTION IS
FROM SOME PORTERS AND PARDON-PEDLARS

THE WORKS OF MR. FRANCIS
RABELAIS

DOCTOR IN PHYSICK. CONTAINING FIVE BOOKS
OF THE LIVES, HEROICK DEEDS AND SAYINGS
OF GARGANTUA AND HIS SONNE PANTAGRUEI

*Together with the Pantagrueline Prognostication, the Oracle of
the Divine Bachuc, and response of the bottle*

*Hereunto are annexed the Navigations unto the Sounding Isle and the
Isle of the Apedefts: as likewise the Philosophical cream
with a Limosin Epistle all done by*

MR. FRANCIS RABELAIS

*In the French tongue and now faithfully translated into **English***

Εὐνοεί, εὔλογε καὶ εὖ πράττε.

1653

Illustrated by W. HEATH ROBINSON

Complete in One Volume

MCMXXXI
THE NAVARRE SOCIETY LONDON

Reprinted 1948

PRINTED IN GREAT BRITAIN

VOLUME I:—THE TABLE

THE FIRST BOOK

THE SECOND BOOK

THE THIRD BOOK

LIST OF ILLUSTRATIONS

xvii

TO THE HONOURED, NOBLE
TRANSLATOUR OF RABELAIS

RABELAIS whose wit prodigiously was made
All men, professions, actions to invade,
With so much furious vigour, as if it
Had liv'd ore each of them and each had quit:
Yet with such happy slight and carelesse skill
As, like the serpent, doth with laughter kill;
So that although his noble leaves appear
Antick and Gottish, and dull souls forbear
To turn them o're, lest they should only finde
Nothing but savage Monsters of a minde;
No shapen beauteous thoughts; yet when the wise
Seriously strip him of his wilde disguise,
Melt down his drosse, refine his massie ore,
And polish that which seem'd rough-cast before,
Search his deep sense, unveil his hidden mirth,
And make that fiery which before seem'd earth;
(Conquering those things of highest consequence,
What's difficult of language or of sense)
He will appear some noble table writ,
In th' old Egyptian Hieroglyphick wit;
Where though you Monsters and Grotescoes see,
You meet all mysteries of Philosophie.
For he was wise and Sovereignly bred
To know what mankinde is, how't may be led:
He stoop'd unto them, like that wise man, who
Rid on a stick when's children would do so.
For we are easie sullen things, and must
Be laught aright, and cheated into trust,

3

Whil'st a black piece of Flegme, that laies about
Dull menaces, and terrifies the rout.
And Cajoles it, with all its peevish strength
Pitiously stretch'd and botch'd up into length,
Whil'st the tir'd rabble sleepily obey
Such opiate talk, and snore away the day.
By all his noise as much their mindes releeves,
As catterwalling of wilde cats frights theeves.
    But Rabelais was another thing, a man
Made up of all that Art and Nature can
Forme from a fiery Genius, he was one
Whose soul so universally was throwne
Through all the Arts of life, who understood
Each stratagem by which we stray from good
So that he best might solid vertue teach,
As some 'gainst sinnes of their own bosomes preach :
He from wise choice did the true meanes preferre,
In the fooles coat acting th' Philosopher.
    Thus hoary Esop's beasts did mildly tame
Fierce man, and moralize him into shame ;
Thus brave Romances, while they seeme to lay
Great traines of lust, Platonick love display ;
Thus would old Sparta, if a seldome chance
Shew'd a drunk slave, teach children temperance ;
Thus did the later Poets nobly bring
The scene to height, making the foole the King.
    And, noble Sir, you vigorously have trod
In this hard path, unknown, un-understood
By its own countreymen, 'tis you appeare
Our full enjoyment which was our despaire,
Scattering his mists, cheering his Cynick frowns,
(For radiant brightnesse now dark Rabelais crownes,)
Leaving your brave Heroick cares, which must
Make better mankinde and embalme your dust,
So undeceiving us that now we see
All wit in Gascone and in Cromartie,
Besides that *Rabelais* is conveigh'd to us,
And that our Scotland is not barbarous.

J. DE LA SALLE.

RABLOPHILA

THE FIRST DECADE

The Commendation

Musa ! canas *nostrorum* in testimonium *Amorum,*
  Et GARGANTUEAS perpetuato *faces.*
Utque homini *tali* resultet nobilis ECCHO :
  Quicquid *Fama* canit, PANTAGRUELIS erit.

THE ARGUMENT

Here I intend *mysteriously* to sing
  With a pen pluck'd from *Fame's* own wing.
Of *Gargantua* that learn'd Breech-wiping King.

DECADE THE FIRST

I

Help me, propitious STARRES ; a mighty *blaze*
  Benumm's me ! I must sound the *praise*
Of him hath turn'd this *crabbed* work in such heroick *pnrase.*

II

What *wit* would not court *martyrdom* to hold
  Upon his head a *Laurel* of *gold,*
Where for each rich *conceit* a *Pumpion-pearle* is told :

III

And such a one is this, Art's *Master-piece,*
  A thing ne're equal'd by old *Greece :*
A thing ne're match'd as yet, a real *Golden-fleece.*

IV

Vice is a *souldier* fights against *mankinde ;*
  Which you may *look* but never *finde :*
For 'tis an *envious* thing, with *cunning interlin'a.*

5

V

And thus he rails at *drinking* all before 'um,
　　And for lewd women does *be-whore* 'um,
And brings their *painted-faces* and *black patches* to th' *Quorum*.

VI

To drink he was a furious *enemy*
　　Contented with a SIX PENY—
(With *Diamond-hatband, silver spurs, six horses*.) PYE—

VII

And for Tobacco's *pate-rotunding* smoke,
　　Much had he said and much more spoke,
But 'twas not *then* found out, so the *designe* was *broke*.

VIII

Muse! Fancy! Faith! come now arise *aloud*,
　　Assembled in a *blew-veyn'd* cloud,
And this tall infant in *Angelick* armes now *shroud*.

IX

To praise it further I would now begin
　　Were 't now a *thorough-faire* and *Inne*,
It *harbours* vice, though 't be to catch it in a *ginne*.

X

Therefore, my *Muse*, draw up thy flowing *saile*,
　　And *acclamate* a gentle HAILE
With all thy *Art* and *Metaphors*, which must *prevail*.

Jam prima Oceani pars est *prœterita nostri.*
　Imparibus restat danda secunda modis.
Quam si prœstiterit mentem Dæmon malus *addam,*
　Cum sapiens totus prodierit RABELAIS.
　　　　　　　　　　　　　　　　MALEVOLUS.

RABELAIS TO THE READER

Good friends, my Readers, who peruse this Book,
Be not offended, whil'st on it you look :
Denude your selves of all deprav'd affection,
For it containes no badnesse, nor infection :
'Tis true that it brings forth to you no birth
Of any value, but in point of mirth ;
Thinking therefore how sorrow might your minde
Consume, I could no apter subject finde ;
    One inch of joy surmounts of grief a span ;
    Because to laugh is proper to the man.

THE AUTHORS PROLOGUE TO THE FIRST BOOK .

Most Noble and Illustrious Drinkers, and you thrice precious Pockified blades, (for to you, and none else do I dedicate my writings) Alcibiades, in that Dialogue of Plato's, which is entituled *The Banquet*, whil'st he was setting forth the praises of his Schoolmaster Socrates (without all question the Prince of Philosophers) amongst other discourses to that purpose said, that he resembled the Silenes. Silenes of old were little boxes, like those we now may see in the shops of Apothecaries, painted on the outside with wanton toyish figures, as Harpyes, Satyrs, bridled Geese, horned Hares, saddled Ducks, flying Goats, Thiller Harts, and other suchlike counterfeted pictures at discretion, to excite people unto laughter, as Silenus himself, who was the foster-father of good Bacchus, was wont to do ; but within those capricious caskets were carefully preserved and kept many rich jewels, and fine drugs, such as Balme, Ambergreece, Amamon, Musk, Civet, with several kindes of precious stones, and other things of great price. Just such another thing was Socrates for to have eyed his outside, and esteemed of him by his exterior appearance, you would not have given the peel of an Oinion for him, so deformed he was in body, and ridiculous in his gesture : he had a sharp pointed nose, with the look of a Bull, and countenance of a foole : he was in his carriage simple, boorish in his apparel, in fortune poore, unhappy in his wives, unfit for all offices in the Common-wealth, always laughing, tipling, and merrily carousing to every one, with continual gybes and jeeres, the better by those meanes to conceale his divine knowledge : now opening this boxe you would have found within it a heavenly and inestimable drug, a more than humane understanding, an admirable vertue, matchlesse learning, invincible

8

courage, unimitable sobriety, certaine contentment of minde, perfect assurance, and an incredible misregard of all that, for which men commonly do so much watch, run, saile, fight, travel, toyle and turmoile themselves.

Whereunto (in your opinion) doth this little flourish of a preamble tend ? For so much as you, my good disciples, and some other jolly fooles of ease and leasure, reading the pleasant titles of some books of our invention, as Gargantua, Pantagruel, Whippot, the dignity of Codpeeces, of Pease and Bacon with a Commentary, etc., are too ready to judge, that there is nothing in them but jests, mockeries, lascivious discourse, and recreative lies ; because the outside (which is the title) is usually (without any farther enquiry) entertained with scoffing and derision : but truly it is very unbeseeming to make so slight account of the works of men, seeing your selves avouch that it is not the habit makes the Monk, many being Monasterially accoutred, who inwardly are nothing lesse then monachal, and that there are of those that weare Spanish caps, who have but little of the valour of Spaniards in them. Therefore is it, that you must open the book, and seriously consider of the matter treated in it, then shall you finde that it containeth things of farre higher value than the boxe did promise ; that is to say, that the subject thereof is not so foolish, as by the Title at the first sight it would appeare to be.

And put the case that in the literal sense, you meet with purposes merry and solacious enough, and consequently very correspondent to their inscriptions, yet must not you stop there as at the melody of the charming Syrens, but endeavour to interpret that in a sublimer sense, which possibly you intended to have spoken in the jollitie of your heart ; did you ever pick the lock of a cupboard to steal a bottle of wine out of it ? Tell me truly, and if you did call to minde the countenance which then you had ? or, did you ever see a Dog with a marrow-bone in his mouth, (the beast of all other, saies Plato, lib. 2, *de Republica*, the most Philosophical) if you have seene him, you might have remarked with what devotion and circumspectnesse he wards and watcheth it ; with what care he keeps it : how fervently he holds it : how prudently he gobbets it : with what affection he breaks it : and with what diligence he sucks it : to what end all this ? what moveth him to take all these paines ? what are the hopes of his labour ? what doth he expect to reap thereby ? nothing but a little marrow : True it is, that this little is more ravoury and delicious than the great quantities of other sorts of meat, because the marrow (as Galen testifieth, 3. *facult. nat.* and 11, *de usu partium*) is a nourishment most perfectly elaboured by nature.

In imitation of this Dog, it becomes you so be wise, to smell, feele and have in estimation these faire goodly books, stuffed with high conceptions, which though seemingly easie in the pursuit, are in the cope and encounter somewhat difficult ; and then like him you must, by a sedulous Lecture, and frequent meditation, break the bone, and suck out the marrow ; that is, my allegorical sense, or the things I to my self propose to be signified by these Pythagorical Symbols, with assured hope, that in so doing, you will at last attaine to be both well-advised and valiant by the reading of them : for in the perusal of this Treatise, you shall finde another kinde of taste, and a doctrine of a more profound and abstruse consideration, which will disclose unto you the most glorious Sacraments, and dreadful mysteries, as well in what concerneth your Religion, as matters of the publike State, and Life œconomical.

Do you beleeve upon your conscience, that Homer whil'st he was a couching his *Iliads* and *Odysses*, had any thought upon those Allegories, which Plutarch, Heraclides Ponticus, Fristatius, Cornutus squeesed out of him, and which Politian filched againe from them : if you trust it, with neither hand nor foot do you come neare to my opinion, which judgeth them to have beene as little dreamed of by Homer, as the Gospel-sacraments were by Ovid in is *Metamorphosis*, though a certaine gulligut Fryer and true bacon-picker would have undertaken to prove it, if perhaps he had met with as very fools as himself, (and as the Proverb saies) a lid worthy of such a kettle : if you give no credit thereto, why do not you the same in these jovial new chronicles of mine ; albeit when I did dictate them, I thought upon no more then you, who possibly were drinking (the whil'st) as I was ; for in the composing of this lordly book, I never lost nor bestowed any more, nor any other time then what was appointed to serve me for taking of my bodily refection, that is, whil'st I was eating and drinking. And indeed that is the fittest, and most proper hour, wherein to write these high matters and deep Sciences : as Homer knew very well, the Paragon of all Philologues, and Ennius, the Father of the Latine Poets (as Horace calls him) although a certain sneaking jobernol alledged that his Verses smelled more of the wine than oile.

So saith a Turlupin or a new start-up grub of my books, but a turd for him. The fragrant odour of the wine ; O how much more dainty, pleasant, laughing, celestial and delicious it is, then that smell of oile ! And I will glory as much when it is said of me, that I have spent more on wine then oile, as did Demosthenes, when it was told him, that his expense on oile was greater than on wine ; I truly hold it for an honour and praise to be called and reputed a Frolick Gualter, and a Robin goodfellow ; for under this name am I welcome in all choise companies of Pantagruelists : it was upbraided to Demosthenes by an envious surly knave, that his Orations did smell like the sarpler or wrapper of a foul and filthy oile-vessel ; for this cause interpret you all my deeds and sayings in the perfectest sense ; reverence the cheese-like brain that feeds you with these faire billevezees, and trifling jollities, and do what lies in you to keep me alwayes merry. Be frolic now my lads, cheer up your hearts, and joyfully read the rest, with all the ease of your body and profit of your reines ; but hearken joltheads, you viedazes, or dickens take ye, remember to drink a health to me for the like favour again, and I will pledge you instantly, *Tout aresmetys.*

THE FIRST BOOK

CHAPTER I

Of the Genealogy and Antiquity of Gargantua

I MUST referre you to the great Chronicle of Pantagruel for the
knowledge of that Genealogy, and Antiquity of race by which
Gargantua is come unto us ; in it you may understand more at
large how the Giants were born in this world, and how from
them by a direct line issued Gargantua the father of Pantagruel :
and do not take it ill, if for this time I passe by it, although the
subject be such, that the oftener it were remembered, the more
it would please your worshipfull Seniorias ; according to which
you have the authority of Plato in Philebo and Gorgias ; and of
Flaccus, who saies that there are some kindes of purposes (such
as these are without doubt) which the frequentlier they be
repeated, still prove the more delectable.

Would to God every one had as certaine knowledge of his
Genealogy since the time of the Arke of Noah until this age.   I
think many are at this day Emperours, Kings, Dukes, Princes,
and Popes on the earth, whose extraction is from some porters,
and pardon-pedlars as on the contrary, many are now poor
wandring beggars, wretched and miserable, who are descended
of the blood and lineage of great Kings and Emperours,
occasioned (as I conceive it) by the transport and revolution of
Kingdomes and Empires, from the Assyrians to the Medes,

from the Medes to the Persians, from the Persians to the Macedonians, from the Macedonians to the Romans, from the
Romans to the Greeks, from the Greeks to the French, etc.

And to give you some hint concerning my self, who speaks
unto you, I cannot think but I am come of the race of some rich
King or Prince in former times, for never yet saw you any man
that had a greater desire to be a King, and to be rich, then I
have, and that onely that I may make good chear, do nothing,
nor care for any thing, and plentifully enrich my friends, and all
honest and learned men : but herein do I comfort myself, that
in the other world I shall be so, yea and greater too then at this
present I dare wish : as for you, with the same or a better conceit consolate your selves in your distresses, and drink fresh
if you can come by it.

To returne to our weathers, I say, that by the sovereign gift
of heaven, the Antiquity and Genealogy of Gargantua hath been
reserved for our use more full and perfect then any other except
that of the Messias, whereof I mean not to speak ; for it belongs
not unto my purpose, and the Devils (that is to say) the false
accusers, and dissembled gospellers will therein oppose me.
This Genealogy was found by John Andrew in a meadow,
which he had near the Pole-arch, under the Olive-tree, as you
go to Marsay : where, as he was making cast up some ditches,
the diggers with their mattocks struck against a great brazen
tomb, and unmeasurably long, for they could never finde the
end thereof, by reason that it entered too farre within the
Sluces of Vienne ; opening this Tomb in a certain place thereof,
sealed on the top with the mark of a goblet, about which was
written in Hetrurian letters H I C B I B I T U R ; they found
nine Flaggons set in such order as they use to ranke their
kyles in Gasconie, of which that which was placed in the middle,
had under it a big, fat, great, gray, pretty, smoll, mouldy, little
pamphlet, smelling stronger, but no better than roses. In that
book the said Genealogy was found written all at length, in a
Chancery hand, not in paper, not in parchment, nor in wax, but
in the bark of an elme-tree, yet so worne with the long tract of
time, that hardly could tree letters together be there perfectly
discerned.

I (though unworthy) was sent for thither, and with much
help of those Spectacles, whereby the art of reading dim writings, and letters that do not clearly appear to the sight, is
practised, as Aristotle teacheth it, did translate the book as you
may see in your pantagruelising, that is to say, in drinking

stiffly to your own hearts desire ; and reading the dreadful and horrifick acts of Pantagruel : at the end of the book there was a little Treatise entituled the Antidoted Fanfreluches, or a Galimatia of extravagant conceits. The rats and mothes or (that I may not lie) other wicked beasts, had nibled off the beginning, the rest I have hereto subjoyned, for the reverence I beare to antiquity.

CHAPTER II

The Antidoted Fanfreluches: or, a Galimatia of extravagant Conceits found in an ancient Monument

No sooner did the Cymbrians overcommer
Pass through the air to shun the dew of summer
But at his coming streight great tubs were fill'd ;
With pure fresh Butter down in showers distill'd
Wherewith when water'd was his Grandam heigh
Aloud he cryed, Fish it, Sir, I pray ye ;
Because his beard is almost all beray'd,
Or that he would hold to 'm a scale he pray'd.

To lick his slipper, some told was much better,
Then to gaine pardons and the merit greater,
In th' interim a crafty chuff approaches,
From the depth issued, where they fish for Roches ;
Who said, Good sirs, some of them let us save,
The Eele is here, and in this hollow cave
You'll finde, if that our looks on it demurre,
A great wast in the bottome of his furre.

13

To read this chapter when he did begin,
Nothing but a calves hornes were found therein ;
I feel (quoth he) the Miter which doth hold
My head so chill, it makes my braines take cold.
Being with the perfume of a turnup warm'd,
To stay by chimney hearths himself he arm'd,
Provided that a new thill horse they made
Of every person of a hair-braind head.
They talked of the bunghole of Saint Knowles,
Of Gilbathar and thousand other holes ;
If they might be reduc'd t' a scarry stuffe,
Such as might not be subject to the cough :
Since ev'ry man unseemly did it finde,
To see them gaping thus at ev'ry winde :
For, if perhaps they handsomely were clos'd,
For pledges they to men might be expos'd.

In this arrest by Hercules the raven
Was flayed at her returne from Lybia haven,
Why am not I said Minos there invited,
Unlesse it be my self, not one's omitted :
And then it is their minde, I do no more
Of Frogs and Oysters send them any store ;
In case they spare my life and prove but civil,
I give their sale of distaffs to the Devil.

To quell him comes Q. R. who limping frets
At the safe passe of trixie crackarets,
The boulter, the grand Cyclops cousin, those
Did massacre whil'st each one wip'd his nose :
Few ingles in this fallow ground are bred,
But on a tanners mill are winnowed :
Run thither all of you th' alarmes sound clear,
You shall have more then you had the last year.

Short while thereafter was the bird of Jove
Resolv'd to speak, though dismal it should prove ;
Yet was afraid, when he saw them in ire,
They should or'throw quite flat down dead th' empire
He rather chus'd the fire from heaven to steale,
To boats where were red Herrings put to sale ;
Then to be calm 'gainst those who strive to brave us,
And to the Massorets fond words enslave us.

14

THE FIRST BOOK OF DR. FRANCIS RABELAIS

All this at last concluded galantly,
In spite of Ate and her hern-like thigh,
Who, sitting saw Penthesilea tane,
In her old age, for a cresse-selling quean ;
Each one cry'd out, Thou filthy Collier toad,
Doth it become thee to be found abroad ?
Thou hast the Roman Standard filtch'd away,
Which they in rags of parchment did display.

Juno was borne who under the Rainbow,
Was a bird-catching with her Duck below :
When her with such a grievous trick they plyed,
That she had almost been bethwacked by it :
The bargain was that of that throatfull she
Should of Prosperina have two egges free ;
And if that she thereafter should be found,
She to a Haw-thorn hill should be fast bound

Seven moneths thereafter, lacking twenty two,
He, that of old did Carthage town undo :
Did bravely midd'st them all himself advance,
Requiring of them his inheritance ;
Although they justly made up the division,
According to the shoe-welt-lawes decision ;
By distributing store of brews and beef
To those poor fellows, that did pen the Brief.

But th' year will come signe of a Turkish Bowe,
Five spindles yarnd, and three pot-bottomes too,
Wherein of a discourteous King the dock
Shall pepper'd be under an Hermits frock,
Ah that for one she hypocrite you must
Permit so many acres to be lost :
Cease, cease, this visard may become another,
Withdraw your selves unto the Serpents brother.

'Tis in times past, that he who is shall reigne
With his good friends in peace now and againe ;
No rash nor heady Prince shall then rule crave,
Each good will its arbitrement shall have :
And the joy promised of old as doome
To the heavens guests, shall in its beacon come :

Then shall the breeding mares, that benumm'd were,
Like royall palfreys ride triumphant there.

And this continue shall from time to time,
Till Mars be fettred for an unknown crime,
Then shall one come who others will surpasse,
Delightful, pleasing, matchlesse, full of grace ;
Chear up your hearts, approach to this repast,
All trusty friends of mine for hee's deceast,
Who would not for a world return againe,
So highly shall time past be cri'd up then.

He who was made of waxe shall lodge each member
Close by the hinges of a block of timber :
We then no more shall Master, master, whoot
The swagger, who th' alarum bell holds out ;
Could one seaze on the dagger which he bears,
Heads would be free from tingling in the eares,
To baffle the whole storehouse of abuses,
And thus farewell Apollo and the Muses.

CHAPTER III

How Gargantua was carried Eleven Moneths in his Mothers Belly

GRANGOUSIER was a good fellow in his time, and notable jester ;
he loved to drink neat, as much as any man that then was in the
world, and would willingly eate salt meal : to this intent he
was ordinarily well furnished with gammons of Bacon, both of

Westphalia, Mayence and Bayone ; with store of dried Neats tongues, plenty of Links, Chitterlings and Puddings in their season ; together with salt Beef and mustard, a good deale of hard rows of powdered mullet called Botargos, great provision of Sauciges, not of Bolonia (for he feared the Lombard boccone) but of Bigorre, Longaulnay, Brene, and Rouargue. In the vigor of his age he married Gargamelle, daughter to the King of the Parpaillons, a jolly pug, and well mouthed wench. These two did often times do the two backed beast together, joyfully rubbing and frolling their Bacon 'gainst one another, insofarre, that at last she became great with childe of a faire sonne, and went with him unto the eleventh moneth, for so long, yea longer, may a woman carry her great belly, especially when it is some master-piece of nature, and a person predestinated to the performance, in his due time, of great exploits ; as Homer saies, that the childe, which Neptune begot upon the Nymph, was borne a whole year after the conception, that is, in the twelfth moneth ; for, as Aulus Gellius saith, libr. 3. this long time was suitable to the majesty of Neptune, that in it the childe might receive his perfect forme : for the like reason Jupiter made the night, wherein he lay with Alcmena, last fourty eight houres, a shorter time not being sufficient for the forging of Hercules, who cleansed the world of the Monstres and Tyrants, wherewith it was supprest. My masters, the ancient pantagruelists have confirmed that which I say, and withall declared it to be not onely possible, but also maintained the lawful birth and legitimation of the infant borne of a woman in the eleventh moneth after the decease of her husband, Hypocrates, *lib. de alimento.* Plinius, lib. 7. cap. 5. Plautus, in his *Cistelleria.* Marcus Varro in his Satyr inscribed, *The Testament,* alledging to this purpose the authority of Aristotle : Censorinus *lib. de die natali.* Arist. lib. 7. cap 3 and 4 *de natura animalium.* Gellius, lib. 3. cap. 16. Servius, in his exposition upon this verse of Virgil's *Eclogues,* " *Matri longa decem,*" etc., and a thousand other fooles, whose number hath been increased by the Lawyers *ff. de suis, et Leg. intestato paragrapho fin.* and in *Auth. de restitu. et ea quæ patit in xi mense ;* moreover upon these grounds they have foysted in their Robidilardick, or Lapiturolive Law. Gallus *ff. de libr. et posth. L. sept. ff. de stat. hom.* And some other Lawes, which at this time I dare not name ; by means whereof the honest widows may without danger play at the close buttock game with might and maine, and as hard as they can for the space of the first two moneths after the decease of their husbands. I pray you, my good lusty springal lads, if you finde any of these females, that are worth the paines of untying the cod-peece-point, get up, ride upon them, and bring them to me; for if they happen within the third moneth to conceive, the childe shall be heire to the deceased, *if, before he died, he had no other children, and the mother shall passe for an honest woman.*

When she is known to have conceived, thrust forward boldly, spare her not, whatever betide you, seeing the paunch is full; as Julia, the daughter of the Emperour Octavian never prostituted her self to her belly-bumpers, but when she found her self with childe, after the manner of Ships that receive not their steers-man, till they have their ballast and lading; and if any blame them for this their retaconniculation, and reiterated lechery upon their pregnancy and big belliednesse, seeing beasts in the like exigent of their fullnesse, will never suffer the male-masculant to incroach them: their answer will be, that those are beasts, but they are women, very well skilled in the pretty vales, and small fees of the pleasant trade and mysteries of superfetation: as Populius heretofore answered, according to the relation of Macrobius, lib. 2. *Saturnal.* If the Devill would not have them to bagge, he must wring hard the spigot, and stop the bung-hole.

CHAPTER IV

How Gargamelle, being great with Gargantua, did eate a huge Deale of Tripes

THE occasion and manner how Gargamelle was brought to bed, and delivered of her childe, was thus: and, if you do not beleeve it, I wish your bum-gut fall out, and make an escapade. Her bum-gut, indeed, or fundament escaped her in an afternoone, on the third day of February, with having eaten at dinner too many godebillios. Godebillios are the fat tripes of coiros, coiros are beeves fatned at the cratch in Oxe stalls, or in the fresh guimo meadows, guimo meadows are those, that for their fruitfulnesse may be mowed twice a yeare, of those fat beeves they had killed three hundred sixty seven thousand and fourteen, to be salted at Shrovetide, that in the entring of the Spring they might have plenty of poudred beef, wherewith to season their mouths at the beginning of their meales, and to taste their wine the better.

They had abundance of tripes, as you have heard, and they were so delicious, that every one licked his fingers, but the mischife was this, that for all men could do, there was no possibility to keep them long in that relish ; for in a very short while they would have stunk, which had been an undecent thing : it was therefore concluded that they should be all of them gulched up, without losing any thing ; to this effect they invited all the Burguers of Sainais, of Suille, of the Rocheclermand, of Vaugaudry, without omitting the Boudray, Monpensier, the Guedevede, and other their neighbours, all stiffe drinkers, brave fellows, and good players at the kyles. The good man Grangousier took great pleasure in their company, and commanded there should be no want nor pinching for any thing : neverthelesse he bade his wife eate sparingly, because she was near her time, and that these tripes were no very commendable meat : they would faine (said he) be at the chewing of ordure, that would eat the case wherein it was. Notwithstanding these admonitions, she did eate sixteen quarters, two bushels, three Pecks and a pipkin full : O the fair fecality, wherewith she swelled, by the ingrediency of such shitten stuffe !

After dinner they all went out in a hurle, to the grove of the willows, where on the green grasse, to the sound of the merry Flutes, and pleasant Bagpipes, they danced so gallantly, that it was a sweet and heavenly sport to see them so frolick.

CHAPTER V

The Discourse of the Drinkers

THEN did they fall upon the chat of victuals and some belly furniture to be snatched at in the very same place, which purpose was no sooner mentioned, but forthwith began flaggons to go, gammons to trot, goblets to fly, great bowles to ting, glasses to ring, draw, reach, fill, mixe, give it me without water, so my friend, so, whip me off this glasse neatly, bring me hither some claret, a full weeping glasse till it run over, a cessation and truce with thirst. Ha, thou false Fever, wilt thou not be gone ? by my figgins, godmother, I cannot as yet enter in the humour of being merry, nor drink so currantly as I would. You have catch'd a cold, gamer, yea forsooth, Sir ; by the belly of Sanct Buf, let us talk of our drink, I never drink but at my hours, like the Pope's Mule, and I never drink but in my breviary, like a faire father Gardien. Which was first, thirst or drinking ? Thirst, for who in the time of innocence would have drunk without being athirst ? nay, Sir, it was drinking ; for *privatio præsupponit habitum.* I am learned, you see : *Fœcundi calices quem non fecere disertum ?* we poor innocents drink but too much without thirst : not I truly, who am a sinner, for I never drink without thirst, either present or future, to prevent it, as you know, I drink for the thirst to come ; I drink eternally, this is to me an eternity of drinking, and drinking of eternity ; let us sing, let us drink, and tune up our round-lays ; where is my funnel ? What, it seems I do not drink but by an Attourney ? do you wet yourselves to dry, or do you dry to wet you ? pish, I understand not the rhethorick (Theorick, I should say) but I help my self somewhat by the practice. Baste, enough, I sup, I wet, I humect, I moisten my gullet, I drink, and all for fear of dying ; drink alwayes and you shall never die : if I drink not, I am a ground dry, gravelled and spent, I am stark dead without drink, and my soul ready to flie inso some marish amongst Frogs ; the soul never dwells in a dry place, drouth kills it. O you butlers, creators of new formes, make me of no drinker a drinker, a perennity and everlastingnesse of sprinkling, and bedewing me through these my parched and sinnewy bowels ; he drinks in vaine, that feels not the pleasure of it ; this entereth into my veines, the pissing tooles and urinal vessels shall have nothing of it. I would willingly wash the tripes of the calf, which I apparelled this morning. I have pretty well now balasted my stomack, and stuft my paunch : if the papers of my bonds and bills could drink as well as I do, my creditors would not want for wine when they come to see me, or when they are to make any formal exhibition of their rights to what of me they can demand ; this hand of yours spoyles your nose, O how many other such will enter here before this go out, what, drink so shallow, it is enough to break both girds and pettrel, this is called a cup of dissimulation, or flaggonal hypocrisie.

RING, DRAW, REACH, FILL AND MIXE

31

What difference is there between a bottle and a flaggon ?
great difference, for the bottle is stopped and shut up with a
stoppel, but the flaggon with a vice, bravely and well plaid upon
the words, Our fathers drank lustily, and emptied their cans;
well cack'd, well sung ; come, let us drink : will you send nothing to the river, here is one going to wash the tripes : I drink
no more than a spurge, I drink like a Templer Knight : and I,
tanquam sponsus, and I, *sicut terra sine aqua*, give me a synony-
mon for a gammon of bacon ? it is the compulsory of drinkers :
it is a pully ; by a pully-rope wine is let down into a cellar, and
by a gammon into the stomach, hei ! now boyes hither, some
drink, some drink, there is no trouble in it, *respice personam,
pone pro duos, bus non est in usu.* If I could get up as well as I
can swallow down, I had been long ere now very high in the aire.

Thus became Tom Tosse-pot rich, thus went in the Taylors
stitch : thus did Bacchus conquer th' Inde thus Philosophy,
Melinde : a little raine allayes a great deale of winde : long
tipling breaks the thunder. But if there came such liquor from
my ballock, would you not willingly thereafter suck the udder
whence it issued ; here, page, fill ; I prethee, forget me not
when it comes to my turne, and I will enter the election I have
made of thee into the very register of my heart, sup, Guillot,
and spare not, there is yet somewhat in the pot. I appeale
from thirst, and disclaim its jurisdiction. Page sue out my
appeale in forme, this remnant in the bottome of the glasse
must follow its Leader. I was wont heretofore to drink out
all, but now I leave nothing. Let us not make too much haste,
it is requisite we carry all along with us ; hey day, here are
tripes fit for our sport, and in earnest excellent Godebillios
of the dun Oxe (you know) with the black streak. O for God's
sake let us lash them soundly, yet thriftily. Drink, or I will.
No, no, drink I beseech you ; sparrows will not eate unlesse
you bob them on the taile, nor can I drink if I be not fairly
spoke to. The concavities of my body are like another Hell
for their capacity. Lagonædatera, there is not a corner, nor
cunniborow in all my body where this wine doth not ferret out
my thirst. Ho, this will bang it soundly, but this shall banish
it utterly. Let us winde our hornes by the sound of flaggons
and bottles, and cry aloud, that whoever hath lost his thirst,
come not hither to seek it. Long clysters of drinking are to be
voided without doors : the great God made the Planets, and
we make the platters neat. I have the word of the Gospel in
my mouth, Sitio. The stone called Asbestos, is not more

unquenchable, than the thirst of my paternitie. Appetite comes with eating saies Angeston, but the thirst goes away with drinking. I have a remedy against thirst, quite contrary to that which is good against the biting of a mad dog. Keep running after a Dog, and he will never bite you, drink alwayes before the thirst, and it will never come upon you. There I catch you, I awake you. Argus had a hundred eyes for his sight, a butler should have (like Briareus) a hundred hands wherewith to fill us wine indefatigably. Hey now lads, let us moisten our selves, it will be time to dry hereafter. White wine here, wine boyes, poure out all in the name of Lucifer, fill here you, fill and fill (pescods on you) till it be full. My tongue peels. Lanstrinque, to thee, Countreyman, I drink to thee good fellow, camarade to thee, lustie, lively, Ha, la, la, that was drunk to some purpose, and bravely gulped over. *O lachryma Christi*, it is of the best grape; 'faith, pure Greek, Greek, O the fine white wine, upon my conscience it is a kinde of taffatas wine, hin, hin, it is of one eare, well wrought, and of good wooll; courage, camrade, up thy heart billy, we will not be beasted at this bout, for I have got one trick, *ex hoc in hoc*, there is no inchantment, nor charme there, every one of you hath seene it, my prentiship is out, I am a free man at this trade. I am prester mast, (Prish)-Brum I should say master past. O the drinkers, those that are a dry, O poore thirsty souls, good Page my friend, fill me here some, and crowne the wine, I pray thee, like a Cardinal, *Natura abhorret vacuum*. Would you say that a flie could drink in this, this is after the fashion of Swisserland, clear off, neat, supernaculum, come, therefore blades to this divine liquor, and celestial juyce, swill it over heartily, and spare not, it is a decoction of Nectar and Ambrosia.

CHAPTER VI

How Gargantua was borne in a strange Manner

WHILST they were on this discourse, and pleasant tattle of drinking, Gargamelle began to be a little unwell in her lower parts; whereupon Grangousier arose from off the grasse, and fell to comfort her very honestly and kindly, suspecting that she was in travel, and told her that it was best for her to sit down upon the grasse under the willows, because she was like very shortly to see young feet, and that therefore it was convenient she should pluck up her spirits, and take a good heart of new at the fresh arrival of her baby, saying to her withal, that although the paine was somewhat grievous to her, it would be but of short continuance, and that the succeeding joy would quickly remove that sorrow, in such short that she should not so much as remember it. On with a sheeps courage (quoth he), dispatch this boy, and we will speedily fall to work for the making of another. Ha (said she) so well as you speak at your own ease, you that are men ; well then, in the name of God, i 'le do my best, seeing that you will have it so, but would to God that it were cut off from you : What ? (said Grangousier) Ha (said she), you are a good man indeed, you understand it well enough ; what, my member ? (said he) by the goats blood, if it please you that shall be done instantly, cause bring hither a knife ; alas, (said she), the Lord forbid, I pray Jesus to forgive me, I did not say it from my heart, therefore let it alone, and do not do it neither more nor lesse any kinde of harme for my speaking so to you ; but I am like to have work enough to do to day, and all for your member, yet God blesse you and it.

Courage, courage (said he) take you no care of the matter, let the four formost oxen do the work. I will yet go drink one whiffe more, and if in the meane time any thing befall you that may require my presence, I will be so near to you, that, at the first whistling in your fist, I shall be with you forthwith : a little while after she began to groane, lament and cry, then suddenly came the midwives from all quarters, who groping her below, found some peloderies, which was a certaine filthy stuffe, and of a taste truly bad enough, this they thought had been the childe, but it was her fundament, that was slipt out with the mollification of her streight intrall, which you call the bum-gut, and that meerly by eating of too many tripes, as we have shewed you before : whereupon an old ugly trot in the company, who had the repute of an expert she-Physician, and was come from Brispaille, near to Saint Gnou, three score years before, made her so horrible a restrictive and binding medicine, and whereby all her *larris*, arse-pipes and conduits were so opilated, stopped, obstructed, and contracted, that you could hardily have opened and enlarged them with your teeth, which is a terrible thing to think upon ; seeing the Devill at the masse at Saint Martins was puzled with the like task, when with

AN UGLY OLD TROT

25

his teeth he had lengthened out the parchment whereon he wrote the tittle tattle of two young mangy whoores ; by this inconvenient the cotyledons of her matrix were presently loosed, through which the childe sprung up and leapt, and so entering into the hollow veine, did climbe by the diaphragm even above her shoulders, where that veine divides it self into two, and from thence taking his way towards the left side, issued forth at her left eare ; as soone as he was borne, he cried not as other babes use to do, *miez, miez, miez, miez,* but with a high, sturdy, and big voice shouted aloud, Some drink, some drink, some drink, as inviting all the world to drink with him ; the noise hereof was so extreamly great, that it was heard in both the Countreys at once, of Beauce and Bibarois.

I doubt me, that you do not thoroughly beleeve the truth of this strange nativity ; though you believe it not, I care not much : but an honest man, and of good judgement beleeveth still what is told him, and that which he findes written.

Is this beyond our Law ? or our faith against reason or the holy Scripture ? For my part, I finde nothing in the sacred Bible that is against it ; but tell me, if it had been the will of God, would you say that he could not do it ? Ha, for favour sake, (I beseech you) never emberlucock or inpulregafize your spirits with these vaine thoughts and idle conceits ; for I tell you, it is not impossible with God, and if he pleased all women henceforth should bring forth their children at the eare ; was not Bacchus engendred out of the very thigh of Jupiter ? did not Roquetaillade come out at his mothers heele and Crocmoush from the slipper of his nurse ? was not Minerva born of the braine, even through the eare of Jove ? Adonis of the bark of a Myrretree ; and Castor and Pollux of the doupe of that Egge which was laid and hatched by Leda ? But you would wonder more, and with farre greater amazement, if I should now present you with that chapter of Plinius, wherein he treateth of strange births, and contrary to nature, and yet am not I so impudent a lier as he was. Reade the seventh book of his *Natural History*, chapt 3., and trouble not my head any more about this

CHAPTER VII

*After what Manner Gargantua had his Name given him,
and how he tippled, bibbed, and curried the Canne*

THE good man Grangousier drinking and making merry with
the rest, heard the horrible noise which his sonne had made as he
entered into the light of this world, when he cried out, Some
drink, some drink, some drink ; whereupon he said in French,
Que grand tu as et souple le gousier, that is to say, How great and
nimble a throat thou hast ; which the company hearing said,
that verily the childe ought to be called Gargantua ; because it
was the first word that after his birth his father had spoken in
imitation, and at the example, of the ancient Hebrewes, whereunto he condescended, and his mother was very well pleased
therewith ; in the meanwhile to quiete the childe, they gave
him to drink a tirelaregot, that is, till his throat was like to
crack with it ; then was he carried to the Font, and there
baptized, according to the manner of good Christians.

Immediately thereafter were appointed for him seventeen
thousand, nine hundred, and thirteen Cowes of the townes of
Pautille and Breemond to furnish him with milk in ordinary,
for it was impossible to finde a nurse sufficient for him in all the
Countrey, considering the great quantity of milk that was
requisite for his nourishment ; although there were not wanting
some Doctors of the opinion of Scotus, who affirmed that his
own mother gave him suck, and that she could draw out of her
breasts one thousand, four hundred, two pipes, and nine pailes
of milke at every time.

Which indeed is not probable, and this point hath been found
duggishly scandalous and offensive to tender eares, for that it
savoured a little of Heresie, thus was he handled for one yeare
and ten moneths, after which time by the advice of Physicians,
they began to carry him, and then was made for him a fine
little cart drawn with Oxen, of the invention of Jan Denio,
wherein they led him hither and thither with great joy, and he
was worth the seeing ; for he was a fine boy, had a burly
physnomie, and almost ten chins ; he cried very little, but
beshit himself every hour : for to speak truly of him, he was

wonderfully flegmatick in his posteriors, both by reason of his natural complexion, and the accidental disposition which had befallen him by his too much quaffing of the septembral juyce. Yet without a cause did not he sup one drop ; for if he happened to be vexed, angry, displeased, or sorry ; if he did fret, if he did weep, if he did cry, and what grievous quarter soever he kept, in bringing him some drink, he would be instantly pacified, reseated in his own temper, in a good humour againe, and as still and quiet as ever. One of his governesses told me (swearing by her fig) how he was so accustomed to this kinde of way, that, at the sound of pintes and flaggons, he would on a sudden fall into an extasie, as if he had then tasted of the joyes of Paradise : so that they upon consideration of this his divine complexion, would every morning, to cheare him up, play with a knife upon the glasses, on the bottles with their stopples, and on the pottle-pots with their lids and covers, at the sound whereof he became gay, did leap for joy, would loll and rock himself in the cradle, then nod with his head, monocording with his fingers, and barytonising with his taile.

CHAPTER VIII

How they apparelled Gargantua

BEING of this age, his father ordained to have clothes made to him in his owne livery, which was white and blew. To work then went the Tailors, and with great expedition were those clothes made, cut, and sewed, according to the fashion that was then in request. I finde by the ancient Records or Pancarts, to be seene in the chamber of accounts, or Count of the

HE WOULD FALL INTO AN EXTASIE

29

exchequer at Montsoreo, that he was accoutred in manner as followeth. To make him every shirt of his were taken up nine hundred ells of Chatelero linnen, and two hundred for the guissets, in manner of cushions, which they put under his arm-pits ; his shirt was not gathered nor plaited, for the plaiting of shirts was not found out, till the seamsters (when the point of their needles was broken) began to work and occupie with the taile ; there were taken up for his doublet, eight hundred and thirteen ells of white Satin, and for his points fifteen hundred and nine dogs skins and a half. Then was it that men began to tie their breeches to their doublets, and not their doublets to their breeches : for it is against nature, as hath most amply been shewed by Ockam upon the exponibles of Master Hautechaussade.

For his breeches were taken up eleven hundred and five ells, and a third of white broad cloth ; they were cut in forme of pillars, chamfered, channel'd and pinked behinde, that they might not over-heat his reines : and were within the panes, puffed out with the lining of as much blew damask as was need-ful : and remark, that he had very good Leg-harnish, pro-portionable to the rest of his stature.

For his Codpeece were used sixteen ells, and a quarter of the same cloth, and it was fashioned on the top like unto a Trium-phant Arch, most gallantly fastened with two enamell'd Clasps, in each of which was set a great Emerauld, as big as an Orange ; for, as sayes Orpheus, *lib. de lapidibus*, and Plinius, *libr. ultimo*, it hath an erective vertue and comfortative of the natural member. The exiture, out-jecting or out-standing of his Codpeece, was of the length of a yard, jagged and pinked, and withal bagging, and strouting out with the blew damask lining, after the manner of his breeches ; but had you seen the faire Embroyderie of the small needle-work purle, and the curiously interlaced knots, by the Goldsmiths Art, set out and trimmed with rich Diamonds, precious Rubies, fine Turquoises, costly Emeraulds, and Persian pearles ; you would have com-pared it to a faire Cornucopia, or Horne of abundance, such as you see in Anticks, or as Rhea gave to the two Nymphs, Amalthea and Ida, the Nurses of Jupiter.

And like to that Horne of abundance, it was still gallant, succulent, droppie, sappie, pithie, lively, alwayes flourishing, alwayes fructifying, full of juice, full of flower, full of fruit, and all manner of delight. I avow God, it would have done one good to have seen him, but I will tell you more of him in the book which I have made of the dignity of Codpieces. One thing I will tell you, that, as it was both long and large, so was it well furnished and victualled within, nothing like unto the hypocritical Codpieces of some fond Wooers, and Wench-courters, which are stuffed only with wind, to the great prejudice of the female sexe.

For his shoes, were taken up foure hundred and six elles of blew Crimson-velvet, and were very neatly cut by parallel lines, joyned in uniforme cylindres : for the soling of them were made use of eleven hundred Hides of brown Cowes, shapen like the taile of a Keeling.

For his coate were taken up eighteen hundred elles of blew velvet, died in grain, embroidered in its borders with faire Gilliflowers, in the middle decked with silver purle, intermixed with plates of gold, and store of pearles, hereby shewing, that in his time he would prove an especial good fellow, and singular whip-can.

His girdle was made of three hundred elles and a halfe of silken serge, half white and halfe blew, if I mistake it not. His sword was not of Valentia, nor his dagger of Saragosa, for his father could not endure these *hidalgos borrachos maranisados como diablos :* but he had a faire sword made of wood, and the dagger of borled leather, as well painted and guilded as any man could wish.

His purse was made of the cod of an Elephant, which was given him by Herre Præcontal, Proconsul of Lybia.

For his Gown were employed nine thousand six hundred elles, wanting two thirds, of blew velvet, as before, all so diagonally purled, that by true perspective issued thence an unnamed colour, like that you see in the necks of Turtle-doves or Turkie-cocks, which wonderfully rejoyceth the eyes of the beholders. For his Bonnet or Cap were taken up three hundred two elles, and a quarter of white velvet, and the forme thereof was wide and round, of the bignesse of his head ; for his father said, that the Caps of the Mirabaise fashion, made like the cover of a pastie, would one time or other bring a mischief on those that wore them. For his Plume, he wore a faire great blew feather, plucked from a Onocrotal of the countrey of Hircania the wilde, very prettily hanging downe over his right eare : for the Jewel or broach which in his Cap he carried, he had in a Cake of gold, weighing three score and eight marks, a faire piece enamell'd, wherein was portrayed a mans body with two heads, looking towards one another, foure armes, foure feet, two arses, such as Plato, in *Symposio*, sayes was the mystical beginning of mans nature ; and about it was written in Ionick letters, Ἀγάπη οὐ ζητεῖ τὰ ἑαυτῆς, or rather, Ἀνὴρ καὶ γυνὴ ζυγάδα ἄνθρωπος ἰδιαίτατα, that is, *Vir et Mulier junctim propriissime homo.* To wear about his neck, he had a golden chaine, weighing twenty five thousand and sixty three marks of gold, the links thereof being made after the manner of great berries, amongst which were set in work green Jaspers ingraven, and cut Dragon-like, all invironed with beams and sparks, as king Nicepsos of old was wont to weare them, and it reached down to the very bust of the rising of his belly, whereby he reaped great benefit all his life long, as the Greek Physicians know well enough. For his Gloves were put in work sixteen Otters skins, and three of lougarous or men-eating wolves, for the bordering of them : and of this stuffe were they made, by the appointment of the Cabalists of Sanlono. As for the Rings which his father would have him to weare to renew the ancient mark of Nobility, He had on the forefinger of his left hand a Carbuncle as big as an Ostrige's Egge, inchased very daintily in gold of the finenesse of a Turkie Seraph. Upon the middle finger of the same hand, he had a Ring made of foure metals together, of the strongest fashion that ever was seen ; so that the steel did not crash against the gold, nor the silver crush the copper. All this was made by Captain Chappius, and Alcofribas his good agent. On the medical finger of his right hand, he had a Ring made Spirewayes, wherein was set a perfect baleu rubie, a pointed Diamond, and a Physon Emerald, of an inestimable value ; for Hans-carvel, the king of Melindas Jeweller, esteemed them at the rate of threescore nine millions, eight hundred ninety foure thousand and eighteen French Crowns of Berrie, and at so much did the foucres of Auspurg prize them.

CHAPTER IX

The Colours and Liveries of Gargantua

GARGANTUAS colours were white and blew, as I have shewed you before, by which his father would give us to understand, that his sonne to him was a heavenly joy, for the white did signifie gladnesse, pleasure, delight, and rejoycing, and the blew celestial things. I know well enough, that in reading this you laugh at the old drinker, and hold this exposition of colours to be very extravagant, and utterly disagreeable to reason, because white is said to signifie faith, and blew constancy. But without moving, vexing, heating or putting you in a chafe, (for the weather is dangerous) answer me if it please you ; for no other compulsory way of arguing will I use towards you, or any else ; only now and then I will mention a word or two of my bottle. What is it that induceth you ? what stirs you up to believe, or who told you that white signifieth faith, and blew, constancy ? An old paultry book, say you, sold by the hawking Pedlars and Balladmongers, entituled *The Blason of Colours :* Who made it ? whoever it was, he was wise in that he did not set his name to it : but, besides, I know not what I should rather admire in him, his presumption or his sottish-nesse : his presumption and overweening, for that he should without reason, without cause, or without any appearance of truth, have dared to prescribe by his private authority, what things should be denotated and signified by the colour : which is the custome of Tyrants, who will have their will to bear sway in stead of equity ; and not of the wise and learned, who with the evidence of reason satisfie their Readers : His sottishnesse and want of spirit, in that he thought, that without any other demonstration or sufficient argument, the world would be pleased to make his blockish, and ridiculous impositions the rule of their devices. In effect, (according to the Proverb, To a shitten taile failes never ordurre), he hath found (it seems) some simple Ninnie in those rude times of old, when the wearing of high round Bonnets was in fashion, who gave some trust to his writings, according to which they carved and ingraved their apophthegms and motos's, trapped and caparisoned their Mules and Sumpter-horses, apparelled their Pages, quartered their breeches, bordered their gloves, fring'd the courtains and vallens of their beds, painted their ensignes, composed songs, and which is worse, placed many deceitful juglings, and un-worthy base tricks undiscoveredly, amongst the very chastest Matrons, and most reverend Sciences. In the like darknesse and mist of ignorance, are wrapped up these vainglorious Courtiers, and name-transposers, who going about in their impresa's, to signifie *esperance*, (that is, hope) have portrayed a sphere and birds pennes for peines ! *Ancholie* (which is the flower colombine) for melancholy : A waning Moon or Cressant, to shew the increasing or rising of ones fortune ; A bench rotten and broken, to signifie bankrout : *non* and a *corslet* for *non dur habit*, (otherwise *non durabit*, it shall not last) *un lit sans ciel*, that is, a bed without a testerne, for *un licencie*, a graduated person, as, Batchelour in Divinity, or utter Barrester at law ; which are æquivocals so absurd and witlesse, so barbarous and clownish, that a foxes taile should be fastened to the neck-piece of, and a Vizard, made of a Cowsheard, given to every one that henceforth should offer, after the restitution of learning, to make use of any such fopperies in France, by the same reasons (if reasons I should call them, and not ravings rather, and idle triflings about words), might I cause paint a panier, to signifie that I am in peine : a Mustard-pot, that my heart tarries much for't : one pissing upwards for a Bishop : the bottom of a paire of breeches for a vessel full of farthings— a Codpiece for the office of the Clerks of the sentences, decrees or judgements, or rather (as the English beares it), for the taile of a Codfish ; and a dogs turd, for the dainty turret, wherein lies the love of my sweet heart. Farre otherwise did heretofore the Sages of Egypt, when they wrote by letters, which they called Hieroglyphicks, which none understood who were not skilled in the vertue, propertie and nature of the things represented by them : of which Orus Apollon hath in Greek composed two books, and Polyphilus in his dream of love, set down more : In France you have a taste of them, in the device or impresa of my Lord Admiral, which was carried before that time by Octavian Augustus. But my little skiffe alongst these unpleasant gulphs and sholes, will saile no further, therefore must I return to the Port from whence I came : yet do I hope one day to write more at large of these things and to shew both by Philosophical arguments and authorities received and approved of by and from all antiquity, what, and how many colours there are in nature, and what may be signified by every one of them, if God save the mould of my Cap which is my best Winepot, as my Grandame said.

CHAPTER X

Of that which is signified by the Colours, White and Blew

THE white therefore signifieth joy, solace and gladnesse, and that not at random, but upon just and very good grounds : which you may perceive to be true if laying aside all prejudicate affections, you will but give eare to what presently I shall expound unto you.

Aristotle saith, that supposing two things contrary in their kinde, as good and evill, vertue and vice, heat and cold, white and black, pleasure and pain, joy and grief : And so of others, if you couple them in such manner, that the contrary of one kinde may agree in reason with the contrary of the other, it must follow by consequence, that the other contrary must answer to the remnant opposite to that wherewith it is conferred ; as for example, vertue and vice are contrary in one kinde, so are good and evil : if one of the contraries of the first kinde, be consonant to one of those of the second, as vertue and goodnesse, for it is clear that vertue is good, so shall the other two contraries, (which are evil and vice) have the same connexion, for vice is evil.

This Logical rule being understood, take these two contraries, joy and sadnesse : then these other two, white and black, for they are Physically contrary ; if so be, then, that black do signifie grief by good reason then should white import joy. Nor is this signification instituted by humane imposition, but by the universal consent of the world received, which Philosophers call Jus Gentium, the Law of Nations, or an uncontrolable right of force in all countreyes whatsoever : for you know well enough, that all people and all languages and nations, (except the ancient Syracusans and certain Argives, who had crosse and thwarting soules) when they mean outwardly to give evidence of their sorrow, go in black ; and all mourning is done with black, which general consent is not without some argument, and reason in nature, the which every man may by himself very suddenly comprehend, without the instruction of any ; and this we call the Law of nature : By vertue of the same natural instinct, we know that by white all the world hath understood joy, gladnesse, mirth, pleasure, and

35

delight. In former times, the Thracians and Grecians did mark their good, propitious, and fortunate dayes with white stones : and their sad, dismal, and unfortunate ones with black ; is not the night mournful, sad and melancholick ? it is black and dark by the privation of light ; doth not the light comfort all the world ? and it is more white then any thing else, which to prove, I could direct you to the book of Laurentius Valla against Bartolus : but an Evangelical testimony I hope will content you, Matth. 17. it is said, that at the transfiguration of our Lord, *Vestimenta ejus facta sunt alba sicut lux,* his apparel was made white like the light by which lightsome whitenesse he gave his three Apostles to understand the Idea and figure of the eternal joyes ; for by the light are all men comforted, according to the word of the old woman, who although she had never a tooth in her head, was wont to say, *Bona lux :* and Tobit, chap. 5. after he had lost his sight, when Raphael saluted him answered, " What joy can I have that do not see the light of Heaven ? " In that colour did the Angels testifie the joy of the whole world at the resurrection of our Saviour, John 20. and at his Ascension Acts 1. with the like colour of vesture did St John the Evangelist, Apoc. 4. 7. see the faithful clothed in the heavenly and blissed Jerusalem.

Reade the ancient both Greek and Latine histories and you shall finde that the towne of Alba (the first patern of Rome), was founded, and so named by reason of a white sow that was seen there : You shall likewise finde in those stories, that when any man, after he had vanquished his enemies, was by decree of the Senate to enter into Rome triumphantly, he usually rode in a chariot drawn by white horses : which in the ovation triumph was also the custome ; for by no signe or colour would they so significantly expresse the joy of their coming, as by the white. You shall there also finde, how Pericles, the General of the Athenians would needs have that part of his Army, unto whose lot befel the white beanes, to spend the whole day in mirth, pleasure and ease whilest the rest were a fighting. A thousand other examples and places could I alledge to this purpose, but that it is not here where I should do it.

By understanding hereof, you may resolve one Problem, which Alexander Aphrodiseus hath accounted unanswerable, why the Lion, who with his only cry and roaring affrights all beasts, dreads and feareth only a white cock ? For (as Proclus saith *libro de Sacrificio et Magia*) it is because the presence of the vertue of the sunne, which is the Organ and Promptuarie of all terrestrial and syderial light doth more symbolize and agree with a white cock as well in regard of that colour as of his property and specifical quality then with a Lion. He saith furthermore that Devils have been often seen in the shape of Lions, which at the sight of a white cock have presently vanished. This is the cause why Galli or Gallices (so are the Frenchmen called, because they are naturally white as milk, which the Greeks call Gala) do willingly weare in their Caps white feathers for by nature they are of a candid disposition, merrie, kinde, gracious and well-beloved, and for their cognizance and armes have the whitest flower of any, the Flower de luce or Lilie. If you demand, how, by white, nature would have us understand joy and gladnesse ? I answer, that the analogy and uniformity is thus, for, as the white doth outwardly disperse and scatter the rayes of the sight, whereby the optick spirits are manifestly dissolved, according to the opinion of Aristotle in his Problemes and perspective Treatises ; as you may likewise perceive by experience, when you passe over mountains covered with snow, how you will complain that you cannot see well : as Xenophon writes to have hapned to his men, and as Galen very largely declareth, lib. 10. *de usu partium :* Just so the heart with excessive joy is inwardly dilated, and suffereth a manifest resolution of the vital spirits, which may go so farre on, that it may thereby be deprived of its nourishment, and by consequence of life itself. By this Pericharie or extremity of gladnesse, as Galen saith, lib. 12. *method* lib. 5. *de locis affectis*, and lib. 2. *de symptomatum causis*. And as it hath come to passe in former times, witnesse Marcus Tullius, lib. 1. *quæst Tuscul.* Verrius, Aristotle, Titus Livius. in his relation of the battel of Cannae, Plinius, lib. 7. cap. 32. and 34. A. Gellius, lib. 3. c. 15, and many other Writers, of Diagoras the Rhodian, Chilon, Sophocles, Dionysius the tyrant of Sicilie, Philippides, Philemon, Polycrates, Philistion, M. Juventi, and others who died with joy, and as Avicen speaketh, in 2 *canon et lib. de virib. cordis*, of the Saffron, that it doth so rejoyce the heart, that, if you take of it excessively, it will by a superfluous resolution and dilatation deprive it altogether of life. Here peruse Alex. Aphrodiseus lib. 1. *Probl.* cap. 19, and that for a cause. But what ? it seems I am entred further into this point then I intended at the first ; Here, therefore, will I strike saile, referring the rest to that book of mine, which handleth this matter to the full. Mean while, in a word I will tell you, that blew doth certainly signifie Heaven and heavenly things, by the same very tokens and symbols, that white signifieth joy and pleasure.

CHAPTER XI

Of the Youthful Age of Gargantua

GARGANTUA from three yeares upwards unto five, was brought up and instructed in all convenient discipline, by the commandment of his father; and spent that time like the other little children of the countrey, that is, in drinking, eating and sleeping: in eating, sleeping and drinking: and in sleeping, drinking and eating: still he wallowed and rowled up and down himself in the mire and dirt: he blurred and sullied his nose with filth: he blotted and smutch't his face with any kinde of scurvie stuffe, he trode down his shoes in the heele: At the flies he did oftentimes yawn, and ran very heartily after the Butterflies, the Empire whereof belonged to his father. He pissed in his shoes, shit in his shirt, and wiped his nose on his sleeve: He did let his snot and snivel fall in his pottage, and dabled, padled, and slabbered every where: He would drink in his slipper, and ordinarily rub his belly against a Panier: He sharpened his teeth with a top, washed his hands with his broth, and combed his head with a bole: He would sit down betwixt two stooles, and his arse to the ground, would cover himself with a wet sack, and drink in eating of his soupe: He did eate his Cake sometimes without bread, would bite in laughing, and laugh in biting; Oftentimes did he spit in the basin, and fart for fatnesse; pisse against the Sunne, and hide himself in the water for fear of raine. He would strike out of the cold iron, be often in the dumps, and frig and wriggle it. He would flay the Fox, say the Apes Paternoster, return to his sheep, and turn the Hogs to the Hay: He would beat the Dogs before the Lion, put the Plough before the Oxen, and claw where it did not itch; He would pump one to draw somewhat out of him, by griping all would hold fast nothing, and alwayes eat his white bread first. He shoo'd the Geese, kept a self-tickling to make himself laugh, and was very stedable in the Kitchen: made a mock at the gods, would cause sing Magnificat at Matines, and found it very convenient so to do ; He would eat cabbage, and shite beets, knew flies in a dish of milk, and would make them lose their feet : He would scrape paper, blur parchment, then run away as hard as he could : He would pul at the Kids leather, or vomit up his dinner, then reckon without his Host ; He would beat the bushes without catching the birds, thought the Moon was made of green cheese, and that bladders are lanternes : out of one sack he would take two moutures or fees for grinding ; would act the Asses part to get some bran, and of his fist would make a Mallet : He took the cranes at the first leap, and would have the Mail-coats to be made link after link : He alwayes looked a given horse in the mouth, leaped from the cock to the asse, and put one ripe between two green : By robbing Peter he payed Paul, he kept the Moon from the wolves, and hoped to catch Larks if ever the Heavens should fall : He did make of necessity vertue, of such bread such pottage, and cared as little for the peeled as for the shaven : Every morning he did cast up his gorge, and his fathers little dogs eat out of the dish with him, and he with them : He would bite their eares, and they would scratch his nose : he would blow in their arses, and they would lick his chaps. But hearken, good fellows, the spigot ill betake you, and whirle round your braines, if you do not give eare : This little Lecher was alwayse groping his Nurses and Governesses, upside down, arswersie, topsiturvie, harrii-bourrquet, with a Yacco haick, hyek gio, handling them very rudely in jumbling and tumbling them to keep them going ; for he had already begun to exercise the tooles, and put his Codpiece in practice ; which Codpiece, or Braguette, his Governesses did every day deck up and adorn with faire nosegayes, curious rubies, sweet flowers, and fine silken tufts, and very pleasantly would passe their time, in taking you know what between their fingers, and dandling it, till it did revive and creep up to the bulk and stiffenesse of a suppository, or streat magdaloen, which is a hard rowled up salve spread upon leather.   Then did they burst out in laughing, when they saw it lift up its eares, as if the sport had liked them ; one of them would call it her little dille, her staffe of love, her quillety, her faucetin, her dandilollie :   Another, her peen, her jolly kyle, her bableret, her membretoon, her quickset Imp : another again, her branch of coral, her female adamant, her placket-racket, her cyprian scepter, her jewel for Ladies : and some of the other women would give it these names, my bunguetee, my stopple too, my busherusher, my gallant wimble, my pretty boarer, my coney-borow-ferret, my little piercer, my augretine, my dangling hangers, down right to it, stiffe and stout, in and to, my pusher, dresser, pouting stick, my hony pipe, my pretty pillicock, linkie pinkie, futilletie, my lustie andouille, and crimson chitterlin, my little couille bredouille my pretty rogue, and so forth : It belongs to me, said one : It is mine, said the other : What, quoth a third, shall I have no share in it ? by my faith, I will cut it then. Ha, to cut it, (said the other), would hurt him ; Madam, do you cut little children's things ? were his cut off, he would be then *Monsieur sans queue*, the curtail'd Master. And that he might play and sport himself after the manner of the other little children of the countrey, they made him a faire weather whirljack, of the wings of the windmil of Myrebalais.

CHAPTER XII

Of Gargantuas Wooden Horses

AFTERWARDS, that he might be all his lifetime a good Rider, they made to him a faire great horse of wood, which he did make leap, curvete, yerk out behinde, and skip forward, all at a time : to pace, trot, rack, gallop, amble, to play the hobbie, the hackney-guelding : go the gate of the camel, and of the wilde asse. He made him also change his colour of hair, as the Monks of Coultibo, (according to the variety of their holy-days) use to do their clothes, from bay, brown, to sorrel, dapple-gray, mouse-dun, deer-colour, roan, cow-colour, gingioline skued colour, pybal'd, and the colour of the savage elk.

Himself of an huge big post made a hunting nag; and another for daily service, of the beam of a Vinepress : and of a great Oak made up a mule, with a footcloth, for his chamber. Besides this, he had ten or twelve spare horses, and seven horses for post ; and all these were lodged in his own chamber, close by his bed-side. One day the Lord of Breadinbag came to visit his father in great bravery, and with a gallant traine : and at the same time, to see him came likewise the Duke of Freemeale, and the Earl of Wetgullet. The house truly for so many guests at once was somewhat narrow, but especially the stables ; whereupon the steward and harbinger of the said Lord Breadinbag, to know if there were any other empty stables in the house, came to Gargantua, a little young lad, and secretly asked him where the stables of the great horses were, thinking that children would be ready to tell all ? Then he led them up along the stairs of the Castle, passing by the second Hall unto a broad great Gallery, by which they entred into a large Tower, and as they were going up at another paire of staires, said the harbinger to the steward, This childe deceives us, for the stables are never on the top of the house : You may be mistaken, (said the steward,) for I know some places at Lyons, at the Basmette, at Chaunon, and elsewhere, which have their stables at the very tops of the houses, so it may be, that behinde the house there is a way to come to this ascent, but I will question with him further. Then said he to Gargantua, My pretty little boy, whither do you lead us ? To the stable, (said he), of my great horses, we are almost come to it, we have but these staires to go up at, then leading them alongst another great Hall, he brought them into his chamber, and opening the door said unto them, This is the stable that you ask for : this is my gennet, this is my gelding, this is my courser, and this is my hackney, and laid on them with a great Leaver : I will bestow upon you, (said he), this Frizeland horse, I had him from Francfort, yet will I give him you ; for he is a pretty little nagge, and will go very well, with a tessel of goosehawk, halfe a dozen of spaniels, and a brace of grey-hounds, thus are you King of the hares and partirdges for all this winter. By St John, (said they), now we are payed, he hath gleeked us to some purpose, bobbed we are now for ever ; I deny it, (said he), he was not here above three dayes judge you now, whether they had most cause, either to hide their heads for shame, or to laugh at the jest : as they were going down again thus amazed, he asked them, Will you have a whimwham ? What is that, said they ? It is (said he) five turds to make you a muzzel : To day (said the steward) though we happen to be rosted, we shall not be burnt, for we are pretty well quipped and larded in my opinion. O my jolly daper boy, thou has given us a gudgeon, I hope to see thee Pope before I die : I think so, (said he) my self ; and then shall you be a puppie, and this gentle popinjeay a perfect papelard, that is, dissembler ; Well, well, (said the harbinger). But, (said Gargantua), guesse how many stitches there are in my mother's smock : Sixteen, (quoth the harbinger). You do not speak gospel, (said Gargantua,) for there is sent before, and sent behinde, and you did not reckon them ill, considering the two under holes. When, (said the harbinger ?) Even then (said Gargantua), when they made a shovel of your nose to take up a quarter of dirt, and of your throat a funnel, wherewith to put it into another vessel, because the bottom of the old one was out. Cocksbod, (said the steward), we have met with a Prater. Farewell (Master tatler) God keep you, so goodly are the words which you come out with, and so fresh in your mouth, that it had need to be salted.

Thus going down in great haste, under the arch of the staires they let fall the great Leaver, which he had put upon their backs, whereupon Gargantua said, What a deedle ! you are (it seems), but bad horsemen, that suffer your bilder to faile you, when you need him most, if you were to go from hence to Chausas, whether had you rather ride on a gesling, or lead a sow in a Leash ? I had rather drink, (said the harbinger), with this they entered into the lower Hall, where the company was, and relating to them this new story, they made them laugh like a swarm of flies.

CHAPTER XIII

How Gargantuas wonderful Understanding, became known to his Father Grangousier, by the Invention of a Torchecul or Wipebreech

ABOUT the end of the fifth yeare, Grangousier returning from the conquest of the Canarians, went by the way to see his sonne Gargantua. There was he filled with joy, as such a father might be at the sight of such a childe of his : and whilest he kist him and embrac'd him, he asked many childish questions of him about divers matters, and drank very freely with him, and with his governesses, of whom in great earnest, he asked amongst other things, whether they had been careful to keep him clean and sweet ? To this Gargantua answered, that he had taken such a course for that himself, that in al the countrey there was not to be found a cleanlier boy than he. How is that (said Grangousier) ? I have (answered Gargantua), by a long and curious experience, found out a means to wipe my bum, the most lordly, the most excellent, and the most convenient that ever was seen ? What is that (said Grangousier) how is it ? I will tell you by and by (said Gargantua). Once I did wipe me with a gentlewomans velvet-mask, and found it to be good ; for the softnesse of the silk was very voluptuous and pleasant to my fundament. Another time with one of their Hoods, and in like manner that was comfortable. At another time with a ladies Neck-kerchief, and after that I wiped me with some ear-pieces of hers made of Crimson sattin, but there was such a number of golden spangles in them (turdie round things, a pox take them) that they fetched away all the skin of my taile with a vengeance. Now I wish St Anthonies fire burn the bum-gut of the Goldsmith that made them, and of her that wore them : This hurt I cured by wiping my self with a Pages cap, garnished with a feather after the Suitsers fashion.

Afterwards, in dunging behinde a bush, I found a Marchcat, and with it wiped my breech, but her clawes were so sharp that they scratched and exculcerated all my perinee ; Of this I recovered the next morning thereafter, by wiping my self with my mother's gloves, of a most excellent perfume and sent of the Arabian Benin. After that I wiped me with sage, with fennil, with anet, with marjoram, with roses, with gourd-leaves, with beets, with colewort, with leaves of the vine-tree, with mallowes, wool-blade, (which is a tail-scarlet), with latice and with spinage leaves. All this did very great good to my leg. Then with Mercurie, with pursley, with nettles, with comfrey, but that gave me the bloody flux of Lumbardie, which I healed by wiping me with my braguette ; Then I wiped my taile in the sheets, in the coverlet, in the curtains, with a cushion, with Arras hangings, with a green carpet, with a table cloth, with a napkin, with a handkerchief, with a combing cloth, in all which I found more pleasure then do the mangy dogs when you rub them. Yea, but (said Grangousier), which torchecul didst thou finde to be the best ? I was coming to it (said Gargantua), and by and by shall you heare the *tu autem*, and know the whole mysterie and knot of the matter : I wiped my self with hay, with straw, with thatch-rushes, with flax, with wooll, with paper, but,

> Who his foule taile with paper wipes,
> Shall at his ballocks leave some chips.

What (said Grangousier), my little rogue, hast thou been at the pot, that thou dost rime already ? Yes, yes, my lord the king (answered Gargantua), I can rime gallantly, and rime till I become hoarse with Rheum. Heark, what our Privy sayes to the Skyters :

> Shittard
> Squirtard
> Crackard
>   Turdous :
> Thy bung
> Hath flung
> Some dung
>   On us !
> Filthard
> Cackard
> Stinkard,
>   St Antonie's fire seize on
>   thy toane
> If thy
> Dirty
> Dounby
>   Thou do not wipe ere
>   thou be gone.

Will you have any more of it ? Yes, yes (answered Grangousier). Then said Gargantua,

A ROUNDLAY

> In shiting yesday I did know
> The sesse I to my arse did owe :
> The smell was such came from that slunk,
> That I was with it all bestunk :
> O had but then some brave Signor
> Brought her to me I waited for,
>   in shiting !

I would have cleft her watergap,
And join'd it close to my flipflap,
Whilset she had with her fingers guarded
My foule Nockandrow, all bemerded
in shiting.

Now say that I can do nothing, by the Merdi, they are not of my making, but I heard them of this good old grandam, that you see here, and ever since have retained them in the budget of my memory.

Let us return to our purpose, (said Grangousier). What, (said Gargantua), to skite ? No, (said Grangousier), but to wipe our taile ; But, (said Gargantua), will not you be content to pay a punchion of Britton-wine, if I do not blank and gravel you in this matter, and put you to a nonplus ? Yes, truly (said Grangousier).

There is no need of wiping ones taile (said Gargantua), but when it is foule ; foule it cannot be unlesse one have been a skiting ; skite then we must before we wipe our tailes. O my pretty little waggish boy (said Grangousier), what an excellent wit thou hast ? I will make thee very shortly proceed Doctor in the jovial quirks of gay learning, and that, by G—, for thou hast more wit than age ; now, I prethie go on in this torche-culatife, or wipe-bummatory discourse, and by my beard I swear, for one puncheon, thou shalt have threescore pipes, I mean of the good Breton wine, not that which grows in Britain, but in the good countrey of Verron. Afterwards I wiped my bum (said Gargantua), with a kerchief, with a pillow, with a pantoufle, with a pouch, with a pannier, but that was a wicked and unpleasant torchecul ; then with a hat, of hats, note, that some are shorne, and others shaggie, some velveted, others covered with taffities, and others with sattin, the best of all these is the shaggie hat, for it makes a very neat abstersion of the fecal matter.

Afterwards I wiped my taile with a hen, with a cock, with a pullet, with a calves skin, with a hare, with a pigeon, with a cormorant, with an Atturneyes bag, with a montero, with a coife, with a faulconers lure ; but, to conclude, I say and main-tain, that of all torcheculs, arsewisps, bumfodders, tail-napkins, bunghole cleansers and wipe-breeches, there is none in the world comparable to the neck of a goose, that is well douned, if you hold her head betwixt your legs ; and beleeve me therein upon mine honour, for you will thereby feele in your nockhole a most wonderful pleasure, both in regard of the softnesse of the said doune, and of the temperate heat of the goose, which is easily communicated to the bum-gut, and the rest of the inwards, insofarre as to come even to the regions of the heart and braines ; And think not, that the felicity of the heroes and demigods in the Elysian fields consisteth either in their Asphodele, Ambrosia, or Nectar, as our old women here used to say ; but in this, (according to my judgment) that they wipe their tailes with the neck of a goose, holding her head betwixt their legs, and such is the opinion of Master John of Scotland, alias Scotus.

CHAPTER XIV

How Gargantua was taught Latine by a Sophister

THE good man Grangousier having heard this discourse, was ravished with admiration, considering the high reach, and marvellous understanding of his sonne Gargantua, and said to his governesses, Philip king of Macedon knew the great wit of his sonne Alexander, by his skilful managing of a horse ; for his horse Bucephalus was so fierce and unruly, that none durst adventure to ride him, after that he had given to his Riders such devillish falls, breaking the neck of this man, the other mans leg, braining one, and putting another out of his jaw-bone. This by Alexander being considered, one day in the hippodrome, (which was a place appointed for the breaking and managing of great horses), he perceived that the fury of the horse proceeded meerly from the feare he had of his own shadow, whereupon getting on his back, he run him against the Sun, so that the shadow fell behinde, and by that meanes tamed the horse, and brought him to his hand : whereby his father, knowing the divine judgement that was in him, caused him most carefully to be instructed by Aristotle, who at that

time was highly renowned above all the philosophers of Greece ;
after the same manner I tell you, that by this only discourse,
which now I have here had before you with my sonne Gargantua,
I know that his understanding doth participate of some divinity,
and that if he be well taught, and have that education which is
fitting, he will attain to a supreme degree of wisdome.   Therefore will I commit him to some learned man, to have him
indoctrinated according to his capacity, and will spare no cost.
Presently they appointed him a great Sophister-Doctor, called
Master Tubal Holophernes, who taught him his A B C so well,
that he could say it by heart backwards ; and about this he
was five yeares and three moneths.   Then read he to him
Donat, Facet, Theodolet, and Alanus *in parabolis :* About this
he was thirteen years, six moneths, and two weeks ; but you
must remark, that in the mean time he did learn to write in
Gottish characters, and that he wrote all his books, for the Art
of printing was not then in use, and did ordinarily carry a great
pen and inkhorne, weighing about seven thousand quintals
(that is, 700,000 pound weight), the penner whereof was as big
and as long, as the great pillars of Enay, and the horne was
hanging to it in great iron chaines, it being of the widenesse of
a tun of merchand ware.   After that he read unto him the
book *de modis significandi*, with the Commentaries of Hurtbise,
of Fasquin, of Tropifeu, of Gualhaut, of Jhon Calf, of Billonio,
of Berlinguandus, and a rabble of others, and herein he spent
more than eighteen yeares and eleven monethes, and was so
well versed in it, that to try masteries in School disputes with
his condisciples, he would recite it by heart backwards and
did sometimes prove on his fingers ends to his mother, *quod de
modis significandi non erat scientia.*   Then did he reade to him
the compost, for knowing the age of the Moon, the seasons of the
year, and tides of the sea, on which he spent sixteen yeares and
two moneths, and that justly at the time that his said Præceptor
died of the French Pox, which was in the yeare one thousand
foure hundred and twenty.   Afterwards he got an old coughing fellow to teach him, named Master Jobelin Bride, or muzled
doult, who read unto him Hugotio, Flebard, Grecisme, the
doctrinal, the parts, the *quid est*, the *supplementum*, Marmotretus *De moribus in mensa servandis*, Seneca *de quatuor
virtutibus cardinalibus*, Passavantus *cum commentar :* and *dormi
securè* for the holydays, and some other of such like mealie
stuffe, by reading whereof he became as wise as any we ever
since baked in an Oven.

MASTER JOBELIN BRIDE

48

CHAPTER XV

How Gargantua was put under other Schoolmasters

AT the last his father perceived, that indeed he studied hard, and that although he spent all his time in it, did neverthelesse profit nothing, but which is worse, grew thereby foolish, simple, doted and blockish, whereof making a heavie regret to Don Philip of Marays, Viceroy or depute King of Papeligosse, he found that it were better for him to learne nothing at all, then to be taught such like books, under such Schoolmasters, because their knowledge was nothing but brutishnesse, and their wisdome but blunt foppish toyes, serving only to bastardize good and noble spirits, and to corrupt all the flower of youth. That it is so, take, (said he), any young boy of this time, who hath only studied two yeares, if he have not a better judgement, a better discourse, and that expressed in better termes then your sonne, with a compleater carriage and civility to all manner of persons, account me for ever hereafter a very clounch, and bacon-slicer of Brene. This pleased Grangousier very well, and he commanded that it should be done. At night at supper, the said Des Marays brought in a young page of his, of Vilie-gouges, called Eudemon so neat, so trim, so handsom in his apparel, so spruce, with his haire in so good order, and so sweet and comely in his behaviour, that he had the resemblance of a little Angel more then of a humane creature. Then he said to Grangousier, Do you see this young boy ? he is not as yet twelve yeares old ; let us try, (if it please you), what difference there is betwixt the knowledge of the doting Mateologians of old time, and the young lads that are now. The trial pleased Grangousier, and he commanded the Page to begin. Then Eudemon, asking leave of the Vice-King his master so to do, with his cap in his hand, a clear and open countenance, beautiful and ruddie lips, his eyes steadie, and his looks fixed upon Gargantua, with a youthful modesty ; standing up streight on his feet, began very gracefully to commend him ; first for his vertue and good manners ; secondly for his knowledge ; thirdly for his nobility ; fourthly for his bodily accomplishments : and, in the fifth place, most sweetly exhorted him to reverence his father with all due observancy, who was so careful to have him well brought up. In the end he prayed him, that he would vouchsafe to admit of him amongst the least of his servants ; for other favour at that time desired he none of heaven, but that he might do him some grateful and acceptable service ; all this was by him delivered with such proper gestures, such distinct pronunciation, so pleasant a delivery, in such exquisite fine termes, and so good Latine, that he seemed rather a Gracchus, a Cicero, an Æmilius of the time past, then a youth of this age : but all the countenance that Gargantua kept was, that he fell to crying like a Cow, and cast down his face, hiding it with his cap, nor could they possibly draw one word from him, no more then a fart from a dead Asse ; whereat his father was so grievously vexed, that he would have killed Master Jobelin, but the said Des Marays withheld him from it by faire persuasions, so that at length he pacified his wrath. Then Grangousier commanded he should be payed his wages, that they should whittle him up soundly, like a Sophister with good drink, and then give him leave to go all the devils in hell : at least (said he), to day, shall it not cost his hoste much, if by chance he should die as drunk as a Suitser. Master Jobelin being gone out of the house, Grangousier consulted with the Viceroy what School-master they should choose for him, and it was betwixt them resolved, that Ponocrates, the tutor of Eudemon, should have the charge, and that they should go altogether to Paris, to know what was the study of the young men of France at that time.

" Comme un Anglais."—Rabelais.

CHAPTER XVI

How Gargantua was sent to Paris, and of the huge great Mare that he rode on ; how she destroyed the Ox-flies of the Beauce

IN the same season Fayoles, the fourth King of Numidia, sent out of the countrey of Africk to Grangousier, the most hideously great Mare that ever was seen, and of the strangest forme, for you know well enough how it is said, that Africk always is productive of some new thing : she was as big as six elephants, and had her feet cloven into fingers, like Julius Cæsars horse, with slouch-hanging eares, like the goats in Languedoc, and a little horne on her buttock, she was of a burnt sorel hue, with a little mixture of daple gray spots, but above all she had a horrible taile ; for it was little more or lesse, then every whit as great as the Steeple-pillar of St Mark beside Langes : and squared as that is, with tuffs, and ennicroches or haire-plaits wrought within one another, no otherwise then as the beards are upon the eares of corne.

If you wonder at this, wonder rather at the tails of the Scythian Rams, which weighed above thirty pounds each, and of the Surian sheep, who need, (if Tenaud say true), a little cart at their heeles to beare up their taile, it is so long and heavy You female Lechers in the plaine countreys have no such tailes. And she was brought by sea in three Carricks and a Brigantine unto the harbour of Olone in Thalmondois.   When Grangousier saw her, Here is, (said he), what is fit to carry my sonne to Paris. So now, in the name of God, all will be well, he will in times coming be a great Scholar, if it were not (my masters), for the beasts, we should live like Clerks : The next morning (after they had drunk, you must understand) they took their journey ; Gargantua, his Pedagogue Ponocrates, and his traine, and with them Eudemon the young Page, and because the weather was faire and temperate, his father caused to be made for him a paire of dun boots, Babin calls them buskins : Thus did they merrily passe their time in travelling on their high way, always making good chear, and were very pleasant till they came a little above Orleans, in which place there was a forrest of five and thirty leagues long, and seventeen in breadth, or thereabouts. This forrest was most horribly fertile and copious in dorflies, hornets and wasps, so that it was a very Purgatory for the poor mares, asses and horses : But Gargantuas mare did avenge herself handsomly of all the outrages therein committed upon beasts of her kinde, and that by a trick whereof they had no suspicion ; for as soon as ever they were entred into the said forest, and that the wasps had given the assault, she drew out and unsheathed her taile, and therewith skirmishing, did so sweep them, that she overthrew all the wood alongst and athwart, here and there, this way and that way, longwise and sidewise, over and under, and felled every where the wood with as much ease, as a mower doth the grasse, in such sort that never since hath there been there, neither wood, nor Dorflies : for all the countrey was thereby reduced to a plain champian-field : which Gargantua took great pleasure to behold, and said to his company no more but this, *Je trouve beau ce*, I finde this pretty ; whereupon that countrey hath been ever since that time called Beauce : but all the breakfast the mare got that day, was but a little yawning and gaping, in memory whereof the Gentlemen of Beauce, do as yet to this day break their fast with gaping, which they finde to be very good, and do spit the better for it ; at last they came to Paris, where Gargantua refresh't himself two or three dayes, making very merry with his folkes, and enquiring what men of learning there were then in the city, and what wine they drunk there.

THE MOST HIDEOUSLY GREAT MARE

53

CHAPTER XVII

*How Gargantua payed his welcome to the Parisians, and how he
took away the great Bells of our Ladies Church*

SOME few dayes after that they had refresh't themselves, he
went to see the city, and was beheld of every body with great
admiration ; for the People of Paris are so sottish, so badot, so
foolish and fond by nature, that a jugler, a carrier of indulgences,
a sumpter-horse, or mule with cymbals, or tinkling bells, a
blinde fidler in the middle of a crosse lane, shall draw a greater
confluence of people together, then an Evangelical Preacher :
and they prest so hard upon him, that he was constrained to
rest himself upon the towers of our Ladies Church ; at which
place, seeing so many about him, he said with a loud voice, I
beleeve that these buzzards will have me to pay them here my
welcom hither, and my *Proficiat* ; it is but good reason, I will
now give them their wine, but it shall be only in sport ; Then
smiling, he untied his faire Braguette, and drawing out his
mentul into the open aire, he so bitterly all-to-bepist them, that
he drowned two hundred and sixty thousand, foure hundred
and eighteen, besides the women and little children : some,
neverthelesse, of the company escaped this piss-flood by meer
speed of foot, who when they were at the higher end of the
university, sweating, coughing, spitting, and out of breath, they
began to swear and curse, some in good hot earnest, and others
in jest, Carimari, carimari : golynoly, golynoly : by my sweet
Sanctesse, we are wash't in sport, a sport truly to laugh at, in
French, *Par ris*, for which that city hath been ever since called
Paris, whose name formerly was Leucotia, (as Strabo testifieth,
lib. quarto) from the Greek word λευκοτης, whitenesse, because
of the white thighs of the Ladies of that place, and forasmuch
as at this imposition of a new name, all the people that were
there, swore every one by the Sancts of his parish, the Parisians,
which are patch'd up of all nations, and all pieces of countreyes,
are by nature both good Jurers, and good Jurists, and somewhat overweening ; where upon Joanninus de Barrauco *libro
de copiositate reverentiarum*, thinks that they are called
Parisians, from the Greek word παρρησία, which signifies

boldnesse and liberty in speech. This done, he considered the great bells, which were in the said tours, and made them sound very harmoniously, which, whilest he was doing, it came into his minde, that they would serve very well for tingling Tantans, and ringing Campanels, to hang about his mares neck, when she should be sent back to his father, (as he intended to do) loaded with Brie cheese, and fresh herring; and indeed he forthwith carried them to his lodging. In the mean while there came a master begar of the Fryers of S. Anthonie, to demand in his canting way the usual benevolence of some hoggish stuffe, who, that he might be heard afar off, and to make the bacon, he was in quest of, shake in the very chimneys, made account to filch them away privily. Neverthelesse, he left them behinde very honestly, not for that they were too hot, but that they were somewhat too heavy for his carriage. This was not he of Bourg, for he was too good a friend of mine. All the city was risen up in sedition, they being, (as you know,) upon any slight occasion, so ready to uproars and insurrections, that forreign nations wonder at the patience of the Kings of France, who do not by good justice restrain them from such tumultuous courses, seeing the manifold inconveniences which thence arise from day to day. Would to God I knew the shop, wherein are forged these divisions, and factious combinations, that I might bring them to light in the confraternities of my parish ! Beleeve for a truth, that the place wherein the people gathered together, were thus sulfured, hopurymated, moiled and bepist, was called Nesle, where then was, (but now is no more,) the Oracle of Leacotia : There was the case proposed, and the inconvenience shewed of the transporting of the bells : after they had well ergoted pro and con, they concluded in Baralipton, that they should send the oldest and most sufficient of the facultie unto Gargantua, to signifie unto him the great and horrible prejudice they sustain by the want of those bells ; and notwithstanding the good reasons given in by some of the University, why this charge was fitter for an Oratour then a Sophister, there was chosen for this purpose our Master Janotus de Bragmardo.

CHAPTER XVIII

How Janotus de Bragmardo was sent to Gargantua,
to recover the great Bells

MASTER JANOTUS with his haire cut round like a dish *a la*
cæsarine, in his most antick accoustrement Liripipionated with
a graduates hood, and, having sufficiently antidoted his stomach
with Ovenmarmalades, that is, bread and holy water of the
Cellar, transported himself to the lodging of Gargantua, driving
before him three red muzled beadles, and dragging after him
five or six artlesse masters, all throughly bedaggled with the
mire of the streets. At their entry Ponocrates met them, who
was afraid, seeing them so disguised, and thought they had
been some maskers out of their wits, which moved him to
enquire of one of the said artlesse masters of the company, what
this mummery meant ? it was answered him, that they desired
to have their bells restored to them. As soon as Ponocrates
heard that, he ran in all haste to carry the newes unto Gargantua, that he might be ready to answer them, and speedily
resolve what was to be done. Gargantua being advertised
hereof, called apart his Schoolmaster Ponocrates, Philotimus
Steward of his house, Gymnastes his Esquire, and Eudemon,
and very summarily conferred with them, both of what he
should do, and what answer he should give. They were all of
opinion that they should bring them unto the goblet-office,
which is the Buttery, and there make them drink like Roysters,
and line their jackets soundly : and that this cougher might
not be puft up with vain-glory, by thinking the bells were
restored at his request, they sent, (whilest he was chopining
and plying the pot,) for the Major of the City, the Rector of the
facultie, and the Vicar of the Church, unto whom they resolved
to deliver the bells, before the Sophister had propounded his
commission ; after that, in their hearing, he should pronounce
his gallant Oration, which was done, and they being come,
the Sophister was brought into a full hall, and began as followeth, in coughing.

CHAPTER XIX

The Oration of Master Janotus de Bragmardo, for recovery of the Bells

HEM, hem, Gudday, Sirs, Gudday *et vobis*, my masters, it were but reason that you should restore to us our bells ; for we have great need of them. Hem, hem, aihfuhash, we have often-times heretofore refused good money for them of those of London in Cahors, yea and of those of Bourdeaux in Brie, who would have bought them for the substantifick quality of the elementary complexion, which is intronificated in the terrestreity of their quidditative nature, to extraneize the blasting mists, and whirlwindes upon our Vines ; indeed not ours, but these round about us ; for if we lose the piot and liquour of the grape, we lose all both sense and law. If you restore them unto us at my request, I shall gaine by it six basketfuls of sauciges, and a fine paire of breeches, which will do my legs a great deal of good, or else they will not keep their promise to me. Ho by gob, *domine*, a paire of breeches is good, *et vir sapiens non abhorrebit eam.* Ha, ha, a paire of breeches is not so easily got, I have experience of it my self. Consider, *Domine*, I have been these eighteen dayes in matagrabolising this brave speech, *Reddite quæ sunt Cæsaris, Cæsari, et quæ sunt Dei, Deo. Ibi jacet lepus*, by my faith, *Domine*, if you will sup with me in *cameris*, by cox body, *charitatis, nos faciemus bonum cherubin ; ego occidit unum purcum, et ego habet bonum vino* : but of good wine we cannot make bad Latine. Well, *de parte Dei datè nobis bellas nostras* ; Hold, I give you in the name of the facultie a *Sermones de utino*, that *utinam* you would give us our bells. *Vultis etiam pardonos ? Per diem vos habebitis, et nihil payabitis.* O Sir *Domine, bellagivaminor nobis* ; verily, *est bonum vobis.* They are useful to every body, if they fit your mare well, so do they do our facultie ; *quæ comparata est jumentis insipientibus, et similis facta est eis, Psalmo nescio quo* ; yet did I quote it in my note-book, *et est unum bonum* Achilles, a good defending argument, hem, hem, hem, haikhash ; for I prove unto you that you should give me them. *Ego sic argumentor, Omnis bella bellabilis in Bellerio bellando, bellans bellative, bellare facit, bellabiliter bellantes : parisius habet*

57

bellas ; ergo gluc. Ha, ha, ha, this is spoken to some purpose ; it is *in tertio primæ,* in *Darii,* or elsewhere. By my soul, I have seen the time that I could play the devil in arguing, but now I am much failed, and henceforward want nothing but a cup of good wine, a good bed, my back to the fire, my belly to the table, and a good deep dish. Hei *domine,* I beseech you, *in nomine Patris, Filii, et Spiritûs sancti, Amen,* to restore unto us our bells : and God keep you from evil, and our Lady from health ; *qui vivit et regnat per omnia secula seculorum. Amen.* Hem, hashchehhawksash, qzrchremhemhash, *verum enim vero quandoquidem, dubio procul, ædepol, quoniam, ità certè, medius fidius* ; A Town without bells is like a blinde man without a staffe, an Asse without a crupper, and a Cow without Cymbals ; therefore be assured, until you have restored them unto us, we will never leave crying after you, like a blinde man that hath lost his staffe, braying like an Asse without a crupper, and making a noise like a Cow without Cymbals : A certain Latinisator, dwelling near the Hospital, said since, producing the authority of one Taponnus, I lie, it was Pontanus the secular Poet, who wish't those bells had been made of feathers, and the clapper of a foxtail, to the end they might have begot a chronicle in the bowels of his braine, when he was about the composing of his carmini-formal lines : but nac petetin petetac tic torche Lorgne, or Rot kipipur kipipot put pantse malf. He was declared an Heretick ; We make them as of wax. And no more saith the deponent. *Valete et plaudite. Calepinus recensui.*

CHAPTER XX

How the Sophister carried away his Cloth, and how he had a Suite in Law against the other Masters

THE Sophister had no sooner ended, but Ponocrates and Eudemon burst out into a laughing so heartily, that they had almost split with it, and given up the ghost, in rendering their souls to God : even just as Crassus did, seeing a lubberly Asse eate thistles ; and as Philemon, who, for seeing an Asse eat those figs which were provided for his own dinner, died with force of laughing ; together with them Master Janotus fell a laughing, too as fast as he could, in which mood of laughing they continued so long, that their eyes did water by the vehement concussion of the substance of the braine, by which these lachrymal humidities, being prest out, glided through the optick nerves, and so to the full represented Democritus Heraclitising, and Heraclitus Democritising.

When they had done laughing, Gargantua consulted with the prime of his retinue, what should be done. There Ponocrates was of opinion, that they should make this faire Orator drink again, and seeing he had shewed them more pastime, and made them laugh more then a natural soule could have done, that they should give him ten baskets full of sauciges, mentioned in his pleasant speech, with a paire of hose, three hundred great billets of logwood, five and twenty hogsheads of wine, a good large down-bed, and a deep capacious dish, which he said were necessary for his old age; All this was done as they did appoint : only Gargantua, doubting that they could not quickly finde out breeches fit for his wearing, because he knew not what fashion would best become the said Orator, whether the martingal fashion of breeches, wherein is a spunghole with a draw-bridge, for the more easie caguing : or the fashion of the Marriners, for the greater solace and comfort of his kidneyes : or that of the Switsers, which keeps warm the bedondaine or belly-tabret : or round breeches with streat cannions, having in the seat a piece like a Cods taile ; all which considered for feare of over-heating his reines, he caused to be given him seven elles of white cloth for the linings. The wood was carried by the Porters, the Masters of Arts carried the sauciges and the dishes, and Master Janotus himself would carry the cloth. One of the said Masters, (called Jesse Bandouille,) shewed him that it was not seemly nor decent for one of his condition to do so, and that therefore he should deliver it to one of them : Ha, said Janotus, Baudet, Baudet, or, Blockhead, Blockhead, thou dost not conclude *in modo et figura* ; for loe, to this end serve the suppositions *et parva Logicalia* : *pannus, pro quo supponit?* *Confusè.* (said Bandouille,) *et distributivè.* I do not ask thee, (said Janotus,) Blockhead, *quomodo supponit,* but *pro quo?* It is, Blockhead, *pro tibiis meis,* and therefore I will carry it, *Egomet sicut suppositum portat appositum* ; so did he carry it away very close and covertly, as Patelin, the Buffoon, did his cloth. The best was, that when this cougher, in a full act or assembly held at the Mathurins, had with great confidence required his breeches and sauciges, and that they were flatly denied him, because he had them of Gargantua, according to the informations thereupon made, he shewed them that this was gratis, and out of his liberality, by which they were not in any sort quit of their promises. Notwithstanding this, it was answered him, that he should be content with reason, without expectation of any other bribe there. Reason, (said Janotus) we use none of it here, unluckie traitors, you are not worth the hanging : the earth beareth not more arrant Villains then you are, I know it well enough ; Halt not before the lame ; I have practised wickednesse with you : By Gods rattle I will inform the king of the enormous abuses that are forged here, and carried underhand by you, and let me be a Leper, if he do not burn you alive like Sodomites, Traitors, Hereticks and Seducers, enemies to God and vertue.

Upon these words they framed articles against him : he on the other side warned them to appear. In summe, the Processe was retained by the Court, and is there as yet. Hereupon the Magisters made a vow, never to decrott themselves in rubbing off the dirt of either their shoes or clothes : Master Janotus with his Adherents vowed never to blow or snuffe their noses, until judgement were given by a definitive sentence ; by these vows do they continue unto this time both dirty and snottie ; for the Court hath not garbeled, sifted, and fully looked into all the pieces as yet. The judgment or decree shall be given out and pronounced at the next Greek Calends, that is, never : as you know that they do more then nature, and contrary to their own articles : The articles of Paris maintain, that to God alone belongs infinite, and nature produceth nothing that is immortal ; for she putteth an end and period to all things by her engendered, according to the saying, *Omnia orta cadunt, etc.* But these thick mist-swallowers make the suits in law depending before them both infinite and immortal ; in doing whereof, they have given occasion to, and verified the saying of Chilo the Lacedemonian, consecrated to the Oracle at Delphos, that misery is the inseparable companion of law-debates ; and that pleaders are miserable ; for sooner shall they attain to the end of their lives, then to the final decision of their pretended rights

CHAPTER XXI

The study of Gargantua, according to the Discipline of his Schoolmasters the Sophisters

THE first day being thus spent, and the bells put up again in their own place, the Citizens of Paris, in acknowledgement of this courtesie, offered to maintain and feed his Mare as long as he pleased, which Gargantua took in good part, and they sent her to graze in the forrest of Biere. I think she is not there now. This done, he with all his heart submitted his study to the discretion of Ponocrates ; who for the beginning appointed that he should do as he was accustomed, to the end he might understand by what meanes, in so long time, his old Masters had made him so sottish and ignorant. He disposed therefore of his time in such fashion, that ordinarily he did awake betwixt eight and nine a clock, whether it was day or not, (for so had his ancient governours ordained,) alledging that which David saith *Vanum est vobis ante lucem surgere.* Then did he tumble and tosse, wag his legs, and wallow in the bed sometime, the better to stirre up, and rouse his vital spirits, and apparelled himself according to the season : but willingly he would weare a great long gown of thick freeze, furred with fox-skins. Afterwards he combed his head with an Alman combe, which is the foure fingers and the thumb ; for his Præceptor said, that to comb himself otherwayes, to wash and make himself neat, was to lose time in this world. Then he dung'd, pist, spued, belched, cracked, yawned, spitted, coughed, yexed, sneezed and snotted himself like an Arch-deacon ; and, to suppresse the dew and bad aire, went to breakfast, having some good fried tripes, faire rashers on the coales, excellent gamons of bacon, store of fine minced meat, and a great deal of sippet brewis, made up of the fat of the beef-pot, laid upon bread, cheese, and chop't parsley strewed together. Ponocrates shewed him, that he ought not to eat so soon after rising out of his bed, unlesse he had performed some exercise beforehand : Gargantua answered, What ! have not I sufficiently well exercised my self ? I have wallowed and rolled my self six or seven turns in my bed, before I rose : is not that enough ? Pope Alexander did so, by the advice of a Jew his physician, and lived till his dying day in despite of his enemies. My first Masters have used me to it, saying that to breakfast made a good memory, and therefore they drank first. I am very well after it, and dine but the better : and Master Tubal, (who was the first Licentiat at Paris,) told me, that it was not enough to run apace, but to set forth betimes ; so doth not the total welfare of our humanity depend upon perpetual drinking in a rible rable, like ducks, but on drinking early in the morning : *unde versus,*

> To rise betimes is no good houre,
> To drink betimes is better sure.

After that he had throughly broke his fast, he went to Church, and they carried to him in a great basket, a huge impantoufled or thick-covered breviary, weighing what in grease, clasps, parchment and cover, little more or lesse then eleven hundred and six pounds. There he heard six and twenty or thirty Masses : This while, to the same place came his orison-mutterer impaletocked, or lap't up about the chin, like a tufted whoop, and his breath pretty well antidoted with store of the vine-tree-sirrup : with him he mumbled all his Kiriels, and dunsical breborions, which he so curiously thumbed and fingered, that there fell not so much as one graine to the ground ; as he went from the Church, they brought him upon a Dray drawn with oxen, a confused heap of Patenotres and Aves of Sante Claude, every one of them being of the bignesse of a hat-block ; and thus walking through the cloysters, galleries or garden, he said more in turning them over, then sixteen Hermites would have done. Then did he study some paltry half-houre with his eyes fixed upon his book ; but, (as the Comick saith,) his minde was in the kitchin. Pissing then a full Urinal, he sate down at table ; and because he was naturally flegmatick, he began his meale with some dozens of gammons, dried neat tongues, hard rowes of mullet called Botargos, Andouilles or sauciges, and such other forerunners of wine ; in the mean while, foure of his folks did cast into his mouth one after another continually mustard by whole shovels full. Immediately after that, he drank a horrible draught of white wine for the ease of his kidneys. When that was done he ate according to the season meat agreeable to his appetite and then left off eating when his belly began to strout, and was like to crack for fulnesse ; as for his drinking, he had in that neither end nor rule ; for he was wont to say, that the limits and bounds of drinking were, when the cork of the shoes of him that drinketh swelleth up half a foot high.

CHAPTER XXII

The Games of Gargantua

THEN blockishly mumbling with a set on countenance a piece of scurvie grace, he wash't his hands in fresh wine, pick't his teeth with the foot of a hog, and talked jovially with his Attendants : then the Carpet being spred, they brought plenty of cardes, many dice, with great store and abundance of checkers and chesse-boards.

There he played

At Flusse.
At Primero.
At the beast.
At the rifle.
At trump.
At the prick and spare not
At the hundred.
At the peenie.
At the unfortunate woman.
At the fib.
At the passe ten.
At one and thirtie.
At post and paire, or even and sequence.
At three hundred.
At the unluckie man.
At the last couple in hell.
At the hock.
At the surlie.
At the lanskenet.
At the cukoe.
At puffe, or let him speak that hath it.
At take nothing and throw out.

At the marriage.
At the frolick or jack daw.
At the opinion.
At who doth the one, doth the other.
At the sequences.
At the ivory bundles.
At the tarots.
At losing load him.
At he's gulled and *esto*.
At the torture.
At the handruf.
At the click.
At honours.
At love.
At the chesse.
At Reynold the fox.
At the squares.
At the cowes.
At the lottery.
At the chance or mum-chance.
At three dice or maniest bleaks.
At the tables.

At nivinivinack.
At the lurch.
At doublets or queens-game.
At the failie.
At the French tictac.
At the long tables or fer-keering.
At feldown.
At Tods body.
At needs must.
At the dames or draughts.
At bob and mow.
At primus secundus.
At Mark-knife.
At the keyes.
At span-counter.
At even or odd.
At crosse or pile.
At bal and huckle-bones.
At ivory balls.
At the billiards.
At bob and hit.
At the owle.
At the charming of the hare.
At pull yet a little.
At trudgepig.
At the magatapies.
At the horne.
At the flower'd or shrove-tide oxe.
At the madge-owlet.
At pinch without laugh-ing.
At prickle me tickle me.
At the unshoing of the Asse.
At the cocksesse.
At hari hohi.
At I set me down.
At earle beardie.
At the old mode.

At draw the spit.
At put out.
At gossip lend me your sack.
At the ramcod ball.
At thrust out the harlot.
At Marseil figs.
At nicknamrie.
At stick and hole.
At boke or him, or flaying the fox.
At the branching it.
At trill madam, or graple my Lady.
At the cat selling.
At blow the coale.
At the rewedding.
At the quick and dead judge.
At unoven the iron.
At the false clown.
At the flints, or at the nine stones.
At to the crutch hulch back.
At the Sanct is found.
At hinch, pinch and laugh not.
At the leek.
At Bumdockdousse.
At the loose gig.
At the hoop.
At the sow.
At belly to belly.
At the dales or straths
At the twigs.
At the quoits.
At I'm for that.
At tilt at weekie.
At nine pins.
At the cock quintin.
At tip and hurle.
At the flat bowles.

At the veere and tourn.
At rogue and ruffian.
At bumbatch touch.
At the mysterious trough.
At the short bowles.
At the daple gray.
At cock and crank it.
At break-pot.
At my desire.
At twirlie whirlietrill.
At the rush bundles.
At the short staffe.
At the whirling gigge.
At hide and seek, or are you all hid.
At the picket.
At the blank.
At the pilfrers.
At the caveson.
At prison barres.
At have at the nuts.
At cherrie-pit.
At rub and rice.
At whip-top.
At the casting top.
At the hobgoblins.
At the O wonderful.
At the soilie smutchie.
At fast and loose.
At scutchbreech.
At the broom-beesome.
At St. Cosme, I come to adore thee.
At the lustie brown boy.
At I take you napping.
At faire and softly passeth lent.
At the forked oak.
At trusse.
At the wolfes taile.
At bum to busse, or nose in breech

At Geordie give me my lance.
At swaggie, waggie or shoggieshou.
At stook and rook, sheare, and threave.
At the birch.
At the musse.
At the dillie dilli darling.
At oxe moudie.
At purpose in purpose.
At nine lesse.
At blinde-man-buffe.
At the fallen bridges.
At bridled nick.
At the white at buts.
At thwack swinge him.
At apple, peare, plum.
At mumgi.
At the toad.
At cricket.
At the pounding stick.
At jack and the box.
At the queens.
At the trades.
At heads and points.
At the vine-tree hug.
At black be thy fall.
At ho the distaffe.
At Joane Thomson.
At the boulting cloth.
At the oats seed.
At greedie glutton.
At the morish dance.
At feebie.
At the whole frisk and gambole.
At battabum, or riding of the wilde mare.
At Hinde the Plowman.
At the good mawkin.
At the dead beast.
At climbe the ladder Billie.

At the dying hog.
At the salt doup.
At the pretty pigeon.
At barley break.
At the bavine.
At the bush leap.
At crossing.
At bo-peep.
At the hardit arsepursie.
At the harrowers nest.
At forward hey.
At the fig.
At gunshot crack.

At mustard peel.
At the gome.
At the relapse.
At jog breech, or prick him forward.
At knockpate.
At the Cornish cough.
At the crane-dance.
At slash and cut.
At bobbing, or the flirt on the nose.
At the larks.
At filipping.

After he had thus well played, reveled, past and spent his time, it was thought fit to drink a little, and that was eleven glassefuls the man, and immediately after making good cheer again, he would stretch himself upon a faire bench, or a good large bed, and there sleep two or three houres together, without thinking or speaking any hurt. After he was awakened he would shake his eares a little. In the mean time they brought him fresh wine, there he drank better than ever. Ponocrates shewed him, that it was an ill diet to drink so after sleeping. It is, (answered Gargantua,) the very life of the Patriarchs and holy Fathers; for naturally I sleepe salt, and my sleep hath been to me in stead of so many gamons of bacon. Then began he to study a little, and out came the patenotres or rosary of beads; which the better and more formally to dispatch, he got up on an old mule, which had served nine Kings, and so mumbling with his mouth, nodding and dodling his head, would go see a coney ferretted or caught in a ginne; At his return he went into the Kitchin, to know what roste meat was on the spit, and what otherwayes was to be drest for supper: and supped very well upon my conscience: and commonly did invite some of his neighbours that were good drinkers, with whom carousing and drinking merrily, they told stories of all sorts from the old to the new. Amongst others, he had for domesticks the Lords of Fou, of Gourville, of Griniot, and of Marigny. After supper were brought in upon the place the faire wooden Gospels, and the books of the foure Kings, that is to say, many paires of tables and cardes: or the faire flusse, one, two, three: or at all to make short work: or else they went to see the wenches thereabouts, with little small banquets, intermixed with collations and reer-Suppers. Then did he sleep without un-brideling, until eight a clock in the next morning.

CHAPTER XXIII

How Gargantua was instructed by Ponocrates, and in such sort disciplinated, that he lost not one hour of the Day

WHEN Ponocrates knew Gargantuas vicious manner of living, he resolved to bring him up in another kinde ; but for a while he bore with him, considering that nature cannot endure a sudden change, without great violence. Therefore to begin his work the better, he requested a learned Physician of that time, called Master Theodorus, seriously to perpend, (if it were possible,) how to bring Gargantua unto a better course ; the said physician purged him canonically with Anticyrian ellebore, by which medicine he cleansed all the alteration, and perverse habitude of his braine. By this meanes also Ponocrates made him forget all that he had learned under his ancient Præceptors, as Timotheus did to his disciples, who had been instructed under other Musicians. To do this the better, they brought him into the company of learned men, which were there, in whose imitation he had a great desire and affection to study otherwayes, and to improve his parts. Afterwards he put himself into such a road and way of studying, that he lost not any one houre in the day, but employed all his time in learning, and honest knowledge. Gargantua awaked them about foure a clock in the morning ; whilest they were in rubbing of him, there was read unto him some chapter of the holy Scripture aloud and clearly, with a pronunciation fit for the matter, and hereunto was appointed a young page borne in Basche, named Anagnostes. According to the purpose and argument of that lesson, he oftentimes gave himself to worship, adore, pray, and send up his supplications to that good God, whose Word did shew his majesty and marvellous judgement. Then went he into the secret places to make excretion of his natural digestions : there his master repeated what had been read, expounding unto him she most obscure and difficult points ; in returning, they considered the face of the sky, if it was such as they had observed it the night before, and into what signes the Sun was entering, as also the Moon for that day. This done, he was apparelled, combed, curled, trimmed and perfumed, during which time they repeated to him the lessons of the day before : he himself said them by heart, and upon them would ground some practical cases concerning the estate of man, which he would prosecute sometimes two or three houres, but ordinarily they ceased as soon as he was fully clothed. Then for three good houres he had a lecture read unto him. This done, they went forth, still conferring of the substance of the lecture, either unto a field near the University called the Brack, or unto the medowes where they played at the ball, the long-tennis, and at the Piletrigone, (which is a play wherein we throw a triangular piece of iron at a ring, to pass it,) most gallantly exercising their bodies, as formerly they had done their mindes. All their play was but in liberty, for they left off when they pleased, and that was commonly when they did sweat over all their body, or were otherwayes weary. Then were they very well wiped and rubbed, shifted their shirts, and, walking soberly, went to see if dinner was ready. Whilest they stayed for that, they did clearly and eloquently pronounce some sentences that they had retained of the lecture. In the mean time Master Appetite came, and then very orderly sate they down at table ; at the beginning of the meale, there was read some pleasant history of the warlike actions of former times, until he had taken a glasse of wine. Then, (if they thought good,) they continued reading, or began to discourse merrily together; speaking first of the vertue, propriety, efficacy and nature of all that was served in at the table; of bread, of wine, of water, of salt, of fleshes, fishes, fruits, herbs, roots, and of their dressing, by meanes whereof, he learned in a little time all the passages competent for this, that were to be found in Plinie, Athenæus, Dioscorides, Julius Pollux, Galen, Porphirie, Oppian, Polybius, Heliodore, Aristotle, Elian, and others. Whilest they talked of these things, many times to be the more certain, they caused the very books to be brought to the table, and so well and perfectly did he in his memory retain the things above said, that in that time there was not a Physician that knew half so much as he did. Afterwards they conferred of the lessons read in the morning, and ending their repast with some conserve or marmalade of quinces : he pick't his teeth with mastick tooth-pickers, wash't his hands and eyes with faire fresh water, and gave thanks unto God in some fine Canticks, made in praise of the divine bounty and munificence. This done, they brought in cards, not to play but to learn a thousand pretty tricks, and new inventions, which were all grounded upon Arithmetick : by this means he fell in love with that numerical science, and every day after dinner and supper he past his time in it as pleasantly, as he was wont to do at cardes and dice : so that at last he understood so well both the Theory and Practical part thereof, that Tunstal the Englishman, who had written very largely of that purpose, confessed that verily in comparison of him he had no skill at all. And not only in that, but in the other Mathematical Sciences, as Geometrie, Astronomie, Musick, etc. For in waiting on the concoction, and attending the digestion of his food, they made a thousand pretty instruments and Geometrical figures, and did in some measure practise the Astronomical canons.

After this they recreated themselves with singing musically, in foure or five parts, or upon a set theme or ground at random, as it best pleased them ; in matter of musical instruments, he learned to play upon the Lute, the Virginals, the Harp, the Allman Flute with nine holes, the Viol, and the Sackbut. This houre thus spent, and digestion finished, he did purge his body of natural excrements then betook himself to his principal study for three houres together, or more, as well to repeat his matutinal lectures, as to proceed in the book wherein he was, as also to write handsomly, to draw and forme the Antick and Romane letters. This being done they went out of their house and with them a young gentleman of Touraine, named the Esquire Gymnast, who taught him the Art of riding; changing then his clothes, he rode a Naples courser, a Dutch roussin, a Spanish gennet, a barbed or trapped steed. then a light fleet horse, unto whom he gave a hundred carieres, made him go the high saults, bounding in the aire, free the ditch with a skip, leap over a stile or pale, turne short in a ring both to the right and left hand. There he broke not his lance; for it is the greatest foolery in the world, to say, I have broken ten lances at tilt or in fight, a Carpenter can do even as much; but it is a glorious and praise-worthy action, with one lance to break and overthrow ten enemies : therefore with a sharp, stiffe, strong and well-steeled lance, would he usually force up a door, pierce a harnesse, beat down a tree, carry away the ring, lift up a cuirasier saddle, with the male-coat and gantlet; all this he did in compleat armes from head to foot. As for the prancing flourishes, and smack-ing popismes, for the better cherishing of the horse, commonly used in riding, none did them better than he. The cavallerize of Ferrara was but as an Ape compared to him. He was singularly skilful in leaping nimbly from one horse to another, without putting foot to ground, and these horses were called desultories : he could likewise from either side, with a lance in his hand, leap on horseback without stirrups, and rule the horse at his pleasure without a bridle, for such things are useful in military engagements. Another day he exercised the battel-axe, which he so dextrously wielded, both in the nimble, strong and smooth management of that weapon, and that in all the feats practiseable by it, that he passed Knight of Armes in the field, and at all Essayes.

Then tost he the pike, played with the two-handed sword, with the back-sword, with the Spanish tuck, the dagger, poiniard, armed, unarmed, with a buckler, with a cloak, with a targuet. Then would he hunt the hart, the roebuck, the Beare, the fallow Deer, the wilde Boare, the Hare, the Phesant, the Partridge and the Bustard. He played at the baloon, and made it bound in the aire, both with fist and foot. He wrestled, ran, jumped, not at three steps and a leap, (called the hops,) nor at clochepied, (called the hares leap,) nor yet at the Almanes ; for, (said Gymnast,) these jumps are for the warres altogether unprofitable, and of no use, but at one leap he would skip over a ditch, spring over a hedge, mount six paces upon a wall, romp and grapple after this fashion up against a window, of the full height of a lance. He did swim in deep waters on his belly, on his back, sidewise, with all his body, with his feet only, with one hand in the air, wherein he held a book, crossing thus the bredth of the river of Seine, without wetting it, and dragged along his cloak with his teeth, as did Julius Cæsar; then with the help of one hand he entred forcibly into a boat, from whence he cast himself again headlong into the water, sounded the depths, hollowed the rocks, and plunged into the pits and gulphs. Then turned he the boat about, governed it, led it swiftly or slowly with the stream and against the stream, stopped it in his course guided it with one hand, and with the other laid hard about him with a huge great Oare, hoised the saile, hied up along the mast by the shrouds, ran upon the edge of the decks, set the compasse in order, tackled the boulins, and steer'd the helme. Coming out of the water, he ran furiously up against a hill, and with the same alacrity and swiftnesse ran down again; he climbed up at trees like a cat, and leaped from the one to the other like a squirrel; he did pull down the great boughes and branches, like another Milo; then with two sharp well-steeled daggers, and two tried bodkins, would he run up by the wall to the very top of a house like a cat; then suddenly came down from the top to the bottom, with such an even composition of members, that by the fall he would catch no harme.

He did cast the dart, throw the barre, put the stone, practise the javelin, the boarspear or partisan, and the halbard; he broke the strongest bowes in drawing, bended against his breast the greatest crosse-bowes of steele, took his aime by the eye with the hand-gun, and shot well, traversed and planted the canon, shot at but-marks, at the papgay from below upwards, or to a height from above downwards, or to a descent; then before him, sidewise, and behinde him, like the Parthians. They tied a cable rope to the top of a high Tower, by one end whereof hanging near the ground, he wrought himself with his hands to the very top: Then upon the same tract came down so sturdily and firme that you could not on a plaine meadow have run with more assurance. They set up a great pole fixed upon two trees, there would he hang by his hands, and with them alone, his feet touching at nothing, would go back and fore along the foresaid rope with so great swiftnesse, that hardly could one overtake him with running; and then to exercise his breast and lungs, he would shout like all the Devils in hell. I heard him once call Eudemon from St. Victors gate to Monmartre. Stentor had never such a voyce at the siege of Troy.

Then for the strengthening of his nerves or sinewes, they made him two great sows of lead, each of them weighing eight thousand and seven hundred kintals, which they called Alteres; those he took up from the ground, in each hand one, then lifted them up over his head, and held them so without stirring three quarters of an hour and more, which was an inimitable force; he fought at Barriers with the stoutest and most vigorous Champions; and when it came to the cope, he stood so sturdily on his feet, that he abandoned himself unto the strongest, in case they could remove him from his place, as Milo was wont to do of old; in whose imitation likewise he held a Pomgranat in his hand, to give it unto him that could take it from him: The time being thus bestowed, and himself rubbed, cleansed, wiped, and refresht with other clothes, he returned fair and softly; and passing througd certain meadows, or other grassie places, beheld the trees and plants, comparing them with what is written of them in the books of the Ancients, such as Theophrast, Dioscorides, Marinus, Plinie, Nicander, Macer, and Galen, and carried home to the house great handfuls of them, whereof a young page called Rizotomos had charge; together with little Mattocks, Pick-axes, Grubbing-hooks, Cabbies, Pruning-knives, and other instruments requisite for herborising. Being come to their lodging, whilest supper was making ready they repeated certain passages of that which hath been read, and sate down at table. Here remark, that his dinner was sober and thrifty, for he did then eat only to prevent the gnawings of his stomack, but his supper was copious and large; for he took then as much as was fit to maintaine and nourish him; which indeed is the true diet prescribed by the Art of good and sound Physick. Although a rabble of logger-headed Physicians, nuzzeled in the brabling shop of Sophisters, counsel the contrary; during that repast was continued the lesson read at dinner as long as they thought good: the rest was spent in good discourse, learned and profitable. After that they had given thanks, he set himself to sing vocally, and play upon harmonious instruments, or otherwayes passed his time at some pretty sports, made with cards or dice, or in practising the feats of Legerdermain, with cups and balls. There they stayed some nights in frolicking thus, and making themselves merrie till it was time to go to bed; and on other nights they would go make visits unto learned men, or to such as had been travellers in strange and remote countreys. When it was full night before they retired themselves, they went unto the most open place of the house to see the face of the sky, and there beheld the comets, if any were, as likewise the figures, situations, aspects, oppositions and conjunctions of the both fixed starres and planets.

Then with his Master did he briefely recapitulate after the manner of the Pythagoreans, that which he had read, seen, learned, done and understood in the whole course of that day.

Then prayed they unto God the Creator, in falling down before him, and strengthening their faith towards him, and glorifying him for his boundlesse bounty, and, giving thanks unto him for the time that was past, they recommended themselves to his divine clemency for the future, which being done, they went to bed, and betook themselves to their repose and rest.

CHAPTER XXIV

How Gargantua spent his Time in rainie Weather

IF it happened that the weather were any thing cloudie, foul and rainie, all the forenoon was employed, as before specified, according to custom, with this difference only, that they had a good clear fire lighted, to correct the distempers of the aire : but after dinner, instead of their wonted exercitations they did abide within, and, by way of Apotherapie, (that is, a making the body healthful by exercise,) did recreate themselves in botteling up of hay, in cleaving and sawing of wood, andin threshing sheaves of corn at the Barn. Then they studied the Art of painting or carving ; or brought into use the antick play of tables, as Leonicus hath written of it, and as our good friend Lascaris playeth at it. In playing they examined the passages of ancient Authors, wherein the said play is mentioned, or any metaphore drawn from it. They went likewise to see the drawing of mettals, or the casting of great ordnance : how the Lapidaries did work, as also the Goldsmiths and Cutters of precious stones : nor did they omit to visit the Alchymists, money-coiners, Upholsters, Weavers, Velvet-workers, Watchmakers, Looking-glasse-framers, Printers, Organists, and other such kinde of Artificers, and every where giving them some what to drink, did learne and consider the industry and invention of the trades. They went also to heare the public lectures the solemn commencements, the repetitions, the acclamations the pleadings of the gentle Lawyers, and Sermons of Evangelical Preachers. He went through the Halls and places appointed for fencing, and there played against the Masters themselves at all weapons, and shewed them by experience, that he knew as much in it as (yea more then) they. And in stead of herborising, they visited the shops of Druggists, Herbalists, and Apothecaries, and diligently considered the fruits, roots, leaves, gums, seeds, the grease and ointments of some forreign parts, as also how they did adulterate them. He went to see the Juglers, Tumblers, Mountebanks and Quacksalvers, and considered their cunning, their shifts, their summer-saults and smooth tongue, especially of those of Chauny in Picardie, who are naturally great praters, and brave givers of fibs in matter of green apes. At their return they did eate more soberly at supper then at other times, and meates more desiccative and extenuating ; to the end that the intemperate moisture of the aire, communicated to the body by a necessary confinitie, might by this means be corrected, and that they might not receive any prejudice for want of their ordinary bodily exercise. Thus was Gargantua governed, and kept on in this course of education, from day to day profiting, as you may understand such a young man of his age may of a pregnant judgement with good discipline well continued. Which although at the beginning it seemed difficult, became a little after so sweet, so easie, and so delightful, that it seemed rather the recreation of a King than the study of a Scholar. Neverthelesse Ponocrates, to divert him from this vehement intension of the spirits, thought fit, once in a month, upon some faire and clear day to go out of the city betimes in the morning, either towards Gentilly, or Boulogne, or to Montrouge, or Charanton bridge, or to Vanves, or St. Clou, and there spent all the day long in making the greatest chear that could be devised, sporting, making merry, drinking healths, playing, singing, dancing, tumbling in some faire medow, unnestling of sparrowes, taking of quailes, and fishing for frogs and crabs ; but although that day was past without books or lecture, yet it was not spent without profit ; for in the said medowes they usually repeated certain pleasant verses of Virgils Agriculture, of Hesoid and of Politian s husbandrie, would set abroach some wittie Latine Epigrams, then immediately turned them into roundlays and songs for dancing in the French language. In their feasting, they would sometimes separate the water from the wine that was therewith mixed, as Cato teacheth *de re rustica*, and Plinie with an ivie cup : would wash the wine in a basin full of water, then take it out again with a funnel as pure as ever. They made the water go from one glasse to another, and contrived a thousand little automaterie Engines, that is to say, moving of themselves

CHAPTER XXV

How there was great Strife and Debate raised betwixt the Cake-Bakers of Lerne, and those of Gargantuas Countrey, where-upon were waged great Warres

AT that time, which was the season of Vintage, in the beginning, of Harvest, when the countrey shepherds were set to keep the Vines, and hinder the Starlings from eating up the grapes ; as some cake-bakers of Lerne happened to passe along in the broad high way, driving unto the City ten or twelve horses loaded with cakes, the said shepherds courteously intreated them to give them some for their money, as the price then ruled in the market ; for here it is to be remarked, that it is a celestial food to eate for breakfast hot fresh cakes with grapes, especially the frail clusters, the great red grapes, the muscadine, the verjuice grape and the luskard, for those that are costive in their belly ; because it will make them gush out, and squirt the length of a Hunters staffe, like the very tap of a barrel ; and often-times thinking to let a squib, they did all-to-besquatter and conskite themselves, whereupon they are commonly called the Vintage thinkers. The Bunsellers or Cake-makers were in nothing inclinable to their request ; but (which was worse) did injure them most outragiously, calling them pratling gablers, lickorous gluttons, freckled bittors, mangie rascals, shiteabed scoundrels, drunken roysters, slie knaves, drowsie loiterers, slapsauce fellows, slabberdegullion druggels, lubbardly lowts, cosening foxes, ruffian rogues, paultrie customers, sycophant-varlets, drawlatch hoydons, flouting milksops, jeering companions, staring clowns, forlorn snakes, ninnie lobcocks, scurvie sneaksbies, fondling fops, base lowns, sawcie coxcombs, idle lusks, scoffing Braggards, noddie meacocks, blockish grutnols, doddi-poljolt-heads, jobernol goosecaps, foolish loggerheads, slutch calf-lollies, grouthead gnat-snappers, lob-dotterels, gaping changelings, codshead loobies, woodcock slangams, ninnie-hammer flycatchers, noddiepeak simpletons ; Turdie gut, shitten shepherds, and other such like defamatory epithets, saying further, that it was not for them to eate of these dainty cakes, but might very well content themselves with the course unraunged bread, or to eat of the great brown household loaf. To which provoking words, one amongst them, called Forgier, (an honest fellow of his person, and a notable springal,) made answer very calmly thus : How long is it since you have got hornes, that you are become so proud ? indeed formerly you were wont to give us some freely, and will you not now let us have any for our money ? This is not the part of good neighbours, neither do we serve you thus when you come hither to buy our good corn, wherof you make your cakes and buns ; besides that, we would have given you to the bargain some of our grapes, but, by his zounds, you may chance to repent it and possibly have need of us at another time, when we shall use you after the like manner, and therefore remember it. Then Marquet, a prime man in the confraternity of the cakebakers, said unto him, Yea Sir, thou art pretty well crest-risen this morning, thou didst eat yesternight too much millet and bolymoug, come hither, Sirrah, come hither, I will give thee some cake : whereupon Forgier dreading no harm, in all simplicity went towards him, and drew a sixpence out of his leather sachel, thinking that Marquet would have sold him some of his cakes ; but, in stead of cakes, he gave him with his whip such a rude lash overthwart the legs, that the marks of the whipcord knots were apparent in them ; then would have fled away, but Forgier cried out as loud as he could, O murther, murther, help, help, help, and in the mean time threw a great cudgel after him, which he carried under his arme, wherewith he hit him in the coronal joynt of his head, upon the crotaphick arterie of the right side thereof, so forcibly, that Marquet fell down from his mare, more like a dead then living man. Meanwhile the farmers and countrey-swaines, that were watching their walnuts near to that place, came running with their great poles and long staves, and laid such load on these cake-bakers, as if they had been to thresh upon green rie. The other shepherds and shepherdesses, hearing the lamentable shout of Forgier, came with their slings and slackies following them, and throwing great stones at them, as thick as if it had been haile. At last they overtook them and took from them about foure or five dosen of their cakes; nevertheless they payed for them the ordinary price, and gave them over and above one hundred egges, and three baskets full of mulberries. Then did the cakebakers help to get up to his mare Marquet, who was most shrewdly wounded, and forthwith returned to Lerne, changing the resolution they had to go to Pareille, threatening very sharp and boisterously the cowherds, shepherds, and farmers of Sevile and Sinays. This done, the shepherds and shepherdesses made merry with these cakes and fine grapes, and sported themselves together at the sound of the pretty small pipe, scoffing and laughing at those vainglorious cake-bakers, who had that day met with a mischief for want of crossing themselves with a good hand in the morning. Nor did they forget to apply to Forgiers leg some faire great red medicinal grapes, and so handsomely drest it and bound it up that he was quickly cured.

CHAPTER XXVI

How the Inhabitants of Lerne, by the Commandment of Picrochole their King, assaulted the Shepherds of Gargantua, unexpectedly and on a sudden

THE Cake-bakers, being returned to Lerne, went presently, before they did either eat or drink, to the Capitol, and there before their King called Picrochole, the third of that name, made their complaint, shewing their paniers broken, their caps all crumpled, their coats torn, their cakes taken away, but, above all Marquet most enormously wounded, saying, that all that mischief was done by the shepherds and herdsmen of Grangousier, near the broad high way beyond Sevile : Picrochole incontinent grew angry and furious ; and without asking any further what, how, why or wherefore, commanded the ban and arriere ban to be sounded throughout all his countrey, that all his vassals of what condition soever, should upon paine of the halter, come in the best armes they could, unto the great place before the Castle, at the houre of noone, and, the better to strengthen his designe, he caused the drum to be beat about the town. Himself, whilest his dinner was making ready, went to see his artillery mounted upon the carriage, to display his colours, and set up the great royal standard, and loaded waines with store of ammunition both for the field and the belly, armes and victuals : at dinner he dispatch't his commissions, and by his expresse Edict my Lord Shagrag was appointed to command the Vanguard, wherein were numbered sixteen thousand and fourteen harquebusiers or fire-locks, together with thirty thousand and eleven Voluntier-adventurers. The great Touquedillion, Master of the horse, had the charge of the ordnance, wherein were reckoned nine hundred and fourteen brazen pieces, in cannons, double cannons, basilisks, serpentines, culverins, bombards or murtherers, falcons, bases or passe-volans, spiroles and other sorts of great guns. The Reerguard was committed to the Duke of Scrapegood : In the maine battel was the King, and the Princes of his Kingdome. Thus being hastily furnished, before they would set forward, they sent three hundred light horsemen under the conduct of Captain

Swillwind, to discover the countrey, clear the avenues, and see whether there was any ambush laid for them : but, after they had made diligent search, they found all the land round about in peace and quiet, without any meeting or convention at all ; which Picrochole understanding, commanded that every one should march speedily under his colours : then immediately in all disorder, without keeping either rank or file, they took the fields one amongst another, wasting, spoiling, destroying and making havock of all wherever they went, not sparing poor nor rich, priviledged nor unpriviledged places, Church nor laity, drove away oxen and cowes, bulls, calves, heifers, wethers, ewes, lambs, goats, kids, hens, capons, chickens, geese, ganders, goslings, hogs, swine, pigs and such like. Beating down the walnuts, plucking the grapes, tearing the hedges, shaking the fruit-trees, and committing such incomparable abuses, that the like abomination was never heard of. Neverthelesse, they met with none to resist them, for every one submitted to their mercy, beseeching them, that they might be dealt with courteously, in regard that they had alwayes carried themselves, as became good and loving neighbours, and that they had never been guilty of any wrong or outrage done upon them, to be thus suddenly surprised, troubled, and disquieted, and that if they would not desist, God would punish them very shortly ; to which expostulations and remonstrances no other answer was made, but that they would teach them to eat cakes.

CHAPTER XXVII

*How a Monk of Sevile saved the Closse of the Abbey from
being ransacked by the Enemie*

So much they did, and so farre they went pillaging and stealing,
that at last they came to Seville, where they robbed both men
and women, and took all they could catch : nothing was either
too hot or too heavie for them.   Although the plague was there
in the most part of all the houses, they neverthelesse entered
every where, then plundered and carried away all that was
within, and yet for all this not one of them took any hurt, which
is a most wonderful case.   For the Curates, Vicars, Preachers,
Physicians, Chirurgions and Apothecaries, who went to visit,
to dresse, to cure, to heale, to preach unto, and admonish those
that were sick, were all dead of the infection ; and these devillish
robbers and murtherers caught never any harme at all.
Whence comes this to passe, (my masters) I beseech you think
upon it ? the town being thus pillaged, they went unto the
Abbey with a horrible noise and tumult, but they found it shut
and made fast against them ; whereupon the body of the army
marched forward towards a passe or ford called the Gue de
Vede, except seven companies of foot, and two hundred lanciers,
who staying there, broke down the walls of the Closse, to waste,
spoile and make havock of all the Vines and Vintage within
that place.   The Monks (poor devils) knew not in that extremity to which of all their Sancts they should vow themselves ;
nevertheless, at all adventures they rang the bells *ad capitulum
capitulantes* : there it was decreed, that they should make a
faire Procession, stuffed with good lectures, prayers and
letanies, *contra hostium insidias*, and jollie responses *pro pace*.
    There was then in the Abbey a claustral Monk, called Freer
Jhon of the funnels and gobbets, in French *des entoumeures*,
young, gallant, frisk, lustie, nimble, quick, active, bold, adventurous, resolute, tall, lean, wide-mouthed, long-nosed, a faire
dispatcher of morning prayers, unbridler of masses, and runner-
over of vigils ; and to conclude summarily in a word, a right
Monk, if ever there was any, since the Monking world monked a
Monkerie : for the rest a Clerk even to the teeth in matter

THEY FELL DOWN BEFORE HIM LIKE HAY BEFORE A MOWER

81

of breviary. This Monk hearing the noise that the enemy made within the inclosure of the Vineyard, went out to see what they were doing; and perceiving that they were cutting and gathering the grapes, whereon was grounded the foundation of all their next yeares wine, returned unto the quire of the Church where the other Monks were, all amazed and astonished like so many Bell-melters, whom when he heard sing, im, nim, pe, ne, ne ne, ne, nene, tum, ne, num, num, ini, i mi, co, o, no, o, o, neno, ne, no, no, no, rum, nenum, num: It is well shit, well sung, (said he). By the vertue of God, why do not you sing Paniers farewell, Vintage is done: The devil snatch me, if they be not already within the middle of our Closse, and cut so well both Vines and Grapes, that by cods body, there will not be found for these foure yeares to come so much as a gleaning in it. By the belly of Sanct James, what shall we (poor devils) drink the while? Lord God! *da mihi potum.* Then said the prior of the Convent, What should this drunken fellow do here, let him be carried to prison for troubling the divine service: Nay, said the Monk, the wine service, let us behave our selves so that it be not troubled; for you your self my Lord Prior, love to drink of the best, and so doth every honest man. Never yet did a man of worth dislike good wine, it is a monastical apophthegme. But these responses that you chant here, by G—, are not in season; wherefore is it, that our devotions were instituted to be short in the time of Harvest and Vintage, and long in the Advent, and all the winter? The late friar, Massepelosse, of good memory, a true zealous man, or else I give my self to the devil, of our religion, told me, and I remember it well, how the reason was, that in this season we might presse and make the wine, and in Winter whiffe it up. Heark you, my masters, you that love the wine, Cops body, follow me; for Sanct Antonie burn me as freely as a fagot, if they get leave to taste one drop of the liquor, that will not now come and fight for relief of the Vine. Hogs belly, the goods of the church! Ha, no, no: what the devil, Sanct Thomas of England was well content to die for them; if I died in the same cause, should not I be a Sanct likewise? Yes. Yet shall I not die there for all this, for it is I that must do it to others and send them a packing. As he spake this, he threw off his great Monks habit, and laid hold upon the staffe of the crosse, which was made of the heart of a sorbaple-tree, it being of the length of a lance, round, of a full gripe, and a little poudred with lilies called flower de luce, the workmanship whereof was almost all defaced and worn out. Thus went he out in a faire long-skirted jacket, putting his frock scarfewayes athwart his breast, and in this equipage, with his staffe, shaft or truncheon of the cross, laid on so lustily, brisk and fiercely upon his enemies, who without any order, or ensigne, or trumpet, or drum, were busied in gathering the grapes of the Vineyard. For the Cornets, Guidons, and Ensigne-bearers, had laid down their standards, banners, and colours by the wallsides : the Drummers had knockt out the heads of their Drums on one end, to fill them with grapes : the Trumpeters were loaded with great bundles of bunches, and huge knots of clusters : In summe, every one of them was out of aray, and all in disorder. He hurried therefore upon them so rudely, without crying gare or beware, that he overthrew them like hogs, tumbled them over like swine, striking athwart and alongst, and by one means or other so laid about him, after the old fashion of fencing, that to some he beat out their braines, to others he crushed their armes, battered their legs, and bethwacked their sides till their ribs cracked with it ; to others again he unjoynted the spondyles or knuckles of the neck, disfigured their chaps, gashed their faces, made their cheeks hang flapping on their chin, and so swinged and belammed them, that they fell down before him like hay before a Mower : to some others he spoiled the frame of their kidneys, marred their backs, broke their thigh-bones, pash't in their noses, poached out their eyes, cleft their mandi-bules, tore their jaws, dung in their teeth into their throat, shook asunder their omoplates or shoulder-blades, sphacelated their shins, mortified their shanks, inflamed their ankles, heaved off of the hinges their ishies, their sciatica or hip-gout, dislocated the joints of their knees squattered into pieces the boughts or pestles of their thighs, and so thumped, mawled and be-laboured them every where, that never was corne so thick and threefold thresht upon by Plowmens flailes, as were the pitifully disjoynted members of their mangled bodies, under the merci-lesse baton of the crosse. If any offered to hide himself amongst the thickest of the Vines, he laid him squat as a flounder, bruised, the ridge of his back and dash't his reines like a dog. If any thought by flight to escape, he made his head to flie in pieces by the Lambdoidal commissure, which is a seame in the hinder part of the scull. If any one did scramble up into a tree, thinking there to be safe, he rent up his perinee, and impaled him in at the fundament. If any of his old acquaintance happened to cry out, Ha Fryar Jhon my friend,

Fryar, Jhon, quarter, quarter, I yield my self to you, to you I render my self : So thou shalt (said he,) and must whether thou wouldest or no, and withal render and yield up thy soul to all the devils in hell, then suddenly gave them dronos, that is, so many knocks, thumps, raps, dints, thwacks and bangs, as sufficed to warne Pluto of their coming, and dispatch them a going : if any was so rash and full of temerity as to resist him to his face, then was it he did shew the strength of his muscles, for without more ado he did transpierce him by running him in at the breast, through the mediastine and the heart. Others again, he so quashed and bebumped, that with a sound bounce under the hollow of their short ribs, he overturned their stomachs so that they died immediately ; to some with a smart souse on the Epigaster, he would make their midrif swag, then redoubling the blow, gave them such a homepush on the navel, that he made their puddings to gush out. To others through their ballocks he pierced their bum-gut, and left not bowel, tripe nor intral in their body, that had not felt the impetuosity, fiercenesse and fury of his violence. Beleeve that it was the most horrible spectacle that ever one saw : Some cried unto Sanct Barbe, others to St. George ; O the holy Lady Nytouch, said one, the good Sanctesse ; O our Lady of Succours, said another, help, help ; others cried, Our Lady of Cunaut, of Loretto, of good tidings on the other side of the water St. Mary over ; some vowed a pilgrimage to St. James, and others to the holy handkerchief at Chamberrie, which three moneths after that burnt so well in the fire, that they could not get one thread of it saved : others sent up their vowes to St. Cadouin, others to St. Jhon d'Angelie, and to St. Eutropius of Xaintes : others again invoked St. Mesmes of Chinon, St Martin of Candes, S Cloud of Sinays, the holy relicks of Laurezay, with a thousand other jolly little Sancts and Santrels : Some died without speaking, others spoke without dying ; some died in speaking, others spoke in dying. Others shouted as loud as they could, Confession, Confession, *Confiteor, miserere, in manus* ; so great was the cry of the wounded, that the Prior of the Abbey with all his Monks came forth, who when they saw these poor wretches so slain amongst the Vines, and wounded to death, confessed some of them ; but whilest the Priests were busied in confessing them, the little Monkies ran all to the place where Friar Jhon was, and asked him, wherein he would be pleased to require their assistance ? To which he answered, that they should cut the throats of those he had thrown down upon the ground.

They presently leaving their outer habits and cowles upon the railes, began to throttle and make an end of those whom he had already crushed : Can you tell with what instruments they did it ? with faire gullies, which are little hulchback't demi-knives, the iron toole whereof is two inches long, and the wooden handle one inch thick, and three inches in length, wherewith the little boyes in our countrey cut ripe walnuts in two, (while they are yet in the shell,) and pick out the kernel, and they found them very fit for the expediting of that wezand-slitting exploit. In the mean time Friar Jhon, with his formidable baton of the Crosse, got to the breach which the enemies had made, and there stood to snatch up those that endeavoured to escape : Some of the Monkito's carried the standards, banners, ensignes, guidons and colours into their cells and chambers, to make garters of them. But when those that had been shriven, would have gone out at the gap of the said breach, the sturdy Monk quash't and fell'd them down with blowes, saying, These men have had confession and are penitent soules, they have got their absolution, and gained the pardons : they go into Paradise as streight as a sickle, or as the way is to Faye, (like Crooked-Lane at Eastcheap.) Thus by his prowesse and valour were discomfited all those of the army that entred into the Closse of the Abbey, unto the number of thirteen thousand, six hundred, twenty and two, besides the women and little children, which is alwayes to be understood. Never did Maugis the Hermite bear himself more valiantly with his bourdon or Pilgrims staffe against the Saracens, of whom is written in the Acts of the foure sons of Haymon, then did this Monk against his enemies with the staffe of the Crosse.

CHAPTER XXVIII

How Picrochole stormed and took by Assault the rock Clermond, and of Grangousiers Unwillingnesse and Aversion from the Undertaking of Warre

WHILEST the Monk did thus skirmish, as we have said, against those which were entered within the Closse ; Picrochole in great haste passed the ford of Vede, (a very especial passe,) with all his souldierie, and set upon the rock Clermond, where there was made him no resistance at all : and, because it was already night, he resolved to quarter himself and his army in that town, and to refresh himself of his pugnative choler. In the morning he stormed and took the Bulwarks and Castle, which afterwards he fortified with rampiers, and furnished with all ammunition requisite, intending to make his retreat there, if he should happen to be otherwise worsted ; for it was a strong place, both by Art and Nature, in regard of the stance and situation of it. But let us leave them there, and return to our good Gargantua, who is at Paris very assiduous and earnest at the study of good letters, and athletical exercitations, and to the good old man Grangousier his father, who after supper warmeth his ballocks by a good, clear, great fire, and, waiting upon the broyling of some chestnuts, is very serious in drawing scratches on the hearth, with a stick burnt at the one end, wherewith they did stirre up the fire, telling to his wife and the rest of the family pleasant old stories and tales of former times. Whilest he was thus employed, one of the shepherds which did keep the Vines, (named Pillot) came towards him, and to the full related the enormous abuses which were committed, and the excessive spoil that was made by Picrochole, King of Lerne, upon his lands and territories, and how he had pillaged, wasted and ransacked all the countrey, except the inclosure at Sevile, which Friar Jhon des Entoumeures to his great honour had preserved : and that at the same present time the said King was in the rock Clermond ; and there with great industry and circumspection, was strengthening himself and his whole army. Halas, halas, alas, (said Grangousier,) what is this good people? do I dream, or is it true that they tell me ? Picrochole my ancient friend of old time, of my own kinred and alliance, comes he to invade me ? what moves him ? what provokes him ? what sets him on ? what drives him to it ? who hath given him this counsel ? Ho, ho, ho, ho, ho, my God, my Saviour, help me, inspire me, and advise me what I shall do. I protest, I swear before thee, so be thou favourable to me, if ever I did him or his subjects any damage or displeasure, or committed any the least robbery in his countrey ; but on the contrary I have succoured and supplied him with men, money, friendship and counsel upon any occasion, wherein I could be steadable for the improvement of his good ; that he hath therefore at this nick of time so outraged and wronged me, it cannot be but by the malevolent and wicked spirit. Good God, thou knowest my courage, for nothing can be hidden from thee ; if perhaps he be grown mad, and that thou hast sent him hither to me for the better recovery and re-establishment of his brain ; grant me power and wisdom to bring him to the yoke of thy holy will by good discipline. Ho, ho, ho, ho, my good people, my friends and my faithful servants, must I hinder you from helping me ? alas, my old age required henceforward nothing else but rest, and all the dayes of my life I have laboured for nothing so much as peace : but now I must (I see it well) load with armes my poor, weary and feeble shoulders ; and take in my trembling hand the lance and horseman's mace, to succour and protect my honest subjects : reason will have it so ; for by their labour am I entertained, and with their sweat am I nourished, I, my children and my family. This notwithstanding, I will not undertake warre, until I have first tried all the wayes and means of peace, that I resolve upon.

Then assembled he his counsel, and proposed the matter as it was indeed, whereupon it was concluded, that they should send some discreet man unto Picrochole, to know wherefore he had thus suddenly broken the Peace, and invaded those lands unto which he had no right nor title. Furthermore, that they should send for Gargantua, and those under his command, for the preservation of the countrey, and defence thereof now at need. All this pleased Grangousier very well, and commanded that so it should be done. Presently therefore he sent the Basque his Lackey, to fetch Gargantua with all diligence, and wrote to him as followeth.

CHAPTER XXIX

*The Tenor of the Letter which Grangousier wrote to his Sonne
Gargantua*

THE fervency of thy studies did require, that I should not in a
long time recall thee from that Philosophical rest thou now
enjoyest ; if the confidence reposed in our friends and ancient
confederates had not at this present disappointed the assurance
of my old age : But seeing such is my fatal destiny, that I
should be now disquieted by those in whom I trusted most :
I am forced to call thee back to help the people and goods,
which by the right of nature belong unto thee ; for even as
armes are weak abroad if there be not counsel at home : so is
that study vaine, and counsel unprofitable, which in a due and
convenient time is not by vertue executed and put in effect.
My deliberation is not to provoke, but to appease ; not to
assault, but to defend : not to conquer, but to preserve my
faithful subjects and hereditary dominions : into which Picrochole is entred in a hostile manner without any ground or cause,
and from day to day persueth his furious enterprise with that
height of insolence that is intolerable to free-born spirits.   I
have endeavoured to moderate his tyrannical choler, offering
him all that which I thought might give him satisfaction : and
oftentimes have I sent lovingly unto him, to understand wherein, by whom, and how he found himself to be wronged.   But
of him could I obtaine no other answer, but a meer defiance,
and that in my lands he did pretend only to the right of a civil
correspondency and good behaviour, whereby I knew that the
eternal God hath left him to the disposure of his own free will
and sensual appetite, which cannot chuse but be wicked, if by
divine grace it be not continually guided : and to contain him
within his duty, and bring him to know himself, hath sent him
hither to me by a grievous token.   Therefore, my beloved son,
as soon as thou canst, upon sight of these letters, repaire hither
with all diligence, to succour not me so much (which neverthelesse by natural Piety thou oughtest to do,) as thine own
People, which by reason thou mayst save and preserve.   The

A VERY WISE AND DISCREET MAN

exploit shall be done with as little effusion of blood as may be ; and, if possible, by meanes far more expedient, such as military policy, devices and stratagems of warre, we shall save all the souls, and send them home as merry as crickets unto their own houses. My dearest Son, the peace of Jesus Christ our Redeemer be with thee ; salute from me Ponocrates, Gymnastes and Eudemon ; the twentieth of September. Thy Father Grangousier.

CHAPTER XXX

How Ulrich Gallet was sent unto Picrochole

THE letters being dictated, signed, and sealed, Grangousier ordained that Ulrich Gallet, Master of the requests, (a very wise and discreet man, of whose prudence and sound judgement he had made trial in several difficult and debateful matters,) to go unto Picrochole, to shew what had been decreed amongst them. At the same houre departed the good man Gallet, and having past the ford, asked at the Miller that dwelt there, in what condition Picrochole was : who answered him, that his souldiers had left him neither cock nor hen, that they were retired and shut up into the rock Clermond, and that he would not advise him to go any further for feare of the Scouts, because they were enormously furious ; which he easily beleeved, and therefore lodged that night with the Miller. The next morning he went with a Trumpeter to the gate of the Castle, and required the guards he might be admitted to speak with the King of somewhat that concerned him. These words being told unto the King, he would by no means consent that they should open the gate ; but getting upon the top of the bulwark, said unto the Ambassadour, What is the news ? what have you to say ? then the Ambassadour began to speak as followeth.

CHAPTER XXXI

The Speech made by Gallet to Picrochole

THERE cannot rise amongst men a juster cause of grief, then when they receive hurt and damage, where they may justly expect for favour and good will ; and not without cause, (though without reason,) have many, after they had fallen into such a calamitous accident, esteemed this indignity lesse supportable then the losse of their own lives, in such sort, that if they have not been able by force of armes, nor any other means, by reach of wit or subtilty, to stop them in their course, and restrain their fury, they have fallen into desperation, and utterly deprived themselves of this light. It is therefore no wonder if King Grangousier my Master be full of high displeasure, and much disquieted in minde upon thy outragious and hostile coming : but truly it would be a marvel, if he were not sensible of, and moved with the incomparable abuses and injuries perpetrated by thee and thine upon those of his countrey, to- wards whom there hath been no example of inhumanity omitted ; which in it self is to him so grievous for the cordial affection, wherewith he hath alwayes cherished his subjects, that more it cannot be to any mortal man ; yet in this, (above humane apprehension,) it is to him the more grievous, that these wrongs and sad offences hath been committed by thee and thine, who time out of minde, from all antiquity, thou and thy Predecessors, have been in a continual league and amity with him, and all his Ancestors ; which, even until this time, you have as sacred together inviolably preserved, kept and enter- tained, so well, that not he and his only, but the very barbarous Nations of the Poictevins, Bretons, Manceaux, and those that dwell beyond the isles of the Canaries, and that of Isabella, have thought it as easie to pull down the firmament, and to set up the depths above the clouds, as to make a breach in your alliance ; and have been so afraid of it in their enterprises, that

91

they have never dared to provoke, incense or indamage the one for feare of the other. Nay, which is more, this sacred league hath so filled the world, that there are few Nations at this day inhabiting throughout all the continent and isles of the Ocean, who have not ambitiously aspired to be received into it, upon your own covenants and conditions, holding your joynt confederacie in as high esteem as their own territories and dominions in such sort ; that from the memory of man, there hath not been either Prince or league so wilde and proud, that durst have offered to invade, I say not your countreys, but not so much as those of your confederates : and if by rash and headie counsel they have attempted any new designe against them, as soon as they heard the name and title of your alliance, they have suddenly desisted from their enterprises. What rage and madnesse therefore doth now incite thee, all old alliance infringed, all amity trod under foot, and all right violated, thus in a hostil manner to invade his countrey, without having been by him or his in any thing prejudiced, wronged, or provoked. Where is faith ? where is law ? where is reason ? where is humanity ? where is the feare of God ? dost thou think that these atrocious abuses are hidden from the eternal spirits, and the supreme God, who is the just rewarder of all our undertakings ? if thou so think, thou deceivest thy self ; for all things shall come to passe, as in his incomprehensible judgement he hath appointed. Is it thy fatal destiny, or influences of the stars that would put an end to thy so long enjoyed ease and rest ? for that all things have their end and period, so as that when they are come to the superlative point of their greatest height, they are in a trice tumbled down again, as not being able to abide long in that state. This is the conclusion and end of those who cannot by reason and temperance moderate their fortunes and prosperities. But if it be predestinated that thy happinesse and ease must now come to an end, must it needs be by wronging my king ? him by whom thou wert established ? If thy house must come to ruine, should it therefore in its fall crush the heels of him that set it up ? The matter is so unreasonable, and so dissonant from common sense, that hardly can it be conceived by humane understanding, and altogether incredible unto strangers, till by the certain and undoubted effects thereof it be made apparent, that nothing is either sacred or holy to those, who having emancipated themselves from God and reason, do meerly follow the perverse affections of their own depraved nature. If any wrong had been done by us to thy subjects and dominions : if we had favoured thy ill-willers : if we had not assisted thee in thy need : if thy name and reputation had been wounded by us : or (to speak more truly) if the calumniating spirit, tempting to induce thee to evil, had by false illusions and deceitful fantasies, put into thy conceit the impression of a thought, that we had done unto thee any thing unworthy of our ancient correspondence and friendship, thou oughtest first to have enquired out of the truth, and afterwards by a seasonable warning to admonish us thereof ; and we should have so satisfied thee, according to thine own hearts desire, that thou shouldest have had occasion to be contented. But, O eternal God, what is thy enterprise ? wouldest thou like a perfidious tyrant, thus spoile and lay waste my Masters Kingdome ? has thou found him so silly and blockish, that he would not : or so destitute of men and money, of counsel and skill in military discipline, that he cannot withstand thy unjust invasion ? March hence presently, and to-morrow some time of the day retreat unto thine own countrey, without doing any kinde of violence or disorderly act by the way : and pay withal a thousand besans of gold, (which, in English money, amounteth to five thousand pounds) for reparation of the damages thou hast done in his countrey : halfe thou shalt pay to morrow, and the other halfe at the ides of May next coming, leaving with us in the meantime for hostages, the Dukes of Turnebank, Lowbuttock and Smalltrash, together with the Prince of Itches, and Viscount of Snatch-bit.

CHAPTER XXXII

How Grangousier to buy Peace, caused the Cakes to be restored

WITH that the good man Gallet held his peace, but Picrochole
to all his discourse answered nothing but Come and fetch them,
come and fetch them : they have ballocks faire and soft, they
will knead and provide some cakes for you.   Then returned he
to Grangousier, whom he found upon his knees bare-headed,
crouching in a little corner of his cabinet, and humbly praying
unto God, that he would vouchsafe to asswage the choler of
Picrochole, and bring him to the rule of reason without proceeding by force.   When the good man came back, he asked
him, Ha, my friend, my friend, what newes do you bring me ?
There is neither hope nor remedy, (said Gallet) the man is
quite out of his wits, and forsaken of God.   Yea, but (said
Grangousier,) my friend, what cause doth he pretend for his
outrages ?   He did not shew me any cause at all (said Gallet,)
only that in a great anger, he spoke some words of cakes.   I
cannot tell if they have done any wrong to his Cake-bakers.
I will know, (said Grangousier,) the matter throughly, before
I resolve any more upon what is to be done ; then sent he to
learn concerning that businesse, and found by true information,
that his men had taken violently some cakes from Picrocholes
people, and that Marquets head was broken with a slackie or
short cudgel : that neverthelesse all was well paid, and that the
said Marquet had first hurt Forgier with a stroke of his whip
athwart the legs ; and it seemed good to his whole counsel, that
he should defend himself with all his might.   Notwithstanding
all this (said Grangousier,) seeing the question is but about a few
cakes, I will labour to content him ; for I am very unwilling
to wage warre against him.   He enquired then what quantity of
cakes they had taken away, and understanding, that it was but
some foure or five dozen, he commanded five cart-loads of them
to be baked that same night ; and that there should be one full
of cakes made with fine butter, fine yolks of egges, fine saffron
and fine spice, to be bestowed upon Marquet, unto whom likewise he directed to be given seven hundred thousand and
three Philips, (that is, at three shillings the piece, one hundred
five thousand pounds and nine shillings of English money) for

reparation of his losses and hindrances, and for satisfaction of the Chirurgion that had dressed his wound : and furthermore settled upon him and his for ever in freehold the Apple Orchard called La Pomardiere ; for the conveyance and passing of all which was sent Gallet, who by the way as they went made them gather near the willow-trees great store of boughs, canes and reeds, wherewith all the Cariers were injoyned to garnish and deck their carts, and each of them to carry one in his hand, as himself likewise did, thereby to give all men to understand that they demanded but Peace, and that they came to buy it.

Being come to the gate, they required to speak with Picrochole from Grangousier. Picrochole would not so much as let them in, nor go to speak with them, but sent them word that he was busie, and that they should deliver their minde to Captain Touquedillon, who was then planting a piece of Ordnance upon the wall. Then said the good man unto him, My Lord, to ease you of all this labour and to take away all excuses why you may not return unto our former alliance, we do here presently restore unto you the Cakes upon which the quarrel arose ; five dozen did our people take away, they were well payed for : we love Peace so well, that we restore unto you five cart-loads, of which this cart shall be for Marquet, who doth most complain ; besides, to content him entirely, here are seven hundred thousand and three Philips, which I deliver to him : and for the losses he may pretend to have sustained, I resigne for ever the farme of the Pomardiere, to be possessed in fee-simple by him and his for ever, without the payment of any duty, or acknowledgement of homage, fealtie, fine or service whatsoever : and here is the tenor of the deed, and, for Gods sake, let us live henceforward in Peace, and withdraw your selves merrily into your own countrey from within this place, unto which you have no right at all, as your selves must needs confesse, and let us be good friends as before. Touquedillon related all this to Picrochole, and more and more exasperated his courage, saying to him, These clowns are afraid to some purpose : by G——, Grangousier conskites himself for feare ; the poor drinker he is not skilled in warfare, nor hath he any stomach for it, he knows better how to empty the flaggons, that is his Art. I am of opinion that it is fit we send back the carts and the money ; and for the rest, that very speedily we fortifie our selves here, then prosecute our fortune. But what do they think to have to do with a ninnie-whoop, to feed you thus with cakes ? You may see what it is ; the good usage, and great familiarity which you have had with them heretofore, hath made you contemptible in their eyes. Anoint a villain, he will prick you : prick a villain, and he will anoint you. Sa, sa, sa, (said Picrochole,) by St. James you have given a true character of them. One thing I will advise you, (said Touquedillon,) we are here but badly victualled, and furnished with mouth-harnesse very slenderly : if Grangousier should come to besiege us, I would go presently, and pluck out of all your souldiers heads and mine own all the teeth except three to each of us, and with them alone we should make an end of our provision, but too soon we shall have, (said Picrochole,) but too much sustenance and feeding-stuffe : came we hither to feed or to fight ? To fight, indeed (said Touquedillon,) yet from the panch comes the dance, and, where famine rules, force is exiled. Leave off your prating (said Picrochole,) and forthwith seize upon what they have brought. Then took they money and cakes, oxen and carts, and sent them away without speaking one word, only that they would come no more so near, for a reason that they would give them the morrow after. Thus without doing any thing, returned they to Grangousier, and related the whole matter unto him, subjoyning that there was no hope left to draw them to Peace, but by sharp and fierce warres.

CHAPTER XXXIII

How same Statesmen of Picrochole, by haire-brain'd
Counsel put him in extreme danger

THE carts being unloaded, and the money and cakes secured, there came before Picrochole the Duke of Small-trash, the Earle Swash-buckler, and Captain Durtaille, who said unto him, Sir, . this day we make you the happiest, the most warlike and chivalrous Prince that ever was since the death of Alexander of Macedonia. Be covered, be covered, (said Picrochole.) Grammercie (said they) we do but our duty : The manner is thus, you shall leave some Captain here to have the charge of this Garrison, with a Party competent for keeping of the place, which besides its natural strength, is made stronger by the rampiers and fortresses of your devising. Your Army you are to divide into two parts, as you know very well how to do. One part thereof shall fall upon Grangousier and his forces, by it shall he be easily at the very first shock routed, and then shall you get money by heaps, for the Clown hath store of ready coine : Clown we call him, because a noble and generous Prince hath never a penny, and that to hoard up treasure is but a clownish trick. The other part of the Army in the mean time shall draw towards Onys, Xaintonge, Angoulesme and Gascony : then march to Perigourt, Medos, and Elanes, taking whereever vou come without resistance, townes, castles, and forts : Afterwards to Bayonne, St. Jhon de Luz, to Fuentarabia, where you shall seize upon all the ships, and coasting along Galicia and Portugal, shall pillage all the maritime places, even unto Lisbone, where you shall be supplied with all necessaries befitting a Conquerour. By copsodie Spain will yield, for they are but a race of Loobies : then are you to passe by the streights of Gibraltar, where you shall erect two pillars more stately then those of Hercules, to the perpetual memory of your name, and the narrow entrance there shall be called the Picrocholinal sea.

Having past the Picrocholinal sea, behold, Barbarossa yields himself your slave : I will (said Picrochole) give him faire quarter and spare his life. Yea, (said they) so that he be content to be christened. And you shall conquer the Kingdomes of Tunes, of Hippos, Argier, Bomine, Corode, yea all Barbary. Furthermore, you shall take into your hands Majorca, Minorca, Sardinia, Corsica, with the other Islands of the Ligustick and Balearian seas. Going alongst on the left hand, you shall rule all Gallia Norbenensis, Provence, the Allobrogians, Genua, Florence, Luca, and then God bi wy Rome ; By my faith (said Picrochole,) I will not then kisse his pantuffle.

Italy being thus taken, behold, Naples, Calabria, Apulia and Sicilie all ransacked, and Malta too. I wish the pleasant Knights of the Rhodes heretofore would but come to resist you, that we might see their urine. I would (said Picrochole) very willingly go to Loretta. No, no, (said they) that shall be at our return ; from thence we will saile Eastwards, and take Candia, Cyprus, Rhodes, and the Cyclade Islands, and set upon Morea. It is ours by St. Trenian, the Lord preserve Jerusalem ; for the great Soldan is not comparable to you in power : I will then (said he) cause Solomons Temple to be built : No, (said they) not yet, have a little patience, stay a while, be never too sudden in your enterprises. Can you tell what Octavian Augustus said ? *Festina lentè* ; it is requisite that you first have the lesser Asia, Caria, Lycia, Pamphilia, Cilicia Lydia, Phrygia, Mysia, Bithynia, Carazia, Satalia, Samagaria, Castamena, Luga, Sanasta, even unto Euphrates. Shall we see, (said Picrochole,) Babylon and Mount Sinai ? There is no need (said they) at this time ; have we not hurried up and down, travelled and toyled enough, in having transfreted and past over the Hircanian sea, marched alongst the two Armenias, and the three Arabias ? By my faith (said he) we have played the fooles, and are undone : Ha, poor soules ! What's the matter, said they ? What shall we have (said he) to drink in these deserts ? For Julian Augustus, with his whole Army died there for thirst, as they say. We have already (said they), given order for that. In the Siriack sea you have nine thousand and fourteen great ships laden with the best wines in the world : they arrived at Port Joppa, there they found two and twenty thousand Camels, and sixteen hundred Elephants, which you shall have taken at one hunting about Sigelmes, when you entered into Lybia : and, besides this, you had all the Mecca Caravane. Did not they furnish you sufficiently with wine ? Yes, but (said he) we did not drink it fresh : By the vertue, (said they) not of a fish, a valiant man, a Conquerour, who pretends and aspires to the Monarchy of the world, cannot alwayes

THE EARLE SWASH-BUCKLER

have his ease. God be thanked, that you and your men are come safe and sound unto the banks of the river Tigris; But (said he) what doth that part of our Army in the mean time, which overthrows that unworthy Swill-pot Grangousier? They are not idle (said they) we shall meet with them by and by, they shall have won you Britany, Normandy, Flanders, Haynault, Brabant, Artois, Holland, Zealand; they have past the Rhine over the bellies of the Switsers and Lanskenets, and a Party of these hath subdued Luxemburg, Lorrain, Champaigne, and Savoy, even to Lions, in which place they have met with your forces, returning from the naval Conquests of the Mediterranean sea: and have rallied again in Bohemia, after they had plundered and sacked Suevia, Wittemberg, Bavaria, Austria, Moravia, and Styria. Then they set fiercely together upon Lubeck, Norway, Swedeland, Rie, Denmark, Gitland, Greenland, the Sterlins, even unto the frozen sea; this done, they conquered the isles of Orkney, and subdued Scotland, England, and Ireland. From thence sailing through the sandie sea, and by the Sarmates, they have vanquished and overcome Prussia, Poland, Lituania, Russia, Walachia, Transilvania, Hungarie, Bulgaria, Turquieland, and are now at Constantinople. Come (said Picrochole,) let us go joyn with them quickly, for I will be Emperour of Trebezonde also: shall we not kill all these dogs, Turks and Mahumetans? What a devil should we do else, said they: and you shall give their goods and lands to such as shall have served you honestly: Reason (said he) will have it so, that is but just, I give unto you the Caramania, Surie, and all the Palestine. Ha, Sir, (said they) it is out of your goodnesse: Grammercie, we thank you, God grant you may alwayes prosper. There was there present at that time an old Gentleman well experienced in the warres, a sterne souldier, and who had been in many great hazards, named Echephron, who hearing this discourse, said, I do greatly doubt that all this enterprise will be like the tale or interlude of the pitcher full of milk, wherewith a Shoemaker made himself rich in conceit: but, when the pitcher was broken, he had not whereupon to dine: what do you pretend by these large Conquests? what shall be the end of so many labours and crosses? Thus it shall be (said Picrochole) that when we are returned, we shall sit down, rest and be merry: But (said Echephron,) if by chance you should never come back, for the voyage is long and dangerous, were it not better for us to take our rest now, then unnecessarily to expose our selves to so many dangers?

O (said Swashbuckler,) by G—, here is a good dotard, come, let us go hide our selves in the corner of a chimney, and there spend the whole time of our life amongst ladies, in threading of pearles, or spinning like Sardanapalus : He that nothing ventures, hath neither horse nor mule, (sayes Solomon) : He who adventureth too much (said Echephron) loseth both horse and mule, answered Malchon. Enough (said Picrochole,) go forward : I feare nothing, but these devillish legions of Grangousier, whilest we are in Mesopotamia, will come on our backs, and charge up our reer, what course shall we then take ? what shall be our remedy ? A very good one, (said Durtaille) a pretty little commission, which you must send unto the Mus- coviters, shall bring you into the field in an instant foure hundred and fifty thousand choise men of warre. O that you would but make me your Lieutenant General, I should for the lightest faults of any inflict great punishments. I fret, I charge, I strike, I take, I kill, I slay, I play the devil. On, on, (said Picrochole) make haste, my lads, and let him that loves me, follow me.

CHAPTER XXXIV

How Gargantua left the City of Paris, to succour his Countrey, and how Gymnast encountered with the Enemy

IN this same very houre Gargantua who was gone out of Paris, as soon as he had read his fathers letters, coming upon his mare had already past the Nunnerie-bridge himself, Ponocrates, Gymnast and Eudemon, who all three, the better to inable them to go along with him, took Post-horses ; the rest of his traine came after him by even journeys at a slower pace, bringing with them all his books and philosophical instruments ; as soon as he had alighted at Parille, he was informed by a farmer of Gouget, how Picrochole had fortified himself within the rock Clermond, and had sent Captain Tripet with a great army to set upon the wood of Vede and Vaugaudry, and that they had already plundered the whole countrey, not leaving cock nor hen, even as farre as to the wine-presse of Billiard. These strange and almost incredible newes of the enormous abuses,

thus committed over all the land, so affrighted Gargantua,
that he knew not what to say nor do : but Ponocrates counselled him to go unto the Lord of Vauguyon, who at all times
had been their friend and confederate, and that by him they
should be better advised in their businesse ; which they did
incontinently, and found him very willing and fully resolved
to assist them, and therefore was of opinion that they should
send some one of his company, to scout along and discover the
countrey, to learn in what condition and posture the enemy
was, that they might take counsel, and proceed according to
the present occasion. Gymnast offered himself to go ; whereupon it was concluded, that for his safety, and the better
expedition, he should have with him some one that knew the
wayes, avenues, turnings, windings, and rivers thereabout.
Then away went he and Prelingot, (the Querry or Gentleman
of Vauguyon's Horse,) who scouted and espied as narrowly
as they could upon all quarters without any feare. In the
meantime Gargantua took a little refreshment, ate somewhat
himself, the like did those who were with him, and caused to give
to his mare a Picotine of Oats, that is, threescore and fourteen
quarters and three bushels. Gymnast and his Camerade rode
so long, that at last they met with the enemies forces, all
scattered and out of order, plundering, stealing, robbing and
pillaging all they could lay hands on : and, as far off as they
could perceive him, they ran thronging upon the back of one
another in all haste towards him, to unload him of his money,
and untrusse his Portmantles. Then cried he out unto them,
(My Masters,) I am a poor devil, I desire you to spare me, I have
yet one Crown left, come, we must drink it, for it is *aurum
potabile* and this horse here shall be sold to pay my welcome ;
afterwards take me for one of your own, for never yet was there
any man that knew better how to take, lard, rost and dresse,
yea, by G— to teare asunder and devoure a hen, then I that am
here ; and for my Proficiat I drink to all good fellowes. With
that he unscrued his Borracho, (which was a great Dutch
leathern bottle), and without putting in his nose drank very
honestly : the maroufle Rogues looked upon him, opening their
throats a foot wide, and putting out their tongues like Grey-
hounds, in hopes to drink after him : but Captain Tripet, in the
very nick of that their expectation, came running to him to see
who it was. To him Gymnast offered his bottle, saying, Hold,
Captain, drink boldly and spare not ; I have been thy taster,
it is wine of La Faye Monjau. What ? (said Tripet) this fellow

gybes and flowts us; Who art thou? (said Tripet) I am (said Gymnast) a poor devil, (*pauvre diable*). Ha, (said Tripet) seeing thou art a poor devil, it is reason that thou shouldest be permitted to go whithersoever thou wilt, for all poor devils passe every where without toll or taxe; but it is not the custome of poor devils to be so wel mounted, therefore, Sir devil, come down, and let me have your horse, and if he do not carry me well, you, Master devil, must do it: for I love a life that such a devil as you should carry me away.

CHAPTER XXXV

How Gymnast very souply and cunningly killed Captain Tripet, and others of Picrocholes men

WHEN they heard these words, some amongst them began to be afraid, and blest themselves with both hands, thinking indeed that he had been a devil disguised: insomuch that one of them, named good Jhon, Captain of the trained bands of the Countrey bumpkins, took his Psalter out of his Codpiece, and cried out aloud, *Hagios ho theos* If thou be of God speak: if thou be of the other spirit avoid hence, and get thee going: yet he went not away: which words being heard by all the souldiers that were there, divers of them being a little inwardly terrified, departed from the place: all this did Gymnast very well remark and consider, and therefore making as if he would have alighted from off his horse, as he was poysing himself on the mounting side, he most nimbly (with his short sword by his thigh,) shifting his foot in the stirrup, performed the stirrup-leather feat, whereby after the inclining of his body downwards, he forwith lanch't himself aloft in the aire, and placed both his feet together on the saddle, standing upright with his back turned towards the horse's head. Now (said he) my case goes backward. Then suddenly in the same very posture wherein he was, he fetched a gambole upon one foot, and turning to the left hand, failed not to carry his body perfectly round, just into its former stance, without missing one jot. Ha (said Tripet,) I will not do that at this time, and not without cause. Well, (said Gymnast) I have failed, I will undo this leap : then with a marvellous strength and agility, turning towards the right hand he fetch't another frisking gambole, as before, which done, he set his right hand thumb upon the hinde bowe of the saddle, raised himself up, and sprung in the aire, poysing and upholding his whole body, upon the muscle and nerve of the said thumb : and so turned and whirled himself about three times : at the fourth, reversing his body, and overturning it upside down, and foreside back, without touching any thing he brought himself betwixt the horses two eares, springing with all his body into the aire, upon the thumb of his left hand, and in that posture turning like a windmill, did most actively do that trick which is called the Millers Passe. After this, clapping his right hand flat upon the middle of the saddle, he gave himself such a jerking swing, that he thereby seated himself upon the crupper, after the manner of Gentlewomens sitting on horse-back : this done, he easily past his right leg over the saddle, and placed himself like one that rides in croup : But, said he, it were better for me to get into the saddle ; then putting the thumbs of both hands upon the crupper before him, and there-upon leaning himself, as upon the only supporters of his body, he incontinently turned heels over head in the aire, and streight found himself betwixt the bowe of the saddle in a good settlement. Then with a summer-sault springing into the aire again, he fell to stand with both his feet close together upon the saddle, and there made above a hundred frisks, turnes and demi-pommads, with his armes held out acrosse, and in so doing, cried out aloud, I rage, I rage, devils, I am stark mad ; devils, I am mad, hold me, devils, hold me, hold, devils, hold, hold.

Whilest he was thus vaulting, the Rogues in great astonish-ment said to one another, By cocks death he is a goblin or a devil thus disguised, *Ab hoste maligno libera nos, Domine,* and ran away in a ful flight, as if they had been routed, looking now and then behinde them, like a dog that carrieth away a goose-

"THIS TREE SHALL SERVE ME BOTH FOR A STAFFE AND LANCE"

105

wing in his mouth. Then Gymnast spying his advantage, alighted from his horse, drew his sword, and laid on great blows upon the thickest, and highest-crested among them, and overthrew them in great heaps, hurt, wounded and bruised, being resisted by no body, they thinking he had been a starved devil, as well in regard of his wonderful feats in vaulting, which they had seen, as for the talk Tripet had with him, calling him poor devil : only Tripet would have traiterously cleft his head with his horsemans sword, or lanse-knight fauchion ; but he was well armed, and felt nothing of the blow, but the weight of the stroke ; whereupon turning suddenly about, he gave Tripet a home-thrust, and upon the back of that, whilest he was about to ward his head from a slash, he ran him in at the breast with a hit, which at once cut his stomack, the fifth gut called the Colon, and the half of his liver, wherewith he fell to the ground, and in falling gushed forth above foure pottles of pottage, and his soule mingled with the pottage.

This done, Gymnast withdrew himself, very wisely considering, that a case of great adventure and hazard, should not be pursued unto its utmost period, and that it becomes all Cavaliers modestly to use their good fortune, without troubling or stretching it too farre : wherefore getting to horse, he gave him the spurre, taking the right way unto Vauguyon, and Prelingot with him.

CHAPTER XXXVI

*How Gargantua demolished the Castle at the Forde of Vede,
and how they past the Ford*

As soon as he came, he related the estate and condition wherein they had found the enemie, and the stratagem which he alone had used against all their multitude, affirming that they were but rascally rogues, plunderers, thieves and robbers, ignorant of all military discipline, and that they might boldly set forward unto the field ; it being an easie matter to fell and strike them down like beasts. Then Gargantua mounted his great Mare, accompanied as we have said before, and finding in his way a high and great tree, (which commonly was called by the name of St. Martins tree, because heretofore St. Martin planted a pilgrims staffe there, which in tract of time grew to that height and greatnesse,) said, This is that which I lacked; this tree shall serve me both for a staffe and lance: with that he pulled it up easily, plucked off the boughs, and trimmed it at his pleasure: in the meantime his Mare pissed to ease her belly, but it was in such abundance, that it did overflow the countrey seven leagues, and all the pisse of that urinal flood, ran glib away towards the Ford of Vede, wherewith the water was so swollen, that all the forces the enemy had there, were with great horrour drowned, except some who had taken the way on the left hand towards the hills. Gargantua, being come to the place of the wood of Vede, was informed by Eudemon, that there was some remainder of the enemy within the Castle which to know, Gargantua cried out as loud as he was able, Are you there, or are you not there? if you be there, be there no more; and if you are not there, I have no more to say. But a ruffian gunner, whose charge was to attend the Portcullis over the gate, let flie a cannon-ball at him, and hit him with that shot most furiously on the right temple of his head, yet did him no more hurt, then if he had but cast a prune or kernel of a wine-grape at him: What is this? (said Gargantua) do you throw at us grape-kernels here? the vintage shall cost you dear, thinking indeed that the bullet had been the kernel of a grape, or raisin-kernel.

Those who were within the Castle, being till then busie at the pillage, when they heard this noise, ran to the towers and fortresses, from whence they shot at him above nine thousand and five and twenty falconshot and harcabusades, aiming all at his head, and so thick did they shoot at him, that he cried out, Ponocrates my friend, these flies here are like to put out mine eyes, give me a branch of those willow-trees to drive them away, thinking that the bullets and stones shot out of the great ordnance had been but dunflies. Ponocrates looked and saw that there were no other flies, but great shot which they had shot from the Castle. Then was it that he rusht with his great tree against the Castle, and with mighty blowes over-threw both towers and fortresses, and laid all level with the ground, by which means all that were within were slain and broken in pieces. Going from thence they came to the bridge at the Mill, where they found all the Ford covered with dead bodies, so thick, that they had choaked up the Mill, and stopped the current of its water, and these were those that were destroyed in the Urinal deluge of the Mare. There they were at a stand, consulting how they might passe without hindrance by these dead carcasses. But Gymnast said, if the devils have past there, I will passe well enough. The devils have past there (said Eudemon,) to carry away the damned soules. By St. Rhenian (said Ponocrates) then by necessary consequence he shall passe there : Yes, yes, (said Gymnastes) or I shall stick in the way : then setting spurs to his horse, he past through freely, his horse not fearing, nor being any thing affrighted at the sight of the dead bodies ; for he had accustomed him (according to the doctrine of the great Ælian) not to feare armour, nor the carcasses of dead men ; and that not by killing men as Diomedes did the Thracians, or as Ulysses did in throwing the Corpses of his enemies at his horses feet as Homer saith, but by putting a Jack-a-lent amongst his hay, and making him go over it ordinarily, when he gave him his oates. The other three followed him very close, except Eudemon only, whose horses foreright or far forefoot sank up to the knee in the paunch of a great fat chuffe, who lay there upon his back drowned, and could not get it out : there was he pestered, until Gargantua with the end of his staffe thrust down the rest of the villains tripes into the water, whilest the horse pulled out his foot ; and (which is a wonderful thing in Hippiatrie,) the said horse was throughly cured of a ringbone which he had in that foot, by this touch of the burst guts of that great loobie.

CHAPTER XXXVII

How Gargantua in combing his Head, made the great Cannon-Balls fall out of his Haire

BEING come out of the river of Vede, they came very shortly after to Grangousiers Castle, who waited for them with great longing ; at their coming they were entertained with many congies, and cherished with embraces, never was seen a more joyful company ; for *supplementum supplementi Chronicorum* saith, that Gargamelle died there with joy ; for my part, truly I cannot tell, neither do I care very much for her, nor for any-body else. The truth was, that Gargantua, in shifting his clothes, and combing his head with a combe, which was nine hundred foot long of the Jewish Canne-measure, and whereof the teeth were great tusks of Elephants, whole and entire, he made fall at every rake above seven balls of bullets, at a dozen the ball, that stuck in his haire, at the razing of the Castle of the wood of Vede, which his father Grangousier seeing, thought they had been lice, and said unto him, What, my dear sonne, hast thou brought us this farre some short-winged hawkes of the Colledge of Montague ? I did not mean that thou shouldest reside there ; Then answered Ponocrates, My soveraign Lord, think not that I have placed him in that lowsie Colledge, which they call Montague ; I had rather have put him amongst the grave-diggers of Sanct Innocent, so enormous is the cruelty and villany that I have known there : for the Galley-slaves are far better used amongst the Moors and Tartars, the murtherers in the criminal dungeons, yea the very dogs in your house, then are the poor wretched Students in the aforesaid Colledge ; and if I were King of Paris, the devil take me if I would not set it on fire, and burne both Principal and Regents, for suffering this inhumanity to be exercised before their eyes : then, taking up one of these bullets, he said, These are cannon-shot, which your sonne Gargantua hath lately received by the treachery of your enemies, as he was passing before the Wood of Vede.

But they have been so rewarded, that they are all destroyed in the ruine of the Castle, as were the Philistines by the policy of Samson, and those whom the tower of Silohim slew, as it is written in the thirteenth of Luke; My opinion is, that we pursue them whilest the luck is on our side, for occasion hath all her haire on her forehead, when she is past, you may not recal her, she hath no tuft whereby you can lay hold on her, for she is bald in the hind-part of her head, and never returneth again. Truly (said Grangousier,) it shall not be at this time; for I will make you a feast this night, and bid you welcome.

This said, they made ready supper, and of extraordinary besides his daily fare, were rosted sixteen oxen, three heifers, two and thirty calves, threescore and three fat kids, fourscore and fifteen wethers, three hundred farrow pigs or sheats sowced in sweet wine or must, eleven score partridges, seven hundred snites and woodcocks, foure hundred Loudun and Cornwalcapons, six thousand pullets, and as many pigeons, six hundred crammed hens, fourteen hundred leverets, or young hares and rabbets, three hundred and three buzzards, and one thousand and seven hundred cockrels. For venison, they could not so suddenly come by it, only eleven wilde bores, which the Abbot of Turpenay sent, and eighteen fallow deer which the Lord of Gramount bestowed; together with seven score pheasants, which were sent by the Lord of Essars; and some dozens of queests, coushots, ringdoves, and woodculvers; River-fowle, teales and awteales, bitterns, courtes, plovers, francolins, briganders, tyrasons, young lapwings, tame ducks, shovelers, woodlanders, herons, moore-hens, criels, storks, canepetiers, oranges, flamans, which are phænicopters, or crimson-winged sea-fowles, terrigoles, turkies, arbens, coots, solingeese, curlews, termagants, and water-wagtails, with a great deal of cream, curds and fresh cheese, and store of soupe, pottages, and brewis with great variety. Without doubt there was meat enough, and it was handsomly drest by Snapsauce, Hotchpot and Brayverjuice, Grangousiers Cooks. Jenkin Trudg-apace and Cleanglasse were very careful to fill them drink.

CHAPTER XXXVIII

How Gargantua did eate up six Pilgrims in a Sallet

THE story requireth, that we relate that which happened unto six Pilgrims, who came from Sebastian near to Nantes: and who for shelter that night, being afraid of the enemy, had hid

AND LAID ALL LEVEL WITH THE GROUND

III

themselves in the garden upon the chichling pease, among the cabbages and lettices. Gargantua finding himself somewhat dry, asked whether they could get any lettice to make him a sallet ; and hearing that there were the greatest and fairest in the countrey (for they were as great as plum-trees, or as walnut-trees,) he would go thither himself, and brought thence in his hand what he thought good, and withal carried away the six Pilgrims who were in so great feare, that they did not dare to speak nor cough.

Washing them therefore first at the fountain, the Pilgrims said one to another softly, What shall we do ? we are almost drowned here amongst these lettice, shall we speak ? but if we speak, he will kill us for spies : and, as they were thus deliberating what to do, Gargantua put them with the lettice into a platter of the house, as large as the huge tun of the White Friars of the Cistertian order, which done, with oile, vineger and salt he ate them up, to refresh himself a little before supper ; and had already swallowed up five of the Pilgrims, the six being in the platter, totally hid under a lettice, except his bourdon or staffe that appeared, and nothing else. Which Grangousier seeing, said to Gargantua, I think that is the horne of a shell-snail, do not eat it. Why not, (said Gargantua) they are good all this moneth, which he no sooner said, but, drawing up the staffe, and therewith taking up the Pilgrim, he ate him very well, then drank a terrible draught of excellent white wine, The Pilgrims, thus devoured, made shift to save themselves as well as they could, by withdrawing their bodies out of the reach of the grinders of his teeth, but could not escape from thinking they had been put in the lowest dungeon of a prison. And when Gargantua whiffed the great draught, they thought to have been drowned in his mouth, and the flood of wine had almost carried them away into the gulf of his stomack. Neverthelesse skipping with their bourdons, as St. Michaels Palmers use to do, they sheltered themselves from the danger of that inundation under the banks of his teeth. But one of them by chance, groping or sounding the countrey with his staffe, to try whether they were in safety or no, struck hard against the cleft of a hollow tooth, and hit the mandibulary sinew, or nerve of the jaw, which put Gargantua to very great pain, so that he began to cry for the rage that he felt ; to ease himself therefore of his smarting ache, he called for his tooth-picker, and rubbing towards a young walnut-tree, where they lay skulking, unnestled you my Gentlemen Pilgrims.

OUR PRIOR

For he caught one by the legs, another by the scrip, another by the pocket, another by the scarf, another by the band of the breeches, and the poor fellow that had hurt him with the bourdon, him he hooked to him by the Codpiece, which snatch neverthelesse did him a great deal of good, for it pierced unto him a pockie botch he had in the groine, which grievously tormented him ever since they were past Ancenis. The Pilgrims thus dislodged ran away athwart the Plain a pretty fast pace, and the paine ceased, even just at the time when by Eudemon he was called to supper, for all was ready. I will go then (said he) and pisse away my misfortune ; which he did do in such a copious measure, that, the urine, taking away the feet from the Pilgrims, they were carried along with the stream unto the bank of a tuft of trees : upon which, as soon as they had taken footing, and that for their self-preservation they had run a little out of the road, they on a sudden fell all six, except Fourniller, into a trap that had been made to take wolves by a train : out of which neverthelesse they escaped by the industry of the said Fourniller, who broke all the snares and ropes. Being gone from thence, they lay all the rest of that night in a lodge near unto Coudry, where they were comforted in their miseries, by the gracious words of one of their company, called Sweertogo who shewed them that this adventure had been foretold by the Prophet David, *Psalm. Quum exsurgerent homines in nos, fortè vivos deglutisseut nos ;* when we were eaten in the sallet, with salt, oile and vineger. *Quum irasceretur furor eorum in nos, forsitan aqua absorbuisset nos ;* when he drank the great draught, *Torrentem pertransivit anima nostra ;* when the stream of his water carried us to the thicket, *Forsitan pertransisset anima nostra aquam intolerabilem ;* that is, the water of his Urine, the flood whereof cutting our way, took our feet from us. *Benedictus Dominus qui non dedit nos in captionem dentibus eorum ; anima nostra sicut passer erepta est de laqueo venantium ;* when we fell in the trap, *Laqueus contritus est,* by Fourniller, *et nos liberati sumus, adjutorium nostrum, etc.*

CHAPTER XXXIX

How the Monk was feasted by Gargantua, and of the jovial
Discourse they had at Supper

WHEN Gargantua was set down at table, after all of them had somewhat stayed their stomacks by a snatch or two of the first bits eaten heartily ; Grangousier began to relate the source and cause of the warre, raised between him and Picrochole : and came to tell how Friar Jhon of the Funnels, had triumphed at the defence of the close of the Abbey, and extolled him for his valour above Camillus, Scipio, Pompey, Cæsar and Themistocles. Then Gargantua desired that he might be presently sent for, to the end that with him they might consult of what was to be done ; whereupon, by a joynt consent, his steward went for him, and brought him along merrily, with his staffe of the Crosse, upon Grangousiers mule : when he was come, a thousand huggings, a thousand embracements, a thousand good dayes were given : Ha, Friar Jhon, my friend, Friar Jhon, my brave cousin, Friar Jhon from the devil : let me clip thee (my heart) about the neck, to me an armesful ; I must gripe thee (my ballock), till thy back crack with it. Come (my cod) let me coll thee till I kill thee ; And Friar Jhon, the gladdest man in the world, never was man made welcomer, never was any more courteously and graciously received then Friar Jhon. Come, come, (said Gargantua), a stool here close by me at this end. I am content, (said the monk), seeing you will have it so. Some water (page); fill, my boy, fill, it is to refresh my liver; give me some, (childe) to gargle my throat withal. *Depositâ cappâ*, (said Gymnast) let us pull off this frock. Ho, by G——, Gentleman, (said the Monk) there is a chapter *in statutis ordinis*, which opposeth my laying of it down. Pish (said Gymnast) a fig for your chapter, this frock breaks both your shoulders, put it off. My friend (said the monk) let me alone with it; for by G——, I'le drink the better that it is on : It makes all my body jocund; if I should lay it aside the waggish Pages would cut to themselves garters out of it, as I was once served at Coulaines; and, which is worse, I shall lose my appetite : but if in this habit I sit down at table, I will drink by G——, both to thee and thy horse, and so courage, frolick, God save the company : I have already sup't, yet will I eat never a whit the lesse for that; for I have a paved stomack, as hollow as a But of malvoisie, or St. Benedictus boot, and alwayes open like a Lawyers pouch. Of all fishes, but the tench, take the wing of a Partridge, or the thigh of a Nunne. Doth not he die like a good fellow that dies with a stiff catso ? Our Prior loves exceedingly the white of a capon : In that (said Gymnast), he doth not resemble the foxes; for of the capons, hens, and pullets which they carry away, they never eat the white : Why ? said the Monk. Because (said Gymnast) they have no Cooks to dresse them; and if they be not competently made ready, they remaine red and not white, the rednesse of meats being a token that they have not got enough of the fire, whether by boyling, roasting, or otherwise, except the shrimps, lobsters, crabs, and crayfishes, which are cardinalised with boyling; by Gods feast-gazers (said the monk), the Porter of our Abbey, then hath not his head well-boyled, for his eyes are as red as a mazer made of an alder tree. The thigh of this leveret is good for those that have the gout. To the purpose of the truel, what is the reason, that the thighs of a gentlewoman are alwayes fresh and coole : This Probleme (said Gargantua) is neither in Aristotle, in Alexander Aphrodiseus, nor in Plutarch. There are three causes (said the monk) by which this place is naturally refreshed. Primò, because the water runs all along by it. Secundò, because it is a shadie place, obscure and dark, upon which the Sun never shines. And thirdly, because it is continually flabbell'd, blown upon and aired by the north-windes of the hole arstick, the fan of the smock, and flipflap of the Codpiece. And lustie my lads, some bousing liquor, Page !

FRIAR JOHN

117

so : Crack, crack, crack. O how good is God that gives us of this excellent juice ! I call him to witnesse, if I had been in the time of Jesus Christ, I would have kept him from being taken by the Jewes in the garden of Olivet : and the devil faile me, if I should have failed to cut off the hams of these Gentlemen Apostles, who ran away so basely after they had well supped, and left their good Master in the lurch. I hate that man worse than poison that offers to run away, when he should fight and lay stoutly about him. Oh that I were but King of France for fourescore or a hundred years ! By G— I should whip like curtail-dogs these runawayes of Pavie : A plague take them, why did they not chuse rather to die there, then to leave their good Prince in that pinch and necessity ? Is it not better and more honourable to perish in fighting valiantly, then to live in disgrace by a cowardly running away ? We are like to eate no great store of goslings this yeare, therefore, friend, reach me some of that rosted pig there.

Diavolo, is there no more must ? No more sweet wine ? *Germinavit radix Jesse. Je renie ma vie, j'enrage de soif ;* I renounce my life, I rage for thirst, this wine is none of the worst ; what wine drink you at Paris ? I give myself to the devil, if I did not once keep open house at Paris for all commers six moneths together ; Do you know Father Claud of the high kildrekins : Oh the good fellow that he is, But I do not know what flie has stung him of late, he is become so hard a student ; for my part, I study not at all. In our Abbey we never study for feare of the mumps, (which disease in horses is called the mourning in the chine ;) Our late Abbot was wont to say, that it is a monstrous thing to see a learned Monk by G—, Master, my friend, *Magis magnos clericos non sunt magis magnos sapientes.* You never saw so many hares as there are this year. I could not any where come by a gosse-hawk, nor tassel of falcon : my Lord Beloniere promised me a Lanner, but wrote to me not long ago, that he was become pursie. The Partridges will so multiply henceforth, that they will go near to eat up our eares : I take no delight in the stalking-horse ; for I catch such cold, that I am like to founder myself at that sport ; if I do not run, toile, travel, and trot about, I am not well at ease. True it is, that in leaping over hedges and bushes, my frock leaves alwayes some of its wool behind it. I have recovered a dainty grey-hound ; I give him to the devil, if he suffer a hare to escape him. A groom was leading him to my Lord Hunt-little, and I robbed him of him ; did I ill ? No, Friar Jhon (said Gymnast), no,

by all the devils there are, no : So (said the monk), do I attest
these same devils so long as they last, or rather, vertue G—,
what could that gowtie Limpard have done with so fine a dog ?
by the body of G—, he is better pleased, when one presents him
with a good yoke of oxen. How now (said Ponocrates) you
swear, Friar Jhon ; it is only (said the monk) but to grace and
adorn my speech ; they are colours of a Ciceronian Rhetorick.

CHAPTER XL

Why Monks are the Out-casts of the World ; and wherefore
some have bigger Noses than others ?

BY the faith of a Christian (said Eudemon) I do wonderfully
dote, and enter in a great extasie, when I consider the honesty
and good fellowship of this Monk ; for he makes us here all
merry. How is it then that they exclude the Monks from all
good companies ? calling them feast-troublers, marrers of
mirth, and disturbers of all civil conversation, as the bees drive
away the drones from their hives ; *Ignavum fucos pecus* (said
Maro) *á præsepibus arcent.* Hereunto answered Gargantua,
There is nothing so true, as that the frock and cowle draw unto
it self the opprobries, injuries and maledictions of the world,
just as the winde called Cecias attracts the clouds : the peremptory reason is, because they eat the ordure and excrements of

the world, that is to say, the sins of the people, and, like dung-chewers, and excrementitious eaters, they are cast into the privies and secessive places, that is, the Covents and Abbeys separated from Political conversation, as the jakes and retreats of a house are : but if you conceive how an Ape in a family is alwayes mocked, and provokingly incensed, you shall easily apprehend how Monks are shunned of all men, both young and old. The Ape keeps not the house as a dog doth : He drawes not in the plow as the oxe : He yields neither milk nor wooll as the sheep : he carrieth no burthen as a horse doth ; that which he doth, is only to conskite, spoile and defile all, which is the cause wherefore he hath of all men mocks, frumperies and bastonadoes.

After the same manner a Monk (I mean those lither, idle, lazie Monks) doth not labour and work, as do the Peasant and Artificer : doth not ward and defend the countrey, as doth the man of warre : cureth not the sick and diseased, as the Physician doth : doth neither preach nor teach, as do the Evangelical Doctors and Schoolmasters : doth not import com-modities and things necessary for the Commonwealth, as the Merchant doth : therefore is it, that by and of all men they are hooted at, hated and abhorred. Yea, but (said Grangousier,) they pray to God for us. Nothing lesse, (answered Gargantua.) True it is, that with a tingle tangle jangling of bells they trouble and disquiet all their neighbours about them : Right, (said the Monk,) a masse, a matine, a vespre well rung are half said. They mumble out great store of Legends and Psalmes, by them at all not understood : they say many patenotres, interlarded with ave-maries, without thinking upon, or apprehending the meaning of what it is they say, which truly I call mocking of God, and not prayers. But so help them God, as they pray for us, and not for being afraid to lose their victuals, their manchots, and good fat pottage. All true Christians, of all estates and conditions, in all places and at all times send up their prayers to God, and the Mediatour prayeth and intercedeth for them, and God is gracious to them. Now such a one is our good Friar Jhon, therefore every man desireth to have him in his company, he is no bigot or hypocrite, he is not torne and divided betwixt reality and appearance, no wretch of a rugged and peevish disposition, but honest, jovial, resolute, and a good fellow : he travels, he labours, he defends the oppressed, com-forts the afflicted, helps the needie, and keeps the close of the Abbey.

Nay (said the Monk) I do a great deal more then that; for whilest we are in dispatching our matines and anniversaries in the quire, I make withal some crossbowe-strings, polish glasse-bottles and boults; I twiste lines and weave purse nets, wherein to catch coneys; I am never idle; but now hither come, some drink, some drink here, bring the fruit. These chesnuts are of the wood of Estrox, and with good new wine are able to make you a fine cracker and composer of bum-sonnets. You are not as yet (it seems) well moistened in this house with this sweet wine and must, by G— I drink to all men freely, and at all Fords like a Proctor or Promoters horse. Friar Jhon, (said Gymnast) take away the snot that hangs at your nose. Ha, ha, (said the monk,) am not I in danger of drowning, seeing I am in water even to the nose? No, no, *quare? quia*, though some water come out from thence, there never goes in any; for it is well antidoted with pot-proof-armour, and sirrup of the Vine-leaf.

O my friend, he that hath winter-boots made of such leather, may boldly fish for oysters, for they will never take water. What is the cause (said Gargantua) that Friar Jhon hath such a faire nose? Because (said Grangousier) that God would have it so, who frameth us in such forme, and for such end, as is most agreeable with his divine Will, even as a Potter fashioneth his vessels. Because (said Ponocrates) he came with the first to the faire of noses, and therefore made choice of the fairest and the greatest. Pish, (said the Monk) that is not the reason of it, but, according to the true Monastical Philosophy, it is because my Nurse had soft teats, by virtue whereof, whilest she gave me suck, my nose did sink in as so much butter. The hard breasts of Nurses make children short-nosed. But hey gay, *Ad formam nasi cognoscitur ad te levavi*. I never eat any confections, Page, whilest I am at the bibbery; Item, bring me rather some tosts.

CHAPTER XLI

How the Monk made Gargantua sleep, and of his Houres and Breviaries

SUPPER being ended, they consulted of the businesse in hand, and concluded that about midnight they should fall unawares upon the enemie, to know what manner of watch and ward they kept, and that in the mean while they should take a little rest, the better to refresh themselves. But Gargantua could not sleep by any meanes, on which side soever he turned himself. Whereupon the Monk said to him, I never sleep soundly, but when I am at Sermon or Prayers. Let us therefore begin, you and I, the seven penitential Psalmes, to try whether you shall not quickly fall asleep. The conceit pleased Gargantua very well, and, beginning the first of these Psalmes, as soon as they came to the words, *Beati quorum*, they fell asleep both the one and the other. But the Monk for his being formerly accustomed to the houre of Claustral matines, failed not to awake a little before midnight, and being up himself awaked all the rest, in singing aloud, and with a full clear voice, the song :

> Awake, O Reinian, Ho, awake ;
>   Awake, O Reinian, Ho :
> Get up, you no more sleep must take,
>   Get up ; for we must go.

When they were all rowsed and up, he said, My Masters, it is a usual saying, that we begin matines with coughing, and supper with drinking ; let us now (in doing clean contrarily) begin our matines with drinking, and at night before supper we shall cough as hard as we can. What ? (said Gargantua) to drink so soon after sleep, this is not to live according to the diet and prescript rule of the Physicians, for you ought first to scoure and cleanse your stomack of all its superfluities and excrements. O well physicked, (said the Monk) a hundred devils leap into my body, if there be not more old drunkards, then old Physicians : I have made this paction and covenant with my appetite, that it alwayes lieth down, and goes to bed with my self, (for to that I every day give very good order,) then the next morning it also riseth with me, and gets up when I am awake. Minde you your charges, (Gentlemen), or tend your cures as much as you will ; I will get me, to my Drawer, (in termes of falconrie, my tiring.) What drawer or tiring do you mean ? (said Gargantua). My breviary (said the Monk,) for just as the Falconers, before they feed their hawks, do make them draw at a hens leg, to purge their braines of flegme, and sharpen them to a good appetite : so by taking this merry little breviary, in the morning I scoure all my lungs, and am presently ready to drink.

After what manner (said Gargantua), do you say these fair houres and prayers of yours ? After the manner of Whipfield, said the Monk, by three Psalmes, and three Lessons, or nothing at all, he that will : I never tie my self to houres, prayers and sacraments : for they are made for the man, and not the man for them : therefore it is that I make my Prayers in fashion of stirrup-leathers ; I shorten or lengthen them when I think good. *Brevis oratio penetrat cœlos et longa potatio evacuat scyphos* : where is that written ? by my faith (said Ponocrates,) I cannot tell my (pillicock,) but thou art more worth than gold : Therein (said the Monk) I am like you : but, *venite, apotemus.* Then made they ready store of Carbonadoes, or rashers on the coales, and good fat soupes, or brewis with sippets ; and the Monk drank what he pleased. Some kept him company, and the rest did forbear for their stomachs were not as yet opened. Afterwards every man began to arme and befit himself for the field ; and they armed the Monk against his will ; for he desired no other armour for back and breast, but his frock, nor any other weapon in his hand, but the staffe of the Crosse : yet at their pleasure was he completely armed cap-a-pe, and mounted upon one of the best horses in the Kingdome, with a good slashing shable by his side, together with Gargantua, Ponocrates, Gymnast, Eudemon, and five and twenty more of the most resolute and adventurous of Grangousiers house, all armed at proof with their lances in their hands, mounted like St. George, and every one of them having a harquebusier behinde him.

CHAPTER XLII ·

How the Monk encouraged his Fellow-Champions, and how he hanged upon a Tree

THUS went out those valiant champions on their adventure, in full resolution, to know what enterprise they should undertake, and what to take heed of, and look well to, in the day of the great and horrible battel. And the Monk encouraged them, saying, My children, do not feare nor doubt, I will conduct you safely : God and Sanct Benedict be with us. If I had strength answerable to my courage, by Sdeath, I would plume them for

you like ducks. I feare nothing but the great ordnance ; yet
I know of a charm by way of Prayer, which the sub-sexton of
our Abbey taught me, that will preserve a man from the
violence of guns, and all manner of fire-weapons and engines,
but it will do me no good, because I do not believe it. Neverthelesse, I hope my staffe of the crosse shall this day play
devillish pranks amongst them ; by G— whoever of our Party
shall offer to play the duck, and shrink when blowes are a
dealing, I give myself to the devil, if I do not make a Monk of
him in my stead, and hamper him within my frock, which is
a sovereign cure against cowardise. Did you never heare of my
Lord Meurles his grey-hound, which was not worth a straw in
the fields ; he put a frock about his neck, by the body of G—
there was neither hare nor fox that could escape him, and which
is more, he lined all the bitches in the countrey, though before
that he was feeble-reined, and *ex frigidis et maleficiatis*. The
Monk uttering these words in choler, as he past under a walnut-
tree, in his way towards the Causey, he broached the vizor
of his helmet, on the stump of a great branch of the said tree :
nevertheless, he set his spurres so fiercely to the horse, who
was full of mettal, and quick on the spurre, that he bounded
forwards, and the Monk, going about to ungrapple his vizor,
let go his hold of the bridle, and so hanged by his hand upon
the bough, whilest his horse stole away from under him. By
this meanes was the Monk left, hanging on the walnut-tree,
and crying for help, murther, murther, swearing also that he
was betrayed : Eudemon perceived him first, and calling
Gargantua said, Sir, come and see Absalom hanging. Gargantua being come, considered the countenance of the Monk,
and in what posture he hanged ; wherefore he said to Eudemon,
You were mistaken in comparing him to Absalom ; for Absalom
hung by his haire, but this shaveling Monk hangeth by the
eares. Help me (said the Monk) in the devils name, is this a
time for you to prate ? you seem to me to be like the decretalist
preachers, who say, that whosoever shall see his neighbour in
the danger of death, ought upon paine of trisulk excommunication, rather choose to admonish him to make his Confession to
a Priest, and put his conscience in the state of Peace, then
otherwise to help and relieve him.

And therefore when I shall see them fallen into a river, and
ready to be drowned, I shall make them a faire long sermon
de contemptu mundi, et fuga seculi ; and when they are stark
dead, shall then go to their aid and succour in fishing after

I SHALL MAKE THEM A FAIRE LONG SERMON

125

them : Be quiet (said Gymnast,) and stirre not my minion ; I am now coming to unhang thee, and to set thee at freedome, for thou art a pretty little gentle Monachus ; *Monachus in claustro non valet ova duo ; sed quando est extra bene valet triginta :* I have seen above five hundred hanged, but I never saw any have a better countenance in his dangling and pendilatory swagging ; truly, if I had so good a one, I would willingly hang thus all my life-time ; What ? (said the Monk) have you almost done preaching ; help me, in the name of God, seeing you will not in the name of the other spirit, or by the habit which I wear you shall repent it, *tempore et loco prælibatis.*

Then Gymnast alighted from his horse, and, climbing up the walnut-tree, lifted up the Monk with one hand, by the gushets of his armour under the arm-pits, and with the other undid his vizor from the stump of the broken branch, which done, he let him fall to the ground and himself after. As soon as the Monk was down, he put off all his armour, and threw away one piece after another about the field, and taking to him again his staffe of the Crosse, remounted up to his horse, which Eudemon had caught in his running away. Then went they on merrily, riding along on the high way.

CHAPTER XLIII

How the Scouts and Fore-Party of Picrochole were met with by Gargantua, and how the Monk slew Captain Draw-forth, and then was taken Prisoner by his Enemies

PICROCHOLE at the relation of those who had escaped out of the broile and defeat, wherein Tripet was untriped, grew very angry that the devils should have so run upon his men, and held all that night a counsel of warre, at which Rashcalf and Touch-faucet concluded his power to be such, that he was able to defeat all the devils of hell, if they should come to justle with his forces. This Picrochole did not fully beleeve, though he doubted not much of it : Therefore sent he under the command and conduct of the Count Draw-forth, for discovering of the Countrey, the number of sixteen hundred horsemen, all well mounted upon light horses for skirmish, and throughly be-

sprinkled with holy water ; and every one for their field-mark
or cognizance had the signe of a starre in his scarf, to serve at all
adventnres, in case they should happen to incounter with
devils ; that by the vertue, as well of that Gregorian water,
as of the starres which they wore, they might make them dis-
appear and evanish.

In this equipage they made an excursion upon the countrey,
till they came near to the Vauguyon, (which is the valley of
Guyon) and to the spittle, but could never finde any body to
speak unto ; whereupon they returned a little back, and took
occasion to passe above the aforesaid hospital, to try what
intelligence they could come by in those parts, in which resolution riding on, and by chance in a pastoral lodge, or shepherds
cottage near to Coudray, hitting upon the six Pilgrims, they
carried them way-bound and manacled, as if they had been
spies, for all the exclamations, adjurations and requests that
they could make. Being come down from thence towards
Seville, they were heard by Gargantua, who said then unto
those that were with him, Camerades and fellow souldiers, we
have here met with an encounter, and they are ten times in
number more then we : shall we charge them or no ? What a
devil (said the Monk), shall we do else ? Do you esteem men
by their number, rather then by their valour and prowes ?
With this he cried out, Charge, devils, charge ; which when the
enemies heard, they thought certainly that they had been very
devils, and therefore even then began all of them to run away
as hard as they could drive, Draw-forth only excepted, who
immediately setled his lance on its rest, and therewith hit the
Monk with all his force on the very middle of his breast, but,
coming against his horrifick frock, the point of the iron, being
with the blow either broke off or blunted, it was in matter of
execution, as if you had struck against an Anvil with a little
wax-candle.

Then did the Monk, with his staffe of the Crosse, give him
such a sturdie thump and whirret betwixt his neck and
shoulders, upon the Acromion bone, that he made him lose
both sense and motion, and fall down stone dead at his horses
feet ; and, seeing the signe of the starre which he wore scarf-
wayes, he said unto Gargantua, These men are but priests,
which is but the beginning of a Monk ; by St. Jhon, I am a
perfect Monk, I will kill them to you like flies.

Then ran he after them at a swift and full gallop, till he
overtook the reere, and felled them down like tree-leaves,

striking athwart and alongst and every way. Gymnast presently asked Gargantua if they should pursue them? To whom Gargantua answered, By no means; for, according to right military discipline, you must never drive your enemy unto despair, for that such a strait doth multiply his force, and increase his courage, which was before broken and cast down; neither is there any better help, or outgate of relief for men that are amazed, out of heart, toiled and spent, then to hope for no favour at all. How many victories have been taken out of the hands of the Victors by the vanquished, when they would not rest satisfied with reason, but attempt to put all to the sword, and totally to destroy their enemies, without leaving so much as one to carry home newes of the defeat of his fellowes? Open therefore unto your enemies all the gates and wayes, and make to them a bridge of silver rather than faile, that you may be rid of them. Yea, but (said Gymnast) they have the monk: Have they the Monk? (said Gargantua.) Upon mine honour then it will prove to their cost; but to prevent all dangers, let us not yet retreat, but halt here quietly, as in an ambush; for I think I do already understand the policie and judgement of our enemies, they are truly more directed by chance and meer fortune, then by good advice and counsel. In the mean while, whilest these made a stop under the walnut-trees, the Monk pursued on the chase, charging all he overtook, and giving quarter to none, until he met with a trouper, who carried behinde him one of the poor Pilgrims, and there would have rifled him. The Pilgrim, in hope of relief at the sight of the Monk, cried out, Ha, my Lord Prior, my good friend, my Lord Prior, save me, I beseech you, save me; which words being heard by those that rode in the van, they instantly faced about, and seeing there was no body but the Monk that made this great havock and slaughter among them, they loded him with blows as thick as they use to do an Asse with wood: but of all this he felt nothing, especially when they struck upon his frock, his skin was so hard. Then they committed him to two of the Marshals men to keep, and looking about, saw nobody coming against them, whereupon they thought that Gargantua and his Party were fled: then was it that they rode as hard as they could towards the walnut-trees to meet with them, and left the Monk there all alone, with his two aforesaid men to guard him. Gargantua heard the noise and neighing of the horses, and said to his men, Camerades, I hear the track and beating of the enemies horse-feet, and withall perceive that some of them come in a troupe and full body against us; let us rallie and close here, then set forward in order, and by this means we shall be able to receive their charge, to their losse and our honour.

CHAPTER XLIV

How the Monk rid himself of his Keepers, and how Picrocholes Forlorne Hope was defeated

THE Monk seeing them break off thus without order, conjectured that they were to set upon Gargantua and those that were with him, and was wonderfully grieved that he could not succour them; then considered he the countenance of the two keepers in whose custody he was, who would have willingly runne after the troops to get some booty and plunder, and were always looking towards the valley unto which they were going; farther, he syllogized, saying, These men are but badly skilled in matters of warre, for they have not required my paroll, neither have they taken my sword from me; suddenly hereafter he drew his brackmard or horsemans sword, wherewith he gave the keeper which held him, on the right side such a sound slash, that he cut clean thorough the jugularie veins, and the sphagitid or transparent arteries of the neck, with the forepart of the throat called the gargareon, even unto the two Adenes, which are throat kernels; and redoubling the blow, he opened the spinal marrow betwixt the second and third verteber; there fell down that keeper stark dead to the ground. Then the Monk, reining his horse to the left, ranne upon the other, who seeing his fellow dead, and the Monk to have the advantage of him, cried with a loud voice, Ha, my Lord Prior, quarter, I yeeld, my Lord Prior, quarter, quarter, my good friend, my Lord Prior : and the Monk cried likewise, my Lord Posterior, my friend, my Lord Posterior, you shall have it upon

your posteriorums : Ha, said the keeper, my Lord Prior, my
Minion, my Gentile Lord Prior, I pray God make you an Abbot.
By the habit (said the Monk), which I weare, I will here make
you a Cardinal ; What do you use to pay ransomes to religious
men ? you shall therefore have by and by a red hat of my
giving : and the fellow cried, Ha, my Lord Prior, my Lord
Prior, my Lord Abbot that shall be, my Lord Cardinal, my
Lord all, ha, ha, hes, no my Lord Prior, my good little Lord the
Prior, I yeeld, render and deliver my self up to you : and I
deliver thee (said the Monk), to all the Devils in hell ; then
at one stroak he cut off his head, cutting his scalp upon the
temple-bones, and lifting up in the upper part of the scul the
two triangularie bones called sincipital, or the two bones
bregmatis, together with the sagittal commissure or dart-like
seame which distinguisheth the right side of the head from the
left, as also a great part of the coronal or forehead-bone, by
which terrible blow likewise he cut the two meninges or filmes
which inwrap the braine, and made a deep wound in the braine's
two posterior ventricles, and the cranium or skull abode hanging upon his shoulders by the skin of the pericranium behinde,
in forme of a Doctors bonnet, black without and red within.
Thus fell he down also to the ground stark dead.

And presently the Monk gave his horse the spurre, and
kept the way that the enemy held, who had met with Gargantua
and his companions in the broad highway, and were so
diminished of their number, for the enormous slaughter that
Gargantua had made with his great tree amongst them, as also
Gymnast, Ponocrates, Eudemon, and the rest, that they began
to retreat disorderly and in great haste, as men altogether
affrighted and troubled in both sense and understanding ;
and, as if they had seen the very proper species and forme of
death before their eyes ; or rather as when you see an Asse with
a brizze or gad-bee under his taile, or flie that stings him, run
hither and thither without keeping any path or way, throwing
down his load to the ground, breaking his bridle and reines,
and taking no breath nor rest, and no man can tell what ailes
him, for they see not any thing touch him : so fled these people
destitute of wit, without knowing any cause of flying, onely
pursued by a panick terror, which in their mindes they had
conceived. The Monk, perceiving that their whole intent was
to betake themselves to their heels, alighted from his horse,
and got upon a big large rock, which was in the way, and with
his great Brackmard sword laid such a load upon those runa-

wayes, and with maine strength fetching a compasse with his arme without feigning or sparing, slew and overthrew so many, that his sword broke in two peces, then thought he within himself that he had slaine and killed sufficiently, and that the rest should escape to carry newes ; therefore, he took up a battle-axe of those that lay there dead, and got upon the rock againe, passing his time to see the enemy thus flying, and to tumble himself amongst the dead bodies, only that he suffered none to carry Pike, Sword, Lance nor Gun with him, and those who carried the Pilgrims bound, he made to alight, and gave their horses unto the said Pilgrims, keeping them there with him under the hedge, and also Touchfaucet, who was then his prisoner.

CHAPTER XLV

How the Monk carried along with him the Pilgrims, and of the good Words that Grangousier gave them

THIS skirmish being ended, Gargantua retreated with his men, excepting the Monk, and about the dawning of the day they came unto Grangousier, who in his bed was praying unto God for their safety and victory : and seeing them all safe and sound, he embraced them lovingly, and asked what was become of the Monk ? Gargantua answered him, that without doubt the enemies had the Monk : then have they mischief and ill luck (said Grangousier) which was very true ; therefore is it a common proverb to this day, to give a man the Monk (or as in French, *luy bailler le moine*), when they would expresse the doing unto one a mischief ; then commanded he a good breakfast to be provided for their refreshment : when all was ready, they called Gargantua, but he was so agrieved that the Monk was not to be heard of, that he would neither eate nor drink : in the meane while, the Monk comes, and from the gate of the outer Court cries out aloud, Fresh wine, fresh wine Gymnast my friend ; Gymnast went out and saw that it was Frier Jhon who brought along with him six pilgrims and Touchfaucet prisoners ; whereupon Gargantua likewise went forth to meet him, and all of them made him the best welcome that possibly they could, and brought him before Grangousier, who asked him of all his adventures: the Monk told him all, both how he was taken, how he rid himself of his keepers, of the slaughter he had made by the way, and how he had rescued the Pilgrims, and brought along with him Captain Touchfaucet. Then did they altogether fall to banqueting most merrily; in the meane time Grangousier asked the Pilgrims what countreymen they were, whence they came, and whither they went? Sweertogo in the name of the rest answered, My Sovereign Lord, I am of Saint Genou in Berrie, this man is of Patvau, this other is of Onzay, this of Argy, this of St. Nazarand, and this man of Villebrenin; we come from Saint Sebastian near Nantes, and are now returning, as we best may, by easie journeys; Yea, but said Grangousier, what went you to do at Saint Sebastian? We went, said Sweertogo, to offer up unto that Sanct our vowes against the Plague. Ah poor men (said Grangousier) do you think that the plague comes from Saint Sebastian? Yes truly, (answered Sweertogo), our Preachers tell us so indeed; But is it so? (said Grangousier) do the false Prophets teach you such abuses? do they thus blaspheme the Sancts and holy men of God, as to make them like unto the Devils, who do nothing but hurt unto mankinde, as Homer writeth, that the Plague was sent into the camp of the Greeks by Apollo, and as the poets feign a great rabble of Vejoves and mischievous gods. So did a certain Cafard or dissembling religionaire preach at Sinay, that Saint Antonie sent the fire into mens legs, that Saint Eutropius made men hydropick; Saint Clidas, fooles, and that Saint Genou made them goutish: but I punished him so exemplarily, though he called me Heretick for it, that since that time no such hypocritical rogue durst set his foot within my territories; and truly I wonder that your king should suffer them in their sermons to publish such scandalous doctrine in his dominions; for they deserve to be chastised with greater severity then those who by magical art, or any other device, have brought the pestilence into a countrey; the pest killeth but the bodies, but such abominable Imposters empoyson our very souls. As he spake these words, in came the Monk very resolute, and asked them, Whence are you, you poor wretches? of Saint Genou, (said they). And how (said the Monk) does the Abbot Gulligut the good drinker, and the Monks, what cheere make they? by G— body they'll have a fling at your wives, and breast them to some purpose, whilest you are upon your roaming rant and gadding Pilgrimage. Hin, hen, said Sweertogo, I am not afraid of mine, for he that shall see her by day will never break his neck to come to her in the night-time. Yea, marry (said the Monk) now you have hit it, let her be as ugly as ever was Proserpina, she will once by the Lord G— be overturned, and get her skin-coat shaken, if there dwell any Monks near to her, for a good Carpenter will make use of any kinde of timber: let me be pepper'd with the pox, if you finde not all your wives with childe at your returne ; for the very shadow of the steeple of an Abbey is fruitful : It is (said Gargantua) like the water of Nilus in Egypt, if you beleeve Strabo and Plinie, lib. 7. cap. 3. What vertue will there be then (said the Monk) in their bullets of concupiscence, their habits and their bodies ?

Then (said Grangousier), Go your wayes, poor men in the name of God the Creatour, to whom I pray to guide you perpetually, and henceforward be not so ready to undertake these idle and unprofitable journeys ; Look to your families, labour every man in his vocation, instruct your children, and live as the good Apostle St. Paul directeth you : in doing whereof, God, his Angels and Sancts, will guard and protect you, and no evil or plague at any time shall befal you. Then Gargantua led them into the hall to take their refection : but the Pilgrims did nothing but sigh, and said to Gargantua, O how happy is that land which hath such a man for their Lord ! we have been more edified and instructed by the talk which he hath had with us, then by all the Sermons that ever were preached in our town. That is (said Gargantua) that which Plato saith, lib. 5. *de republ.*, That those Commonwealths are happy, whose Rulers philosophate, and whose Philosophers rule. Then caused he their wallets to be filled with victuals, and their bottles with wine, and gave unto each of them a horse to ease them upon the way, together with some pence to live by.

CHAPTER XLVI

*How Grangousier did very kindly entertain Touchfaucet
his Prisoner*

Touchfaucet was presented unto Grangousier, and by him
examined upon the enterprise and attempt of Picrochole, what
it was he could pretend to, or aim at, by the rustling stirre,
and tumultuary coyle of this his sudden invasion : whereunto
he answered, that his end and purpose was to conquer all the
countrey, if he could, for the injury done to his cake-bakers :
It is too great an undertaking (said Grangousier ;) and (as the
Proverb is), He that gripes too much, holds fast but little :
the time is not now as formerly, to conquer the Kingdomes of
our neighbour Princes, and to build up our own greatnesse upon
the losse of our nearest Christian brother : this imitation of
the ancient Herculeses, Alexanders, Hannibals, Scipios, Cæsars,
and other such heroes is quite contrary to the Profession of the
Gospel of Christ, by the which we are commanded to preserve,
keep, rule, and govern every man his own countrey and lands,
and not in a hostile manner to invade others, and that which
heretofore the Barbars and Saracens called prowesse, and
valour, we do now call robbing, theevery and wickednes ; It
would have been more commendable in him to have contained
himself within the bounds of his own territories, royally governing them, then to insult and domineer in mine, pillaging and
plundering every where like a most unmerciful enemy ; for
by ruling his own with discretion, he might have increas't his
greatnesse, but by robbing me he cannot escape destruction ;
Go your wayes in the name of God, prosecute good enterprises,
shew your King what is amisse, and never counsel him with
regard unto your own particular profit, for the public losse
will swallow up the private benefit. As for your ransome, I

do freely remit it to you, and will that your armes and horse be restored to you ; so should good neighbours do, and ancient friends ; seeing this our difference is not properly warre, as Plato, lib. 5. *de repub.* would not have it called warre but sedition, when the Greeks took up armes against one another, and that therefore when such combustions should arise amongst them, his advice was to behave themselves in the managing of them with all discretion and modesty. Although you call it warre, it is but superficial, it entereth not into the closet and inmost cabinet of our hearts ; for neither of us hath been wronged in his honour, nor is there any question betwixt us in the main, but only how to redresse by the by some petty faults committed by our men ; I mean, both yours and ours, which although you knew you ought to let passe ; for these quarrelsome persons deserve rather to be contemned then mentioned, especially seeing I offered them satisfaction according to the wrong. , God shall be the just Judge of our variances, whom I beseech by death rather to take me out of this life, and to permit my goods to perish and be destroyed before mine eyes, then that by me or mine he should in any sort be wronged. These words uttered, he called the Monk, and before them all spoke thus unto him : Friar Jhon, my good friend, is it you that took prisoner the captain Touchfaucet here present ? Sir (said the monk) seeing himself is here, and that he is of the yeares of discretion, I had rather you should know it by his confession then by any words of mine. Then said Touchfaucet, My sovereign Lord, it is he indeed that took me, and I do therefore most freely yield my self his prisoner. Have you put him to any ransom ? said Grangousier to the monk. No, (said the Monk,) of that I take no care : How much would you have for having taken him ? nothing, nothing, (said the monk,) I am not swayed by that, nor do I regard it ; Then Grangousier commanded, that in presence of Touchfaucet, should be delivered to the Monk for taking him, the summe of threescore and two thousand saluts (in English money, fifteen thousand and five hundred pounds) which was done, whilest they made a collation or little banquet to the said Touchfaucet, of whom Grangousier asked, if he would stay with him, or if he loved rather to return to his King ? Touchfaucet answered, that he was content to take whatever course he would advise him to. Then (said Grangousier) return unto your King, and God be with you.

Then he gave him an excellent sword of a Vienne blade with a golden scabbard wrought with Vine-branch-like flourishes, of faire Goldsmiths work, and a coller or neckchain of gold, weighing seven hundred and two thousand merks (at eight ounces each,) garnished with precious stones of the finest sort, esteemed at a hundred and sixty thousand ducats, and ten thousand crownes more, as an honourable donative, by way of present.

After this talk, Touchfaucet got to his horse, and Gargantua for his safety allowed him the guard of thirty men at armes, and six score archers to attend him under the conduct of Gymnast, to bring him even unto the gate of the rock Clermond, if there were need. As soon as he was gone, the Monk restored unto Grangousier the three-score and two thousand saluts, which he had received, saying, Sir it is not as yet the time for you to give such gifts, stay till this warre be at an end, for none can tell what accidents may occurre, and war begun without good provision of money before-hand for going through with it, is but as a breathing of strength, and blast that will quickly passe away ; coine is the sinews of warre. Well then (said Grangousier) at the end I will content you by some honest recompence, as also all those who shall do me good service.

CHAPTER XLVII

How Grangousier sent for his Legions, and how Touchfaucet slew Rashcalf, and was afterwards executed by the command of Picrochole

ABOUT this same time those of Besse, of the old Market, of St. James bourg, of the draggage of Parille, of the Rivers, of the rocks St. Pol, of the Vaubreton, of Pautille, of the Brahemont, of Clainbridge, of Cravant, of Grammont, of the town at the Badgerholes, of Huymes, of Serge, of Husse, of St. Lovant, of Panzoust, of the Coldraux, of Vernon, of Coulaines, of Chose, of Varenes, of Bourgueil, of the Bouchard Claud, of the Croulay, of Narsie, of Cand, of Monsoreau, and other bordering places, sent Ambassadours unto Grangousier, to tell him that they were advised of the great wrongs which Picrochole had done him, and in regard of their ancient confederacy, offered him what assistance they could afford, both in men, money, victuals and ammunition, and other necessaries for warre ; The money, which by the joynt agreement of them all was sent unto him, amounted to six-score and fourteen millions, two crowns and a half of pure gold. The forces wherewith they did assist him, did consist in fifteen thousand cuirasiers, two and thirty thousand light horsemen, fourscore and nine thousand dragoons, and a hundred and forty thousand voluntier adventurers. These had with them eleven thousand and two hundred cannons, double cannons, long pieces of Artillery called Basilisks, and smaller sized ones, known by the name of spirols, besides the mortar-pieces and granadoes. Of pioneers they had seven and forty thousand, all victualled and payed for six moneths and four dayes of advance ; which offer Gargantua did not altogether refuse, nor wholly accept of : but, giving them hearty thanks, said that he would compose and order the warre by such a device, that there should not be found great need to put so many honest men to trouble in the managing of it ; and there-fore was content at that time to give order only for bringing along the legions, which he maintained in his ordinary Garison-townes of the Deviniere, of Chavignie, of Gravot, and of the Quinquenais, amounting to the number of two thousand cuirasiers, threescore and six thousand foot-souldiers, six and twenty thousand dragoons, attended by two hundred pieces of great ordnance, two and twenty thousand Pioneers, and six thousand light horsemen, all drawn up in troupes, so well befitted and accommodated with their commissaries, sutlers, ferriers, harnasse-makers, and other such like necessary members in a military camp ; so fully instructed in the Art of warfare, so perfectly knowing and following their colours, so ready to hear and obey their Captains, so nimble to run, so strong at their charging, so prudent in their adventures, and every day so well disciplined, that they seemed rather to be a consort of organ-pipes, or mutual concord of the wheels of a clock, then an infantry and cavalry, or army of souldiers.

Touchfaucet immediately after his return presented himself before Picrochole, and related unto him at large all that he had done and seen, and at last endeavoured to perswade him with strong and forcible arguments, to capitulate and make an agreement with Grangousier, whom he found to be the honestest man in the world, saying further, that it was neither right nor reason thus to trouble his neighbours, of whom they had never received any thing but good : and in regard of the main point, that they should never be able to go through stitch with that warre, but to their great damage and mischief : for the forces of Picrochole were not so considerable, but that Grangousier could easily overthrow them.

He had not well done speaking, when Rashcalf said out aloud, Unhappy is that prince, which is by such men served, who are so easily corrupted, as I know Touchfaucet is ; for I see his courage so changed, that he had willingly joyned with our enemies to fight against us and betray us, if they would have received him ; but as vertue is of all, both friends and foes, praised and esteemed, so is wickednes soon known and suspected, and although it happen the enemies to make use thereof for their profit, yet have they alwayes the wicked, and the traitors in abomination.

Touchfaucet being at these words very impatient, drew out his sword, and therewith ran Rashcalf through the body, a little under the nipple of his left side, whereof he died presently, and pulling back his sword out of his body said boldly, So let him perish, that shall a faithful servant blame. Picrochole incontinently grew furious, and seeing Touchfaucets new sword and his scabbard so richly diapred with flourishes of most excellent workmanship, said, Did they give thee this weapon, so felloniously therewith to kill before my face my so good friend Rashcalf ? then immediately commanded he his guard to hew him in pieces, which was instantly done, and that so cruelly, that the chamber was all died with blood : Afterwards he appointed the corps of Rashcalf to be honourably buried, and that of Touchfaucet, to be cast over the walls into the ditches.

The newes of these excessive violences were quickly spread through all the Army ; whereupon many began to murmure against Picrochole, insofarre that Pinchpennie said to him, My sovereign Lord, I know not what the issue of this enterprise will be ; I see your men much dejected, and not well resolved in their mindes, by considering that we are here very ill provided of victuall, and that our number is already much diminished by three or four sallies. Furthermore, great supplies and recruits come daily in to your enemies : but we so moulder away, that, if we be once besieged, I do not see how we can escape a total destruction ; Tush, pish, (said Picrochole) you are like the Melun eeles, you cry before they come to you ; Let them come, let them come, if they dare.

CHAPTER XLVIII

How Gargantua set upon Picrochole, within the rock Clermond, and utterly defeated the Army of the said Picrochole

GARGANTUA had the charge of the whole Army, and his father Grangousier stayed in his Castle, who encouraging them with good words, promised great rewards unto those that should do any notable service. Having thus set forward, as soon as they had gained the Passe at the Ford of Vede, with boats and bridges speedily made they passed over in a trice, then considering the situation of the town, which was on a high and advantageous place, Gargantua thought fit to call his counsel, and passe that night in deliberation upon what was to be done : But Gymnast said unto him, My sovereign Lord, such is the nature and complexion of the Frenches, that they are worth nothing, but at the first push, then are they more fierce then devils ; but if they linger a little, and be wearied with delays, they'll prove more faint and remisse than women : my opinion is therefore, that now presently after your men have taken breath, and some small refection, you give order for a resolute assault, and that we storme them instantly. His advice was found very good, and for effectuating thereof, he brought forth his army into the plain field, and placed the reserves on the skirt or rising of a little hill. The Monk took along with him six companies of foot, and two hundred horsemen well armed, and with great diligence crossed the marish, and valiantly got up on the top of the green hillock, even unto the high-way which leads to Loudin. Whilest the assault was thus begun, Picrocholes men could not tell well what was best, to issue out and receive the Assailants, or keep within the town and not to stirre : Himself in the mean time, without deliberation, sallied forth in a rage with the cavalry of his guard, who were forthwith received, and royally entertained with great cannon-shot, that fell upon them like haile from the high grounds, on which the Artillery was planted ; whereupon the Gargantuists betook themselves unto the valleys, to give the ordnance leave to play, and range with the larger scope.

Those of the town defended themselves as well as they

could, but their shot past over us, without doing us any hurt at all : Some of Picrocholes men, that had escaped our Artillery, set most fiercely upon our souldiers, but prevailed little ; for they were all let in betwixt the files, and there knock't down to the ground, which their fellow-souldiers seeing, they would have retreated, but the Monk having seised upon the Passe, by the which they were to return, they run away and fled in all the disorder and confusion that could be imagined.

Some would have pursued after them, and followed the chase, but the Monk withheld them, apprehending that in their pursuit the Pursuers might lose their ranks, and so give occasion to the besieged to sallie out of the town upon them. Then staying there some space, and none coming against him, he sent the Duke Phrontist, to advise Gargantua to advance towards the hill up on the left hand, to hinder Picrocholes retreat at that gate, which Gargantua did with all expedition, and sent thither foure brigades under the conduct of Sebast, which had no sooner reach't the top of the hill, but they met Picrochole in the teeth, and those that were with him scattered.

Then charged they upon them stoutly, yet were they much indamaged by those that were upon the walles, who galled them with all manner of shot, both from the great ordnance, small guns and bowes. Which Gargantua perceiving, he went with a strong Partie to their relief, and with his Artillery began to thunder so terribly upon that canton of the wall, and so long, that all the strength within the town, to maintain and fill up the breach, was drawn thither. The Monk, seeing that quarter which he kept besieged, void of men and competent guards, and in a manner altogether naked and abandoned, did most magnanimously on a sudden lead up his men towards the fort, and never left it till he had got up upon it, knowing, that such as came to the reserve in a conflict, bring with them alwayes more feare and terrour, then those that deal about them with their hands in the fight.

Neverthelesse he gave no alarm till all his souldiers had got within the wall, except the two hundred horsemen, whom he left without to secure his entry, then did he give a most horrible shout, so did all these who were with him, and immediately thereafter without resistance, putting to the edge of the sword the guard that was at that gate, they opened it to the horsemen with whom most furiously they altogether ran towards the East-gate, where all the hurlie burlie was, and coming close upon them in the reer, overthrew all their forces. The besieged seeing that the Gargantuists had won the town upon them, and that they were like to be secure in no corner of it, submitted themselves unto the mercy of the Monk, and asked for quarter, which the Monk very nobly granted to them, yet made them lay down their armes ; then shutting them up within Churches, gave order to seise upon all the staves of the Crosses, and placed men at the doores to keep them from coming forth ; then opening that East-gate, he issued out to succour and assist Gargantua : but Picrochole, thinking it had been some relief coming to him from the towne, adventured more forwardly then before, and was upon the giving of a most desperate home-charge, when Gargantua cried out, Ha, Friar Jhon, my friend, Friar Jhon, you are come in a good houre ; which unexpected accident so affrighted Picrochole and his men, that giving all for lost, they betook themselves to their heels, and fled on all hands. Gargantua chased them till they came near to Vau-gaudry, killing and slaying all the way, and then sounded the retreat.

CHAPTER XLIX

How Picrochole in his Flight fell into great Misfortunes,
and what Gargantua did after the Battel

PICHROCHOLE thus in despaire, fled towards the Bouchard island, and in the way to Riveere his horse stumbled and fell down, whereat he on a sudden was so incensed, that he with his sword without more ado killed him in his choler ; then not finding any that would remount him, he was about to have taken an Asse at the Mill that was thereby : but the Millers men did so baste his bones, and so soundly bethwack him, that they made him both black and blew with strokes ; then, stripping him of all his clothes, gave him a scurvie old canvas jacket wherewith to cover his nakednesse. Thus went along this poor cholerick wretch, who passing the water at Porthuaux, and relating his misadventurous disasters, was foretold by an old Lourpidon hag, that his Kingdome should be restored to him at the coming of the Cocklicranes, which she called Coque-cigrues. What is become of him since we cannot certainly tell, yet was I told that he is now a porter at Lyons, as testie and pettish in humour as ever he was before, and would be always with great lamentation enquiring at all strangers of the coming of the Cocklicranes, expecting assuredly, (according to the old womans prophecie), that at their coming he shall be re-established in his Kingdom. The first thing Gargantua did after his return into the town was to call the Muster-roll of his men, which when he had done, he found that there were very few either killed or wounded, only some few foot of captain Tolmeres company, and Ponocrates who was shot with a musket-ball through the doublet. Then he caused them all at and in their several posts and divisions to take a little refresh-ment, which was very plenteously provided for them in the best drink and victuals that could be had for money, and gave order to the Treasurers and Commissaries of the Army, to pay for and defray that repast, and that there should be no outrage at all, nor abuse committed in the town, seeing it was his own. And furthermore commanded, that immediately after the souldiers had done with eating and drinking for that time sufficiently, and to their own hearts desire, a gathering should be beaten for bringing them altogether, to be drawn up on the Piazza before the Castle, there to receive six moneths pay compleatly, all which was done. After this by his direction, were brought before him in the said place, all those that re-mained of Picrocholes party, unto whom in the presence of the Princes, Nobles, and Officers of his Court and Army, he spoke as followeth.

WAS FORETOLD BY AN OLD LOURPIDON HAG, THAT HIS KINGDOME
SHOULD BE RESTORED TO HIM AT THE COMING OF THE
COCKLICRANES

143

CHAPTER L

Gargantuas Speech to the Vanquished

OUR forefathers and Ancestors of all times, have been of this
nature and disposition, that, upon the winning of a battel, they
have chosen rather for a signe and memorial of their triumphs
and victories, to erect trophies and monuments in the hearts of
the vanquished by clemencie, then by architecture in the lands
which they had conquered; for they did hold in greater estimation, the lively remembrance of men purchased by liberality,
then the dumb inscription of arches, pillars and pyramides,
subject to the injury of stormes and tempests, and to the envie
of every one. You may very well remember of the courtesie,
which by them was used towards the Bretons, in the battel of
St. Aubin of Cormier, and at the demolishing of Partenay.
You have heard, and hearing admire their gentle comportment
towards those at the barreers of Spaniola, who had plundered,
wasted and ransacked the maritime borders of Olone and
Talmondois. All this hemisphere of the world was filled with
the praises and congratulations which your selves and your
fathers made, when Alpharbal King of Canarre, not satisfied
with his own fortunes, did most furiously invade the land of
Onyx, and with cruel Piracies molest all the Armorick islands,
and confine regions of Britanie; yet was he in a set naval
fight justly taken and vanquished by my father, whom God
preserve and protect. But what? whereas other Kings and
Emperours, yea those who entitle themselves Catholiques,
would have dealt roughly with him, kept him a close prisoner,
and put him to an extream high ransom: he intreated him
very courteously, lodged him kindly with himself in his own
Palace, and out of his incredible mildnesse and gentle disposition
sent him back with a safe conduct, loaden with gifts, loaden
with favours, loaden with all offices of friendship: what fell
out upon it? Being returned into his countrey, he called a
Parliament, where all the Princes and States of his Kingdom
being assembled, he shewed them the humanity which he had
found in us, and therefore wished them to take such course by
way of compensation therein, as that the whole world might be

edified by the example, as well of their honest graciousnesse to us, as of our gracious honesty towards them. The result hereof was, that it was voted and decreed by an unanimous consent, that they should offer up entirely their Lands, Dominions and Kingdomes, to be disposed of by us according to our pleasure.

Alpharbal in his own person, presently returned with nine thousand and thirty eight great ships of burden, bringing with him the treasures, not only of his house and royal lineage, but almost of all the countrey besides ; for he imbarking himself, to set saile with a West-North-East winde, every one in heaps did cast into the ship gold, silver, rings, jewels, spices, drugs, and aromatical parfumes, parrets, pelicans, monkies, civet-cats, black-spotted weesils, porcupines, etc. He was accounted no good Mothers son, that did not cast in all the rare and precious things he had.

Being safely arrived, he came to my said father, and would have kist his feet : that action was found too submissively low, and therefore was not permitted, but in exchange he was most cordially embraced : he offered his presents, they were not received, because they were too excessive : he yielded himself voluntarily a servant and vassal, and was content his whole posterity should be liable to the same bondage ; this was not accepted of, because it seemed not equitable : he surrendered by vertue of the decree of his great Parliamentarie councel, his whole Countreys and Kingdomes to him, offering the Deed and Conveyance, signed, sealed and ratified by all those that were concerned in it ; this was altogether refused, and the parchments cast into the fire. In end, this free good will, and simple meaning of the Canarriens wrought such tendernesse in my fathers heart, that he could not abstain from shedding teares, and wept most profusely : then, by choise words very congruously adapted, strove in what he could to diminish the estimation of the good offices which he had done them, saying, that any courtesie he had conferred upon them was not worth a rush, and what favour so ever he had shewed them, he was bound to do it. But so much the more did Alpharbal augment the repute thereof. What was the issue ? whereas for his ransom in the greatest extremity of rigour, and most tyrannical dealing, could not have been exacted above twenty times a hundred thousand crownes, and his eldest sons detained as hostages, till that summe had been payed, they made themselves perpetual tributaries, and obliged to give us every year two millions of gold at foure and twenty carats fine : The first year we received the whole sum of two millions : the second yeare of their own accord they payed freely to us three and twenty hundred thousand crowns ; the third year six and twenty hundred thousand ; the fourth year, three millions, and do so increase it alwayes out of their own good will, that we shall be constrained to forbid them to bring us any more. This is the nature of gratitude and true thankfulnesse. For time, which gnawes and diminisheth all things else, augments and increaseth benefits ; because a noble action of liberality, done to a man of reason, doth grow continually, by his generous thinking of it, and remembring it.

Being unwilling therefore any way to degenerate from the hereditary mildnesse and clemencie of my Parents, I do now forgive you, deliver you from all fines and imprisonments, fully release you, set you at liberty, and every way make you as frank and free as ever you were before. Moreover, at your going out of the gate, you shall have every one of you three moneths pay to bring you home into your houses and families, and shall have a safe convoy of six hundred cuirasiers and eight thousand foot under the conduct of Alexander, Esquire of my body, that the Clubmen of the Countrey may not do you any injury. God be with you. I am sorry from my heart that Picrochole is not here ; for I would have given him to understand, that this warre was undertaken against my will, and without any hope to increase either my goods or renown : but seeing he is lost, and that no man can tell where nor how he went away, it is my will that his Kingdome remain entire to his sonne ; who, because he is too young, (he not being yet full five yeares old,) shall be brought up and instructed by the ancient Princes, and learned men of the Kingdom. And because a Realm thus desolate, may easily come to ruine ; if the covetousnesse and avarice of those, who by their places are obliged to administer justice in it, be not curbed and restrained : I ordain and will have it so, that Ponocrates be overseer and superintendent above all his governours, with whatever power and authority is requisite thereto, and that he be continually with the childe, until he finde him able and capable to rule and govern by himself.

Now I must tell you, that you are to understand how a too feeble and dissolute facility in pardoning evil-doers, giveth them occasion to commit wickednesse afterwards more readily, upon this pernicious confidence of receiving favour ; I consider,

HE CAUSED TO BE HONOURABLY BURIED IN BLACK-SOILE-VALLEY

147

that Moses, the meekest man that was in his time upon the earth, did severely punish the mutinous and seditious people of Israel : I consider likewise, that Julius Cæsar, who was so gracious an Emperour, that Cicero said of him, that his fortune had nothing more excellent than that he could ; and his vertue nothing better than that he would alwayes save and pardon every man : He notwithstanding all this, did in certain places most rigorously punish the authors of rebellion ; After the example of these good men, it is my will and pleasure, that you deliver over unto me, before you depart hence, first, that fine fellow Marquet, who was the prime cause, origin and ground-work of this warre, by his vain presumption and overweening : secondly, his fellow cake-bakers, who were neglective in check-ing and reprehending his idle hairebrain'd humour in the instant time : and lastly, all the Councillors, Captains, Officers and Domesticks of Picrochole, who had been incendiaries or fomenters of the warre, by provoking, praising or counselling him to come out of his limits thus to trouble us.

CHAPTER LI

How the victorious Gargantuists were recompensed after the Battel

WHEN Gargantua had finished his speech, the seditious men whom he required, were delivered up unto him, except Swash-buckler, Durtaille, and Smaltrash, who ran away sixe houres before the battel, one of them as farre as to Lainielneck at one course, another to the valley of Vire, and the third even unto Logroine, without looking back, or taking breath by the way ; and two of the Cake-bakers who were slaine in the fight, Gargantua did them no other hurt, but that he appointed them to pull at the presses of his Printing-house, which he had newly set up : then those who died there he caused to be honourably buried in Black-soile-valley, and Burn-hag-field, and gave order that the wounded should be drest and had care of in his great hospital or Nosocome. After this, considering the great pre-judice done to the towne and its inhabitants, he re-imbursed their charges, and repaired all the losses that by their confession upon oath could appear they had sustained : and for their better defence and security in times coming against all sudden uproars and invasions, commanded a strong cittadel to be built there with a competent Garison to maintaine it; at his departure he did very graciously thank all the souldiers of the brigades that had been at this overthrow, and sent them back to their winter-quarters in their several stations, and Garisons; the Decumane Legion onely excepted, whom in the field on that day he saw do some great exploit, and their Captains also, whom he brought along with himself unto Grangousier.

At the sight and coming of them, the good man was so joyful, that it is not possible fully to describe it; he made them a feast the most magnificent, plentiful, and delicious that ever was seen since the time of the king Assuerus; at the taking up of the table he distributed amongst them his whole cupboard of plate, which weighed eight hundred thousand and fourteen Besants of gold, in great antick vessels, huge pots, large basins, big tasses, cups, goblets, candlesticks, comfit-boxes, and other such plate, all of pure massie gold besides the precious stones, enameling and workmanship, which by all mens estimation was more worth then the matter of the gold; then unto ever one of them out of his coffers caused he to be given the summe of twelve hundred thousand crownes ready money: and further he gave to each of them for ever and in perpetuity (unlesse he should happen to decease without heirs) such Castles and neighbouring lands of his as were most commodious for them: to Ponocrates he gave the rock Clermond; to Gymnast, the Coudray; to Eudemon, Monpensier, Rivan, to Tolmere; to Ithibolle, Montsaureau; to Acamas, Cande; Varenes, to Chirovacte; Gravot, to Sebast; Quinquenais, to Alexander; Legre, to Sophrone, and so of his other places.

CHAPTER LII

How Gargantua caused to be built for the Monk the Abbey of Theleme

THERE was left onely the Monk to provide for, whom Gargantua would have made Abbot of Seville, but he refused it ; he would have given him the Abby of Bourgueil, or of Sanct Florent, which was the better, or both, if it pleased him ; but the Monk gave him a very peremptory answer, that he would never take upon him the charge nor government of Monks. For how shall I be able (said he) to rule over others, that have not full power and command of my self : if you think I have done you, or may hereafter do any acceptable service, give me leave to found an Abby after my owne minde and fancie ; the motion pleased Gargantua very well, who thereupon offered him all the Countrey of Theleme by the river of Loire, till within two leagues of the great forest of Port-huaut : the Monk then requested Gargantua to institute his religious order contrary to all others. First then (said Gargantua) you must not build a wall about your convent, for all other Abbies are strongly walled and mured about : See (said the Monk), and not without cause, (seeing wall and mure signifie but one and the same thing ;) where there is mur before and mur behinde, there is store of murmur, envie and mutual conspiracie. Moreover, seeing there are certain convents in the world, whereof the custome is, if any woman come in (I mean chaste and honest women) they immediately sweep the ground which they have trod upon : therefore was it ordained that if any man or woman entered into religious orders, should by chance come within this new Abbey, all the roomes should be thoroughly washed and cleansed through which they had passed ; and because in all other Monasteries and Nunneries all is compassed, limited, and regulated by houres, it was decreed that in this new structure there should be neither Clock nor Dial, but that according to the opportunities, and incident occasions, all their hours should be disposed of ; for (said Gargantua) the greatest losse of time, that I know, is to count the hours, what good comes of it ? now can there be any greater dotage in the world

then for one to guide and direct his courses by the sound of a
Bell, and not by his owne judgement and discretion.

Item, Because at that time they put no women into
Nunneries, but such as were either purblinde, blinkards, lame,
crooked, ill-favoured, mis-shapen, fooles, senselesse, spoyled
or corrupt; nor encloystered any men, but those that were
either sickly, subject to defluxions, ill-bred lowts, simple sots,
or peevish trouble-houses: but to the purpose; (said the
monk) A woman that is neither faire nor good, to what use
serves she? To make a Nunne of, said Gargantua: Yea,
said the Monk, and to make shirts and smocks; therefore was
it ordained, that into this religious order should be admitted
no women that were not faire, well featur'd, and of a sweet
disposition; nor men that were not comely, personable and
well conditioned.

Item, Because in the convents of women men come not
but under-hand, privily, and by stealth, it was therefore
enacted, that in this house there shall be no women in case
there be not men, nor men in case there be not women.

Item, Because both men and women, that are received into
religious orders after the expiring of their noviciat or probation-
year, were constrained and forced perpetually to stay there all
the days of their life, it was therefore ordered, that all whatever,
men or women, admitted within this Abbey, should have full
leave to depart with peace and contentment, whensoever it
should seem good to them so to do.

Item, for that the religious men and women did ordinarily
make three Vows, to wit, those of chastity, poverty and
obedience, it was therefore constituted and appointed, that in
this Convent they might be honourably married, that they
might be rich, and live at liberty. In regard to the legitimat
time of the persons to be initiated, and years under, and above,
which they were not capable of reception, the women were to be
admitted from ten till fifteen, and the men from twelve till
eighteen.

CHAPTER LIII

How the Abbey of the Thelemites was built and endowed

FOR the fabrick and furniture of the Abbey, Gargantua caused to be delivered out in ready money seven and twenty hundred thousand, eight hundred and one and thirty of those golden rams of Berrie, which have a sheep stamped on the one side, and a flowred crosse on the other ; and for every yeare, until the whole work were compleated, he allotted threescore nine thousand crowns of the Sunne, and as many of the seven starres, to be charged all upon the receit of the custom.   For the foundation and maintenance thereof for ever, he settled a perpetual fee-farm-rent of three and twenty hundred, threescore and nine thousand, five hundred and fourteen rose nobles, exempted from all homage, fealty, service or burden whatsoever, and payable every yeare at the gate of the Abbey ; and of this by letters pattent passed a very good grant.   The Architecture was in a figure hexagonal, and in such a fashion, that in every one of the six corners there was built a great round tower of threescore foot in diameter, and were all of a like forme and bignesse.   Upon the north-side ran along the river of Loire, on the bank whereof was situated the tower called Arctick : going towards the East, there was another called Calaer, the next following Anatole, the next Mesembrine, the next Hesperia, and the last Criere.   Every tower was distant from other the space of three hundred and twelve paces.   The whole Ædifice was every where six stories high, reckoning the Cellars under ground for one ; the second was arched after the fashion of a basket-handle ; the rest were seeled with pure wainscot, flourished with Flanders fret-work, in the forme of the foot of a lamp ; and covered above with fine slates, with an indorsement of lead, carrying the antick figures of little puppets, and animals of all sorts, notably well suited to one another, and guilt, together with the gutters, which, jetting without the walls from betwixt the crosse barres in a diagonal figure, painted with gold and azur, reach'd to the very ground, where they ended into great conduit-pipes, which carried all away unto the river from under the house.

YOUR SALARIE IS AT THE GIBET-FOOT

This same building was a hundred times more sumptuous and magnificent then ever was Bonnivet, Chambourg or Chantillie; for there were in it nine thousand, three hundred and two and thirty chambers, every one whereof had a withdrawing room, a handsom closet, a wardrobe, an oratory, and neat passage, leading into a great and spacious hall. Between every tower, in the midst of the said body of building, there was a paire of winding (such as we now call lantern) staires, whereof the steps were part of Porphyrie, (which is a dark red marble, spotted with white,) part of Numidian stone, (which is a kind of yellowishly streaked marble upon various colours,) and part of Serpentine marble, (with light spots on a dark green ground) each of these steps being two and twenty foot in length, and three fingers thick, and the just number of twelve betwixt every rest, or, (as we now terme it), landing place. In every resting place were two faire antick arches where the light came in : and by those they went into a Cabinet, made even with and of the bredth of the said winding, and the re-ascending above the roofs of the house, ended conically in a pavillion : By that vize or winding, they entered on every side into a great hall, and from the halls into the chambers ; from the Arctick tower unto the Criere, were the faire great libraries in Greek, Latine, Hebrew, French, Italian and Spanish, respectively distributed in their several cantons, according to the diversity of these languages. In the midst there was a wonderful scalier or winding-staire, the entry whereof was without the house, in a vault or arch six fathom broad. It was made in such symmetrie and largenesse, that six men at armes with their lances in their rests might together in a breast ride all up to the very top of all the Palace. From the tower Anatole to the Mesembrine were faire spacious galleries, all coloured over and painted with the ancient prowesses, histories and descriptions of the world. In the midst thereof there was likewise such another ascent and gate, as we said there was on the river-side. Upon that gate was written in great antick letters, that which followeth.

CHAPTER LIV

The Inscription set upon the great Gate of Theleme

HERE enter not vile bigots, hypocrites,
Externally devoted Apes, base snites,
Puft up, wry-necked beasts, worse then the Huns
Or Ostrogots, forerunners of baboons :
Curst snakes, dissembled varlots, seeming Sancts,
Slipshod caffards, beggars pretending wants,
Fat chuffcats, smell-feast knockers, doltish gulls,
Out-strouting cluster-fists, contentious bulls,
Fomenters of divisions and debates,
Elsewhere, not here, make sale of your deceits.

> Your filthy trumperies
> Stuff't with pernicious lies,
>   (Not worth a bubble)
>   Would do but trouble,
> Our earthly Paradise,
> Your filthy trumperies.

Here enter not Atturneys, Barristers,
Nor bridle champing law-Practitioners :
Clerks, Commissaries, Scribes nor Pharisees,
Wilful disturbers of the Peoples ease :
Judges, destroyers, with an unjust breath,
Of honest men, like dogs, ev'n unto death.
Your salarie is at the gibet-foot :
Go drink there ; for we do not here fly out
On those excessive courses, which may draw
A waiting on your courts by suits in law.

> Law-suits, debates and wrangling
> Hence are exil'd, and jangling.
>   Here we are very
>   Frolic and merry.
> And free from all intangling,
> Law-suits, debates and wrangling

Here enter not base pinching Usurers,
Pelf-lickers, everlasting gatherers.
Gold-graspers, coine-gripers, gulpers of mists :
Niggish deformed sots, who, though your chests
Vast summes of money should to you affoard,
Would ne'erthelesse adde more unto that hoard,
And yet not be content, you cluntchfist dastards,
Insatiable fiends, and Plutoes bastards.
Greedie devourers, chichie sneakbill rogues,
Hell-mastiffs gnaw your bones, you rav'nous dogs.

> You beastly looking fellowes,
> Reason doth plainly tell us,
>   That we should not
>   To you allot
> Roome here, but at the Gallowes,
> You beastly looking fellowes.

Here enter not fond makers of demurres
In love adventures, peevish, jealous curres,
Sad pensive dotards, raisers of garboyles,
Hags, goblins, ghosts, firebrands of houshold broyls,
Nor drunkards, liars, cowards, cheaters, clowns,
Theeves, cannibals, faces o'recast with frowns,
Nor lazie slugs, envious, covetous :
Nor blockish, cruel, nor too credulous.
Here mangie, pockie folks shall have no place,
No ugly lusks, nor persons of disgrace.

> Grace, honour, praise, delight,
> Here sojourn day and night.
>   Sound bodies lin'd
>   With a good minde,
> Do here pursue with might
> Grace, honour, praise, delight.

Here enter you, and welcom from our hearts,
All noble sparks, endow'd with gallant parts.
This is the glorious place, which bravely shall
Afford wherewith to entertain you all.
Were you a thousand, here you shall not want
For any thing ; for what you 'l ask we 'l grant.

Stay here, you lively, jovial, handsom, brisk,
Gay, witty, frolick, chearful, merry, frisk,
Spruce, jocund, courteous, furtherers of trades,
And in a word, all worthy gentile blades.

    Blades of heroick breasts
    Shall taste here of the feasts,
      Both privily
      And civilly
    Of the celestial guests,
    Blades of heroick breasts.

Here enter you, pure, honest, faithful, true,
Expounders of the Scriptures old and new.
Whose glosses do not blind our reason, but
Make it to see the clearer, and who shut
Its passages from hatred, avarice,
Pride, factious cov'nants, and all sort of vice.
Come, settle here a charitable faith,
Which neighbourly affection nourisheth.
And whose light chaseth all corrupters hence,
Of the blist Word, from the aforesaid sense.

    The Holy Sacred Word
    May it alwayes afford
      T' us all in common
      Both man and woman
    A sp'ritual shield and sword,
    The holy sacred Word.

Here enter you all Ladies of high birth,
Delicious, stately, charming, full of mirth,
Ingenious, lovely, miniard, proper, faire,
Magnetick, graceful, splendid, pleasant, rare,
Obliging, sprightly, vertuous, young, solacious,
Kinde, neat, quick, feat, bright, compt, ripe,
    choice, dear, precious.
Alluring, courtly, comely, fine, compleat,
Wise, personable, ravishing and sweet.
Come joyes enjoy, the Lord celestial
Hath giv'n enough, wherewith to please us all.

Gold give us, God forgive us,
And from all woes relieve us.
  That we the treasure
  May reap of pleasure.
And shun what e're is grievous,
Gold Give us, God forgive us.

CHAPTER LV

What manner of Dwelling the Thelemites had

IN the middle of the lower Court there was a stately fountain of faire Alabaster, upon the top thereof stood the three Graces, with their cornucopias, or hornes of abundance, and did jert out the water at their breasts, mouth, eares, eyes, and other open passages of the body ; the inside of the buildings in this lower Court stood upon great pillars of Cassydonie stone, and Porphyrie marble, made arch-wayes after a goodly antick fashion. Within those were spacious galleries, long and large, adorned with curious pictures, the hornes of Bucks and Unicornes : with Rhinoceroses, water-horses called Hippopotames, the teeth and tusks of Elephants, and other things well worth the beholding. The lodging of the Ladies (for so we may call those gallant women) took up all from the tower Arctick unto the gate Mesembrine : the men possessed the rest, before the said lodging of the Ladies, that they might have their recreation between the two first towers. On the out-side, were placed the tilt-yard, the barriers or lists for turnements, the hippodrome or riding Court, the theater or publike play-house, and Natatorie or place to swim in, with most admirable bathes in three stages, situated above one another, well furnished with all necessary accommodation, and store of myrtle-water. By the river-side was the faire garden of pleasure ; and in the midst of that the glorious labyrinth. Between the two other towers were the Courts for the tennis and the baloon. Towards the tower Criere stood the Orchard full of all fruit-trees, set and ranged in a quincuncial order. At the end of that was the great Park, abounding with all sort of Venison. Betwixt the third couple of towers were the buts and marks for shooting with a snap-work gun, an ordinary bowe for common archery, or with a Crosse bowe. The office-houses were without the tower Hesperie, of one story high. The stables were beyond the offices, and before them stood the falconrie, managed by ostridge-keepers and Falconers, very expert in the art, and it was yearly supplied and furnished by the Canadians, Venetians, Sarmates (now called Moscoviters) with all sorts of most excellent hawks, eagles, gerfalcons, gosehawkes, sacres, lanners, falcons, sparhawks, Marlins, and other kindes of them, so gentle and perfectly well manned, that flying of themselves sometimes from the Castle for their own disport, they would not faile to catch whatever they encountred. The Venerie where the Beagles and Hounds were kept, was a little farther off drawing towards the Park.

All the halls, chambers, and closets or cabinets, were richly hung with tapestrie, and hangings of divers sorts, according to the variety of the seasons of the year. All the pavements and floors were covered with green cloth : the beds were all embroidered : in every back-chamber or withdrawing room there was a looking-glasse of pure crystal set in a frame of fine gold, garnished all about with pearles, and was of such greatnesse, that it would represent to the full the whole lineaments and proportion of the person that stood before it. At the going out of the halls, which belong to the Ladies lodgings, were the perfumers and trimmers, through whose hands the gallants past when they were to visit the Ladies ; those sweet Artificers did every morning furnish the Ladies chambers with the spirit of roses, orange-flower-water and Angelica ; and to each of them gave a little precious casket vapouring forth the most odoriferous exhalations of the choicest aromatical sents.

CHAPTER LVI

How the Men and Women of the Religious Order of Theleme were apparelled

THE Ladies at the foundation of this order, were apparelled after their own pleasure and liking ; but since that of their own accord and free will they have reformed themselves, their accoutrement is in manner as followeth. They wore stockins of scarlet crimson, or ingrained purple die, which reached just three inches above the knee, having a list beautified with exquisite embroideries, and rare incisions of the Cutter's art. Their garters were of the colour of their bracelets, and circled the knee a little both over and under. Their shoes, pumps and slippers were either of red, violet, or crimson-velvet, pinked and jagged like Lobster wadles.

Next to their smock they put on the pretty kirtle or vasquin of pure silk chamlet : above that went the taffatie or tabie vardingale, of white, red, tawnie, gray, or of any other colour ; Above this taffatie petticoat they had another of cloth of tissue or brocado, embroidered with fine gold, and interlaced with needle-work, or as they thought good, and according to the temperature and disposition of the weather had their upper coats of sattin, damask or velvet, and those either orange, tawnie, green, ash-coloured, blew, yelow, bright, red, crimson or white, and so forth ; or had them of cloth of gold, cloth of silver, or some other choise stuffe, inriched with purple, or embroidered according to the dignity of the festival dayes and times wherein they wore them.

Their gownes, being still correspondent to the season, were either of cloth of gold frizled with a silver-raised work : of red sattin, covered with gold purle ; of tabie, or taffatie, white, blew, black, tawnie, etc., of silk serge, silk chamlot, velvet, cloth of silver, silver tissue, cloth of gold, gold wire, figured velvet, or figured sattin tinselled and overcast with golden threads, in divers variously purfled draughts.

In the summer some dayes in stead of gowns they wore light handsome mantles, made either of the stuffe of the aforesaid attire, or like Moresco rugs, of violet, velvet frizled, with a raised work of gold upon silver purle, or with a knotted cord-work of gold embroiderie, every where garnished with little Indian pearles. They alwayes carried a faire Pannache, or plume of feathers, of the colour of their muffe, bravely adorned and tricked out with glistening spangles of gold. In the winter-time, they had their taffatie gownes of all colours, as above-named : and those lined with the rich furrings of hinde-wolves, or speckled linxes, black-spotted weesils, martlet-skins of Calabria, sables, and other costly furres of an inestimable value. Their beads, rings, bracelets, collars, carcanets and neck-chaines were all of precious stones, such as carbuncles, rubies, baleus, diamonds, saphirs, emeralds, turkoises, garnets, agates, berilles, and excellent margarits. Their head-dressing also varied with the season of the yeare, according to which they decked themselves. In winter it was of the French fashion, in the spring of the Spanish ; in summer of the fashion of Tuscanie, except only upon the holy dayes and Sundayes, at which times they were accoutred in the French mode, because they accounted it more honourable, and better befitting the garb of a matronal pudicity.

The men were apparelled after their fashion ; their stockins were of tamine or of cloth-serge, of white, black, scarlet, or some other ingrained colour : their breeches were of velvet, of the same colour with their stockins, or very near, embroidered and cut according to their fancy ; their doublet was of cloth of gold, of cloth of silver, of velvet, sattin, damask, taffaties, etc., of the same colours, cut, embroidered, and suitably trimmed up in perfection : the points were of silk of the same colours, the tags were of gold well enameled : their coats and jerkins were of cloth of gold, cloth of silver, gold, tissue or velvet embroi-dered, as they thought fit : their gownes were every whit as costly as those of the Ladies : their girdles were of silk, of the colour of their doublets ; every one had a gallant sword by his side, the hilt and handle whereof were gilt, and the scabbard of velvet, of the colour of his breeches, with a chape of gold, and pure Goldsmiths work : the dagger was of the same : their caps or bonnets were of black velvet, adorned with jewels and buttons of gold ; upon that they wore a white plume, most prettily and minion-like, parted by so many rowes of gold spangles, at the end whereof hung dangling in a more sparkling resplendencie faire rubies, emeralds, diamonds, etc., but there was such a sympathy betwixt the gallants and the Ladies, that every day they were apparelled in the same livery : and that

they might not misse, there were certain Gentlemen appointed
to tell the youths every morning what vestments the ladies
would on that day weare; for all was done according to the
pleasure of the Ladies. In these so handsome clothes, and
abiliaments so rich, think not that either one or other of either
sex did waste any time at all; for the Masters of the wardrobes
had all their raiments and apparel so ready for every morning,
and the chamber-Ladies so well skilled, that in a trice they
would be dressed, and compleatly in their clothes from head
to foot. And to have those accoutrements with the more conveniency, there was about the wood of Theleme a row of houses
of the extent of half a league, very neat and cleanly, wherein
dwelt the Goldsmiths, Lapidaries, Jewellers, Embroiderers,
Tailors, Gold-drawers, Velvet-weavers, Tapestrie-makers and
Upholsterers, who wrought there every one in his own trade,
and all for the aforesaid jollie Friars and Nuns of the new stamp,
they were furnished with matter and stuffe from the hands of
the Lord Nausiclete, who every year brought them seven ships
from the Perlas and Cannibal-islands, laden with ingots of gold,
with raw silk, with pearles and precious stones. And if any
margarites (called unions), began to grow old, and lose somewhat of their natural whitenesse and lustre, those with their
Art they did renew, by tendering them to eat to some pretty
cocks, as they use to give casting into hawkes.

CHAPTER LVII

How the Thelemites were governed, and of their Manner of living

ALL their life was spent not in lawes, statutes or rules, but
according to their own free will and pleasure. They rose out

of their beds, when they thought good : they did eat, drink, labour, sleep, when they had a minde to it, and were disposed for it. None did awake them, none did offer to constrain them to eat, drink, nor to do any thing ; for so had Gargantua established it. In all their rule, and strictest tie of their order, there was but this one clause to be observed,

DO WHAT THOU WILT.

Because men that are free, well-borne, well-bred, and conversant in honest companies, have naturally an instinct and spurre that prompteth them unto vertuous actions, and withdraws them from vice, which is called honour. Those same men, when by base subjection and constraint they are brought under and kept down, turn aside from that noble disposition, by which they formerly were inclined to vertue, to shake off and break that bond of servitude, wherein they are so tyrannously inslaved ; for it is agreeable with the nature of man to long after things forbidden, and to desire what is denied us.

By this liberty they entered into a very laudable emulation, to do all of them what they saw did please one ; if any of the gallants or Ladies should say, Let us drink, they would all drink : if any one of them said, Let us play, they all played ; if one said, Let us go a walking into the fields, they went all : if it were to go a hawking or a hunting, the Ladies mounted upon dainty well-paced nags, seated in a stately palfrey saddle, carried on their lovely fists, miniardly begloved every one of them, either a sparhawk, or a Laneret, or a Marlin, and the young gallants carried the other kinds of Hawkes : so nobly were they taught, that there was neither he nor she amongst them, but could read, write, sing, play upon several musical instruments, speak five or sixe several languages, and compose in them all very quaintly, both in Verse and Prose : never were seen so valiant Knights, so noble and worthy, so dextrous and skilful both on foot and a horseback, more brisk and lively, more nimble and quick, or better handling all manner of weapons then were there. Never were seene Ladies so proper and handsome, so miniard and dainty, lesse froward, or more ready with their hand, and with their needle, in every honest and free action belonging to that sexe, then were there ; for this reason, when the time came, that any man of the said Abbey, either at the request of his parents, or for some other

cause, had a minde to go out of it, he carried along with him
one of the Ladies, namely her whom he had before that chosen
for his Mistris, and were married together : and if they had
formerly in Theleme lived in good devotion and amity, they
did continue therein and increase it to a greater height in their
state of matrimony : and did entertaine that mutual love till
the very last day of their life, in no lesse vigour and fervency,
then at the very day of their wedding.   Here must not I forget
to set down unto you a riddle, which was found under the
ground, as they were laying the foundation of the Abbey,
ingraven in a copper plate, and it was thus as followeth.

CHAPTER LVIII

A Propheticall Riddle

Poor mortals, who wait for a happy day,
Cheer up your hearts, and hear what I shall say :
If it be lawful firmly to beleeve,
That the celestial bodies can us give
Wisdom to judge of things that are not yet :
Or if from Heav'n such wisdom we may get,
As may with confidence make us discourse
Of years to come, their destinie and course ;
I to my hearers give to understand,
That this next Winter, though it be at hand,
Yea and before, there shall appear a race
Of men, who loth to sit still in one place
Shall boldly go before all peoples eyes,
Suborning men of divers qualities,
To draw them unto covenants and sides,
In such a manner, that whate're betides,
They 'l move you, if you give them eare (no doubt)
With both your friends and kindred to fall out.
They 'l make a vassal to gain-stand his lord,
And children their own Parents, in a Word,
All reverence shall then be banished :
No true respect to other shall be had :
They 'l say that every man should have his turn,

THE VERIEST LOWT OF ALL SHALL BE THEIR JUDGE

Both in his going forth, and his return ;
And hereupon there shall arise such woes,
Such jarrings, and confused toos and froes,
That never were in history such coyles
Set down as yet, such tumults and garboyles.
Then shall you many gallant men see by
Valour stirr'd up, and youthful fervencie,
Who trusting too much in their hopeful time,
Live but a while, and perish in their prime.
Neither shall any who this course shall run,
Leave off the race which he hath once begun,
Till they the heavens with noise by their contention
Have fill'd, and with their steps the earth's dimension.
Then those shall have no lesse authority,
That have no faith, then those that will not lie ;
For all shall be governed by a rude,
Base, ignorant, and foolish multitude ;
The veriest lowt of all shall be their Judge,
O horrible, and dangerous deluge !
Deluge I call it, and that for good reason,
For this shall be omitted in no season ;
Nor shall the earth of this foule stirre be free,
Till suddenly you in great store shall see
The waters issue out, with those streams the
Most moderate of all shall moist'ned be,
And justly too ; because they did not spare
The flocks of beasts that innocentest are,
But did their sinews, and their bowels take,
Not to the gods a sacrifice to make,
But usually to serve themselves for sport :
And now consider, I do you exhort,
In such commotions so continual,
What rest can take the globe terrestrial ?
Most happy then are they, that can it hold,
And use it carefully as precious gold,
By keeping it in Goole, whence it shall have
No help but him, who being to it gave.
And to increase his mournful accident,
The Sunne, before it set in th' occident ;
Shall cease to dart upon it any light,
More then in an eclipse, or in the night.
So that at once its favour shall be gone,
And liberty with it be left alone.

And yet, before it come to ruine thus,
Its quaking shall be as impetuous
As Ætna's was, when Titan's sons lay under,
And yeeld, when lost, a fearful sound like thunder.
Inarime did not more quickly move,
When Typheus did the vast huge hills remove,
And for despite into the sea them threw.
   Thus shall it then be lost by wayes not few,
And changed suddenly, when those that have it
To other men that after come shall leave it.
Then shall it be high time to cease from this
So long, so great, so tedious exercise ;
For the great waters told you now by me,
Will make each think where his retreat shall be ;
And yet before that they be clean disperst,
You may behold in th' aire, where nought was erst,
The burning heat of a great flame to rise,
Lick up the water, and the enterprise.
   It resteth after those things to declare,
That those shall sit content, who chosen are,
With all good things, and with celestial man,
And richly recompensed every man :
The others at the last all strip't shall be,
That after this great work all men may see
How each shall have his due, this is their lot ;
O he is worthy-praise that shrinketh not.

No sooner was this ænigmatical monument read over, but Gargantua, fetching a very deep sigh, said unto those that stood by, It is not now only (I perceive) that People called to the faith of the Gospel, and convinced with the certainty of Evangelical truths, are persecuted ; but happy is that man that shall not be scandalized, but shall alwayes continue to the end, in aiming at that mark, which God by his dear Son hath set before us, without being distracted or diverted by his carnal affections and depraved nature.

The Monk then said, What do you think in your conscience is meant and signified by this riddle ?   What ? (said Gargantua) the progresse and carrying on of the divine truth.   By St. Goderan (said the monk) that is not my exposition ; it is the stile of the Prophet Merlin : make upon it as many grave allegories and glosses as you will, and dote upon it you and the rest of the world as long as you please : for my part, I can conceive no other meaning in it, but a description of a set at tennis in dark and obscure termes. The suborners of men are the Makers of matches, which are commonly friends. After the two chases are made, he that was in the upper end of the tennis-court goeth out, and the other cometh in. They beleeve the first, that saith the ball was over or under the line. The waters are the heats that the players take till they sweat again. The cords of the rackets are made of the guts of sheep or goats. The Globe terrestrial is the tennis-ball. After playing, when the game is done, they refresh themselves before a clear fire, and change their shirts : and very willingly they make all good cheer, but most merrily those that have gained : And so, farewel.

FINIS

THE SECOND BOOK OF THE WORKS OF ∽ ∽ MR.
FRANCIS RABELAIS ∽ ∽ DOCTOR IN PHY-
SICK ∽ ∽ TREATING OF THE HEROICK DEEDS,
AND ∽ ∽ SAYINGS OF THE GOOD ∽ ∽ PANTA-
GRUEL ∽ ∽ WRITTEN ORIGINALLY IN THE ∽ ∽
FRENCH TONGUE ∽ ∽ AND NOW FAITHFULLY
TRANSLATED INTO ∽ ∽ ENGLISH

FOR THE READER

THE Reader here may be pleased to take notice, that the Copy of Verses
by the title of Rablophila, premised to the first book of this Translation,
being but a kinde of mock Poem, in imitation of somewhat lately published,
(as to any indifferent Observer will easily appear, by the false quantities
in the Latine, the abusive strain of the English, and extravagant sub-
scription to both,) and as such, by a friend of the translators, at the desire
of some frolick Gentlemen of his acquaintance (more for a trial of skill,
then prejudicacie to any,) composed in his jollity, to please their fancies,
was only ordained to be prefixed to a dozen of books, and no more, thereby
to save the labour of transcribing so many, as were requisite for satisfying
the curiosity of a company of just that number ; and that therefore the
charging of the whole Impression with it is meerly to be imputed to the
negligence of the Presse-men, who receiving it about the latter end of the
night, were so eager before the next morning to afford compleat books,
that as they began, they went on, without animadverting what was recommended to their discretion ;   This is hoped will suffice to assure the
ingenuous Reader, that in no treatise of the Translators, (whether Original
or Translatitious) shall willingly be offered the meanest rub to the reputation of any worthy Gentleman, and that however Providence dispose of
him, no misfortune shall be able to induce his minde to any complacency
in the disparagement of another.

Again.

The Pentateuch of Rabelais, mentioned in the title-page of the first
book of this Translation, being written Originally in the French Tongue,
(as it comprehendeth some of its bruskest dialects,) with so much in-
geniositie, and wit, that more impressions have been sold thereof in that
language, then of any other book, that hath been set forth at any time
within these fifteen hundred yeares : so difficult nevertthelesse to be turned
into any other speech, that many prime spirits in most of the Nations of
Europe, since the yeare 1573, (which was fourescore yeares ago) after
having attempted it, were constrained with no small regret to give it over,
as a thing impossible to be done, is now in its Translation thus farre

advanced, and the remainder faithfully undertaken with the same hand to be rendered into English by a Person of quality, who (though his lands be sequestred, his house garrisoned, his other goods sold, and himself detained a Prisoner of warre at London, for his having been at Worcester fight) hath, at the most earnest intreaty of some of his especial friends, well acquainted with his inclination to the performance of conducible singularities promised, besides his version of these two already published, very speedily to offer up unto this Isle of Britaine the virginity of the Translation of the other three most admirable books of the aforesaid Author ; provided that by the plurality of judicious and understanding men it be not declared, he hath already proceeded too farre, or that the continuation of the rigour whereby he is dispossest of all his both real and personal estate, by pressing too hard upon him, be not an impediment thereto, and to other more eminent undertakings of his, as hath beene oftentimes very fully mentioned by the said Translatour, in several original Treatises of his own penning, lately by him so numerously dispersed, that there is scarce any, who being skilful in the English Idiome, or curious of any new ingenious invention, hath not either read them, or heard of them.

MR. HUGH SALEL TO RABELAIS

If profit mix'd with pleasure may suffice,
T' extoll an Authors worth above the skies,
Thou certainly for both must praised be :
I know it ; for thy judgement hath in the
Contexture of this book set down such high
Contentments, mingled with utility,
That (as I think) I see Democritus
Laughing at men as things ridiculous :
   Insist in thy designe ; for, though we prove
   Ungrate on earth, thy merit is above.

THE AUTHOR'S PROLOGUE TO THE SECOND BOOK

Most Illustrious and thrice valourous Champions, Gentlemen and others, who willingly apply your mindes to the entertainment of pretty conceits, and honest harmlesse knacks of wit : You have not long ago seen, read and understood the great and inestimable Chronicle of the huge and mighty Gyant Gargantua, and like upright Faithfullists, have firmly beleeved all to be true that is contained in them, and have very often passed your time with them amongst Honourable Ladies and Gentle-women, telling them faire long stories, when you were out of all other talk, for which you are worthy of gret apraise and sempiternal memory : and I do heartily wish that every man would lay aside his own businesse, meddle no more with his Profession nor Trade, and throw all affaires concerning himself behinde his back, to attend this wholly, without distracting or troubling his minde with any thing else, until he have learned them without book ; that if by chance the Art of printing should cease, or in case that in time to come all books should perish, every man might truly teach them unto his children, and deliver them over to his successors and survivors from hand to hand, as a religious Cabal ; for there is in it more profit, then a rabble of great pockie Loggerheads are able to discern, who surely understand far lesse in these little merriments, then the fool Raclet did in the institutions of Justinian.

I have known great and mighty Lords, and of those not a few, who, going a Deer-hunting, or a hawking after wilde Ducks, when the chase had not encountered with the blinks, that were cast in her way to retard her course, or that the Hawk did but plaine and smoothly fly without moving her wings, perceiving the prey by force of flight to have gained bounds of her, have been much chafed and vexed, as you understand well enough ; but the comfort unto which they had refuge, and that they might not take cold, was to relate the inestimable deeds of the said Gargantua. There are others in the world, (these are no flimflam stories, nor tales of a tub,) who being much troubled with the toothache, after they had spent their goods upon Physicians, without receiving at all any ease of their pain, have found no more ready remedy, then to put the said Chronicles betwixt two pieces of linnen cloth made somewhat hot, and so apply them to the place that smarteth, synapising them with a little powder of projection, otherwayes called doribus.

But what shall I say of those poor men, that are plagued with the Pox and the Gowt ? O how often have we seen them, even immediately after they were anointed and thoroughly greased, till their faces did glister like the Keyhole of a powdering tub, their teeth dance like the jacks of a paire of little Organs or Virginals, when they are played upon, and that they foamed from their very throats like a boare, which the Mongrel Mastiffe-hounds have driven in, and overthrown among the foyles : what did they then ? All their consolation was to have some page of the said jollie book read unto them : and we have seen those who have given themselves to a hundred punchions of old devils, in case that they did not feele a manifest ease and asswagement of paine, at the hearing of the said book read, even when they were kept in a purgatory of torment ; no more nor lesse then women in travel use to finde their sorrow abated, when the life of St. Margarite is read unto them : is this nothing ? finde me a book in any language, in any faculty or science whatsoever, that hath such vertues, properties and prerogatives, and I will be content to pay you a quart of tripes. No, my Masters, no, it is peerlesse, incomparable, and not to be matched ; and this am I resolved for ever to maintaine even unto the fire *exclusive*. And those that will pertinaciously hold the contrary opinion, let them be accounted Abusers, Predestinators, Impostors and Seducers of the People; it is very true, that there are found in some gallant and stately books, worthy of high estimation, certain occult and hid properties; in the number of which are reckoned Whippot, Orlando furioso, Robert the devil, Fierabras, William without feare, Huon of Bourdeaux, Monteville, and Matabrune; but they are not comparable to that which we speak of; and the world hath well known by infallible experience the great emolument and utility which it hath received by this Gargantuine Chronicle; for the Printers have sold more of them in two moneths time, then there will be bought of Bibles in nine years.

I therefore (your humble slave) being very willing to increase your solace and recreation a little more, do offer you for a Present another book of the same stamp, only that it is a little more reasonable and worthy of credit then the other was; for think not (unless you wilfully will erre against your knowledge) that I speak of it as the Jewes do of the Law; I was not born under such a Planet, neither did it ever befall me to lie, or affirme a thing for true that was not: I speak of it like a lustie frolick Onocrotarie, I should say Crotenotarie of the martyrised lovers, and Croquenotarie of love. *Quod vidimus, testamur.* It is of the horrible and dreadful feats and prowesses of Pantagruel, whose menal servant I have been since I was a page, till this houre that by his leave I am permitted to visit my Cow-countrey, and to know if any of my kindred there be alive.

And therefore, to make an end of this Prologue, even as I give myselfe to an hundred Pannier-fulls of faire devils, body and soul, tripes and guts, in case that I lie so much as one single word in this whole History: After the like manner, St. Anthonies fire burne you; Mahoom's disease whirle you; the squinance with a stitch in your side, and the Wolfe in your stomack trusse you, the bloody flux seize upon you, the curst sharp inflammations of wilde fire, as slender and thin as Cowes haire, strengthened with quick silver, enter into your fundament, and like those of Sodom and Gomorrha, may you fall into sulphur, fire and bottomlesse pits, in case you do not firmly beleeve all that I shall relate unto you in this present Chronicle.

MAY YOU FALL INTO SULPHUR, FIRE AND BOTTOMLESSE PITS

173

THE SECOND BOOK

CHAPTER I

Of the Original and Antiquity of the great Pantagruel

It will not be an idle nor unprofitable thing, seeing we are
at leasure to put you in minde of the Fountain and Original
Source, whence is derived unto us the good Pantagruel; for
I see that all good Historiographers have thus handled their
Chronicle; not only the Arabians, Barbarians and Latines, but
also the gentle Greeks, who were eternal drinkers. You must
therefore remark, that at the beginning of the world, (I speak
of a long time, it is above fourty quarantaines, or fourty times
fourty nights, according to the supputation of the ancient
Druids) a little after that Abel was killed by his brother Cain,
the earth, imbrued with the blood of the just, was one year so
exceeding fertil in all those fruits which it usually produceth
to us, and especially in Medlars, that ever since, throughout
all ages it hath been called the year of the great medlars, for
three of them did fill a bushel: in it the Calends were found by
the Grecian Almanacks, there was that yeare nothing of the
moneth of March in the time of Lent, and the middle of August
was in May: in the moneth of October, as I take it, or at
least September, (that I may not erre, for I will carefully take
heed of that) was the week so famous in the Annals, which they
call the week of the three Thursdayes; for it had three of them
by meanes of the irregular leap-yeares, (called Bissextils)
occasioned by the Sunnes having tripped and stumbled a little
towards the left hand, like a debtor afraid of Serjeants, coming
right upon him to arrest him: and the Moon varied from her
course above five fathom, and there was manifestly seen the
motion of trepidation in the firmament of the fixed starres, called
Aplanes, so that the middle Pleiade, leaving her fellows, declined
towards the Equinoctial, and the starre named Spica left the
constellation of the Virgin to withdraw herself towards the
balance, known by the name of Libra, which are cases very
terrible, and matters so hard and difficult, that Astrologians

174

cannot set their teeth in them; and indeed their teeth had been
pretty long if they could have reached thither.

However account you it for a truth, that every body then
did most heartily eat of those medlars, for they were faire to
the eye, and in taste delicious : but even as Noah, that holy
man, (to whom we are so much beholding, bound and obliged,
for that he planted to us the Vine, from whence we have that
nectarian, delicious, precious, heavenly, joyful and deifick
liquour, which they call the piot or tiplage) was deceived in the
drinking of it, for he was ignorant of the great vertue and
power thereof : so likewise the men and women of that time
did delight much in the eating of that faire great fruit, but
divers and very different accidents did ensue thereupon ; for
there fell upon them all in their bodies a most terrible swelling,
but not upon all in the same place, for some were swollen in the
belly, and their belly strouted out big like a great tun, of whom
it is written, *Ventrem omnipotentem,* who were all very honest
men, and merry blades : and of this race came St. Fatgulch and
Shrove-tuesday. Others did swell at the shoulders, who in
that place were so crump and knobbie, that they were therefore
called Montifers, (which is as much to say as Hill-carriers,) of
whom you see some yet in the world of divers sexes and degrees :
of this race came Æsop, some of whose excellent words and
deeds you have in writing : some other puffes did swell in
length by the member, which they call the Labourer of nature,
in such sort that it grew marvellous long, fat, great, lustie,
stirring and Crest-risen, in the Antick fashion, so that they
made use of it as of a girdle, winding it five or six times about
their waste : but if it happened the foresaid member to be in
good case, spooming with a full saile bunt faire before the
winde, then to have seen those strouting Champions, you would
have taken them for men that had their lances setled on their
Rest, to run at the ring or tilting whintam : of these beleeve
me the race is utterly lost and quite extinct, as the women say ;
for they do lament continually, that there are none extant now
of those great, etc. you know the rest of the song. Others did
grow in matter of ballocks so enormously, that three of them
would well fill a sack, able to contain five quarters of wheat,
from them are descended the ballocks of Lorraine, which never
dwell in Codpieces, but fall down to the bottome of the breeches.
Others grew in the legs, and to see them, you would have said
they had been Cranes, or the reddish-long-bill'd-stork-likt-
scrank-legged sea-fowles, called Flamans, or else men walking

upon stilts or scatches: the little Grammar schoolboyes (known by the name of Grimos,) called those leg-grown slangams Jambus, in allusion to the French word *Jambe*, which signifieth a leg. In others, their nose did grow so, that it seemed to be the beak of a Limbeck, in every part thereof most variously diapred with the twinkling sparkles of Crimson-blisters budding forth, and purpled with pimples all enameled with thick-set wheales of a sanguine colour, bordered with gueules, and such have you see the Chanon, or Prebend Panzoul, and Woodenfoot the Physician of Angiers: of which race there were few that liked the Ptisane, but all of them were perfect lovers of the pure septembral juice; Naso and Ovid had their extraction from thence, and all those of whom it is written, *Ne reminiscaris*. Others grew in eares, which they had so big, that out of one would have been stuffe enough got to make a doublet, a paire of breeches and a jacket, whilest with the other they might have covered themselves as with a Spanish Cloak: and they say, that in Bourbonois this race remaineth yet. Others grew in length of body, and of those came the Giants, and of them Pantagruel.

And the first was Chalbroth
who begat Sarabroth
who begat Faribroth
who begat Hurtali, that was a brave eater of pottage, and reigned in the time of the flood
who begat Nembroth
who begat Atlas, that with his shoulders kept the sky from falling.
who begat Goliah
who begat Erix, that invented the Hocus pocus playes of Legerdemain.
who begat Titius
who begat Eryon
who begat Polyphemus
who begat Cacos
who begat Etion, the first man that ever had the pox, for not drinking fresh in Summer as Bartachin witnesseth.
who begat Enceladus
who begat Ceus
who begat Tiphæus
who begat Alæus
who begat Othus

who begat Ægeon
who begat Briareus that had a hundred hands.
who begat Porphyrio
who begat Adamastor
who begat Anteus
who begat Agatho
who begat Porus, against whom fought Alexander the great
who begat Aranthas
who begat Gabbara, that was the first inventor of the drinking
    of healths.
who begat Goliah of Secondille
who begat Offot, that was terribly well nosed for drinking at
    the barrel-head.
who begat Artachæus
who begat Oromedon
who begat Gemmagog, the first inventor of Poulan shoes,
    which are open on the foot, and tied over the instep with
    a latchet.
who begat Sisyphus
who begat the Titans, of whom Hercules was born.
who begat Enay, the most skilful man that ever was, in matter
    of taking the little wormes (called Cirons) out of the
    hands.
who begat Fierabras, that was vanquished by Oliver Peer of
    France, and Rowlands Camrade.
who begat Morgan, the first in the world that played at dice
    with spectacles.
who begat Fracassus, of whom Merlin Coccaius hath written,
    and of him was borne Ferragus.
who begat Hapmouche, the first that ever invented the drying
    of neats tongues in the Chimney; for, before that,
    people salted them, as they do now gammons of
    bacon.
who begat Bolivorax
who begat Longis
who begat Gayoffo, whose ballocks were of poplar, and his
    pr... of the servise or sorb-apple-tree.
who begat Maschefain
who begat Bruslefer
who begat Angoulevent
who begat Galehaut the inventor of flaggons.
who begat Mirelangaut
who begat Gallaffre

M

who begat Salourdin
who begat Roboast
who begat Sortibrant of Conimbres.
who begat Brusbant of Mommiere
who begat Bruyer that was overcome by Ogier the Dane Peer
 of France.
who begat Mabrun
who begat Foutasnon
who begat Haquelebas
who begat Vitdegrain
who begat Grangousier
who begat Gargantua
who begat the noble Pantagruel my Master.

  I know that reading this passage, you will make a doubt
within your selves, and that grounded upon very good reason ;
which is this, how it is possible that this relation can be true,
seeing at the time of the flood all the world was destroyed,
except Noah, and seven persons more with him in the Ark, into
whose number Hurtali is not admitted ; doubtlesse the demand
is well made, and very apparent, but the answer shall satisfie
you, or my wits is not rightly caulked : and because I was not
at that time to tell you any thing of my own fancie, I will
bring unto you the authority of the Massorets, good honest
fellows, true ballokeering blades, and exact Hebraical bag-
pipers, who affirm that verily the said Hurtali was not within
the Ark of Noah, (neither could he get in, for he was too big)
but he sate astride upon it, with one leg on the one side, and
another on the other, as little children use to do upon their
wooden horses : or as the great Bull of Berne, which was
killed at Marinian, did ride for his Hackney the great murthering
piece called the Canonpevier, a pretty beast of a faire and
pleasant amble without all question.
  In that posture, he after God, saved the said Ark from
danger, for with his legs he gave it the brangle that was needful,
and with his foot turned it whither he pleased, as a ship
answereth her rudder. Those that were within sent him up
victuals in abundance by a Chimney, as people very thankfully
acknowledging the good that he did them ; and sometimes
they did talk together as Icaromenippus did to Jupiter, according to the report of Lucian. Have you understood all this
well ? drink then one good draught without water ; for if you
beleeve it not : no truly do I not, quoth she.

CHAPTER II

Of the Nativity of the most dread and redoubted Pantagruel

GARGANTUA at the age of foure hundred, fourescore fourty and foure yeares begat his sonne Pantagruel, upon his wife named Badebec, daughter to the king of the Amaurots in Utopia, who died in childe-birth, for he was so wonderfully great and lumpish, that he could not possibly come forth into the light of the world without thus suffocating his mother. But that we may fully understand the cause and reason of the name of Pantagruel which at his Baptism was given him, you are to remark, that in that yeare there was so great drought over all the countrey of Affrick, that there past thirty and six moneths, three weeks, foure dayes, thirteen houres, and a little more without raine, but with a heat so vehement, that the whole earth was parched and withered by it : neither was it more scorched and dried up with heat in the dayes of Eliah, then it was at that time ; for there was not a tree to be seen, that had either leafe or bloom upon it : the grasse was without verdure or greennesse, the rivers were drained, the fountaines dried up, the poore fishes abandoned and forsaken by their proper element, wandring and crying upon the ground most horribly : the birds did fall down from the aire for want of moisture and dew, wherewith to refresh them : the wolves, foxes, harts, wild-boares, fallow-deer, hares, coneys, weesils, brocks, badgers, and other such beasts were found dead in the fields with their mouths open ; in respect of men, there was the pity, you should have seen them lay out their tongues like hares that have been run six houres : many did throw themselves into the wells : others entred within a Cowes belly to be in the shade ; those Homer calls Alibants : all the Countrey was idle, and could do no vertue : it was a most lamentable case to have seen the labour of mortals in defending themselves from the vehemencie of this horrifick drought ; for they had work enough to do to save the holy water in the Churches from being wasted ; but there was such order taken by the counsel of my Lords the Cardinals, and of our holy Father, that none did dare to take above one lick : yet, when any one came into the Church, you should have seen above twenty poor thirsty fellows hang upon him that was the distributer of the water, and that with a wide open throat, gaping for some little drop, (like the rich glutton in Luke,) that might fall by, lest any thing should be lost. O how happy was he in that yeare, who had a coole Cellar under ground, well plenished with fresh wine !

The Philosopher reports in moving the question, wherefore it is that the sea-water is salt ? that at the time when Phœbus gave the government of his resplendent chariot to his sonne Phaeton, the said Phaeton, unskilful in the Art, and not knowing how to keep the ecliptick line betwixt the two tropicks of the latitude of the Sunnes course, strayed out of his way, and came so near the earth, that he dried up all the Countreys that were under it, burning a great part of the Heavens, which the Philosophers call *via lactea*, and the Huffsnuffs, St. James his way, although the most coped, lofty, and high-crested Poets affirme that to be the place where Juno's milk fell, when she gave suck to Hercules.

The earth at that time was so excessively heated, that it fell into an enormous sweat, yea such a one as made it sweat out the sea, which is therefore salt, because all sweat is salt ; and this you cannot but confesse to be true, if you will taste of your own, or of those that have the pox, when they are put into sweating, it is all one to me. Just such another case fell out this same yeare : for on a certain Friday, when the whole people were bent upon their devotions, and had made goodly Processions, with store of Letanies, and faire preachings, and beseechings of God Almighty, to look down with his eye of mercy upon their miserable and disconsolate condition, there was even then visibly seen issue out of the ground great drops of water, such as fall from a puff-bagg'd man in a top sweat, and the poore Hoydons began to rejoyce, as if it had been a thing very profitable unto them ; for some said that there was not one drop of moisture in the aire, whence they might have any rain, and that the earth did supply the default of that. Other learned men said, that it was a showre of the Antipodes, as Seneca saith in his fourth book *Quæstionum naturalium*, speaking of the source and spring of Nilus : but they were deceived, for the Procession being ended, when every one went about to gather of this dew, and to drink of it with full bowles, they found that it was nothing but pickle, and the very brine of salt, more brackish in taste then the saltest water of the sea : and because in that very day Pantagruel was borne, his father gave him that name ; for *Panta* in Greek is as much to say as all, and *Gruel* in the Hagarene language doth signifie thirsty; inferring hereby, that at his birth the whole world was a-dry and thirstie, as likewise foreseeing that he would be some day Suprem Lord and Sovereign of the thirstie Ethrappels, which was shewn to him at that very same hour by a more evident signe; for when his mother Badebec was in the bringing of him forth, and that the midwives did wait to receive him, there came first out of her belly threescore and eight Tregeneers (that is, Salt-sellers), every one of them leading in a Halter a mule heavy loaden with salt: after whom issued forth nine Dromedaries, with great loads of gammons of bacon, and dried neats tongues on their backs: then followed seven Camels loaded with links and chitterlings, Hogs puddings and salciges: after them came out five great waines, full of leeks, garlick, onions and chibots, drawn with five and thirty strong Cart horses, which was six for every one, besides the Thiller. At the sight hereof the said midwives were much amazed, yet some of them said, Lo, here is good provision, and indeed we need it; for we drink but lazily, as if our tongues walked on crutches, and not lustily like Lansman dutches: truly this is a good signe, there is nothing here but what is fit for us, these are the spurres of wine that set it a going. As they were tatling thus together after their own manner of chat, behold out comes Pantagruel all haire like a Beare, whereupon one of them inspired with a prophetical Spirit said, This will be a terrible fellow, he is borne with all his haire, he is undoubtedly to do wonderful things, and, if he live, he shall have age.

CHAPTER III

*Of the Grief wherewith Gargantua was moved at the Decease
of his Wife Badebec*

WHEN Pantagruel was borne, there was none more astonished
and perplexed then was his father Gargantua ; for of the one
side, seeing his wife Badebec dead, and on the other side his
sonne Pantagruel borne, so faire and so great, he knew not
what to say nor what to do : and the doubt that troubled his
braine was to know whether he should cry for the death of his
wife, or laugh for the joy of his sonne : he was *hinc indé* choaked
with sophistical arguments, for he framed them very well *in
modo et figura*, but he could not resolve them, remaining pestered
and entangled by this means, like a mouse catch't in a trap, or
kite snared in a ginne : Shall I weep, (said he ?) Yes, for
why ? my so good wife is dead, who was the most this, the most
that, that ever was in the world : never shall I see her, never
shall I recover such another, it is unto me an inestimable
losse ! O my good God, what had I done that thou shouldest
thus punish me ? why didst thou not take me away before her ?
seeing for me to live without her is but to languish. Ah
Badebec, Badebec, my minion, my dear heart, my sugar, my
sweeting, my honey, my little C... (yet it had in circumference
full six acres, three rods, five poles, foure yards, two foot, one
inche and a half of good woodland measure) my tender peggie,
my Codpiece darling, my bob and hit, my slipshoe-lovie, never
shall I see thee ! Ah, poor Pantagruel, thou hast lost thy good

mother, thy sweet nurse, thy well-beloved Lady ! O false death, how injurious and despightful hast thou been to me ? how malicious and outrageous have I found thee ? in taking her from me, my well-beloved wife, to whom immortality did of right belong. With these words he did cry like a Cow, but on a sudden fell a laughing like a Calfe, when Pantagruel came into his minde. Ha, my little sonne, (said he) my childilollie, fedlifondie, dandlichuckie, my ballockie, my pretty rogue ; O how jollie thou art, and how much am I bound to my gracious God, that hath been pleased to bestow on me a sonne, so faire, so spriteful, so lively, so smiling, so pleasant, and so gentle ! Ho, ho, ho, ho, how glad I am ? Let us drink, ho, and put away melancholy : bring of the best : rense the glasses, lay the cloth, drive out these dogs, blow this fire, light candles, shut that door there, cut this bread in sippets for brewis, send away these poore folks in giving them what they ask, hold my gown, I will strip my self into my doublet, (*én cuerpo*) to make the Gossips merry, and keep them company.

As he spake this, he heard the Letanies and the mementos of the Priests that carried his wife to be buried, upon which he left the good purpose he was in, and was suddenly ravished another way, saying, Lord God, must I again contrist my self ? this grieves me ; I am no longer young, I grow old, the weather is dangerous ; I may perhaps take an ague, then shall I be foiled, if not quite undone ; by the faith of a Gentleman, it were better to cry lesse, and drink more.

My wife is dead, well, by G——, (*da jurandi*) I shall not raise her again by my crying : she is well, she is in Paradise at least, if she be no higher : she prayeth to God for us, she is happy, she is above the sense of our miseries, nor can our calamities reach her : what though she be dead, must not we also die ? the same debt which she hath paid, hangs over our heads ; nature will require it of us, and we must all of us some day taste of the same sauce ; let her passe then, and the Lord preserve the Survivors ; for I must now cast about how to get another wife. But I will tell you what you shall do, (said he) to the Midwives in France called wise women (where be they, good folks ? I cannot see them,) go you to my wife's interrement, and I will the while rock my sonne ; for I finde my self somewhat altered and distempered, and should otherwayes be in danger of falling sick ; but drink one good draught first, you will be the better for it ; and beleeve me upon mine honour, they at his request went to her burial and funeral obsequies :

HO, HO, HO, HO, HOW GLAD I AM!

in the mean while, poor Gargantua staying at home, and willing to have somewhat in remembrance of her to be engraven upon her tomb, made this Epitaph in the manner as followeth.

> Dead is the noble Badebec,
> Who had a face like a Rebeck;
> A Spanish body, and a belly
> Of Swisserland; she'd dy'd, I tell ye,
> In childe-birth: pray to God, that her
> He pardon wherein she did erre.
> Here lies her body, which did live
> Free from all vice, as I beleeve;
> And did decease at my bed-side,
> The yeare and day in which she dy'd.

CHAPTER IV

Of the Infancie of Pantagruel

I FINDE by the ancient Historiographers and Poets, that divers have been borne in this world after very strange manners, which would be too long to repeat : reade therefore the seventh chapter of Pliny, if you have so much leisure : yet have you never heard of any so wonderful as that of Pantagruel; for it is a very difficult matter to beleeve, how in the little time he was in his mothers belly, he grew both in body and strength. That which Hercules did was nothing, when in his Cradle he

slew two serpents ; for those serpents were but little and weak :
but Pantagruel, being yet in the Cradle, did farre more admirable things, and more to be amazed at. I passe by here the
relation of how at every one of his meales he supped up the milk
of foure thousand and six hundred Cowes : and how to make
him a skellet to boil his milk in, there were set a work all the
Braziers of Somure in Anjou, of Villedieu in Normandy, and of
Bramont in Lorraine : and they served in this whitepot-meat
to him in a huge great Bell, which is yet to be seen in the city of
Bourges in Berrie, near the Palace ; but his teeth were already
so well grown, and so strengthened with vigour, that of the
said Bell he bit off a great morsel, as very plainly doth appeare
till this houre.

One day in the morning, when they would have made him
suck one of his Cows, (for he never had any other Nurse, as the
History tells us) he got one of his armes loose from the swadling
bands, wherewith he was kept fast in the Cradle, laid hold on
the said Cow under the left fore hamme, and grasping her to
him ate up the udder and half of her paunch, with the liver
and the kidneys, and had devoured all up, if she had not cried
out most horribly, as if the wolves had held her by the legs,
at which noise company came in, and took away the said Cow
from Pantagruel ; yet could they not so well do it, but that the
quarter whereby he caught her was left in his hand, of which
quarter he gulp't up the flesh in a trice, even with as much ease
as you would eate a salcige ; and that so greedily with desire
of more, that when they would have taken away the bone from
him, he swallowed it down whole, as a Cormorant would do a
little fish ; and afterwards began fumblingly to say, Good,
good, good, for he could not yet speak plaine ; giving them to
understand thereby, that he had found it very good, and that
he did lack but so much more ; which when they saw that
attended him, they bound him with great cable-ropes, like
those that are made at Tain, for the carriage of salt to Lyons :
or such as those are, whereby the great French ship rides at
Anchor, in the Road of Newhaven in Normandie.

But on a certain time, a great Beare, which his father had
bred, got loose, came towards him, began to lick his face, for
his Nurses had not throughly wiped his chaps, at which unexpected approach being on a sudden offended, he as lightly
rid himself of those great cables, as Samson did of the haulser
ropes wherewith the Philistines had tied him, and by your
leave, takes me up my Lord the Beare, and teares him to you in

pieces like a pullet, which served him for a gorge-ful or good warme bit for that meale.

Whereupon Gargantua fearing lest the childe should hurt himself, caused foure great chaines of iron to be made to binde him, and so many strong wooden arches unto his Cradle, most firmly stocked and mortaised in huge frames : of those chaines you have one at Rochel, which they draw up at night betwixt the two great towers of the Haven : Another is at Lyons : A third at Angiers : And the fourth was carried away by the devils to binde Lucifer, who broke his chaines in those dayes, by reason of a cholick that did extraordinarily torment him, taken with eating a Serjeants soule fried for his breakfast, and therefore you may beleeve that which Nicholas de Lyra saith upon that place of the Psalter, where it is written, *Et Og Regem Basan*, that the said Og, being yet little, was so strong and robustious, that they were faine to binde him with chaines of iron in his Cradle ; thus continued Pantagruel for a while very calme and quiet, for he was not able so easily to break those chaines, especially having no room in the Cradle to give a swing with his armes. But see what happened once upon a great Holiday, that his father Gargantua made a sumptuous banquet to all the Princes of his Court : I am apt to beleeve, that the menial officers of the house were so imbusied on waiting each on his proper service at the feast, that nobody took care of poor Pantagruel, who was left *à reculorum*, behinde-hand all alone, and as forsaken. What did he ? Heark what he did, good people : he strove and essayed to break the chaines of the Cradle with his armes, but coold not, for they were too strong for him : then did he keep with his feet such a stamping stirre, and so long, that at last he beat out the lower end of his Cradle, which notwithstanding was made of a great post five foot in square : and, as soon as he had gotten out his feet, he slid down as well as he could till he had got his soales to the ground ; and then with a mighty force he rose up, carrying his Cradle upon his back, bound to him like a Tortoise that crawles up against a wall ; and to have seen him, you would have thought it had been a great Carrick of five hundred tunne upon one end. In this manner he entred into the great Hall where they were banquetting, and that very boldly, which did much affright the companie ; yet because his armes were tied in, he could not reach any thing to eate, but with great pain stooped now and then a little, to take with the whole flat of his tongue some lick, good bit, or morsel.

Which when his father saw, he knew well enough that they had left him without giving him any thing to eate, and therefore commanded that he should be loosed from the said chains, by the counsel of the Princes and Lords there present : besides that, also the Physicians of Gargantua said, that if they did thus keep him in the Cradle, he would be all his life-time subject to the stone. When he was unchained they made him to sit down, where after he had fed very well, he took his Cradle, and broke it into more than.five hundred thousand pieces with one blow of his fist, that he struck in the midst of it, swearing that he would never come into it again.

CHAPTER V

Of the Acts of the noble Pantagruel in his youthful Age

Thus grew Pantagruel from day to day, and to every ones eye waxed more and more in all his dimensions, which made his father to rejoyce by a natural affection : therefore caused he to be made for him, whilest he was yet little, a pretty Crossbowe, wherewith to shoot at small birds, which now they call the great Crossebowe at Chantelle. Then he sent him to the school to learn, and to spend his youth in vertue : in the prosecution of which designe he came first to Poictiers, where, as he studied and profited very much, he saw that the Scholars were oftentimes at leisure, and knew not how to bestow their time, which moved him to take such compassion on them, that one day he took from a long ledge of rocks (called there Passelourdin,) a huge great stone, of about twelve fathom square, and fourteen handfuls thick, and with great ease set it upon foure pillars in the midst of a field, to no other end, but that the said Scholars, when they had nothing else to do, might passe their time in getting up on that stone, and feast it with store of gammons, pasties and flaggons, and carve their names upon it with a knife, in token of which deed till this houre the stone is called the lifted stone : and in remembrance hereof there is none entered into the Register and matricular Book of the said University, or accounted capable of taking any degree therein, till he have first drunk in the Caballine fountain of Croustelles, passed at Passelourdin, and got up upon the lifted stone.

Afterwards reading the delectable Chronicles of his Ancestors, he found that Jafrey of Lusinian, called Jafrey with the great tooth, Grandfather to the Cousin in law of the eldest Sister of the Aunt of the Son in law of the Uncle of the good daughter of his Stepmother, was interred at Maillezais ; therefore one day he took Campos, (which is a little vacation from study to play a while,) that he might give him a visit as unto an honest man : and going from Poictiers with some of his companions, they passed by the Guge, visiting the noble Abbot Ardillon : then by Lusinian, by Sansay, by Celles, by Coalonges, by Fontenay the Conte, saluting the learned Tiraqueau, and from thence arrived at Maillezais, where he went to see the Sepulchre of the said Jafrey with the great tooth ; which made him somewhat afraid, looking upon the picture, whose lively draughts did set him forth in the representation of a man in an extreme fury, drawing his great Malchus faulchion half way out of his scabbard : when the reason hereof was demanded, the Chanons of the said place told him, that there was no other cause of it, but that *Pictoribus atque Poetis, etc.*, that is to say, that Painters and Poets have liberty to paint and devise what they list after their own fancie : but he was not satisfied with their answer, and said, He is not thus painted without a cause ; and I suspect that at his death there was some wrong done him, whereof he requireth his Kinred to take revenge ; I will enquire further into it, and then do what shall be reasonable ; then he returned not to Poictiers, but would take a view of the other Universities of France : therefore going to Rochel, he took shipping and arrived at Bourdeaux, where he found no great exercise, only now and then he would see some Marriners and Lightermen a wrestling on the key or strand by the river side : From thence he came to Tholouse, where he learned to dance very well, and to play with the two-handed sword, as the fashion of the Scholars of the said University is to bestir themselves in games, whereof they may have their hands full : but he stayed not long there, when he saw that they did cause burne their regents alive like red herring, saying, Now God

THUS GREW PANTAGRUEL FROM DAY TO DAY

190

forbid that I should die this death; for I am by nature sufficiently dry already, without heating my self any further.

He went then to Montpellier, where he met with the good wives of Mirevaux, and good jovial company withal, and thought to have set himself to the study of Physick; but he considered that that calling was too troublesome and melancholick, and that Physicians did smell of glisters like old devils. There he resolved he would studie the lawes; but seeing that there were but three scauld, and one baldpated Legist in that place, he departed from thence, and in his way made the bridge of Gard, and the Amphitheater of Neems in lesse then three houres, which neverthelesse seems to be a more divine then humane work. After that he came to Avignon, where was not above three dayes before he fell in love; for the women there take great delight in playing at the close buttock-game, because it is Papal ground; which his Tutor and Pedagogue Epistemon perceiving, he drew him out of that place, and brought him to Valence in the Dauphinee, where he saw no great matter of recreation, only that the Lubbards of the Town did beat the Scholars, which so incensed him with anger, that when upon a certain very faire Sunday, the people being at their public dancing in the streets, and one of the Scholars offering to put himself into the ring to partake of that sport, the foresaid lubbardly fellowes would not permit him the admittance into their society, He taking the Scholars part, so belaboured them with blowes, and laid such load upon them, that he drove them all before him, even to the brink of the river Rhosne, and would have there drowned them, but that they did squat to the ground, and there lay close a full halfe league under the river. The hole is to be seen there yet.

After that he departed from thence, and in three strides and one leap came to Angiers, where he found himself very well, and would have continued there some space, but that the plague drove them away. So from thence he came to Bourges, where he studied a good long time, and profited very much in the faculty of the Lawes, and would sometimes say, that the books of the Civil Law were like unto a wonderfully precious, royal and triumphant robe of cloth of gold, edged with dirt; for in the world are no goodlier books to be seen, more ornate, nor more eloquent then the texts of the Pandects, but the bordering of them, that is to say, the glosse of Accursius, is so scurvie, vile, base, and unsavourie, that it is nothing but filthinesse and villany.

THE SECOND BOOK OF DR. FRANCIS RABELAIS

Going from Bourges, he came to Orleans, where he found store of swaggering Scholars that made him great entertainment at his coming, and with whom he learned to play at tennis so well, that he was a Master at that game; for the Students of the said place make a prime exercise of it; and sometimes they carried him unto Cupids houses of commerce (in that city termed Islands, because of their being most ordinarily environed with other houses, and not contiguous to any,) there to recreate his person at the sport of Poussavant, which the wenches of London call the Ferkers in and in. As for breaking his head with over-much study, he had an especial care not to do it in any case, for feare of spoiling his eyes; which he the rather observed, for that it was told him by one of his teachers, (there called Regents,) that the paine of the eyes was the most hurtful thing of any to the sight: for this cause when he one day was made a Licentiate, or Graduate in law, one of the Scholars of his acquaintance, who of learning had not much more then his burthen, though in stead of that he could dance very well, and play at tennis, made the blason and device of the Licentiates in the said University, saying,

> So you have in your hand a racket,
> A tennis-ball in your Cod-placket,
> A Pandect law in your caps tippet,
> And that you have the skill to trip it
> In a low dance, you will b' allow'd
> The grant of the Licentiates hood.

CHAPTER VI

How Pantagruel met with a Limousin, who too affectedly did counterfeit the French Language

Upon a certain day, I know not when, Pantagruel walking after supper with some of his fellow-Students without that gate of the City, through which we enter on the rode to Paris, encountered with a young spruce-like Scholar that was coming upon the same very way, and after they had saluted one another, asked him thus; My friend, from whence comest thou now? the

Scholar answered him : From the alme, inclyte and celebrate Academie, which is vocitated Lutetia. What is the meaning of this (said Pantagruel) to one of his men ? It is (answered he) from Paris. Thou comest from Paris then (said Pantagruel,) and how do you spend your time there, you my Masters the Students of Paris ? the Scholar answered, We transfretate the Sequan at the dilucul and crepuscul ; we deambulate by the compites and quadrives by the Urb : we despumate the Latial verbocination ; and like verisimilarie amorabons, we captat the benevolence of the omnijugal, omniform, and omnigenal fœminine sexe : upon certain diecules we invisat the Lupanares, and in a venerian extase inculcate our veretres into the penitissime recesses of the pudends of these amicabilis-sim meretricules : then do we cauponisate in the meritory taberns of the pineapple, the castle, the magdalene, and the mule, goodly vervecine spatules perforaminated with petrocile ; and if by fortune there be rarity, or penury of pecune in our marsupies ; and that they be exhausted of ferruginean mettal, for the shot we dimit our codices, and oppugnerat our vesti-ments, whilest we prestolate the coming of the Tabellaries from the Penates and patriotick Lares : to which Pantagruel answered, What devillish language is this ? by the Lord, I think thou art some kind of Heretick : My Lord, no, said the Scholar ; for libentissimally, as soon as it illucesceth any minutule slice of the day, I demigrate into one of these so well architected minsters, and there irrorating my self with faire lustral water, I mumble off little parcels of some missick precation of our sacrificuls : and submurmurating my horarie precules, I elevate and absterge my anime from its nocturnal inquinations : I revere the Olympicols. I latrially venere the supernal Astripotent : I dilige and redame my proxims : I observe the decalogical precepts, and, according to the faculta-tule of my vires, I do not discede from them one late unguicule ; neverthelesse it is veriforme, that because Mammona doth not supergurgitate any thing in my loculs, that I am somewhat rare and lent to supererogate the elemosynes to those egents, that hostially queritate their stipe.

Prut, tut, (said Pantagruel), what doth this foole meane to say ? I think he is upon the forging of some diabolical tongue, and that inchanter-like he would charme us ; to whom one of his men said, Without doubt (Sir) this fellow would counterfeit the language of the Parisians, but he doth only flay the Latine, imagining by so doing that he doth highly Pindarize it in most

"AND SO LET HIM GO"

194

eloquent termes, and strongly conceiteth himself to be therefore a great Oratour in the French, because he disdaineth the common manner of speaking. To which Pantagruel said, Is it true ? the Scholar answered, My worshipful Lord, my genie is not apt nate to that which this flagitious Nebulon saith, to excoriate the cutule of our vernacular Gallick, but viceversally I gnave opere, and by vele and rames enite to locupletate it, with the Latinicome redundance. By G— (said Pantagruel), I will teach you to speak : but first come hither, and tell me whence thou art ? To this the Scholar answered, The primeval origin of my aves and ataves was indigenarie of the Lemovick regions, where requiesceth the corpor of the hagiotat St. Martial ; I understand thee very well (said Pantagruel), when all comes to all, thou art a Limousin, and thou wilt here by thy affected speech counterfeit the Parisiens : well now, come hither, I must shew thee a new trick, and handsomely give thee the combfeat : with this he took him by the throat, saying to him, Thou flayest the Latine ; by St. John, I will make thee flay the foxe, for I will now flay thee alive ; then began the poor Limousin to cry ; Haw, gwid Maaster, haw, Laord, my halp and St. Marshaw, haw, I'm worried : Haw, my thropple, the bean of my cragg is bruck ! Haw, for gauads seck, lawt my lean, Mawster ; waw, waw, waw : Now (said Pantagruel) thou speakest naturally, and so let him go, for the poor Limousin had totally berayed, and throughly conshit his breeches, which were not deep and large enough, but round streat caniond gregs, having in the seat a piece like a keelings taile, and therefore in French called *de chausses à queüe de merlus.* Then (said Pantagruel) St. Alipantin, what civette ? fi to the devil with this Turnepeater, as he stinks, and so let him go : but this hug of Pantagruels with such a terrour to him all the dayes of his life, and took such deep impression in his fancie, that very often, distracted with sudden affrightments, he would startle and say that Pantagruel held him by the neck ; besides that it procured him a continual drought and desire to drink, so that after some few years he died of the death Roland, in plain English called thirst, a work of divine vengeance, shewing us that which saith the Philosopher and Aulus Gellius, that it becometh us to speak according to the common language : and that we should, (as said Octavian Augustus) strive to shun all strange and un-known termes with as much heedfulnesse and circumspection, as Pilots of ships use to avoid the rocks and banks in the sea.

CHAPTER VII

*How Pantagruel came to Paris, and of the choise
Books of the Library of St. Victor*

AFTER that Pantagruel had studied very well at Orleans, he
resolved to see the great University at Paris ; but before his
departure, he was informed, that there was a huge big bell at
St. Anian in the said town of Orleans, under the ground, which
had been there above two hundred and fourteen years ; for
it was so great that they could not by any device get it so much
as above the ground, although they used all the meanes that are
found in Vitruvius *de Architectura*, Albertus *de re œdificatoria*,
Euclid, Theon, Archimedes, and Hero *de ingeniis* : for all that
was to no purpose, wherefore condescending heartily to the
humble request of the Citizens and Inhabitants of the said
Town, he determined to remove it to the tower that was erected
for it : with that he came to the place where it was, and lifted
it out of the ground with his little finger, as easily as you would
have done a Hawks bell, or Bell-weathers tingle tangle ; but
before he would carry it to the foresaid tower or steeple,
appointed for it, he would needs make some Musick with it
about the Town, and ring it alongst all the streets, as he carried
it in his hand, wherewith all the people were very glad ; but
there happened one great inconveniency, for with carrying it so,
and ringing it about the streets, all the good Orleans wine turned
instantly, waxed flat, and was spoiled, which no body there

did perceive till the night following ; for every man found himself so altered, and a-dry with drinking these flat wines, that
they did nothing but spit, and that as white as Maltha cotton,
saying ; We have of the Pantagruel, and our very throats are
salted.   This done, he came to Paris with his retinue, and at
his entry every one came out to see him (as you know well
enough, that the people of Paris is sottish by nature, by B.
flat, and B. sharp,) and beheld him with great astonishment,
mixed with no less feare, that he would carry away the Palace
into some other countrey, *à remotis*, and farre from them, as
his father formerly had done the great peal of Bells at our
Ladies Church, to tie about his Mare's neck.   Now after
he had stayed there a pretty space, and studied very well in
all the seven liberal Arts, he said it was a good towne to live in,
but not to die ; for that the grave-digging rogues of St.
Innocent used in frostie nights to warme their bums with dead
mens bones.   In his abode there he found the Library of St.
Victor, a very stately and magnifick one, especially in some
books which were there, of which followeth the Repertory and
Catalogue, *Et primò,*

The for Godsake of Salvation.
The Codpiece of the Law.
The Slipshoe of the Decretals.
The Pomegranate of Vice.
The Clew-bottom of Theologie.
The Duster or Foxtail-flap of Preachers, composed by
    Turlupin.
The Churning Ballock of the Valiant.
The Henbane of the Bishops.
Marmotretus de baboonis et apis, cum Commento Dorbellis.
Decretum Universitatis Parisiensis super gorgiasitate mulier-
    cularum ad placitum.
The Apparition of Sancte Geltrud to a nun of Poissie, being
    in travel, at the bringing forth of a childe.
Ars honestè fartandi in societate, per Marcum Corvinum.
The Mustard-pot of Penance.
The Gamashes, aliàs the Boots of Patience.
Formicarium artium.
De brodiorum usu, et honestate quartandi per Sylvestrem
    prioratem Jacobinum.
The coosened or gulled in Court.
The Fraile of the Scriveners.

The Marriage-packet.
The cruizie or crucible of Contemplation.
The Flimflams of the Law.
The Prickle of Wine.
The Spurre of Cheese.
Ruboffatorium scholarium.
Tartaretus de modo cacandi.
The Bravades of Rome.
Bricot de differentiis Browsarum.
The tail-piece-cushion, or close-breech of Discipline.
The cobled Shoe of Humility.
The Trevet of good thoughts.
The Kettle of Magnanimity.
The cavilling intanglements of Confessors.
The Snatchfare of the Curats.
Reverendi patris fratris Lubini, provincialis Bavardiæ, de
    gulpendis lardslicionibus libri tres.
Pasquilli doctoris marmorei, de capreolis cum artichoketa
    comedendis, tempore Papali ab Ecclesia interdicto.
The Invention of the Holy Crosse, personated by six wilie
    Priests.
The Spectacles of Pilgrims bound for Rome.
Majoris de modo faciendi puddinos.
The Bagpipe of the Prelates.
Beda de optimitate triparum.
The Complaint of the Barresters upon the reformation of
    Confites.
The Furred Cat of the Sollicitors and Atturneys.
Of Pease and Bacon, *cum Commento.*
The Small Vales or Drinking Money of the Indulgences.
Præclarissimi juris utriusque Doctoris Maistre pilloti, etc.,
    Scrapfarthingi de botchandis gloss Accursianæ Triflis
    repetitio enucidiluculissima.
Stratagemata Francharchæri de Baniolet.
Carlbumpkinus de re militari cum figuris Tevoti.
De usu et utilitate flayandi equos et equas, authore Magistro
    nostro de quebecu.
The sawcinesse of Countrey-Stuarts.
M. N. Rostocostojam Bedanesse de mustarda post prandium
    servienda, libri quatuordecim, apostillati per M. Vauril-
    lonis.
The covillage or wench-tribute of Promooters.
Quæstio subtilissima, utrum Chimæra in vacuo bombinans

posset comedere secundas intentiones ; et fuit debatuta per decem hebdomadas in Consilio Constantiensi.

The bridle-champer of the Advocates.

Smutchudlamenta Scoti.

The rasping and hard-scraping of the Cardinals.

De calcaribus removendis, Decades undecim, per M. Albericum de rosata.

Ejusdem de castramentandis criminibus libri tres.

The entrance of Antonie de leve into the territories of Brasil.

Marforii, bacalarii, cubantis Romæ, de peelandis aut un-skinnandis blurrandisque Cardinalium mulis.

The said Authors Apologie against those who alledge that the Popes mule doth eat but at set times.

Prognosticatio quæ incipit Silvii Triquebille, balata per M. N., the deep dreaming gull Sion.

Boudarini Episcopi de emulgentiarum profectibus Æneades novem, cum privilegio Papali ad triennium et postea non.

The shitabranna of the maids.

The bald arse or peeld breech of the widows

The cowle or capouch of the Monks.

The Mumbling Devotion of the Cœlestine Fryars.

The passage-toll of beggarlinesse.

The teeth-chatter or gum-didder of lubberly lusks.

The paring-shovel of the Theologues.

The drench-horne of the Masters of Arts.

The scullions of Olcam the uninitiated Clerk.

Magistri N. Lickdishetis, de garbellisiftationibus horarum canonicarum, libri quadriginta.

Arsiversitatorium confratriarum, incerto authore.

The gulsgoatonie or rasher of cormorants and ravenous feeders.

The Rammishnesse of the Spaniards supergivuregondigaded by Fryar Inigo.

The muttring of pitiful wretches.

Dastardismus rerum Italicarum, authore Magistro Burnegad.

R. Lullius de Batisfolagiis Principum.

Calibistratorium caffardiæ, authore M. Jacobo Hocstraten hereticometra.

Codtickler de Magistro nostrandorum Magistro nostratorum-que beuvetis, libri octo galantissimi.

The Crackarades of balists or stone-throwing Engines, contrepate Clerks, Scriveners, Brief-writers, Rapporters, and Papal Bull-dispatchers lately compiled by Regis.

A perpetual Almanack for those that have the gowt and
the pox.

Manera sweepandi fornacellos per Mag. Eccium.

The shable or cimeterre of Merchants.

The pleasures of the Monachal life.

The hotchpot of Hypocrites.

The history of the Hobgoblins.

The ragamuffianisme of the pensionary maimed souldiers.

The gulling fibs and counterfeit shewes of Commissaries.

The litter of Treasurers.

The juglingatorium of Sophisters.

Antipericatametanaparbeugedamphicribationes toordi-
cantium.

The periwinkle of ballad-makers.

The push-forward of the Alchimists.

The niddie noddie of the sachel-loaded seekers, by Friar
Bindfastatis.

The shackles of Religion.

The racket of swag-waggers.

The leaning-stock of old age.

The muzzle of Nobility.

The Apes pater noster.

The Crickets and Hawks bells of Devotion.

The pot of the Emberweeks.

The mortar of the politick life.

The flap of the Hermites.

The riding-hood or Monterg of the Penitentiaries.

The trictrac of the knocking Friars.

Blockheadodus de vita and honestate bragadochiorum.

Lyrippii Sorbonici moralisationes, per M. Lupoldum.

The Carrier-horse-bells of Travellers.

The bibbings of the tipling Bishops.

Dolloporediones Doctorum Coloniensium adversus Reuclin.

The Cymbals of Ladies.

The Dungers martingale.

Whirlingfriskorum Chasemarkerorum per fratrem Crack-
woodloguetis.

The clouted patches of a stout heart.

The mummerie of the racket-keeping Robin-good-fellows.

Gerson de auferibilitate Papæ ab Ecclesia.

The Catalogue of the nominated and graduated persons.

Jo. Dytebrodii de terribilitate excommunicationis libellus
acephalos.

Ingeniositas invocandi diabolos et diabolas, per M. Guin-
golphum.

The hotchpotch or gallimafree of the perpetually begging
Friars.

The Whinings of Cajetan.

Muddisnowt Doctoris cherubici de origine roughfootedarum
et wryneckedorum ritibus libri septem.

Sixty-nine fat breviaries.

The night-Mare of the five orders of Beggars.

The skinnery of the new start-ups extracted out of the
fallow-butt, incornifistibulated and plodded upon in the
Angelick summe.

The raver and idle talker in cases of conscience.

The fat belly of the Presidents.

The bafling flowter of the Abbots.

Sutoris adversus eum qui vocaverat eum Slabsauceatorem,
et quod Slabsauceatores non sunt damnati ab Ecclesia.

Cacatorium medicorum.

The chimney-sweeper of Astrologie.

Campi clysteriorum per paragraph C.

The bumsquibcracker of Apothecaries.

The kissebreech of Chirurgerie.

Justinianus de Whiteleperotis tollendis.

Antidotarium animæ.

Merlinus Coccaius de patria diabolorum.

The Practice of iniquity by Cleuraunes Sadden.

The Mirrour of basenesse, by Radnecu Waldenses.

The ingrained rogue, by Dwarsencas Eldenu.

The mercilesse Cormorant, by Hoxinidno the Jew.

Of which library some books are already printed and the rest
are now at the presse, in this noble city of Tubinge.

CHAPTER VIII

*How Pantagruel being at Paris received Letters from his
Father Gargantua, and the Copy of them*

PANTAGRUEL studied very hard, as you may well conceive, and
profited accordingly ; for he had an excellent understanding,

THE SECOND BOOK OF DR. FRANCIS RABELAIS

and notable wit, together with a capacity in memory, equal to the measure of twelve oyle budgets, or butts of Olives. And as he was there abiding one day, he received a letter from his father in manner as followeth.

Most dear sonne, amongst the gifts, graces and prerogatives, with which the Soveraign Plasmator God Almighty hath endowed and adorned human Nature at the beginning, that seems to me most singular and excellent, by which we may in a mortal estate attain to a kinde of immortality, and in the course of this transitory life perpetuate our name and seed, which is done by a progeny issued from us in the lawful bonds of Matrimony : whereby that in some measure is restored unto us, which was taken from us by the sin of our first Parents, to whom it was said, that because they had not obeyed the Commandment of God their Creator, they should die, and by death should be brought to nought that so stately frame and Plasmature, wherein the man at first had been created.

But by this meanes of seminal propagation there continueth in the children what was lost in the Parents, and in the grand-children that which perished in their fathers, and so successively until the day of the last judgement, when Jesus Christ shall have rendered up to God the Father his Kingdom in a peaceable condition, out of all danger and contamination of sin ; for then shall cease all generations and corruptions, and the elements leave off their continual transmutations, seeing the so much desired peace shall be attained unto and enjoyed, and that all things shall be brought to their end and period ; and, therefore not without just and reasonable cause do I give thanks to God my Saviour and Preserver, for that he hath inabled me to see my bald old age reflourish in thy youth : for when at his good pleasure, who rules and governs all things, my soul shall leave this mortal habitation, I shall not account my self wholly to die, but to passe from one place unto another : considering that, in and by that, I continue in my visible image living in the world, visiting and conversing with people of honour, and other my good friends, as I was wont to do : which conversation of mine, although it was not without sin, (because we are all of us trespassers, and therefore ought continually to beseech his divine Majesty to blot our transgressions out of his memory), yet was it by the help and grace of God, without all manner of reproach before men.

Wherefore, if those qualities of the minde but shine in thee, wherewith I am endowed, as in thee remaineth the perfect image of my body, thou wilt be esteemed by all men to be the perfect guardian and treasure of the immortality of our name : but if otherwise, I shall truly take but small pleasure to see it, considering that the lesser part of me, which is the body, would abide in thee : and the best, to wit, that which is the soule, and by which our name continues blessed amongst men, would be degenerate and abastardised : This I do not speak out of any distrust that I have of thy vertue, which I have heretofore already tried, but to encourage thee yet more earnestly to proceed from good to better : and that which I now write unto thee is not so much, that thou shouldest live in this vertuous course, as that thou shouldest rejoyce in so living and having lived, and cheer up thy self with the like resolution in time to come ; to the prosecution and accomplishment of which enterprise and generous undertaking thou mayest easily remember how that I have spared nothing, but have so helped thee, as if I had had no other treasure in this world, but to see thee once in my life compleatly well bred and accomplished, as well in vertue, honesty and valour, as in all liberal knowledge and civility : and so to leave thee after my death as a mirrour, representing the person of me thy father, and if not so excellent, and such in deed as I do wish thee, yet such in my desire.

But although my deceased father of happy memory Grangousier, had bent his best endeavours to make me profit in all perfection and Political knowledge, and that my labour and study was fully correspondent to, yea, went beyond his desire : neverthelesse, as thou mayest well understand, the time then was not so proper and fit for learning as it is at present, neither had I plenty of good masters such as thou hast had ; for that time was darksome, obscured with clouds of ignorance, and savouring a little of the infelicity and calamity of the Gothes, who had, whereever they set footing, destroyed all good literature, which in my age hath by the divine goodnesse been restored unto its former light and dignity, and that with such amendment and increase of the knowledge, that now hardly should I be admitted unto the first forme of the little Grammar-school-boyes : I say, I, who in my youthful dayes was, (and that justly) reputed the most learned of that age ; which I do not speak in vain boasting, although I might lawfully do it in writing unto thee, in verification whereof thou hast the authority of Marcus Tullius in his book of old age, and the sentence of Plutarch, in the book intituled, how a man may praise himself with envie : but to give thee an emulous encouragement to strive yet further.

Now is it that the mindes of men are qualified with all manner of discipline, and the old sciences revived, which for many ages were extinct : now it is, that the learned languages are to their pristine purity restored, viz. Greek, (without which a man may be ashamed to account himself a scholar,) Hebrew, Arabick, Chaldæan and Latine. Printing likewise is now in use, so elegant, and so correct, that better cannot be imagined, although it was found out but in my time by divine inspiration, as by a diabolical suggestion on the other side was the invention of Ordnance. All the world is full of knowing men, of most learned Schoolmasters, and vast Libraries : and it appears to me as a truth, that neither in Plato's time, nor Cicero's, nor Papinian's, there was ever such conveniency for studying, as we see at this day there is : nor must any adventure henceforward to come in publick, or present himself in company, that hath not been pretty well polished in the shop of Minerva : I see robbers, hangmen, free-booters, tapsters, ostlers, and such like, of the very rubbish of the people, more learned now, then the Doctors and Preachers were in my time.

What shall I say ? the very women and children have aspired to this praise and celestial Manna of good learning : yet so it is, that in the age I am now of, I have been constrained to learn the Greek tongue, which I contemned not like Cato, but had not the leasure in my younger yeares to attend the study of it : and take much delight in the reading of Plutarchs *Morals*, the pleasant *Dialogues* of Plato, the *Monuments* of Pausanias, and the *Antiquities* of Athenæus, in waiting on the houre wherein God my Creator shall call me, and command me to depart from this earth and transitory pilgrimage. Wherefore (my sonne) I admonish thee, to imploy thy youth to profit as well as thou canst, both in thy studies and in vertue. Thou art at Paris, where the laudable examples of many brave men may stirre up thy minde to gallant actions, and hast likewise for thy Tutor and Pædagogue the learned Epistemon, who by his lively and vocal documents may instruct thee in the Arts and Sciences.

I intend, and will have it so, that thou learn the Languages perfectly : first of all, the Greek, as Quintilian will have it : secondly, the Latine ; and then the Hebrew, for the holy Scripture-sake : and then the Chaldee and Arabick likewise, and that thou frame thy stile in Greek in imitation of Plato, and, for the Latine, after Cicero. Let there be no history which thou shalt not have ready in thy memory ; unto the prosecuting of which designe, books of Cosmographie will be very conducible, and help thee much. Of the liberal Arts of Geometry, Arithmetick and Musick, I gave thee some taste when thou wert yet little, and not above five or six yeares old ; proceed further in them, and learn the remainder if thou canst. As for Astronomy, study all the rules thereof, let passe neverthelesse, the divining and judicial Astrology, and the Art of Lullius, as being nothing else but plain abuses and vanities. As for the Civil Law, of that I would have thee to know the texts by heart, and then to conferre them with Philosophie.

Now in matter of the knowledge of the works of Nature, I would have thee to study that exactly, and that so there be no sea, river nor fountain, of which thou doest not know the fishes, all the fowles of the aire, all the several kindes of shrubs and trees, whether in forrests or orchards : all the sorts of herbes and flowers that grow upon the ground : all the various mettals that are hid within the bowels of the earth ; together with all the diversity of precious stones, that are to be seen in the Orient and South parts of the world, let nothing of all these be hidden from thee. Then faile not most carefully to peruse the books of the Greek, Arabian and Latine Physicians, not despising the Talmudists and Cabalists ; and by frequent Anatomies get thee the perfect knowledge of the other world, called the Microcosme, which is man : and at some houres of the day apply thy minde to the study of the holy Scriptures : first in Greek, the New Testament, with the Epistles of the Apostles ; and then the Old Testament in Hebrew. In brief, let me see thee an Abysse, and bottomlesse pit of knowledge : for from hence forward, as thou growest great and becomest a man, thou must part from this tranquillity and rest of study, thou must learn chivalrie, warfare, and the exercises of the field, the better thereby to defend my house and our friends, and to succour and protect them at all their needs against the invasion and assaults of evil doers.

Furthermore, I will that very shortly thou try how much thou hast profited, which thou canst not better do, then by maintaining publickly Theses and Conclusions in all Arts, against all persons whatsoever, and by haunting the company of learned men, both at Paris and otherwhere. But because as the wise man Solomon saith, Wisdome entereth not into a malicious minde ; and that knowledge without conscience is

HE SEEMED TO HAVE BEEN A-FIGHTING WITH MASTIFFE-DOGS

but the ruine of the soule, it behooveth thee to serve, to love, to feare God, and on him to cast all thy thoughts and all thy hope, and by faith formed in charity to cleave unto him, so that thou mayest never be separated from him by thy sins. Suspect the abuses of the world : set not thy heart upon vanity ; for this life is transitory, but the Word of the Lord endureth for ever. Be serviceable to all thy neighbours, and love them as thy self : reverence thy Præceptors : shun the conversation of those whom thou desireth not to resemble, and receive not in vaine the graces which God hath bestowed upon thee : and when thou shalt see that thou hast attained to all the knowledge that is to be acquired in that part, return unto me, that I may see thee, and give thee my blessing before I die. My sonne, the peace and grace of our Lord be with thee. Amen.

From Utopia the 17 day of the moneth of March.
Thy father Gargantua.

These letters being received and read, Pantagruel pluck't up his heart, took a fresh courage to him, and was inflamed with a desire to profit in his studies more then ever, so that if you had seen him, how he took paines, and how he advanced in learning, you would have said that the vivacity of his spirit amidst the books, was like a great fire amongst dry wood, so active it was, vigorous and indefatigable.

CHAPTER IX

How Pantagruel found Panurge, whom he loved all his Lifetime

ONE day as Pantagruel was taking a walk without the City, towards St. Antonies Abbey, discoursing and philosophating with his own servants and some other scholars, he met with a young man of very comely stature, and surpassing handsome in all the lineaments of his body, but in several parts thereof most pitifully wounded ; in such bad equipage in matter of his apparel, which was but tatters and rags, and every way so far out of order, that he seemed to have been a fighting with mastiffe-dogs, from whose fury he had made an escape, or, to say better, he looked in the condition wherein he then was, like an Apple-gatherer of the countrey of Perche.

As farre off as Pantagruel saw him, he said to those that stood by : Do you see that man there, who is a coming hither upon the road from Charanton-bridge ? by my faith, he is only poor in fortune ; for I may assure you, that by his Physiognomie it appeareth, that nature hath extracted him from some rich and noble race, and that too much curiosity hath thrown him upon adventures, which possibly have reduced him to this indigence, want and penurie. Now as he was just amongst them, Pantagruel said unto him, Let me intreat you, (friend) that you may be pleased to stop here a little, and answer me to that which I shall ask you, and I am confident you will not think your time ill bestowed ; for I have an extream desire, (according to my ability), to give you some supply in this distresse, wherein I see you are ; because I do very much commiserate your case, which truly moves me to great pity ; Therefore (my friend) tell me, who you are ? whence you come ? whither you go ? what you desire ? and what your name is ? the companion answered him in the Dutch tongue, thus.

'Junker, Gott geb euch glück und heil zuvor. Lieber Junker, ich lasz euch wissen, das da ihr mich von fragt, ist ein arm und erbärmlich Ding, und wer viel darvon zu sagen, welches euch verdrüssig zu hören, und mir zu erzelen wer, wiewol die Poeten und Oratorn vorzeiten haben gesagt in ihren Sprüchen und Sentenzen, dasz die gedechtniss des Elends und Armuth vorlängst erlitten ist eine grosse Lust.' My friend (said Pantagruel,) I have no skill in that gibberish of yours; therefore, if you would have us to understand you, speak to us in some other language; then did the drole answer him thus.

'Albarildim gotfano dechmin brin alabo dorido falbroth ringuam albaras. Nin portzadikin almucatin milko prin alelmin en thoth dalheben ensouim : kuthim al dum alkatim nim broth dechoth porth min michais im endoth, pruch dalmaisoulum hol moth danfrihim lupaldas in voldemoth. Nin hur diavosth mnarbotim dalgousch palfrapin duch im scoth pruch galeth dal chinon, min foulchrich al conin brutathen doth dal prin.' Do you understand none of this, said Pantagruel to the company ? I beleeve (said Epistemon,) that this is the language of the Antipodes, and such a hard one that the devil himself knowes not what to make of it. Then, said Pantagruel, Gossip, I know not if the walls do comprehend the meaning of your words, but none of us here doth so much as understand one syllable of them. Then said my blade again.—

'Signor mio, voi vedete per essempio, che la cornamusa non suona mai, s'ella non ha il ventre pieno. Cosi io parimente non vi saprei contare le mie fortune, se prima il tribulato ventre non ha la solita refettione. Al quale è adviso che le mani et li denti habbiano perso il loro ordine naturale et del tutto annichilati.' To which Epistemon answered as much of the one as of the other, and nothing of either. Then said Panurge.

'My Lord, if the Generosity of your Mind be suitable to your Body, you would naturally have Pity of me. For Nature made us equal; But Fortune has exalted some, and other some has depressed. Nevertheless, tho' Virtue is despised, and worthy Men depressed ; yet till the end none can be pronounced Happy.' Yet lesse said Pantagruel ; then said my jollie Panurge.

'Jona andie guaussa goussy etan beharda er remedio beharde versela ysser landa. Anbat es otoy y es nausu ey nessassust gourray proposian ordine den. Non ysseno bayta facheria egabe gen herassy badia sadassu noura assia. Aran hondavan gualde cydassu naydassuna. Estou oussyc eg vinan soury hien er darstura eguy harm. Genicoa plasar vadu.' Are you there (said Eudemon) Genicoa ? to this (said Carpalin,) St. Trinian's rammer unstitch your bum, for I had almost understood it. Then answered Panurge.

'Prust frest frinst sorgdmand strochdi drhds pag brlelang Gravot Chavigny Pomardiere rusth pkaldracg Deviniere pres

Nays. Couille kalmuch monarch drupp del meupplist rincq drlnd dodelb up drent loch minc stz rinq jald de vins ders cordelis bur jocst stzampenards.' Do you speak Christian (said Epistemon) or the Buffoon language, otherwise called patelinois ? Nay, it is the puzlatory tongue (said another) which some call Lanternois. Then said Panurge.

' Heere, ik en spreeke anders geen taele dan kersten taele : my dunkt noghtans, al en seg ik u niet een wordt, mynen noot verklaert genoegh wat ik begeere : geeft my uyt bermher-tigheit yets waar van ik gevoet magh zyn.' To which answered Pantagruel, As much of that : then said Panurge.

' Sennor, de tanto hablar yo soy cansado, porque yo suplico a vuestra reverentia que mire a los preceptos evangelicos, para que ellos movan vuestra reverentia a lo que es de conscientia ; y si ellos non bastaren, para mouer vuestra reverentia a piedad, yo suplico que mire a la piedad natural, la qual yo creo que le movera como es de razon : y con esso non digo mas.' Truly, my friend, I doubt not but you can speak divers languages, but tell us that which you would have us to do for you in some tongue, which you conceive we may understand ? Then said the companion.

' Min Herre, endog ieg med ingen tunge talede, ligesom bærn, oc uskellige creatuure : Mine klædebon oc mit legoms magerhed uduiser alligeuel klarlig huad ting mig best behof gioris, som er sandelig mad oc dricke : Huorfor forbarme dig ofuer mig, oc befal at giue mig noguet, af huilcket ieg kand slyre min giæendis mage, ligeruiis som mand *Cerbero* en suppe forsetter : Saa skalt du lefue længe oc lycksalig.' I think really (said Eusthenes) that the Gothes spoke thus of old, and that, if it pleased God, we would all of us speak so with our tailes. Then again said Panurge.

' Adon, scalom lecha : im ischar harob hal hebdeca bime-herah thithen li kikar lehem : chanchat ub laah al Adonai cho nen ral.' To which answered Epistemon, At this time have I understood him very well ; for it is the Hebrew tongue most rhetorically pronounced. Then again said the Gallant.

' Despota, tinyn panagathe, diati sy mi ouk artodotis ? horas gar limo analiscomenon eme athlion, ka en to metaxy me ouk eleis oudamos, zetis de par emou ha ou chre. Ke homos philologi pantes homologousi tote logous te ke remata peritta hyparchin, opote pragma afto pasi delon esti. Entha gar anankei monon logi isin, hina pragmata (hon peri amphis-betoumen), me prosphoros epiphenete.' What ? (said Carpalim)

Pantagruels footman, it is Greek, I have understood him : and how ? hast thou dwelt any while in Greece ? Then said the drole again.

'Agonou dont oussys vous desdagnez algorou : nou den farou zamist vous mariston ulbrou, fousques voubrol tant bredaguez moupreton dengoulhoust, daguez daguez non cropys fost pardonnoflist nougrou. Agou paston tol nalprissys hourtou los echatonous, prou dhouquys, brol pany gou den bascrou noudous caguons goulfren goul oustaroppassou.' Methinks I understand him (said Pantagruel) for either it is the language of my countrey of Utopia, or sounds very like it : and as he was about to have begun some purpose, the companion said,

'Jam toties vos per sacra, perque deos deasque omnes obtestatus sum, ut si quæ vos pietas permovet, egestatem meam solaremini, nec hilum proficio clamans et ejulans. Sinite, quæso, sinite, viri impii, quo me fata vocant abire ; nec ultra vanis vestris interpellationibus obtundatis, memores veteris illius adagii, quo venter famelicus auriculis carere dicitur.' Well, my friend, (said Pantagruel) but cannot you speak French ? that I can do (Sir) very well, (said the companion,) God be thanked : it is my natural language and mother tongue, for I was borne and bred in my younger yeares in the garden of France, to wit, Touraine : Then (said Pantagruel) tell us what is your name, and from whence you are come ; for, by my faith, I have already stamped in my minde such a deep impression of love towards you, that, if you will condescend unto my will, you shall not depart out of my company, and you and I shall make up another couple of friends, such as Æneas and Achates were ; Sir (said the companion) my true and proper christen name is Panurge, and now I come out of Turkie, to which countrey I was carried away prisoner at that time, when they went to Metelin with a mischief : and willingly would I relate unto you my fortunes, which are more wonderful than those of Ulysses were : but seeing that it pleaseth you to retain me with you, I most heartily accept of the offer, protesting never to leave you, should you go to all the devils in hell ; we shall have therefore more leisure at another time, and a fitter opportunity wherein to report them ; for at this present I am in a very urgent necessity to feed, my teeth are sharp, my belly empty, my throat dry, and my stomack fierce and burning : all is ready, if you will but set me to work, it will be as good as a balsamum for sore eyes to see me gulch

and raven it, for Gods sake, give order for it. Then Pantagruel
commanded that they should carry him home, and provide
him good store of victuals, which being done, he ate very well
that evening, and (capon-like) went early to bed, then slept
until dinner-time the next day, so that he made but three steps
and one leap from the bed to the board.

CHAPTER X

*How Pantagruel judged so equitably of a Controversie, which was
wonderfully obscure and difficult : that by Reason of his just
Decree therein, he was reputed to have a most admirable
Judgement*

PANTAGRUEL, very well remembring his fathers letter and
admonitions, would one day make trial of his knowledge.
Thereupon in all the Carrefours, that is, throughout all the
foure quarters, streets and corners of the City, he set up Conclusions to the number of nine thousand seven hundred sixty
and foure, in all manner of learning, touching in them the
hardest doubts that are in any science. And first of all, in the
fodder-street he held dispute against all the Regents or Fellowes
of Colledges, Artists or Masters of Arts, and Oratours, and did
so gallantly, that he overthrew them. and set them all upon
their tailes, he went afterwards to the Sorbone, where he maintained argument against all the Theologians or Divines, for
the space of six weeks, from foure a clock in the morning until
six in the evening, except an interval of two houres to refresh
themselves, and take their repast : and at this were present
the greatest part of the Lords of the Court, the Masters of
Requests, Presidents, Counsellors, those of the Accompts,
Secretaries, Advocates and others : as also the Sheriffes of the
said town, with the Physicians and Professors of the canon-
law ; amongst which it is to be remarked, that the greatest part
were stubborn jades, and in their opinions obstinate ; but he
took such course with them, that for all their Ergo's and
fallacies, he put their backs to the wall, gravelled them in the
deepest questions, and made it visibly appear to the world,
that compared to him, they were but monkies, and a knot of

mufled calves : Whereupon every body began to keep a bustling noise, and talk of his so marvellous knowledge, through
all degrees of persons in both sexes, even to the very Laun-
dresses, Brokers, Rostmeatsellers, Penknife-makers and others,
who, when he past along in the street, would say, This is he ;
in which he took delight, as Demosthenes the prince of Greek
Oratours did, when an old crouching wife, pointing at him
with her fingers, said, That is the man.

Now at this same very time there was a processe or suit in
law, depending in Court between two great Lords, of which one
was called my Lord Kissebreech, Plaintiffe of one side, and
the other my Lord Suckfist, Defendant of the other ; whose
Controversie was so high and difficult in Law, that the Court
of Parliament could make nothing of it. And therefore by the
Commandment of the King there were assembled foure of the
greatest and most learned of all the Parliaments of France,
together with the great Councel, and all the principal Regents
of the Universities, not only of France, but of England also
and Italy, such as Jason, Philippus Decius, Petrus de Petroni-
bus, and a rabble of other old Rabbinists : who being thus met
together, after they had thereupon consulted for the space of six
and fourty weeks, finding that they could not fasten their teeth
in it, nor with such clearnesse understand the case, as that they
might in any manner of way be able to right it, or take up the
difference betwixt the two aforesaid Parties, it did so greviously
vex them, that they most villanously conshit themselves for
shame. In this great extremity, one amongst them named
Du Douhait, the learnedst of all, and more expert and prudent
then any of the rest, whilest one day they were at their wits end,
all-to-be-dunced and philogrobolized in their braines, said unto
them : We have been here (my Masters,) a good long space
without doing any thing else, then trifle away both our time
and money, and can neverthelesse finde neither brim nor
bottome in this matter ; for the more we study about it, the
lesse we understand therein, which is a great shame and disgrace
to us, and a heavy burthen to our consciences ; yea such, that
in my opinion we shall not rid our selves of it without dishonour,
unlesse we take some other course, for we do nothing but doat
in our consultations.

See therefore what I have thought upon : you have heard
much talking of that worthy personage named Master Pantagruel, who hath been found to be learned above the capacity
of this present age, by the proofs he gave in those great dis-

THE PLAINTIFF

214

putations, which he held publickly aganist all men : my opinion is, that we send for him, to conferre with him about this businesse ; for never any man will encompasse the bringing of it to an end, if he do it not.

Hereunto all the Counsellors and Doctors willingly agreed, and according to that their result having instantly sent for him, they intreated him to be pleased to canvass the processe, and sift it thoroughly, that after a deep search and narrow examination of all the points thereof, he might forthwith make the report unto them, such as he shall think good in true and legal knowledge : to this effect they delivered into his hands the bags wherein were the Writs and Pancarts concerning that suit, which for bulk and weight were almost enough to lade foure great couillard or stoned Asses ; but Pantagruel said unto them, Are the two Lords, between whom this debate and processe is, yet living ? It was answered him, Yes : To what a devil then (said he,) serve so many paultry heapes, and bundles of papers and copies which you give me ? is it not better to heare their Controversie from their own mouthes, whilest they are face to face before us, then to reade these vile fopperies, which are nothing but trumperies, deceipts, diabolical cosenages of Cepola, pernicious slights and subversions of equity ? for I am sure, that you, and all those thorough whose hands this processe hath past, have by your devices added what you could to it *pro et contra* in such sort, that although their difference perhaps was clear and easie enough to determine at first, you have obscured it, and made it more intricate, by the frivolous, sottish, unreasonable and foolish reasons and opinions of Accursius, Baldus, Bartolus, de Castro, de Imola, Hippolytus Panormo, Bertachin, Alexander, Curtius, and those other old Mastiffs, who never understood the least law of the Pandects, they being but meer blockheads and great tithe-calvs, ignorant of all that which was needful for the understanding of the lawes ; for (as it is most certain) they had not the knowledge either of the Greek or Latine tongue, but only of the Gothick or Barbarian ; the lawes neverthelesse, were first taken from the Greeks, according to the testimony of Ulpian. *L. poster. de origine juris*, which we likewise may perceive by that all the lawes are full of Greek words and sentences : and then we finde that they are reduced into a Latine stile, the most elegant and ornate, that whole language is able to afford, without excepting that of any that ever wrote therein, nay, not of Salust, Varo, Cicero, Seneca, Titus Livius, nor Quintilian ;

how then could these old dotards be able to understand aright the text of the lawes, who never in their time had looked upon a good Latine book, as doth evidently enough appear by the rudenesse of their stile, which is fitter for a Chimney-sweeper, or for a Cook or a Scullion, than for a Jurisconsult and Doctor in the Lawes ?

Furthermore, seeing the Lawes are excerpted out of the middle of moral and natural Philosophie, how should these fooles have understood it, that have, by G—, studied lesse in Philosophie then my Mule ? in respect of humane learning, and the knowledge of Antiquities and History, they were truly laden with those faculties as a toad is with feathers. And yet of all this the Lawes are so full, that without it they cannot be understood, as I intend more fully to shew unto you in a peculiar Treatise, which on that purpose I am about to publish. Therefore if you will that I take any medling in this processe, first, cause all these papers to be burnt ; secondly, make the two Gentlemen come personally before me ; and afterwards, when I shall have heard them, I will tell you my opinion freely without any feignednes or dissimulation whatsoever.

Some amongst them did contradict this motion, as you know that in all companies there are more fooles then wise men, and that the greater part alwayes surmounts the better, as saith Titus Livius, in speaking of the Carthaginians : but the foresaid Du Douet held the contrary opinion, maintaining that Pantagruel had said well, and what was right, in affirming that these records, bills of inquest, replies, rejoinders, exceptions, depositions, and other such diableries of truth-intangling Writs, were but Engines wherewith to overthrow justice, and unnecessarily to prolong such suits as did depend before them ; and that therefore the devil would carry them all away to hell, if they did not take another course, and proceeded not in times coming according to the Prescripts of Evangelical and Philosophical equity. In fine, all the papers were burnt, and the two Gentlemen summoned and personally convented ; at whose appearance before the Court, Pantagruel said unto them, Are you they, that have this great difference betwixt you ? Yes, (my Lord) said they : Which of you (said Pantagruel,) is the Plaintiffe ? It is I, said my Lord Kissebreech. Go to then, my friend, (said he) and relate your matter unto me from point to point, according to the real truth, or else (by cocks body), if I finde you to lie so much as in one word, I will make you shorter by the head, and take it from off your shoulders, to shew others by your example, that in justice and judgement men ought to speak nothing but the truth ; therefore take heed you do not adde nor impare any thing in the Narration of your case. Begin.

CHAPTER XI

How the Lords of Kissebreech and Suckfist did plead before Pantagruel without an Atturney

THEN began Kissebreech in manner as followeth : My Lord, it is true, that a good woman of my house carried egges to the market to sell : Be covered, Kissebreech, said Pantagruel : Thanks to you, my Lord, said the Lord Kissebreech ; but to the purpose.   There passed betwixt the two tropicks the summe of three pence towards the zenith and a halfpenny, forasmuch as the Riphæan mountaines had been that yeare opprest with a great sterility of counterfeit gudgions, and shewes without substance, by meanes of the babling tattle, and fond fibs, seditiously raised between the gibblegablers, and Accursian gibberish-mongers, for the rebellion of the Swissers, who had assembled themselves to the full number of the bum-bees, and myrmidons, to go a handsel-getting on the first day of the new yeare, at that very time when they gave brewis to the oxen, and deliver the key of the coales to the Countrey-girles, for serving in of the oates to the dogs.   All the night long they did nothing else (keeping their hands still upon the pot) but dispatch both on foot and horseback, leaden-sealed Writs or letters, (to wit, Papal Commissions commonly called Bulls,) to stop the boats : for the Tailors and Seamsters would have made of the stollen shreds and clippings a goodly sagbut to cover the face of the Ocean, which then was great with childe of a potfull of cabbidge, according to the opinion of the hay-bundle-makers : but the physicians said, that by the Urine they could discern no manifest signe of the Bustards pace, nor how to eat double-tongued mattocks with mustard, unlesse the Lords and Gentlemen of the Court should be pleased to give by B.mol expresse command to the pox, not to run about any longer, in gleaning up of Coppersmiths and Tinkers ; for the Jobernolls had already a pretty good beginning in their dance of the Brittish gig, called the *estrindore*, to a perfect diapason, with one foot in the fire, and their head in the middle, as good man Ragot was wont to say.

Ha (my masters,) God moderates all things, and disposeth of them at his pleasure, so that against unluckie fortune a Carter broke his frisking whip, which was all the winde-instrument he had : this was done at his return from the little paultry town, even then when Master Amtitus of Cresseplots was licentiated, and had past his degrees in all dullerie and blockishnesse, according to this sentence of the Canonists, *Beati Dunces, quoniam ipsi stumblaverunt.* But that which makes lent to be so high, by St. Fiacre of Bry, is for nothing else, but that the Pentecost never comes, but to my cost ; yet on afore there, hoe, a little rain stills a great winde, and we must think so, seeing that the Serjeant hath propounded the matter so farre above my reach, that the Clerks and Secondaries could not with the benefit thereof lick their fingers feathered with gaunders, so orbicularly as they were wont in other things to do. And we do manifestly see, that every one acknowledgeth himself to be in the errour, wherewith another hath been charged, reserving only those cases whereby we are obliged to take an ocular inspection in a perspective glasse of these things, towards the place in the Chimney, where hangeth the signe of the wine of fourty girths, which have been alwayes accounted very necessary for the number of twenty pannels and pack-saddles of the bankrupt Protectionaries of five yeares respit ; howsoever at least he that would not let flie the owle before the Cheesecakes, ought in law to have discovered his reason why not, for the memory is often lost with a wayward shooing : Well, God keep Theobald Mitain from all danger. Then said Pantagruel, Hold there : Ho, my friend, soft and faire, speak at leisure, and soberly without putting your self in choler ; I understand the case, go on. Now then (my Lord) said Kissebreech, the foresaid good woman, saying her gaudez and audi nos, could not cover her selfe with a treacherous back-blow, ascending by the wounds and passions of the priviledges of the Universities, unlesse by the vertue of a warming-pan she had Angelically fomented every part of her body, in covering them with a hedge of garden-beds then giving in a swift un-avoidable thrust very near to the place where they sell the old rags, whereof the Painters of Flanders make great use, when they are about neatly to clap on shoes on grashoppers, locusts, cigals, and such like flie-fowles, so strange to us, that I am wonderfully astonished why the world doth not lay, seeing it is so good to hatch.

Here the Lord of Suckfist would have interrupted him and spoken somewhat, whereupon Pantagruel said unto him, St ! by St Antonies belly, doth it become thee to speak without command ? I sweat here with the extremity of labour and exceeding toile I take to understand the proceeding of your mutual difference, and yet thou comest to trouble and disquiet me : peace, in the devils name, peace, thou shalt be permitted to speak thy belly full, when this man hath done, and no sooner. Go on, (said he) to Kissebreech, speak calmly, and do not over-heat your self with too much haste.

I perceiving then (said Kissebreech,) that the pragmatical sanction did make no mention of it, and that the holy Pope to every one gave liberty to fart at his own ease, if that the blankets had no streaks, wherein the liars were to be crossed with a ruffianlike crue : and the rain-bow being newly sharpened at Milan to bring forth larks, gave his full consent that the good woman should tread down the heel of the hipgut-pangs, by vertue of a solemn protestation put in by the little testiculated or codsted fishes, which to tell the truth, were at that time very necessary for understanding the syntax and construction of old boots.   Therefore John Calfe, her Cosen gervais once removed with a log from the woodstack, very seriously advised her not to put her selfe into the hazard of quagswagging in the Lee, to be scowred with a buck of linnen clothes, till first she had kindled the paper : this counsel she laid hold on, because he desired her to take nothing, and throw out, for *Non de ponte vadit, qui cum sapientia cadit :* matters thus standing, seeing the Masters of the chamber of Accompts, or members of that Committee, did not fully agree amongst themselves in casting up the number of the Almanie whistles, whereof were framed those spectacles for Princes, which have been lately printed at Antwerp : I must needs think that it makes a bad return of the Writ, and that the adverse Party is not to be beleeved, *in sacer verbo dotis ;* for that having a great desire to obey the pleasure of the King, I armed my self from toe to top with belly furniture, of the soles of good venison-pasties, to go see how my grape-gatherers and vintagers had pinked and cut full of small holes their high coped-caps, to lecher it the better, and play at in and in.   And indeed the time was very dangerous in coming from the Faire, in so farre that many trained bowe-men were cast at the muster, and quite rejected, although the chimney-tops

THE LORD SUCKFIST PLEADED BEFORE PANTAGRUEL

220

were high enough, according to the proportion of the windgalls in the legs of horses, or of the Malaunders, which in the esteem of expert Farriers is no better disease, or else the story of Ronypatifam, or Lamibaudichon, interpreted by some to be the tale of a tub, or of a roasted horse, savours of Apocrypha, and is not an authentick history ; and by this means there was that yeare great abundance throughout all the countrey of Artois, of tawny buzzing beetles, to the no small profit of the Gentlemen-great-stick-faggot-carriers, when they did eate without disdaining the cocklicranes, till their belly was like to crack with it again : as for my own part, such is my Christian charity towards my neighbours, that I could wish from my heart every one had as good a voice, it would make us play the better at the tennis and the baloon. And truly (my Lord) to expresse the real truth without dissimulation, I cannot but say, that those petty subtile devices, which are found out in the etymologizing of patins, would descend more easily into the river of Seine, to serve for ever at the Millars bridge upon the said water, as it was heretofore decreed by the King of the Canarrians, according to the sentence or judgement given thereupon, which is to be seen in the Registry and Records within the Clerks office of this house.

And therefore (my Lord) I do most humbly require, that by your Lordship there may be said and declared upon the case what is reasonable, with costs, damages, and interests. Then said Pantagruel, My friend, is this all you have to say ? Kissebreech answered, Yes, (my Lord) for I have told all the *tu autem*, and have not varied at all upon mine honour in so much as one single word. You then, (said Pantagruel) my Lord of Suckfist, say what you will, and be brief, without omitting neverthelesse any thing that may serve to the purpose.

CHAPTER XII

How the Lord of Suckfist pleaded before Pantagruel

THEN began the Lord Suckfist in manner as followeth : My Lord, and you my masters, if the iniquity of men were as easily seene in categoricall judgement, as we can discerne flies in a milk-pot, the worlds four oxen had not been so eaten up with Rats, nor had so many eares upon the earth beene nibled away so scurvily ; for although all that my adversary hath spoken be of a very soft and downy truth, in so much as concernes the Letter and History of the factum : yet neverthelesse the crafty slights, cunning subtilties, slie cozenages, and little troubling intanglements are hid under the Rose-pot, the common cloak and cover of all fraudulent deceits.

Should I endure, that, when I am eating my pottage equall with the best, and that without either thinking or speaking any manner of ill, they rudely come to vexe, trouble, and perplex my braines with that antick Proverb, which saith,

> Who in his pottage-eating drinks will not
> When he is dead and buried, see one jot.

And good Lady, how many great Captaines have we seen in the day of battel, when in open field the Sacrament was distributed in lunchions of the sanctified bread of the Confraternity, the more honestly to nod their heads, play on the lute, and crack with their tailes, to make pretty little platforme leaps, in keeping level by the ground : but now the world is unshackled from the corners of the packs of Leycester. One flies out lewdly and becomes debauch't, another likewise five, four and two, and that at such randome, that, if the Court take not some course therein, it will make as bad a season in matter of gleaning this yeare, as ever it made, or it will make goblets. If any poor creature go to the stoves to illuminate his muzzle with a Cowshard, or to buy winter-boots, and that the Serjeants passing by, or those of the watch, happen to receive the decoction of a clystere, or the fecal matter of a close-stool, upon their rustling-wrangling-clutter-keeping masterships, should any because of that make bold to clip the shillings and testers, and try the wooden dishes ? sometimes, when we think one thing, God does another ; and, when the Sunne is wholly set, all beasts are in the shade : let me never be beleeved again, if I do not gallantly prove it by several people that have seen the light of the day.

In the yeare thirty and six, buying a Dutch curtail, which was a middle sized horse, both high and short, of a wool good enough, and died in graine, as the Goldsmiths assured me, although the Notarie put an etc. in it ; I told really, that I was not a Clerk of so much learning as to snatch at the Moon with

my teeth; but as for the Butter-firkin, where Vulcanian deeds
and evidences were sealed, the rumour was, and the report
thereof went currant, that salt-beefe will make one finde the
way to the wine without a candle, though it were hid in the
bottom of a Colliers sack, and that with his drawers on he were
mounted on a barbed horse furnished with a fronstal, and such
armes, thighs, and leg-pieces as are requisite for the well frying
and broyling of a swaggering sawcinesse. Here is a sheeps
head, and it is well they make a proverb of this, that it is good
to see black Cowes in burnt wood, when one attains to the
enjoyment of his love. I had a consultation upon this point
with my Masters the Clerks, who for resolution concluded in
frisesomorum, that there is nothing like to mowing in the
summer, and sweeping clean away in water, well garnished with
paper, ink, pens and penknives of Lyons upon the river of
Rosne, dolopym dolopof, tarabin tarabas, tut, prut, pish: for
incontinently after that armour begins to smell of garlick,
the rust will go near to eat the liver, not of him that weares it,
and then do they nothing else but withstand others courses,
and wryneckedly set up their bristles 'gainst one another, in
lightly passing over their afternoons sleep, and this is that which
maketh salt so dear. My Lords, beleeve not, when the said
good woman had with bird-lime caught the shovelar fowle,
the better before a Serjeants witnesse, to deliver the younger
sons portion to him, that the sheeps pluck, or hogs haslet, did
dodge and shrink back in the Usurers purses, or that there could
be any thing better to preserve one from the Cannibals, then to
take a rope of onions, knit with three hundred turneps, and a
little of a Calves Chaldern of the best allay that the Alchymists
have provided, and that they daub and do over with clay, as
also calcinate and burne to dust these pantoffles, muf in muf out,
mouflin mouflard, with the fine sauce of the juice of the rabble
rout, whilest they hide themselves in some petty moldwarphole,
saving alwayes the little slices of bacon. Now if the dice will
not favour you with any other throw but ambesace, and the
chance of three at the great end, mark well the ace, then take
me your dame, settle her in a corner of the bed, and whisk me
her up drilletrille, there, there, toureloura la la; which when
you have done, take a hearty draught of the best, *despicando
grenovillibus*, in despight of the frogs, whose faire course be-
buskined stockins shall be set apart for the little green geese,
or mued goslings, which, fatned in a coope, take delight to sport
themselves at the wagtaile game, waiting for the beating of the

mettal, and heating of the waxe by the slavering drivellers of consolation.

Very true it is, that the foure oxen which are in debate, and whereof mention was made, were somewhat short in memory : neverthelesse, to understand the gamme aright, they feared neither the Cormorant nor Mallard of Savoy, which put the good people of my countrey in great hope, that their children sometime should become very skilful in Algorisme ; therefore is it, that by a law rubrick and special sentence thereof, that we cannot faile to take the wolfe, if we make our hedges higher then the wind-mill, whereof somewhat was spoken by the Plaintiffe. But the great Devil did envie it, and by that means put the high Dutches farre behinde, who played the devils in swilling down and tipling at the good liquour, trink, meen herr, trink, trink, by two of my table men in the corner-point I have gained the lurch ; for it is not probable, nor is there any appearance of truth in this saying, that at Paris upon a little bridge the hen is proportionable ; and were they as copped and high-crested as marish whoops, if veritably they did not sacrifice the Printers pumpet-balls at Moreb, with a new edge set upon them by text letters, or those of a swift-writing hand, it is all one to me, so that the head-band of the book breed not moths or wormes in it. And put the case, that at the coupling together of the buck-hounds, the little puppies should have waxed proud before the Notarie could have given an account of the serving of his Writ by the Cabalistick Art, it will necessarily follow (under correction of the better judgement of the Court,) that six acres of medow ground of the greatest breadth will make three butts of fine ink, without paying ready money ; considering that at the Funeral of King Charles, we might have had the fathom in open market for one and two, that is, deuce ace : this I may affirm with a safe conscience, upon my oath of wooll.

And I see ordinarily in all good bagpipes, that when they go to the counterfeiting of the chirping of small birds, by swinging a broom three times about a chimney, and putting his name upon record, they do nothing but bend a Crossebowe backward, and winde a horne, if perhaps it be too hot, and that by making it fast to a rope he was to draw, immediately after the sight of the letters, the Cowes were restored to him. Such another sentence after the homeliest manner was pronounced in the seventeenth yeare, because of the bad government of Louzefougarouse, whereunto it may please the Court to have regard. I desire to be rightly understood ; for truly I say not, but that in all equity, and with an upright conscience, those may very well be dispossest, who drink holy water, as one would do a weavers shuttle, whereof suppositories are made to those that will not resigne, but on the termes of ell and tell, and giving of one thing for another. *Tunc* (my Lords) *quid juris pro minoribus ?* for the common custom of the Salick law is such, that the first incendiarie or fire-brand of sedition, that flayes the Cow, and wipes his nose in a full consort of musick, without blowing in the Coblers stitches, should in the time of the night-mare sublimate the penury of his member by mosse gathered when people are like to foundre themselves at the messe at midnight, to give the estrapade to these white-wines of Anjou, that do the feat of the leg in lifting it (by horse-men called the Gambetta,) and that neck to neck, after the fashion of Britanie, concluding as before with costs, damages and interests.

After that the Lord of Suckfist had ended, Pantagruel said to the Lord of Kissebreech, My friend, have you a minde to make any reply to what is said ? No, (my Lord) answered Kissebreech ; for I have spoke all I intended, and nothing but the truth, therefore put an end for Gods sake to our difference, for we are here at great charge.

CHAPTER XIII

How Pantagruel gave Judgement upon the Difference of the two Lords

THEN Pantagruel rising up, assembled all the Presidents, Counsellors and Doctors that were there, and said unto them : Come now (my Masters) you have heard (*vivæ vocis oraculo*) the Controversie that is in question ; what do you think of it ? They answered him, We have indeed heard it, but have not understood the devil so much as one circumstance of the case ; and therefore we beseech you, *unâ voce*, and in courtesie request you, that you would give sentence as you think good, and, *ex nunc prout ex tunc*, we are satisfied with it, and do ratifie it with our full consents : Well, my Masters (said Pantagruel) seeing you are so well pleased, I will do it : but I do not truly finde the case so difficult as you make it : your paragraph *Caton* : the law *Frater*, the law *Gallus*, the law *Quinque pedum*, the

226

law *Vinum*, the law *Si Dominus*, the law *Mater*, the law *Mulier bona*, the law *Si quis*, the law *Pomponius*, the law *Fundi*, the law *Emptor*, the law *Prœtor*, the law *Venditor*, and a great many others, are farre more intricate in my opinion. After he had spoke this, he walked a turn or two about the hall, plodding very profoundly, as one may think ; for he did groan like an Asse, whilest they girth him too hard, with the very intensiveness of considering how he was bound in conscience to do right to both parties, without varying or accepting of persons. Then he returned, sate down, and began to pronounce sentence as followeth.

Having seen, heard, calculated and well considered of the difference between the Lords of Kissebreech and Suckfist, the Court saith unto them, that in regard of the sudden quaking, shivering and hoarinesse of the flickermouse, bravely declining from the estival soltice, to attempt by private means the surprisal of toyish trifles in those, who are a little unwell for having taken a draught too much, through the lewd demeanour and vexation of the beetles, that inhabit the diarodal climate of an hypocritical Ape on horseback, bending a Crossebowe backwards. The Plaintiffe truly had just cause to calfet, or with Ockam, to stop the chinks of the gallion, which the good woman blew up with winde, having one foot shod and the other bare, reimbursing and restoring to him, low and stiffe in his conscience, as many bladder-nuts and wilde pistaches as there is of haire in eighteen Cowes, with as much for the embroiderer, and so much for that. He is likewise declared innocent of the case priviledged from the Knapdardies, into the danger whereof it was thought he had incurred ; because he could not jocundly and with fulnesse of freedom untrusse and dung, by the decision of a paire of gloves perfumed with the sent of bum-gunshot, at the walnut-tree taper, as is usual in his countrey of Mirebalois. Slacking therefore the top-saile, and letting go the boulin with the brazen bullets, wherewith the Mariners did by way of protestation bake in paste-meat, great store of pulse interquilted with the dormouse, whose hawks bells were made with a puntinaria, after the manner of Hungary or Flanders lace, and which his brother in law carried in a Panier, lying near to three chevrons or bordered gueules, whilest he was clean out of heart, drooping and crest-fallen by the too narrow sifting, canvassing and curious examining of the matter, in the angularly doghole of nastie scoundrels, from whence we shoot at the vermiformal popingay with the flap made of a foxtaile.

But in that he chargeth the Defendant, that he was a botcher, cheese-eater, and trimmer of mans flesh imbalmed, which in the arsiversie swagfall tumble was not found true, as by the Defendant was very well discussed.

The Court therefore doth condemn and amerce nim in three porringers of curds, well cemented and closed together, shining like pearles, and Codpieced after the fashion of the Countrey, to be payed unto the said Defendant about the middle of August in May : but, on the other part the Defendant shall be bound to furnish him with hay and stubble, for stopping the caltrops of his throat, troubled and impulregafized, with gabardines garbeled shufflingly, and friends as before without costs and for cause.

Which sentence being pronounced, the two Parties departed both contented with the decree, which was a thing almost incredible ; for it never came to passe since the great rain, nor shall the like occur in thirteen jubilees hereafter, that two Parties, contradictorily contending in judgment, be equally satisfied and well pleased with the definitive sentence. As for the Counsellors, and other Doctors in the law, that were there present, they were all so ravished with admiration at the more then humane wisdom of Pantagruel, which they did most clearly perceive to be in him, by his so accurate decision of this so difficult and thornie cause, that their spirits, with the extremity of the rapture, being elevated above the pitch of actuating the organs of the body, they fell into a trance and sudden extasie, wherein they stayed for the space of three long houres, and had been so as yet in that condition, had not some good people fetched store of vinegar and rose-water, to bring them again unto their former sense and understanding, for the which God be praised every where : And so be it

CHAPTER XIV

How Panurge related the Manner how he escaped out of the hands of the Turks

THE great wit and judgement of Pantagruel, was immediately after this made known unto all the world, by setting forth his

praises in print, and putting upon record this late wonderful
proof he hath given thereof amongst the Rolls of the Crown,
and Registers of the Palace, in such sort, that every body began
to say, that Solomon, who by a probable guesse only, without
any further certainty, caused the childe to be delivered to its
own mother, shewed never in his time such a Masterpiece of
wisdom, as the good Pantagruel hath done ; happy are we
therefore that have him in our Countrey. And indeed they
would have made him thereupon Master of the Requests, and
President in the Court : but he refused all, very graciously
thanking them for their offer, for (said he) there is too much
slavery in these offices, and very hardly can they be saved
that do exercise them, considering the great corruption that is
amongst men : which makes me beleeve, if the empty seats of
Angels be not fil'd with other kind of people then those, we
shall not have the final judgement these seven thousand sixty
and seven jubilees yet to come, and so Cusanus will be
deceived in his conjecture : Remember that I have told you
of it, and given you faire advertisement in time and place
convenient.

But if you have any hogsheads of good wine, I willingly will
accept of a present of that, which they very heartily did do, in
sending him of the best that was in the City, and he drank
reasonably well, but poor Panurge bibbed and bowsed of it
most villainously, for he was as dry as a red-herring, as lean as
a rake, and like a poor, lank, slender cat, walked gingerly as
if he had trod upon egges : so that by some one being
admonished, in the midst of his draught of a large deep bowle,
full of excellent Claret, with these words, Faire and softly,
Gossip, you suck up as if you were mad ; I give thee to the
devil, (said he) thou hast not found here thy little tipling sippers
of Paris, that drink no more then the little bird called a spink
or chaffinch, and never take in their beak ful of liquour, till they
be bobbed on the tailes after the manner of the sparrows.
O companion, if I could mount up as well as I can get down, I
had been long ere this above the sphere of the Moon with
Empedocles. But I cannot tell what a devil this meanes.
This wine is so good and delicious, that the more I drink thereof,
the more I am athirst ; I beleeve that the shadow of my Master
Pantagruel engendereth the altered and thirsty men, as the
Moon doth the catarres and defluxions ; at which word the
company began to laugh : which Pantagruel perceiving, said,
Panurge, What is that which moves you to laugh so ? Sir,

AS LEAN AS A RAKE

230

said he, I was telling them that these devillish Turks are very
unhappy, in that they never drink one drop of wine, and that
though there were no other harme in all Mahomets Alcoran,
yet for this one base point of abstinence from wine, which
therein is commanded, I would not submit my self unto their
law.   But now tell me, (said Pantagruel) how you escaped out
of their hands.   By G—, Sir, said Panurge, I will not lie to
you in one word.

The rascally Turks had broached me upon a spit all larded
like a rabbet, (for I was so dry and meagre, that otherwise,
of my flesh they would have made but very bad meat) and in
this manner began to rost me alive.   As they were thus roasting
me, I recommended my self unto the divine grace, having in my
minde the good St. Lawrence, and alwayes hoped in God that
he would deliver me out of this torment, which came to passe,
and that very strangely ; for as I did commit my self with all
my heart unto God, crying, Lord God, help me, Lord God, save
me, Lord God, take me out of this paine and hellish torture,
wherein these traiterous dogs detain me for my sincerity in the
maintenance of thy law : the roster or turn-spit fell asleep
by the divine will, or else by the vertue of some good Mercury,
who cunningly brought Argus into a sleep for all his hundred
eyes : when I saw that he did no longer turne me in roasting,
I looked upon him, and perceived that he was fast asleep, then
took I up in my teeth a firebrand by the end where it was not
burnt, and cast it into the lap of my roaster, and another did I
throw as well as I could under a field-couche, that was placed
near to the chimney, wherein was the straw-bed of my Master
turnspit ; presently the fire took hold in the straw, and from
the straw to the bed, and from the bed to the loft, which was
planked and seeled with firre, after the fashion of the foot of a
lamp : but the best was, that the fire which I had cast into
the lap of my paultry roaster burnt all his groine, and was
beginning to seize upon his cullions, when he became sensible
of the danger, for his smelling was not so bad, but that he felt
it sooner than he could have seen day-light : then suddenly
getting up, and in a great amazement running to the window,
he cried out to the streets as high as he could, *dal baroth, dal
baroth, dal baroth*, which is as much to say as, Fire, fire, fire :
incontinently turning about, he came streight towards me, to
throw me quite into the fire, and to that effect had already cut
the ropes, wherewith my hands were tied, and was undoing the
cords from off my feet, when the Master of the house hearing

him cry, Fire, and smelling the smoke from the very street where he was walking with some other Baashaws and Musta-phaes, ran with all the speed he had to save what he could, and to carry away his Jewels ; yet such was his rage (before he could well resolve how to go about it,) that he caught the broach whereon I was spitted, and therewith killed my roaster stark dead, of which wound he died there for want of government or otherwise ; for he ran him in with the spit a little above the navel, towards the right flank, till he pierced the third lappet of his liver, and, the blow slanting upwards from the midriffe or diaphragme, through which it had made penetration, the spit passed athwart the pericardium, or capsule of his heart, and came out above at his shoulders, betwixt the spondyls or turning joints of the chine of the back, and the left homoplat, which we call the shoulder-blade.

True it is, (for I will not lie,) that, in drawing the spit out of my body, I fell to the ground near unto the Andirons, and so by the fall took some hurt, which indeed had been greater, but that the lardons, or little slices of bacon, wherewith I was stuck, kept off the blow. My Baashaw then seeing the case to be desperate, his house burnt without remission, and all his goods lost, gave himselfe over unto all the devils in hell, calling upon some of them by their names, Gringoth, Astaroth, Rappalus, and Gribouillis, nine several times, which when I saw, I had above six pence worth of feare, dreading that the devils would come even then to carry away this foole, and seeing me so near him would perhaps snatch me up too : I am already (thought I) halfe rosted, and my lardons will be the cause of my mischief ; for these devils are very lickorous of lardons, according to the authority which you have of the Philosopher Jamblicus, and Murmault, in the Apology of Bossutis, adulterated *pro magistros nostros :* but for my better security I made the signe of the Crosse ; crying, *Hageos, athanatos, ho theos,* and none came : at which my rogue Baashaw being very much aggrieved, would in transpiercing his heart with my spit have killed himself ; and to that purpose had set it against his breast, but it could not enter, because it was not sharp enough ; whereupon I per-ceiving that he was not like to work upon his body the effect which he intended, although he did not spare all the force he had to thrust it forward, came up to him and said, Master Bugrino, thou dost here but trifle away thy time, or rashly lose it, for thou wilt never kill thy self thus as thou doest : well thou mayest hurt or bruise somewhat within thee, so as to make thee languish all thy life-time most pitifully amongst the hands of the Chirurgions ; but if thou wilt be counselled by me, I will kill thee clear out-right, so that thou shalt not so much as feel it, and trust me, for I have killed a great many others, who have found themselves very well after it : Ha, my friend, said he, I prethee do so, and for thy paines I will give thee my Cod-piece ; take, here it is, there are six hundred Seraphs in it, and some fine Diamonds, and most excellent Rubies. And where are they (said Epistemon ?) By St. John (said Panurge) they are a good way hence, if they alwayes keep going : but where is the last yeares snow ? this was the greatest care that Villon the Parisien Poet took. Make an end (said Pantagruel) that we may know how thou didst dresse thy Baashaw : By the faith of an honest man (said Panurge) I do not lie in one word. I swadled him in a scurvie swathel-binding, which I found lying there half burnt, and with my cords tied him royster-like both hand and foot, in such sort that he was not able to winse ; then past my spit thorough his throat, and hanged him thereon, fastening the end thereof at two great hooks or cramp-irons, upon which they did hang their Halberds ; and then kindling a faire fire under him, did flame you up my Milourt, as they use to do dry herrings in a chimney : with this, taking his budget, and a little javelin that was upon the foresaid hooks, I ran away a faire gallop-rake, and God he knows how I did smell my shoulder of mutton.

When I was come down into the street, I found every body come to put out the fire with store of water, and seeing me so halfe-roasted, they did naturally pity my case, and threw all their water upon me, which by a most joyful refreshing of me, did me very much good : then did they present me with some victuals, but I could not eat much, because they gave me no-thing to drink but water after their fashion. Other hurt they did me none, only one little villainous Turkie knobbreasted rogue came thiefteously to snatch away some of my lardons, but I gave him such a sturdie thump and sound rap on the fingers with all the weight of my javelin, that he came no more the second time. Shortly after this, there came towards me a pretty young Corinthian wench, who brought me a box full of Conserves, of round Mirabolan plums, called Emblicks, and looked upon my poor Robin with an eye of great compassion, as it was flea-bitten and pinked with the sparkles of the fire from whence it came, for it reached no further in length, (beleeve me) then my knees ; but note, that this roasting cured me entirely of a Sciatick, whereunto I had been subject above seven yeares before, upon that side, which my roaster, by falling asleep, suffered to be burnt.

Now whilest they were thus busie about me, the fire triumphed, never ask, How ? for it took hold on above two thousand houses, which one of them espying cried out, saying, By Mahooms belly, all the City is on fire, and we do neverthelesse stand gazing here, without offering to make any relief : upon this every one ran to save his own ; for my part, I took my way towards the gate. When I was got upon the knap of a little hillock, not farre off, I turned me about as did Lots wife, and, looking back, saw all the City burning in a faire fire, whereat I was so glad, that I had almost beshit my selfe for joy : but God punished me well for it : How ? said Pantagruel : Thus, said Panurge ; for when with pleasure I beheld this jolly fire, jesting with my self, and saying, Ha ! poor flies, ha ! poor mice, you will have a bad winter of it this yeare, the fire is in your reeks, it is in your bed-straw,—out came more then six, yea more then thirteen hundred and eleven dogs great and small, altogether out of the town, flying away from the fire ; at the first approach they ran all upon me, being carried on by the sent of my leacherous half-roasted flesh, and had even then devoured me in a trice, if my good Angel had not well inspired me with the instruction of a remedy, very sovereign against the tooth-ache. And wherefore (said Pantagruel) wert thou afraid of the toothache, or paine of the teeth ? wert thou not cured of thy rheumes ? By Palme-sunday, (said Panurge) is there any greater pain of the teeth, then when the dogs have you by the legs ? But on a sudden (as my good angel directed me) I thought upon my lardons, and threw them into the midst of the field amongst them : then did the dogs run, and fight with one another at faire teeth, which should have the lardons : by this means they left me, and I left them also bustling with, and hairing one another. Thus did I escape frolick and lively, grammercie roastmeat and cookery.

CHAPTER XV

How Panurge shewea a very new Way to build the Walls of Paris

PANTAGRUEL one day to refresh himself of his study, went a walking towards St. Marcels suburbs, to see the extravagancie of the Gobeline building, and to taste of their spiced bread. Panurge was with him, having alwayes a flaggon under his gown, and a good slice of a gammon of bacon; for without this he never went, saying, that it was as a Yeoman of the guard to him, to preserve his body from harme. Other sword carried he none; and when Pantagruel would have given him one, he answered, that he needed none, for that it would but heat his milt. Yea, but (said Epistemon) if thou shouldest be set upon, how wouldest thou defend thy self? With great buskinades or brodkin blowes, answered he, provided thursts were forbidden. At their return, Panurge considered the walls of the City of Paris, and in derision said to Pantagruel, See what faire walls here are! O how strong they are, and well fitted to keep geese in a mue or coop to fatten them! by my beard they are competently scurvie for such a City as this is; for a Cow with one fart would go near to overthrow above six fathoms of them. O my friend (said Pantagruel) doest thou know what Agesilaus said, when he was asked, Why the great city of Lacedemon was not inclosed with walls? Lo here (said he) the walls of the City, in shewing them the inhabitants and Citizens thereof, so strong, so well armed, and so expert in military discipline; signifying thereby, that there is no wall but of bones, and that Towns and Cities cannot have a surer wall, nor better fortification, then the prowesse and vertue of

WAS PICKING UP AND GATHERING SOME STICKS IN THE SAID FORREST

236

the Citizens and Inhabitants ; so is this City so strong, by the great number of warlike people that are in it, that they care not for making any other walls. Besides, whosoever would go about to wall it, as Strasbourg, Orleans, or Ferrara, would finde it almost impossible, the cost and charges would be so excessive. Yea, but (said Panurge) it is good, nevertheless, to have an out-side of stone, when we are invaded by our enemies, were it but to ask, Who is below there ? As for the enormous expence, which you say would be needful for undertaking the great work of walling this City about, if the Gentlemen of the Town will be pleased to give me a good rough cup of wine, I will shew them a pretty, strange and new way, how they may build them good cheap. How (said Pantagruel ?) Do not speak of it then (answered Panurge,) and I will tell it you. I see that the sine quo nons, kallibistris, or contrapunctums of the women of this Countrey are better cheap then stones : of them should the walls be built, ranging them in good symmetrie by the rules of Architecture, and placing the largest in the first ranks, then sloping downwards ridgewayes, like the back of an Asse. The middle sized ones must be ranked next, and last of all the least and smallest. This done, there must be a fine little interlacing of them, like points of Diamonds, as is to be seen in the great Tower of Bourges, with a like number of the nudinnudo's, nilnisistando's, and stiffe bracmards, that dwell in amongst the claustral Codpieces. What devil were able to overthrow such walls ? there is no metal like it to resist blowes, in so farre that if culverin-shot should come to grease upon it, you would incontinently see distil from thence the blessed fruit of the great pox, as small as raine : beware in the name of the devils, and hold off ; furthermore, no thunderbolt or lightning would fall upon it, for why ? they are all either blest or consecrated : I see but one inconveniency in it : Ho, ho, ha, ha, ha ! (said Pantagruel,) and what is that ? It is, that the flies would be so lickorish of them, that you would wonder, and would quickly gather there together, and there leave their ordure and excretions, and so all the work would be spoiled. But see how that would be remedied, they must be wiped and made rid of the flies with faire foxtailes, or good great viedazes (which are asse-pizzles) of Provence. And to this purpose I will tell you (as we go to supper,) a brave example set down by *Frater Lubinus libro de compotationibus mendicantium ;* in the time that the beasts did speak, which is not yet three dayes since. A poor Lion, walking through the forrest of Bieure, and saying his own little private devotions, past under a tree, where there was a roguish Collier gotten up to cut down wood, who seeing the lion, cast his hatchet at him, and wounded him enormously in one of his legs, whereupon the lion halting, he so long toiled and turmoiled himself in roaming up and down the forrest to finde helpe, that at last he met with a Carpenter, who willingly look't upon his wound, cleansed it as well as he could, and filled it with mosse, telling him that he must wipe his wound well, that the flies might not do their excrements in it, whilest he should go search for some yarrow or millefoile, commonly called the Carpenters herbe. The Lion, being thus healed, walked along in the forrest, at what time a sempiternous Crone and old Hag was picking up and gathering some sticks in the said forrest, who seeing the lion coming towards her, for feare fell down backwards, in such sort, that the winde blew up her gown, coats and smock, even as farre as above her shoulders ; which the lion perceiving, for pity ran to see whether she had taken any hurt by the fall, and thereupon considering her how do you call it said, O poor woman, who hath thus wounded thee ? which words when he had spoken, he espied a fox, whom he called to come to him, saying, Gossip Renard, hau, hither, hither, and for cause : when the fox was come, he said unto him, My gossip and friend, they have hurt this good woman here between the legs most villainously, and there is a manifest solution of continuity, see how great a wound it is, even from the taile up to the navel, in measure foure, nay full five handfuls and a half : this is the blow of an hatchet, I doubt me it is an old wound, and therefore that the flies may not get into it, wipe it lustily well and hard, I prethy, both within and without ; thou hast a good taile, and long, wipe, my friend, wipe, I beseech thee, and in the mean while I will go get some mosse to put into it ; for thus ought we to succour and help one another, wipe it hard, thus, my friend, wipe it well, for this wound must be often wiped, otherwise the Party cannot be at ease : go to, wipe well, my little gossip, wipe, God hath furnished thee with a taile, thou hast a long one, and of a bignesse proportionable, wipe hard, and be not weary. A good wiper, who, in wiping continually, wipeth with his wipard, by wasps shall never be wounded : wipe, my pretty minion, wipe, my little bullie, I will not stay long. Then went he to get store of mosse ; and, when he was a little way off, he cried out in speaking to the fox thus, Wipe well still, gossip, wipe, and let it never grieve thee to wipe well, my little gossip, I will put thee into service to be wiper to Don Pedro de Castille, wipe, only wipe, and no more. The poor fox wiped as hard as he could, here and there, within and without; but the false old trot did so fizzle and fist, that she stunk like a hundred devils, which put the poor fox to a great deal of ill ease, for he knew not to what side to turn himself, to escape the unsavoury perfume of this old womans postern blasts, and whilest to that effect he was shifting hither and thither, without knowing how to shun the annoyance of those unwholesom gusts, he saw that behinde there was yet another hole, not so great as that which he did wipe, out of which came this filthy and infectious aire. The Lion at last returned, bringing with him of mosse more then eighteen packs would hold, and began to put into the wound, with a staffe which he had provided for that purpose, and had already put in full sixteen packs and a half, at which he was amazed: What a devil? (said he) this wound is very deep, it would hold above two cart-loads of mosse. The fox perceiving this, said unto the Lion, O gossip Lion, my friend, I pray thee, do not put in all thy mosse there, keep somewhat, for there is yet here another little hole, that stinks like five hundred devils; I am almost choaked with the smell thereof, it is so pestiferous and impoisoning.

Thus must these walls be kept from the flies, and wages allowed to some for wiping of them. Then said Pantagruel, How dost thou know that the privy parts of women are at such a cheap rate? for in this City there are many vertuous, honest and chaste women besides the maids: *Et ubi prenus*, said Panurge? I will give you my opinion of it, and that upon certain and assured knowledge. I do not brag that I have bumbasted four hundred and seventeen, since I came into this City, though it be but nine dayes ago: but this very morning I met with a good fellow, who in a wallet, such as Æsops was, carried two little girles of two or three yeares old at the most, one before, and the other behinde: he demanded almes of me, but I made him answer, that I had more cods then pence; afterwards I asked him, Good man, these two girles, are they maids? Brother, said he, I have carried them thus these two yeares, and in regard of her that is before, whom I see continually, in my opinion she is a Virgin, neverthelesse I will not put my finger in the fire for it; as for her that is behinde, doubtlesse I can say nothing. Indeed (said Pantagruel) thou art a gentile companion, I will have thee to be apparelled in my livery, and therefore caused him to be clothed most gallantly according

GOOD MAN, THESE TWO GIRLES ARE THEY MAIDS?

to the fashion that then was, only that Panurge would have the Codpiece of his breeches three foot long, and in shape square, not round, which was done, and was well worth the seeing. Oftentimes was he wont to say, that the world had not yet known the emolument and utility that is in wearing great Codpieces ; but time would one day teach it them, as all things have been invented in time. God keep from hurt (said he) the good fellow whose long Codpiece or Braguet hath saved his life : God keep from hurt him, whose long Braguet hath been worth to him in one day, one hundred threescore thousand and nine Crowns ! God keep from hurt him, who by his long Braguet hath saved a whole City from dying by famine. And by G— I will make a book of the commodity of long Braguets, when I shall have more leisure. And indeed he composed a faire great book with figures, but it is not printed as yet that I know of

CHAPTER XVI

Of the Qualities and Conditions of Panurge

PANURGE was of a middle stature, not too high, nor too low, and had somewhat an Aquiline nose, made like the handle of a rasor : he was at that time five and thirty years old or thereabouts, fine to gild like a leaden dagger ; for he was a notable cheater and cony-catcher, he was a very gallant and proper man of his person, only that he was a little leacherous, and naturally subject to a kinde of disease, which at that time they called lack of money : it is an incomparable grief, yet, notwithstanding he had three-score and three tricks to come by it at his need, of which the most honourable and most ordinary was in manner of thieving, secret purloining and filching ; for he was a wicked lewd rogue, a cosener, drinker, royster, rover, and a very dissolute and debautch'd fellow, if there were any in Paris ; otherwise, and in all matters else, the best and most vertuous man in the world ; and he was still contriving some plot, and devising mischief against the Serjeants and the watch.

At one time he assembled three or foure especial good hacksters and roaring boyes, made them in the evening drink like Templers, afterwards led them till they came under St. Genevieve, or about the Colledge of Navarre, and at the houre that the watch was coming up that way, which he knew by putting his sword upon the pavement, and his eare by it, and, when he heard his sword shake, it was an infallible signe that the watch was near at that instant : then he and his companions took a tumbrel or dung-cart, and gave it the brangle, hurling it with all their force down the hill, and so overthrew all the poor watchmen like pigs, and then ran away upon the other side ; for in lesse then two dayes he knew all the streets, lanes and turnings in Paris, as well as his *Deus det*.

At another time he made in some faire place, where the said watch was to passe, a traine of gun-powder, and, at the very instant that they went along, set fire to it, and then made himself sport to see what good grace they had in running away, thinking that St. Antonies fire had caught them by the legs. As for the poor Masters of Arts, he did persecute them above all others : when he encountered with any of them upon the street, he would not never faile to put some trick or other upon them, sometimes putting the bit of a fried turd in their graduate hoods : At other times pinning on little fox-tails, or hares-eares behind them, or some other such roguish prank. One day that they were appointed all to meet in the fodder-street, he made a Borbonesa tart, or filthy and slovenly compound, made of store of garlick, of Assa fætida, of Castoreum, of dogs turds very warm, which he steeped, temper'd and liquifi'd in the corrupt matter of pockie biles, and pestiferous botches, and, very early in the morning, therewith anointed all the pavement, in such sort, that the devil could not have endured it, which made all these good people there to lay up their gorges, and vomit what was upon their stomachs before all the world, as if they had flayed the fox ; and ten or twelve of them died of the plague, fourteen became lepers, eighteen grew lousie, and above seven and twenty had the pox, but he did not care a button for it. He commonly carried a whip under his gowne wherewith he whipt without remission the pages, whom he found carrying wine to their Masters, to make them mend their pace. In his coat he had above six and twenty little fabs and pockets alwayes full, one with some lead-water, and a little knife as sharp as a glovers needle, wherewith he used to cut purses : Another with some kinde of bitter stuffe, which he threw into the eyes of those he met : another with clotburrs, penned with little geese or capons feathers, which he cast upon the gowns and caps of honest people, and often made them faire hornes, which they wore about all the City, sometimes all their life. Very often also upon the womens French hoods would he stick in the hind-part somewhat made in the shape of a mans member. In another, he had a great many little hornes full of fleas and lice, which he borrowed from the beggars of St. Innocent, and cast them with small canes or quills to write with, into the necks of the daintiest Gentlewomen that he could finde, yea even in the Church, for he never seated himself above in the quire, but alwayes sate in the body of the Church amongst the women, both at Masse, at Vespres, and at Sermon. In another, he used to have good store of hooks and buckles, wherewith he would couple men and women together, that sate in company close to one another, but especially those that wore gownes of crimson taffaties, that when they were about to go away, they might rent all their gownes. In another, he had a squib furnished with tinder, matches, stones to strike fire, and all other tackling necessary for it : in another, two or three burning glasses, wherewith he made both men and women sometimes mad, and in the Church put them quite out of countenance ; for he said that there was but an Antistrophe, or little more difference then of a literal inversion between a woman, *folle a la messe*, and *molle a la fesse;* that is, foolish at the Masse, and of a pliant buttock.

In another, he had a good deal of needles and thread, wherewith he did a thousand little devillish pranks. One time at the entry of the Palace unto the great Hall, where a certain gray Friar or Cordelier was to say Masse to the Counsellors : He did help to apparel him, and put on his vestments, but in the accoutring of him, he sowed on his alb, surplice or stole, to his gowne and shirt, and then withdrew himself, when the said Lords of the Court, or Counsellors came to heare the said Masse ; but when it came to the *Ite missa est*, that the poor Frater would have laid by his stole or surplice (as the fashion then was) he plucked off withal both his frock and shirt which were well sowed together, and therby stripping himself up to the very shoulders, shewed his *bel vedere* to all the worla, together with his Don Cypriano, which was no small one, as you may imagine ; and the Friar still kept haling, but so much the more did he discover himself, and lay open his backparts, till one of the Lords of the Court said, How now, what's the matter ? will this faire Father make us here an offering of his taile to kisse it ? nay, St. Antonies fire kisse it for us. From thenceforth it was ordained that the poor fathers should never disrobe themselves any more before the world, but in their vestry-room, or sextry, as they call it ; especially in the presence of women, lest it should tempt them to the sin of longing, and disordinate desire. The people then asked, why it was the Friars had so long and large genitories ? the said Panurge resolved the Probleme very neatly, saying, That which makes Asses to have such great eares, is that their dams did put no biggins on their heads, as Alliaco mentioneth in his suppositions : by the like reason, that which makes the genitories or generation-tooles of those so faire Fraters so long is, for that they weare no bottomed breeches, and therefore their jolly member, having no impediment, hangeth dangling at liberty, as farre as it can reach, with a wigle-wagle down to their knees, as women carry their patinotre beads : and the cause wherefore they have it so correspondently great is, that in this constant wig-wagging the humours of the body descend into the said member : for, according to the Legists, Agitation and continual motion is cause of attraction.

Item, he had another pocket full of itching powder, called stone-allum, whereof he would cast some into the backs of those women whom he judged to be most beautiful and stately, which did so ticklishly gall them, that some would strip themselves in the open view of the world, and others dance like a cock upon hot embers, or a drumstick on a taber : others again ran about the streets, and he would run after them : to such as were in the stripping veine he would very civilly come to offer his attendance, and cover them with his cloak, like a courteous and very gracious man.

Item, in another he had a little leather bottle full of old oile, wherewith, when he saw any man or woman in a rich new handsome suit, he would grease, smutch and spoile all the best parts of it under colour and pretence of touching them, saying, This is good cloth, this is good sattin, good taffaties : Madam, God give you all that your noble heart desireth ; you have a new suit, pretty Sir ; and you a new gown, sweet Mistris, God give you joy of it, and maintain you in all prosperity ! and with this would lay his hand upon their shoulder, at which touch such a villainous spot was left behinde, so enormously engraven to perpetuity in the very soule, body and reputation, that the devil himself could never have taken it away. Then upon his departing, he would say, Madam, take heed you do not fall, for there is a filthy great hole before you, whereinto if you put your foot, you will quite spoile your selfe : another he had all full of Euphorbium, very finely pulverised. In that powder did he lay a faire handkerchief curiously wrought, which he had stollen from a pretty Seamstresse of the Palace, in taking away a lowse from off her bosome, which he had put there himself : and when he came into the company of some good Ladies, he would trifle them into a discourse of some fine workmanship of bone-lace, then immediately put his hand into their bosome asking them, And this work, is it of Flanders, or of Hainault ? and then drew out his handkerchief, and said, hold, hold, look what work here is, it is of Foutignan or of Fontarabia, and shaking it hard at their nose, made them sneeze foure houres without ceasing : in the mean while he would fart like a horse, and the women would laugh and say, How now, do you fart, Panurge ? No, no, Madam (said he,) I do but tune my taile to the plain song of the Musick, which you make with your nose. In another he had a picklock, a pellican, a cramp iron, a crook, and some other iron tooles, wherewith there was no door nor coffer which he would not pick open. He had another full of little cups, wherewith he played very artificially, for he had his fingers made to his hand, like those of Minerva or Arachne, and had heretofore cried Triacle. And when he changed a teston, cardecu, or any other piece of money, the changer had been more subtil then a fox, if Panurge had not at every time made five or six sols, (that is some six or seven pence,) vanish away invisibly, openly and manifestly, without making any hurt or lesion, whereof the changer should have felt nothing but the winde.

CHAPTER XVII

*How Panurge gained the Pardons, and married the old Women,
and of the Suit in Law which he had at Paris*

ONE day I found Panurge very much out of countenance,
melancholick and silent, which made me suspect that he had
no money ; whereupon I said unto him, Panurge, you are sick,
as I do very well perceive by your physiognomie, and I know
the disease, you have a flux in your purse ; but take no care.
I have yet seven pence half penny, that never saw father nor
mother, which shall not be wanting, no more than the pox, in
your necessity : whereunto he answered me, Well, well, for
money, one day I shall have but too much ; for I have a
Philosophers stone, which attracts money out of mens purses,
as the adamant doth iron ; but will you go with me to gain the
pardons, said he ?   By my faith (said I) I am no great pardon-
taker in this world ; if I shall be any such in the other, I cannot
tell ; yet let us go in Gods name, it is but one farthing more
or lesse.   But (said he) lend me then a farthing upon interest.
No, no, (said I) I will give it you freely, and from my heart.
Grates vobis dominos, said he.

So we went along, beginning at St. Gervase, and I got the
pardons at the first boxe only, for in those matters very little
contenteth me : then did I say my small suffrages, and the
prayers of St. Brigid, but he gained them at all the boxes, and
alwayes gave money to every one of the Pardoners ; from
thence we went to our Ladies Church, to St. Johns, to St.
Antonies, and so to the other Churches, where there was a
banquet of pardons.   For my part, I gained no more of them :
but he at all the boxes kissed the relicks, and gave at every
one : to be brief, when we were returned, he brought me to
drink at the Castle-tavern, and there shewed me ten or twelve
of his little bags full of money, at which I blest my self, and
made the signe of the Crosse, saying, Where have you recovered
so much money in so little time ? unto which he answered me,
that he had taken it out of the basins of the pardons ; for in
giving them the first farthing (said he) I put it in with such
slight of hand, and so dexterously, that it appeared to be a

three-pence ; thus with one hand I took three-pence, nine-pence, or six-pence at the least, and with the other as much, and so thorough all the Churches where we have been.   Yea, but (said I) you damn your self like a snake, and are withal a thief and sacrilegious person.   True (said he) in your opinion, but I am not of that minde ; for the Pardoners do give me it, when they say unto me in presenting the relicks to kisse, *Centuplum accipies*, that is, that for one penny I should take a hundred ; for *accipies* is spoken according to the manner of the Hebrewes, who use the future tense in stead of the imperative, as you have in the law, *Diliges Dominum*, that is, *Dilige :* even so when the Pardon-bearer sayes to me, *Centuplum accipies*, his meaning is, *Centuplum accipe ;* and so doth Rabbi Kimy, and Rabbi Aben Ezra expound it, and all the Massorets, *et ibi Bartholus*.   Moreover, Pope Sixtus gave me fifteen hundred francks of yearly pension (which in English money is a hundred and fifty pounds) upon his Ecclesiastical revenues and treasure, for having cured him of a canckrous botch, which did so torment him, that he thought to have been a cripple by it all his life. Thus I do pay my self at my owne hand (for otherwise I get nothing) upon the said Ecclesiastical treasure.   Ho, my friend (said he) if thou didst know what advantage I made, and how well I feathered my nest, by the Popes bull of the Croisade, thou wouldest wonder exceedingly.   It was worth to me above six thousand florins (in English coine six hundred pounds), and what a devil is become of them ?- (said I) for of that money thou hast not one half penny.   They returned from whence they came (said he) they did no more but change their Master.

But I employed at least three thousand of them (that is, three hundred pounds English,) in marrying, not young Virgins ; for they finde but too many husbands, but great old sempiternous trots, which had not so much as one tooth in their heads ; and that out of the consideration I had, that these good old women had very well spent the time of their youth in playing at the close-buttock-game to all commers, serving the foremost first, till no man would have any more dealing with them.   And by G—, I will have their skin-coat shaken once yet before they die ; by this meanes, to one I gave a hundred florins, to another six score, to another three hundred, according to that they were infamous, detestable and abominable ; for, by how much the more horrible and execrable they were, so much the more must I needs have given them, otherwayes the devil would not have jum'd them.   Presently I went to

TO ONE I GAVE A HUNDRED FLORINS

248

some great and fat woodporters, or such like, and did my selfe make the match, but before I did shew him the old Hags, I made a faire muster to him of the Crownes, saying, Good fellow, see what I will give thee, if thou wilt but condescend to dufle, dinfredaille, or lecher it one good time : then began the poor rogues to gape like old mules, and I caused to be provided for them a banquet, with drink of the best, and store of spiceries, to put the old women in rut and heat of lust. To be short, they occupied all, like good soules, only to those that were horribly ugly and ill-favoured, I caused their head to be put within a bag, to hide their face.

Besides all this, I have lost a good deal in suits of law : And what lawsuits couldest thou have ? (said I) thou hast neither house nor lands. My friend, (said he) the Gentlewomen of this City had found out, by the instigation of the devil of hell, a manner of high-mounted bands, and neckerchiefs for women, which did so closely cover their bosomes, that men could no more put their hands under ; for they had put the slit behinde, and those neckcloths were wholly shut before, whereat the poor sad contemplative lovers were much discontented. Upon a faire Tuesday, I presented a Petition to the Court, making my self a Party against the said Gentlewomen, and shewing the great interest that I pretended therein, protesting that by the same reason, I would cause the Codpeece of my breeches to be sowed behinde, if the Court would not take order for it. In summe, the Gentlewomen put in their defences, shewed the grounds they went upon, and constituted their Atturney for the prosecuting of the cause, but I pursued them so vigorously, that by a sentence of the Court it was decreed, those high neckclothes should be no longer worne, if they were not a little cleft and open before ; but it cost me a good summe of money. I had another very filthy and beastly processe against the dung-farmer (called master Fifi) and his Deputies, that they should no more reade privily the pipe, punchon, nor quart of sentences, but in faire full day, and that in the fodder schools, in face of the Arrian Sophisters, where I was ordained to pay the charges, by reason of some clause mistaken in the relation of the Serjeant. Another time I framed a complaint to the Court against the mules of the Presidents, Counsellors and others, tending to this purpose, that when in the lower Court of the Palace they left them to champ on their bridles : some bibs were made for them, that with their drivelling they might not spoile the pavement, to the end, that the Pages of

THEN BEGAN THE POOR ROGUES TO GAPE LIKE OLD MULES

the Palace might play upon it with their dice, or at the game of coxbody, at their own ease, without spoiling their breeches at the knees ; and for this I had a faire decree, but it cost me deare.   Now reckon up what expence I was at in little banquets, which from day to day I made to the Pages of the Palace, and to what end, said I ?   My friend (said he) thou hast no passe-time at all in this world.   I have more then the King, and if thou wilt joyne thy self with me, we will do the devil together. No, no, (said I) by St. Adauras, that will I not, for thou wilt be hanged one time or another.   And thou (said he) wilt be interred sometime or other ; now which is most honourable, the aire or the earth ?   Ho, grosse pecore, whilest the Pages are at their banqueting, I keep their mules, and to some one I cut the stirrup-leather of the mounting side, till it hang but by a thin strap or thread, that, when the great puffe-guts of the Counsellor or some other hath taken his swing to get up, he may fall flat on his side like a pork, and so furnish the Spectators with more then a hundred francks worth of laughter.   But I laugh yet further, to think how at his home-coming the Master-page is to be whipt like green rie, which makes me not to repent what I have bestowed in feasting them.   In brief, he had (as I said before) threescore and three wayes to acquire money, but he had two hundred and fourteen to spend it, besides his drinking.

CHAPTER XVIII

How a great Scholar of England would have argued against Pantagruel, and was overcome by Panurge

In that same time, a certain learned man, named Thaumast, hearing the fame and renown of Pantagruels incomparable knowledge, came out of his own countrey of England, with an intent only to see him, to try thereby, and prove, whether his knowledge in effect was so great as it was reported to be.   In this resolution, being arrived at Paris, he went forthwith unto the house of the said Pantagruel, who was lodged in the Palace of St. Denys, and was then walking in the garden thereof with Panurge, philosophizing after the fashion of the Peripateticks. At his first entrance he startled, and was almost out of his wits for feare, seeing him so great, and so tall. Then did he salute him courteously as the manner is, and said unto him, Very true it is, (saith Plato the Prince of Philosophers,) that if the image and knowledge of wisdom were corporeal and visible to the eyes of mortals, it would stirre up all the world to admire her : which we may the rather beleeve, that the very bare report thereof, scattered in the air, if it happen to be received into the eares of men, who for being studious, and lovers of vertuous things, are called Philosophers, doth not suffer them to sleep nor rest in quiet, but so pricketh them up, and sets them on fire, to run unto the place where the person is, in whom the said knowledge is said to have built her Temple, and uttered her Oracles, as it was manifestly shewn unto us in the Queen of Sheba, who came from the utmost borders of the East and Persian sea, to see the order of Solomons house, and to heare his wisdom ; in Anacharsis, who came out of Scythia, even unto Athens, to see Solon ; in Pythagoras, who travelled farre to visit the Memphitical Vaticinators ; in Platon, who went a great way off to see the Magicians of Egypt, and Architus of Tarentum ; in Apollonius Tianeus, who went as farre as unto Mount Caucasus, passed along the Scythians, the Massagetes, the Indians, and sailed over the great river Phison, even to the Brachmans to see Hiarchas ; as likewise unto Babylon, Chaldea, Media, Assyria, Parthia, Syria, Phœnicia, Arabia, Palestina and Alexandria, even unto Æthiopia, to see the Gymnosophists: the like example have we of Titus Livius, whom to see and heare, divers studious persons came to Rome, from the Confines of France and Spaine ; I dare not reckon my self in the number of those so excellent persons, but well would be called studious, and a lover, not only of learning, but of learned men also ; and indeed, having heard the report of your so inestimable knowledge, I have left my countrey, my friends, my kindred and my house, and am come thus farre, valuing at nothing the length of the way, the tediousnesse of the sea, nor strangenesse of the land, and that only to see you, and to conferre with you about some passages in Philosophy, of Geomancie, and of the Cabalistick Art ; whereof I am doubtful, and cannot satisfie my minde ; which if you can resolve, I yield my self unto you for a slave henceforward, together with all my posterity, for other gift have I none, that I can esteem a recompence sufficient for so great a favour : I will reduce them into writing, and to morrow publish them to all the learned men in the City, that we may dispute publickly before them.

But see in what manner, I mean that we shall dispute : I will not argue *pro et contra*, as do the sottish Sophisters of this town, and other places : likewise I will not dispute after the manner of the Academicks by declamation ; nor yet by numbers, as Pythagoras was wont to do, and as Picus de la Mirandula did of late at Rome : but I will dispute by signes only without speaking, for the matters are so abstruse, hard and arduous, that words proceeding from the mouth of man will never be sufficient for unfolding of them to my liking. May it therefore please your Magnificence to be there, it shall be at the great Hall of Navarre at seven o'clock in the morning. When he had spoke these words, Pantagruel very honourably said unto him, Sir, of the graces that God hath bestowed upon me, I would not deny to communicate unto any man to my power ; for whatever comes from him is good, and his pleasure is, that it should be increased, when we come amongst men worthy and fit to receive this celestial manna of honest literature : in which number, because that in this time (as I do already very plainly perceive,) thou holdest the first rank, I give thee notice, that at all houres thou shalt finde me ready to condescend to every one of thy requests, according to my poor ability : although I ought rather to learn of thee, then thou of me, but, as thou hast protested, we will conferre of these doubts together, and will seek out the resolution, even unto the bottom of that undrainable Well, where Heraclitus sayes the truth lies hidden : and I do highly commend the manner of arguing which thou hast proposed, to wit, by signes without speaking ; for by this means thou and I shall understand one another well enough, and yet shall be free from this clapping of hands, which these blockish Sophisters make, when any of the Arguers hath gotten the better of the Argument : Now to morrow I will not faile to meet thee at the place and houre that thou hast appointed, but let me intreat thee, that there be not any strife or uproare between us, and that we seek not the honour and applause of men, but the truth only : to which Thaumast answered, The Lord God maintain you in his favour and grace, and instead of my thankfulnesse to you, poure down his blessings upon you, for that your Highnesse and magnificent greatnesse hath not disdained to descend to the grant of the request of my poor basenesse, so farewel till to morrow ! Farewel, said Pantagruel. Gentlemen, you that read this present discourse, think not that ever men were more elevated and transported in their thoughts, then all this night were both

THAUMAST

254

Thaumast and Pantagruel ; for the said Thaumast said to the
Keeper of the house of Cluny, where he was lodged, that in all
his life he had never known himself so dry, as he was that night.
I think (said he) that Pantagruel held me by the throat ;
Give order, I pray you, that we may have some drink, and see
that some fresh water be brought to us, to gargle my palat :
on the other side, Pantagruel stretched his wits as high as he
could, entring into very deep and serious meditations, and did
nothing all that night but dote upon, and turn over the book of
Beda, *de numeris et signis ;* Plotin's book, *de inenarrabilibus ;*
the book of Proclus, *de magia ;* the book of Artemidorus,
περὶ Ὀνειροκριτικῶν ; of Anaxagoras, περὶ Σημείων ; Dinarius, περὶ
Ἀφατῶν ; the books of Philistion ; Hipponax, περὶ Ἀνεκφωντῶν,
and a rabble of others, so long, that Panurge said unto
him,

My Lord leave all these thoughts and go to bed ; for I
perceive your spirits to be so troubled by a too intensive bending of them, that you may easily fall into some Quotidian fever
with this so excessive thinking and plodding : but, having first
drunk five and twenty or thirty good draughts, retire your self
and sleep your fill : for in the morning I will argue against, and
answer my master the Englishman ; and if I drive him not
ad metam non loqui, then call me Knave : Yea, but (said he)
my friend Panurge, he is marvellously learned, how wilt thou
be able to answer him ? Very well, (answered Panurge) I
pray you talk no more of it, but let me alone ; is any man so
learned as the devils are ? No, indeed (said Pantagruel)
without God's especial grace : Yet for all that (said Panurge)
I have argued against them, gravelled and blanked them in
disputation, and laid them so squat upon their tailes that I
have made them look like Monkies ; therefore be assured, that
to morrow I will make this vain-glorious Englishman to skite
vineger before all the world. So Panurge spent the night with
tipling amongst the pages, and played away all the points of his
breeches at *primus secundus,* and at peck point, in French
called *La Vergette.* Yet when the condescended on time was
come, he failed not to conduct his Master Pantagruel to the
appointed place, unto which (beleeve me) there was neither
great nor small in Paris but came, thinking with themselves
that this devillish Pantagruel, who had overthrown and
vanquished in dispute all these doting fresh-water Sophisters,
would now get full payment and be tickled to some purpose ;
for this Englishman is a terrible bustler and horrible coyle-

keeper. We will see who will be Conquerour, for he never met with his match before.

Thus all being assembled, Thaumast stayed for them, and then when Pantagruel and Panurge came into the hall, all the School-boyes, Professors of Arts, Senior-Sophisters, and Batchelors began to clap their hands, as their scurvie custome is. But Pantagruel cried out with a loud voice, as if it had been the sound of a double cannon, saying, Peace, with a devil to you, peace! By God—you rogues, if you trouble me here, I will cut off the heads of every one of you : at which words they remained all daunted and astonished, like so many ducks, and durst not do so much as cough, although they had swallowed fifteen pounds of feathers : withal they grew so dry with this only voice, that they laid out their tongues a full half foot beyond their mouthes, as if Pantagruel had salted all their throats. Then began Panurge to speak, saying to the Englishman, Sir, are you come hither to dispute contentiously in those Propositions you have set down, or, otherwayes but to learn and know the truth ? To which answered Thaumast, Sir, no other thing brought me hither but the great desire I had to learn, and to know that of which I have doubted all my life long, and have neither found book nor man able to content me in the resolution of those doubts which I have proposed : and, as for disputing contentiously, I will not do it, for it is too base a thing, and therefore leave it to those sottish Sophisters, who in their disputes do not search for the truth, but for contradiction only and debate. Then said Panurge, if I who am but a mean and inconsiderable disciple of my Master my lord Pantagruel, content and satisfie you in all and every thing, it were a thing below my said Master, wherewith to trouble him : therefore is it fitter he be Chair-man, and sit as a Judge and Moderator of our discourse and purpose, and give you satisfaction in many things, wherein perhaps I shall be wanting to your expectation. Truly (said Thaumast) it is very well said : begin then. Now you must note that Panurge had set at the end of his long Codpiece a pretty tuft of red silk, as also of white, green and blew, and within it had put a faire orange.

CHAPTER XIX

How Panurge put to a Non-plus the Englishman, that argued by Signes

EVERY body then taking heed, and hearkening with great silence, the Englishman lift up on high into the aire his two hands severally, clunching in all the tops of his fingers together, after the manner, which, *à la Chinonnese*, they call the hen's arse, and struck the one hand on the other by the nailes foure several times : then he, opening them, struck the one with the flat of the other, till it yielded a clashing noise, and that only once : again in joyning them as before he struck twice, and afterwards foure times in opening them ; then did he lay them joyned, and extended the one towards the other, as if he had been devoutly to send up his prayers unto God. Panurges suddenly lifted up in the aire his right hand, and put the thumb thereof into the nostril of the same side, holding his foure fingers streight out, and closed orderly in a parallel line to the point of his nose, shutting the left eye wholly, and making the other wink with a profound depression of the eye-brows and eye-lids. Then lifted up he his left hand, with hard wringing and stretching forth his foure fingers, and elevating his thumb, which he held in a line directly correspondent to the situation of his right hand, with the distance of a cubit and a halfe between them. This done, in the same forme he abased towards the ground both the one and the other hand ; Lastly, he held them in the midst, as aiming right at the English mans nose. And if Mercurie, said the English man, there Panurge interrupted him, and said, You have spoken Mask.

Then made the English man this signe, his left hand all open he lifted up into the aire, then instantly shut his fist the foure fingers thereof, and his thumb extended at length he placed upon the gristle of his nose; presently after, he lifted up his right hand all open, and all open abased and bent it downwards, putting the thumb thereof in the very place where the little finger of the left hand did close in the fist, and the foure right hand fingers he softly moved in the aire: then contrarily he did with the right hand what he had done with the left, and with the left what he had done with the right.

Panurge, being not a whit amazed at this, drew out into the aire his Trismegist Codpiece with the left hand, and with his right drew forth a trunchion of a white oxe-rib, and two pieces of wood of a like forme, one of black eben, and the other of incarnation brasil, and put them betwixt the fingers of that hand in good symmetrie; then knocking them together, made such a noise as the Lepers of Britanie use to do with their clappering clickets, yet better resounding, and farre more harmonious, and with his tongue contracted in his mouth did very merrily warble it, always looking fixedly upon the English man. The Divines, Physicians and Chirurgions, that were there, thought that by this signe he would have inferred that the English man was a Leper: the Counsellors, Lawyers and Decretalists conceived, that by doing this he would have concluded some kinde of mortal felicity to consist in Leprosie, as the Lord maintained heretofore.

The English man for all this was nothing daunted, but holding up his two hands in the aire, kept them in such forme, that he closed the three master-fingers in his fist, and passing his thumbs through his indical, or foremost and middle fingers, his auricularie or little fingers remained extended and stretched out, and so presented he them to Panurge; then joyned he them so, that the right thumb touched the left, and the left little finger touched the right. Hereat Panurge, without speaking one word, lift up his hands and made this signe.

He put the naile of the forefinger of his left hand, to the naile of the thumb of the same, making in the middle of the distance as it were a buckle, and of his right hand shut up all the fingers into his fist, except the forefinger, which he often thrust in and out through the said two others of the left hand: then stretched he out the forefinger, and middle finger or medical of his right hand, holding them asunder as much as he could, and thrusting them towards Thaumast. Then did he put the thumb of his left hand upon the corner of his left eye, stretching out all his hand like the wing of a bird, or the finne of a fish, and moving it very daintily this way and that way, he did as much with his right hand upon the corner of his right eye. Thaumast began then to waxe somewhat pale, and to tremble, and made him this signe.

With the middle finger of his right hand he struck against the muscle of the palme or pulp, which is under the thumb : then put he the forefinger of the right hand in the like buckle of the left, but he put it under and not over, as Panurge did. Then Panurge knocked one hand against another, and blowed in his palme, and put again the forefinger of his right hand into the overture or mouth of the left, pulling it often in and out ; then held he out his chinne, most intentively looking upon Thaumast. The people there which understood nothing in the other signes, knew very well what therein he demanded (without speaking a word to Thaumast,) What do you mean by that ? In effect, Thaumast then began to sweat great drops, and seemed to all the Spectators a man strangely ravished in high contemplation. Then he bethought himself, and put all the nailes of his left hand against those of his right, opening his fingers as if they had been semicircles, and with this signe lift up his hands as high as he could. Whereupon Panurge presently put the thumb of his right hand under his jawes, and the little finger thereof in the mouth of the left hand, and in this posture made his teeth to sound very melodiously, the upper against the lower. With this Thaumast, with great toile and vexation of spirit rose up, but in rising let a great bakers fart, for the bran came after, and, pissing withal very strong vineger, stunk like all the devils in hell : the company began to stop their noses ; for he had conskited himself with meer anguish and perplexity. Then lifted he up his right hand, clunching it in such sort, that he brought the ends of all his fingers to meet together, and his left hand he laid flat upon his breast : whereat Panurge drew out his long Codpiece with his tuffe, and stretched it forth a cubit and a half, holding it in the aire with his right hand, and with his left took out his orange, and, casting it up into the aire seven times, at the eight he hid it in the fist of his right hand, holding it steadily up on high, and then began to shake his faire Codpiece, shewing it to Thaumast.

After that Thaumast began to puffe up his two cheeks like a player on a bagpipe, and blew as if he had been to puffe up a pigs bladder; whereupon Panurge put one finger of his left hand in his nockandrow, by some called St. Patricks hole, and with his mouth suck't in the aire, in such a manner as when one eats oysters in the shell, or when we sup up our broth; this done, he opened his mouth somewhat, and struck his right hand flat upon it, making therewith a great and a deep sound, as if it came from the superficies of the midriffe through the trachiartere or pipe of the lungs, and this he did for sixteen times; but Thaumast did alwayes keep blowing like a goose. Then Panurge put the forefinger of his right hand into his mouth, pressing it very hard to the muscles thereof; then he drew it out, and withal made a great noise, as when little boyes shoot pellets out of the pot-canons made of the hollow sticks of the branch of an aulder-tree, and he did it nine times.

Then Thaumast cried out, Ha, my Masters, a great secret; with this he put in his hand up to the elbow; then drew out a dagger that he had, holding it by the point downwards; whereat Panurge took his long Codpiece, and shook it as hard as he could against his thighes, then put his two hands intwined in manner of a combe upon his head, laying out his tongue as farre as he was able, and turning his eyes in his head, like a goat that is ready to die. Ha, I understand (said Thaumast) but what? making such a signe, that he put the haft of his dagger against his breast, and upon the point thereof the flat of his hand, turning in a little the ends of his fingers; whereat Panurge held down his head on the left side and put his middle finger into his right eare, holding up his thumb bolt upright; then he crost his two armes upon his breast, and coughed five times, and at the fifth time he struck his right foot against the ground: then he lift up his left arme, and closing all his fingers into his fist, helde his thumbe against his forehead, striking with his right hand six times against his breast. But Thaumast, as not content therewith, put the thumb of his left hand upon the top of his nose, shutting the rest of his said hand, whereupon Panurge set his two Master-fingers upon each side of his mouth, drawing it as much as he was able, and widening it so, that he shewed all his teeth: and with his two thumbs pluck't down his two eye-lids very low, making therewith a very ill-favour'd countenance, as it seemed to the company.

CHAPTER XX

How Thaumast relateth the Vertues ana Knowledge of Panurge

THEN Thaumast rose up, and, putting off his cap, did very kindly thank the said Panurge, and with a loud voice said unto all the people that were there, My Lords, Gentlemen and others, at this time may I to some good purpose speak that evangelical word, *Et ecce plus quam Salomon hic :* You have here in your presence an incomparable treasure, that is, my Lord Pantagruel, whose great renown hath brought me hither, out of the very heart of England, to conferre with him about the insoluble problemes, both in Magick, Alchymie, the Caballe, Geomancie, Astrologie and Philosophie, which I had in my minde : but at present I am angry, even with fame it self, which I think was envious to him, for that it did not declare the thousandth part of the worth that indeed is in him : You have seen how his disciple only hath satisfied me, and hath told me more than I asked of him : besides, he hath opened unto me, and resolved other inestimable doubts, wherein I can assure you he hath to me discovered the very true Well, Fountain, and Abysse of the Encyclopedia of learning ; yea in such a sort, that I did not think I should ever have found a man that could have made his skill appear, in so much as the first elements of that concerning which we disputed by signes, without speaking either word or half word. But in fine, I will reduce into writing that which we have said and concluded, that the world may not take them to be fooleries, and will thereafter cause them to be printed, that every one may learne as I have done. Judge then what the master had been able to say, seeing the disciple hath done so valiantly ; for, *Non est discipulus super Magistrum.* Howsoever God be praised, and I do very humbly thank you, for the honour that you have done us at this Act : God reward you for it eternally : the like thanks gave Pantagruel to all the company, and, going from thence, he carried Thaumast to dinner with him, and beleeve that they drank as much as their skins could hold, or, as the phrase is, with unbuttoned bellies (for in that age they made fast their bellies with buttons, as we do now the colars of our doublets or jerkins,) even till they

neither knew where they were, nor whence they came. Blessed
Lady, how they did carouse it, and pluck (as we say) at the
kids leather : and flaggons to trot, and they to toote, Draw,
give (page) some wine here, reach hither, fill with a devil, so !
There was not one but did drink five and twenty or thirty
pipes, can you tell how ? even *Sicut terra sine aqua ;* for the
weather was hot, and besides, that they were very dry. In
matter of the exposition of the Propositions set down by
Thaumast : and the signification of the signes, which they used
in their disputation, I would have set them down for you
according to their own relation : but I have been told that
Thaumast made a great book of it imprinted at London,
wherein he hath set down all without omitting any thing, and
therefore at this time I do passe by it.

CHAPTER XXI

How Panurge was in Love with a Lady of Paris

PANURGE began to be in great reputation in the city of Paris,
by means of this disputation, wherein he prevailed against the
English man, and from thenceforth made his Codpiece to be
very useful to him, to which effect he had it pinked with pretty
little Embroideries after the Romanesca fashion ; and the
world did praise him publickly, in so farre that there was a song
made of him, which little children did use to sing, when they
were to fetch mustard : he was withal made welcome in all
companies of Ladies and Gentlewomen, so that at last he became
presumptuous, and went about to bring to his lure one of the
greatest Ladies in the City : and indeed leaving a rabble of
long prologues and protestations, which ordinarily these dolent
contemplative Lent-lovers make, who never meddle with the

flesh; one day he said unto her, Madam, it would be a very great benefit to the Commonwealth, delightful to you, honourable to your progeny, and necessary for me, that I cover you for the propagating of my race, and, beleeve it, for experience will teach it you : the lady at this word thrust him back above a hundred leagues, saying, You mischievous foole, is it for you to talk thus unto me ? whom do you think you have in hand ? be gone, never to come in my sight again ; for if one thing were not, I would have your legs and armes cut off. Well (said he) that were all one to me, to want both legs and armes, provided you and I had but one merry bout together, at the branglebuttock-game ; for here within is (in shewing her his long Codpiece) Master John Thursday, who will play you such an Antick, that you shall feel the sweetnesse thereof even to the very marrow of your bones : He is a gallant, and doth so well know how to finde out all the corners, creeks and ingrained inmates in your carnal trap, that after him there needs no broom, he 'l sweep so well before, and leave nothing to his followers to work upon : whereunto the Lady answered, Go, villain, go, if you speak to me one such word more, I will cry out, and make you to be knocked down with blowes. Ha, (said he), you are not so bad as you say, no, or else I am deceived in your physiognomie, for sooner shall the earth mount up unto the Heavens, and the highest Heavens descend unto the Hells, and all the course of nature be quite perverted, then that in so great beauty and neatnesse as in you is, there should be one drop of gall or malice : they say indeed, that hardly shall a man ever see a faire woman that is not also stubborn : yet that is spoke only of those vulgar beauties, but yours is so excellent, so singular, and so heavenly, that I beleeve nature hath given it you as a paragon, and master-piece of her Art, to make us know what she can do, when she will imploy all her skill, and all her power. There is nothing in you but honey, but sugar, but a sweet and celestial Manna : to you it was, to whom Paris ought to have adjudged the golden Apple, not to Venus, no, nor to Juno, nor to Minerva ; for never was there so much magnificence in Juno, so much wisdom in Minerva, nor so much comelinesse in Venus, as there is in you. O heavenly gods and godesses ! how happy shall that man be to whom you will grant the favour to embrace her, to kisse her, and to rub his bacon with hers ? by G— that shall be I, I know it well ; for she loves me already her belly full, I am sure of it, and so was I predestinated to it by the Fairies : and therefore that we lose no time, put on, thrust out your gamons, and would have embraced her, but she made as if she would put out her head at the window, to call her neighbours for help. Then Panurge on a sudden ran out, and, in his running away, said, Madam, stay here till I come again, I will go call them my self, do not you take so much paines : thus went he away not much caring for the repulse he had got, nor made he any whit the worse cheer for it. The next day he came to the Church, at the time she went to Masse. At the door he gave her some of the holy water, bowing himself very low before her, afterwards he kneeled down by her very familiarly, and said unto her, Madam, know that I am so amorous of you, that I can neither pisse nor dung for love : I do not know (Lady,) what you mean, but if I should take any hurt by it, how much you would be to blame ? Go, said she, go, I do not care, let me alone to say my prayers. I, but, (said he,) equivocate upon this ; *a beau mont le viconte*, or, to faire mount the pric-cunts : I cannot, said she : It is, said he, *a beau con le vit monte*, or to a faire C . . . the pr . . . mounts : and, upon this pray to God to give you that which your noble heart desireth, and I pray you give me these patenotres. Take them (said she) and trouble me no longer : this done, she would have taken off her patenotres, which were made of a kinde of yellow stone called Cestrin, and adorned with great spots of gold, but Panurge nimbly drew out one of his knives, wherewith he cut them off very handsomly, and, whilest he was going away to carry them to the Brokers, he said to her, Will you have my knife ? No, no, said she : But (said he) to the purpose, I am at your commandment, body an goods, tripes and bowels.

In the mean time, the Lady was not very well content with the want of her patenotres, for they were one of her implements to keep her countenance by in the Church : then thought with her self, this bold flowting Royster is some giddy, fantastical, light-headed foole of a strange countrey ; I shall never recover my patenotres again, what will my husband say, he will no doubt be angry with me ; but I will tell him, that a thief hath cut them off from my hands in the Church, which he will easily beleeve, seeing the end of the riban left at my girdle. After dinner Panurge went to see her, carrying in his sleeve a great purse full of Palace-crowns, called counters, and began to say unto her, Which of us two loveth other best, you me, or I you ? whereunto she answered, As for me, I do not hate you ; for as God commands, I love all the world : But to the purpose, (said he) are not you in love with me ? I have (said she) told you so many times already, that you should talk so no more to me, and if you speak of it again, I will teach you, that I am not one to be talked unto dishonestly : get you hence packing, and deliver me my patenotres, that my husband may not ask me for them.

How now, (Madame) said he, your patenotres ? nay, by mine oath, I will not do so but I will give you others ; had you rather have them of gold well enameled in great round knobs, or after the manner of love-knots, or otherwise all massive, like great ingots, or if you had rather have them of Ebene, of Jacinth, or of grained gold, with the marks of fine Turkoises, or of faire Topazes, marked with fine Saphirs or of baleu Rubies, with great marks of Diamonds of eight and twenty squares ? No, no, all this is too little ; I know a faire bracelet of fine Emeralds, marked with spotted Ambergris, and at the buckle a Persian pearle as big as an Orange : it will not cost above five and twenty thousand ducates, I will make you a present of it, for I have ready coine enough, and withal he made a noise with his counters as if they had been French Crownes.

Will you have a piece of velvet, either of the violet colour, or of crimson died in graine, or a piece of broached or crimson sattin ? will you have chaines, gold, tablets, rings ? You need no more but say, Yes, so farre as fifty thousand ducates may reach, it is but as nothing to me ; by the vertue of which words he made the water come in her mouth : but she said unto him, No, I thank you, I will have nothing of you. By G—, said he, but I will have somewhat of you ; yet shall it be that which shall cost you nothing, neither shall you have a jot the lesse, when you have given it, hold, (shewing his long Codpiece) this is Master John Goodfellow, that askes for lodging, and with that would have embraced her ; but she began to cry out, yet not very loud. Then Panurge put off his counterfeit garb, changed his false visage, and said unto her, You will not then otherwayes let me do a little ? a turd for you, You do not deserve so much good, nor so much honour : but by G—, I will make the dogs ride you ; and with this he ran away as fast as he could, for feare of blowes, whereof he was naturally fearful.

CHAPTER XXII

*How Panurge served a Parisian Lady a Trick that pleased
her not very well*

Now you must note that the next day was the great festival
of Corpus Christi, called the Sacre, wherein all women put on
their best apparel, and on that day the said Lady was cloathed
in a rich gown of crimson-sattin, under which she wore a very
costly white velvet petticoat.

The day of the Eve (called the vigile) Panurge searched so
long of one side, and another, that he found a hot or salt bitch,
which when he had tied her with his girdle, he led to his chamber,
and fed her very well all that day and night. In the morning
thereafter he killed her, and took that part of her which the
Greek geomanciers know, and cut it into several small pieces,
as small as he could ; then, carrying it away as close as might be,
he went to the place where the Lady was to come along, to
follow the Procession, as the custome is upon the said holy day ;
and when she came in, Panurge sprinkled some holy water on
her, saluting her very courteously : then a little while after she
had said her petty devotions, he sate down close by her upon
the same bench, and gave her this roundlay in writing, in
manner as followeth.

A ROUNDLAY

For this one time, that I to you my love
Discovered, you did too cruel prove
To send me packing, hoplesse, and so soon,
Who never any wrong to you had done
In any kinde of action, word or thought :
So that, if my suit lik'd you not, you ought
T' have spoke more civilly, and to this sense,
My friend, be pleased to depart from thence,
           For this one time.

What hurt do I wish you to remark
With favour and compassion how a spark

Of your great beauty hath inflam'd my heart
With deep affection, and that for my part,
I only ask that you with me would dance
The brangle gay in feats of dalliance,
For this one time.

And as she was opening this paper to see what it was, Panurge very promptly and lightly scattered the drug that he had upon her in divers places, but especially in the plaits of her sleeves, and of her gowne : then said he unto her, Madam, the poor lovers are not alwayes at ease : as for me, I hope that those heavy nights, those paines and troubles, which I suffer for love of you, shall be a deduction to me of so much paine in Purgatory : yet at the least pray to God to give me patience in my misery. Panurge had no sooner spoke this, but all the dogs that were in the Church, came running to this Lady with the smell of the drugs that he had strowed upon her, both small and great, big and little, all came, laying out their member, smelling to her, and pissing every where upon her, it was the greatest villainy in the world. Panurge made the fashion of driving them away : then took his leave of her, and withdrew himself into some Chappel or Oratory of the said Church, to see the sport ; for these villainous dogs did compisse all her habiliaments, and left none of her attire unbesprinkled with their staling, in so much that a tall grey-hound pist upon her head, others in her sleeves, others on her crupper-piece, and the little ones pissed upon her pataines ; so that all the women that were round about her had much ado to save her. Whereat Panurge very heartily laughing, he said to one of the Lords of the City, I beleeve that same Lady is hot, or else that some grey-hound hath covered her lately. And when he saw that all the dogs were flocking about her, yarring at the retardment of their accesse to her, and every way keeping such a coyle with her, as they are wont to do about a proud or salt bitch, he forthwith departed from thence, and went to call Pantagruel : not forgetting in his way alongst the streets, thorough which he went, where he found any dogs to give them a bang with his foot, saying, Will you not go with your fellowes to the wedding ? Away, hence, avant, avant, with a devil avant ! And being come home, he said to Pantagruel, Master, I pray you come and see all the dogs of the countrey, how they are assembled about a Lady, the fairest in the City, and would dufle and line her : whereunto Pantagruel willingly condescended and saw the mystery, which he found very pretty and strange : But the best was at the Procession, in which were seen above six hundred thousand and fourteen dogs about her, which did very much trouble and molest her, and whithersoever she past, those dogs that came afresh, tracing her footsteps, followed her at the heeles, and pist in the way where her gown had touched. All the world stood gazing at this spectacle, considering the countenance of those dogs, who leaping up got about her neck, and spoiled all her gorgeous accoutrements, for the which she could finde no remedy, but to retire unto her house, which was a Palace. Thither she went, and the dogs after her ; she ran to hide her self, but the Chamber-maids could not abstaine from laughing. When she was entered into the house, and had shut the door upon her self, all the dogs came running, of half a league round, and did so well bepisse the gate of her house, that there they made a stream with their urine, wherein a duck might have very well swimmed, and it is the same current that now runs at St. Victor, in which Gobelin dieth scarlet, for the specifical vertue of these pisse-dogs, as our master Doribus did heretofore preach publickly. So may God help you ; a mill would have ground corne with it ; yet not so much as those of Basacle at Toulouse.

CHAPTER XXIII

How Pantagruel departed from Paris, hearing Newes, that the Dipsodes had invaded the Land of the Amaurots : and the Cause wherefore the Leagues are so short in France

A LITTLE while after Pantagruel heard newes that his father Gargantua had been translated into the land of the Fairies by Morgue, as heretofore were Oger and Arthur, as also, that, the report of his translation being spread abroad, the Dipsodes had issued out beyond their borders, with inrodes had wasted a great part of Utopia, and at that very time had besieged the great City of the Amaurots : whereupon departing from Paris without bidding any man farewel, for the businesse required diligence, he came to Rowen.

Now Pantagruel in his journey, seeing that the leagues of that little territory about Paris called France were very short in regard of those of other Countreys, demanded the cause and reason of it from Panurge, who told him a story which Marotus of the Lac, Monachus, set down in the acts of the Kings of Canarre, saying, that in old times Countreys were not distinguished into leagues, miles, furlongs, nor parasanges, until that king Pharamond divided them, which was done in manner as followeth. The said King chose at Paris a hundred faire, gallant, lustie, briske young men, all resolute and bold adventurers in Cupids duels, together with a hundred comely, pretty, handsome, lovely and well-complexioned wenches of Picardie, all which he caused to be well entertained, and highly fed for the space of eight dayes : then, having called for them, he delivered to every one of the young men his wench, with store of money to defray their charges, and this injunction besides to go unto divers places here and there, and wheresoever they should biscot and thrum their wenches, that they setting a stone there, it should be accounted a league ; thus went away those brave fellowes and sprightly blades most merrily and because they were fresh, and had been at rest, they very often jum'd and fanfreluched almost at every fields end, and this is the cause why the leagues about Paris are so short ; but when they had gone a great way, and were now as weary as poor devils, all the oile in their lamps being almost spent, they did not chinke and dufle so often, but contented themselves, (I mean for the men's part,) with one scurvie paultry bout in a day, and this is that, which makes the leagues in Britany, Delanes, Germany, and other more remote Countreys so long : other men give other reasons for it, but this seems to me of all other the best. To which Pantagruel willingly adhered. Parting from Rowen, they arrived at Honfleur, where they took shipping, Pantagruel, Panurge, Epistemon, Eusthenes and Carpalin.

In which place, waiting for a favourable winde, and caulking their ship, he received from a Lady of Paris, which he had formerly kept, and entertained a good long time, a letter directed on the out-side thus, To the best beloved of the faire women, and least loyal of the valiant men. P.N.T.G.R.L.

CHAPTER XXIV

A Letter which a Messenger brought to Pantagruel from a Lady of Paris, together with the Exposition of a Posie, written in a gold Ring

WHEN Pantagruel had read the superscription, he was much amazed, and therefore demanded of the said messenger the name of her that had sent it : then opened he the letter, and found nothing written in it, nor otherwayes inclosed, but only a gold ring, with a square table-diamond. Wondering at this, he called Panurge to him, and shewed him the case ; whereupon Panurge told him, that the leafe of paper was written upon, but with such cunning and artifice, that no man could see the writing at the first sight, therefore to finde it out he set it by the fire, to see if it was made with Sal Ammoniack soaked in water ; then put he it into the water, to see if the letter was written with the juice of Tithymalle : after that he held it up against the candle, to see if it was written with the juice of white onions.

Then he rubbed one part of it with oile of nuts, to see if it were not written with the lee of a fig-tree : and another part of it with the milk of a woman giving suck to her eldest daughter, to see if it was written with the blood of red toads, or green earth-frogs : Afterwards he rubbed one corner with the ashes of a Swallowes nest, to see if it were not written with the dew that is found within the herb Alcakengie, called the winter-cherry. He rubbed after that one end with eare-wax, to see if it were not written with the gall of a Raven : then did he dip it into vinegar, to try if it was not written with the juice of the garden Spurge : After that he greased it with the fat of a bat or flitter-mouse, to see if it was not written with the sperm of a whale, which some call ambergris : Then put it very fairly into a basin full of fresh water, and forthwith took it out, to see whether it were written with stone-allum : But after all experiments, when he perceived that he could finde out nothing, he called the messenger, and asked him, Good fellow, the lady that sent thee hither, did she not give thee a staffe to bring with thee ? thinking that it had been according to the conceit whereof Aulus Gellius maketh mention, and the messenger answered him, No, Sir. Then Panurge would have caused his head to be shaven, to see whether the Lady had written upon his bald pate, with the hard lie whereof sope is made, that which she meant; but perceiving that his hair was very long, he forbore, considering that it could not have grown to so great a length in so short a time.

Then he said to Pantagruel, Master, by the vertue of G— I cannot tell what to do nor say in it; for to know whether there be any thing written upon this or no, I have made use of a good part of that which Master Francisco di Nianto the Tuscan sets down, who hath written the manner of reading letters that do not appear; that which Zoroastes published, *Peri grammaton acriton;* and Calphurnius Bassus, *de literis illegibilibus:* but I can see nothing, nor do I beleeve that there is any thing else in it then the Ring: let us, therefore, look upon it. Which when they had done, they found this in Hebrew written within, *Lamach sabathani;* whereupon they called Epistemon, and asked him what that meant? To which he answered, that they were Hebrew words, signifying, Wherefore hast thou forsaken me? upon that Panurge suddenly replied, I know the mystery, do you see this diamond? it is a false one; this, then is the exposition of that which the Lady meanes, *Diamant faux,* that is, false lover, why hast thou forsaken me? which interpretation Pantagruel presently understood, and withal remembering, that at his departure he had not bid the Lady farewel, he was very sorry, and would faine have returned to Paris, to make his peace with her; but Epistemon put him in minde of Æneas's departure from Dido, and the saying of Heraclitus of Tarentum, That the ship being at anchor when need requireth, we must cut the cable rather then lose time about untying of it, and that he should lay aside all other thoughts, to succour the City of his Nativity, which was then in danger; and indeed within an houre after that, the winde arose at the north-north-west, wherewith they hoised saile, and put out, even into the maine sea, so that within few dayes, passing by Porto Sancto, and by the Maderas, they went ashore in the Canarie islands; parting from thence, they passed by Capobianco, by Senege, by Capoverde, by Gambre, by Sagres, by Melli, by the Cap di Buona Speranza, and set ashore againe in the Kingdom of Melinda; parting from thence, they sailed away with a tramontan or northerly winde, passing by Meden, by Uti, by Uden, by Gelasim, by the isles of the Fairies, and alongst the Kingdom of Achorie, till at last they

TO THE BEST BELOVED OF THE FAIRE WOMEN

arrived at the port of Utopia, distant from the city of the Amaurots three leagues and somewhat more.

When they were ashore, and pretty well refreshed, Pantagruel said, Gentlemen, the City is not farre from hence, therefore were it not amisse, before we set forward, to advise well what is to be done, that we be not like the Athenians, who never took counsel until after the fact: Are you resolved to live and die with me? Yes, Sir, said they all, and be as confident of us, as of your own fingers. Well (said he) there is but one thing that keeps my minde in great doubt and suspense, which is this, that I know not in what order nor of what number the enemie is, that layeth siege to the City; for if I were certain of that, I should go forward, and set on with the better assurance. Let us therefore consult together, and bethink our selves by what meanes we may come to this intelligence: whereunto they all said, Let us go thither and see, and stay you here for us, for this very day, without further respite do we make account to bring you a certain report thereof.

My self (said Panurge) will undertake to enter into their camp, within the very midst of their guards, unespied by their watch, and merrily feast and lecher it at their cost, without being known of any to see the Artillery and the Tents of all the Captaines, and thrust my self in with a grave and magnifick carriage, amongst all their troopes and companies, without being discovered; the devill would not be able to peck me out with all his circumventions: for I am of the race of Zopyrus.

And I (said Epistemon) know all the plots and stratagems of the valiant Captaines, and warlike Champions of former ages, together with all the tricks and subtilties of the Art of warre; I will go, and though I be detected and revealed, I will escape, by making them beleeve of you whatever I please, for I am of the race of Sinon.

I (said Eusthenes) will enter and set upon them in their trenches, in spight of their Centries, and all their guards; for I will tread upon their bellies, and break their legs and armes, yea though they were every whit as strong as the devil himself; for I am of the race of Hercules.

And I (said Carpalin) will get in there, if the birds can enter, for I am so nimble of body, and light withal, that I shall have leaped over their trenches, and ran clean through all their camp before that they perceive me; neither do I feare shot, nor arrow, nor horse, how swift soever, were he the Pegasus of

Persee or Pacolet, being assured that I shall be able to make a safe and sound escape before them all, without any hurt : I will undertake to walk upon the eares of corne, or grasse in the meddows, without making either of them do so much as bow under me ; for I am of the race of Camilla the Amazone.

CHAPTER XXV

How Panurge, Carpalin, Eusthenes, and Epistemon (the Gentle-men Attendants of Pantagruel,) vanquished and discomfitted six hundred and threescore Horsemen very cunningly

As he was speaking this, they perceived six hundred and three-score light horsemen, gallantly mounted, who made an outrode thither, to see what ship it was that was newly arrived in the harbour, and came in a full gallop to take them if they had been able : Then said Pantagruel, My Lads, retire your selves unto the ship, here are some of our enemies coming apace, but I will kill them here before you like beasts, although they were ten times so many ; in the meane time withdraw your selves, and take your sport at it. Then answered Panurge, No, Sir, there is no reason that you should do so, but on the contrary retire you unto the ship, both you and the rest, for I alone will here discomfit them ; but we must not linger, come, set forward ; whereunto the others said, It is well advised, Sir, withdraw your self and we will help Panurge here, so shall you know what we are able to do : Then said Pantagruel, Well, I am content,

274

but if that you be too weak, I will not faile to come to your assistance. With this Panurge took two great cables of the ship, and tied them to the kemstock or capstane which was on the deck towards the hatches, and fastened them in the ground, making a long circuit, the one further off, the other within that. Then said he to Epistemon, Go aboard the ship, and, when I give you a call, turn about the capstane upon the orlop diligently, drawing unto you the two cable-ropes: and said to Eusthenes, and to Carpalin, My bullies, stay you here, and offer your selves freely to your enemies, do as they bid you, and make as if you would yield unto them, but take heed you come not within the compasse of the ropes, be sure to keep your selves free of them; and presently he went aboard the ship, and took a bundle of straw, and a barrel of gun-powder, strowed it round about the compasse of the cordes, and stood by with a brand of fire or match lighted in his hand. Presently came the horsemen with great fury, and the foremost ran almost home to the ship, and by reason of the slipperinesse of the bank, they fell, they and their horses, to the number of foure and fourty, which the rest seeing came on, thinking that resistance had been made them at their arrival. But Panurge said unto them, My Masters, I beleeve that you have hurt your selves, I pray you pardon us, for it is not our fault, but the slipperinesse of the sea-water, that is alwayes flowing; we submit our selves to your good pleasure; so said likewise his two other fellowes, and Epistemon that was upon the deck; in the mean time Panurge withdrew him selfe, and seeing that they were all within the compasse of the cables, and that his two companions were retired, making room for all those horses which came in a croud, thronging upon the neck of one another to see the ship, and such as were in it, cried out on a sudden to Epistemon, Draw, draw: then began Epistemon to winde about the capstane, by doing whereof the two cables so intangled and impestered the legs of the horses, that they were all of them thrown down to the ground easily, together with their Riders: but they seeing that, drew their swords, and would have cut them: whereupon Panurge set fire to the traine, and there burnt them up all like damned souls, both men and horses, not one escaping save one alone, who being mounted on a fleet Turkie courser, by meere speed in flight got himself out of the circle of the ropes; but when Carpalin perceived him, he ran after him with such nimblenesse and celerity, that he overtook him in lesse then a hundred paces; then leaping close behinde him upon the crupper of his horse, clasped him in his armes, and brought him back to the ship.

This exploit being ended, Pantagruel was very jovial, and wondrously commended the industry of these Gentlemen, whom he called his fellow-souldiers, and made them refresh themselves, and feed well and merrily upon the sea-shore, and drink heartily with their bellies upon the ground, and their prisoner with them, whom they admitted to that familiarity : only that the poor devil was somewhat afraid that Pantagruel would have eaten him up whole, which, considering the widenesse of his mouth, and capacity of his throat, was no great matter for him to have done ; for he could have done it easily as you would eate a small comfit, he shewing no more in his throat, then would a graine of millet-seed in the mouth of an Asse.

CHAPTER XXVI

How Pantagruel and his Company were weary in eating still salt Meats : and how Carpalin went a hunting to have some Venison

THUS as they talked and chatted together, Carpalin said, And by the belly of St. Quenet, shal we never eat any venison ? this salt meat makes me horribly dry, I will go fetch you a quarter of one of those horses which we have burnt, it is well roasted already : as he was rising up to go about it, he perceived under the side of a wood a fair great roe-buck, which was come out of his Fort (as I conceive) at the sight of Panurge's fire : him did he pursue and run after with as much vigour and swiftnesse, as if it had been a bolt out of a Crossbowe, and caught him in a moment ; and whilest he was in his course, he with his hands took in the aire foure great bustards, seven bitterns, six and twenty gray partridges, two and thirty red legged ones, sixteen pheasants, nine woodcocks, nineteen herons, two and thirty coushots and ring-doves ; and with his feet killed ten or twelve hares and rabbets, which were then at relief, and pretty big withal, eighteen rayles in a knot together, with fifteen young wilde boares, two little Bevers, and three great foxes : so striking the kid with his fauchion athwart the head he killed him, and bearing him on his back, he in his return took up his hares, rayls, and young wild boares, and as far off as he could be heard, cried out, and said, Panurge, my friend, vineger, vineger: then the good Pantagruel, thinking he had fainted, commanded them to provide him some vineger; but Panurge, knew well that there was some good prey in hands, and forth-with shewed unto noble Pantagruel, how he was bearing upon his back a faire roe-buck, and all his girdle bordered with hares; then immediately did Epistemon make in the name of the nine Muses, nine antick wooden spits: Eusthenes did help to flay, and Panurge placed two great cuirasier saddles in such sort that they served for Andirons, and making their prisoner to be their Cook, they roasted their venison by the fire, wherein the horse-men were burnt; and making great chear with a good deal of vineger, the devil a one of them did forbear from his victuals, it was a triumphant and incomparable spectacle to see how they ravened and devoured. Then said Pantagruel, Would to God, every one of you had two paires of little Anthem or Sacring bells hanging at your chin, and that I had at mine the great clocks of Renes, of Poitiers, of Tours, and of Cambray, to see what a peale they would ring with the wagging of our chaps; But, said Panurge, it were better we thought a little upon our businesse, and by what meanes we might get the upper hand of our enemies: That is well remembered, said Pantagruel; therefore spoke he thus to the prisoner, My friend, tell us here the truth and do not lie to us at all, if thou wouldest not be flayed alive, for it is I that eate the little children: relate unto us at full the order, the number and the strength of the Army: to which the prisoner answered, Sir, know for a truth that in the army there are three hundred giants, all armed with armour of proof, and wonderful great: neverthelesse, not fully so great as you, except one that is their head, named Loup-garou, who is armed from head to foot with Cyclopical anvils; further-more, one hundred threescore and three thousand foot, all armed with the skins of hobgoblins, strong and valiant men; eleven thousand foure hundred men at armes or cuirasiers: three thousand six hundred double cannons, and harquebusiers without number; fourscore and fourteen thousand Pioneers; one hundred and fifty thousand whores, faire like goddesses (that is for me, said Panurge,) whereof some are Amazons, some Lionnoises, others Parisiennes, Taurangelles, Angevines, Poicte-vines, Normandes, and high Dutch, there are of them of all Countreys, and all languages.

Yea, but (said Pantagruel) is the King there? Yes Sir,

THE POOR DEVIL WAS SOMEWHAT AFRAID

278

(said the prisoner) he is there in person, and we call him Anarchus, King of the Dipsodes, which is as much to say as thirsty people, for you never saw men more thirsty, nor more willing to drink, and his tent is guarded by the Giants: It is enough (said Pantagruel) come brave boyes, are you resolved to go with me? To which Panurge answered, God confound him that leaves you: I have already bethought myself how I will kill them all like pigs, and so the devil one leg of them shall escape; but I am somewhat troubled about one thing: and what is that? said Pantagruel: It is, (said Panurge) how I shall be able to sct forward to the jusling and bragmardising of all the whores that be there this afternoon, in such sort, that there escape not one unbumped by me, breasted and jum'd after the ordinary fashion of man and woman, in the Venetian conflict. Ha, ha, ha, ha, said Pantagruel.

And Carpalin said; The devil take these sink-holes, if by G— I do not bumbast some one of them: Then said Eusthenes, What shall not I have any, whose paces since we came from Rowen, were never so well winded up, as that my needle could mount to ten or eleven a clock till now, that I have it hard, stiffe and strong, like a hundred devils? Truly, (said Panurge,) thou shalt have of the fattest, and of those that are most plump, and in the best case.

How now? (said Epistemon), every one shall ride, and I must lead the Asse, the devil take him that will do so, we will make use of the right of warre, *Qui potest capere, capiat:* No, no, said Panurge, but tie thine Asse to a crook, and ride as the world doth: And the good Pantagruel laughed at all this, and said unto them, You reckon without your host; I am much afraid, that before it be night, I shall see you in such taking, that you will have no great stomach to ride, but more like to be rode upon, with sound blowes of pike and lance: Baste, (said Epistemon), enough of that, I will not faire to bring them to you, either to roste or boile, to fry or put in paste; they are not so many in number, as were in the army of Xerxes, for he had thirty hundred thousand fighting men, if you will beleeve Herodotus and Trogus Pompeius: and yet Themistocles with a few men overthrew them all: for Gods sake take you no care for that. Cobsminnie, Cobsminnie, (said Panurge) my Codpiece alone shall suffice to overthrow all the men; and my St. Sweephole, that dwells within it, shall lay all the women squat upon their backs. Up then my lads (said Pantagruel) and let us march along.

CHAPTER XXVII

*How Pantagruel set up one Trophee in Memorial of their Valour,
and Panurge another in Remembrance of the Hares: how
Pantagruel likewise with his Farts begat little Men, and with
his Fisgs little Women: and how Panurge broke a great
Staffe over two Glasses*

BEFORE we depart hence, (said Pantagruel) in remembrance
of the exploit that you have now performed, I will in this place
erect a faire Trophee : then every man amongst them with
great joy, and fine little Countrey-songs, set up a huge big
post, whereunto they hanged a great cuirasier saddle, the
fronstal of a barbed horse, bridle bosses, pullie-pieces for the
knees, stirrup-leathers, spurres, stirrups, a coat of male, a
corslet tempered with steel, a battel-axe, a strong, short and
sharp horsemans sword, a gantlet, a horsemans mace, gushet-
armour for the arme-pits, leg-harnesse, and a gorget, with all
other furniture needful for the decorement of a triumphant
arch, in signe of a Trophee. And then Pantagruel, for an
eternal memorial, wrote this victorial Ditton, as followeth.

> Here was the prowesse made apparent of
> Foure brave and valiant champions of proof,
> Who without any armes but wit, at once,
> (Like Fabius, or the two Scipions)
> Burn't in a fire six hundred and threescore
> Crablice, strong rogues ne're vanquished betore.
> By this each King may learn, rook, pawn, and Knight,
> That slight is much more prevalent then might.

> For victory,
> (As all men see)
> Hangs on the Dittie
> Of that Committie,
> Where the great God
> Hath his abode :

> Nor doth he it to strong and great men give,
> But to his elect, as we must beleeve ;
> Therefore shall he obtaine wealth and esteem,
> Who thorough faith doth put his trust in him.

Whilest Pantagruel was writing these foresaid verses, Panurge halved and fixed upon a great stake the hornes of a roe-buck, together with the skin, and the right forefoot thereof, the eares of three levrets, the chine of a coney, the jawes of a hare, the wings of two bustards, the feet of foure queest-doves, a bottle or borracho full of vineger, a horne wherein to put salt, a wooden spit, a larding stick, a scurvie kettle full of holes, a dripping pan to make sauce in, an earthen salt-cellar, and a goblet of Beauvais. Then in imitation of Pantagruels verses and Trophee, wrote that which followeth :

> Here was it that foure jovial blades sate down
> To a profound carowsing, and to crown
> Their banquet with those wines, which please best great
> Bacchus, the Monarch of their drinking state :
> Then were the reines and furch of a young hare,
> With salt and vineger, displayed there,
> Of which to snatch a bit or two, at once
> They all fell on like hungry scorpions :

> For th' Inventories
> Of Defensories
> Say that in heat
> We must drink neat
> All out, and of
> The choicest stuffe ;

> But it is bad to eat of young hares flesh,
> Unlesse with vineger we it refresh :
> Receive this tenet then without controll,
> That vineger of that meat is the soul.

Then (said Pantagruel,) Come, my lads, let us be gone, we have stayed here too long about our victuals ; for very seldom doth it fall out, that the greatest eaters do the most martial exploits, there is no shadow like that of flying colours, no smoke like that of horses, no clattering like that of armour : at this Epistemon began to smile, and said, There is no shadow like that of the kitchin, no smoke like that of pasties, and no clattering like that of goblets : unto which answered Panurge, There is no shadow like that of courtaines, no smoke like that of womens breasts, and no clattering like that of ballocks : then forthwith rising up he gave a fart, a leap, and a whistle, and most joyfully cried out aloud, Ever live Pantagruel : when Pantagruel saw that, he would have done as much ; but with the fart that he let, the earth trembled nine leagues about, wherewith and with the corrupted aire, he begot about three and fifty thousand little men, ill favoured dwarfes, and with one fisg that he let, he made as many little women, crouching down, as you shall see in divers places, which never grow but like Cowes tailes downwards, or like the Limosin radishes, round. How now (said Panurge), are your farts so fertile and fruitful ? by G— here be brave farted men, and fisgued women, let them be married together, they will beget fine hornets and dorflies ; so did Pantagruel, and called them Pygmies ; those he sent to live in an island thereby, where since that time they are increased mightily : but the cranes make warre with them continually, against which they do most couragiously defend themselves ; for these little ends of men and dandiprats (whom in Scotland they call whiphandles, and knots of a tarre-barrel) are commonly very teastie and cholerick : the Physical reason whereof is, because their heart is near their spleen.

At this same time, Panurge took two drinking glasses that were there, both of one bignesse, and filled them with water up to the brim, and set one of them upon one stool, and the other upon another, placing them about five foot from one another : then he took the staffe of a javelin, about five foot and a half long, and put it upon the two glasses, so that the two ends of the staffe did come just to the brims of the glasses : This done, he took a great stake or billet of wood, and said to Pantagruel, and to the rest : My Masters, behold, how easily we shall have the victory over our enemies ; for just as I shall break this staffe here upon these glasses, without either breaking or crazing of them, nay, which is more, without spilling one drop of the water that is within them, even so shall we break the heads of our Dipsodes, without receiving any of us any

282

wound or losse in our person or goods : but that you may not think there is any witchcraft in this, hold (said he to Eusthenes) strike upon the midst as hard as thou canst with this log : Eusthenes did so, and the staffe broke in two pieces, and not one drop of the water fell out of the glasses : Then said he, I know a great many such other tricks, let us now therefore march boldly, and with assurance.

CHAPTER XXVIII

How Pantagruel got the Victory very strangely over the Dipsodes and the Giants

AFTER all this talk, Pantagruel took the prisoner to him, and sent him away, saying, Go thou unto thy King in his Camp, and tell him tidings of what thou hast seen, and let him resolve to feast me to-morrow about noon ; for as soon as my galleys shall come, which will be to-morrow at furthest ; I will prove unto him by eighteen hundred thousand fighting men, and seven thousand Giants, all of them greater then I am, that he hath done foolishly and against reason, thus to invade my countrey, wherein Pantagruel feigned that he had an army at sea ; but the Prisoner answered, that he would yield himself to be his slave, and that he was content never to return to his own people, but rather with Pantagruel to fight against them, and for Gods sake besought him, that he might be permitted so to do : whereunto Pantagruel would not give consent, but commanded him to depart thence speedily, and be gone, as he had told him, and to that effect gave him a box full of Euphorbium, together with some grains of the black chameleon thistle, steeped into aqua vitæ, and made up into the condiment of a wet sucket, commanding him to carry it to his King, and to say unto him, that if he were able to eate one ounce of that without drinking after it, he might then be able to resist him, without any feare or apprehension of danger.

The Prisoner then besought him with joynt hands, that in the houre of the battel he would have compassion upon him : whereat Pantagruel said unto him, After that thou hast delivered all unto the King, put thy whole confidence in God, and he will not forsake thee ; because although for my part I be mighty, as thou mayest see, and have an infinite number of men in armes, I do neverthelesse trust neither in my force nor in mine industry, but all my confidence is in God my Protectour, who doth never forsake those that in him do put their trust and confidence. This done, the Prisoner requested him that he would afford him some reasonable composition for his ransom : to which Pantagruel answered, that his end was not to rob nor ransom men, but to enrich them, and reduce them to total liberty ; Go thy way, (said he) in the peace of the living God, and never follow evil company, lest some mischief befall thee. The Prisoner being gone, Pantagruel said to his men, Gentlemen, I have made this Prisoner believe that we have an army at sea, as also that we will not assault them till to-morrow at noon, to the end, that they doubting of the great arrival of our men, may spend this night in providing and strengthening themselves, but in the mean time my intention is, that we charge them about the houre of the first sleep.

Let us leave Pantagruel here with his Apostles, and speak of King Anarchus and his army. When the prisoner was come, he went unto the King, and told him how there was a great Giant come, called Pantagruel, who had overthrown, and made to be cruelly roasted all the six hundred and nine and fifty horsemen, and he alone escaped to bring the news : besides that, he was charged by the said Giant to tell him, that the next day about noon he must make a dinner ready for him, for at that houre he was resolved to set upon him : then did he give him that boxe wherein were those confitures ; but as soon as he had swallowed down one spoonful of them, he was taken with such a heat in the throat, together with an ulceration in the flap of the top of the winde-pipe, that his tongue peel'd with it, in such sort that for all they could do unto him, he found no ease at all, but by drinking only without cessation ; for as soon as ever he took the goblet from his head, his tongue was on a fire, and therefore they did nothing but still poure in wine into his throat with a funnel, which when his Captains, Bashawes and guard of his body did see, they tasted of the same drugs, to try whether they were so thirst-procuring and alterative or no : but it so befell them as it had done their King, and they plied the flaggon so well, that the noise ran throughout all the Camp, how the Prisoner was returned, that the next day they were to have an assault, that the King and his Captains did already prepare themselves for it, together with his guards, and that with carowsing lustily, and quaffing as hard as they could, every man therefore in the army began to tipple, ply the pot, swill and guzzle it as fast as they could. In summe, they drunk so much, and so long, that they fell asleep like pigs, all out of order throughout the whole camp.

Let us now return to the good Pantagruel, and relate how he carried himself in this businesse. Departing from the place of the Trophies, he took the mast of their ship in his hand like a Pilgrims staffe, and put within the top of it two hundred and seven and thirty poinsons of white wine of Anjou, the rest was of Rowen, and tied up to his girdle the bark all full of salt, as easily as the Lanskennets carry their little panniers, and so set onward on his way with his fellow-souldiers. When he was come near to the enemies Camp, Panurge said unto him, Sir, if you would do well, let down this white wine of Anjou from the scuttle of the mast of the ship, that we may all drink thereof, like Britains.

Hereunto Pantagruel very willingly consented, and they drank so neat, that there was not so much as one poor drop left, of two hundred and seven and thirty punchons, except one Boracho or leathern bottle of Tours, which Panurge filled for himself, (for he called that his vade mecum,) and some scurvie lees of wine in the bottom, which served him instead of vineger. After they had whitled and curried the canne pretty handsomely, Panurge gave Pantagruel to eate some devillish drugs, compounded of Lithotripton, (which is a stone-dissolving ingredient,) nephrocatarticon, (that purgeth the reines) the marmalade of Quinces, (called Codiniac) a confection of Cantharides, (which are green flies breeding on the tops of olive-trees) and other kindes of diuretick or pisse-procuring simples. This done, Pantagruel said to Carpalin, Go into the city, scrambling like a cat up against the wall, as you can well do, and tell them, that now presently they come out, and charge their enemies as rudely as they can, and having said so, come down taking a lighted torch with you, wherewith you shall set on fire all the tents and pavillions in the Camp, then cry as loud as you are able with your great voice, and then come away from thence. Yea, but, said Carpalin, were it not good to cloy all their ordnance ? No, no, (said Pantagruel,) only blow up all their powder. Carpalin obeying him, departed suddenly, and did as he was appointed by Pantagruel, and all the Combatants came forth that were in the City, and, when he had set fire in the tents and pavillions, he past so lightly through them, and so highly and profoundly did they snort and sleep, that they never perceived him. He came to the place where their Artillery was, and set their munition on fire: but here was the danger, the fire was so sudden, that poor Carpalin had almost been burnt; and, had it not been for his wonderful agility, he had been fried like a roasting pig: but he departed away so speedily, that a bolt or arrow out of a Crossebowe could not have had a swifter motion. When he was clear of their trenches, he shouted aloud, and cried out so dreadfully, and with such amazement to the hearers, that it seemed all the devils of hell had been let loose: at which noise the enemies awaked, but can you tell how? even no lesse astonished then are Monks, at the ringing of the first peale to Matins, which in Lusonnois is called Rubbalock.

In the meantime Pantagruel began to sowe the salt that he had in his bark, and, because they slept with an open gaping mouth, he filled all their throats with it, so that those poor wretches were by it made to cough like foxes. Ha, Pantagruel, how thou addest greater heat to the firebrand that is in us. Suddenly Pantagruel had will to pisse, by meanes of the drugs which Panurge had given him, and pist amidst the camp so well and so copiously, that he drowned them all, and there was a particular deluge, ten leagues round about, of such considerable depth, that the history saith, if his fathers great mare had been there, and pist likewise, it would undoubtedly have been a more enormous deluge than that of Deucalion; for she did never pisse, but she made a river, greater then is either the Rhosne, or the Danow, which those that were come out of the City seeing, said, They are all cruelly slain, see how the blood runs along: but they were deceived in thinking Pantagruels urine had been the blood of their enemies; for they could not see but by the light of the fire of the pavillions, and some small light of the Moon.

The enemies after that they were awaked, seeing on one side the fire in the Camp, and on the other the inundation of the urinal deluge, could not tell what to say, nor what to think; some said, that it was the end of the world, and the final judgement, which ought to be by fire: Others again thought that the sea-gods, Neptune, Protheus, Triton, and the rest of them, did persecute them, for that indeed they found it to be like sea-water and salt.

O who were able now condignely to relate, how Pantagruel did demean himself against the three hundred Giants; O my Muse, my Calliope, my Thalia, inspire me at this time, restore unto me my spirits; for this is the Logical bridge of asses here is the pitfall, here is the difficultie, to have ability enough to expresse the horrible battel that was fought; Ah, would to God that I had now a bottle of the best wine, that ever those drank, who shall read this so veridical history.

CHAPTER XXIX

How Pantagruel discomfitted the three hundred Giants armed with Free Stone, and Loupgarou their Captain

THE Giants seeing all their Camp drowned, carried away their King Anarchus upon their backs, as well as they could, out of the Fort, as Æneas did to his father Anchises, in the time of the conflagration of Troy. When Panurge perceived them, he said to Pantagruel, Sir, yonder are the Giants coming forth against you, lay on them with your mast gallantly like an old Fencer: for now is the time that you must shew your self a brave man and an honest. And for our part we will not faile you; I my self will kill to you a good many boldly enough; for why, David killed Goliath very easily, and then this great lecher Eusthenes, who is stronger then foure oxen, will not spare himself. Be of good courage therefore, and valiant, charge amongst them with point and edge, and by all manner of meanes. Well (said Pantagruel,) of courage I have more then for fifty francks, but let us be wise, for Hercules first never

LOUPGAROU

undertook against two ; That is well cack'd, well scummered, (said Panurge) do you compare your self with Hercules ? You have by G— more strength in your teeth, and more sent in your bum than ever Hercules had in all his body and soule : so much is a man worth as he esteems himself. Whilest they spake those words behold, Loupgarou was come with all his Giants, who seeing Pantagruel in a manner alone, was carried away with temerity and presumption, for hopes that he had to kill the good man ; whereupon he said to his companions the Giants, You Wenchers of the low countrey, by Mahoom, if any of you undertake to fight against these men here, I will put you cruelly to death : it is my will that you let me fight single. In the mean time you shall have good sport to look upon us : then all the other Giants retired with their King, to the place where the flaggons stood, and Panurge and his Camerades with them, who counterfeited those that have had the pox, for he wreathed about his mouth, shrunk up his fingers, and with a harsh and hoarse voice said unto them, I forsake -od, (fellow souldiers) if I would have it to be beleeved, that we make any warre at all ; Give us somewhat to eat with you, whilest our Masters fight against one another ; to this the King and Giants joyntly condescended, and accordingly made them to banquet with them. In the meantime Panurge told them the follies of Turpin, the examples of St. Nicholas, and the tale of a tub. Loupgarou then set forward towards Pantagruel, with a mace all of steel, and that of the best sort, weighing nine thousand seven hundred kintals, and two quarterons, at the end whereof were thirteen pointed diamonds, the least whereof was as big as the greatest bell of our Ladies Church at Paris, there might want perhaps the thicknesse of a naile, or at most, that I may not lie, of the back of those knives which they call cut-lugs or eare-cutters, but for a little off or on, more or lesse, it is no matter, and it was inchanted in such sort, that it could never break, but contrarily all that it did touch, did break immediately. Thus then as he approached with great fiercenesse and pride of heart, Pantagruel, casting up his eyes to heaven, recommended himself to God with all his soule, making such a Vow as followeth.

O thou Lord God, who hast alwayes been my Protectour, and my Saviour, thou seest the distresse wherein I am at this time : nothing brings me hither but a natural zeale, which thou hast permitted unto mortals, to keep and defend themselves, their wives and children, countrey and family, in case

WHEN MY LORDS THE DEVILS HAD A MINDE TO RECREATE THEMSELVES
UPON THE WATER

thy own proper cause were not in question, which is the faith ; for in such a businesse thou wilt have no coadjutors, only a Catholick Confession and service of thy Word, and hast forbidden us all arming and defence ; for thou art the Almighty, who in thine owne cause, and where thine own businesse is taken to heart, canst defend it far beyond all that we can conceive, thou who hast thousand thousands of hundreds of millions of legions of Angels, the least of which is able to kill all mortal men, and turn about the Heavens and earth at his pleasure, as heretofore it very plainly appeared in the army of Sennacherib, if it may please thee therefore at this time to assist me, as my whole trust and confidence is in thee alone, I vow unto thee, that in all Countreys whatsoever, wherein I shall have any power or authority, whether in this of Utopia, or elsewhere, I will cause thy holy Gospel to be purely, simply and entirely preached, so that the abuses of a rabble of hypocrites and false prophets, who by humane constitutions, and depraved inventions, have impoisoned all the world, shall be quite exterminated from about me. This Vow was no sooner made, but there was heard a voice from heaven, saying, *Hoc fac, et vinces :* that is to say, Do this, and thou shalt overcome.

Then Pantagruel, seeing that Loupgarou with his mouth wide open was drawing near to him, went against him boldly, and cried out as loud as he was able, Thou diest, villain, thou diest !—purposing by his horrible cry to make him afraid, according to the discipline of the Lacedemonians. Withal, he immediately cast at him out of his bark, which he wore at his girdle, eighteen cags, and foure bushels of salt, wherewith he filled both his mouth, throat, nose and eyes : at this Loupgarou was so highly incensed, that most fiercely setting upon him, he thought even then with a blow of his mace to have beat out his braines : but Pantagruel was very nimble, and had alwayes a quick foot, and a quick eye, and therefore with his left foot did he step back one pace, yet not so nimbly, but that the blow, falling upon the bark, broke it in foure thousand, forescore and six pieces, and threw all the rest of the salt about the ground : Pantagruel, seeing that, most gallantly displayed the vigour of his armes, and, according to the Art of the axe, gave him with the great end of his mast a home thrust a little above the breast ; then bringing along the blow to the left side, with a slash struck him between the neck and shoulders : After that, advancing his right foot, he gave him a push upon the couillons, with the upper end of his said mast, wherewith breaking the scuttle, on the top thereof he spilt three or four puncheons of wine that were left therein.

Upon that Loupgarou thought that he had pierced his bladder, and that the wine that came forth had been his urine. Pantagruel, being not content with this, would have doubled it by a side-blow ; but Loupgarou, lifting up his mace, advanced one step upon him, and with all his force would have dash't it upon Pantagruel, wherein (to speak the truth) he so sprightfully carried himself, that if God had not succoured the good Pantagruel, he had been cloven from the top of his head to the bottom of his milt. But the blow glanced to the right side, by the brisk nimblenesse of Pantagruel, and his mace sank into the ground above threescore and thirteen foot, through a huge rock, out of which the fire did issue greater than nine thousand and six tuns. Pantagruel, seeing him busie about plucking out his mace, which stuck in the ground between the rocks, ran upon him, and would have clean cut off his head, if by mischance his mast had not touched a little against the stock of Loupgarous mace, which was inchanted, as we have said before : by this meanes his mast broke off about three handfuls above his hand, whereat he stood amazed like a Bell-Founder, and cried out, Ah Panurge, where are thou ? Panurge seeing that, said to the King and the Giants, By G— they will hurt one another, if they be not parted ; but the giants were as merry as if they had been at a wedding : then Carpalin would have risen from thence to help his Master ; but one of the Giants said unto him, By Golfarin the Nephew of Mahoon, if thou stir hence, I will put thee in the bottom of my breeches, in stead of a Suppository, which cannot chuse but do me good ; for in my belly I am very costive, and cannot well cagar without gnashing my teeth, and making many filthy faces. Then Pantagruel, thus destitute of a staffe, took up the end of his mast, striking athwart and alongst upon the Giant, but he did him no more hurt then you would do with a filip upon a Smiths Anvil. In the time Loupgarou was drawing his mace out of the ground, and having already plucked it out, was ready therewith to have struck Pantagruel, who being very quick in turning, avoided all his blowes, in taking only the defensive part in hand, until on a sudden he saw, that Loupgarou did threaten him with these words, saying, Now, villain, will not I faile to chop thee as small as minced meat, and keep thee henceforth from ever making any more poor men athirst ; for then without any more ado, Pantagruel struck him such a blow with his foot against the belly, that he made him fall backwards, his heels over his head and dragged him thus along at flay-buttock above a flight-shot. Then Loupgarou cried out, bleeding at the throat, Mahoon, Mahoon, Mahoon, at which noise all the Giants arose to succour him : But Panurge said unto them, Gentlemen, do not go, if you will beleeve me, for our Master is mad, and strikes athwart and alongst, he cares not where, he will do you a mischief ; but the Giants made no account of it, seeing that Pantagruel had never a staffe.

And when Pantagruel saw those Giants approach very near unto him, he took Loupgarou by the two feet, and lift up his body like a pike in the aire, wherewith (it being harnished with Anvils) he laid such heavy load amongst those Giants armed with free stone, that striking them down as a mason doth little knobs of stones, there was not one of them that stood before him, whom he threw not flat to the ground, and by the breaking of this stony armour there was made such a horrible rumble, as put me in minde of the fall of the butter-tower of St. Stephens at Bourge, when it melted before the Sunne. Panurge, with Carpalin and Eusthenes, did cut in the mean time the throats of those that were struck down ; in such sort that there escaped not one. Pantagruel to any mans sight was like a Mower, who with his sithe (which was Loupgarou,) cut down the meddow grasse (to wit the giants,) but with this fencing of Pantagruel, Loupgarou lost his head, which happened when Pantagruel struck down one whose name was Riflandouille or pudding-plunderer, who was armed cap-a-pe with grison stones, one chip whereof splintring abroad cut off Epistemon's neck clean and faire : for otherwise the most part of them were but lightly armed with a kinde of sandie brittle stone, and the rest with slaits : at last when he saw that they were all dead, he threw the body of Loupgarou, as hard as he could against the City, where falling like a frog upon his belly, in the great piazza thereof, he with the said fall killed a singed he-cat, a wet she-cat, a farting duck, and a prideled goose.

CHAPTER XXX

*How Epistemon, who had his Head cut off, was finely healed by
Panurge, and of the Newes which he brought from the Devils,
and of the damned People in Hell*

THIS Gigantal victory being ended, Pantagruel withdrew himself to the place of the flaggons, and called for Panurge and the
rest, who came unto him safe and sound, except Eusthenes,
whom one of the Giants had scratched a little in the face,
whilest he was about the cutting of his throat, and Epistemon,
who appeared not at all : whereat Pantagruel was so aggrieved,
that he would have killed himself : but Panurge said unto him,
Nay, Sir, stay a while, and we will search for him amongst the
dead, and finde out the truth of all : thus as they went seeking
after him, they found him stark dead, with his head between his
armes all bloody.   Then Eusthenes cried out, Ah cruel death !
hast thou taken from me the perfectest amongst men ?   At
which words Pantagruel rose up with the greatest grief that
ever any man did see, and said to Panurge, Ha, my friend, the
prophecy of your two glasses, and the javelin staffe, was a great
deal too deceitful, but Panurge answered, My dear bullies all,
weep not one drop more, for he being yet all hot, I will make
him as sound as ever he was ; in saying this, he took the head,
and held it warme fore-gainst his Codpiece, that the winde might
not enter into it, Eusthenes and Carpalin carried the body to
the place where they had banqueted, not out of any hope that
ever he would recover, but that Pantagruel might see it.
Neverthelesse Panurge gave him very good comfort, saying,
If I do not heale him, I will be content to lose my head (which
is a fooles wager), leave off therefore crying, and help me.
Then cleansed he his neck very well with pure white wine, and
after that, took his head, and into it synapised some powder

of diamerdis, which he alwayes carried about him in one of his bags. Afterwards, he anointed it with I know not what ointment, and set it on very just, veine against veine, sinew against sinew, and spondyle against spondyle, that he might not be wry-necked, (for such people he mortally hated) this done, he gave it round about some fifteen or sixteen stitches with a needle, that it might not fall off again, then on all sides, and every where he put a little ointment on it, which he called resuscitative.

Suddenly Epistemon began to breath, then opened his eyes, yawned, sneezed, and afterwards let a great houshold fart; whereupon Panurge said, Now certainly he is healed, and therefore gave him to drink a large full glasse of strong white wine, with a sugred toast. In this fashion was Epistemon finely healed, only that he was somewhat hoarse for above three weeks together, and had a dry cough of which he could not be rid, but by the force of continual drinking: and now he began to speak, and said, that he had seen the divel, had spoken with Lucifer familiarly, and had been very merry in hell, and in the Elysian fields, affirming very seriously before them all, that the devils were boone companions, and merry fellowes: but in respect of the damned, he said he was very sorry that Panurge had so soon called him back into this world again; for (said he) I took wonderful delight to see them: How so? said Pantagruel: because they do not use them there (said Epistemon) so badly as you think they do: their estate and condition of living is but only changed after a very strange manner; for I saw Alexander the great there, amending and patching on clowts upon old breeches and stockins, whereby he got but a very poor living.

Xerxes was a Cryer of mustard.
Romulus, a Salter and patcher of patines.
Numa, a nailsmith.
Tarquin, a Porter.
Piso, a clownish swaine.
Sylla, a Ferrie-man.
Cyrus, a Cowheard.
Themistocles, a glasse-maker.
Epaminondas, a maker of Mirrours or Looking-glasses.
Brutus and Cassius, Surveyors or Measurers of land.
Demosthenes, a Vine-dresser.
Cicero, a fire-kindler.

TRAJAN WAS A FISHER OF FROGS

296

Fabius, a threader of beads.
Artaxerxes, a rope-maker.
Æneas, a Miller.
Achilles was a scauld-pated maker of hay-bundles.
Agamemnon, a lick-box.
Ulysses, a hay-mower.
Nestor, a Deer-keeper or Forrester.
Darius a Gold-finder, or Jakes-farmer.
Ancus Martius, a ship-trimmer.
Camillus, a foot-post.
Marcellus, a sheller of beans.
Drusus, a taker of money at the doors of play-houses.
Scipio Africanus, a Crier of Lee in a wooden slipper.
Asdrubal, a Lanterne-maker.
Hannibal, a Kettlemaker and seller of eggeshels.
Priamus, a seller of old clouts.
Lancelot of the lake was a flayer of dead horses.

All the Knights of the round Table were poore day-labourers, employed to rowe over the rivers of Cocytus, Phlegeton, Styx, Acheron and Lethe, when my Lords, the devils had a minde to recreate themselves upon the water, as in the like occasion are hired the boatmen at Lions, the gondeleers of Venice, and oares at London ; but with this difference, that these poor Knights have only for their fare a bob or flirt on the nose, and in the evening a morsel of course mouldie bread.

Trajan was a fisher of frogs.
Antoninus, a Lackey.
Commodus, a Jeat-maker.
Pertinax, a peeler of wall-nuts.
Lucullus, a maker of rattles and Hawks bells.
Justinian, a Pedlar.
Hector, a Snap-sauce Scullion.
Paris was a poore beggar.
Cambyses, a Mule-driver.

Nero, a base blinde fidler, or player on that instrument which is called a windbroach : Fierabras was his serving-man who did him a thousand mischievous tricks, and would make him eat of the brown bread, and drink of the turned wine, when himself did both eate and drink of the best.

Julius Cæsar and Pompey were boat-wrights and tighters of ships.

Valentine and Orson did serve in the stoves of hell, and were sweat-rubbers in hot houses.

FIERABRAS WAS HIS SERVING-MAN

Giglan and Govian were poor Swine-herds.

Jafrey with the great tooth was a tinder-maker and seller of matches.

Godfrey de bullion, a Hood-maker.

Jason was a Bracelet-maker.

Don Pietro de Castille, a Carrier of Indulgences.

Morgan, a beer-Brewer.

Huon of Bourdeaux, a Hooper of barrels.

Pyrrhus, a Kitchin-Scullion.

Antiochus, a Chimney-sweeper.

Octavian, a Scraper of parchment.

Nerva, a Mariner.

Pope Julius was a Crier of pudding pyes, but he left off wearing there his great buggerly beard.

John of Paris was a greaser of boots.

Arthur of Britain, an ungreaser of caps.

Pierce Forrest, a Carrier of fagots.

Pope Boniface the eighth, a Scummer of pots.

Pope Nicholas the third, a Maker of paper.

Pope Alexander, a rat-catcher.

Pope Sixtus, an Anointer of those that have the pox.

What, (said Pantagruel) have they the pox there too ı Surely (said Epistemon) I never saw so many : there are there, I think, above a hundred millions ; for beleeve, that those who have not had the pox in this world, must have it in the other.

Cotsbody (said Panurge) then I am free ; for I have been as farre as the hole of Gibraltar, reached unto the outmost bounds of Hercules, and gathered of the ripest.

Ogier the Dane was a Furbisher of armour.

The King Tigranes, a mender of thatched houses.

Galien Restored, a taker of Moldwarps.

The foure sons of Aymon were all tooth-drawers.

Pope Calixtus was a barber of a womans *Sine quo non*.

Pope Urban, a bacon-pecker.

Melusina was a Kitchin drudge-wench.

Mattabrune, a Laundresse.

Cleopatra, a Crier of onions.

Helene, a broker for Chamber-maids.

Semiramis, the Beggars lice-killer.

Dido did sell mushroms.

Pentasilea sold cresses.

Lucretia was an Ale-house-keeper.

Hortensia, a Spinstresse.

Livia, a grater of verdigreece.

After this manner, those that had been great Lords and Ladies here, got but a poor scurvie wretched living there below. And on the contrary, the Philosophers and others, who in this world had been altogether indigent and wanting, were great lords there in their turne. I saw Diogenes there strout it out most pompously, and in great magnificence, with a rich purple gown on him, and a golden Scepter in his right hand. And which is more, he would now and then make Alexander the Great mad, so enormously would he abuse him, when he had not well patched his breeches ; for he used to pay his skin with sound bastonadoes ; I saw Epictetus there most gallantly apparelled after the French fashion, sitting under a pleasant Arbour, with store of handsom Gentlewomen, frolicking, drinking, dancing, and making good cheare, with abundance of Crowns of the Sunne. Above the lattice were written these verses for his device :

> To leap and dance, to sport and play,
> And drink good wine both white and brown :
> Or nothing else do all the day,
> But tell bags full of many a Crown.

When he saw me, he invited me to drink with him very courteously, and I being willing to be entreated, we tipled and chopined together most theologically. In the mean time came Cyrus to beg one farthing of him for the honour of Mercurie, therewith to buy a few onions for supper ? No, no, said Epictetus, I do not use in my almes-giving to bestow farthings, hold, thou Varlet, there 's a crown for thee, be an honest man : Cyrus was exceeding glad to have met with such a bootie ; but the other poor rogues, the Kings that are there below, as Alexander, Darius, and others stole it away from him by night. I saw Pathelin, Treasurer of Rhadamantus, who in cheapening the pudding-pyes that Pope Julius cried, asked him, How much a dozen ? Three blanks (said the Pope) : Nay (said Pathelin) three blowes with a cudgel. Lay them down here you rascal, and go fetch more : the poor Pope went away weeping, who when he came to his Master the Pye-maker, told him that they had taken away his pudding-pyes ; whereupon his Master gave him such a sound lash with an eele-skin, that his own would have been worth nothing to make bag-pipe-bags of. I saw master John Le maire there personate the Pope in such fashion, that he made all the poor Kings and Popes of this world kisse his feet, and taking great state upon him, gave them his benediction, saying, Get the pardons, rogues, get the pardons, they are good cheap : I absolve you of bread and pottage, and dispense with you to be never good for any thing : then, calling Caillet and Triboulet to him, he spoke these words, My Lords the Cardinals dispatch their bulls, to wit, to each of them a blow with a Cudgel upon the reines, which accordingly was forthwith performed.

I heard Master Francis Villon ask Xerxes, How much the messe of mustard ? A farthing, said Xerxes : to which the said Villon answered, The pox take thee for a villain : as much of square-ear'd wheat is not worth half that price, and now thou offerest to inhance the price of victuals : with this he pist in his pot as the mustard-makers of Paris used to do. I saw the trained bowe-man of the bathing tub, (known by the name of the Francarcher de baignolet) who being one of the trustees of the Inquisition, when he saw Pierce Forrest making water against a wall, in which was painted the fire of St. Antonie, declared him heretick, and would have caused him to be burnt alive, had it not been for Morgant, who for his Proficiat and other small fees gave him nine tuns of beer. Well (said Pantagruel), reserve all these faire stories for another time, only tell us how the Usurers are there handled : I saw them (said Epistemon) all very busily employed in seeking of rustie pins, and old nailes in the kennels of the streets, as you see poor wretched rogues do in this world ; but the quintal, or hundred weight of this old iron ware is there valued but at the price of a cantle of bread, and yet they have but a very bad dispatch and riddance in the sale of it : thus the poor Misers are sometimes three whole weeks without eating one morsel or crumb of bread, and yet work both day and night, looking for the faire to come : neverthelesse, of all this labour, toile and misery, they reckon nothing, so cursedly active they are in the prosecution of that their base calling, in hopes at the end of the yeare, to earne some scurvie penny by it.

Come, (said Plantagruel) let us now make our selves merry one bout, and drink (my lads) I beseech you, for it is very good drinking all this moneth : then did they uncase their flaggons by heaps and dozens, and with their leaguer-provision made excellent good chear : but the poor King Anarchus could not all this while settle himselfe towards any fit of mirth ; whereupon Panurge said, Of what trade shall we make my Lord the King

ALL VERY BUSILY EMPLOYED IN SEEKING OF RUSTIE PINS

here, that he may be skilful in the Art, when he goes thither to sojourn amongst all the devils of hell ? Indeed (said Pantagruel) that was well advised of thee, do with him what thou wilt : I give him to thee : Grammercie (said Panurge) the present is not to be refused, and I love it from you.

CHAPTER XXXI

How Pantagruel entered into the City of the Amaurots, and how Panurge married King Anarchus to an old Lantern-carrying Hag, and made him a Cryer of Green Sauce

AFTER this wonderful victory, Pantagruel sent Carpalin unto the city of the Amaurots, to declare and signifie unto them, how the King Anarchus was taken prisoner, and all the enemies of the City overthrown, which news when they heard, all the inhabitants of the City came forth to meet him in good order, and with a great triumphant pomp, conducting him with a heavenly joy into the City, where innumerable bone-fires were set on, thorough all the parts thereof, and faire round tables, which were furnished with store of good victuals, set out in the middle of the streets ; this was a renewing of the golden age in the time of Saturn, so good was the cheere which then they made.

But Pantagruel having assembled the whole Senate, and Common Councelmen of the town, said (My Masters) we must now strike the iron whilest it is hot ; it is therefore my will, that before we frolick it any longer, we advise how to assault and take the whole Kingdom of the Dipsodes : to which effect let those that will go with me provide themselves against to-morrow after drinking ; for then will I begin to march, not that I need any more men then I have to help me to conquer it ; for I could make it as sure that way as if I had it already, but I see this City is so full of inhabitants, that they scarce can turn in the streets ; I will, therefore, carry them as a Colonie into Dipsodie, and will give them all that Countrey, which is faire, wealthie, fruitful and pleasant, above all other Countreys in the world, as many of you can tell who have been there heretofore. Every one of you, therefore that will go along, let him provide himself as I have said. This counsel and resolution being published in the City, the next morning there assembled in the piazza, before the Palace, to the number of eighteen hundred fifty six thousand and eleven, besides women and little children : thus began they to march straight into Dipsodie, in such good order as did the people of Israel, when they departed out of Egypt, to passe over the red sea.

But before we proceed any further in this purpose, I will tell you how Panurge handled his prisoner the King Anarchus ; for having remembred that which Epistemon had related, how the Kings and rich men in this world were used in the Elysian fields, and how they got their living there by base and ignoble trades ; he therefore one day apparelled his King in a pretty little canvass doublet, all jagged and pinked like the tippet of a light horsemans cap, together with a paire of large Mariners breeches, and stockins without shoes ; For (said he) they would but spoile his sight ; and a little peach-coloured bonnet, with a great capons feather in it : I lie, for I think he had two : and a very handsome girdle of a sky-colour and green, (in French called *pers et vert*) saying, that such a livery did become him well, for that he had alwayes been perverse, and in this plight bringing him before Pantagruel, said unto him, Do you know this royster ? No indeed, said Pantagruel : It is (said Panurge) my Lord the King of the three batches, or threadbare sovereign : I intend to make him an honest man. These devillish Kings which we have here are but as so many calves, they know nothing, and are good for nothing, but to do a thousand mischiefs to their poor subjects, and to trouble all the world with warre for their unjust and detestable pleasure : I will put him to a trade, and make him a crier of green sauce : Go to, begin and cry, Do you lack any green sauce ? and the poor wretch cried : That is too low (said Panurge,) then took him by the eare, saying, Sing higher in Ge. sol. re. ut : So, so (poor wretch) thou hast a good throat : thou wert never so happy as to be no longer King : and Pantagruel made himself merry with all this ; for I dare boldly say, that he was the best little gaffer that was to be seen between this and the end of a staffe. Thus was Anarchus made a good Crier of green sauce. Two dayes thereafter Panurge married him with an old Lanterne-carrying Hag, and he himselfe made the wedding with fine sheeps-heads, brave haslets with mustard, gallant salligots with garlick, of which he sent five horse-loads unto Pantagruel, which he ate up all, he found them so appetizing : and for their drink, they had a kinde of small well-watered wine, and some sorbapple-cider : and, to make them dance, he hired a blinde man, that made musick to them with a windbroach.

After dinner he led them to the Palace, and shewed them to Pantagruel, and said, pointing to the married woman, You need not feare that she will crack. Why ? said Pantagruel : Because, said Panurge, she is well slit and broke up already ; What do you mean by that ? said Pantagruel : Do not you see ? said Panurge, that the chestnuts which are roasted in the fire, if they be whole, they crack as if they were mad ; and, to keep them from cracking, they make an incision in them, and slit them ; so this new bride is in her lower parts well slit before, and therefore will not crack behinde.

Pantagruel gave them a little lodge near the lower street, and a mortar of stone wherein to bray and pound their sauce, and in this manner did they do their little businesse, he being as pretty a Crier of green sauce, as ever was seene in the Countrey of Utopia. But I have been told since, that his wife doth beat him like plaister, and the poor sot dare not defend himself, he is so simple.

CHAPTER XXXII

How Pantagruel with his Tongue covered a whole Army, and what the Author saw in his Mouth

THUS as Pantagruel with all his Army had entered into the Countrey of the Dipsodes, every one was glad of it, and incontinently rendred themselves unto him, bringing him out of their own good wills the Keyes of all the Cities where he went, the Almirods only excepted, who being resolved to hold out against him, made answer to his Heraulds, that they would not yield but upon very honourable and good conditions.

What ? (said Pantagruel) do they ask any better termes, then the hand at the pot, and the glasse in their fist ? Come, let us go sack them, and put them all to the sword : then did they put themselves in good order, as being fully determined to give an assault, but by the way passing through a large field, they were overtaken with a great shower of raine, whereat they began to shiver and tremble, to croud, presse and thrust close to one another. When Pantagruel saw that, he made their Captains tell them, that it was nothing, and that he saw well above the clouds, that it would be nothing but a little dew ; but howsoever, that they should put themselves in order, and he would cover them : then did they put themselves in a close

THE POOR SOT DARE NOT DEFEND HIMSELF

order, and stood as near to other as they could : and Pantagruel drew out his tongue only half-wayes and covered them all, as a hen doth her chickens. In the mean time I, who relate to you these so veritable stories, hid myself under a burdock-leafe, which was not much lesse in largenesse then the arch of the bridge of Montrible, but when I saw them thus covered, I went towards them to shelter my self likewise ; which I could not do, for that they were so (as the saying is) ' At the yards end there is no cloth left.' Then as well as I could, I got upon it, and went along full two leagues upon his tongue, and so long marched, that at last I came into his mouth : but, oh gods and goddesses, what did I see there ? Jupiter confound me with his trisulk lightning if I lie : I walked there as they do in Sophie and Constantinople, and saw there great rocks, like the mountains in Denmark, I believe that those were his teeth. I saw also faire meddows, large forrests, great and strong Cities, not a jot lesse than Lyons or Poictiers. The first man I met with there, was a good honest fellow planting coleworts, whereat being very much amazed, I asked him, My friend, what dost thou make here ? I plant coleworts, said he ; but how, and wherewith, said I ? Ha, Sir, said he, every one cannot have his ballocks as heavy as a mortar, neither can we be all rich : thus do I get my poor living, and carry them to the market to sell in the City which is here behinde. Jesus ! (said I) is there here a new world ? Sure, (said he) it is never a jot new, but it is commonly reported, that without this there is an earth, whereof the inhabitants enjoy the light of a Sunne and a Moone, and that it is full of, and replenished with very good commodities ; but yet this is more ancient that that : Yea, but (said I) my friend, what is the name of that City, whither thou carriest thy Coleworts to sell ? It is called Aspharage, (said he) and all the indwellers are Christians, very honest men, and will make you good chear. To be brief, I resolved to go thither, Now in my way, I met with a fellow that was lying in wait to catch pigeons, of whom I asked, (My friend) from whence came these pigeons ? Sir, (said he) they come from the other world : then I thought, that when Pantagruel yawned, the pigeons went into his mouth in whole flocks, thinking that it had been a pigeon-house.

Then I went into the City, which I found faire, very strong, and seated in a good aire ; but at my entry the guard demanded of me my passe or ticket : whereat I was much astonished, and asked them, (My Masters) is there any danger of the plague here ?   O Lord, (said they) they die hard by here so fast, that the cart runs about the streets ; Good God ! (said I) and where ? whereunto they answered that it was in Larinx and Phærinx, which are two great Cities, such as Rowen and Nants, rich and of great trading : and the cause of the plague was by a stinking and infectious exhalation, which lately vapoured out of the abismes, whereof there have died above two and twenty hundred and three-score thousand and sixteen persons within this sevennight ; then I considered, calculated and found, that it was a rank and unsavoury breathing, which came out of Pantagruels stomack, when he did eat so much garlick, as we have aforesaid.

Parting from thence, I past amongst the rocks, which were his teeth, and never left walking, till I got up on one of them ; and there I found the pleasantest places in the world, great large tennis-Courts, faire galleries, sweet meddows, store of Vines, and an infinite number of banqueting summer out-houses in the fields, after the Italian fashion, full of pleasure and delight, where I stayed full foure moneths, and never made better cheer in my life as then.   After that I went down by the hinder teeth to come to the chaps ; but in the way I was robbed by thieves in a great forrest, that is in the territory towards the eares : then (after a little further travelling) I fell upon a pretty petty village, (truly I have forgot the name of it) where I was yet merrier than ever, and got some certain money to live by.   Can you tell how ? by sleeping ; for there they hire men by the day to sleep, and they get by it sixpence a day, but they that can snort hard get at least nine pence. How I had been robbed in the valley, I informed the Senators, who told me that, in very truth, the people of that side were bad livers, and naturally theevish, whereby I perceived well, that as we have with us the Countreys cisalpine and transalpine, that is, behither and beyond the mountains, so have they there the Countreys cidentine and tradentine, that is, behither and beyond the teeth : but it is farre better living on this side, and the aire is purer.   There I began to think, that it is very true which is commonly said, that the one half of the world knoweth not how the other half liveth ; seeing none before my self had ever written of that Countrey, wherein are above five and twenty Kingdoms inhabited, besides deserts, and a great arme of the sea : concerning which purpose, I have composed a great book intituled the History of the Throttias, because they dwell in the throat of my Master Pantagruel.

At last I was willing to return, and, passing by his beard, I cast my self upon his shoulders, and from thence slid down to the ground, and fell before him: as soon as I was perceived by him, he asked me, Whence comest thou, Alcofribas? I answered him, Out of your mouth, my Lord: and how long hast thou been there? said he. Since the time (said I) that you went against the Almirods; That is, about six moneths ago, said he: and wherewith didst thou live? what didst thou drink? I answered, My Lord, of the same that you did, and of the daintiest morsels that past through your throat I took toll: Yea, but, said he, where didst thou shite? In your throat (my lord) said I. Ha, ha, thou art a merry fellow, said he. We have with the help of God conquered all the land of the Dipsodes; I will give thee the Chastelleine, or Lairdship of Salmigondin. Grammercy, my Lord, said I, you gratifie me beyond all that I have deserved of you.

CHAPTER XXXIII

How Pantagruel became sick, and the Manner how he was recovered

A WHILE after this the good Pantagruel fell sick, and had such an obstruction in his stomack, that he could neither eate nor drink: and because mischief seldome comes alone, a hot pisse seised on him, which tormented him more then you would beleeve: His Physicians neverthelesse helped him very well, and with store of lenitives and diuretick drugs made him pisse away his paine: his urine was so hot, that since that time it is not yet cold, and you have of it in divers places of France, according to the course that it took, and they are called the hot baths, as

At Coderets.
At Limoŭs.
At Dast.
At Ballervie.
At Neric.
At Bourbonansie, and elsewhere in Italie.
At Mongros.
At Appone.
At Sancto Petro de Padua.
At St. Helen.
At Casa Nuova.
At St. Bartolomee, in the County of Boulogne.
At the Porrette, and a thousand other places.

And I wonder much at a rabble of foolish Philosophers and Physicians, who spend their time in disputing, whence the heat of the said waters cometh, whether it be by reason of Borax, or sulphur, or allum, or salt-peter that is within the mine: for they do nothing but dote, and better were it for them, to rub their arse against a thistle, then to waste away their time thus in disputing of that, whereof they know not the original; for the resolution is easie, neither need we to enquire any further, than that the said baths came by a hot pisse of the good Pantagruel.

Now to tell you after what manner he was cured of his principal disease; I let passe how for a minorative, or gentle potion, he took foure hundred pound weight of Colophoniack Scammonee, six score and eighteen cart-loads of Cassia: an eleven thousand and nine hundred pound weight of Rubarb, besides other confuse jumblings of sundry drugs: You must understand, that by the advice of the Physicians it was ordained, that what did offend his stomach should be taken away; and therefore they made seventeen great balls of copper, each whereof was bigger then that which is to be seen on the top of St. Peters needle at Rome, and in such sort, that they did open in the midst, and shut with a spring. Into one of them entered one of his men, carrying a Lanterne and a torch lighted, and so Pantagruel swallowed him down like a little pill: into seven others went seven Countrey-fellows, having every one of them a shovel on his neck: into nine others entred nine wood-carriers, having each of them a basket hung at his neck, and so were they swallowed down like pills : when they were in his stomack, every one undid his spring, and came out of their cabins : the first whereof was he that carried the Lantern, and so they fell more then half a league into a most horrible gulph, more stinking and infectious then ever was Mephitis, or the marishes of the Camerina, or the abominably unsavoury lake of Sorbona, whereof Strabo maketh mention. And had it not been, that they had very well antidoted their stomach, heart and wine-pot, which is called the noddle, they had been altogether suffocated and choaked with these destestable vapours. O what a perfume ! O what an evaporation wherewith to bewray the mask or muflers of young mangie queans: after that with groping and smelling they came near to the fecal matter and the corrupted humours ; finally, they found a montjoy or heap of ordure and filth : then fell the pioneers to work to dig it up, and the rest with their shovels filled the baskets ; and when all was cleansed, every one retired himself into his ball.

This done, Pantagruel enforcing himself to a vomit, very easily brought them out, and they made no more shew in his mouth, then a fart in yours : but when they came merrily out of their pills, I thought upon the Grecians coming out of the Trojan horse : by this meanes was he healed, and brought unto his former state and convalescence ; and of these brazen pills, or rather copper-balls, you have one at Orleans, upon the steeple of the Holy Crosse Church.

CHAPTER XXXIV

The Conclusion of this present Book, and the Excuse of the Author

Now (my masters) you have heard a beginning of the horrifick history of my Lord and Master Pantagruel : Here will I make an end of the first book ; My head akes a little, and I perceive that the Registers of my braine are somewhat jumbled and disordered with this septembral juice. You shall have the rest of the history at Franckfort mart next coming, and there shall you see how Panurge was married and made a Cuckold within a moneth after his wedding : how Pantagruel found out the Philosophers stone, the manner how he found it, and the way how to use it : how he past over the Caspian mountaines, and how he sailed thorough the Atlantick sea, defeated the Cannibals, and conquered the isles of Perles, how he married

WHEATH·ROBINSON·

WHO DISGUISE THEMSELVES LIKE MASKERS TO DECEIVE THE WORLD

312

the daughter of the King of India, called Prestian, how he fought against the devil, and burnt up five chambers of hell, ransacked the great black chamber, threw Proserpina into the fire, broke five teeth to Lucifer, and the horne that was in his arse. How he visited the regions of the Moon, to know whether indeed the Moon were not entire and whole, or if the women had three quarters of it in their heads, and a thousand other little merriments all veritable. These are brave things truly ; Good night, Gentlemen, *Perdonate mi*, and think not so much upon my faults, that you forget your own.

If you say to me, (Master) it would seem that you were not very wise in writing to us these flimflam stories, and pleasant fooleries : I answer you, that you are not much wiser to spend your time in reading them : neverthelesse, if you read them to make your selves merry, as in manner of pastime I wrote them, you and I both are farre more worthy of pardon, then a great rabble of squint-minded fellowes, dissembling and counterfeit Saints, demure lookers, hypocrites, pretended zealots, tough Fryars, buskin-Monks, and other such sects of men, who disguise themselves like Maskers to deceive the world, for, whilest they give the common people to understand, that they are busied about nothing but contemplation and devotion in fastings, and maceration of their sensuality ; and that only to sustain and aliment the small frailty of their humanity : it is so far otherwise, that on the contrary (God knows) what cheer they make, *Et Curios simulant, sed bacchanalia vivunt*. You may read it in great letters, in the colouring of their red snowts, and gulching bellies as big as a tun, unlesse it be when they perfume themselves with sulphur ; as for their study, it is wholly taken up in reading of Pantagruelin books, not so much to passe the time merrily, as to hurt some one or other mischievously, to wit, in articling, sole-articling, wry-neckifying, buttock-stirring, ballocking, and diabliculating, that is, culumniating ; wherein they are like unto the poor rogues of a village, that are busie in stirring up and scraping in the ordure and filth of little children, in the season of cherries and guinds, and that only to find the kernels, that they may sell them to the druggists, to make thereof pomander oile. Fly from these men, abhorre and hate them as much as I do, and upon my faith you will finde your selves the better for it. And if you desire to be good Pantagruelists (that is to say, to live in peace, joy, health, making your selves alwayes merry) never trust those men that alwayes peep out at one hole.

313

THE THIRD BOOK OF THE WORKS OF ◦ ◦ MR.
FRANCIS RABELAIS ◦ ◦ DOCTOR IN PHY
SICK ◦ ◦ CONTAINING THE HEROICK DEEDS
OF ◦ ◦ PANTAGRUEL THE SON OF GAR-
GANTUA ◦ ◦ NOW FAITHFULLY TRANSLATED
INTO ENGLISH ◦ ◦ BY THE UNIMITABLE PEN
OF ◦ ◦ SIR THOMAS URWHART, K^t & BAR. ◦ ◦
THE TRANSLATOR OF THE TWO FIRST ◦ ◦
BOOKS

FRANCIS RABELAIS

TO THE SOUL OF THE DECEASED

QUEEN OF NAVARRE

ABSTRACTED Soul, ravish'd with Ecstasies,
Gone back, and now familiar in the Skies,
Thy former Host, thy Body, leaving quite
Which to obey thee always took delight ;
Obsequious, ready. Now from motion free,
Senseless, and as it were, in Apathy.
Would'st thou not issue forth, for a short space,
From that Divine, Eternal, Heav'nly Place,
To see the Third Part, in this Earthly Cell,
Of the brave Acts of good Pantagruel.

THE AUTHOR'S PROLOGUE TO THE THIRD BOOK

GOOD People, most Illustrious Drinkers, and you thrice-precious Gouty
Gentlemen. Did you ever see Diogenes the Cynic Philosopher ? If you
have seen him, you then had your Eyes in your Head, or I am very much
out of my Understanding and Logical Sense. It is a gallant thing to see
the clearness of (Wine, Gold) the Sun. I'll be judg'd by the Blind, born
so, renowned in the Sacred Scriptures ; who having at his choice to ask
whatever he would from Him who is Almighty, and whose Word in an
Instant is effectually performed, ask'd nothing else but that he might see.
Item, you are not young, which is a competent Quality for you to Philo-
sophat more than Physically in Wine (not in vain) and henceforwards to
be of the Bacchick Council ; to the end that opening there, you may give

your Opinion faithfully of the Substance, Colour, excellent Odour, Eminency, Propriety, Faculty, Virtue, and effectual Dignity of the said blessed and desired Liquor.

If you have not seen him (as I am easily induced to believe that you have not) at least you have heard some talk of him. For through the Air, and the whole extent of this Hemisphere of the Heavens, hath his Report and Fame, even until this present time, remained very memorable and renowned. Then all of you are derived from the Phrygian Blood (if I be not deceived). If you have not so many Crowns as Midas had, yet have you something (I know not what) of him, which the Persians of old esteemed more of in all their Otacusts, and which was more desired by the Emperor Antónine, and gave occasion thereafter to the Basilisco at Roan to be Surnamed Goodly Ears. If you have not heard of him, I will presently tell you a Story to make your Wine relish: Drink then, so, to the purpose; hearken now whilst I give you notice, (to the end that you may not, like Infidels, be by your simplicity abused) that in his time he was a rare Philosopher, and the chearfullest of a thousand: If he had some Imperfection, so have you, so have we; for there is nothing (but God) that is perfect: Yet so it was, that by Alexander the Great (altho' he had Aristotle for his Instructor and Domestick) was he held in such Estimation, that he wish'd, if he had not been Alexander, to have been Diogenes the Sinopian.

When Philip King of Macedon enterprised the Siege and Ruin of Corinth, the Corinthians having received certain Intelligence by their Spies, that he with a numerous Army in Battle Rank was coming against them, were all of them (not without cause) most terribly afraid; and therefore were not neglective of their duty, in doing their best Endeavours to put themselves in a fit posture to resist his Hostile Approach, and defend their own City.

Some from the Fields brought into the Fortified Places their Moveables, Bestial, Corn, Wine, Fruit, Victuals, and other necessary Provision.

Others did fortifie and rampire their Walls, set up little Fortresses, Bastions, squared Ravelins, digged Trenches, cleansed Countermines, fenced themselves with Gabions, contrived Platforms, emptied Casemates, barricado'd the false Brayes, erected the Cavalliers, repaired the Countrescrafes, plaister'd the Courtines, lengthned Ravelins, stopt Parapets, mortaised Barbacans, assured the Port-culleys, fasten'd the Herses, Sarasinesks and Cataracks, placed their Centries, and doubled their Patrouilee.

Every one did Watch and Ward, and not one was exempted from carrying the Basket.

Some polish'd Corselets, varnish'd Backs and Breasts, clean'd the Head-pices, Mail-Coats, Brigandines, Salads, Helmets, Murrions, Jacks, Gushets, Gorgets, Hoguines, Brassers and Cuissars, Corselets, Haubergeons, Shields, Bucklers, Targuets, Greves, Gantlets and Spurs.

Others made ready Bows, Slings, Cross-bows, Pellets, Catapults,

Migrames or Fire-balls, Firebrands, Balists, Scorpions, and other such Warlike Engines, expugnatorie, and destructive to the Helle-polists.

They sharpned and prepared Spears, Staves, Pikes, Brown Bills, Halberts, Long Hooks, Lances, Zagages, Quarter-staves, Eel-spears, Partisans, Trout-staves, Clubs, Battle-axes, Maces, Darts, Dartlets, Glaves, Javelins, Javelots, and Trunchions.

They set Edges upon Cimeters, Cutlasses, Badelans, Backswords, Tucks, Rapiers, Bayonets, Arrowheads, Dags, Daggers, Mandousians, Poigniards, Whinyards, Knives, Skenes, Sables, Chipping Knives, and Raillons.

Every Man exercis'd his Weapon, every Man scour'd off the Rust from his natural Hanger : Nor was there a Woman amongst them (tho' never so reserv'd or old) who made not her Harnish to be well furbish'd ; as you know the Corinthian Women of old were reputed very couragious Combatants.

Diogenes seeing them all so warm at work, and himself not employed by the Magistrates in any business whatsoever, he did very seriously (for many days together, without speaking one word) consider and contemplate the Countenance of his Fellow-Citizens.

Then on a sudden, as if he had been roused up and inspired by a Martial Spirit, he girded his Cloak, scarfways, about his Left Arm, tuck'd up his Sleeves to the Elbow, truss'd himself like a Clown gathering Apples, and giving to one of his old acquaintance his Wallet, Books, and Opistographs, away went he out of Town towards a little Hill or Promontory of Corinth call'd Cranie ; and there on the Strand, a pretty level place, did he roul his Jolly Tub, which serv'd him for an House to shelter him from the Injuries of the Weather : There, I say, in a great vehemency of his Spirit, did he turn it, veer it, wheel it, whirl it, frisk it, jumble it, shuffle it, huddle it, tumble it, hurry it, joult it, justle it, overthrow it, evert it, invert it, subvert it, overturn it, beat it, thwack it, bump it, batter it, knock it, thrust it, push it, jerk it, shock it, shake it, toss it, throw it, overthrow it upside down, topsiturvy, arsiturvy, tread it, trample it, stamp it, tap it, ting it, ring it, tingle it, toul it, sound it, resound it, stop it, shut it, unbung it, close it, unstopple it. And then again, in a mighty bustle, he bandy'd it, slubber'd it, hack'd it, whitled it, weigh'd it, darted it, hurl'd it, stagger'd it, reel'd it, swindg'd it, brangl'd it, totter'd it, lifted it, heav'd it, transform'd it, transfigur'd it, transpos'd it, transplaced it, rear'd it, rais'd it, hois'd it, wash'd it, dighted it, cleans'd it, rins'd it, nail'd it, settled it, fasten'd it, shackl'd it, fetter'd it, level'd it block'd it, tugg'd it, tew'd it, carry'd it, ebdasht it, beray'd it, parch'd it, mounted it, broach'd it, nick'd it, notch'd it, bespatter'd it, deck'd it, adorn'd it, trimm'd it, garnish'd it, gaged it, furnish'd it, boar'd it, pierc'd it, trap'd it, rumbled it, slid it down the Hill, and precipitated it from the very height of the Cranie ; then from the foot to the top (like another Sisyphus with his Stone) bore it up again, and every way so bang'd it and belabour'd it, that it was ten thousand to one he had not struck the bottom of it out.

Which when one of his Friends had seen, and ask'd him why he did so toil his Body, perplex his Spirit, and torment his Tub : The Philosopher's Answer was, That not being employed in any other Charge by the Republick, he thought it expedient to thunder and storm it so tempestuously upon his Tub, that amongst a People so fervently busie, and earnest at work, he alone might not seem a loitering Slug, and lazye Fellow. To the same Purpose may I say of my self,

> Tho' I be rid from Fear,
> I am not void of Care.

For perceiving no Account to be made of me, towards the Discharge of a Trust of any great Concernment, and considering that through all the Parts of this most noble Kingdom of France, both on this and the other side of the Mountains, every one is most diligently exercised and busied ; some, in the fortifying of their own Native Country, for its Defence ; others, in the repulsing of their Enemies by an offensive War ; and all this with a Policy so excellent, and such admirable Order, so manifestly profitable for the future, whereby France shall have its Frontiers most magnifically enlarged, and the Frenches assured of a long and well-grounded Peace ; that very little withholds me from the Opinion of good Heraclitus, which affirmeth War to be the Father of all good things ; and therefore do I believe that War is in Latin called *Bellum*, not by Antiphrasis, as some Patchers of old rusty Latin would have us to think ; because in War there is little Beauty to be seen, but absolutely and simply ; for that in War appeareth all that is good and graceful, and that by the Wars is purged out all manner of Wickedness and Deformity. For Proof whereof, the wise and pacifick Solomon could no better represent the unspeakable Perfection of the Divine Wisdom, than by comparing it to the due Disposure and Ranking of an Army in Battle Array, well provided and ordered.

Therefore, by reason of my weakness and Inability, being reputed by my Compatriots unfit for the Offensive part of Warfare ; and on the other side, being no way employed in matter of the Defensive, altho' it had been but to carry Burthens, fill Ditches, or break Clods, either whereof had been to me indifferent, I held it not a little disgraceful to be only an idle Spectator of so many valorous, eloquent and warlike Persons, who in the view and sight of all Europe act this notable Interlude or Tragi-Comedy, and not make some Effort towards the Performance of this, nothing at all remains for me to be done. In my opinion, little Honour is due to such as are meer Lookers on, liberal of their Eyes, and of their Purse parsimonious ; who conceal their Crowns, and hide their Silver, scratching their Head with one Finger like grumbling Puppies, gaping at the Flyes like Tythe Calves ; clapping down their Ears like Arcadian Asses at the Melody of Musicians, who with their very Countenances in the depth of silence, express their consent to the Prosopopeie.

AND ASK'D HIM WHY HE DID SO TOIL HIS BODY

THE THIRD BOOK OF DR. FRANCIS RABELAIS

Having made this Choice and Election, it seem'd to me that my Exercise therein would be neither unprofitable nor troublesome to any, whilst I should thus set a-going my Diogenical Tub, which is all that is left me safe from the Shipwrack of my former Misfortunes.

At this dingle dangle wagging of my Tub, what would you have me to do ? By the Virgin that tucks up her Sleeve, I know not as yet : Stay a little till I suck up a Draught of this Bottle ; it is my true and only Helicon ; it is my Caballine Fountain ; it is my sole Entousiasm. Drinking thus, I meditate, discourse, resolve and conclude. After that the Epilogue is made, I laugh, I write, I compose, and drink again. Ennius drinking, wrote ; and writing, drank. Aeschylus (if Plutarch in his Symposiacs merit any Faith) drank composing ; and drinking, composed. Homer never wrote fasting, and Cato never wrote till after he had drunk. These Passages I have brought before you, to the end you may not say that I live without the Example of Men well praised, and better prised. It is good and fresh enough, even (as if you would say) it is entring upon the Second Degree. God, the good God Sabaoth (that is to say, the God of Armies) be praised for it eternally. If you, after the same manner would take one great Draught, or two little ones, whilst you have your Gown about you, I truly find no kind of Inconveniency in it, provided you send up to God for all some small scantling of Thanks.

Since then my Luck or Destiny is such as you have heard, (for it is not for every body to go to Corinth) I am fully resolved to be so little idle and unprofitable, that I will set my self to serve the one and the other sort of People. Amongst the Diggers, Pioniers, and Rampire-builders, I will do as did Neptune and Apollo at Troy under Laomedon, or as did Renault of Mountauban in his latter days : I will serve the Masons, I'll set on the Pot to boil for the Bricklayers : and whilst the minced Meat is making ready at the sound of my small Pipe, I'll measure the muzzle of the musing Dotards. Thus did Amphion, with the Melody of his Harp, found, build, and finish the great and renowned City of Thebes.

For the Use of the Warriours, I am about to broach off new my Barrel to give them a taste, (which by two former Volumes of mine, if by the deceitfulness and falsehood of Printers they had not been jumbled, marr'd, and spoil'd, you would have very well relish'd) and draw unto them of the growth of our own trippery Pastimes, a gallant third-part of a Gallon, and consequently a jolly chearful Quart of Pantagruelick Sentences, which you may lawfully call (if you please) Diogenical ; and shall have me (seeing I cannot be their Fellow-Soldier) for their faithful Butler, refreshing and cheering, according to my little power, their return from the Alarms of the Enemy ; as also, for an indefatigable Extoller of their Martial Exploits and Glorious Atchievements. I shall not fail therein, *par lapathium acutum de dieu*, if Mars fail not in Lent, which the cunning Lecher (I warrant you) will be loth to do.

I remember nevertheless to have read, that Ptolemee the Son of Lagus one day, among the many Spoils and Booties, which by his Victories he had acquired, presenting to the Egyptians, in the open view of the People, a Bactrian Camel all black, and a party-colour'd Slave, in such sort, as that the one half of his Body was black, and the other white, not in partition of Breadth by the Diaphragma, as was that Woman consecrated to the Indian Venus, whom the Tyanean Philosopher did see between the River Hydaspes and Mount Caucasus, but in a perpendicular Dimension of Altitude; which were things never before that seen in Egypt. He expected, by the shew of these Novelties, to win the Love of the People. But what happened thereupon? At the production of the Camel they were all affrighted, and offended at the sight of the party-colour'd Man; Some scoff'd at him, as a detestible Monster brought forth by the Errour of Nature. In a word; of the hope which he had to please these Egyptians, and by such means to encrease the Affection which they naturally bore him, he was altogether frustrate and disappointed; understanding fully by their Deportments, that they took more pleasure and delight in things that were proper, handsom and perfect, than in mishapen, monstrous and ridiculous Creatures; since which time he had both the Slave and the Camel in such dislike, that very shortly thereafter, either through Negligence, or for want of ordinary Sustenance, they did exchange their Life with Death.

This Example, My Cake will be Dough, and for my Venus I shall have but some deformed Puppy, putteth me in a suspence between Hope and Fear, misdoubting that for the Contentment which I aim at, I will but reap what shall be most distasteful to me; instead of serving them, I shall but vex them, and offend them whom I purpose to exhilirate; resembling in this dubious adventure Euclion's Cook, so renowned by Plautus in his Pot; and by Ausonius in his Griphon, and by divers others; which Cook, for having by his scraping discover'd a Treasure, had his Hide well curry'd. Put the case I get no Anger by it, tho' formerly such things fell out, and the like may occur again: Yet, by Hercules, it will not. So I perceive in them all one and the same specifical Form, and the like individual Proprieties, which our Ancestors call'd Pantagruelism; by virtue whereof, they will bear with any thing that floweth from a good, free, and loyal Heart. I have seen them ordinarily take Good-will in part of Payment, and remain satisfied therewith, when one was not able to do better. Having dispatch'd this point, I return to my Barrel.

Up, my Lads to this Wine; spare it not: Drink, Boys, and trowl it off at full Bowls: If you do not think it good, let it alone. I am not like those officious and importunate Sots, who by Force, Outrage and Violence constrain an easie good-natur'd Fellow to whiffle, quaff, carouse, and what is worse. All honest Tiplers, all honest gouty Men, all such as are a-dry, coming to this little Barrel of mine, need not drink thereof, if it please them not: But if they have a mind to it, and that the Wine prove agreeable to the Tastes of their worshipful Worships, let them drink frankly, freely and boldly, with out paying any thing and welcome. This is my Decree, my Statute and Ordinance: And let none fear there shall be any want of Wine, as at the Marriage of Cana in Galilee; for how much soever you shall draw forth at the Faucet, so much shall I tun in at the Bung. Thus shall the Barrel remain inexhaustible; it hath a lively Spring, and perpetual Current. Such was the Beverage contained within the Cup of Tantalus, which was figuratively represented amongst the Bracman Sages. Such was in Iberia the Mountain of Salt, so highly written of by Cato. Such was the Branch of Gold consecrated to the subterranean Goddess, which Virgil treats of so sublimely. It is a true Cornu-copia of Merriment and Railery. If at any time it seem to you to be emptied to the very Lees, yet shall it not, for all that, be drawn wholly dry: Good Hope remains there at the bottom, as in Pandora's Bottle; and not Despair, as in the Punction of the Danaids. Remark well what I have said, and what manner of People they be whom I do invite; for to the end that none be deceived, I (in imitation of Lucilius, who did protest that he wrote only to his own Tarentias and Consentious) have not pierced this Vessel for any else, but you honest Men, who are Drinkers of the First Edition, and Gouty Blades of the highest degree. The great Dorophages, Bribe-mongers, have (on their hands) Occupation enough, and enough on the hooks, for their Venison. There may they follow their Prey; here is no Garbage for them. You Pettifoggers, Garbellers, and Masters of Chicanery, speak not to me, I beseech you, in the Name of, and for the Reverence you bear to the Four Hips that ingender'd you, and to the Quickning Peg which at that time conjoined them. As for Hypocrites, much less; altho' they were all of them unsound in Body, pockify'd, scurfie, furnish'd with unquenchable Thirst, and insatiable Eating; because indeed they are not of good, but of evil, and of that evil from which we daily pray to God to deliver us. And albeit we see them sometimes counterfeit Devotion, yet never did Old Age make pretty Moppet. Hence Mastiffs, Dogs in a Doublet; get you behind, aloof Villains, out of my Sunshine; Currs, to the Devil. Do you jog hither, wagging your Tails, to pant at my Wine, and bepiss my Barrel? Look here is the Cudgel, which Diogenes, in his last Will, ordained to be set by him after his Death, for beating away, crushing the Reins, and breaking the Backs of these Bustuary Hobgoblins, and Cerberian Hell-Hounds. Pack you hence therefore, you Hyppocrites, to your Sheep-dogs; Get you gone, you Dissemblers, to the Devil. Hey! What, are you there yet? I renounce my part of Papimanie. If I snatch you, Grr, Grrr, Grrrrrr. Avant, Avant! Will you not be gone? May you never shit till you be soundly lash'd with Stirrup-leather, never piss but by the Strapado, nor be otherways warmed, than by the Bastinado.

THE THIRD BOOK

CHAPTER I

How Pantagruel transported a Colony of Utopians into Dypsodie

PANTAGRUEL having wholly subdued the Land of Dypsodie, transported thereunto a Colony of Utopians, to the number of 9876543210 Men, besides the Women and little Children, Artificers of all Trades, and Professors of all Sciences; to people, cultivate and improve that Country, which otherways was ill inhabited, and in the greatest part thereof but a meer Desert and Wilderness; and did transport them so much for the excessive multitude of Men and Women which were in Utopia multiplied (for number) like Grashoppers upon the face of the Land. You understand well enough, nor is it needful further to explain it to you, that the Utopian Men had so rank and fruitful Genitories, and that the Utopian Women carried Matrixes so ample, so glutonous, so tenaciously retentive, and so Architectonically cellulated, that at the end of every Ninth Month, Seven Children at the least (what Male, what Female) were brought forth by every marry'd Woman, in imitation of the People of Israel in Egypt, if Anthony de Lyra be to be trusted. Nor yet was this Transplantation made so much for the Fertility of the Soil, the Wholsomness of the Air, or Commodity of the Country of Dypsodie, as to retain that Rebellious People within the Bounds of their Duty and Obedience, by this new Transport of his ancient and most faithful Subjects, who from all time out of mind, never knew, acknowledged, owned or served any other Sovereign Lord but him; and who likewise from the very instant of their Birth, as soon as they were entred into this World, had, with the Milk of their Mothers and Nurses, suck'd in the Sweetness, Humanity and Mildness of his Government, to which they were all of them so nourished and habituated, that there was nothing surer, than that they would sooner abandon their Lives, than swerve from this singular and primitive Obedience naturally due to their Prince, whithersoever they should be dispersed or removed.

And not only should they, and their Children successively descending from their Blood, be such, but also would keep and maintain in this same Fealty, and obsequious Observance, all the Nations lately annexed to his Empire : Which so truly came to pass, that therein he was not disappointed of his Intent. For if the Utopians were, before their Transplantation thither, dutiful and faithful Subjects, the Dypsodes, after some few days conversing with them, were every whit as (if not more) loyal than they ; and that by virtue of I know not what natural Fervency incident to all Human Creatures at the beginning of any labour wherein they took delight ; solemnly attesting the Heavens, and Supreme Intelligences, of their being only sorry, that no sooner unto their knowledge had arrived the great Renown of the good Pantagruel.

Remark therefore here (honest Drinkers) that the manner of preserving and retaining Countries newly conquer'd, in Obedience, is not (as hath been the erroneous Opinion of some Tyrannical Spirits, to their own Detriment and Dishonour) to pillage, plunder, force, spoil, trouble, oppress, vex, disquiet, ruin and destroy the People, ruling, governing, and keeping them in awe with Rods of Iron ; and (in a word) eating and devouring them, after the fashion that Homer calls an Unjust and Wicked King, $\theta\eta\mu\delta\beta\rho\rho\nu$, that is to say, a Devourer of his People.

I will not bring you, to this Purpose, the Testimony of ancient Writers ; it shall suffice, to put you in mind of what your Fathers have seen thereof, and your selves too, if you be not very Babes. New-born, they must be given suck to, rock'd in a Cradle, and dandled. Trees newly planted must be supported, under-propp'd, strengthned and defended against all Tempests, Mischiefs, Injuries and Calamities. And one lately saved from a long and dangerous Sickness, and new upon his Recovery, must be forborn, spared and cherished, in such sort, that they may harbour in their own Breasts this Opinion, That there is not in the World a King or a Prince, who does not desire fewer Enemies, and more Friends.

Thus Osiris, the great King of the Egyptians, conquer'd almost the whole Earth, not so much by Force of Arms, as by easing the People of their Troubles, teaching them how to live well and honestly, giving them good Laws, and using them with all possible Affability, Courtesy, Gentleness and Liberality :

Therefore was he by all Men deservedly entituled, Great King Evergetes, (that is to say, Benefactor), which Style he obtained by virtue of the Command of Jupiter to Pamyla.

And in effect, Hesiod, in his Hierarchy, placed the good Dæmons (call them Angels, if you will, or Geniuses) as Intercessors and Mediators betwixt the Gods and Men, they being of a degree inferiour to the Gods, but superiour to Men; and for that through their Hands the Riches and Benefits we get from Heaven are dealt to us; and that they are continually doing us good, and still protecting us from evil. He saith, that they exercise the Offices of Kings; because to do always good, and never ill, is an Act most singularly Royal.

Just such another was the Emperor of the Universe, Alexander the Macedonian. After this manner was Hercules Sovereign Possessor of the whole Continent, relieving Men from monstrous Oppressions, Exactions and Tyrannies; governing them with Discretion, maintaining them in Equity and Justice, instructing them with seasonable Policies and wholsom Laws, convenient for, and suitable to the Soil, Climate and Disposition of the Country, supplying where was wanting, abating what was superfluous, and pardoning all that was past, with a sempiternal forgetfulness of all preceding Offences, as was the Amnestie of the Athenians, when by the Prowess, Valour and Industry of Thrasybulus the Tyrants were exterminated; afterwards at Rome by Cicero exposed, and renewed under the Emperor Aurelian. These are the Philtres, Allurements, Jynges, Inveiglements, Baits and Enticements of Love, by the means whereof that may be peaceably revived, which was painfully acquired. Nor can a Conqueror reign more happily, whether he be a Monarch, Emperor, King, Prince or Philosopher, than by making his Justice to second his Valour. His Valour shows it self in Victory and Conquest; his Justice will appeal in the Good-will and Affection of the People, when he maketh Laws, publisheth Ordinances, establisheth Religion, and doth what is right to every one, as the noble Poet Virgil writes of Octavian Augustus:

Victorque volentes
Per populos dat jura.

Therefore is it that Homer, in his *Iliads* calleth a good Prince and great King, κοσμήτορα λαῶν, that is, The Ornament of the People.

Such was the Consideration of Numa Pompilius the Second King of the Romans, a just Politician and wise Philosopher, when he ordained that to God Terminus, on the Day of his Festival call'd Terminales, nothing should be sacrificed that had died ; teaching us thereby, that the Bounds, Limits and Frontiers of Kingdoms should be guarded, and preserved in Peace, Amity and Meekness, without polluting our hands with Blood and Robbery : Who doth otherways, shall not only lose what he hath gained, but also be loaded with this Scandal and Reproach, That he is an unjust and wicked Purchaser, and his Acquests perish with him ; *Juxta illud malæ parta, male dilabuntur.* And altho' during his whole Life-time, he should have peaceable Possession thereof ; yet if what hath been so acquired moulder away in the Hands of his Heirs, the same Opproby, Scandal and Imputation will be charged upon the Defunct, and his Memory remain accursed, for his unjust and unwarrantable Conquest ; *Juxta illud, de male quæsitis vix gaudet tertius hæres.*

Remark likewise, Gentlemen, you Gouty Feoffees, in this main Point worthy of your Observation, how, by these means, Pantagruel of one Angel made two ; which was a Contingency opposite to the Council of Charlemaine, who made two Devils of one, when he transplanted the Saxons into Flanders, and the Flemins into Saxony. For not being able to keep in such Subjection the Saxons, whose Dominion he had joined to the Empire, but that ever and anon they would break forth into open Rebellion, if he should casually be drawn into Spain, or other remote Kingdom : He caused them to be brought unto his own Country of Flanders, the Inhabitants whereof did naturally obey him ; and transported the Haynaults and Flemens, his ancient loving Subjects, into Saxony, not mistrusting their Loyalty, now that they were transplanted into a strange Land. But it hapned that the Saxons persisted in their Rebellion and primitive Obstinacy ; and the Flemens dwelling in Saxony did imbibe the stubborn Manners and Conditions of the Saxons.

CHAPTER II

*How Panurge was made Laird of Salmygondin in Dypsodie,
and did waste his Revenue before it came in*

WHILST Pantagruel was giving Order for the Government of all
Dypsodie, he assigned to Panurge the Lairdship of Salmygondin,
which was yearly worth 6789106789 Royals of certain Rent,
besides the uncertain Revenue of the Locusts and Periwinkles,
amounting one year with another to the value of 435768, or
2435769 French Crowns of Berry. Sometimes it did amount to
1230554321 Seraphs when it was a good Year, and that Locusts
and Periwinkles were in request ; but that was not every Year.

Now his Worship, the new Laird, husbanded this his Estate
so providently well and prudently, that in less than fourteen
days he wasted and dilapidated all the certain and uncertain
Revenue of his Lairdship for three whole Years : Yet did not
he properly dilapidate it, as you might say, in founding of
Monasteries, building of Churches, erecting of Colleges, and
setting up of Hospitals, or casting his Bacon-Flitches to the
Dogs ; but spent it in a thousand little Banquets and jolly
Collations, keeping open House for all Comers and Goers ; yea,
to all good Fellows, young Girls, and pretty Wenches ; felling
Timber, burning the great Logs for the sale of the Ashes,
borrowing Money before-hand, buying dear, selling cheap, and
eating his Corn (as it were) whilst it was but Grass.

Pantagruel being advertised of this his Lavishness, was in
good sooth no way offended at the matter, angry nor sorry ;

for I once told you, and again tell it you, that he was the best, little, great Good-man that ever girded a Sword to his Side ; he took all things in good part, and interpreted every Action to the best Sense : He never vexed nor disquieted himself with the least pretence of Dislike to any thing ; because he knew that he must have most grosly abandoned the Divine Mansion of Reason, if he had permitted his Mind to be never so little grieved, afflicted or altered at any occasion whatsoever. For all the Goods that the Heaven covereth, and that the Earth containeth in all their Dimensions and Heighth, Depth, Breadth, and Length, are not of so much worth, as that we should for them disturb or disorder our Affections, trouble or perplex our Senses or Spirits.

He drew only Panurge aside, and then making to him a sweet Remonstrance and mild Admonition, very gently represented before him in strong Arguments, That if he should continue in such an unthrifty course of Living, and not become a better Mesnagier, it would prove altogether impossible for him, or at least hugely difficult at any time to make him Rich. Rich ! answered Panurge, Have you fixed your Thoughts there ? Have you undertaken the Task to enrich me in this World ? Set your Mind to live merrily in the Name of God and good Folks, let no other Cark nor Care be harboured within the Sacro sanctified Domicile of your Celestial Brain. May the Calmness and Tranquility thereof be never incommodated with, or over-shadowed by any frowning Clouds of sullen Imaginations and displeasing Annoyance. For if you live joyful, merry, jocund and glad, I cannot be but rich enough. Every body cries up thrift, thrift, and good Husbandry ; but many speak of Robin Hood that never shot in his Bow ; and talk of that Vertue of Mesnagery, who know not what belong to it. It is by me that they must be advised. From me therefore take this Advertisement and Information, that what is imputed to me for a Vice, hath been done in imitation of the University and Parliament of Paris, places in which is to be found the true Spring and Source of the lively Idea of Pantheology, and all manner of Justice. Let him be counted an Heretick that doubteth thereof, and doth not firmly believe it : Yet they in one day eat up their Bishop, or the Revenue of the Bishoprick (is it not all one) for a whole year ; yea, sometimes for two. This is done on the day he makes his Entry, and is installed : Nor is there any place for an Excuse ; for he cannot avoid it, unless he would be houted at and stoned for his Parsimony.

It hath been also esteemed an act flowing from the Habit of the Four Cardinal Vertues. Of Prudence in borrowing Money before-hand ; for none knows what may fall out ; who is able to tell if the World shall last yet three years ? But although it should continue longer, is there any Man so foolish, as to have the Confidence to promise himself three years ?

> What fool so confident to say
> That he shall live one other day ?

Of Commutative Justice, in buying dear (I say upon Trust) and selling Goods cheap, (that is, for ready Money) what says Cato in his Book of Husbandry to this purpose ? The Father of a Family (says he) must be a perpetual Seller ; by which means it is impossible but that at last he shall become rich, if he have of vendible Ware enough still ready for Sale.

Of Distributive Justice it doth partake, in giving Entertainment to good (remark good) and gentle Fellows, whom fortune had Shipwrack'd (like Ulysses) upon the Rock of a hungry Stomach without provision of Sustenance : And likewise to the good (remark the good) and young Wenches : For according to the Sentence of Hippocrates, Youth is impatient of Hunger, chiefly if it be vigorous, lively, frolick, brisk, stirring and bouncing ; which wanton Lasses willingly, and heartily devote themselves to the pleasure of Honest Men ; and are in so far both Platonick and Ciceronian, that they do acknowledge their being born into this World, not to be for themselves alone, but that in their proper Persons their Acquaintance may claim one share, and their Friends another.

The vertue of Fortitude appears therein by the cutting down and overthrowing of the great Trees, like a second Milo making Havock of the dark Forests, which did serve only to furnish Dens, Caves, and shelter to Wolves, with Boars and Foxes ; and afford Receptacles, withdrawing Corners and Refuges to Robbers, Thieves and Murtherers ; lurking holes and sculking places for Cut-throat Assassinators ; secret obscure shops for Coiners of false Money, and safe Retreats for Hereticks, laying them even and level with the plain Champion Fields and pleasant Heathy Ground, at the sound of the Hautbois and Bagpipes playing, reeks with the high and stately Timber, and preparing Seats and Benches for the Eve of the dreadful day of Judgment.

I gave thereby proof of my Temperance in eating my Corn

whilst it was but Grass, like an Hermit feeding upon Sallets and Roots, and so affranchising my self from the Yoak of sensual Appetites to the utter disclaiming of their Sovereignty, I might the better reserve somewhat in store, for the relief of the lame, blind, cripple, maimed, needy, poor and wanting Wretches.

In taking this course I save the expence of the weed-grubbers, who gain Money; of the Reapers in Harvest-time, who drink lustily, and without water; of Gleaners, who will expect their Cakes and Bannocks; of Threshers, who leave no Garlick, Scallions, Leeks nor Onyons in our Gardens (by the authority of Thestilis in Virgil); and of the Millers, who are generally Thieves; and of the Bakers, who are little better; is this small Saving or Frugality? besides the mischief and damage of the Field-mice, the decay of Barns, and the destruction usually made by Weesils and other Vermin.

Of Corn in the Blade. You may make good Green-sauce of a light concoction, and easie Digestion, which recreates the Brain, and exhilerates the Animal Spirits, rejoyceth the Sight, openeth the Appetite, delighteth the Taste, comforteth the Heart, tickleth the Tongue, cheareth the Countenance, striking a fresh and lively Colour, strengthning the Muscles, tempers the Blood, disburthens the Midrif, refresheth the Liver, disobstructs the Spleen, easeth the Kidneys, suppleth the Reins, quickens the Joynts of the Back, cleanseth the Urine-Conduits, dilates the Spermatick Vessels, shortens the Cremasters, purgeth the Bladder, puffeth up the Genitories, correcteth the Prepuce, hardens the Nut, and rectifies that Member. It will make you have a current Belly to trot, fart, dung, piss, sneeze, cough, spit, belch, spew, yawn, snuff, blow, breath, snort, sweat, and set taunt your Robin, with a thousand other rare Advantages. I understand you very well (says Pantagruel) you would thereby infer, that those of a mean Spirit and shallow Capacity, have not the skill to spend much in a short time: You are not the first in whose conceit that Heresie hath entred: Nero maintained it, and above all Mortals admired most his Unkle Caius Caligula, for having in a few days, by a most wonderful pregnant Invention totally spent all the Goods and Patrimony which Tiberius had left him.

But instead of observing the Sumptuous Supper-curbing Laws of the Romans, to wit, the Orchia, the Fannia, the Didia, the Licinia, the Cornelia, the Lepidiana, the Antia, and of the Corinthians; by which they were inhibited, under pain of great

Punishment, not to spend more in one year, than their annual Revenue did amount to. You have offered up the Oblation of Protervia, which was with the Romans such a Sacrifice as the Paschal Lamb was amongst the Jews, wherein all that was eatable was to be eaten, and the remainder to be thrown into the fire, without reserving anything for the next day. I may very justly say of you, as Cato did of Albidius, who after that he had by a most extravagant Expence wasted all the Means and Possessions he had to one only House, he fairly set it on Fire, that he might the better say, *Consummatum est.* Even just as since his time St. Thomas Aquinas did when he had eaten up the whole lamprey, although there was no necessity in it.

CHAPTER III

How Panurge praiseth the Deblors and Borrowers

But, quoth Pantagruel, when will you be out of Debt ? At the next ensuing Term of the Greek Calends, answered Panurge, when all the World shall be content, and that it be your fate to become your own Heir. The Lord forbid that I should be out of Debt, as if, indeed, I could not be trusted. Who leaves not some Leaven over Night, will hardly have Past the next Morning.

Be still indebted to some body or other, that there may be some body always to pray for you ; that the Giver of all good things may grant unto you a blessed, long, and prosperous Life, fearing if Fortune should deal crosly with you, that it might be his chance to come short of being paid by you ; he will always

WHO LENDETH NOTHING IS AN UGLY AND WICKED CREATURE

speak good of you in every Company, ever and anon purchase
new Creditors unto you ; to the end that through their means
you may make a shift by borrowing from Peter to pay Paul,
and with other Folks Earth fill up his Ditch. When of old in
the Region of the Gauls, by the Institution of the Druids, the
Servants, Slaves and Bondmen were burnt quick at the Funerals
and Obsequies of their Lords and Masters ; had not they fear
enough, think you, that their Lords and Masters should die ?
For per force, they were to die with them for Company. Did
not they uncessantly send up their Supplications to their great
God Mercury, as likewise unto Dis the Father of Wealth, to
lengthen out their Days, and preserve them long in Health ?
Were not they very careful to entertain them well, punctually
to look unto them, and to attend them faithfully and circumspectly ? For by those means were they to live together at
least until the hour of Death. Believe me, your Creditors with
a more fervent Devotion will beseech Almighty God to prolong
your Life, they being of nothing more afraid than that you
should die ; for that they are more concerned for the Sleeve
than the Arm, and love Silver better than their own Lives ; as
it evidently appeareth by the Usurers of Landerousse, who not
long since hanged themselves, because the price of the Corn
and Wines was fallen, by the return of a gracious Season.

To this Pantagruel answering nothing, Panurge went on in
his Discourse, saying, Truly, and in good sooth (Sir,) when I
ponder my Destiny aright, and think well upon it, you put me
shrewdly to my Plunges, and have me at a Bay in twitting me
with the Reproach of my Debts and Creditors ; And yet did I,
in this only respect and consideration of being a Debtor,
esteem my self worshipful, reverend and formidable. For
against the Opinion of most Philosophers, that of nothing
ariseth nothing ; yet, without having bottomed on so much as
that which is called the First Matter, did I out of nothing become
such Maker and Creator, that I have created—what ? a gay
number of fair and jolly Creditors. Nay, Creditors (I will
maintain it, even to the very Fire it self exclusively) are fair
and goodly Creatures. Who lendeth nothing is an ugly and
wicked Creature, and an accursed imp of the Infernal Old Nick.
And there is made, what ? Debts : A thing most precious and
dainty, of great Use and Antiquity. Debts, (I say) surmount-
ing the number of Syllables which may result from the Combinations of all the Consonants, with each of the Vowels heretofore projected, reckoned and calculated by the Noble Xeno-

crates. To judge of the perfection of debtors by the Numerosity of their Creditors, is the readiest way for entring into the Mysteries of Practical Arithmetick.

You can hardly imagine how glad I am, when every Morning I perceive my self environed and surrounded with Brigades of Creditors ; humble, fawning, and full of their Reverences : And whilst I remark, that, as I look more favourably upon, and give a chearfuller Countenance to one than to another, the Fellow thereupon buildeth a conceit that he shall be the first dispatched, and the foremost in the Date of Payment ; and he valueth my Smiles at the rate of ready Money. It seemeth unto me, that I then act and personate the God of the Passion of Saumure, accompanied with his Angels and Cherubims.

These are my Flatterers, my Soothers, my Claw-backs, my Smoothers, my Parasites, my Saluters, my givers of good Morrows, and perpetual Orators ; which makes me verily think, that the supreamest height of Heroick Vertue, described by Hesiode, consisteth in being a Debtor, wherein I held the first Degree in my Commencement. Which Dignity, though all Human Creatures seem to aim at, and aspire thereto, few nevertheless, because of the Difficulties in the way, and Incumbrances of hard Passages are able to reach it, as is easily perceivable by the ardent desire and vehement longing harboured in the Breast of every one, to be still creating more Debts, and new Creditors.

Yet doth it not lie in the power of every one to be a Debtor. To acquire Creditors is not at the disposure of each Man's Arbitriment. You nevertheless would deprive me of this sublime Felicity. You ask me when I will be out of Debt. Well, to go yet further on, and possibly worse in your Conceit, may Sanct Bablin, the good Sanct, snatch me, if I have not all my Life-time held Debt to be as an Union or Conjunction of the Heavens with the Earth, and the whole Cement whereby the Race of Mankind is kept together ; yea, of such Vertue and Efficacy, that, I say, the whole Progeny of Adam would very suddenly perish without it. Therefore, perhaps, I do not think amiss, when I repute it to be the great soul of the Universe, which (according to the Opinion of the Academicks) vivifyeth all manner of things. In Confirmation whereof, that you may the better believe it to be so, represent unto your self, without any prejudicacy of Spirit, in a clear and serene Fancy, the Idea and Form of some other world than this ; take if you please, and lay hold on the thirtieth of those which the Philosopher Methrodorus did enumerate, wherein it is to be supposed there is no Debtor or Creditor, that is to say, a World without Debts.

There amongst the Planets will be no regular Course, all will be in disorder. Jupiter reckoning himself to be nothing indebted unto Saturn, will go near to detrude him out of his Sphere, and with the Homerick Chain will he like to hang up the Intelligences, Gods, Heavens, Dæmons, Heroes, Devils, Earth and Sea together with the other Elements. Saturn no doubt combining with Mars will reduce that so disturbed World into a Chaos of Confusion.

Mercury then would be no more subjected to the other Planets ; he would scorn to be any longer their Camillus, as he was of old termed in the Hetrurian Tongue ; for it is to be imagined that he is no way a Debtor to them.

Venus will be no more Venerable, because she shall have lent nothing. The Moon will remain bloody and obscure : For to what end should the Sun impart unto her any of his Light ? He owed her nothing. Nor yet will the Sun shine upon the Earth, nor the Stars send down any good Influence, because the Terrestrial Globe hath desisted from sending up their wonted Nourishment by Vapours and Exhalations, where-with Heraclitus said the Stoicks proved Cicero maintained they were cherished and alimented. There would likeways be in such a World no manner of Symbolization, Alteration, nor Transmutation amongst the Elements ; for the one will not esteem it self obliged to the other, as having borrowed nothing at all from it. Earth then will not become Water, Water will not be changed into Air, of Air will be made no Fire, and Fire will afford no Heat unto the Earth ; the Earth will produce nothing but Monsters, Titans, Giants ; no Rain will descend upon it, nor Light shine thereon ; no Wind will blow there, nor will there be in it any Summer or Harvest. Lucifer will break loose, and issuing forth of the depth of Hell, accompanied with his Furies, Fiends and Horned Devils, will go about to unnestle and drive out of Heaven all the Gods, as well of the greater as of the lesser Nations. Such a World without lending, will be no better than a Dog-kennel, a place of Contention and Wrangling, more unruly and irregular than that of the Rector of Paris ; a Devil of an Hurly-burly, and more disordered con-fusion, than that of the Plagues of Douay. Men will not then salute one another ; it will be but lost labour to expect Aid or Succour from any, or to cry, Fire, Water, Murther, for none will put to their helping Hand. Why ? He lent no Money,

LUCIFER WILL BREAK LOOSE

335

there is nothing due to him. No body is concerned in his Burning, in his Shipwrack, in his Ruine, or in his Death; and that because he hitherto had lent nothing, and would never thereafter have lent any thing. In short, Faith, Hope and Charity would be quite banish'd from such a world; for Men are born to relieve and assist one another; and in their stead should succeed and be introduced Defiance, Disdain and Rancour, with the most execrable Troop of all Evils, all Imprecations and all Miseries. Whereupon you will think, and that not amiss, that Pandora had there spilt her unlucky Bottle. Men unto Men will be Wolves, Hobthrushers and Goblins, (as were Lycaon, Bellorophon, Nebuchadonosor), Plunderers, High-way Robbers, Cut-throats, Rapperees, Murtherers, Poysoners, Assassinators, lewd, wicked, malevolent, pernicious Haters, set against every body, like to Ismael, Metabus, or Timon the Athenian, who for that cause was named Misanthropos; in such sort, that it would prove much more easie in Nature to have Fish entertained in the Air, and Bullocks fed in the bottom of the Ocean, than to support or tolerate a rascally Rabble of People that will not Lend. These Fellows (I vow) do I hate with a perfect Hatred; and if conform to the pattern of this grievous, peevish and perverse World which lendeth nothing, you figure and liken the little World, which is Man, you will find in him a terrible justling Coyle and Clutter: The Head will not lend the sight of his Eyes to guide the Feet and Hands; the Legs will refuse to bear up the Body; the Hands will leave off working any more for the rest of the Members; the Heart will be weary of its continual Motion for the beating of the Pulse, and will no longer lend his Assistance; the Lungs will withdraw the use of their Bellows; the Liver will desist from conveying any more Blood through the Veins for the good of the whole; the Bladder will not be indebted to the Kidneys, so that the Urine thereby will be totally stopped. The Brains, in the interim, considering this unnatural course, will fall into a raving Dotage, and with-hold all feeling from the Sinews, and Motion from the Muscles: Briefly, in such a World without Order and Array, owing nothing, lending nothing, and borrowing nothing, you would see a more dangerous Conspiration than that which Æsope exposed in his Apologue. Such a World will perish undoubtedly; and not only perish, but perish very quickly. Were it Æsculapius himself, his Body would immediately rot, and the chafing Soul full of Indignation takes its flight to all the Devils of Hell after my Money.

CHAPTER IV

Panurge continueth his Discourse in the praise of
Borrowers and Lenders

ON the contrary, be pleased to represent unto your Fancy another World, wherein every one lendeth, and every one oweth, all are Debtors, and all Creditors. O how great will that Harmony be, which shall thereby result from the regular Motions of the Heavens! Methinks I hear it every whit as well as ever Plato did. What Sympathy will there be amongst the Elements! O how delectable then unto Nature will be our own Works and Productions? Whilst Ceres appeareth loaden with Corn, Bacchus with Wines, Flora with Flowers, Pomona with Fruits, and Juno fair in a clear Air, wholsom and pleasant: I lose my self in this high Contemplation.

Then will among the Race of Mankind Peace, Love, Benevolence, Fidelity, Tranquility, Rest, Banquets, Feastings, Joy, Gladness, Gold, Silver, single Money, Chains, Rings, with other Ware, and Chaffer of that nature be found to trot from hand to hand; no Suits at Law, no Wars, no Strife, Debate, nor Wrangling: none will be there a Usurer, none will be there a Pinch-penny, a Scrape-good Wretch, or churlish hard-hearted Refuser. Good God! Will not this be the Golden Age in the Reign of Saturn? The true Idea of the Olympick Regions, wherein all Vertues cease; Charity alone ruleth, governeth, domineereth and triumpheth. All will be fair and goodly People there, all just and vertuous.

O happy World! O People of that World most happy! Yea, thrice and four times blessed is that People! I think in very deed that I am amongst them, and swear to you, by my good Forsooth, that if this glorious aforesaid World had a Pope, abounding with Cardinals, that so he might have the Association of a Sacred College, in the space of very few years you should be sure to see the Sancts much thicker in the Roll, more numerous, wonder-working and mirifick, more Services, more Vows, more Staves and Wax-Candles than are all those in the Nine Bishopricks of Britany, St. Yves only excepted. Consider (Sir) I pray you, how the noble Patelin, having a mind to deify, and extol even to the Third Heavens the Father of William Josseaume, said no more but this, And he did lend his Goods to those who were desirous of them.

O the fine Saying! Now let our Microcosm be fancied conform to this Model in all its Members; lending, borrowing and owing, (that is to say) according to its own Nature: For Nature hath not to any other end created man, but to owe, borrow and lend; no greater is the Harmony amongst the Heavenly Spheres, than that which shall be found in its well-ordered Policy. The Intention of the Founder of this Microcosm is, to have a Soul therein to be entertained, which is lodged there, as a Guest with its Host, it may live there for a while. Life consisteth in Blood, Blood is the Seat of the Soul; therefore the chiefest Work of Microcosm is, to be making Blood continually.

At this Forge are exercised all the Members of the Body; none is exempted from Labour, each operates apart, and doth its proper Office. And such is their Hierarchy, that perpetually the one borrows from the other, the one lends the other, and the one is the others Debtor. The Stuff and Matter convenient which Nature giveth to be turned into Blood is Bread and Wine. All kind of nourishing Victuals is understood to be comprehended in these two, and from hence in the Gothish Tongue is called Companage. To find out this Meat and Drink, to prepare and boil it, the Hands are put to Work, the Feet do walk and bear up the whole Bulk of the Corporal Mass; the Eyes guide and conduct all; the Appetite in the Orifice of the Stomach, by Means of little sowrish black Humour (called Melancholy) which is transmitted thereto from the Milt, giveth warning to shut in the Food. The Tongue doth make the first Essay, and tastes it; the Teeth do chaw it, and the Stomach doth receive, digest and chylifie it; the Mesaraick Veins suck out of it what is good and fit, leaving behind the Excrements, which are, through special Conduits for that purpose, voided by an expulsive Faculty; thereafter it is carried to the Liver, where it being changed again, it by the vertue of that new Transmutation becomes Blood. What Joy, conjecture you, will then be found amongst those Officers, when they see this Rivolet of Gold, which is their sole Restorative? No greater is the Joy of Alchimists, when after long Travel, Toil and Expence, they see in their Furnaces the Transmutation: Then is it that every Member doth prepare it self, and strive a-new to purifie and to refine this Treasure. The Kidneys through the emulgent Veins draw that aquosity from thence which you call Urine, and there send it away through the Ureters to be slipt downwards; where, in a lower Receptacle, and proper for it, to wit, (the Bladder) it is kept, and stayeth there until an opportunity to void it out in his due time. The Spleen draweth from the Blood its Terrestrial part, viz., The Grounds, Lees or thick Substance setled in the bottom thereof, which you term Melancholy: The Bottle of the Gall substracts from thence all the superfluous Choler; whence it is brought to another Shop or Work-house to be yet better purified and fined, that is, the Heart, which by its agitation of Diastolick and Systolick Motions so neatly subtilizeth and inflames it, that in the right side Ventricle it is brought to perfection, and through the Veins is sent to all the Members; each parcel of the Body draws it then unto its self, and after its own fashion is cherished and alimented by it: Feet, Hands, Thighs, Arms, Eyes, Ears, Back, Breast, yea, all; and then it is, that who before were Lenders, now become Debtors. The Heart doth in its left side Ventricle so thinnifie the Blood, that it thereby obtains the Name of Spiritual; which being sent through the Arteries to all the Members of the Body, serveth to warm and winnow the other Blood which runneth through the Veins: The Lights never cease with its Lappets and Bellows to cool and refresh it; in acknowledgment of which good the Heart through the Arterial Vein imparts unto it the choicest of its Blood: At last it is made so fine and subtle within the Rete Mirabilis, that thereafter those Animal Spirits are framed and composed of it; by means whereof the Imagination, Discourse, Judgment, Resolution, Deliberation, Ratiocination and Memory have their Rise, Actings and Operations.

Cops body, I sink, I drown, I perish, I wander astray, and quite fly out of my self, when I enter into the Consideration of the profound Abyss of this World, thus lending, thus owing. Believe me, it is a Divine thing to lend, to owe an Heroick Vertue. Yet is not this all; this little world thus lending, owing and borrowing, is so good and charitable, that no sooner is the above-specified Alimentation finished, but that it forth-with projecteth, and hath already forecast, how it shall lend to those who are not as yet born, and by that Loan endeavour, what it may, to eternize it self, and multiply in Images like the Pattern, that is, Children. To this end every Member doth of the choicest and most precious of its Nourishment, pare and cut off a Portion, then instantly dispatcheth it downwards to that Place, where Nature hath prepared for it very fit Vessels and Receptacles, through which descending to the Genitories by long Ambages, Circuits and Flexuosities, it receiveth a Competent Form, and Rooms apt enough both in the Man and Woman for the future Conservation and perpetuating of Human Kind. All this is done by Loans and Debts of the one unto the other; and hence have we this word, the Debt of Marriage. Nature doth reckon Pain to the Refuser, with a most grievous Vexation to his Members, and an outragious Fury amidst his Senses. But on the other part, to the Lender a set Reward, accompanied with Pleasure, Joy, Solace, Mirth, and merry Glee.

CHAPTER V

How Pantagruel altogether abhorreth the Debtors and Borrowers

I UNDERSTAND you very well, (quoth Pantagruel) and take you to be very good at Topicks, and thoroughly affectioned to your own Cause : But preach it up, and patrocinate it ; prattle on it, and defend it as much as you will, even from hence to the next Whitsontide, if you please so to do ; yet, in the end, will you be astonish'd to find how you shall have gained no ground at all upon me, nor perswaded me, by your fair Speeches and smooth Talk, to enter never so little into the Thraldom of Debt. You shall owe to none (saith the Holy Apostle) any thing save Love, Friendship, and a mutual Benevolence.

You serve me here I confess, with fine Graphides and Diatyposes, Descriptions and Figures, which truly please me very well : But let me tell you, if you will represent unto your Fancy an impudent blustering Bully, and an importunate Borrower, entring afresh and newly into a Town already advertised of his Manners, you shall find that at his Ingress the Citizens will be more hideously affrighted and amazed, and in a greater terror and fear, dread and trembling, than if the Pest it self should step into it in the very same Garb and Accoutrement wherein the Tyanæan Philosopher found it within the City of Ephesus. And I am fully confirmed in the Opinion, that the Persians erred not, when they said, That the second Vice was to Lye, the first being that of owing Money. For in very truth,

Debts and Lying are ordinarily joined together. I will never-theless not from hence infer, that none must owe any thing, or lend any thing. For who so rich can be that sometimes may not owe ? or who can be so poor, that sometimes may not lend ?

Let the Occasion notwithstanding in that Case (as Plato very wisely saith, and ordaineth in his Laws) be such, that none be permitted to draw any Water out of his Neighbour's Well, until first they, by continual digging and delving into their own proper Ground, shall have hit upon a kind of Potter's Earth, which is called Ceramite, and there had found no Source or drop of Water ; for that sort of Earth, by reason of its Substance, which is fat, strong, firm and close ; so retaineth its Humidity, that it doth not easily evaporate it by any outward excursion or evaporation.

In good sooth, it is a great shame to chuse rather to be still borrowing in all places from every one, than to work and win. Then only, in my judgment, should one lend, when the diligent, toiling and industrious Person is no longer able by his Labour to make any Purchase unto himself or otherwise, when by mischance he hath suddenly fallen into an unexpected loss of his Goods.

Howsoever, let us leave this Discourse, and from hence-forwards do not hang upon Creditors, nor tie your self to them ; I make account, for the time past, to rid you freely of them, and from their bondage to deliver you. The least I should in this Point, (quoth Panurge) is to thank you, tho' it be the most I can do : And if Gratitude and Thanksgiving be to be estimated and prized by the Affection of the Benefactor, that is to be done infinitely and sempiternally ; for the love which you bear me of your own accord and free grace, without any merit of mine, goeth far beyond the reach of any price or value ; it transcends all weight, all number, all measure ; it is endless and everlast-ing ; therefore should I offer to commensurate and adjust it, either to the size and proportion of your own noble and gracious Deeds, or yet to the Contentment and Delight of the obliged Receivers, I would come off but very faintly and flaggingly. You have verily done me a great deal of good, and multiplied your Favours on me more frequently than was fitting to one of my Condition. You have been more bountiful towards me than I have deserved, and your Courtesies have by far sur-passed the extent of my Merits, I must needs confess it. But it is not, as you suppose, in the proposed Matter : For there it is not where I itch; it is not there where it fretteth, hurts or vexeth me; for henceforth being quit and out of Debt, what Countenance will I be able to keep? You may imagine that it will become me very ill, for the first Month; because I have never hitherto been brought up or accustomed to it, I am very much afraid of it. Furthermore, there shall not one hereafter, Native of the Country of Salmigondy, but he shall level the Shot towards my Nose; all the backcracking Fellows of the World, in discharging of their Postern Petarades, use commonly to say, *Voilà pour les quitters;* that is, For the quit. My Life will be of very short continuance, I do foresee it, I recommend to you the making of my Epitaph; for I perceive I will die confected in the very stinch of Farts. If at any time to come, by way of restorative to such good Women as shall happen to be troubled with the grievous Pain of the Wind-Cholick, the ordinary Medicaments prove nothing effectual, the Mummy of all my befarted Body will streight be as a present Remedy appointed by the Physicians; whereof they taking any small modicum, it will incontinently for their Ease afford them a Rattle of Bum-shot, like a Sal of Muskets.

Therefore would I beseech you to leave me some few Centuries of Debts: as King Lewis XI. exempting from Suits in Law the Reverend Milles d'Illiers Bishop of Chartre, was by the said Bishop most earnestly sollicited to leave him some few for the exercise of his Mind. I had rather give them all my Revenue of the Periwinkles, together with the other Incomes of the Locusts, albeit I should not thereby have any parcel abated from off the principal Sums which I owe. Let us wave this matter (quoth Pantagruel) I have told it you over again

CHAPTER VI

Why New-marry'd Men were privileged from going to the Wars

BUT, in the interim, ask'd Panurge, by what Law was it constituted, ordained and established, that such as should plant a new Vineyard, those that should build a new House, and the new-married Men should be exempted and discharged from the Duty of Warfare for the first Year ? By the Law, (answer'd Pantagruel) of Moyses. Why (reply'd Panurge) the lately marry'd ? As for the Vine-Planters, I am now too old to reflect on them ; my Condition, at this present, induceth me to remain satisfied with the Care of Vintage, finishing and turning the Grapes into Wine : Nor are these pretty new Builders of Dead Stones written or prick'd down in my Book of Life ; it is all with Live Stones that I set up and erect the Fabricks of my Architecture, to wit, Men. It was, according to my opinion, (quoth Pantagruel) to the end, first, That the fresh married Folks should for the first Year reap a full and compleat Fruition of their Pleasures in their mutual exercise of the Act of Love, in such sort, that in waiting more at leisure on the Production of Posterity, and propagating of their Progeny, they might the better encrease their Race, and make provision of new Heirs. That if in the Years thereafter the Men should, upon their undergoing of some Military Adventure, happen to be kill'd, their Names and Coats of Arms might continue with their Children in the same Families : And next that, the Wives thereby coming to know whether they were barren or fruitful, (for one Year's Trial, in regard of the Maturity of Age wherein of old they married, was held sufficient for the Discovery) they might pitch the more suitably, in case of their first Husband's decease, upon a second Match. The Fertile Women to be wedded to those who desire to multiply their Issue ; and the Steril ones to such other Mates, as misregarding the storing of their own Lineage, chuse them only for their Virtues, Learning, Genteel Behaviour, Domestick Consolation, Management of the House, and Matrimonial Conveniences and Comforts, and such like. The Preachers of Varennes (saith Panurge) detest and abhor the Second Marriages, as altogether foolish and dishonest.

Foolish and dishonest, (quoth Pantagruel). A Plague take

such Preachers! Yea, but (quoth Panurge) the like Mischief also befal the Fryar, Charmer, who in a full Auditory, making a Sermon at Perille, and therein abominating the Reiteration of Marriage, and the entring again into the Bonds of a Nuptial Tie, did swear and heartily give himself to the swiftest Devil in Hell, if he had not rather chuse, and would much more willingly undertake the unmaidening or depucelating of a hundred Virgins, than the simple Drudgery of one Widow. Truly, I find your Reason in that Point right good, and strongly grounded.

But what would you think, if the Cause why this Exemption or Immunity was granted, had no other Foundation, but that, during the whole space of the said first Year, they so lustily bobb'd it with their Female Consorts, (as both Reason and Equity require they should do) that they had drained and evacuated their Spermatick Vessels; and were become thereby altogether feeble, weak, emasculated, drooping and flaggingly pithless; yea, in such sort, that they, in the Day of Battle, like Ducks which plunge over Head and Ears, would sooner hide themselves behind the Baggage, than in the Company of valiant Fighters and daring Military Combatants, appear where stern Bellona deals her Blows, and moves a bustling Noise of Thwacks and Thumps. Nor is it to be thought that under the Standard of Mars they will so much as once strike a fair Stroke, because their most considerable Knocks have been already jerk'd and whirrited within the Curtains of his Sweet-heart Venus.

In confirmation whereof, amongst other Relicks and Monuments of Antiquity, we now as yet often see, that in all great Houses, after the expiring of some few Days, these young married Blades are readily sent away to visit their Uncles, that in the absence of their Wives, reposing themselves a little, they may recover their decayed Strength by the recruit of a fresh Supply, the more vigorous to return again and face about to renew the duelling Shock and Conflict of an amorous Dalliance: Albeit (for the greater part) they have neither Uncle nor Aunt to go to.

Just so did the King Crackart, after the Battle of the Cornets, not cashier us, (speaking properly) I mean me and the Quaile-caller, but for our Refreshment remanded us to our Houses; and he is as yet seeking after his own. My Grandfather's Godmother was wont to say to me when I was a Boy;

Patonisters et Oraisons
  Sont pour ceux-là qui les retiennent.
Un fiffre en frenaisons
  Est plus fort que deux qui en viennent.

Not Orisons nor Patrenotres
  Shall ever disorder my Brain :
One Cadet, to the Field as he flutters,
  Is worth two when they end the Campaign.

That which prompteth me to that opinion, is, that the Vine-
Planters did seldom eat of the Grapes, or drink of the Wine of
their Labour, 'till the first Year was wholly elapsed : During all
which time also the Builders did hardly inhabit their new
structur'd Dwelling-places, for fear of dying suffocated through
want of Respiration ; as Galen hath most learnedly remarked,
in the Second Book of the *Difficulty of Breathing*. Under
favour, Sir, I have not asked this Question without Cause
causing, and Reason truly very ratiocinant. Be not offended,
I pray you.

CHAPTER VII

*How Panurge had a Flea in his Ear, and forbore to wear
any longer his magnificent Codpiece*

PANURGE, the day thereafter, caused pierce his Right Ear, after
the Jewish Fashion, and thereto clasped a little Gold Ring, of a
Fearny-like kind of Workmanship, in the Beazil or Collet whereof was set and enchased a Flea ; and to the end you may be rid
of all Doubts, you are to know that the Flea was black. O
what a brave thing it is, in every case and circumstance of a
Matter, to be throughly well informed ! The Sum of the
Expence hereof, being cast up, brought in, and laid down upon

his Council-board Carpet, was found to amount to no more quarterly than the Charge of the Nuptials of a Hircanian Tigress; even as you would say 600000 Maravedis. At these vast Costs and excessive Disbursements, as soon as he perceiv'd himself to be out of Debt, he fretted much; and afterwards, as Tyrants and Lawyers used to do, he nourish'd and fed her with the Sweat and Blood of his Subjects and Clients.

He then took four French Ells of a coarse brown Russet Cloth, and therein apparelling himself, as with a long, plain-seamed and single-stitch'd Gown, left off the wearing of his Breeches, and tied a pair of Spectacles to his Cap. In this Equipage did he present himself before Pantagruel; to whom this Disguise appeared the more strange, that he did not, as before, see that goodly, fair and stately Codpiece, which was the sole Anchor of Hope, wherein he was wonted to rely, and last Refuge he had 'midst all the Waves and boisterous Billows, which a stormy Cloud in a cross Fortune would raise up against him. Honest Pantagruel, not understanding the Mystery, ask'd him, by way of Interrogatory, what he did intend to personate in that new-fangl'd Prosopopeia? I have (answer'd Panurge) a Flea in mine Ear, and have a mind to marry. In a good time (quoth Pantagruel) you have told me joyful Tidings; yet would not I hold a redhot Iron in my Hand for all the Gladness of them. But it is not the fashion of Lovers to be accoutred in such dangling Vestments, so as to have their Shirts flagging down over their Knees, without Breeches, and with a long Robe of a dark-brown mingled Hue, which is a Colour never used, in Talarian Garments, amongst any Persons of Honour, Quality, or Virtue. If some Heretical Persons and Schismatical Sectaries have at any time formerly been so arrayed and cloathed, (tho' many have imputed such a kind of Dress to Cosenage, Cheat, Imposture, and an Affectation of Tyranny upon credulous Minds of the rude Multitude) I will nevertheless not blame them for it, nor in that Point judge rashly or sinistrously of them; every one overflowingly aboundeth in his own Sense and Fancy: Yea, in Things of a Foreign Consideration, altogether extrinsecal and indifferent, which in and of themselves are neither commendable nor bad, because they proceed not from the Interior of the Thoughts and Heart, which is the Shop of all Good and Evil. Of Goodness, if it be upright, and that its Affections be regulated by the pure and clean Spirit of Righteousness; and on the other side, of Wickedness, if its Inclinations, straying beyond the Bounds of

IN THIS EQUIPAGE DID HE PRESENT HIMSELF BEFORE PANTAGRUEL.

347

Equity, be corrupted and depraved by the Malice and Suggestions of the Devil. It is only the Novelty and Newfangledness thereof which I dislike, together with the Contempt of common Custom, and the Fashion which is in use.

The Colour (answer'd Panurge) is convenient, for it is conform to that of my Council-board Carpet; therefore will I henceforth hold me with it, and more narrowly and circumspectly than ever hitherto I have done, look to my Affairs and Business. Seeing I am once out of Debt, you never yet saw Man more unpleasing than I will be, if God help me not. Lo, here be my Spectacles. To see me afar off, you would readily say, that it were Fryar Burgess. I believe certainly, that in the next ensuing Year, I shall once more preach the Croisade, Bounce Buckram. Do you see this Russet? Doubt not but there lurketh under it some hid Property and occult Virtue, known to very few in the World. I did not take it on before this Morning; and nevertheless, am already in a rage of Lust, made after a Wife, and vehemently hot upon untying the Codpiece-point, I itch, I tingle, I wriggle, and long exceedingly to be married; that without the danger of Cudgel blows, I may labour my Female Copes-mate with the hard push of a Bull-horned Devil. O the provident and thrifty Husband that I then will be! After my Death, with all Honour and Respect due to my Frugality, will they burn the Sacred Bulk of my Body, on purpose to preserve the Ashes thereof, in memory of the choicest Pattern that ever was, of a perfectly wary and compleat Housholder. Cops-body, this is not the Carpet whereon my Treasurer shall be allowed to play false in his Accompts with me, by setting down an X for a V, or an L for an S; for in that case, should I make a hail of Fisticuffs to fly into his Face. Look upon me (Sir) both before and behind it is made after the manner of a Toge, which was the ancient fashion of the Romans in time of Peace. I took the Mode, Shape and Form thereof in Trajan's Column at Rome, as also in the Triumphant Arch of Septimus Severus. I am tired of the Wars, weary of wearing Buffcoats, Cassocks, and Hoquetons. My Shoulders are pitifully worn and bruised with the carrying of Harness; let Armour cease, and the Long-Robe bear sway; at least it must be so for the whole space of the succeeding Years. If I be married as yesterday, by the Mosaick Law, you evidenced, in what concerneth the Breeches: my Great-Aunt Laurence did long ago tell me, that the Breeches were only ordained for the Use of the Codpiece, and to no other end;

which I, upon a no less forcible Consequence, give credit to every whit as well, as to the Saying of the fine Fellow Galen, who in his Ninth Book Of the Use and Employment of our Members, alledgeth, That the Head was made for the Eyes: for Nature might have placed our Heads in our Knees or Elbows; but having beforehand determined that the Eyes should serve to discover things from afar, she, for the better enabling them to execute their designed Office, fixed them in the Head (as on the top of a long Pole) in the most eminent Part of all the Body: no otherwise than we see the Phares, or high Towers erected in the Mouths of Havens, the Navigators may the farther off perceive with ease the Lights of the nightly Fires and Lanterns. And because I would gladly, for some short while, (a Year at least) take a little Rest and Breathing-time from the toilsom Labour of the Military Profession, that is to say, be marry'd; I have desisted from wearing any more a Codpiece, and consequently have laid aside my Breeches: For the Codpiece is the principal and most especial Piece of Armour that a Warriour doth carry; and therefore do I maintain even to the Fire (exclusively, understand you me) that no Turks can properly be said to be armed Men, in regard that Codpieces are by their Law forbidden to be worn.

CHAPTER VIII

Why the Codpiece is held to be the chief piece of Armour amongst Warriours

WILL you maintain (quoth Pantagruel) that the Codpiece is the chief piece of a Military Harness? It is a new kind of Doctrine very Paradoxical: For we say at Spurs begins the arming of a Man. Sir, I maintain it, (answered Panurge) and not wrongfully do I maintain it. Behold how Nature having a fervent desire after its Production of Plants, Trees, Shrubs, Herbs, Sponges, and plant Animals, to eternize, and continue them unto all Succession of Ages (in their several Kinds, or Sorts at least, although the Individuals perish) unruinable, and in an everlasting Being, hath most curiously armed and fenced their Buds, Sprouts, Shoots, and Seeds, wherein the above-mentioned perpetuity consisteth, by strengthning, covering, guarding, and fortifying them with an admirable industry, with Husks, Cases, Scurfs, and Swads, Hulls, Cods, Stones, Films, Cartels, Shells, Ears, Rinds, Barks, Skins, Ridges, and Prickles, which serve them instead of strong, fair, and natural Codpieces : As is manifestly apparent in Pease, Beans, Fasels, Pomegranates, Peaches, Cottons, Gourds, Pumpions, Melons, Corn, Lemons, Almonds, Walnuts, Filberts, and Chestnuts ; as likewise in all Plants, Slips, or Sets whatsoever, wherein it is plainly and evidently seen, that the Sperm and *Semenæ* is more closely veiled, over-shadowed, corroborated, and throughly harnessed than any other part, portion, or parcel of the whole.

Nature nevertheless did not after that manner provide for the sempiternizing of Human Race : But on the contrary created Man naked, tender, and frail, without either offensive or defensive Arms ; and that in the Estate of Innocence, in the first Age of all, which was the Golden Season ; not as a Plant, but living Creature, born for Peace, not War, and brought forth into the World with an unquestionable Right and Title to the plenary fruition and enjoyment of all Fruits and Vegetables ; as also to a certain calm and gentle Rule and Dominion over all kinds of Beasts, Fowls, Fishes, Reptils, and Insects. Yet afterwards it hapning in the time of the Iron Age, under the Reign of Jupiter, when to the multiplication of mischievous Actions, Wickedness and Malice began to take root and footing within the then perverted Hearts of Men, that the Earth began to bring forth Nettles, Thistles, Thorns, Bryars, and such other stubborn and rebellious Vegetables to the Nature of Man ; nor scarce was there any Animal, which by a fatal Disposition did not then revolt from him, and tacitly conspire, and covenant with one another to serve him no longer, (nor in case of their ability to resist) to do him any manner of Obedience, but rather (to the uttermost of their Power) to annoy him with all the hurt and harm they could. The Man then, that he might maintain his primitive Right and Prerogative, and continue his Sway and Dominion over all, both Vegetable and Sensitive Creatures ; and knowing of a truth, that he could not be well accommodated as he ought, without the servitude and subjection of several Animals, bethought himself, that of necessity he must needs put on Arms, and make provision of Harness against Wars and Violence. By the holy Saint Babingoose, (cried out Pantagruel) you can become, since the last Rain, a great

Lifre lofre, Philosopher, I should say. Take notice, Sir (quoth Panurge) when Dame Nature had prompted him to his own Arming, what part of the Body it was, where, by her Inspiration, he clapped on the first Harness : It was forsooth by the double pluck of my little Dog the Ballock, and good Senor Don Priapos Stabostando, which done, he was content, and sought no more. This is certified by the Testimony of the great Hebrew Captain Philosopher Moyses, who affirmeth, That he fenced that Member with a brave and gallant Cod-piece, most exquisitely framed, and by right curious Devices of a notably pregnant Invention, made up and composed of Fig-tree-leaves, which by reason of their solid stiffness, incisory notches, curled frisling, sleeked smoothness, large ampleness, together with their colour, smell, vertue, and faculty, were exceeding proper, and fit for the covering and arming of the Sachels of Generation, the hideously big Lorram Cullions being from thence only excepted ; which swaggering down to the lowermost bottom of the Breeches, cannot abide (for being quite out of all order and method) the stately fashion of the high and lofty Codpiece ; as is manifest, by the Noble Valentin Viardiere, whom I found at Nancie, on the first Day of May (the more flauntingly to gallantrize it afterwards) rubbing his Ballocks, spread out upon a Table after the manner of a Spanish Cloak. Wherefore it is, that none should henceforth say, who would not speak improperly, when any Country-Bumpkin hyeth to the Wars, Have a care (my Roysters) of the Wine-pot, that is the Scull, but have a care (my Royster) of the Milk-pot ; that is, the Testicles. By the whole Rabble of the horned Fiends of Hell, the Head being cut off, that single Person only thereby dieth : But if the Ballocks be marred, the whole Race of Human Kind would forthwith perish, and be lost for ever.

This was the motive which incited the goodly Writer Galen, Lib. 1, *De Spermate*, to aver with boldness, That it were better (that is to say, a less evil) to have no Heart at all, than to be quite destitute of Genitories : For there is laid up, conserved, and put in store, as in a Successive Repository, and Sacred Ware-house, the *Seminæ*, and Original Source of the whole Off-spring of Mankind. Therefore would I be apt to believe, for less than a hundred Franks, that those are the very same Stones, by means whereof Deucalion and Pyrrha restored the Humane Race, in peopling with Men and Women the World, which a little before that, had been drowned in the overflowing Waves of a Poetical Deluge. This stirred up the valiant

Justinian, L. 1. 4. *De Cagotis tollendis*, to collocate his *Summum Bonum, in Braguibus, et Braguetis*. For this, and other Causes, the Lord Humphry de Merville, following of his King to a certain warlike Expedition, whilst he was in trying upon his own Person a new suit of Armour, for of his old rusty Harness he could make no more use, by reason that some few Years since, the Skin of his Belly was a great way removed from his Kidneys, his Lady thereupon in the profound musing of a contemplative Spirit, very maturely considering that he had but small care of the Staff of Love, and Packet of Marriage, seeing he did no otherwise arm that part of the Body, then with Links of Mail, advised him to shield, fence, and gabionate it with a big tilting Helmet, which she had lying in her Closet, to her otherways utterly unprofitable. On this Lady was penned these subsequent Verses ; which are extant in the Third Book of the Shitbrana of paultry Wenches.

> When Yoland saw her Spouse, equipt for Fight,
> And, save the Codpiece, all in Armour dight,
> My dear, she cry'd, Why, pray, of all the rest,
> Is that expos'd, you know I love the best ?
> Was she to blame for an ill-manag'd fear ?
> Or rather pious, conscionable Care :
> Wise Lady, She ! in hurly-burly Fight,
> Can any tell where random blows may hit ?

Leave off then (Sir) from being astonished, and wonder no more at this new manner of decking and trimming up of my self as you now see me.

CHAPTER IX

How Panurge asketh Counsel of Pantagruel whether he should marry, Yea or No

To this Pantagruel replying nothing, Panurge prosecuted the Discourse he had already broached, and therewithal fetching, as far from the bottom of his Heart, a very deep sigh, said, My Lord and Master, you have heard the Design I am upon, which is to marry, if by some disastrous mischance, all the Holes in

PANURGE ASKETH COUNSEL OF PANTAGRUEL WHETHER HE SHOULD MARRY the World be not shut up, stopped, closed, and bush'd. I humbly beseech you for the Affection which of a long time you have born me, to give me your best Advice therein. Then (answered Pantagruel) seeing you have so decreed, taken deliberation thereon, and that the matter is fully determined, what need is there of any further Talk thereof, but forthwith to put it into execution what you have resolved. Yea, but (quoth Panurge) I would be loath to act anything therein without your Counsel had thereto. It is my Judgment also (quoth Pantagruel) and I advise you to it. Nevertheless (quoth Panurge) if I understood aright that it were much better for me to remain a Batchelor as I am, than to run headlong upon new hairbrain'd Undertakings of Conjugal Adventure, I would rather choose not to marry. Quoth Pantagruel, Then do not marry. Yea, but (quoth Panurge) would you have me so solitarily drive out the whole course of my Life, without the Comfort of a Matrimonial Consort ? You know it is written, *Væ soli*, and a single Person is never seen to reap the Joy and Solace that is found with married Folks. Then marry, in the Name of God, quoth Pantagruel. But if (quoth Panurge) my Wife should make me a Cuckold ; as it is not unknown unto you, how this hath been a very plentiful Year in the production of that kind of Cattel ; I would fly out, and grow impatient, beyond all measure and mean. I love Cuckolds with my Heart, for they seem unto me to be of a right honest Conversation, and I, truly, do very willingly frequent their Company : But should I die for it, I would not be one of their number, that is a Point for me of a two-sore prickling Point. Then do not marry, (quoth Pantagruel) for without all Controversie, this Sentence of Seneca is infallibly true, What thou to others shalt have done, others will do the like to thee. Do you (quoth Panurge) aver that without all exceptions ? Yes, truly, (quoth Pantagruel) without all exception. Ho, ho (says Panurge) by the Wrath of a little Devil, his meaning is, either in this World, or in the other, which is to come. Yet seeing I can no more want a Wife, then a blind Man his Staff, the Funnel must be in agitation, without which manner of Occupation I cannot live. Were it not a great deal better for me to apply and associate my self to some one honest, lovely, and vertuous Woman, then (as I do) by a new change of Females every Day, run a hazard of being Bastinadoed, or (which is worse) of the Great Pox, if not of both together : For never (be it spoken, by their Husbands leave and favour) had I enjoyment yet of an honest Woman. Marry then in God's Name, quoth Pantagruel. But if (quoth Panurge) it were the Will of God, and that my Destiny did unluckily lead me to marry an honest Woman who should beat me, I would be stor'd with more than two third parts of the Patience of Job, if I were not stark mad by it, and quite distracted with such rugged Dealings: for it hath been told me, that those exceeding honest Women have ordinarily very wicked Head-pieces; therefore it is that their Family lacketh not for good Vinegar. Yet in that case should it go worse with me, if I did not then in such sort bang her Back and Breast, so thumpingly bethwack her Gillets, to wit, her Arms, Legs, Head, Lights, Liver, and Milt, with her other Intrails, and mangle, jag, and slash her Coats, so after the Cross-billet fashion, that the greatest Devil of Hell should wait at the Gate for the reception of her damned Soul. I could make a shift for this Year to wave such molestation and disquiet, and be content to lay aside that trouble, and not to be engaged in it.

Do not marry then, answered Pantagruel. Yea, but (quoth Panurge) considering the Condition wherein I now am, out of Debt and Unmarried; mark what I say, free from all Debt, in an ill hour, (for were I deeply on the Score, my Creditors would be but too careful of my Paternity) but being quit, and not married, no Body will be so regardful of me, or carry towards me a Love like that which is said to be in a Conjugal Affection. And if by some mishap I should fall sick, I would be lookt to very waywardly. The wise Man saith, Where there is no Woman (I mean the Mother of a Family, and Wife in the Union of a lawful Wedlock) the Crazy and Diseased are in danger of being ill used, and of having much brabling and strife about them: as by clear Experience hath been made apparent in the Persons of Popes, Legates, Cardinals, Bishops, Abbots, Priors, Priests and Monks: But there, assure your self, you shall not find me. Marry then in the Name of God, answered Pantagruel. But if (quoth Panurge) being ill at ease, and possibly thro' that Distemper, made unable to discharge the Matrimonial Duty that is incumbent to an active Husband, my Wife, impatient of that drooping Sickness, and faint Fits, of a pining Languishment, should abandon and prostitute herself to the Embraces of another Man, and not only then not help and assist me in my extremity and need, but withal flout at, and make sport of that my grievous Distress and Calamity; or peradventure, (which is worse) imbezzle my goods and steal from me, as I have seen it oftentimes befal unto the lot of many other Men, it were enough to undo me utterly, to fill brimful the Cup of my Misfortune, and makes me play the Mad-pate Reeks of Bedlam. Do not marry then (quoth Pantagruel). Yea, but (saith Panurge) I shall never by any other means come to have lawful Sons and Daughters, in whom I may harbour some hope of perpetuating my Name and Arms, and to whom also I may leave and bequeath my Inheritances and purchased Goods, (of which latter sort you need not doubt, but that in some one or other of these Mornings, I will make a fair and goodly show) that so I may chear up and make merry, when otherways I should be plunged into a pievish sullen Mood of pensive sullenness, as I do perceive daily by the gentle and loving Carriage of your kind and gracious Father towards you ; as all honest Folks used to do at their own Homes, and private Dwelling-Houses. For being free from Debt, and yet not married, if casually I should fret and be angry, although the cause of my Grief and Displeasure were never so just, I am afraid instead of Consolation, that I should meet with nothing else but Scoffs, Frumps, Gibes, and Mocks at my disastrous Fortune. Marry then in the Name of God, quoth Pantagruel.

CHAPTER X

How Pantagruel representeth unto Panurge the difficulty of giving Advice in the matter of Marriage ; and to that purpose mentioneth somewhat of the Homerick and Virgilian Lotteries

YOUR Counsel (quoth Panurge) under your Correction and Favour, seemeth unto me not unlike to the Song of Gammer Yeabynay ; it is full of Sarcasms, Mockqueries, bitter Taunts, nipping Bobs, derisive Quips, biting Jerks, and contradictory Iterations, the one part destroying the other. I know not (quoth Pantagruel) which of all my Answers to lay hold on ; for your Proposals are so full of ifs and buts, that I can ground nothing on them, nor pitch upon any solid and positive Determination satisfactory to what is demanded by them. Are not you assured within your self of what you have a mind to ?

the chief and main point of the whole matter lieth there ; all the rest is merely casual, and totally dependeth upon the fatal Disposition of the Heavens.

We see some so happy in the fortune of this Nuptial Encounter, that their Family shineth (as it were) with the radiant Effulgency of an Idea, Model or Representation of the Joys of Paradise ; and perceive others again to be so unluckily match'd in the Conjugal Yoak, that those very basest of Devils, which tempt the Hermits that inhabit the Deserts of Thebaida and Montserrat, are not more miserable than they. It is therefore expedient, seeing you are resolved for once to take a trial of the state of Marriage, that, with shut Eyes, bowing your Head, and kissing the Ground, you put the business to a Venture, and give it a fair hazard in recommending the success of the residue to the disposure of Almighty God. It lieth not in my Power to give you any other manner of Assurance, or otherways to certifie you of what shall ensue on this your Undertaking. Nevertheless (if it please you) this you may do, Bring hither Virgil's Poems, that after having opened the Book, and with our Fingers sever'd the Leaves thereof three several times, we may, according to the number agreed upon betwixt our selves, explore the future Hap of your intended Marriage : For frequently, by a Homerick Lottery, have many hit upon their Destinies ; as is testified in the Person of Socrates, who, whilst he was in Prison, hearing the Recitation of this Verse of Homer, said of Achilles, in the Ninth of the *Iliads*,

Ἤματί κεν τριτάτῳ Φθίην ἐρίβωλον ἱκοίμην.

We, the third day, to fertile Pthia came.

Thereby foresaw that on the third subsequent day he was to die : Of the truth whereof he assured Æschines, as Plato, *in Critone* ; Cicero, *in primo de Divinatione* : Diogenes Laertius, and others have to the full recorded in their Works. The like is also witnessed by Opilius Macrinus, to whom, being desirous to know if he should be the Roman Emperor, befell, by chance of Lot, this sentence in the Eighth of the *Iliads*,

Ὦ γέρον, ἦ μάλα δή σε νέοι τείρουσι μαχηταί,
Σὴ δὲ βίη λέλυται, χαλεπὸν δέ σε γῆρας ὀπάζει.

Dotard, new Warriours urge thee to be gone,
Thy Life decays, and old Age weighs thee down.

In Fact, he being then somewhat ancient, had hardly enjoyed the Sovereignty of the Empire for the space of Fourteen Months, when by Heliogabalus (then both young and strong) he was disposess'd thereof, thrust out of all, and killed. Brutus also doth bear witness of another Experiment of this nature, who willing, through this exploratory way by Lot, to learn what the Event and Issue should be of the Pharsalian Battle, wherein he perished, he casually encountred on this Verse, said of Patroclus in the Sixteenth of the *Iliads*,

Ἀλλά με μοῖρ ὀλοὴ, καὶ Λητοῦς ἔκτανεν υἱός.

Fate, and Latona's Son have shot me dead.

And accordingly Apollo was the Field-word in the dreadful Day of that Fight. Divers notable things of old have likeways been foretold and known by casting of Virgilian Lots; yea, in matters of no less importance than the obtaining of the Roman Empire, as it happened to Alexander Severus, who trying his Fortune at the said kind of Lottery, did hit upon this Verse written in the Sixth of the *Æneids*,

Tu regere imperio populos, Romane, memento.

Know, Roman, that thy business is to Reign.

He within very few Years thereafter was effectually and in good earnest created and installed Roman Emperor. A semblable Story thereto is related of Adrian, who being hugely perplexed within himself, out of a longing Humour to know in what Accompt he was with the Emperor Trajan, and how large the measure of that Affection was which he did bear unto him, had recourse after the manner above specified, to the Maronian Lottery, which by hap-hazard tender'd him these Lines out of the Sixth of the *Æneids*,

Quis procul ille autem ramis insignis olivæ
Sacra ferens ? nosco crines incanaque menta
Regis Romani.

But who is he, conspicuous from afar,
With Olive Boughs, that doth his Offerings bear ?
By the white Hair and Beard I know him plain,
The Roman King.

Shortly thereafter was he adopted by Trajan, and succeeded to him in the Empire. Moreover to the Lot of the praise-worthy Emperor Claudius befel this Line of Virgil, written in the Sixth of his *Æneids*,

> *Tertia dum Latio regnantem viderit æstas,*
>
> Whilst the third Summer saw him reign, a King
> In Latium.

And in effect he did not reign above two Years. To the said Claudian also, enquiring concerning his Brother Quintilius, whom he proposed as a Colleague with himself in the Empire, hapned the Responce following in the Sixth of the *Æneids*,

> *Ostendent terris hunc tantum fata.*
>
> Whom Fate let us see,
> And would no longer suffer him to be.

And it so fell out ; for he was killed on the Seventeenth Day after he had attained unto the management of the Emperial Charge. The very same Lot also, with the like misluck, did betide the Emperor Gordian the younger. To Claudius Albinus, being very sollicitous to understand somewhat of his future Adventures, did occur this Saying, which is written in the Sixth of the *Æneids*,

> *Hic rem Romanam magno turbante tumultu*
> *Sistet Eques, etc.*
>
> The Romans boiling with tumultuous rage,
> This Warriour shall the dangerous Storm asswage :
> With Victories he the Carthaginian mauls,
> And with strong hand shall crush the Rebel Gauls.

Likeways when the Emperor D. Claudius, Aurelian's Predecessor, did with great eagerness research after the Fate to come of his Posterity, his hap was to alight on this Verse in the first of the *Æneids*,

> *Hic ego nec metas rerum, nec tempora pono.*
>
> No bounds are to be set, no limits here.

Which was fulfilled by the goodly Genealogical Row of his Race. When Mr. Peter Amy did in like manner explore and make trial, if he should escape the Ambush of the Hobgoblins, who lay in wait all to bemawl him, he fell upon this Verse in the Third of the *Æneids*,

> *Heu fuge crudeles terras, fuge littus avarum !*
>
> Oh flee the bloody Land, the wicked Shoar !

Which Counsel he obeying, safe and sound forthwith avoided all these Ambuscades.

Were it not to shun Prolixity, I could enumerate a thousand such like Adventures, which conform to the Dictate and Verdict of the Verse, have by that manner of Lot-casting encounter befallen to the curious Researchers of them. Do not you nevertheless imagine, lest you should be deluded, that I would upon this kind of Fortune flinging Proof infer an uncontrolable, and not to be gainsaid Infallibility of Truth.

CHAPTER XI

How Pantagruel sheweth the Trial of ones Fortune by throwing of Dice to be unlawful

IT would be sooner done (quoth Panurge) and more expediently, if we should trie the matter at the chance of three fair Dice. (Quoth Pantagruel) That sort of Lottery is deceitful, abusive, illicitous, and exceedingly scandalous ; never trust in it ; the accursed Book of the Recreation of Dice was a great while ago excogitated in Achaia near Bourre, by that ancient Enemy to Mankind, the Infernal Calumniator, who before the Statue or Massive Image of the Bourraick Hercules, did of old, and doth in several places of the World as yet, make many simple Souls to err and fall into his snares. You know how my Father Gargantua hath forbidden it over all his Kingdoms and Dominions ; how he hath caused to burn the Moulds and Draughts thereof, and altogether suppressed, abolished, driven forth and cast it out of the Land, as a most dangerous Plague and Infection to any well-polished State or Commonwealth. What I have told you of Dice, I say the same of the Play at Cockall. It is a Lottery of the like Guile and Deceitfulness ; and therefore do not for convincing of me, alledge in opposition to this my Opinion, or bring in the Example of the fortunate Cast of Tiberius, within the Fountain of Appona, at the Oracle of Gerion. These are the baited Hooks by which the Devil attracts and draweth unto him the foolish Souls of silly People into eternal Perdition. Nevertheless to satisfie your Humour in some measure, I am content you throw three Dice upon this

Table, that according to the number of the Blots which shall happen to be cast up, we may hit upon a Verse of that Page, which in the setting open of the Book you shall have pitched upon.

Have you any Dice in your Pocket ? A whole Bag full, answered Panurge, that is Provision against the Devil, as is expounded by Merlin Coccajus, Lib. 2. *De Patria Diabolorum*, the Devil would be sure to take me napping, and very much at unawares, if he should find me without Dice. With this the three Dice being taken out, produced and thrown, they fell so pat upon the lower Points, that the Cast was Five, Six, and Five. These are (quoth Panurge) Sixteen in all. Let us take the Sixteenth Line of the Page, the number pleaseth me very well ; I hope we shall have a prosperous and happy Chance. May I be thrown amidst all the Devils of Hell, even as a great Bowl cast athwart at a Set of Nine Pins, or Cannon-ball shot among a Battalian of Foot, in case so many times I do not boult my future Wife the first Night of our Marriage. Of that, forsooth, I make no doubt at all : (quoth Pantagruel.) You needed not to have rapped forth such a horrid Imprecation, the sooner to procure Credit for the Performance of so small a business, seeing possibly the first Bout will be amiss, and that you know is usually at Tennis called Fifteen. At the next justling Turn you may readily amend that Fault, and so compleat your Reckoning of Sixteen. Is it so (quoth Panurge) that you understand the matter ? and must my Words be thus interpreted ? Nay, believe me, never yet was any Solecism committed by that valiant Champion, who often hath for me in Belly-dale stood Centry at the Hypogastrian Crany. Did you ever hitherto find me in the Confraternity of the Faulty ? Never I trow ; never, nor ever shall, for ever and a day. I do the Feat like a goodly Friar, or Father Confessor without Default : And therein am I willing to be judged by the Players. He had no sooner spoke these Words, than the Works of Virgil were brought in : But before the Book was laid open, Panurge said to Pantagruel, My Heart, like the Furch of a Hart in Rut, doth beat within my Breast. Be pleased to feel and grope my Pulse a little on this Artery of my Left Arm ; at its frequent Rise and Fall you would say that they swinge and belabour me after the manner of a Probationer posed, and put to a peremptory Trial in the Examination of his Sufficiency for the Discharge of the Learned Duty of a Graduate in some Eminent Degree in the Colledge of the Sorbonists.

But would not you hold it expedient, before we proceeded any further, that we should invocate Hercules and the Tenitian Goddesses, who in the Chamber of Lots are said to Rule, sit in Judgment, and bear a Presidential Sway ? Neither him nor them, (answered Pantagruel) only open up the Leaves of the Book with your Fingers, and set your Nails awork.

CHAPTER XII

How Pantagruel doth explore by the Virgilian Lottery what Fortune Panurge shall have in his Marriage

THEN at the opening of the Book in the Sixteenth Row of the Lines of the disclosed Page, did Panurge encounter upon this following Verse :

Nec Deus hunc mensa Dea nec Dignata cubili est.

The God him from his Table banished,
Nor would the Goddess have him in her Bed.

This Response (quoth Pantagruel) maketh not very much for your benefit or advantage : for it plainly signifies and denoteth, that your Wife shall be a Strumpet, and your self by consequence a Cuckold ; the Goddess, whom you shall not find propitious nor favourable unto you, is Minerva, a most redoubtable and dreadful Virgin, a powerful and fulminating Goddess, an enemy to Cuckolds, and effeminate Youngsters, to Cuckold-makers and Adulterers : the God is Jupiter, a terrible and Thunder-striking God from Heaven ; and withal, it is to be remarked, that conform to the Doctrine of the ancient

Hetrurians, the Manubes (for so did they call the darting Hurls, or slinging Casts of the Vulcanian Thunderbolts) did only appertain to her, and to Jupiter her Father Capital. This was verified in the Conflagration of the Ships of Ajax Oileus, nor doth the fulminating Power belong to any other of the Olympick Gods; Men therefore stand not in such fear of them. Moreover, I will tell you, and you may take it as extracted out of the profoundest Mysteries of Mythology, that when the Giants had enterprized the waging of a War against the Power of the Cœlestial Orbs, the Gods at first did laugh at those attempts, and scorn'd such despicable Enemies, who were in their conceit, not strong enough to cope in Feats of Warfare with their Pages : but when they saw by the Gigantine labour the high Hill Pelion set on lofty Ossa, and that the Mount Olympus was made shake to be erected on the top of both.

Then was it that Jupiter held a Parliament, or General Convention, wherein 'twas unanimously resolved upon, and condescended to by all the Gods, that they should worthily and valiantly stand to their Defence. And because they had often seen Battles lost by the cumbersom Letts and disturbing Incumbrances of Woman, confusedly hudled in amongst Armies, it was at that time Decreed and Enacted, That they should expel and drive out of Heaven into Ægypt, and the Confines of Nile, that whole Crue of Goddesses disguised in the shapes of Weezels, Polecats, Bats, Shrew-Mice, Ferrets, Fulmarts, and other such-like odd Transformations, only Minerva was reserved to participate with Jupiter in the horrifick ful· minating Power, as being the Goddess both of War and Learning, of Arts and Arms, of Counsel and Dispatch, a Goddess arm'd from her Birth, a Goddess dreaded in Heaven, in the Air, by Sea and Land. By the Belly of St. Buff (quoth Panurge) should I be Vulcan, whom the Poet blazons ! Nay, I am neither a Cripple, Coiner of False-Money, nor Smith, as he was.

My Wife possibly will be as comely and handsom as ever was his Venus, but not a Whore like her, nor I a Cuckold like him.

The crook-legg'd slovenly Slave made himself to be declared a Cuckold, by a definitive Sentence and Judgment, in the open view of all the Gods : For this cause ought you to interpret the aforemention'd Verse quite contrary to what you have said. This Lot importeth, that my Wife will be honest, virtuous, chast, loyal, and faithful; not armed, surly, waiward, cross, giddy, humourous, heady, hair-brain'd, or extracted out of the Brains, as was the Goddess Pallas : Nor shall this fair jolly Jupiter be my Corrival, he shall never dip his Bread in my Broth, tho' we shou'd sit together at one Table.

Consider his Exploits and gallant Actions ; he was the manifest Ruffian, Wencher, Whoremonger, and most infamous Cuckold-maker that ever breath'd : He did always lecher it like a Boar ; and no wonder, for he was foster'd by a Sow in the Isle of Candia, (if Agathocles the Babylonian be not a Lyar) and more rammishly lascivious than a Buck ; whence it is that he is said, by others, to have been suckled and fed with the Milk of the Amalthæan Goat. By the virtue of Acheron, he justled, bulled and lastauriated in one day the third part of the World, Beasts and People, Floods and Mountains, that was in Europa.

For this grand subagitary Atchievement, the Animonians caused, draw, delineate, and paint him in the figure and shape of a Ram, ramming, and horned Ram. But I know well enough how to shield and preserve my self from that horned Champion : He will not, trust me, have to deal in my Person, with a sottish, dunsical Amphytrion ; nor with a silly witless Argus, for all his hundred Spectacles ; nor yet with the cowardly Meacock Acrisius ; the simple Goosecap Lyrus of Thebes ; the doating Blockhead Agenor ; the flegmatick Pea-Goose Æsop ; rough-footed Lycaon ; the luskish mishapen Corytus of Tuscany ; nor with the large-back'd and strong-rein'd Atlas : Let him alter, change, transform, and meta-morphose himself into a hundred various shapes and figures ; into a Swan, a Bull, a Satyr, a Shour of Gold, or into a Cuckow, as he did when he unmaiden'd his Sister Juno ; into an Eagle, Ram, or Dove, as when he was enamour'd of the Virgin Phthia, who then dwelt in the Ægean Territory ; into Fire, a Serpent ; yea, even into a Flea, into Epicurian and Democratical Atomes, or more Magistronostralistically, into those sly Intentions of the Mind, which in the Schools are call'd Second Notions, I'll catch him in the nick, and take him napping.

And would you know what I would do unto him, even that which to his Father Cœlum, Saturn did, (Seneca foretold it of me, and Lactantius hath confirm'd it) what the Goddess Rhea did to Athis ; I would make him two Stone lighter, rid him of his Cyprian Cimbals, and cut so close and neatly by the Breech, that there should not remain thereof so much as one ———, so cleanly would I shave him ; and disable him for ever from being Pope ; for *Testiculos non habet*. Hold there, said Pantagruel ; *Hoc*, soft and fair (my Lad) enough of that, cast up, turn over the Leaves, and try your Fortune for the second time. Then did he fall upon this ensuing Verse :

Membra quatit, gelidusque coit formidine sanguis.

His Joints and Members quake, he becomes pale,
And sudden Fear doth his cold Blood congeal.

This importeth (quoth Pantagruel) that she will soundly bang your Back and Belly. Clean and quite contrary (answer'd Panurge) it is of me that he prognosticates, in saying, that I will beat her like a Tyger, if she vex me. Sir Martin Wagstaff will perform that Office ; and in default of a Cudgel, the Devil gulp him, if I shou'd not eat her up quick, as Candaul the Lydian King did his Wife, whom he ravened and devoured.

You are very stout, says Pantagruel, and couragious Hercules himself durst hardly adventure to scuffle with you in this your raging Fury : Nor is it strange ; for the Jan is worth two, and two in fight against Hercules are too too strong. Am I a Jan ? quoth Panurge. No, no, (answer'd Pantagruel) my mind was only running upon the lurch and tricktrack. Thereafter did he hit, at the third opening of the Book, upon this Verse :

Fœmineo prædæ, et spoliorum ardebat amore.

After the Spoil and Pillage (as in Fire)
He burnt with a strong Feminine Desir

This portendeth (quote Pantagruel) that she will steal your Goods, and rob you. Hence this, according to these three drawn Lots, will be your future Destiny, (I clearly see it) you will be a Cuckold, you will be beaten, and you will be robb'd. Nay, it is quite otherwise, (quoth Panurge) for it is certain that this Verse presageth, that she will love me with a perfect liking : Nor did the Satyr-writing Poet lye in proof hereof, when he affirmed, That a Woman burning with extream Affection, takes sometimes pleasure to steal from her Sweetheart. And what I pray you ? a Glove, a Point, or some such trifling Toy of no importance, to make him keep a gentle kind of stirring in the research and quest thereof : In like manner, these small scolding Debates, and petty brabling Contentions, which frequently we see spring up, and for a certain space boil very hot betwixt a couple of high-spirited Lovers, are nothing else but recreative Diversions for their Refreshment, Spurs to, and Incentives of a more fervent Amity than ever. As for Example : We do

sometimes see Cutlers with Hammers mawl their finest Whet-
stones, therewith to sharpen their Iron Tools the better.

And therefore do I think, that these three Lots make much
for my advantage ; which if not, I from their Sentence totally
appeal.   There is no appellation (quoth Pantagruel) from the
Decrees of Fate or Destiny, of Lot or Chance ; as is recorded by
our ancient Lawyers, witness Baldus, *lib. ult. cap. de Leg.*
The reason hereof is, Fortune doth not acknowledge a Superiour,
to whom an Appeal may be made from her, or any of her
Substitutes.   And in this case, the Pupil cannot be restored
to his Right in full, as openly by the said Author is alledged
in *L. ait prætor, Paragr. ult. H. de minor.*

CHAPTER XIII

*How Pantagruel adviseth Panurge to try the future good or
bad Luck of his Marriage, by Dreams*

Now seeing we cannot agree together in the manner of expounding or interpreting the Sense of the Virgilian Lots, let us
bend our course another way, and try a new sort of Divination.
Of what kind ? (asked Panurge.) Of a good Ancient and
Authentick Fashion, (answer'd Pantagruel) it is by Dreams :
For in Dreaming, such Circumstances and Conditions being
thereto adhibited, as are clearly enough described by Hippocrates in lib. Περὶ ἐδυπνίων, by Plato, Plotin, Iamblicus,
Sinesius, Aristotle, Xenophon, Galen, Plutarch, Artemidorus,

Valdianus, Herophilus, G. Calaber, Theocritus, Pliny, Athenæus, and others, the Soul doth often times foresee what is to come.

How true this is, you may conceive by a very vulgar and familiar Example ; as when you see that at such a time as Sucking Babes, well nourished, fed and foster'd with good Milk, sleep soundly and profoundly, the Nurses in the interim get leave to sport themselves, and are licentiated to recreate their Fancies at what Range to them shall seem most fitting and expedient ; their Presence, Sedulity and Attendance on the Cradle, being, during all that space, held unnecessary.

Even just so, when our Body is at rest, that the Concoction is every-where accomplish'd, and that till it awake, it lacks for nothing, our Soul delighteth to disport it self, and is well pleased in that Frolick to take a Review of its Native Country, which is the Heavens, where it receiveth a most notable Participation of its first Beginning, with an Imbuement from its Divine Source, and in Contemplation of that Infinite and Intellectual Sphere, whereof the Centre is every-where, and the Circumference in no place of the universal World, to wit, God, according to the Doctrine of Hermes Trismegistus, to whom no new thing hap'neth, whom nothing that is past escapeth, and unto whom all things are alike present, remarketh not only what is preterit, and gone in the inferiour Course and Agitation of sublunary Matters, but withal taketh notice what is to come ; then bringing a Relation of those future Events unto the Body by the outward Senses and exterior Organs, it is divulged abroad unto the hearing of others. Whereupon the Owner of that Soul deserveth to be termed a Vaticinator, or Prophet.

Nevertheless, the truth is, that the Soul is seldom able to report those things in such Sincerity as it hath seen them, by reason of the Imperfection and Frailty of the Corporeal Senses, which obstruct the effectuating of that Office ; even as the Moon doth not communicate unto this Earth of ours that Light which she receiveth from the Sun with so much Splendour, Heat, Vigour, Purity, and Liveliness as it was given her. Hence it is required, for the better reading, explaining and unfolding of these Somniatory Vaticinations and Predictions of that nature, that a dexterous, learned, skilful, wise, industrious, expert, rational and peremptory Expounder or Interpreter be pitch'd upon, such a one as by the Greeks is call'd Onirocrit, or Oniropolist.

For this cause, Heraclitus was wont to say, that nothing is

by Dreams revealed to us, that nothing is by Dreams concealed from us, and that only we thereby may have a mystical Signification and secret Evidence of Things to come, either for one prosperous or unlucky Fortune, or for the favourable or disasterous Success of another. The Sacred Scriptures testify no less, and Profane Histories assure us of it, in both which are exposed to our view a thousand several kinds of strange Adventures, which have befallen pat according to the nature of the Dream, and that as well to the Party Dreamer, as to others. The Atlantick People, and those that inhabit the Land of Thasos (one of the Cyclades) are of this grand Commodity deprived ; for in their Countries none yet ever dreamed. Of this sort, Cleon of Daulia, Thrasymedes ; and in our days the learned Frenchman Villanovanus, neither of all which knew what Dreaming was.

Fail not therefore to morrow, when the jolly and fair Aurora, with her rosie Fingers, draweth aside the Curtains of the Night, to drive away the sable Shades of Darkness, to bend your Spirits wholly to the task of sleeping sound, and thereto apply your self. In the mean while, you must denude your Mind of every Human Passion or Affection, such as are Love and Hatred, Fear and Hope ; for as of old the great Vaticinator, most famous and renowned Prophet Proteus, was not able in his Disguise or Transformation into Fire, Water, a Tyger, a Dragon, and other such-like uncouth Shapes and Visors to presage any thing that was to come, 'till he was restored to his own first natural and kindly Form. Just so doth Man ; for at his reception of the Art of Divination, and Faculty of Prognosticating future Things, that part in him which is the most Divine, (to wit, the νοῦς, or Mens) must be calm, peaceable, untroubled, quiet, still, husht, and not imbusied or distracted with Foreign, Soul-disturbing Perturbations. I am content, (quoth Panurge :) But I pray you, Sir, must I this Evening, e're I go to Bed, eat much or little ? I do not ask this without Cause : For if I sup not well, large, round and amply, my sleeping is not worth a forked Turnep ; all the Night long I then but dose and rave, and in my slumbering Fits talk idle Nonsence, my Thoughts being in a dull brown Study, and as deep in their Dumps as is my Belly hollow.

Not to sup (answer'd Pantagruel) were best for you, considering the state of your Complexion, and healthy Constitution of your Body. A certain very ancient Prophet named Amphiaraus, wished such as had a mind by Dreams to be imbued with any Oracles, for four and twenty Hours to taste no Victuals, and to abstain from Wine three days together ; yet shall not you be put to such a sharp, hard, rigorous and extream sparing Diet.

I am truly right apt to believe, that a Man whose Stomach is repleat with various Cheer, and in a manner surfeited with drinking, is hardly able to conceive aright of Spiritual things ; yet am not I of the Opinion of those, who after long and pertinacious Fastings, think by such means to enter more profoundly into the Speculation of Celestial Mysteries. You may very well remember how my Father Gargantua, (whom here for Honour-sake I name) hath often told us, That the Writings of abstinent, abstemious, and long-fasting Hermits, were every whit as saltless, dry, jejune and insipid, as were their Bodies when they did compose them. It is a most difficult thing for the Spirits to be in a good plight, serene and lively, when there is nothing in the Body but a kind of Voidness and Inanity : seeing the Philosophers with the Physicians jointly affirm, that the Spirits which are styled Animal, spring from, and have their constant practice in and through the Arterial Blood, refin'd and purify'd to the Life within the admirable Net, which, wonderfully framed, lieth under the Ventricles and Tunnels of the Brain. He gave us also the Example of the Philosopher, who, when he thought most seriously to have withdrawn himself unto a solitary Privacy, far from the rustling clutterments of the tumultuous and confused World, the better to improve his Theory, to contrive, comment and ratiocinate, was, notwithstanding his uttermost endeavours to free himself from all untoward Noises, surrounded and environ'd about so with the barking of Currs, bawling of Mastiffs, bleating of Sheep, prating of Parrots, tattling of Jackdaws, grunting of Swine, girning of Boars, yelping of Foxes, mewing of Cats, cheeping of Mice, squeaking of Weasils, croaking of Frogs, crowing of Cocks, kekling of Hens, calling of Partridges, chanting of Swans, chattering of Jays, peeping of Chickens, singing of Larks, creaking of Geese, chirping of Swallows, clucking of Moorfowls, cucking of Cuckows, bumbling of Bees, rammage of Hawks, chirming of Linets, croaking of Ravens, screeching of Owls, wicking of Pigs, gushing of Hogs, curring of Pigeons, grumbling of Cushet-doves, howling of Panthers, curkling of Quails, chirping of Sparrows, crackling of Crows, nuzzing of Camels, wheening of Whelps, buzzing of Dromedaries, mumbling of Rabets, cricking of Ferrets, humming of

Wasps, mioling of Tygers, bruzzing of Bears, sussing of Kitnings, clamring of Scarfes, whimpring of Fullmarts, boing of Buffalos, warbling of Nightingales, quavering of Meavises, drintling of Turkies, coniating of Storks, frantling of Peacocks, clattering of Magpies, murmuring of Stock-doves, crouting of Cormorants, cigling of Locusts, charming of Beagles, guarring of Puppies, snarling of Messens, rantling of Rats, guerieting of Apes, snuttering of Monkies, pioling of Pelicans, quecking of Ducks, yelling of Wolves, roaring of Lions, neighing of Horses, crying of Elephants, hissing of Serpents, and wailing of Turtles ; that he was much more troubled, than if he had been in the middle of the Crowd at the Fair of Fontenoy or Niort.

Just so it is with those who are tormented with the grievous Pangs of Hunger ; the Stomach begins to gnaw, (and bark as it were) the Eyes to look dim, and the Veins, by greedily sucking some Refection to themselves from the proper Substance of all the Members, of a fleshy Consistence ; violently pull down and draw back that vagrant roaming Spirit, careless and neglecting of his Nurse and natural Host, which is the Body. As when a Hawk upon the Fist, willing to take her Flight by a soaring aloft into the open spacious Air, is on a sudden drawn back by a Leash tied to her Feet.

To this purpose also did he alledge unto us the Authority of Homer, the Father of all Philosophy, who said, that the Grecians did not put an end to their mournful mood for the Death of Patroclus, the most intimate Friend of Achilles, till Hunger in a rage declared her self, and their Bellies protested to furnish no more Tears unto their Grief. For from Bodies emptied and macerated by long Fasting, there could not be such supply of Moisture and brackish Drops, as might be proper on that Occasion.

Mediocrity at all times is commendable ; nor in this case are you to abandon it. You may take a little Supper, but thereat must you not eat of a Hare, nor of any other Flesh : You are likewise to abstain from Beans, from the Preak, (by some called the Polyp) as also from Coleworts, Cabbage, and all other such like windy Victuals, which may endanger the troubling of your Brains, and the dimming or casting a kind of Mist over your Animal Spirits : For as a Looking-glass cannot exhibit the Semblance or Representation of the Object set before it, and exposed, to have its Image to the life expressed, if that the polish'd sleekedness thereof be darken'd by gross Breathings, dampish Vapours, and foggy, thick, infectious

EUDEMON

371

Exhalations; even so the Fancy cannot well receive the impression of the likeness of those things, which Divination doth afford by Dreams, if any way the Body be annoyed or troubled with the fumish steam of Meat, which it had taken in a while before; because betwixt these two there still hath been a mutual Sympathy and Fellow-feeling, of an indissolubly-knit Affection. You shall eat good Eusebian and Bergamot-Pears, one Apple of the short-shank Pepin-kind, a parcel of the little Plums of Tours, and some few Cherries of the growth of my Orchard: Nor shall you need to fear, that thereupon will ensue some doubtful Dreams, fallacious, uncertain, and not to be trusted to, as by some Peripatetick Philosophers hath been related; for that, say they, Men do more copiously in the Season of Harvest feed on Fruitages, than at any other time. The same is mystically taught us by the ancient Prophets and Poets, who alledge, That all vain and deceitful Dreams lie hid and in covert, under the Leaves which are spread on the Ground: By reason that the Leaves fall from the Trees, in the Autumnal Quarter: For the natural fervour, which abounding in ripe, fresh, recent Fruits, cometh by the quickness of its ebullition, to be with ease evaporated into the Animal parts of the dreaming Person (the Experiment is obvious in most) is a pretty while before it be expired, dissolved, and evanished. As for your Drink, you are to have it of the fair, pure Water of my Fountain.

The Condition (quoth Panurge) is very hard: Nevertheless, cost what price it will, or whatsoever come of it, I heartily condescend thereto; protesting that I shall to morrow break my Fast betimes, after my somniatory Exercitations; furthermore, I recommend my self to Homer's two Gates, to Morpheus, to Iselon, to Phautasus, and unto Phabetor. If they in this my great need succour me, and grant me that assistance which is fitting, I will, in honour of them all, erect a jolly, gentiel Altar, composed of the softest Down. If I were now in Laconia, in the Temple of Juno, betwixt Oetile and Thalamis, she suddenly would disintangle my Perplexity, resolve me of my Doubts, and chear me up with fair and jovial Dreams in a deep Sleep. Then did he say thus unto Pantagruel: Sir, were it not expedient for my purpose, to put a Branch or two of curious Laurel betwixt the Quilt and Bolster of my Bed, under the Pillow on which my Head must lean? There is no need at all of that (quoth Pantagruel) for besides that it is a thing very Superstitious, the Cheat thereof hath been at large discovered unto us, in the Writings of Serapion, Ascalonites, Antiphon, Philochorus, Artemon, and Fulgentius Placiades. I could say as much to you of the left Shoulder of a Crocodile, as also of a Camelion, without prejudice be it spoken to the Credit which is due to the Opinion of old Democritus; and likewise of the Stone of the Bactrians, called Eumerites, and of the Hamonian Horn: for so by the Æthiopians is termed a certain precious Stone, coloured like Gold, and in the fashion, shape, form, and proportion of a Ram's Horn, as the Horn of Jupiter Hammon is reported to have been: They over and above assuredly affirming, that the Dreams of those who carry it about them are no less veritable and infallible, than the Truth of the Divine Oracles. Nor is this much unlike to what Homer and Virgil wrote of these two Gates of Sleep: to which you have been pleased to recommend the management of what you have in hand. The one is of Ivory, which setteth in confused, doubtful, and uncertain Dreams; for thro' Ivory, how small and slender it soever be, we can see nothing, the density, opacity, and close compactedness of its material parts, hindring the penetration of the visual Rays, and the reception of the Speciesses of such things as are visible: The other is of Horn, at which an entry is made to sure and certain Dreams, even as through Horn, by reason of the diaphanous splendour, and bright transparency thereof, the Species of all Objects of the sight distinctly pass, and so without confusion appear, that they are clearly seen. Your meaning is, and you would thereby infer (quoth Fryar Jhon) that the Dreams of all horned Cuckolds (of which number Panurge, by the help of God, and his future Wife, is without controversie to be one) are always true and infallible.

CHAPTER XIV

Panurge's Dream, with the Interpretation thereof

At Seven a Clock of the next following Morning, Panurge did not fail to present himself before Pantagruel, in whose Chamber were at that time Epistemon, Fryar John of the Funnels, Ponocrates, Eudemon, Carpalin, and others, to whom, at the entry of Panurge, Pantagruel said, Lo, here cometh our

Dreamer. That word (quoth Epistemon) in ancient times cost
very much, and was dearly sold to the Children of Jacob.
Then, said Panurge, I have been plunged into my dumps so
deeply, as if I had been lodged with Gaffer Noddy-cap : dreamed
indeed I have, and that right lustily ; but I could take along
with me no more thereof, that I did goodly understand, save
only, that I in my Vision had a pretty, fair, young, gallant,
handsom Woman, who no less lovingly and kindly treated and
entertained me, hugg'd, cherish'd, cocker'd, dandled, and made
much of me, as if I had been another neat dillidarling Minion,
like Adonis : Never was Man more glad than I was then, my
Joy at that time was incomparable ; she flattered me, tickled
me, stroaked me, groped me, frizled me, curled me, kissed me,
embraced me, laid her Hands about my Neck, and now and
then made jestingly, pretty little Horns above my Forehead :
I told her in the like disport, as I did play the fool with her,
that she should rather place and fix them in a little below
mine Eyes, that I might see the better what I should stick at,
with them : For being so situated, Momus then would find no
fault therewith, as he did once with the position of the Horns
of Bulls. The wanton, toying Girl, notwithstanding any
Remonstrance of mine to the contrary, did always drive and
thrust them further in : Yet thereby (which to me seemed
wonderful) she did not do me any hurt at all. A little after,
though I know not how, I thought I was transformed into a
Tabor, and she into a Chough.

My sleeping there being interrupted, I awaked in a start,
angry, displeased, perplexed, chafing, and very wroth. There
have you a large Platter-ful of Dreams, make thereupon good
Chear, and, if you please, spare not to interpret them according
to the Understanding which you may have in them. Come
Carpalin, let us to Breakfast. To my sence and meaning,
(quoth Pantagruel) if I have skill or knowledge in the Art of
Divination by Dreams, your Wife will not really, and to the
outward appearance of the World, plant, or set Horns, and
stick them fast in your Forehead, after a visible manner, as
Satyrs use to wear and carry them ; but she will be so far from
preserving herself Loyal in the discharge and observance of a
Conjugal Duty, that on the contrary she will violate her plighted
Faith, break her Marriage-Oath, infringe all Matrimonial
Tyes, prostitute her Body to the Dalliance of other Men, and
so make you a Cuckold. This point is clearly and manifestly
explained and expounded by Artemidorus, just as I have

NEVER WAS MAN MORE GLAD THAN I WAS THEN

375

related it. Nor will there be any metamorphosis, or transmutation made of you into a Drum, or Tabor, but you will surely be as soundly beaten as e're was Tabor at a merry Wedding: Nor yet will she be changed into a Chough, but will steal from you, chiefly in the Night, as is the nature of that thievish Bird. Hereby may you perceive your Dreams to be in every jot conform and agreeable to the Virgilian Lots: A Cuckold you will be, beaten and robbed. Then cryed out Father John with a loud Voice: He tells the truth; upon my Conscience, thou wilt be a Cuckold, an honest one, I warrant thee; O the brave Horns that will be born by thee! Ha, ha, ha. Our good Master de Cornilius, God save thee, and shield thee; wilt thou be pleased to preach but two words of a Sermon to us, and I will go through the Parish Church to gather up Alms for the Poor.

You are (quoth Panurge) very far mistaken in your Interpretation; for the matter is quite contrary to your sence thereof; my Dream presageth, that I shall by Marriage be stored with plenty of all manner of Goods, the hornifying of me shewing, that I will possess a Cornucopia, that Amalthæan Horn, which is called, The Horn of Abundance, whereof the fruition did still portend the Wealth of the Enjoyer. You possibly will say, that they are rather like to be Satyrs Horns; for you of these did make some mention. *Amen, Amen, Fiat, fiat, ad differentiam papæ.* Thus shall I have my Touch-her-home still ready; my Staff of Love sempiternally in a good case, will, Satyr-like, be never toyled out; a thing which all Men wish for, and send up their Prayers to that purpose, but such a thing as nevertheless is granted but to a few; hence doth it follow by a consequence as clear as the Sun-beams, that I will never be in the danger of being made a Cuckold, for the defect hereof is, *Causa sine qua non*; yea, the sole cause (as many think) of making Husbands Cuckolds. What makes poor scoundrel Rogues to beg (I pray you)? Is it not because they have not enough at home, wherewith to fill their Bellies, and their Poaks? What is it makes the Wolves to leave the Woods? Is it not the want of Flesh Meat? What maketh Women Whores? you understand me well enough: And herein may I very well submit my Oᵢinion to the Judgement of learned Lawyers, Presidents, Counsellors, Advocates, Procurers, Attorneys, and other Glossers and Commentators on the venerable Rubrick, *De Frigidis, et maleficiatis.* You are in truth, Sir, as it seems to me (excuse my boldness if I have transgressed) in a most palpable and absurd Error, to attribute my Horns to Cuckoldry : Diana wears them on her Head after the manner of a Cressant, is she a Cucquean for that ? How the Devil can she be cuckolded, who never yet was married ? Speak somewhat more correctly, I beseech you, least she being offended, furnish you with a pair of Horns, shapen by the Pattern of those which she made for Actæon. The goodly Bacchus also carries Horns ; Pan, Jupiter Hammon, with a great many others, are they all Cuckolds ? If Jove be a Cuckold, Juno is a Whore : this follows by the Figure Metalepsis. As to call a Child in the presence of his Father and Mother, a Bastard, or Whore's Son, is tacitly and underboard, no less than if he had said openly, the Father is a Cuckold, and his Wife a Punk. Let our Discourse come nearer to the purpose : The Horns that my Wife did make me are Horns of Abundance, planted and grafted in my Head for the increase and shooting up of all good things : This will I affirm for truth, upon my Word, and pawn my Faith and Credit both upon it ; as for the rest, I will be no less joyful, frolick, glad, cheerful, merry, jolly, and gamesom than a well-bended Tabor in the Hands of a good Drummer, at a Nuptial Feast, still making a noise, still rowling, still buzzing and cracking. Believe me, Sir, in that consisteth none of my least good Fortunes. And my Wife will be jocund, feat, compt, neat, quaint, dainty, trim, trick'd up, brisk, smirk and smug, even as a pretty little Cornish Chough : who will not believe this, let Hell or the Gallows be the Burden of his Christmas Carol.

I remark (quoth Pantagruel) the last point or particle which you did speak of, and having seriously conferred it with the first, find that at the beginning you were delighted with the sweetness of your Dream ; but in the end and final closure of it, you startingly awaked, and on a sudden were forthwith vexed in Choler, and annoyed. Yea, (quoth Panurge) the reason of that was, because I had fasted too long. Flatter not your self (quoth Pantagruel) all will go to ruine : Know for a certain truth, that every Sleep that endeth with a starting, and leaves the Person irksom, grieved, and fretting, doth either signifie a present Evil, or otherways presageth, and portendeth a future imminent mishap. To signifie an Evil, that is to say, to shew some Sickness hardly curable, a kind of pestilentious, or malignant Bile, Botch, or Sore, lying and lurking, hid, occult, and latent within the very Center of the Body, which many times doth by the means of Sleep (whose Nature is to reinforce,

and strengthen the Faculty and Vertue of Concoction) begin
according to the Theorems of Physick to declare itself, and
moves toward the outward Superficies. At this sad stirring is
the Sleeper's rest and ease disturbed and broken, whereof the
first feeling and stinging smart admonisheth, that he must
patiently endure great pain and trouble, and thereunto provide
some Remedy : As when we say proverbially to incense Hornets,
to move a stinking Puddle, and to awake a sleeping Lyon,
instead of these more usual Expressions, and of a more familiar
and plain meaning, to provoke angry Persons, to make a thing
the worse by meddling with it, and to irritate a testy cholerick
Man when he is at quiet. On the other part, to presage or
foretel an Evil, especially in what concerneth the Exploits of
the Soul, in matter of Somnial Divinations, is as much as to
say, that it giveth us to understand, that some dismal Fortune
or Mischance is destinated and prepared for us, which shortly
will not fail to come to pass. A clear and evident example hereof
is to be found in the Dream, and dreadful awaking of Hecuba,
as likewise in that of Euridice, the Wife of Orpheus, neither of
which was sooner finished, (saith Cunius) but that incontinently
thereafter they awaked in a start, and were affrighted horribly ;
thereupon these Accidents ensued, Hecuba had her Husband
Priamus, together with her Children, slain before her Eyes,
and saw then the Destruction of her Country ; and Euridice
died speedily thereafter, in a most miserable manner. Æneas
dreaming that he spoke to Hector a little after his Decease, did
on a sudden in a great start awake, and was afraid : now hereupon did follow this event ; Troy that same Night was spoil'd,
sack'd, and burnt. At another time the same Æneas, dreaming
that he saw his familiar Geniuses and Penates, in a ghastly
fright and astonishment awaked, of which terrour and amazement the issue was, that the very next day subsequent, by a
most horrible Tempest on the Sea, he was like to have perished,
and been cast away. Moreover, Turnus being prompted,
instigated, and stirred up, by the fantastick Vision of an infernal
Fury, to enter into a bloody War against Æneas, awaked in a
start much troubled and disquieted in Spirit, in sequel whereof,
after many notable and famous Routs, Defeats and Discom-
fitures in open Field, he came at last to be killed in a single
Combat, by the said Æneas. A thousand other Instances I
could afford, if it were needful, of this matter. Whilst I relate
these Stories of Æneas, remark the saying of Fabius Pictor,
who faithfully averred, That nothing had at any time befallen

unto, was done, or enterprized by him, whereof he preallably had not notice, and beforehand fore-seen it to the full, by sure Predictions, altogether founded on the Oracles of Somnial Divination. To this there is no want of pregnant Reasons, no more than of Examples : For if Repose and Rest in sleeping be a special Gift and Favour of the Gods, as is maintained by the Philosophers, and by the Poet attested in these Lines :

> Then Sleep, that heavenly Gift, came to refresh,
> Of humane Labourers, the wearied Flesh.

Such a Gift or Benefit can never finish or terminate in Wrath and Indignation, without portending some unlucky Fate, and most disastrous Fortune to ensue ; otherways it were a Molestation, and not an Ease ; a Scourge and not a Gift, at least, proceeding from the Gods above, but from the infernal Devils our Enemies, according to the common vulgar Saying.

Suppose the Lord, Father, or Master of a Family, sitting at a very sumptuous Dinner, furnished with all manner of good Cheer, and having at his entry to the Table his Appetite sharp set upon his Victuals, whereof there was great plenty, should be seen to rise in a start, and on a sudden fling out of his Chair, abandoning his Meat, frighted, appalled, and in a horrid Terrour, who should not know the cause hereof would wonder, and be astonished exceedingly : But what ? He heard his Male Servants cry, Fire, fire, fire, fire : his Serving Maids and Women yell, Stop Thief, stop Thief ; and all his Children shout as loud as ever they could, Murther, O Murther, Murther. Then was it not high time for him to leave his Banqueting, for application of a Remedy in hast, and to give speedy Order for succouring of his distressed Household. Truly, I remember, that the Cabalists and Massorats, Interpreters of the Sacred Scriptures, in treating how with verity one might judge of Evangelical Apparitions (because oftentimes the Angel of Satan is disguized and transfigured into an Angel of Light) said, That the difference of these two mainly did consist in this : The favourable and comforting Angel useth in his appearing unto Man at first to terrifie and hugely affright him ; but in the end he bringeth Consolation, leaveth the Person who hath seen him, joyful, well-pleased, fully content, and satisfied : On the other side, the Angel of Perdition, that wicked, devilish, and malignant Spirit, at his appearance unto any Person, in the beginning cheareth up the Heart of his Beholder, but at last forsakes him, and leaves him troubled, angry, and perplexed.

CHAPTER XV

*Panurge's Excuse and Exposition of the Monastick
Mystery concerning Pouder'd Reef*

THE Lord save those who see, and do not hear, (quoth Panurge)
I see you well enough, but know not what it is that you have
said : The Hunger-starved Belly wanteth Ears : For lack
of Victuals, before God, I roar, bray, yell and fume as in a
furious Madness. I have performed too hard a Task to day,
an extraordinary Work indeed : He shall be craftier, and do
far greater Wonders than ever did Mr. Mush, who shall be able
any more this year to bring me on the Stage of Preparation for
a dreaming Verdict. Fy ; not to sup at all, that is the Devil.
Pox take that Fashion. Come Friar John, let us go break our
Fast ; for if I hit on such a round Refection in the Morning, as
will serve throughly to fill the Mill-hopper and Hogshide of my
Stomach, and furnish it with Meat and Drink sufficient, then
at a pinch, as in the case of some extream necessity which
presseth, I could make a shift that day to forbear Dining.
But not to Sup : A Plague rot that base Custom, which is an
Error offensive to Nature. That Lady made the Day for
Exercise, to travel, work, wait on and labour in each his
Negotiation and Employment ; and that we may with the
more Fervency and Ardour prosecute our business, she sets
before us a clear burning Candle, to wit, the Suns Resplendency :
And at Night, when she begins to take the Light from us,
she thereby tacitly implies no less, than if she would have
spoken thus unto us : My Lads and Lasses, all of you are good
and honest Folks, you have wrought well to day, toiled and
turmoiled enough, the Night approacheth, therefore cast off
these moiling Cares of yours, desist from all your swinking
painful Labours, and set your Minds how to refresh your
Bodies in the renewing of their Vigour with good Bread, choice
Wine, and store of wholsom Meats ; then may you take some
Sport and Recreation, and after that lie down and rest your
selves, that you may strongly, nimbly, lustily, and with the
more Alacrity to morrow attend on your Affairs as formerly.
    Falconers in like manner, when they have fed their Hawks,

will not suffer them to fly on a full Gorge, but let them on a Pearch abide a little, that they may rouse, bait, tour and soar the better. That good Pope, who was the first Instituter of Fasting, understood this well enough; for he ordained that our Fast should reach but to the hour of Noon; all the remainder of that day was at our disposure, freely to eat and feed at any time thereof. In ancient times there were but few that dined, as you would say, some Churchmen, Monks and Canons; for they have little other Occupation; each day is a Festival unto them; who diligently heed the Claustral Proverb, *De missa ad mensam*. They do not use to linger and defer their sitting down and placing of themselves at Table, only so long as they have a mind in waiting for the coming of the Abbot; so they fell to without Ceremony, Terms or Conditions; and every body supped, unless it were some vain, conceited, dreaming Dotard. Hence was a Supper called *Cœna*, which sheweth that it is common to all sorts of People. Thou knowest it well, Friar John. Come let us go, my dear Friend, in the name of all the Devils of the Infernal Regions, let us go: The gnawings of my Stomach, in this rage of Hunger, are so taring, that they make it bark like a Mastiff. Let us throw some Bread and Beef into his Throat to pacifie him, as once the Sibyl did to Cerberus. Thou likest best Monastical Browess, the prime, the flower of the Pot. I am for the solid, principal Verb that comes after: The good brown Loaf, always accompany'd with a round slice of the Nine-lecture-poudred Labourer. I know thy meaning, (answered Friar John) this Metaphor is extracted out of the Claustral Kettle; the Labourer is the Ox, that hath wrought and done the Labour; after the fashion of Nine Lectures, that is to say, most exquisitely well and throughly boil'd. These holy Religious Fathers, by a certain Cabalistick Institution of the Ancients, not written, but carefully by Tradition conveyed from hand to hand, rising betimes to go to Morning Prayers, were wont to flourish, that their matutinal Devotion with some certain notable Preambles before their entry into the Church, viz., They dunged in the Dungeries, pissed in the Pisseries, spit in the Spitteries, melodiously coughed in the Cougheries, and doted in their Doteries, that to the Divine Service they might not bring any thing that was unclean or foul.

These things thus done, they very zealously made their repair to the Holy Chapel, (for so was, in their canting Language, termed the Covent Kitchin) where they with no small earnestness, had care that the Beef-Pot should be put on the Crook for the Breakfast of the Religious Brothers of our Lord and Saviour; and the Fire they would kindle under the Pot themselves. Now the Matines consisting of Nine Lessons, was so incumbent on them, that they must have risen the rather for the more expedite dispatching of them all. The sooner that they rose, the sharper was their Appetite, and the Barking of their Stomachs, and the Gnawings increase in the like proportion, and consequently made these godly Men thrice more a hungred and a-thirst, than when their Matines were hem'd over only with three Lessons.

The more betimes they rose by the said Cabal, the sooner was the Beef Pot put on; the longer that the Beef was on the Fire, the better it was boiled; the more it boiled, it was the tenderer; the tenderer that it was, the less it troubled the Teeth, delighted more the Palate, less charged the Stomach, and nourished our good Religious Men the more substantially; which is the only end and prime intention of the first Founders, as appears by this, That they eat not to live, but live to eat, and in this World have nothing but their Life. Let us go, Panurge.

Now have I understood thee, (quoth Panurge) my Plushcod Friar, my Caballine and Claustral Ballock. I freely quit the Costs, Interest and Charges, seeing you have so egregiously commented upon the most especial Chapter of the Culinary and Monastick Cabal. Come along, my Carpalin, and you Friar John, my Leather-dresser: Good morrow to you all, my good Lords: I have dreamed too much to have so little. Let us go. Panurge had no sooner done speaking, than Epistemon with a loud Voice said these Words: It is a very ordinary and common thing amongst Men to conceive, foresee, know and presage the misfortune, bad luck or disaster of another; but to have the understanding, providence, knowledge and prediction of a Man's own mishap is very scarce and rare to be found any where. This is exceeding judiciously and prudently deciphered by Esop in his Apologues, who there affirmeth, That every Man in the World carrieth about his Neck a Wallet, in the Fore-bag whereof were contained the Faults and Mischances of others, always exposed to his view and knowledge; and in the other Scrip thereof, which hangs behind, are kept the Bearers proper Transgressions, and inauspicious Adventures, at no time seen by him, nor thought upon, unless he be a Person that hath a favourable Aspect from the Heavens.

CHAPTER XVI

*How Pantagruel adviseth Panurge to consult with the
Sibyl of Panzoust*

A LITTLE while thereafter Pantagruel sent for Panurge, and
said unto him, The Affection which I bear you being now
inveterate, and setled in my Mind by a long continuance of
time, prompteth me to the serious consideration of your
Welfare and Profit; in order whereto remark what I have
thought thereon : It hath been told me that at Panzoust near
Crouly, dwelleth a very famous Sibyl, who is endowed with the
skill of foretelling all things to come. Take Epistemon in
your Company, repair towards her, and hear what she will say
unto you. She is possibly (quoth Epistemon) she is some
Canidia, Sagane or Pythonisse, either whereof with us is
vulgarly called a Witch. I being the more easily induced to
give Credit to the truth of this Character of her, that the place
of her Abode is vilely stained with the abominable repute of
abounding more with Sorcerers and Witches, than ever did the
Plains of Thessaly. I should not, to my thinking, go thither
willingly, for that it seems to me a thing unwarrantable, and
altogether forbidden in the Law of Moyses.

We are not Jews, (quoth Pantagruel) nor is it a matter
judiciously confess'd by her, nor authentically proved by
others that she is a Witch. Let us for the present suspend our
Judgment, and defer till after your return from thence, the
sifting and garbeling of those Niceties. Do we know but that
she may be an Eleventh Sibyl, or a Second Cassandra ? But
although she were neither, and she did not merit the Name or
Title of any of these Renowned Prophetesses, what Hazard, in

the Name of God, do you run, by offering to talk and confer
with her of the instant Perplexity and Perturbation of your
Thoughts ? Seeing especially (and which is most of all) she
is in the Estimation of those that are acquainted with her,
held to know more, and to be of a deeper reach of Understanding, than is either customary to the Country wherein she liveth,
or to the Sex whereof she is. What hindrance, hurt or harm
doth the laudable desire of Knowledge bring to any Man, were
it from a Sot, a Pot, a Fool, a Stool, a Winter Mittam, a Truckle
for a Pully, the Lid of a Goldsmiths Crucible, an Oil-Bottle,
or old Slipper ? You may remember to have read, or heard at
least, that Alexander the Great, immediately after his having
obtained a glorious Victory over the King Darius in Arbeles,
refused in the Presence of the splendid and illustrious Courtiers
that were about him, to give Audience to a poor certain despic-
able-like Fellow, who through the Sollicitation and Mediation
of some of his Royal Attendants was admitted humbly to beg
that Grace and Favour of him : But sore did he repent, although
in vain, a thousand and ten thousand times thereafter, the
surly State which he then took upon him to the Denial of so
just a Suit, the Grant whereof would have been worth unto him
the value of a Brace of potent Cities. He was indeed Victorious
in Persia, but withal so far distant from Macedonia, his Hereditary Kingdom, that the Joy of the one did not expel the
extream Grief, which through occasion of the other he had
inwardly conceived ; for not being able with all his Power to
find or invent a convenient Mean and Expedient, how to get or
come by the certainty of any News from thence ; both by
reason of the huge remoteness of the places from one to another,
as also because of the impeditive Interposition of many great
Rivers, the interjacent Obstacle of divers wild Deserts, and
obstructive Interjection of sundry almost inaccessible Mountains. Whilst he was in this sad quandary and solicitous
pensiveness, which, you may suppose, could not be of a small
Vexation to him ; considering that it was a matter of no great
difficulty to run over his whole Native Soil, possess his Country,
seize on his Kingdom, install a new King in the Throne, and
plant thereon Foreign Colonies, long before he could come to
have any Advertisement of it. For obviating the Jeopardy
of so dreadful Inconveniency, and putting a fit Remedy thereto,
a certain Sydonian Merchant of a low Stature, but high Fancy,
very poor in shew, and to the outward appearance of little or
no Account, having presented himself before him, went about

to affirm and declare, that he had excogitated and hit upon a ready mean and way, by the which those of his Territories at home should come to the certain notice of his Indian Victories, and himself be perfectly informed of the state and condition of Egypt and Macedonia within less than five days. Whereupon the said Alexander, plunged into a sullen animadvertency of Mind, through his rash Opinion of the Improbability of performing a so strange and impossible-like Undertaking, dismissed the Merchant without giving ear to what he had to say, and villify'd him. What could it have cost him to hearken unto what the honest Man had invented and contrived for his good ? What Detriment, Annoyance, Damage, or Loss could he have undergone to listen to the Discovery of that Secret, which the good Fellow would have most willingly revealed unto him ? Nature, I am perswaded, did not without a cause frame our Ears open, putting thereto no Gate at all, nor shutting them up with any manner of Inclosures, as she hath done unto the Tongue, the Eyes, and other such out-jetting parts of the Body : The Cause, as I imagine, is, to the end that every Day and every Night, and that continually, we may be ready to hear, and by a perpetual hearing apt to learn : For of all the Senses, it is the fittest for the reception of the knowledge of Arts, Sciences and Disciplines ; and it may be, that Man was an Angel, (that is to say, a Messenger sent from God) as Raphael was to Toby. Too suddenly did he contemn, despise and misregard him ; but too long thereafter, by an untimely and too late Repentance did he do Penance for it. You say very well, (answered Epistemon) yet shall you never for all that induce me to believe, that it can tend any way to the Advantage or Commodity of a Man, to take Advice and Counsel of a Woman, namely, of such a Woman, and the Woman of such a Country. Truly I have found (quoth Panurge) a great deal of good in the Counsel of Women, chiefly in that of the Old Wives amongst them ; who for every time I consult with them, I readily get a Stool or two extraordinary, to the great Solace of my Bum-gut passage. They are as Sloth-hounds in the Infallibility of their Scent, and in their Sayings no less Sententious than the Rubricks of the Law. Therefore in my Conceit it is not an improper kind of speech to call them Sage or Wise Women. In confirmation of which Opinion of mine, the customary style of my Language alloweth them the Denomination of Presage Women. The Epithet of Sage is due unto them, because they are surpassing dextrous in the knowledge of most things. And I give them the Title of Presage, for that they Divinely foresee, and certainly foretel future Contingencies, and Events of things to come. Sometimes I call them not Maunettes, but Monettes, from their wholsom Monitions. Whether it be so, ask Pythagoras, Socrates, Empedocles, and our Master Ortuinus. I furthermore praise and commend above the Skies the ancient memorable Institution of the pristine Germans, who ordained the Responses and Documents of Old Women to be highly extolled, most cordially reverenced, and prised at a rate, in nothing inferiour to the weight, test and standard of the Sanctuary : And as they were respectfully prudent in receiving of these sound Advices, so by honouring and following them did they prove no less fortunate in the happy Success of all their Endeavours Witness the old Wife Antinia, and the good Mother Villed, in the days of Vespasian. You need not any way doubt, but that Feminine Old Age is always fructifying in Qualities Sublime, I would have said Sibylline. Let us go, by the help ; let us go, by the Vertue. God, let us go. Farewel, Friar John, I recommend the care of my Codpiece to you. Well, (quoth Epistemon) I will follow you, with this Protestation nevertheless, that if I happen to get a sure Information, or otherways find that she doth use any kind of Charm or Enchantment in her Responses, it may not be imputed to me for a blame to leave you at the Gate of her House, without accompanying you any further in.

CHAPTER XVII

How Panurge spoke to the Sibyl of Panzoust

THEIR Voyage was three days journeying, on the third whereof was shewn unto them the House of the Vaticinatress standing on the knap or top of a Hill, under a large and spacious Walnut-tree. Without great difficulty they enter'd into that straw-thatch'd Cottage, scurvily built, naughtily movabled, and all besmoaked. It matters not, (quoth Epistemon) Heraclitus the grand Scotist, and tenebrous darksome Philosopher, was nothing astonish'd at his Introit into such a coarse and paultry

Habitation; for he did usually shew forth unto his Sectators and Disciples, That the Gods made as cheerfully their Residence in these mean homely Mansions, as in sumptuous magnifick Palaces, replenish'd with all manner of delight, pomp, and pleasure. I withal do really believe, that the Dwelling-place of the so famous and renowned Hecate, was just such another petty Cell as this is, when she made a Feast therein to the valiant Theseus. And that of no other better Structure was the Coat or Cabin of Hyræus, or Oænopion, wherein Jupiter, Neptune and Mercury were not ashamed, all three together, to harbour and sojourn a whole Night, and there to take a full and hearty Repast; for the payment of the Shot they thankfully pissed Orion.

They finding the ancient Woman at a corner of her own Chimney, Epistemon said, She is indeed a true Sibyl, and the lively Pourtraict of one represented by the τῇ καμινοῖ of Homer. The old Hag was in a pitiful bad plight and condition, in matter of the outward state and complexion of her Body, the ragged and totter'd Equipage of her Person, in the point of Accoutrement, and beggarly poor Provision of Fare for her Diet and Entertainment; for she was ill apparelled, worse nourished, toothless, blear-ey'd, crook-shoulder'd, snotty, her Nose still dropping, and her self still drooping, faint, and pithless. Whilst in this wofully wretched case she was making ready for her Dinner, Porridge of wrinkled green Colworts, with a bit skin of yellow Bacon, mixed with a twice before cooked sort of watrish, unsavoury Broth, extracted out of bare and hollow Bones. Epistemon said, By the Cross of a Groat, we are to blame, nor shall we get from her any Response at all, for we have not brought along with us the Branch of Gold. I have (quoth Panurge) provided pretty well for that, for here I have it within my Bag, in the substance of a Gold Ring, accompanied with some fair Pieces of small Money. No sooner were these Words spoken, when Panurge coming up towards her, after the Ceremonial Performance of a profound and humble Salutation, presented her with six Neats-Tongues dried in the Smoke, a great Butter-pot full of fresh Cheese, a Boracho furnished with good Beverage, and a Rams Cod stored with Single-Pence newly coined: At last he, with a low Curtsie, put on her Medical Finger a pretty handsom Golden-Ring, whereinto was right artificially inchased a precious Toadstone of Beausse. This done, in few words, and very succinctly did he set open and expose unto her the motive reason of his coming, most civilly and courteously entreating her, that she might be pleased to vouchsafe to give him an ample and plenary Intelligence, concerning the future good luck of his intended Marriage.

The Old Trot for a while remained silent, pensive and grining like a Dog; then, after she had set her wither'd Breech upon the bottom of a Bushel, she took into her Hands three old Spindles, which when she had turned and whirled betwixt her Fingers very diversly, and after several fashions, she pryed more narrowly into, by the tryal of their Points; the sharpest whereof she retained in her Hand, and threw the other two under a Stone-Trough; after this, she took a pair of Yarn-Windles, which she nine times unintermittedly veered, and frisked about, then at the ninth revolution or turn, without touching them any more, maturely perpending the manner of their motion, she very demurely waited on their repose and cessation from any farther stirring. In sequel whereof, she pulled off one of her wooden Pattens, put her Apron over her Head, as a Priest uses to do his Amice, when he is going to sing Mass, and with a kind of antick, gaudy, party-colour'd String, knit it under her Neck. Being thus covered and muffled, she whiff'd off a lusty good Draught out of the Boracho, took three several Pence forth of the Ram Cod Fob, put them into so many Walnut-shells, which she set down upon the bottom of a Feather-pot; and then, after she had given them three Whisks of a Broom Besom athwart the Chimney, casting into the Fire half a Bevin of long Heather, together with a Branch of dry Lawrel, she observed with a very hush, and coy silence, in what form they did burn, and saw, that although they were in a flame, they made no kind of noise, or crackling din, hereupon she gave a most hideous and horribly dreadful shout, muttering betwixt her Teeth some few barbarous Words, of a strange termination.

This so terrified Panurge, that he forthwith said to Epistemon, The Devil mince me into a Gally-mafry, if I do not tremble for fear. I do not think but that I am now inchanted; for she uttereth not her Voice in the terms of any Christian Language. O look, I pray you, how she seemeth unto me, to be by three full spans higher than she was when she began to hood her self with her Apron.

What meaneth this restless wagging of her slouchy Chaps? What can be the signification of the uneven shrugging of her hulchy Shoulders? To what end doth she quaver with her

Lips, like a Monkey in the dismembring of a Lobster? My Ears through horrour glow; ah! how they tingle. I think I hear the skreaking of Proserpina; the Devils are breaking loose to be all here. O the foul, ugly, and deformed Beasts! Let us run away! By the Hook of God, I am like to die for fear! I do not love the Devils; they vex me, and are unpleasant Fellows. Now let us fly, and betake us to our heels. Farewel, Gammer; Thanks and Grammercy for your Goods. I will not marry, no, believe me, I will not; I fairly quit my Interest therein, and totally abandon and renounce it, from this time forward, even as much as at present. With this, as he endeavoured to make an escape out of the Room, the old Crone did anticipate his flight, and make him stop: The way how she prevented him was this; whilst in her Hand she held the Spindle, she flung out to a Back-yard close by her Lodge, where after she had peeled off the Barks of an old Sycamore three several times, she very summarily, upon eight Leaves which dropt from thence, wrote with the spindle-point some curt, and briefly couched Verses, which she threw into the Air, then said unto them, Search after them if you will; find them if you can; the fatal Destinies of your Marriage written in them.

No sooner had she done thus speaking, when she did withdraw her self into her lurking Hole, where, on the upper Seat of the Porch, she tuck'd up her Gown, her Coats and Smock, as high as her Arm-pits, and gave them a full inspection of the Nockandroe: Which being perceiv'd by Panurge, he said to Epistemon, Gods Bodikins, I see the Sibyl's Hole. She suddenly then bolted the Gate behind her, and was never since seen any more. They jointly ran in haste after the fallen and dispersed Leaves, and gathered them at last, tho' not without great labour and toil, for the Wind had scatter'd them amongst the Thorn-bushes of the Valley. When they had ranged them each after other in their due Places, they found out their Sentence, as it is metrified in this Ocstatick:

> Thy Fame upheld,
>   Even so, so:
> And she with Child
>   Of thee: No.
> Thy Good End
>   Suck she shall,
> And flay thee, Friend,
>   But not all.

CHAPTER XVIII

*How Pantagruel and Panurge did diversly Expound the
Verses of the Sibyl of Panzoust*

THE Leaves being thus collected, and orderly disposed, Epistemon and Panurge returned to Pantagruel's Court, partly well
pleased, and other part discontented; glad for their being
come back, and vexed for the trouble they had sustained by the
way, which they found to be craggy, rugged, stony, rough, and
ill adjusted. They made an ample and full Relation of their
Voyage, unto Pantagruel; as likewise of the Estate and Condition of the Sibyl. Then having presented to him the Leaves of
the Sycamore, they shew him the short and twattle Verses that
were written in them. Pantagruel having read and considered
the whole sum and substance of the Matter, fetch'd from his
Heart a deep and heavy Sigh, then said to Panurge; You are
now, forsooth, in a good taking, and have brought your Hogs
to a fine Market : The Prophecy of the Sibyl doth explain and
lay out before us, the same very Predictions which have been
denotated, foretold, and presaged to us by the Decree of the
Virgilian Lots, and the Verdict of your own proper Dreams;
to wit, that you shall be very much disgraced, shamed, and
discredited by your Wife : for that she will make you a Cuckold
in prostituting her self to others, being big with Child by
another than you ; will steal from you a great deal of your
Goods, and will beat you, scratch, and bruise you, even from
plucking the Skin in apart from off you ; will leave the Print
of her Blows in some Member of your Body. You understand
as much (answer'd Panurge) in the veritable Interpretation,
and Expounding of recent Prophecies, as a Sow in the Matter
of Spicery. Be not offended (Sir, I beseech you) that I speak
thus boldly ; for I find my self a little in Choler, and that not
without cause, seeing it is the contrary that is true ; take heed,
and give attentive ear unto my words : The Old Wife said,
That as the Bean is not seen till first it be unhusk'd, and that its
swad or hull be shaled, and pilled from off it : so is it that my
Virtue and transcendent Worth will never come by the Mouth
of Fame, to be blazed abroad proportionable to the height,

extent, and measure of the excellency thereof, until preallably I get a Wife, and make the full half of a married Couple. How many times have I heard you say, that the Function of a Magistrate, or Office of Dignity, discovereth the Merits, Parts and Endowments of the Person so advanced and promoted, and what is in him; that is to say, we are then best able to judge aright of the Deservings of a Man, when he is called to the management of Affairs: For when before he lived in a private Condition, we could have no more certain knowledge of him, than of a Bean within his Husk. And thus stands the first Article explained: otherways could you imagine, that the good Fame, Repute, and Estimation of an Honest Man, should depend upon the Tail of a Whore?

Now to the meaning of the Second Article: My Wife will be with Child, (here lies the prime Felicity of Marriage) but not of me. Copsbody, that I do believe indeed: It will be of a pretty little Infant: O how heartily I shall love it! I do already dote upon it; for it will be my dainty Fedle-darling, my genteel Dilli-minion. From thenceforth no Vexation, Care, or Grief, shall take such deep impression in my Heart, how hugely great or vehement soever it otherways appear; but that it shall evanish forthwith, at the sight of that my future Babe; and at the hearing of the Chat and Prating of its Childish Gibbrish: And blessed be the Old Wife. By my truly, I have a mind to settle some good Revenue or Pension upon her, out of the readiest Encrease of the Lands of my Salmigondinois; not an inconstant and uncertain Rentseek, like that of witless, giddy-headed Batchelors, but sure and fixed, of the nature of the well-payed Incomes of Regenting Doctors.

If this Interpretation doth not please you, think you my Wife will bear me in her Flanks: Conceive with me, and be of me delivered, as Women use in Childbed to bring forth their Young ones; so as that it may be said, Panurge is a second Bacchus, he hath been twice born; he is re-born, as was Hypolitus, as was Proteus, one time of Thetis; and secondly, of the Mother of the Philosopher Apollonius; as were the two Palices, near the Flood Samethoe in Sicily; his Wife was big of Child with him. In him is renewed and begun again the Palintocy, and of the Megariens, and the Palingenesie of Democritus. Fie upon such Errors; to hear Stuff of that nature, rends my Ears.

The words of the third Article are; She will suck me at my

best End. Why not? that pleaseth me right well. You know the thing, I need not tell you, that it is my intercrural Pudding with one end. I swear and promise, that in what I can, I will preserve it sappy, full of juice, and as well victualled for her use as may be; she shall not suck me, I believe, in vain, nor be destitute of her Allowance; there shall her *justum* both in Peck and Lippy be furnish'd to the full eternally. You expound this Passage allegorically, and interpret it to Theft and Larceny. I love the Exposition, and the Allegory pleaseth me; but not according to the Sense whereto you stretch it. It may be that the Sincerity of the Affection which you bear me, moveth you to harbour in your Breast those refractory Thoughts concerning me, with a Suspicion of my Adversity to come. We have this Saying from the Learned, That a marvellously fearful thing is Love, and that true Love is never without Fear. But (Sir) according to my Judgment, you do understand both of and by your self, that here Stealth signifieth nothing else, no more than in a thousand other places of Greek and Latin, Old and Modern Writings, but the sweet fruits of amorous Dalliance, which Venus liketh best, when reap'd in secret, and cull'd by fervent Lovers filchingly.

Why so? I prithee tell: Because when the Feat of the Loose-Coat Skirmish happeneth to be done under-hand and privily, between two well-disposed, athwart the Steps of a Pair of Stairs, lurkingly, and in covert, behind a Suit of Hangings, or close hid and trussed upon an unbound Faggot, it is more pleasing to the Cyprian Goddess, (and to me also, I speak this without prejudice to any better, or more sound Opinion) than to perform that Culbusting Art, after the Cynick manner, in the view of the clear Sunshine, or in a rich Tent, under a precious stately Canopy, within a glorious and sublime Pavilion, or yet on a soft Couch betwixt rich Curtains of Cloth of Gold, without affrightment, at long intermediate Respits, enjoying of Pleasures and Delights a Belly-full, all at great ease, with huge fly-flap Fan of Crimson Sattin, and a Bunch of Feathers of some East Indian Ostrich, serving to give chase unto the Flyes all round about: whilst, in the interim, the Female picks her Teeth with a stiff Straw, pick'd even then from out of the bottom of the Bed she lies on.

If you be not content with this my Exposition, are you of the mind that my Wife will suck and sup me up, as people use to gulp and swallow Oysters out of the Shell? Or as the Cilician Women, according to the Testimony of Dioscorides, were wont to do the Grain of Alkermes? Assuredly that is an Error. Who seizeth on it, doth neither gulch up, nor swill down; but takes away what hath been packed up, catcheth, snatcheth, and plies the Play of Hey pass, Repass.

The Fourth Article doth imply, That my Wife will flay me, but not all. O the fine Word! You interpret this to beating Strokes and Blows. Speak wisely: Will you eat a Pudding? Sir, I beseech you to raise up your Spirits above the low-sized pitch of earthly Thoughts, unto that height of sublime Contemplation, which reacheth to the Apprehension of the Mysteries and Wonders of Dame Nature. And here be pleased to condemn your self, by a renouncing of those Errors which you have committed very grosly, and somewhat perversely, in expounding the Prophetick Sayings of the Holy Sibyl. Yet put the case (albeit I yield not to it) that by the instigation of the Devil, my Wife should go about to wrong me, make me a Cuckold downwards to the very Breech, disgrace me otherways, steal my goods from me, yea, and lay violently her hands upon me; she nevertheless should fail of her Attempts, and not attain to the proposed end of her unreasonable Undertakings.

The Reason which induceth me hereto, is grounded totally on this last Point, which is extracted from the profoundest Privacies of a Monastick Pantheology, as good Friar Arthur Wagtaile told me once upon a Monday morning; as we were (if I have not forgot) eating a Bushel of Trotter-pies; and I remember well it rained hard: God give him the good Morrow.

The Women at the beginning of the World, or a little after conspired to flay the Men quick, because they found the Spirit of Mankind inclined to domineer it, and bear rule over them upon the face of the whole Earth; and in pursuit of this their Resolution, promised, confirmed, sworn and covenanted amongst them all, by the pure Faith they owe to the nocturnal Sanct Rogero. But O the vain Enterprises of Women! O the great Fragility of that Sex Feminine! They did begin to flay the Man, or pill him, (as says Catullus) at that Member which of all the Body they loved best; to wit, the nervous and cavernous Cane; and that above five thousand years ago; yet have they not of that small part alone flayed any more till this hour but the Head: In meer despite whereof the Jews snip off that parcel of the Skin in Circumcision, choosing far rather to be called Clip-yards,

Raskals, than to be flayed by Women, as are other Nations. My Wife, according to this Female Covenant, will flay it to me, if it be not so already. I heartily grant my Consent thereto, but will not give her leave to flay it all : Nay, truly will I not, my noble King. Yea, but (quoth Epistemon) you say nothing of her most dreadful Cries and Exclamations, when she and we both saw the Lawrel-bough burn without yielding any noise or crackling. You know it is a very dismal Omen, an inauspicious sign, unlucky judice, and token formidable, bad, disastrous, and most unhappy, as is certified by Propertius, Tibullus, and quick Philosopher Porphyrius, Eustachius on the *Iliads*, of Homer, and by many others.

Verily, verily, (quoth Panurge) brave are the Allegations which you bring me, and Testimonies of two-footed Calves. These Men were Fools, as they were Poets ; and Dotards, as they were Philosophers ; full of Folly, as they were of Philosophy.

CHAPTER XIX

How Pantagruel praiseth the Counsel of Dumb Men

PANTAGRUEL, when this Discourse was ended, held for a pretty while his Peace, seeming to be exceeding sad and pensive ; then said to Panurge, The malignant Spirit misleads, beguileth and seduceth you. I have read that in times past the surest and most veritable Oracles were not those which either were delivered in Writing, or utter'd by word of Mouth in speaking : For many times, in their Interpretation, right witty, learned and ingenious Men have been deceived thro' Amphibolories, Equivokes, and Obscurity of Words, no less than by the brevity of their Sentences. For which cause Apollo, the God of Vaticination, was surnamed Λοξίας. Those which were represented then by Signs and outward Gestures were accounted the truest and the most infallible. Such was the Opinion of Heraclitus : And Jupiter did himself in this manner give forth in Amon frequently Predictions. Nor was he single in this Practice ; for Apollo did the like amongst the Assyrians. His prophesying thus unto those People, moved them to paint him with a large long Beard, and Cloaths beseeming an old setled Person, of a most posed, stayed and grave Behaviour ; not naked, young and beardless, as he was pourtrayed most usually amongst the Græcians. Let us make trial of this kind of Fatidicency : and go you take Advice of some dumb Person without any speaking. I am content, (quoth Panurge). But says Pantagruel, it were requisite that the Dumb you consult with be such as have been deaf from the hour of their Nativity, and consequently dumb ; for none can be so lively, natural, and kindly dumb, as he who never heard.

How is it, (quoth Panurge) that you conceive this matter ? If you apprehend it so, that never any spoke, who had not before heard the Speech of others, I will from that Antecedent bring you to infer very logically a most absurd and paradoxical Conclusion. But let it pass ; I will not insist on it. You do not then believe what Herodotus wrote of two Children, who at the special Command and Appointment of Psammeticus King of Egypt, having been kept in a pretty Country Cottage, where they were nourished and entertained in a perpetual Silence, did at last, after a certain long space of time, pronounce this word *Bec*, which in the Phrygian Language signifieth Bread. Nothing less (quoth Pantagruel) do I believe, than that it is a meer abusing of our Understandings to give Credit to the words of those, who say that there is any such thing as a Natural Language. All Speeches have had their primary Origin from the Arbitrary Institutions, Accords and Agreements of Nations in their respective Condescendments to what should be noted and betokened by them. An Articulate Voice (according to the Dialecticians) hath naturally no signification at all ; for that the sence and meaning thereof did totally depend upon the good will and pleasure of the first Deviser and Imposer of it. I do not tell you this without a Cause ; for Bartholus, Lib. 5. *de Verb. Oblig.* very seriously reporteth that even in his time there was in Cugubia one named Sir Nello de Gabrielis, who although he by a sad mischance became altogether deaf, understood nevertheless every one that talked in the Italian Dialect howsoever he expressed himself ; and that only by looking on his external Gestures, and casting an attentive Eye upon the divers motions of his Lips and Chaps. I have read, I remember also, in a very literate and eloquent Author, that Turidates King of Armenia, in the days of Nero, made a Voyage to Rome, where he was received with great Honour and Solemnity, and with all manner of Pomp and Magnificence : Yea, to the end there might be a sempiternal Amity and Correspondence preserved betwixt him and the Roman Senate ; there was no remarkable thing in the whole city which was not shown unto him.

At his Departure the Emperor bestowed upon him many ample Donatives of an inestimable Value : And besides, the more entirely to testifie his Affection towards him, heartily intrusted him to be pleased to make choice of any whatsoever thing in Rome was most agreeable to his Fancy ; with a Promise juramentally confirmed, That he should not be refused of his Demand. Thereupon, after a suitable Return of Thanks for a so gracious Offer, he required a certain Jack-pudding, whom he had seen to act his part most egregiously upon the Stage, and whose meaning (albeit he knew not what it was he had spoken) he understood perfectly enough by the Signs and Gesticulations which he had made. And for this Suit of his, in that he asked nothing else, he gave this Reason, That in the several wide and spacious Dominions, which were reduced under the Sway and Authority of his Sovereign Government, there were sundry Countries and Nations much differing from one another in Language, with whom, whether he was to speak unto them, or give any Answer to their Requests, he was always necessitated to make use of divers sorts of Truchmen and Interpreters : Now with this Man alone, sufficient for supplying all their places, will that great Inconveniency hereafter be totally removed ; seeing he is such a fine Gesticulator, and in the Practice of Chirology an Artist so compleat, expert and dextrous, that with his very Fingers he doth speak. Howsoever you are to pitch upon such a dumb Bone as is deaf by Nature, and from his Birth ; to the end that his Gestures and Signs may be the more vively and truly Prophetick, and not counterfeit by the intermixture of some adulterate Lustre and Affectation. Yet whether this dumb Person shall be of the Male or

Female Sex is in your Option, lieth at your Discretion, and altogether dependeth on your own Election.

I would more willingly (quoth Panurge) consult with and be advised by a dumb Woman, were it not that I am afraid of two things. The first is, That the greater part of Women, whatever it be that they see, do always represent unto their Fancies, think and imagine, that it hath some relation to the sugred entring of the goodly Ithyphallos, and graffing in the Cleft of the overturned Tree, the quick-set Imp of the Pin of Copulation. Whatever Signs, Shews or Gestures we shall make, or whatever our Behaviour, Carriage or Demeanour shall happen to be in their view and Presence, they will interpret the whole in reference to the act of Androgynation, and the culbatizing Exercise, by which means we shall be abusively disappointed of our Designs, in regard that she will take all our Signs for nothing else but Tokens and Representations of our Desire to entice her unto the Lists of a Cyprian Combat, or Catsenconny Skirmish.

Do you remember what hapned at Rome two hundred and threescore Years after the Foundation thereof ? A young Roman Gentleman encountring by chance at the Foot of Mount Celion with a beautiful Latin Lady named Verona, who from her very Cradle upwards had always been both deaf and dumb, very civilly asked her, (not without a Chironomatick Italianising of his Demand, with various Jectigation of his Fingers, and other Gesticulations, as yet customary amongst the Speakers of that Country) what Senators in her Descent from the top of the Hill she had met with going up thither. For you are to conceive, that he knowing no more of her Deafness than Dumbness, was ignorant of both. She in the mean time, who neither heard nor understood so much as one word of what he had said, streight imagin'd, by all that she could apprehend in the lovely Gesture of his manual Signs, that what he then required of her was, what her self had a great mind to, even that which a Young Man doth naturally desire of a Woman. Then was it, that by Signs (which in all occurrences of Venerial Love are incomparably more attractive, valid and efficacious than Words) she beckned to him to come along with her to her House ; which when he had done, she drew him aside to a privy Room, and then made a most lively alluring Sign unto him, to shew that the Game did please her. Whereupon, without any more Advertisement, or so much as the uttering of one Word on either side, they fell to, and bringuardised it lustily.

The other Cause of my being averse from consulting with dumb Women, is, that to our Signs they would make no answer at all, but suddenly fall backwards in a divarication posture, to intimate thereby unto us the reality of their consent to the supposed motion of our tacit Demands. Or if they should chance to make any contre-signs responsory to our Propositions, they would prove so foolish, impertinent, and ridiculous, that by them our selves should easily judge their thoughts to have no excursion beyond the duffling Academy. You know very well how at Croquiniole, when the religious Nun, sister Fatbum, was made big with Child by the young Stifly-Stantor, her Pregnancy came to be known, and she cited by the Abbess, and in a full Convention of the Convent, accused of Incest. Her excuse was, That she did not consent thereto, but that it was done by the violence and impetuous force of the Friar Stifly-stand-to't. Hereto the Abbess very austerely replying, Thou naughty wicked Girl, why didst thou not cry, a Rape, a Rape, then should all of us run to thy Succour. Her answer was, That the Rape was committed in the Dorter, where she durst not cry, because it was a place of sempiternal Silence. But (quoth the Abbess) thou roguish Wench, why didst not thou then make some sign to those that were in the next Chamber beside thee ? To this she answered, That with her Buttocks she made a sign unto them, as vigorously as she could, yet never one of them did so much as offer to come to her help and assistance. But (quoth the Abbess) thou scurvy Baggage, why didst not thou tell it me immediately after the perpetration of the Fact, that so we might orderly, regularly, and canonically have accused him ? I would have done so, had the case been mine, for the clearer manifestation of mine Innocency. I truly, Madam, would have done the like with all my Heart and Soul, (quoth Sister Fatbum) but that fearing I should remain in Sin, and in the hazard of Eternal Damnation, if prevented by a sudden Death, I did confess my self to the Father Fryar before he went out of the Room, who for my Penance, enjoyned me not to tell it, or reveal the matter unto any. It were a most enormous and horrid Offence, detestable before God and the Angels, to reveal a Confession : such an abominable Wickedness would have possibly brought down fire from Heaven, wherewith to have burnt the whole Nunnery, and sent us all headlong to the bottomless Pit, to bear company with Corah, Dathan, and Abiram. You will not (quoth Pantagruel) with all your Jesting make me laugh ; I know that all Monks,

W HEATH ROBINSON

GOATSNOSE

Fryars, and Nuns had rather violate and infringe the highest of the Commandments of God, than break the least of their Provincial Statutes. Take you therefore Goatsnose, a Man very fit for your present purpose ; for he is, and hath been, both dumb and deaf from the very remotest Infancy of his Child-hood.

CHAPTER XX

How Goatsnose by signs maketh answer to Panurge

GOATSNOSE being sent for, came the day thereafter to Panta-gruel's Court ; at his arrival to which Panurge gave him a fat Calf, the half of a Hog, two Punchions of Wine, one Load of Corn, and thirty Franks of small Money : Then having brought him before Pantagruel, in presence of the Gentlemen of the Bedchamber, he made this sign unto him. He yawned a long time, and in yawning made without his Mouth with the thumb of his right Hand the figure of the Greek Letter *Tau* by frequent Reiterations. Afterwards he lifted up his Eyes to Heaven-wards, then turned them in his Head like a Shee-goat in the painful fit of an absolute Birth, in doing whereof he did cough and sigh exceeding heavily : This done, after that he had made demonstration of the want of his Codpiece, he from under his shirt took his Placket-racket in a full gripe, making it there-withal clack very melodiously betwixt his Thighs : Then no sooner had he with his Body stooped a little forwards, and bowed his left Knee, but that immediately thereupon holding both his Arms on his Breast, in a loose faintlike Posture, the one over the other, he paused a-while.

Goatsnose looked wistly upon him, and having heedfully enough viewed him all over, he lifted up into the Air his left Hand, the whole fingers whereof he retained first-ways closed together, except the Thumb and the Forefinger, whose Nails he softly joyned and coupled to one another. I understand (quoth Pantagruel) what he meaneth by that sign : It denotes Marriage, and withal the number thirty, according to the Pro-fession of Pythagorians, you will be married. Thanks to you (quoth Panurge) in turning himself towards Goatsnose, my little Sewer, pretty Mastersmate, dainty Baily, curious Ser-geant-Marshal, and jolly Catchpole-leader. Then did he lift higher up than before his said left Hand, stretching out al! the five Fingers thereof, and severing them as wide from one another as he possibly could get done. Here (says Pantagruel) doth he more amply and fully insinuate unto us, by the Token which he sheweth forth of the Quinary number, that you shall be married. Yea, that you shall not only be affianced, betrothed, wedded, and married, but that you shall furthermore cohabit, and live jollily and merrily with your Wife; for Pythagoras called five the Nuptial Number, which together with Marriage, signifieth the Consummation of Matrimony, because it is composed of a ternary, the first of the odd, and binary, the first of the even Numbers, as of a Male and Female knit and united together. In very deed it was the fashion of old in the City of Rome at Marriage Festivals to light five wax Tapers, nor was it permitted to kindle any more at the magnifick Nuptials of the most Potent and Wealthy; nor yet any fewer at the penurious Weddings of the Poorest and most Abject of the World. Moreover in times past, the Heathen or Paynims implored the Assistance of five Deities, or of one helpful (at least) in five several good Offices to those that were to be married: Of this sort were the Nuptial Jove, Juno, President of the Feast, the fair Venus, Pitho the Goddess of Eloquence and Perswasion, and Diana, whose aid and succour was required to the labour of Child-bearing. Then shouted Panurge, O the gentile Goatsnose, I will give him a Farm near Gnais, and a Wind-mill hard by Mirebalais. Hereupon the dumb Fellow sneezeth with an impetuous vehemency, and huge concussion of the Spirits of the whole Body, withdrawing himself in so doing with a jerting turn towards the left Hand. By the Body of a Fox new slain (quoth Pantagruel) what is that? This maketh nothing for your Advantage; for he betokeneth thereby that your marriage will be inauspicious and unfortunate. This snezing (according to the Doctrine of Terpsion, is the Socratick Demon) if done towards the right side, it imports and portendeth, that boldly, and with all assurance, one may go whither he will, and do what he listeth, according to what deliberation he shall be pleased to have thereupon taken: his entries in the beginning, progress in his proceedings, and success in the events and issues will be all lucky, good, and happy. The quite contrary thereto is thereby implied and presaged, if it be done towards the left. You (quoth Panurge) do take always the matter at the worst, and continually, like another Davus, casteth in new Disturbances and Obstructions;

nor ever yet did I know this old paultry Terpsion worthy of citation, but in points only of Cosenage and Imposture. Nevertheless (quoth Pantagruel) Cicero hath written I know not what to the same purpose in his Second Book of Divination.

Panurge then turning himself to Goatsnose made this sign unto him. He inverted his Eye-lids upwards, wrinched his Jaws from the right to the left side, and drew forth his Tongue half out of his Mouth; this done, he posited his left Hand wholly open (the mid-finger wholly excepted, which was perpendicularly placed upon the Palm thereof) and set it just in the room where his Codpiece had been. Then did he keep his right Hand altogether shut up in a fist, save only the Thumb, which he streight turned backwards directly under the right Arm-pit, and setled it afterwards on that most eminent part of the Buttocks which the Arabs call the Alkatim. Suddenly thereafter he made this interchange, he held his right Hand after the manner of the left, and posited it on the place wherein his Codpiece sometime was, and retaining his left Hand in the form and fashion of the right, he placed it upon his Alkatim: This altering of Hands did he reiterate nine several times; at the last whereof he reseated his Eyelids into their own first natural Position. Then doing the like also with his Jaws and Tongue, he did cast a squinting look upon Goatsnose, diddering and shivering his Chaps, as Apes use to do now-a-days, and Rabbets, whilst almost starved with Hunger, they are eating Oats in the Sheaf.

Then was it that Goatsnose lifting up into the Air his right Hand wholly open and displayed, put the Thumb thereof, even close unto its first Articulation, between the two third Joints of the middle and ring Fingers, pressing about the said Thumb thereof very hard with them both, and whilst the remanent Joints were contracted and shrunk in towards the Wrist, he stretched forth with as much straitness as he could, the fore and little Fingers. That Hand thus framed and disposed of, he laid and posited upon Panurge's Navel, moving withal continually the aforesaid Thumb, and bearing up, supporting, or under-propping that Hand upon the above specified, and fore and little Fingers, as upon two Legs. Thereafter did he make in this posture his Hand by little and little, and by degrees and pauses, successively to mount from athwart the Belly to the Stomach, from whence he made it to ascend to the Breast, even upwards to Panurge's Neck, still gaining ground, till having reached his Chin he had put within the concave of his

Mouth his afore-mentioned Thumb : Then fiercely brandishing the whole Hand, which he made to rub and grate against his Nose, he heaved it further up, and made the fashion, as if with the Thumb thereof he would have put out his Eyes. With this Panurge grew a little angry, and went about to withdraw, and rid himself from this ruggedly untoward dumb Devil. But Goatsnose in the mean time prosecuting the intended purpose of his Prognosticatory Response, touched very rudely with the above-mentioned shaking Thumb, now his Eyes, then his Forehead, and after that, the borders and corners of his Cap. At last Panurge cried out, saying, Before God, Master-Fool, if you do not let me alone, or that you will presume to vex me any more, you shall receive from the best hand I have a Mask, wherewith to cover your rascally scoundred Face, your paultry shitten Varlet. Then said Fryar Jhon, He is Deaf, and doth not understand what thou sayest unto him. Bulliballock, make sign to him of a hail of Fisticuffs upon the Muzzle.

What the Devil (quoth Panurge) means this busie restless Fellow ? What is it that this Polypragmonetick Ardeloine to all the Fiends of Hell doth aim at ? He hath almost thrust out mine Eyes, as if he had been to potch them in a Skillet with Butter and Eggs, by G—, *da Jurandi*, I will feast you with flirts and raps on the Snout, interlarded with a double row of bobs and finger filipings ? Then did he leave him in giving him by way of *Salvo* a Volley of Farts for his Farewel. Goatsnose perceiving Panurge thus to slip away from him, got before him, and by meer strength enforcing him to stand, made this sign unto him. He let fall his right Arm towards his knee on the same side as low as he could, and raising all the fingers of that Hand into a close fist, past his dexterer Thumb betwixt the foremost and mid-fingers thereto belonging. Then scrubbing and swindging a little with his left Hand almost, and upon the uppermost in the very bought of the Elbow of the said dexter Arm, the whole Cubit thereof by leisure fair, and softly, at these thumpatory warnings, did raise and elevate it self even to the Elbow, and above it, on a sudden did he then let it fall down as low as before : And after that, at certain intervals and such spaces of time, raising and abasing it, he made a shew thereof to Panurge. This so incensed Panurge, that he forthwith lifted his Hand to have strucken him the dumb Royster, and given him a sound whirret on the Ear, but that the respect and reverence which he carried to the Presence of Pantagruel restrained his Choler, and kept his Fury within bounds and limits. Then said Pantagruel, If the bare signs now vex and trouble you, how much more grievously will you be perplexed and disquieted with the real things, which by them are represented and signified? All Truths agree, and are consonant with one another; this dumb Fellow Prophesieth and Foretelleth that you will be married, cuckolded, beaten and robbed. As for the marriage (quoth Panurge) I yield thereto, and acknowledge the verity of that point of his Prediction; as for the rest I utterly abjure and deny it: and believe, Sir, I beseech you, if it may please you so to do, that in the matter of Wives and Horses, never any Man was predestinated to a better Fortune than I.

CHAPTER XXI

How Panurge consulteth with an old French Poet, named Raminagrobis

I NEVER thought (said Pantagruel) to have encountred with any Man so headstrong in his Apprehensions, or in his Opinions so wilful, as I have found you to be, and see you are. Nevertheless, the better to clear and extricate your Doubts, let us try all courses, and leave no stone unturn'd, nor wind unsailed by. Take good heed to what I am to say unto you. The Swans, which are Fowls consecrated to Apollo, never chant but in the hour of their approaching Death, especially in the Meander Flood, which is a River that runneth along some of the Territories of Phrygia. This I say, because Elianus and Alexander

Wyndius write, that they had seen several Swans in other Places die, but never heard any of them sing or chant before their Death. However, it passeth for current, that the imminent Death of a Swan is presaged by his foregoing Song, and that no Swan dieth until preallably he have sung.

After the same manner Poets, who are under the Protection of Apollo, when they are drawing near their latter end, do ordinarily become Prophets, and by the inspiration of that God sing sweetly, in vaticinating things which are to come. It hath been likewise told me frequently, That old decrepit Men upon the Brinks of Charon's Banks, do usher their Disease with a Disclosure, all at ease (to those that are desirous of such Informations) of the determinate and assured truth of future Accidents and Contingencies. I remember also, that Aristophanes, in a certain Comedy of his, calleth Folks Sibyls, Ο δὲ γέρων σιβυλλιᾷ, for as when being upon a Peer by the Shore, we see afar off Mariners, Seafaring Men, and other Travellers alongst the curled Waves of Azure Thetis, within their Ships, we then consider them in silence only, and seldom proceed any further than to wish them a happy and prosperous Arrival : But when they do approach near to the Haven, and come to wet their Keels within their Harbour, then both with Words and Gestures we salute them, and heartily congratulate their Access safe to the Port wherein we are our selves. Just so the Angels, Heroes, and good Dæmons (according to the Doctrin of Platonicks) when they see Mortals drawing near unto the Harbour of the Grave, as the most sure and calmest Port of any, full of Repose, Ease, Rest, Tranquility ; free from the Troubles and Sollicitudes of this tumultuous and tempestuous World ; then is it that they with alacrity hale and salute them, cherish and comfort them, and speaking to them lovingly, begin even then to bless them with Illuminations, and to communicate unto them the abstrusest Mysteries of Divination. I will not offer here to confound your Memory by quoting antick Examples of Isaac, of Jacob, of Patroclus towards Hector, of Hector towards Achilles, of Polymnester towards Agamemnon, of Hecuba, of the Phodian renowned by Possidonius, of Calanus the Indian towards Alexander the Great, of Orodes towards Mezentius, and of many others ; it shall suffice for the present, that I commemorate unto you the learned and valiant Knight and Cavalier William of Ballay, late Lord of Langey, who died on the Hill of Tarara, the 10th of January, in the Climacterick Year of his Age, and of our Supputation 1543, according to the

Roman Account. The last three or four Hours of His life he did employ in the serious utterance of a very pithy Discourse, whilst with a clear Judgment and Spirit void of all Trouble, he did foretel several important Things, whereof a great deal is come to pass, and the rest we wait for. Howbeit, his Prophecies did at that time seem unto us somewhat strange, absurd, and unlikely; because there did not then appear any sign of Efficacy enough to engage our Faith to the Belief of what he did prognosticate.

We have here, near to the Town of Villomer, a Man that is both Old and a Poet, to wit, Raminagrobis, who to his second Wife espoused my Lady Broadsow, on whom he begot the fair Basoche; it hath been told me, he is a dying, and so near unto his latter end, that he is almost upon the very last moment, point, and article thereof; repair thither as fast as you can, and be ready to give an attentive ear to what he shall chant unto you: it may be that you shall obtain from him what you desire, and that Apollo will be pleased, by his means, to clear your Scruples. I am content (quoth Panurge) let us go thither Epistemon, and that both instantly and in all haste, lest otherways his Death prevent our coming. Wilt thou come along with us, Fryar Jhon? Yes, that I will, (quoth Fryar Jhon) right heartily to do thee a Courtesy, my Billy-ballocks; for I love thee with the best of my Milt and Liver. Thereupon, incontinently, without any further lingring to the Way, they all three went, and quickly thereafter (for they made good speed) arriving at the Poetical Habitation, they found the jolly Old Man, albeit in the Agony of his Departure from this World, looking chearfully, with an open Countenance, splendid Aspect, and Behaviour full of Alacrity. After that Panurge had very civilly saluted him, he in a free Gift did present him with a Gold Ring, which he even then put upon the Medical Finger of his Left-Hand, in the Collet or Bezle whereof was inchased an Oriental Saphir, very fair and large. Then, in imitation of Socrates, did he make an Oblation unto him of a fair White Cock; which was no sooner set upon the Tester of his Bed, than that with a high-raised Head and Crest, lustily shaking his Feather-Coat, he crowed Stentoriphonically loud. This done, Panurge very courteously required of him, that he would vouchsafe to favour him with the Grant and Report of his Sense and Judgment, touching the future Destiny of his intended Marriage. For answer hereto, when the honest Old Man had forthwith commanded Pen, Paper and Ink to be

OLD DECREPIT MEN UPON THE BRINKS OF CHARON'S BANKS

407

brought unto him, and that he was at the same Call conveniently served with all the three, he wrote these following verses :

> Take, or not take her,
>   Off, or on :
> Handy-dandy is your Lot.
> When her Name you write, you blot.
> 'Tis undone, when all is done,
> Ended e're it was begun :
> Hardly Gallop, if you Trot,
> Set not forward when you run,
> Nor be single, tho' alone,
>   Take, or not take her.

> Before you Eat, begin to Fast ;
> For what shall be, was never past.
> Say, unsay, gainsay, save your Breath ;
> Then wish at once her Life and Death.
>   Take, or not take her.

These Lines he gave out of his own Hands unto them, saying unto them, Go, my Lads, in Peace, the Great God of the highest Heavens be your Guardian and Preserver ; and do not offer any more to trouble or disquiet me with this or any other Business whatsoever. I have this same very day (which is the last both of May and of me) with a great deal of labour, toil and difficulty, chased out of my House a rabble of filthy, unclean, and plaguily pestilentious Rake-hells, black Beasts, dusk, dun, white, ash-colour'd, speckled, and a foul Vermin of other hues, whose obtrusive importunity would not permit me to die at mine own ease : for by fraudulent and deceitful pricklings, ravenous, Harpy-like graspings, waspish stingings, and such-like unwelcom Approaches, forged in the Shop of I know not what kind of Insatiabilities ; they went about to withdraw, and call me out of those sweet Thoughts, wherein I was already beginning to repose my self, and acquiesce in the Contemplation and Vision ; yea, almost in the very touch and taste of the Happiness and Felicity which the good God hath prepared for his faithful Saints and Elect in the other Life, and State of Immortality. Turn out of their Courses, and eschew them, step forth of their ways, and do not resemble them : mean while, let me be no more troubled by you, but leave me now in silence, I beseech you.

CHAPTER XXII

How Panurge Patrocinates and Defendeth the Order of the Begging Fryars

PANURGE, at his issuing forth of Raminagrobis's Chamber, said as if he had been horribly affrighted, By the Virtue of God, I believe that he is an Heretick, the Devil take me, if I do not; he doth so villanously rail at the Mendicant Fryars, and Jacobins; who are the two Hemispheres of the Christian World; by whose Gyronomonick Circumbilvaginations, as by two Celivagous Filopendulums, all the Autonomatick Metagrobolism of the Romish Church, when tottering and emblustricated with the Gibble-gabble Gibbrish of this odious Error and Heresy, is homocentrically poised. But what harm, in the Devil's Name, have these poor Devils the Capucins and Minims done unto him? Are not these beggarly Devils sufficiently wretched already? Who can imagine that these poor Snakes, the very Extracts of Ichthyophagy, are not throughly enough besmoaked and besmeared with Misery, Distress, and Calamity? Dost thou think, Fryar Jhon, by thy Faith, that he is in the State of Salvation? He goeth, before God, as surely damn'd to Thirty thousand Baskets-full of Devils, as a Pruning-Bill to the lopping of a Vine-Branch.

To revile with opprobrious Speeches the good and couragious Props and Pillars of the Church, is that to be called a Poetical Fury? I cannot rest satisfied with him, he sinneth grosly, and blasphemeth against the true Religion. I am very much offended at his scandalizing Words, and contumelious Obloquy.

I do not care a straw (quoth Fryar Jhon) for what he hath said ; for altho' everybody should twit and jerk them, it were but a just Retaliation, seeing all Persons are served by them with the like Sauce : therefore do I pretend no interest therein. Let us see nevertheless what he hath written. Panurge very attentively read the Paper which the Old Man had penn'd, then said to his two Fellow-Travellers, The poor Drinker doateth : Howsoever, I excuse him ; for that I believe he is now drawing near to the end, and final closure of his Life : Let us go make his Epitaph.

By the Answer which he hath given us, I am not, I protest, one jot wiser than I was. Hearken here, Epistemon, my little Bully, dost thou not hold him to be very resolute in his Respon-sory Verdicts ? He is a witty, quick and subtle Sophister : I will lay an even Wager, that he is a miscreant Apostate. By the Belly of a stalled Oxe, how careful he is not to be mistaken in his Words.

He answer'd but by Disjunctives, therefore can it not be true which he saith ; for the verity of such-like Propositions is inherent only in one of its two Members. O the cozening Pratler that he is ! I wonder if Santiago of Bressure be one of these cogging Shirks. Such was of old (quoth Epistemon) the Custom of the grand Vaticinator and Prophet Teresias, who used always (by way of a Preface) to say openly and plainly, at the beginning of his Divinations and Predictions, that what he was to tell, would either come to pass, or not : And such is truly the Style of all prudently presaging Prognosticators. He was, nevertheless, (quoth Panurge) so unfortunately mis-adventrous in the Lot of his own Destiny, that Juno thrust out both his Eyes.

Yes, (answer'd Epistemon) and that meerly out of a spight and spleen, for having pronounced his Award more veritably than she, upon the Question which was merrily proposed by Jupiter. But (quoth Panurge) what Arch-Devil is it that hath possess'd this Master Raminagrobis, that so unreasonably, and without any occasion, he should have so snappishly and bitterly inveighed against these poor honest Fathers, Jacobins, Minors, and Minims ? It vexeth me grievously, I assure you ; nor am I able to conceal my Indignation. He hath transgressed most enormously ; his Soul goeth infallibly to thirty thousand Panniers-full of Devils.

I understand you not (quoth Epistemon) and it disliketh me very much, that you should so absurdly and perversely interpret that of the Fryar Mendicants, which by the harmless Poet was spoken of black Beasts, dun, and other sorts of other coloured Animals. He is not, in my opinion, guilty of such a sophistical and fantastick Allegory, as by that Phrase of his, to have meant the Begging Brothers; he in downright terms speaketh absolutely and properly of Fleas, Punies, Hand-worms, Flyes, Gnats, and other such-like scurvy Vermin, whereof some are black, some dun, some ash-coloured, some tawny, and some brown and dusky, all noisom, molesting, tyrannous, cumbersom, and unpleasing Creatures, not only to sick and diseased Folks, but to those also who are of a sound, vigorous, and healthful Temperament and Constitution. It is not unlike, that he may have the Ascarids, and the Lumbricks and Worms within the Intrails of his Body. Possibly doth he suffer (as is frequent and usual amongst the Ægyptians, together with all those who inhabit the Erythræan Confines, and dwell along the Shores and Coasts of the Red-Sea) some sour prickings, and smart stingings in his Arms and Legs of those little speckled Dragons, which the Arabians call Meden. You are to blame for offering to expound his Words otherways, and wrong the ingenuous Poet, and outragiously abuse and miscall the said Fraters, by an imputation of baseness un-deservedly laid to their charge. We still should in such-like Discourses of fatiloquent Soothsayers, interpret all things to the best. Will you teach me (quoth Panurge) how to discern Flyes among Milk, or shew your Father the way how to beget Children? He is, by the Virtue of God, an arrant Heretick, a resolute formal Heretick; I say, a rooted combustible Here-tick, one as fit to burn as the little wooden Clock at Rochel. His Soul goeth to thirty thousand Carts-full of Devils. Would you know whither? Cocksbody, my Friend, streight under Proserpina's Close-stool, to the very middle of the self-same infernal Pan, within which she, by an excrementitious evacua-tion, voideth the fecal stuff of her stinking Clysters, and that just upon the left side of the great Cauldron of three fathom height, hard by the Claws and Talons of Lucifer, in the very darkest of the Passage which leadeth towards the Black Chamber of Demigorgon. Oh, the Villain!

CHAPTER XXIII

How Panurge maketh the motion of a Return to Raminagrobis

LET us return (quoth Panurge) not ceasing, to the uttermost
of our Abilities, to ply him with wholsom Admonitions, for the
furtherance of his Salvation. Let us go back, for God's sake ;
let us go, in the Name of God : it will be a very meritorious
Work, and of great Charity in us to deal so in the matter, and
provide so well for him, that albeit he come to lose both Body
and Life, he may at least escape the risk and danger of the
eternal Damnation of his Soul. We will, by our holy Perswa-
sions, bring him to a sense and feeling of his Escapes, induce
him to acknowledge his Faults, move him to a cordial Repentance of his Errors, and stir up in him such a sincere Contrition
of Heart for his Offences, as will prompt him with all earnestness to cry Mercy, and to beg Pardon at the Hands of the good
Fathers, as well of the absent, as of such as are present :
Whereupon we will take Instrument formally and authentically
extended, to the end he be not, after his Decease, declared an
Heretick, and condemned, as were the Hobgoblins of the
Provost's Wife of Orleans, to the undergoing of such Punishments, Pains and Tortures, as are due to, and inflicted on those
that inhabit the horrid Cells of the infernal Regions ; and withal
encline, instigate and perswade him to bequeath and leave in
Legacy (by way of an Amends and Satisfaction for the Outrage
and Injury done) to those good Religious Fathers, throughout
all the Convents, Cloisters and Monasteries of this Province,
many Bribes, a great deal of Mass-singing, store of Obits, and
that sempiternally, on the Anniversary-Day of his Decease,

O THE TERRIBLE COYL THAT THEY KEEP!

413

every one of them all be furnished with a quintuple Allowance : and that the great Borracho, replenish'd with the best Liquor, trudge apace along the Tables, as well of the young Duckling, Monkitos, Lay-Brothers, and lowermost degree of the Abbey-Lubbards, as of the learned Priests, and reverend Clerks. The very meanest of the Novices, and Mitiants unto the Order, being equally admitted to the benefit of those Funerary and Obsequial Festivals, with the aged Rectors, and professed Fathers ; this is the surest ordinary means, whereby from God he may obtain forgiveness.

Ho, ho, I am quite mistaken, I digress from the purpose, and fly out of my Discourse, as if my Spirits were a wool-gathering. The Devil take me, if I go thither. Vertue, God, the Chamber is already full of Devils. O what a swindging, thwacking Noise is now amongst them ! O the terrible Coyl that they keep ! Hearken, do you not hear the rustling thumping bustle of their Stroaks and Blows, as they scuffle with one another, like true Devils indeed, who shall gulp up the Raminagrobis Soul, and be the first Bringer of it, whilst it is hot, to Monsieur Lucifer. Beware, and get you hence : For my part, I will not go thither : the Devil roast me if I go. Who knows but that these hundred mad Devils may in the hast of their rage and fury of their Impatience, take a *quid* for a *quo*, and instead of Raminagrobis snatch up poor Panurge frank and free ? Though formerly, when I was deep in Debt, they always failed. Get you hence : I will not go thither. Before God, the very bare apprehension thereof is like to kill me. To be in the place where there are greedy, famished, and hunger-starved Devils ; amongst factious Devils : Amidst trading and trafficking Devils : O the Lord preserve me ! Get you hence, I dare pawn my Credit on it, that no Jacobin, Cordelier, Carmel Capucin, Theatin, or Minim, will bestow any personal Presence at his Interment. The wiser they, because he hath ordained nothing for them in his latter Will and Testament.

The Devil take me, if I go thither : if he be damned, to his own loss and hindrance be it. What the Duce moved him to be so snappish and depravedly bent against the good Fathers of the true Religion ? Why did he cast them off, reject them. and drive them quite out of his Chamber, even in that very nick of time when he stood in greatest need of the aid, suffrage, and assistance of their devout Prayers, and holy Admonitions ? Why did not he by Testament leave them, at least, some jolly Lumps and Cantles of substantial Meat, a parcel of Cheekpuffing Victuals, and a little Belly-Timber, and Provision for the Guts of these poor Folks, who have nothing but their Life in this World.

Let him go thither, who will; the Devil take me, if I go; for if I should, the Devil would not fail to snatch me up. Cancro: Ho, the Pox! Get you hence, Fryar Jhon; art thou content that Thirty thousand Waineload of Devils should get away with thee at this same very instant? If thou be, at my Request, do these Three things: First, Give me thy Purse; for besides, that thy Money is marked with Crosses, and the Cross is an Enemy to Charms, the same may befall to thee, which not long ago happened to Jhon Dodin, Collector of the Excise of Coudray, at the Ford of Vede, when the Soldiers broke the Planks. This money'd Fellow meeting at the very brink of the Bank of the Ford, with Fryar Adam Crankcod, a Franciscan Observantin of Mirebeau, promised him a new Frock, provided, that in the transporting of him over the Water, he would bear him upon his Neck and Shoulders, after the manner of carrying dead Goats: for he was a lusty, strong-limb'd, sturdy Rogue.

The Condition being agreed upon, Friar Crankcod trusseth himself up to his very Ballock, and layeth upon his Back like a fair little Saint Christopher, the load of the said Supplicant Dodin, and so carry'd him gayly and with a good Will; as Æneas bore his Father Anchises through the Conflagration of Troy, singing in the mean while a prety *Avemaris Stella*. When they were in the very deepest place of all the Foord, a little above the Master-wheel of the Water-Mill, he asked if he had any Coin about him. Yes, (quoth Dodin) a whole Bag full; and that he needed not to mistrust his Ability in the performance of the Promise, which he had made unto him concerning a new Frock. How! (quoth Friar Crankcod) thou knowest well enough, that by the express Rules, Canons and Injunctions of our Order, we are forbidden to carry on us any kind of Money: Thou art truly unhappy, for having made me in this point to commit a heinous Trespass. Why didst thou not leave thy Purse with the Miller? Without fail thou shalt presently receive thy Reward for it; and if ever hereafter I may but lay hold upon thee within the Limits of our Chancel at Mirebeau, thou shalt have the *Miserere* even to the *Vitulos*. With this suddenly discharging himself of his Burthen, he throws me down your Dodin headlong.

Take example by this Dodin, my dear Friend Friar Jhon,

to the end that the Devils may the better carry thee away at thine own ease. Give me thy Purse. Carry no manner of Cross upon thee. Therein lieth an evident and manifestly apparent Danger: For if you have any Silver coined with a Cross upon it, they will cast thee down headlong upon some Rocks; as the Eagles use to do with the Tortoises for the breaking of their Shells, as the bald Pate of the Poet Eschilus can sufficiently bear witness. Such a Fall would hurt thee very sore my Sweet Bully, and I would be very sorry for it; or otherways they will let thee fall, and tumble down into the high swollen Waves of some capacious Sea, I know not where; but I warrant thee far enough hence, (as Icarus fell) which from thy Name would afterwards get the Denomination of the Funnelian Sea.

Secondly, Out of Debt: For the Devils carry a great liking to those that are out of Debt. I have sore felt the experience thereof in mine own Particular; for now the lecherous Varlets are always wooing me, courting me, and making much of me, which they never did when I was all to pieces. The Soul of one in Debt is insipid, dry, and heretical altogether.

Thirdly, With the Cowl and Domino de Grobis, return to Raminagrobis; and in case, being thus qualify'd, Thirty Thousand Boats full of Devils forthwith come not to carry thee quite away, I shall be content to be at the charge of paying for the Pinte and Fagot. Now if for the more Security thou wouldst have some associate to bear thee Company, let not me be the Comrade thou searchest for, think not to get a Fellow-Traveller of me; nay, do not, I advise thee for the best. Get you hence; I will not go thither; the Devil take me if I go. Notwithstanding all the Fright that you are in, (quoth Friar Jhon) I would not care so much, as might possibly be expected I should, if I once had but my Sword in my Hand. Thou hast verily hit the Nail on the Head, (quoth Panurge) and speakest like a Learned Doctor, subtile, and well skilled in the Art of Devilry.

At the time when I was a Student in the University of Tolouse, that same Reverend Father in the Devil, Picarris, Rector of the Diabological Faculty, was wont to tell us, that the Devils did naturally fear the bright glancing of Swords, as much as the Splendour and Light of the Sun. In confirmation of the Verity whereof he related this Story, That Hercules at his Descent into Hell to all the Devils of those Regions, did not by half so much terrifie them with his Club and Lion's Skin, as afterwards Æneas did with his clear shining Armour upon him, and his Sword in his Hand well furbished and un-rusted, by the Aid, Counsel, and Assistance of the Sibylla Cumana. That was perhaps the reason why the Senior Jhon Jacomo di Trivulcio, whilst he was a dying at Chartres, called for his cutlass, and died with a Drawn Sword in his Hand, laying about him alongst and athwart around the Bed, and every where within his reach, like a stout, doughty, valorous and Knight-like Cavalier : By which resolute manner of Fence he scared away and put to flight all the Devils that were then lying in wait for his Soul at the passage of his Death. When the Massorets and Cabalists are asked, Why it is that none of all the Devils do at any time enter into the Terestrial Paradise ? Their answer hath been, is, and will be still, That there is a Cherubin standing at the Gate thereof with a Flame-like glistering Sword in his Hand. Although to speak in the true Diabological Sense or Phrase of Toledo, I must needs confess and acknowledge, that veritably the Devils cannot be killed, or die by the stroke of a Sword. I do nevertheless avow and maintain, according to the Doctrine of the said Diabology, that they may suffer a Solution of Continuity ; (as if with thy Shable thou should'st cut athwart the Flame of a burning Fire, or the gross opacous Exhalations of a thick and obscure Smoak) and cry out, like very Devils, at their Sense and Feeling of this Dissolution, which in real deed I must averr and affirm is devilishly painful, smarting and dolorous.

When thou seest the impetuous Shock of two Armies, and vehement Violence of the Push in their horrid Encounter with one another ; dost thou think, Balockasso, that so horrible a noise as is heard there proceedeth from the Voice and Shouts of Men ? The dashing and joulting of Harnish ? The clatter-ing and clashing of Armies ? The hacking and slashing of Battle Axes ? The justling and crashing of Pikes ? The bustling and breaking of Lances ? The clamour and Shrieks of the Wounded ? The sound and din of Drums ? The Clangour and Shrilness of Trumpets ? The neighing and rushing in of Horses ? With the fearful Claps and thundering of all sorts of Guns, from the Double Canon to the Pocket Pistol inclusively ? I cannot, Goodly, deny, but that in these various things which I have rehearsed, there may be somewhat occasionative of the huge Yell and Tintamarre of the two engaged Bodies.

But the most fearful and tumultuous Coil and Stir, the terriblest and most boisterous Garboil and Hurry, the chiefest rustling Black Sanctus of all, and most principal Hurly Burly, springeth from the grievously plangorous howling and lowing of Devils, who Pell-mell, in a hand-over-head Confusion, waiting for the poor Souls of the maimed and hurt Soldiery, receive unawares some Stroaks with Swords, and so by those means suffering a Solution of, and Division in the Continuity of their Aerial and Invisible Substances : As if some Lackey, snatching at the Lardslices, stuck in a piece of Roast meat on the Spit, should get from Mr. Greazyfist a good rap on the Knuckles with a Cudgel, they cry out and shout like Devils. Even as Mars did, when he was hurt by Diomedes at the Siege of Troy, who (as Homer testifieth of him) did then raise his voice more horrifically loud, and sonoriferously high, than ten thousand Men together would have been able to do. What maketh all this for our present purpose ? I have been speaking here of well-furbished Armour and bright shining Swords. But so is it not (Friar Jhon) with thy Weapon ; for by a long discontinuance of Work, cessation from Labour, desisting from making it officiate, and putting it into that practice wherein it had been formerly accustomed ; and in a word, for want of Occupation, it is, upon my Faith, become more rusty than the Key-hole of an old Poudering-Tub. Therefore it is expedient that you do one of these two, either furbish your Weapon bravely, and as it ought to be, or otherwise have a care that in the rusty case it is in, you do not presume to return to the House of Raminagrobis. For my part, I vow I will not go thither, the Devil take me if I go.

CHAPTER XXIV

How Panurge consulteth with Epistemon

HAVING left the Town of Villomere, as they were upon their return towards Pantagruel, Panurge in addressing his Discourse to Epistemon, spoke thus : My most ancient Friend and Gossip, thou seest the perplexity of my Thoughts, and knowest many Remedies for the Removal thereof ; art thou not able to help and succour me ? Epistemon thereupon taking the Speech in hand, represented unto Panurge, how the open Voice and common Fame of the whole Country did run upon no other Discourse, but the derision and mockery of his new Disguise ; wherefore his Counsel unto him was that he would in the first place be pleased to make use of a little Hellebore, for the purging of his Brain of that peccant humour, which thro' that extravagant and fantastick Mummery of his had furnished the People with a too just occasion of flouting and gibing, jeering and scoffing him ; and that next he would resume his ordinary Fashion of Accoutrement, and go apparelled as he was wont to do. I am (quoth Panurge) my dear Gossip Epistemon, of a mind and resolution to Marry, but am afraid of being a Cuckold, and to be unfortunate in my Wedlock : For this cause have I made a Vow to young St. Francis, (who at Plessiletours is much reverenced of all Women, earnestly cried unto by them, and with great Devotion ; for he was the first Founder of the Confraternity of good Men, whom they naturally covet, affect and long for) to wear Spectacles in my Cap, and to carry no Codpiece in my Breeches, until the present Inquietude and Perturbation of my Spirits be fully setled.

Truly (quoth Epistemon) that is a pretty jolly Vow, of Thirteen to a Dozen : It is a shame to you, and I wonder much at it, that you do not return unto your self, and recall your Senses from this their wild swarving, and straying abroad to that rest and stilness which becomes a vertuous Man. This whimsical Conceit of yours brings me to the remembrance of a solemn Promise made by the Shaghaired Argives, who having in their Controversy against the Lacedæmonians for the Territory of Tyree lost the Battle, which they hoped should have decided it for their Advantage, vowed to carry never any hair on their Heads, till preallably they had recovered the loss of both their Honour and Lands : As likewise to the memory of the Vow of a pleasant Spaniard called Michel Doris, who vowed to carry in his Hat a piece of the Shin of his Leg, till he should be revenged of him who had struck it off. Yet do not I know which of these two deserveth most to wear a Green and Yellow Hood with a Hares Ears tied to it, either the aforesaid vainglorious Champion, or that Euguerrant, who having forgot the art and manner of writing Histories, set down by the Samosatian Philosopher, maketh a most tediously long Narrative and Relation thereof : For at the first reading of such a profuse Discourse, one would think it had been broached for the introducing of a Story of great importance and moment concerning the waging of some formidable War, or the notable change and mutation of potent States and Kingdoms ; but in conclusion, the world laugheth at the capricious Champion, at the Englishman who had affronted him, as also at their Scribler Euguerrant, more driveling at the Mouth than a Mustard-pot. The Jest and Scorn thereof is not unlike to that of the Mountain of Horace, which by the Poet was made to cry out and lament most enormously as a Woman in the Pangs and Labour of Child-birth, at which deplorable and exorbitant Cries and Lamentations the whole Neighbourhood being assembled in expectation to see some marvellous monstrous Production, could at last perceive no other but the paultry ridiculous Mouse.

Your mousing (quoth Panurge) will not make me leave my musing why Folks should be so frumpishly disposed, seeing I am certainly perswaded that some flout, who merit to be flouted at ; yet as my Vow imports so will I do. It is now a long time since, by Jupiter Philos, we did swear Faith and Amity to one another : Give me your Advice, and tell me your Opinion freely, should I marry or no ? Truly (quoth Epistemon) the case is hazardous, and the danger so eminently apparent, that I find my self too weak and insufficient to give you a punctual and peremptory resolution therein ; and if ever it was true, the Judgment is difficult in matters of the Medicinal Art, what was said by Hippocrates of Lango, it is certainly so in this case. True it is, that in my Brain there are some rowling Fancies, by means whereof somewhat may be pitched upon of a seeming efficacy to the disintangling your mind of those dubious Apprehensions wherewith it is perplexed ; but they do not throughly satisfie me. Some of the Platonick Sect affirm, that whosoever is able to see his proper Genius, may know his own Destiny. I understand not their Doctrine ; nor do I think that you adhere to them ; there is a palpable Abuse. I have seen the experience of it in a very curious Gentleman of the Country of Estrangowre. This is one of the Points. There is yet another not much better. If there were any Authority now in the Oracles of Jupiter Ammon ; of Apollo in Lebadia, Delphos, Delos, Cyrra, Patara, Tegires, Preneste, Lycia, Colophon, or in the Castalian Fountain ; near Antioch in Syria ; between the Branchidians ; of Bacchus in Dodona ; of Mercure in Phares near Parras ; of Apis in Egypt ; of Serapis in Canoire ; of Faunus in Menalia, and Albunes near Tivoly ; of Tiresias in Orchomenie ; of Mosus in Silicia ; of Orpheus in Lisbos ; and of Trophonius in Lucadia. I would in that case advise you, and possibly not, to go thither for their Judgment concerning the Design and Enterprize you have in hand. But you know that they are all of them become as dumb as so many Fishes, since the Advent of that Saviour King, whose coming to this World hath made all Oracles and Prophecies to cease ; as the approach of the Suns radiant Beams expelleth Goblins, Bugbears, Hobthrushes, Broams, Schriech Owl-Mates, Nightwalking Spirits, and Tenebrions. These now are gone ; but although they were as yet in continuance, and in the same Power, Rule and Request that formerly they were, yet would not I counsel you to be too credulous in putting any Trust in their Responses : Too many Folks have been deceived thereby. It stands furthermore upon Record, how Agrippina did charge the fair Lollia with the Crime of having interrogated the Oracle of Apollo Clarius, to understand if she should be at any time married to the Emperor Claudius ; for which Cause she was first banished, and thereafter put to a shameful and ignominious Death.

But (saith Panurge) let us do better ; the Ogygian Islands are not far distant from the Haven of Sammalo : Let us, after that we shall have spoken to our King, make a Voyage thither. In one of these four Isles, to wit, that which hath its primest Aspect towards the Sun setting, it is reported, (and I have read in good Antick and Authentick Authors) that there reside many Soothsayers, Fortune-tellers, Vaticinators, Prophets, and Diviners of things to come ; that Saturn inhabiteth that place, bound with fair Chains of Gold, and within the Concavity of a Golden Rock, being nourished with Divine Ambrosie and

Nectar, which are daily in great store and abundance transmitted to him from the Heavens, by I do not well know what kind of Fowls (it may be that they are the same Ravens, which in the Deserts are said to have fed St. Paul, the first Hermit) he very clearly foretelleth unto every one, who is desirous to be certified of the condition of his Lot, what his Destiny will be, and what future chance the Fates have ordained for him : For the Parques, or Weerd Sisters do not twist, spin, or draw out a Thread ; nor yet doth Jupiter perpend, project, or deliberate any thing, which the good old Cœlestial Father knoweth not to the full, even whilst he is asleep : This will be a very summary Abbreviation of our Labour, if we but hearken unto him a little upon the serious debate and canvassing of this my perplexity. That is (answered Epistemon) a Gullery too evident, a plain Abuse and Fib too fabulous. I will not go, not I, I will not go.

CHAPTER XXV

How Panurge consulteth with Her Trippa

NEVERTHELESS, (quoth Epistemon, continuing his Discourse) I will tell you what you may do, if you will believe me, before we return to our King : Hard by here, in the Brown-wheat-Island, dwelleth Her Trippa ; you know how by the Arts of Astrology, Geomancy, Chiromancy, Metopomancy, and others of a like stuff and nature, he foretelleth all things to come : Let us talk a little, and confer with him about your Business. Of that (answered Panurge) I know nothing : But of this much concerning him I am assured, that one day, and that not long since, whilst he was prating to the Great King, of Cœlestial, Sublime, and Transcendent Things, the Lackqueys and Foot-boys of the Court, upon the upper Steps of Stairs between two Doors, jumbled, one after another, as often as they listed, his Wife ; who is passable fair, and a pretty snug Hussie. Thus he who seemed very clearly to see all Heavenly and Terrestrial Things without Spectacles, who discoursed boldly of Adventures past, with great confidence opened up present Cases and Accidents, and stoutly professed the presaging of all future Events and Contingencies, and was not able with all the Skill

HER TRIPPA

423

and Cunning that he had, to perceive the Bumbasting of his Wife, whom he reputed to be very chast ; and hath not till this Hour, got Notice of any thing to the contrary. Yet let us go to him, seeing you will have it so : for surely we can never learn too much. They on the very next ensuing Day, came to Her Trippa's Lodging. Panurge, by way of Donative, presented him with a long Gown lined all thorough with Wolves-skins, with a short Sword mounted with a gilded Hilt, and covered with a Velvet Scabbard, and with fifty good single Angells : Then in a familiar and friendly way did he ask of him his Opinion touching the Affair. At the very first Her Trippa looking on him very wistly in the face, said unto him : Thou hast the Metoposcopy, and Physiognomy of a Cuckold ; I say, of a notorious and infamous Cuckold. With this casting an eye upon Panurge's right Hand in all the parts thereof, he said, This rugged Draught which I see here, just under the Mount of Jove, was never yet but in the Hand of a Cuckold. Afterwards, he with a White Lead Pen, swiftly, and hastily drew a certain number of diverse kinds of Points, which by Rules of Geomancy he coupled and joyned together, then said, Truth it self is not truer, than that it is certain, thou wilt be a Cuckold, a little after thy Marriage. That being done, he asked of Panurge the Horoscope of his Nativity ; which was no sooner by Panurge tendred unto him, than that, erecting a Figure, he very promptly and speedily formed and fashion'd a compleat Fabrick of the Houses of Heaven, in all their parts, whereof when he had considered the Situation and the Aspects in their Triplicities, he fetched a deep sigh, and said : I have clearly enough already discovered unto you the Fate of your Cuck-oldry, which is unavoidable, you cannot escape it ; and here have I got of new a further assurance thereof, so that I may now hardily pronounce, and affirm without any scruple or hesitation at all, that thou wilt be a Cuckold ; that furthermore, thou wilt be beaten by thine own Wife, and that she will purloyn, filch, and steal of thy Goods from thee ; for I find the Seventh House, in all its Aspects, of a malignant Influence, and every one of the Planets threatning thee with Disgrace, according as they stand seated towards one another, in relation to the Horned Signs of Aries, Taurus, and Capricorn : In the Fourth House I find Jupiter in a Decadence, as also in a Tetragonal Aspect to Saturn, associated with Mercury, Thou wilt be soundly pepper'd, my good honest Fellow, I warrant thee. I will be : (answered Panurge) a Plague rot thee, thou old Fool, and doating Sot, how graceless and unpleasant thou art.

When all Cuckolds shall be at a General Rendezvous, thou shouldst be their Standard-bearer. But whence comes this Ciron-worm betwixt these two Fingers? This Panurge said, putting the Fore-finger of his Left-hand, betwixt the Fore and Mid-finger of the Right, which he thrust out towards Her Trippa, holding them open after the manner of two Horns, and shutting into a Fist his Thum, with the other Fingers. Then in turning to Epistemon, he said, Lo here the true Ollus of Martial, who addicted and devoted himself wholly to the observing the Miseries, Crosses, and Calamities of others, whilst his own Wife, in the interim, did keep an open Baudy-house.

This Varlet is poorer than ever was Irus, and yet he is a proud, vaunting, arrogant, self-conceited, over-weening, and more insupportable than seventeen Devils; in one word, Πτωχαλάζιον; which term of old was applied to the like beggarly strutting Coxcombs.

Come, let us leave this Madpash Bedlam, this hairbrain'd Fop, and give him leave to rave and dose his Belly-full, with his private and intimately acquainted Devils; who, if they were not the very worst of all the infernal Fiends, would never have daigned to serve such a knavish, barking Curr as this is. He hath not learn'd the first Precept of Philosophy, which is, Know thy self: For whilst he braggeth and boasteth, that he can discern the least Mote in the Eye of another, he is not able to see the huge Block that puts out the sight of both his Eyes. This is such another Polypragmon, as is by Plutarch described: He is of the Nature of the Lamian Witches, who in foreign Places, in the Houses of Strangers, in Publick, and amongst the Common People, had a sharper and more piercing Inspection into their Affairs than any Lync; but at home, in their own proper dwelling Mansions, were blinder than Mold-Warbs, and saw nothing at all: For their Custom was, at their return from abroad, when they were by themselves in private, to take their Eyes out of their head, from whence they were as easily removable as a Pair of Spectacles from their Nose, and to lay them up in a wooden Slipper, which for that purpose did hang behind the Door of their Lodging.

Panurge had no sooner done speaking, when Her Trippa took into his Hand a Tamarisk Branch. In this (quoth Epistemon) he doth very well, right, and like an Artist; for Nicander calleth it the Divinatory Tree. Have you a mind (quoth Her Trippa) to have the truth of the matter yet more fully and amply disclosed unto you by Pyromancy, by Aeromancy, (whereof Aristophanes in his *Clouds* maketh great estimation) by Hydromancy, by Leconomancy, of old in prime request amongst the Assyrians, and throughly tried by Hermolaus Barbarus : Come hither, and I will shew thee, in this Platter-full of fair Fountain-water, thy future Wife lechering, and sercroupierising it with two swaggering Ruffians, one after another. Yea, but have a special care, (quoth Panurge) when thou comest to put thy Nose within my Arse, that thou forget not to pull off thy Spectacles. Her Trippa going on in his Discourse, said by Catoptromancy, likewise held in such account by the Emperor Didius Julianus, That by means thereof, he ever and anon foresaw all that which at any time did happen or befal unto him : Thou shalt not need to put on thy Spectacles ; for in a Mirror thou wilt see her as clearly and manifestly Nebrundiated, and Billibodring-it, as if I should shew it in the Fountain of the Temple of Minerva near Parras. By Coscinomancy, most religiously observed of old, amidst the Ceremonies of the ancient Romans. Let us have a Sieve and Shiers, and thou shalt see Devils. By Alphitomancy, cried up by Theocritus in his *Pharmeketria.* By Alentomancy, mixing the Flower of Wheat with Oatmeal. By Astragalomancy, whereof I have the Plots and Models all at hand ready for the Purpose. By Tyromancy, whereof we make some Proof in a great Brehemont Cheese, which I here keep by me. By Giromancy, if thou shouldst turn round Circles, thou mightest assure thy self from me, that they would fall always on the wrong side. By Sternomancy, which maketh nothing for thy Advantage, for thou hast an ill-proportion'd Stomach. By Libanomancy, for the which we shall need but a little Frankincense. By Gastromancy, which kind of ventral Fatiloquency was for a long time together used in Ferrara by Lady Giacoma Rodogina, the Eugastrimythian Prophetess. By Cephalomancy, often practised amongst the High-Germans, in their boiling of an Asse's Head upon burning Coals. By Ceromancy, where, by the means of Wax dissolved into Water, thou shalt see the Figure, Pourtrait and lively Representation of thy future Wife, and of her Fredin Fredaliatory Bellythumping Blades. By Capnomancy ; O the gallantest and most excellent of all Secrets ! By Axionomancy, we want only a Hatchet and a Jeat-stone to be laid together upon a quick Fire of hot Embers. O how bravely Homer was versed in the Practice hereof towards Penelope's Suitors! By Onymancy, for that we have Oil and Wax. By Tephromancy, thou wilt see the Ashes thus aloft dispersed, exhibiting thy Wife in a fine Posture. By Botomancy, for the nonce I have some few Leaves in reserve. By Sicomancy; O Divine Art in Fig-tree Leaves! By Icthiomancy, in ancient times so celebrated, and put in use by Tiresias and Polydamas, with the like certainty of event as was tried of old at the Dinaditch within that Grove consecrated to Apollo, which is in the Territory of the Lycians. By Choiramancy: Let us have a great many Hogs, and thou shalt have the Bladder of one of them. By Cheromomancy, as the Bean is found in the Cake at the Epiphany Vigil. By Anthropomancy, practised by the Roman Emperor Heliaga-bolus; it is somewhat irksom, but thou wilt endure it well enough, seeing thou art destinated to be a Cuckold. By a Sibylline Stichomancy. By Onomatomancy: How do they call thee! Chawturd, (quoth Panurge) or yet by Alectryo-mancy. If I should here with a Compass draw a Round, and in looking upon thee, and considering thy Lot, divide the Cir-cumference thereof into four and twenty equal Parts, then form a several Letter of the Alphabet upon every one of them; and lastly, posit a Barley-Corn or two upon each of these so disposed Letters, I durst promise upon my Faith and Honesty, that if a Young Virgin Cock be permitted to range alongst and athwart them, he should only eat the Grains which are set and placed upon these Letters, A. C.u.c.k.o.l.d. T.h.o.u. s.h.a.l.t. b.e. And that as fatidically, as under the Emperor Valence, most perplexedly desirous to know the Name of him who should be his Successor to the Empire, the Cock Vaticinating and Alec-tryomantick, ate up the Pickles that were posited on the Letters T.h.e.o.d. Or for the more certainty, will you have a trial of your Fortune by the Art of Aruspiciny? by Augury? or by Extispicine? By Turdispicine, quoth Panurge; or yet by the Mystery of Negromancy? I will, if you please, suddenly set up again, and revive some one lately deceased, as Apol-lonius of Tyan did to Achilles, and the Pythoniss in the Presence of Saul; which Body so raised up, and requickned, will tell us the Sum of all you shall require of him; no more nor less than at the Invocation of Erictho, a certain defunct Person, foretold to Pompey the whole Progress and Issue of the fatal Battle fought in the Pharsalian Fields? Or if you be afraid of the Dead, as commonly all Cuckolds are, I will make use of the Faculty of Sciomancy. Go, get thee gone, (quoth Panurge) thou frantick Ass, to the Devil, and be bugger'd, filthy Bordachio that thou art, by some Albanian, for a Steeple-crown'd Hat. Why the Devil didst not thou counsel me as well to hold an Emerald, or the Stone of a Hyena under my Tongue? Or to furnish and provide my self with Tongues of Whoops, and Hearts of Green Frogs? Or to eat of the Liver or Milt of some Dragon? To the end that by those means I might, at the chanting and chirping of Swans and other Fowls, understand the Substance of my future Lot and Destiny, as did of old the Arabians in the Country of Mesopotamia? Fifteen Brace of Devils seize upon the Body and Soul of this horned Renegado, miscreant Cuckold, the Inchanter, Witch, and Sorcerer of Antichrist to all the Devils of Hell.

Let us return towards our King: I am sure he will not be well pleased with us, if he once come to get notice that we have been in the Kennel of this muffled Devil. I repent my being come hither. I would willingly dispense with a Hundred Nobles, and Fourteen Yeomans, on condition that he who not long since did blow in the bottom of my Breeches, should instantly with his squirting Spittle inluminate his Mustaches. O Lord God now! how the Villain hath besmoaked me with Vexation and Anger, with Charms and Witchcraft, and with a terrible Coyl and Stir of Infernal and Tartarian Devils! The Devil take him: Say Amen; and let us go drink. I shall not have any Appetite for my Victuals (how good Cheer soever I make) these two days to come, hardly these four.

CHAPTER XXVI

How Panurge consulteth with Fryar Jhon, of the Funnels

PANURGE was indeed very much troubled in Mind, and disquieted at the words of Her Trippa, and therefore as he passed by the little Village of Hugmes, after he had made his Address to Fryar Jhon, in pecking at, rubbing and scratching his own left Ear, he said unto him, Keep me a little jovial and merry, my dear and sweet Bully, for I find my Brains altogether metagrabolized and confounded, and my Spirits in a most dunsical puzzle at the bitter talk of this Devilish, Hellish, Damned Fool : Hearken, my dainty Cod.

Mellow C.	Orange-tawny C.	Absolute C.
Lead-coloured C.	Imbroidered C.	Well-set C.
Knurled C.	Glazed C.	Gemel C.
Suborned C.	Interlarded C.	Turkish C.
Desired C.	Burger-like C.	Burning C.
Stuffed C.	Impoudred C.	Thwacking C.
Speckled C.	Ebenized C.	Convulsive C.
Finely metal'd C.	Brasiliated C.	Restorative C.
Arabian-like C.	Organized C.	Masculinating C.
Trussed up, Grey-	Passable C.	Incarnative C.
hound-like C.	Trunkified C.	Sigillative C.
Mounted C.	Furious C.	Sallying C.
Sleeked C.	Packed C.	Plump C.
Diapred C.	Hooded C.	Thundering C.
Spotted C.	Varnished C.	Lechering C.
Master C.	Renowned C.	Fulminating C.
Seeded C.	Matted C.	Sparkling C.
Lusty C.	Genetive C.	Ramming C.
Jupped C.	Gigantal C.	Lusty C.
Milked C.	Oval C.	Urgent C.
Calfeted C.	Claustral C.	Handsom C.
Raised C.	Viril C.	Prompt C.
Odd C.	Stayed C.	Fortunate C.
Steeled C.	Massive C.	Boxewood C.
Stale C.	Manual C.	Latten C.

Unbridled C.
Hooked C.
Researched C.
Encompassed C.
Strouting out C.
Jolly C.
Lively C.
Gerundive C.
Franked C.
Polished C.
Powder'd Beef C.
Positive C.
Spared C.
Bold C.
Lascivious C.
Gluttonous C.
Resolute C.
Cabbage-like C.
Courteous C.
Fertil C.
Whizzing C.
Neat C.
Common C.
Brisk C.
Quick C.
Barelike C.
Partitional C.
Patronymick C.
Cockney C.
Auromercuriated C.
Robust C.
Membrous C.
Strong C.
Twin C.
Belabouring C
Gentil C.
Stirring C.
Confident C.
Nimble C.
Roundheaded C.
Figging C.
Helpful C.
Spruce C.

Plucking C.
Ramage C.
Appetizing C.
Succourable C.
Redoubtable C.
Affable C.
Memorable C.
Palpable C.
Barbable C.
Tragical C.
Transpontine C.
Digestive C.
Active C.
Vital C.
Magistral C.
Monachal C.
Subtil C.
Hammering C.
Clashing C.
Tingling C.
Usual C.
Exquisite C.
Trim C.
Succulent C.
Factious C.
Clammy C.
Fat C.
High-priced C.
Requisite C.
Laycod C.
Hand-filling C.
Insuperable C.
Agreeable C.
Formidable C.
Profitable C.
Notable C.
Musculous C.
Subsidiary C.
Satyrick C.
Repercussive C.
Odoriferous C.
Pranked C.
Jocund C.

Routing C.
Purloining C.
Frolick C.
Wagging C.
Ruffling C.
Jumbling C.
Rumbling C.
Thumping C.
Bumping C.
Cringeling C.
Houshold C.
Pretty C.
Astrolabian C.
Algebraical C.
Venust C.
Aromatizing C.
Trixy C.
Paillard C.
Gaillard C.
Broaching C.
Adle C.
Syndicated C.
Boulting C.
Snorting C.
Pilfring C.
Shaking C.
Bobbing C.
Chiveted C.
Fumbling C.
Topsiturvying C.
Raging C.
Piled up C.
Filled up C.
Manly C.
Idle C.
Affecting C.
Affected C.
Grapled C.
Stuffed C.
Well-fed C.
Flourished C.
Fallow C.
Graspful C.

Sudden C.
Swillpow C.
Crushing C.
Fine C.
Fierce C.
Brawny C.
Compt C.
Repaired C.
Soft C.
Wild C.
Renewed C.
Quaint C.
Starting C.
Fleshy C.
Auxiliary C.
New-vamped C.
Improved C.
Malling C.
Sounding C.
Batled C.
Burly C.
Seditious C.
Wardian C.
Protective C.

Twinkling C.
Able C.
Algoristical C.
Creaking C.
Dilting C.
Ready C.
Vigorous C.
Scoulking C.
Superlative C.
Clashing C.
Wagging C.
Scriplike C.
Encremaster'd C.
Berumpling C.
Jogging C.
Nobbing C.
Touzing C.
Tumbling C.
Fambling C.
Overturning C.
Shooting C.
Culeting C.
Jagged C.
Pinked C.

Arsiversing C.
Polished C.
Slasht C.
Hamed C.
Leisurely C.
Cut C.
Smooth C.
Depending C.
Independent C.
Lingring C.
Rapping C.
Reverend C.
Nodding C.
Disseminating C.
Bouncing C.
Levelling C.
Fly-flap C.
Perinæ tegminal C.
Squat-couching C.
Short-hung C.
The hypogastrian C
Witness bearing C.
Testigerous C.
Instrumental C.

My Harcabuzing Cod, and Buttockstirring Ballock, Fryar Jhon, my Friend : I do carry a singular respect unto thee, and honour thee with all my Heart, thy Counsel I hold for a choice and delicate Morsel, therefore have I reserved it for the last Bit. Give me thy advice freely, I beseech thee ; Should I marry, or no ? Fryar Jhon very merrily, and with a sprightly chearfulness made this Answer to him : Marry, in the Devil's Name, Why not : What the Devil else shouldst thou do, but marry ? Take thee a Wife, and furbish her Harnish to some tune : Swinge her Skin-coat, as if thou wert beating on Stock-fish, and let the repercussion of thy Clapper from her resounding Metal, make a Noise, as if a double Peal of Chiming-Bells were hung at the Cremasters of thy Ballock. As I say Marry, so do I understand, that thou shouldst fall to work as speedily amayst be : yea, my meaning is, that thou oughtest to be so quick and forward therein, as on this same very day, before Sunset, to cause, proclaim thy Banes of Matrimony, and make provision of Bedsteads. By the Blood of a Hog's-pudding, till when wouldst thou delay the acting of a Husband's part ? Dost thou not know, and is it not daily told unto thee, that the end of the World approacheth ? We are nearer it by three Poles, and half a Fathom, then we were two days ago. The Antichrist is already born, at least it is so reported by many : the truth is, that hitherto the effects of his wrath have not reached further than to the scratching of his Nurse and Governesses : his Nails are not sharp enough as yet, nor have his Claws attained to their full growth ; he is little.

Crescat ; Nos qui vivimus, multiplicemur. It is written so, and it is holy stuff, I warrant you : The truth whereof is like to last as long as a Sack of Corn may be had for a penny, and a Punction of pure Wine for Three-pence. Would thou be content to be found with thy Genitories full in the Day of Judgment ? *Dum veneris judicari.* Thou hast (quoth Panurge) a right, clear, and neat Spirit, Fryar Jhon, my Metropolitan Cod ; thou speakest in very deed pertinently, and to purpose : That belike was the reason which moved Leander of Abydos in Asia, whilst he was swimming through the Hellespontick Sea, to make a Visit to his Sweetheart Hero of Sestus in Europe, to pray unto Neptune, and all the other Marine Gods, thus :

> Now, whilst I go, have pity on me,
> And at my back returning drown me.

He was loath, it seems, to die with his Cods over-gorged : He was to be commended, therefore do I promise, that from henceforth no Malefactor shall by Justice be executed within my Jurisdiction of Salmigondinois, who shall not, for a day or two at least before, be permitted to culbut, and foraminate, Onocrotalwise, that there remain not in all his Vessels, to write a great Greek Y ; such a precious thing should not be foolishly cast away ; he will perhaps therewith beget a Male, and so depart the more contentedly out of this Life, that he shall have left behind him one for one.

CHAPTER XXVII

How Fryar Jhon merrily, and sportingly counselleth Panurge

By Saint Rigomet (quoth Fryar Jhon) I do advise thee to no-thing, (my dear Friend Panurge) which I would not do my self, were I in thy place : only have a special care, and take good heed thou soulder well together the Joynts of the double backed and two bellied Beast, and fortifie thy Nerves so strongly, that there be no discontinuance in the Knocks of the Venerian thwacking, else thou art lost, poor Soul : for if there pass long intervals betwixt the Priapising feats, and that thou make an intermission of too large a time, that will befall thee, which betides the Nurses, if they desist from giving suck to Children, they lose their Milk ; and if continually thou do not hold thy Aspersory Tool in exercise, and keep thy Mentul going, thy Lactinician Nectar will be gone, and it will serve thee only as a Pipe to piss out at, and thy Cods for a Wallet of lesser value than a Beggars Scrip. This is a certain truth I tell thee, Friend, and doubt not of it ; for my self have seen the sad experiment thereof in many, who cannot now do what they would, because before they did not what they might have done : *Ex desuetudine amittuntur Privilegia :* Nonusage often-times destroys ones Right, say the learned Doctors of the Law : therefore, my Billy, encertain as well as possibly thou canst, that Hypogastrian, lower sort of Troglodytick People that their chief pleasure may be placed in the case of sempiternal labour-ing. Give order that henceforth they live not like idle Gentlemen, idle upon their Rents and Revenues, but that they may work for their livelyhood, by breaking ground within the Paphian Trenches. Nay truly (answered Panurge) Fryar Jhon, my left Ballock, I will believe thee, for thou dealest plain with me, and fallest downright square upon the business, without going about the Bush with frivolous circumstances, and unnecessary reservations. Thou with the splendour of piercing Wit, hast dissipated all the louring Clouds of anxious Apprehensions and Suspicions, which did intimidate and terrifie me : therefore the Heavens be pleased to grant to thee, at all She-conflicts, a stiff-standing Fortune. Well then, as thou hast said, so will I do, I will, in good Faith marry ; in that point there shall be no failing, I promise thee, and shall have always by me pretty Girls clothed with the Name of my Wives Waiting-Maids, that lying under thy Wings, thou mayest be Night-Protector of their Sister-hood.

Let this serve for the first part of the Sermon. Hearken (quoth Fryar Jhon) to the Oracle of the Bells of Varenes ; What say they ? I hear and understand them (quoth Panurge) their Sound is by my Thirst, more uprightly fatidical, than that of Jove's Great Kettles in Dodona. Hearken ; Take thee a Wife, take thee a Wife, and marry, marry, marry : for if thou marry, thou shalt find good therein, herein, here in a Wife thou shalt find good ; so marry, marry. I will assure thee, that I shall be married, all the Elements invite and prompt me to it : let this Word be to thee a Brazen Wall, by diffidence not to be broken thorough. As for the Second part of this our Doctrine : Thou seemest in some measure to mistrust the readiness of my Paternity, in the practising of my Placket-Racket within the Aphrodisian Tennis-Court at all times fitting, as if the stiff God of Gardens were not favourable to me. I pray thee, favour me so much as to believe, that I still have him at a beck, attending always my Commandments, docile, obedient, vigorous, and active in all things, and every-where, and never stubborn or refractory to my will or pleasure.

I need no more, but to let go the Reins, and slacken the Leash, which is the Bellypoint, and when the Game is shewn unto him, say, Hey, Jack, to thy Booty, he will not fail even then to flesh himself upon his Prey, and tuzle it to some purpose. Hereby you may perceive, although my future Wife were as unsatiable and gluttonous in her Voluptuousness, and the Delights of Venery, as ever was the Empress Messalina, or yet the Marchioness in England ; and I desire thee to give

I DO ADVISE THEE TO NOTHING, (MY DEAR FRIEND PANURGE) WHICH I
WOULD NOT DO MY SELF

435

credit to it, that I lack not for what is requisite to overloy the Stomach of her Lust, but have wherewith aboundingly to please her.

I am not ignorant that Solomon said, who indeed of that matter speaketh Clerklike, and learnedly : As also how Aristotle after him declared for a truth, That for the greater part, the Lechery of a Woman is ravenous and unsatisfiable : Nevertheless, let such as are my Friends, who read those Passages, receive from me for a most real verity, that I for such a Gill, have a fit Jack ; and that, if Womens things cannot be satiated, I have an Instrument indefatigable ; an Implement as copious in the giving, as can in craving be their Vade Mecums. Do not here produce ancient Examples of the Paragons of Paillardise, and offer to match with my Testiculatory Ability, the Priapæan Prowess of the fabulous Fornicators, Hercules, Proculus, Cæsar, and Mahomet, who in his Alcoran doth vaunt, that in his Cods he had the vigour of Threescore Bully Ruffians ; but let no zealous Christian trust the Rogue, the filthy ribald Rascal is a Lyar. Shall thou need to urge Authorities, or bring forth the Instance of the Indian Prince, of whom Theophrastus, Plinius, and Athenæus testifie, that with the help of a certain Herb, he was able, and had given frequent Experiments thereof, to toss his sinewy Piece of Generation, in the Act of carnal Concupiscence, above threescore and ten times in the space of four and twenty Hours. Of that I believe nothing, the number is supposititious, and too prodigally foisted in : Give no Faith unto it, I beseech thee, but prithee trust me in this, and thy credulity therein shall not be wronged ; for it is true, and *Probatum est*, that my Pionier of Nature, the sacred Ithyphallian Champion, is of all stiff-intruding Blades the primest : Come hither my Ballockette, and hearken, Didst thou ever see the Monk of Castres Cowl ? When in any house it was laid down, whether openly in view of all, or covertly out of the sight of any, such was the ineffable Vertue thereof for excitating and stirring up the people of both Sexes unto Lechery, that the whole Inhabitants and Indwellers, not only of that, but likeways of all the circumjacent places thereto, within three Leagues around it, did suddenly enter into Rut, both Beasts and Folk, Men and Women, even to the Dogs and Hogs, Rats and Cats.

I swear to thee, that many times heretofore I have perceived, and found in my Codpiece a certain kind of Energy, or efficacious Vertue, much more irregular, and of a greater Anomaly, then what I have related : I will not speak to thee either of

House or Cottage, nor of Church or Market, but only tell thee, that once at the Representation of the Passion, which was acted at Saint Mexents, I had no sooner entred within the Pit of the Theatre, but that forthwith, by the vertue and occult property of it, on a sudden all that were there, both Players and Spectators, did fall into such an exorbitant Temptation of Lust, that there was not Angel, Man, Devil, nor Deviless, upon the place, who would not then have Bricollitched it with all their Heart and Soul.

The Prompter forsook his Copy, he who played Michael's part, came down to rights, the Devils issued out of Hell, and carried along with them most of the pretty little Girls that were there; yea, Lucifer got out of his Fetters; in a word: Seeing the huge Disorder, I disparked my self forth of that inclosed place, in imitation of Cato the Censor, who perceiving by reason of his presence, the Floralian Festivals out of order, withdrew himself.

CHAPTER XXVIII

How Friar Jhon comforteth Panurge in the doubtful matter of Cuckoldry

I UNDERSTAND thee well enough, said Friar Jhon; but time makes all things plain. The most durable Marble or Porphyr is subject to Old Age and Decay. Though for the present thou possibly be not weary of the Exercise, yet is it like, I will hear thee confess a few years hence, that thy Cods hang dangling downwards for want of a better Truss. I see thee waxing a little hoar-headed already; thy Beard by the Distinctions of grey, white tawny and black, hath to my thinking the resemblance of a Map of the Terrestrial Globe, or Geographical Chart. Look attentively upon, and take Inspection of what I shall show unto thee. Behold there Asia, here are Tygris and Euphrates: Lo there Africk; here is the Mountain of the Moon, yonder thou mayst perceive the Fenny Marsh of Nilus. On this side lieth Europe: Dost thou not see the Abby of Tileme? This little Tuft, which is altogether white, is the Hyperborean Hills. By the thirst of my Throple Friend,

437

when Snow is on the Mountains, I say the Head and Chin, there is not then any considerable Heat to be expected in the Valleys and Low-Countries of the Codpiece. By the Kibes of thy Heels (quoth Panurge) thou dost not understand the Topicks. When Snow is on the tops of the Hills, Lightning, Thunder, Tempest, Whirlwinds, Storms, Hurricanes, and all the Devils of Hell rage in the Valleys. Wouldst thou see the experience thereof, go to the Territory of the Swissers, and earnestly perpend with thy self there the Situation of the Lake of Wendel-berlick, about four Leagues distant from Berne, on the Syon-side of the Land. Thou twittest me with my Grey Hairs, yet considerest not how I am of the Nature of Leeks, which with a white Head carry a green, fresh, streight, and vigorous Tail.

The truth is nevertheless, (why should I deny it) that I now and then discern in my self some indicative Signs of Old Age. Tell this, I prithee, to no body, but let it be kept very close and secret betwixt us two : for I find the Wine much sweeter now, more savoury to my taste, and unto my Palate of a better relish than formerly I was wont to do ; and withal, besides mine accustomed manner, I have a more dreadful Apprehension than I ever heretofore have had of lighting on bad Wine. Note and observe that this doth argue and portend I know not what of the West and Occident of my time, and signifieth that the South and Meridian of mine Age is past. But what then ? My Gentle Companion, that doth but betoken that I will here-after drink so much the more. That is not, the Devil hale it, the thing that I fear ; nor is it there where my Shoe pinches. The thing that I doubt most, and have greatest reason to dread and suspect, is, that through some long absence of our King Pantagruel (to whom I must needs bear Company, should he go to all the Devils of Barathrum) my future Wife shall make me a Cuckold. This is, in truth, the long and the short on't : For I am by all those whom I have spoke to menac'd and threatned with a Horned Fortune ; and all of them affirm, it is the Lot to which from Heaven I am predestinated. Every one (answered Friar Jhon) that would be a Cuckold, is not one : If it be thy Fate to be hereafter of the number of that Horned Cattle, then may I conclude with an Ergo, thy Wife will be beautiful, and Ergo, thou wilt be kindly used by her : Likewise with this Ergo thou shalt be blessed with the fruition of many Friends and Well-willers : And finally with this other Ergo thou shalt be saved, and have a place in Paradise. These are

Monachal Topicks and Maxims of the Cloister : Thou mayst take more liberty to sin : Thou shalt be more at ease than ever : There will be never the less left for thee, nothing diminished, but thy Goods shall increase notably ; And if so be it was preordinated for thee, wouldst thou be so impious as not to acquiesce in thy Destiny ?   Speak thou jaded Cod,

Faded C.
Mouldy C.
Musty C.
Paultery C.
Senseless C.
Foundred C.
Distempred C.
Fleeted C.
Cloyed C.
Squeezed C.
Resty C.
Pounded C.
Loose C.
Coldish C.
Cut off C.
Beveraged C.
Scarified C.
Dasht C.
Slasht C.
Infeebled C.
Whore-hunting C.
Berayed C.
Inveigled C.
Dangling C.
Stupid C.
Seedless C.
Soaked C.
Lowting C.
Discouraged C.
Surfeited C.
Peevish C.
Translated C.
Forlorn C.
Unsavoury C.
Worm-eaten C.
Overtoiled C.

Miserable C.
Steeped C.
Kneaded with cold
   Water C.
Appealant C.
Swagging C.
Withered C.
Broken reined C.
Defective C.
Crestfallen C.
Felled C.
Wrangling C.
Gangreened C.
Crustrisen C.
Ragged C.
Quelled C.
Bragadochio C.
Beggarly C.
Trepanned C.
Bedusked C.
Emasculated C.
Corked C.
Transparent C.
Vile C.
Antidated C.
Chopped C.
Pinked C.
Cup-glassified C.
Fruitless C.
Riven C.
Pursie C.
Fusty C.
Jadish C.
Fistulous C.
Languishing C.
Maleficiated C.

Peckled C.
Churned C.
Filiped C.
Singlefied C.
Begrimed C.
Wrinkled C.
Fainted C.
Extenuated C.
Grim C.
Wasted C.
Inflamed C.
Unhinged C.
Scurfie C.
Stradling C.
Putrefied C.
Maimed C.
Overlechered C.
Druggely C.
Mitified C.
Goat-ridden C.
Weakned C.
Asse-ridden C.
Puff-pasted C.
St. Anthonified C.
Untriped C.
Blasted C.
Rangling tasted C.
Rooted out C.
Costive C.
Hailed on C.
Cuffed C.
Buffeted C.
Whirreted C.
Robbed C.
Neglected C.
Lame C.

Confused C.

Unsavoury C.

Overthrown C.

Boulted C.

Trod under C.

Desolate C.

Declining C.

Stinching C.

Sorrowful C.

Murthered C.

Matachin-like C

Besotted C.

Customerless C.

Minced C.

Exulcerated C.

Deteriorated C.

Chil C.

Scrupulous C.

Crazed C.

Tasteless C.

Hacked C.

Flaggy C.

Scrubby C.

Drained C.

Haled C.

Lolling C.

Drenched C.

Burst C.

Stirred up C.

Mitred C.

Pedling furnished C.

Rusty C.

Exhausted C.

Perplexed C.

Unhelved C.

Fizled C.

Leprous C.

Bruised C.

Spadonick C.

Boughty C.

Mealy C.

Corrected C.

Slit C.

Skittish C.

Spungy C.

Botched C.

Dejected C.

Jagged C.

Pining C.

Deformed C.

Mischieved C.

Cobled C.

Imbased C.

Ransacked C.

Despised C.

Mangy C.

Abased C.

Supine C.

Mended C.

Dismayed C

Harsh C.

Beaten C.

Barred C.

Abandoned C.

Confounded C.

Lowtish C.

Hectick C.

Worn out C.

Ill-favoured C.

Duncified C.

Macerated C.

Paralytick C.

Degraded C.

Benummed C.

Bat-like C.

Fart-shotten C.

Sun-burnt C.

Pacified C.

Blunted C.

Belammed C.

Fabricant C.

Perused C.

Emasculated C.

Roughly handled C.

Examined C.

Crakt C.

Waiward C.

Hagled C.

Gleaning C.

Ill-favoured C.

Pulled C.

Drooping C.

Faint C.

Parched C.

Paultry C.

Cankred C.

Void C.

Vexed C.

Bestunk C.

Crooked C.

Brabling C.

Rotten C.

Anxious C.

Clouted C.

Tired C.

Proud C.

Fractured C.

Melancholy C.

Coxcombly C.

Base C.

Bleaked C.

Detested C.

Diaphanous C.

Unworthy C.

Checked C.

Mangled C.

Flapping C.

Patched C.

Stupified C.

Annihilated C.

Spent C.

Foiled C.

Aguish C.

Disfigured C.

Disabled C.

Forcedless C.

Censured C.

Cut C.

Rifled C.

Undone C.
Turned over C.
Harried C.
Flawed C.
Froward C.
Ugly C.
Drawn C.
Riven C.
Distasteful C.
Hanging C.
Broken C.
Limber C.
Effeminate C.
Kindled C.
Evacuated C.
Grieved C.
Carking C.
Disorderly C.
Empty C.
Disquieted C.
Besysted C.
Confounded C.
Hooked C.
Diverous C.
Wearied C.
Sad C.
Cross C.
Vain-glorious C.
Poor C.
Brown C.
Shrunk-in C.
Abhorred C.
Troubled C.
Scornful C.
Dishonest C.
Reproved C.
Cocketed C.
Filthy C.
Shred C.
Born down C.
Sparred C.
Abashed C.
Unseasonable C.

Opprest C.
Grated C.
Falling away C.
Smalcut C.
Disordered C.
Lattised C.
Ruined C.
Exasperated C.
Rejected C.
Chawned C.
Short-winded C.
Branchless C.
Chapped C.
Failing C.
Deficient C.
Lean C.
Consumed C.
Used C.
Puzled C.
Allayed C.
Spoiled C.
Clagged C.
Palsey-strucken C.
Amazed C.
Bedunsed C.
Extirpated C.
Banged C.
Stripped C.
Hoary C.
Winnowed C.
Decayed C.
Disastrous C.
Unhandsom C.
Stummed C.
Barren C.
Wretched C.
Feeble C.
Cast down C.
Stopped C.
Kept under C.
Stubborn C.
Ground C.
Retchless C.

Weather-beaten C.
Flayed C.
Bauld C.
Tossed C.
Cleft C.
Meagre C.
Dumpified C.
Supprest C.
Hagged C.
Jawped C.
Havocked C.
Astonished C.
Dulled C.
Slow C.
Plucked up C.
Constipated C.
Blown C.
Blockify'd C.
Pommeled C.
All-to-be mawl'd C.
Fallen away C.
Unlucky C.
Steril C.
Beshitten C.
Appeased C.
Caitive C.
Woful C.
Unseemly C.
Heavy C.
Weak C.
Prostrated C.
Uncomely C.
Naughty C.
Laid flat C.
Suffocated C.
Held down C
Barked C.
Hairless C.
Spotted C.
Crumpled C.
Flamping C.
Hooded C.
Wormy C.

Besysted C.
Faulty C.
Bemealed C.
Mortified C.
Scurvy C.
Bescabbed C.
Torn C.
Subdued C.
Sneaking C.
Bare C.
Swart C.
Smutched C.
Raised up C.
Chopped C.
Flirted C.
Blained C.
Blotted C.
Sunk in C.
Gastly C.
Unpointed C.
Beblistered C.
Wizened C.
Begger-plated C.

Douf C.
Clarty C.
Lumpish C.
Abject C.
Side C.
Choaked up C.
Backward C.
Prolix C.
Adamitical C.
Frumpled C.
Stale C.
Corrupted C.
Beflowred C.
Amated C.
Blackish C.
Underlaid C.
Loathing C.
Ill-filled C.
Bobbed C.
Mated C.
Tawny C.
Whealed C.

Besmeared C.
Hollow C.
Pantless C.
Guizened C.
Demiss C.
Refractory C.
Rensie C.
Frowning C.
Limping C.
Revealed C.
Rammish C.
Gaunt C.
Beskimmered C.
Scraggy C.
Lank C.
Swashring C.
Moyling C.
Swinking C.
Harried C.
Tugged C.
Towed C.
Misused C.

Balockatso to the Devil, my dear Friend Panurge, seeing it is so decreed by the Gods, wouldst thou invert the course of the Planets, and make them retrograde ? Wouldst thou disorder all the Cœlestial Spheres ? Blame the Intelligencies, blunt the Spindles, joynt the Wherves, slander the Spinning Quills, reproach the Bobbins, revile the Clew-bottoms, and finally ravel and untwist all the threads of both the warp and the waft of the weer'd Sister Parques ? What a Pox to thy Bones dost thou mean, stony Cod ? Thou wouldst if thou couldst, a great deal worse than the Gyants of old intended to have done. Come hither, Billicullion ; whither wouldst thou be jealous without cause, or be a Cuckold and know nothing of it ? Neither the one nor the other (quoth Panurge) would I choose to be ; But if I get an inkling of the matter, I will provide well enough, or there shall not be one stick of Wood within five hundred Leagues about me, whereof to make a Cudgel. In good Faith (Fryar Jhon) I speak now seriously unto thee, I think it will be my best not to marry ; Hearken to what the Bells do tell me, now that we are nearer to them : Do not Marry, Marry not,

W.HEATH.ROBINSON

HANS CARVEL

443

not, not, not, not; Marry, Marry not, not, not, not, not: If thou Marry, thou wilt miscarry, carry, carry, thou'lt repent it, resent it, sent it: If thou Marry, thou a Cuckold, a Cou-cou-Cuckoe, Cou-cou-Cuckold thou shalt be. By the worthy Wrath of God, I begin to be angry; this Campanilian Oracle fretteth me to the Guts, a March-Hare was never in such a Chaff as I am. O how I am vexed! you Monks and Fryars of the Cawl-pated and Hood-patted Fraternity, have you no Remedy nor Salve against this Malady of Graffing Horns in Heads? Hath Nature so abandon'd Human-kind, and of her help left us so destitute, that married Men cannot know how to sail through the Seas of this mortal Life, and be safe from the Whirpools, Quicksands, Rocks and Banks that lie alongst the Coast of Cornwall.

I will (said Fryar Jhon) shew thee a Way, and teach thee an Expedient, by means whereof thy Wife shall never make thee a Cuckold without thy knowledge, and thine own consent. Do me the favour, I pray thee, (quoth Panurge) my pretty, soft, downy Cod; now tell it, Billy, tell it, I beseech thee. Take (quoth Fryar Jhon) Hans Carvel's Ring upon thy Finger, who was the King of Melinda's chief Jeweller; besides that, this Hans Carvel had the Reputation of bei g very skilful and expert in the Lapidary's Profession, he was a studious, learned, and ingenious Man, a Scientifick Person, full of Know-ledge, a great Philosopher, of a sound Judgment, of a prime Wit, good Sense, clear spirited, an honest Creature, Courteous, Charitable, Giver of Alms, and of a Jovial Humour, a Boon Companion and a Merry Blade, if ever there was any in the World: He was somewhat Gorbellied, had a little Shake in his Head, and in effect unwieldy of his Body: in his Old Age he took to Wife the Bailiff of Concordat's Daughter, a young, fair, jolly, gallant, spruce, frisk, brisk, neat, feat, smirk, smug, compt, quaint, gay, fine, trixy, trim, decent, proper, graceful, handsom, beautiful, comly; and kind, a little too much to her Neighbours and Acquaintance.

Hereup n it fell out, after the expiring of a scantling of Weeks, that Master Carvel became as jealous as a Tygar, and entred into a very profound Suspicion that his new-marry'd Gixy did keep a Buttock-stirring with others: To prevent which inconveniency, he did tell her many tragical Stories of the total Ruine of several Kingdoms by Adultery; did read unto her the Legend of Chast Wives; then made some Lectures to her in the praise of the choice Virtue of Pudicity, and did present her with a Book in Commendation of Conjugal Fidelity, wherein the Wickedness of all Licentious Women was odiously detested ; and withal, he gave her a Chain enrich'd with pure Oriental Saphires Notwithstanding all this, he found her always more and more enclin'd to the reception of her Neighbour Cope-Mates, that day by day his Jealousy encreased ; in sequel whereof, one night as he was lying by her, whilst in his Sleep the rambling Fancies of the lecherous Deportments of his Wife, did take up the Celluls of his Brain, he dream'd that he encountred with the Devil, to whom he had discovered to the full the buzzing of his Head, and suspicion that his Wife did tread her Shooe awry ; the Devil, he thought, in this perplexity, did, for his comfort, give him a Ring, and therewithal did kindly put it on his Middle-finger, saying, Hans Carvel, I give thee this Ring ; whilst thou carriest it upon that Finger, thy Wife shall never carnally be known by any other than thy self, without thy special knowledge and consent. Grammercy (quoth Hans Carvel) my Lord Devil ; I renounce Mahomet, if ever it shall come off my Finger. The Devil vanished, as is his custom ; and then Hans Carvel, full of Joy, awaking, found that his Middle-finger was as far as it could reach within the What-d'ye-call-it of his Wife. I did forget to tell thee, how his Wife, as soon as she had felt the Finger there, said, in recoiling her Buttocks, Off, yes, nay, tut, pish, tush, aye, Lord, that is not the Thing which should be put up in that Place. With this, Hans Carvel thought that some pilfering Fellow was about to take the Ring from him. Is not this an infallible and sovereign Antidote ? Therefore, if thou wilt believe me, in imitation of this Example, never fail to have continually the Ring of thy Wife's Commodity upon thy Finger. When that was said, their Discourse and their Way ended.

CHAPTER XXIX

How Pantagruel Convocated together a Theologian, Physician, Lawyer, and Philosopher, for extricating Panurge out of the Perplexity wherein he was

No sooner were they come into the Royal Palace, but they, to the full, made Report unto Pantagruel of the Success of their

Expedition ; they shew him the Response of Raminagrobis. When Pantagruel had read it over and over again, the oftner he perused it, being the better pleased therewith ; he said, in addressing his Speech to Panurge, I have not as yet seen any Answer framed to your Demand, which affordeth me more Contentment : For in this his succinct Copy of Verses, he summarily, and briefly, yet fully enough expresseth, how he would have us to understand, that every one in the Project and Enterprise of Marriage, ought to be his own Carver, sole Arbitrator of his proper Thoughts, and from himself alone take counsel in the main and peremptory closure of what his Determination should be, in either his assent to, or dissent from it. Such always hath been my opinion to you ; and when at first you spoke thereof to me, I truly told you this very same thing : but tacitly you scorned my Advice, and would not harbour it within your mind I know for certain, and therefore may I with the greater confidence utter my conception of it, that Philauty, or Self-love, is that which blinds your judgment, and deceiveth you.

Let us do otherwise, and that is this : Whatever we are, or have, consisteth in three things ; the Soul, the Body, and the Goods : Now for the preservation of these three, there are three sorts of learned Men ordained, each respectively to have care of that one which is recommended to his charge. Theologues are appointed for the soul, Physicians for the Welfare of the Body, and Lawyers for the Safety of our Goods : Hence it is, that it is my Resolution to have on Sunday next with me at Dinner, a Divine, a Physician, and a Lawyer, that with those three assembled thus together, we may in every Point and Particle confer at large of your Perplexity. By St. Picot (answer'd Panurge) we never shall do any good that way : I see it already, and you see your self, how the World is vilely abused, as when with a Fox-tail one claps another's Breech, to cajole him We give our Souls to keep to the Theologues, who for the greater part are Hereticks : Our Bodies we commit to the Physicians, who never themselves take any Physick : And then we intrust our Goods to Lawyers, who never go to Law against one another. You speak like a Courtier, (quoth Pantagruel) but the first Point of your Assertion is to be denied : For we daily see how good Theologues make it their chief Business, their whole and sole Employment, by their Deeds, their Words, and Writings, to extirpate Errors and Heresies out of the Hearts of Men ; and in their stead profoundly plant the

true and lively Faith. The second Point you spoke of I commend : For whereas the Professors of the Art of Medicine give
so good Order to the Prophylactick, or Conservative part of
their Faculty, in what concerneth their proper Healths, that
they stand in no need of making use of the other Branch, which
is the Curative, or Therapeutick, by Medicaments. As for the
third, I grant it to be true : For learned Advocates and Counsellors at Law are so much taken up with the Affairs of others
in their Consultations, Pleadings, and such like Patrocinations
of those who are their Clients, that they have no leisure to
attend any Controversies of their own. Therefore, on the next
ensuing Sunday, let the Divine be our godly Father Hippothadee, the Physician our honest Master Rondibilis, and the
Legist our good Friend Bridlegoose : Nor will it be (to my
thinking) amiss, that we enter into the Pythagorick Field, and
chuse for an Assistant to the three aforenamed Doctors, our
ancient faithful Acquaintance, the Philosopher Trouillogan ;
especially seeing a perfect Philosopher, such as is Trouillogan,
is able positively to resolve all whatsoever Doubts you can
propose. Carpalin, have you a care to have them here all four
on Sunday next at Dinner, without fail.

I believe (quoth Epistemon) that throughout the whole
Country, in all the Corners thereof, you could not have pitch'd
upon such other four ; which I speak not so much in regard of
the most excellent Qualifications and Accomplishments wherewith all of them are endowed, for the respective Discharge and
Management of each his own Vocation and Calling, (wherein,
without all doubt or controversy, they are the Paragons of the
Land, and surpass all others) as for that Rondibilis is married
now, who before was not : Hippothadee was not before, nor
is yet : Bridlegoose was married once, but is not now : And
Trouillogan is married now, who wedded was to another Wife
before. Sir, if it may stand with your good liking, I will ease
Carpalin of some parcel of his labour, and invite Bridlegoose
my self, with whom I of a long time have had a very intimate
familiarity, and unto whom I am to speak on the behalf of a
pretty hopeful Youth, who now studieth at Tholouse, under
the most learned, virtuous Doctor Boissonnet. Do what you
deem most expedient, (quoth Pantagruel) and tell me, if my
Recommendation can in any thing be steadable for the pro-
moval of the good of that Youth, or otherwise serve for the
bettering of the Dignity and Office of the worthy Boissonnet,
whom I do so love and respect, for one of the ablest and most

sufficient in his way, that any-where are extant. Sir, I will use therein my best Endeavours, and heartily bestir my self about it.

CHAPTER XXX

How the Theologue, Hippothadee, giveth Counsel to Panurge in the Matter and Business of his Nuptial Enterprize

THE Dinner on the subsequent Sunday was no sooner made ready, than that the aforenamed invited Guests gave thereto their Appearance, all of them; Bridlegoose only excepted, who was the Deputy-Governor of the Fonsbeton. At the ushering in of the Second Service, Panurge making a low Reverence, spake thus: Gentlemen, the Question I am to propound unto you, shall be uttered in very few words; Should I marry, or no? If my Doubt herein be not resolved by you, I shall hold it altogether insolvable, as are the *Insolubilia de Aliaco;* for all of you are elected, chosen, and culled out from amongst others, every one in his own Condition and Quality, like so many picked Peas on a Carpet.

The Father Hippothadee, in obedience to the Bidding of Pantagruel, and with much Courtesy to the Company, answer'd exceeding modestly after this manner: My Friend, you are pleased to ask Counsel of us; but first you must consult with your self. Do you find any trouble or disquiet in your Body, by the importunate stings and pricklings of the Flesh? That I do (quoth Panurge) in a hugely strong and almost irresistable measure: Be not offended, I beseech you, good Father, at the freedom of my Expression. No truly, Friend, not I (quoth Hippothadee) there is no reason why I should be displeased therewith: But in this Carnal Strife and Debate of yours, have you obtained from God the Gift and special Grace of Continency? In good faith, not, (quoth Panurge.) My Counsel to you in that Case (my Friend) is, that you marry, (quoth Hippothadee) for you should rather chuse to marry once, than to burn still in Fires of Concupiscence. Then Panurge, with a jovial Heart and a loud Voice, cried out, That is spoke gallantly, without circumbilivaginating about and about, and never hit it in its centred Point. Grammercy, my good Father. In truth I am resolved now to marry, and without fail I shall do it quickly. I invite you to my Wedding : By the Body of a Hen, we shall make good Cheer, and be as merry as Crickets : You shall wear the Bridegroom's Colours ; and if we eat a Goose, my Wife shall not rost for me. I will intreat you to lead up the first Dance of the Bride-Maids, if it may please you to do me so much Favour and Honour. There resteth yet a small Difficulty, a little Scruple, yea, even less than nothing, whereof I humbly crave your Resolution ; Shall I be a Cuckold, Father, yea, or no ? By no means (answer'd Hippothadee) will you be Cuckolded, if it please God. O the Lord help us now, (quoth Panurge) Whither are we driven to, good Folks ? To the Conditionals, which, according to the Rules and Precepts of the Dialectick Faculty, admit of all Contradictions and Impossibilities. If my Transalpine Mule had Wings, my Transalpine Mule would fly. If it please God I shall not be a Cuckold, but I shall be a Cuckold if it please him. Good God, if this were a Condition which I knew how to prevent, my Hopes should be as high as ever, nor would I despair : But you here send me to God's Privy-Council, to the Closet of his little Pleasures. You, my French Countrymen, Which is the Way you take to go thither ?

My honest Father, I believe it will be your best not to come to my Wedding : The Clutter and dingle-dangle Noise of Marriage Guests will but disturb you, and break the serious Fancies of your Brain. You love Repose, with Solitude and Silence ; I really believe you will not come : And then you dance but indifferently, and would be out of Countenance at the first Entry. I will send you some good Things to your Chamber, together with the Bride's Favour, and there you may drink our Health, if it may stand with your good liking. My Friend, (quoth Hippothadee) take my Words in the Sense wherein I mean them, and do not mis-interpret me. When I tell you, if it please God, do I to you any wrong therein ? Is it an ill expression ? Is it a Blaspheming Clause or Reserve any way scandalous unto the World ? Do not we thereby honour the Lord God Almighty, Creator, Protector and Con-server of all things ? Is not that a mean, whereby we do acknowledge him to be the sole Giver of all whatsoever is good ? Do not we in that manifest our Faith, that we believe all things to depend upon his infinite and incomprehensible Bounty ? and that without Him nothing can be produced, nor after its Production be of any value, force, or power, without the concurring aid and favour of his assisting Grace ? Is it not a canonical and authentick Exception, worthy to be premised to all our Undertakings ? Is it not expedient, that what we propose unto our selves, be still referred to what shall be disposed of by the Sacred Will of God, unto which all things must acquiesce in the Heavens, as well as on the Earth ? Is not that verily a sanctifying of his holy Name ? My Friend, you shall not be a Cuckold, if it please God ; nor shall we need to despair of the knowledge of his good Will and Pleasure herein, as if it were such an abstruse and mysteriously hidden Secret, that, for the clear understanding thereof, it were necessary to consult with those of his Celestial Privy-Council, or expresly make a voyage unto the Empirean Chamber, where Order is given for the effectuating of his most holy Pleasures.

The Great God hath done us this good, that he hath declared and revealed them to us openly and plainly, and described them in the Holy Bible : There you will find that you shall never be a Cuckold, that is to say, your Wife shall never be a Strumpet, if you make choice of one of a commendable Extraction, descended of honest Parents, and instructed in all Piety and Virtue : Such a one as hath not at any time haunted or frequented the Company or Conversation of those that are of corrupt and depraved Manners ; one loving and fearing God, who taketh a singular delight in drawing near to him by Faith, and the cordial observing of his Sacred Commandments : And finally, one who standing in awe of the Divine Majesty, of the Most High, will be loth to offend Him, and lose the favourable Kindness of his Grace, through any defect of Faith, or transgression against the Ordinances of his Holy Law, wherein Adultery is most rigorously forbidden, and a close adherence to her Husband alone most strictly and severely enjoin'd : yea, in such sort, that she is to cherish, serve and love him above any thing, next to God, that meriteth to be loved. In the interim, for the better schooling of her in these Instructions, and that the wholsom Doctrin of a Matrimonial Duty may take the deeper root in her Mind, you must needs carry your self so on your part, and your behaviour is to be such, that you are to go before her in a good Example, by entertaining her unfeignedly with a Conjugal Amity, by continually approving your self in all your Words and Actions a faithful and discreet Husband ; and by living not only at home, and privately with your own Household and Family, but in the face also of all Men, and open view of the World, devotely, virtuously and chastly, as you would have her on her side to deport and demean her self towards you, as becomes a godly, loyal, and respectful Wife, who maketh conscience to keep inviolably the Tie of a Matrimonial Oath.

For as that Looking-glass is not the best, which is most deck'd with Gold and Precious-stones, but that which representeth to the Eye the liveliest Shapes of Objects set before it; even so that Wife should not be most esteemed who richest is, and of the noblest Race, but she who fearing God, conforms her self nearest unto the Humour of her Husband.

Consider how the Moon doth not borrow her Light from Jupiter, Mars, Mercury, or any other of the Planets, nor yet from any of those Splendid Stars which are set in the spangled Firmament; but from her Husband only, the bright Sun, which she receiveth from him more or less, according to the manner of his Aspect, and variously bestowed Eradiations. Just so should you be a Pattern to your Wife in Virtue, goodly Zeal, and true Devotion; that by your Radiance in darting on her the Aspect of an Exemplary Goodness, she, in your imitation, may outshine the Luminaries of all other Women. To this effect, you daily must implore God's Grace to the protection of you both. You would have me then (quoth Panurge, twisting the Whiskers of his Beard on either side with the Thumb and Fore-Finger of his Left-Hand) to espouse and take to Wife the prudent and frugal Woman described by Solomon: Without all doubt she is dead, and truly, to my best remembrance, I never saw her; the Lord forgive me. Nevertheless, I thank you, Father; Eat this slice of Marchpane, it will help your Digestion; then shall you be presented with a Cup of Claret Hypocras, which is right healthful and stomached. Let us proceed.

CHAPTER XXXI

How the Physician Rondibilis counselleth Panurge

PANURGE, continuing his Discourse, said, The first word which was spoken by him who guelded the Lubbardly quaffing Monks of Saussiniac, after that he had unstoned Fryar Corcil, was this, To the rest. In like manner, I say, To the rest. Therefore I beseech you, my good Master Rondibilis, should I marry or not? By the raking pace of my Mule, quoth Rondibilis, I know not what Answer to make to this Problem of yours.

You say that you feel in you the pricking Stings of Sensuality, by which you are stirred up to Venery. I find in our Faculty of Medicine, and we have founded our Opinion therein upon the deliberate Resolution and final Decision of the ancient Platonicks, that Carnal Concupiscence is cooled and quelled five several ways.

First, By the means of Wine. I shall easily believe that, (quoth Friar Jhon) for when I am well whitled with the Juyce of the Grape, I care for nothing else so I may sleep. When I say (quoth Rondibilis) that Wine abateth Lust, my meaning is, Wine immoderately taken; for by Intemperancy proceeding from the excessive drinking of Strong Liquor, there is brought upon the Body of such a Swilldown Bouser a chilness in the Blood, a slackening in the Sinews, a Dissipation of the Genera-

RONDIBILIS

453

tive Seed, a numbness and hebetation of the Senses, with a
perversive wriness and Convulsion of the Muscles; all which
are great Lets and Impediments to the Act of Generation.
Hence it is that Bacchus, the God of Bibbers, Tiplers and
Drunkards is most commonly painted Beardless, and clad in a
Woman's Habit, as a person altogether Effeminate, or like a
libbed Eunuch. Wine nevertheless taken moderately worketh
quite contrary Effects, as is implied by the old Proverb, which
saith, That Venus takes cold when not accompanied with Ceres
and Bacchus. This Opinion is of great Antiquity, as appeareth
by the Testimony of Diodorus the Sicilian, and confirmed by
Pausanias, and universally held amongst the Lampsacians,
that Don Priapos was the Son of Bacchus and Venus.

Secondly, The Fervency of Lust is abated by certain Drugs,
Plants, Herbs, and Roots, which make the Taker cold, maleficiated, unfit for, and unable to perform the Act of Generation;
as hath been often experimented in the Water-Lilly, Heraclea,
Agnus Castus, Willow-twigs, Hemp-stalks, Woodbind, Honey-
suckle, Tamarisk, Chastree, Mandrake, Bennet, Kecbugloss,
the Skin of a Hippopatam, and many other such, which by
convenient Doses, proportion'd to the peccant Humour and
Constitution of the Patient, being duly and seasonably received
within the Body, what by their Elementary Virtues on the one
side, and peculiar Properties on the other, do either benumb,
mortifie and beclumpse with Cold the prolifick Semence; or
scatter and disperse the Spirits, which ought to have gone
along with, and conducted the Sperm to the places destinated
and appointed for its Reception. Or lastly, Shut up, stop and
obstruct the Ways, Passages and Conduits through which the
Seed should have been expelled, evacuated and ejected. We
have nevertheless of those Ingredients, which being of a contrary Operation, heat the Blood, bend the Nerves, unite the
Spirits, quicken the Senses, strengthen the Muscles, and thereby
rouze up, provoke, excite and inable a Man to the vigorous
Accomplishment of the Feat of Amorous Dalliance. I have no
need of those, (quoth Panurge) God be thanked, and you my
good Master. Howsoever I pray you take no exception or
offence at these my Words; for what I have said was not out of
any ill will I did bear to you, the Lord he knows.

Thirdly, The Ardour of Letchery is very much subdued and
mated by frequent Labour and continual Toiling: For by
painful Exercises and laborious Working, so great a Dissolution
is brought upon the whole Body, that the Blood which runneth

alongst the Channels of the Veins thereof, for the Nourishment and Alimentation of each of its Members, hath neither time, leisure nor power to afford the Seminal Resudation or super-fluity of the third Concoction, which Nature most carefully reserves for the conservation of the Individual, whose Pre-servation she more heedfully regardeth than the propagat-ing of the Species, and the multiplication of Humane Kind. Whence it is, that Diana is said to be chast, because she is never idle, but always busied about her Hunting ; for the same reason was a Camp, or Leaguer of old called *Castrum*, as if they would have said *Castum :* Because the Soldiers, Wrestlers, Runners, Throwers of the Bar, and other such-like Athletick Champions, as are usually seen in a Military Circumvallation, do uncessantly travel and turmoil, and are in a perpetual stir and agitation. To this purpose Hippocrates also writeth in his Book, *De Aere, Aqua, et locis :* That in his time there were People in Scythia as impotent as Eunuchs, in the discharge of a Venerian Exploit ; because that without any cessation, pause, or respit, they were never from off Horseback, or otherways assiduously employed in some troublesom and molesting Drudgery.

On the other part, in opposition and repugnancy hereto, the Philosophers say, That Idleness is the Mother of Luxury : When it was asked Ovid, Why Egistus became an Adulterer ? He made no other answer but this : Because he was idle. Who were able to rid the World of Loytring and Laziness, might easily frustrate and disappoint Cupid of all his Designs, Aims, Engines, and Devices, and so disable and appall him, that his Bow, Quiver, and Darts should from henceforth be a meer needless Load and Burthen to him : For that it could not then lie in his power to strike, or wound any of either Sex, with all the Arms he had. He is not, I believe, so expert an Archer, as that he can hit the Cranes flying in the Air, or yet the young Stags, skipping through the Thickets, as the Parthians knew well how to do ; that is to say, People moyling, sinking, and hurrying up and down, restless, and without repose. He must have those husht, still, quiet, lying at a stay, lither, and full of ease, whom he is able, though his Mother help him, to touch, much less to pierce with all his Arrows : In confirmation hereof, Theophrastus being asked on a time, What kind of Beast or Thing he judged a toyish, wanton Love to be ? He made Answer, That it was a Passion of idle and sluggish Spirits. From which pretty Description of tickling Love-tricks that of Diogenes's hatching was not very discrepant, when he defined

Leachery, Occupation of Folks destitute of all other Occupation.

For this cause the Syconian Engraver, Canachus, being desirous to give us to understand, that Sloath, Drouziness, Negligence, and Laziness were the prime Guardians and Governesses of Ribaldry, made the Statue of Venus (not standing, as other Stone-Cutters had used to do, but) sitting.

Fourthly, The tickling pricks of Incontinency are blunted by an eager Study ; for from thence proceedeth an incredible resolution of the Spirits, that oftentimes there do not remain so many behind as may suffice to push and thrust forwards the Generative Resudation to the places thereto appropriated, and therewithal inflate the Cavernous Nerve ; whose Office is to ejaculate the Moisture for the Propagation of Humane Progeny. Least you should think it is not so, be pleased but to contemplate a little the Form, Fashion, and Carriage of a Man exceeding earnestly set upon some Learned Meditation, and deeply plunged therein, and you shall see how all the Arteries of his Brains are stretched forth, and bent like the String of a Cross-bow, the more promptly, dexterously, and copiously to suppeditate, furnish, and supply him with store of Spirits, sufficient to replenish, and fill up the Ventricles, Seats, Tunnels, Mansions, Receptacles, and Celluls of the common Sense ; of the Imagination, Apprehension, and Fancy ; of the Ratiocination, Arguing, and Resolution ; as likewise of the Memory, Recordation, and Remembrance ; and with great alacrity, nimbleness, and agility to run, pass, and course from the one to the other, through those Pipes, Windings, and Conduits, which to skilful Anatomists are perceivable, at the end of the Wonderful Net, where all the Arteries close in a terminating Point : Which Arteries taking their rise and origine from the left Capful of the Heart, bring through several Circuits, Ambages, and Anfractuosities, the Vital, to subtilize and refine them to the Ætherial Purity of Animal Spirits. Nay, in such a studiously musing Person, you may espy so extravagant Raptures of one, as it were, out of himself, that all his Natural Faculties for that time will seem to be suspended from each their proper charge and office, and his exteriour Senses to be at a stand. In a word, you cannot otherways choose than think, that he is by an extraordinary Extasie quite transported out of what he was, or should be ; and that Socrates did not speak improperly, when he said, That Philosophy was nothing else but a Meditation upon Death. This possibly is the reason, why Democritus deprived himself of the sense of Seeing, prizing at a much lower rate the loss of his Sight, than the diminution of his Contemplations; which he frequently had found disturbed by the vagrant, flying-out strayings of his unsetled and roving Eyes. Therefore is it, that Pallas, the Goddess of Wisdom, Tutress, and Guardianess of such as are diligently studious, and painfully industrious, is, and hath been still accounted a Virgin. The Muses upon the same Consideration are esteemed perpetual Maids : And the Graces for the like reason, have been held to continue in a sempiternal Pudicity.

I remember to have read, that Cupid on a time being asked of his Mother Venus, why he did not assault and set upon the Muses, his Answer was, That he found them so fair, so sweet, so neat, so wise, so learned, so modest, so discreet, so courteous, so vertuous, and so continually busied and employed : One in the Speculation of the Stars; another in the Supputation of Numbers; the Third in the Dimension of Geometrical Quantities; the Fourth in the Composition of Heroick Poems; the Fifth in the jovial Interludes of a Comick Strain; the Sixth in the stately Gravity of a Tragick Vein; the Seventh in the Melodious Disposition of Musical Airs; the Eighth in the compleatest manner of Writing Histories, and Books on all sort of Subjects; and the Ninth in the Mysteries, Secrets, and Curiosities of all Sciences, Faculties, Disciplines, and Arts whatsoever, whether Liberal or Mechanick; that approaching near unto them, he unbended his Bow, shut his Quiver, and extinguished his Torch, through meer shame and fear, that by mischance he might do them some hurt or prejudice : Which done, he thereafter put off the Fillet wherewith his Eyes were bound, to look them in the Face, and to hear their Melody and Poetick Odes. There took he the greatest pleasure in the World ; that many times he was transported with their Beauty and pretty Behaviour, and charmed asleep by the Harmony : so far was he from assaulting them, or interrupting their Studies. Under this Article may be comprised, what Hippocrates wrote in the aforecited Treatise concerning the Scythians, as also that in a Book of his entituled, *Of Breeding and Production ;* where he hath affirmed, all such men to be unfit for Generation, as have their Parotid Arteries cut; whose Situation is beside the Ears : For the reason given already, when I was speaking of the resolution of the Spirits, and of that Spiritual Blood, whereof the Arteries are the sole and proper Receptacles ; and that likewise he doth maintain a large portion of the Parastatick Liquor, to issue and descend from the Brains and Backbone.

Fifthly, By the too frequent reiteration of the Act of Venery. There did I wait for you (quoth Panurge) and shall willingly apply it to my self, whilst any one that pleaseth may, for me, make use of any of the four preceding. That is the very same thing (quoth Fryar Jhon) which Father Scyllino, Prior of Saint Victor, at Marseilles, calleth by the Name of Maceration, and taming of the Flesh. I am of the same Opinion; and so was the Hermite of Saint Radegonde, a little above Chinon: For (quoth he) the Hermites of Thebaida can no more aptly or expediently macerate and bring down the Pride of their Bodies, daunt and mortifie their letcherous Sensuality, or depress and overcome the stubbornness and rebellion of the Flesh, than by duffling and fanferluching it Five and twenty, or Thirty times a day. I see Panurge, quoth Rondibilis, neatly featured, and proportioned in all the Members of his Body, of a good temperament in his Humors, well complexioned in his Spirits, of a competent Age, in an opportune Time, and of a reasonably forward Mind to be married: Truly, if he encounter with a Wife of the like Nature, Temperament, and Constitution, he may beget upon her Children worthy of some Transpontine Monarchy; and the sooner he marry, it will be the better for him, and the more conducible for his Profit, if he would see and have his Children in his own time well provided for. Sir, my worthy Master (quoth Panurge) I will do it, do not you doubt thereof; and that quickly enough, I warrant you. Nevertheless, whilst you were busied in the uttering of your Learned Discourse, this Flea which I have in mine Ear, hath tickled me more than ever. I retain you in the Number of my Festival Guests, and promise you, that we shall not want for Mirth and good Chear enough; yea, over and above the ordinary Rate. And, if it may please you, desire your Wife to come along with you, together with her She-Friends and Neighbours: That is to be understood, and there shall be fair Play.

CHAPTER XXXII

How Rondibilis declareth Cuckoldry to be naturally one of the Appendances of Marriage

THERE remaineth as yet, quoth Panurge going on in his Discourse, one small scruple to be cleared : You have seen heretofore, I doubt not, in the Roman Standards, *S. P. Q. R.* Si, Peu, Que, Rien : Shall not I be a Cuckold ? By the Haven of Safety, cried out Rondibilis, what is this you ask of me ? If you shall be a Cuckold : My Noble Friend, I am married, and you are like to be so very speedily : Therefore be pleased from my Experiment in the matter, to write in your Brain, with a Steel-pen, this subsequent Ditton, There is no married Man who doth not run the hazard of being made a Cuckold. Cuckoldry naturally attendeth Marriage ; the Shadow doth not more naturally follow the Body, than Cuckoldry ensueth after Marriage, to place fair Horns upon the Husband's Heads.

And when you shall happen to hear any Man pronounce these three words : He is married : If you then say he is, hath been, shall be, or may be a Cuckold, you will not be accounted an unskilful Artist in framing of true Consequences. Tripes and Bowels of all the Devils, (cryes Panurge) what do you tell me ? My dear Friend (answer'd Rondibilis) as Hippocrates, on a time, was in the very nick of setting forwards from Lango to Polystilo, to visit the Philosopher Democritus, he wrote a familiar Letter to his Friend Dionoys, wherein he desired him, That he would, during the interval of his absence, carry his Wife to the House of her Father and Mother, who were an honourable Couple, and of good Repute ; because I would not have her at my Home (said he) to make abode in Solitude : yet notwithstanding this her Residence beside her Parents, do not fail (quoth he) with a most heedful care and circumspection to pry into her ways, and to espy what Places she shall go to with her Mother, and who those be that shall repair unto her : Not (quoth he) that I do mistrust her Virtue, or that I seem to have any diffidence of her Pudicity, and chast Behaviour ; for of that I have frequently had good and real Proofs : but I must freely tell you, She is a Woman ; there lies the Suspicion.

My worthy Friend, the Nature of Women is set forth before our Eyes, and represented to us by the Moon, in divers other things, as well as in this, that they squat, sculk, constrain their own Inclinations, and with all the Cunning they can, dissemble and play the Hypocrite in the sight and presence of their Husbands ; who come no sooner to be out of the way, but that forthwith they take their advantage, pass the time merrily, desist from all labour, frolick it, gad abroad, lay aside their counterfeit Garb, and openly declare and manifest the interiour of their Dispositions ; even as the Moon, when she is in Conjunction with the Sun, is neither seen in the Heavens, nor on the Earth, but in her Opposition, when remotest from him, shineth in her greatest fulness, and wholly appeareth in her brightest splendour whilst it is Night : Thus Women are but Women.

When I say Womankind, I speak of a Sex so frail, so variable, so changeable, so fickle, inconstant, and imperfect, that, in my opinion, Nature, (under favour nevertheless of the prime Honour and Reverence which is due unto her) did in a manner mistake the Road which she had traced formerly, and stray exceedingly from that Excellence of Providential Judgment, by the which she had created and formed all other things, when she built, framed, and made up the Woman. And having thought upon it a hundred and five times, I know not what else to determin therein, save only that in the devising, hammering, forging and composing of the Woman, she hath had a much tenderer regard, and by a great deal more respectful heed to the delightful Consortship, and sociable Delectation of the Man, than to the Perfection and Accomplishment of the individual Womanishness, or Muliebrity. The divine Philosopher Plato was doubtful in what Rank of living Creatures to place and collocate them, whither amongst the Rational Animals, by elevating them to an upper Seat in the Specifical Classis of Humanity ; or with the Irrational, by degrading them to a lower Bench on the opposite side, of a Brutal Kind, and meer Bestiality : For Nature hath posited in a privy, secret, and intestine place of their Bodies, a sort of Member, (by some not impertinently termed an Animal) which is not to be found in Men. Therein sometimes are ingendred certain Humours so saltish, brackish, clammy, sharp, nipping, tearing, prickling, and most eagerly tickling, that by their stinging Acrimony, rending Nitrosity, figging Itch, wrigling Mordicancy, and smarting Salsitude (for the said Member is altogether sinewy, and of a most quick and lively feeling) their whole Body is shaken and ebrangled, their Senses totally ravished and transported, the Operations of their Judgment and Understanding utterly confounded, and all disordinate Passions and Perturbations of the Mind thoroughly and absolutely allowed, admitted, and approved of ; yea, in such sort, that if Nature had not been so favourable unto them, as to have sprinkled their Forehead with a little Tincture of Bashfulness and Modesty, you should see them in a so frantick mood run mad after Letchery, and hye apace up and down with haste and Lust, in quest of, and to fix some Chamber-Standard in their Paphian Ground, that never did the Pretides, Mimallonides, nor Lyæan Thyads, deport themselves in the time of their Bacchanalian Festivals, more shamelesly, or with a so affronted and brazen-faced Impudency ; because this terrible Animal is knit unto, and hath an union with all the chief and most principal Parts of the Body, as to Anatomists is evident. Let it not here be thought strange that I should call it an Animal, seeing therein I do no otherwise than follow and adhere to the Doctrin of the Academick and Peripatetick Philosophers. For if a proper Motion be a certain mark and infallible token of the Life and Animation of the Mover, (as Aristotle writeth) and that any such thing as moveth of it self ought to be held Animated, and of a Living Nature; then assuredly Plato with very good reason did give it the Denomination of an Animal ; for that he perceived and observed in it the proper and self-stirring motions of Suffocation, Precipitation, Corrugation, and of Indignation, so extremely violent, that often-times by them is taken and removed from the Women all other Sense and Moving whatsoever, as if she were in a swooning Lipothymy, benumming Sincop, Epileptick, Apoplectick Palsey, and true resemblance of a pale-fac'd Death.

Furthermore, in the said Member there is a manifest discerning Faculty of Scents and Odours very perceptible to Women, who feel it fly from what is rank and unsavoury, and follow fragrant and Aromatick Smells. It is not unknown to me how Cl. Gallen striveth with might and main to prove, that these are not proper and particular Notions proceeding intrinsecally from the thing it self, but accidentally, and by chance. Nor hath it escaped my notice, how others of that Sect have laboured hardly, yea, to the utmost of their Abilities, to demonstrate that it is not a sensitive discerning or perception in it of the difference of Wafts and Smells, but meerly a various

461

manner of Virtue and Efficacy, passing forth and flowing from
the diversity of odoriferous Substances applied near unto it.
Nevertheless, if you will studiously examine, and seriously
ponder and weigh in Critolaus's Balance the strength of their
Reasons and Arguments, you shall find that they, not only in
this, but in several other Matters also of the like nature, have
spoken at random, and rather out of an ambitious Envy to
check and reprehend their Betters, than for any design to make
enquiry into the solid Truth.

I will not launch my little Skif any further into the wide
Ocean of this Dispute, only will I tell you, that the Praise and
Commendation is not mean and slender, which is due to those
honest and good Women, who living chastly and without blame,
have had the power and virtue to curb, range, and subdue that
unbridled, heady and wild Animal, to an obedient, submissive
and obsequious yielding unto Reason. Therefore here will I
make an end of my Discourse thereon, when I shall have told
you, that the said Animal being once satiated (if it be possible
that it can be contented or satisfied) by that Aliment, which
Nature hath provided for it out of the Epididymal Store-house
of Man, all its former and irregular and disorder'd Motions are
at an end, laid and asswaged, all its vehement and unruly
Longings lulled, pacified and quieted, and all the furious and
raging Lusts, Appetites and Desires thereof appeased, suppressed, calmed and exstinguished. For this cause, let it seem
nothing strange unto you, if we be in a perpetual danger of being
Cuckolds ; that is to say, such of us as have not wherewithal
fully to satisfie the Appetite and Expectation of that voracious
Animal. Ods fish ! (quoth Panurge) have you no preventive
Cure in all your Medicinal Art for hindring one's Head to be
Hornygraffed at home, whilst his Feet are plodding abroad ?
Yes that I have, my gallant Friend, (answer'd Rondibilis) and
that which is a sovereign Remedy, whereof I frequently make
use my self ; and that you may the better relish, it is set down
and written in the Book of a most famous Author, whose Renown is of a standing of two thousand Years, hearken and take
good heed. You are (quoth Panurge) by Cockshobby, a right
honest Man, and I love you with all my heart : Eat a little of
this Quince-Pye, it is very proper and convenient for the
shutting up of the Orifice of the Ventricle of the Stomach ;
because of a kind of astringent Stypticity which is in that sort
of Fruit, and is helpful to the first Concoction. But what ?
I think I speak Latin before Clerks. Stay, fill, I give you some-

what to drink out of this Nestorian Goblet. Will you have another Draught of White Hippocras ? Be not afraid of the Squinzy, No : There is neither Squinant, Ginger, nor Grains in it ; only a little Choice Cinnamon, and some of the best refined Sugar, with the delicious White-wine of the Growth of that Vine, which was set in the Slips of the great Sorbaple, above the Walnut-tree.

CHAPTER XXXIII

Rondibilis the Physician's Cure of Cuckoldry

AT that time (quoth Rondibilis) when Jupiter took a View of the State of his Olympick House and Family, and that he had made the Calendar of all the Gods and Goddesses, appointing unto the Festival of every one of them its proper Day and Season, establishing certain fixed Places and Stations for the pronouncing of Oracles, and relief of travelling Pilgrims; and ordaining Victims, Immolations and Sacrifices suitable and correspondent to the Dignity and Nature of the worshipped and adored Deity. Did not he do (asked Panurge) therein, as Tintouille the Bishop of Auxerre is said once to have done ? This Noble Prelate loved entirely the pure Liquor of the Grape, as every honest and judicious Man doth ; therefore was it that he had an especial care and regard to the Bud of the Vine-tree, as to the Great-Grand-father of Bacchus. But so it is, that for sundry Years together he saw a most pitiful Havock,

Desolation and Destruction made amongst the Sprouts, Shootings, Buds, Blossoms and Sciens of the Vines, by hoary Frosts, Dank-fogs, hot Mists, unseasonable Colds, chill Blasts, thick Hail, and other calamitous Chances of foul Weather happening, as he thought, by the dismal Inauspiciousness of the Holidays of St. George, St. Mary, St. Paul, St. Eutrope, Holy Rood, the Ascension, and other Festivals, in that time when the Sun passeth under the Sign of Taurus ; and thereupon harboured in his Mind this Opinion, That the aforenamed Saints were Saint Hail-flingers, Saint Frost-senders, Saint Fog-mongers, and Saint Spoilers of the Vine-buds ; for which cause he went about to have transmitted their Feasts from the Spring to the Winter, to be celebrated between Christmas and Epiphany, (so the Mother of the three Kings call'd it) allowing them with all honour and reverence the liberty then to freeze, hail and rain as much as they would ; for that he knew that at such a time Frost was rather profitable than hurtful to the Vine-buds, and in their steads to have placed the Festivals of St. Christopher, St. John the Baptist, St. Magdalene, St. Anne, St. Domingo, and St. Lawrence ; yea, and to have gone so far as to collocate and transpose the middle of August, in and to the beginning of May ; because, during the whole space of their Solemnity, there was so little danger of hoary Frosts and cold Mists, that no Artificers are then held in greater request, than the Afforder of Refrigerating Inventions, Makers of Junkets, fit Disposers of cooling Shades, Composers of green Arbours, and Refreshers of Wine.

Jupiter (said Rondibilis) forgot the poor Devil Cuckoldry, who was then in the Court of Paris, very eagerly solliciting a pedling Suit at Law for one of his Vassals and Tenants ; within some few days thereafter, (I have forgot how many) when he got full notice of the Trick, which in his absence was done unto him, he instantly desisted from prosecuting Legal Processes, in the behalf of others, full of sollicitude to pursue after his own Business, lest he should be fore-closed : And thereupon he appeared personally at the Tribunal of the great Jupiter, displayed before him the importance of his preceding Merits, together with the acceptable Services, which, in obedience to his Commands, he had formerly performed ; and therefore, in all humility, begged of him, that he would be pleased not to leave him alone amongst all the sacred Potentates, destitute and void of Honour, Reverence, Sacrifices, and Festival Ceremonies. To this Petition, Jupiter's Answer was excusatory,

That all the Places and Offices of his House were bestowed. Nevertheless, so importuned was he by the continual Supplications of Monsieur Cuckoldry, that he, in fine, placed him in the Rank, List, Roll, Rubrick and Catalogue; and appointed Honours, Sacrifices, and Festival Rites to be observed on Earth in great Devotion, and tendred to him with Solemnity.

The Feast, because there was no void, empty, nor vacant Place in all the Calendar, was to be celebrated jointly with, and on the same Day that had been consecrated to the Goddess Jealousy: His Power and Dominion should be over Married Folks, especially such as had handsom Wives: His Sacrifices were to be, Suspicion, Diffidence, Mistrust, a lowring, powting Sullenness, Watchings, Wardings, Researchings, Plyings, Explorations, together with the Waylayings, Ambushes, narrow Observations, and malicious Doggings of the Husband's Scouts and Espials of the most privy Actions of their Wives. Herewithal every married Man was expresly and rigorously commanded to reverence, honour and worship him; to celebrate and solemnize his Festival with twice more respect than that of another Saint or Deity, and to immolate unto him, with all sincerity and alacrity of Heart, the above-mention'd Sacrifices and Oblations, under pain of severe Censures, Threatnings, and Comminations of these subsequent Fines, Mulcts, Amerciaments, Penalties and Punishments to be inflicted on the Delinquents; that Monsieur Cuckoldry should never be favourable nor propitious to them; that he should never help, aid, supply, succour, nor grant them any subventitious Furtherance, auxiliary Suffrage, or adminicular Assistance; that he should never hold in any Reckoning, Account, or Estimation; that he should never daign to enter within their Houses, neither at the Doors, Windows, nor any other Place thereof; that he should never haunt nor frequent their Companies or Conversations; how frequently soever they should invocate him, and call upon his Name; and that not only he should leave and abandon them to rot alone with their Wives in a sempiternal Solitariness, without the benefit of the Diversion of any Copesmate or Corrival at all; but should withal shun and eschew them, fly from them, and eternally forsake and reject them as impious Hereticks and sacrilegious Persons, according to the accustomed manner of other Gods, towards such as are too slack in offering up the Duties and Reverences which ought to be performed respectively to their Divinities: As is evidently apparent in Bacchus towards negligent Vinedressers; in Ceres against idle Flow-men and Tillers of the Ground; in Pomona to unworthy Fruiterers and Coster-mongers; in Neptune towards dissolute Mariners and Sea-faring Men; in Vulcan towards loytering Smiths and Forge-men; and so throughout the rest.

Now, on the contrary, this infallible Promise was added, that unto all those who should make a Holy Day of the above-recited Festival, and cease from all manner of worldly Work and Negotiation, lay aside all their own most important Occasions, and to be so wretchless, heedless, and careless of what might concern the management of their proper Affairs, as to mind nothing else but a suspicious espying and prying into the secret Deportments of their Wives, and how to koop, shut up, hold at under, and deal cruelly and austeerly with them, by all the Harshness and Hardships that an implacable, and every way inexorable Jealousie can devise and suggest, con-form to the sacred Ordinances of the afore-mentioned Sacrifices and Oblations, he should be continually favourable to them, should love them, sociably converse with them, should be Day and Night in their Houses, and never leave them destitute of his Presence. Now I have said, and you have heard my Cure.

Ha, ha, ha, (quoth Carpalin laughing) this is a Remedy yet more apt and proper than Hans Carvel's Ring: The Devil take me if I do not believe it. The Humour, Inclination and Nature of Women is like the Thunder, whose force in its Bolt, or otherways, burneth, bruiseth, and breaketh only hard, massive and resisting Objects, without staying or stopping at soft, empty and yielding matters: For it pasheth into pieces the Steel Sword, without doing any hurt to the Velvet Scabbard which insheatheth it: It rusheth also, and consumeth the Bones, without wounding or endammaging the Flesh, where-with they are vailed and covered: Just so it is, that Women for the greater part never bend the Contention, Subtilty, and contradictory Disposition of their Spirits, unless it be to do what is prohibited and forbidden.

Verily, (quoth Hippothadee) some of our Doctors averr for a Truth, that the first Woman of the World, whom the Hebrews call Eve, had hardly been induced or allured into the temptation of eating of the Fruit of the Tree of Life, if it had not been forbidden her so to do. And that you may give the more credit to the Validity of this Opinion, consider how the cautelous and wily Tempter did commemorate unto her, for an antecedent to his Enthymeme, the Prohibition which was made to taste it, as being desirous to infer from thence, It is forbidden thee : therefore thou shouldst eat of it, else thou canst not be a Woman.

CHAPTER XXXIV

How Women ordinarily have the greatest longing after things prohibited

WHEN I was (quoth Carpalin) a Whoremaster at Orleans, the whole Art of Rhetorick in all its Tropes and Figures, was not able to afford unto me a Colour or Flourish of greater force and value ; nor could I by any other form or manner of Elocution pitch upon a more perswasive Argument for bringing young beautiful married Ladies into the Snares of Adultery, through alluring and inticing them to tast with me of Amorous Delights, than with a lively Sprightfulness to tell them in down-right terms, and to remonstrate to them (with a great shew of Detestation of a Crime so horrid) how their Husbands were jealous. This was none of my Invention : It is written, and we have Laws, Examples, Reasons and daily Experiences confirmative of the same. If this Belief once enter into their Noddles, their Husbands will infallibly be Cuckolds ; yea, by G—, will they, (without swearing) although they should do like Semiramis, Pasiphae, Egesta, the Women of the Isle Mandez in Egypt, and other such like Queanish flurting Harlots, mentioned in the Writings of Herodotus, Strabo, and such like Puppies.

Truly, (quoth Ponocrates) I have heard it related, and it hath been told me for a Verity, that Pope Jhon 22. passing on a day through the Abby of Toucherome, was in all Humility required and besought by the Abbess, and other discreet Mothers of the said Convent, to grant them an Indulgence, by means whereof they might confess themselves to one another, alledging, That Religious Women were subject to some petty secret Slips and Imperfections, which would be a foul and burning shame for them to discover and to reveal to Men, how Sacerdotal soever their Function were : but that they would freelier, more familiarly, and with greater chearfulness, open to each other their Offences, Faults, and Escapes, under the Seal of Confession. There is not any thing (answered the Pope) fitting for you to impetrate of me, which I would not most willingly condescend unto : But I find one Inconvenience ; you know, Confession should be kept secret, and Women are not able to do so. Exceeding well (quoth they) most Holy Father, and much more closely than the best of Men.

The said Pope on the very same day, gave them in keeping a pretty Box, wherein he purposely caused a little Linnet to be put, willing them very gently and courteously to lock it up in some sure and hidden place ; and promising them, by the Faith of a Pope, that he should yield to their Request, if they would keep secret what was inclosed within that deposited Box : Enjoyning them withal, not to presume one way nor other, directly or indirectly, to go about the opening thereof, under pain of the highest Ecclesiastical Censure, Eternal Excommunication. The Prohibition was no sooner made, but that they did all of them boil with a most ardent desire to know, and see what kind of thing it was that was within it : They thought long already, that the Pope was not gone, to the end they might joyntly, with the more leisure and ease apply themselves to the Box-opening Curiosity.

The Holy Father, after he had given them his Benediction, retired and withdrew himself to the Pontifical Lodgings of his own Palace ; but he was hardly gone three Steps from without the Gates of their Cloyster, when the good Ladies throngingly, and as in a hudled Crowd, pressing hard on the Backs of one another, ran thrusting and shoving who should be first at the setting open of the forbidden Box, and descrying of the *Quod latitat* within.

On the very next day thereafter, the Pope made them another Visit, of a full design, purpose, and intention (as they imagined) to dispatch the Grant of their sought and wished-for Indulgence : But before he would enter into any Chat or Communing with them, he commanded the Casket to be brought unto him : it was done so accordingly ; but by your leave, the Bird was no more there. Then was it, that the Pope did represent to their Maternities, how hard a matter and difficult it was for them to keep Secrets revealed to them in Confession, unmanifested to the Ears of others ; seeing for the space of Four and twenty hours they were not able to lay up in secret a Box, which he had highly recommended to their Discretion, Charge and Custody.

Welcome, in good Faith, my dear Master, welcome : It

HER SCOLDING WAS BUT IN VAIN

469

did me good to hear you talk, the Lord be praised for all. I do not remember to have seen you before now, since the last time that you acted at Montpelliers, with our ancient Friends, Anthony Saporra, Guy Bourguyer, Balthasar Noyer, Tolly, Jhon Quentin, Francis Robinet, Jhon Perdrier, and Francis Rabelais, the Moral Comedy of him who had espoused and married a Dumb Wife. I was there, quoth Epistemon, the good honest Man, her Husband, was very earnestly urgent to have the Fillet of her Tongue untied, and would needs have her speak by any means : At his Desire some pains were taken on her, and partly by the industry of the Physician, other part by the expertness of the Surgeon, the Encyliglotte, which she had under her Tongue, being cut, she spoke and spoke again ; yea, within few hours she spoke so loud, so much, so fiercely, and so long, that her poor Husband returned to the same Physician for a Recipe to make her hold her Peace : There are (quoth the Physician) many proper Remedies in our Art, to make dumb Women speak, but there are none, that ever I could learn therein, to make them silent. The only Cure which I have found out, is their Husband's Deafness. The Wretch became within few Weeks thereafter, by Vertue of some Drugs, Charms or Enchantments, which the Physician had prescribed unto him, so deaf, that he could not have heard the thundring of Nineteen hundred Canons at a Salvo. His Wife perceiving, that indeed he was as deaf as a Door-nail, and that her Scolding was but in vain, sith that he heard her not, she grew stark mad.

Some time after, the Doctor asked for his Fee of the Husband ; who answered, That truly he was deaf, and so was not able to understand what the tenure of his Demand might be. Whereupon the Leech bedusted him with a little, I know not what, sort of Powder ; which rendred him a Fool immediately : so great was the stultificating Vertue of that strange kind of pulverized Dose. Then did this Fool of a Husband, and his mad Wife joyn together, falling on the Doctor and the Surgeon, did so scratch, bethwack, and bang them, that they were left half dead upon the place, so furious were the Blows which they received : I never in my Life-time laughed so much, as at the acting of that Buffoonry.

Let us come to where we left off, (quoth Panurge) your Words being translated from the Clapper-dudgions to plain English, do signifie, that it is not very inexpedient that I marry, and that I should not care for being a Cuckold. You have there hit the Nail on the Head. I believe, Master Doctor, that on the day of my Marriage you will be so much taken up with your Patients, or otherways so seriously employed, that we shall not enjoy your Company : Sir, I will heartily excuse your absence.

Stercus et urina medici sunt prandia prima,
Ex aliis paleas ex istis collige grana.

You are mistaken (quoth Rondibilis) in the Second Verse of our Distich ; for it ought to run thus :

Nobis sunt signa nobis sunt prandia digna.

If my Wife at any time prove to be unwell, and ill at ease, I will look upon the Water which she shall have made in an Urinal-glass, (quoth Rondibilis) grope her Pulse, and see the disposition of her Hypogaster, together with her Umbilicary Parts. According to the Prescript Rule of Hippocrates, 2 *Aph.* 35. before I proceed any further in the Cure of her Distemper. No, no, (quoth Panurge) that will be but to little purpose ; such a Feat is for the Practice of us that are Lawyers, who have the Rubrick, *De Ventre inspiciendo :* Do not therefore trouble your self about it, (Master Doctor) I will provide for her a Plaister of warm Guts. Do not neglect your more urgent occasions otherwhere, for coming to my Wedding, I will send you some supply of Victuals to your own House, without putting you to the trouble of coming abroad, and you shall always be my special Friend. With this approaching somewhat nearer to him, he clapp'd into his Hand, without the speaking of so much as one word, four Rose Nobles. Rondibilis did shut his Fist upon them right kindly ; yet as if it had displeased him to make acceptance of such Golden Presents ; he in a start, as if he had been wroth, said, He, he, he, he, he, there was no need of any thing, I thank you nevertheless ; From wicked Folks I never get enough ; and I from honest People refuse nothing. I shall be always, Sir, at your Command. Provided that I pay you well, quoth Panurge. That (quoth Rondibilis) is understood.

CHAPTER XXXV

How the Philosopher Trouillogan handleth the difficulty of Marriage

As this Discourse was ended, Pantagruel said to the Philosopher Trouillogan, Our loyal, honest, true and trusty Friend, the Lamp from hand to hand is come to you ; it falleth to your turn to give an Answer, Should Panurge, pray you, marry, yea or no ? He should do both, quoth Trouillogan. What say you, asked Panurge ? That which you have heard, answered Trouillogan. What have I heard ? replied Panurge. That which I have said, replied Trouillogan. Ha, ha, ha, are we come to that pass, quoth Panurge ? Let it go nevertheless, I do not value it at a rush, seeing we can make no better of the Game. But howsoever tell me, should I marry or no ? Neither the one nor the other, answered Trouillogan. The Devil take me, quoth Panurge, if these odd Answers do not make me dote, and may he snatch me presently away, if I do understand you. Stay awhile until I fasten these Spectacles of mine on this left Ear, that I may hear you better. With this Pantagruel perceived at the Door of the great Hall, (which was that day their Dining-Room) Gargantua's little Dog, whose Name was Kyne ; for so was Toby's Dog called, as is recorded. Then did he say to these who were there present, Our King is not far off, let us all rise. That word was scarcely sooner uttered, than that Gargantua with his Royal Presence graced that banqueting and stately Hall. Each of their Guests arose to do their King that Reverence and Duty which became them. After that Gargantua had most affably saluted all the Gentlemen there present, he said, Good Friends, I beg this favour of you, and therein you

472

will very much oblige me, that you leave not the places where you sate, nor quit the Discourse you were upon.

Let a Chair be brought hither unto this end of the Table, and reach me a Cup full of the strongest and best Wine you have, that I may drink to all the Company. You are in Faith, all welcom, Gentlemen. Now let me know what Talk you were about. To this Pantagruel answered, That at the beginning of the Second Service Panurge had proposed a Problematick Theme, to wit, Whether he should marry, or not marry? That Father Hippothadee, and Doctor Rondibilis had already dispatched their Resolutions thereupon; and that just as his Majesty was coming in, the faithful Trouillogan, in the delivery of his Opinion, hath thus far proceeded, that when Panurge asked, whether he ought to marry, yea or no, at first he made this Answer, Both together. When this same Question was again propounded, his second Answer was, Not the one nor the other. Panurge exclaimeth, that those Answers are full of Repugnancies and Contradictions, protesting that he understands them not, nor what it is that can be meaned by them. If I be not mistaken, quoth Gargantua, I understand it very well: The Answer is not unlike to that which was once made by a Philosopher in ancient times, who being interrogated, if he had a Woman, whom they named him, to his Wife; I have her, quoth he, but she hath not me; possessing her, by her I am not possest. Such another Answer, quoth Pantagruel, was once made by a certain bouncing Wench of Sparta, who being asked, if at any time she had had to do with a Man? No, (quoth she) but sometimes Men have to do with me. Well then (quoth Rondibilis) let it be a Neuter in Physick; as when we say a body is Neuter, when it is neither sick nor healthful; and a Mean in Philosophy; that by an Abnegation of both Extreams, and this by the Participation of the one and of the other: Even as when lukewarm Water is said to be both hot and cold; or rather, as when Time makes the Partition, and equally divides betwixt the two, a while in the one, another while, as long, in the other opposite extremity. The holy Apostle, (quoth Hippothadee) seemeth, as I conceive, to have more clearly explained this Point, when he said, Those that are married, let them be as if they were not married; and those that have Wives, let them be as if they had no Wives at all. I thus interpret (quoth Pantagruel) the having and not having of a Wife. To have a Wife, is to have the use of her in such a way as Nature hath ordained, which is for the Aid, Society and

Solace of Man, and propagating of his Race : To have no Wife is not to be uxorious, play the Coward, and be lazy about her, and not for her sake to distain the Lustre of that Affection which Man owes to God ; or yet for her to leave those Offices and Duties which he owes unto his Country, unto his Friends and Kindred ; or for her to abandon and forsake his precious Studies, and other businesses of Account, to wait still on her Will, her Beck, and her Buttocks. If we be pleased in this Sense to take having and not having of a Wife, we shall indeed find no Repugnancy nor Contradiction in the Terms at all.

THE WORKS OF
MR. FRANCIS RABELAIS

THE WORKS OF MR. FRANCIS
RABELAIS

DOCTOR IN PHYSICK. CONTAINING FIVE BOOKS OF THE LIVES, HEROICK DEEDS AND SAYINGS OF GARGANTUA AND HIS SONNE PANTAGRUEL

Together with the Pantagrueline Prognostication, the Oracle of the Divine Bacbuc, and response of the bottle

Hereunto are annexed the Navigations unto the Sounding Isle and the Isle of the Apedefts: as likewise the Philosophical cream with a Limosin Epistle all done by

MR. FRANCIS RABELAIS

In the French tongue and now faithfully translated into English

Εὐνοεῖ, εὔλογε καὶ εὖ πράττε.

1653

Illustrated by W. HEATH ROBINSON

The Second Part

THE NAVARRE SOCIETY LONDON

Printed in Great Britain.

VOLUME II:—THE TABLE

THE THIRD BOOK (*Continued*)

▼

THE FOURTH BOOK

THE TABLE OF THE FOURTH BOOK ix

THE FIFTH BOOK

LETTERS WRITTEN BY FRANCIS RABELAIS, M.D., during his stay in Italy, in the Year 1536.

LIST OF ILLUSTRATIONS

xv

THE THIRD BOOK

(*Continued*)

CHAPTER XXXVI

A Continuation of the Answer of the Ephectick and Pyrronian Philosopher Trouillogan

You speak wisely, quoth Panurge, if the Moon were Green Cheese ; such a Tale once piss'd my Goose : I do not think but that I am let down into that dark Pit, in the lowermost bottom whereof the truth was hid, according to the saying of Heraclitus. I see no whit at all, I hear nothing, understand as little, my Senses are altogether dull'd and blunted ; truly I do very shrewdly suspect that I am enchanted. I will now alter the former style of my Discourse, and talk to him in another Strain. Our trusty Friend, stir not, nor imburse any ; but let us vary the Chance, and speak without Disjunctives : I see already that these loose and ill-joined Members of an Enunciation do vex, trouble, and perplex you.

Now go on, in the Name of God, Should I marry ?

TROUILLOGAN. There is some likelyhood therein.

PANURGE. But if I do not marry ?

TROUIL. I see in that no Inconvenience.

PAN. You do not ?

TROUIL. None, truly, if my Eyes deceive me not.

PAN. Yea, but I find more than Five Hundred.

TROUIL. Reckon them.

PAN. This is an Impropriety of Speech, I confess ; for I do no more thereby, but take a certain for an uncertain Number, and posit the determinate Term for what is indeterminate. When I say therefore Five Hundred, my meaning is, many.

TROUIL. I hear you.

PAN. Is it possible for me to live without a Wife, in the Name of all the Subterranean Devils ?

TROUIL. Away with these filthy Beasts.

PAN. Let it be then in the Name of God; for my Sal-migondinish People use to say, To lie alone without a Wife, is certainly a bruitish Life. And such a Life also was it assevered to be by Dido in her Lamentations.

TROUIL. At your Command.

PAN. By the Pody Cody, I have fished fair; where are we now? But will you tell me? Shall I marry?

TROUIL. Perhaps.

PAN. Shall I thrive or speed well withal?

TROUIL. According to the Encounter.

PAN. But if in my Adventure I encounter aright, as I hope I will, shall I be fortunate?

TROUIL. Enough.

PAN. Let us turn the clean contrary way, and brush our former Words against the Wool; what if I encounter ill?

TROUIL. Then blame not me.

PAN. But, of Courtesie, be pleased to give me some Advice: I heartily beseech you, what must I do?

TROUIL. Even what thou wilt.

PAN. Wishy, washy; Trolly, Trolly.

TROUIL. Do not invocate the Name of any thing, I pray you.

PAN. In the Name of God, let it be so: My Actions shall be regulated by the Rule and Square of your Counsel: What is it that you advise and counsel me to do?

TROUIL. Nothing.

PAN. Shall I marry?

TROUIL. I have no hand in it.

PAN. Then shall I not marry?

TROUIL. I cannot help it.

PAN. If I never marry, I shall never be a Cuckold.

TROUIL. I thought so.

PAN. But put the case that I be married.

TROUIL. Where shall we put it?

PAN. Admit it be so then, and take my meaning in that Sence.

TROUIL. I am otherways employed.

PAN. By the death of a Hog, and Mother of a Toad, O Lord, if I durst hazard upon a little Fling at the swearing Game, though privily and under Thumb, it would lighten the burthen of my Heart, and ease my Lights and Reins exceedingly; a little Patience nevertheless is requisite. Well then, if I marry, I shall be a Cuckold.

TROUIL. One would say so.

PAN. Yet if my Wife prove a vertuous, wise, discreet and chaste Woman, I shall never be Cuckolded.

TROUIL. I think you speak congruously.

PAN. Hearken.

TROUIL. As much as you will.

PAN. Will she be discreet and chaste ? This is the only Point I would be resolved in ?

TROUIL. I question it.

PAN. You never saw her ?

TROUIL. Not that I know of.

PAN. Why do you then doubt of that which you know not ?

TROUIL. For a Cause.

PAN. And if you should know her.

TROUIL. Yet more.

PAN. Page, my pretty little Darling, take here my Cap, I give it thee : Have a care you do not break the Spectacles that are in it ; go down to the lower Court, Swear there half an hour for me, and I shall in compensation of that Favour swear hereafter for thee as much as thou wilt. But who shall Cuckold me ?

TROUIL. Some body.

PAN. By the Belly of the wooden Horse at Troy, Master Somebody, I shall bang, belam thee, and claw thee well for thy labour.

TROUIL. You say so.

PAN. Nay, nay, that Nick in the dark Cellar, who hath no white in his Eye, carry me quite away with him, if, in that case, whensoever I go abroad from the Palace of my Domestick Residence, I do not with as much Circumspection, as they use to ring Mares in our Country to keep them from being sallied by Stoned Horses, clap a Bergamasco Lock upon my Wife.

TROUIL. Talk better.

PAN. It is *Bien chien chié chanté*, well cacked, and cackled ; shitten, and sung in matter of Talk : Let us resolve on somewhat.

TROUIL. I do not gainsay it.

PAN. Have a little patience, seeing I cannot on this side draw any Blood of you. I will try, if with the Launcet of my Judgment, I be able to bleed you in another Vein. Are you married, or are you not ?

TROUIL. Neither the one nor the other, and both together.

PAN. O the good God help us ; by the Death of a Buffle-ox, I sweat with the toyl and travel that I am put to, and find my

Digestion broke off, disturbed, and interrupted for all my Phrenes, Metaphrenes, and Diaphragmes, Back, Belly, Midrif, Muscles, Veins, and Sinews are held in a suspence, and for a while discharged from their proper Offices, to stretch forth their several Powers and Abilities, for Incornifistibulating, and laying up into the Hamper of my Understanding, your various Sayings and Answers.

TROUIL. I shall be no hinderer thereof.

PAN. Tush, for shame : Our faithful Friend, speak, Are you married ?

TROUIL. I think so.

PAN. You were also married before you had this Wife.

TROUIL. It is possible.

PAN. Had you good Luck in your first Marriage ?

TROUIL. It is not impossible.

PAN. How thrive you with this Second Wife of yours ?

TROUIL. Even as it pleaseth my Fatal Destiny.

PAN. But what in good earnest ? tell me : Do you prosper well with her ?

TROUIL. It is likely.

PAN. Come on, in the Name of God : I vow, by the Burthen of Saint Christopher, that I had rather undertake the fetching of a Fart forth of the Belly of a dead Ass, than to draw out of you a positive and determinate Resolution : yet shall I be sure at this time to have a snatch at you, and get my Claws over you. Our trusty Friend, let us shame the Devil of Hell, and confess the verity : Were you ever a Cuckold ? I say, you who are here, and not that other you who playeth below in the Tennis-Court ?

TROUIL. No, if it was not predestinated.

PAN. By the Flesh, Blood, and Body, I swear, reswear, forswear, abjure, and renounce, he evades and avoids, shifts, and escapes me, and quite slips and winds himself out of my Gripes and Clutches.

At these words Gargantua arose, and said, Praised be the good God in all things, but especially for bringing the World into that height of Refinedness, beyond what it was when I first came to be acquainted therewith, that now the Learnedst and most prudent Philosophers are not ashamed to be seen entring in at the Porches and Frontispieces of the Schools of the Pyrronian, Aporetick, Sceptick, and Ephectick Sects : Blessed be the Holy Name of God, veritably, it is like henceforth to be found an Enterprize of much more easie undertaking, to

4

catch Lyons by the Neck, Horses by the Main, Oxen by the Horns, Bulls by the Muzzle, Wolves by the Tail, Goats by the Beard, and flying Birds by the Feet, then to intrap such Philosophers in their words. Farewel, my worthy, dear, and honest Friends.

When he had done thus speaking, he withdrew himself from the Company ; Pantagruel, and others with him would have followed and accompanied him, but he would not permit them so to do. No sooner was Gargantua departed out of the Banquetting-Hall, than that Pantagruel said to the invited Guests : Plato's Timee, at the Beginning always of a solemn Festival Convention, was wont to count those that were called thereto ; we on the contrary, shall at the Closure and End of this Treatment, reckon up our Number, One, Two, Three ; Where is the Fourth ? I miss my Friend Bridlegoose : Was not he sent for ? Epistemon answered, That he had been at his House to bid and invite him ; but could not meet with him : For that a Messenger from the Parliament of Mirlingois, in Mirlingues, was come from him, with a Writ of Summons, to cite and warn him personally to appear before the Reverend Senators of the High Court there, to vindicate and justifie himself at the Bar, of the Crime of Prevarication laid to his charge, and to be peremptorily instanced against him in a certain Decree, Judgment, or Sentence lately awarded, given and pronounced by him : and that therefore he had taken Horse, and departed in great hast from his own House ; to the end, that without peril or danger of falling into a default, or contumacy, he might be the better able to keep the perfixed and appointed time.

I will (quoth Pantagruel) understand how that matter goeth ; it is now above forty Years, that he hath been constantly the Judge of Fonsbeton : During which space of time, he hath given four thousand Definitive Sentences : Of two thousand three hundred and nine whereof, although appeal was made by the Parties whom he had judicially condemned from his inferiour Judicatory, to the Supream Court of the Parliament of Mirlingois, in Mirlingues they were all of them nevertheless confirmed, ratified and approved of by an Order, Decree, and final Sentence of the said Sovereign Court, to the casting of the Appellants, and utter overthrow of the Suits wherein they had been foiled at Law, for ever and a day : That now in his old Age he should be personally summoned, who in all the foregoing time of his Life, hath demeaned himself so unblamably in the Discharge of the Office and Vocation he had been called unto; it cannot assuredly be, that such a change hath happened without some notorious Misfortune and Disaster: I am resolved to help and assist him in Equity and Justice to the uttermost extent of my Power and Ability. I know the Malice, Despight, and Wickedness of the World to be so much more now-a-days exasperated, increased, and aggravated by what it was not long since, that the best Cause that is, how just and equitable soever it be, standeth in great need to be succoured, aided and supported. Therefore presently, from this very instant forth, do I purpose, till I see the event and closure thereof, most heedfully to attend and wait upon it, for fear of some under-hand tricky Surprizal, Cavilling, Pettifoggery, or fallacious quirks in Law, to his detriment, hurt, or disadvantage.

Then Dinner being done, and the Tables drawn and removed, when Pantagruel had very cordially and affectionately thanked his invited Guests, for the favour which he had enjoyed of their Company, he presented them with several rich and costly Gifts, such as Jewels, Rings set with precious Stones, Gold and Silver Vessels, with a great deal of other sort of Plate besides; and lastly, taking of them all his Leave, retired himself into an inner Chamber.

CHAPTER XXXVII

How Pantagruel perswaded Panurge to take Counsel of a Fool

WHEN Pantagruel had withdrawn himself, he by a little sloping Window in one of the Galleries perceived Panurge in a Lobbey not far from thence, walking alone, with the Gesture, Carriage, and Garb of a fond Dotard, raving, wagging, and shaking his Hands, dandling, lolling, and nodding with his Head, like a Cow bellowing for her Calf; and having then called him nearer, spoke unto him thus: You are at this present (as I think) not unlike to a Mouse intangled in a Snare, who the more that she goeth about to rid and unwind her self out of the Gin wherein she is caught, by endeavouring to clear and deliver her feet from the Pitch whereto they stick, the fouler she is bewrayed with it, and the more strongly pestered therein ; even so is it with you : For the more that you labour, strive, and inforce your self to disincumber, and extricate your Thoughts out of the implicating Involutions and Fetterings of the grievous and lamentable Gins and Springs of Anguish and Perplexity ; the greater difficulty there is in the relieving of you, and you remain faster bound than ever : nor do I know for the removal of this Inconveniency, any Remedy but one.

Take heed ; I have often heard it said in a vulgar Proverb, The Wise may be instructed by a Fool. Seeing the Answers and Responses of sage and judicious Men, have in no manner of way satisfied you, take advice of some Fool ; and possibly by so doing, you may come to get that Counsel which will be agreeable to your own Heart's desire and contentment. You know how by the Advice and Counsel and Prediction of Fools, many Kings, Princes, States, and Commonwealths have been preserved, several Battels gained, and divers doubts of a most perplexed Intricacy resolved : I am not so diffident of your Memory, as to hold it needful to refresh it with a Quotation of Examples ; nor do I so far undervalue your Judgment, but that I think it will acquiesce in the Reason of this my subsequent Discourse.

As he who narrowly takes heed to what concerns the dextrous Management of his private Affairs, domestick Businesses and those Adoes which are confined within the streight-lac'd compass of one Family : who is attentive, vigilant, and active in the œconomick Rule of his own House ; whose frugal Spirit never strays from home ; who loseth no occasion, whereby he may purchace to himself more Riches, and build up new heaps of Treasure on his former Wealth ; and who knows warily how to prevent the inconveniences of Poverty, is called a worldly wise Man, though perhaps in the se ond Judgment of the Intelligences which are above, he be esteemed a Fool. So on the contrary, is he most like (even in the thoughts of all Cœlestial Spirits) to be not only sage, but to presage Events to come by Divine Inspiration, who laying quite aside those Cares which are conducible to his Body, or his Fortunes, and as it were departing from himself, rids all his Senses of Terene Affections, and clears his Fancies of those plodding Studies, which harbour in the Minds of thriving Men : All which neglects of Sublunary Things are vulgarly imputed Folly.

After this manner, the Son of Picus, King of the Latins,

that great Southsayer Faunus, was called Fatuus, by the witless Rabble of the common People. The like we daily see practised amongst the Commick Players, whose Drammatick Rolls, in distribution of the Personages, appoint the acting of the Fool to him who is the wisest of the Troop. In approbation also of this fashion, the Mathematicians allow the very same Horoscope to Princes, and to Sots. Whereof a right pregnant instance by them is given in the Nativities of Æneas and Choræbus ; the latter of which two is by Euphorion said to have been a Fool : and yet had with the former the same Aspects, and Heavenly Genethlick Influences.

I shall not, I suppose, swerve much from the purpose in hand, if I relate unto you, what Jhon Andrew said upon the Return of a Papal Writ, which was directed to the Mayor of Rochel ; and Burgesses after him by Panorm, upon the same Pontifical Canon ; Barbatia, on the Pandects, and recently by Jason, in his Councels, concerning Seiny Jhon the noted Fool of Paris, and Caillets, fore-great Grandfather. The Case is this :

At Paris, in the Roast-meat Cookery of the Petit Chastelet, before the Cook-Shop of one of the Roast-meat Sellers of that Lane, a certain hungry Porter was eating his Bread, after he had by Parcels kept it a while above the Reek and Steam of a fat Goose on the Spit, turning at a great Fire, and found it so besmoaked with the Vapour, to be savoury ; which the Cook observing, took no notice, till after having ravined his Penny Loaf, whereof no Morsel had been unsmoakified, he was about discamping and going away ; but by your leave, as the Fellow thought to have departed thence shot-free, the Master-Cook laid hold upon him by the Gorget, demanded payment for the Smoak of his Roast-meat. The Porter answered, that he had sustained no loss at all ; that by what he had done there was no Diminution made of the Flesh, that he had taken nothing of his, and that therefore he was not indebted to him in any thing : As for the Smoak in question, that, although he had not been there, it would howsoever have been evaporated : Besides that, before that time it had never been seen nor heard, that Roast-meat Smoak was sold upon the Streets of Paris. The Cook hereto replied, That he was not obliged nor any way bound to feed and nourish for nought a Porter whom he had never seen before with the Smoak of his Roast-meat ; and thereupon swore, that if he would not forthwith content and satisfie him with present Payment for the Repast which he had thereby

got, that he would take his crooked Staves from off his Back ;
which instead of having Loads thereafter laid upon them,
should serve for Fuel to his Kitchen Fires. Whilst he was
going about so to do, and to have pulled them to him by one
of the bottom Rungs, which he had caught in his Hand, the
sturdy Porter got out of his Gripes, drew forth the knotty
Cudgel, and stood to his own Defence. The Altercation waxed
hot in Words, which moved the gaping Hoydons of the sottish
Parisians to run from all parts thereabouts to see what the issue
would be of that babling Strife and Contention. In the interim
of this Dispute, to very good purpose Seiny Jhon the Fool and
Citizen of Paris, hapned to be there, whom the Cook perceiving,
said to the Porter, Wilt thou refer and submit unto the noble
Seiny Jhon, the Decision of the Difference and Controversie
which is betwixt us ? Yes, by the blood of a Goose, answered
the Porter, I am content. Seiny Jhon the Fool, finding that
the Cook and Porter had compromised the Determination of
their Variance and Debate to the Discretion of his Award and
Arbitriment ; after that the Reasons on either side whereupon
was grounded the mutual fierceness of their brawling Jar had
been to the full displayed and laid open before him, commanded
the Porter to draw out of the Fab of his Belt a piece of Money,
if he had it. Whereupon the Porter immediately without
delay, in Reverence to the Authority of such a Judicious
Umpire, put the tenth part of a Silver Phillip into his Hand.
This little Phillip Seiny Jhon took, then set it on his left
Shoulder, to try by feeling if it was of a sufficient weight ;
after that, laying it on the palm of his Hand he made it ring
and tingle, to understand by the Ear if it was of a good Alloy
in the Metal whereof it was composed : Thereafter he put it to
the Ball or Apple of his left Eye, to explore by the sight if it
was well stamped and marked ; all which being done, in a
profound Silence of the whole doltish People, who were there
Spectators of this Pageantry, to the great hope of the Cooks,
and despair of the Porters Prevalency in the Suit that was in
agitation, he finally caused the Porter to make it sound several
times upon the Stall of the Cooks Shop. Then with a Presidential Majesty holding his Bable (Scepter-like) in his Hand,
muffling his Head with a Hood of Martern Skins, each side
whereof had the resemance of an Ape's Face, sprucified up
with Ears of pasted Paper, and having about his Neck a
bucked Ruff, raised, furrowed, and ridged, with Ponting Sticks
of the shape and fashion of small Organ-Pipes ; he first, with

all the force of his Lungs, coughed two or three times, and then with an audible Voice pronounced this following Sentence, The Court declareth, That the Porter, who ate his Bread at the Smoak of the Roast, hath civilly paid the Cook with the Sound of his Money : And the said Court Ordaineth, That every one return to his own Home, and attend his proper Business, without Cost and Charges, and for a Cause. This Verdict, Award and Arbitriment of the Parisian Fool, did appear so equitable, yea, so admirable to the aforesaid Doctors, that they very much doubted, if the Matter had been brought before the Sessions for Justice of the said Place, or that the Judges of the Rota at Rome had been Umpires therein ; or yet that the Areopagites themselves had been the Deciders thereof, if by any one part, or all of them together, it had been so judicially sententiated and awarded. Therefore advise, if you will be counselled by a Fool.

CHAPTER XXXVIII

How Triboulet is set forth and blazed by Pantagruel and Panurge

BY my Soul, (quoth Panurge) that Overture pleaseth me exceedingly well ; I will therefore lay hold thereon, and embrace it. At the very motioning thereof, my very Right Entrail seemeth to be widened and enlarged, which was but just now hard bound, contracted and costive : But as we have hitherto made choice of the purest and most refined Cream of Wisdom and Sapience for our Counsel, so would I now have to preside and bear the prime Sway in our Consultation, as were a Fool in the supreme degree. Triboulet (quoth Pantagruel) is compleatly foolish, as I conceive. Yes, truly, (answer'd Panurge) he is properly and totally a Fool. a

PANTAGRUEL.	PANURGE.
Fatal F.	Mercurial F.
Natural F.	Lunatick F.
Celestial F.	Erratick F.
Jovial F.	Excentrick F.
Ætherial and Junonian F.	Latinized F.
Arctick F.	Ordinary F.
Heroick F.	Transcendent F.
Genial F.	Rising F.
Inconstant F.	Papal F.
Earthly F.	Consistorian F.
Solacious and Sporting F.	Conclavist F.
Jocund and Wanton F.	Bullist F.
Pimpled F.	Synodal F.
Freckled F.	Episcopal F.
Bell-tinging F.	Doctoral F.
Laughing and Lecherous F.	Monachal F.
Nimming and Filching F.	Fiscal F.
Unpressed F.	Extravagant F.
First-broached F.	Writhed F.
Augustal F.	Canonical F.
Cesarine F.	Such another F.
Imperial F.	Graduated F.
Royal F.	Commensal F.
Patriarchal F.	Primolicentiated F.
Original F.	Trainbairing F.
Loyal F.	Supererrogating F.
Ducal F.	Collateral F.
Common F.	Haunch and Side F.
Lordly F.	Nestling, Ninny, and Youngling F.
Palatin F.	Flitting, Giddy, and Unsteddy F.
Principal F.	
Pretorian F.	Brancher, Novice, and Cockney F.
Elected F.	Hagard, Cross, and Froward F.
Courtly F.	Gentle, Mild, and Tractable F.
Primipilary F.	Mail-coated F.
Triumphant F.	Pilfring and Purloining F.
Vulgar F.	Tail-grown F.
Domestick F.	Gray-peckled F.

PANTAGRUEL.	PANURGE.
Exemplary F.	Doating and Raving F.
Rare Outlandish F.	Singular and Surpassing F
Satrapal F.	Special and Excelling F.
Civil F.	Metaphysical F.
Popular F.	Ingrained F.
Familiar F.	City F.
Notable F.	Basely accoutred F.
Favourized F.	Mast-headed F.
Scatical F.	Modal F.
Predicamental and Cata-gorick F.	Second Notial F.
Predicable and Enuncia-tory F.	Micher pincrust F
Decumane and Super-lative F.	Heteroclit F.
Dutiful and Officious F.	Summist F.
Optical and Perspective F.	Abbridging F.
Algoristick F.	Morrish F.
Algebraical F.	Leaden-sealed F.
Cabalistical and Massoreti-cal F.	Mandatory F.
Talmudical F.	Compassionate F.
Algamalized F.	Titulary F.
Compendious F.	Crooching, Showking Ducking F.
Abbreviated F.	Grim, Stern, Harsh, and Wayward F.
Hyperbolical F.	Well-hung and timbred F.
Anatomastical F.	Ill-claued, pounced and pawed F.
Allegorical F.	Well-stoned F.
Tropological F.	Crabbed and Unpleasing F.
Pleonasmical F	Winded and Tainted F.
Capital F.	Kitchin-haunting F.
Hairbrained F.	Lofty and Stately F.
Cordial F.	Spitrack F.
Intimate F.	Architrave F.
Hepatick F.	Pedestal F.
Cushotten and Swilling F.	Tetragonal F.
Splenetick F.	Renowned F.
Windy F.	Chearful and Buxom F.
Legitimate F.	Solemn F.

PANTAGRUEL.	PANURGE.
Azymathal F.	Annual F.
Almicautarized F.	Festival F.
Proportioned F.	Recreative F.
Chinnified F.	Boorish and Counterfeit F
Swollen and Puffed up F.	Pleasant F.
Overcockrifedlid and Lified F.	Privileged F.
Corallery F.	Rustical F.
Eastern F.	Barytonant F.
Sublime F.	Pink and Spot-poudered F
Crimson F.	Musket-proof F.
Proper and Peculiar F.	Pedantick F.
Ever ready F.	Strouting F.
Diapatonal F.	Wood F.
Resolute F.	Greedy F.
Hieroglyphical F.	Senseless F.
Authentick F.	Godderlich F.
Worty F.	Obstinate F.
Precious F.	Contradictory F.
Fanatick F.	Pedagogical F.
Fantastical F.	Daft F.
Symphatick F.	Drunken F.
Panick F.	Peevish F.
Limbicked and Distilled F.	Prodigal F.
Comportable F.	Rash F.
Wretched and Heartless F.	Plodding F.
Rheumatick F.	Prating F.
Flaunting and Bragga-dochio F.	Catechetick F.
Egregious F.	Cacodoxical F.
Humorous and Caprici-ous F.	Meridional F.
Rude, Gross, and Absurd F.	Nocturnal F.
Large-measured F.	Occidental F.
Bable F.	Trifling F.
Downright F.	Astrological and Figure-flinging F.
Broad-lifted F.	Cenethliack and Horo-scopal F.
Downsical-bearing F.	Knavish F.
Stale and Overworn F.	Idiot F.
Saucy and Swaggering F.	Blockish F.

PANTAGRUEL.	PANURGE.
Full-bulked F.	Beetle-headed F
Gallant and Vain-glorious F.	Crotesk F.
Gorgeous and Gawdy F.	Impertinent F.
Continual and Intermitting F.	Quarrelsom F.
Rebasing and Roundling F.	Unmannerly F.
Prototypal and Precedenting F.	Captious and Sophistical F.
Fooded F.	Soritick F.
Thick and threefold F.	Catholoproton F.
Damasked F.	Hoti and Diots F.
Fearny F.	Aplos and Catati F
Unleavened F.	

PANTAG. If there was any reason why at Rome the Quirinal Holiday, of old, was call'd, The Feast of Fools; I know not why we may not for the like cause institute in France the Tribouletick Festivals, to be celebrated and solemnized over all the Land.

PANUR. If all Fools carried Cruppers.

PANTAG. If he were the God Fatuus, of whom we have already made mention, the Husband of the Goddess Fatua, his Father would be Good Day, and his Grandmother Good Even.

PANUR. If all Fools paced, albeit he be somewhat wrylegg'd, he would overlay at least a Fathom at every Rake. Let us go toward him, without any further lingring or delay, we shall have, no doubt, some fine Resolution of him. I am ready to go, and long for the issue of our Progress impatiently. I must needs (quoth Pantagruel) according to my former Resolution of him, be present at Bridlegoose's Tryal: Nevertheless, whilst I shall be upon my Journey towards Mirelingues, which is on the other side of the River of Loire, I will dispatch Carpalin to bring along with him from Blois the Fool Triboulet. Then was Carpalin instantly sent away, and Pantagruel at the same time, attended by his Domesticks, Panurge, Epistemon, Ponocrates, Fryar Jhon, Gymnast, Rysotome, and others marched forward on the High Road to Mirelingues.

CHAPTER XXXIX

How Pantagruel was present at the Tryal of Judge Bridlegoose
who decided Causes and Controversies in Law, by the Chance
and Fortune of the Dice

On the Day following, precisely at the Hour appointed, Pantagruel came to Mirelingues: At his Arrival, the Presidents,
Senators and Counsellors prayed him to do them the honour
to enter in with them, to hear the Dicision of all the Causes,
Arguments and Reasons, which Bridlegoose in his own Defence
would produce, why he had pronounced a certain Sentence
against the Subsidy-Assessor, Toucheronde; which did not
seem very equitable to that Centumviral Court. Pantagruel
very willingly condescended to their Desire; and accordingly
entring in, found Bridlegoose sitting within the middle of the
Inclosure of the said Court of Justice; who immediately, upon
the coming of Pantagruel, accompanied with the Senatorian
Members of that worshipful Judicatory, arose, went to the Bar,
had his Indictment read; and for all his Reasons, Defences,
and Excuses, answer'd nothing else, but that he was become
Old, and that his Sight of late was very much failed, and become
dimmer than it was wont to be, instancing therewithal many
Miseries and Calamities which Old Age bringeth along with it,
and are concomitant to wrinkled Elders; which not, *par Archi*

15

d'lxxvi. *C. tanta :* by reason of which Infirmity, he was not able so distinctly and clearly to discern the Points and Blots of the Dice, as formerly he had been accustomed to do : Whence it might very well have happened, said he, as old dim-sighted Isaac took Jacob for Esau, that I after the same manner, at the Decision of Causes and Controversies in Law, should have been mistaken in taking a *Quatre* for a *Cinque,* or *Tre* for a *Deuce :* This, I beseech your Worship (quoth he) to take into your serious Consideration, and to have the more favourable opinion of my Uprightness (notwithstanding the Prevarication whereof I am accused, in the Matter of Toucherondy's Sentence) that at the time of that Decree's pronouncing, I only had made use of my small Dice ; and your Worships (said he) knew very well, how by the most Authentick Rules of the Law, it is provided, That the Imperfections of Nature should never be imputed unto any for Crimes and Transgressions ; as appeareth, *F. de re Mil. L. qui cum uno F. de Reg. Jur. L. fere F. de œdit. edict. per totum, F. de term. Mo. L. Divus Adrianus,* resolved by *LU. RO. ML. Si. Vero. F. Sol. Mat.* And who would offer to do otherwise, should not thereby accuse the Man, but Nature, and the All-seeing Providence of God, as is evident in *L. Maximum Vitium C. de Liber prœter.*

What kind of Dice (quoth Trinquamelle, Grand-President of the said Court) do you mean, my Friend Bridlegoose ? The Dice (quoth Bridlegoose) of Sentences at Law, Decrees, and peremptory Judgments, *Alea Judiciorum,* whereof is written, *Per Doct.* 26 *qu.* 2. *Ca. Sors L. nec emptio F. de contrahen. empt. L. quod debetur. F. de pecu, et ibi Bart.* And which your Worships do, as well as I, use, in this glorious Sovereign Court of yours : so do all other righteous Judges, in their Decision of Processes, and Final Determination of Legal Differences, observing that which hath been said thereof by *D. Henri. Ferraudet, et not. Gl. MC. si de sort. il et L. sed cum ambo F. de rud. ubi Doc.* Where mark, that Chance and Fortune, are good, honest, profitable and necessary for ending of, and putting a final Closure to Dissentions and Debates in Suits at Law. The same hath more clearly been declared by *Bal. Barto. et Alex. C. communia de L. Si duo.* But how is it that you do these things ? (asked Trinquamelle.) I very briefly (quoth Bridlegoose) shall answer you, according to the Doctrin and Instructions of *L. ampliorem par in refutatoriis C. de Apell.* Which is conform to what is said in *Il. 1. L. 2. F. quod met. cau gaudent. brevitate moderni.* My Practice is therein the same

W.HEATH·ROBINSON·

BRIDLEGOOSE

with that of your other Worships, and as the Custom of the Judicatory requires, unto which our Law commandeth us to have regard, and by the Rule thereof still to direct and regulate our Actions and Procedures. *Ut not. extra de consuet. C. ex literis et ibi Jano :* For having well and exactly seen, surveyed, overlooked, reviewed, recognized, read, and read over again, turned and tossed over, seriously perused and examined the Bills of Complaint, Accusations, Impeachments, Indictments, Warnings, Citations, Summonings, Comparitions, Appearances, Mandates, Commissions, Delegations, Instructions, Informations, Inquests, Preparatories, Productions, Evidences, Proofs, Allegations, Depositions, cross Speeches, Contradictions, Supplications, Requests, Petitions, Enquiries, Instruments of the Deposition of Witnesses, Rejoinders, Replies, Confirmations of former Assertions, Duplies, Triplies, Answers to Rejoinders, Writings, Deeds, Reproaches, disabling of Exceptions taken, Grievances, Salvation-Bills, Re-examination of Witnesses, Confronting of them together, Declarations, Denunciations, Libels, Certificates, Royal Missives, Letters of Appeal, Letters of Attorney, Instruments of Compulsion, Delinatories, Anticipatories, Evocations, Messages, Dimissions, Issues, Exceptions, dilatory Pleas, Demurs, Compositions, Injunctions, Reliefs, Reports, Returns, Confessions, Acknowledgments, Exploits, Executions, and other such-like Confects and Spiceries, both at the one and the other Side, as a good Judge ought to do, conform to what hath been noted thereupon. *Sper. de ordinario. Paragr. 3. et Tit. de Offi. O. in Paragr. fin. et de Prescriptis Præsent. a Parag. 1.* I posit on the end of a Table, in my Closet, all the Poaks and Bags of the Defendant, and then allow unto him the first hazard of the Dice ; according to the usual manner of your other Worships. And it is mentioned, *L. Favorabiliores F. de Reg. Jur. et in d. cum sunt eo. Tit. Lib.* 6. which saith, *Quum sunt partium Jura obscura, reo potius favendum est quam actori.* That being done, I thereafter lay down upon the other end of the same Table, the Bags and Sachels of the Plaintiff, (as your other Worships are accustomed to do) *Visum Visu,* just over-against one another ; for, *Opposita juxta se potest clarius elucescunt : ut not. in L. Parag. Videamus F. de his qui sunt sui vel alieni juris et in L. Munerum. Mixta F. de mun. et hon.* Then do I likeways, and semblably throw the Dice for him, and forthwith livre him his Chance. But, (quoth Trinquamelle) my Friend, how come you to know, understand and resolve the Obscurity of these various and seeming contrary Passages in Law, which are laid claim to by the Suitors, and pleading Parties ? Even just (quoth Bridlegoose) after the fashion of your other Worships ; to wit, when there are many Bags on the one side, and on the other, I then use my little small Dice (after the customary manner of your other Worships) in obedience to the Law. *Semper in stipulationibus F. de Reg. Jur.* The Law verified, verifieth that, *Eo. tit. semper in obscuris quod minimum est sequimur :* Canonized in *C. in obscuris eod. Tit. Lib.* 6. I have other large great Dice, fair, and goodly ones, which I employ in the fashion that your other Worships use to do, when the Matter is more plain, clear and liquid ; that is to say, when there are fewer Bags. But when you have done all these fine things (quoth Trinquamelle) how do you, my Friend, award your Decrees, and pronounce Judgment ? Even as your other Worships (answer'd Bridlegoose) for I give out Sentence in his favour, unto whom hath befallen the best Chance by Dice ; Judiciary, Tribunian, Pretorial, what comes first: So our Laws command. *F. qui pot. in Pig. L. Potior. L. Creditor. C. de Cons. L. 1. et de Reg. Jur. on U. Qui prior est iure*

CHAPTER XL

How Bridlegoose giveth Reasons, why he looked upon those Law-Actions which he decided by the Chance of the Dice

YEA, but (quoth Trinquamelle) my Friend, seeing it is by the Lot, Chance, and Throw of the Dice, that you award your Judgments and Sentences, why do not you livre up these fair Throws and Chances the very same Day and Hour, without any further procrastination or delay, that the controverting Party-pleaders appear before you ? To what use can those Writings serve you, those Papers, and other Procedures contained in the Bags and Poaks of the Law-Suitors ? To the very same use (quoth Bridlegoose) that they serve your other Worships, They are behooful unto me, and serve my turn in three things very exquisite, requisite, and authentical. First, For Formality sake, the omission whereof, that it maketh all whatever is done, to be of no force nor value, is excellently well proved, by *Spec. tit. de inst. edi. et tit. de rescript. præsent.* Besides, that it is not unknown to you, who have had many more Experiments thereof than I, how oftentimes in Judicial Proceedings, the Formalities utterly destroy the Materialities and Substances of the Causes and Matters agitated ; for *Forma mutata, mutatur substantia F. ad exh. L. Julianus F. ad leg. Pals. si is qui Quadraginta. Et extra de deci. C. ad. audientiam. Et de Cel. Miss. C. in quadam.*

Secondly, They are useful and steadable to me, (even as unto your other Worships) in lieu of some other honest and healthful Exercise. The late Master Othoman Vadat, a prime Physician, as you would say, *Cod. de Comit. et Archi. Lib.* 12. hath frequently told me, That the lack and default of Bodily Exercise, is the chief, if not the sole and only cause of the little Health, and short Lives of all Officers of Justice, such as your Worships and I am. Which Observation was singularly well, before him, noted and remarked by Bortholus in *Lib.* 1. *C. de Sent. quæ pro eo quod :* therefore is it, that the Practice of such-like Exercitations is appointed to be laid hold on by your other Worships, and consequently not to be denied unto me, who am of the same Profession : *Quia accessurum naturam sequitur principalis, de Reg. Jur. L.* 7. *et L. cum principalis, et L. nihil dolo F. eo tit. F. de fide juss. L. fide juss. et extra de Officio de L. Cap.* 1. Let certain honest, and recreative Sports and Plays of Corporeal Exercises be allowed and approved of ; and so far *Ut omnes obed. in prius Coll.* 7. *et F. de præscript. ver. L. gratuitatem et L.* 1. *Cod. de Spe. L.* 11. Such also is the Opinion of D. Thom. *in Secunda, Secundæ Q.* 168. Quoted in very good purpose, by D. at de Rosa ; who, *Fuit magnus Practicus*, and a solemn Doctor, as Barbaria attesteth in *Principiis Consil.* Wherefore the Reason is evidently and clearly deduced, and set down before us, in *Gloss. in præmio F. par ne autem tertii Interpone tuis interdum gaudia curis.* In very deed, one, in the Year a Thousand four hundred fourscore and sixth, having a Business concerning the Portion and Inheritance of a younger Brother, depending in the Court and Chamber of the four High Treasurers of France, whereinto as soon as ever I got leave to enter by a Pecuniary Permission of the Usher thereof, as your other Worships know very well, that *Pecunia obediant omnia ;* and there says Baldus, in *L. Singularia. F. si cert. pet. et lol. in L. receptitia Cod. de constit. pecuni. et card. in cler.* 1. *de Baptism.* I found them all recreating and diverting themselves at the Play called Musse, either before or after Dinner ; to me, truly, it is a thing altogether indifferent, whether of the two it was, provided that *Hic not.* that the Game of the Musse is honest, healthful, ancient, and lawful : *A Muscho inventore, de quo Cod. deperhœre L. si post motam : et Muscarii.* Such as play and sport it at the Musse, are excusable in and by Law, *Lib.* 1. *C. de excus. artific. lib.* 10. And at the very same time was Master Tielman Picquet, one of the Players of that Game of Musse : There is nothing that I do better remember ; for he laughed heartily, when his Fellow-Members of the aforesaid Judicial Chamber, spoiled their Caps in swindging of his Shoulders ; he, nevertheless, did even then say unto them, that the banging and flapping of him to the wast, and havock of their Caps, should not at their return from the Palace to their own Houses, excuse them from their Wives : *Part.* 1. *extra de præsum. et ibi glos.* Now *resolutory loquendo,* I should say, according to the stile and phrase of your other Worships, that there is no Exercise, Sport, Game, Play, nor Recreation in all this Palatine, Palacial, or Parliamentary World, more ariomatizing and fragrant, than to empty and void Bags and Purses : turn over Papers and Writings : quote Margins and Backs of Scrolls and Rolls ; fill Panniers, and take inspections of Causes : *Ex Bart. et Joan de prad in L. falsa de condit. et Demost. F.*

Thirdly, I consider as your own Worships use to do, that Time ripeneth and bringeth all things to maturity, that by Time every thing cometh to be made manifest and patent, and that Time is the Father of Truth and Vertue. *Gloss. in J. cod. de Servit. authent. de restit. et ea quæ pa. et spe tit. de requis cons.* Therefore is it, that after the manner and fashion of your other Worships, I defer, protract, delay, prolong, intermit, surcease, pause, linger, suspend, prorogate, drive out, wyre-draw, and shift off the Time of giving a Definitive Sentence, to the end that the Suit or Process, being well vanned and winnowed, tost and canvassed to and fro ; narrowly, precisely, and nearly garbelled, sifted, searched, and examined : And on all Hands exactly argued, disputed and debated, may, by success of Time come at last to its full ripeness and maturity : By means wherof, when the fatal hazard of the Dice ensueth thereupon, the Parties cast or condemned by the said Aleatory Chance, will with much greater patience, and more mildly and gently endure and bear up the disastrous Load of their Misfortune, than if they had been sentenced at their first arrival unto the Court : As, *Not. gl. F. de excus. tut. L. tria onera.*

Portatur leviter quod portas quisque libenter. On the other part, to pass a Decree or Sentence, when the action is raw, crude, green, unripe, and unprepared as at the beginning, a danger would ensue of a no less inconveniency, than that, which the Physicians have been wont to say, befalleth to him in whom an Imposthume is pierced before it be ripe ; or unto any other whose Body is purged of a strong predominating Humour, before its digestion : For as it is written, *In Authent. hæc consist. in nos. de constit. princip.* So is the same repeated, *In gloss. in C. cæterum extr. quod medicamenta morbis exhibent, hoc jura negotiis.* Nature furthermore admonisheth and teacheth us, to gather and reap, eat and feed on Fruits when they are ripe, and not before. *Instit. de re di paragr. is ad quem et F. de action. empt. L. Julianus.* To marry likewise our Daughters when they are ripe, and no sooner. *F. de donation inter vir. et uxor. L. cum his status paragr. si quia sponsa et 21. q. C. sic ut dicit. gl.*

> *Jam matura thoro plenis adoleverat annis*
> *Virginitas.*

And in a word, she instructeth us to do nothing of any considerable Importance, but in a full maturity and ripeness, *23 q. 2. paragr. ult. et 23. de C. ultimo.*

CHAPTER XLI

How Bridlegoose relateth the History of the Reconcilers of Parties at variance in matters of Law

I REMEMBER to the same purpose (quoth Bridlegoose, in continuing his Discourse) that in the time when at Poictiers I was
a Student of Law under Crocadium Juris, there was at Smerva
one Peter Dandin, a very honest Man, careful Labourer of the
Ground, fine singer in a Church-Desk, of good Repute and
Credit, and older than the most aged of all your Worships,
who was wont to say, that he had seen the great and goodly
good Man the Council of Lateran, with his wide and broad
brimmed red Hat : As also, that he had beheld and looked upon
the fair and beautiful Pragmatical Sanction, his Wife, with her
huge Rosary or Patenotrian Chapelet of Jeat-beads, hanging
at a large Sky-coloured Ribbond. This honest Man compounded, attoned and agreed more Differences, Controversies
and Variances at Law than had been determined, voided, and
finished during his time in the whole Palace of Poictiers, in
the Auditory of Montmorillon, and in the Town-house of the
old Partenay. This amicable Disposition of his rendred him
Venerable, and of great Estimation, Sway, Power and Authority
throughout all the neighbouring places of Chauvinie, Nouaille,
Vivonne, Mezeaux, Estables, and other bordering and circumjacent Towns, Villages, and Hamlets : All their Debates were
pacified by him ; he put an end to their brabling Suits at Law,
and wrangling Differences. By his Advise and Counsels were
Accords and Reconcilements no less firmly made, than if the
Verdict of a Sovereign Judge had been interposed therein,
although, in very deed, he was no Judge at all, but a right
honest Man, as you may well conceive. *Arg. in L. si Anius
F. de Jure jur. et de verbis obligatorii sit continuus.*
There was not a Hog killed within three Parishes of him,
whereof he had not some part of the Haslet and Puddings.
He was almost every day invited either to a Marriage, Banquet,
Christning Feast, an Uprising or Women-Churching Treatment,
a Birth-day's Anniversary Solemnity, a merry Frollick Gossip-
ing, or otherways to some delicious Entertainment in a Tavern,
to make some Accord and Agreement between Persons at odds,

and in debate with one another. Remark what I say; for he never yet setled and compounded a Difference betwixt any two at Variance, but he streight made the Parties agreed and pacified, to drink together, as a sure and infallible Token and Symbol of a perfect and compleatly well cemented Reconciliation, sign of a sound and sincere Amity and proper Mark of a new Joy and Gladness to follow thereupon. *Ut Not. per F. de Peri et com. rei. ven. L.* 1. He had a Son whose Name was Tenot Dandin, a lusty young sturdy frisking Royster, so help me God, who likewise (in imitation of his Peace-making Father) would have undertaken and medled with the taking up of Variances, and deciding of Controversies betwixt disagreeing and contentious Parties, Pleaders as you know.

> *Sæpe solet similis filius esse patri.*
> *Et sequitur leviter filia matris iter.*

Ut ait gloss. vi, quæst. 1. *C. siquis g. de cons. disc. v. C.* 2. *fin. et est. int. per dict. cod. de impu. et aliis substit. L. vir. et L. Legitimæ. F. de stat. hom. gloss. in L. quod si nolit. de adi L. quisquis C. ad leg. Jure Majest. excipio filiusà moniali susceptos ex Monacho per gloss. in C. impudicas* 27. *questione.* And such was his Confidence to have no worse Success than his Father, he assumed unto himself the Title of Law-strife-setler. He was likeways in these pacificatory Negotiations so active and vigilant; for *Vigilantibus Jura subveniunt ex L. pupillus F. quæ in fraud. cred. et ibi L. non enim et instit. m. proœm.* That when he had smelt, heard, and fully understood; *ut F. si quando paufec. L. Agaso q. in verbo offecit, id est nasum ad culum posuit.* That there was any where in the Country a debatable matter at Law, he would incontinently thrust in his Advice, and so forwardly intrude his Opinion in the business, that he made no Bones of making offer, and taking upon him to decide it, how difficult soever it might happen to be, to the full contentment and Satisfaction of both Parties: It is written, *Qui non laborat non manducat.* And the said *Gl. F. de damn. infect. L. si quamvis:* And *Currere* plus quæ le pas *vetulam compellit egestas. Gloss. F. de lib. agnosco. L. si quis pro quo facit. L. si plures C. de Codd. incert.* But so huge great was his Misfortune in this his Undertaking, that he never composed any difference, how little soever you may imagine it might have been, but that instead of reconciling the Parties at odds, he did incense, irritate, and exasperate them to a higher point

THIS AMICABLE DISPOSITION OF HIS RENDRED HIM VENERABLE, AND
OF GREAT ESTIMATION

of Dissention and Enmity than ever they were at before. Your Worships know I doubt not that,

Sermo datur cunctis animi sapientia paucis.

Gl. F. de alien. in mun. caus. fa. lib. 2. This administred unto the Tavern-keepers, Wine-drawers and Vintners of Smerva an occasion to say, that under him they had not in the space of a whole year so much Reconciliation-Wine (for so were they pleased to call the good Wine of Leguge) as under his Father they had done in one half hours time. It hapned a little while thereafter, that he made a most heavy regret thereof to his Father, attributing the Causes of his bad Success in pacificatory Enterprizes to the Perversity, Stubbornness, froward, cross and backward Inclinations of the People of his time, roundly boldly and irreverently upbraiding, that if but a score of Years before the World had been so wayward, obstinate, pervicacious, implacable, and out of all Square, Frame and Order as it was then, his Father had never attained to, and acquired the Honour and Title of Strife-appeaser, so irrefragably, inviolably and irrevocably as he hath done ; in doing whereof Tenot did heinously transgress against the Law which prohibiteth Children to reproach the Actions of their Parents. *Per gl. et Barth. L.* 3. *paragr. si quis F. de cond. ob caus. et authent. de Nupt. par sed quod sancitum Col.* 3. *ment.* To this the honest old Father answered thus : My Son Dandin, when Don Oportet taketh place, this is the course which we must trace, *Gl. C. de Appel. L. eos etiam:* For the Road that you went upon was not the way to the Fullers Mill, nor in any part thereof was the Form to be found wherein the Hare did sit. Thou hast not the skill and dexterity of setling and composing Differences. Why ? Because thou takest them at the beginning, in the very Infancy and Bud as it were, when they are green, raw, and indigestible ; yet I know handsomly and featly how to compose and settle them all. Why ? Because I take them at their Decadence, in their Weaning, and when they are pretty well digested. So saith *Gl. dulcior est fructus post multa pericula ductus. L. non moriturus C. de contrahend. et comit. stip.* Didst thou ever hear the vulgar Proverb, Happy is the Physician whose coming is desired at the declension of a Disease ? For the Sickness being come to a Crisis, is then upon the decreasing hand, and drawing towards an end, although the Physician should not repair thither for the Cure thereof ;

whereby though Nature wholly do the work, he bears away the Palm and Praise thereof. My Pleaders after the same manner, before I did interpose my Judgment in the reconciling of them, were waxing faint in their Contestations, their Altercation Heat was much abated, and in declining from their former Strife, they of themselves inclined to a firm Accommodation of their Differences ; because there wanted Fuel to that Fire of burning, Rancour and despightful Wrangling, whereof the lower sort of Lawyers were the Kindlers : That is to say, their Purses were emptied of Coin, they had not a Win in their Fab, nor Penny in their Bag, wherewith to sollicit and present their Actions,

Deficiente pecu deficit omne, nia.

There wanted then nothing but some Brother to supply the place of a Paranymph, Braul-broker, Proxenete or Mediator, who acting his part dextrously, should be the first broacher of the Motion of an Agreement, for saving both the one and the other Party from that hurtful and pernicious Shame, whereof he could not have avoided the Imputation, when it should have been said, that he was the first who yielded and spoke of a Reconcilement ; and that therefore his Cause not being good, and being sensible where his Shoe did pinch him, was willing to break the Ice, and make the greater haste to prepare the way for a Condescendment to an amicable and friendly Treaty. Then was it that I came in pudding time, (Dandin my Son) nor is the fat of Bacon more relishing to boiled Pease, than was my Verdict then agreeable to them : This was my Luck, my Profit and good Fortune. I tell thee, my Jolly Son Dandin, that by this Rule and Method I could settle a firm Peace, or at least clap up a Cessation of Arms and Truce for many years to come betwixt the Great King and the Venetian State ; the Emperor and the Cantons of Swisserland ; the English and the Scots ; and betwixt the Pope and the Ferrarians. Shall I go yet further : Yea, as I would have God to help me, betwixt the Turk and the Sophy, the Tartars and the Muscoviters. Remark well what I am to say unto thee, I would take them at that very instant nick of time, when both those of the one and the other side should be weary and tired of making War, when they had voided and emptied their own Cashes and Coffers of all Treasure and Coin, drained and exhausted the Purses and Bags of their Subjects, sold and morgaged their Domains and proper Inheritances, and totally wasted, spent and consumed the

Munition, Furniture, Provision and Victuals that were necessary for the continuance of a Military Expedition. There I am sure, by God, or by his Mother, that would they, would they, in spight of all their Teeths, they should be forced to take a little Respit and Breathing-time, to moderate the Fury and cruel Rage of their ambitious Aims. This is the Doctrine in *Gl.* 37. *d. c. Si quando.*

Odero, si potero, si non invitus amabo.

CHAPTER XLII

How Suits at Law are bred at first, and how they come afterward to their perfect growth

FOR this Cause (quoth Bridlegoose, going on in his Discourse) I temporise and apply my self to the Times, as your other Worships use to do, waiting patiently for the Maturity of the Process, full Growth and Perfection thereof in all its Members ; to wit, the Writings and the Bags. *Arg. in L. fin. Major. C. commodus, et de cons. de* 1. *c. solemnitates, et ibi gl.* A Suit in Law at its Production, Birth and first beginning, seemeth to me as unto your other Worships, shapeless, without Form or Fashion, incompleat, ugly and imperfect, even as a Bear, at his first coming into the World, hath neither Hands, Skin, Hair nor Head, but is meerly an inform, rude and ill-favoured piece and lump of Flesh ; and would remain still so, if his Dam out of the abundance of her Affection to her hopeful Cub, did not with much licking put his Members into that figure and shape which Nature had provided for those of an Arctick and Ursinal kind. *Ut Not. Doct. F. ad L. aliquia* 2. *in si.* Just so when I see, as your other Worships do, Processes and Suits in Law at their first bringing forth, to be numberless, without shape, deformed and disfigured ; for that then they consist only of one or two Writings, or Copies of Instruments, through which Defect they appear unto me as to your other Worships, foul, loathsom, filthy and mis-shapen Beasts. But when there are heaps of these Legiformal Papers packed, piled, laid up together, impoaked, insacheled, and put up in Bags, then is it that with a good reason we may term that Suit, to which, as pieces, parcels, parts, portions and members thereof, they do pertain and belong, well-formed and fashioned, big-limmed, strong set, and in all and each of its Dimensions most compleatly membred : Because *forma dat. esse. rei L. si is qui F. ad leg. falcid. in C. cum delicta extra de rescript. Barbaria consil. Lib.* 2. And before him, *Balsus in C. ult. extra decons. et L. Julianus exhib. et F. ad L. quæsitum F. de log.* 3. The manner is such as is set down *in gl. p. quæst.* 1. *C. Paulus.*

Debile principiam melior fortuna sequetur.

Like your other Worships, also the Sergeants, Catchpoles, Pursevants, Messengers, Summoners, Apparitors, Ushers, Doorkeepers, Pettifoggers, Attorneys, Proctors, Commissioners, Justices of the Peace, Judge Delegates, Arbitrators, Overseers, Sequestrators, Advocates, Inquisitors, Jurors, Searchers, Examiners, Notaries, Tabellions, Scribes, Scriveners, Clerks, Pregnatories, Secondaries, and Expedanean Judges, *de quibus tit. est L.* 3. *C.* by sucking very much, and that exceeding forcibly, and licking at the Purses of the pleading Parties, they, to the Suits already begot and engendred, form, fashion and frame Head, Feet, Claws, Talons, Beaks, Bills, Teeth, Hands, Veins, Sinews, Arteries, Muscles, Humours, and so forth, through all the Simulary and Dissimilary Parts of the whole ; which Parts, Particles, Pendicles and Appurtenances, are the Law-poaks and Bags, *Gl. de Cons. d.* 3. *C. accepisti qualis vestis erit, talia cornua gerit. Hic notandum est.* That in this respect the Pleaders, Litigants and Law-Suiters are happier than the Officers, Ministers, and Administrators of Justice : For *beatus est dare quam accipere. F. Com. L.* 3. *extra de celeb. Miss. cum Matthœ et* 24. *Quæst.* 1. *Cap. Od. Gl.*

Affectum dantis pensat censura tonantis.

Thus becometh the Action or Process, by their care and industry, to be of a compleat and goodly bulk, well shaped, framed, formed, and fashioned according to the Canonical Gloss.

Accipe, sume, cape, sunt verba placentia Papæ.

Which Speech hath been more clearly explained by Alb. de Res. *in verbo Roma.*

Roma manus rodit, quas rodere non valet, odit.
Dantes custodit, non dantes spernit, et odit.

The Reason whereof is thought to be this :

Ad præsens ova, cras pullis sunt meliora.

Ut est Gl. in L. quum H. F. de Transact. Nor is this all, for the inconvenience of the contrary is set down in *H. C. de Allu. L. F.*

Quum labor in damno est, crescit mortalis egestas.

In confirmation whereof we find, that the true Etymology and Exposition of the word Process is Purchase, viz. of good store of Money to the Lawyers, and of many Poaks, *id est, Prou-Sacks*, to the Pleaders, upon which Subject we have most Cœlestial Quips, Gybes, and Girds.

Litigando jura crescunt, litigando jus acquiritur.

Item Gl. in Cap. illud extrem. de præsumpt. et C. de prob. L. instram. L. non Epistolis L. non nudis.

Et si non prosunt singula, multa juvant.

Yea, but (asked Trinquamelle) how do you proceed (my Friend) in Criminal Causes the culpable and guilty Party being taken and seized upon, *Flagrante Crimine?* Even as your other Worships use to do (answered Bridlegoose :) First, I permit the Plaintiff to depart from the Court, enjoyning him not to presume to return thither, till he preallably, should have taken a good sound and profound Sleep, which is to serve for the prime Entry and Introduction to the legal carrying on of the Business. In the next place, a formal Report is to be made to me of his having slept. Thirdly, I issue forth a Warrant to convent him before me. Fourthly, He is to produce a sufficient and authentick Attestation, of his having thoroughly and entirely sleeped, conform to the *Gloss.* 22. *Quest.* 7. *Si quis cum.*

Quandoque bonus dormitat Homerus.

Being thus far advanced in the Formality of the Process, I find that this Consopiating Act engendreth another Act, whence ariseth the articulating of a Member ; that again produceth a Third Act, fashionative of another Member ; which Third bringing forth a Fourth, Procreative of another Act: New

THEY, TO THE SUITS ALREADY BEGOT AND ENGENDRED, FORM HEAD,
FEET, CLAWS

31

Members in a no fewer Number are shapen and framed, one still breeding, and begetting another (as Link after Link, the Coat of Mail at length is made) till thus, Piece after Piece, by little and little, like Information upon Information, the Process be compleatly well formed, and perfect in all his Members. Finally, having proceeded this length, I have recourse to my Dice, nor is it to be thought, that this interruption, respit, or interpellation, is by me occasioned without very good reason inducing me thereunto, and a notable Experience of a most convincing and irrefragable force.

I remember, on a time, that in the Camp at Stockholm, there was a certain Gascon named Gratinauld, Native of the Town of Saint Sever, who having lost all his Money at Play, and consecutively being very angry thereat, as you know, *Pecunia est alius sanguis ut ait Anto. de Burtio, MC accedens 2. extra ut lit. non contest. et Bald. in L. si tuis C de op. Lib. per not. et L. advocati. C. de advo. diu. Jud. pecunia est vita hominis et optimus fide jusser in necessitatibus :* Did, at his coming forth of the Gaming-House, in the presence of the whole Company that was there, with a very loud Voice, speak in his own Language these following words : Pap. cap. de bious nillots que maux depipes rous tresire : aresque de pergudes sont les mires bingt, et quovatre bagnelles, ta pla donne rien pies cruz et Patacts, Scy de Gum de bons aulx, qui boille trequar ambe Jou à Belsambiz. Finding that none would make him any Answer, he passed from thence to that part of the Leaguer, where the huff, snuff, honder-sponder, swash-buckling High-Germans were, to whom he renewed these very Terms, provoking them to fight with him ; but all the Return he had from them to his stout Challenge was only, Der Gasconner that schich, usz. mitt. cim. iedem zesclage aberer ist genegrer au staclen darum liebem fram ve hend serg au inverm hausraut. Finding also, that none of that Band of Teutonick Soldiers offered himself to the Combat ; he passed to that quarter of the Leaguer where the French Free-booting Adventurers were encamped, and reiterating unto them, what he had before repeated to the Dutch Warriours, challenged them likewise to fight with him, and therewithal made some pretty little Gasconado frisking Gambols, to oblige them the more cheerfully and gallantly to cope with him in the Lists of a Duellizing Engagement ; but no answer at all was made unto him. Whereupon the Gascon despairing of meeting with any Antagonists, departed from thence, and laying himself down, not far from the Pavilions of the grand Christian Cavalier Crissie, fell fast asleep. When he had throughly slept an hour or two, another adventurous and all-hazarding Blade of the Forlorn Hope of the lavishing wasting Gamesters, having also lost all his Moneys, sallied forth with a Sword in his Hand, of a firm Resolution to fight with the aforesaid Gascon, seeing he had lost as well as he.

Ploratur lachrymis amissa pecunia veris,

Saith the *Gl. de pœnitent. distinct. 2. C. sunt plures.* To this effect, having made enquiry and search for him throughout the whole Camp, and in sequel thereof found him asleep, he said unto him, Up, ho, good Fellow, in Name of all the Devils of Hell, rise up, rise up, get up ; I have lost my Money as well as thou hast done, let us therefore go fight lustily together, grapple and scuffle it to some purpose : Thou may'st see that ; and look, my Tuck is no longer than thy Rapier. The Gascon, altogether astonish'd at his unexpected Provocation, without altering his former Dialect, spoke thus : Cap de Saint Arnault, qu'au segs tu qui me rebeillez ? Que mande taberne te gire : Ho Saint Siobe Cab de Gascoigne tapla do my Jou, quand à quest ta quam me bringu estæ. The ventrous Royster inviteth him again to the Duel ; but the Gascon, without condescending to his Desire, said only this : Hepauvres Jet' esquinerie ares que son plat reposat : vene impaur que te pansat comme Jou peusse truquete. Thus, in forgetting his Loss, he forgot the eagerness which he had to fight. In conclusion, after that the other had likewise slept a little, they, instead of fighting, and possibly killing one another, went jointly to a Sutler's Tent, where they drank together very amicably, each upon the pawn of his Sword. Thus, by a little Sleep, was pacified the ardent Fury of two warlike Champions. There, Gossip, comes the Golden Word of Jhon Andr. *in Cap. ult. de Sent. et rejudic. L. Sexto.*

Sedendo, et dormiendo fit anima prudens.

CHAPTER XLIII

How Pantagruel excuseth Bridlegoose, in the Matter of
Sentencing Actions at Law, by the Chance of the Dice

WITH this Bridlegoose held his peace. Whereupon Trinquamelle bid them withdraw from the Court : Which accordingly was done ; and then directed his Discourse to Pantagruel
after this manner : It is fitting (most Illustrious Prince) not
only by reason of the deep Obligations wherein this present
Parliament, together with the whole Marquisate of Merlingues,
stand bound to your Royal Highness, for the innumerable
Benefits, which as effects of meer Grace, they have received
from your incomparable Bounty ; but for that excellent Wit
also, prime Judgment, and admirable Learning wherewith
Almighty God, the Giver of all Good Things, hath most richly
qualified and endowed you, we tender and present unto you
the Decision of this new, strange, and Paradoxical Case of
Bridlegoose, who in your presence, to your both hearing and
seeing, hath plainly confessed his final Judging and Determinat-
ing of Suits of Law, by the meer Chance and Fortune of the
Dice : Therefore do we beseech you, that you may be pleased
to give Sentence therein, as unto you shall seem most just and
equitable. To this Pantagruel answered : Gentlemen, It is not
unknown to you, how my Condition is somewhat remote from
the Profession of deciding Law-Controversies ; yet seeing you
are pleased to do me the Honour to put that Task upon me,
instead of undergoing the Office of a Judge, I will become your
humble Supplicant : I observe, Gentlemen, in this Bridlegoose,
several things, which induce me to represent before you, that
it is my opinion he should be pardoned. In the first place, his
Old Age ; secondly, his Simplicity : To both which Qualities
our Statute and Common Laws, Civil and Municipal together,
allow many Excuses for any Slips or Escapes, which through
the invincible Imperfection of either, have been inconsiderately
stumbled upon by a Person so qualified. Thirdly, Gentlemen,
I must needs display before you another Case, which in Equity
and Justice maketh much for the advantage of Bridlegoose ;
to wit, that this one, sole, and single fault of his, ought to be
quite forgotten, abolished, and swallowed up, by that immense

and vast Ocean of just Dooms and Sentences, which heretofore
he hath given and pronounced : His Demeanours for these
forty Years and upwards, that he hath been a Judge, having
been so evenly balanced in the Scales of Uprightness, that Envy
it self, till now, could not have been so impudent as to accuse
and twit him with any Act worthy of a Check or Reprehension :
As if a Drop of the Sea were thrown into the Loire, none could
perceive, or say, that by this single Drop, the whole River
should be salt and brackish.

Truly, it seemeth unto me, that in the whole Series of
Bridlegoose's Juridical Decrees, there hath been, I know not
what, of extraordinary savouring of the unspeakable Benignity
of God, that all those his preceding Sentences, Awards, and
Judgments, have been confirmed and approved of by your
selves, in this your own Venerable and Sovereign Court : For
it is usual (as you know well) with Him whose Ways are in-
scrutable, to manifest his own ineffable Glory, in blunting the
Perspicacy of the Eyes of the Wise, in weakening the Strength
of potent Oppressors, in depressing the Pride of rich Extor-
tioners, and in erecting, comforting, protecting, supporting,
upholding, and shoaring up the poor, feeble, humble, silly, and
foolish Ones of the Earth. But waving all these Matters, I
shall only beseech you, not by the Obligations which you pretend to owe to my Family, for which I thank you ; but for
that constant and unfeigned Love and Affection which you
have always found in me, both on this and on the other side of
Loire, for the Maintenance and Establishment of your Places,
Offices, and Dignities, that for this one time you would pardon
and forgive him, upon these two Conditions : First, That he
satisfie, or put a sufficient Surety for the Satisfaction of the
Party wronged by the Injustice of the Sentence in question :
For the fulfilment of this Article, I will provide sufficiently.
And Secondly, That for his subsidiary Aid in the weighty
Charge of administering Justice, you would be pleased to appoint
and assign unto him some pretty, little, virtuous Counseller,
younger, learneder, and wiser than he, by the Square and Rule
of whose Advice he may regulate, guide, temper and moderate in
times coming, all his Judiciary Procedures, or otherways, if you
intend totally to depose him from his Office, and to deprive him
altogether of the State and Dignity of a Judge, I shall cordially
intreat you to make a Present and free Gift of him to me, who
shall find in my Kingdoms Charges and Employments enough
wherewith to imbusie him, for the bettering of his own For-

tunes, and furtherance of my Service. In the mean time, I implore the Creator, Saviour and Sanctifier of all good things, in their Grace, Mercy and Kindness, to preserve you all now and evermore, World without end.

These Words thus spoken, Pantagruel vailing his Cap, and making a Leg, with such a Majestick Garb as became a Person of his paramount Degree and Eminency, farewell d Trinquamelle the President, and Master-Speaker of that Merlinguesian Parliament, took his leave of the whole Court, and went out of the Chamber ; at the Door whereof finding Panurge, Epistemon, Fryar Jhon, and others, he forthwith, attended by them, walked to the utter Gate, where all then immediately took Horse to return towards Gargantua. Pantagruel by the Way related to them, from point to point, the manner of Bridlegoose's sententiating Differences at Law. Fryar Jhon said, that he had seen Peter Dandin, and was acquainted with him at that time when he sojourned in the Monastery of Fontaine le Conte, under the Noble Abbot Ardillon. Gymnast likewise affirmed, that he was in the Tent of the Grand Christian Cavallier de Cressie, when the Gascon, after his Sleep, made answer to the Adventurer. Panurge was somewhat incredulous in the Matter of Believing, that it was morally possible Bridlegoose should have been for such a long space of Time so continually fortunate in that Aleatory way of deciding Law-Debates. Epistemon said to Pantagruel, Such another Story, not much unlike to that, in all the Circumstances thereof, is vulgarly reported of the Provost of Montlehery. In good sooth, such a perpetuity of good Luck is to be wonder'd at. To have hit right twice or thrice in a Judgment so given by Hap-hazard, might have fallen out well enough, especially in Controversies that were ambiguous, intricate, abstruse, perplexed, and obscure.

CHAPTER XLIV

How Pantagruel relateth a strange History of the Perplexity of Human Judgment

SEEING you talk (quoth Pantagruel) of dark, difficult, hard and knotty Debates, I will tell you of one controverted before Cneius Dolobella, Proconsul in Asia. The Case was this :

A Wife in Smyrna had of her first Husband a Child named Abece ; he dying, she, after the expiring of a Year and a Day, married again, and to her Second Husband bore a Boy call'd Edege : A pretty long time thereafter it happened (as you know the Affection of Step-fathers and Step-dams is very rare, towards the Children of the first Fathers and Mothers deceased) that this Husband, with the help of his Son Edege, secretly, wittingly, willingly and treacherously murthered Abece. The Woman came no sooner to get Information of the Fact, that it might not go unpunished, she caused kill them both, to revenge the Death of her first Son. She was Apprehended, and carried before Cneius Dolobella, in whose Presence she, without dissembling any thing, confessed all that was laid to her Charge ; yet alledged, that she had both Right and Reason on her side for the killing of them. Thus was the State of the Question. He found the Business so dubious and intricate, that he knew not what to determin therein, nor which of the Parties to encline to. On the one hand, it was an execrable Crime to cut off at once both her Second Husband and her Son. On the other hand, the Cause of the Murther seemed to be so natural, as to be grounded upon the Law of Nations, and the rational Instinct of all the People of the World ; seeing they two together had feloniously and murtherously destroyed her first Son : Not that they had been in any manner of way wronged, outraged or injured by him, but out of an avaricious intent to possess his Inheritance. In this doubtful Quandary and Uncertainty what to pitch upon, he sent to the Areopagites then sitting at Athens, to learn and obtain their Advice and Judgment. That judicious Senate very sagely perpending the Reasons of his Perplexity, sent him word to summon her personally to compear before him, a precise hundred Years thereafter, to answer to some Interrogatories touching certain Points, which were not contained in the Verbal Defence : Which Resolution of theirs did import, that it was, in their opinion, a so difficult and inextricable a Matter, that they knew not what to say or judge therein. Who had decided that Plea by the Chance and Fortune of the Dice, could not have erred nor awarded amiss, on which side soever he had past his casting and condemnatory Sentence : If against the Woman, she deserved Punishment for usurping Sovereign Authority, by taking that Vengeance at her own hand, the inflicting whereof was only competent to the Supream Power, to administer Justice in Criminal Cases : If for her, the just Resentment of a so atrocious Injury done unto her, in murthering her innocent Son, did fully excuse and vindicate her of any Trespass or Offence about that Particular committed by her. But this continuation of Bridlegoose for so many Years, still hitting the Nail on the Head, never missing the Mark, and always judging aright, by the meer throwing of the Dice, and the Chance thereof, is that which most astonisheth and amazeth me.

To answer (quoth Epistemon) categorically to that which you wonder at, I must ingeniously confess and avow that I cannot ; yet conjecturally to guess at the reason of it, I would refer the Cause of that marvellously long-continued happy Success in the Judiciary Results of his Definitive Sentences to the favourable Aspect of the Heavens, and Benignity of the Intelligences ; who, out of their love to Goodness, after having contemplated the pure Simplicity and sincere Unfeignedness of Judge Bridlegoose in the acknowledgment of his Inabilities, did regulate that for him by Chance, which by the profoundest Act of his maturest Deliberation he was not able to reach unto. That likewise which possibly made him to diffide in his own Skill and Capacity, notwithstanding his being an expert and understanding Lawyer, for any thing that I know to the contrary, was the Knowledge and Experience which he had of the Antenomies, Contrarieties, Antilogies, Contradictions, Traversings and Thwartings of Laws, Customs, Edicts, Statutes, Orders and Ordinances, in which dangerous Opposition, Equity and Justice being structured and founded on either of the opposite Terms, and a Gap being thereby opened for the ushering in of Injustice and Iniquity, through the various Interpretations of Self-ended Lawyers, being assuredly perswaded that the Infernal Calumniator, who frequently transformeth himself into the likeness of a Messenger or Angel of Light, maketh use of these cross Glosses and Expositions in the Mouths and Pens of his Ministers and Servants, the perverse Advocates, bribing Judges, Law-monging Attorneys, prevaricating Counsellors, and other such-like Law-wrestling Members of a Court of Justice, to turn by those means Black to White, Green to Grey, and what is Streight to a Crooked ply ; for the more expedient doing whereof, these Diabolical Ministers make both the Pleading Parties believe that their Cause is just and righteous ; for it is well known, that there is no Cause, how bad soever, which doth not find an Advocate to patrocinate and defend it, else would there be no Process in the World, no Suits at Law, nor Pleadings at the Bar. He did in these Extremities, as I

AND TREACHEROUSLY MURTHERED ABECE

conceive, most humbly recommend the Direction of his Judicial Proceedings to the Upright Judge of Judges, God Almighty ; did submit himself to the Conduct and Guideship of the Blessed Spirit, in the Hazard and Perplexity of the Definitive Sentence ; and by this Aleatory Lot, did, as it were, implore and explore the Divine Decree of his Good Will and Pleasure, instead of that which we call the Final Judgment of a Court. To this effect, to the better attaining to his Purpose, which was to judge righteously, he did in my opinion throw and turn the Dice, to the end, that by the Providence aforesaid, the best Chance might fall to him whose Action was uprightest, and back'd with greatest Reason ; in doing whereof, he did not stray from the Sense of Talmudists, who say, that there is so little harm in that manner of searching the Truth, that in the Anxiety and Perplexedness of Human Wits, God oftentimes manifesteth the secret Pleasure of his Divine Will.

Furthermore, I will neither think nor say, nor can I believe, that the Unstreightness is so irregular, or the Corruption so evident, of those of the Parliament of Mirlingois in Mirlingues, before whom Bridlegoose was Arraigned for Prevarication, that they will maintain it to be a worse Practice to have the Decision of a Suit at Law referred to the Chance and Hazard of a Throw of the Dice, hab nab, or luck as it will, than to have it remitted to, and past by the Determination of those whose Hands are full of Blood, and Hearts of wry Affections. Besides that, their principal Direction in all Law-matters, comes to their Hands from one Tribonian, a wicked, miscreant, barbarous, faithless, and perfidious Knave, so pernicious, unjust, avaricious and perverse in his ways, that it was his ordinary custom to sell Laws, Edicts, Declarations, Constitutions and Ordinances, as at an Outroop or Putsale, to him who offered most for them. Thus did he shape Measures for the Pleaders, and cut their Morsels to them by and out of these little Parcels, Fragments, Bits, Scantlings and Shreds of the Law now in use, although concealing, suppressing, disanulling and abolishing the remainder, which did make for the total Law ; fearing that if the whole Law were made manifest and laid open to the knowledge of such as are interested in it, and the learned Books of the ancient Doctors of the Law, upon the Exposition of the Twelve Tables, and Prætorian Edicts, his villanous Pranks, Naughtiness, and vile Impiety, should come to the publick Notice of the World. Therefore were it better in my conceit, that is to say, less inconvenient, that Parties at Variance in any Juridicial

Case, should in the dark march upon Caltropes, than to submit the Determination of what is their Right to such unhallowed Sentences and horrible Decrees: As Cato in his time wished and advised, that every Judiciary Court should be paved with Caltropes.

CHAPTER XLV

How Panurge taketh Advice of Triboulet

ON the sixth Day thereafter Pantagruel was returned Home, at the very same hour that Triboulet was by Water come from Blois. Panurge, at his Arrival, gave him a Hog's Bladder puffed up with Wind, and resounding, because of the hard Pease that were within it: Moreover, he did present him with a gilt Wooden Sword, a hollow Budget made of a Tortoise-shell, an Osier Watled Wicker-Bottle-full of Briton Wine, and five and twenty Apples of the Orchard of Blanduco.

If he be such a Fool (quoth Carpalin) as to be won with Apples, there is no more Wit in his Pate, than in the Head of an Ordinary Cabbage. Triboulet girded the Sword and Script to his side, took the Bladder in his Hand, ate some few of the Apples, and drunk up all the Wine. Panurge very wistly and

heedfully looking upon him, said, I never yet saw a Fool, (and
I have seen ten thousand Franks worth of that kind of Cattle)
who did not love to drink heartily, and by good long Draughts.
When Triboulet had done with his Drinking, Panurge laid out
before him, and exposed the Sum of the Business, wherein
he was to require his Advice in eloquent and choicely-sorted
Terms, adorned with Flourishes of Rhetorick. But before he
had altogether done, Triboulet with his Fist gave him a bouncing
Whirret between the Shoulders, rendred back into his Hand
again the empty Bottle, fillipped and flirted him on the Nose
with the Hog's Bladder; and lastly, for a final Resolution,
shaking and wagging his Head strongly and disorderly, he
answer'd nothing else but this, By God, God; mad Fool;
beware the Monk: Buzansay, Hornepipe. These Words thus
finished, he slipt himself out of the Company, went aside, and
ratling the Bladder, took a huge Delight in the melody of the
rickling, crackling Noise of the Pease: After which time, it lay
not in the power of them all to draw out of his Chaps the
Articulate Sound of one Syllable; insomuch that when Panurge went about to interrogate him further, Triboulet drew
his Wooden Sword, and would have struck him therewith. I
have fish'd fair now (quoth Panurge) and brought my Pigs
to a fine Market. Have I not got a brave Determination of all
my Doubts, and a Response in all things agreeable to the
Oracle that gave it? He is a great Fool that is not to be
denied; yet is he a greater Fool who brought him hither to me.
That Bolt (quoth Carpalin) levels point-blank at me; but of
the three, I am the greatest Fool, who did impart the Secret
of my Thoughts to such an Idiot Ass, and Native Ninny.

Without putting our selves to any stir or trouble in the
least, (quoth Pantagruel) let us maturely and seriously consider and perpend the Gestures and Speech which he hath made
and uttered: In them veritably (quoth he) have I remarked
and observed some excellent and notable Mysteries, yea, of
such important worth and weight, that I shall never henceforth
be astonished, nor think strange, why the Turks, with a great
deal of worship and reverence, honour and respect Natural
Fools, equally with their Primest Doctors, Mufties, Divines and
Prophets. Did not you take heed (quoth he) a little before he
opened his Mouth to speak, what a shogging, shaking and
wagging his Head did keep? By the approved Doctrine of
the ancient Philosophers, the customary Ceremonies of the
most expert Magicians, and the received Opinions of the

TRIBOULET

43

learnedest Lawyers, such a brangling Agitation and Moving should by us all be judged to proceed from, and be quickned and suscitated by the coming and Inspiration of the Prophetizing and Fatidical Spirit, which entring briskly, and on a sudden, into a shallow Receptacle of a debil Substance (for as you know, and as the Proverb shews it, a little Head containeth not much Brains) was the cause of that Commotion. This is conform to what is avouched by the most skilful Physicians, when they affirm, that Shakings and Tremblings fall upon the Members of a Humane Body, partly because of the Heaviness and violent Impetuosity of the Burthen and Load that is carried, and other part, by reason of the Weakness and Imbecillity that is in the vertue of the bearing Organ : A manifest Example whereof appeareth in those, who fasting, are not able to carry to their Head a great Goblet full of Wine without a trembling and a shaking in the Hand that holds it. This of old was accounted a Prefiguration and a mystical pointing out of the Pythian Divineress, who used always before the uttering of a Response from the Oracle, to shake a Branch of her Domestick Lawrel. Lampridius also testifieth that the Emperor Heliogabulus, to acquire unto himself the Reputation of a Soothsayer, did, on several Holy Days of prime solemnity, in the Presence of the Fanatick Rabble, make the Head of his Idol, by some slight within the Body thereof, publickly to shake. Plautus, in his *Asserie*, declareth likewise, that Saurius, whithersoever he walked like one quite distracted of his Wits, keepeth such a furious lolling and mad-like shaking of his Head, that he commonly affrighted those who casually met with him in his Way. The said Author in another place shewing a Reason why Charmides shook and brangled his Head, averred that he was transported, and in an Extasie. Catullus after the same manner maketh mention in his *Berecynthia* and *Atys*, of the place wherein the Menades, Bacchical Women, She-Priests of the Lyæan God, and demented Prophetesses, carrying Ivy Boughs in their Hands, did shake their Heads. As in the like case amongst the Gauls, the gelded Priests of Cibyle were wont to do in the celebrating of some Festivals, which according to the Sense of the ancient Theologues, have from thence had their Denomination ; for κύβεσθαι signifieth to turn round, whirl about, shake the Head, and play the part of one that is wry-necked.

Semblably Titus Livius writeth, that in the Solemnization time of the Bacchanalian Fobedays at Rome, both Men and

44

Women seemed to Prophetize and Vaticinate, because of an affected kind of wagging of the Head, shrugging of the Shoulders, and Jectigation of the whole Body, which they used then most punctually. For the common Voice of the Philosophers, together with the Opinion of the People, asserteth for an irrefragable Truth, that Vaticination is seldom by the Heavens bestowed on any, without the Concomitancy of a little Phrensie, and a Head-shaking, not only when the said presaging Vertue is infused, but when the Person also therewith inspired declareth and manifesteth it unto others. The learned Lawyer Julien, being asked on a time, if that Slave might be truly esteemed to be healthful and in a good plight, who had not only convers'd with some furious, maniack and enraged People, but in their Company had also prophesied, yet without a Noddle-shaking Concussion, answered, That seeing there was no Head-wagging at the time of his Predictions, he might be held for sound and competent enough. Is it not daily seen how School-masters, Teachers, Tutors and Instructors of Children, shake the Heads of their Disciples (as one would do a Pot in holding it by the Lugs), that by this Erection, Vellication, stretching and pulling their Ears, (which according to the Doctrine of the sage Egyptians, is a Member consecrated to the Memory) they may stir them up to recollect their scatter'd Thoughts, bring home those Fancies of theirs, which perhaps have been extravagantly roaming abroad upon strange and uncouth Objects, and totally range their Judgments, which possibly by disordinate Affections have been made wild, to the Rule and Pattern of a wise, discreet, vertuous and Philosophical Discipline : All which Virgil acknowledgeth to be true, in the branglement of Apollo Cynthius.

CHAPTER XLVI

*How Pantagruel and Panurge diversely interpret
the Words of Triboulet*

He says you are a Fool ; and what kind of Fool ? A mad Fool, who in your old Age would enslave your self to the Bondage of Matrimony, and shut your Pleasures up within a Wedlock, whose Key some Ruffian carries in his Codpiece. He says furthermore, beware of the Monk. Upon mine Honour, it gives me in my mind, that you will be cuckolded by a Monk. Nay, I will engage mine Honour, which is the most precious Pawn I could have in my Possession, although I were sole and peaceable Dominator over all Europe, Asia, and Africk, that if you marry, you will surely be one of the horned Brotherhood of Vulcan. Hereby may you perceive how much I do attribute to the wise Foolery of our Morosoph Triboulet. The other Oracles and Responses did in the general prognosticate you a Cuckold, without descending so near to the point of a particular Determination, as to pitch upon what Vocation, amongst the several sorts of Men, he should profess who is to be the Copesmate of your Wife, and Hornifyer of your proper self. Thus noble Triboulet tells it us plainly, from whose Words we may gather with all ease imaginary, that your Cuckoldry is to be infamous, and so much the more scandalous, that your Conjugal Bed will be incestuously contaminated with the Filthiness of a Monkery Letcher. Moreover he says, that you will be the Hornepipe of Buzansay. That is to say, well horned, hornified and cornuted : And as Triboulet's Unkle asked from Lewis the Twelfth, for a younger Brother of his own who lived at Blois, the Hornepipes of Buzansay, for the Organ Pipes, through the mistake of one Word for another : Even so, whilst you think to marry a wise, humble, calm, discreet and honest Wife, you shall unhappily stumble upon one witless, proud, lowd, obstreperous, bawling, clamorous, and more unpleasant than any Buzansay-hornepipe. Consider withal, how he flirted you on the Nose with the Bladder, and gave you a sound thumping Blow with his Fist upon the ridge of the Back. This denotates and presageth, that you shall be banged, beaten and filliped by her ; and that also she will steal of your Goods from you, as you stole the Hogs Bladder from the little boys of Vaubreton. Flat contrary (quoth Panurge) not that I would impudently exempt my self from being a Vassal in the Territory of Folly ; I hold of that Jurisdiction, and am subject thereto, I confess it ; and why should I not ? for the whole World is foolish. In the old Lorrain Language (*fou* for *oou*) All and Fool were the same thing. Besides it is avouched by Solomon, that infinite is the number of Fools : From an Infinity nothing can be deducted or abated, nor yet by the Testimony of Aristotle, can any thing thereto be added or subjoyned. Therefore were I a mad Fool, if being a Fool I should not hold my self a Fool. After the same manner of speaking, we may aver the number of the mad and enraged Folks to be infinite. Avicenne maketh no Bones to assert, that the several kinds of Madness are infinite.

Though this much of Triboulet's words tend little to my Advantage, how be it the Prejudice which I sustain thereby be common with me to all other Men, yet the rest of his Talk and Gesture maketh altogether for me. He said to my Wife, Be wary of the Monkey ; that is as much, as if he should be chery, and take as much delight in a Monkey as ever did the Lesbia of Catullus in her Sparrow ; who will for his Recreation pass his time no less joyfully at the exercise of snatching Flies, than heretofore did the merciless Flycatcher Domitian. Withal he meant by another part of his Discourse, that she should be of a Jovial Country-like Humour, as gay and pleasing as a harmonious Hornepipe of Saulian or Buzansay. The veridical Triboulet did therein hint at what I liked well, as perfectly knowing the Inclinations and Propensions of my Mind, my natural Disposition, and the Biass of my interior Passions and Affections : For you may be assured, that my Humour is much better satisfied and contented with the pretty frolick rural discheveled Shepheardesses, whose Bums through their course Canvas Smocks smell of the Claver-grass of the Field, than with those great Ladies in Magnifick Courts, with their Flandan, Topknots, and Sultana's, their Polvil, Postillo's and Cosmeticks. The homely sound likeways of a Rustical Hornepipe, is more agreeable to my Ears, than the curious Warbling and musical Quavering of Lutes, Teorbes, Viols, Rebecks and Violins. He gave me a lusty rapping thwack on my Back. What then ? Let it pass in the Name and for the Love of God, as an Abatement of, and Deduction from so much of my future Pains in Purgatory. He did it not out of any evil intent : He thought belike to have hit some of the Pages : He is an honest Fool, and an innocent Changeling. It is a Sin to harbour in the heart any bad Conceit of him. As for my self, I heartily pardon him. He flirted me on the Nose : In that there is no harm ; for it importeth nothing else, but that betwixt my Wife and me there will occur some toyish wanton Tricks. which usually happen to all new married Folks.

CHAPTER XLVII

*How Pantagruel and Panurge resolved to make a Visit
to the Oracle of the Holy Bottle*

THERE is as yet another Point (quoth Panurge) which you have
not at all considered on, although it be the chief and principal
Head of the matter. He put the Bottle in my Hand, and
restored it me again. How interpret you that Passage ?
What is the meaning of that ? He possibly (quoth Pantagruel)
signifieth thereby, that your Wife will be such a Drunkard,
as shall daily take in her Liquor kindly, and ply the Pots and
Bottles apace. Quite otherways (quoth Panurge) for the
Bottle was empty. I swear to you, by the prickling brambly
Thorn of St. Fiacre in Brie, that our unique Morosoph, whom I
formerly termed the Lunatick Triboulet, referreth me, for
attaining to the final Resolution of my Scruple to the Response-
giving Bottle : Therefore do I renew afresh the first Vow which
I made, and here in your Presence protest and make Oath by
Styx and Acheron, to carry still Spectacles in my Cap, and never
to wear a Codpiece in my Breeches, until upon the Enterprize
in hand of my Nuptial Undertaking, I shall have obtained an
Answer from the Holy Bottle. I am acquainted with a prudent
understanding, and discreet Gentleman, and besides a very
good Friend of mine, who knoweth the Land, Country, and
Place where its Temple and Oracle is built and posited : He
will guide and conduct us thither sure and safely. Let us go
thither, I beseech you : Deny me not, and say not, Nay ;
reject not the Suit I make unto you, I intreat you. I will be to
you an Achates, a Damis, and heartily accompany you all
along in the whole Voyage, both in your going forth and coming

back. I have of a long time known you to be a great lover of Peregrination, desirous still to learn new things, and still to see what you had never seen before.

Very willingly (quoth Pantagruel) I condescend to your Request. But before we enter in upon our Progress towards the Accomplishment of so far a Journey, replenished and fraught with eminent Perils, full of innumerable Hazards, and every way stored with evident and manifest Dangers. What Dangers (quoth Panurge) interrupting him ? Dangers fly back, run from, and shun me whither soever I go seven Leagues around : As in the Presence of the Soveraign a subordinate Magistracy is eclipsed ; or as Clouds and Darkness quite evanish at the bright coming of a Radiant Sun ; or as all Sores and Sicknesses did suddenly depart, at the approach of the Body of St. Martin Aquande : Nevertheless (quoth Pantagruel) before we adventure to set forwards on the Road of our projected and intended Voyage, some few Points are to be discussed, expedited and dispatched. First, Let us send back Triboulet to Blois, (which was instantly done, after that Pantagruel had given him a Frize Coat.) Secondly, Our Design must be backed with the Advice and Counsel of the King my Father. And Lastly, It is most needful and expedient for us, that we search for, and find out some Sibylle to serve us for a Guide, Truchman, and Interpreter. To this Panurge made answer, That his Friend Xenomanes would abundantly suffice for the plenary Discharge and Performance of the Sibyl's Office ; and that furthermore, in passing through the Lanternatory Revelling Country, they should take along with them a learned and profitable Lantern, which would be no less useful to them in their Voyage, than was that of the Sibyl to Æneas in his Descent to the Elysian Fields. Carpalin in the interim, as he was upon the conducting away of Triboulet, in his passing by, hearkened a little to the Discourse they were upon, then spoke out, saying, Ho, Panurge, Master Freeman, take my Lord Debitis at Calais alongst with you, for he is Goudfallot, a good Fellow : He will not forget those who have been Debitors ; These are Lanterns : Thus shall you not lack for both Fallot and Lantern. I may safely with the little Skill I have (quoth Pantagruel) prognosticate, that by the way we shall engender no Melancholy ; I clearly perceive it already : The only thing that vexeth me is, that I cannot speak the Lanternatorie Language. I shall (answered Panurge) speak for you all ; I understand it every whit as well as I do mine own

Maternal Tongue, I have been no less used to it than to the vulgar French.

> *Briz marg dalgotbric nubstze zos,*
> *Isquebsz prusq albork crinqz zacbac.*
> *Misbe dilbarkz morp nipp stancz bos,*
> *Strombtz, Panurge walmap quost gruszbac.*

Now guess, Friend Epistemon, what this is. They are (quoth Epistemon) Names of errand Devils, paissant Devils, and rampant Devils. These words of thine, dear friend of mine, are true (quoth Panurge) yet are they Terms used in the Language of the Court of the Lanternish People. By the way as we go upon our Journey I will make to thee a pretty little Dictionary, which notwithstanding shall not last you much longer than a pair of new Shoes : thou shalt have learned it sooner than thou canst perceive the Dawning of the next subsequent Morning. What I have said in the foregoing Tetrastick is thus translated out of the Lanternish Tongue into our Vulgar Dialect.

> All Miseries attended me, whilst I
> A Lover was, and had no good thereby :
> Of better Luck the married People tell,
> Panurge is one of those, and knows it well.

There is little more then (quoth Pantagruel) to be done, but that we understand what the Will of the King my Father will be therein, and purchase his Consent.

CHAPTER XLVIII

How Gargantua sheweth, that the Children ought not to marry without the special knowledge and Advice of their Fathers and Mothers

No sooner had Pantagruel entred in at the Door of the Great Hall of the Castle, than that he encountred full but with the good honest Gargantua coming forth from the Council Board, unto whom he made a succinct and summary Narrative of what had pass'd and occurred worthy of his Observation in his Travels abroad, since their last Interview : Then, acquainting him with the Design he had in hand, besought him that it might stand with his good Will and Pleasure to grant him leave to prosecute and go thorough-stitch with the Enterprize which he had undertaken. The good Man Gargantua having in one hand two great bundles of Petitions, indorsed and answered ; and in the other some remembrancing Notes and Bills, to put him in mind of such other Requests of Supplicants, which albeit presented, had nevertheless been neither read nor heard, he gave both to Ulrich Gallet, his ancient and faithful Master of Requests ; then drew aside Pantagruel, and with a Countenance more serene and jovial than customary, spoke to him thus : I praise God, and have great reason so to do, my most dear Son, that he hath been pleased to entertain in you a constant Inclination to vertuous Actions. I am well content that the Voyage which you have motioned to me be by you accomplished, but withal, I could wish you would have a mind and desire to marry, for that I see you are of competent years. Panurge in the mean while was in a readiness of preparing and providing for Remedies, Salves and Cures against all such Lets, Obstacles and Impediments as he could in the height of his Fancy conceive might by Gargantua be cast in the way of their Itinerary Design. It is your Pleasure (most dear Father) that you speak ? (answered Pantagruel). For my part I have not yet thought upon it. In all this Affair I wholly submit and rest in your good liking and Paternal Authority : For I shall rather pray unto God that he would throw me down stark dead at your Feet, in your Pleasure, than that against your pleasure I should be found married alive. I never yet heard that by any Law, whether Sacred or Profane, yea, amongst the rudest and most barbarous Nations in the World, it was allowed and approved of that Children may be suffered and tolerated to marry at their own good Will and Pleasure, without the Knowledge, Advice or Consent asked and had thereto of their Fathers, Mothers, and nearest Kindred. All Legislators every where upon the face of the whole Earth, have taken away and removed this Licentious Liberty from Children, and totally reserved it to the Discretion of the Parents.

My dearly beloved Son (quoth Gargantua) I believe you, and from my Heart thank God for having endowed you with the Grace of having both a perfect notice of, and entire liking to laudable and praise-worthy things; and that through the Windows of your exterior Senses he hath vouchsafed to transmit unto the interiour faculties of your Mind, nothing but what is good and vertuous. For in my time there hath been found on the Continent a certain Country, wherein are I know not what kind of Pastophorian Mole-catching Priests, who albeit averse from engaging their proper Persons into a Matrimonial Duty, like the Pontifical Flamens of Cibele in Phrygia, as if they were Capons and not Cocks; full of Lasciviousness, Salacity and Wantonness, who yet have nevertheless, in the matter of Conjugal Affairs, taken upon them to prescribe Laws and Ordinances to married Folks. I cannot goodly determine what I should most abhor, detest, loath and abominate, whether the Tyrannical Presumption of those dreaded Sacerdotal Molecatchers, who not being willing to contain and coop up themselves within the Grates and Treillices of their own mysterious Temples, do deal in, meddle with, obtrude upon, and thrust their Sickles into Harvests of Secular Businesses quite contrary, and diametrically opposite to the Quality, State and Condition of their Callings, Professions and Vocations; or the superstitious Stupidity and senceless Scrupulousness of married Folks, who have yielded Obedience, and submitted their Bodies, Fortunes and Estates to the Discretion and Authority of such odious, perverse, barbarous, and unreasonable Laws. Nor do they see that which is clearer than the Light and Splendour of the Morning Star, how all these Nuptial and Connubial Sanctions, Statutes and Ordinances have been decreed, made and instituted, for the sole Benefit, Profit and Advantage of the Flaminal Mysts, and mysterious Flamens, and nothing at all for the good Utility or Emolument of the silly hoodwinked married People; which administreth unto others a sufficient Cause for rendring these Churchmen suspicious of Iniquity, and of an unjust and fraudulent manner of dealing, no more to be connived at nor countenanced, after that it be well weighed in the Scales of Reason, than if with a reciprocal Temerity the Laicks by way of Compensation would impose Laws to be followed and observed by those Mysts and Flamens; how they should behave themselves in the making and Performance of their Rites and Ceremonies, and after what manner they ought to proceed in the offering up, and immolating of their various Oblations, Victims and Sacrifices; seeing that besides the Edecimation and Tithhaling of their Goods, they cut off and take Parings, Shreddings and Clippings of the Gain proceeding from the Labour of their Hands, and Sweat of their Brows, therewith to entertain themselves the better. Upon which Consideration in my Opinion, their Injunctions and Commands would not prove so pernicious and impertinent as those of the Ecclesiastick Power, unto which they had tendred their blind Obedience.

For as you have very well said, there is no place in the World where legally a Licence is granted to the Children to marry without the Advice and Consent of their Parents and Kindred. Nevertheless by those wicked Laws and Mole-catching Customs, whereat there is a little hinted in what I have already spoken to you, there is no scurvy, mezely, leprous or pocky Ruffian, Pander, Knave, Rogue, Skelm, Robber or Thief, pilloried, whipped and burn-marked in his own Country for his Crimes and Felonies, who may not violently snatch away and ravish what Maid soever he had a mind to pitch upon, how noble, how fair, how rich, honest and chast soever she be, and that out of the House of her own Father, in his own Presence, from the Bosom of her Mother, and in the sight and despight of her Friends and Kindred looking on a so woful Spectacle, provided that the Rascal Villain be so cunning as to associate unto himself some Mystical Flamen, who according to the Covenant made betwixt them two, shall be in hope some day to participate of the Prey.

Could the Goths, the Scyths, or Messagets do a worse or more cruel Act to any of the Inhabitants of a Hostile City, when after the loss of many of their most considerable Commanders, the expense of a great deal of Money, and a long Siege, they shall have stormed and taken it by a violent and impetuous Assault ? May not these Fathers and Mothers (think you) be sorrowful and heavy-hearted, when they see an unknown Fellow, a Vagabond Stranger, a barbarous Lowt, a rude Curr, rotten, fleshless, putrified, scraggy, bily, botchy, poor, a forlorn Caitif and miserable Snake, by an open Rapt, snatch away before their own Eyes their so fair, delicate, neat, well-behavoured, richly provided for, and healthful Daughters, on whose Breeding and Education they had spared no Cost nor Charges, by bringing them up in an honest Discipline to all the honourable and vertuous Employments becoming one of their Sex, descended of a noble Parentage, hoping by those commendable and industrious means in an opportune and convenient time to bestow them on the worthy Sons of their well-deserving Neighbours and ancient Friends, who had nourished, entertained, taught, instructed and schooled their Children with the same Care and Sollicitude, to make them Matches fit to attain to the Felicity of a so happy Marriage; that from them might issue an Off-spring and Progeny no less Heirs to the laudable Endowments and exquisite Qualifications of their Parents whom they every way resemble, than to their Personal and Real Estates, Moveables and Inheritances? How doleful, trist and plangorous would such a Sight and Pageantry prove unto them? You shall not need to think that the Collachrymation of the Romans, and their Confederates, at the Decease of Germanicus Drusus, was comparable to this Lamentation of theirs? Neither would I have you to believe, that the Discomfort and Anxiety of the Lacedæmonians, when the Greek Helen, by the Perfidiousness of the Adulterous Trojan Paris was privily stóllen away out of their Country, was greater or more pitiful than this ruthful and deplorable Collugency of theirs? You may very well imagine that Ceres, at the Ravishment of her Daughter Proserpina, was not more attristed, sad nor mournful than they. Trust me, and your own Reason, that the loss of Osyris was not so regreatable to Isis; nor did Venus so deplore the Death of Adonis; nor yet did Hercules so bewail the straying of Hylas; nor was the Rapt of Polyxena more throbbingly resented and condoled by Pryamus and Hecuba, than this aforesaid Accident would be sympathetically bemoaned, grievous, ruthful, and anxious to the wofully desolate and disconsolate Parents.

Notwithstanding all this, the greater part of so vilely abused Parents, are so timerous and afraid of Devils and Hobgoblins, and so deeply plunged in Superstition, that they dare not gainsay nor contradict, much less oppose and resist those unnatural and impious Actions, when the Molecatcher hath been presen at the perpetrating of the Fact, and a Party Contracter and Covenanter in that detestable Bargain. What do they do then? They wretchedly stay at their own miserable Homes, destitute of their well-beloved Daughters; the Fathers cursing the days and the hours wherein they were married; and the Mothers howling and crying that it was not their fortune to have brought forth Abortive Issues, when they hapned to be delivered of such unfortunate Girls; and in this pitiful plight spend at best the remainder of their Time with Tears and Weeping for those their Children of, and from whom they expected (and with good reason should have obtained and reaped) in these latter days of theirs, Joy and Comfort. Other Parents there have been, so impatient of that Affront and Indignity put upon them and their Families, that, transported with the Extremity of Passion, in a mad and frantick mood, through the Vehemency of a grievous Fury and raging Sorrow, have drowned, hanged, killed, and otherways put violent hands on themselves. Others again of that Parental Relation, have upon the reception of the like Injury, been of a more magnanimous and heroick Spirit, who (in imitation, and at the Example of the Children of Jacob, revenging upon the Sichemits the Rapt of their Sister Dina) having found the Rascally Ruffian in the Association of his mystical Molecatcher closely and in hugger-mugger, conferring, parlying, and coming with their Daughters, for the suborning, corrupting, depraving, perverting and enticing these innocent, unexperienced Maids into filthy Lewdnesses, have, without any further Advisement on the matter, cut them instantly into pieces, and thereupon forthwith thrown out upon the Fields their so dismembered Bodies, to serve for Food unto the Wolves and Ravens. Upon the chivalrous, bold and couragious Atchievement of a so valiant, stout and man-like Act, the other Mole-catching Symmists have been so highly incensed, and have so chafed, fretted and fumed thereat, that Bills of Complaint and Accusations having been in a most odious and detestible manner put in before the competent Judges, the Arm of Secular Authority hath with much Importunity and Impetuosity been by them implored and required, they proudly contending, that the Servants of God would become contemptible, if exemplary Punishment were not speedily taken upon the Persons of the Perpetrators of such an enormous, horrid, sacrilegious, crying, heinous, and execrable Crime.

Yet neither by Natural Equity, by the Law of Nations, nor by any Imperial Law whatsoever, hath there been found so much as one Rubrick, Paragraph, Point or Tittle, by the which any kind of Chastisement or Correction hath been adjudged due to be inflicted upon any for their Delinquency in that kind. Reason opposeth, and Nature is repugnant : For there is no vertuous Man in the World, who, both naturally and with good reason, will not be more hugely troubled in Mind, hearing of the news of the Rapt, Disgrace, Ignominy and Dishonour of his Daughter, than of her Death. Now any Man finding in hot Blood, one who with a fore-thought Felony hath murthered his Daughter, may, without tying himself to the Formalities and Circumstances of a Legal Proceeding, kill him on a sudden, and out of hand, without incurring any hazard of being attainted and apprehended by the Officers of Justice for so doing. What wonder is it then ? or how little strange should it appear to any rational Man, if a Lechering Rogue, together with his Mole-catching Abetter, be entrapped in the flagrant Act of suborning his Daughter, and stealing her out of his House (though her self consent thereto) that the Father in such a case of Stain and Infamy by them brought upon his Family, should put them both to a shameful Death, and cast their Carcasses upon Dunghils to be devoured and eaten up by Dogs and Swine, or otherwise fling them a little further off to the direption, tearing and rending asunder of their Joynts and Members by the wild Beasts of the Field.

Dearly beloved Son, have an especial Care, that after my Decease none of these Laws be received in any of your King-doms ; for whilst I breath, by the Grace and Assistance of God I shall give good Order.

Seeing therefore you have totally referred unto my Dis-cretion the Disposure of you in Marriage, I am fully of an Opinion, that I shall provide sufficiently well for you in that Point. Make ready and prepare your self for Panurge's Voyage : Take along with you Epistemon, Friar Jhon, and such others as you will choose : Do with my Treasures what unto your self shall seem most expedient : None of your Actions, I promise you, can in any manner of way displease me. Take out of my Arcenal Thalasse, whatsoever Equipage, Furniture or Provision you please, together with such Pilots, Mariners and Truchmen, as you have a mind to ; and with the first fair and favourable Wind set sail and make out to Sea in the Name of God our Saviour. In the mean while, during your Absence, I shall not be neglective of providing a Wife for you, nor of those Preparations, which are requisite to be made for the more sumptuous solemnising of your Nuptials with a most splendid Feast, if ever there was any in the World, since the days of Assuerus.

CHAPTER XLIX

How Pantagruel did put himself in a readiness to go to Sea ; and of the Herb named Pantagruelion

WITHIN very few days after that Pantagruel had taken his leave of the good Gargantua, who devoutly prayed for his Sons happy Voyage, he arrived at the Sea-Port, near to Sammalo, accompanied with Panurge, Epistemon, Friar Jhon of the Funnels, Abbot of Theleme, and others of the Royal House, especially with Xenomanes the great Traveller, and Thwarter of dangerous ways, who was come at the bidding and appointment of Panurge, of whose Castlewick of Salmigondin he did hold some petty Inheritance by the Tenure of a Mesnefee. Pantagruel being come thither, prepared and made ready for launching a Fleet of Ships, to the number of those which Ajax of Salamine had of old equipped, in Convoy of the Græcian Soldiery against the Trojan State. He likewise picked out for his use so many Mariners, Pilots, Sailors, Interpreters, Artificers, Officers and Soldiers, as he thought fitting ; and therewithal made Provision of so much Victuals of all sorts, Artillery, Munition of divers kinds, Cloaths, Moneys, and other such Luggage, Stuff, Baggage, Chaffer and Furniture, as he deemed needful for carrying on the Design of a so tedious, long and perillous Voyage. Amongst other things, it was observed, how he caused some of his Vessels to be fraught and loaded with a great quantity of an Herb of his called Pantagruelion, not only of the green and raw sort of it, but of the confected also, and of that which was notably well befitted for present use after the fashion of Conserves. The Herb Pantagruelion hath a little Root somewhat hard and ruff, roundish, terminating

in an obtuse and very blunt Point, and having some of its
Veins, Strings or Filaments coloured with some spots of white,
never fixeth it self into the ground above the profoundness
almost of a Cubit, or Foot and a half ; from the Root thereof
proceedeth the only Stalk, orbicular, canelike, green without,
whitish within, and hollow like the Stem of Smyrgium, *Olus
Atrum*, Beans and Gentian, full of long Threds, streight, easie
to be broken, jogged, snipped, nicked and notched a little after
the manner of Pillars and Columns, slightly farrowed, chamfered, guttred and channel'd, and full of Fibres, or Hairs like
Strings, in which consisteth the chief Value and Dignity of the
Herb, especially in that part thereof which is termed *Mesa*,
as he would say the Mean ; and in that other which hath got
the Denomination of *Milasea*. Its height is commonly of
five or six Foot ; yet sometimes it is of such a tall Growth, as
doth surpass the length of a Lance, but that is only when it
meeteth with a sweet, easie, warm, wet and well-soaked Soil,
(as is the ground of the Territory of Olone, and that of Rasea,
near to Preneste in Sabinia) and that it want not for Rain
enough about the Season of the Fishers Holydays, and the
Estival Solstice. There are many Trees whose Height is by it
very far exceeded, and you might call it *Dendromalache* by the
Authority of Theophrastus. The Plant every year perisheth ;
the Tree, neither in the Trunk, Root, Bark or Boughs, being
durable.

From the Stalk of this Pantagruelion Plant there issue forth
several large and great Branches, whose Leaves have thrice
as much length as breadth, always green, roughish and rugged
like the Alcanet, or Spanish Buglose, hardish, slit round about
like unto a Sickle, or as the Saxifragum, Betony, and finally
ending as it were in the Points of a Macedonian Spear, or of such
a Lancet as Surgeons commonly make use of in their Phle-
botomizing Tiltings. The figure and shape of the Leaves
thereof is not much different from that of those of the Ash-
tree, or of Egrimony ; the Herb it self so being like the Eupa-
torian Plant, that many skilful Herbalists have called it the
Domestick Eupator, and the Eupator the wild Pantagruelion.
These Leaves are in equal and parallel Distances spread around
the Stalk, by the number in every Rank either of Five or Seven,
Nature having so highly favoured and cherish'd this Plant,
that she hath richly adorned it with these two odd, divine and
mysterious Numbers. The Smell thereof is somewhat strong,
and not very pleasing to nice, tender, and delicate Noses :

The Seed inclosed therein mounteth up to the very top of its Stalk, and a little above it.

This is a numerous Herb; for there is no less abundance of it than of any other whatsoever. Some of these Plants are Spherical, some Romboid, and some of an oblong shape, and all of those either black, bright-coloured or tawny, rude to the touch, and mantled with a quickly-blasted-away Coat, yet such a one is of a delicious Taste and Savour to all shrill and sweetly singing Birds, such as Linnets, Goldfinches, Larks, Canary-Birds, Yellowhammers, and others of that Airy chirping Quire; but it would quite extinguish the Natural Heat and Procreative Vertue of the Semence of any Man, who would eat much, and often of it. And although, that, of old, amongst the Greeks there was certain kinds of Fritters and Pancakes, Buns and Tarts made thereof, which commonly for a licquorish Daintiness were presented the Table after Supper, to delight the Palat, and make the Wine relish the better. Yet is it of a difficult Concoction, and offensive to the Stomach; for it engendreth bad and unwholsom Blood, and with its exorbitant Heat woundeth them with grievous, hurtful, smart and noysom Vapours. And as in divers Plants and Trees there are two Sexes, Male and Female, which is perceptible in Lawrels, Palms, Cypresses, Oaks, Holmes, the Daffadil, Mandrake, Fearn, the Agarick, Mushrum, Birthwort, Turpentine, Pennyroyal, Peony, Rose of the Mount, and many other such like. Even so, in this Herb there is a Male which beareth no Flower at all, yet it is very copious of, and abundant in Seed. There is likeways in it a Female, which hath great store and plenty of whitish Flowers, serviceable to little or no purpose; nor doth it carry in it Seed of any worth at all, at least comparable to that of the Male. It hath also a larger Leaf, and much softer than that of the Male; nor doth it altogether grow to so great a height. This Pantagruelion is to be sown at the first coming of the Swallows, and is to be plucked out of the Ground when the Grashoppers begin to be a little hoarse.

CHAPTER L

How the famous Pantagruelion ought to be prepared and wrought

THE Herb Pantagruelion in September, under the Autumnal Equinox, is dressed and prepared several ways, according to the various Fancies of the People, and Diversity of the Climates wherein it groweth. The first Instruction which Pantagruel gave concerning it, was, to divest and dispoil the Stalk and Stem thereof of all its Flowers and Seeds, to macerate and mortifie it in Pond, Pool, or Lakewater, which is to be made run a little for five days together, if the Season be dry, and the Water hot ; or for full nine or twelve days, if the weather be cloudish, and the Water cold : Then must it be parched before the Sun, till it be drained of its Moisture : After this it is in the Shadow, where the Sun shines not, to be peeled, and its Rind pulled off : Then are the Fibres and Strings thereof to be parted, (wherein, as we have already said, consisteth its prime Vertue, Price, and Efficacy) and severed from the woody part thereof, which is improfitable, and serveth hardly to any other use, than to make a clear and glistering Blaze, to kindle the Fire, and for the Play, Pastime, and Disport of little Children, to blow up Hogs Bladders, and make them rattle. Many times some use is made thereof by tipling, sweet-lipped Bibbers, who out of it frame Quills and Pipes, through which they with their Liquor-attractive Breath suck up the new dainty Wine from the Bung of the Barrel. Some modern Pantagruelists, to shun and avoid that manual Labour, which such a separating and partitional Work would of necessity require, employ certain Catarractick Instruments, composed and formed after the same manner that the froward, pettish and angry Juno did hold the Fingers of both her Hands interwovenly clenched together, when she would have hindred the Childbirth Delivery of Alcmena, at the Nativity of Hercules ; and athwart those Cataracts they break and bruise to very Trash the woody parcels, thereby to preserve the better the Fibres, which are the precious and excellent parts. In, and with this sole Operation do these acquiesce and are contented, who, contrary to the received Opinion of the whole Earth, and in a manner para- doxical to all Philosophers, gain their Livelihoods backwards, and by recoiling. But those that love to hold it at a higher rate, and prize it according to its Value, for their own greater Profit, do the very same which is told us of the Recreation of the three fatal Sister Parques, or of the nocturnal Exercise of the noble Circe ; or yet of the Excuse which Penelope made to her fond wooing Youngsters and effeminate Courtiers, during the long absence of her Husband Ulysses.

By these means is this Herb put into a way to display its inestimable Vertues, whereof I will discover a part : (for to relate all is a thing impossible to do) I have already interpreted and exposed before you the Denomination thereof. I find that Plants have their Names given and bestowed upon them after several ways : Some got the Name of him who first found them out, knew them, sowed them, improved them by Culture, qualified them to a tractability, and appropriated them to the uses and subserviences they were fit for : As the Mercuriale from Mercury, Panacee from Panace the Daughter of Esculapius, Armois from Artemis, who is Diana ; Eupatorie from the King Eupator ; Telephion from Telephus : Euphorbium from Euphorbus, King Juba's Physician ; Clymenos from Clymenus ; Alchibiadium from Alcibiades ; Gentiane from Gentius King of Sclavonia, and so forth, through a great many other Herbs and Plants. Truly, in ancient Times, this Prerogative of imposing the Inventors Name upon an Herb found out by him, was held in a so great account and estimation, that as a Controversie arose betwixt Neptune and Pallas, from which of them two that Land should receive its Denomination, which had been equally found out by them both together, though thereafter it was called and had the Appellation of Athens, from Athnee, which is Minerva : Just so would Lynceus King of Scythia have treacherously slain the young Triptolemus, whom Ceres had sent to shew unto Mankind the Invention of Corn, which until then had been utterly unknown, to the end, that after the murther of the Messenger (whose Death he made account to have kept secret) he might, by imposing with the less suspicion of false-dealing, his own Name upon the said found out Seed, acquire unto himself an immortal Honour and Glory, for having been the Inventor of a Grain so profitable and necessary to, and for the use of Humane Life. For the wickedness of which Treasonable Attempt he was by Ceres transformed into that wild Beast, which by some is called a Lynx, and by others an Ounce. Such also was the Ambition of others upon the like occasion, as appeareth by that, very sharp Wars, and of a long continuance, have been made of old betwixt some Residentary Kings in Cappadocia, upon this only Debate, of whose Name a certain Herb should have the Appellation ; by reason of which difference, so troublesom and expensive to them all, it was by them called Polemonion, and by us for the same Cause termed Make-bate.

Other Herbs and Plants there are, which retain the Names of the Countries from whence they were transported : As the Median Apples from Media, where they first grew ; Punick

Apples from Punicia, (that is to say, Carthage;) Ligusticum (which we call Louage) from Liguria the Coast of Genoua; Rubarb from a Flood in Barbary (as Ammianus attesteth) called Ru; Sautonica from a Region of that Name; Fenugreek from Greece; Gastanes from a Country so called; Persicarie from Persia; Sabine from a Territory of that Appellation; Stæchas from the Stæchad Islands; Spica Celtica from the Land of the Celtick Gauls; and so throughout a great many other, which were tedious to enumerate. Some others again have obtained their Denominations by way of Antiphrasis, or Contrariety; as, Absinth, because it is contrary to ψίντος; for it is bitter to the taste in drinking; Holosteon, as if it were all Bones, whilst on the contrary, there is no frailer, tenderer or britler Herb in the whole Production of Nature than it.

There are some other sorts of Herbs, which have got their Names from their Vertues and Operations; as Aristolochie, because it helpeth Women in Childbirth; Lichen, for that it cureth the Disease of that Name; Mallow, because it mollifieth; Callithricum, because it maketh the Hair of a bright Colour; Alyssum, Ephemerum, Bechium, Nasturtium, Aneban, and so forth through many more.

Other some there are which have obtained their Names from the admirable Qualities which are found to be in them; as Heliotropium (which is the Marigold) because it followeth the Sun; so that at the Sun rising it displayeth and spreads it self out, at his ascending it mounteth, at his declining it waineth; and when he is set it is close shut: Adianton, because although it grow near unto watry Places, and albeit you should let it lie in Water a long time, it will nevertheless retain no Moisture or Humidity: Hierachia, Eringium, and so throughout a great many more. There are also a great many Herbs, and Plants, which have retained the very same Names of the Men and Women who have been metamorphosed and transformed in them; as from Daphne, the Lawrel is called also Daphne; Myrrhe, from Myrrha the Daughter of Cinarus; Pythis, from Pythis; Cinara (which is the Artichoak) from one of that Name; Narcissus, with Saffran, Similax, and divers others.

Many Herbs likewise have got their Names of those things which they seem to have some resemblance: as Hippuris, because it hath the likeness of a Horse's Tail; Alopecuris, because it representeth in similitude the Tail of a Fox; Psyllion,

EXCEEDING ODIOUS AND HATEFUL TO THIEVES AND ROBBERS

63

from a Flea which it resembleth; Delphinium, for that it is
like a Dolphin Fish; Bugloss is so called, because it is an Herb
like an Oxe's Tongue; Iris, so called, because in its Flowers
it hath some resemblance of the Rainbow; Myosata, because it
is like the Ear of a Mouse; Coronopus, for that it is of the
likeness of a Crow's Foot; A great many other such there
are, which here to recite were needless. Furthermore, as
there are Herbs and Plants which have had their Names from
those of Men, so by a reciprocal Denomination have the Sirnames of many Families taken their Origin from them; as
the Fabii, *à fabiis*, Beans; the Pisons, *à pisis*, Peas; the
Lentuli, from Lentils; the Cicerons, *à Ciceribus, vel Ciceris*,
a sort of Pulse call'd Cichepeason, and so forth. In some
Plants and Herbs, the resemblance or likeness hath been taken
from a higher Mark or Object; as when we say, Venus Navil,
Venus Hair, Venus Tub, Jupiter's Beard, Jupiter's Eye, Mars's
Blood, the Hermodactyl or Mercury's Fingers, which are all of
them Names of Herbs, as there are a great many more of the
like Appellation. Others again have received their Denomination from their Forms; such as the Trefoil, because it is three-
leaved; Pentaphylon, for having five Leaves; Serpolet,
because it creepeth along the Ground; Helixine, Petast,
Myrobalon, which the Arabians call Been, as if you would say
an Ackorne, for it hath a kind of resemblance thereto, and
withall is very oily.

CHAPTER LI

Why it is called Pantagruelion, and of the admirable Virtues thereof

By such like means of attaining to a Denomination (the fabulous
ways being only from thence excepted; for the Lord forbid
that we should make use of any Fables in this a so venerable
History) is this Herb call'd Pantagruelion; for Pantagruel
was the Inventor thereof: I do not say, of the Plant it self,
but of a certain Use which it serves for, exceeding odious and
hateful to Thieves and Robbers, unto whom it is more con-
trarious and hurtful than the Strangle-weed, Choakfitch, is
to the Flax, the Cat's-tail to the Brakes, the Sheavegrass to the

Mowers of Hay, the Fitches to the Chickny-Pease, the Darnel to Barley, the Hatchet Fitch to the Lentil Pulse, the Antramium to the Beans, Tares to Wheat, Ivy to Walls, the Water-Lilly to lecherous Monks, the Birchin Rod to the Scholars of the College of Navarre in Paris, Colewort to the Vine-tree, Garlick to the Loadstone, Onions to the Sight, Fearn-seed to Women with Child, Willow-grain to vicious Nuns, the Yew-three Shade to those that sleep under it, Wolfsbane to Wolves and Libbards, the Smell of Fig-tree to mad Bulls, Hemlock to Goslings, Purslane to the Teeth, or Oil to Trees : For we have seen many of those Rogues, by virtue and right application of this Herb, finish their Lives, short and long, after the manner of Phillis Queen of Thracia, of Benosus Emperor of Rome, of Amata King Latinus's Wife, of Iphus, Autolicus, Lycambe, Arachne, Phædra, Leda, Achius King of Lydia, and many thousands more ; who were chiefly angry and vexed at this Disaster therein, that without being otherways sick, evil disposed in their Bodies, by a Touch only of the Pantagruelion, they came on a sudden to have the Passage obstructed, and their Pipes (through which were wont to bolt so many jolly Sayings, and to enter so many luscious Morsels) stopped, more cleaverly, than ever could have done the Squinancy.

Others have been heard most wofully to lament, at the very instant when Atropos was about to cut the thread of their Life, that Pantagruel held them by the George. But (well-a-day) it was not Pantagruel; he never was an Executioner : It was the Pantagruelion, manufactured and fashioned into an Halter, and serving in the Place and Office of a Crevat. In that verily they solæcised, and spoke improperly, unless you would excuse them by a Trope, which alloweth us to posit the Inventor in the place of the thing invented ; as when Ceres is taken for Bread, and Bacchus put instead of Wine. I swear to you here, by the good and frolick Words which are to issue out of that Wine-bottle which is a cooling below in the Copper Vessel full of Fountain Water, that the noble Pantagruel never snatch'd any Man by the Throat, unless it was such a one as was altogether careless and neglective of those obviating Remedies, which were preventive of the Thirst to come.

It is also termed Pantagruelion by a Similitude : For Pantagruel, at the very first minute of his Birth, was no less tall than this Herb is long, whereof I speak unto you, his measure having been then taken the more easie, that he was born in the Season of the great Drowth, when they were busiest in the gathering of the said Herb, to wit, at that time when Icarus's Dog, with his fiery bawling and barking at the Sun, maketh the whole World Troglodytick, and enforceth People every-where to hide themselves in Dens and subterranean Caves. It is likewise call'd Pantagruelion, because of the notable and singular Qualities, Virtues and Properties thereof: For as Pantagruel hath been the Idea, Pattern, Prototype and Exemplary of all Jovial Perfection and Accomplishment, (in the truth whereof, I believe there is none of you, Gentlemen Drinkers, that putteth any question) so in this Pantagruelion have I found so much Efficacy and Energy, so much Compleatness and Excellency, so much Exquisiteness and Rariety, and so many admirable Effects and Operations of a transcendent Nature, that if the Worth and Virtue thereof had been known, when those Trees, by the Relation of the Prophet, made Election of a Wooden King to rule and govern over them, it without all doubt would have carried away from all the rest the Plurality of Votes and Suffrages.

Shall I yet say more? If Oxilus the Son of Orius had begotten this Plant upon his Sister Hamadryas, he had taken more Delight in the Value and Perfection of it alone, than in all his eight Children, so highly renowned by our ablest Mythologians, that they have sedulously recommended their Names to the never-failing Tuition of an eternal Remembrance. The eldest Child was a Daughter, whose Name was Vine; the next born was a Boy, and his Name was Fig-tree; the third was call'd Walnut-tree; the fourth Oak; the fifth Sorbable-tree; the sixth Ash; the seventh Poplar; and the last had the Name of Elm, who was the greatest Surgeon in his time. I shall forbear to tell you, how the Juice or Sap thereof, being poured and distilled within the Ears, killeth every kind of Vermin, that by any manner of Putrefaction cometh to be bred and ingendred there; and destroyeth also any whatsoever other Animal that shall have entred in thereat. If likewise you put a little of the said Juice within a Pale or Bucket full of Water, you shall see the Water instantly turn and grow thick therewith, as if it were Milk-Curds, whereof the Virtue is so great, that the Water thus curded, is a present Remedy for Horses subject to the Cholick, and such as strike at their own Flanks: The Root thereof well boiled, mollifieth the Joints, softneth the hardness of shrunk in Sinews, is every way comfortable to the Nerves, and good against all Cramps and Convulsions, as likewise all cold and knotty Gouts. If

W. HEATH ROBINSON

THE ELDEST CHILD WAS A DAUGHTER, WHOSE NAME WAS VINE

you would speedily heal a burning, whether occasion'd by Water or Fire, apply thereto a little raw Pantagruelion, that is to say, take it so as it cometh out of the Ground, without bestowing any other Preparation or Composition upon it : but have a special care to change it for some fresher in lieu thereof, as soon as you shall find it waxing dry upon the Sore.

Without this Herb, Kitchens would be detested, the Tables of Dining-Rooms abhorred, although there were great Plenty and Variety of most dainty and sumptuous Dishes of Meat set down upon them ; and the choicest Beds also, how richly soever adorned with Gold, Silver, Amber, Ivory, Porphyr, and the mixture of most precious Metals, would without it yield no Delight or Pleasure to the Reposers in them : Without it Millers could neither carry Wheat, nor any other kind of Corn to the Mill ; nor would they be able to bring back from thence Flour, or any other sort of Meal whatsoever. Without it, how could the Papers and Writs of Lawyers Clients be brought to the Bar ? Seldom is the Mortar, Lime, or Plaister, brought to the Work-house without it. Without it, how should the Water be drawn out of a Draw-Well ? In what case would Tabellions, Notaries, Copists, Makers of Counterpanes, Writers, Clerks, Secretaries, Scriveners, and such-like Persons, be without it ? Were it not for it, what would become of the Toll-rates and Rent-rolls ? Would not the Noble Art of Printing perish without it ? Whereof could the Chassis or Paper-Windows be made ? How should the Bells be rung ? The Altars of Isis are adorned therewith ; the Pastophorian Priests are therewith clad and accoutred ; and whole Human Nature covered and wrapped therein, at its first position and production in, and into this World : All the Lunifick Trees of Seres, the Bumbast and Cotton Bushes in the Territories near the Persian Sea and Gulf of Bengala ; the Arabian Swans, together with the Plants of Maltha, do not all of them cloath, attire, and apparel so many Persons as this one Herb alone. Soldiers are now-adays much better sheltered under it, than they were in former times, when they lay in Tents covered with Skins. It overshadows the Theatres and Amphitheatres from the Heat of a scorching Sun : It begirdeth and encompasseth Forests, Chases, Parks, Copses, and Groves, for the pleasure of Hunters : It descendeth into the Salt and Fresh of both Sea and River-Waters, for the profit of Fishers : By it are Boots of all sizes, Buskins, Gamashes, Brodkins, Gambados, Shooes, Pumps, Slippers, and every cobled Ware wrought and made steddable for the Use of Man : By it the Butt and Rover-bows are strong, the Cross-bows bended, and the Slings made fixed : And as it were an Herb every whit as holy as the Verveine, and reverenced by Ghosts, Spirits, Hobgoblins, Fiends and Phantoms, the Bodies of deceased Men are never buried without it.

I will proceed yet further : By the means of this fine Herb, the invisible Substances are visibly stopped, arrested, taken, detained, and, Prisoner-like, committed to their receptive Jails. Heavy and ponderous Weights are by it heaved, lifted up, turned, veered, drawn, carried, and everyway moved quickly, nimbly, and easily, to the great Profit and Emolument of Human Kind. When I perpend with my self these and such-like marvellous Effects of this wonderful Herb, it seemeth strange unto me, how the Invention of so useful a Practice did escape, through so many by-past Ages, the Knowledge of the ancient Philosophers, considering the inestimable Utility which from thence proceeded ; and the immense Labour, which without it, they did undergo in their pristine Elucubrations. By virtue thereof, through the retention of some Aërial Gusts, are the huge Rambarges, mighty Gallions, the large Floyts, the Chiliander, the Myriander Ships launched from their Stations, and set a-going at the Pleasure and Arbitriment of their Rulers, Conners and Steersmen. By the help thereof, those remote Nations, whom Nature seemed so unwilling to have discovered to us, and so desirous to have kept them still *in abscondito*, and hidden from us, that the Ways through which their Countries were to be reached unto, were not only totally unknown, but judged also to be altogether impermeable and inaccessible, are now arrived to us, and we to them.

Those Voyages outreached Flights of Birds, and far surpassed the Scope of Feather'd Fowls, how swift soever they had been on the Wing, and notwithstanding that advantage which they have of us in swimming through the Air. Taproban hath seen the Heaths of Lapland, and both the Java's the Riphæan Mountains, wide distant Phæbol shall see Theleme, and the Islanders drink of the Flood Euphrates : By it the chill-mouthed Boreas hath surveyed the parched Mansions of the torrid Auster, and Eurus visited the Regions which Zephirus hath under his Command ; yea, in such sort have Interviews been made, by the assistance of this Sacred Herb, that maugre Longitudes and Latitudes, and all the Variations of the Zones. The Periæcian People, and the Antoecian, Amphiscian,

Heteroscian, and Periscian, had oft tendred and received mutual Visits to and from other, upon all the Climates. These strange Exploits bred such Astonishment to the Celestial Intelligences, to all the Marine and Terrestrial Gods, that they were on a sudden all afraid: From which Amazement, when they saw how, by means of this bless'd Pantagruelion, the Arctick People look'd upon the Antarctick, scoured the Antlantick Ocean, passed the Tropicks, pushed through the Torrid Zone, measured all the Zodiack, sported under the Equinoctial, having both Poles level with their Horizon; they judged it high time to call a Council, for their own Safety and Preservation.

The Olympick Gods being all and each of them affrighted at the sight of such Atchievements, said, Pantagruel hath shapen Work enough for us, and put us more to a Plunge, and nearer our Wits end, by this sole Herb of his, than did of old the Aloids, by overturning Mountains. He very speedily is to be married, and shall have many Children by his Wife: It lies not in our Power to oppose this Destiny; for it hath passed through the Hands and Spindles of the Fatal Sisters, Necessity's inexorable Daughters. Who knows but by his Sons may be found out an Herb of such another Virtue, and prodigious Energy, as that by the Aid thereof, in using it aright according to their Father's Skill, they may contrive a way for Human Kind to pierce into the high Aërian Clouds, get up unto the Spring-head of the Hail, take an Inspection of the Snowy Sources, and shut and open as they please the Sluces from whence proceed the Floodgates of the Rain; then prosecuting their Ætherial Voyage, they may step in unto the Lightning Work-house and Shop, where all the Thunderbolts are forged, where seizing on the Magazin of Heaven, and Storehouse of our Warlike Fire Munition, they may discharge a bouncing Peal or two of thundring Ordnance, for Joy of their Arrival to these new supernal Places; and charging those Tonitrual Guns afresh, turn the whole force of that Artillery against our selves, wherein we most confided: Then is it like they will set forward to invade the Territories of the Moon, whence passing through both Mercury and Venus, the Sun will serve them for a Torch, to shew the Way from Mars to Jupiter and Saturn: We shall not then be able to resist the Impetuosity of their Intrusion, nor put a stoppage to their entring in at all whatever Regions, Domicils or Mansions of the Spangled Firmament they shall have any mind to see, to stay in, to travel through for their

PIERCE INTO THE HIGH AËRIAN CLOUDS

71

Recreation: All the Celestial Signs together, with the Constellations of the Fixed Stars, will jointly be at their Devotion then : Some will take up their Lodging at the Ram, some at the Bull, and others at the Twins ; some at the Crab, some at the Lion Inn, and others at the Sign of the Virgin : some at the Balance, others at the Scorpion, and others will be quartered at the Archer ; some will be harboured at the Goat, some at the Water-pourer's Sign, some at the Fishes; some will lie at the Crown, some at the Harp, some at the Golden Eagle, and the Dolphin ; some at the Flying Horse, some at the Ship ; some at the great, some at the little Bear ; and so throughout the glistning Hostories of the whole twinkling Asteristick Welkin : There will be Sojourners come from the Earth, who longing after the Tast of the sweet Cream, of their own scumming off, from the best Milk of all the Dairy of the Galaxy, will set themselves at Table down with us, drink of our Nectar and Ambrosia, and take to their own Beds at Night for Wives and Concubines our fairest Goddesses, the only means whereby they can be Deify'd. A Junto hereupon being convocated, the better to consult upon the manner of obviating a so dreadful Danger, Jove, sitting in his Presidential Throne, asked the Votes of all the other Gods ; which after a profound Deliberation amongst themselves on all Contingencies, they freely gave at last, and then resolved unanimously to withstand the Shock of all whatsoever sublunary Assaults.

CHAPTER LII

How a certain kind of Pantagruelion is of that nature,
that the Fire is not able to consume it

I HAVE already related to you great and admirable things ; but if you might be induced to adventure upon the hazard of believing some other Divinity of this Sacred Pantagruelion, I very willingly would tell it you. Believe it if you will, or otherwise believe it not, I care not which of them you do, they are both alike to me, it shall be sufficient for my Purpose to have told you the Truth, and the Truth I will tell you : But to enter in thereat, because it is of a knaggy, difficult and rugged access, this is the Question which I ask of you, If I had put within this Bottle two Pints, the one of Wine, and the other of Water, throughly and exactly mingled together, how would you unmix them ? After what manner would you go about to sever them, and separate the one Liquor from the other, in such sort, that you render me the Water apart, free from the Wine, and the Wine also pure, without the intermixture of one drop of Water ; and both of them in the same measure, quantity and taste that I had embottled them ? Or to state the Question otherways, If your Carmen and Mariners, intrusted for the Provision of your Houses, with the bringing of a certain considerable number of Tuns, Punchions, Pipes, Barrels and Hogsheads of Graves Wine, or of the Wine of Orleans, Beanne and Mirevaux, should drink out the half, and afterwards with Water fill up the other empty halves of the Vessels as full as before ; as the Limosins use to do in their Carriages by Wains and Carts of the Wines of Argenton and Sangaultier. After that, how would you part the Water from the Wine, and purifie them both in such a case ? I understand you well enough ; your meaning is, that I must do it with an Ivy Funnel ; That it is written, it is true, and the Verity thereof explored by a thousand Experiments ; you have learned to do this Feat before I see it : But those that have never known it, nor at any time have seen the like, would hardly believe that it were possible. Let us nevertheless proceed.

But put the case we were now living in the Age of Sylla, Marius, Cæsar, and other such Roman Emperors ; or that we were in the time of our ancient Druids, whose Custom was to burn and calcine the dead Bodies of their Parents and Lords, and that you had a mind to drink the Ashes or Cinders of your Wives or Fathers in the infused Liquor of some good White-wine, as Artemisia drunk the Dust and Ashes of her Husband Mausolus ; or otherways, that you did determin to have them reserved in some fine Urn, or Reliquary Pot, how would you save the Ashes apart, and separate them from those other Cinders and Ashes into which the Fuel of the Funeral and bustuary Fire hath been converted ? Answer if you can; by my Figgins, I believe it will trouble you so to do.

Well, I will dispatch, and tell you, that if you take of this Celestial Pantagruelion so much as is needful to cover the Body of the Defunct, and after that you shall have inwrapped and bound therein as hard and closely as you can the Corps of the said deceased Persons, and sowed up the Folding-sheet with thread of the same stuff, throw it into the Fire, how great or ardent soever it be it matters not a straw, the Fire through this Pantagruelion will burn the Body, and reduce to Ashes the Bones thereof, and the Pantagruelion shall be not only not consumed nor burnt, but also shall neither lose one Atom of the Ashes inclos'd within it, nor receive one Atom of the huge bustuary heap of Ashes resulting from the blazing Conflagration of things combustible laid round about it, but shall at last, when taken out of the Fire, be fairer, whiter, and much cleaner than when you did put it in at first : Therefore it is called Asbeston, which is as much as to say incombustible. Great plenty is to be found thereof in Carpasia, as likewise in the Climate Diasienes, at very easie rates. O how rare and admirable a thing it is, that the Fire which devoureth, consumeth and destroyeth all such things else, should cleanse, purge and whiten this sole Pantagruelion Carpasian Asbeston ! If you mistrust the Verity of this Relation, and demand for further Confirmation of my Assertion a visible Sign, as the Jews, and such incredulous Infidels use to do ; take a fresh Egg, and orbicularly (or rather ovally) infold it within this Divine Pantagruelion ; when it is so wrapped up, put it in the hot Embers of a Fire, how great or ardent soever it be, and having left it there as long as you will, you shall at last, at your taking it out of the Fire, find the Egg roasted hard, and as it were burnt, without any Alteration, Change, Mutation, or so much as a Calefaction of the Sacred Pantagruelion : For less than a Million of Pounds Sterling, modified, taken down and moderated to the twelfth part of one Four Pence Half-penny Farthing, you are able to put it to a trial, and make Proof thereof.

Do not think to overmatch me here, by paragoning with it, in the way of a more eminent Comparison, the Salamander. That is a Fib ; for albeit a little ordinary Fire, such as is used in Dining-Rooms and Chambers, gladden, chear up, exhilerate and quicken it, yet may I warrantably enough assure, that in the flaming fire of a Furnace, it will, like any other animated Creature, be quickly suffocated, choaked, consumed and destroyed. We have seen the Experiment thereof, and Galen many Ages ago hath clearly demonstrated and confirmed it, Lib. 3. *De tempera mentis.* And Dioscorides maintaineth the same Doctrine, Lib. 2. Do not here instance in competition with this Sacred Herb the Feather Allum, or the wooden Tower of Pyrce, which Lucius Sylla was never able to get burnt ; for the' Archelaus, Governor of the Town for Mithridates King of Pontus, had plaistered it all over on the out-side with the said Allum. Nor would I have you to compare therewith the Herb, which Alexander Cornelius called Fonem, and said that it had some resemblance with that Oak which bears the Misselto ; and that it could neither be consumed, nor receive any manner of prejudice by Fire, nor by Water, no more than the Misselto, of which was built (said he) the so renowned Ship *Argos.* Search where you please for those that will believe it, I in that Point desire to be excused. Neither would I wish you to parallel therewith (although I cannot deny but that it is, of a very marvellous Nature) that sort of Tree which groweth alongst the Mountains of Brianson and Ambrun, which produceth out of his Root the good Agarick ; from its Body it yieldeth unto us a so excellent Rosin, that Galen hath been bold to equal it to the Turpentine : Upon the delicate Leaves thereof it retaineth for our use that sweet Heavenly Honey, which is called the Manna : And although it be of a gummy, oily, fat and greasie Substance, it is notwithstanding unconsumable by any Fire. It is in Greek and Latin called Larix. The Alpinesi name it Melze. The Antenodites and Venetians term it Larege ; which gave occasion to that Castle in Piedmont to receive the Denomination of Larignum, by putting Julius Cæsar to a stand at his return from amongst the Gauls.

Julius Cæsar commanded all the Yeomens, Boors, Hinds, and other Inhabitants in, near unto, and about the Alps and Piedmont, to bring all manner of Victuals and Provisions for an Army to those places, which on the Military Road he had appointed to receive them for the use of his marching Soldiery ; to which Ordinance all of them were obedient, save only those as were within the Garrison of Larignum ; who, trusting in the natural Strength of the Place, would not pay their Contribution. The Emperor purposing to chastise them for their refusal, caused his whole Army to march streight towards that Castle, before the Gate whereof was erected a Tower, built of huge big Sparrs and Rafters of the Larch Tree, fast bound together with Pins and Pegs of the same Wood, and inter-

changeably laid on one another, after the fashion of a Pile or
Stack of Timber, set up in the Fabrick thereof to such an apt
and convenient heighth, that from the Parapet above the Portcullis they thought with Stones and Leavers to beat off and
drive away such as should approach thereto.

When Cæsar had understood that the chief Defence of those
within the Castle did consist in Stones and Clubs, and that it
was not an easie matter to sling, hurl, dart, throw, or cast them
so far as to hinder the Approaches, he forthwith commanded
his Men to throw great store of Bavins, Faggots and Fascines
round about the Castle ; and when they had made the Heap
of a competent height to put them all in a fair Fire, which was
thereupon incontinently done ; the Fire put amidst the Faggots
was so great and so high, that it covered the whole Castle, that
they might well imagine the Tower would thereby be altogether
burnt to Dust, and demolished. Nevertheless, contrary to all
their Hopes and Expectations, when the Flame ceased, and
that the Faggots were quite burnt and consumed, the Tower
appeared as whole, sound and entire as ever. Cæsar, after a
serious Consideration had thereof, commanded a Compass tc
be taken, without the distance of a Stones cast from the Castle
round about it there, with Ditches and Entrenchments to form
a Blockade ; which when the Loringians understood, they
rendred themselves upon Terms : And then, by a Relation
from them it was that Cæsar learned the admirable Nature and
Vertue of this Wood ; which, of it self, produceth neither Fire,
Flame, nor Coal ; and would therefore in regard of that rare
Quality of Incombustibility, have been admitted into this
Rank and Degree of a true Pantagruelional Plant ; and that
so much the rather, for that Pantagruel directed that all the
Gates, Doors, Angiports, Windows, Gutters, frettized and
embowed Cielings, Cans, and other whatsoever wooden Furni-
ture in the Abby of Theleme should be all materiated of this
kind of Timber. He likewise caused to cover therewith the
Sterns, Stems, Cook-rooms or Laps, Hatches, Decks, Coursies,
Bends and Walls of his Carricks, Ships, Gallions, Galloys,
Brigantines, Foysts, Frigats, Crears, Barks, Floyts, Pinks,
Pinnaces, Hoys, Catches, Capers, and other Vessels of his
Thalassian Arcenal ; were it not that the Wood or Timber of
the Larch-tree, being put within a large and ample Furnace full
of huge vehemently flaming Fire, proceeding from the Fuel
of other sorts and kinds of Wood, cometh at last to be corrupted,
consumed, dissipated and destroyed, as are Stones in a Lime-

kill : But this Pantagruelion Asbeston is rather by the Fire renewed and cleansed, than by the Flames thereof consumed or changed. Therefore,

Arabians, Indians, Sabæans,
Sing not in Hymns and Iö Pæans ;
Your Incense, Myrrh, or Ebony :
Come, here, a nobler Plant to see ;
And carry home, at any rate,
Some Seed, that you may propagate.
If in your Soil it takes, to Heaven
A thousand thousand Thanks be given ,
And say with France, it goodly goes
Where the Pantagruelion grows.

THE END OF THE THIRD BOOK

PANTAGRUEL'S VOYAGE ◦ ◡ ◦ TO THE ◦ ◦ ◦
ORACLE OF THE BOTTLE ◦ ◦ ◦ BEING
THE ◦ ◦ ◦ FOURTH AND FIFTH BOOKS ◦ ◦ ◦
OF ◦ ◦ ◦ THE WORKS ◦ ◦ ◦ OF ◦ ◦ ◦
FRANCIS RABELAIS, M.D. ◦ ◦ ◦ WITH ◦ ◦ ◦
THE *PANTAGRUELIAN* PROGNOSTICATION, AND
OTHER ◦ ◦ ◦ PIECES IN VERSE AND PROSE
BY THAT AUTHOR: ALSO ◦ ◦ ◦ HIS HISTORI-
CAL LETTERS. COMPLEATING ALL HIS WORKS
◦ ◦ ◦ THAT ARE EXTANT. NEVER BEFORE
PRINTED IN *ENGLISH*

TO THE HONOURABLE

HUGH HARE ESQ.

SIR, I would not imitate those Authors who fly for Protection to Persons
that are unable, or unwilling to grant it. Your Love for Learning prompt-

ing You to countenance the Well-meant Endeavours of Studious Men, You have condescended to extend Your Favours even to me. This, Sir, made me so presumptuous as to relish no other Method of owning the Debt I cannot pay, and at the same time prepossessing the Reader in my Favour, than by dedicating this Translation of the best Work of France's greatest Wit to You, who have made the Copy of the Masterpiece of one of Italy's best Historians outshine the beautiful Original. For, whatever my Performance be, most Readers will as little doubt its being good, because offer'd to so great a Judge, as they would be apt to mistrust a Child's Legitimacy, to whom they saw a Man of Nice Honour stand Godfather. Indeed, as Those who have no Children may be thought more oblig'd to be thus Trustees for those of others, and make amends for not begetting any: so those whose Pens produce nothing, seem more engag'd to take care of the Off-spring of other mens Brains, than those whose fertile Minds, like Yours, are like to people the learned World with manly and charming Productions. Yet this do's not excuse the latter from appearing in Behalf of those who stand in need of their charitable good Word, when usher'd in to the World. Besides, as He who never had any Progeny is less likely to secure a good Fame to that of others, than a Person whose honourable Offspring evinces his Capacity for such a Christian-like Office ; so he who never writ can hardly so effectually save a Book from Damnation, as one who having enrich'd the Public with valuable Pieces, is acknowledg'd a competent Judge in the matter. Till Occasion calls, and you consent to leave the Study of the best Ancients and Moderns, to devote Your Self wholly to what You love more than Your Ease, I mean Your Country, it hopes, Sir, to be oblig'd to You for such Presents, the Product of the hours, that divide those during which You either bless Your Friends with your Conversation, or Your Self with that of a Consort, whose outward Graces are attended with all the Beauties of the Mind. May Your Happiness, like Your Vertues, admit of no Allay ; Be still the Joy of a Noble Father, who doubly lives, while he sees the Heir to his Honours, already like himself, adorn'd with the most essential Nobility, when he sees in You so ripe a Judgment, so calm and sedate a Mind, in so flourishing a Youth, so universal a Learning without any Tincture of Affectation or Pedantry, so great a Knowledge of the World without the least Acquaintance with its Vices ; and, above all, so charming a Modesty, that Vertue which shuns a Lustre, yet heightens that of every other. But that Darling of Yours causes me to draw a Veil over those other Accomplishments, which, as they endear You to all Mankind, would have made me ambitious of owning my self Your Admirer, tho I were not otherwise bound to profess myself with all imaginable Zeal and Respect, Sir, your most humble and most oblig'd Servant,

PETER MOTTEUX.

THE TRANSLATOR'S PREFACE

READER, I don't know what kind of a Preface I must write to find thee Courteous, an Epithete too often bestow'd without a Cause. The Author of this Work has been as sparing of what we call Good Nature, as most Readers are now adays. So I'm afraid his Translator and Commentator is not to expect much more than has been shew'd them. What's worse, there are but two sorts of takin? Prefaces, as there are but two kinds of Prologues to Plays ; for, Mr. Bays was doubtless in the right, when he said, That if Thunder and Lightning could not fright an Audience into Complaisance, the sight of the Poet with a Rope about his Neck, might work them into Pity. Some indeed have bullied many of you into an applause, and rail'd at your Faults, that you might think them without any ; and others, more safely, have spoken kindly of you, that you might think, or at least speak as favourably of them, and be flatter'd into Patience. Now I fancy there's nothing less difficult to attempt than the first Method ; for in this blessed Age, 'tis as easy to find a Bully without Courage, as a Whore without Beauty, or a Writer without Wit ; though those Qualifications are so necessary in their respective Professions : The mischief is, that you seldom allow any to rail besides your selves, and cannot bear a Pride which shocks your own. As for wheedling you into a liking of a Work, I must confess it seems the safest way ; but tho' Flattery pleases you well when 'tis particular, you hate it, as little concerning you, when 'tis general. Then we Knights of the Quill are a stiff-neck'd Generation, who as seldom care to seem to doubt the worth of our Writings, and their being lik'd, as we love to flatter more than one at a time ; and had rather draw our Pens, and stand up for the Beauty of our Works (as some errant Fools us'd to do for that of their Mistresses) to the last Drop of our Ink. And truly this Submission which sometimes wheedles you into Pity, as seldom decoys you into Love, as the awkward cringing of an antiquated Fop, as moneyless as he's ugly affects an experienc'd Fair One. Now as we little value your Pity, as a Lover his Mistresses, well satisfy'd that 'tis only a less uncivil way of dismissing us. But what if neither of these two ways will work upon you ; of which doleful Truth some of our Play-wrights stand so many living Monuments ? Why, then truly I can think on no other way at present, but blending the two into one ; and from this Marriage of Huffing and Cringing, there will result a new kind of careless Medley, which, perhaps, will work upon both sorts of Readers ; those who are to be hector'd, and those whom we must creep to. At least 'tis like to please by its novelty, and 'twill not be the first Monster that has pleas'd you when regular Nature could not do it.

If uncommon Mirth, lively Wit, and deep Learning, wove into wholsom Satire, a bold, good, and vast Design admirably pursu'd, Truth set out in its true light, and a Method how to arrive to its Oracle, can recommend a Work, I am sure this has enough to please any reasonable Man. The three Books publish'd some time since, which are in a manner an entire Work, were kindly receiv'd : Yet in the French they come far short of these two, which are also intire Pieces ; for the Satire is all general here, much more obvious, and consequently more entertaining. Even my long explanatory Preface was not thought improper, tho' I was so far from being allow'd time to make it methodical, that at first only a few Pages were intended ; yet as fast as they were printed I wrote on, till it prov'd at last like one of those Towns built little at first, then inlarg'd, where you see promiscuously an odd variety of all sorts of irregular Buildings. I hope the Remarks I give now will not please less ; for, as I have translated the Work which they explain, I had more time to make them, though as little to write them. It would be needless to give here a large Account of my Performance ; for, after all, you Readers care no more for this or that Apology or Pretence of Mr. Translator, if the Version do's not please you, than we do for a blundering Cook's Excuse after he has spoilt a good Dish in the Dressing. Nor can the first pretend to much Praise, besides that of giving his Author's Sense in its full extent, and copying his Stile, if 'tis to be coppied ; since he has no share in the Invention or Disposition of what he translates. Yet there was no small difficulty in doing Rabelais Justice in that double respect ; the obsolete Words and turns of Phrase, and dark Subjects, often as darkly treated, make the sense hard to be understood even by a Frenchman, and it cannot be easy to give it the free and easy Air of an Original ; for even what seems most common Talk in one Language, is what's often the most difficult to be made so in another ; and Horace's Thoughts of Comedy may well be apply'd to this :

> *Creditur, ex medio quia res arcessit, habere*
> *Sudoris minimum ; sed habet Comœdia tantum*
> *Plus oneris, quanto veniæ minus,*

Far be it from me for all this to value my self upon hitting the Words of Cant in which my drolling Author is so luxuriant ; for tho' such Words have stood me in good stead, I scarce can forbear thinking my self unhappy in having insensibly hoarded up so much Gibberish and Billingsgate Trash in my Memory ; nor could I forbear asking of my self, as an Italian Cardinal said on another account, *D'onde hai hai tu pigliato tante Coglionerie ?* Where the Devil didst thou rake up all these Fripperies ?

It was not less difficult to come up to the Author's sublime Expression. Nor would I have attempted such a Task, but that I was ambitious of giving a view of the most valuable Work of the greatest Genius of his Age, to the Mecœnas and best Genius of This. For I'm not overfond of so ungrateful a Task as Translating, and would rejoice to see less Versions and more Originals, so the matter were not as bad as many of the first are through want of Incouragement. Some indeed have deservedly gain'd Esteem by Translating ; yet not many condescend to translate, but such as cannot invent; though, to do the first well, requires often as much Genius as to do the latter.

I wish, Reader, thou mayest be as willing to do my Author Justice, as I have strove to do him Right. Yet if thou art a Brother of the Quill, 'tis ten to one thou art too much in love with thy own dear Productions, to admire those of one of thy Trade: However I know three or four who have not such a mighty Opinion of themselves, but I'll not name them, lest I be oblig'd to place myself among them. If thou art one of those, who, tho' they never write, criticise every one that does; avaunt—— Thou 'rt a profess'd Enemy of Mankind and of thy self, who wilt never be pleas'd, nor let any body be so, and know'st no better way to Fame, than by striving to lessen that of others; tho', would'st thou write, thou mightest be soon known, even by the Butter-women, and fly through the World in Band-boxes. If thou art of the Dissembling Tribe, 'tis thy Office to rail at those Books which thou hugg'st in a Corner. If thou art one of those Eves-droppers who would have their Moroseness be counted Gravity, thou 'lt condemn a Mirth which thou'rt past relishing; and I know no other way to quit the Score, than by writing (as like enough I may) something as dull, or duller than thy self, if possible. If thou art one of those Critics in Dressing, those Extempore's of Fortune, who having lost a Relation, and got an Estate, in an instant set up for Wit and every Extravagance, thou 'lt either praise or discommend this Book, according to the Dictates of some less foolish than thyself, perhaps of one of those who, being lodg'd at the Sign of the Box and Dice, will know better things, than to recommend to thee a Work, which bids thee beware of his Tricks. This Book might teach thee to leave thy Follies; but some will say, it do's not signify much to some Fools whether they are so or not; for when was there ever a Fool that thought himself one? If thou art one of those who would put themselves upon us for Learned Men in Greek and Hebrew, yet are meer Blockheads in English, and patch together old Pieces of the Ancients, to get themselves Cloaths out of them, thou art too severely maul'd in this Work to like it. Who then will, some will cry? Nay, besides these, many Societies that make a great Figure in the world are reflected on in this Book; which caus'd Rabelais to study to be dark, and even bedaub it with many loose Expressions, that he might not be thought to have any other Design than to droll; in a manner bewraying his Book that his Enemies might not bite it. Truly, tho' now the Riddle is expounded, I would advise those who read it, not to reflect on the Author, lest he be thought to have been before hand with them, and they be rank'd among those who have nothing to shew for their Honesty, but their Money; nothing for their Religion, but their Dissembling, or a fat Benefice; nothing for their Wit, but their Dressing; for their Nobility, but their Title; for their Gentility, but their Sword; for their Courage, but their Huffing; for their Preferment, but their Assurance; for their Learning, but their Degrees; or for their Gravity, but their Wrinkles or Dulness. They had better laugh at one another here, as 'tis the Custom of the World. Laughing is the end of all Professions ; the Miser may hoard, the Spend-thrift squander, the Politician plot, the Lawyer wrangle, and the Gamester cheat ; still their main Design is, to be able to laugh at one another ; and here they may do it at a cheap and easy rate. After all, should this Work fail to please the greater number of Readers, I am sure it cannot miss being lik'd by those who are for witty Mirth, and a chirping Bottle ; tho' not by those solid Sots, who seem to have drudg'd all their Youth long, only that they might enjoy the sweet Blessing of getting Drunk every night in their Old Age. But those Men of Sense and Honour, who love Truth, and the good of Mankind in general above all other things, will undoubtedly countenance this Work. I'll not gravely insist upon its usefulness, having said enough of it in the Preface to the First Part. I'll only add, That as Homer in his *Odysses* makes his Hero wander Ten Years through most parts of the then known World, so Rabelais, in a Three-months Voyage makes Pantagruel take a View of almost all sorts of People and Professions : with this difference however between the Ancient Mythologist and the Modern, That while the *Odysses* has been compar'd to a setting Sun, in respect to the *Iliads*, Rabelais's last Work, which is this *Voyage to the Oracle of the Bottle*, (by which he means Truth) is justly thought his Masterpiece ; being writ with more Spirit, Salt, and Flame, than the First Part of his Works. At near 70 Years of Age, his Genius, far from being drain'd, seem'd to have acquir'd fresh Vigor, and new Graces ; the more it exerted it self ; like those Rivers which grow more deep, large, majestic and useful by their Course. Those who accuse the French of being as sparing of their Wit, as lavish of their Words, will find an ENGLISHMAN in our Author. I must confess indeed that my Countrymen, and other Southern Nations, temper the one with the other, in a manner, as they do their Wine with Water, often just dashing the latter with a little of the first. Now here, Men love to drink their Wine pure ; nay, sometimes it will not satisfy, unless in its very Quintessence, as in Brandies ; though an Excess of this betrays want of Sobriety, as much as an Excess of Wit betrays a want of Judgment. But I must conclude, lest I be justly tax'd with wanting both. I will only add, That as every Language has its peculiar Graces, seldom or never to be acquir'd by a Foreigner, I cannot think I have given my Author those of the English in every place : But as none compell'd me to write, I fear to ask a Pardon, which yet the generous Temper of this Nation makes me hope to obtain. Albinus, a Roman who had written in Greek, desir'd in his Preface to be forgiven his Faults of Language ; but Cato ask'd in derision, Whether any had forc'd him to write in a Tongue of which he was not an absolute Master ? Lucullus wrote an History in the same Tongue, and said, He had scatter'd some false Greek in it, to let the World know it was the Work of a Roman. I 'll not say as much of my Writings, in which I study to be as little incorrect as the hurry of Business, and shortness of Time will permit ; but I may better say, as Tully did of the History of his Consulship, which he also had written in Greek, That what

Errors may be found in the Diction, are crept in against my Intent. Indeed Livius Andronicus, and Terence, the one a Greek, the other a Carthaginian, wrote successfully in Latin, and the latter is perhaps the most perfect Model of the Purity and Urbanity of that Tongue : But I ought not to hope for the Success of those great Men. Yet am I ambitious of being as subservient to the useful Diversion of the Ingenious of this Nation as I can, which I have endeavour'd in this Work ; with Hopes to attempt some greater Tasks, if ever I am happy enough to have more Leisure. In the mean time it will not displease me if 'tis known that this is given by one, who, though born and educated in France, has the Love and Veneration of a Loyal Subject for this Nation : One, who by a Fatality, which with many more made him say,

Nos patriam fugimus et dulcia linquimus arva,

Is oblig'd to make the Language of these happy Regions as natural to him as he can, and thankfully say with the rest, under this Protestant Government,

Deus nobis hæc otia fecit.

ON RABELAIS, EXPLAIN'D BY MR. MOTTEUX, AND HIS TRANSLATION OF THE TWO LAST BOOKS

I

Before the Reign of Avarice and Lust,
When Virtue with unborrow'd Lustre shone,
Men were by instinct Temperate and Just,
And Law and Physic useless and unknown.

II

But quickly, ah ! too quickly Vice prevail'd ;
On Arts and Rule distemper'd Mortals thought ;
Health in the Mind and in the Body fail'd,
And ev'ry Hour new Desolations brought.

III

Through ev'ry Vein the gliding Poison ran,
No Cure succeeded for no Cure could please ;
What Miracle could e're restore the Man
That loath'd the Med'cine, charm'd with the Disease ?

IV

In vain Physicians labour'd to beguile
The stubborn Patient by a kind Deceit ;
In vain was all the Moral Sages Toil
To gain the Sinner by a pious Cheat.

THE FOURTH BOOK OF DR. FRANCIS RABELAIS

V

Rab'lais at last the noble Secret found ;
But, wanting either Courage or Good-will,
He hid the precious Talent under Ground,
And all but Mirth and Wit was secret still.

VI

Charm'd with the Influence of that pow'rful Spell
The languid Patient rear'd his drooping Head ;
Down sunk th' ill Genius to his native Hell,
And all his Train of grim Attendants fled.

VII

Straight all the Humours trace their wonted Rounds,
Through ev'ry Nerve the Brain shoots dancing Rays,
The Heart again with sprightly Force rebounds,
And the whole Engine vigorously plays.

VIII

Motteux has now unscreen'd the Mystic Veil,
Which Artful Rab'lais o're the Treasure drew :
To him who gives what th' other did conceal,
An equal Praise, but greater thanks are due.

IX

Pedants and Quacks now leave their Queen of Whims,
Cits, Clowns and Courtiers wince, then kiss the Rod,
The Fiery Bigot calmly reads his Crimes,
And Popehawk's batter'd where he sits as God.

X

Daring th' Attempt, and glorious the Success,
For any other than Motteux would be,
Rab'lais's Wit with equal Force t' express,
And make the Copy with the Text agree.

XI

But what in others Arrogance had been,
Is but a noble Ardor in his Mind :
New Beauties now in ev'ry Line are seen,
The Stile's enliven'd, and the Sense refin'd.

J. MITCHELL, M.D.

THE FOURTH BOOK OF DR. FRANCIS RABELAIS

ON MR. MOTTEUX'S TRANSLATION OF THE TWO LAST BOOKS OF RABELAIS, AND HIS KEY TO THE WHOLE

WHEN tasteless France provok'd out Author's Gall,
And Rab'lais moulded on the dusty stall,
The Great Physician wrote with Artful Rage,
To cure the vicious Palate of the Age.
Bitter the Med'cine was, but kindly He,
To make it relish, gave it an Allay :
Sweet'ned with seeming Nonsense, down it went ;
'Twas tempered well, and answer'd his intent.
Drench'd with a Dose of Satire, all the Age
Recover'd in a Laugh ; such Pleasantry and Rage
Were wisely mingled in the double-meaning Page.
Mirth seem'd predominant, and most it work'd ;
The Fable tickled, but the Moral lurk'd.
Too deep it lay, for Men of shallow Sense
To fathom ; or to find its Excellence.
Rab'lais, the greatest Genius of his Time,
Tho' artfully he hid it, wrote sublime :
And such the Thought, and such the Satire is,
It must be found b' a Genius great as his.
  And see ! 'tis found ! Motteux, with searching Eye
Has div'd into the hidden Mystery.
Motteux, whom France and England jointly claim ;
Their Claims are just, and both their Pleas the same :
Language They urge ; That no Distinction show'th,
He truly seems a Native of them Both.
Much Rab'lais owes, nor less is England's Debt ;
England can read, and Rab'lais now is Great.
Thick lay the Mist, but now there shines through all
The Life and Beauties of the Great Original.
The Mist is gone ; and every beauteous Line
Does with New Graces, pointed Glories, shine.
So in thick Clouds the Trojan Heroe stood ;
The Clouds dispers'd, and shew'd a beauteous God.
Around him all his Mother's Graces mov'd ;
The Crowd admiring gaz'd, and stricken Dido lov'd.

ROBERT GALE.

New-College in Oxon.

THE FOURTH BOOK OF DR. FRANCIS RABELAIS

TO MR. MOTTEUX, ON HIS TRANSLATION OF THE TWO LAST BOOKS OF RABELAIS, AND HIS KEY TO THE WHOLE

WHEN in an happy Age of circling Time,
To raise the Glory of some envy'd Clime
Nature intends a Genius ; and to strain
Something Divine with less Allay of Man ;
She rests a Century for the vast Design,
And culls Ideas exquisitely fine,
Till all Perfections in one Soul combine.
To such Expence it does her Skill engage,
One must suffice a Nation, crown an Age.
   Such was the mighty Rab'lais, in whose Mind
No scatter'd Gleams of trivial Sense we find,
But view the Pourtraiture of Human kind.
All Nature's System ! Miniature of Man !
   Through every Line th' infernal Genius ran,
And shew'd a vast, an universal Vein.
But long his Sense, not Fogs, but Shades did shrow'd ;
And as a priest must be to every God,
To guard the Shrine, and draw aside the Cloud ;
Many had strove t' invade the Mystery,
But we at last the destin'd Flamen see ;
You come, and Rab'lais opens to your Key.
'Tis true, upon his Basis stands your Praise,
'Tis from his Brow that you derive your Bays :
But 'tis as when with a peculiar Grace
Great Kneller copies an illustrious Face ;
Each stroke is Titian, and the mighty Fair
Viewing the Piece, is fearful to compare.
Others had view'd the wealthy Mine before,
And brought the Bullion to our English Shore,
And stampt it, but allay'd it with their own ;
Faint was the Mark, and Rab'lais dimly shone.
Tho' that which can but his least Image bear
Must be Divine, inevitably rare.
Thus mighty Jove, when Nectar warm'd his Blood,
On some inferior Nymph the Grace bestow'd,
The Nymph retain'd the Vigour of the God :
And wheresoe're th' Æthereal Genius reigns,
Transmits Divinity through all her Veins.
Nor can the Mould so much the God destroy,
But, through some Grace, Jove sparkles in the Boy.
But you admit, Sir, no Allay of Fame ;
You met your Author with an equal Flame,

Transfus'd his Air, his Genius in your Lines ;
Through every Page the British Rab'lais shines,
Nor sinks below the French, through all the whole,
You, as you share his Country, share his Soul.
Take then our Thanks, the Work's divinely done ;
And those whose first Attempts have nobly flown,
Must veil their Lawrels, and the Conquest own.
'Tis worthy such an Age, and such a Reign,
Where Wit's upon the stretch, her utmost strain ;
An Age where all compleated Glories join,
Where Fields with Heroes, Courts and Beauties shine.
Nor does the Wreath upon the learned Brow
Less fresh, or fast, than on the Hero, grow.
Methinks I see suspended in the Air,
Not Phœbus, (no ; we banish him the Chair,)
But some Poetic Angel from the Sky,
Betwixt the Rival Nations, hold on high
The dubious Lawrel ! Here Great Dryden stands,
And there Boileau, whose undisputed Hands
Reach for the Prize. Thus strive the mighty Pair ;
But here some Spirit, friendly to the Fair,
From the French Poet does the Bays remove,
(Who durst Heav'ns nearest type defame) to prove,
That Charming Sex has Advocates above.
Here Tate ! whose Soul's more eminently taught
To trace the Grandeur of the Roman Thought ;
Who best their Air and Sense, and Vigour shews,
And makes them match their Eagle with their Muse.
Here Congreve ! whose young Genius cou'd disdain
Nature's slow Compute, and the steps of Man.
Who rose full Zenith, born into his Reign !

Go on, ye British Bards, and only write
With the same Vigour that your King does fight.
Let your Thoughts reach his Actions, match'd his Pow'r,
The Lawrel's won ; for none can higher soar.
And as the Hero conquer'd on the Boyn,
We, from the Banks of the deserted Seine,
Will bring the Muses, the Illustrious Nine ;
To nobler Pleasures upon Isis Stream,
Or the delicious Banks of sacred Cham ;
And all shall join to weild the Monarch's Fame.

II. DENNE.

Trin. Coll. Camb.

THE AUTHOR'S EPISTLE DEDICATORY

TO THE MOST ILLUSTRIOUS PRINCE

AND MOST REVEREND

ODET, CARDINAL DE CHASTILLON

You know, Most Illustrious Prince, how often I have been and am daily prest by Great Numbers of eminent Persons, to proceed in the Pantagruelian Fables; they tell me that many languishing, sick, and disconsolate Persons perusing them, have deceiv'd their Grief, passed their Time merrily, and been inspir'd with new Joy and Comfort. I commonly answer, That I aim'd not at Glory and Applause, when I diverted my self with writing; but only design'd to give by my Pen, to the absent who labour under Affliction, that little Help which at all times I willingly strive to give to the Present that stand in need of my Art and Service. Sometimes I at large relate to them, how Hippocrates in several places, and particularly in Lib. 6. *Epidem.* describing the Institution of the Physician his Disciple, and also Soranus of Ephesus, Orbasius, Galen, Hali, Abbas, and other Authors, have descended to Parliculars in the Prescription of his Motions, Deportment, Looks, Countenance, Gracefulness, Civility, Cleanliness of Face, Cloaths, Beard, Hair, Hands, Mouth, even his very Nails; as if he were to play the Part of a Lover, in some Comedy, or enter the Lists to fight some Enemy. And indeed the Practice of Physic is properly enough compar'd by Hippocrates to a Fight, and also to a Farce acted between three Persons, the Patient, the Physician, and the Disease. Which Passage has sometimes put me in mind of Julia's saying to Augustus her Father. One day she came before him in a very gorgeous loose lascivious Dress; which very much displeas'd him, though he did not much discover his Discontent. The next Day, she put on another, and in modest Garb, such as the Chast Roman Ladies wore, came into his presence. The kind father could not then forbear expressing the Pleasure which he took to see her, so much alter'd, and said to her, Oh! how much more this Garb becomes, and is commendable in the Daughter of Augustus! But she, having her Excuse ready, answered, This day, Sir, I drest my self to please my Father's Eye; yesterday to gratifie that of my Husband. Thus, disguis'd in Looks and Garb, nay even, as formerly was the Fashion, with a rich and pleasant Gown with four Sleeves, which was called Philonium, according to Petrus Alexandrinus in 6. *Epidem.* a Physician might answer to such as might find the Metamorphosis indecent: Thus have I accoutred my self, not that I am proud of appearing in such a Dress; but for the sake of my Patient, whom alone I wholly design to please, and no ways offend or dissatisfie. There is also a Passage in our Father Hippocrates, in the Book I have nam'd, which causes some to sweat, dispute, and labour; not indeed to know whether the Physician's frowning, discontented, and morose Look render the Patient sad, and his joyful, serene, and pleasing Countenance rejoyce him, for Experience teaches us that this is most certain; but whether such Sensations of Grief, or Pleasure, are produc'd by the Apprehension of the Patient, observing his Motions and Qualities in his Physician, and drawing from thence Conjectures of the end, and catastrophe of his Disease, as by his pleasing Look, joyful and desirable Events, and by his sorrowful and unpleasing Air, sad and dismal Consequences; or whether those Sensations be produced by a transfusion of the serene or gloomy, aerial or terrestial, joyful or melancholic Spirits of the Physician, into the Person of the Patient, as it is the Opinion of Plato, Averroes and others.

Above all things the best Authors have given particular Directions to Physicians about the Words, Discourse, and Converse, which they ought to have with their Patients, every one aiming at one Point, that is, to rejoyce them without offending God, and in no ways whatsoever to vex or displease them. Which causes Herophilus much to blame that Physician, who being ask'd by a Patient of his, Shall I die? impudently made him this Answer:

> Patroclus dy'd, whom all allow,
> By much, a better Man than you.

Another who had a mind to know the state of his Distemper, asking him after our merry Patelin's way: Well, Doctor, do's not my Water tell you I shall die? He foolishly answer'd, No; if Latona the Mother of those lovely Twins, Phœbus and Diana, begot thee. Galen, lib. 4. *Comment.* 6. *Epidem.* blames much also Quinus his Tutor, who, a certain noble Man of Rome, his Patient, saying to him, You have been at breakfast, my Master, your Breath smells of Wine; answered arrogantly, Yours smells of Fever, which is the better of the two? Wine or a putrid Fever? But the Calumny of certain Cannibals, Misanthropes, perpetual Eaves-droppers, has been so foul and excessive, that it had conquered my Patience; and I had resolv'd not to write one jot more. For the least of their Detractions were, that my Books are all stuffed with various Heresies, of which nevertheless they could not show one single Instance; much indeed of Comical and facetious fooleries, neither offending God nor the King: (And truly I own they are the subject, and only Theme of these Books.) But of Heresie, not a word, unless they interpreted wrong and against all use of Reason, and common Language, what, I had rather suffer a thousand Deaths, if it were possible, than have thought: as who should make Bread to be Stone, a Fish to be a Serpent, and an

Egg to be a Scorpion. This, my Lord, emboldned me once to tell you as I was complaining of it in your Presence, that if I did not esteem my self a better Christian, than they show themselves towards me, and if my Life, Writings, Words, nay Thoughts betray'd to me one single spark of Heresie, or I should in a detestable manner fall into the Snares of the Spirit of Detraction, Διάβολος, that by their means raises such Crimes against me; I would then like the Phœnix gather dry Wood, kindle a Fire, and burn my self in the midst of it. You were then pleas'd to say to me, That King Francis of Eternal Memory, had been made sensible of those false Accusations: And that having caused my Books, (mine, I say, because several false, and infamous have been wickedly laid to me,) to be carefully and distinctly read to him by the most learned and faithful Anagnost in this Kingdom, he had not found any Passage suspitious; and that he abhorr'd a certain envious, ignorant, hypocritical Informer, who grounded a mortal Heresie on an N put instead of an M by the carelessnes of the Printers.

As much was done by his Son, our most gracious, virtuous and blessed Sovereign, Henry, whom Heaven long preserve; so that he granted you his Royal Privilege, and particular Protection, for me against my slandering Adversaries.

You kindly condescended since, to confirm me these happy News at Paris, and also lately when you visited my Lord Cardinal du Bellay, who for the benefit of his Health, after a lingring Distemper, was retired to St. Maur, that Place (or rather Paradise) of Salubrity, Serenity, Conveniency, and all desirable Country-pleasures.

Thus, my Lord, under so glorious a Patronage, I am emboldened once more to draw my Pen, undaunted now and secure; with hopes that you will still prove to me against the Power of Detraction, a second Gallic Hercules in Learning, Prudence, and Eloquence, and Alexicacos in Virtue, Power, and Authority; you, of whom I may truly say what the wise Monarch Solomon saith of Moses that great Prophet, and Captain of Israel, *Ecclesiast.* 45. A Man fearing and loving God, who found favour in the sight of all flesh, whose Memorial is blessed. God made him like to the glorious Saints, and magnified him so, that his Enemies stood in fear of him; and for him made Wonders: made him glorious in the sight of Kings, gave him a Commandment for his People, and by him shew'd his light; he sanctified him in his faithfulness, and meekness, and chose him out of all Men. By him he made us to hear this Voice, and caused by him the Law of Life and Knowledge to be given.

Accordingly, if I shall be so happy as to hear any one commend those merry Composures, they shall be adjur'd by me to be oblig'd, and pay their Thanks to you alone, as also to offer their Prayers to Heaven for the continuance and encrease of your Greatness; and to attribute no more to me, than my humble and ready Obedience to your Commands: For by your most honourable Incouragement, you at once have inspir'd me with Spirit, and with Invention; and without you my Heart had fail'd me, and the Fountain-head of my Animal Spirits had been dry. May the Lord keep you in his blessed Mercy.

My Lord, Your most humble and most devoted Servant,

FRANCIS RABELAIS,
Physician.

Paris this 28th of
January, MDLII.

THE AUTHOR'S PROLOGUE TO THE FOURTH BOOK

Good People, God save and keep you : Where are you ? I can't see you ; stay—I'll saddle my Nose with Spectacles—Oh, Oh ! 'twill be fair anon, I see you. Well, you have had a good Vintage, they say ; this is no bad News to Frank you may swear ; you have got an infallible Cure against Thirst, rarely perform'd of you, my Friends ! You, your Wives, Children, Friends, and Families are in as good Case as Heart can wish ; 'tis well, 'tis as I'd have it : God be praised for it, and if such be his Will, may you long be so. For my part I am thereabouts, thanks to his blessed Goodness ; and by the means of a little Pantagruelism, (which you know is a certain Jollity of Mind pickled in the scorn of Fortune) you see me now Hale, and Cheery, as sound as a Bell, and ready to drink, if you will. Would you know why I'm thus, Good People ? I'll e'en give you a positive answer—such is the Lord's Will, which I obey and revere ; it being said in his Word, in great Derision to the Physician, neglectful of his own Health, Physician, heal thy self.

Galen had some knowledge of the Bible, and had convers'd with the Christians of his time, as appears Lib. 11. *De Usu Partium;* Lib. 2. *de differentiis Pulsuum,* cap. 3. and *ibid.* Lib. 3. cap. 2. and Lib. *de rerum affectibus* (if it be Galen's) yet 'twas not for any such Veneration of Holy Writ that he took Care of his own Health. No, 'twas for fear of being twitted with the Saying so well known among Physicians,

Ἰατρὸς ἄλλων, αὐτὸς βρύων.

He boasts of healing Poor and Rich,
Yet is himself all over Itch.

This made him boldly say, that he did not desire to be esteem'd a Physician, if from his twenty eighth Year to his old Age he had not liv'd in perfect Health, except some ephemerous Fevers, of which he soon rid himself ; yet he was not naturally of the soundest Temper, his Stomach being evidently bad. Indeed, as he s ith, Lib. 5. *de Sanitate tuendâ,* that Physician will hardly be thought very careful of the Health of others, who neglects his own. Asclepiades boasted yet more than this ; for he said that he had articled with Fortune not to be reputed a Physician, if he could be said to have been sick, since he began to practise Physic, to his latter Age, which he reach'd, lusty in all his Members, and victorious over Fortune, till at last the old Gentleman unluckily tumbled down from the Top of a certain ill-propp'd and rotten Stair-Case ; and so there was an end of him.

If by some Disaster Health is fled from your Worships to the right or to the left, above or below, before or behind, within or without, far or near, on this side or t'other side, wheresoever it be, may you presently, with the help of the Lord meet with it ; having found it, may you immediately claim it, seize it and secure it. The Law allows it ; the King would have it so : nay, you have my Advice for 't ; neither more nor less than the Law-Makers of Old did fully impower a Master to claim and seize his run-away Servant where-ever he might be found. Ods-bodikins, is it not written and warranted by the Ancient Customs of this so noble, so rich, so flourishing Realm of France, That the Dead seizes the Quick ? See what has been declar'd very lately in that Point by that Learned, Wise, Courteous, and Just Civilian Andrè Tiraquell, one of the Judges in the most Honourable Court of Parliament at Paris. Health is our Life, as Antiphron the Sicyonian wisely has it, without Health Life is no Life, 'tis not living Life. Ἀβίος βίος, βίος ἀβίοτος. Without Health Life is only a Languishment and an Image of Death. Therefore, you that want your Health, that is to say, that are Dead, seize the Quick; secure Life to your selves, that is to say, Health.

I have this hope in the Lord, that he will hear our Supplications, considering with what Faith and Zeal we Pray, and that he will grant this our Wish, because 'tis moderate and mean. Mediocrity was held by the ancient Sages to be Golden, that is to say, precious, prais'd by all Men, and pleasing in all Places. Read the Sacred Bible, you 'll find, the Prayers of those who ask'd moderately were never unanswer'd. For Example, little dapper Zacheus, whose Body and Reliques the Monks of St. Garlick, near Orleans, boast of having, and nickname him St. Sylvanus: he only wished to see our Blessed Saviour near Jerusalem. 'Twas but a small Request, and no more than any Body then might pretend to. But alas! he was but low built, and one of so diminutive a Size among the Croud couldn't so much as get a Glimpse of him: well then he struts, stands on Tip-Toes, bustles and bestirring his stumps, shoves and makes way, and with much ado clambers up a Sycamore. Upon this, the Lord who knew his sincere Affection, presented himself to his sight and was not only seen by him, but heard also: Nay, what's more, he came to his House, and blest his Family.

One of the Sons of the Prophets in Israel, felling Wood near the River Jordan, his Hatchet forsook the Helve and fell to the Bottom of the River; so he pray'd to have it again ('twas but a small Request, mark ye me,) and having a strong Faith, he did not throw the Hatchet after the Helve, as some Spirits of Contradiction say by way of scandalous Blunder, but the Helve after the Hatchet, as you all properly have it. Presently two great Miracles were seen, up springs the Hatchet from the Bottom of the Water, and fixes it self to its old Acquaintance the Helve. Now had he wish'd to coach it to Heaven in a Fiery Chariot like Elias, to multiply in Seed like Abraham, be as rich as Job, strong as Sampson, and beautiful as Absalom, would he have obtain'd it, d'ye think? I' troth, my Friends, I question it very much.

Now I talk of moderate Wishes in point of Hatchet (But hark 'e me, be sure you don't forget when we ought to drink) I'll tell you what's written among the Apologues of wise Æsop the Frenchman, I mean the Phrygian and Trojan, as Max. Planudes makes him; from which People, according to the most faithful Chroniclers, the noble French are descended: Ælian writes that he was of Thrace, and Agathias after Herodotus, that he was of Samos; 'tis all one to Frank.

In his time liv'd a poor honest Country Fellow of Gravot, Tom Wellhung by Name, a Wood-cleaver by Trade, who in that low Drudgery made shift so, to pick up a sorry Lively-hood. It happen'd that he lost his Hatchet. Now tell me who had ever more Cause to be vex'd than poor Tom? Alas, his whole Estate and Life depended on his Hatchet; by

MY HATCHET, LORD JUPITER, MY HATCHET

95

his Hatchet he earn'd many a fair Penny of the best Wood-mongers or Log-merchants, among whom he went a Jobbing; for want of his Hatchet he was like to starve, and had Death but met him six Days after without a Hatchet, the grim Fiend would have mow'd him down in the twinkling of a Bedstaff. In this sad Case he began to be in a heavy Taking, and call'd upon Jupiter with most eloquent Prayers (for you know, Necessity was the Mother of Eloquence) with the Whites of his Eyes turn'd up towards Heaven, down on his Marrowbones, his Arms rear'd high, his Fingers stretched wide, and his Head bare, the poor Wretch without ceasing was roaring out by way of Litany at every Repetition of his Supplications, my Hatchet, Lord Jupiter, my Hatchet, my Hatchet; only my Hatchet, O Jupiter, or Money to buy another, and nothing else; Alas, my poor Hatchet!

Jupiter happen'd then to be holding a grand Council about certain urgent Affairs, and old Gammer Cybele was just giving her Opinion, or if you had rather have it so, it was Young Phœbus the Beau: but in short, Tom's Out-cry and Lamentations were so loud that they were heard with no small Amazement at the Council Board, by the whole Consistory of the Gods. What a Devil have we below, quoth Jupiter, that howls so horridly? By the Mud of Styx, haven't we had all along, and haven't we here still enough to do to set to rights a World of damn'd puzzling Businesses of Consequence? We made an end of the Fray between Presthan King of Persia, and Soliman the Turkish Emperor; we have stopp'd up the Passages between the Tartars and the Moscovites; answer'd the Xeriff's Petition, done the same to that of Golgots Rays; the State of Parma's dispatch'd, so is that of Maydemburg, that of Mirandola, and that of Africa, that Town on the Mediterranean which we call Aphrodisium; Tripoli by carelesness has got a new Master, her hour was come.

Here are the Gascons cursing and damning, demanding the Restitution of their Bells.

In Yonder Corner are the Saxons, Easterlings, Ostrogoths, and Germans, Nations formerly invincible, but now Aberkeids, Bridled, Curb'd and brought under by a Paultry Diminutive crippled Fellow: they ask us Revenge, Relief, Restitution of their former good Sense and Ancient Liberty.

But what shall we do with this same Ramus and this Galland with a Pox to 'em, who surrounded with a swarm of their Scullions, Blackguard, Ragamuffins, Sizers, Vouchers and Stipulators, set together by the Ears, the whole University of Paris? I am in a sad quandary about it, and for the Heart's Blood of me can't tell yet with whom of the two to side.

Both seem to be notable Fellows, and as true Cods as ever piss'd; the one has Rose-Nobles, I say fine and weighty ones; the other would gladly have some too. The one knows something: the other's no Dunce. The one loves the better sort of Men, the other's belov'd by 'em. The one is an old cunning Fox, the other with Tongue and Pen, Tooth and Nail, falls foul on the ancient Orators and Philosophers, and barks at them like a Cur.

What think'st thou of it, say, thou bawdy Priapus ? I have found thy Council just before now, *Et habet tua mentula mentem.*

King Jupiter, answer'd Priapus, standing up and taking off his Cowle, his Snout uncas'd and rear'd up, fiery and stiffly propt, since you compare the one to a yelping snarling Cur, and the other to a sly Reynard the Fox, my Advice is with submission, that without fretting or puzling your Brains any farther about 'em, without any more ado you e'en serve 'em both as in the Days of Yore you did the Dog and the Fox. How ? ask'd Jupiter, when ? who were they ? where was it ? You have a rare Memory for ought I see, return'd Priapus l This right Worshipful Father Bacchus, whom we have here Nodding with his Crimson Phyz, to be reveng'd on the Thebans, had got a Fairy Fox, who whatever Mischief he did, was never to be caught or wrong'd by any Beast that wore a Head.

The Noble Vulcan here present had fram'd a Dog of Monesian Brass, and with long puffing and Blowing put the Spirit of Life into him : he gave it you, you gave it to Miss Europa, Miss Europa gave it Minos, Minos gave it Procris, Procris gave it Cephalus. He was also of the Fairy Kind, so that like the Lawyers of our Age, he was too hard for all other sorts of Creatures, nothing could scape the Dog : Now who should happen to meet but these two ? What do you think they did ? Dog by his Destiny was to take Fox, and Fox by his Fate was not to be taken.

The Case was brought before your Council ; you protested that you would not act against the Fates ; and the Fates were contradictory. In short, the End and Result of the matter was, that to reconcile two Contradictions was an impossibility in Nature. The very Pang put you into a sweat, some drops of which happening to light on the Earth, produced what the Mortals call Collyflowers. All our Noble Consistory for want of a Categorical Solution were seized with such a horrid Thirst, that above seventy eight Hogsheads of Nectar were swill'd down at that sitting. At last you took my Advice, and transmogriphy'd 'em into Stones, and immediately got rid of your Perplexity, and a Truce with Thirst was proclaim'd thro' this vast Olympus. This was the year of flabby Cods, near Teumessus between Thebes and Chalcis.

After this manner, 'tis my Opinion that you should petrifie this Dog and this Fox. The Metamorphosis will not be incongruous ; for they both bear the Name of Peter. And because, according to the Lymosin Proverb, To make an Oven's Mouth there must be three stones, you may associate them with Master Peter du Coignet, whom you formerly petrified for the same Cause. Then those three dead Pieces shall be put in an equilateral Trigone, somewhere in the great Temple at Paris, in the middle of the Porch, if you will, there to perform the Office of Extinguishers, and with their Noses put out the lighted Candles, Torches, Tapers and Flambeaux ; since, while they liv'd, they still lighted ballock-like the Fire of

Faction, Division, Ballock Sects, and wrangling among those idle bearded Boys, the Students. And this will be an everlasting Monument to show that those puny self-conceited Pedants, Ballock-framers, were rather contemn'd than condemned by you Dixi, I have said my Say.

You deal too kindly by them, said Jupiter, for ought I see Monsieur Priapus. You don't use to be so kind to every Body, let me tell you: For as they seek to eternize their Names, it would be much better for them to be thus changed into hard Stones, than to return to Earth and Putrefaction. But now to other Matters: Yonder behind us towards the Tuscan Sea, and the Neighbourhood of Mount Appennin, do you see what Tragedies are stirr'd up by certain topping Ecclesiastical Bullies? This hot Fit will last its time, like the Limoisns Ovens, and then will be cool'd, but not so fast.

We shall have Sport enough with it, but I foresee one Inconveniency; for methinks we have but little store of Thunder-Ammunition, since the time that you, my Fellow Gods, for your Pastime, lavish'd them away to bombard New Antioch, by my particular permission; as since, after your Example, the Stout Champions, who had undertaken to hold the Fortress of Dindenarois against all Comers, fairly wasted their powder with shooting at Sparrows; and then, not having wherewith to defend themselves in time of Need, valiantly surrendred to the Enemy, who were already packing up their Awls, full of Madness and despair, and thought on nothing but a shameful Retreat. Take care this be remedied, Son Vulcan; Rouse up your drowsie Cyclopes, Asteropes, Brontes, Arges, Polyphemus, Steropes, Pyracmon, and so forth; set them at work, and make them drink as they ought.

Never spare Liquor to such as are at hot work. Now let us despatch this bawling Fellow below; you Mercury, go see who it is? and know what he wants. Mercury look'd out at Heaven's Trap-door, through which, as I am told, they hear what's said here below; by the way, one might well enough mistake it for the Scuttle of a Ship; tho' Icaromenippus said it was like the Mouth of a Well; the light-heel'd Deity saw that it was honest Tom, who ask'd for his lost Hatchet; and accordingly he made his report to the Synod. By Jove, said Jupiter, we are finely hop'd up, as if we had now nothing else to do here but to restore lost Hatchets. Well, he must then have it for all this, for so 'tis written in the Book of Fate, (Do you hear?) as well as if it was worth the whole Dutchy of Milan. The truth is, the Fellow's Hatchet is as much to him as a Kingdom to a King. Come, come, let no more words be scattered about it, let him have his Hatchet again.

Now, let us make an end of the difference betwixt the Levites and Mole-catcher of Landerousse. Whereabouts were we? Priapus was standing in the Chimney-corner, and having heard what Mercury had reported, said in a most courteous and jovial manner, King Jupiter, while by your Order and particular Favour, I was Garden-keeper general on Earth; I observed that this word Hatchet is equivocal to many

COME, COME, SAID JUPITER TO MERCURY

99

things : for it signifies a certain Instrument, by the means of which Men fell and cleave Timber. It also signifies (at least I am sure it did formerly) a Female soundly and frequently Thumpthumpriggletickletwiddletoby'd : thus I perceived that every Cock of the Game us'd to call his Doxie his Hatchet, for with that same Tool (this he said lugging out and exhibiting his nine Inch Knocker) they so strongly and resolutely shove and drive in their Helves, that the females remain free from a fear Edidemical amongst their Sex, viz. that from the bottom of the Male's Belly the said Instrument should dangle at his Heel for want of Feminine props. And I remember, (for I have a Member, and a Memory too, ay, and a fine Memory, large enough to fill a Butter Firkin) : I remember, I say, that one Day of Tubilustre (Horn Fair) at the Festivals of Goodman Vulcan in May, I heard Josquin Des prez, Olkegan, Hobreths, Agricola, Brumel, Camelin, Vigoris, dela Fage, Bruyer, Prioris, Seguin, dela Rue, Midy, Moulu, Mouton, Gascoigne, Loiset, Compere, Penet, Fevin, Roufee, Richard Fort, Rousseau, Consilion, Constantio, Festi, Jacquet, and Bercan melodiously singing the following Catch on a pleasant Green.

> Long John to bed went to his Bride,
> And laid a Mallet by his side :
> What means this Mallet, John, saith she.
> Why ! 'tis to wedge thee home, quoth he.
> Alas ! cried she, the Man's a Fool :
> What need you use a wooden Tool ?
> When lusty John do's to me come,
> He never shoves but with his Bum.

Nine Olympiads and an Interclary Year after (I have a rare Member, I would say Memory, but I often make Blunders in the symbolisation and colligance of those two Words) I heard Adrian Viellard, Gombert, Janequin, Arcader, Claudin, Certon, Machicourt, Auxerre, Villiers, Sandrin, Sohier, Hesdin, Morales, Passereau, Maille, Maillart, Jacotin, Hurteur, Verdelot, Carpentras, l'Heriner, Cadeac, Doublet, Vermunt, Bouteiller, Lupi, Pagnier, Millet, Du Mollin, Alaire, Maraut, Morpin, Gendre, and other merry lovers of Musick, in a private Garden, under some fine shady Trees round about a Bulwark of Flaggons, Gammons, Pasty's, with several coated Quails, and lac'd Mutton, waggishly singing.

> Since Tools without their Hafts are useless Lumber,
> And Hatchets without Helves are of that Number ;
> That one may go in t'other, and may match it,
> I'll be the Helve, and thou shalt be the Hatchet.

Now would I know what kind of Hatchet this Bawling Tom wants ? This threw all the venerable Gods and Goddesses into a fit of Laughter like any Microcosm of Flyes ; and even set limping Vulcan a hopping and jumping smoothly three or four times for the sake of his dear. Come, come, said Jupiter to Mercury, run down immediately, and cast at the poor fellow's Feet three Hatchets; his own, another of Gold, and a third of Massie Silver, all of one size: then having left it to his Will to take his choice, if he take his own, and be satisfied with it, give him t'other two. If he take another, chop his Head off with his own; and henceforth serve me all those Losers of Hatchets after that manner. Having said this, Jupiter, with an awkward turn of his Head, like a Jackanapes swallowing of Pills, made so dreadful a Phyz, that all the vast Olympus quak'd again. Heaven's Foot-Messenger, thanks to his low crown'd narrow brim'd Hat, and plume of Feathers, Heel pieces, and running Stick with Pigeon Wings, flings himself out at Heaven's Wicket thro' the idle Desarts of the Air, and in a trice nimbly alights upon the Earth, and throws at Friend Tom's Feet the three Hatchets; saying to him, Thou hast bawl'd long enough to be a dry, thy Prayers and Request are granted by Jupiter; see which of these three is thy Hatchet, and take it away with thee. Wellhung lifts up the Golden Hatchet, peeps upon it, and finds it very heavy; then staring on Mercury, cries Codszouks this is none of mine; I won't ha't. The same he did with the Silver one, and said, 'Tis not this neither, you may e'en take them again. At last, he takes up his own Hatchet, examines the end of the Helve, and finds his Mark there; then ravish'd with Joy, like a Fox that meets some straggling Poultry, and sneering from the tip of the Nose, he cried by the Mass, This is my Hatchet, Master God, if you will leave it me, I will sacrifice to you a very good and huge Pot of Milk, brim full, cover'd with fine Strawberries next Ides of May.

Honest Fellow, said Mercury, I leave it thee, take it, and because thou hast wish'd and chosen moderately, in point of Hatchet, by Jupiter's command, I give thee these two others; thou hast now wherewith to make thy self rich: be honest. Honest Tom gave Mercury a whole Cart-load of Thanks, and rever'd the most great Jupiter. His old Hatchet he fastens close to his Leathern Girdle; and girds it above his Breech like Martin of Cambray: The two others, being more heavy, he lays on his Shoulder. Thus he plods on trudging over the Fields, keeping a good Countenance amongst his Neighbours and Fellow-Parishioners, with one merry Saying or other after Patelin's way. The next Day having put on a clean white Jacket, he takes on his Back the two precious Hatchets, and comes to Chinon, the famous City, noble City, ancient City, yea the first City in the World, according to the Judgment and Assertion of the most learned Massoreths. At Chinon he turned his Silver Hatchet into fine Testons, Crownpieces and other white Cash; his golden Hatchet into fine Angels, curious Ducats, substantial Ridders, Spankers, and Rose Nobles. Then with them purchases a good Number of Farms, Barns, Houses, Out-Houses, Thatch-Houses, Stables, Meadows, Orchards, Fields, Vineyards, Woods, arable Lands, Pastures, Ponds, Mills, Gardens, Nurseries, Oxen, Cows, Sheep, Goats, Swine, Hogs, Asses, Horses, Hens, Cocks, Capons, Chickens, Geese, Ganders, Ducks, Drakes, and a World of all other Necessaries, and in a short time became the richest Man in the Country, nay, even richer than that limping Scrapegood Maulevrier.

His Brother Bumpkins and the Yeomen, and other Country-Puts there-abouts, perceiving his good Fortune, were not a little amaz'd, insomuch, that their former Pity of poor Tom was soon chang'd into an Envy of his so great and unexpected Rise ; and as they could not for their Souls devise how this came about, they made it their business to pry up and down, and lay their Heads together, to enquire, seek and inform themselves by what Means, in what Place, on what Day, what Hour, how, why and wherefore he had come by this great Treasure.

At last, hearing it was by Losing his Hatchet, Ha, ha ! said they, was there no more to do, but to lose a Hatchet, to make us rich ? Mum for that ; 'tis as easie as pissing a Bed, and will cost but little ; Are then at this time the Revolutions of the Heavens, the Constellations of the Firmament, and Aspects of the Planets such, that whosoever shall lose a Hatchet, shall immediately grow rich ? Ha, ha, ha, by Jove, you shall e'en be lost, an 't please you, my dear Hatchet. With this they all fairly lost their Hatchets out of hand. The Devil of one that had a Hatchet left ; he was not his Mother's Son, that did not lose his Hatchet. No more was Wood fell'd or cleav'd in that Country thro' want of Hatchets. Nay, the Æsopian Apologue even saith, that certain petty Country Gents, of the lower Class, who had sold Wellhung their little Mill and little Field, to have wherewithal to make a Figure at the next Muster, having been told that this Treasure was come to him by that only means, sold the only Badge of their Gentility, their Swords, to purchase Hatchets to go lose them, as the silly Clodpates did, in hopes to gain store of Chink by that Loss.

You would have truly sworn they had been a parcel of your petty spiritual Usurers, Rome-bound, selling their All, and borrowing of others to buy store of Mandates a Pennyworth of a new made Pope.

Now they cry'd out and bray'd, and pray'd, and bawl'd, and lamented, and invok'd Jupiter ; my Hatchet ! my Hatchet ! Jupiter, my Hatchet, on this side, my Hatchet, on that side, my Hatchet, ho, ho, ho, ho, Jupiter, my Hatchet. The Air round about rung again with the Cries and Howlings of these rascally Losers of Hatchets.

Mercury was nimble in bringing them Hatchets ; to each offering that which he had lost, another of Gold, and a third of Silver.

Every He still was for that of Gold, giving Thanks in abundance to the great Giver Jupiter ; but in the very nick of time, that they bow'd and stoop'd to take it from the Ground, whip, in a trice, Mercury lopp'd off their Heads, as Jupiter had commanded ; and of Heads, thus cut off, the Number was just equal to that of the lost Hatchets.

You see how it is now ; you see how it goes with those who in the simplicity of their Hearts wish and desire with Moderation. Take warning by this, all you greedy, fresh-water Shirks, who scorn to wish for any thing under Ten Thousand Pounds : and do not for the future run on impudently, as I have sometimes heard you wishing, Would to God, I had now one hundred seventy eight Millions of Gold ; Oh ! how I should tickle it off ? The Dewse on you, what more might a King, an Emperor, or a Pope wish for ? For that reason, indeed, you see that after you have made such hopeful Wishes, all the good that comes to you of it, is the Itch or the Scab, and not a Cross in your Breeches to scare the Devil that tempts you to make these Wishes ; no more than those two Mumpers, Wishers after the Custom of Paris ; one of whom only wish'd to have in good old Gold as much as hath been spent, bought and sold in Paris since it's first Foundations were laid, to this Hour ; all of it valued at the Price, Sale and Rate of the dearest Year in all that space of Time. Do you think the Fellow was bashful ? Had he eaten sowre Plums unpeil'd ? Were his Teeth on edge, I pray you ? The other wish'd Our Lady's Church brim full of Steel Needles, from the Floor to the top of the Roof, and to have as many Ducats as might be cram'd into as many Bags as might be sow'd with each and every one of those Needles, till they were all either broke at the Point or Eye. This is to wish with a Vengeance ! What think you of it ? What did they get by 't, in your Opinion ? Why, at Night both my Gentlemen had kyb'd Heels, a Tetter in the Chin, a Church yard Cough in the Lungs, a Catarrh in the Throat, a swinging Bile at the Rump, and the Devil of one musty Crust of a brown George the poor Dogs had to scoure their Grinders with. Wish therefore for Mediocrity, and it shall be given unto you, and over and above yet ; that is to say, provided you bestir your selves manfully, and do your best in the mean time.

Ah, but say you, God might as soon have given me seventy eight thousand as the thirteenth part of one half ; for he is Omnipotent, and a Million of Gold is no more to him than one Farthing ? Oh, ho, pray tell me who taught you to talk at this rate of the Power and Predestination of God, poor silly People ? Peace, Tush, St, St, St, fall down before his sacred Face, and own the Nothingness of your Nothing.

Upon this, O ye that labour under the Affliction of the Gout, I ground my Hopes firmly believing, that if so it pleases the Divine Goodness, you shall obtain Health ; since you wish and ask for nothing else, at least for the present. Well, stay yet a little longer, with half an Ounce of Patience.

The Genouese do not use, like you, to be satisfied with wishing Health alone, when after they have all the live-long Morning been in a brown study, talk'd, ponder'd, ruminated, and resolv'd in their Counting-Houses, of whom and how they may squeeze the Ready, and who by their Craft must be hook'd in, wheadled, bubbl'd, sharp'd, over-reach'd and chous'd, they go to the Exchange, and greet one another with a *sanita* and *guadagno, Messer ;* Health and Gain to you, Sir. Health alone will not go down with the greedy Curmudgeons, they over and above must wish for Gain, with a Pox to 'em ; ay, and for the fine Crowns, or *scudi di guadagno ;* whence, Heaven be praised, it happens many a time, that the silly Wishers and Woulders are baulk'd and get neither. Now, my Lads, as you hope for good Health, cough once aloud with lungs of Leather ; Take me off three swinging Bumpers ; Prick up your Ears ; and you shall hear me tell Wonders of the noble and good Pantagruel.

THE FOURTH BOOK

CHAPTER I

*How Pantagruel went to Sea, to visit the Oracle of Bacbuc,
alias the Holy Bottle*

IN the Month of June, on Vesta's Holidays, the very numerical
Day on which Brutus conquering Spain, taught its strutting
Dons to truckle under him, and that niggardly Miser Crassus
was routed and knock'd on the head by the Parthians, Pantagruel took his leave of the good Gargantua, his Royal Father.
The old Gentleman, according to the laudable Custom of the
Primitive Christians, devoutly pray'd for the happy Voyage
of his Son and his whole Company, and then they took Shipping
at the Port of Thalassa. Pantagruel had with him Panurge,
Fryar Jhon des Entomeures, alias of the Funnels, Epistemon,
Gymnast, Eusthenes, Rhizotome, Carpalin, *cum multis aliis*,
his ancient Servants and Domestics. Also Xenomanes, the
great Traveller, who had cross'd so many dangerous Roads,

Dikes, Ponds, Seas, and so forth, and was come sometime before, having been sent for by Panurge.

For certain good Causes and Considerations him thereunto moving, he had left with Gargantua, and marked out in his great and universal hydrographical Chart, the Course which they were to steer to visit the Oracle of the Holy Bottle, Bacbuc. The number of Ships was such as I described in the Third Book, convoy'd by a like number of Triremes, Men of War, Gallions and Felucca's well rigg'd, caulk'd, and stor'd with a good quantity of Pantagruelion.

All the Officers, Droggermen, Pilots, Captains, Mates, Boatswains, Midshipmen, Quartermasters, and Sailors, met in the *Thalamege*, Pantagruel's principal Flag-Ship, which had in her Stern a huge large Bottle, half Silver well polish'd, the other half Gold inamell'd with Carnation, whereby it was easy to guess that White and Red were the Colours of the noble Travellers, and that they went for the Word of the Bottle.

On the Stern of the Second was a Lantern like those of the Ancients, industriously made with Diaphanous Stone, implying that they were to pass by Lanternland. The Third Ship had for her Device a fine deep China Ewre. The Fourth a double-handed Jar, much like an ancient Urn. The Fifth a famous Kan made of Sperm of Emerald. The Sixth, a Monk's Mumping-Bottle made of the four Metals together. The Seventh an Ebony Funnel all imboss'd and wrought with Gold after the Tauchic manner. The Eighth, an Ivy Goblet very precious, inlaid with Gold. The Ninth, a Cup of fine Obriz Gold. The Tenth, a Tumbler of aromatic Agaloch (you call it Lignum Aloes) edg'd with Cyprian Gold, after the Azemine make. The Eleventh, a Golden Vine-Tub of Mozaic Work. The Twelfth a Runlet of unpolish'd Gold, covered with a small Vine of large Indian Pearl of Topiarian Work. Insomuch that there was no Man, however in the Dumps, musty, sour-look'd, or melancholic he were, not even excepting that Blubbering Whiner Heraclitus, had he been there, but seeing this noble Convoy of Ships and their Devices, must have been seiz'd with present Gladness of Heart, and smiling at the Conceit, have said, that the Travellers were all honest Topers, true Pitcher-men; and have judged by a most sure Prognostication, that their Voyage both outward and homeward bound, would be performed in Mirth and perfect Health.

In the *Thalamege* where was the general Meeting, Pantagruel made a short but sweet Exhortation, wholly back'd with

Authorities from Scripture upon Navigation; which being ended, with an audible Voice Prayers were said in the presence and hearing of all the Burghers of Thalassa, who had flock'd to the Mole to see them take Shipping. After the Prayers, was melodiously sung a Psalm of the Holy King David, which begins, When Israel went out of Ægypt; and that being ended, Tables were plac'd upon Deck, and a Feast speedily serv'd up. The Thalassians who had also born a Chorus in the Psalm, caused store of Belly-timber to be brought out of their Houses. All drank to them, they drank to all; which was the cause that none of the whole Company gave up what they had eaten, nor were sea-sick with a Pain at the Head and Stomach, which Inconveniency they could not so easily have prevented by drinking, for some time before, Salt-Water, either alone or mixt with Wine, using Quinces, Citron-peel, Juice of Pomgranats, sourish Sweet-meats, fasting a long time, covering their Stomachs with Paper, or following such other idle Remedies as foolish Physicians prescribe to those that go to Sea.

Having often renewed their Tiplings, each Mother's Son retir'd on board his own Ship, and set Sail all so fast with a merry Gale at South-East, to which Point of the Compass the chief Pilot, James Brayer by name, had shap'd his Course, and fixt all things accordingly. For seeing that the Oracle of the Holy Bottle lay near Catay in the upper India, his Advice, and that of Xenomanes also, was, not to steer the Course which the Portuguese use, while sailing thro' the Torrid Zone, and Cape Bona Speranza at the South Point of Africk beyond the Equinoctial Line, and losing sight of the Northern Pole their Guide, they make a prodigious long Voyage; but rather to keep as near the Parallel of the said India as possible, and to tack to the westward of the said Pole, so that winding under the North, they might find themselves in the Latitude of the Port of Olone, without coming nearer it, for fear of being shut up in the frozen Sea; whereas following this Canonical Turn by the said Parallel, they must have that on the Right to the Eastward, which at their departure was on their Left.

This prov'd a much shorter Cut; for without Shipwreck, Danger, or loss of Men, with uninterrupted good Weather, except one day near the Island of the Macreons, they perform'd in less than four Months the Voyage of Upper India, which the Portuguese, with a thousand Inconveniences and innumerable Dangers, can hardly complete in three Years. And it is my

Opinion, with Submission to better Judgments, that this Course was perhaps steer'd by those Indians who sail'd to Germany, and were honourably receiv'd by the King of the Swedes, while Quintus Metellus Celer was Proconsul of the Gauls, as Corn. Nepos, Pomponius Mela, and Pliny after them, tell us.

CHAPTER II

How Pantagruel bought many Rarities in the Island of Medamothy

THAT Day and the two following, they neither discovered Land nor any thing new ; for they had formerly sailed that way ; but on the fourth they made an Island call'd Medamothy, of a fine and delightful Prospect, by reason of the vast number of Light-Houses and high Marble Towers in its Circuit, which is not less than that of Canada. Pantagruel enquiring who govern'd there, heard that it was King Philophanes, absent at that time upon account of the Marriage of his Brother Philo-theamon with the Infanta of the Kingdom of Engys.

Hearing this, he went ashoar in the Harbour, and while every Ship's Crew water'd, pass'd his time in viewing divers Animals, Fishes, Birds, and other exotic and foreign Merchandises which were along the Walks of the Mole, and in the Markets of the Port. For it was the third Day of the great and famous Fair of the place, to which the chief Merchants of Africa and Asia resorted. Out of these Fryar Jhon bought him two rare Pictures, in one of which, the Face of a Man that brings in an Appeal, was drawn to the Life, and in the other a Servant that wants a Master, with every needful particular Action, Countenance, Looks, Gate, Feature, and Deportment ; being an Original, by Master Charles Charmois, principal Painter to King Megistus ; and he paid for them in the Court fashion, with Congé and Grimace. Panurge bought a large Picture, copied and done from the Needle-work formerly wrought by Philomela, shewing to her Sister Progne how her Brother-in-law Tereus had by force hansell'd her Copy-hold, and then cut out her Tongue, that she might not (as Women will) tell Tales. I vow and swear by the Handle of my Paper Lantern, that it was a gallant, a mirific, nay a most admirable

Piece. Nor do you think, I pray you, that in it was the Picture of a Man playing the Beast with two Backs with a Female ; this had been too silly and gross ; no, no ; 'twas another-guise thing, and much plainer. You may, if you please, see it at Theleme, on the left hand as you go into the high Gallery. Epistemon bought another wherein were painted to the Life, the Idea's of Plato, and the Atoms of Epicurus Rhizotome purchased another, wherein Echo was drawn to the Life. Pantagruel caused to be bought by Gymnast, the Life and Deeds of Achilles in Seventy-eight Pieces of Tapestry four fathom long, and three fathom broad, all of Phrygian Silk imboss'd with Gold and Silver ; the Work beginning at the Nuptials of Peleus and Thetis, continuing to the Birth of Achilles ; his Youth describ'd by Statius Papinius ; his warlike Atchievements celebrated by Homer ; his Death and Exequies written by Ovid and Quintus Calaber ; and ending at the appearance of his Ghost, and Polyxene's Sacrifice rehearsed by Euripides.

He also caus'd to be bought three fine young Unicorns ; one of them a Male of a Chestnut colour, and two grey dappled Females ; also a Tarand whom he bought of a Scythian of the Geloni's Country.

A Tarand is an Animal as big as a Bullock, having a Head like a Stag, or a little bigger, two stately Horns with large Branches, cloven Feet, Hair long like that of a furr'd Muscovite, I mean a Bear ; and a Skin almost as hard as Steel Armor. The Scythian said that there are but few Tarands to be found in Scythia, because it varieth its Colour according to the diversity of the Places where it grazes and abides, and repre-sents the Colour of the Grass, Plants, Trees, Shrubs, Flowers, Meadows, Rocks, and generally of all things near which it comes. It hath this common with the Sea-Pulp or Polypus, with the Thoes, with the Wolves of India, and with the Chamæ-leon, which is a kind of Lizard so wonderful, that Democritus hath written a whole Book of its Figure, and Anatomy, as also of its Virtue and Propriety in Magic. This I can affirm, that I have seen it change its Colour not only at the approach of things that have a Colour, but by its own voluntary Impulse, according to its Fear or other Affections ; as for example, upon a green Carpet, I have seen it certainly become green ; but having remain'd there some time, it turned yellow, blue, tann'd, and purple in course, in the same manner as you see a Turkey-cock's Comb change colour according to its Passions.

But what we found most surprizing in this Tarand, is, that not only its Face and Skin, but also its Hair could take whatever Colour was about it. Near Panurge with his Kersy Coat, its Hair used to turn grey ; near Pantagruel with his Scarlet Mantle, its Hair and Skin grew red ; near the Pilot drest after the fashion of the Isiacs of Anubis in Ægypt, its Hair seem'd all white ; which two Colours the Chamælion cann't borrow. When the Creature was free from any Fear or Affection, the Colour of its Hair was just such as you see that of the Asses of Meung.

CHAPTER III

How Pantagruel receiv'd a Letter from his Father Gargantua, and of the strange way to have speedy News from far distant places

WHILE Pantagruel was taken up with the purchase of those foreign Animals, the noise of ten Guns and Culverins, together with a loud and joyful Cheer of all the Fleet was heard from the Mole. Pantagruel look'd towards the Haven, and perceiv'd that this was occasion'd by the arrival of one of his Father Gargantua's Celoces, or Advice-Boat, named the *Chelidonia*, because on the Stern of it was carv'd in Corinthian Brass a Sea-Lark, which is a Fish as large as a Dare-Fish of Loire, all Flesh and no Bone, with cartilaginous Wings (like a Bat's) very long and broad, by the means of which, I have seen them fly about three Fathom above Water, about a Bow-shot. At Marseilles 'tis call'd Lendole. And indeed that Ship was as light as a Lark, so that it seem'd rather to fly on the Sea than to sail. Malicorn, Gargantua's Esq : Carver, was come in her, being sent expresly by his Master to have an account of his Son's Health and Circumstances, and to bring him Credentials. When Malicorn had saluted Pantagruel, before the Prince opened the Letters, the first thing he said to him was, Have you here the Gozal, the heavenly Messenger ? Yes, Sir, said he, here it is swadled up in this Basket. It was a grey Pigeon taken out of Gargantua's Dove-house, whose Young-ones were just hatch'd when the Advice-Boat was going off.

If any ill fortune had befallen Pantagruel, he would have fasten'd some black Ribbon to its Feet ; but because all things had succeeded happily hitherto, having caus'd it to be undress'd, he ty'd to its Feet a white Ribbon, and without any further delay, let it loose. The Pigeon presently flew away cutting the Air with an incredible Speed, as you know that there is no Flight like a Pigeons, especially when it hath Eggs or Young-ones, thro' the extreme Care which Nature hath fix'd in it to relieve and be with its Young ; insomuch that in less than two hours it compass'd in the Air, the long Tract which the Advice-Boat with all her Diligence, with Oars and Sails, and a fair Wind, had gone thro' in no less than three Days and three Nights, and was seen (as it went into the Dove-house) in its Nest. Whereupon Gargantua hearing that it had the white Ribbon on, was joyful and secure of his Son's welfare. This was the Custom of the noble Gargantua and Pantagruel, when they would have speedy News of something of great concern, as the Event of some Battle either by Sea or Land ; the surrendring or holding out of some strong Place ; the determination of some Difference of moment ; the safe or unhappy Delivery of some Queen or great Lady ; the Death or Recovery of their sick Friends or Allies, and so forth. They used to take the Gozal, and had it carried from one to another by the Post, to the Places whence they desired to have News. The Gozal bearing either a black or white Ribbon, according to the Occurrences and Accidents, us'd to remove their Doubts at its Return, making in the space of one Hour, more way thro' the Air, than thirty Post-Boys could have done in one natural Day. May not this be said to redeem and gain Time with a vengeance, think you ? For the like Service therefore, you may believe as a most true thing, that in the Dove-houses of their Farms, there were to be found all the Year long, store of Pigeons hatching Eggs or rearing their Young. Which may be easily done in Aviaries and Voleries, by the help of Saltpeter and the sacred Herb Vervain.

HE ALSO CAUS'D TO BE BOUGHT THREE FINE YOUNG UNICORNS

III

The Gozal being let fly, Pantagruel perus'd his Father Gargantua's Letter, the Contents of which were as followeth.

My Dearest Son,—The Affection that naturally a Father bears a beloved Son, is so much increased in me, by reflecting on the particular Gifts which by the Divine Goodness have been heaped on thee, that since thy departure, it hath often banished all other Thoughts out of my Mind ; leaving my Heart wholly possess'd with Fear, lest some Misfortune has attended thy Voyage : for thou knowest that Fear was ever the Attendant of true and sincere Love. Now because (as Hesiod saith) A good beginning of any thing is the half of it ; or, well begun's half done, according to the old Saying ; to free my Mind from this Anxiety, I have expressly dispatch'd Malicorn, that he may give me a true account of thy Health at the beginning of thy Voyage. For if it be good and such as I wish it, I shall easily foresee the rest.

I have met with some diverting Books, which the Bearer will deliver thee, thou mayst read them when thou wantest to unbend and ease thy Mind from thy better Studies : He will also give thee at large the News at Court. The Peace of the Lord be with thee. Remember me to Panurge, Fryar Jhon, Epistemon, Xenomanes, Gymnast, and thy other principal Domestics. Dated at our Paternal Seat this 13th day of June. Thy Father and Friend, Gargantua.

CHAPTER IV

How Pantagruel writ to his Father Gargantua, and sent him several curiosities

PANTAGRUEL having perused the Letter, had a long Conference with the Esquire Malicorn, insomuch that Panurge at last interrupting them, ask'd him, Pray Sir, when do you design to drink ? When shall we drink ? When shall the worshipful Esquire drink ? What a Devil have you not talk'd long enough to drink ? 'Tis a good Motion, answer'd Pantagruel ; go, get us something ready at the next Inn ; I think 'tis the Centaur. In the mean time he writ to Gargantua as followeth, to be sent by the aforesaid Esquire.

Most Gracious Father,—As our Senses and animal Faculties are more discompos'd at the News of Events unexpected, tho' desir'd (even to an immediate dissolution of the Soul from the Body) than if those Accidents had been foreseen ; so the coming of Malicorn hath much surprized and disordered me. For I had no hopes to see any of your Servants, or to hear from you, before I had finished our Voyage, and contented my self with the dear Remembrance of your August Majesty, deeply impress'd in the hindmost Ventricle of my Brain, often representing you to my Mind.

But since you have made me happy beyond expectation, by the perusal of your gracious Letter, and the Faith I have in your Esquire, hath reviv'd my Spirits by the News of your welfare ; I am as it were compell'd to do what formerly I did freely, that is, first to praise the blessed Redeemer, who by his Divine Goodness preserves you in this long enjoyment of perfect Health ; then to return you eternal Thanks for the fervent Affection which you have for me your most humble Son and unprofitable Servant.

Formerly a Roman, named Furnius, said to Augustus, who had received his Father into Favour, and Pardoned him after he had sided with Anthony, That by that Action the Emperor had reduc'd him to this Extremity, That for want of Power to be grateful, both while he liv'd and after it, he should be oblig'd to be tax'd with Ingratitude. So I may say, That the excess of your fatherly Affection, drives me into such a streight, that I shall be forced to live and die ungrateful ; unless that Crime be redress'd by the Sentence of the Stoics, who say, That there are three parts in a Benefit, the one of the Giver, the other of the Receiver, the third of the Remunerator ; and that the Receiver rewards the Giver when he freely receives the Benefit, and always remembers it ; as on the contrary, That Man is most ungrateful who despises and forgets a Benefit. Therefore being overwhelmed with infinite Favours, all proceeding from your extreme Goodness, and on the other side wholly uncapable of making the smallest Return, I hope at least to free my self from the imputation of Ingratitude, since they can never be blotted out of my mind ; and my Tongue shall never cease to own, that to thank you as I ought transcends my Capacity.

As for us, I have this assurance in the Lord's Mercy and Help, that the end of our Voyage will be answerable to its beginning, and so it will be entirely perform'd in Health and

Mirth. I will not fail to set down in a Journal a full account of our Navigation, that at our Return you may have an exact Relation of the whole.

I have found here a Scythian Tarand, an Animal strange and wonderful for the Variations of Colour on its Skin and Hair, according to the distinction of neighbouring Things, it is as tractable and easily kept as a Lamb ; be pleased to accept of it.

I also send you three young Unicorns, which are the tamest of Creatures.

I have confer'd with the Esquire, and taught him how they must be fed ; these cannot graze on the Ground, by reason of the long Horn on their Forehead, but are forced to brouze on Fruit-trees, or on proper Racks, or to be fed by Hand with Herbs, Sheaves, Apples, Pears, Barly, Rye, and other Roots being plac'd before them.

I am amazed that ancient Writers should report them to be so wild, furious, and dangerous, and never seen alive : Far from it, you will find that they are the mildest Things in the World, provided they are not maliciously offended. Likewise, I send you the Life and Deeds of Achilles in curious Tapestry ; assuring you that whatever Rarities of Animals, Plants, Birds, or precious Stones, and others, I shall be able to find and purchase in our Travels, shall be brought to you, God willing, whom I beseech by his blessed Grace, to preserve you. From Medamothy, this 16th of June. Panurge, Fryar Jhon, Epistemon, Xenomanes, Gymnast, Eusthenes, Rhizotome, and Carpalin, having most humbly kissed your Hand, return your Salute a thousand times. Your most dutiful Son and Servant,

Pantagruel.

While Pantagruel was writing this Letter, Malicorn was made welcome by all with a thousand goodly Good-morrows and How-d'ye's ; they clung about him so, that I cannot tell you how much they made of him, how many Humble Services, how many from my Love and to my Love were sent with him. Pantagruel having writ his Letters, sat down at Table with him, and afterwards presented him with a large Chain of Gold weighing eight hundred Crowns ; between whose septenary Links, some large Diamonds, Rubies, Emeralds, Turky-Stones, and Unions were alternatively set in. To each of his Bark's Crew, he order'd to be given five hundred Crowns. To Gargantua his Father, he sent the Tarand cover'd with a Cloth of Gold, brocaded with Satin ; and the Tapestry containing the

Life and Deeds of Achilles ; with the three Unicorns in friz'd
Cloth of Gold Trappings. And so they left Medamothy.
Malicorn to return to Gargantua ; Pantagruel to proceed in his
Voyage, during which, Epistemon read to him the Books which
the Esquire had brought : And because he found them jovial
and pleasant, I shall give you an account of them, if you
earnestly desire it.

CHAPTER V

*How Pantagruel met a Ship with Passengers returning
from Lantern-Land*

ON the fifth Day we began already to wind by little and little
about the Pole, going still farther from the Equinoctial Line,
we discovered a Merchant-man to the windward of us. The
Joy for this was not small on both sides, we in hopes to hear
News from Sea, and those in the Merchant-man from Land.
So we bore upon 'em, and coming up with them, we hal'd them,
and finding them to be Frenchmen of Xaintonge, back'd our
Sails and lay by to talk to them. Pantagruel heard that they
came from Lantern-Land, which added to his Joy, and that of
the whole Fleet. We enquir'd about the state of that Country,
and the way of living of the Lanterns ; and were told, that
about the latter end of the following July, was the time pre-
fix'd for the meeting of the general Chapter of the Lanterns ;
and that if we arrived there at that time, as we might easily,
we should see a handsom, honourable, and jolly Company of
Lanterns ; and that great preparations were making, as if they
intended to Lanternise there to the purpose. We were told

also, That if we touch'd at the great Kingdom of Gebarin, we should be honourably received and treated by the Sovereign of that Country, King Ohabé, who, as well as all his Subjects, speaks Touraine French.

While we were listning to these News, Panurge fell out with one Dingdong a Drover or Sheep-merchant of Taillebourg. The occasion of the Fray was thus.

This same Dingdong seeing Panurge without a Codpiece, with his Spectacles fastened to his Cap, said to one of his Comrades, Prithee look, is not there here a fine Medal of a Cuckold ? Panurge by reason of his Spectacles, as you may well think, heard more plainly by half with his Ears than usually ; which caused him (hearing this) to say to the saucy Dealer in Mutton, in a kind of Pet,

How the Devil should I be one of the hornify'd Fraternity, since I am not yet a Brother of the Marriage-noose, as thou art, as I guess by thy ill-favour'd Phyz ?

Yea verily, quoth the Grazier, I am married, and would not be otherwise for all the pairs of Spectacles in Europe ; nay, not for all the magnifying Gimcracks in Africa ; for I have got me the cleverest, prettiest, handsomest, properest, neatest, tightest, honestest, and soberest piece of Woman's-Flesh for my Wife, that is in all the whole Country of Xaintonge, I'll say that for her, and a Fart for all the rest. I bring her home a fine and eleven Inch long Branch of red Coral, for her Christmas-Box ; what hast thou to do with it ? What's that to thee ? Who art thou ? Whence comest thou, O dark Lantern of Antichrist ? Answer if thou art of God ? I ask thee, by the way of Question, said Panurge to him very seriously, if with the consent and countenance of all the Elements, I had Gingumbob'd, Codpiec'd, and Thumpthumpriggledtickledtwidl'd thy so clever, so pretty, so handsom, so proper, so neat, so tight, so honest, and so Sober Female Importance, insomuch that the stiff Deity that has no forecast, Priapus, (who dwells here at Liberty, all subjection of fastned Codpieces or Bolts, Bars, and Locks abdicated) remain'd sticking in her natural Christmas-box in such a lamentable manner, that it were never to come out, but eternally should stick there, unless thou didst pull it out with thy Teeth ; what wouldst thou do ? Wouldst thou everlastingly leave it there, or wouldst thou pluck it out with thy Grinders ? Answer me, O thou Ram of Mahomet, since thou art one of the Devil's Gang. I would, reply'd the Sheepmonger, take thee such a woundy Cut on this Spectacle-bearing Lug of thine, with my trusty Bilbo, as would smite thee dead as a Herring. Thus having taken Pepper in the Nose, he was lugging out Sword; but alas, curs'd Cows have short Horns, it stuck in the Scabbard; as you know that at Sea, cold Iron will easily take rust, by reason of the excessive and nitrous Moistness. Panurge so smitten with Terror, that his Heart sunk down to his Midriff, scour'd off to Pantagruel for help: But Fryar Jhon laid hand on his slashing Scymiter that was new ground, and would certainly have dispatch'd Dingdong to rights, had not the Skipper and some of his Passengers beseech'd Pantagruel not to suffer such an Outrage to be committed on board his Ship. So the matter was made up, and Panurge and his Antagonist shak'd Fists, and drank in course to one another, in token of a perfect Reconciliation.

CHAPTER VI

How the Fray being over, Panurge cheapened one of Dingdong's Sheep

THIS Quarrel being hush'd, Panurge tipp'd the wink upon Epistemon and Fryar Jhon, and taking them aside; Stand at some distance out of the way, said he, and take your share of the following Scene of Mirth; you shall have rare Sport anon, if my Cake ben't Dough, and my Plot do but take. Then addressing himself to the Drover, he took off to him a Bumper of good Lantern Wine. The other pledg'd him briskly and courteously. This done, Panurge earnestly entreated him to sell him one of his Sheep: But the other answered him, Is it come to that, Friend and Neighbour, would you put Tricks upon Travellers? Alas, how finely you love to play upon poor Folk! Nay, you seem a rare Chapman, that's the truth on't. Oh what a mighty Sheep-Merchant you are! In good faith you look liker one of the Diving Trade than a Buyer of Sheep. Adzookers, what a Blessing it would be to have one's Purse well lin'd with Chink near your Worship at a Tripe-House when it begins to thaw! Humph, Humph, did not we know you well, you might serve one a slippery Trick! Pray do but see, good People, what a mighty Conjurer the Fellow would be reckon'd. Patience, said Panurge; but, waving that, be so kind as to sell me one of your Sheep, come, how much? What do you mean, Master of mine, answered the other? They are long Wool Sheep, from these did Jason take his Golden Fleece. The Gold of the House of Burgundy was drawn from them. Zwoons, Man, they are Oriental Sheep, Topping Sheep, Fatted Sheep, Sheep of Quality. Be it so, said Panurge, but sell me one of them, I beseech you, and that for a cause, paying you ready Money upon the Nail, in good and lawful Occidental Currant Cash; wilt say how much? Friend, Neighbour, answered the Seller of Mutton, hark'e me a little, on the other Ear.

PANURGE. On which side you please; I hear you.

DINGDONG. You are a going to Lantern-Land, they say.

PANURGE. Yea verily.

DING. To see Fashions?

PANURGE. Even so.

DING. And be merry?

PANURGE. And be Merry.

DING. Your Name is, as I take it, Robin Mutton?

PANURGE. As you please for that, sweet Sir.

DING. Nay, without Offence.

PANURGE. So I would have it.

DING. You are, as I take it, the King's Jester, aren't you?

PANURGE. Ay, ay, any thing.

DING. Give me your Hand,—Humph, Humph, you go to see Fashions, you are the King's Jester, your Name is Robin Mutton! Do you see this same Ram? His Name too is Robin. Here Robin, Robin, Robin: Baea, Baea, Baea; Hath he not a rare Voice?

PANURGE. Ay marry has he, a very fine and harmonious Voice.

DING. Well, this Bargain shall be made between you and me, Friend, and Neighbour, we will get a pair of Scales, then you Robin Mutton shall be put into one of them, and Tup Robin into the other. Now I'll hold you a Peck of Busch Oysters, that in Weight, Value, and Price, he shall outdo you, and you shall be found light in the very numerical manner, as when you shall be hang'd and suspended.

Patience, said Panurge, but you would do much for me, and your whole Posterity, if you would Chaffer with me for him, or some other of his Inferiors. I beg it of you; good your Worship, be so kind. Hark 'e, Friend of mine, answered the other, with the Fleece of these your fine Roan Cloth is to be made, your Lemster superfine Wooll is mine Arse to 't; meer Flock in comparison : of their Skin the best Cordivant will be made, which shall be sold for Turky and Montelimart, or for Spanish Leather at least. Of the Guts shall be made Fiddle and Harp Strings, that will sell as dear as if they came from Munican or Aquileia. What do you think on 't, hah ? If you please, sell me one of them, said Panurge, and I am yours for ever. Look, here's ready Cash. What's the Price ? This he said, exhibiting his Purse stuffed with new Henricuses.

CHAPTER VII

Which if you read, you'll find how Panurge bargain'd with Dingdong

NEIGHBOUR, my Friend, answer'd Dingdong, they are Meat for None but Kings and Princes; their Flesh is so delicate, so savory, and so dainty, that one would swear, it melted in the Mouth. I bring them out of a Country where the very Hogs, God be with us, live on nothing but Mirabolans. The Sows in their Styes when they lie in, (saving the honour of this good Company) are fed only with Orange Flowers. But, said Panurge, drive a Bargain with me for one of them, and I will pay you for't like a King, upon the honest Word of a true Trojan : come come, what do you ask ? Not so fast, Robin, answer'd the Trader, these Sheep are lineally descended from the very Family of the Ram that wafted Phrixus and Helle over the Sea, since call'd the Hellespont. A Pox on't, said Panurge, you are *Clericus vel Addiscens !* *Ita* is a Cabbage, and *Verè* a Leek, answered the Merchant. But rr, rrr, rrrr, rrrrr, hoh Robin, rr, rrrrrrr, you don't understand that Gibberish, do you ? Now I think on't, over all the Fields, where they piss, Corn grows as fast as if the Lord had piss'd there ; they need neither be till'd, nor dung'd. Besides, Man, your Chymists extract the best Saltpetre in the World out of their Urine : nay, with their very Dung (with reverence be it spoken) the Doctors in our Country make Pills that cure seventy eight Kinds of Diseases ; the least of which is the Evil of St. Eutropius of Xaintes, from which good Lord deliver us ! Now what do you think on't, Neighbour, my Friend ? The truth is, they cost me Money, that they do ! Cost what they will, cry'd Panurge, trade with me for one of them, paying you well. Our Friend, quoth the quack-like Sheep-man, do but mind the Wonders of Nature that are found in those Animals, even in a Member which one would think were of no use. Take me but these Horns, and bray them a little with an Iron Pestle, or with an Andiron, which you please, 'tis all one to me; then bury them where-ever you will, provided it be where the Sun may shine, and water them frequently; in a few Months I'll engage you will have the best Asparagus in the World, not even excepting those of Ravenna. Now come and tell me whether the Horns of you other Knights of the Bulls Feather, have such a Virtue and wonderful Propriety ?

Patience, said Panurge : I don't know whether you be a Scholar or no, pursued Dingdong : I have seen a World of Scholars, I say great Scholars that were Cuckolds, I'll assure you. But hark you me, if you were a Scholar, you should know that in the most inferiour Members of those Animals (which are the Feet), there is a Bone (which is the Heel) the Astragalus, if you will have it so, wherewith, and with that of no other Creature breathing, except the Indian Ass, and the Dorcades of Libya, they us'd in old Times to play at the Royal Game of Dice, whereat Augustus the Emperor won above fifty thousand Crowns one Evening. Now such Cuckolds as you will be hang'd e're you get half so much as it. Patience, said Panurge, but let us dispatch. And when, my Friend and Neighbour, continu'd the canting Sheep-seller, shall I have duly prais'd the inward Members, the Shoulders, the Legs, the Knuckles, the Neck, the Breast, the Liver, the Spleen, the Tripes, the Kidneys, the Bladder, wherewith they make Foot-balls, the Ribs, which serve in Pigmy-land to make little Cross-bows to pelt the Cranes with Cherry-stones ; the Head which with a little Brimstone serves to make a miraculous Decoction to loosen and ease the Belly of Costive Dogs. A Turd on 't, said the Skipper to his preaching Passenger, what a fidle fadle have we here ? There is too long a Lecture by half, sell him one if thou wilt ; if thou won't, don't let the Man lose more time. I hate a gibble gabble and a rimble ramble Talk, I am for a Man of Brevity. I will for your sake, reply'd the Holder-forth : but then he shall give me three Livres French Money for each, and pick and chuse. 'Tis a woundy Price, cry'd Panurge, in our Country I could have five, nay six for the Money; see that you do not overreach me, Master. You are not the first Man whom I have known, to have fallen, even sometime to the endangering, if not breaking of his own Neck, for endeavouring to rise all at once. A Murrain seize thee for a blockheaded Booby, cry'd the angry Seller of Sheep; by the worthy Vow of our Lady of Charroux: the worst in this Flock is four times better than those which the Coraxians in Tuitania, a Country of Spain, us'd to sell for a Gold Talent each; and how much do'st thou think, thou Hyberinan Fool, that a Talent of Gold was worth? Sweet Sir, you fall into a Passion I see, return'd Panurge: Well, hold, here is your Money. Panurge having paid his Money, chose him out of all the Flock a fine topping Ram, and as he was hawling it along crying out and bleating, all the rest hearing and bleating in Consort star'd, to see whither their Brother-Ram should be carried. In the mean while the Drover was saying to his Shepherds, Ah! How well the Knave could chuse him out a Ram, the Whoreson has Skill in Cattle; on my honest Word I reserv'd that very piece of Flesh for the Lord of Cancale, well knowing his Disposition; for the good Man naturally is overjoy'd when he holds a good siz'd handsom Shoulder of Mutton, instead of a left-handed Racket in one Hand, with a good sharp Carver in the other; got wot how he belabours himself then.

CHAPTER VIII

How Panurge caus'd Dingdong and his Sheep to be drowned in the Sea

On a sudden, you would wonder how the thing was so soon done; for my part I can't tell you, for I had not leisure to mind it; our Friend Panurge without any further tittle tattle, throws you his Ram over-board into the middle of the Sea bleating and making a sad Noise. Upon this all the other Sheep in the Ship crying and bleating in the same Tone made all the haste they could to leap nimbly into the Sea one after another, and great was the Throng who should leap in first after their Leader. It was impossible to hinder them; for you know that it is in the Nature of Sheep always to follow the first, wheresoever it goes; which makes Aristotle, lib. 9. *de Hist. Animal.* mark them for the most silly and foolish Animals in the World. Dingdong at his Wit's end, and stark staring mad like a Man who saw his Sheep destroy and drown themselves before his Face, strove to hinder and keep them back with might and main, but all in vain; they all, one after t' other, frisk'd and jump'd into the Sea, and were lost : at last he laid hold on a huge sturdy one by the Fleece upon the Deck of the Ship, hoping to keep it back, and so to save that and the rest; but the Ram was so strong that it proved too hard for him, and carried its Master into the Herring-Pond, in spight of his Teeth ; where 'tis supposed he drank somewhat more than his fill : so that he was drowned, in the same manner, as one-eyed Polyphemus's Sheep carried out of the Den Ulysses and his Companions : The like happen'd to the Shepherds and all their Gang, some laying hold on their beloved Tup, this by the Horns, t' other by the Legs, a third by the Rump, and others by the Fleece ; till in fine they were all of them forc'd to Sea, and drowned like so many Rats. Panurge on the Gunnel of the Ship with an Oar in his Hand, not to help them, you may swear, but to keep them from swimming to the Ship, and saving themselves from drowning, preach'd and canted to them all the while like any little Fryar Maillard, or another Fryar John Burgess, laying before them Rhetorical common Places concerning the Miseries of this Life, and the Blessings and Felicity of the next ; assuring them that the Dead were much happier than the Living in this Vale of Misery, and promising to erect a stately Cenotaphe and Honorary Tomb to every one of them on the highest summit of Mount Cenis at his return from Lantern-Land ; wishing them nevertheless, in case they were not yet dispos'd to shake Hands with this Life, and did not like their salt Liquor, they might have the good Luck to meet with some kind Whale which might set them ashoar safe and sound, on some bless'd Land of Gotham after a famous Example.

The Ship being clear'd of Dingdong and his Tups : Is there ever another sheepish Soul left lurking on board, cried Panurge ? Where are those of Toby Lamb, and Robin Ram, that sleep whilst the rest are a feeding ? Faith, I can't tell my self. This was an old Coaster's Trick : What think'st thou of it, Fryar Jhon, hah ? Rarely perform'd, answer'd Fryar Jhon, only methinks that as formerly in War on the Day of Battel, a double Pay was commonly promis'd the Soldiers for that Day ; for if they overcame, there was enough to pay them ;

and if they lost, it would have been shameful for them to demand it, as the cowardly Foresters did after the Battle of Cerizoles : Likewise, my Friend, you ought not to have paid your Man, and the Money had been sav'd. A Fart for the Money, said Panurge, have I not had above fifty thousand Pounds worth of Sport ? Come now, let's be gone, the Wind is fair, hark you me, my Friend Jhon, never did Man do me a good Turn but I return'd or at least acknowledg'd it : No, I scorn to be ungrateful, I never was, nor ever will be : Never did Man do me an ill one without ruing the Day that he did it, either in this World or the next. I am not yet so much of a Fool neither. Thou damn'st thyself like any old Devil, quoth Fryar Jhon. It is written *Mihi vindictam*, etc., matter of Breviary, Mark ye me ; that's holy Stuff.

CHAPTER IX

How Pantagruel arrived at the Island of Ennasin, and of
the strange ways of being akin in that Country

WE had still the Wind at South South West, and had been a whole Day without making Land. On the third Day, at the Flyes up-rising, which, you know, is some two or three Hours after the Sun's, we got sight of a Triangular Island, very much like Sicily for its Form and Situation. It was called the Island of Alliances.

The People there are much like your Carrot-pated Poitevins, save only that all of them, Men, Women, and Children, have their Noses shap'd like an Ace of Clubs. For that reason the ancient Name of the Country was Ennasin. They were all akin, as the Mayor of the Place told us, at least they boasted so.

You People of the other World, esteem it a wonderful thing, that, out of the Family of the Fabii at Rome, on a certain Day, which was the 13th of February, at a certain Gate, which was the Porta Carmentalis, since nam'd Scelerata, formerly situated at the foot of the Capitol, between the Tarpeian Rocks and the Tyber, march'd out against the Veientes of Etruria, three hundred and six Men bearing Arms, all related to each other, with five thousand other Soldiers, every one of them their Vassals, who were all slain near the River Cremera, that comes out of the Lake of Beccano.   Now from this same Country of Ennasin, in case of need, above three hundred thousand all Relations, and of one Family, might march out.   Their degrees of Consanguinity and Alliance are very strange, for being thus akin and allied to one another, we found that none was either Father or Mother, Brother or Sister, Uncle or Aunt, Nephew or Neece, Son-in-Law or Daughter-in-Law, God-Father or God-Mother to the other, unless truly, a tall flat-nos'd old Fellow, who, as I perceiv'd, call'd a little shitten-ars'd Girl of three or four Years old, Father, and the Child call'd him Daughter.

Their distinction of degrees of Kindred was thus ; a Man us'd to call a Woman my Lean Bit ; the Woman call'd him my Porpus.   Those, said Fryar Jhon, must needs stink damnably of Fish, when they have rubb'd their Bacon one with t' other. One smiling on a young bucksom Baggage, said, Good morrow, dear Curry-Comb : she to return him his Civility, said, The like to you my Steed.   Hah ! hah ! hah ! said Panurge, that 's pretty well i' faith, for indeed it stands her in good stead to Curry-comb this Steed.   Another greeted his Buttock with a Farewel my Case : she reply'd, Adieu Tryal.   By St. Winifred's Placket, cry'd Gymnast, this Case has been often try'd. Another ask'd a she Friend of his, How is 't, Hatchet ? she answer'd him, At your service, dear Helve.   Odds Belly, saith Carpalin, this Helve and this Hatchet are well match'd.   As we went on, I saw one who, calling his she Relation, styl'd her my Crum, and she call'd him my Crust.

Quoth one to a brisk, plump, juicy Female, I am glad to see you, dear Tap : so am I to find you so merry, sweet Spiggot, reply'd she.   One call'd a Wench his Shovel, she call'd him her Peal.   One nam'd his, my Slipper, and she him, my Foot. Another my Boot, she my Shasoon.

In the same degree of Kindred, one call'd his, my Butter, she call'd him, my Eggs ; and they were akin just like a Dish of Butter'd Eggs.   I heard one call his, my Tripe, and she him, my Faggot : Now I could not for the Heart's Blood of me pick out or discover what Parentage, Alliance, Affinity, or Consanguinity was between them, with reference to our Custom,

HOW 'ST MY TOP?

125

only they told us that she was Faggot's Tripe; (*Tripe de Faggot* means the smallest Sticks in a Faggot.) Another complementing his Convenient, said, Yours, my Shell; she reply'd, I was yours before, sweet Oyster: I reckon, said Carpalin, she hath gutted his Oyster. Another long-shank'd ugly Rogue, mounted upon a pair of high-heel'd wooden Slippers, meeting a strapping, fusty-squabb'd Dowdy, says to her, how 'st my Top? She was short upon him, and arrogantly reply'd, never the better for you, my Whip: By St. Anthony's Hog, said Xenomanes, I believe so, for how can this Whip be sufficient to lash this Top.

A College-Professor well provided with Cod, and powdered and prink'd up, having a while discoursed with a great Lady, taking his leave with these Words, Thank you Sweet Meat; she cry'd There needs no Thanks, Sour Sauce. Saith Pantagruel, this is not altogether incongruous, for sweet Meat must have sour Sauce. A wooden Loggerhead said to a young Wench, 'Tis long since I saw you Bag; all the better, cry'd she, Pipe: Set 'em together, said Panurge, then blow in their Arses, 'twill be a Bag-pipe. We saw after that a diminutive hump-back'd Gallant, pretty near us, taking leave of a She-relation of his, thus, Fare thee well, Friend Hole; she repartee'd, Save thee, Friend Peg. Quoth Fryar Jhon, what could they say more, were he all Peg, and she all Hole: But now would I give something to know if every cranny of the Hole, can be stopp'd up with that same Peg.

A Baudy Batchelor talking with an old Trout, was saying, Remember it, Rusty Gun. I won't fail, said she, Scourer. Do you reckon these two to be akin, said Pantagruel to the Mayor? I rather take them to be Foes; in our Country a Woman would take this as a mortal Affront. Good people of t' other World, reply'd the Mayor, you have few such and so near Relations as this Gun and Scourer are to one another; for they both came out of one Shop. What, was the Shop their Mother, quoth Panurge? What Mother, said the Mayor, does the Man mean? That must be some of your World's Affinity: we have here neither Father nor Mother: Your little paltry Fellows that live on t' other side the Water, poor Rogues, booted with Wisps of Hay, may indeed have such, but we scorn it. The good Pantagruel stood gazing and listning, but at these words he had like to have lost all Patience; ὡς καὶ νῦν ὁ ἑρμηνευτὴς Π. Μ.

Having very exactly viewed the Situation of the Island,

and the way of living of the Ennased Nation, we went to take a Cup of the Creature at a Tavern where there happen'd to be a Wedding after the manner of the Country, bating that shocking custom there was special good Chear.

While we were there, a pleasant Match was struck up betwixt a Female call'd Pear, (a tight thing as we thought, but by some who knew better things, said to be quaggy and flabby) and a young soft Male, call'd Cheese, somewhat sandy. In our Country indeed we say, *Il ne fut onc tel marriage, qu'est de la Poire et du Fromage*, There's no Match like that made between the Pear and the Cheese ; and in many other Places good store of such Bargains have been driven. Besides, when the women are at their last Prayers, 'tis to this day a noted Saying, That after Cheese comes nothing.

In another Room I saw them marrying a old greasy Boot to a young pliable Buskin. Pantagruel was told, that young Buskin took old Boot to have and to hold, because she was of special Leather, in good case, and wax'd, sear'd, liquor'd, and greas'd to the purpose, even tho' it had been for the Fisherman that went to Bed with his Boots on. In another Room below, I saw a young Brogue taking a young Slipper for better for worse : Which, they told us was neither for the sake of her Piety, Parts, or Person, but for the fourth comprehensive P, Portion ; the Spankers, Spur-royals, Rose-nobles, and other Coriander Seed, with which she was quilted all over.

CHAPTER X

How Pantagruel went ashoar at the Island of Chely,
where he saw King St. Panigon

WE sail'd right before the Wind, which we had at West, leaving those odd Alliancers with their Ace of Clubs Snouts, and having taken height by the Sun, stood in for Chely, a large, fruitful wealthy, and well-peopled Island. King St. Panigon first of the Name, reign'd there, and attended by the Princes his Sons, and the Nobles of his Court, came as far as the Port to receive Pantagruel, and conducted him to his Palace, near the Gate of which, the Queen attended by the Princesses her Daughters and the Court Ladies, received us. Panigon directed her and all her Retinue to salute Pantagruel and his Men with a Kiss; for such was the civil Custom of the Country; and they were all fairly buss'd accordingly, except Fryar Jhon, who step'd aside and sneak'd off among the King's Officers. Panigon us'd all the Entreaties imaginable, to persuade Pantagruel to tarry there that Day and the next, but he would needs be gone, and excus'd himself upon the opportunity of Wind and Weather, which being oftener desir'd than enjoy'd, ought not to be neglected when it comes. Panigon having heard these reasons, let us go; but first made us take off some five and twenty or thirty Bumpers each.

Pantagruel returning to the Port, miss'd Fryar Jhon, and ask'd why he was not with the rest of the Company? Panurge could not tell how to excuse him, and would have gone back to the Palace to call him, when Fryar Jhon overtook them, and merrily cry'd, Long live the noble Panigon; as I love my Belly, he minds good Eating, and keeps a noble House, and a dainty Kitchen; I have been there, Boys, every thing goes about by Dozens, I was in good hopes to have stuft my Puddings there like a Monk. What! always in a Kitchen, Friend, said Pantagruel? By the Belly of St. Cramcapon, quo' the Fryar, I understand the Customs and Ceremonies which are us'd there, much better than all the formal Stuff, antic Postures, and nonsensical Fiddle-faddle that must be us'd with those Women; *magni, magna, shittencumshita,* Cringes, Grimaces, Scrapes, Bows, and Congées; Double Honours this way, triple Salutes that way, the Embrace, the Grasp, the Squeeze, the Hug, the Leer, the Smack, *baso las manos de vostra merce, de vostra maesta.* Your most *tarabin, tarabas, Stront,* that's downright Dutch, why all this ado? I don't say but a Man might be for a bit by the bye and away, to be doing as well as his Neighbours; but this little nasty Cringing and Curtising made me as mad as any March Devil. You talk of kissing Ladies; by the worthy and sacred Frock I wear, I seldom venture upon 't, lest I be serv'd as was the Lord of Guyercharois. What was it, said Pantagruel, I know him, he is one of the best Friends I have?

He was invited to a sumptuous Feast, said Fryar Jhon, by a Relation and Neighbour of his, together with all the Gentlemen and Ladies in the Neighbourhood. Now some of the latter, expecting his coming, drest the Pages in Women's Cloaths, and finify'd them like any Babies, then order'd them to meet my Lord at his coming, near the Draw-bridge ; so the complementing Monsieur came, and there kiss'd the peticoated Lads with great formality. At last the Ladies who minded Passages in the Gallery, burst out with Laughing, and made signs to the Pages to take off their Dress ; which the good Lord having observed, the Devil a bit he durst make up to the true Ladies to kiss them, but said, That since they had disguis'd the Pages, by his Great-grandfather's Helmet, these were certainly the very Footmen and Grooms still more cunningly disguis'd. Ods-fish, *da jurandi*, why do not we rather remove our Humanities into some good warm Kitchen of God, that noble Laboratory ? and there admire the turning of the Spits, the harmonious rattling of the Jacks and Fenders, criticize on the position of the Lard, the Temperature of the Potages, the preparation for the desert, and the order of the Wine-service ? *Beati Immaculati in via*, matter of Breviary, my Masters.

CHAPTER XI

Why Monks love to be in Kitchens

THIS, said Epistemon, is spoke like a true Monk, I mean like a right monking Monk, not a bemonk'd monastical Monkling. Truly you put me in mind of some Passages that happen'd at Florence some twenty Years ago in a Company of studious Travellers, fond of visiting the Learned, and seeing the Antiquities of Italy, among whom I was. As we view'd the Situation and Beauty of Florence, the Structure of the Dome, the Magnificence of the Churches, and Palaces, we strove to outdo one another in giving them their due ; when a certain Monk of Amiens, Bernard Lardon by name, quite angry, scandaliz'd, and out of all Patience, told us, I don't know what the Devil you can find in this same Town, that's so much cry'd up ; for my part I have look'd and por'd and star'd as well as the best of you, I think my Eye-sight's as clear as another body's, and what can one see after all ? There are fine Houses indeed, and that's all : But the Cage does not feed the Birds : God and Monsieur St. Bernard our good Patron be with us, in all this same Town I have not seen one poor Lane of Roasting Cooks, and yet I have not a little look'd about, and sought for so necessary part of a Commonwealth; Ay, and I dare assure you that I have pry'd up and down with the exactness of an Informer; as ready to number both to the Right and Left, how many, and on what side, we might find most Roasting Cooks, as a Spy would be to reckon the Bastions of a Town: Now at Amiens, in four, nay five times less Ground than we have trod in our Contemplations, I could have shown you above fourteen Streets of Roasting Cooks, most ancient, savoury, and aromatic. I can't imagine what kind of Pleasure you can have taken in gazing on the Lions and Africans, (so methinks you call their Tigres) near the Belfrey, or in ogling the Porcupines and Estridges in the Lord Philip Strozzi's Palace. Faith and Troth, I had rather see a good fat Goose at the Spit. This Porphyry, those Marbles are fine; I say nothing to the contrary: But our Cheese-cakes at Amiens are far better in my mind: These ancient Statues are well made, I am willing to believe it; but by St. Ferreol of Abbeville, we have young Wenches in our Country which please me better a thousand times.

What is the reason, ask'd Fryar John, that Monks are always to be found in Kitchens; and Kings, Emperors and Popes are never there? Is there not, said Rhizotome, some latent Vertue and specific Propriety hid in the Kettles and Pans, which, as the Loadstone attracts Iron, draws the Monks there; and cannot attract Emperors, Popes, and Kings? or is it a natural Induction and Inclination fix'd in the Frocks and Cowls, which of it self leads and forceth those good Religious Men into Kitchens, whether they will or no? He would speak of Forms following Matter, as Averroës names them, answer'd Epistemon: Right, said Fryar Jhon.

I'll not offer to solve this Problem, said Pantagruel; for it is somewhat ticklish, and you can hardly handle it without coming off scurvily; but I'll tell you what I have heard.

Antigonus King of Macedon one day coming into one of the Tents, where his Cooks use to dress his Meat, and finding there Poet Antagoras frying a Conger, and holding the Pan himself, merrily ask'd him, Pray, Mr. Poet, was Homer frying Congers when he writ the Deeds of Agamemnon? Antagoras readily answer'd, But do you think, Sir, that when Agamemnon did them, he made it his business to know if any in his Camp were frying Congers? The King thought it an Indecency that a Poet shou'd be thus frying in a Kitchen; and the Poet let the King know, that it was a more indecent thing for a King to be found in such a place : I 'll clap another Story upon the Neck of this, quoth Panurge, and will tell you what Briton Villandray answer'd one day to the Duke of Guise.

They were saying that at a certain Battel of King Francis against Charles V., Briton arm'd Capape to the Teeth, and mounted like St. George ; yet sneak'd off, and play'd least in sight during the Engagement. Blood and Oons, answer'd Briton, I was there and can prove it easily ; nay, even where you, my Lord, dar'd not have been. The Duke began to resent this as too rash and sawcy ; but Briton easily appeas'd him, and set them all a laughing. I gad, my Lord, quoth he, I kept out of harm's way ; I was all the while with your Page Jack, sculking in a certain Place where you had not dar'd hide your Head as I did. Thus discoursing they got to their Ships, and left the Island of Chely.

CHAPTER XII

How Pantagruel pass'd by the Land of Petifogging, and of the strange way of living among the Catchpoles

STEERING our Course forwards the next Day we pass'd by Pettifogging, a Country all blurr'd and blotted, so that I could hardly tell what to make on 't. There we saw some Pettifoggers and Catchpoles, Rogues that will hang their Father for a Groat. They neither invited us to eat or drink, but with a multiplied train of Scrapes and Cringes, said they were all at our service, for the *Legem pone.*

One of our Droggermen related to Pantagruel their strange

way of living, diametrically oppos'd to that of our modern
Romans : for at Rome a world of Folks get an honest lively-
hood by Poysoning, Drubbing, Lambasting, Stabbing and
Murthering, but the Catchpoles earn theirs by being thrash'd,
so that if they were long without a tight Lambasting, the poor
Dogs with their Wives and Children would be starv'd. This is
just, quoth Panurge, like those who, as Galen tells us, cannot
erect the Cavernous Nerve towards the Equinoctial Circle,
unless they are soundly flogg'd. By St. Patrick's Slipper, who
ever should jirk me so, would soon instead of setting me right,
throw me off the Saddle, in the Devil's Name.

The way is this, said the Interpreter, when a Monk, Levite,
close-fisted Usurer or Lawyer owes a grudge to some neighbouring Gentleman, he sends to him one of those Catchpoles
or Apparitors, who nabs, or at least cites him, serves a Writ or
Warrant upon him ; thumps, abuses and affronts him impudently by natural Instinct, and according to his pious Instructions ; in so much that if the Gentleman hath but any Guts in
his Brains, and is not more stupid than a Girin Frog, he will
find himself oblig'd either to apply a Foggot-stick or his Sword
to the Rascal's Jobbornol, give him the gentle Lash, or make
him cut a Caper out at the Window by way of Correction.
This done, Catchpole is rich for four months at least, as if
Bastinadoes were his real harvest ; for the Monk, Levite,
Usurer or Lawyer will reward him roundly, and my Gentleman
must pay him such swinging Damages, that his Acres may bleed
for 't, and he be in danger of miserably rotting within a Stone
Doublet, as if he had struck the King.

Quoth Panurge, I know an excellent Remedy against this,
us'd by the Lord of Basché. What is it ? said Pantagruel.
The Lord of Basché, said Panurge, was a brave honest noble-
spirited Gentleman, who at his return from the long War in
which the Duke of Ferrara, with the help of the French, bravely
defended himself against the Fury of Pope Julius II. was every
Day cited, warn'd and prosecuted at the Suit and for the Sport
and Fancy of the fat Prior of St. Louant.

One Morning as he was at breakfast with some of his
Domesticks (for he lov'd to be sometimes among them) he sent
for one Loir his Baker and his Spouse, and for one Oudart the
Vicar of his Parish, who was also his Butler, as the Custom was
then in France ; then said to them before his Gentleman and
other Servants, You all see how I am daily plagu'd with these
rascally Catchpoles, truly if you do not lend me your helping

Hand, I am finally resolv'd to leave the Country, and go fight for the Sultan, or the Devil, rather than be thus eternally teas'd. Therefore to be rid of their damn'd Visits, hereafter, when any of them come here, be ready you Baker and your Wife, to make your personal appearance in my great Hall in your wedding Cloaths, as if you were going to be affianc'd ; here take these Ducats, which I give you to keep you in a fitting Garb. As for you, Sir Oudart, be sure you make your personal appearance there in your fine Surplice and Stole, not forgetting your Holy Water, as if you were to wed them. Be you there also Trudon, said he to his Drummer, with your Pipe and Tabor. The Form of Matrimony must be read, and the Bride kiss'd, then all of you, as the Witnesses use to do in this Country, shall give one another the remembrance of the Wedding, (which you know is to be a Blow with your Fist, bidding the Party struck remember the Nuptials by that Token) this will but make you have the better Stomach to your Supper : but when you come to the Catchpole's turn, thrash him thrice and three-fold, as you would a Sheaf of Green Corn, don't spare him, maul him, drub him, lambast him, swinge him off, I pray you. Here, take these Steel Gantlets, covered with Kid, Head, Back, Belly, and Sides, give him Blows innumerable ; he that gives him most, shall be my best Friend. Fear not to be call'd to an account about it, I'll stand by you ; for the Blows must seem to be given in jest, as it is Customary amongst us at all Weddings.

Ay, but how shall we know the Catchpole, said the Man of God, all sorts of People daily resort to this Castle ? I have taken care of that, reply'd the Lord. When some Fellow either on foot or on a scurvy Jade, with a large broad Silver Ring on his Thumb comes to the Door, he is certainly a Catchpole : the Porter having civilly let him in, shall ring the Bell, then be all ready, and come into the Hall, to act the Tragi-Comedy, whose Plot I have now laid for you.

The numerical Day, as Chance would have it, came an old fat ruddy Catchpole ; having knock'd at the Gate, and then piss'd, as most Men will do, the Porter soon found him out, by his large greasie Spatterdashes, his Jaded hollow flank'd Mare, his Bag full of Writs and Informations dangling at his Girdle, but above all, by the large Silver Hoop on his left Thumb.

The Porter was civil to him, admitted him in kindly, and rung the Bell briskly. As soon as the Baker and his Wife heard it, they clapp'd on their best Clothes, and made their personal appearance in the Hall, keeping their Gravities like a new made

Judge. The Domine put on his Surplice and Stole, and as he came out of his Office, met the Catchpole, had him in there, and made him suck his Face a good while, while the Gantlets were drawing on all Hands, and then told him, you are come just in Pudding time, my Lord is in his right Cue ; we shall feast like kings anon, here's to be swinging doings, we have a Wedding in the House, here, drink and cheer up, pull away.

While these two were at it hand to fist, Basché, seeing all his People in the Hall in their proper Equipage, sends for the Vicar. Oudart comes with the Holy Water Pot, follow'd by the Catchpole, who as he came into the Hall, did not forget to make good store of aukward Cringes, and then serv'd Basché with a Writ. Basché gave him Grimace for Grimace, slipp'd an Angel into his Mutton Fist, and pray'd him to assist at the Contract and Ceremony. Which he did. When it was ended, Thumps and Fisticuffs began to fly about among the Assistants ; but when it came to the Catchpole's turn, they all lay'd on him so unmercifully with their Gantlets, that they at last settled him, all stunn'd, and batter'd, bruis'd, and mortifi'd, with one of his Eyes black and blue, eight Ribs bruis'd, his Brisket sunk in, his Omoplates in four quarters, his under Jaw-bone in three pieces, and all this in jest and no harm done. God wot how the Levite belabour'd him, hiding within the long Sleeve of his Canonical Shirt, his huge Steel Gantlet lin'd with Ermin, for he was a strong built Ball, and an old Dog at Fisticuffs. The Catchpole, all of a bloody Tiger-like hue, with much ado, crawl'd home to l'Isle Bouchart, well pleas'd and edifi'd however with Basché's kind reception, and with the help of the good Surgeons of the place, liv'd as long as you'd have him. From that time to this not a word of the Business ; the Memory of it was lost with the sound of the Bells that rung for Joy at his Funeral.

CHAPTER XIII

*How, like Master Francis Villon, the Lord of Basché
commended his Servants*

THE Catchpole being pack'd off on blind Sorrel (so he call'd
his one Ey'd Mare) Basché sent for his Lady, her Women and
all his Servants into the Arbour of his Garden ; had Wine
brought, attended by good store of Pasties, Hams, Fruit, and
other Table-Ammunition for a Nuncion, drank with them joyfully, and then told them this Story.

Master Francis Villon, in his old Age, retir'd to St. Maixent
in Poitou, under the Patronage of a good honest Abbot of the
place. There to make sport for the Mob, he undertook to get
the *Passion* acted after the Way and in the Dialect of the
Country. The Parts being distributed, the Play having been
rehears'd, and the Stage prepar'd, he told the Mayor and
Aldermen, that the Mystery might be ready after Niort Fair,
and that there only wanted Properties and Necessaries, but

chiefly Clothes fit for the Parts ; so the Mayor and his Brethren took care to get them.

Villon, to dress an old Clownish Father Grey-beard, who was to represent God the Father, begg'd of Fryar Stephen Tickletoby, Sacristan to the Franciscan Fryars of the Place, to lend him a Cope and a Stole. Tickletoby refus'd him, alledging that by their Provincial Statutes, it was rigorously forbidden to give or lend any thing to Players. Villon reply'd, That the Statute reached no farther than Farces, Drolls, Anticks, loose and dissolute Games, and that he ask'd no more than what he had seen allow'd at Brussels and other Places. Tickletoby, notwithstanding, peremptorily bid him provide himself elsewhere if he would, and not to hope for any thing out of his Monastical Wardrobe. Villon gave an account of this to the Players, as of a most abominable Action ; adding, that God would shortly revenge himself, and make an Example of Tickletoby.

The Saturday following he had notice given him, that Tickletoby upon the Filly of the Convent (so they call a young Mare that was never leap'd yet) was gone a mumping to St. Ligarius, and would be back about two in the Afternoon. Knowing this, he made a Cavalcade of his Devils of the *Passion* through the Town. They were all rigg'd with Wolves, Calves, and Rams Skins, lac'd and trimm'd with Sheeps Heads, Bulls Feathers, and large Kitchen Tenter-Hooks, girt with broad Leathern Girdles, whereat hang'd dangling huge Cow-Bells and Horse-Bells, which made a horrid din. Some held in their Claws black sticks full of Squibs and Crackers ; others had long lighted pieces of Wood, upon which at the corner of every Street they flung whole handfuls of Rosin-dust, that made a terrible Fire and Smoak : having thus led them about, to the great diversion of the Mob, and the dreadful fear of the little Children, he finally carried them to an Entertainment at a Summer-House without the Gate that leads to St. Ligarius.

As they came near the Place, he spy'd Tickletoby afar off, coming home from Mumping, and told them in Maceronic Verse,

Hic est Mumpator natus de gente Cucowli,
Qui solet antiquo scrappas portare bisacco.

A Plague on his Fryarship (said the Devils then) the lowsie Beggar would not lend a poor Cope to the Fatherly Father, let us fright him. Well said, cry'd Villon; but let us hide our selves till he comes by, and then charge home briskly with your Squibs and burning Sticks. Tickletoby being come to the Place, they all rush'd on a sudden into the Road to meet him, and in a frightful manner threw Fire from all sides upon him and his Filly Foal, ringing and tingling their Bells, and howling like so many real Devils, hho, hho, hho, hho, brrou, rrou, rrourrs, rrrourrs, hoo, hou, hou, hho, hho, hhoi, Fryar Stephen, don't we play the Devils rarely? The Filly was soon scar'd out of her seven Senses, and began to start, to funk it, to squirt it, to trot it, to fart it, to bound it, to gallop it, to kick it, to spurn it, to calcitrate it, to winse it, to frisk it, to leap it, to curvet it, with double Jirks and bum-motions; in so much that she threw down Tickletoby, tho' he held fast by the Tree of the Pack-Saddle with might and main: now his Straps and Stirrups were of Cord, and on the right side, his Sandal was so entangled and twisted, that he could not for the Hearts Blood of him get out his Foot. Thus he was dragg'd about by the Filly through the Road, scratching his bare Breech all the way, she still multiplying her Kicks against him, and straying for fear, over Hedge and Ditch; in so much that she trepann'd his thick Skull so, that his Cockle Brains were dash'd out near the Osanna or High Cross. Then his Arms fell to pieces, one this way, and t' other that way, and even so were his Legs serv'd at the same time: Then she made a bloody havock with his Puddings, and being got to the Convent, brought back only his right Foot and twisted Sandal, leaving them to guess what was become of the rest.

Villon seeing that things had succeeded as he intended, said to his Devils, you will act rarely, Gentlemen Devils, you will act rarely; I dare engage you 'll top your Parts. I defie the Devils of Saumur, Douay, Montmorillon, Langez, St. Espain, Angers; nay, by Gad, even those of Poictiers, for all their bragging and vapouring, to match you.

Likewise, Friends, said Basché, I foresee, that hereafter you will act rarely this Tragical Farce, since the very first time you have so skilfully hamper'd, bethwack'd, belamm'd, and be-bump'd the Catchpole. From this Day I double your Wages. As for you, my Dear (said he to his Lady) make your Gratifica-tions as you please; you are my Treasurer, you know. For my part, first and foremost, I drink to you all. Come on, box it about, 'tis good and cool. In the second place, you, Mr. Steward, take this Silver Bason, I give it you freely. Then

you, my Gentleman of the Horse, take these two Silver gilt
Cups, and let not the Pages be Horse-whipp'd these three
Months. My Dear, let them have my best white Plumes of
Feathers with the Gold Buckles to them. Sir Oudart, this
Silver Flaggon falls to your share : this other I give to the
Cooks. To the Valets de Chambre, I give this Silver Basket ;
to the Grooms this Silver gilt Boat ; to the Porter these two
Plates : to the Hostlers these ten Porringers. Trudon, take
you these Silver Spoons and this Sugar-box. You Footmen,
take this large Salt. Serve me well, and I'll remember you.
For on the word of a Gentleman, I had rather bear in War one
hundred Blows on my Helmet in the Service of my Country,
than be once cited by these Knavish Catchpoles, meerly to
humour this same gorbelly'd Prior.

CHAPTER XIV

A further Account of Catchpole's who were drubb'd at Basché's House

FOUR Days after, another young long-shank'd raw-bon'd
Catchpole coming to serve Basché with a Writ at the Fat
Prior's request, was no sooner at the Gate, but the Porter
smelt him out, and rung the Bell ; at whose second pull, all
the Family understood the Mystery. Loire was kneading his
Dough, his Wife was sifting Meal ; Oudart was toping in his
Office ; the Gentlemen were playing at Tennis ; the Lord
Basché at In and Out with my Lady ; the Waitingmen and
Gentlewomen at Push-Pin ; the Officers at Lanterlue, and the
Pages at Hot-cockles, giving one another smart Bangs. They
were all immediately inform'd that a Catchpole was hous'd.

Upon this, Oudart put on his Sacerdotal, and Loire and his
Wife their Nuptial Badges. Trudon Pip'd it, and then Taber'd
it like mad, all made haste to get ready, not forgetting the
Gantlets. Basché went into the outward Yard ; there the
Catchpole meeting him, fell on his Marrowbones beg'd of him
not to take it ill, if he serv'd him with a Writ at the Suit of the
fat Prior ; and in a pathetic Speech, let him know that he was
a publick Person, a Servant to the Monking Tribe, Apparitor

W. HEATH ROBINSON.

GOD KNOWS HOW HE GOT TO L'ISLE BOUCHART

139

to the Abbatial Mytre, ready to do as much for him, nay, for the least of his Servants, whensoever he would employ and use him.

Nay, truly, said the Lord, you shall not serve your Writ till you have tasted some of my good Quinquenays Wine, and been a Witness to a Wedding which we are to have this very Minute. Let him drink and refresh himself, added he, turning towards the Levitical Butler, and then bring him into the Hall. After which, Catchpole well stuffed and moisten'd, came with Oudart to the place where all the Actors in the Farce stood ready to begin. The sight of their Game set them a laughing, and the Messenger of Mischief grinn'd also for Company's sake. Then the Mysterious Words were mutter'd to and by the Couple, their Hands join'd, the Bride buss'd, and all besprinkled with Holy Water. While they were bringing Wine and Kickshaws, Thumps began to trot about by dozens. The Catchpole gave the Levite several blows. Oudart, who had his Gantlet hid under his Canonical Shirt, draws it on like a Mitten, and then with his clench'd Fist, souce he fell on the Catchpole, and maul'd him like a Devil; the junior Gantlets dropt on him likewise like so many battering Rams. Remember the Wedding by this, by that, by these blows, said they. In short, they stroak'd him so to the purpose that he piss'd Blood out at Mouth, Nose, Ears, and Eyes, and was bruis'd, sore, batter'd, bebump'd, and crippled at the Back, Neck, Breast, Arms, and soforth. Never did the Batchellors at Avignon in Carnival time play more melodiously at Raphe, than was then play'd on the Catchpole's Microcosm : at last down he fell.

They threw a great deal of Wine on his Snout, ty'd round the Sleeve of his Doublet a fine yellow and green Favour, and got him upon his snotty Beast, and God knows how he got to l'Isle Bouchart, where I cannot truly tell you whether he was dress'd and look'd after or no, both by his Spouse and the able Doctors of the Country, for the thing never came to my Ears.

The next Day they had a third part to the same Tune, because it did not appear by the lean Catchpole's Bag, that he had serv'd his Writ. So the fat Prior sent a new Catchpole at the head of a brace of Bums for his *Guard du Corps* to summon my Lord. The Porter ringing the Bell, the whole Family was overjoy'd, knowing that it was another Rogue. Basché was at Dinner with his Lady and the Gentlemen, so he sent for the Catchpole, made him sit by him, and the Bums by the Women, and made them eat till their Bellies crack'd with their Breeches unbutton'd. The Fruit being serv'd, the Catchpole arose from Table, and before the Bums cited Basché, Basché kindly ask'd him for Copy of the Warrant, which the other had got ready: he then takes Witness and a Copy of the Summons. To the Catchpole and his Bums he order'd four Ducats for Civility Money. In the mean time all were withdrawn for the Farce. So Trudon gave the Alarm with his Tabor. Basché desir'd the Catchpole to stay and see one of his Servants married, and witness the Contract of Marriage, paying him his Fee. The Catchpole slap dash was ready, took his Ink-horn, got Paper immediately, and his Bums by him.

Then Loire came into the Hall at one Door, and his Wife with the Gentlewomen at another in Nuptial Accoutrements. Oudart, in *Pontificalibus*, takes them both by the Hands, asketh them their Will; giveth them the Matrimonial Blessing, and was very Liberal of Holy Water. The Contract Written, Sign'd, and Register'd, on one side was brought Wine and Comfits; on the other, White and Orange-tauny-colour'd Favours were distributed; on another, Gantlets privately handed about.

CHAPTER XV

How the Ancient Custom at Nuptials is renewed by the Catchpole

THE Catchpole having made shift to get down a swinging Streaker of Briton Wine, said to Basché, Pray, Sir, what do you mean? You do not give one another the Memento of the Wedding. By St. Joseph's Wooden Shoe all good Customs are forgot. We find the Form, but the Hare's scamper'd; and the Nest, but the Birds are flown. There are no true

Friends now-a-days. You see how in several Churches the Ancient Laudable Custom of Tippling on account of the Blessed St. O. O. at Christmas is come to nothing. The World is in its Dotage, Dooms-day is certainly coming all so fast. Now come on ; the Wedding, the Wedding, the Wedding, remember it by this. This he said, striking Basché and his Lady, then her Women and the Levite. Then the Tabor beat a Point of War, and the Gantlets began to do their Duty, insomuch that the Catchpole had his Crown crack'd in no less than nine places. One of the Bums had his right Arm put out of joint, and the other his upper Jaw-bone or Mandibule dislocated ; so that it hid half his Chin, with a denundation of the Uvula and sad loss of the molar, masticatory, and canine Teeth. Then the Tabor beat a Retreat ; the Gantlets were carefully hid in a trice, and Sweet-meats afresh distributed to renew the Mirth of the Company. So they all drank to one another, and especially to the Catchpole and his Bums. But Oudart curs'd and damn'd the Wedding to the Pit of Hell, complaining that one of the Bums had utterly disincornifistibulated his nether Shoulder-blade. Nevertheless he scorn'd to be thought a Flincher, and made shift to tope to him on the square.

The Jawless Bum shrug'd up his Shoulders, join'd his Hands, and by signs beg'd his Pardon ; for speak he could not. The sham Bridegroom made his moan. That the crippled Bum had struck him such a horrid thump with his Shoulder-of-Mutton-Fist on the nether Elbow, that he was grown quite efperruquanchuzelubelouzerireliced down to his very heel, to the no small loss of Mrs. Bride.

But what harm had poor I done (cry'd Trudon, hiding his left Eye with his Kerchief, and shewing his Tabor crack'd on one side) they were not satisfied with thus poching, black-and-bluing, and morrambouzevezengouzequoquemorgasacbaque-vezinemaffreliding my poor Eyes, but they have also broke my harmless Drum. Drums indeed are commonly beaten at Weddings ; (and 'tis fit they should) but Drummers are well entertained, and never beaten. Now let Belzebub e'en take the Drum to make his Devilship a Night-cap. Brother, said the lame Catchpole, never fret thy self, I will make thee a Present of a fine, large, old Patent, which I have here in my Bag, to patch up thy Drum, and for Madam St. Ann's sake I pray thee forgive us. By 'r Lady of River, the blessed Dame, I meant no more harm than the Child unborn. One of the Querries, who hopping and halting like a mumping Cripple, mimick'd the good limping Lord de la Roche Posay, directed his Discourse to the Bum with the pouting Jaw, and told him, What, Mr. Manbound, was it not enough thus to have morcrocastebezasteverestegrigeligoscopapopondrillated us all in our upper Members with your botch'd Mittens, but you must also apply such Morderegripippiatabirofreluchamburelurecaquelurintimpaniments on our Shin-Bones with the hard Tops and Extremities of your cobbl'd Shoes ? Do you call this Children's Play ? By the Mass 'tis no Jest. The Bum wringing his Hands, seem'd to beg his Pardon, muttering with his Tongue, mon, mon, mon, vrelon, von, von, like a dumb Man. The Bride crying laught, and laughing cry'd, because the Catchpole was not satisfied with drubbing her without choice or distinction of Members, but had also rudely rous'd and tous'd her, pull'd off her Topping, and not having the Fear of her Husband before his Eyes, treacherously trepignemanpenillorifrizonoufresturfumbledtumbled and squeez'd her lower Parts. The Devil go with it, said Basché, there was much need indeed that this same Master King (this was the Catchpole's Name) should thus break my Wife's Back ; however I forgive him now ; these are little Nuptial Caresses. But this I plainly perceive, that he cited me like an Angel, and drubb'd me like a Devil. He hath something in him of Fryar Thumpwell. Come, for all this I must drink to him, and to you likewise his trusty Esquires. But said his Lady, Why hath he been so very liberal of his manual Kindness to me, without the least Provocation ? I assure you, I by no means like it ; but this I dare say for him, that he hath the hardest Knuckles that ever I felt on my Shoulders. The Steward held his left Arm in a Scarf, as if it had been rent and torn in twain : I think it was the Devil, said he, that mov'd me to assist at these Nuptials ; shame on ill luck, I must needs be meddling, with a Pox, and now see what I have got by the Bargain, both my Arms are wretchedly engoulevezinemassdandbruis'd. Do you call this a Wedding ? By St. Bridget's Tooth, I had rather be at that of a Tom T—dman ; this is o' my word e'en just such another Feast as was that of the Lapithes, describ'd by the Philosopher of Samosate. One of the Bums had lost his Tongue. The two other, tho' they had more need to complain, made their excuse as well as they could, protesting that they had no ill design in this Dumbfounding ; begging that for Goodness sake they would forgive them ; and so, tho' they could hardly budge a foot, or wag along, away they crawl'd. About a Mile from

Basché's Seat, the Catchpole found himself somewhat out of sorts. The Bums got to l'Isle Bouchart, publickly saying, That since they were born, they had never seen an honester Gentleman than the Lord of Basché, or civiller People than his, and that they had never been at the like Wedding (which I verily believe) but that it was their own faults, if they had been tickled off, and toss'd about from Post to Pillar, since themselves had began the Beating. So they liv'd I can't exactly tell you how many Days after this. But from that time to this it was held for a certain Truth, That Basché's Money was more pestilential, mortal, and pernicious to the Catchpoles and Bums, than were formerly the Aurum Tholosanum, and the Sejan Horse to those that possessed them. Ever since this he lived quietly, and Basché's Wedding grew into a common Proverb.

CHAPTER XVI

How Fryar Jhon made tryal of the Nature of the Catchpoles

THIS Story would seem pleasant enough, said Pantagruel, were we not to have always the Fear of God before our Eyes. It had been better, said Epistemon, if those Gantlets had fallen upon the fat Prior : Since he took a pleasure in spending his Money, partly to vex Basché, partly to see those Catchpoles bang'd, good lusty Thumps would have done well on his shav'd Crown, considering the horrid Concussions now-adays among those puny Judges. What harm had done those poor Devils the Catchpoles. This puts me in mind, said Pantagruel, of an ancient Roman named L. Neratius ; he was of noble Blood, and for some time was rich ; but had this tyrannical Inclination, that whenever he went out of doors, he caus'd his Servants to fill their Pockets with Gold and Silver, and meeting in the Street your Spruce Gallants and better sort of Beaux, without the least Provocation, for his Fancy he us'd to strike them hard on the Face with his Fist, and immediately after that, to appease them and hinder them from complaining to the Magistrates, he would give them as much Money as satisfied them according to the Law of the Twelve Tables. Thus he us'd to spend his Revenue, beating People for the Price of his

A REDSNOUT CATCHPOLE

Money. By St. Bennet's sacred Boot, quoth Fryar Jhon, I will know the truth of it presently.

This said, he went on shoar, put his Hand in his Fob, and took out twenty Ducats, then said with a loud Voice in the hearing of a shoal of the Nation of Catchpoles, Who will earn twenty Ducats, for being beaten like the Devil? Io, Io, Io, said they all; you will cripple us for ever, Sir, that's most certain, but the Money is tempting. With this they were all thronging who should be first, to be thus preciously beaten. Fryar Jhon singled him out of the whole Knot of these Rogues-in-grain, a red-snout Catchpole, who upon his right Thumb wore a thick broad Silver Hoop, wherein was set a good large Toad-stone. He had no sooner pick'd him out from the rest, but I perceiv'd that they all mutter'd and grumbl'd; and I heard a young thin-jaw'd Catchpole, a notable Scholar, a pretty Fellow at his Pen, and, according to publick Report, much cry'd up for his Honesty at Doctor's-Commons, making his complaint, and muttering; because this same crimson Phyz carry'd away all the Practice, and that if there were but a score and a half of Bastinado's to be got, he would certainly run away with eight and twenty of them. But all this was look'd upon to be nothing but mere Envy.

Fryar Jhon so unmercifully thrash'd, thump'd, belabour'd Red-snout, Back and Belly, Sides, Legs and Arms, Head, Feet, and so forth, with the home and frequently repeated application of one of the best Members of a Faggot, that I took him to be a dead Man; then he gave him the twenty Ducats, which made the Dog get on his Legs, pleas'd like a little King or two. The rest were saying to Fryar Jhon, Sir, Sir, Brother Devil, if it please you to do us the favour to beat some of us for less Money, we are all at your Devilship's command, Bags, Papers, Pens and all. Red-snout cry'd out against them, saying with a loud Voice, Body of me, you little Prigs, will you offer to take the Bread out of my Mouth? will you take my Bargain over my Head? would you draw and inveigle from me my Clients and Customers? Take notice, I summon you before the Official this day se'night; I will law and claw you like any old Devil, that I will.——Then turning himself towards Fryar Jhon, with a smiling and joyful Look, he said to him, Reverend Father in the Devil, if you have found me a good Hide, and have a mind to divert your self once more, by beating your humble Servant, I will bate you half in half this time, rather than lose your Custom, do not spare me, I beseech you;

I am all, and more than all yours, good Mr. Devil, Head, Lungs, Tripes, Guts and Garbage, and that at a Peniworth, I 'll assure you. Fryar Jhon ne'er heeded his Proffers, but e'en left them. The other Catchpoles were making Addresses to Panurge, Epistemon, Gymnast, and others, entreating them charitably to bestow upon their Carcasses a small beating, for otherwise they were in danger of keeping a long Fast : but none of them had a Stomach to it. Some time after, seeking fresh Water for the Ship's Company, we met a couple of old Female Catchpoles of the place, miserably howling and weeping in Consort. Pantagruel had kept on board, and already had caus'd a Retreat to be sounded, thinking they might be related to the Catchpole that was bastinado'd. We ask'd them the occasion of their Grief. They reply'd, That they had too much cause to weep ; for that very hour, from an exalted Triple Tree, two of the honestest Gentlemen in Catchpole-land had been made to cut a Caper on nothing. Cut a Caper on nothing ? said Gymnast, my Pages use to cut Capers on the Ground ; to cut a Caper on nothing should be hanging and choaking, or I am out. Ay, ay, said Fryar Jhon, you speak of it like St. Jhon de la Palisse.

We ask'd them, why they treated those worthy Persons with such a choaking Hempen Sallet ? They told us, they had only borrow'd, *alias* stoln, the Tools of the Mass, and hid them under the Handle of the Parish. This is a very allegorical way of speaking said Epistemon.

CHAPTER XVII

How Pantagruel came to the Islands of Tohu and Bohu, and of the
strange Death of Widenostrils the Swallower of Windmils

THAT Day Pantagruel came to the two Islands of Tohu and
Bohu, where the Devil a bit we could find any thing to fry
with : For, one Widenostrils, a huge Giant had swallowed
every individual Pan, Skillet, Kettle, Frying-pan, Dripping-pan,
and Brass and Iron Pot in the Land, for want of Windmils,
which were his daily Food. Whence it happen'd that somewhat
before Day, about the Hour of his Digestion, the Greedy Churl
was taken very ill, with a kind of a Surfeit or crudity of Stomach,
occasion'd (as the Physicians said) by the weakness of the
concocting Faculty of his Stomach, naturally dispos'd to
digest whole Windmils at a Gust ; yet unable to consume
perfectly the Pans and Skillets, though it had indeed pretty
well digested the Kettles and Pots, as they said they knew
by the Hypostases and Encoresmes of four Tubs of second-
hand Drink, which he had evacuated at two different times that
Morning. They made use of divers Remedies according to Art,
to give him ease : But all would not do, the Distemper prevailed over the Remedies, insomuch that the famous Widenostrils dy'd that Morning, of so strange a Death, that I think
you ought no longer to wonder at that of the Poet Æschylus's.
It had been foretold him by the Soothsayers, that he would dye
on a certain Day, by the ruin of something that should fall on
him ; that fatal Day being come in its Turn, he remov'd himself
out of Town, far from all Houses, Trees, or any other things that
can fall, and indanger by their ruin ; and stay'd in a large
Field, trusting himself to the open Sky, there very secure
as he thought, unless indeed the Sky should happen to fall,
which he held to be impossible. Yet they say that the Larks
are much afraid of it, for if it should fall, they must all be
taken.

The Celtx that once liv'd near the Rhine, (they are our
noble valiant French) in ancient Times were also afraid of the
Sky's falling ; for being ask'd by Alexander the Great, What
they fear'd most in this World, hoping well they would say that
they fear'd none but him, considering his great Atchievements,

FOR, ONE WIDENOSTRILS, A HUGE GIANT HAD SWALLOWED EVERY PAN,
SKILLET, KETTLE, FRYING-PAN AND DRIPPING-PAN IN THE LAND, FOR
WANT OF WINDMILS, HIS DAILY FOOD

they made answer, That they fear'd nothing but the Sky's falling; however, not refusing to enter into a Confederacy with so brave a King: If you believe Strabo, Lib. 7. and Arrian, Lib. 1.

Plutarch also in his Book of the Face that appears on the Body of the Moon, speaks of one Phœnaces who very much fear'd the Moon should fall on Earth, and piti'd those that live under that Planet, as the Æthiopians and Taprobanians, if so heavy a Mass ever happened to fall on them; and would have fear'd the like of Heaven and Earth, had they not been duly propp'd up and born by the Atlantic Pillars, as the Ancients believ'd, according to Aristotle's Testimony, Lib. 5. *Metaphis*. Notwithstanding all this, poor Æschylus was kill'd by the fall of the Shell of a Tortoise, which falling from betwixt the Claws of an Eagle high in the Air, just on his Head, dash'd out his Brains.

Neither ought you to wonder at the death of another Poet, I mean old jolly Anacreon, who was choak'd with a Grape-stone: nor at that of Fabius the Roman Prætor, who was smothered with a single Goat's-hair as he was supping up a Porringer of Milk. Nor at the death of that bashful Fool, who by holding in his Wind, and for want of letting out a Bum-gunshot, dy'd suddenly in the presence of the Emperor Claudius. Nor at that of the Italian, buried on the Via Flaminia at Rome, who, in his Epitaph, complains that the bite of a She-Puss on his little Finger was the cause of his death. Nor of that of Q. Lecanius Bassus, who died suddenly of so small a prick with a Needle on his left Thumb, that it could hardly be descern'd. Nor of Quenelault a Norman Physician, who dy'd suddenly at Montpellier, meerly for having sideways took a Worm out of his Hand with a Pen-knife. Nor of Philomenes, whose Servant having got him some new Figs, for the first Course of his Dinner, whilst he went to fetch Wine, a straggling well-hung Ass got into the House, and seeing the Figs on the Table, without further Invitation soberly fell to: Philomenes coming into the Room, and nicely observing with what Gravity the Ass eat its Dinner, said to his Man, who was come back; Since thou hast set Figs here for this reverend Guest of ours to eat, methinks it's but reason thou also give him some of this Wine to drink. He had no sooner said this, but he was so excessively pleased, and fell into so exorbitant a fit of Laughter, that the use of his Spleen took that of his Breath utterly away, and he immediately dy'd. Nor of Spurius Saufeius, who dy'd supping up a soft

Egg as he came out of a Bath. Nor of him who, as Boccace tells us, dy'd suddenly by picking his Grinders with a Sagestalk. Nor of Philipot Placut, who being brisk and hale, fell dead as he was paying an old Debt ; which causes perhaps many not to pay theirs, for fear of the like Accident. Nor of the Painter Zeuxis, who kill'd himself with laughing at the sight of the Antick Jobbernol of an old Hag drawn by him. Nor, in short, of a thousand more of which Authors write, as Verrius, Pliny, Valerius, J. Baptista, Fulgosius, and Bacabery the elder. In short, Gaffer Widenostrils choak'd himself with eating a huge lump of fresh Butter at the Mouth of a hot Oven, by the Advice of Physicians.

They likewise told us there, that the King of Cullan in Bohu had routed the Grandees of King Mecloth, and made sad work with the Fortresses of Belima.

After this, we sail'd by the Islands of Nargues and Zargues ; also by the Islands of Teleniabin and Geneliabin, very fine and fruitful in Ingredients for Clisters : and then by the Islands of Enig and Evig, on whose account formerly the Landgrave of Hesse was swindg'd off with a vengeance.

CHAPTER XVIII

How Pantagruel met with a great Storm at Sea

THE next Day we espied nine Sail that came spooning before the Wind ; they were full of Dominicans, Jesuits, Capuchins, Hermits, Austins, Bernardins, Celestins, Theatins, Egnatins, Amadeans, Cordeliers, Carmelites, Minims, and the Devil and all of other holy Monks and Fryars, who were going to the Council of Chesil, to sift and garble some Articles of Faith against the new Hereticks ; Panurge was overjoy'd to see them, being most certain of good Luck, for that Day, and a long Train of others. So, having courteously saluted the goodly Fathers, and recommended the Salvation of his precious Soul to their Devout Prayers and private Ejaculations, he caus'd seventy eight dozen of Westphalia Hams, Unites of Pots of Caviar, Tens of Bolonia Sawsages, Hundreds of Botargoes, and Thousands of fine Angels, for the Souls of the Dead, to be thrown on board their Ships. Pantagruel seem'd metagraboliz'd, dozing, out of sorts, and as melancholick as a Cat; Fryar Jhon, who soon perceiv'd it, was enquiring of him whence should come this unusual Sadness? When the Master, whose Watch it was, observing the fluttering of the Ancient above the Poop, and seeing that it began to overcast, judg'd that we should have Wind, therefore he bid the Boatswain call Hands upon Deck, Officers, Sailors, Fore-mast Men, Swabbers, and Cabbin-boys, and even the Passengers; made 'em first settle their Top-sails, take in their Spreet-sail; then he cry'd, in with your Top-sails, lower the Fore-sail, Tallow under the Parrels, brade up close all them Sails, strike your Top-masts to the Cap, make all sure with your Sheeps-feet, lash your Guns fast. All this was nimbly done. Immediately it blow'd a Storm, the Sea began to roar, and swell Mountain high: the Rut of the Sea was great, the Waves breaking upon our Ships Quarter, the North-West Wind bluster'd and overblow'd; boisterous Gusts; dreadful Clashings and deadly Scuds of Wind whistled through our Yards, and made our Shrouds rattle again. The Thunder grumbled so horribly, that you would have thought Heaven had been tumbling about our Ears; at the same time it Lighten'd, Rain'd, Hail'd; the Sky lost its transparent hue, grew dusky, thick and gloomy, so that we had no other Light than that of the Flashes of the Lightning and rending of the Clouds: the Hurricans, Flaws, and sudden Whirlwinds began to make a Flame about us by the Lightnings, Fiery Vapours, and other Aerial Ejaculations. Oh! how our Looks were full of Amazement and Trouble, while the sawcy Winds did rudely lift up above us the Mountainous Waves of the Main. Believe me, it seem'd to us a lively Image of the Chaos, where Fire, Air, Sea, Land, and all the Elements were in a refractory Confusion. Poor Panurge, having, with the full Contents of the inside of his Doublet, plentifully fed the Fish, greedy enough of such odious Fare, sat on the Deck all in a heap, with his Nose and Arse together, most sadly cast down, moping and half dead; invok'd and call'd to his Assistance all the blessed he and she Saints he could muster up, swore and vow'd to confess in Time and Place convenient, and then bawl'd out frightfully, Steward, Maistre d'Hostel, see hoe, my Friend, my Father, my Uncle, pr'ythee let's have a Piece of Powder'd Beef or Pork, we shall drink but too much anon, for ought I see, eat little and drink the more shall hereafter be my Motto, I fear. Would to our dear Lord, and to our blessed, worthy, and sacred Lady, I

ONE PHŒNACES WHO VERY MUCH FEAR'D THE MOON SHOULD FALL ON EARTH

153

were now, I say, this very Minute of an Hour, well on shoar on *Terra firma*, hale and easie. O twice and thrice happy those that plant Cabbages! O Destinies, why did you not Spin me for a Cabbage Planter? O how few are they to whom Jupiter hath been so favourable as to predestinate them to plant Cabbage! They have always one Foot on the Ground, and the other not far from it. Dispute who will of Felicity, and *summum bonum*, for my part, whosoever plants Cabbages, is now by my Decree proclaim'd most happy; for as good a reason as the Philosopher Pyrho being in the same Danger, and seeing a Hog near the Shoar eating some scatter'd Oats, declar'd it happy in two respects, first, because it had plenty of Oats, and besides that was on Shoar. Hah, for a Divine and Princely Habitation, commend me to the Cows Floor.

Murther! This Wave will sweep us away, blessed Saviour! O, my Friends! a little Vinegar. I sweat again with meer Agony. Alas, the Misen-Sail's split, the Gallery's wash'd away, the Masts are sprung, the Main-Top-Mast Head dives into the Sea; the Keel is up to the Sun; our Shrouds are almost all broke, and blown away. Alas! Alas! Where is our main Course? *Ael is verlooren by Godt*, our Top-Mast is run adrift. Alas! Who shall have this Wreck? Friend, lend me here behind you one of these Wales. Your Lanthorn is fallen, my Lads. Alas! don't let go the Main-tack, nor the Bowlin. I hear the Block crack, is it broke? For the Lord's sake, let us save the Hull, and let all the Rigging be damn'd. Be be be bous, bous, bous. Look to the Needle of your Compass, I beseech you, good Sir Astrophel, and tell us, if you can, whence comes this Storm, my Heart's sunk down below my Midriff. By my troth I am in a sad fright; bou, bou, bou, bous, bous, I am lost for ever. I conskite my self for meer Madness and Fear. Bou, bou, bou, bou, Otto to to to to ti. Bou, bou, bou, ou, ou, ou, bou, bou, bous. I sink, I'm drowned, I'm gone, good People, I'm drowned.

CHAPTER XIX

What Countenances Panurge and Fryar Jhon kept during the Storm

PANTAGRUEL having first implor'd the help of the Great and Almighty Deliverer, and pray'd publickly with fervent Devotion, by the Pilot's Advice held titely the Mast of the Ship. Fryar Jhon had stripp'd himself to his Wastcoat, to help the Seamen. Epistemon, Ponocrates, and the rest did as much. Panurge alone sate on his Breech upon Deck, weeping, and howling. Fryar Jhon espy'd him, going on the Quarter-Deck, and said to him: Odzoons, Panurge the Calf, Panurge the Whiner, Panurge the Brayer, would it not become thee much better to lend us here a helping Hand, than to lie lowing like a Cow, as thou dost, sitting on thy Stones like a bald breech'd Baboon? Be, be, be, bous, bous, bous, return'd Panurge, Fryar John, my Friend, my good Father, I am drowning, my dear Friend! I drown; I am a dead Man, my dear Father in God, I am a dead Man, my Friend: your cutting Hanger cannot save me from this: Alas! Alas! We are above *Ela*. Above the pitch, out of Tune, and off the Hinges. Be, be, be, bou, bous. Alas! we are now above *G sol re ut*. I sink, I sink, hah, my Father, my Uncle, my All. The Water is got into my Shoes by the Collar; bous, bous, bous, paisch, hu, hu, hu, he, he, he, ha, ha, I drown. Alas! Alas! Hu, hu, hu, hu, hu, hu, hu, be be bous, bous, bobous, bobous, ho, ho, ho, ho, ho. Alas! Alas! Now am I like your Tumblers, my Feet stand higher than my Head: Would to Heaven I were now with those good, holy Fathers, bound for the Council, whom we met this Morning, so Godly, so Fat, so Merry, so Plump and Comely. Holos, holos, holas, alas, alas. This Devilish Wave (*mea culpa, Deus*) I mean this Wave of God will sink our Vessel. Alas, Fryar Jhon, my Father, my Friend, Confession, here I am down on my Knees, *Confiteor*; your holy Blessing. Come hither and be damn'd thou pitiful Devil and help us (said Fryar Jhon) who fell a swearing and cursing like a Tinker; in the Name of thirty Legions of black Devils, come, will you come? Don't let us swear at this time, said Panurge, Holy Father, my Friend, don't swear, I beseech you; to morrow as much as you please. Holos, holos, alas, our Ship leaks. I drown, alas, alas, I will give eighteen hundred thousand Crowns to any one that will set me on shoar all beray'd, and dedaub'd as I am now, if ever there was a Man in my Country in the like pickle. *Confiteor*, alas! a word or two of Testament or Codicil at least. A thousand Devils seize the Cuckoldy Cow-hearted Mungril, cry'd Fryar Jhon; Ods Belly, art thou talking here of making thy Will, now we are in danger, and it behoveth us to bestir our Stumps lustily, or never. Wilt thou come, ho Devil? Midship-man my Friend, O the rare Lieutenant, here Gymnast, here on the Poop. We are by the Mass, all beshit now, our Light is out. This is hastening to the Devil as fast as it can.—Alas, bou, bou, bou, bou, bou, alas, alas, alas, alas, said Panurge, was it here we were born to perish? Oh! hoh! Good People, I drown, I die. *Consummatum est.* I am sped.— Magna, gna, gna, said Fryar Jhon. Fye upon him, how ugly the shitten Howler looks.—Boy, Younker, see hoyh.—Mind the Pumps, or the Devil choak thee.—Hast thou hurt thy self? Zoons, here fasten it to one of these Blocks. On this side in the Devil's Name, hay—so my Boy.—Ah Fryar Jhon, said Panurge, good Ghostly Father, dear Friend, don't let us swear, you sin. Oh ho, Oh ho, be be be bous, bous, bhous, I sink, I die, my Friends. I die in Charity with all the World. Farewell, *In manus.* Bohous, bhous, bhousowwauwaus. St. Michael of Aure! St. Nicholas! now, now or never. I here make you a solemn Vow and to our Saviour, that if you stand by me but this time, I mean if you set me ashoar out of this

I SINK, I SINK, HAH, MY FATHER, MY UNCLE, MY ALL

Danger, I will build you a fine large little Chappel or two between Cande and Monsoreau, where neither Cow nor Calf shall feed. Oh ho, oh ho. Above eighteen Palefuls or two of it are got down my Gullet, bous, bhous, bhous, bhous, how damn'd bitter and salt it is.—By the virtue (said Fryar Jhon) of the Blood, the Flesh, the Belly, the Head, if I hear thee again howling, thou Cuckoldly Cur, I'll maul thee worse than any Sea-Wolf. Ods fish, why don't we take him up by the Lugs, and throw him over-board to the bottom of the Sea? Here, Sailor, ho honest Fellow. Thus, thus, my Friend, hold fast above.—In truth here is a sad Lightning and Thundering; I think that all the Devils are got loose, 'tis Holy-day with 'em, or else Madam Proserpine is in Child's labour, all the Devils dance a Morrice.

W·H·R·

CHAPTER XX

How the Pilots were forsaking their Ships in the greatest stress of Weather

OH, said Panurge, you sin, Fryar Jhon, my former Crony, former, I say, for at this time I am no more, you are no more: It goes against my Heart to tell it you; for I believe this swearing doth your Spleen a great deal of good; as it is a great ease to a Wood-Cleaver to cry hem, at every Blow; and as one who plays at Nine-Pins, is wonderfully help'd, if, when he hath not thrown his Bowl right, and is like to make a bad cast, some ingenious stander-by leans and screws his Body half way about, on that side which the Bowl should have took to hit the Pins. Nevertheless you offend, my sweet Friend. But what do you think of eating some kind of Cabirotadoes ? Wouldn't this secure us from this Storm ? I have read that the Ministers of the Gods Cabiri so much celebrated by Orpheus, Apollonius, Pherecides, Strabo, Pausanias, and Herodotus, were always secure in time of Storm. He doats, he raves, the poor Devil, said Fryar Jhon. A thousand, a million, nay, a hundred millions of Devils seize the hornifi'd Doddipole. Lend's a Hand here, hoh, Tiger, wouldst thou ? Here on the Starboard side ; Ods me, thou Buffolo's-Head stuffed with Relicks, what Ape's *Pater Noster* art thou muttering and chattering here between thy Teeth ? That Devil of a Sea-calf is the Cause of all this Storm, and is the only Man who doth not lend a helping hand. By G— if I come near thee, I 'll fetch thee out by the Head and Ears with a vengeance, and chastise thee like any Tempestative Devil. Here Mate, my Lad, hold fast till I have made a double Knot. O' brave Boy ! Would to Heaven thou wert Abbot of Talemouze, and that he that is, were Guardian of Croullay. Hold Brother Ponocrates, you will hurt your self Man. Epistemon, pr'ythee stand off out of the Hatchway. Methinks I saw the Thunder fall there but just now. Con the Ship, so ho——Mind your Steerage. Well said, thus, thus, steady, keep her thus, get the Long-Boat clear.—Steady. Ods fish, the Beakhead is stav'd to pieces. Grumble, Devils, fart, belch, shite a T—d o' the Wave. If this be Weather, the Devil's a Ram. Nay, by G— a little more would have wash'd me clear away into the Current. I think all the Legions of Devils hold here their Provincial Chapter, or are Polling, Canvasing and Wrangling for the Election of a new Rector.—Starboard ; well said.—Take heed ; have a care of your Noddle, Lad, in the Devil's Name. So ho, Starboard, Starboard. Be, be, be, bous, bous, bous, cry'd Panurge, bous, bous, be, be, be, bous, bous, I am lost. I see neither Heaven nor Earth ; of the four Elements we have here only Fire and Water left. Bou, bou, bou, bous, bous, bous. Would it were the pleasure of the worthy Divine Bounty, that I were at this present Hour in the Close at Sevillé, or at Innocent's the Pastry-Cook, over against the painted Wine-Vault at Chinon, though I were to strip to my Doublet, and bake the petty Pasties my self.

Honest Man, could not you throw me ashoar, you can do a world of good things, they say. I give you all Salmigondinois, and my large Shoar full of Whilks, Cockles and Periwinkles, if by your Industry, I ever set Foot on firm Ground. Alas, alas, I drown. Hark'ee, my Friends, since we cannot get safe into

Port, let us come to an Anchor into some Road, no matter whither. Drop all your Anchors, let us be out of danger, I beseech you. Here honest Tar, get you into the Chains and heave the Lead, an't please you. Let us know how many Fathom Water we are in. Sound, Friend, in the Lord Harry's Name. Let us know, whether a Man might here drink easily without stooping. I am apt to believe One might. Helm a lee, hoh, cry'd the Pilot. Helm a lee, a Hand or two at the Helm, About Ships with her, Helm a lee, Helm a lee.—Stand off from the Leech of the Sail.—Hoh, Belay, here make fast below, hoh, Helm a lee, lash sure the Helm a lee, and let her drive. Is it come to that, said Pantagruel, our good Saviour then help us. Let her lie under the Sea, cry'd James Brayer, our chief Mate, let her drive. To Prayers, to Prayers, let all think on their Souls, and fall to Prayers ; nor hope to scape but by a Miracle. Let us, said Panurge, make some good pious kind of Vow, alas, alas, alas, bou, bou, be be be bous, bous, bous, Oho, Oho, Oho, Oho, let us make a Pilgrim ; come, come, let every Man club his Penny towards it, come on. Here, here, on this side, said Fryar Jhon in the Devil's Name. Let her drive, for the Lord's sake unhang the Rudder, hoh, let her drive, let her drive, and let us drink, I say of the best and most cheering, d' ye hear Steward, produce, exhibit, for d' ye see this, and all the rest will as well go to the Devil out of hand. A Pox on that Wind-broaker Æolus with his Fluster-blusters, Sirrah, Page, bring me here my Drawer (for so he call'd his Breviary) stay a little here, hawl, Friend, thus——Odzoons here's a deal of Hail and Thunder to no purpose. Hold fast above, I pray you. When have we All-Saints Day ? I believe 'tis the unholy Holiday of all the Devil's Crew. Alas, said Panurge, Fryar Jhon damns himself here as black as Butter-milk for the noance. Oh what a good Friend I lose in him. Alas, alas, there is anothergats Bout than last Year's. We are falling out of Scylla into Charybdis. Oho ! I drown. *Confiteor*, one poor Word or two by way of Testament, Fryar Jhon, my Ghostly Father, good Mr. Abstractor, my Crony, my Achates, Xenomanes, my All. Alas I drown, two Words of Testament here upon this Ladder.

I BELIEVE 'TIS THE UNHOLY HOLIDAY OF ALL THE DEVIL'S CREW

CHAPTER XXI

*A continuation of the Storm, with a short discourse on the
Subject of making Testaments at Sea*

To make ones last Will, said Epistemon, at this time that we
ought to bestir our selves, and help our Seamen, on the penalty
of being drown'd, seems to me as idle and ridiculous a Maggot
as that of some of Cæsar's Men, who at their coming into the
Gauls, were mightily busi'd in making Wills and Codicils,
bemoan'd their Fortune, and the absence of their Spouses and
Friends at Rome, when it was absolutely necessary for them
to run to their Arms, and use their utmost Strength against
Ariovistus their Enemy.

This also is to be as silly as that jolt-headed Loblolly of a
Carter, who having laid his Waggon fast in a Slough, down on
his Marrow-bones, was calling on the strong-back'd Deity
Hercules, might and main, to help him at a dead lift, but all the
while forgot to goad on his Oxen, and lay his Shoulder to the
Wheels, as it behoved him, as if a Lord have mercy upon us
alone, would have got his Cart out of the Mire.

What will it signify to make your Will now ? For either
we shall come off, or drown for't. If we scape, it will not
signify a Straw to us; for Testaments are of no value or
Authority, but by the Death of the Testators. If we are
drown'd, will it not be drown'd too ? Pr'ythee who will
transmit it to the Executors ? Some kind Wave will throw it
ashoar, like Ulysses, reply'd Panurge, and some King's daughter,
going to Fetch a Walk in the Fresco on the Evening, will find
it, and take care to have it prov'd and fulfill'd ; nay, and have
some stately Cenotaph erected to my Memory, as Dido had to
that of her good Man Sichæus, Æneas to Deiphobus upon the
Trojan Shoar near Rhœte ; Andromache to Hector in the City
of Buthrot ; Aristotle to Hermias and Eubulus ; the Athenians

to the Poet Euripides; the Romans to Drusus in Germany, and to Alexander Severus their Emperor in the Gauls; Argentier to Callaischre, Xenocrates to Lisidices; Timares to his Son Teleutagoras; Eupolis and Aristodice to their Son Theotimus; Onestes to Timocles; Callimachus to Sopolis the Son of Dioclides; Catullus to his Brother; Statius to his Father; Germain of Brie to Herveé the Breton Tarpawlin. Art thou mad, said Fryar Jhon, to run on at this rate? Help here, in the name of Five hundred thousand Millions of Cart-loads of Devils, help; may a Shanker gnaw thy Mustacho's, and three rows of Pock-royals and Collyflowers cover thy Bum and Turd-barrel instead of Breeches and Codpiece. Codsooks, our Ship is almost overset. Ods death, how shall we clear her? 'Tis well if she don't founder. What a devilish Sea there runs? She 'll neither try, nor hull, the Sea will overtake her, so we shall never scape, the Devil scape me. Then Pantagruel, was heard to make a sad Exclamation, saying with a loud Voice, Lord save us, we perish: Yet not as we would have it, but thy holy Will be done. The Lord and the blessed Virgin be with us said Panurge: Holos, alas, I drown, be be be bous, be bous bous: *In manus.* Good Heaven, send me some Dolphin to carry me safe on shoar, like a pretty little Arion: I shall make shift to sound the Harp if it be not unstrung. Let nineteen Legions of black Devils seize me, said Fryar Jhon, (the Lord be with us, whisper'd Panurge between his chattering Teeth), If I come down to thee, I'll shew thee to some purpose, that the Badge of thy Humanity dangles at a Calf's Breech, thou ragged-horn'd Cuckoldy Booby; mgna, mgnan, mgnan: Come hither and help us, thou great weeping Calf, or may thirty millions of Devils leap on thee; wilt thou come, Sea-calf? Fye, how ugly the howling Whelp looks! What, always the same Ditty? Come on now my bonny Drawer; (this he said opening his Breviary) come forward, thou and I must be somewhat serious for a while, let me peruse thee stiffly: *Beatus vir qui non abiit.* Pshaw, I know all this by heart; let's see the Legend of Monsieur St. Nicholas.

Horrida tempestas montem turbavit acutum,

Tempest was a mighty Flogger of Lads at Mountague-College: If Pedants be damn'd for whipping poor little innocent Wretches their Scholars, he is, upon my Honour, by this time fix'd within Ixion's Wheel, lashing the croptear bobtail'd Cur that gives it Motion. If they are sav'd for having whipp'd innocent Lads, he ought to be above the——

CHAPTER XXII

An End of the Storm

SHOAR, shoar, cry'd Pantagruel, land to, my Friends, I see Land, pluck up a good Spirit Boys, 'tis within a kenning, so we are not far from a Port——I see the Sky clearing up to the Northwards——Look to the South-east ! Courage, my Hearts, said the Pilot, now she'll bear the hullock of a Sail, the Sea is much smoother, some Hands aloft, to the main Top——Put the Helm a weather——Steady, steady—Hawl your aftermisen Bowlins—Haul, haul, haul—Thus, thus, and no nearer. Mind your Steerage, bring your main Tack aboard——Clear your Sheets ; clear your Bowlins ; port, port, helm a-lee—Now, to the Sheet on the starboard-side, thou Son of a Whore. Thou art mightily pleas'd, honest Fellow, quoth Fryar Jhon, with hearing him make mention of thy Mother. Loff, loff, cry'd the Quartermaster that con'd the Ship, keep her full, loff the Helm. Loff, it is, answer'd the Steerman ; keep her thus——Get the Bonnets fix'd——Steady, steady.

That 's well said, said Fryar Jhon, now this is something like a Tanzy. Come, come, come, Children, be nimble——Good—— Loff, loff——Thus——Helm a weather. That's well said and thought on. Methinks the Storm is almost over. It was high time, faith ; however the Lord be thanked——Our Devils begin to scamper——Out with all your Sails——Hoist your Sails——

Hoist——That's spoke like a Man, Hoist, hoist——Here agod's name honest Ponocrates, thou 'rt a lusty Fornicator, the Whore-son will get none but boys, Eusthenes, thou art a notable Fellow——Run up to the Foretop-Sail——Thus, thus—— Well said, i-faith, thus, thus. I dare not fear any thing all this while, for it is Holiday. Vea, vea, vea! Husah! This Shout of the Seamen is not amiss, and pleases me, for it is Holiday: Keep her full, thus——Good. Chear up my merry Mates all, cry'd out Epistemon, I see already Castor on the Right. Be, be, bous, bous, bous, said Panurge, I am much afraid it is the Bitch Helen. 'Tis truly Mixarchagenas, return'd Epistemon, if thou likest better that Denomination which the Argives give him. Ho, ho! I see Land too; let her bear it with the Har-bour; I see a good many People on the Beach; I see a Light on an Obeliscolychny. Shorten your Sails, said the Pilot, fetch the Sounding-line, we must double that Point of Land, and mind the Sands——We are clear of them, said the Sai ors. Soon after, away she goes, quoth the Pilot, and so doth the rest of our Fleet: Help came in good season.

By St. John, said Panurge, this is spoke somewhat like: Oh the sweet Word! There 's the Soul of Musick in 't. Mgna, mgna, mgna, said Fryar Jhon: If ever thou tast a Drop on 't, let the Devil's Dam tast me, thou ballocky Devil. Here honest Soul, here's a full Sneaker of the very best. Bring the Flaggons, dost hear, Gymnast, and that same large Pasty Jambic, Gammonic, as you will have it——Take heed you pilot her in right.

Chear up, cry'd out Pantagruel, chear up, my Boys: Let's be our selves again, do you see yonder close by our Ship, two Barks, three Sloops, five Ships, eight Pinks, four Yawls, and six Frigots, making towards us, sent by the Good People of the neighbouring Island to our relief. But who is this Ucalegon below, that cries and makes such a sad moan? Were it not that I hold the Mast firmly with both my Hands, and kept it streighter than two hundred Tacklings.—I'd.—It is (said Fryar Jhon) that poor Devil Panurge, who is troubled with a Calf's Ague; he quakes for fear when his Belly's full. If, said Pantagruel, he hath been afraid during this dreadful Hurricane, and dangerous Storm, provided (waving that) he hath done his part like a Man, I do not value him a jot the less for it. For as to fear in all Encounters, is the mark of a heavy, and cowardly Heart, as Agamemnon did, who for that reason, is ignominiously tax'd by Achilles with having Dogs Eyes, and a Stags Heart ; so not to fear when the case is evidently dreadful, is a sign of want or smalness of Apprehension.

Now if any thing ought to be feared, in this Life, next to offending God, I will not say it is Death ; I will not meddle with the Disputes of Socrates and the Academies, that Death of it self is neither bad nor to be fear'd : But I will affirm that this kind of death by Shipwreck is to be fear'd or nothing is. For, as Homer saith, it is a grievous, dreadful, and an unnatural thing to perish at Sea. And indeed Æneas, in the Storm that took his Fleet near Sicily, was griev'd that he had not dy'd by the Hand of the brave Diomedes, and said that those were three, nay four times happy who perish'd with Troy. No Man here hath lost his Life ; the Lord our Saviour be eternally prais'd for it : but, in truth, here is a Ship sadly out of order. Well, we must take care to have the Damage repair'd. Take heed we do not run a ground and billage her.

CHAPTER XXIII

How Panurge play'd the Good Fellow when the Storm was over

WHAT Cheer ho ? fore and aft ? quoth Panurge, Oh, ho ! All is well, the Storm is over. I beseech ye, be so kind as to let me be the first that is set on shoar ; for I would by all means a little untruss a Point.—Shall I help you still, here, let me see, I 'll coyle this Rope ; I have plenty of Courage, and of Fear as little as may be. Give it me yonder, honest Tar—No, no, I have not a bit of Fear. Indeed that same Decumane Wave that took us fore and aft somewhat alter'd my Pulse.——Down with your Sails, well said, how now, Fryar Jhon, you do nothing ? Is it time for us to drink now ? Who can tell but St. Martin's running Footman Belzebuth may still be hatching us some further Mischief ? Shall I come and help you again ? Pork and Pease choak me, if I do not heartily repent, tho' too late, not having followed the doctrine of the good Philosopher, who tells us, That to walk by the Sea, and to navigate by the Shoar, are very safe and pleasant things ; just as 'tis to go on foot when we hold our Horse by the Bridle.—Hah, hah, hah, by G— all goes well.—Shall I help you here too ? Let me see, I 'll do this as it should be, or the Devil 's in 't.

Epistemon (who had the inside of one of his Hands all flea'd and bloody, having held a Tackling with might and main) hearing what Pantagruel had said, told him, You may believe my Lord, I had my share of Fear, as well as Panurge, yet I spar'd no Pains in lending my helping Hand. I consider'd, that since by fatal and unavoidable Necessity, we must all die, it is the blessed Will of God that we die this or that Hour, and this or that kind of death; nevertheless we ought to implore, invoke, pray, beseech, and supplicate him: but yet we must not stop there; it behoveth us also to use our Endeavours on our side, and, as the Holy Writ saith, to co-operate with him.

You know what C. Flaminius the Consul said, when by Hanibal's Policy he was penn'd up near the Lake of Peruse alias Thrasymene, Friends (said he to his Soldiers) you must not hope to get out of this place barely by Vows or Prayers to the Gods; no, 'tis by Fortitude and Strength we must escape, and cut ourselves a Way with the Edge of our Swords, through the midst of our Enemies.

Salust likewise makes M. Portius Cato say this, The help of the Gods is not obtain'd by idle Vows, and Womanish Complaints; 'tis by Vigilance, Labour, and repeated Endeavours that all things succeed according to our Wishes and Designs.

If a Man in time of Need and Danger is negligent, heartless, and lazy, in vain he implores the Gods; they are then justly angry and incens'd against him. The Devil take me, said Fryar Jhon (I'll go his halves, quoth Panurge) if the Close of Sevillé had not been all gather'd, vintag'd, glean'd, and destroy'd, if I had only sung *Contra hostium insidias* (matter of Breviary) like all the rest of the Monking Devils, and had not bestir'd my self to save the Vineyard as I did, dispatching the Truant Piccaroons of Lerné with the Staff of the Cross.

Let her sink or swim a God's name, said Panurge, all 's one to Fryar Jhon, he doth nothing; his Name is Fryar Jhon Doelittle; for all he sees me here a sweating and puffing to help with all my Might this honest Tar, first of the Name.——Hark you me, dear Soul, a word with you—but pray be not angry; How thick do you judge the Planks of our Ship to be? Some two good Inches and upwards, return'd the Pilot, don't fear. Odskilderkins, said Panurge, it seems then we are within two Fingers breadth of Damnation. Is this one of the nine Comforts of Matrimony? Ah, dear Soul, you do well to measure the Danger by the Yard of Fear. For my part I have none on 't, my Name is William Dreadnought. As for Heart, I have more than enough on 't ; I mean none of your Sheeps Heart ; but of Wolf's Heart, the Courage of a Bravoe ; by the Pavilion of Mars, I fear nothing but Danger.

CHAPTER XXIV

How Panurge was said to have been afraid, without reason, during the Storm

GOOD morrow, Gentlemen, said Panurge, Good morrow to you all, You are in very good Health, thanks to Heaven, and your selves : You are all heartily welcome, and in good time. Let us go on shoar—Here, Coxen, get the Ladder over the Gunnel, Man the Sides, Man the Pinnace, and get her by the Ships side.— Shall I yet lend you a hand here ? I am stark mad for want of Business, and would work like any two Yoaks of Oxen.— Truly this is a fine Place, and these look like a very good People.—Children, do you want me still in any thing, do not spare the Sweat of my Body, for godsake. Adam (that is Man) was made to labour and work, as the Birds were made to fly, our Lord's Will is that we get our Bread with the Sweat of our Brows, not idling and doing nothing, like this Tatterdemallion of a Monk here, this Fryar Jack, who is fain to drink to hearten himself up, and dies for fear.—Rare Weather.—I now find the Answer of Anacharsis, the noble Philosopher, very proper ; being ask'd what Ship he reckon'd the safest ; he reply'd, that which is in the Harbour : he made a yet better Repartie, said Pantagruel, when some Body enquiring which is greater, the Number of the Living, or that of the Dead ? He ask'd them, amongst which of the two they reckon'd those that are at Sea ? ingeniously implying, that they are continually in danger of Death, dying live, and living die. Portius Cato also said that there were but three things of which he would repent ; that is, if ever he had trusted his Wife with his Secret, if he had idled away a Day, and if he had ever gone by Sea, to a Place which he could visit by Land. By this dignified Frock of mine, said Fryar Jhon to Panurge, Friend, thou hast been afraid during the Storm, without cause or reason ; for thou wert not

THE DEVIL WAS SICK, THE DEVIL A MONK WOU'D BE

born to be drowned, but rather to be hang'd, and exalted in the Air, or to be roasted in the midst of a jolly Bonfire. My Lord, would you have a good Cloak for the Rain ? Leave me off your Wolf and Badger-skin Mantle : Let Panurge but be flead, and cover your self with his Hide. But do not come near the Fire, nor near your Blacksmith's Forges a God's Name, for in a Moment you would see it in Ashes. Yet be as long as you please in the Rain, Snow, Hail, nay, by the Devil's Maker, throw your self or dive down to the very bottom of the Water, I 'll engage you 'll not be wet at all. Have some winter Boots made of it, they 'll never take in a drop of Water ; make Bladders of it to lay under Boys, to teach them to swim, instead of Corks, and they will learn without the least danger. His Skin then, said Pantagruel, should be like the Herb called, True Maidens Hair, which never takes wet nor moistness, but still keeps dry, though you lay it at the bottom of the Water as long as you please, and for that reason is call'd Adiantos.

Friend Panurge, said Fryar Jhon, I pray thee never be afraid of Water, thy Life for mine, thou art threatn'd with a contrary Element. Ay, ay, reply'd Panurge, but the Devil's Cooks dote sometimes, and are apt to make horrid Blunders as well as others, often putting to boil in Water what was design'd to be roasted on the Fire, like the head Cooks of our Kitchen, who often lard Partridges, Queests and Stock-doves with intent to roast them, one wou'd think, but it happens sometimes, that they e'en turn the Patridges into the Pot to be boil'd with Cabbages, the Queests with Leek Porrage, and the Stockdoves with Turnips.

But hark you me, good Friends, I protest before this noble Company, that as for the Chappel which I vow'd to Monsieur St. Nicholas, between Cande, and Monsoreau, I honestly mean that it shall be a Chappel, alias a Lymbeck of Rose-water, which shall be where neither Cow nor Calf shall be fed, for between you and I, I intend to throw it to the bottom of the Water. Here is a rare Rogue for yee, said Eusthenes ; here 's a pure Rogue, a Rogue in grain, a Rogue enough, a Rogue and a half. He is resolv'd to make good the Italian Proverb, *Passato el pericolo è gabato el Santo.*

> The Devil was sick, the Devil a Monk wou'd be ;
> The Devil was well, and the Devil a Monk he 'd be.

THE DEVIL WAS WELL, AND THE DEVIL A MONK HE'D BE

171

CHAPTER XXV

*How after the Storm, Pantagruel went on Shoar in the
Islands of the Macreons*

IMMEDIATELY after, we went a shoar at the Port of an Island,
which they call'd the Island of the Macreons ; the good People
of the Place receiv'd us very honourably. An old Macrobius
(so they call'd their eldest Elderman) desir'd Pantagruel to
come to the Town-house to refresh himself, and eat something,
but he would not budge a foot, from the Mole, till all his Men
were landed. After he had seen them, he gave order they
should all change Cloaths, and that some of all the Stores in
the Fleet, should be brought on shoar, that every Ship's Crew
might live well, which was accordingly done ; and God wot how
they all top'd, and carrouz'd ; the People of the Place brought
them Provisions in abundance. The Pantagruelists return'd
them more : As the truth is, their's were somewhat damag'd by
the late Storm. When they had well stuffed the insides of their
Doublets, Pantagruel desired every one to lend their help to
repair the Damage, which they readily did. It was easie
enough to refit there ; for all the Inhabitants of the Island
were Carpenters, and all such Handicrafts as are seen in the
Arsenal at Venice. None but the largest Island was inhabited,
having three Ports, and ten Parishes ; the rest being over-run
with Wood, and Desart, much like the Forest of Arden. We
entreated the old Macrobius to shew us what was worth seeing
in the Island, which he did ; and in the Desart and dark
Forest, we discover'd several old ruined Temples, Obeliscs,
Pyramids, Monuments, and ancient Tombs, with diverse
Inscriptions, and Epitaphs, some of them in Hieroglyphic
Characters, others in the Gothic Dialect, some in the Arabic,
Agarenian, Sclavonian, and other Tongues : of which Epistemon took an exact Account. In the interim Panurge said to
Fryar Jhon, Is this the Island of the Macreons ? Macreon
signifies in Greek an old Man, or one much stricken in Years.
What's that to me, said Fryar Jhon, how can I help it ? I was
not in the Country when they Christen'd it. Now I think on 't,
quoth Panurge, I believe the Name of Makerel [that's a Bawd
in French] was deriv'd from it ; for, procuring is the Province

of the old, as Buttock-riggling is that of the young. Therefore
I don't know but this may be the Bawdy or Mackrel Island, the
Original and Prototype of the Island of that Name at Paris.
Let 's go and drudge for Cock-Oysters. Old Macrobius ask'd
in the Ionick Tongue, how, and by what Industry and Labour
Pantagruel got to their Port that Day, there having been such
blustering Weather, and such a dreadful Storm at Sea. Pantagruel told him, that the Almighty Preserver of Mankind had
regarded the Simplicity, and sincere Affection of his Servants,
who did not travel for Gain or Sordid Profit, the sole design of
their Voyage being a studious desire to know, see, and visit
the Oracle of Bacbuc, and take the Word of the Bottle upon
some Difficulties offer'd by one of the Company ; nevertheless
this had not been without great Affliction, and evident danger
of Shipwrack. After that, he ask'd him what he judg'd to be
the cause of that terrible Tempest, and if the adjacent Seas
were thus frequently subject to Storms, as in the Ocean are
the Ratz of Sammaieu, Maumusson, and in the Mediterranean
Sea the Gulph of Sataly, Montargentan, Piombino, Capo Melio
in the Morea, the Streights of Gibraltar, Faro di Messina, and
others.

CHAPTER XXVI

How the good Macrobius gave us an Account of the
Mansion, and Decease of the Heroes

THE good Macrobius then answer'd, Friendly Strangers, this
Island is one of the Sporades, not of your Sporades that lie in
the Carpathian Sea, but one of the Sporades of the Ocean ; in
former times rich, frequented, wealthy, populous, full of Traffic,
and in the Dominions of the Ruler of Britain ; but now by
course of Time, and in these latter Ages of the World, poor and
desolate as you see. In this dark Forest, above seventy eight
thousand Persian Leagues in compass, is the Dwelling-place of
the Dæmons and Heroes, that are grown old, and we believe
that some one of them dy'd yesterday ; since the Comet, which
we saw for three Days before together, shines no more : And
now 'tis likely, that at his Death there arose this horrible
Storm ; for while they are alive, all Happiness attends both
this and the adjacent Islands, and a settled Calm and Serenity.
At the Death of every one of them we commonly hear in the
Forest loud and mournful Groans, and the whole Land is
infested with Pestilence, Earthquakes, Inundations and other
Calamities ; the Air with Fogs and Obscurity, and the Sea with
storms and hurricanes. What you tell us seems to me likely
enough, said Pantagruel ; for as a Torch or Candle, as long as it
hath Life enough and is lighted, shines round about, disperses
its Light, delights those that are near it, yields them its Service
and Clearness, and never causes any Pain or Displeasure ; but
as soon as 'tis extinguished, its Smoak and Evaporation infects
the Air, offends the Bystanders, and is noisom to all : So, as
long as those noble and renowned Souls inhabit their Bodies,
Peace, Profit, Pleasure, and Honour never leave the Places
where they abide ; but as soon as they leave them, both the
Continent and the adjacent Islands are annoyed with great
Commotions ; in the Air, Fogs, Darkness, Thunder, Hail ;
Tremblings, Pulsations, Arietations of the Earth ; Storms and
Hurricanes at Sea ; together with sad Complaints amongst
the People, Broaching of Religions, Changes in Governments,
and Ruins of Common-wealths.

We had a sad Instance of this lately, said Epistemon, at the

174

Death of that valiant and learned Knight William du Bellay, during whose Life France enjoy'd so much Happiness, that all the rest of the World look'd upon it with Envy, sought Friendship with it, and stood in awe of its Power ; but soon after his Decease it hath for a considerable time been the Scorn of the rest of the World.

Thus, said Pantagruel, Anchises being dead at Drepany in Sicily, Æneas was dreadfully toss'd and endanger'd by a Storm ; and perhaps for the same reason Herod, that Tyrant and cruel King of Judea, finding himself near the Pangs of a horrid kind of Death (for he dy'd of a Phthiriasis, devour'd by Vermin and Lice ; as before him dy'd L. Scylla, Pherecides the Syrian Preceptor, Pythagoras, the Greek Poet Alcmæon and others) and foreseeing that the Jews would make Bonfires at his Death, caus'd all the Nobles and Magistrates to be summoned to his Seraglio out of all the Cities, Towns, and Castles of Judæa, fraudulently pretending that he had some things of moment to impart to them. They made their personal appearance ; whereupon he caus'd them all to be shut up in the Hippodrome of the Seraglio ; then said to his Sister Salome, and Alexander her Husband ; I am certain that the Jews will rejoice at my Death, but if you will observe and perform what I will tell you, my Funeral shall be honourable, and there will be a general Mourning. As soon as you shall see me dead, let my Guards, to whom I have already given strict Commission to that purpose, kill all the Noblemen and Magistrates that are secur'd in the Hippodrome. By these means all Jewry shall in spite of themselves be oblig'd to mourn and lament, and Foreigners will imagine it to be for my Death, as if some heroic Soul had left her Body. A desperate Tyrant wish'd as much, when he said, When I dye, let Earth and Fire be mix'd together ; which was as much as to say, Let the whole World perish : Which Saying the Tyrant Nero alter'd, saying While I live, as Suetonius affirms it. This detestable Saying, of which Cicero, lib. 3. *de Finib.* and Seneca, lib. 2. *de Clementia,* make mention, is ascrib'd to the Emperor Tiberius, by Dion Nicæus, and Suidas.

CHAPTER XXVII

Pantagruel's Discourse of the Decease of Heroic Souls ; and of the dreadful Prodigies that happen'd before the Death of the late Lord de Langey

I WOULD not, continu'd Pantagruel, have miss'd the Storm that hath thus disorder'd us, were I also to have miss'd the Relation of these things told us by this good Macrobius. Neither am I unwilling to believe what he said of a Comet that appears in the Sky some Days before such a Decease. For some of those Souls are so Noble, so precious, and so heroic, that Heaven gives us notice of their Departing, some days before it happens. And as a prudent Physician seeing by some Symptoms that his Patient draws towards his End, some Days before, gives notice of it to his Wife, Children, Kindred, and Friends, that, in that little time he hath yet to live, they may admonish him to settle all things in his Family, to tutor and instruct his Children as much as he can, recommend his Relict to his Friends, in her Widdowhood, declare what he knows to be necessary about a Provision for the Orphans, that he may not be surpriz'd by Death without making his Will, and may take care of his Soul and Family. In the same manner the Heavens, as it were, joyful for the approaching reception of those blessed Souls, seem to make Bonfires by those Comets and blazing Meteors, which they at the same time kindly design should Prognosticate to us here, that in few days one of those venerable Souls, is to leave her Body and this terrestrial Globe. Not altogether unlike this, was what was formerly done at Athens by the Judges of the Areopagus. For when they gave their Verdict to cast or clear the Culprits that were try'd before them, they us'd certain Notes according to the substance of the Sentences ; by Θ, signifying Condemnation to Death ; by T, Absolution ; by A, Ampliation or a Demur, when the Case was not sufficiently examin'd. Thus having publickly set up those Letters, they eas'd the Relations and Friends of the Prisoners, and such others as desir'd to know their Doom, of their Doubts. Likewise by these Comets, as in ætherial Characters, the Heavens silently say to us, Make haste, Mortals, if you would know or learn of these blessed Souls any thing concerning the publick Food or your private Interest ; for their Catastrophe is near, which being past, you will vainly wish for them afterwards.

The good-natur'd Heavens still do more ; and, that Mankind may be declared unworthy of the enjoyment of those renown'd Souls, they fright and astonish us with Prodigies, Monsters, and other foreboding Signs, that thwart the Order of Nature.

Of this we had an instance several Days before the Decease of the heroic Soul of the learned and valiant Chevalier de Langey, of whom you have already spoken. I remember it, said Epistemon, and my heart still trembles within me when I think on the many dreadful Prodigies that we saw five or six Days before he dy'd. For the Lords of D'assier, Chemant, one-ey'd Mailly, St. Ayl, Villeneufue-la-Guyart, Master Gabriel, Physician of Savillan, Rabelais, Cobuau, Massuau, Majorici, Bullou, Cercu, alias Bourgmaistre, Francis Proust, Ferron, Charles Girard, Francis Bourré, and many other Friends and Servants to the Deceased, all dismay'd, gaz'd on each other, without uttering one word ; yet not without foreseeing that France wou'd, in a short time, be depriv'd of a Knight so accomplish'd and necessary for its Glory and Protection, and that Heaven claim'd him again as its due. By the tufted Tip of my Cowle, cry'd Fryar Jhon, I am e'en resolv'd to become a Scholar before I die : I have a pretty good Headpiece of my own, you must own : Now pray give me leave to ask you a civil Question ; Can these same Hero's and Demi-gods, you talk of, die ? May I never be damn'd, if I was not so much a Lobcock as to believe they had been Immortal, like so many fine Angels ; Heav'n forgive me ! but this most Reverend Father, Macroby, tells us, They die at last. We all must, return'd Pantagruel.

The Stoicks held them all to be Mortal, except one, who alone is Immortal, Impassible, Invisible. Pindar plainly saith, That there is no more Thread, that is to say, no more Life spun from the Distaff and Flax of the hard-hearted Fates, for the Goddesses Hamadryades, than there is for those Trees that are preserv'd by them, which are good sturdy downright Oaks, whence they derived their Original, according to the Opinion of Callimachus, and Pausanias in Phoci ; with whom concurs Martianus Capella. As for the Demi-gods, Fauns, Satyrs, Sylvans, Hobgoblins, Ægpanes, Nymphs, Heroes, and Dæmons, several Men have, from the total Sum, which is the Result of the divers Ages calculated by Hesiod, reckon'd their Life to be 9720 Years, that Sum, consisting of four special Numbers orderly arising from one, the same added together, and multiplied by four every way, amounts to forty ; these forties being reduced into Triangles by five times, make up the total of the foresaid Number. See Plutarch, in his Book about the Cessation of Oracles.

This, said Fryar Jhon, is not Matter of Breviary ; I may believe as little or as much of it as you and I please. I believe, said Pantagruel, that all Intellectual Souls are exempted from Atropos's Scissers. They are all Immortal, whether they be of Angels, of Dæmons, or Human : Yet I 'll tell you a Story concerning this, that 's very strange, but is written and affirmed by several learned Historians.

CHAPTER XXVIII

How Pantagruel related a very sad Story of the Death of the Hero's

EPITHERSES the Father of Æmilian the Rhetorician, sailing from Greece to Italy, in a Ship freighted with divers Goods and Passengers, at Night the Wind fail'd 'em near the Echinades, some Islands that lie between the Morea and Tunis, and the vessel was driven near Paxos. When they were got thither, some of the Passengers being asleep, others awake, the rest eating and drinking, a Voice was heard that call'd aloud Thamous ; which Cry surpriz'd them all. This same Thamous was their Pilot, an Egyptian by Birth, but known by Name only to some few Travellers. The Voice was heard a second time calling Thamous, in a frightful Tone ; and none making answer, but trembling and remaining silent, the Voice was heard a third time, more dreadful than before.

This caus'd Thamous to answer, Here am I ; What do'st thou call me for ? What wilt thou have me do ? Then the Voice, louder than before, bad him publish, when he should come to Paloda, That the Great God Pan was dead.

Epitherses related, that all the Mariners and Passengers, having heard this, were extremely amaz'd and frighted ; and that consulting among themselves, whether they had best conceal or divulge what the Voice had enjoyn'd, Thamous said, His Advice was, That if they happen'd to have a fair Wind, they shou'd proceed, without mentioning a word on 't ; but if they chanc'd to be becalm'd, he wou'd publish what he had heard : Now when they were near Paloda they had no Wind, neither were they in any Current. Thamous then getting up on the top of the Ship's Fore-castle, and casting his Eyes on the Shore, said that he had been commanded to proclaim, That the great God Pan was dead. The Words were hardly out of his Mouth, when deep Groans, great Lamentations, and Shrieks, not of one Person, but of many together, were heard from the Land.

The News of this, (many being present then) was soon spread at Rome ; insomuch that Tiberius, who was then Emperor, sent for this Thamous, and having heard him, gave credit to his Words ; and enquiring of the Learned in his Court, and at Rome, who was that Pan ? He found, by their Relation, that he was the Son of Mercury and Penelope ; as Herodotus, and Cicero in his Third Book of the Nature of the Gods, had written before.

For my part, I understand it of that Great Saviour of the Faithful, who was shamefully put to Death at Jerusalem, by the Envy and Wickedness of the Doctors, Priests and Monks of the Mosaic Law. And methinks my Interpretation is not improper ; for He may lawfully be said, in the Greek Tongue, to be Pan, since He is our All. For all that we are, all that we live, all that we have, all that we hope, is Him, by Him, from Him, and in Him ; He is the Good Pan, the Great Shepherd ; who, as the loving Shepherd Corydon affirms, hath not only a tender Love and Affection for his Sheep, but also for their Shepherds. At His Death, Complaints, Sighs, Fears and Lamentations were spread through the whole Fabrick of the Universe, whether Heaven, Land, Sea, or Hell.

The Time also concurs with this Interpretation of mine ; for this Most Good, Most Mighty Pan, Our only Saviour, died near Jerusalem, during the Reign of Tiberius Cæsar. Pantagruel having ended this Discourse, remain'd silent, and full of

Contemplation ; a little while after, we saw the Tears flow out
of his Eyes as big as Ostridge's Eggs. God take me presently,
if I tell you one single syllable of a Lye in the Matter.

CHAPTER XXIX

How Pantagruel sail'd by the Sneaking-Island where Shrovetide reign'd

THE Jovial Fleet being refitted and repair'd, new Stores taken
in, the Macreons over-and-above satisfy'd, and pleas'd with the
Money spent there by Pantagruel, our Men in better Humour
yet than they us'd to be if possible, we merrily put to Sea the
next Day near Sun-set, with a delicious fresh Gale.

Xenomanes shew'd us afar off the Sneaking-Island, where
reign'd Shrovetide, of whom Pantagruel had heard much Talk
formerly ; for that reason, he wou'd gladly have seen him in
Person, had not Xenomanes advis'd him to the contrary :
First, because this wou'd have been much out of our Way ; and
then, for the Lean Chear which he told us, was to be found at
that Prince's Court, and indeed all over the Island.

You can see nothing there for your Money (said he) but a
huge Greedy-guts, a tall woundy Swallower of Hotwardens and
Muscles, a Long-shank'd Mole-catcher, an over-grown Bottler
of Hay, a Mossy-chin'd, Demi-giant with a double-shaven
Crown, of Lantern-breed ; a very great Loitering Noddy-
peak'd Youngster, Banner-bearer to the Fish-eating Tribe,
Dictator of Mustard-land, Flogger of little Children, Calciner
of Ashes, Father and Foster-father to Physicians, swarming with
Pardons, Indulgences and Stations, a very honest Man, a good
Catholick, and as brim-full of Devotion as ever he can hold :
He weeps the three-fourth parts of the Day, and never assists
at any Weddings ; but, give the Devil his due, he 's the most
industrious Larding-stick and Scure-maker in forty Kingdoms.

About Six Years ago, as I pass'd by Sneaking-Land, I
brought home a large Scure from thence, and made a Present of
it to the Butchers of Quande, who set a great Value upon them,
and that for a Cause. Sometime or other, if ever we live to
come back to our own Country, I will shew you two of them

THE FOURTH BOOK OF DR. FRANCIS RABELAIS

fasten'd on the great Church-Porch. His usual Food is pickled
Coats of Mail, salt Helmets and Headpieces, and salt Sallads;
which sometimes makes him piss Pins and Needles. As for
his Cloathing, 'tis comical enough o' conscience, both for make
and colour; for he wears Gray and Gold, nothing before, and
nought behind, with the Sleeves of the same.

You will do me a Kindness, said Pantagruel, if, as you have
described his Cloaths, Food, Actions, and Pastimes, you will
also give me an Account of his Shape, and Disposition in all his
Parts. Prithee do, dear Cod, said Fryar Jhon, for I have found
him in my Breviary, and then follow the Moveable Holy-days.
With all my Heart, answer'd Xenomanes : We may chance to
hear more of him, as we touch at the Wild Island, the Dominion
of the Squob Chitterlings his Enemies, against whom he is
eternally at Odds; and were it not for the help of the noble
Carnaval their Protector, and good Neighbour, this Meagre-
look'd Lozelly Shrovetide would long before this have made sad
Work among them, and rooted them out of their Habitation.
Are these same Chitterlings, said Fryar Jhon, Male or Female,
Angels or Mortals, Women or Maids ? They are, reply'd
Xenomanes, Female in Sex, Mortal in Kind, some of them
Maids, others not. The Devil have me, said Fryar Jhon, if I
been't for them. What a shameful Disorder in Nature is it
not, to make War against Women. Let's go back, and hack
the Villain to pieces.——What ! meddle with Shrovetide, cry'd
Panurge : In the Name of Belzebub, I am not yet so weary of
my Life : No, I 'm not yet so mad as that comes to. *Quid
juris ?* Suppose we shou'd find our selves pent up between the
Chitterlings and Shrovetide ? between the Anvil and the
Hammers ? Shankers and Bubo's; stand off; Gadzooks, let 's
make the best of our Way. I bid you Good-night, sweet Mr.
Shrovetide ; I recommend to you the Chitterlings, and pray
don't forget the Puddings.

CHAPTER XXX

How Shrovetide is anatomiz'd and describ'd by Xenomanes

As for the Inward Parts of Shrovetide, said Xenomanes, his Brain is (at least it was in my time) in Bigness, Colour, Substance, and Strength, much like the Left-Cod of a He-hand-worm.

The Ventricles of his said Brain, like an Augre.

The Worm-like Excrescence, like a Christmas-Box.

The Membranes, like a Monk's Cowle.

The Funnel, like a Mason's Chissel.

The Fornix, like a Casket.

The Glandula pinealis, like a Bag-pipe.

The Rete Admirable, like a Gutter.

The Dug-like Processes, like a Patch.

The Tympanums, like a Whirly-Gig.

The Rocky bones, like a Goose-wing.

The Nape of the Neck, like a Paper Lanthorn.

The Nerves, like a Pipkin.

The Uvula, like a Sack-butt.

The Palate, like a Mitten.

The Spittle, like a Shuttle.

The Almonds, like a Telescope.

The Bridge of his Nose, like a Wheel-barrow.

The Head of the Larynx, like a Vintage Basket.
The Stomach, like a Belt.
The Pylorus, like a Pitchfork.
The Windpipe, like an Oyster-knife.
The Throat, like a Pincushion stuff'd with Oakham.
The Lungs, like a Prebend's Fur-gown.
The Heart, like a Cope.
The Mediastin, like an earthen Cup.
The Pleura, like a Crows-bill.
The Arteries, like a Watch-coat.
The Midriff, like a Mounteer-Cap.
The Liver, like a double-tongu'd Mattock.
The Veins, like a Sash-window.
The Spleen, like a Catcal.
The Guts, like a Trammel.
The Gall, like a Coopers Ads.
The Entrails, like a Gantlet.
The Mesentery, like an Abbot's Myter.
The Hungry Gut, like a Button.
The Blind Gut, like a Breast-plate.
The Colon, like a Bridle.
The Arse-Gut, like a Monk's Leathern Bottle.
The Kidneys, like a Trowel.
The Loyns, like a Padlock.
The Ureters, like a Pot-hook.
The Emulgent Veins, like two Gilly-flowers.
The Spermatick Vessels, like a Cully-mully-puff.
The Parastata's, like an Ink-pot.
The Bladder, like a Stone-bow.
Its Neck, like a Mill-Clapper.
The Mirach, or lower Parts of the Belly, like a High-crown'd
    Hat.
The Siphach, or its Inner Rind, like a Wooden Cuff.
The Muscles, like a pair of Bellows.
The Tendons, like a Hawking Glove.
The Ligaments, like a Tinker's Budget.
The Bones, like three-corner'd Cheese-Cakes.
The Marrow, like a Wallet.
The Cartilages, like a Field Tortoise, *alias* a Mole.
The Glandules in the Mouth, like a Pruning-Knife.
The Animal Spirit, like swinging Fisty-cuffs.
The Blood fermenting, like a multiplication of flurts on the Nose.
The Urin, like a Fig-pecker.

The Sperm like a hundred of Tenpenny-Nails.

And his Nurse told me, That being married to Mid-Lent, he only begot a good Number of Local Adverbs, and certain double Fasts.

His Memory he had like a Scarf.

His Common Sense, like a buzzing of Bees.

His Imagination, like the Chime of a Set of Bells.

His Thoughts, like a flight of Starlings.

His Conscience, like the unnesting of a parcel of young Herns.

His Deliberations, like a Set of Organs.

His Repentance, like the Carriage of a double Canon.

His Undertakings, like the Ballast of a Galion.

His Understanding, like a torn Breviary.

His Notions, like Snails crawling out of Strawberries.

His Will, like three Filberts in a Porrenger

His Desire, like six Trusses of Hay.

His Judgment, like a Shoing-horn.

His Discretion, like the Truckle of a Pully.

His Reason, like a Cricket.

CHAPTER XXXI

Shrovetide's outward Parts Anatomiz'd

SHROVETIDE, continued Xenomanes, is somewhat better proportioned in his outward Parts, excepting the seven Ribs which he had over and above the common Shape of Men.

His Toes were like a Virginal on an Organ.

His Nails, like a Gimlet.

His Feet, like a Guitar.

His Heels, like a Club.

The Soles of his Feet, like a Crucible.

His Legs, like a Hawk's Lure.

His Knees, like a Joynt-Stool.

His Thighs, like a Steel Cap.

His Hips, like a Wimble.

His Belly, as big as a Tun, button'd after the old Fashion, with a Girdle riding over the middle of his Bosom.

His Navel, like a Cymbal.

His Groyn, like a Minc'd Pye.

His Member, like a Slipper.

His Purse, like an Oyl-Cruet.

His Genitals, like a Joyners Plainer.

Their Erecting Muscles, like a Racket.

The Perineum, like a Flageolet.

His Arse-hole, like a Crystal-Looking-Glass.

His Bum, like a Harrow.

His Loyns, like a Butter-pot.

The Peritonæum, or Caul wherein his Bowels were wrapp'd, like a Billiard-Table.

His Back, like an overgrown rack-bent Cross-Bow.

The Vertibræ, or Joynts of his Back-bone, like a Bag-pipe.

His Ribs, like a Spinning-Wheel.

His Brisket, like a Canopy.

His Shoulder-Blades, like a Mortar.

His Breast, like a Game at Nine-pins.

His Paps, like a Horn-Pipe.

His Arm-pits, like a Chequer.

His Shoulders, like a Hand-barrow.

His Arms, like a Riding-Hood.

His Fingers, like a Brotherhood's Andirons.

The Fibulæ, or lesser Bones of his Legs, like a pair of Stilts.

His Shin-bones, like Sickles.

His Elbows, like a Mouse-Trap.

His Hands, like a Curry-Comb.

His Neck, like a Talboy.

His Throat, like a Felt to distil Hippocras.

The Knob in his Throat, like a Barrel, where hang'd two brazen Wens, very fine and harmonious, in the shape of an Hour-Glass.

His Beard, like a Lanthorn.

His Chin, like a Mushrom.

His Ears, like a pair of Gloves.

His Nose, like a Buskin.

His Nostrils, like a Forehead-Cloth.

His Eye-brows, like a Dripping-pan.

On his left Brow, was a mark of the shape and bigness of an Urinal.

His Eye-lids, like a Fiddle.

His Eyes, like a Comb-box.

His Optick Nerves, like a Tinder-box.

His Forehead, like a false Cup.

His Temples, like the Cock of a Cistern.
His Cheeks, like a pair of Wooden Shoes.
His Jaws, like a Cawdle Cup.
His Teeth, like a Hunter's Staff. Of such Colts Teeth as his, you will find one at Colonges les Royaux in Poictou, and two at la Brosse in Xaintonge, on the Celler-door.
His Tongue, like a Jews-Harp.
His Mouth, like a Horse-Cloth.
His Face imbroider'd like a Mule's Pack-Saddle.
His Head contriv'd like a Still.
His Skull, like a Pouch.
The Suturæ, or Seams of his Skull, like the Annulus Piscatoris, or the Fisher's Signet.
His Skin, like a Gabardine.
His Epidermis, or outward Skin, like a Boulting-Cloth.
His Hair, like a Scrubbing-Brush.
His Fur, such as abovesaid.

CHAPTER XXXII

A Continuation of Shrovetide's Countenance

Tis a wonderful thing, continued Xenomanes, to hear and see the State of Shrovetide.
If he chanc'd to Spit, it was whole Baskets full of Goldfinches.
If he blow'd his Nose, it was pickl'd Grigs.
When he Wept, it was Ducks with Onion Sauce.
When he Trembl'd, it was large Venison Pasties.

When he did Sweat, it was Old Ling with Butter Sauce.
When he Belch'd, it was Bushels of Oysters.
When he Sneez'd, it was whole Tubs full of Mustard.
When he Cough'd, it was Boxes of Marmalade.
When he Sob'd, it was Water-Cresses.
When he Yawn'd, it was Pots full of Pickl'd Pease.
When he Sigh'd, it was dry'd Neats Tongues.
When he Whistled, it was a whole Scuttle full of Green Apes.
When he Snoar'd, it was a whole Pan-full of fry'd Beans.
When he Frown'd, it was Sows'd-Hogs-Feet.
When he Spoke, it was coarse brown Russet-Cloth ; so little it was like Crimson Silk, with which Parisatis desir'd that the Words of such as spoke to her Son Cyrus, King of Persia, should be interwoven.
When he Blow'd, it was Indulgence Money-boxes.
When he Wink'd, it was Butter'd Buns.
When he Grumbled, it was March Cats.
When he Nodded, 'twas Iron-bound Waggons.
When he made Mouths, it was broken Staves.
When he Mutter'd, it was Lawyers Revels.
When he Hopp'd about, it was Letters of License and Protections.
When he stepp'd back, it was Sea Cockle-shells.
When he Slabber'd, it was common Ovens.
When he was Hoarse, it was an entry of Morrice-Dancers.
When he broke Wind, it was Dun-Cows-Leather Spatterdashes.
When he Funk'd, it was Wash'd-Leather Boots.
When he scratch'd himself, it was new Proclamations.
When he Sung, it was Pease in Cods.
When he Evacuated, it was Mushroms and Morilles.
When he Puffed, it was Cabbages with Oyl, *alias* Caules Ambolif.
When he Talk'd, it was the last Years Snow.
When he Dreamt, it was of a Cock and a Bull.
When he gave nothing, so much for the Bearer.
If he Thought to himself, it was Whimsies and Maggots.
If he Doz'd, it was Leases of Lands.

What is yet more strange, he us'd to work doing Nothing, and did nothing, tho' he work'd ; carous'd sleeping, and slept carousing, with his Eyes open like the Hares in our Country, for fear of being taken Napping by the Chitterlings, his inveterate Enemies ; biting he laugh'd, and laughing bit ; eat nothing fasting, and fasted eating nothing ; mumbled upon Suspicion, drank by Imagination ; swam on the tops of high Steeples, dry'd his Cloaths in Ponds and Rivers ; fish'd in the Air, and there us'd to catch Decumane Lobsters ; hunted at the bottom of the Herring-Pond, and caught there Ibices, Stamboucs, Shamois, and other wild Goats ; us'd to put out the Eyes of all the Crows which he took sneakingly ; fear'd nothing but his own Shadow, and the Cries of fat Kids ; us'd to gad abroad some Days like a Truant School-boy ; play'd with the Ropes of Bells on Festival Days of Saints ; made a Mallet of his Fist, and writ on hairy Parchment Prognostications and Almanacks with his huge Pincase.

Is that the Gentleman, said Fryar Jhon, he is my Man : this is the very Fellow I look'd for ; I 'll send him a Challenge immediately. This is, said Pantagruel, a strange and monstrous sort of a Man, if I may call him a Man. You put me in mind of the Form and Looks of Amodunt and Dissonance. How were they made, said Fryar Jhon ? may I be peel'd like a raw Onion if ever I heard a Word of them. I 'll tell you what I read of them in some ancient Apologues, reply'd Pantagruel.

Physis (that is to say Nature) at her first Burthen, begat Beauty, and Harmony, without Carnal Copulation, being of her self very Fruitful and Prolifick : Antiphysis, who ever was the Counterpart of Nature, immediately out of a malicious Spight against her for Beatiful and Honourable Productions, in opposition, begot Amodunt and Dissonance, by Copulation with Tellumon. Their heads were round like a Football, and not gently flatted on both sides like the common shape of Men. Their ears stood prick'd up like those of Asses ; their Eyes, as hard as those of Crabs, and without Brows, star'd out of their Heads, fix'd on Bones like those of our Heels ; their Feet were round like Tennis-balls ; their Arms and Hands turn'd backwards towards their Shoulders, and they walk'd on their Heads, continually turning round like a Ball, topsie-turvy Heels over Head.

Yet (as you know that Apes esteem their Young the handsomest in the World) Antiphysis extoll'd her Off-spring, and, strove to prove, that their Shape was handsomer and neater, than that of the Children of Physis ; saying that thus to have Spherical Heads, and Feet, and walk in a circular Manner, wheeling round, had something in it of the Perfection of the Divine Power, which makes all Beings eternally turn in that fashion ; and that to have our Feet uppermost, and the Head below them, was to imitate the Creator of the Universe, the

Hair being like the Roots, and the Legs like the Branches of Man ; for Trees are better planted in the Earth by the Roots, than they could be by their Branches. By this Demonstration, she imply'd that her Children were much more to be prais'd, for being like a standing Tree, than those of Physis that made the Figure of a Tree upside down : As for the Arms and Hands, she pretended to prove that they were more justly turn'd towards the Shoulders, because that part of the Body ought not to be without a Defence, while the fore-part is duly fenc'd with Teeth, which a Man cannot only use to chew, but also to defend himself against those Things that offend him. Thus by the Testimony, and Astipulation of the brute Beasts, she drew all the witless Herd, and Mob of Fools into her Opinion, and was admir'd by all brainless and nonsensical People.

Since that, she begot the hypocritical Tribes of evesdropping Dissemblers, superstitious Popemongers and Priest-ridden Biggots, the Frantic Pistolets, the Scrapers of Benefices, Apparitors with the Devil in them, and other Grinders and Squeezers of Livings, your mad Herb-stinking Hermits, gulliguted Dunces of the Cowl, Church-vermin, false Zealots, Devourers of the Substance of Men, and many more other deform'd and ill-favour'd Monsters, made in spite of Nature.

CHAPTER XXXIII

How Pantagruel discover'd a Monstrous Physetere, or Whirlpool near the Wild Island

ABOUT Sun-set coming near the Wild Island, Pantagruel spy'd afar off a huge monstrous Physetere, a sort of a Whale (which some call a Whirlpool,) that came right upon us neighing, snorting, rais'd above the Waves higher than our Main-Tops, and spouting Water all the way into the Air, before it self, like a large River falling from a Mountain : Pantagruel showed it to the Pilot, and to Xenomanes.

By the Pilot's Advice the Trumpets of the *Thalamege* were sounded, to warn all the Fleet to stand close and look to themselves : this Alarm being given, all the Ships, Gallions, Frigats,

Brigantines, (according to their Naval Discipline) placed themselves in the Order and Figure of a Y. (Upsilon,) the Letter of Pythagoras, as Cranes do in their flight, and like an Angle, in whose Cone and Basis the *Thalamege* plac'd her self ready to fight smartly : Fryar Jhon with the Granadeers, got on the Forecastle.

Poor Panurge began to cry and howl worse than ever ; Babillebabou, said he, shrugging up his Shoulders, quivering all over with Fear, There will be the Devil upon Dun. This is a worse Business than That t' other Day ; let us fly, let us fly ; Old Nick take me if it is not Leviathan, describ'd by the noble Prophet Moses, in the Life of Patient Job. It will swallow us all, Ships and Men, Shag, Rag, and Bobtail, like a Dose of Pills. Alas, it will make no more of us, and we shall hold no more room in its hellish Jaws, than a Sugar-plum in an Asse's Throat. Look, look, 'tis upon us, let's wheel off, whip it away and get ashoar. I believe 'tis the very individual Sea Monster, that was formerly design'd to devour Andromeda ; we are all undone. Oh ! for some valiant Perseus here now to kill the Dog.

I'll do its Business presently, said Pantagruel ; fear nothing. Odds-belly, said Panurge, remove the cause of my Fear then ; when, the Devil, would you have a Man be afraid, but when there is so much Cause ? If your Destiny be such as Fryar Jhon was saying a while ago (reply'd Pantagruel) you ought to be afraid of Pyrois, Eöus, Æthon, and Phlegon, the Sun's Coach-Horses, that breathe Fire at the Nostrils, and not of Physeters, that spout nothing but Water at the Snout and Mouth. Their Water will not endanger your Life ; and that Element will rather save and preserve, than hurt or endanger you.

Ay, ay, trust to that, and hang me, quoth Panurge, yours is a very pretty Fancy ; Od's Fish, did I not give you a sufficient account of the Elements Transmutation, and the Blunders that are made of Roast for Boyl'd, and Boyl'd for Roast ? Alas, here 'tis : I'll go hide my self below. We are dead Men every Mother's Son of us ; I see upon our Main-Top that merciless Hagg Atropos with her Scissers new ground, ready to cut our Threads all at one Snip. Oh ! how dreadful and abominable thou art ! Thou hast drown'd a good many, besides us, who never made their Brags of it. Did it but spout good brisk, dainty, delicious White-wine, instead of this damn'd bitter Salt-water, one might better bear with it, and there would be some cause to be patient; like that English Lord, who being doom'd to die, and had leave to chuse what kind of Death he would, chose to be drown'd in a Butt of Malmsy. Here it is.—Oh, oh, Devil, Sathanas, Leviathan; I can't abide to look upon thee, thou art so abominably ugly.— Go to the Bar; go take the Pettifoggers.

CHAPTER XXXIV

How the monstrous Physetere was slain by Pantagruel

THE Physetere coming between the Ships and the Gallions, threw Water by whole Tuns upon them, as if it had been the Catadupes of the Nile in Ethiopia. On the other side, Arrows, Darts, Gleaves, Javelins, Spears, Harping-irons, and Partizans flew upon it like Hail. Fryar Jhon did not spare himself in it. Panurge was half dead for Fear. The Artillery roar'd and thunder'd like mad, and seem'd to gall it in good earnest, but did but little good; for the great Iron and Brass Cannon-shot entring its Skin, seem'd to melt like Tiles in the Sun.

Pantagruel then considering the weight and exigency of the matter, stretched out his Arms, and shew'd what he could do. You tell us, and it is recorded that Commodus the Roman Emperor could shoot with a Bow so dextrously that at a good distance he would let fly an Arrow through a Child's Fingers, and never touch them. You also tell us of an Indian Archer, who liv'd when Alexander the Great conquer'd India, and was so skilful in drawing the Bow, that at a considerable distance he would shoot his Arrows through a Ring, tho' they were three Cubits long, and their Iron so large and weighty that with them he us'd to pierce Steel Cutlasses, thick Shields, Steel Breastplates, and generally what he did hit, how firm, resisting, hard, and strong soever it were. You also tell us Wonders of the Industry of the ancient Francks, who were preferr'd to all others in point of Archery, and when they hunted either black or dun Beasts, us'd to rub the head of their Arrows with Hellebore, because the Flesh of the Venison struck with such an Arrow was more tender, dainty, wholsom, and delicious (paring off nevertheless the part that was touch'd round about.) You also talk of the Parthians who us'd to shoot backwards more dextrously than other Nations forwards ; and also celebrate the Skill of the Scythians in that Art, who sent once to Darius King of Persia an Ambassador that made him a Present of a Bird, a Frog, a Mouse and five Arrows, without speaking one Word ; and being ask'd what those Presents meant, and if he had Commission to say any thing, answer'd that he had not ; Which puzzl'd and gravell'd Darius very much ; till Gobrias, one of the seven Captains that had kill'd the Magi explain'd it, saying to Darius, By these Gifts and Offerings the Scythians silently tell you, that except the Persians like Birds fly up to Heaven, like Mice hide themselves near the Centre of the Earth, or like Frogs dive to the very bottom of Ponds and Lakes, they shall be destroyed by the Power and Arrows of the Scythians.

The noble Pantagruel was without Comparison, more admirable yet in the Art of Shooting and Darting ; for with his dreadful Piles and Darts, nearly resembling the huge Beams that support the Bridges of Nantes, Saumur, Bergerac, and at Paris the Millers and the Changers Bridges, in length, size, weight and Ironwork, he at a Mile's distance would open an Oyster and never touch the edges ; he would snuff a Candle without putting it out ; would shoot a Magpy in the Eye, take off a Boot's Under-soal, or a Riding-hood's Lining, without soiling them a bit ; turn over every Leaf of Fryar Jhon's Breviary one after another, and not tear one.

With such Darts, of which there was good store in his Ship, at the first blow he ran the Physetere in at the Forehead so furiously, that he pierced both its Jaws and Tongue, so that from that time to this it no more open'd its Guttural Trapdoor, nor drew and spouted Water. At the second blow he put out its right Eye, and at the third its left; and we had all the pleasure to see the Physetere bearing those three Horns in its Forehead, somewhat leaning forwards in an equilateral Triangle.

Mean while it turn'd about to and fro, staggering and straying like one stunn'd, blinded, and taking his leave of the World. Pantagruel not satisfied with this, let fly another Dart, which took the Monster under the Tail likewise sloping; then with three other on the Chyne in a perpendicular Line divided its Flank from the Tail to the Snout at an equal distance; then he larded it with fifty on one side, and after that to make even work, he darted as many on its other side; so that the Body of the Physetere seem'd like the hulk of a Gallion with three Masts, join'd by a competent Dimension of its Beams, as if they had been the Ribs and Chainwales of the Keel, which was a pleasant Sight. The Physetere then giving up the Ghost, turn'd it self upon its Back, as all dead Fishes do, and being thus overturn'd with the Beams and Darts upside down in the Sea, it seem'd a Scolopendria, or Centipede, as that Serpent is describ'd by the ancient Sage Nicander.

CHAPTER XXXV

How Pantagruel went on shoar at the Wild Island, the ancient Abode of the Chitterlings

THE Boat's Crew of the Ship *Lantern* tow'd the Physetere a-shore on the neighbouring Shore (which happen'd to be the Wild-Island) to make an Anatomical Dissection of its Body, and save the Fat of its Kidneys, which, they said, was very useful and necessary for the Cure of a certain Distemper which they call'd Want of Money. As for Pantagruel, he took no manner of notice of the Monster; for he had seen many such, nay bigger, in the Gallick Ocean: Yet he condescended to land in the Wild-Island, to dry and refresh some of his Men (whom the Physetere had wetted and bedawb'd) at a small Desert Seaport towards the South, seated near a fine pleasant Grove, out of which flow'd a delicious Brook of fresh, clear and purling Water;

here they pitch'd their Tents, and set up their Kitchens, nor did they spare Fuel.

Every one having shifted as they thought fit, Fryar Jhon rang the Bell, and the Cloth was immediately laid, and Supper brought in. Pantagruel eating chearfully with his Men, much about the second Course, perceiv'd certain little sly Chitterlings clammering up a high Tree near the Pantry, as still as so many Mice : Which made him ask Xenomanes what kind of Creatures these were, taking them for Squirrels, Weesels, Martins, or Hermins. They are Chitterlings, reply'd Xenomanes : This is Wild-Island, of which I spake to you this Morning : There hath been an irreconcileable War this long time between them and Shrovetide their malicious and ancient Enemy : I believe that the Noise of the Guns, which we fir'd at the Physetere, hath alarm'd 'em, and made them fear their Enemy was come with his Forces to surprise them, or lay the Island waste, as he hath often attempted to do, tho' he still came off but bluely, by reason of the Care and Vigilance of the Chitterlings, who (as Dido said to Æneas's Companions, that wou'd have landed at Carthage without her Leave or Knowledge) were forc'd to watch and stand upon their Guard, considering the Malice of their Enemy, and the Neighbourhood of his Territories.

Pray, dear Friend, said Pantagruel, if you find that by some honest Means we may bring this War to an end, and reconcile them together, give me Notice of it ; I will use my Endeavours in it, with all my Heart, and spare nothing on my side to moderate and accommodate the Points in dispute between both Parties.

That 's impossible at this time, answer'd Xenomanes. About four Years ago, passing *incognito* by this Country I endeavour'd to make a Peace, or at least a long Truce among them ; and I had certainly brought them to be good Friends and Neighbours, if both one and the other Parties would have yielded to one single Article. Shrovetide would not include in the Treaty of Peace the Wild Puddings, nor the Highland Sausages, their ancient Gossips and Confederates. The Chitterlings demanded, that the Fort of Caques might be under their Government, as is the Castle of Sulloaoir, and that a parcel of I don't know what stinking Villains, Murtherers, Robbers, that held it then, should be expell'd. But they could not agree in this ; and the Terms that were offer'd, seem'd too hard to either Party. So the Treaty broke off, and nothing was done. Nevertheless, they became less severe, and gentler Enemies than they were before: But since the Denunciation of the National Council of Chesil, whereby they were roughly handled, hamper'd, and cited, whereby also Shrovetide was declared filthy, beshitten, and beray'd, in case he made any League or Agreement with them, they are grown wonderful inveterate, incens'd, and obstinate against one another; and there is no way to remedy it: You might sooner reconcile Cats and Rats, or Hounds and Hares together.

CHAPTER XXXVI

How the Wild Chitterlings laid an Ambuscado for Pantagruel

WHILE Xenomanes was saying this, Fryar Jhon spy'd twenty five or thirty young slender-shap'd Chitterlings, posting as fast as they could towards their Town, Citadel, Castle, and Fort of Chimney; and said to Pantagruel, I smell a Rat; there will be here the Devil upon two sticks, or I am much out. These worshipful Chitterlings may chance to mistake you for Shrovetide, tho' you are not a bit like him. Let us once in our Lives leave our Junketing for a while, and put our selves in a posture to give 'em a Belly-full of Fighting, if they wou'd be at that Sport. There can be no false-Latin in this, said Xenomanes; Chitterlings are still Chitterlings, always double-hearted and treacherous.

Pantagruel then arose from Table, to visit and scoure the Thicket, and return'd presently, having discover'd on the Left an Ambuscade of Squob-Chitterlings ; and on the Right, about half a League from thence, a large Body of huge Giant-like arm'd Chitterlings rang'd in Battalia along a little Hill, and marching furiously towards us, at the sound of Bag-pipes, Sheep's-paunches, and Bladders, the merry Fifes and Drums, Trumpets and Clarions, hoping to catch us, as Moss caught his Mare. By the conjecture of Seventy eight Standards which we told, we guess'd their Number to be Two and forty thousand, at a modest Computation.

Their Order, proud Gate, and resolute Looks, made us judg that they were none of your raw paultry Links, but old Warlike Chitterlings and Sausages. From the foremost Ranks to the Colours they were all arm'd *Cap-a-pié* with Small-Arms, as we reckon'd them at a distance, yet very sharp and case-harden'd. Their Right and Left Wings were lin'd with a great number of Forest-Puddings, heavy Patty-pans, and Horse-Sausages, all of them tall and proper Islanders, Banditti, and Wild.

Pantagruel was very much daunted, and not without cause, tho' Epistemon told him, that it might be the Use and Custom of the Chitterlingonians to welcom and receive in Arms their foreign Friends ; as the Noble Kings of France are received, and saluted at their first coming into the chief Cities of the Kingdom, after their advancement to the Crown. Perhaps, said he, it may be the usual Guard of the Queen of the Place ; who having Notice given her, by the Junior Chitterlings of the Forlorn-hope, whom you saw on the Tree, of the arrival of your fine and pompous Fleet, hath judg'd that it was without doubt some rich and potent Prince, and is come to visit you in Person.

Pantagruel little trusting to this, call'd a Council to have their Advice at large in this doubtful Case. He briefly shew'd them how this way of Reception with Arms, had often, under colour of Compliment and Friendship been fatal to the Parties so receiv'd. Thus, said he, the Emperor Antonius Caracalla at one time destroy'd the Citizens of Alexandria ; and at another time cut off the Attendants of Artabanus King of Persia, under colour of Marrying his Daughter : Which, by the way, did not pass unpunish'd ; for a while after, this cost him his life.

Thus Jacob's Children destroy'd the Sichemites, to revenge the Rape of their Sister Dina. By such another hypocritical

HAVING DISCOVER'D AN AMBUSCADE OF SQUOB-CHITTERLINGS

197

trick, Galienus the Roman Emperor put to Death the Military Men in Constantinople. Thus, under colour of Friendship, Antonius inticed Artavasdes King of Armenia, then having caused him to be bound in heavy Chains, and shackled, at last put him to Death.

We find a thousand such Instances in History; and King Charles the VIth is justly commended for his Prudence to this Day, in that, coming back Victorious over the Ghenters and other Flemmings, to his good City of Paris, and when he came to Bourget, (a League from thence) hearing that the Citizens with their Mallets (whence they got their name of Maillotins) were march'd out of a Town in Battalia Twenty thousand strong, he would not go into the Town, till they had laid down their Arms, and retired to their respective Homes, tho' they protested to him, that they had taken Arms with no other design, than to receive him with the greater Demonstration of Honour and Respect.

CHAPTER XXXVII

How Pantagruel sent for Colonel Mawl-Chitterling, and Colonel Cut-Pudding; with a Discourse well worth your hearing, about the Names of Places and Persons

THE Resolution of the Council was, That, let things be how they wou'd, it behov'd the Pantagruelists to stand upon their Guard. Therefore Carpalim and Gymnast were order'd, by Pantagruel, to go for the Soldiers that were on-board the Cup-Gally, under the Command of Colonel Mawl-Chitterling, and those on-board the Vine-Tub-Frigat, under the Command of Colonel Cut-Pudding the Younger. I'll ease Gymnast of that trouble, said Panurge, who wanted to be upon the Run: You may have occasion for him here. By this worthy Frock of mine, quoth Fryar Jhon, thou hast a mind to slip thy Neck out of the Collar, and absent thy self from the Fight, thou White-liver'd Son of a Dunghil; upon my Virginity, thou 'lt never come back. Well, there can be no great loss in thee; for thou would'st do nothing here but Houl, Bray, Weep, and dishearten the good Sholdiers. I'll certainly come back, (said Panurge) Fryar Jhon, my ghostly Father, and speedily too:

Do but take care that these plaguy Chitterlings don't board our Ships ; all the while you 'll be a Fighting, I 'll Pray heartily for your Victory, after the Example of the valiant Captain and Guide of the People of Israel, Moses. Having said this, he wheel'd off.

Then said Epistemon to Pantagruel, The Denomination of these two Colonels of yours, Mawl-Chitterling and Cut-Pudding, promiseth us Assurance, Success and Victory, if those Chitterlings should chance to set upon us. You take it rightly, said Pantagruel ; and it pleaseth me to see you foresee and prognosticate our Victory, by the Names of our Colonels.

This way, of foretelling by Names, is not New ; it was in Old-times celebrated, and religiously observ'd by the Pythagoreans. Several great Princes and Emperors have formerly made good Use of it. Octavianus Augustus, Emperor of the Romans, meeting on a day a Country Fellow nam'd Eutychius (that is, Fortunate) driving an Ass nam'd Nicon (that is, in Greek, Victorian) mov'd by the Signification of the Ass's and Ass-drivers Names, remain'd assur'd of all Prosperity and Victory.

The Emperor Vespasian, being once all alone at Prayers in the Temple of Serapis, at the sight and unexpected coming of a certain Servant of his nam'd Basilides, (that is, Royal) whom he had left sick a great way behind, took hopes and assurance of obtaining the Empire of the Romans. Regilian was chosen Emperor by the Soldiers, for no other reason, but the Signification of his Name. See the *Cratyle* of the divine Plato ; (By my Thirst I will read it, said Rhizotome ; I hear you so often quote it) see how the Pythagoreans, by reason of the Names and Numbers, conclude, that Patroclus was to fall by the hand of Hector, Hector by Achilles, Achilles by Paris, Paris by Philoctetes. I am quite lost in my Understanding, when I reflect upon the admirable Invention of Pythagoras, who by the Number, either Even or Odd, of the Syllables of every Noun, would tell you of what side a Man was Lame, Hulch-back'd, Blind, Gouty, troubled with the Palsy, Pleurisy, or any other Distemper incident to Human Kind, allotting Even Numbers to the Right, and Odd ones to the Left-side of the Body.

Indeed, said Epistemon, I saw this way of Syllabizing try'd at Xaintes, at a general Procession, in the Presence of that good, virtuous, learned and just President Brian Vallée, Lord of Douhait. When there went by a Man or Woman that was either Lame, Blind of one Eye, or Hump-back'd, he had an

Account brought him of his or her Name, and if the Syllables of the Name were of an Odd Number, immediately, without seeing the Persons, he declar'd them to be Deform'd, Blind, Lame, or Crooked of the Right-side; and of the Left, if they were Even in Number : And such indeed we ever found them.

By this Syllabical Invention, said Pantagruel, the Learned have affirm'd, that Achilles kneeling, was wounded by the Arrow of Paris in the Right-Heel, for his Name is of Odd Syllables : (Here we ought to observe, that the Ancients us'd to kneel the Right-Foot.) And that Venus was also wounded before Troy in the Left-Hand; for her Name in Greek is 'Αφροδίτη, of four Syllables; Vulcan Lam'd of his Left-Foot, for the same reason; Philip King of Macedon, and Hannibal, Blind of the Right-Eye : Not to speak of Sciatica's, Broken-Bellies, and Hemicrania's, which may be distinguish'd by this Pythagorean Reason.

But returning to Names : Do but consider how Alexander the Great, Son to King Philip, of whom we spoke just now, compass'd his Undertaking, meerly by the Interpretation of a Name. He had besieged the strong City of Tyre, and for several Weeks batter'd it with all his Power : but all in vain; his Engines and Attempts were still baffled by the Tyrians : Which made him finally resolve to raise the Siege, to his great Grief, foreseeing the great Stain which such a shameful Retreat would be to his Reputation. In this Anxiety and Agitation of Mind he fell asleep, and dreamt that a Satyr was come into his Tent, capering, skipping, and tripping it up and down with his Goatish Hoofs, and that he strove to lay hold on him. But the Satyr still slipt from him, till at last, having penn'd him up into a Corner, he took him. With this he awak'd; and telling his Dream to the Philosophers and Sages of his Court, they let him know, that it was a Promise of Victory from the Gods, and that he should soon be Master of Tyre; the word *Satyros* divided into two being *Sa Tyros*, and signifying Tyre is thine; and in truth, at the next On-set he took the Town by Storm, and by a compleat Victory, reduc'd that stubborn People to Subjection.

On the other hand, see how by the Signification of one word, Pompey fell into despair. Being overcome by Cæsar at the Battle of Pharsalia, he had no other way left to escape but by flight; which attempting by Sea, he arriv'd near the Island of Cyprus, and perceiv'd on the Shore, near the City of Paphos, a beautiful and stately Palace : Now asking the Pilot what was the name of it, he told him, that it was call'd Κακοβασιλέα, that is, Evil-King; which struck such a Dread and Terror in him, that he fell into Despair, as being assured of losing shortly his Life; insomuch that his Complaints, Sighs and Groans were heard by the Mariners and other Passengers. And indeed, a while after, a certain strange Peasant, call'd Achillas, cut off his Head.

To all these Examples might be added what happen'd to L. Paulus Æmilius, when the Senate elected him Emperor, that is, Chief of the Army which they sent against Perses King of Macedon; that Evening returning Home to prepare for his Expedition, and kissing a little Daughter of his call'd Tracia, she seem'd somewhat sad to him. What is the matter, said he, my Chicken; why is my Trasia thus sad and melancholy? Daddy (reply'd the Child) Persa is dead; this was the Name of a little Bitch which she lov'd mightily. Hearing this, Paulus took assurance of a Victory over Perses.

If Time would permit us to discourse of the Sacred Hebrew Writ, we might find a hundred noted Passages evidently shewing how religiously they observ'd Proper Names, and their Significations. He had hardly ended this Discourse, when the two Colonels arrived with their Soldiers, all well arm'd and resolute. Pantagruel made them a short Speech, intreating them to behave themselves bravely, in case they were attackt; for he cou'd not yet believe that the Chitterlings were so treacherous, but he bad them by no means to give the first Offence; giving them Carnaval for the Watch-word.

W·H·R·

CHAPTER XXXVIII

How Chitterlings are not to be slighted by Men

You shake your empty Noddles now, jolly Topers, and don't believe what I tell you here any more than if it were some Tale of a Tub : Well, well, I can't help it. Believe it if you will ; if you won't, let it alone. For my part, I very well know what I saw. It was in the wild Island, in our Voyage to the Holy Bottle, I tell you the Time and Place, what would you have more ? I would have you call to mind the strength of the ancient Giants that undertook to lay the high Mountain Pelion on the top of Ossa, and set among those the shady Olympus, to dash out the Gods Brains, unnestle them, and scour their Heavenly Lodgings. Their's was no small strength, you may well think, and yet they were nothing but Chitterlings from the Waste downwards, or at least, Serpents, not to tell a Lye for the matter.

The Serpent that tempted Eve too was of the Chitterling kind, and yet it is recorded of him, that he was more subtle than any Beast of the Field. Even so are Chitterlings : Nay, to this very Hour they hold in some Universities that this same Tempter was the Chitterling call'd Ithyphallus, or Standing, into which was transform'd bawdy Priapus, Arch-Seducer of Females in Paradise, that is, a Garden in Greek.

Pray now tell me, Who can tell but that the Switzers, now so bold and warlike, were formerly Chitterlings ? For my part, I would not take my Oath to the contrary. The Him-antopodes, a Nation very famous in Ethiopia, according to Pliny's Description, are Chitterlings, and nothing else. If all this will not satisfie your Worships, or remove your Incredulity, I would have you forthwith (I mean drinking first, that nothing be done rashly) visit Lusignan, Parthenay, Vouant, Mervant, and Ponzauges in Poictou. There you will find a Cloud of Witnesses, not of your Affidavit-Men of the right stamp, but Credible, time out of mind, that will take their Corporal Oath, on Rigome's Knuckle-bone, that Mellusine their first Founder, or Foundress, which you please, was Woman from the Head to the Prick-purse, and thence downwards was a Serpentine

Chitterling, or, if you 'll have it otherwise, a Chitterlingdiz'd Serpent. She nevertheless had a genteel and noble Gate, imitated to this very Day by your Hop-Merchants of Britanny in their *Paspié* and Country Dances.

What do you think was the cause of Erichthonius's being the first Inventor of Coaches, Litters, and Chariots ? Nothing but because Vulcan had begot him with Chitterlingdiz'd Legs, which to hide, he chose to ride in a Litter rather than on Horseback ; for Chitterlings were not yet in esteem at that time.

The Scythian Nymph Ora was likewise half Woman and half Chitterling ; and yet seem'd so beautiful to Jupiter, that nothing could serve him but he must give her a touch of his Godship's Kindness ; and accordingly had a brave Boy by her call'd Colaxes, and therefore, I would have you leave off shaking your empty Noddles at this, as if it were a Story, and firmly believe that nothing is truer than the Gospel.

CHAPTER XXXIX

How Fryar Jhon joyn'd with the Cooks to fight the Chitterlings

FRYAR JHON, seeing these furious Chitterlings thus boldly march up, said to Pantagruel ; here will be a rare Battel of Hobby-Horses, a pretty kind of Puppet-show Fight for ought I see ; Oh ! What mighty Honour and wonderful Glory will attend our Victory ? I would have you only be a bare Spectator of this Fight, and for any thing else leave me and my Men to deal with them. What men ? said Pantagruel. Matter of Breviary, reply'd Fryar Jhon : How came Potiphar who was Head Cook of Pharaoh's Kitchens, he that bought Joseph, and whom the said Joseph might have made a Cuckold, if he had not been a Joseph ; how came he I say, to be made General of all the Horse in the Kingdom of Egypt ? Why was Nabuzardan, King Nebuchadonozor's Head-Cook chosen, to the Exclusion of all other Captains, to besiege and destroy Jerusalem ? I hear you, reply'd Pantagruel ; By St. Christopher's Whiskers, said Fryar Jhon, I dare lay a Wager that it was because they had formerly engaged Chitterlings, or Men as little valu'd ; whom to rout, conquer, and destroy, Cooks are without comparison, more fit than Cuirassiers and Gens d'Armes arm'd at all Points, or all the Horse and Foot in the world.

You put me in mind said Pantagruel, of what is written amongst the Facetious and merry Sayings of Cicero. During the more than Civil Wars between Cæsar and Pompey, tho' he was much Courted by the first, he naturally lean'd more to the side of the latter ; now one day, hearing that the Pompejans in a certain Rencontre had lost a great many Men, he took a Fancy to visit their Camp. There he perceiv'd little Strength, less Courage, but much disorder. From that time, foreseeing that things would go ill with them, as it since happen'd, he began to Banter now one and then another, and be very Free of his cutting Jests : so some of Pompey's Captains playing the good Fellows to shew their assurance, told him, Do you see how many Eagles we have yet ? (They were then the Devise of the Romans in War) They might be of use to you, reply'd Cicero, if you had to do with Magpies.

Thus seeing we are to fight Chitterlings, pursued Pantagruel, you infer thence that it is a Culinary War, and have a mind to joyn with the Cooks. Well, do as you please. I'll stay here in the mean time, and wait for the event of the Battel.

Fryar Jhon went that very moment among the Sutlers into the Cooks Tents, and told them in a pleasing manner, I must see you Crown'd with Honour and Triumph this day, my Lads ; To your Arms are reserv'd such Atchievements, as never yet were perform'd within the Memory of Man. Od's Belly, do they make nothing of the valiant Cooks ? Let us go fight yonder fornicating Chitterlings, I'll be your Captain : But first let's drink, Boys—come on—Let us be of good Cheer. Noble Captain, return'd the Kitchen Tribe, this was spoken like your self, bravely offer'd : Huzza ! we are all at your Excellency's Command, and will live and dye by you. Live, live, said Fryar Jhon, a God's Name ; but dye by no means. That's the Chitterlings lot, they shall have their Belly full on 't :

Come on then let us put our selves in Order; Nabuzardan's the word.

CHAPTER XL

How Fryar Jhon fitted up the Sow ; and of the Valiant Cooks that went into it

THEN by Fryar Jhon's Order the Engineers and their Work-men fitted up the great Sow that was in the Ship *Leathern-Bottle.* It was a wonderful Machine, so contriv'd, that by the means of large Engines that were round about it in Rows, it throw'd forked Iron Bars, and four squar'd Steel Boults ; and in its Hold two hundred Men at least could easily fight, and be shelter'd. It was made after the Model of the Sow of Riole, by the means of which Bergerac was re-taken from the English in the Reign of Charles the sixth.

Here are the Names of the Noble and Valiant Cooks who went into the Sow, as the Greeks did into the Trojan Horse.

Sowre Sauce	Grisp Pig.	Sop in Pan.
Sweet Meat.	Greasy Slouch.	Pick-foul.
Greedy Gut.	Fatgut.	Mustard-pot.
Licorish Chops.	Bray-mortar.	Calfs Pluck.
Sows'd Pork.	Lick-sawce.	Hogs Haslet.
Slap Sawce.	Hog's Foot.	Chopt-phiz.
Cock-Broth.	Hodgepodge.	Gallymaufrey.
Slipslop.	Carbonadoe.	

All these Noble Cooks in their Coat of Arms did bear in a Field Gules, a Larding-pin Vert, charg'd with a Chevron Argent.

Lard, Hogs Lard.	Pinch Lard.	Snatch Lard.
Nible Lard.	Top Lard.	Gnaw Lard.
Filch Lard.	Pick Lard.	Scrape Lard.
Fat Lard.	Save Lard.	Chew Lard.

Gaillard (by Syncope) born near Rambioullet : The said

Culinary Doctor's name was Gaillard-lard; in the same manner as you use to Idolatrous for Idololatrous.

Stiff Lard.	Cut Lard.	Waste Lard.
Watch Lard.	Mince Lard.	Ogle-Lard.
Sweet Lard.	Dainty Lard.	Weigh Lard.
Eat Lard.	Fresh Lard.	Gulch Lard.
Snap Lard.	Rusty Lard.	Eye Lard.
Catch Lard.		

Names unknown among the Marranes and Jews.

Balloky.	Thirsty.	Porridge Pot.
Pick Sallat.	Kitchin Stuff.	Lick Dish.
Broyl Rasher.	Verjuice.	Salt Gullet.
Conny Skin.	Save Dripping.	Snail Dresser.
Dainty Chops.	Water-Creese.	Soupe-Monger.
Pye Wright.	Scrape Turnip.	Browis Belly.
Pudding-pan.	Trivet.	Chine Picker.
Toss-pot.	Monsieur Ragoust.	Suck Gravy.
Mustard Sawce.	Crack Pipkin.	Macaroon.
Claret Sawce.	Scrape Pot.	Scure Maker.
Swill Broth.		

Smell-Smock, he was afterwards taken from the Kitchin and remov'd to Chamber Practice, for the Service of the Noble Cardinal Hunt Venison.

Rot Rost.	Hogs Gullet.	Fox Tail.
Dishclout.	Sir Loyne.	Fly Flap.
Save Sewet.	Spit Mutton.	Old Grizle.
Fire Fumbler	Friter Fryer.	Ruff Belly.
Pillicock.	Flesh Smith.	Saffron Sawce.
Long Tool.	Cram Gut.	Strutting Tom.
Prick Pride.	Tuzzymussy.	Slash'd Snout.
Prick-Madam.	Jacket Liner.	Smutty Face.
Pricket.	Guzzle Drink.	

Mondam that first invented Madam's Sawce, and for that Discovery, was thus called in the Scotch-French Dialect.

Loblolly.	Scum Pot.	Swallow-pitcher.
Slabber Chops.	Sloven.	Wafer-Monger.

Trencher-man.	Rinse Pot.	Scurvy Phiz.
Goodman Goosecap.	Drink-spiller.	Pudding-bag.
Munch Turnip.	Snap Gobbet.	Pig-sticker.
Gully Guts.		

Robert, he invented Robert's Sawce, so good and necessary for Roasted Coneys, Ducks, Fresh Pork, Poach'd Eggs, Salt Fish, and a thousand other such Dishes.

Cold Eel.	Frying-pan.	Big Snout.
Thornback.	Man-of Dough.	Lick-finger.
Gurnard.	Sawce-Doctor.	Titt Bit.
Grumbling Gut.	Waste Butter.	Sauce-box.
Alms-scrip.	Shitbreech.	All Fours.
Taste all.	Thick Brawn.	Whimwham.
Scrap Merchant.	Tom T——d.	Basterost.
Belly-timberman.	Mouldy Crust.	Gaping Hoyden.
Hashee.	Hasty.	Calf Pluck.
Frig-palat.	Red Herring.	Leather Breeches.
Powdering-tub.	Cheese Cake.	

All these Noble Cooks went into the Sow, Merry, Cheery, Hale, Brisk, old Dogs at Mischief, and ready to fight stoutly; Fryar Jhon, ever and anon waving his huge Scimiter, brought up the Reer, and double-lock'd the Doors on the inside.

CHAPTER XLI

How Pantagruel broke the Chitterlings at the Knees

THE Chitterlings advanc'd so near, that Pantagruel perceiv'd that they stretched their Arms, and already began to charge their Lances, which caus'd him to send Gymnast to know what they meant, and why they thus, without the least provocation, came to fall upon their old trusty Friends, who had neither said nor done the least ill thing to them. Gymnast being advanc'd near their Front, bow'd very low, and said to them as loud as ever he could; We are Friends, we are Friends; all, all of us your Friends, yours, and at your command, we are for Carnaval your old Confederate. Some have since told me, that he mistook and said Cavernal instead of Carnaval.

Whatever it was, that word was no sooner out of his Mouth, but a huge wild Squob-Sawsage, starting out of the Front of their main Body, would have grip'd him by the Collar. By the Helmet of Mars, said Gymnast, I'll swallow thee, but thou shalt only come in in chips and slices; for, big as thou art, thou could'st never come in whole. This spoke, he lugs out his trusty Sword, Kiss-mine-Arse, (so he call'd it) with both his Fists, and cut the Sawsage in twain. Bless me, how fat the foul Thief was! It puts me in mind of the huge Bull of Berne that was slain at Marignan when the drunken Switzers were so mawl'd there. Believe me, it had little less than four inches Lard on its Paunch.

The Sawsage's job being done, a Crowd of others flew upon Gymnast, and had most scurvily drag'd him down, when Pantagruel with his Men came up to his relief. Then began the Martial Fray, higledy pickledy. Mawl Chitterling did mawl Chitterlings, Cut Pudding did cut Puddings; Pantagruel did break the Chitterlings at the Knees; Fryar Jhon play'd at least in sight within his Sow, viewing and observing all things; when the Patty-pans that lay in Ambuscado, most furiously sallied out upon Pantagruel.

Fryar Jhon, who lay snug all this while, by that time perceiving the Rout and Hurly-burly, set open the Doors of his Sow, and sallied out with his merry Greeks, some of them arm'd with Iron Spits, others with Andirons, Racks, Fire-

Shouvels, Frying pans, Kettles, Grid Irons, Oven-Forks, Tongs, Dripping-pans, Brooms, Iron-pots, Mortars, Pestles, all in Battle array like so many House-breakers, hollowing and roaring out all together most frightfully, Nabuzardan, nabuzardan, nabuzardan. Thus shouting and hooting they fought like Dragons, and charg'd through the Patty-pans, and Sawsages. The Chitterlings perceiving this fresh reinforcement, and that the others would be too hard for 'em, betook themselves to their Heels, scampering off with full speed, as if the Devil had been come for them. Fryar John with an Iron Crow knock'd them down as fast as Hops; his Men too were not sparing on their side. Oh! What a woeful Sight it was! The field was all over strow'd with heaps of dead or wounded Chitterlings; and History relates, that had not Heav'n had a hand in it, the Chitterling Tribe had been totally routed out of the World, by the Culinary Champions. But there happened a wonderful thing, you may believe as little or as much of it as you please.

From the North flew towards us a huge, fat, thick, grizly Swine, with long and large Wings like those of a Windmil, its Plumes red Crimson, like those of a Phenicoptere (which in Languedoc they call Flaman) its Eyes were red and flaming like a Carbuncle, its Ears green like a Prasin Emerald, its Teeth like a Topaze, its Tail long and black like Jet, its Feet white, diaphanous, and transparent like a Diamond, somewhat broad and of the splay-kind, like those of Geese, and as Queen Dick's us'd to be at Tholose in the Days of Yore. About its Neck it wore a Gold Collar round which were some Ionian Characters whereof I could pick out but two words ΣΥΣ AOHNAN : Hog teaching Minerva.

The Sky was clear before, but at that Monster's appearance, it chang'd so mightily for the worse, that we were all amaz'd at it. As soon as the Chitterlings perceiv'd the flying Hog, down they all threw their Weapons and fell on their Knees, lifting up their Hands joyn'd together, without speaking one word, in a posture of Adoration. Fryar Jhon and his Party kept on mincing, felling, braining, mangling, and spitting the Chitterlings like mad; But Pantagruel sounded a Retreat, and all Hostility ceas'd. The Monster, having several times hover'd backwards and forwards between the two Armies, with a Tail-shot voided above twenty seven Buts of Mustard on the ground; then flew away through the Air, crying all the while, Carnaval, Carnaval, Carnaval.

CHAPTER XLII

How Pantagruel held a treaty with Niphleseth
Queen of the Chitterlings

THE Monster being out of sight, and the two Armies remaining silent, Pantagruel demanded a parly with the Lady Niphleseth, Queen of the Chitterlings who was in her Chariot by the Standards, and it was easily granted. The Queen alighted, courteously receiv'd Pantagruel, and was glad to see him. Pantagruel complain'd to her of this Breach of Peace: But she civilly made her excuse, telling him that a false information had caus'd all this mischief, her Spies having brought her word, that Shrovetide their mortal foe was landed, and spent his time in examining the Urin of Physeteres.

She therefore intreated him to pardon them their Offence, telling him, that Sir-reverence was sooner found in Chitterlings than Gall; and offering, for her self, and all her Successors, to hold of him and his the whole Island and Country, to obey him in all his Commands, be Friends to his Friends, and Foes to his Foes; and also to send every Year, as an Acknowledgment of their Homage, a Tribute of Seventy eight thousand Royal Chitterlings, to serve him at his first Course at Table, six Months in the Year: which was punctually perform'd. For, the next Day, she sent the aforesaid quantity of Royal Chitterlings to the good Gargantua, under the Conduct of young Niphleseth Infanta of the Island.

The good Gargantua made a Present of them to the great King of Paris: But by change of Air, and for want of Mustard (the natural Balsam and Restorer of Chitterlings) most of them died. By the great King's particular Grant, they were buried in heaps, in a part of Paris, to this day call'd *La Rue pavée d'Andouilles*, (The Street pav'd with Chitterlings.) At the Request of the Ladies at his Court, young Niphleseth **was** preserv'd, honourably us'd, and since that marry'd to heart's content; and was the Mother of many Children, for which heav'n be prais'd.

Pantagruel civilly thank'd the Queen, forgave all Offences, refus'd the Offer she had made of her Country, and gave her a pretty little Knife: After that, he ask'd several nice Questions concerning the Apparition of that Flying-Hog? She answer'd, That it was the Idea of Carnaval, their Tutelary God, in time of War, first Founder and Original of all the Chitterling-race, for which reason he resembled a Hog, for Chitterlings drew their Extraction from Hogs.

Pantagruel asking to what Purpose, and curative Indication, he had voided so much Mustard on the Earth? The Queen reply'd, That Mustard was their Sangreal, and celestial Balsam, of which laying but a little in the wounds of the fallen Chitterlings, in a very short time the Wounded were heal'd, and the Dead restor'd to Life. Pantagruel held no further Discourse with the Queen, but retir'd a Shipboard: The like did all the Bon Companions with their Implements of Destruction, and their huge Sow.

CHAPTER XLIII

How Pantagruel went into the Island of Ruach

Two Days after, we arriv'd at the Island of Ruach ; and I swear to you, by the Celestial Hen and Chickens, that I found the way of Living of the People so strange and Wonderful, that I can't for the heart's blood of me half tell it you. They live on nothing but Wind, eat nothing but Wind, and drink nothing but wind : They have no other Houses but Weather-cocks : They sow no other Seeds but the three sorts of Wind-flowers, Rue, and Herbs that may make one break wind to the purpose, these scoure them off carefully. The Common Sort of People, to feed themselves, make use of Feather, Paper or Linnen Fans, according to their Abilities. As for the Rich, they live by the means of Wind-mills.

When they wou'd have some noble Treat, the Tables are spread under one or two Wind-mills : There they feast as merry as Beggars ; and during the Meal, their whole Talk is commonly of the Goodness, Excellency, Salubrity and Rarity of Winds ; as you jolly Topers, in your Cups, Philosophize and Argue upon Wines. The one praises the South-East ; the other the South-West : This the West and by South, and this the East and by North ; another the West, and another the East ; and so of the rest. As for Lovers, and Amorous Sparks, no Gale for them like a Smock-Gale. For the Sick, they use Bellows, as we use Clysters among us.

Oh ! (said to me a little diminutive swoln Bubble) that I had now but a Bladderfull of that same good Languedoc Wind, which they call Cierce. The famous Physician Scurron, passing one day by this Country, was telling us that it was so strong, that it will make nothing of overturning a loaded Waggon : Oh ! what good wou'd it not do my oedipodic Legg. The biggest are not the best ; but, said Panurge, rather would I had here a large Butt of that same good Languedoc Wine that grows at Mireveux, Canteperdrix, and Frontignan.

I saw a good likely sort of a Man there, much resembling Ventrose, tearing and fuming in a grievous fret, with a tall burly Groom, and a pimping little Page of his laying them on, like the Devil, with a Buskin : Not knowing the cause of his

Anger, at first I thought that all this was by the Doctor's Advice, as being a thing very healthy to the Master to be in a Passion, and to his Man to be bang'd for 't. But at last I heard him taxing his Man with stealing from him, like a Rogue as he was, the better half of a large Leathern Bag of an excellent Southerly Wind, which he had carefully lay'd up, like a hidden Reserve, against the Cold Weather.

They neither Exonerate, Piss, nor Spit in that Island ; but to make amends, they Belch, Fizle, Funk, and give Tailshots in abundance. They are troubled with all manner of Distempers : And indeed, all Distempers are engendred and proceed from Ventosities, as Hippocrates demonstrates, lib. *de Flatibus.* But the most epidemical among them, is the Wind-Colick. The Remedies which they use are large Blisters, whereby they void store of Windiness. They all dye of Dropsies and Tympanies, the Men farting, and the Women fizling, so that their Soul takes her leave at the back-door.

Some time after, walking in the Island, we met three hare-brain'd airy Fellows, who seem'd mightily pufft up, and went to take their Pastime, and view the Pluvers who live on the same Diet as themselves, and abound in the Island. I observ'd, that as you true Topers, when you travell, carry Flasks, Leathern Bottles, and small Runlets along with you, so each of them had at his Girdle a pretty little Pair of Bellows. If they happen'd to want Wind, by the help of those pretty Bellows they immediately drew some fresh and cool, by Attraction, and Reciprocal Expulsion : For, as you well know, Wind, essentially defin'd, is nothing but fluctuating and agitated Air.

A while after, we were commanded, in the King's Name, not to receive, for three hours, any Man or Woman of the Country on board our Ships. Some having stole from him a rousing Fart of the very individual Wind which old Goodman Æolus the Snoarer gave Ulysses, to conduct his Ship, when ever it should happen to be becalm'd : Which Fart the King kept religiously, like another Sangreal, and perform'd a world of wonderfull Cures with it, in many dangerous Diseases, letting loose and distributing to the Patient only as much of it as might frame a Virginal Fart ; that is, if you must know, what our Sanctimonials, *alias* Nuns, in their Dialect, call Ringing backwards.

CHAPTER XLIV

How a small Rain lays a high Wind

PANTAGRUEL commended their Government, and way of Living, and said to their Hypenemian Mayor, If you approve Epicurus's Opinion, placing the *summum bonum* in Pleasure, (I mean, Pleasure that's easie, and free from toil) I esteem you happy ; for your Food being Wind, costs you little or nothing, since you need but blow. True, Sir, return'd the Mayor ; but alas, nothing is perfect here below : For too often, when we are at Table feeding on some good blessed Wind of God, as on Celestial Manna, merry as so many Fryars, down drops on a sudden some small Rain, which lays our Wind, and so robs us of it ; thus many a Meal lost for want of Meat.

Just so, quoth Panurge, Jenin Toss-pot of Quinquenois, evacuating some Wine of his own burning on his Wife's Posteriors, laid the ill fum'd Wind that blow'd out of their Centre, as out of some Magisterial Æolipyle. Here's a kind of a Whim on that Subject which I made formerly :

> One Evening, when Toss-pot had been at his Buts,
> And Joane his fat Spouse cram'd with Turnips her Guts,
> Together they pigg'd ; nor did Drink so besot him,
> But he did what was done when his Daddy begot him.
> Now when, to recruit, he'd fain have been snoaring,
> Joane's Back-door was filthily puffing and roaring :
> So for spight he bepiss'd her, and quickly did find,
> That a very small Rain lays a very high Wind.

We are also plagu'd yearly with a very great Calamity, cry'd the Mayor ; for a Giant call'd Widenostrils, who lives in the Island of Tohu, comes hither every Spring to purge, by the Advice of his Physicians, and swallows us, like so many Pills, a great number of Windmills and of Bellows also, at which his Mouth waters exceedingly.

Now this is a sad Mortification to us here, who are fain to fast over three or four whole Lents every Year for this, besides certain petty Lents, Ember-Weeks, and other Orison and

W HEATH·ROBINSON·

THEY LIVE ON NOTHING BUT WIND

215

Starving-tides. And have you no Remedy for this ? ask'd Pantagruel. By the Advice of our Mezarims, reply'd the Mayor, about the time that he uses to give us a Visit, we Garrison our Windmills with good store of Cocks and Hens. So the first time that the greedy Thief swallow'd them, they had like to have done his business at once, for they crow'd and cackl'd in his Maw, and flutter'd up and down athwart and along in his Stomach, which threw the Glutton into a Lipothymy, Cardiac Passion, and dreadful and dangerous Convulsions, as if some Serpent creeping in at his Mouth, had been frisking in his Stomach.

Here is a Comparative *as* altogether incongruous and impertinent, cry'd Fryar Jhon, interrupting them ; for I have formerly heard, that if a Serpent chance to get into a Man's Stomach, it will not do him the least hurt, but will immediately get out, if you do but hang the Patient by the Heels, and lay a Pan full of warm Milk near his Mouth. You were told this, said Pantagruel, and so were those who gave you this Account ; but none ever saw or read of such a Cure. On the contrary, Hippocrates, in his Fifth Book of *Epidem.* writes, That such a case happening in his time, the Patient presently died of a Spasm and Convulsion.

Besides the Cocks and Hens, (said the Mayor, continuing his Story) all the Foxes in the Country whip'd into Widenostril's Mouth, posting after the Poultry, which made such a stir with Reynard at their Heels, that he grievously fell into Fits each minute of an hour.

At last, by the Advice of a Baden Enchanter, at the time of the Paroxysm, he us'd to flea a Fox, by way of Antidote : Since that, he took better Advice, and eases himself with taking a Clyster made with a Decoction of Wheat and Barly-Corns and of Livers of Goslins ; to the first of which the Poultry run, and the Foxes to the latter. Besides, he swallows some of your Badgers or Fox-Dogs, by the way of Pills and Bolus's. This is our misfortune. Cease to fear, good People, cry'd Pantagruel : This huge Widenostrils, this same Swallower of Windmills, is no more, I 'll assure you ; he dy'd, being stifled and choak'd with eating a lump of Fresh Butter, at the Mouth of a hot Oven, by the Advice of his Physicians.

CHAPTER XLV

How Pantagruel went ashoar in the Island of Pope Figg-land

THE next Morning we arriv'd at the Island of Popefiggs, formerly a rich and free People call'd the Gaillardets, but now, alas, miserably poor, and under the Yoke of the Papimen. The Occasion of it was this.

On a certain yearly high Holy-day, the Burger-Master, Syndics and topping Rabbies of the Gaillardets chanc'd to go into the neighbouring Island of Papimany, to see the Festival, and pass away the Time. Now one of them having espy'd the Pope's Picture, (with the Sight of which, according to a laudable Custom, the People were bless'd on High-offering Holy-days) made mouths at it, and cry'd, A Fig for 't, as a sign of manifest Contempt and Derision. To be reveng'd of this affront, the Papimen some Days after, without giving the others the least warning, took Arms, and surpriz'd, destroy'd, and ruin'd the whole Island of the Gaillardets, putting the Men to the Sword, and sparing none but the Women and Children, and those too only on Condition to do what the Inhabitants of Milan were condemn'd to, by the Emperor Frederick Barbarossa.

These had rebell'd against him in his absence, and ignominiously turn'd the Empress out of the City, mounting her a

Horse-back on a Mule call'd Thacor, with her Breech foremost towards the old Jaded Mule's Head, and her Face turn'd towards the Crupper. Now Frederick being return'd, master'd them, and caus'd so careful a Search to be made, that he found out and got the famous Mule Thacor. Then the Hang-man, by his Order, clap'd a Fig into the Mule's Jim-crack, in the Presence of the inslav'd Citts that were brought into the middle of the great Market-place, and proclaim'd, in the Emperor's Name, with Trumpets, That whosoever of them would save his own Life, should publickly pull the Fig out with his Teeth, and after that put it in again in the very individual Cranny whence he had draw'd it, without using his Hands; and that whoever refus'd to do this, should presently swing for 't, and die in his Shoes. Some sturdy Fools, standing upon their Punctilio, chose Honourably to be hang'd, rather than submit to so shameful and abominable a Disgrace; and others, less nice in Point of Ceremony, took heart of grace, and ev'n resolv'd to have at the Fig, and a Fig for 't, rather than make a worse Figure with a Hempen Collar, and die in the Air, at so short Warning: Accordingly, when they had neatly pick'd out the Fig with their Teeth from old Thacor's Snatch-blatch, they plainly shew'd it the Heads-man, saying *Ecco lo Fico !* (Behold the Fig !)

By the same Ignominy, the rest of these poor distress'd Gaillardets sav'd their Bacon, becoming Tributaries and Slaves; and the Name of Pope-Figs was given them, because they had said, A Fig for the Pope's Image. Since this, the poor Wretches never prosper'd; but every Year the Devil was at their Doors, and they were plagu'd with Hail, Storms, Famine, and all manner of Woes, as an everlasting Punishment for the Sin of their Ancestors and Relations. Perceiving the Misery and Calamity of that Generation, we did not care to go further up into the Country, contenting our selves with going into a little Chappel near the Haven, to take some Holy Water. It was dilapidated and ruin'd, wanting also a Cover (like St. Peter at Rome). When we were in, as we dip'd our Fingers in the sanctifi'd Cistern, we spy'd in the middle of that Holy Pickle a Fellow muffled up with Stoles all under Water, like a diving Duck, except the tip of his Snout to draw his Breath. About him, stood three Priests, true shavelings, clean shorn and poll'd, who were muttering strange Words to the Devils out of a Conjuring Book.

Pantagruel was not a little amaz'd at this, and, inquiring

WORK, CLOWN, WORK

what kind of Sport these were at, was told, that, for three Years last past, the Plague had so dreadfully rag'd in the Island, that the better half of it had been utterly depopulated, and the Lands lay Fallow without Owners. Now the Mortality being over, this same Fellow, who was crept into the Holy Tub, having a large piece of Ground; chanc'd to be sowing it with White winter Wheat; at the very Minute of an Hour that a kind of a silly sucking Devil, who could not yet Write or Read, or Hail and Thunder, unless it were on Parsly or Colworts, had got leave of his Master Lucifer to go into this Island of Pope-figs, where the Devils were very familiar with the Men and Women, and often went to take their Pastime.

This same Devil being got thither, directed his Discourse to the Husband-man, and ask'd him what he was doing. The poor Man told him, that he was sowing this Ground with Corn to help him to subsist the next Year. Ay, but the Ground is none of thine, Mr. Plough-jobber, cry'd the Devil, but mine: for, since the time that you mock'd the Pope, all this Land has been proscrib'd, adjudg'd, and abandon'd to us. However, to sow Corn is not my Province; therefore I will give thee leave to sow the Field; that is to say, provided we share the Profit. I will, reply'd the Farmer. I mean, said the Devil, that, of what the Land shall bear, two Lots shall be made, one of what shall grow above Ground, the other of what shall be cover'd with Earth; the right of chusing belongs to me, for I am a Devil of noble and ancient Race; thou art a base Clown. I therefore chuse what shall lye under Ground, take thou what shall be above. When dost thou reckon to reap, hah? About the middle of July, quoth the Farmer. Well, said the Devil, I'll not fail thee then: In the mean time, slave as thou oughtest. Work, Clown, work: I am going to tempt to the pleasing Sin of whoring, the Nuns of Dryfart, the Sham-Saints of the Cowle, and the gluttonish Crew; I am more than sure of these. There needs but meet, and the Job's done; true Fire and Tinder, touch and take; down falls Nun, and up gets Fryar.

CHAPTER XLVI

How a Junior Devil was fool'd by a Husbandman of Popefig-land

In the middle of July, the Devil came to the Place aforesaid, with all his Crew at his Heels, a whole Quire of the younger

Fry of Hell, and having met the Farmer, said to him; Well, Clod-pate, how hast thou done, since I went? Thou and I must now share the Concern. Ay, Master Devil, quoth the Clown, 'tis but reason we should. Then he and his Men began to cut and reap the Corn: and on the other side the Devil's Imps fell to work, grubbing up, and pulling out the Stubble by the Root.

The Country-man had his corn thrash'd, winnow'd it, put it into Sacks, and went with it to Market. The same did the Devil's Servants, and sate them down there by the Man, to sell their Straw. The Country-man sold off his Corn at a good rate, and with the Money fill'd an old kind of a Demy-Buskin, which was fasten'd to his Girdle; but the Devil a Sous the Devils took; far from taking Hansel, they were flouted, and jeer'd by the Country Louts.

Market being over, quoth the Devil to the Farmer, well Clown thou hast chous'd me once, 'tis thy Fault; chouse me twice, 'twill be mine. Nay, good Sir Devil, reply'd the Farmer, how can I be said to have chous'd you, since 'twas your Worship that chose first. The truth is, that by this Trick you thought to cheat me, hoping that nothing would spring out of the Earth for my share, and that you should find whole under Ground the Corn which I had sow'd, and with it tempt the Poor and Needy, the close Hypocrite, or the covetous Gripe, thus making them fall into your Snares. But troth, you must e'n go to School yet, you are no Conjurer, for ought I see: for, the Corn that was sow'd is dead and rotten, its Corruption having caus'd the generation of that which you saw me sell: so you chose the worst, and therefore are curs'd in the Gospel. Well, talk no more on 't, quoth the Devil: what can'st thou sow our Field with for next Year? If a Man would make the best on 't, answer'd the Ploughman, 'twere fit he sow it with Radish. Now cry'd the Devil, thou talkst like an honest Fellow, Bumpkin, well, sow me good store of Radish, I 'll see and keep them safe from Storms, and will not hail a bit on them; but harke'e me, this time I bespeak for my share what shall be above Ground, what 's under shall be thine: Drudge on, Looby, drudge on. I am going to tempt Hereticks, their Souls are dainty Victuals when broil'd in Rashers and well powder'd. My Lord Lucifer has the griping in the Guts, they 'l make a dainty warm Dish for his Honour's Maw.

When the season of Radishes was come, our Devil fail'd not to meet in the Field with a Train of rascally Underlings, all waiting Devils, and finding there the Farmer and his Men, he began to cut and gather the Leaves of the Radishes. After him the Farmer with his Spade digg'd up the Radishes, and clapt them up into Pouches. This done, the Devil, the Farmer, and their Gangs, hy'd them to Market, and there the Farmer presently made good Mony for his Radishes; but the poor Devil took nothing, nay, what was worse, he was made a common laughing-stock by the gaping Hoydons. I see thou hast play'd me a scurvy Trick, thou villainous Fellow, (cry'd the angry Devil,) at last I am fully resolved e'en to make an end of the Business between thee and my self about the Ground, and these shall be the Terms; We 'll chapperclaw each other, and whoever of us two shall first cry hold, shall quit his share of the Field, which shall wholly belong to the Conqueror. I fix the Time for this Tryal of Skill on this day se'night: Assure thy self that I 'll claw thee off like a Devil. I was going to tempt your Fornicators, Bayliffs, Perplexers of Causes, Scriveners, Forgers of Deeds, two-handed Counsellors, prevaricating Sollicitors, and other such Vermine; but they were so civill as to send me word by an Interpreter, that they are all mine already: Besides, our Master Lucifer is so cloy'd with their Souls, that he often sends them back to the smutty Scullions and slovenly Devils, of his Kitchin, and they scarce go down with him, unless now and then, when they are high-season'd.

Some say there is no Breakfast like a Student's, no Dinner like a Lawyer's, no Afternoon's Nunchion like a Vintner's, no Supper like a Tradesman's, no second Supper like a serving Wench's, and none of these Meals together like a frockifi'd Hobgoblin's. All this is true enough; accordingly at my Lord Lucifer's first Course Hobgoblings, *alias* Imps in Cowles, are a standing Dish. He willingly us'd to breakfast on Students; but, alas, I do not know by what ill Luck, they have of late years join'd the Holy Bible to their Studies; so the Devil a one we can get down among us, and I verily believe that unless the Hypocrites of the Tribe of Levi help us in it; taking from the inlightned Book-mongers their St. Paul, either by Threats, Revilings, Force, Violence, Fire and Faggot, we shall not be able to hook-in any more of them, to nibble at below. He dines commonly on Counsellors, Mischief-mongers, Multipliers of Law-Suits, such as wrest and pervert Right and Law, and grind and fleece the Poor: he never fears to want any of these. But who can endure to be wedded to a Dish?

He said t 'other Day at a full Chapter, that he had a great mind to eat the Soul of one of the Fraternity of the Cowle that had forgot to speak for himself, in his Sermon, and he promis'd double Pay, and a large Pension, to any one that should bring him such a Tit-bit piping-hot. We all went a hunting after such a Rarity, but came home without the Prey; for they all admonish the good Women to remember their Convent. As for afternoon Nunchions, he has left them off, since he was so wofully grip'd with the Colic, his Fosterers, Sutlers, Char-Coalmen, and Boyling-Cooks having been sadly mawl'd and pepper'd off in the Northern Countries.

His high Devil ship sups very well on Tradesmen, Usurers, Apothecaries, Cheats, Coyners, and Adulterers of Wares. Now and then when he is on the merry Pin, his second Supper is of serving Wenches, who, after they have by stealth soak'd their Faces with their Masters good Liquor, fill up the Vessel with it at second-hand, or with other stinking Water.

Well, drudge on, Boor, drudge on; I am going to tempt the Students of Trebisonde, to leave Father and Mother, forgo for ever the establish'd and common Rule of living; disclaim and free themselves from obeying their lawful Sovereign's Edicts, live in absolute Liberty, proudly despise every one, laugh at all Mankind, and taking the fine jovial little Cap of Poetic License, become so many pretty Hobgoblins.

CHAPTER XLVII

How the Devil was deceiv'd by an Old Woman of Popefig-land

THE Country Lob trudg'd home very much concern'd and thoughtfull, you may swear; in so much that his good Woman, seeing him thus look moping, ween'd that something had been stolen from him at Market; but when she had heard the cause of his Affliction, and seen his Budget well lin'd with Coyn, she bad him be of good Cheer, assuring him that he 'd be never the worse for the scratching Bout in question, wishing him only to leave her to manage that Business, and not trouble his head about it: for she had already contriv'd how to bring him off cleaverly. Let the worst come to the worst, said the Husbandman, it will be but a scratch, for I 'll yield at the first stroke, and quit the Field. Quit a Fart, reply'd the Wife, he shall have none of the Field, rely upon me and be quiet, let me alone to deal with him. You say he 's a pimping little Devil, that 's enough; I 'll soon make him give up the Field, I 'll warrant you: Indeed had he been a great Devil, it had been somewhat.

The Day that we landed in the Island happen'd to be that which the Devil had fix'd for the Combat. Now the Country-man, having like a good Catholic very fairly confessed himself and received, betimes in the Morning, by the Advice of his Vicar had hid himself, all but the Snout, in the holy Water-stock in the Posture in which we found him : And just as they were telling us this Story, News came that the old Woman had fool'd the Devil, and gain'd the Field : you may not be sorry perhaps to hear how this happen'd.

The Devil, you must know, came to the poor Man's Door and rapping there, cry'd, So hoe, ho the House, hoe Clod-pate, where art thou ? Come out with a vengeance, come out with a wannion, come out and be damn'd ; now for clawing ; then briskly and resolutely entring the House, and not finding the Country Man there, he spy'd his Wife lying on the Ground pitiously weeping and howling : What 's the matter ? ask'd the Devil, where is he ? What does he ? Oh ! that I knew where he is, reply'd Threescore and five, the wicked Rogue, the Butcherly Dog, the Murtherer : he has spoyl'd me, I am undone, I dye of what he has done me. How, cry'd the Devil, what is it : I 'll tickle him off for you by and by. Alas, cry'd the old Dissembler, he told me, the Butcher, the Tyrant, the Tearer of Devils, that he had made a match to scratch with you this Day, and to try his Clawes, he did but just touch me with his little Finger, here betwixt the Legs, and has spoyl'd me for ever. Oh ! I am a dead Woman, I shall never be my self again : do but see ! nay, and besides he talk'd of going to the Smiths to have his Pounces sharpen'd and pointed. Alas, you are undone, Mr. Devil ; good Sir, Scamper quickly, I am sure he won't stay ; save your self, I beseech you : while she said this, she uncover'd her self up to the Chin, after the manner in which the Persian Women met their Children, who fled from the Fight, and plainly shew'd her What de'e call them. The frighted, Devil, seeing the enormous Solution of the Continuity in all its Dimensions, blest himself, cry'd out, *Mahon, Demiourgon, Megæra, Alecto, Persephone :* s'Life, catch

224

OH, I AM A DEAD WOMAN

me here when he comes! I am gone, s'Death what a gash! I resign him the Field.

Having heard the Catastrophe of the Story, we retired a Ship-board, not being willing to stay there any longer. Pantagruel gave to the Poors-Box of the Fabrick of the Church, eighteen thousand Gold Royals in commiseration of the Poverty of the People, and the Calamity of the Place

CHAPTER XLVIII

How Pantagruel went ashoar at the Island of Papimany

HAVING left the desolate Island of the Popefigs, we sailed for the space of a Day very fairly and merrily, and made the blessed Island of Papimany. As soon as we had dropt Anchor in the Road, before we had well-moor'd our Ship with ground Tackle, four Persons in different Garbs row'd towards us in a Skiff. One of them was dress'd like a Monk in his Frock, draggle-tail'd and booted: the other like a Falkoner with a Lure and a long-wing'd Hawk on his Fist; the third like a Sollicitor, with a large Bag, full of Informations, Subpœna's, Breviates, Bills, Writs, Cases, and other Implements of Pettifogging. The fourth look'd like one of your Vine Barbers about Orleans, with a jantee pair of Canvass Trowzers, a Dosser and a Pruning Knife at his Girdle.

As soon as the Boat had clap'd them on board, they all with one Voice ask'd, Have you seen him, good Passengers, have you seen him? Who, ask'd Pantagruel? You know who answer'd they. Who is it, ask'd Fryar Jhon, s'Blood and Oonds, I 'll thrash him thick and threefold? This he said, thinking that they enquir'd after some Robber, Murtherer, or Church-breaker. Oh wonderful, cry'd the four, do not you foreign People know the One? Sirs, reply'd Epistemon,

we do not understand those Terms; but if you will be pleas'd
to let us know who you mean, we'll tell you the truth of the
matter without any more ado. We mean, said they, he that
is; did you ever see him? He that is, return'd Pantagruel,
according to our Theological Doctrine, is God, who said to
Moses, I am that I am : We never saw him, nor can he be
beheld by Mortal Eyes. We meant nothing less than that
supream God who rules in Heaven, reply'd they, we spoke of
the God on Earth, did you ever see him? Upon my Honour,
cry'd Carpalim, they mean the Pope. Ay, ay, answer'd
Panurge, yea verily, Gentlemen, I have seen three of them,
whose sight has not much better'd me. How! cry'd they,
our Sacred Decretals inform us, that there never is more than
one living. I mean successively, one after the other, return'd
Panurge; otherwise I never saw more than one at a time.

O thrice and four times happy People, cry'd they, you are
welcom and more than double-welcom! They then kneel'd
down before us and would have kiss'd our Feet, but we would
not suffer it, telling them, that, should the Pope come thither
in his own Person, 'tis all they could do to him. No, certainly,
answer'd they, for we have already resolv'd upon the matter.
We would kiss his bare Arse, without boggling at it, and eke
his two Pounders; for he has a pair of them, the holy Father,
that he has; we find it so by our fine Decretals, otherwise he
could not be Pope. So that according to our subtile Decretalin
Philosophy, this is a necessary Consequence; he is Pope,
therefore he has Genitories; and, should Genitories no more
be found in the World, the World could no more have a
Pope.

While they were talking thus, Pantagruel enquir'd of one
of their Coxwain's Crew, who those Persons were? he answer'd,
that they were the four Estates of the Island, and added, that
we should be made as welcom as Princes, since we had seen the
Pope. Panurge having been acquainted with this by Pantagruel, said to him in his Ear, I swear and Vow, Sir, 'tis even so,
he that has Patience may compass any thing. Seeing the
Pope had done us no good, now in the Devil's Name, 'twill do
us a great deal. We then went ashoar, and the whole Country,
Men, Women and Children came to meet us as in a solemn
Procession. Our four Estates cry'd out to them with a loud
Voice; they have seen him, they have seen him, they have
seen him. That Proclamation being made, all the Mob kneeled
down before us, lifting up their Hands towards Heaven, and

crying; O happy Men! O most happy. And this Acclamation lasted above a quarter of an Hour.

Then came the Busby of the Place, with all his Pedagogues, Ushers, and Schoolboys, whom he Magisterially flogg'd, as they us'd to whip Children in our Country, formerly when some Criminal was hang'd, that they might remember it. This displeas'd Pantagruel, who said to them: Gentlemen, if you do not leave off whipping these poor Children, I 'm gone. The People were amaz'd hearing his Stentorean Voice; and I saw a little Hump with long Fingers, say to the Hypodidascal; What! In the Name of Wonder, do all those that see the Pope, grow as tall as yon huge Fellow that threatens us? Ah! how I shall think time long, till I have seen him too, that I may grow and look as big. In short, the Acclamations were so great, that Homenas (so they call'd their Bishop) hasten'd thither on an unbridled Mule, with green Trappings, attended by his Aposts (as they said) and his Supposts or Officers, bearing Crosses, Banners, Standards, Canopies, Torches, Holywater Pots, etc. He too wanted to kiss our Feet, (as the good Christian Valsinier did to Pope Clement) saying, that one of their Hipothetes, that 's one of the Scavengers, Scowrers and Commentators of their Holy Decretals, had written, that, in the same manner as the Messiah, so long and so much expected by the Jews, at last appear'd among them; so on some happy Day of God the Pope would come into that Island; and that, while they waited for that blessed Time, if any who had seen him at Rome, or elsewhere, chanc'd to come among them, they should be sure to make much of them, feast them plentifully and treat them with a great deal of reverence. However, we civilly desir'd to be excus'd.

CHAPTER XLIX

How Homenas Bishop of Papimany shew'd us the
Uranopet Decretals

HOMENAS then said to us: 'Tis enjoyn'd us by our Holy
Decretals, to visit Churches first, and Taverns after. Therefore, not to decline that fine Institution, let us go to Church;
we shall afterwards go to Feast our selves. Man of God,
quoth Fryar Jhon, do you go before, we 'll follow you; you
spoke in the matter properly, and like a good Christian; 'tis
long since we saw any such. For my part, this rejoyces my
mind very much, and I verily believe that I shall have the
better Stomach after it: Well, 'tis a happy thing to meet with
good Men! Being come near the Gate of the Church, we
spy'd a huge thick Book, gilt and cover'd all over with Precious
Stones, as Rubies, Emeralds and Pearls, more or at least as
valuable as those which Augustus consecrated to Jupiter
Capitolinus. This Book hang'd in the Air, being fasten'd with
two thick Chains of Gold to the Zoophore of the Porch. We
look'd on it, and admir'd it. As for Pantagruel, he handled it,

and dandled it, and turn'd it as he pleas'd, for he could reach
it without straining; and he protested, that whenever he
touch'd it, he was seiz'd with a pleasant tickling at his Fingers
end, new Life and Activity in his Arms, and a violent temptation in his Mind to beat one or two Sergeants or such Officers,
provided they were not of the Shaveling-kind. Homenas
then said to us, The Law was formerly given to the Jews by
Moses, written by God himself: At Delphos, before the Portal
of Apollo's Temple, this Sentence, ΓΝΩΘΙ ΣΕΑΥΤΟΝ, was found
written with a Divine Hand, and sometime after it was also
seen, and as Divinely written and transmitted from Heaven.
Cybele's Shrine was brought out of Heaven into a Field call'd
Penisunt in Phrygia; so was that of Diana to Tauris, if you
will believe Euripides; the Oriflambe, or Holy Standard,
was transmitted out of Heaven to the Noble and most Christian
Kings of France to fight against the Unbelievers. In the
Reign of Numa Pompilius, second King of the Romans, the
famous Copper Buckler call'd Ancile was seen to descend from
Heaven. At Acropolis near Athens, Minerva's Statue formerly
fell from the Empyreal Heaven. In like manner, the sacred
Decretals, which you see, were written with the Hand of an
Angel of the Cherubin-kind; you Outlandish People will hardly
believe this, I fear. Little enough of Conscience, said Panurge.——And then, continued Homenas, they were miracul-
ously transmitted to us here from the very Heaven of Heavens,
in the same manner as the River Nile is call'd Diipetes, by
Homer the Father of all Philosophy (the holy Decretals always
excepted.) Now because you have seen the Pope, their
Evangelist and everlasting Protector, we will give you leave
to see and kiss them on the Inside, if you think it meet. But
then you must fast three Days before, and Canonically confess, nicely and strictly mustering up, and inventorising your
Sins great and small, so thick that one single Circumstance of
them may not scape you, as our holy Decretals, which you see,
direct. This will take up some time. Man of God, answered
Panurge, we have seen and descry'd Decrees and eke Decretals
enough o' Conscience, some on Paper, other on Parchment
fine and gay like any painted Paper Lantern, some on Vellom,
some in Manuscript, and others in Print; so you need not
take half this Pains to shew us these. We 'll take the Good-
will for the Deed, and thank you as much as if we had. Ay,
marry, said Homenas; but you never saw these that are
Angelically written. Those in your Country, are only Tran-

scripts from ours, as we find it written by one of our old Decretaline Scoliasts. For me; Do not spare me: I do not value the Labour, so I may serve you; do but tell me whether you will be confest, and fast only three short little Days of God? As for Shriving, answer'd Panurge, there can be no great harm in 't; but this same Fasting, Master of mine, will hardly down with us at this time; for we have so very much over-fasted our selves at Sea, that the Spiders have spun their Cobwebs over our Grinders. Do but look on this, good Fryar Jhon des Entomeures, (Homenas then courteously demy-clip'd him about the Neck) some Moss is growing in his Throat, for want of bestirring and exercising his Chaps. He speaks the truth, vouch'd Fryar Jhon; I have so much fasted, that I 'm almost grown Hump-shoulder'd. Come then, let 's go into the Church, said Homenas; and pray forgive us, if for the present we do not sing you a fine High Mass: The hour of Mid-day is past, and after it our sacred Decretals forbid us to sing Mass, I mean your high and lawful Mass. But I 'll say a low and dry one for you. I had rather have one moisten'd with some good Anjou Wine, cry'd Panurge: Fall to, Fall to your Low Mass, and dispatch. Od's Bodikins, quoth Fryar John, it frets me to the Guts, that I must have an empty Stomach at this time of day; For had I eaten a good breakfast, and fed like a Monk, if he should chance to sing us the *Requiem æternam dona eis, domine,* I had then brought thither Bread and Wine for the Traits passes, (those that are gone before.) Well, Patience; Pull away, and save a Tide; short and sweet, I pray you, and this for a Cause.

CHAPTER L

*How Homenas shew'd us the Arch-Type, or Representation
of a Pope*

Mass being mumbled over, Homenas took a huge bundle of
Keys out of a Trunk near the Head Altar, and put Thirty two
of them into so many Key-holes, put back so many Springs,
then with Fourteen more master'd so many Padlocks, and at
last open'd an Iron-Window strongly barr'd above the said
Altar. This being done, in token of great Mystery, he cover'd
himself with wet Sackcloth, and drawing a Curtain of Crimson
Sattin, shew'd us an Image daub'd over coarsly enough, to my
thinking; then he touch'd it with a pretty long Stick, and
made us all kiss the part of the Stick that had touch'd the
Image. After this, he said to us, What think you of this
Image? It is the Likeness of a Pope, answer'd Pantagruel;
I know it by the Tripple-Crown, his Furr'd Aumusse, his
Rochet, and his Slipper. You are in the right, said Homenas;
it is the Idea of that same good God on Earth, whose coming
we devoutly await, and whom we hope one day to see in this
Country. O happy, wish'd for, and much expected Day;

and happy, most happy, you whose propitious Stars have so far favour'd you, as to let you see the living and real Face of this good God on Earth, by the single Sight of whose Picture we obtain full Remission of all the Sins which we remember, that we have committed, as also a Third part, and Eighteen Quarantaines of the Sins which we have forgot : And indeed we only see it on high Annual Holy days.

This caus'd Pantagruel to say, That it was a Work like those which Dædalus us'd to make ; since, tho' it were deform'd and ill drawn, nevertheless some divine Energy in Point of Pardons lay hid and conceal'd in it. Thus, said Fryar Jhon, at Sevillé, the raskally Beggers being one Evening on a Solemn Holy-day at Supper in the Spittle, one bragg'd of having got Six Blancs, or Two pence halfpenny ; another, Eight Liards, or Two pence ; a third, Seven Carolus's, or Six pence : but an old Mumper made his Vaunts of having got Three Testons, or Five Shillings. Ah, but (cry'd his Comrades) thou hast a Leg of God. As if, continu'd Fryar Jhon, some divine Vertue could lye hid in a stenching ulcerated rotten Shanck. Pray, said Pantagruel, when you are for telling us some such nauseous Tale, be so kind as not to forget to provide a Bason, Fryar Jhon ; I 'll assure you, I had much ado to forbear bringing up my Breakfast : Fy, I wonder a Man of your Coat is not asham'd to use thus the Sacred Name of God, in speaking of things so filthy and abominable : Fy, I say : If among your Monking Tribes such an abuse of Words is allow'd, I beseech you leave it there, and do not let it come out of the Cloysters. Physicians, said Epistemon, thus attribute a kind of Divinity to some Diseases. Nero also extoll'd Mushrooms, and in a Greek Proverb term'd them Divine Food, because with them he had Poyson'd Claudius his Predecessor. But methinks, Gentlemen, this same Picture is not over-like our late Popes : For I have seen them, not with their Pallium, Aumusse or Rochet on, but with Helmets on their Heads, more like the Top of a Persian Turbant : and while the Christian Commonwealth was in Peace, they alone were most furiously and cruelly making War. This must have been then, return'd Homenas, against the Rebellious, Heretical Protestants ; Reprobates who are disobedient to the Holiness of this good God on Earth. 'Tis not only lawful for him to do so, but it is enjoyn'd him by the Sacred Decretals ; for if any dare transgress one single Iota against their Commands, whether they be Emperors, Kings, Dukes, Princes, or Commonwealths, he is immediately to pursue them with Fire and Sword, strip them of all their Goods, take their Kingdoms from them, proscribe them, Anathematize them, and destroy not only their Bodies, those of their Children, Relations and others, but Damn also their Souls to the very bottom of the most hot and burning Caldron in Hell. Here, in the Devil's Name, said Panurge, the People are no Hereticks, such as was our Raminagrobis, and as they are in Germany and England. You are Christians of the best Edition, all pick'd and cull'd, for ought I see. Ay, marry are we, return'd Homenas, and for that reason we shall all be sav'd. Now let us go and bless our selves with Holy-water, and then to Dinner.

CHAPTER LI

Table-Talk in Praise of the Decretals

Now Topers, pray observe, that while Homenas was saying his dry Mass, three Collectors, or Licens'd Beggers of the Church, each of them with a large Basin, went round among the People, saying with a loud Voice: Pray remember the blessed Men who have seen his Face. As we came out of the Temple, they brought their Basins brim full of Papimany Chink to Homenas, who told us, that it was plentifully to feast with; and that of this Contribution and voluntary Tax, one part should be laid out in good Drinking, another in good Eating, and the remainder in both; according to an admirable Exposition hidden in a Corner of their holy Decretals; which was perform'd to a T, and that at a noted Tavern not much unlike that of Will's at Amiens. Believe me, we tickled it off there with copious Cramming, and numerous Swilling.

I made two notable Observations at that Dinner; the one, that there was not one Dish serv'd up, whether of Cabrittas, Capons, Hogs, (of which latter there's great plenty in Papimany) Pigeons, Coneys, Leverets, Turkeys, or others, without abundance of Magistral Stuff; the other, that every Course, and the Fruit also, were serv'd up by unmarried Females of the Place, tight Lasses, I'll assure you, Waggish, Fair, Good-condition'd and Comely, Spruce, and fit for Business: They were clad all in fine long white Albes with two Girts, their Hair interwoven with narrow Tape and purple Ribbond, stuck with Roses, Gilly-flowers, Marjoram, Daffidown-dillies, Thyme, and other sweet Flowers.

At every Cadence, they invited us to drink and bang it about, dropping us neat and gentile Court'sies : Nor was the Sight of them unwelcome to all the Company ; and as for Fryar Jhon, he leer'd on them sideways, like a Cur that steals a Capon. When the first Course was taken off, the Females melodiously sung us an Epode in Praise of the Sacrosanct Decretals ; and then the second Course being serv'd up, Homenas, joyful and cheery, said to one of the She Buttlers, Light here, Claricia. Immediately one of the Girls brought him a Tall-boy brim-full of Extravagant Wine. He took fast hold of it, and fetching a deep Sigh, said to Pantagruel ; My Lord, and you my good Friends, Here 's t' ye, with all my Heart : You are all very Welcome. When he had tipp'd that off, and given the Tall-boy to the pretty Creature, he lifted up his Voice and said ; O most holy Decretals, how good is good Wine found, through your means. This is the best Jest we have had yet, observ'd Panurge ; but 'twould still be a better, if they could turn bad Wine into good.

O Seraphic Sextum ! (continu'd Homenas) how necessary are you not to the Salvation of poor Mortals. O Cherubic Clementinæ ! how perfectly the perfect Institution of a true Christian is contain'd and describ'd in you ! O Angelical Extravagants ! how many poor Souls, that wander up and down in mortal Bodies, throw this vale of Misery, would perish, were it not for you ! When, ha ! when shall this special gift of grace be bestow'd on Man kind, as to lay aside all other Studies and Concerns, to use you, to peruse you, to know you by heart, to practise you, to incorporate you, to turn you into Blood, and incenter you into the deepest Ventricles of their Brains, the inmost Marrow of their Bones, and most intricate Labyrinth of their Arteries ? Then, ha then, and no sooner than then, nor otherwise than thus, shall the World be happy ! While the Old Man was thus running on, Epistemon arose and softly said to Panurge ; For want of a Close stool, I must e'en leave you or a Moment or two ; this Stuff has unbung'd the Orifice of my Mustard-Barrel, but I 'll not tarry long.

Then, ah then, continu'd Homenas, no Hail, Frost, Ice, Snow, Overflowing, or Vis-major : then plenty of all earthly Goods here below. Then uninterrupted and eternal Peace throw the Universe, an End of all Wars, Plunderings, Drudgeries, Robbing, Assassinates, unless it be to destroy these cursed Rebels the Heretics. Oh then, Rejoycing, Cheerfulness, Jollity, Solace, Sports, and delicious Pleasures, over the Face of the Earth. Oh! What great Learning, inestimable Erudition, and Godlike Precepts, are knit, link'd, rivetted and mortais'd in the Divine Chapters of these eternal Decretals?

Oh! How wonderfully, if you read but one Demy Canon, short Paragraph, or single Observation of these Sacrosanct Decretals, how wonderfully, I say, do you not perceive to kindle in your Hearts, a Furnace of Divine Love, Charity towards your Neighbour (provided he be no Heretic,) bold Contempt of all casual and sublunary Things, firm Content in all your Affections, and extatic Elevation of Soul even to the third Heaven!

CHAPTER LII

A Continuation of the Miracles caus'd by the Decretals

WISELY, Brother Timothy, quoth Panurge, did am, did am; he says blew; but for my part I believe as little of it as I can. For, one Day by chance I happen'd to read a Chapter of them at Poictiers, at the most Decretalipotent Scotch Doctor's, and Old Nick turn me into Bumfodder, if this did not make me so Hide-bound and costive, that for four or five Days I hardly scumber'd one poor Butt of Sir-reverence ; and that too was full as dry and hard, I protest, as Catullus tells us were those of his Neighbour Furius.

> *Nec toto decies cacas in anno,*
> *Atque id durius est fabâ, et lapillis :*
> *Quod tu si manibus teras, fricesque*
> *Non unquam digitum inquinare posses.*

Oh, ho, cry'd Homenas, by 'r Lady, it may be you were then in the state of Mortal Sin, my Friend. Well turn'd, cry'd Panurge, this was of a new strain é gad.

One day, said Fryar John, at Sevillé I had apply'd to my Posteriors by the way of Hind-Towel a leaf of an old Clementinæ, which our Rent-gatherer John Guimard had thrown out into the Green of our Cloyster : now the Devil broyl me like a Black-pudding, if I wasn't so abominably plagu'd with Chaps, Chawns and Piles at the Fundament, that the Orifice of my poor Nockandroe was in a most wofull Pickle for I don't know how long. By 'r Lady, cry'd Homenas, 'twas a plain Punishment of God, for the Sin that you had committed in beraying that sacred Book, which you ought rather to have kiss'd and ador'd, I say with an Adoration of Latria, or of Hyperdulia at least : the Panormitan never told a Lye in the matter.

Saith Ponocrates, at Montpelier, John Choüart having bought of the Monks of St. Olary a delicate Set of Decretals written on fine large Parchment of Lamballe, to beat Gold between the Leaves, not so much as a piece that was beaten in them came to good, but all were dilacerated and spoil'd. Mark this, cry'd Homenas, 'twas a Divine Punishment and Vengeance.

At Mans, said Eudemon, Francis Cornu, Apothecary, had turn'd an old set of Extravagantes into waste Paper ; may I never stir, if whatever was lapt up in them was not immediately corrupted, rotten and spoyl'd ; Incense, Pepper, Cloves, Cinnamon, Saffron, Wax, Cassia, Rhubarb, Tamarinds, all, Drugs and Spices, were lost without exception. Mark, mark, quoth Homenas, an effect of Divine Justice. This comes of putting the Sacred Scriptures to such prophane Uses.

At Paris, said Carpalim, Snip Groignet the Taylor had turned an old Clementinæ into Patterns and Measures, and all the Clothes that were cut on them were utterly spoil'd and lost ; Gowns, Hoods, Cloaks, Cassocks, Jerkins, Jackets, Wastcoats,

Capes, Doublets, Petticoats, Corps de Robes, Vardingals, and soforth. Snip thinking to cut a Hood, would cut you out a Codpiece; instead of a Cassock he 'd make you a high crown'd Hat; for a Wastcoat he 'd shape you out a Rochet; on the Pattern of a Doublet he 'd make you a thing like a Frying-pan; then his Journey-men, having stitch'd it up, did jagg it and pink it at the bottom, and so it look'd like a pan to fry Chestnuts; instead of a Cape he made a Buskin; for a Vardingale he shap'd a Montero-Cap; and thinking to make a Cloak, he 'd cut out a pair of your big outstroutting Switzers Breeches, with Panes like the outside of a Tabor. In so much that Snip was condemn'd to make good the Stuffs to all his Customers; and to this Day poor Cabbidge's Hair grows through his Hood, and his Arse through his Pocket-holes. Mark, an effect of Heavenly Wrath and Vengeance, cry'd Homenas.

At Cahusac, said Gymnast, a match being made by the Lords of Estissac and Vicount Lausun to shoot at a Mark, Perotou had taken to pieces a set of Decretals, and set one of the Leaves for the White to shoot at; now I sell, nay, I give and bequeath for ever and aye the Mould of my Doublet to fifteen hundred Hampers full of black Devils, if ever any Archer in the Country (tho' they are singular Marksmen in Gujenne) could hit the White. Not the least bit of the Holy Scrible was contaminated or touch'd; nay, and Sansornin the Elder who held Stakes, swore to us, *Figues dioures*, hard Figs (his greatest Oath) that he had openly, visibly, and manifestly seen the Bolt of Carquelin moving right to the round Circle in the middle of the White, and that just on the point when it was going to hit and enter, it had gone aside above seven Foot and four Inches wide of it towards the Bakehouse.

Miracle! (cry'd Homenas) Miracle, Miracle! Clerica, come Wench, light, light here, Here 's to you all Gentlemen; I vow you seem to me very sound Christians. While he said this, the Maidens began to snicker at his elbow, grinning, giggling and twittering among themselves. Fryar Jhon began to paw, neigh and whinny at the Snout's end, as one ready to leap, or at least to play the Ass, and to get up and ride tantivy to the Devil like a Beggar on Horseback.

Methinks, said Pantagruel, a Man might have been more out of Danger near the White of which Gymnast spoke, than was formerly Diogenes near another. How's that? ask 'd Homenas, what was it? Was he one of our Decretalists? Rarely fallen in again e'gad, said Epistemon returning from

Stool, I see he will hook his Decretals in, tho' by the Head and Shoulders.

Diogenes, said Pantagruel, one Day for Pastime, went to see some Archers that shot at Butts, one of whom was so unskilful, that, when it was his turn to shoot, all the bystanders went aside, lest he should mistake them for the Mark. Diogenes had seen him shoot extremly wide off it, so when the other was taking aim a second time, and the People remov'd at a great distance to the right and left of the White, he placed himself close by the Mark, holding that place to be the safest, and that so bad an Archer would certainly rather hit any other.

One of the Lord d'Estissac's Pages at last found out the Charm, pursued Gymnast, and by his Advice Perotou put in another White made up of some Papers of Pouillac's Law Suit, and then every one shot cleverly.

At Landerousse, said Rhizotome, at John Delif's Wedding were very great doings, as 'twas then the Custom of the Country. After Supper, several Farces, Interludes, and Comical Scenes were acted : they had also several Morrice-dances with Bells and Tabors ; and divers sorts of Masques, and Mummers let in. My School-fellows and I, to grace the Festival to the best of our Power (for fine white and purple Liveries had been given to all of us in the Morning) contriv'd a merry Mask with store of Cockle-shells, shells of Snails, Periwinkles, and such other. Then for want of Cuckoe-pint or Priest-pintle, Lousebur, Clote, and Paper, we made our selves false Faces with the Leaves of an old Sextum, that had been thrown by and lay there for any one that would take it up, cutting out holes for the Eyes, Nose and Mouth. Now did you ever hear the like since you were born, when we had play'd our little Boyish Antick Tricks, and came to take off our sham-faces, we appear'd more hideous and ugly than the little Devils that acted the Passion at Douay : For our Faces were utterly spoyl'd at the places which had been touch'd by those Leaves ; one had there the Small Pox, another God's Token, or the Plague Spot, a third the Crinckums, a fourth the Measles, a fifth Botches, Pushes and Carbuncles ; in short, he came off the least hurt who only lost his Teeth by the bargain. Miracle, bawl'd out Homenas, Miracle !

Hold, hold, cry'd Rhizotome, 'tisn't yet time to clap ; my Sister Kate, and my Sister Ren had put the Crepines of their Hoods, their Ruffles, Snuffekins, and Neck-Ruffs new wash'd, starch'd and iron'd, into that very Book of Decretals ; for, you must know, it was covered with thick Boards and had strong Clasps ; now, by the virtue of God——Hold, interrupted Homenas, what God do you mean ?   There is but one, answer'd Rhizotome. In Heaven, I grant, reply'd Homenas, but we have another here on earth, d' ye see. Ay marry, have me, said Rhizotome, but on my Soul I protest I had quite forgot it— well then, by the virtue of God the Pope, their Pinners, Neck-ruffs, Bibs, Coifs, and other Linnen turn'd as black as a Char-coal-man's Sack. Miracle, cry'd Homenas ! Here, Clerica, light me here, and pr'ythee, Girl, observe these rare Stories. How comes it to pass then, ask'd Fryar Jhon, that People say,

Ever since Decrees had Tails
And Gens-d'Arms lugg'd heavy Mails,
Since each Monk would have a Horse,
All went here from bad to worse.

Depuis que Decrets eurent Ales,
Et Gens-d'Armes porterent Males,
Moines allerent à Cheval,
En ce monde abonda à tout mal.

I understand you, answer'd Homenas ; this is one of the Quirks and little Satyres of the new fangl'd Hereticks.

CHAPTER LIII

How, by the Virtue of the Decretals, Gold is subtilly
drawn out of France to Rome

I WOULD, said Epistemon, it had cost me a Pint of the best Tripe that ever can enter into Gut, so we had but compar'd with the Original, the dreadful Chapter, *Execrabilis. De multa. Si plures. De Annatis per totum. Nisi essent. Cum ad Monasterium. Quod dilectio. Mandatum ;* and certain others that draw every Year out of France to Rome, four hundred thousand Ducats and more.

Do you make nothing of this, ask'd Homenas ? Tho' methinks, after all, 'tis but little if we consider that France

THE FOURTH BOOK OF DR. FRANCIS RABELAIS

the most Christian, is the only Nurse, the See of Rome has. However find me in the whole World a Book, whether of Philosophy, Physic, Law, Mathematicks, or other human Learning, nay, even, by my God, of the Holy Scripture it self, that will draw as much Money thence? None, none, pshaw, tush, blurt, pish, none can: You may look till your Eyes drop out of your Head; nay, till Dooms-day in the afternoon, before you can find another of that Energy; I 'll pass my word for that.

Yet these Devilish Heretics refuse to learn and know it. Burn 'em, tear 'em, nip 'em with hot Pincers, drown 'em, hang 'em, spit 'em at the Bung-hole, pelt 'em, paut 'em, bruise 'em, beat 'em, cripple 'em, dismember 'em, cut 'em, gut 'em, bowel 'em, paunch 'em, thrash 'em, slash 'em, gash 'em, chop 'em, slice 'em, slit 'em, carve 'em, saw 'em, bethwack 'em, pare 'em, hack 'em, hew 'em, mince 'em, flea 'em, boyl 'em, broyl 'em, roast 'em, toast 'em, bake 'em, fry 'em, crucifie 'em, crush 'em, squeeze 'em, grind 'em, batter 'em, burst 'em, quarter 'em, unlimb 'em, bebump 'em, bethump 'em, belamme 'em, belabour 'em, pepper 'em, spitchcock 'em, and carbonade 'em on Grid-irons, these wicked Heretics; Decretalifuges, Decretalicides, worse than Homicides, worse than Parricides, Decretalictones of the Devil of Hell.

As for you other good People, I most earnestly pray and beseech you to believe no other thing, think on, say, undertake, or do no other thing than what 's contain'd in our Sacred Decretals, and their Corallaries, this fine Sextum, these fine Clementinæ, these fine Extravagantes. O Deific Books! So shall you enjoy Glory, Honour, Exaltation, Wealth, Dignities, and Preferments in this World; be rever'd, and dreaded by all, prefer'd, elected, and chosen above all Men.

For, there is not under the Cope of Heaven, a Condition of Men out of which you 'll find Persons fitter to do and handle all things, than those who by Divine Prescience, Eternal Predestination, have applied themselves to the Study of the Holy Decretals.

Would you chuse a worthy Emperor, a good Captain, a fit General in time of War, one that can well forsee all Inconveniencies, avoid all Dangers, briskly and bravely bring his Men on to a Breach or Attack, still be on sure grounds, always overcome without loss of his Men, and know how to make a good use of his Victory? Take me a Decretist.—No, no, I mean a Decretalist. Ho, the foul Blunder, whisper'd Epistemon.

Would you, in time of Peace, find a Man capable of wisely governing the State of a Commonwealth, of a Kingdom, of an Empire, of a Monarchy, sufficient to maintain the Clergy, Nobility, Senate and Commons in Wealth, Friendship, Unity, Obedience, Virtue and Honesty ?   Take a Decretalist.

Would you find a Man, who, by his exemplary Life, Eloquence, and pious Admonitions, may in a short time without effusion of human Blood Conquer the Holy Land, and bring over to the Holy Church the misbelieving Turks, Jews, Tartars, Muscovites, Mammelus, and Sarrabonites ? Take me a Decretalist.

What makes in many Countries, the People rebellious and deprav'd, Pages Sawcy and mischievous, Students sottish and duncical ?   Nothing but that their Governors, Esquires, and Tutors were not Decretalists.

But what, on your Conscience, was it d 'ye think that establish'd, confirm'd and authoris'd these fine Religious Orders with whom you see the Christian World every where adorn'd, grac'd and illustrated as the Firmament is with its glorious Stars ?   The Holy Decretals.

What was it that founded, underpropt, and fix'd, and now maintains, nourishes and feeds the devout Monks and Fryars in Convents, Monasteries and Abbeys, so that did they not daily and mightily pray without ceasing, the World would be in evident danger of returning to its Primitive Chaos ?   The Sacred Decretals.

What makes, and daily encreases the famous and celebrated Patrimony of St. Peter in plenty of all Temporal, Corporeal and Spiritual Blessings ?   The Holy Decretals.

What made the Holy Apostolick See and Pope of Rome in all times, and at this present so dreadful in the Universe, that all Kings, Emperors, Potentates, and Lords willing nilling must depend on him, hold of him, be crown'd, confirm'd, and authoris'd by him, come thither to strike sail, buckle, and fall down before his Holy Slipper, whose Picture you have seen ? The mighty Decretals of God.

I will discover you a great Secret ; The Universities of your World have commonly a Book either open or shut in their Arms and Devises ; what Book do you think it is ?   Truly, I do not know, answer'd Pantagruel, I never read it.   It is the Decretals, said Homenas, without which the Privileges of all Universities would soon be lost.   You must own I have taught you this, ha, ha, ha, ha, ha.

Here Homenas began to belch, to fart, to funk, to laugh, to slaver, and to sweat; and then he gave his huge greasie four-corner'd Cap to one of the Lasses, who clapt it on her pretty Head with a deal of Joy, after she had lovingly buss'd it, as a sure Token that she should be first married. *Vivat*, cry'd Epistemon, *fifat, bibat, pipat.*

O Apocalyptic Secret, continued Homenas! light, light, Clerica, light here with double Lanterns. Now for the Fruit, Virgins.

I was saying then, that giving your selves thus wholly to the study of the Holy Decretals, you'll gain Wealth and Honour in this World; I add, that in the next you'll infallibly be saved in the blessed Kingdom of Heaven, whose Keys are given to Our good God and Decretaliarch. O My good God, whom I adore and never saw, by thy special Grace open unto us, at the Point of Death at least, this most Sacred Treasure of our Holy Mother Church, whose Protector, Preserver, Buttler, Chief Larder, Administrator, and Disposer thou art; and take care, I beseech thee, O Lord, that the precious Works of Supererogation, the goodly Pardons do not fail us in time of need; so that the Devils may not find an opportunity to gripe our precious Souls, and the dreadful Jaws of Hell may not swallow us. If we must pass thro' Purgatory, Thy Will be done. It is in thy Power to draw us out of it when thou pleasest. Here Homenas began to shed huge hot briny Tears, to beat his Breast, and kiss his Thumbs in the shape of a Cross.

CHAPTER LIV

How Homenas gave Pantagruel some Bon-Christian Pears

EPISTEMON, Fryar Jhon, and Panurge seeing this doleful Catastrophe, began under the cover of their Napkins to cry, Meeow, Meeow, Meeow, feining to wipe their Eyes all the while, as if they had wept. The Wenches were doubly diligent, and brought Brimmers of Clementine Wine to every one, besides store of Sweet-meats, and thus the Feasting was reviv'd.

Before we arose from Table, Homenas gave us a great quantity of fair large Pears ; saying, Here, my good Friends, these are singular good Pears ; you 'll find none such anywhere else, I dare warrant. Every Soil bears not every thing, you know : India alone boasts Black Ebony, the best Incense is produced in Sabæa, the Sphragitid Earth at Lemnos ; so this Island is the only Place where such fine Pears grow. You may, if you please, make Seminaries with their Pippins, in your Country.

I like their Taste extremely, said Pantagruel ; if they were slic'd and put into a Pan on the Fire with Wine and Sugar, I fancy they would be very wholsom Meat for the Sick aswell as for the Healthy ; Pray, what do you call 'em ? No other-wise than you 've heard, reply'd Homenas ; we are a plain down-right sort of People, as God wou'd have it, and call Figs, Figs ; Plumbs, Plumbs ; and Pears, Pears. Truly, said Pantagruel, if I live to go home, (which I hope will be speedily, God willing) I 'll set and graff some in my Garden in Touraine by the Banks of the Loire, and will them call Bon-Christian or Good-Christian Pears; for I never saw better Christians than are these good Papimans. I 'd like him two to one better yet, said Fryar Jhon, would he but give us two or three Cart-loads of yon buxom Lasses. Why, what wou'd you do with them, cry'd Homenas ? Quoth Fryar Jhon, No harm, only bleed the kind-hearted Souls straight between the two Great-Toes with certain clever Lancets of the right stamp : By which Operation, Good-Christian Children would be inoculated upon them, and the Breed be multiplied in our Country, in which there are not many over-good, the more 's the pity.

Nay, verily reply'd Homenas, we cannot do this, for you wou'd make them tread their Shoes awry, crack their Pipkins, and spoil their Shapes : You love Mutton, I see ; you 'll run at Sheep ; I know you by that same Nose and Hair of yours, tho' I never saw your Face before. Alas, alas, how kind you are ! And wou'd you indeed Damn your precious Soul ? Our Decretals forbid this : Ah, I wish you had them at your Fingers-end. Patience, said Fryar Jhon : But, *Si tu non vis dare, præsta quæsumus ;* matter of Breviary ; as for that, I defie all the World, and I fear no Man that wears a Head and a Hood, tho' he were a Chrystallin, I mean, a Decretalin Doctor.

Dinner being over, we took our Leave of the Right Reverend Homenas, and of all the good People, humbly giving Thanks ; and to make them amends for their kind Entertainment, promised them, that at our coming to Rome we would make our Applications so effectually to the Pope, that he would speedily be sure to come to Visit them in Person. After this, we went o' Board.

Pantagruel, by an Act of Generosity, and as an Acknowledgment for the Sight of the Pope's Picture, gave Homenas Nine Pieces of double-friz'd Cloth of Gold, to be set before the Grates of the Window. He also caus'd the Church-Box for its Repairs and Fabrick, to be quite fill'd with Double-Crowns of Gold, and order'd Nine hundred and fourteen Angels to be deliver'd to each of the Lasses, who had waited at Table, to buy them Husbands when they could get them.

CHAPTER LV

How Pantagruel, being at Sea, heard various unfrozen Words

WHEN we were at Sea, Junketing, Tipling, Discoursing, and telling Stories, Pantagruel rose and stood up to look out ; then ask'd us, Do you hear nothing, Gentlemen ? Methinks I hear some People talking in the Air ; yet I can see no body ; Hark ! According to his Command we listen'd, and with full Ears suck'd in the Air, as some of you suck Oysters, to find if we could hear some Sound scatter'd through the Sky ; and to lose none of it, like the Emperor Antoninus, some of us laid their Hands hollow next to their Ears : But all this wou'd not do, nor cou'd we hear any Voice. Yet Pantagruel continued to assure us he heard various Voices in the Air, some of Men, and some of Women.

At last we began to fancy that we also heard something, or at least that our Ears tingled ; and the more we listen'd, the plainer we discern'd the Voices, so as to distinguish Articulate Sounds. This mightily frighted us, and not without cause, since we could see nothing, yet heard such various Sounds and Voices of Men, Women, Children, Horses, etc. insomuch that Panurge cry'd out, Cods Belly, there 's no fooling with the Devil ; we are all beshit ; let 's fly. There is some Ambuscado hereabouts. Fryar Jhon, Art thou here, my Love ? I prithee stay by me, old Boy : Hast thou got thy swindging Tool ? See that it do not stick in the Scabbard ; thou never scour'st it half as it should be. We are undone. Hark ! They are Guns, Gad judge me ; Let 's fly, I do not say with Hands and Feet, as Brutus said at the Battle of Pharsalia, I say with Sails and Oars ; Let 's whip it away, I never find my self to have a bit of Courage at Sea : In Cellars and elsewhere I have more than enough : Let 's fly, and save our Bacon. I do not say this, for any Fear that I have : for I dread nothing but Danger, that I don't : I always say it, that shou'dn't. The Free Archer of Baignolet said as much. Let 's hazard nothing therefore, I say, lest we come off bluely. Tack about ! Helm a Lee ! thou Son of a Batchelor. Wou'd I were now well in Quinquenois, tho' I were never to Marry. Haste away ; let 's make all the Sail we can, they 'll be too hard for us we are not able to cope with them ; they are ten to our one, I 'll warrant you ; nay, and they are on their Dunghil, while we do not know the Country. They 'll be the death of us. We 'll lose no Honour by flying ; Demosthenes saith, That the Man that runs away, may fight another time. At least, let us retreat to the Lee-ward. Helm a Lee ! Bring the Main-tack aboard ! Hawl the Bowlins ! Hoist the Top-gallants ! We are all dead Men. Get off, in the Devil's Name, get off.

Pantagruel, hearing the sad Outcry which Panurge made, said, Who talks of Flying ? Let 's first see who they are ; perhaps they may be Friends : I can discover no body yet, tho' I can see a hundred Miles round me : But let 's consider a little ; I have read, that a Philosopher, nam'd Perron, was of Opinion, that there were several Worlds that touch'd each other in an Equilateral Triangle; in whose Centre, he said, was the Dwelling of Truth; and that the words, Ideas, Copies and Images of all things past and to come, resided there; round which was the Age, and that with Success of Time part of them us'd to fall on Mankind like Rheums and Mildews, just as the Dew fell on Gideon's Fleece, till the Age was fulfilled.

I also remember, continu'd he, that Aristotle affirms Homer's Words to be flying, moving, and consequently animated. Besides, Antiphanes said, that Plato's Philosophy was like Words which being spoken in some Country during a hard Winter, are immediately congeal'd, frozen up, and not heard; for what Plato taught young Lads, could hardly be understood by them when they were grown old: Now, continu'd he, we should Philosophise and Search whether this be not the Place where those Words are thaw'd.

You'd wonder very much, should this be the Head and Lyre of Orpheus. When the Thracian Women had torn him to pieces, they threw his Head and Lyre into the River Hebrus; down which they floated to the Euxine Sea, as far as the Island of Lesbos, the Head continually uttering a doleful Song, as it were, lamenting the Death of Orpheus, and the Lyre, with the Wind's impulse, moving its Strings, and harmoniously Accompanying the Voice. Let 's see if we cannot discover them hereabouts.

CHAPTER LVI

How among the Frozen Words, Pantagruel found some Odd ones

THE Skipper made answer; Be not afraid, my Lord, we are on the Confines of the Frozen Sea, on which, about the beginning of last Winter, happen'd a great and bloody Fight between the Arimaspians and the Nephelibates. Then the Words and Cries of Men and Women, the hacking, slashing and hewing of Battle-axes, the shocking, knocking and joulting of Armours and Harnesses, the neighing of Horses, and all other Martial

Din and Noise, froze in the Air: And now the Rigour of the Winter being over, by the succeeding Serenity and Warmth of the Weather, they melt, and are heard.

By jingo, quoth Panurge, the Man talks somewhat like; I believe him; but cou'dn't we see some of 'em? Methinks I have read, that on the edge of the Mountain on which Moses receiv'd the Judaic Law, the People saw the Voices sensibly.— Here, here, said Pantagruel, here are some that are not yet thaw'd. He then throw'd us on the Deck whole handfuls of frozen Words, which seem'd to us like your rough Sugar-Plumbs, of many Colours, like those us'd in Heraldry, some words *Gules*, (This means also Jests and merry Sayings) some *Vert*, some *Azure*, some *Black*, some *Or*, (This means also fair Words;) and when we had somewhat warm'd them between our Hands, they melted like Snow, and we really heard them, but cou'd not understand them, for it was a Barbarous Gibberish; one of them only that was pretty big, having been warm'd between Fryar Jhon's Hands, gave a sound much like that of Chestnuts when they are thrown into the Fire without being first cut, which made us all start. This was the report of a Field-piece in its time, cry'd Fryar Jhon.

Panurge pray'd Pantagruel to give him some more; but Pantagruel told him, that to give Words, was the Part of a Lover. Sell me some then, I pray you, cry'd Panurge. That's the Part of a Lawyer, return'd Pantagruel; I wou'd sooner sell you Silence, tho' at a dearer Rate, as Demosthenes formerly sold it, by the means of his Argentangina or Silver Squinsey.

However, he threw three or four handfulls of them on the Deck, among which I perceiv'd some very sharp Words, and some bloody Words, which, the Pilot said, us'd sometimes to go back and recoil to the Place whence they came, but 'twas with a slit Wesand; we also saw some terrible Words, and some others not very pleasant to the Eye.

When they had been all melted together, we heard a strange Noise, Hin, hin, hin, hin, his, tick, tock, taack, brededin, brededack, frr, frr, frr, bou, bou, bou, bou, bou, bou, bou, bou, track, track, trr, trr, trr, trrr, trrrrrr, on, on, on, on, on, on, ououououon, gog, magog, and I do not know what other barbarous Words, which the Pilot said, were the Noise made by the Charging Squadrons, the Shock and the Neighing of Horses.

Then we heard some large ones go off like Drums and Fifes, and others like Clarions and Trumpets. Believe me, we had very good Sport with them. I wou'd fain have sav'd some merry Odd Words, and have preserved them in Oil, as Ice and Snow are kept, and between clean Straw : But Pantagruel would not let me, saying, that 'tis a folly to hoard up what we are never like to want, or have always at hand, odd, quaint, merry and fat Words of *Gules* never being scarce among all good and jovial Pantagruelists.

Panurge somewhat vex'd Fryar Jhon, and put him in the Pouts ; for he took him at his Word, while he dreamt of nothing less. This caus'd the Fryar to threaten him with such a piece of Revenge as was put upon G. Jousseaume, who having taken the merry Patelin at his Word, when he had overbid himself in some Cloth, was afterwards fairly taken by the Horns like a Bullock, by his jovial Chapman whom he took at his Word like a Man. Panurge well knowing that threaten'd Folks live long, bobb'd, and made mouths at him, in token of Derision ; then cry'd, Wou'd I had here the Word of the Holy Bottle, without being thus oblig'd to go farther in Pilgrimage to her.

CHAPTER LVII

How Pantagruel went ashore at the Dwelling of Gaster the first Master of Arts in the World

THAT Day Pantagruel went ashore in an Island, which for Situation and Government, may be said not to have its fellow. When you just come into it, you find it rugged, craggy, barren, unpleasant to the Eye, painful to the Feet, and almost as inaccessible as the Mountain of Dauphine, which is somewhat like a Toadstool, and was never clim'd, as any can remember, by any but Doyac, who had the charge of King Charles the Eighth's Train of Artillery.

This same Doyac, with strange Tools and Engines, gain'd that Mountain's Top, and there he found an old Ram. It puzzl'd many a wise Head to guess how it got thither. Some said, that some Eagle, or great Horn-Coot, having carry'd it thither while 'twas yet a Lambkin, it had got away and sav'd it self among the Bushes.

As for us, having with much toil and sweat overcome the difficult Ways at the Entrance, we found the Top of the Mountain so fertile, healthful and pleasant, that I thought I was then in the true Garden of Eden, or Earthly Paradise, about whose Situation our good Theologues are in such a quandary, and keep such a pother.

As for Pantagruel, he said, That here was the Seat of Arete (that 's as much as to say, Virtue) describ'd by Hesiod ; this however, with submission to better Judgments. The Ruler of the Place was one Master Gaster, the first Master of Arts in this World ; for if you believe that Fire is the great Master of Arts, as Tully writes, you very much wrong him and your self ; alas, Tully never believ'd this. On the other side, if you fansie Mercury to be the first Inventer of Arts, as our ancient Druids believ'd of old, you are mightily beside the Mark. The Satyrist's Sentence, that affirms Master Gaster to be Master of all Arts, is true. With him peacefully resided old Goody Penia alias Poverty, the Mother of the Ninety Nine Muses, on whom Porus the Lord of Plenty formerly begot Love, that Noble Child, the Mediator of Heaven and Earth, as Plato affirms in *Symposio*.

We were all oblig'd to pay our Homage and swear Allegiance to that mighty Sovereign ; for he is Imperious, Severe, Blunt, Hard, Uneasie, Inflexible ; you cannot make him believe, represent to him, or persuade him any thing.

He do's not hear ; and as the Egyptians said, That Harpocrates the God of Silence nam'd Sigalion in Greek was Astomé, that is, without a Mouth ; so Gaster was created without Ears, even like the Image of Jupiter in Candia.

He only speaks by Signs, but those Signs are more readily obey'd by every one, than the Statutes of Senates, or Commands of Monarchs; neither will he admit the least lett, or delay in his Summons. You say, that when a Lyon roars all the Beasts at a considerable distance round about, as far as his Roar can be heard, are seiz'd with a shivering. This is written, 'Tis true, I have seen it. I assure you, that at Master Gaster's Command, the very Heavens tremble, and all the Earth shakes, his Command is call'd, Do this or die : Needs must whom the Devil drives, there 's no gainsaying of it.

The Pilot was telling us how on a certain Time, after the manner of the Members that mutin'd against the Belly, as Æsop describes it, the whole Kingdom of the Somates went off into a direct Faction against Gaster, resolving to throw off his Yoke, but they soon found their mistake and most humbly submitted, for otherwise they had all been famish'd.

What Companies soever he is in, none dispute with him for Precedence or Superiority, he still goes first, tho' Kings, Emperors, or even the Pope were there. So he held the first Place at the Council of Basle, tho' some will tell you that the Council was tumultuous by the Contentions and Ambition of many for Priority.

Every one is busied, and labours to serve him; and indeed, to make amends for this, he do's this good to Mankind, as to invent for them all Arts, Machines, Trades, Engines, and Crafts; he even instructs Brutes in Arts which are against their Nature, making Poets of Ravens, Jack-Daws, chattering Jays, Parrots and Starlings, and Poetesses of Magpies, teaching them to utter human Languages, Speak and Sing; and All for the Gut. He reclaims and tames Eagles, Gerfaulcons, Faulcons-gentle, Sakers, Lanniers, Gosse-hawks, Spar-hawks, Merlins, Hagards, Passengers, wild rapacious Birds; so that setting them free in the Air, whenever he thinks fit, as high and as long as he pleases, he keeps them suspended, straying, flying, hovering, and courting him above the Clouds: then on a sudden he makes them stoop and come down amain from Heaven next to the Ground; and all for the Gut.

Elephants, Lions, Rhinocerotes, Bears, Horses, Mares, and Dogs, he teaches to Dance, Prance, Vault, Fight, Swim, hide themselves, fetch and carry what he pleases; and all for the Gut.

Salt and fresh-water Fish, Whales, and the Monsters of the Main, he brings up from the bottom of the Deep; Wolves he forces out of the Woods, Bears out of the Rocks, Foxes out of their Holes, and Serpents out of the Ground; and all for the Gut.

In short, he is so unruly, that in his Rage he devours all Men and Beasts; as was seen among the Vascons, when Q. Metellus besieg'd them in the Sertorian Wars; among the Saguntines besieg'd by Hannibal; among the Jews besieg'd by the Romans, and Six hundred more; and all for the Gut. When his Regent Penia takes a Progress, where-ever she moves, all Senates are shut up, all Statutes repeal'd, all Orders and Proclamations vain; she knows, obeys, and has no Law. All shun her, in every Place chusing rather to expose themselves to Shipwracks at Sea, and venture through Fire, Rocks, Caves and Precipices, than be seiz'd by that most dreadful Tormentor.

CHAPTER LVIII

How at the Court of the Master of Ingenuity, Pantagruel detested the Engastrimythes and the Gastrolaters

At the Court of that great Master of Ingenuity, Pantagruel observ'd two sorts of troublesom and too officious Apparitors, whom he very much detested. The first, were call'd Engastrimythes; the others, Gastrolaters.

The first pretended to be descended of the ancient Race of Euricles; and for this brought the Authority of Aristophanes, in his Comedy call'd, *The Wasps;* whence of old they were call'd Euriclians, as Plato writes, and Plutarch in his Book of the *Cessation of Oracles.* In the Holy Decrees 26 Qu. 3. they are stil'd Ventriloqui; and the same Name is given them in Ionian by Hippocrates, in his Fifth Book of *Epid.* as Men who speak from the Belly. Sophocles calls them Sternomantes. These were Southsayers, Enchanters, Cheats, who gull'd the Mob, and seem'd not to speak and give Answers from the Mouth; but from the Belly.

Such a one, about the Year of our Lord 1513, was Jacoba Rodogina, an Italian Woman of mean Extract; from whose Belly, we, as well as an infinite Number of others at Ferrara, and elsewhere, have often heard the Voice of the Evil Spirit speak, low, feeble and small indeed; but yet very distinct, articulate and intelligible, when she was sent for, out of Curiosity, by the Lords and Princes of the Cisalpine Gaul. To remove all manner of Doubt, and be assur'd that this was not a Trick, they us'd to have her stripp'd stark naked, and caus'd her Mouth and Nose to be stopp'd. This Evil Spirit would be call'd Curl'd-Pate, or Cincinnatulo, seeming pleas'd when any call'd him by that Name; at which, he was always ready to answer. If any spoke to him of things past or present, he gave pertinent Answers, sometimes to the Amazement of the Hearers; but, if of things to come, then the Devil was gravell'd, and us'd to Lye as fast as a Dog can trot. Nay, sometimes he seem'd to own his Ignorance, instead of an Answer, letting out a rouzing Fart, or uttering some Words with barbarous and uncouth Inflexions, and not to be understood.

As for the Gastrolaters, they stuck close to one another in

GOODY PENIA.

767

Knots and Gangs. Some of them merry, wanton, and soft as so many Milksops; others lowring, grim, dogged, demure and crabbed, all idle, mortal Foes to Business, spending half their Time in sleeping, and the rest in doing nothing, a Rent-charge and dead unnecessary Weight on the Earth, as Hesiod saith; afraid (as we judg'd) of offending or lessening their Paunch. Others were mask'd, disguis'd, and so oddly dress'd, that 'twould have done you good to have seen them.

There's a Saying, and several Ancient Sages write, That the Skill of Nature appears wonderful in the Pleasure which she seems to have taken in the Configuration of Sea-shells, so great is their Variety, Colours, Streaks, and inimitable Shapes, I protest, the Variety we perceiv'd in the Dresses of the Gastro-latrous Coquillons was not less. They all own'd Gaster for their Supreme God, ador'd him as a God, offer'd him Sacrifices as to their Omnipotent Deity, own'd no other God, serv'd, lov'd, and honour'd him above all things.

You would have thought that the Holy Apostle spoke of those, when he said, Phil. Chap. 3. Many walk of whom I have told you often, and now tell you even weeping, that they are Enemies of the Cross of Christ: whose End is Destruction, whose God is their Belly. Pantagruel compar'd them to the Cyclops Polyphemus, whom Euripides brings in speaking thus, I only Sacrifice to my self (not to the Gods) and to this Belly of mine, the greatest of all the Gods

CHAPTER LIX

Of the ridiculous Statue Manduce; and how, and what the Gastrolaters sacrifice to their Ventripotent God

WHILE we fed our Eyes with the sight of the Phyzzes and Actions of these lozelly Gulligutted Gastrolaters, we on a sudden heard the Sound of a Musical Instrument call'd a Bell, at which all of them plac'd themselves in Rank and File as for some mighty Battel, every one according to his Office, Degree and Seniority.

In this Order, they mov'd towards Master Gaster, after a plump, young, lusty gorbellied Fellow, who on a long Staff fairly gilt, carried a wooden Statue grosly carv'd, and as scurvily daub'd o'er with Paint, such a one as Plautus, Juvenal and Pomp. Festus describe it. At Lions during the Carnaval 'tis call'd Maschecrouste, or Gnaw-crust; they call'd this Manduce.

It was a monstrous, ridiculous, hideous Figure, fit to fright little Children: Its Eyes were bigger than its Belly, and its Head larger than all the rest of its Body, well Mouth-cloven however, having a goodly Pair of wide, broad Jaws, lin'd with two Rows of Teeth, upper Teer and under Teer, which, by the Magic of a small Twine hid in the hollow part of the Golden Staff, were made to clash, clatter and rattle dreadfully one against another, as they do at Metz with St. Clement's Dragon.

Coming near the Gastrolaters, I saw they were follow'd by a great Number of fat Waiters and Tenders laden with Baskets, Dossers, Hampers, Dishes, Wallets, Pots and Kettles: Then under the Conduct of Manduce, and singing I don't know what Dithyrambicks, Crepalocomes and Epenons, opening their Baskets and Pots, they offer'd their God,

White Hippocras with dry Toasts.	Fricasses 9 sorts.	Cold Loins of Veal with Spice.
White-Bread.	Monastical Browess.	Beatille-Pyes.
Brown-Bread.	Gravy-soupe.	Brewess.
Carbonadoes, six sorts.	Hotch-pots.	Marrow-Bones, Toast and Cabbige.
Brawn.	Soft-bread.	Hashes.
Sweet-breads.	Houshold-Bread.	
	Capirotadoes.	
	Zinziberine.	

Eternal Drink intermix'd. Brisk delicate White-wine led the Van, Claret and Champaign follow'd, cool, nay, as cold as the very Ice, I say, fill'd and offer'd in large Silver Cups: Then they offer'd,

Chitterlins garnish'd with Mustard.	Hogs-haslets.	Hams.
Saucidges.	Scotch Collops.	Brawn-heads.
Neats Tongues.	Puddings.	Powder'd Venison, with Turnips.
Hung Beef.	Cervelats.	Pickled Olives.
Chines and Pease.	Bolonia Sawcidges.	

All this associated with Sempiternal Liquor. Then they hous'd within his Muzzle,

Legs of Mutton with Shallots.
Ollas.
Lumber-Pyes, with hot Sauce.
Ribs of Pork, with Onion Sauce.
Roast Capons basted with their own Dripping.
Caponets.
Caviar and Toast.
Fawns, Deer.
Hares, Leverets.
Partridges, and young Partridges.
Pluvers.
Dwarfe-herons.
Teals.
Duckers.
Bittors.
Shovelers.
Curlues.
Wood-hens.
Coots with Leeks
Fat Kids.
Shoulders of Mutton with Capers.
Sir-Loins of Beef.
Breasts of Veal.
Phesants and Phesant poots.
Peacocks.
Storks.
Woodcocks.
Snipes.
Hortolans.
Turkey-Cocks, Hen-Turkeys and Turkey-poots.

Stock-doves and Wood-culvers.
Pigs with Wine Sauce.
Blackbirds, Owsels, and Rayles.
Moor-hens.
Bustards and Bustard poots
Fig-peckers.
Young Guiny-hens.
Flemmings.
Cignets.
A Renforcement of Vinegar intermixt.
Venison Pasties.
Lark Pyes.
Dormise Pyes.
Cabretto Pasties.
Roe-buck Pasties.
Pigeon Pyes.
Kid Pasties.
Capon Pyes.
Bacon Pyes.
Souc'd Hogs-feet.
Fry'd Pasty-crust.
Forc'd Capons.
Parmesan Cheese.
Red and Pale Hip-pocras.
Gold-Peaches
Artichokes.
Dry and wet Sweet-meats 78 sorts.
Boyl'd Hens and fat Capons maronated.
Pullets with Eggs.
Hen-Chickens.
Quails and young Quails.

Rabbets and sucking Rabbets.
Pigeons Squobbs and Squeakers.
Herons and young Herons.
Feldivers.
Olaves.
Thrushes.
Young Sea-Ravens.
Geese, Goslins.
Queests.
Widgeons.
Mavises.
Grouses.
Turtles.
Doe-Conneys
Hedge-hogs.
Snytes.
Then large Puffs.
Thistle-Finches.
Whore's Farts.
Fritters.
Cakes, 16 sorts.
Crisp Wafers.
Quince Tarts.
Curds and Cream.
Whipp'd Cream.
Preserv'd Myra-bolans.
Gellies.
Welch Barrapyclids.
Macaroons.
Tarts, 20 sorts.
Lemon Cream, Ras-berry Cream, etc.
Comfits, 100 Colours.
Cream Wafers.
Cream Cheese.

Vinegar brought up the Reer to wash the Mouth, and for fear of the Squinsy : Also Toast to scower the Grinders.

CHAPTER LX

What the Gastrolaters sacrific'd to their God on interlarded Fish-Days

PANTAGRUEL did not like this pack of Rascally Scoundrels with their manifold Kitchen Sacrifices, and would have been gone, had not Epistemon prevail'd with him to stay and see the End of the Farce ; he then ask'd the Skipper, what the idle Lobcocks us'd to sacrifice to their gorbellied God on interlarded Fish-days ? For his first Course, said the Skipper, they gave him

Caviar.
Botargoes.
Fresh Butter.
Pease soupe.
Spinage.
Fresh Herrings full-
   roed.
Salats, a hundred
   Varieties, of
   Creeses, sodden

Hoptops, Bishops-
Cods, Sellery,
Sives, Rampions,
Jew's Ears, (a sort
of Mushrooms that
sprout out of old
Elders) Sparagus,
Woodbind and a
World of others.

Red-herrings.
Pilchards.
Anchovies.
Fry of Tunny.
Collyflowers.
Beans.
Salt Salmon.
Pickled Griggs.
Oysters in the
   Shell.

Then he must drink or the Devil would gripe him at the Throat ; this therefore they take care to prevent, and nothing 's wanting. Which being done, they gave him Lampreys with Hippocras Sawce,

Gurnards.
Salmon-Trouts.
Barbels great and
   small.
Roaches.
Cockrells.
Menews.

Thornbacks.
Sleeves.
Sturgeons.
Sheath-fish.
Mackerels.
Maids.
Plaice.

Fry'd Oysters.
Cockles.
Prawnes.
Smelts.
Rock-fish.
Gracious Lords.
Sword-fish.

Skate-fish.
Lamprills.
Jegs.
Pickerells.
Millers' Thumbs.
Preeks.
Bret-fish.
Flounders.
Sea-nettles.
Mullets.
Gudgeons.
Dabs and Sandings.
Haddocks.
Carpes.
Pykes.
Botitoes.
Rochets.
Sea-Bears.
Sharplins.
Tunnyes.
Silver Eels.
Chevins.
Cray-fish.
Pallours.

Shrimps.
Congers.
Porposes.
Bases.
Trouts not above a Foot long.
Salmons.
Meagers.
Sea-Breams.
Halibuts.
Soles.
Dog's-tongue or Kind-fool.
Muskles.
Lobsters.
Great Prawnes.
Dace.
Bleaks.
Tenches.
Ombers.
Fresh Cods.
Dried Melwells.
Darefish.
Fausens, and Griggs.

Eel-pouts.
Tortoises.
Serpents, *i.e.* Wood-Eeles.
Dores.
Moor-game.
Golden Carps.
Burbates.
Salmons.
Salmon-perls.
Dolphins.
Barn Trouts.
Shads.
Murenes, a sort of Lampreys.
Graylings.
Smys.
Turbots.
Pearches.
Loaches.
Crab-fish.
Snails and Whelks.
Froggs.

If, when he had cramm'd all this down his Guttural Trapdoor, he did not immediately make the Fish swim again in his Paunch, Death would pack him off in a trice; special care is taken to Antidote his Godship with Vine-tree Syrup. Then is sacrific'd to him, Haberdines, Poor Jack, mingle-mangled mishmash'd, etc.

Eggs fry'd, beaten, butter'd, poach'd, hardened, boyl'd, broyl'd, stew'd, slic'd, roasted in the Embers, toss'd in the Chimney, etc.
Stock-fish.
Green-fish.
Sea-Batts.
Cod's-Ounds.
Sea-Pikes.

Which to concoct and digest the more easily, Vinegar is multiply'd. For the latter part of their Sacrifices they offer,

Rice Milk and hasty Pudding
Butter'd Wheat and Flummery
Watergruel and Milk-Porradge.

Frumenty and Bony-claber.	Figgs.	Chestnuts and Wall-nuts.
Stew'd Prunes, and bak'd Bullies.	Almond-Butter.	Filberds
Pistachoes or Fistick-Nuts.	Skirret-Root.	Parsenips.
	White-Pot.	Artichoakes.
	Raisins.	
	Dates.	

Perpetuity of Soaking with the whole.

'Twas none of their Fault, I 'll assure you, if this same God of theirs was not publickly, preciously and plentifully serv'd in his Sacrifices, better yet than Heliogabalus's Idol; nay, more than Bell and the Dragon in Babylon under King Balshazzar. Yet Gaster had the Manners to own that he was no God, but a poor, vile, wretched Creature. And as King Antigonus, first of the Name, when one Hermodotus, (as Poets will flatter, especially Princes) in some of his Fustian dubb'd him a God, and made the Sun adopt him for his Son, said to him, (My Lasanophore, or in plain English, my Groom of the Close-stool) can give thee the Lye; so Master Gaster very civilly us'd to send back his bigotted Worshipers to his Close-stool, to see, smell, taste, philosophise and examine what kind of Divinity they could pick out of his Sir-reverence.

CHAPTER LXI

How Gaster invented Means to get and preserve Corn

THOSE Gastrolatrous Hobgoblins being withdrawn, Pantagruel carefully minded the famous Master of Arts, Gaster. You know that by the Institution of Nature, Bread has been assign'd him for provision and Food, and that as an addition to this Blessing, he should never want the means to get Bread.

Accordingly, from the beginning he invented the Smith's Art and Husbandry to manure the Ground that it might yield him Corn; he invented Arms, and the Art of War to defend Corn; Physick and Astronomy, with other parts of Mathematicks, which might be useful to keep Corn a great number of Years in safety from the Injuries of the Air, Beasts, Robbers and Purloiners; he invented Water, Wind and Hand-Mills, and a thousand other Engines to grind Corn, and turn it into Meal, Leaven to make the Dough ferment, and the use of Salt to give it a savour, for he knew that nothing bred more Diseases than heavy, unleaven'd, unsavoury Bread.

He found a way to get Fire to Bake it; Hour-glasses, Dials and Clocks to mark the time of its Baking; and as some Countries wanted Corn, he contrived means to convey some out of one Country into another.

He had the Wit to pimp for Asses and Mares, Animals of different Species, that they might Copulate for the Generation of a third, which we call Mules, more strong and fit for hard Service than the other two. He invented Carts and Waggons to draw him along with greater ease; and as Seas and Rivers hindred his Progress, he devis'd Boats, Gallies and Ships (to the astonishment of the Elements) to waft him over to barbarous, unknown, and far distant Nations, thence to bring, or thither to carry Corn.

Besides, seeing that, when he had tilled the Ground, some Years the Corn perish'd in it for want of Rain in due Season, in others rotted, or was drown'd by its excess, sometimes spoil'd by Hail, eat by Worms in the Ear, or beaten down by Storms, and so his Stock was destroy'd on the Ground; we were told that ever since the Days of Yore, he has found out a way to conjure the Rain down from Heaven only with cutting certain Grass, common enough in the Field, yet known to very few, some of which was then shown us : I took it to be the same as the Plant, one of whose Boughs being dipp'd by Jove's Priest into the Agrian Fountain, on the Lycian Mountain in Arcadia in time of Drought, rais'd Vapours which gather'd into Clouds, and then dissolv'd into Rain, that kindly moisten'd the whole Country.

Our Master of Arts was also said to have found a way to keep the Rain up in the Air, and make it fall into the Sea ; also to annihilate the Hail, suppress the Winds, and remove Storms as the Methanensians of Trœzene us'd to do. And as in the Fields Thieves and Plunderers sometimes stole and took by force the Corn and Bread which others had toyl'd to get, he invented the Art of building Towns, Forts, and Castles, to hoard and secure that Staff of Life ; on the other hand, finding none in the Fields, and hearing that it was hoarded up and secur'd in Towns, Forts and Castles, and watch'd with more care than ever were the Golden Pippins of the Hesperides, he turn'd Engenier, and found ways to beat, storm, and demolish Forts and Castles, with Machines, and warlike Thunderbolts, Battering-Rams, Balists, and Catapults, whose shapes were shown us, not over-well understood by our Engeniers, Architects, and other Disciples of Vitruvius, as Master Philebert de l'Orme, King Megistus's principal Architect has own'd to us.

And seeing that sometimes all these Tools of Destruction were baffled by the cunning Subtilty, or the subtle Cunning (which you please) of Fortifiers, he lately invented Cannons, Field-pieces, Culverins, Bombards, Basilisko's, murthering Instruments that dart Iron, Leaden and Brazen Balls, some of them outweighing huge Anvils ; this by the means of a most dreadful Powder, whose Hellish Compound and Effect has even amaz'd Nature, and made her own her self out-done by Art ; the Oxydracan Thunders, Hails and Storms, by which the People of that Name immediately destroy'd their Enemies in the Field, being but meer Pot-guns to these. For, one of our great Guns when us'd, is more dreadful, more terrible, more diabolical, and maims, tears, breaks, slays, mows down, sweeps away more Men, and causes a greater Consternation and Destruction than a hundred Thunderbolts.

CHAPTER LXII

How Gaster invented an Art to avoid being hurt or touch'd by Cannon Balls

GASTER having secur'd himself with his Corn within strong Holds, has sometimes been attack'd by Enemies, his Fortresses, by that thrice threefold curst Instrument, levell'd and destroy'd, his dearly beloved Corn and Bread snatch'd out of his Mouth, and sack'd by a Titannick Force, therefore he then sought means to preserve his Walls, Bastions, Rampiers, and Sconces from Cannon-shot, and to hinder the Bullets from hitting him, stopping them in their flight, or at least from doing him, or the Besiegers and Walls any damage; he show'd us a tryal of this, which has since been us'd by Fronton, and is now common among the Pastimes and harmless Recreations of the Thelemites. I'll tell you how he went to work, and pray for the future be a little more ready to believe what Plutarch affirms to have try'd; Suppose a Herd of Goats were all scampering as if the Devil drove 'em, do but put a bit of Eringo into the Mouth of the hindmost Nanny, and they will all stop stock-still, in the time you can tell three.

Thus Gaster, having caus'd a Brass Faulkon to be charg'd, with a sufficient quantity of Gunpowder, well purg'd from its Sulphur, and curiously made up with fine Camphir, he then had a suitable Ball put into the Piece, with twenty-four little Pellets like Hail-shot, some round, some Pearl fashion, then taking his aim, and levelling it at a Page of his, as if he would have hit him on the Breast, about sixty strides off the Piece, half way between it and the Page in a right Line, he hang'd on a Gibbet by a Rope a very large Side-ride or Iron-like Stone, otherwise call'd Herculean, formerly found on Ida in Phrygia by one Magnes as Nicander writes, and commonly call'd Load-stone: then he gave Fire to the Prime on the Piece's Touch-hole, which in an instant consuming the Powder, the Ball and Hail-shot, were with incredible violence and swiftness hurried out of the Gun at its Muzzle, that the Air might penetrate to its Chamber, where otherwise would have been a Vacuum; which Nature abhors so much that this Universal Machine, Heaven, Air, Land, and Sea would sooner return to

WHEATH. ROBINSON.

EPISTEMON

263

the Primitive Chaos than admit the least void any where. Now the Ball and small Shot which threaten'd the Page with no less than quick Destruction, lost their impetuosity, and remain'd suspended and hovering round the Stone, nor did any one of them, notwithstanding the Fury with which they rush'd, reach the Page.

Master Gaster could do more than all this yet, if you 'll believe me, for he invented a way how to cause Bullets to fly backwards, and recoyl on those that sent 'em, with as great a Force, and in the very numerical Parallel for which the Guns were planted. And indeed, why should he have thought this difficult, seeing the Herb Ethiopis opens all Locks whatsoever, and an Echineis or Remora, a silly weakly Fish, in spight of all the Winds that blow from the 32 Points of the Compass, will in the midst of a Hurricane make you the biggest First Rate remain stock still, as if she were becalm'd, or the blustering Tribe had blown their last ; nay, and with the Flesh of that Fish preserv'd with Salt, you may fish Gold out of the deepest Well that was ever sounded with a Plummet, for it will certainly draw up the precious Metal, since Democritus affirm'd it.

Theophrastus believ'd and experienc'd that there was an Herb at whose single touch an Iron Wedge, tho' never so far driven into a huge Log of the hardest Wood that is, would presently come out, and 'tis this same Herb your Hickways, *alias* Woodpeckers use, when with some mighty Ax any one stops up the hole of their Nests, which they industriously dig and make in the Trunk of some sturdy Tree. Since Stags and Hinds when deeply wounded with Darts, Arrows, and Bolts, if they do but meet the Herb call'd Dittany, which is common in Candia, and eat a little of it, presently the Shafts come out, and all 's well again ; even as kind Venus cur'd her beloved By-blow Æneas, when he was wounded on the right Thigh with an Arrow by Juturna Turnus's Sister. Since the very Wind of Laurels, Fig-trees, or Sea-calves, makes the Thunder sheer off, insomuch that it never strikes them. Since at the sight of a Ram, mad Elephants recover their former Senses ; since mad Bulls coming near wild Fig-trees call'd Caprifici grow tame, and will not budge a foot, as if they had the Cramp. Since the venomous Rage of Vipers is asswag'd, if you but touch them with a Beechen Bough. Since also Euphorion writes, that in the Isle of Samos, before Juno's Temple was built there, he has seen some Beasts call'd Neades, whose Voice made the Neighbouring Places gape and sink into a

Chasm and Abyss. In short, since Elders grow of a more pleasing Sound, and fitter to make Flutes in such places where the crowing of Cocks is not heard, as the Ancient Sages have writ, and Theophrastus relates; as if the crowing of a Cock dull'd, flatten'd and perverted the Wood of the Elder, as it is said to astonish and stupifie with Fear that strong and resolute Animal, a Lion.

I know that some have understood this of wild Elder, that grows so far from Towns or Villages that the crowing of Cocks cannot reach near it; and doubtless that sort ought to be preferr'd to the stenching common Elder that grows about decay'd and ruin'd Places; but others have understood this in a higher Sense, not Literal, but Allegorical, according to the Method of the Pythagoreans. As when it was said that Mercury's Statue could not be made of every sort of Wood, to which Sentence they give this Sense; That God is not to be worshipp'd in a vulgar form, but in a chosen and religious manner.

In the same manner by this Elder, which grows far from places where Cocks are heard, the Ancients meant, that the wise and studious ought not to give their Minds to trivial or vulgar Musick, but to that which is Celestial, Divine, Angelical, more abstracted and brought from remoter Parts, that is from a Region where the crowing of Cocks is not heard; for, to denote a solitary and unfrequented Place, we say, Cocks are never heard to crow there

CHAPTER LXIII

How Pantagruel fell asleep near the Island of Chaneph, and of the Problems propos'd to be solv'd when he wak'd

THE next Day merrily pursuing our Voyage we came in sight of the Island of Chaneph, where Pantagruel's Ship could not arrive, the Wind chopping about, and then failing us, so that we were becalm'd, and could hardly get o' head, tacking about from Starboard to Larboard, and Larboard to Starboard, tho' to our Sails we had added Drablers.

With this Accident we were all out of sorts, moping, drooping, metagrabolized as dull as Dun in the Mire, in C sol fa ut flat out of Tune, off the Hinges, and I don't know howish, without caring to speak one single Syllable to each other.

Pantagruel was taking a Nap, slumbering and nodding on the Quarter-deck, by the Cuddy, with an Heliodorus in his Hand, for still 'twas his custom to sleep better by Book than by Heart.

Epistemon was Conjuring with his Astrolabe to know what Latitude we were in.

Fryar Jhon was got into the Cook-room examining by the Ascendant of the Spits, and the Horoscope of Ragousts and Fricassees what time o' day it might then be.

Panurge (sweet Baby!) held a stalk of Pantagruelion, *alias* Hemp, next his Tongue, and with it made pretty Bubbles and Bladders.

Gymnast was making Tooth-pickers with Lentisk.

Ponocrates, dozing, doz'd, and dreaming dream'd, tickled himself to make himself laugh, and with one Finger scratch'd his Noddle where it did not itch.

Carpalim with a Nut-shell, and a Trencher of Verne (that's a Card in Gascony) was making a pretty little merry Windmill, cutting the Card long-ways into four slips, and fastning them with a Pin to the Convex of the Nut, and its Concave to the tarr'd side of the Gunnel of the Ship.

Eusthenes bestriding one of the Guns, was playing on it with his Fingers, as if it had been a Trump-marine.

Rhizotome with the soft Coat of a Field-Tortoise, *alias*, eclip'd a Mole, was making himself a Velvet Purse.

Xenomanes was patching up an old weather-beaten Lantern with a Hawk's Jesses.

Our Pilot (good Man!) was pulling Maggots out of the Seamen's Noses.

At last Fryar Jhon returning from the Fore-castle, perceiv'd that Pantagruel was awake. Then breaking this obstinate Silence, he briskly and cheerfully asked him, how a Man should kill Time, and raise good Weather, during a Calm at Sea?

Panurge, whose Belly thought his Throat cut, back'd the Motion presently, and ask'd for a Pill to purge Melancholy?

Epistemon also came on, and ask'd how a Man might be ready to bepiss himself with Laughing, when he has no heart to be merry?

Gymnast arising, demanded a Remedy for a dimness of Eyes.

Ponocrates, after he had a while rub'd his Noddle, and shak'd his Ears, ask'd, How one might avoid Dog-sleep? Hold, cry'd Pantagruel, the Peripateticks have wisely made a Rule, that all Problems, Questions and Doubts which are offer'd to be solv'd, ought to be certain, clear, and intelligible; What do you mean by Dog-sleep? I mean, answer'd Ponocrates, to sleep fasting in the Sun at Noon-day, as the Dogs do.

Rhizotome, who lay stooping on the Pump, rais'd his drowsy Head, and lazily yawning, by natural Sympathy, set almost every one in the Ship a yawning too; then ask'd for a Remedy against Oscitations and Gapings?

Xenomanes, half puzzled, and tir'd out with new vamping his antiquated Lantern, ask'd, How the Hold of the Stomach might be so well ballasted and freighted from the Keel to the Main-hatch with Stores well stowed, that our human Vessels might not heeld, or be walt, but well trimm'd, and stiff?

Carpalim twirling his diminutive Wind-mill, ask'd how many Motions are to be felt in Nature before a Gentleman may be said to be hungry?

Eusthenes hearing them talk, came from between Decks, and from the Capstern call'd out to know why a Man that's fasting, bit by a Serpent also fasting, is in greater danger of death, than when Man and Serpent have eat their breakfasts? Why a Man's fasting-spittle is poysonous to Serpents and venomous Creatures?

One single Solution may serve for all your Problems, Gentlemen, answer'd Pantagruel, and one single Medicine for all such Symptoms and Accidents. My Answer shall be short, not to tire you with a long needless Train of pedantick Cant: The Belly has no Ears, nor is it to be fill'd with fair Words; you shall be answer'd to content by Signs and Gestures. As formerly at Rome, Tarquin the Proud, its last King, sent an Answer by Signs to his Son Sextus, who was among the Gabii, (saying this, he pull'd the String of a little Bell, and Fryar Jhon hurried away to the Cook-room.) The Son having sent his Father a Messenger to know how he might bring the Gabii under a close subjection; the King mistrusting the Messenger, made him no Answer, and only took him into his Privy-garden, and in his presence with his Sword lopt off the Heads of the tall Poppies that were there. The Express return'd without any other dispatch, yet having related to the Prince what he had seen his Father do, he easily understood that by those Signs he advis'd him to cut off the Heads of the chief Men in the Town, the better to keep under the rest of the People.

CHAPTER LXIV

How Pantagruel gave no Answer to the Problems

PANTAGRUEL then ask'd, what sorts of People dwell'd in that damn'd Island ? They are, answer'd Xenomanes, all Hypocrites, holy Mountebanks, Tumblers of Beads, Mumblers of *Ave Maries*, spiritual Comedians, sham Saints, Hermits, all of them poor Rogues, who like the Hermit of Lormont, between Blaye and Bordeaux, live wholly on Alms given them by Passengers. Catch me there if you can, cry'd Panurge, may the Devil's Head-cook conjure my Bum-gut into a pair of Bellows, if ever you find me among them. Hermits, sham Saints, living Forms of Mortification, holy Mountebanks, avaunt, in the Name of your Father Sathan get out of my sight ; when the Devil 's a Hog you shall eat Bacon. I shall not forget yet a while our fat Concilipetes of Chesil ; O that Beelzebub and Astaroth had counsell'd them to hang themselves out of the way, and they had done 't, we had not then suffer'd so much by devilish Storms as we did for having seen 'em. Harkee me, dear Rogue, Xenomanes, my Friend, I pr'y thee, are these Hermits, Hypocrites, and Eves-droppers, Maids or Married ? Is there any thing of the Feminine Gender among them ? Could a Body hypocritically take there a small hypocritical Touch ? Will they lye backwards, and let out their fore-rooms ? There 's a fine Question to be ask'd, cry'd Pantagruel ! Yes, yes, answer'd Xenomanes, you may find there many goodly Hypocritesses, jolly spiritual Actresses, kind Hermitesses, Women that have a plaguy deal of Religion ; then there 's the Copies of 'em, little Hypocritillons, Sham-sanctitos, and Hermitillons ; Foh, away with them, cry'd Fryar Jhon, a young Saint an old Devil, (mark this, an old Saying, and as true a one, as a young Whore an old Saint.) Were there not such, continu'd Xenomanes, the Isle of Caneph for want of a multiplication of Progeny, had long ere this been desert and desolate.

Pantagruel sent them by Gymnast in the Pinnace seventy

eight thousand fine pretty little Gold Half-Crowns, of those that are mark'd with a Lantern. After this he ask'd, What 's o' Clock ? Past nine, answer'd Epistemon. 'Tis then the best time to go to Dinner, said Pantagruel, for the sacred Line so celebrated by Aristophanes in his play call'd *Concionatores*, is at hand, never failing when the Shadow is decempedal.

Formerly among the Persians Dinner-time was at a set Hour only for Kings ; as for all others, their Appetite and their Belly was their Clock ; when that chim'd, they thought it time to go to Dinner. So we find in Plautus a certain Parasite making a heavy do, and sadly railing at the Inventors of Hour-glasses and Dials, as being unnecessary things, there being no Clock more regular than the Belly.

Diogenes Being ask'd at what times a Man ought to eat, answer'd, The Rich when he is hungry, the Poor when he has anything to eat. Physicians more properly say, that the Canonical Hours are,

> To rise at five, to dine at nine,
> To sup at five, to sleep at nine.

The famous King Petorsiris's Magick was different—here the Officers for the Gut came in, and got ready the Tables and Cupboards, laid the Cloth, whose sight and pleasant smell were very comfortable ; and brought Plates, Napkins, Salts, Tankards, Flaggons, Tall-boys, Ewers, Tumblers, Cups, Goblets, Basons, and Cisterns.

Fryar Jhon at the head of the Stewards, Sewers, Yeomen of the Pantry, and of the Mouth, Tasters, Carvers, Cup-bearers, and Cupboard-keepers, brought four stately Pasties, so huge that they put me in mind of the four Bastions at Turin ; 'ods Fish, how manfully did they storm them ! What havock did they make with the long Train of Dishes that came after them, how bravely did they stand to their Pan puddings, and pay'd off their Dust ! How merrily did they soak their Noses !

The Fruit was not yet brought in, when a fresh Gale at West and by North began to fill the Main-course, Misen-sail, Fore-sail, Tops, and Top-gallants ; for which Blessing they all sung divers Hymns of Thanks and Praise.

When the Fruit was on the Table, Pantagruel ask'd, Now tell me, Gentlemen, are your Doubts fully resolv'd or no ? I gape and yawn no more, answer'd Rhizotome ; I sleep no longer like a Dog, said Ponocrates ; I have clear'd my Eye-

sight, said Gymnast ; I have broke my Fast, said Eusthenes ;
so that for this whole Day shall be secure from the danger of
my Spittle

Aspes.
Amphisbenes.
Anerudutes.
Abedissimons.
Alhatrafs.
Ammobates.
Apimaos.
Alhatabans.
Aractes.
Asterions.
Alcharates.
Arges.
Spiders.
Cenchres.
Cockatrices.
Dipsades.
Domeses.
Dryinades.
Dragons.
Elopes.
Enhydrides.
Falvises.
Galeotes.
Harmenes.
Handons.
Icles.
Jarraries.
Ilicines.
Pharao's Mice.
Kedusudures.
Sea-hares.
Chalcidic Newts.
Footed Serpents.

Starry Lizards.
Attelabes.
Ascalabotes.
Hæmorrhoids.
Basilisks.
Fitches.
Sucking Water-
    snakes.
Black Wag leg-flies.
Spanish flies.
Catoblepes.
Horn'd Snakes.
Caterpillars.
Manticores.
Mulures.
Mouse-serpents.
Shrew-mice.
Miliares.
Megalaunes.
Spitting Asps.
Porphyri.
Parcades.
Phalangs.
Pemphredons.
Pine-tree-worms.
Rutelæ.
Worms.
Rhagia.
Rhaganes.
Salamanders.
Sloe-worms.
Stellions.
Scorpones.

Crocodiles.
Toads.
Night-mares.
Mad Dogs.
Colotes.
Cychriodes.
Cafezates.
Cauhares.
Snakes.
Cuhersks, Two-
    tongu'd Adders
Amphibious Ser-
    pents.
Scorpions.
Horn-worms.
Scalavotins.
Solofruidars.
Deaf-Asps.
Horse-Leeches.
Salt-haters.
Rot Serpents.
Stink-fish.
Stuphes.
Sabrins.
Blood-sucking-flies.
Hornfretters.
Scolopendres.
Tarantolas.
Blind-worms.
Tetragnathias.
Teristals.
Vipers, etc.

THE MAN'S EMPHATICALLY MAD,
WHO DRINKS THE BEST, YET CAN BE SAD

271

CHAPTER LXV

How Pantagruel past the Time with his Servants

IN what Hierarchy of such venemous Creatures do you place Panurge's future Spouse, ask'd Fryar Jhon ? Art thou speaking ill of Women, cry'd Panurge, thou mangy Scoundrel, thou sorry, noddy-peak'd, shaveling Monk ? By the Cenomanic Paunch and Gixie, said Epistemon, Euripides has written, and makes Andromache say it, that by Industry, and the help of the Gods, Men had found Remedies against all poisonous Creatures ; but none was yet found against a bad Wife.

This flaunting Euripides, cry'd Panurge, was gabbling against Women every foot, and therefore was devour'd by Dogs, as a Judgment from Above ; as Aristophanes observes ——Let 's go on, let him speak that 's next. I can leak now like any Stone-horse, said then Epistemon. I am, said Xenomanes, full as an Egg and round as a Hoop ; my Ship's Hold can hold no more, and will now make shift to bear a steddy Sail. Said Carpalim, A Truce with Thirst, a Truce with Hunger ; they 're strong, but Wine and Meat are stronger. I 'm no more in the Dumps, cry'd Panurge, my Heart 's a Pound lighter. I 'm in the right Cue now, as brisk as a Body-Louse, and as merry as a Beggar. For my part, I know what I do when I drink ; and 'tis a true thing (though 'tis in your Euripides) that is said by that jolly Toper Silenus, of blessed Memory, that

> The Man 's emphatically Mad,
> Who drinks the Best, yet can be sad.

We must not fail to return our humble and hearty Thanks to the Being, who, with this good Bread, this cool delicious Wine, these good Meats and rare Dainties, removes from our Bodies and Winds these Pains and Perturbations, and, at the same time, fills us with Pleasure and with Food.

But methinks, Sir, you did not give an Answer to Fryar Jhon's Question ; which, as I take it, was, how to raise good Weather ? Since you ask no more than this easie Question, answer'd Pantagruel, I 'll strive to give you satisfaction, and some other time we 'll talk of the rest of the Problems, if you will.

WHILE JOLLY COMPANIONS CARROUSE IT TOGETHER,
A FIG FOR THE STORM; IT GIVES WAY TO GOOD WEATHER

Well then, Fryar Jhon ask'd how good Weather might be rais'd : have we not rais'd it ? Look up, and see our full Top-sails ; Hark ! how the Wind whistles through the Shrouds, what a stiff Gale it blows ; observe the rattling of the Tacklings, and see the Sheats, that fasten the Main-sail behind ; the force of the Wind puts them upon the stretch. While we pass'd our time merrily, the dull Weather also pass'd away, and while we rais'd the Glasses to our Mouths, we also rais'd the Wind by a secret sympathy in Nature.

Thus Atlas and Hercules clubb'd to raise and underprop the falling Sky, if you 'll believe the wise Mythologists; but they rais'd it some half an Inch too high ; Atlas to entertain his Guest Hercules more pleasantly, and Hercules to make himself amends for the Thirst which sometime before had tormented him in the Deserts of Africa.——Your good Father, said Fryar Jhon, interrupting him, takes care to free many People from such an Inconveniency ; for I have been told by many venerable Doctors, that his chief Butler Turelupin saves about eighteen hundred Pipes of Wine yearly, to make Servants and all Comers and Goers drink before they are a dry.——As the Camels and Dromedaries of a Caravan, continued Pantagruel, use to drink for the Thirst that 's past, for the present, and for that to come, so did Hercules ; and being thus excessively rais'd, this gave a new Motion to the Sky, which is that of Titubation and Trepidation, about which our crack-brain'd Astrologers make such a pother.——This, said Panurge, makes the Saying good,

> While jolly Companions carrouse it together,
> A fig for the Storm ; it gives way to good Weather.

Nay, continued Pantagruel, some will tell you, that we have not only shortned the time of the Calm, but also much disburthen'd the Ship, not like Æsop's Basket, by easing it of the Provision, but by breaking our Fasts, and that a Man is more Terrestrial and heavy when fasting, than when he has eaten and drank, even as they pretend that he weighs more dead than living. However 'tis you 'll grant they are in the right, who take their Mornings draught, and Breakfast before a long Journey, then say that the Horses will perform the better, and that a Spur in the Head, is worth two in the Flank ; or in the same Horse Dialect,

That a Cup in the Pate
Is a Mile in the Gate.

Don't you know that formerly the Amycleans worshiped the
Noble Father Bacchus above all other Gods, and gave him the
Name of Psila, which in the Dorick Dialect signifies Wings;
for, as the Birds raise themselves by a towering flight with their
Wings above the Clouds; so with the help of soaring Bacchus,
the powerful Juice of the Grape, our Spirits are exalted to a
pitch above themselves, our Bodies are more sprightly, and
their Earthy Parts become soft and pliant.

CHAPTER LXVI

How by Pantagruel's Order the Muses were saluted near
the Isle of Ganabim

THIS fair Wind and as fine Talk brought us in sight of a high
Land, which Pantagruel discovering afar off, shew'd it Xeno-
manes, and ask'd him, do you see yonder to the Leeward a
high Rock with two Tops, much like Mount Parnassus in
Phocis? I do plainly, answer'd Xenomanes, 'tis the Isle of
Ganabim; have you a mind to go ashoar there? No, return'd
Pantagruel. You do well indeed, said Xenomanes, for there
is nothing worth seeing in the Place. The People are all
Thieves; yet there is the finest Fountain in the World, and
a very large Forest towards the right top of the Mountain.
Your Fleet may take in Wood and Water there.

He that spoke last spoke well, quoth Panurge let us not
by any means be so mad as to go among a parcel of Thieves
and Sharpers. You may take my word for 't, this Place is just
such another, as, to my knowledge, formerly were the Islands
of Sark and Herm between the smaller and the greater Britain;
such as were the Poneropolis of Philip in Thrace; Islands
of Thieves, Banditti, Picaroons, Robbers, Ruffians, and
Murtherers, worse than Raw-head and Bloody-bones, and
full as honest as the Senior Fellows of the College of Iniquity,
the very Out-casts of the County-Goal's Common-side. As

you love your self, do not go among 'em; if you go, you 'll come off but bluely, if you come off at all. If you will not believe me, at least believe what the good and wise Xenomanes tells you : for may I never stir if they are not worse than the very Canibals, they would certainly eat us alive. Do not go among 'em, I pray you, 'twere safer to take a Journey to Hell. Hark, by Cob's Body, I hear 'em ringing the Alarm-Bell most dreadfully, as the Gascons about Bourdeaux us'd formerly to do against the Commissaries and Officers for the Tax on Salt, or my Ears tingle. Let 's shear off.

Believe me, Sir, said Fryar Jhon, let 's rather land, we 'll rid the World of that Vermin, and inn there for nothing. Old Nick go with thee for me, quoth Panurge. This rash hair-brain'd Devil of a Fryar fears nothing, but ventures and runs on like a mad Devil as he is, and cares not a Rush what becomes of others ; as if every one was a Monk like his Fryarship ; a Pox on grinning Honour, say I. Go to, return'd the Fryar, thou mangy Noddy-peak l thou forlorn druggle-headed Sneaksby l And may a Million of black Devils Anatomise thy Cockle Brain. The Hen-hearted Rascal is so cowardly, that he berays himself for Fear every Day. If thou art so afraid, Dunghil, don't go, stay here and be hang'd, or go and hide thy Logger-head under Madam Proserpine's Petticoat.

Panurge hearing this, his Breech began to make Buttons, so he slunk in in an instant, and went to hide his Head down in the Bread-room among the musty Biscuits, and the Orts, and Scraps of broken Bread.

Pantagruel in the mean time said to the rest, I feel a pressing retraction in my Soul, which, like a Voice, admonishes me not to land there. Whenever I have felt such a Motion within me, I have found my self happy in avoiding what it directed me to shun, or in undertaking what it prompted me to do, and I never had occasion to repent following its Dictates.

As much, said Epistemon, is related of the Dæmon of Socrates, so celebrated among the Academics. Well then, Sir, said Fryar Jhon, while the Ship's Crew water, have you a mind to have good Sport ? Panurge is got down somewhere in the Hold, where he is crept into some Corner and lurks like a Mouse in a Cranny ; let 'em give the word for the Gunner to fire yon Gun over the Round-house on the Poop ; this will serve to salute the Muses of this Antiparnassus ; besides, the Powder does but decay in it. You are i' th' right, said Pantagruel ; here, give the word for the Gunner.

The Gunner immediately came, and was order'd by Panta-gruel to fire that Gun, and then charge it with fresh Powder, which was soon done ; the Gunners of the other Ships, Frigats, Gallions, and Gallies of the Fleet hearing us fire, gave every one a Gun to the Island ; which made such a horrid Noise, that ou 'd have sworn Heav'n had been tumbling about our Ears.

CHAPTER LXVII

How Panurge beray'd himself for Fear, and of the huge Cat Rodilardus, which he took for a puny Devil

PANURGE like a wild addle-pated giddy Goat, sallies out of the Bread-room in his Shirt, with nothing else about him but one of his Stockings, half on half off, about his Heel, like a rough-footed Pigeon, his Hair and Beard all bepowdered with Crums of Bread, in which he had been over Head and Ears, and a huge and mighty Puss partly wrapt up in his other Stocking. In this Equipage, his Chops moving like a Monkey's who 's a Louse-hunting, his Eyes staring like a dead Pig's, his Teeth chattering, and his Bum quivering, the poor Dog fled to Fryar Jhon, who was then sitting by the Chain-Wales of the Starboard-side of the Ship, and pray'd him heartily to take pity on him, and keep him in the safeguard of his trusty Bilbo, swearing by his share of Papimany that he had seen all Hell broke loose.

Woe 's me, my Jackee (cry'd he) my dear Johny, my old Crony, my Brother, my Ghostly Father, all the Devils keep Holy-day, all the Devils keep their Feast to day, Man ; Pork and Pease choak me, if ever thou sawest such Preparations in thy life for an Infernal Feast. Dost thou see the Smoke of Hell's Kitchens ? (This he said shewing him the Smoke of the Gun-powder above the Ships) thou never sawest so many damn'd Souls since thou wast born ; and so fair, so bewitching they seem, that one would swear they are Stygian Ambrosia. I thought at first, (God forgive me) they had been English Souls, and I don't know but that this Morning, the Isle of Horses near Scotland was sack'd with all the English who had surpris'd it, by the Lords of Termes and Essay.

Fryar Jhon, at the approach of Panurge, was entertain'd

with a kind of Smell that was not like that of Gun-powder, nor altogether so sweet as Musk ; which made him turn Panurge about, and then he saw that his Shirt was dismally bepah'd, and beray'd with fresh Sir-reverence. The retentive Faculty of the Nerve which restrains the Muscle call'd Sphincter ('tis the Arse-hole an 't please you) was relaxated by the violence of the Fear which he had been in during his fantastic Visions. Add to this the thundering Noise of the shooting, which seems more dreadful between Decks than above. Nor ought you to wonder at such a mishap, for one of the Symptoms and Accidents of Fear is, that it often opens the Wicket of the Cupboard wherein second-hand-meat is kept for a time. Let 's illustrate this noble Theme with some Examples.

Messer Pantolfe de la Cassina of Siena, riding Post from Rome, came to Chamberry, and alighting at honest Vinet's, took one of the Pitch-forks in the Stable ; then turning to the Inn-keeper, said to him, *Da Roma in qua io non son andato del Corpo. Di gratia piglia in mano questa forcha, e fa mi paura.* I have not had a Stool since I left Rome ; I pray thee take this Pitch-fork and fright me. Vinet took it, and made several Offers, as if he would in good earnest have hit the Signior, but all in vain ; so the Sienese said to him, *Si tu non fai altramente, tu non fai nulla : Pero sforzati di ad operarli piu guagliardamente ;* If thou dost not go another way to work, thou hadst as good do nothing ; therefore try to bestir thy self more briskly. With this, Vinet lent him such a swinging stoater with the Pitch-fork sowce between the Neck and the Collar of his Jerkin, that down fell Signore on the ground Arsyversy with his spindle-shanks wide straggling over his Pole. Then mine Host sputtering, with a full-mouth'd laugh, said to his Guest, By Belzebub's Bum-gut, much good may do you, Signore Italiano take notice this is *Datum Camberiaci,* given at Chamberry. 'Twas well the Sienese had untruss'd his Points and let down his Drawers ; for this Physick work'd with him as soon as he took it, and as copious was the Evacuation, as that of nine Buffeloes, and fourteen missificating Archlubbers. Which Operation being over, the mannerly Sienese courteously gave mine Host a whole bushel of thanks, saying to him, *Io ti ringratio, bel messere ; cosi faciendo tu m'ai esparagnata la speza d'un Servitiale :* I thank thee, good Landlord ; by this thou hast e'en sav'd me the expence of a Clyster.

I 'll give you another Example of Edward the Fifth, King

of England. Master Francis Villon being banish'd France, fled to him, and got so far into his Favour, as to be privy to all his Houshold Affairs. One day the King being on his Close-stool, show'd Villon the Arms of France, and said to him, Dost thou see what Respect I have for thy French Kings? I have none of their Arms any where but in this Back-side near my Close-stool. Od's Life, said the Buffoon, how Wise, Prudent, and careful of your Health, your Highness is! How carefully your learned Doctor Thomas Linacer looks after you! He saw that, now you grow old, you are enclin'd to be some-what Costive, and every day were fain to have an Apothecary, I mean, a Suppository or Clyster thrust into Royal Nockandro, so he has, much to the purpose, induc'd you to place here the Arms of France; for the very sight of them puts you into such a dreadful fright, that you immediately let fly, as much as would come from eighteen squattering Bonasi of Peonia: and if they were painted in other Parts of your House, by Jingo, you would presently conskite your self where-ever you saw them: Nay, had you but here a picture of the great Oriflamb of France, Od'sbodikins your Tripes and Bowels would be in no small danger of dropping out at the Orifice of your Posteriors.——But henh, henh, *atque iterum* henh.

> A silly Cockney am I not,
> As ever did from Paris come?
> And with a Rope and Sliding-knot
> My Neck shall know what weighs my Bum.

A Cockney of short reach, I say, shallow of Judgment, and judging shallowly to wonder, that you should cause your Points to be untrussed in your Chamber before you came into this Closet; by 'r Lady, at first I thought your Close-stool had stood behind the Hangings, or your Bed, otherwise it seem'd very odd to me you should untruss so far from the Place of Evacuation. But now I find I was a Gull, a Wittal, a Woodcock, a meer Ninny, a Jolt-head, a Noddy, a Changeling, a Calf-lolly, a Doddipole. You do wisely, by the Mass, you do wisely; for had not you been ready to clap your Hind-face on the Mustard-pot as soon as you came within sight of these Arms, mark ye me, Cop's Body, the bottom of your Breeches had supply'd the Office of a Close-stool.

Fryar Jhon stopping the Handle of his Face with his Left-hand, did, with the Fore-finger of the Right, point out Panurge's

Shirt to Pantagruel; who, seeing him in this Pickle, scar'd, appall'd, shivering, raving, staring, beray'd, and torn with the Claws of the famous Cat Rodilardus, could not chuse but laugh, and said to him, Pry'thee what wouldst thou do with this Cat? With this Cat, quoth Panurge, the Devil scratch me, if I did not think it had been a young Soft-chin'd Devil, which, with this same Stocking instead of Mitten, I had snatch'd up in the great Hutch of Hell, as Thievishly as any Sizar of Mountague College cou'd ha' done. The Devil take Tybert, I feel it has all bepink'd my poor Hide, and drawn on it to the Life I don't know how many Lobster's Whiskers: with this he threw his Boar-Cat down.

Go, go, said Pantagruel, be bath'd and clean'd, calm your Fears, put on a clean Shirt, and then your Cloaths. What! do you think I am afraid? cry'd Panurge: Not I, I protest; by the Testicles of Hercules, I am more hearty and stout, tho' I say it that should not, than if I had swallow'd as many Flyes as are put into Plumb-Cakes, and other Paste at Paris, from Midsummer to Christmas.——But what's this? hah! oh, ho, how the Devil came I by this? Do you call this what the Cat left in the Malt, Filth, Dirt, Dung, Dejection, fœcal Matter, Excrement, Stircoration, Sir-reverence, Ordure, Second-hand-meat, Fewmets, Stronts, Scybal or Syparathe? 'Tis Hybernian Saffron, I protest, Hah, hah, hah, 'tis Irish Saffron by Shaint Pawtrick. And so much for this time. *Selah*, Let's drink.

THE FIFTH BOOK OF ✺ ✺ THE WORKS ✺ ✺ OF ✺ ✺
FRANCIS RABELAIS, M.D. ✺ ✺ CONTAINING
THE ✺ ✺ HEROIC DEEDS AND SAYINGS ✺ ✺ OF
THE GOOD ✺ ✺ PANTAGRUEL ✺ ✺ TO WHICH IS
ADDED ✺ ✺ THE *PANTAGRUELIAN* PROGNOSTI-
CATION ; ✺ ✺ *RABELAIS'S* LETTERS, AND
SEVERAL OTHER ✺ ✺ PIECES BY THAT AUTHOR
✺ ✺ *NEVER BEFORE PRINTED IN* ENGLISH

W. HEATH ROBINSON

THE AUTHOR'S PROLOGUE TO THE
FIFTH BOOK

INDEFATIGABLE Topers, and you Thrice precious Martyrs of the Smock,
give me leave to put a serious Question to your Worships, while you are
idly stroaking your Codpieces, and I my self not much better employ'd :

Pray, why is it that People say, that Men are not such Sots now-a-days as they were in the days of Yore? Sot is an old word, that signifies a Dunce, Dullard, Jolthead, Gull, Wittal, or Noddy, one without Guts in his Brains, whose Cockloft is unfurnish'd, and in short, a Fool. Now would I know, Whether you would have us understand by this same Saying, as indeed you logically may, That formerly Men were Fools, and this Generation is grown Wise? How many and what Dispositions made them fools? How many and what Dispositions were wanting to make 'em Wise? Why were they Fools? How should they be Wise? Pray, how came you to know that Men were formerly Fools? How did you find that they are now Wise? Who the Devil made 'em Fools? Who a God's Name made 'em Wise? Who d' ye think are most, those that lov'd Mankind Foolish, or those that love it Wise? How long has it been Wise? How long otherwise? Whence proceeded the foregoing Folly? Whence the following Wisdom? Why did the old Folly end now, and no later? Why did the Modern Wisdom begin now, and no sooner? What were we the worse for the former Folly? What the better for the succeeding Wisdom? How should the Ancient Folly be come to nothing? How should this same new Wisdom be started up and establish'd?

Now answer me, an 't please you; I dare not adjure you in stronger Terms, Reverend Sirs, lest I make your pious fatherly Worships in the least uneasie. Come, pluck up a good Heart, speak the Truth, and shame the Devil. Be cheery, my Lads, and if you are for me, take me off three or five Bumpers to the best, while I make an halt at the first part of the Sermon; then answer my Question. If you are not, avaunt! avoid Satan! For I swear by my great Grandmother's Placket (and that's a horrid Oath!) that if you don't help me to solve that puzzling Problem, I will, nay, I already do repent, having propos'd it: For still I must remain netled and gravell'd, and the Devil a bit I know how to get off. Well, what say you? I' faith, I begin to smell you out. You are not yet dispos'd to give me an Answer; nor I neither, by these Whiskers. Yet to give some Light into the Business, I'll e'en tell you what had been anciently foretold in the Matter, by a Venerable Doc, who being mov'd by the Spirit in a Prophetic Vein, wrote a Book eclip'd *The Prelatical Bagpipe*. What d' ye think the Old Fornicator saith? Hearken, you Old Noddies, hearken now or never.

> The Jubilee's Year, when all, like Fools, were shorn,
> Is about thirty (*Trente*) supernumerary.
> O want of Veneration! Fools they seem'd,
> But, persevering, with long Briefs, at last
> No more they shall be gaping greedy Fools:
> For they shall shell the Shrub's delicious Fruit,
> Whose Flow'r they in the Spring so much had fear'd.

> *L'an Jubile que tout le monde raire*
> *Fadas se feit, est supernumeraire*
> *Au dessus Trente, O peu de reverence!*
> *Fat il sembloit; mais, en perseuerance*

De long Brevets, fat plus ne gloux sera ;
Car le doux fruict ce l' herbe esgous era
Dont tant craignoit la fleur en prime vere.

Now you have it, what do you make on 't ? The Seer is Ancient, the Style Laconic, the Sentences dark, like those of Scotus, though they treat of Matters dark enough in themselves. The best Commentators on that good Father take the Jubilee after the Thirtieth, to be the Years that are included in this present Age till 1550, (there being but one Jubilee every fifty Years.) Men shall no longer be thought Fools next Green Pease Season.

The Fools, whose Number, as Solomon certifies, is infinite, shall go to pot like a parcel of mad Bedlamites as they are ; and all manner of Folly shall have an end, that being also numberless, according to Avicenna, *Maniæ infinitæ sunt species.* Having been driven back and hidden towards the Centre, during the rigour of the Winter, 'tis now to be seen on the Surface, and buds out like the Trees. This is as plain as a Nose in a Man's Face ; you know it by Experience, you see it. And it was formerly found out by that great good Man Hippocrates, *Aphorism. Veræ etenim maniæ, etc.* The World therefore, wisifying it self, shall no longer dread the Flower and Blossoms of Beans every coming Spring ; that is, as you may believe, Bumper in Hand, and Tears in Eyes in the woful time of Lent, which us'd to keep them company.

Whole Cartloads of Books that seem'd florid, flourishing and flowry, gay and gawdy as so many Butterflies ; but in the main were tiresome, dull, soporiferous, irksome, mischievous, crabbed, knotty, puzzling, and dark as those of Whining Heraclytus, as unintelligible as the Numbers of Pythagoras, that King of the Bean according to Horace : Those Books, I say, have seen their best days, and shall soon come to nothing, being deliver'd to the executing Worms, and merciless Petty-Chandlers ; such was their Destiny, and to this they were Predestinated.

In their stead Beans in Cod are started up ; that is, these Merry and Fructifying Pantagruelian Books, so much sought now-a-days, in expectation of the following Jubilee's period ; to the study of which Writings all People have given their Minds ; and accordingly have gain'd the Name of Wise.

Now, I think, I have fairly solv'd and resolv'd your Problem ; then reform and be the better for it. Hem once or twice like Hearts of Oak, stand to your Pan-puddings, and take me off your Bumpers, Nine go downs, and Huzza ! since we are like to have a good Vintage, and Misers hang themselves : Oh ! they 'll cost me an Estate in Hempen Collars if fair Weather hold. For I hereby promise to furnish them with twice as much as will do their Business, on free cost, as often as they will take the pains to dance at a Rope's end, providently to save Charges, to the no small disappointment of the Finisher of the Law.

Now my Friends, that you may put in for a share of this new Wisdom, and shake off the antiquated Folly, this very Moment, scratch me out of your Scrouls, and quite discard the Symbol of the old Philosopher with the Golden Thigh, by which he has forbidden you to eat Beans: For you may take it for a truth granted among all Professors in the Science of good eating, that he enjoyn'd you not to taste of them, only with the same kind intent that a certain fresh-water Physician had, when he did forbid to Amer, late Lord of Camelotiere, Kinsman to the Lawyer of that Name, the Wing of the Partridge, the Rump of the Chicken, and the Neck of the Pigeon, saying, *Ala mala, Rumpum dubium, Collum bonum pelle remotâ.* For the Dunsical Dog-leech was so selfish, as to reserve them for his own dainty Chops, and allowed his poor Patients little more than the bare Bones to pick, lest they should overload their squeamish Stomachs.

To the Heathen Philosopher succeeded a pack of Capusions, Monks, who forbid us the use of Beans, that is, Pantagruelian Books. They seem to follow the Example of Philoxenus and Gnatho, Sicilians of fulsome Memory, the Ancient Master-Builders of their Monastick Cramgut Voluptuousness; who when some dainty Bit was serv'd up at a Feast, filthily us'd to spit on it, that none but their nasty selves might have the stomach to eat of it, though their Lickerish Chops watered never so much after it.

So these hideous, snotty, pthisicky, eves-dropping, musty, moving Forms of Mortification, both in publick and private, curse those dainty Books, and like Toads spit their Venom upon them.

Now though we have in our Mother-Tongue several excellent Works in Verse and Prose, and, Heav'n be prais'd, but little left of the Trash and Trumpery Stuff of those dunsical Mumblers of Avemaries, and the barbarous foregoing Gothick Age; I have made bold to chuse to chirrup and warble my plain Ditty, or as they say, to whistle like a Goose among the Swans, rather than be thought deaf among so many pretty Poets and Eloquent Orators. And thus I am prouder of acting the Clown, or any other underpart among the many Ingenious Actors in that Noble Play; than of herding among those Mutes, who, like so many Shadows and Cyphers, only serve to fill up the House, and make up a Number, gaping and yawning at the Flies, and pricking up their Lugs, like so many Arcadian Asses at the striking up of the Musick, thus silently giving to understand, that their Fopships are tickled in the right Place.

Having taken this Resolution, I thought it would not be amiss to move my Diogenical Tub, that you might not accuse me of living without Example. I see a swarm of our modern Poets and Orators, your Collinets, Marots, Drouets, Saingelais, Salels, Masuels, and many more; who having commenc'd Masters in Apollo's Academy on Mount Parnassus, and drunk Brimmers at the Caballin Fountain, among the Nine merry Muses, have rais'd our Vulgar Tongue and made it a noble and everlasting Structure. Their Works are all Parian Marble, Alebaster, Porphiry, and Royal Ciment, they treat of nothing but Heroick Deeds, mighty Things, grave and difficult Matters, and this in a Crimson Alamode Rhetorical Style.

HAVING BEEN DRIVEN BACK

285

Their Writings are all Divine Nectar, rich, racy, sparkling, delicate and luscious Wine. Nor does our Sex wholly engross this Honour; Ladies have had their share of the Glory: One of them of the Royal Blood of France, whom it were a Prophanation but to name here, surprizes the Age at once by her transcendent and inventive Genius in her Writings, and the admirable Graces of her Style. Imitate those great Examples, if you can, for my part I cannot. Every one, you know, cannot go to Corinth. When Solomon built the Temple, all could not give Gold by handfuls.

Since then 'tis not in my power to improve our Architecture as much as they, I am e'en resolv'd to do like Renault of Montauban; I'll wait on the Masons, set on the Pot for the Masons, cook for the Stonecutters; and since it was not my good luck to be cut out for one of them, I will live and die the Admirer of their Divine Writings.

As for you, little envious Prigs, snarling, bastard, puny Criticks, you'll soon have rail'd your last: Go hang your selves, and chuse you out some well-spread Oak, under whose shade you may swing in state, to the Admiration of the gaping Mob; you shall never want Rope enough. While I here solemnly protest before my Helicon, in the Presence of my Nine Mistresses the Muses, that if I live yet the Age of a Dog, ek'd out with that of three Crows, sound Wind and Limbs, like the old Hebrew Captain Moses, Xenophilus the Musicianer, and Demonax the Philosopher, by Arguments no ways impertinent, and Reasons not to be disputed, I will prove, in the Teeth of a parcel of Brokers and Retailers of Ancient Rhapsodies, and such Trash, That our Vulgar Tongue is not so mean, silly, poor, and contemptible, as they pretend. Nor ought I to be afraid of I know not what Botchers of old thredbare Stuff a hundred and a hundred times clouted up and piec'd together; wretched Bunglers, that can do nothing but new vamp old rusty Saws; beggarly Scavengers, that rake even the muddiest Canals of Antiquity for scraps and bits of Latin, as insignificant as they are often uncertain. Beseeching our Grandees of Witland, that, as when formerly Apollo had distributed all the Treasures of his Poetical Exchequer to his Favourites, little hulchback'd Æsop got for himself the Office of Apologuemonger: In the same manner, since I do not aspire higher, they would not deny me that of Puny Riparographer, or Riffraff-scribler of the Sect of Pyrricus.

I dare swear they will grant me this; for they are all so kind, so good-natur'd, and so generous, that they'll ne're boggle at so small a Request. Therefore both dry and hungry Souls, Pot and Trenchermen, fully enjoying those Books, perusing, quoting them, in their merry Conventicles, and observing the great Mysteries of which they treat, shall gain a singular Profit and Fame; as in the like case was done by Alexander the Great, with the Books of Prime Philosophy compos'd by Aristotle.

O rare! Belly on Belly! what Swillers, what Twisters will there be!

Then be sure, all you that take care not to die of the Pip, be sure, I say, you take my Advice, and stock your selves with good store of such

THE FIFTH BOOK OF DR. FRANCIS RABELAIS

Books, as soon as you meet with them at the Booksellers, and do not only shell those Beans in Cods, but e'n swallow them down like an Opiat Cordial, and let them be in you, I say, let them be within you : Then shall you find, my Bleoved, what good they do to all clever Shellers of Beans.

Here is a good handsome Basketful of them, which I here lay before your Worships ; they were gather'd in the very individual Garden whence the former came. So I beseech you, Reverend Sirs, with as much Respect as e're was paid by Dedicating Author, to accept of the Gift, in hopes of somewhat better against next Visit the Swallows give us.

THE FIFTH BOOK

CHAPTER I

How Pantagruel arriv'd at the Ringing Island, and of the Noise that we heard

PURSUING our Voyage, we sail'd three Days without discovering any thing; on the fourth we made Land. Our Pilot told us, That it was the Ringing Island; and indeed we heard a kind of a confus'd and often-repeated Noise, that seem'd to us at a great distance not unlike the Sound of great, middle-siz'd and little Bells rung all at once, as 'tis customary at Paris, Tours, Gergeau, Nantes, and elsewhere on high Holidays; and the nearer we came to the Land, the louder we heard that Jangling.

Some of us doubted that this was the Dodonoan Kettles, or the Portico call'd Heptaphone in Olympia, or the eternal Humming of the Colossus rais'd on Memnon's Tomb in Thebes of Egypt, or the horrid Din that us'd formerly to be heard about a Tomb at Lipara, one of the Eo ian Islands. But this did not square with Chorography

HE WAS A LITTLE QUEAR OLD FELLOW

W.HEATH ROBINSON.

I don't know, said Pantagruel, but that some Swarms of Bees here-abouts may be taking a Ramble in the Air, and so the Neighbourhood make this dingle-dangle with Pans, Kettles, and Basons, the Coribanting Cymbals of Cybele, Grand-mother of the Gods, to call them back. Let 's hearken ! when we were nearer, among the everlasting Ringing, we heard the indefatigable Singing (as we thought) of some Men. For this Reason, before we offer'd to land on the Ringing Island, Pantagruel was of opinion that we should go in the Pinnace to a small Rock, near which we discover'd an Hermitage, and a little Garden. There we found a diminutive old Hermit, whose Name was Braguibus, born at Glenay. He gave us a full Account of all the Jangling, and regal'd us after a strange sort of a fashion ; four live-long-days did he make us fast, assuring us, That we should not be admitted into the Ringing Island otherwise, because 'twas then one of the four Fasting, or Ember-Weeks. As I love my Belly, quoth Panurge, I by no means understand this Riddle : Methinks this should rather be one of the four Windy-Weeks ; for while we fast, we are only pufft up with Wind. Pray now, good Father Hermit, have not you here some other Pastime besides Fasting : methinks 'tis somewhat of the leanest, we might well enough be without so many Palace-holidays, and those Fasting-Times of yours. In my Donatus, quoth Fryar Jhon, I could find yet but Three Times or Tenses, the Preterit, the Present, and the Future ; doubtless here the fourth ought to be a work of Supererogation. That Time or Tense, said Epistemon, is Aorist, deriv'd from the Preterimperfect Tense of the Greeks, admitted in War, and odd Cases : Patience per force, is a Remedy for a Mad-Dog. Saith the Hermit, 'Tis as I told you, fatal to go against this ; whoever does it, is a rank Heretick, and wants nothing but Fire and Faggot, that 's certain. To deal plainly with you, my dear Pater, cry'd Panurge, being at Sea, I much more fear being wet than being warm, and being drown'd than being burnt.

Well, however, let us fast a God's Name ; yet I have fasted so long, that it has quite undermin'd my Flesh, and I fear that at last the Bastions of this Bodily Fort of mine will fall to ruin. Besides, I am much more afraid of vexing you in this same Trade of Fasting, for the Devil a bit I understand any thing in it, and it becomes me very scurvily, as several People have told me, and I am apt to believe them. For my part, I have no great Stomach to Fasting ; for alas,

'tis as easie as pissing a Bed, and a Trade of which any body
may set up, there needs no Tools. I am much more enclin'd
not to fast for the future; for to do so, there's some Stock
required, and some Tools are set a work. No matter, since
you are so stedfast, and have us fast, let's fast as fast as we
can, and then breakfast in the name of Famine; now we are
come to these esurial idle Days. I vow, I had quite put them
out of my head long ago. If we must fast, said Pantagruel,
I see no other Remedy but to get rid of it as soon as we can,
as we wou'd out of a bad Way. I'll in that space of time somewhat look over my Papers, and examine whether the Marine
Study be as good as ours at Land. For Plato, to describe a
silly, raw, ignorant Fellow, compares him to those that are
bred on Ship-board, as we wou'd do to one bred up in a Barrel,
who never saw any thing but through the Bung-hole. To tell
you the short and long of the matter, our Fasting was most
hideous and terrible; for, the first day we fasted at Fisticuffs,
the second at Cudgels, the third at Sharps, and the fourth at
Blood and Wounds; such was the Order of the Fairies.

CHAPTER II

*How the Ringing Island had been inhabited by the Siticines, who
were become Birds*

HAVING fasted as aforesaid, the Hermit gave us a Letter for
one whom he call'd Albiam Camar, Master Ædituus of the
Ringing Island ; but Panurge greet ng him, call'd him, Master
Antitus.   He was a little quear old Fellow, bald pated, with a
Snout whereat you might easily have lighted a Card-match,
and a Phiz as red as a Cardinal's Cap.   He made us all very
welcome, upon the Hermit's Recommendation, hearing that
we had fasted, as I have told you.

When we had well stuff'd our Puddings, he gave us an
Account of what was Remarkable in the Island ; affirming,
That it had been at first inhabited by the Siticines ; but that
according to the course of Nature, as all things, you know,
are subject to change, they were become Birds.

There I had a full Account of all that Atteius Capito, Paulus
Marcellus, A. Gellius, Atheneus, Suidas, Ammonius and others
had writ of the Siticines and Sicinnists ; and then we thought
we might as easily believe the Transmutations of Nectimene,
Progne, Itys, Alcyone, Antigone, Tereus, and other Birds.
Nor did we think it more reasonable to doubt of the Trans-
mogrification of the Macrobian Children into Swans, or that
of the Men of Pallene in Thrace into Birds, as soon as they
have bath'd themselves in the Tritonic Lake.   After this, the
Devil a word we cou'd get out of him, but of Birds and Cages.

The Cages were spacious, costly, magnificent, and of admirable Architecture.   The Birds were large, fine, and neat
accordingly ; looking as like the Men in my Country, as one
Pea do's like another ; for they eat and drank like Men, muted
like Men, endued or digested like Men, farted like Men, but
stunk like Devils, slept, bill'd and trod their Females like Men,
but somewhat oftener : In short, had you seen and examin'd
'em from Top to Toe, you would have laid your Head to a
Turnip, that they had been meer Men.   However, they were
nothing less, as Master Ædituus told us ; assuring us at the
same time, that they were neither Secular nor Layic ; and

truth is, the diversity of their Feathers and Plumes did not a little puzzle us.

Some of them were all over as white as Swans, others as black as Crows, many as grey as Owls, others black and white like Magpies, some all red like Red-birds, and others purple and white like Pigeons. He call'd the Males, Clerghawks, Monkhawks, Priesthawks, Abbothawks, Bishhawks, Cardinhawks, and one Popehawk, who is a Species by himself. He call'd the Females, Clergkites, Nunkites, Priestkites, Abbesskites, Bishkites, Cardinkites, and Popekites.

However, said he, as Hornets and Drones will get among the Bees, and there do nothing but buzz, eat and spoil every thing; so, for these last Three hundred Years, a vast Swarm of Bigottello's flockt I don't know how among these goodly Birds every fifth Full Moon, and have bemuted, bewray'd, and conskited the whole Island. They are so hard-favoured and monstrous, that none can abide 'em. For their wry Necks make a figure like a crooked Billet; their Paws are hairy like those of rough-footed Pigeons; their Claws and Pounces, Belly and Breech like those of the Stymphalid Harpies. Nor is it possible to root them out; for if you get rid of one, strait four and twenty new ones fly thither.

There had been need of another Monster-hunter, such as was Hercules; for Fryar Jhon had like to have run distracted about it, so much he was nettled and puzzled in the matter. As for the good Pantagruel, he was e'en serv'd as was Messer Priapus, contemplating the Sacrifices of Ceres, for want of Skin.

CHAPTER III

How there is but one Popehawk in the Ringing Island

WE then ask'd Master Ædituus why there was but one Popehawk among such numbers of venerable Birds, multiply'd in all their Species? He answer'd, That such was the first Institution and fatal Destiny of the Stars. That the Clerghawks begot the Priesthawks and Monkhawks, without Carnal Copulation, as some Bees are born of a young Bull. The Priesthawks beget the Bishhawks, the Bishhawks the stately

Cardinhawks, and the stately Cardinhawks, if they live long enough, at last come to be Popehawk.

Of this last Kind, there never is more than one at a time, as in a Bee-hive there is but one King, and in the World is but one Sun.

When the Popehawk dies, another rises in his stead out of the whole Brood of Cardinhawks, that is, as you must understand it all along, without Carnal Copulation, So that there is in that Species an individual Unity, with a perpetuity of Succession, neither more nor less than in the Arabian Phœnix.

'Tis true, that about Two thousand seven hundred and sixty Moons ago, two Popehawks were seen upon the Face of the Earth ; but then you never saw in your lives such a woful Rout and Hurly-burly as was all over this Island. For all these same Birds did so peck, clapperclaw and maul one another all that time, that there was the Devil and all to do, and the Island was in a fair way of being left without Inhabitants. Some stood up for this Popehawk, some for t' other. Some, struck with a Dumbness, were as mute as so many Fishes ; the Devil a Note was to be got out of them ; part of the merry Bells here were as silent as if they had lost their Tongues, I mean their Clappers.

During these troublesom Times, they call'd to their Assistance the Emperors, Kings, Dukes, Earls, Barons, and Commonwealths of the World that live on t 'other side the Water ; nor was this Schism and Sedition at an end, till one of them died, and the Plurality was reduc'd to Unity.

We then ask'd what mov'd those Birds to be thus continually chanting and singing ? He answer'd, That it was the Bells that hang'd on the tops of their Cages. Then he said to us, Will you have me make these Monkhawks whom you see bardocucullated with a Bag, such as you use to still Brandy, sing like any Wood-Larks ? Pray do, said we. He then gave half a dozen pulls to a little Rope, which caus'd a diminutive Bell to give so many Ting-tings, and presently a parcel of Monkhawks ran to him as if the Devil had drove 'em, and fell a singing like mad.

Pray Master, cry'd Panurge, if I also rang this Bell, could I make those other Birds yonder with Red-herring-colour'd Feathers, sing ? Ay, marry wou'd you, return'd Ædituus. With this Panurge hang'd himself (by the Hands, I mean) at the Bell-rope's end, and no sooner made it speak, but those smoak'd Birds hy'd them thither, and began to lift up their

MONKHAWKS

295

Voices, and make a sort of an untowardly hoarse Noise, which I grudge to call Singing. Ædituus indeed told us, That they fed on nothing but Fish, like the Herns and Cormorants of the World, and that they were a fifth kind of Cucullati newly stampt.

He added, That he had been told by Robert Valbringue, who lately pass'd that Way in his Return from Africa, that a sixth kind was to fly hither out of hand, which he call'd Capushawks, more grum, vinegar-fac'd, brainsick, froward, and loathsom, than any kind whatsoever in the whole Island. Africa, said Pantagruel, still uses to produce some new and monstrous Thing.

CHAPTER IV

How the Birds of the Ringing Island were all Passengers

SINCE you have told us, said Pantagruel, how the Popehawk is begot by the Cardinhawks, the Cardinhawks by the Bishhawks, and the Bishhawks by the Priesthawks, and the Priesthawks by the Clerghawks, I would gladly know whence you have these same Clerghawks. They are all of them Passengers, return'd Ædituus, and come hither from t' other World ; part out of a vast Country, call'd Want-o'-bread ; the rest out of another towards the West, which they style, Too-many-of-'em. From these two Countries flock hither every Year, whole Legions of these Clerghawks, leaving their Fathers, Mothers, Friends and Relations.

This happens when there are too many Children, whether Male or Female, in some good Family of the latter Country ; insomuch that the House would come to nothing, if the Paternal Estate were shar'd among them all ; (as Reason requires, Nature directs, and God commands). For this cause, Parents use to rid themselves of that Inconveniency, by packing off the Younger Fry, and forcing them to seek their Fortune in this Isle Bossart, (Crooked Island.) I suppose he means l'Isle Bouchart, near Chinon, cry'd Panurge. No, reply'd t' other, I mean Bossart (Crooked) ; for there is not one in ten among them, but is either crooked, crippled, blinking, limping, ill-favour'd, deform'd, or an unprofitable Load to the Earth.

'Twas quite otherwise among the Heathens, said Pantagruel,

THE LOWER CLASS OF BIRDS

when they us'd to receive a Maiden among the number of Vestals; for Leo Antistius affirms, that it was absolutely forbidden to admit a Virgin into that Order, if she had any Vice in her Soul, or Defect in her Body, tho' it were but the smallest Spot on any part of it. I can hardly believe, continued Edituus, that their Dams on t' other side the Water go Nine Months with them; for they cannot endure them Nine Years, nay, scarce Seven, sometimes in the House; But by putting only a Shirt over the other Cloaths of the Young Urchins, and lopping off I don't well know how many Hairs from their Crowns, mumbling certain apostrophis'd and expiatory Words, they visibly, openly, and plainly, by a Pythagorical Metempsychosis, without the least hurt, transmogrifie them into such Birds as you now see; much after the fashion of the Egyptian Heathens, who us'd to constitute their Isiacs, by shaving them, and making them put on certain Linostoles, or Surplices. However, I don't know, my good Friends, but that these She-things, whether Clergkites, Monkites, and Abesskites, (that should not) instead of singing some plaisant Verses and Charisters, such as us'd to be sung to Oromasis by Zoroaster's Institution, may be bellowing out such Cataretes and Scythropys, (curs'd, lamentable, and wretched Imprecations) as were usually offer'd to the Arimanian Dæmon; being thus in Devotion for their kind Friends and Relations, that transform'd them into Birds, whether when they were Maids, or Thornbacks, in their Prime, or at their last Prayers.

But the greatest number of our Birds come out of Want-o'-bread, which tho' a barren Country, where the Days are of a most tedious lingring length, overstocks this whole Island with the lower Class of Birds. For hither flie the Assaphis that inhabit that Land, either when they are in danger of passing their time scurvily for want of Bellytimber, being unable, or, what 's more likely, unwilling to take heart of grace, and follow some honest lawful Calling, or too proud-hearted and lazy to go to Service in some sober Family. The same is done by your frantick Inamorado's, who when cross'd in their wild Desires, grow stark-staring mad, and chuse this Life suggested to them by their despair, too cowardly to make them swing like their Brother Iphis of doleful Memory. There is another sort, that is, your Jail-birds, who having done some Rogue's Trick, or other heinous Villany, and being sought up and down to be truss'd up, and made to ride the Two or Three-legg'd Mare that groans for them, warily scour off, and come here to save their Bacon ; Because all these sorts of Birds are here provided for, and grow in an instant as fat as Hogs, tho' they came as lean as Rakes ; For having the Benefit of the Clergy, they are as safe as Thieves in a Mill, within this Sanctuary.

But, ask'd Pantagruel, Do these Birds never return to the World where they were hatch'd ? Some do, answer'd Ædituus ; formerly very few, very seldom, very late, and very unwillingly. However, since some certain Eclipses, by the virtue of the Celestial Constellations, a great Croud of them fled back to the World. Nor do we fret or vex our selves a jot about it ; for those that stay, wisely sing, The fewer, the better Cheer ; and all those that flie away first, cast off their Feathers here among these Nettles and Bryars. Accordingly we found some thrown by there ; and as we look'd up and down, we chanc'd to light on what some People will hardly thank us for having discover'd ; and thereby hangs a Tale.

CHAPTER V

Of the Dumb Knighthawks of the Ringing Island

THESE Words were scarce out of his mouth, when some Five and twenty or Thirty Birds flew towards us : They were of a Hue and Feather like which we had not yet seen any thing in the whole Island. Their Plumes were as changeable as the Skin of the Chamelion, and the Flower of Tripolion, or Tenerion. They had all under the Left-Wing a Mark like two Diameters dividing a Circle into Equal Parts, or (if you had rather have it so) like a Perpendicular Line falling on a Right Line. The Marks which each of them bore, were much of the same Shape, but of different Colours ; for some were White, others Green, some Red, others Purple, and some Blue. Who are those, ask'd Panurge, and how do you call them ? They are Mongrels, quoth Ædituus.

We call them Knighthawks, and they have a great number of rich Commanderies, (fat Livings) in your World. Good your Worship, said I, make them give us a Song, an 't please you, that we may know how they sing. They scorn your words, cry'd Ædituus, they are none of your Singing Birds ; but to make amends, they feed as much as the best two of them all. Pray, where are their Hens, where are their Females ? said I. They have none, answer'd Ædituus. How comes it to pass then, ask'd Panurge, that they are thus bescabb'd, bescurf'd, all embroider'd o'er the Phiz with Carbuncles, Pushes, and Pockroyals, some of which undermine the Handles of their Faces. This same Fashionable and Illustrious Disease, quoth Ædituus, is common among that kind of Birds, because they are pretty apt to be toss'd on the Salt Deep.

He then acquainted us with the Occasion of their coming. This, next to us, said he, looks so wistfully upon you, to see whether he may not find among your Company a stately gaudy kind of huge dreadful Birds of Prey, which yet are so untoward, that they ne'er could be brought to the Lure, nor to Perch on the Glove. They tell us that there are such in your World, and that some of them have goodly Garters below the Knee, with an Inscription about them, which condemns him (*qui mal y pense*) who shall think ill of it, to be bewray'd and conskited. Others are said to wear the Devil in a String before their Paunches ; and others a Ram's Skin. All that 's true enough, good Master Ædituus, quoth Panurge, but we have not the honour to be acquainted with their Knightships.

Come on, cry'd Ædituus in a merry mood, we have had Chat enough o' Conscience ! let 's e'en go Drink :——And Eat, quoth Panurge. Eat, reply'd Ædituus, and Drink bravely, old Boy ; Twist like Plough-Jobbers, and Swill like Tinkers ; Pull away and save Tide ; for nothing is so dear or precious as Time, therefore we 'll be sure to put it to a good Use.

He wou'd fain have carried us first to bathe in the Bagnio's of the Cardinhawks, which are goodly delicious Places, and have us lick'd over with precious Ointments by the Alyptes *alias* Rubbers, as soon as we should come out of the Bath. But Pantagruel told him, That he could Drink but too much without that : He then led us into a spacious delicate Refectuary, or Fratrie-room, and told us, Braguibus the Hermit, made you fast four days together ; now, contrarywise, I 'll make you eat and drink of the best, four Days through-stitch before you budge from this place. But hark-ye-me, cry'd Panurge,

mayn't we take a Nap in the mean time ? Ay, ay, answer'd
Ædituus, that 's as you shall think good, for he that sleeps,
drinks. Good Lord ! how we liv'd ! what good Bub ! what
dainty Cheer ! Oh what an honest Cod was this same Ædituus !

CHAPTER VI

How the Birds are cramm'd in the Ringing Island

PANTAGRUEL look'd I don't know howish, and seem'd not very
well pleas'd with the four Days Junketting which Ædituus
enjoyn'd us. Ædituus, who soon found it out, said to him,
You know, Sir, that seven Days before Winter, and seven Days
after, there is no Storm at Sea : For then the Elements are still,
out of respect for the Halcyons, or Kingfishers, Birds sacred to
Thetis, which then lay their Eggs and hatch their Young near
the Shoar. Now here the Sea makes it self amends for this
long Calm ; and whenever some Foreigners come hither, it
grows Boisterous and Stormy for four Days together. We can
give no other reason for it, but that it is a piece of its Civility,
that those who come among us may stay whether they will or
no, and be copiously feasted all the while with the Incomes of
the Ringing. Therefore pray don't think your time lost, for
willing, nilling, you 'll be forc'd to stay ; unless you are resolv'd
to encounter Juno, Neptune, Doris, Æolus and his Fluster-
blusters ; and, in short, all the pack of ill-natur'd left-handed
Godlings and Vejoves. Do but resolve to be cheary, and fall
to briskly.

After we had pretty well staid our Stomachs, with some
tight Snatches, Fryar Jhon said to Ædituus, For ought I see,
you have none but a parcel of Birds and Cages in this Island
of yours, and the Devil-a-bit of one of them all that sets his
Hand to the Plough, or Tills the Land, whose Fat he devours :
Their whole business is to be frolick, to chirp it, to whistle it,
to warble it, to sing it, and roar it merrily Night and Day ;
Pray then, if I may be so bold, Whence comes this Plenty and
Overflowing of all dainty Bits and good Things which we see
among you ? From all the other World, return'd Ædituus,
if you except some part of the Northern Regions, who of late

Years have stirr'd up the Jakes ; Mum ! they may chance e're
long to rue the Day they did so ; their Cows shall have Porrage,
and their Dogs Oats ; there will be work made among them,
that there will : Come, a Fig for' t, let 's drink,——But, pray
what Country Men are you ? Tourain is our Country, answer'd
Panurge ; Cod so, cry'd Ædituus, you were not then hatch'd
of an ill Bird, I 'll say that for you, since the blessed Tourain is
your Mother. For from thence there comes hither every Year
such a vast store of good Things, that we were told by some
Folks of the Place that happen'd to touch at this Island, that
your Duke of Tourain's Income will not afford him to eat his
Belly-full of Beans and Bacon (a Dish spoil'd between Moses
and Pythagoras) because his Predecessors have been more than
liberal to these most holy Birds of ours, that we might here
munch it, twist it, cram it, gorge it, craw it, riot it, junket it,
and tickle it off, stuffing our Puddings with dainty Pheasants,
Partridges, Pullets with Eggs, fat Capons of Loudunois, and
all sorts of Venison and wild Fowl. Come, box it about, tope
on my Friends. Pray do but see yon jolly Birds that are
perch'd together, how Fat, how Plump, and in good Case, they
look with the Income that Tourain yields us ! And in faith they
sing rarely for their good Founders, that 's the truth on 't. You
never saw any Arcadian Birds mumble more fairly than they
do over a Dish, when they see these two gilt Battoons, or when
I ring for them these great Bells that you see above their Cages.
Drink on, Sirs, whip it away, verily Friends, 'tis very fine
drinking to Day, and so 'tis every Day o' the Week ; then drink
on, toss it about ; here 's to you with all my Soul, you are most
heartily welcome : Never spare it, I pray you, fear not we
should ever want good Bub, and Belly-Timber ; for, look here,
though the sky were of Brass, and the Earth of Iron, we should
not want wherewithal to stuff the Gut, though they were to
continue so seven or eight Years longer than the Famine in
Egypt. Let us then with Brotherly Love and Charity refresh
our selves here with the Creature.

Woons, Man, cry'd Panurge, what a rare time you have
on 't in this World ! Pshaw, return'd Ædituus, this is nothing
to what we shall have in t' other : The Elizian Fields will be
the least that can fall to our Lot. Come, in the mean time
let 's drink here, come here 's to thee old Fuddlecap.

Your first Siticines, said I, were superlatively wise, in
devising thus a means for you to compass whatever all Men
naturally covet so much, and so few, or (to speak more properly)

W HEATH ROBINSON

KNIGHTHAWKS

303

none can enjoy together; I mean, a Paradise in this Life, and another in the next; sure you were born wrapt in your Mother's Smickits. O happy Creatures! O more than Men! would I had the luck to fare like you.

CHAPTER VII

How Pantagruel came to the Island of the Apedefers, or Ignoramus's, with long Claws, and crooked Paws, and of terrible Adventures and Monsters there

As soon as we had cast Anchor and had moor'd the Ship, the Pinnace was put over the Ship's side, and Mann'd by the Coxswain's Crew. When the good Pantagruel had prayed publickly, and given Thanks to the Lord that had deliver'd him from so great a Danger, he stept into it with his whole Company, to go on shoar, which was no ways difficult to do; for as the Sea was Calm, and the Winds laid, they soon got to the Cliffs. When they were set on shoar, Epistemon, who was admiring the Situation of the Place, and the strange Shape of the Rocks, discover'd some of the Natives. The first he met, had on a short Purple Gown, a Doublet cut in Pains like a Spanish Leather Jerkin; Half-sleeves of Sattin, and the upper part of them Leather, a Coif like a Black Pot tipp'd with Tin; he was a good likely sort of a Body, and his Name, as we heard afterwards, was Double-fee. Epistemon ask'd him, how they called those strange craggy Rocks and deep Vallies? He told him it was a Colony, brought out of Attorney-land, and call'd Process; and that if we forded the River somewhat further beyond the Rocks, we should come into the Island of the Apedefers. By the Memory of the Decretals, ask'd Fryar Jhon, tell us, I pray you, what you honest Men here live on? Could not a Man take a chirping Bottle with you, to taste your Wine? I can see nothing among you but Parchment, Inkhorns, and Pens. We live on nothing else, return'd Double-fee; and all who live in this Place must come through my Hands, How, quoth Panurge, are you a Shaver then, do you fleece 'em? Ay, ay. their Purse, answer'd Double-fee, nothing else. By the Foot of Pharao, cry'd Panurge, the

De'll a Sous you 'll get of me. However, sweet Sir, be so kind as to shew an honest Man the way to those Apedefers, or Ignorant People, for I come from the Land of the Learned, where I did not learn over much.

Still talking on, they got to the Island of the Apedefers, for they were soon got over the Ford. Pantagruel was not a little taken up with admiring the Structure and Habitation of the People of the Place. For they live in a swindging Wine-press, fifty Steps up to it ; you must know there are some of all sorts, little, great, private, middlesiz'd, and so forth. You go through a large Peristile, alias a long Entry set about with Pillars, in which you see in a kind of Landskip, the Ruins of almost the whole World ; besides so many great Robbers Gibbets, so many Gallows and Racks, that 'tis enough to fright you out of your seven Senses. Double-fee perceiving that Pantagruel was taken up with contemplating those things, Let us go further, Sir, said he to him, all this is nothing yet. Nothing, quoth he, cry'd Fryar Jhon, By the soul of my over-heated Codpiece, Friend Panurge and I here shake and quiver for meer Hunger. I had rather be drinking, than staring on those Ruins. Pray come along, Sir, said Double-fee. He then led us into a little Wine-press that lay backwards in a blind Corner, and was call'd Pithies in the Language of the Country. You need not ask whether Master Jhon and Panurge made much of their sweet selves there ; 'tis enough that I tell you, there was no want of Bolonia Saucidges, Turkypoots, Capons, Bustards, Malmesy, and all other sorts of good Belly-Timber, very well drest.

A pimping Son of ten Fathers, who, for want of a better, who did the Office of a Butler, seeing that Fryar Jhon had cast a Sheep's Eye at a choice Bottle that stood near a Cupboard by it self, at some distance from the rest of the Bottelic Maga-zine, like a Jack in an Office, said to Pantagruel, Sir, I perceive that one of your Men here is making Love to this Bottle, he ogles it, and would fain caress it ; but I beg that none offer to meddle with it ; for 'tis reserv'd for their Worships. How, cry'd Panurge, there are some Grandees here then I see : 'Tis Vintage-time with you, I perceive.

Then Double-fee led us up a private Stair-case, and shew'd us into a Room, whence, without being seen, out at a Loop-hole, we could see their Worships in the great Wine-press, where none could be admitted without their leave. Their Worships, as he call'd them, were about a score of fusty Crack-ropes and Gallowclappers, or rather more, all posted before a Bar, and staring at each other like so many dead Pigs : Their Paws were as long as a Crane's Foot, and their Claws four and twenty Inches long at least ; for you must know, they are injoin'd never to pair off the least Chip of them, so that they grow as crooked as a Welch Hook, or a Hedging Bill.

We saw a swindging Bunch of Grapes that are gather'd and squeez'd in that Country, brought in to them. As soon as it was laid down, they clapp'd it into the Press, and there was not a bit of it out of which each of them did not squeeze some Oil of Gold. Insomuch, that the poor Grape was tri'd with a Witness, and brought off so drain'd and pick'd, and so dry, that there was not the least Moisture, Juice or Substance left in it, for they had prest out its very Quintessence.

Double-fee told us they had not often such huge Bunches, but, let the worst come to the worst, they were sure never to be without others in their Press. But hark you me, Master of mine, ask'd Panurge, Have they not some of different growth ? Ay marry have they, quoth Double-fee ; do you see here this little Bunch, to which they are going to give t' other wrinch ; 'Tis of Tyth-growth you must know ; they crush'd, wrung, squeez'd and strain'd out the very Heart's Blood of it but t' other Day, but it did not bleed freely, the Oil came hard, and smelt of the Priest's Chest ; so that they found there was not much good to be got out of 't. Why then, said Pantagruel, do they put it again into the Press ? Only, answer'd Double-fee, for fear there should still lurk some Juice among the Husks, and Hullings, in the Mother of the Grape. The Devil be damn'd, cry'd Fryar Jhon, do you call these same Folks illiterate Lobcocks, and Dunsical Doddipoles ? May I be broil'd like a Red-herring, if I don't think they are wise enough to skin a Flint, and draw Oil out of a Brick-wall. So they are, said Double-fee, for they sometimes put Castles, Parks, and Forests into the Press, and out of them all extract *Aurum potabile*. You mean *Portabile*, I suppose, cry'd Epistemon, such as may be born. I mean as I said, repli'd Double-fee, *Potabile*, such as may be drunk ; for it makes them drink many a good Bottle more than otherwise they should.

But I cannot better satisfie you as to the growths of the Vine-tree Syrup that is here squeez'd out of Grapes, than in desiring you to look yourself yonder in that Back-yard, where you 'll see above a thousand different growths that lie a waiting to be squeez'd every Moment. Here are some of the publick,

RUINS OF ALMOST THE WHOLE WORLD

307

and some of the private growth; some of the Builders,
Fortifications, Loans, Gifts and Gratuities, Escheats, For-
feitures, Fines and Recoveries, Penal Statutes, Crown-Lands
and Demesne, Privy-Purse, Post-Office, Offerings, Lordships
of Mannors, and a world of other growths for which we want
Names. Pray, quoth Epistemon, tell me of what growth
is that great one with all those little Grapelings about it.
Oh, oh! return'd Double-fee, that plump one is of the Treasury,
the very best growth in the whole Country; whenever any
one of that growth is squeez'd, there is not one of their Worships but gets Juice enough out of it to soak his Nose six
Months together. When their Worships were up, Pantagruel
desir'd Double-fee to take us into that great Wine-press,
which he readily did. As soon as we were in, Epistemon,
who understood all sorts of Tongues, began to shew us many
Devises on the Press, which was large and fine, and made of the
Wood of the Cross (at least Double-fee told us so.) On each
part of it were Names of every thing in the Language of the
Country. The Spindle of the Press was call'd Receipt; the
Trough, Costs and Damages; the Hole for the Vice-pin,
State; the Side-boards, Money paid into the Office; the great
Beam, Respit of homage; the Branches, *Radiatur;* the Side-
beams, *Recuperetur;* the Fats, *Ignoramus;* the two-handled
Baskets, the Rolls; the Treading place, Acquittance; the
Dossers, Validation; the Panniers, Authentic Decrees; the
Pailes, Potentials; the Funnel, *Quietus est.*

By the Queen of the Chitterlings, quoth Panurge, all the
Hieroglyphics of Egypt are mine A—— to this Jargon. Why!
here's a parcel of Words full as analogous as Chalk and Cheese,
or a Cat and a Cart-wheel! But why, pr'y thee, Dear Double-
fee, do they call these worshipful Dons of yours, Ignorant
Fellows? Only, said Double-fee, because they neither are or
ought to be Clerks, and all must be ignorant as to what they
transact here; nor is there to be any other Reason given,
but, The Court hath said it; The Court will have it so; The
Court has decreed it. Cop's Body, quoth Panurge, they might
full as well have call'd 'em Necessity; for Necessity has no Law.

From thence, as he was leading us to see a thousand little
puny Presses, we spy'd another paltry Bar, about which sate
four or five ignorant waspish Churls, of so testy, fuming a
Temper, and so ready to take Pepper in the Nose for Yea and
Nay, that a Dog wou'd not have liv'd with 'em. They were
hard at it with the Lees and Dregs of the Grapes, which they

grip'd over and over again, might and main with their clench'd
Fists. They were call'd Contractors, in the Language of the
Country; These are the ugliest, mishapen, grim-look'd Scrubbs,
said Fryar Jhon, that ever were beheld with or without
Spectacles. Then we pass'd by an infinite number of little
pimping Wine-presses, all full of Vintagemongers, who were
picking, examining, and raking the Grapes with some Instruments call'd Bills of Charge.

Finally, We came into a Hall down Stairs, where we saw
an overgrown curs'd mangy Curr with a pair of Heads, a
Wolf's Belly, and Claws like the Devil of Hell. The Son of a
Bitch was fed with Cost; for he liv'd on a Mulctiplicity of
Fine Amonds, and Amerciaments, by Order of their Worships,
to each of whom the Monster was worth more than the best
Farm in the Land. In their Tongue of Ignorance, they call'd
him Twofold. His Dam lay by him, and her Hair and Shape
was like her Whelp's; only she had four Heads, two Male,
and two Female, and her Name was Fourfold. She was
certainly the most curs'd and dangerous Creature of the
Place, except her Grandam, that had been kept lock'd up
in a Dungeon time out of mind, and her Name was Refusing
of Fees.

Fryar Jhon, who had always twenty Yards of Gut ready
empty, to swallow a Gallimaufry of Lawyers, began to be
somewhat out of humour, and desir'd Pantagruel to remember
he had not din'd, and bring Double-fee along with him. So,
away we went; and as we march'd out at the Back-gate,
whom shou'd we meet but an old Piece of Mortality in Chains;
he was half Ignorant, and half Learned, like an Hermaphrodite
of Satan. The Fellow was all caparison'd with Spectacles,
as a Tortoise is with Shells, and liv'd on nothing but a sort of
Food, which, in their Gibberish, was call'd Appeals. Pantagruel ask'd Double-fee, of what Breed was that Prothonotary,
and what Name they gave him? Double-fee told us, That,
time out of mind, he had been kept there in Chains, to the great
grief of their Worships, who starv'd him; and his Name
was Review. By the Pope's sanctify'd Two-pounders, cry'd
Fryar Jhon, I don't much wonder at the meagre Cheer which
this old Chuff finds among their Worships, do but look a little
on the weather-beaten Scratch Toby, Friend Panurge; by
the sacred Tip of my Cowle, I'll lay Five Pounds to a Hazel-
nut, the foul Thief has the very Looks of Gripe-me-now.
These same Fellows here, ignorant as they be, are as sharp

and knowing as other Folk. But were it my Case, I 'd send him packing with a Squib in his Breech, like a Rogue enough as he is. By my Oriental Barnicles, quoth Panurge, honest Fryar, thou 'rt in the right; for if we but examin that treacherous Review's ill-favour'd Phiz, we find that the filthy Snudge is yet more mischievous and ignorant than these ignorant Wretches here; since they (honest Dunces !) grapple and glean with as little harm and pother as they can, without any long Fiddle-come-farts or Tantalizing in the Case; nor do they dally and demur in your Suit, but, in two or three words, whip-stitch in a trice, they finish the Vintage of the Close, bating you all those damn'd tedious Interlocutories, Examinations and Appointments, which frets to the hearts-blood your Furr'd Law-cats.

CHAPTER VIII

How Panurge related to Master Ædituus, the Fable of the Horse and the Ass

WHEN we had cramm'd and cramm'd again, Ædituus took us into a Chamber that was well furnish'd, hung with Tapestry, and finely gilt. Thither he caus'd to be brought store of Mirabolans, Cashou, Green Ginger preserv'd, with plenty of Hypocrass, and delicious Wine. With these Antidotes, that were like a sweeter Lethe, he invited us to forget the Hardships of our Voyage; and at the same time he sent Plenty of Provisions on board our Ships that rid in the Harbour. After this, we e'en jogg'd to Bed for that Night, but the Devil-a-bit poor Pilgarlic could sleep one wink, the everlasting Jingle-jangle of the Bells kept me awake whether I wou'd or no.

About Midnight Ædituus came to wake us, that we might drink. He himself shew'd us the way, saying, You Men of t' other World say, That Ignorance is the Mother of all Evil; and so far you are right : yet for all that, you don't take the least care to get rid of it, but still plod on, and live in it, with it, and by it ; for which cause, a plaguy-deal of Mischief lights on you every day, and you are right enough serv'd ; you are perpetually ailing somewhat, making a moan, and never right. 'Tis what I was ruminating upon just now. And indeed, Ignorance keeps you here fasten'd in Bed, just as that Bully-rock Mars was detain'd by Vulcan's Art ; for all the while you don't mind that you ought to spare some of your Rest, and be as lavish as you can of the Goods of this famous Island. Come, come, you shou'd have eaten three Breakfasts already ; and take this from me for a certain Truth, That if you wou'd consume the Mouth-Ammunition of this Island, you must rise betimes ; Eat them, they multiply ; Spare them, they diminish.

For Example : Mow a Field in due Season, and the Grass will grow thicker and better ; don't mow it, and in a short time 'twill be floor'd with Moss. Let 's drink, and drink again, my Friends ; come, let 's all carouse it. The leanest of our Birds are now singing to us all ; we 'll drink to them, if you please. Let 's take off one, two, three, nine Bumpers, *Non Zelus, sed Charitas*.

When Day peeping in the East, made the Sky turn from Black to Red, like a boiling Lobster, he wak'd us again, to take a Dish of Monastical Browess. From that time we made but one Meal that only lasted the whole Day ; so that I cannot well tell how I may call it, whether Dinner, Supper, Nunchion, or After-Supper ; only to get a Stomach, we took a turn or two in the Island, to see and hear the blessed Singing-Birds.

At Night Panurge said to Ædituus, Give me leave, sweet Sir, to tell you a merry Story of something that happen'd some three and twenty Moons ago in the Country of Chastel-leraudland.

On the First of April, a certain Gentleman's Groom, Roger by Name, was walking his Master's Horses in some Fallow-Ground. There 'twas his good fortune to find a pretty Shepherdess, feeding her bleating Sheep, and harmless Lambkins, on the Brow of a neighbouring Mountain, in the Shade of an adjacent Grove; Near her, some frisking Kids tript it o'er a green Carpet of Nature's own spreading; and to compleat the Pastoral Landskip, There stood an Ass. Roger, who was a Wag, had a Dish of Chat with her; and after some If's, And's, and But's, Hem's, and Heigh's on her Side, got her in the mind to get up behind him, to go and see his Stable, and there take a Bit by the bye in a Civil way. While they were holding a Parley, the Horse directing his discourse to the Ass, (for all Brute Beasts spoke that Year in divers Places) whisper'd these words in his Ear: Poor Ass, how I pity thee! Thou slavest like any Hack, I read it on thy Crupper; thou do'st well however, since God has created thee to serve Mankind; thou art a very honest Ass: But not to be better Rub'd down, Curri-comb'd, Trap'd, and Fed than thou art, seems to me indeed to be too hard a Lot. Alas! thou art all Rough-coated, in ill Plight; Jaded, Founder'd, Crest-fallen, and Drooping like a Mooting Duck, and feedest here on nothing but coarse Grass, or Bryars, and Thistles: Therefore do but Pace it along with me, and thou shalt see how we noble Steeds, made by Nature for War, are treated; come, thou 'lt lose nothing by coming, I 'll get thee a taste of my Fare. I' troth, Sir, I can but love you and thank you, return'd the Ass; I 'll wait on you, good Mr Steed. Methinks, Gaffer Ass, you might as well have said, Sir Grandpaw Steed. Oh! Cry mercy, good Sir Grandpaw, return'd the Ass; we country Clowns are somewhat gross, and apt to knock Words out of joint: However, an 't please you, I 'll come after your Worship at some distance, lest for taking this Run, my Side shou'd chance to be firk'd and curried with a vengeance, as 'tis but too often, the more 's my sorrow.

The Shepherdess being got behind Roger, the Ass follow'd, fully resolv'd to Bate like a Prince with Roger's Steed. But when they got to the Stable, the Groom who spy'd the grave Animal, order'd one of his Underlings to welcom him with the pitchfork, and curricomb him with a Cudgel. The Ass, who heard this, recommended himself mentally to the God Neptune, and was packing off, thinking, and syllogising within himself thus; Had not I been an Ass, I had not come here among great Lords, when I must needs be sensible that I was only made for the Use of the small Vulgar; Æsop had given me a fair Warning of this, in one of his Fables. Well, I must e'e scamper, or take what follows. With this he fell a Trotting, and Winsing, and Yerking, and Calcitrating *alias* Kicking, and Farting, and Funking, and Curveting and Bounding, and Springing, and Galloping full drive, as if the Devil had been come for him *in propriâ personâ*.

The Shepherdess, who saw her Ass scour off, told Roger that 'twas her Cattle, and desir'd he might be kindly us'd, or else she would not stir her foot over the Threshold. Friend Roger no sooner knew this, but he order'd him to be fetched in, and that my Master's Horses shou'd rather chop Straw for a Week together, than my Mistress's Beast should want his Belly-full of Corn.

The most difficult point was to get him back; for in vain the Youngsters complimented and cox'd him to come; I dare not, said the Ass, I am bashful; and the more they strove by fair means to bring him with them, the more the stubborn Thing was untoward, and flew out at heels; insomuch that they might have been there to this hour, had not his Mistress advis'd 'em to toss Oats in a Sieve, or in a Blanket, and call him; which was done, and made him wheel-about, and say, Oats with a witness, Oats shall go to pot, *adveniat*; Oats will do, there's Evidence in the Case; but none of the Rubbing down, none of the Firking. Thus melodiously Singing, for as you know that Arcadian Bird's Note is very harmonious, he came to the Young Gentlemen of the Horse, *alias* Blackgarb, who brought him into the Stable.

When he was there, they plac'd him next to the great Horse, his Friend, Rubb'd him down, Curricomb'd him, laid clean Straw under him up to his Chin, and there he lay at Rack and Manger; the first stuff'd with sweet Hay, the latter with Oats; which when the Horse-*Valets-de-Chambre* sifted, he clapt down his Lugs to tell them by Signs that he would eat it but too well without sifting, and that he did not deserve so great an honour.

When they had well fed, quoth the Horse to the Ass, Well, poor Ass, how is it with thee now? How do'st thou like this Fare? Thou wer't so nice at first, a body had much ado to get thee hither. By the Fig, answer'd the Ass, which one of our Ancestors eating, Philemon died laughing, this is all sheer Ambrosia, good Sir Grandpaw. But what wou'd you have an Ass say? Methinks all this is yet but half Cheer: Don't your Worships here use now and then to take a Leap? What Leaping do'st thou mean? ask'd the Horse: The Devil leap thee, do'st thou take me for an Ass? I' troth, Sir Grandpaw, quoth the Ass, I am somewhat a Blockhead, you know, and can't for the heart's blood of me learn so fast the Court-way of Speaking of you Gentlemen-horses; I mean, Don't you Stallionize it sometimes here among your metal'd Fillies? Tush, whisper'd the Horse, speak lower; for, by Bucephalus, if the Grooms but hear thee, they 'll maul and belam me and thee thrice and three-fold; so that thou 'lt have but little stomach to a Leaping bout. Cod so, Man, we dare not so much as grow stiff at the tip of the lowermost Snout, tho' 'twere but to leak or so, for fear of being Jirk'd and Paid out of our Letchery. As for any thing else, we are as happy as our Master, and perhaps more. By this Packsaddle, my old Acquaintance, quoth the Ass, I have done with you, a fart for thy Litter and Hay, and a fart for thy Oats; Give me the Thistles of our Fields, since there we Leap when we list: Eat less, and Leap the more, I say; 'tis Meat, Drink, and Cloth to us. Ah! Friend Grandpaw, it wou'd do thy heart good to see us at a Fair, when we hold our Provincial Chapter. Oh! how we Leap it, while our Mistresses are selling their Goslins and other Poultry! With this they parted: *Dixi:* I have done.

Panurge then held his Peace: Pantagruel would have had him to have gone on to the end of the Chapter: But Ædituus said, A Word to the Wise is enough; I can pick out the meaning of that Fable, and know who is that Ass, and who the Horse; but you are a bashful Youth I perceive: Well, know that there 's nothing for you here, scatter no Words. Yet, return'd Panurge, I saw but e'en now a pretty kind of a cooing Abbeykite as white as a Dove, and her I had rather ride than lead. May I never stir, if she is not a Dainty Bit, and very well worth a Sin or two, Heav'n forgive me! I meant no more harm in it than you; may the harm I meant in it befal me presently.

CHAPTER IX

How with much ado we got a sight of the Popehawk

OUR Junketing and Banquetting held on at the same rate the third day, as the two former. Pantagruel then earnestly desir'd to see the Popehawk; but Ædituus told him, it was not such an easie matter to get a sight of him. How, ask'd Pantagruel, has he Plato's Helmet on his Crown, Gyges's Ring on his Pounces, or a Cameleon on his Breast, to make him invisible when he pleases? No, Sir, return'd Ædituus, but he is naturally of pretty difficult access; however I 'll see and take care that you may see him if possible. With this he left us piddling; then within a quarter of an Hour came back, and told us the Popehawk is now to be seen; so he led us, without the least Noise, directly to the Cage wherein he sate drooping, with his Feathers staring about him, attended by a Brace of little Cardinhawks and six lusty fusty Bishhawks.

Panurge star'd at him like a dead Pig, examining exactly his Figure, Size, and Motions. Then with a loud Voice he said, A Curse light on the Hatcher of the ill Bird, o' my word this is a filthy Whoophooper. Tush, speak softly, said Ædituus, By G— he has a pair of Ears, as formerly Michæl de Metiscone remark'd. What then, return'd Panurge, so hath a Whoopcat. So said Ædituus, if he but hear you speak such another blasphemous word, you had as good be damn'd; Do you see that Basin yonder in his Cage? Out of it shall sally Thunderbolts and Lightnings, Storms, Bulls, and the Devil and all, that will sink you down to Peg-Trantums an hundred Fathom under Ground. 'Twere better to drink and be merry, quoth Fryar Jhon.

Panurge was still feeding his Eyes with the sight of the Popehawk, and his Attendants, when somewhere under his Cage he perceiv'd a Madgehowlet; with this he cry'd out, By the Devil's-maker's Master, there 's Roguery in the Case; they put Tricks upon Travellers here more than any where else, and would make us believe that a T———d's a Sugarloaf. What damn'd cousening, gulling, and Coney-catching have we here! Do you see this Madgehowlet? by Minerva, we are all beshit. Odsoons, said Ædituus, speak softly, I tell you, 'tis no Madgehowlet, no she-thing, on my honest word, but a male and a noble Bird.

May we not hear the Popehawk sing, ask'd Pantagruel? I dare not promise that, return'd Ædituus, for he only sings and eats at his own time; so don't I, quoth Panurge, poor Pilgarlic is fain to make every Body's time his own; if they have time, I find time; Come then, let us go drink if you will. Now this is something like a Tansy, said Ædituus; you begin to talk somewhat like, still speak in that fashion, and I 'll secure you from being thought a Heretic. Come on, I am of your mind.

As we went back to have t' other fuddling Bout, we spy'd an old green-headed Bishhawk, who sate moping with his Mate and three jolly Bitter Attendants, all snoring under an Arbor. Near the old Chuff stood a buxom Abbeskite, that sung like any Linet; and we were so mightily tickl'd with her singing, that I vow and swear we could have wish'd all our Members but one turn'd into Ears, to have had more of the Melody. Quoth Panurge, This pretty Cherubin of Cherubins is here breaking her Head with chanting to this huge, fat, ugly-face, who lies grunting all the while like a Hog as he is. I 'll make him change his Note presently in the Devil's Name. With this he rang a Bell that hung over the Bishhawk's Head; but, tho' he rang and rang again, the Devil-a-bit Bishhawk would hear; the louder the sound, the louder his snoring. There was no making him sing. By G——, quoth Panurge, you old Buzzard, if you won't sing by fair means, you shall by foul. Having said this, he took up one of St. Stephen's Loaves, *alias* a Stone, and was going to hit him with it about the middle. But Ædituus cry'd to him, Hold, hold, honest Friend, strike, wound, poyson, kill and murther all the Kings and Princes in the World, by Treachery, or how thou wilt, and as soon as thou wouldst, unnestle the Angels from their Cockloft, Popehawk will pardon thee all this. But never be so mad as to meddle with these sacred Birds, as much as thou lov'st the Profit, Welfare and Life not only of thy self, and thy Friends and Relations alive or dead, but also of those that may be born hereafter to the thousandth Generation; for so long thou wouldst entail Misery upon them. Do but look upon that Basin. Cat-so! let us rather drink then, quoth Panurge. He that spoke last, spoke well, Mr Antitus, quoth Fryar Jhon; while we are looking on these devilish Birds, we do nothing but blaspheme; and while we are taking a Cup, we do nothing but praise God. Come on then, let 's go drink: How well that word sounds!

The third Day (after we had drank, as you must under-stand) Ædituus dismiss'd us. We made him a Present of a pretty little Perguois Knife, which he took more kindly than Artaxerxes did the Cup of cold Water that was given him by a Clown. He most courteously thank'd us, and sent all sorts of Provisions aboard our Ships, wish'd us a prosperous Voyage and Success in our Undertakings, and made us promise and swear by Jupiter of Stone to come back by his Territories. Finally, he said to us, Friends, pray note that there are many

more Stones in the World than Men; take care you don't
forget it.

CHAPTER X

How we arriv'd at the Island of Tools

HAVING well ballasted the Holds of our human Vessels, we
weigh'd Anchor, hois'd up Sail, stow'd the Boats, set the Land,
and stood for the Offing with a fair loom Gale, and for more
haste unparrell'd the Misen-yard, and lanch'd it and the Sail
over her Lee-quarter, and fitted Gives to keep it steady, and
boom'd it out; so in three Days we made the Island of Tools,
that is altogether uninhabited. We saw there a great number
of Trees which bore Mattocks, Pickaxes, Crows, Weeding
Hooks, Scythes, Sickles, Spades, Trowels, Hatchets, Hedging
Bills, Saws, Addes, Bills, Axes, Sheers, Pincers, Bolts, Piercers,
Augres and Wimbles.

Others bore Dags, Daggers, Poniards, Bayonets, Square-
bladed Tucks, Stilettoes, Poinadoes, Skenes, Penknives, Puncheons, Bodkins, Swords, Rapiers, Backswords, Cutlasses,
Semiters, Hangers, Falchions, Glaives, Raillons, Whittles
and Whinyards.

Whoever would have any of these needed but to shake the
Tree, and immediately they dropp'd down as thick as Hops,
like so many ripe Plumbs; nay, what 's more, they fell on a
kind of Grass call'd Scabbard, and sheath'd themselves in it
cleverly. But when they came down there was need of taking
care lest they happen'd to touch the Head, Feet, or other
Parts of the Body. For they fell with the Point downwards,
and in they stuck, or slit the *continuum* of some Member, or
lopp'd it off like a Twig; either of which generally was enough
to have kill'd a Man though he were a hundred Year old, and
worth as many thousand Spankers, Spur-Royals, and Rose-
Nobles.

Under some other Trees, whose Names I can't justly tell you,
I saw some certain sorts of Weeds that grew and sprouted like
Pikes, Lances, Javelins, Javelots, Darts, Dartlets, Halbarts,
Boarspears, Eelspears, Partisans, Tridentes, Prongs, Trout-
staves, Spears, Half-pikes, and Hunting-Staffs. As they

317

sprouted up and chanc'd to touch the Tree, strait they met with their Heads, Points, and Blades, each suitable to its Kind, made ready for them by the Trees over them ; as soon as every individual Wood was grown up, fit for its Steel ; even like the Childrens Coats that are made for them as soon as they can wear them, and you wean them of their Swadling Cloaths ; nor do you mutter, I pray you, at what Plato, Anaxagoras and Democritus have said ; Od's fish ! they were none of your Lower-Form Gimcracks, were they ?

Those Trees seem'd to us Terrestrial Animals, in no wise so different from Brute Beasts as not to have Skin, Fat, Flesh, Veins, Arteries, Ligaments, Nerves, Cartilages, Kernels, Bones, Marrow, Humours, Matrices, Brains and Articulations ; for they certainly have some, since Theophrastus will have it so ; but in this Point they differ'd from other Animals, that their Heads, that is, the Part of their Trunks next to the Root are downwards ; their Hair, that is, their Roots, in the Earth ; and their Feet, that is their Branches, upside down ; as if a Man should stand on his Head with out-stretch'd Legs. And as you, batter'd Sinners, on whom Venus has bestow'd something to remember her, feel the approach of Rains, Winds, Cold, and every change of Weather, at your Ischiatic Legs, and your Omoplates, by means of the perpetual Almanac which she has fix'd there ; so these Trees have notice given them by certain Sensations which they have at their Roots, Stocks, Gums, Paps or Marrow, of the growth of the Staffs under them ; and accordingly they prepare suitable Points and Blades for them beforehand. Yet as all things, except God, are sometimes subject to Error, Nature its self not free from it, when it produceth Monstrous Things ; likewise I observ'd something amiss in these Trees. For a Half-pike that grew up high enough to reach the Branches of one of these Instrument-iferous Trees, happen'd no sooner to touch them, but instead of being join'd to an Iron-head, it impal'd a stubb'd Broom at the Fundament. Well, no matter, 'twill serve to sweep the Chimney. Thus a Pertusan met with a Pair of Garden-shears ; Come, all's good for something, 'twill serve to nip off little Twigs, and destroy Catterpillars. The Staff of a Halbert got the Blade of a Scythe, which made it look like an Her-maphrodite ; happy be lucky, 'tis all a case, 'twill serve for some Mower. Oh 'tis a great Blessing to put our trust in the Lord ! As we went back to our Ships, I spy'd behind I don't know what Bush, I don't know what Folks, doing I don't know what Business, in I don't know what Posture, scowring I don't know what Tools, in I don't know what Manner, and I don't know what Place.

CHAPTER XI

How Pantagruel arriv'd at the Island of Sharping

WE left the Island of Tools to pursue our Voyage, and the next Day stood in for the Island of Sharping, the true Image of Fontainbleau; for the Land is so very lean there, that the Bones, that is the Rocks, shoot through its Skin. Besides, 'tis sandy, barren, and unpleasant. Our Pilot shew'd us there two little square Rocks, which had eight equal Points in the shape of a Cube; they were so white that I might have mistaken them for Alabaster or Snow, had he not assur'd us they were made of Bone.

He told us that twenty chance Devils, very much fear'd in our Country, dwelt there in six different Stories, and that the biggest Twins or Braces of them were call'd Sixes, and the smallest Amb'sace; the rest Cinques, Quaters, Treys and Dewses. When they were conjur'd up, otherwise coupled, they were call'd either Sice - cincq, Sice - quater, Sice - trey, Sice-dewse, and Sice-ace; or Cincq-quater, Cincq-trey, and so forth. I made there a shrewd Observation; would you know

319

what 'tis, Gamesters ? 'Tis that there are very few of you in the World but what call upon and invoke the Devils. For the Dice are no sooner thrown on the Board, and the greedy gazing Sparks have hardly said, two sixes, Frank, but six Devils damn it, cry as many of them ; if Amb's-Ace, then, A Brace of Devils broil me, will they say. Quater Deuse, Tom ; the Dewse take it, cries another, and so on to the end of the Chapter. Nay, they don't forget sometimes to call the Black Cloven-footed Gentlemen by their Christen-names and Sirnames ; and what 's stranger yet, they use them as their greatest Cronies, and make them so often the Executors of their Wills, not only giving themselves, but every Body and every Thing to the Devil, that there 's no doubt but he takes care to seize, soon or late, what 's so zealously bequeath'd him. Indeed 'tis true, Lucifer do's not always immediately appear by his lawful Attornies ; but alas ! 'tis not for want of Good-will ; he is really to be excus'd for his delay, for what the Devil would you have a Devil do ? He and his black Guards are then at some other Places, according to the Priority of the Persons that call on them : Therefore pray let none be so venturesom as to think, that the Devils are deaf and blind.

He then told us, that more Wrecks had happen'd about those Square-rocks, and a greater loss of Body and Goods, than about all the Syrtes, Sylla's and Charibdes, Sirens, Scrophades and Gulphs in the Universe. I had not much ado to believe it, remembring, that formerly amongst the wise Egyptians, Neptune was describ'd in Hieroglyphics by the first Cube, Apollo by an Ace, Diana by a Duce, Minerva by Seven, and so forth.

He also told us that there was a Phial of Sang real, a most divine thing, and known but to a few. Panurge did so sweeten up the Syndics of the Place, that they blest us with the sight of 't : But it was with three times more pother and ado, with more Formalities and antick Tricks, than they shew the Pandects of Justinian at Florence, or the Holy Veronica at Rome. I never saw such a sight of Flambeaux, Torches, and Hagio's, sanctifi'd Tapers, Rush-Lights, and Farthing Candles, in my whole life. After all, that which was shewn us, was only the ill-fac'd Countenance of a roasted Conny.

All that we saw there worth speaking of, was a good Face set upon an ill Game, and the Shells of the two Eggs formerly laid up and hatch'd by Læda, out of which came Castor and Pollux, fair Helen's Brothers. These same Syndics sold us a piece of 'em for a Song, I mean, for a morsel of Bread. Before we went, we bought a parcel of Hats and Caps of the Manufacture of the Place, which, I fear, will turn to no very good account : Nor are those who shall take 'em off our hands more likely to commend their wearing.

CHAPTER XII

How we past through the Wicket, inhabited by Gripe-men-all, Arch-Duke of the Furr'd Law-cats

FROM thence Condemnation was pass'd by us : 'Tis another damn'd barren Island, whereat none for the World car'd to touch. Then we went through the Wicket, but Pantagruel had no mind to bear us company, and 'twas well he did not, for we were nabb'd there, and clapp'd into Lob's-Pound by Order of Gripe-men-all, Arch-Duke of the Furr'd Law-cats, because one of our Company wou'd ha' put upon a Serjeant some Hats of the sharping Island.

The Furr'd Law-cats are most terrible and dreadful Monsters, they devour little Children, and trample over Marble-Stones. Pray tell me, Noble Topers, do they not deserve to have their Snouts slit ? The Hair of their Hides do's n't lie outward, but inwards ; and every Mother's Son of 'em, for his Devise, wears a gaping Pouch, but not all in the same manner ; for some wear it ty'd to their Neck Scarfwise, others upon the Breech, some on the Paunch, others on the Side, and all for a Cause, with Reason and Mystery : They have Claws so very strong, long, and sharp, that nothing can get from 'em, that is once fast between their Clutches : Sometimes they cover their Heads with Mortar-like Caps, at other times with mortify'd Caparisons.

As we enter'd their Den, said a common Mumper to whom we had given half a Teston, Worshipful Culprits, God send you a good Deliverance. Examine well said he, the Countenance of these stout Props and Pillars of this Catch-coin Law and Iniquity ; and pray observe, that if you still live but six Olympiads, and the Age of two Dogs more, you 'll see these Furr'd Law-cats Lords of all Europe, and in peaceful Possession of all the Estates and Dominions belonging to it; unless by Divine Providence what 's got over the Devil's Back is spent under his Belly; or the Goods which they unjustly get, perish with their Prodigal Heirs: Take this from an honest poor Beggar.

Among 'em reigns the Sixth Essence; by the means of which they gripe all, devour all, conskite all, burn all, draw all, hang all, quarter all, behead all, murther all, imprison all, waste all, and ruin all, without the least notice of Right or Wrong: For among them Vice is call'd Virtue; Wickedness, Piety; Treason, Loyalty; Robbery, Justice; Plunder is their Motto; and when acted by them, is approv'd by all Men, except the Hereticks: And all this they do, because they dare; their Authority is Sovereign and Irrefragable.

For a sign of the Truth of what I tell you, you 'll find, that there the Mangers are above the Racks. Remember hereafter, that a Fool told you this; and if ever Plague, Famine, War, Fire, Earthquakes, Inundations, or other Judgments befal the World, do not attribute them to the Aspects and Conjunctions of the Malevolent Planets, to the Abuses of the Court of Roumania, or the Tyranny of Secular Kings and Princes, to the Impostures of the false Zealots of the Cowl, Heretical Bigots, False-Prophets and Broachers of Sects, to the Villany of griping Usurers, Clippers and Coiners, or to the Ignorance, Impudence and Imprudence of Physicians, Surgeons and Apothecaries, nor to the Lewdness of Adulteresses and Destroyers of Byeblows; but charge 'em all wholly and solely to the inexpressible, incredible and inestimable Wickedness and Ruin, which is continually hatch'd, brew'd and practis'd in the Den of those Furr'd Law-cats. Yet 'tis no more known in the World, than the Cabala of the Jews, the more 's the pity; and therefore 'tis not detested, chastis'd, and punish'd, as 'tis fit it shou'd be. But shou'd all their Villany be once display'd in its true Colours, and expos'd to the People, there never was, is, nor will be any Spokesman so sweet-mouth'd, whose fine colloguing Tongue cou'd save 'em; nor any Laws so rigorous and Draconic, that cou'd punish 'em as they deserve; nor yet any Magistrate so powerful, as to hinder their being burnt alive in their Coney-boroughs without Mercy: Even their own Furr'd Kittlings, Friends and Relations would abominate 'em.

For this reason, as Hannibal was solemnly sworn by his Father Amilcar to pursue the Romans with the utmost hatred, as long as ever he liv'd; so, my late Father has enjoin'd me

W HEATH ROBINSON

A LAW-CAT

3²3

to remain here without, till God Almighty's Thunder reduce them there within to Ashes, like other presumptuous Titans, prophane Wretches, and Opposers of God; since Mankind is so inur'd to their Oppressions, that they either do not remember, foresee, or have a Sense of the Woes and Miseries which they have caused; or if they have, either will, dare, or cannot root 'em out.

How! said Panurge, say you so! Catch me there and hang me! Damme, Let's march off! This Noble Beggar has scar'd me worse than the Thunder would do them. Upon this we were filing off! but alas! we found our selves trapp'd: The Door was double-lock'd and barricado'd. Some Messengers of ill News told us, 'twas full as easie to get in there, as to get into Hell, and as hard for some to get out. Ay, there indeed lay the Difficulty: For there is no getting loose without a Pass and Discharge in due Course from the Bench. This for no other reason, than because Folks go easier out of a Church than out of a Spunging-house, and they could not have our Company when they would. The worst on 't was when we got thro' the Wicket, for we were carry'd to get out our Pass or Discharge, before a more dreadful Monster than ever was read of in the Legends of Knight-Errantry: They call'd him Gripe-men-all: I can't tell what to compare it to, better than to a Chymæra, a Sphinx, a Cerberus; or to the Image of Osiris, as the Egyptians represented him, with Three Heads, one of a roaring Lion, t' other of a Fawning Curr, and the last of a Houling Prouling Wolf, twisted about with a Dragon biting his Tail, surrounded with fiery Rays. His Hands were full of Gore, his Talons like those of the Harpies, his Snout like a Hawk's Bill, his Fangs or Tusks like those of an overgrown brindled Wild-Boar, his Eyes were flaming like the Jaws of Hell, all cover'd with Mortars interlac'd with Pestles, and nothing of his Arms was to be seen but his Clutches. His Hutch, and that of the Warren-cats his Collaterals, was a long, spick-and-span new Rack, a top of which, (as the Mumper told us) some large, stately Mangers were fix'd in the Reverse. Over the Chief-Seat was the Picture of an Old Woman holding the Case or Scabbard of a Sickle in her Right-hand, a Pair of Scales in her Left, with Spectacles on her Nose: The Cups of the Balance were a Pair of Velvet-Pouches; the one full of Bullion, which over-pois'd t' other, empty and long, hoisted higher than the middle of the Beam: I 'm of opinion that it was the true Effigies of Justice Gripe-men-all; far different from the Institution of the ancient Thebans, who set up the Statues of their Dicastes without Hands, in Marble, Silver, or Gold, according to their Merit, even after their Death.

When we made our Personal Appearance before him, a sort of I don't-know-what Men, all cloath'd with I don't-know-what Bags and Pouches, with long Scrowls in their Clutches, made us sit down upon a Cricket : (such as Criminals sit on when they are Try'd in France.) Quoth Panurge to 'em, Good my Lords, I 'm very well as I am ; I 'd as lieve stand, an 't please you. Besides, this same Stool is somewhat of the lowest for a Man that has new Breeches and a short Doublet. Sit you down, said Gripe-men-all again, and look that you don't make the Court bid you twice. Now, continu'd he, the Earth shall immediately open its Jaws, and swallow you up to quick Damnation, if you don't answer as you should.

CHAPTER XIII

How Gripe-men-all propounded a Riddle to us

WHEN we were sate, Gripe-men-all, in the middle of his Furr'd-cats, call'd to us in a hoarse, dreadful Voice ; Well, come on, give, give me presently—an Answer. Well, come on, mutter'd Panurge between his Teeth ; give, give me presently—a comforting Dram. Hearken to the Court, continu'd Gripe-men-all.

AN ENIGMA

A Young tight Thing, as Fair as may be,
Without a Dad conceiv'd a Baby ;
And brought him forth, without the Pother
In Labour made by teeming Mother.
Yet the curs'd Brat fear'd not to gripe her,
But gnaw'd for haste her Sides, like Viper.
Then the black Upstart boldly sallies,
And walks and flies o'er Hills and Vallies.
Many fantastick Sons of Wisdom,
Amaz'd, foresaw their own, in his Doom,
And thought, like an old Græcian Noddy,
A Human Spirit mov'd his Body.

ENIGME

Une bien jeune et toute blondeleite
Conceut un fils Ethiopien sans pere ;
Puis l'enfanta sans douleur la tendrette,
Quoy qu'il sortit comme fait la vipere,
L'ayant rongé, en moult grand vitupere,
Tout l'un des Flancs, pour son impatience,
Depuis, passa monts et vaus en fiance,
Par l'Air volant, en terre cheminante ;
Tant qu'estonna l'amy de sapience,
Qui l'estimoit estre humain animante.

Give, give me out of hand—an Answer to this Riddle, quoth Gripe-men-all. Give, give me—leave to tell you, good, good my Lord, answer'd Panurge, That if I had but a Sphinx at home, as Verres one of your Precursors had, I might then solve your Enigma presently ; but verily, good my Lord, I was not there ; and as I hope to be sav'd, am as innocent in the matter as the Child unborn : Foh, give me—a better Answer, cry'd Gripe-men-all, or, by Gold, this shall not serve your turn ; I 'll not be paid in such Coin : If you have nothing better to offer, I 'll let your Rascalship know, that it had been better for you to have fallen into Lucifer's own Clutches, than into ours. Do'st thou see 'em here, Sirrah ? hah ! and do'st thou prate here of thy being Innocent, as if thou could'st be deliver'd from our Racks and Tortures for being so ! Give me—Patience ! thou Widgeon, our Laws are like Cob-webs ; your silly little Flyes are stopt, caught, and destroy'd there ; but your stronger Birds break them, and force and carry them which way they please. Likewise don't think we are so mad as to set up our Nets to snap up your great Robbers and Tyrants : No, they are somewhat too hard for us, there 's no medling with them ; for they would make no more of us, than we make of the little ones : But your paultry, silly, innocent Wretches, must make us amends ; and, by Gold, we will Innocentise your Fopship with a Wannion, you never were so innocentis'd in your days.

Fryar Jhon hearing him run on at that mad rate, had no longer the power to remain silent, but cry'd to Him, High-dey ! Prithee, Mr. Devil in a Coif, would'st thou have a Man tell thee more than he knows ? has-n't the Fellow told you he does not know a word of the business ? his Name 's Twyford. A Plague rot you, won't Truth serve your turns ? Why how-now, Mr. Prate-a-pace, (cry'd Gripe-men-all, taking him short) Marry come up, who made you so saucy as to open your Lips before you were spoken to ? Give me—Patience! By Gold ! this is the first time since I reign, that any one has had the impudence to speak before he was bidden. How came this mad Fellow to break loose ? (Villain, thou lyest, said Fryar Jhon, without stirring his Lips.) Sirrah, Sirrah, continued Gripe-men-all, I doubt thou 'lt have business enough on thy hands, when it comes to thy turn to answer. (Damme, thou lyest, said Fryar Jhon, silently.) Do'st thou think, continu'd my Lord, thou 'rt in the Wilderness of your foolish University, wrangling and bawling among the idle, wandring Searchers and Hunters after Truth ? By Gold, we have here other Fish to fry, we go another-gat's way to work, that we do : By Gold, People here must give Catagorical Answers to what they don't know. By Gold, they must confess they have done those things which they have not and ought not to have done. By Gold, they must protest that they know what they never knew in their Lives : And after all, Patience per Force must be their only remedy, as well as a Mad-Dog's. Here silly Geese are pluck'd, yet cackle not. Sirrah, Give me—an Account, whether you had a Letter of Attorney, or whether you were fee'd, or no, that you offer'd to bawl in another Man's Cause ? I see you had no Authority to speak, and I may chance to have you wed to something you won't like. Oh, you Devils, cry'd Fryar Jhon, Proto-Devils, Panto-Devils, you wou'd wed a Monk, wou'd you ? Ho ha, ho ha, a Heretic, a Heretic, I 'll give thee out for a rank Heretic.

CHAPTER XIv

How Panurge solv'd Gripe-men-all's Riddle

GRIPE-MEN-ALL, as if he had not heard what Fryar Jhon said, directed his Discourse to Panurge, saying to him, Well, what have you to say for your self, Mr. Rogue-enough, hah ! Give, give me out of hand—an Answer. Say ! quoth Panurge, why, what would you have me say ? I say, that we are damnably beshit, since you give no heed at all to the Equity of the Plea, and the Devil sings among you; let this Answer serve for all, I beseech you, and let us go about our business ; I am no longer able to hold out, as gad shall judge me.

Go to, go to, cry'd Gripe-men-all ; When did you ever hear that for these three hundred Years last past any body ever got out of this Weel, without leaving something of his behind him. No, no, get out of the Trap if you can, without losing Leather, Life, or at least some Hair, and you 'll have done more than ever was done yet. For why, this would bring the Wisdom of the Court into question, as if we had took you up for nothing, and dealt wrongfully by you. Well, by hook or by crook we must have something out of you. Look ye, 'tis a folly to make a rout for a fart and a doe; one word 's as good as twenty ; I have no more to say to thee, but that as thou likest thy former Entertainment, thou 'lt tell me more of the next ; for 'twill go ten times worse with thee, unless, by Gold, you give me— a Solution to the Riddle I propounded. Give, give—it, without any more ado, I say.

By Gold, quoth Panurge, 'tis a black Mite, or Weevil, which is born of a white Bean, and sallies out at the hole which he makes, gnawing it : The Mite being turn'd into a kind of a Fly, sometimes walks and sometimes flies over Hills and Dales. Now Pythagoras the Philosopher, and his Sect, besides many others, wondring at its Birth in such a Place, (which makes some argue for equivocal Generation) thought that by a Metempsychosis the Body of that Insect was the Lodging of an Human Soul. Now were you Men here, after your welcom'd Death, according to his Opinion, your Souls wou'd most certainly enter into the Body of Mites or Weevils ; for in your present state of Life you are good for nothing in the World,

THEY FELL TO 'T

but to gnaw, bite, eat, and devour all things ; so in the next you 'll e'en gnaw and devour your Mother's very Sides, as the Vipers do. Now, by Gold, I think I have fairly solv'd and resolv'd your Riddle.

May my Bawble be turn'd into a Nut-cracker, quoth Fryar Jhon, if I could not almost find in my heart to wish that what comes out of my Bunghole were Beans, that these evil Weevils might feed as they deserve.

Panurge then, without any more ado, threw a large Leathern Purse stuff'd with Gold Crowns (*Escus au Soleil*) among them : The Furr'd Law-Cats no sooner heard the jingling of the Chink, but they all began to bestir their Claws, like a parcel of Fiddlers running a Division ; and they fell to 't, squimble squamble, catch that catch can. They all said aloud, These are the Fees, these are the Gloves ; now this is somewhat like a Tanzy : Oh, 'twas a pretty Trial, a sweet Trial, a dainty Trial. O' my word they did not starve the Cause ; these are none of your sniveling *Forma Pauperis's :* No, they are Noble Clients, Gentlemen every Inch of them. By Gold, 'tis Gold, quoth Panurge, good old Gold, I 'll assure you.

Saith Gripe-men-all, the Court, upon a full Hearing, (of the Gold, quoth Panurge) and weighty Reasons given, finds the Prisoners Not guilty : and accordingly orders 'em to be discharg'd out of Custody, paying their Fees. Now, Gentlemen, proceed, go forwards, said he to us ; we have not so much of the Devil in us, as we have of his Hue ; tho' we are Stout, we are Merciful.

As we came out at the Wicket, we were conducted to the Port by a Detachment of certain Highland-Griffins, *scribere cum dashoes,* who advised us, before we came to our Ships, not to offer to leave the place, till we had made the usual Presents, first to the Lady Gripe-men-all, then to all the Furr'd Law-Pusses ; otherwise we must return to the place from whence we came. Well, well, saith Fryar Jhon, we 'll fumble in our Fobs, examine every one of us his Concern, and e'en give the Women their due ; we 'll ne'er boggle or stick out on that account ; as we tickled the Men in the Palm, we 'll tickle the Women in the right place. Pray, Gentlemen, added they, don't forget to leave somewhat behind you for us poor Devils to drink your Healths. O Lawd ! never fear, answer'd Fryar Jhon, I don't remember that I ever went any where yet where the poor Devils are not mention'd and encourag'd.

CHAPTER XV

How the Furr'd Law-Cats live on Corruption

FRYAR JHON had hardly said those Words e're he perceived seventy eight Gallies and Frigats just arriving at the Port. So he hied him thither to learn some News ; and as he ask'd what Goods they had o' board, he soon found that their whole Cargo was Venison, Hares, Capons, Turkeys, Pigs, Swine, Bacon, Kids, Calves, Hens, Ducks, Teals, Geese, and other Poultry and Wildfowl.

He also spy'd among these some Pieces of Velvet, Sattin and Damask. This made him ask the Newcomers whither and to whom they were going to carry those dainty Goods ? They answer'd that they were for Gripe-men-all, and the Furr'd Law-Cats.

Pray, asked he, what 's the true Name of all these Things, in your Country Language ? Corruption, they reply'd. If they live on Corruption, said the Fryar, they 'll perish with their Generation ; May the Devil be damn'd, I have it now : Their Fathers devour'd the good Gentlemen, who, according to their State of Life, us'd to go much a Hunting and Hawking to be the better inur'd to Toil in time of War ; for Hunting is an Image of a Martial Life ; and Xenophon was much in the right on 't, when he affirm'd that Hunting had yielded a great Number of excellent Warriors, as well as the Trojan Horse. For my part I am no Scholar, I have it but by hearsay, yet I believe it. Now the Souls of those brave Fellows, according to Gripe-men-all's Riddle, after their decease, enter into Wild-boars, Stags, Roe-bucks, Herns, and such other Creatures, which they lov'd, and in quest of which they went while they were Men ; and these Furr'd Law-Cats having first destroy'd and devour'd their Castles, Lands, Demesnes, Possessions, Rents, and Revenues, are still seeking to have their Blood and Soul in another Life. What an honest Fellow was that same Mumper who had forewarn'd us of all these things, and bid us take notice of the Mangers above the Racks !

But, said Panurge to the New-Comer, how do you come by all this Venison ? methinks the Great King has issued out a

Proclamation, strictly inhibiting the destroying of Stags, Does, Wild-boars, Roe-bucks, or other Royal Game, on pain of Death. All this is true enough answer'd one for the rest: But the great King is so good and gracious, you must know, and these Furr'd Law-Cats so curst and cruel, so mad and thirsting after Christian Blood, that we have less cause to fear in trespassing against that Mighty Sovereign's Commands, than reason to hope to live, if we do not continually stop the Mouths of these Furr'd Law-Cats with such Bribes and Corruption. Besides, added he, to-morrow Gripe-men-all marries a Furr'd Law-Puss of his to a high and mighty Double-furr'd Law-Tibert.

Formerly we used to call them Chop-hay; but, alas, they are not such neat Creatures now as to eat any, or chew the Cud. We call them Chop-Hares, Chop-Partridges, Chop-Woodcocks, Chop-Pheasants, Chop-Pullets, Chop-Venison, Chop-Connies, Chop-Pigs; for they scorn to feed on coarser Meat. A T—d for their Chops, cry'd Fryar Jhon, next Year we 'll have 'em called Chop-Dung, Chop-Stront, Chop-Filth.

Would you take my Advice, added he to the Company? What is it, answer'd we? Let 's do two things, return'd he; First, let 's secure all this Venison and Wild-fowl, (I mean paying well for them:) for my part I am but too much tir'd already with our Salt-meat, it heats my Flanks so horribly: In the next place let 's go back to the Wicket, and destroy all these devilish Furr'd Law-Cats. For my part, quoth Panurge, I know better things, catch me there, and hang me; No, I am somewhat more inclin'd to be fearful than bold, I love to sleep in a whole Skin.

CHAPTER XVI

How Fryar Jhon talks of rooting out the Furr'd Law-Cats

VERTUE of the Frock, quoth Fryar Jhon, what kind of a Voyage are we making? A shitten one o' my word; the Devil of anything we do but fizzling, farting, funking, squattering, dozing, raving, and doing nothing. Ods Belly, 'tisn't in my Nature to lie idle, I mortally hate it; unless I am doing

some Heroic Deed every foot, I can't sleep one wink o' Nights.
Dam it, did you then take me along with you for your Chaplain,
to sing Mass and shrive you ? By Maunday-Thursday, the
first of ye all that comes to me on such an Account shall be
fitted ; for, the only Penance I 'll enjoin shall be, that he
immediately throw himself headlong overboard into the Sea,
like a wicked Cow-hearted Son of ten Fathers ; this in deduction
of the Pains of Purgatory.

What made Hercules such a famous Fellow d' ye think ?
nothing, but that while he travell'd he still made it his business
to rid the World of Tyrannies, Errors, Dangers, and Drudgeries,
he still put to death all Robbers, all Monsters, all venemous
Serpents and hurtful Creatures. Why then do we not follow
his Example, doing as he did in the Countries through which we
pass ? He destroy'd the Stymphalides, the Lernæan Hydra,
Cacus, Antheus, the Centaurs, and what not ; I am no Clericus,
those that are such, tell me so.

In imitation of that noble Bye-blow, let 's destroy and root
out these wicked Furr'd Law-Cats, that are a kind of Ravenous Devils ; thus we shall remove all manner of Tyranny out
of the Land. Mawmet's Tutor swallow me Body and Soul,
Tripes and Guts, if I would stay to ask your Help or Advice in
the Matter, were I but as strong as he was. Come, he that
would be thought a Gentleman, let him storm a Town : Well
then, shall we go ? I dare swear we 'll do their business for
them with a wet Finger ; they 'll bear it, never fear ; since they
could swallow down more foul Language that came from us,
than ten Sows and their Babies could swill Hogwash. Dam
'em, they don't value all the ill words or dishonour in the World
at a Rush, so they but get the Coin into their Purses, though
they were to have it in a shitten Clout. Come, we may chance
to kill 'em all, as Hercules would have done, had they liv'd
in his time. We only want to be set to work by another
Eurystheus, and nothing else for the present ; unless it be
what I heartily wish them, That Jupiter may give 'em a
short Visit only some two or three Hours long, and walk among
their Lordships in the same Equipage that attended him when
he came last to his Miss Semele, jolly Bacchus's Mother.

'Tis a very great Mercy, quoth Panurge, that you have
got out of their Clutches ; for my part, I have no stomach to
go there again ; I 'm hardly come to my self yet, so scar'd and
appall'd I was ; my Hair still stands up on end when I think
on 't ; and most damnably troubled I was there, for three very

weighty Reasons. First, Because I was troubled. Secondly, Because I was troubled. Thirdly and lastly, Because I was troubled. Hark'n to me a little on thy right side, Fryar John, my left Cod, since thou 'lt not hear at the other; When-ever the Maggot bites thee, to take a Journey down to Hell, and visit the Tribunal of Minos, Eacus, and Rhadamantus, do but tell me, and I 'll be sure to bear thee company, and never leave thee, as long as my Name's Panurge, but will wade over Acheron, Styx, and Cocytus, drink whole Bumpers of Lethe's Water, (tho' I mortally hate that Element) and even pay thy Passage to that bawling cross-grained Ferry-man Caron. But as for that damn'd Wicket, if thou art so weary of thy Life as to go thither again, thou may'st e'en look for some Body else to bear thee company; for I 'll not move one step that way, e'en rest satisfi'd with this positive Answer. By my good-will, I 'll not stir a foot to go thither as long as I live, any more than Calpe will come over to Abyla. (Calpe is a Mountain in Spain, that faces another, called Abyla in Mauritiania, both said to have been sever'd by Hercules.) Was Ulysses so mad as to go back into the Cyclops's Cave to fetch his Sword? No marry was he not. Now, I have left nothing behind me at the Wicket through forgetfulness, why then should I think of going thither?

Well, quoth Fryar Jhon, as good sit still as rise up and fall; what can't be cur'd, must be endur'd. But, pr'ythee, let 's hear one another speak. Come, wert thou not a wise Doctor, to fling away a whole Purse of Gold on those mangy Scoundrels? Hah? A Squinzy choak thee, we were too rich, were we? Had it not been enough to have thrown the Hell-hounds a few cropt Pieces of white Cash?

How could I help it, returned Panurge? Did you not see how Gripe-men-all held his gaping Velvet-Pouch, and every Moment roar'd and bellow'd, By Gold, give, give me out of hand; By Gold, give, give, give me presently. Now, thought I to my self, we shall never come off scotfree; I 'll e'en stop their Mouths with Gold, that the Wicket may be open'd, and we may get out; the sooner the better. And I judged that lowsy Silver would not do the business; for, d' ye see, Velvet-Pouches don't use to gape for little paultry clipt Silver, and small Cash: No, they are made for Gold, my friend Jhon, that they are my dainty Cod. Ah! when thou hast been larded, basted, and roasted, as I was, thou 'lt hardly talk at this rate, I doubt. But now what's to be done—we are enjoyn'd by them to go for-Wards.

The scabby Slabberdegullions still waited for us at the Port, expecting to be greas'd in the Fist as well as their Masters. Now when they perceiv'd that we were ready to put to Sea, they came to Fryar Jhon, and begg'd that we might not forget to gratifie the Apparitors before we went off, according to the Assessment for the Fees at our Discharge. Hell and Damnation, cry'd Fryar Jhon, Are you here still, ye Bloodhounds, ye citing, scribling Imps of Satan? Rot you, Am I not vext enough already, but you must have the Impudence to come and plague me, ye scurvy Fly-catchers you? By Cob's-Body I 'll gratifie your Ruffianships as you deserve, I 'll Apparitorize you presently, with a Wannion, that I will. With this he lugg'd out his slashing Cutlas, and, in a mighty heat, came out of the Ship, to cut the cousening Varlets into Stakes, but they scamper'd away, and got out of sight in a Trice.

However, there was somewhat more to do; for some of our Sailors, having got leave of Pantagruel to go o'shoar, while we were had before Gripe-men-all, had been at a Tavern near the Haven to make much of themselves, and roar it, as Seamen will do when they come into some Port. Now I don't know whether they had paid their Reck'ning to the full or no; but, however it was, an old fat Hostess meeting Fryar Jhon on the Key, was making a woful Complaint, before a Sergeant, Son-in-law to one of the Furr'd Law-Cats, and a Brace of Bums his Assistants.

The Fryar, who did not much care to be tir'd with their impertinent Prating, said to them, Harkee me, ye lubbardly Gnat-snappers, Do you presume to say, that our Seamen are not honest men? I 'll maintain they are, ye Dotterels, and will prove it to your brazen Faces, by Justice; I mean this trusty piece of cold Iron by my side; with this, he lugg'd it out, and flourish'd with it. The forlorn Lobcocks soon shew'd him their Backs, betaking themselves to their heels; But the old fusty Landlady kept her ground, swearing, like any Butter-whore, that the Tarpawlins were very honest Cods; but that they had only forgot to pay for the Bed on which they had lay'n after Dinner, and she ask'd Five-pence French Money for the said Bed. May I never sup, said the Fryar, if it be not Dog-cheap; they are sorry Guests, and unkind Customers, that they are; they don't know when they have a Penniworth, and will not always meet with such Bargains; Come, I my self will pay you the Money, but I would willingly see it first.

The Hostess immediately took him home with her, and

shew'd him the Bed, and having prais'd it for all its good qualifications, said that she thought, as Times went, she was not out of the way, in asking Five-pence for 't. Fryar Jhon then gave her the Five-pence, and she no sooner turn'd her back, but he presently began to rip up the Ticking of the Featherbed and Bolster, and throw'd all the Feathers out at the Window. In the mean time the old Hag came down, and roar'd out for help, crying out Murther, to set all the Neighbourhood in an Uproar. Yet she also fell to gathering the Feathers that flew up and down in the Air, being scatter'd by the Wind. Fryar Jhon let her bawl on, and, without any further ado, march'd off with the Blanket, Quilt, and both the Sheets, which he brought aboard undiscover'd ; for the Air was dark'ned with the Feathers, as it uses sometimes to be with Snow. He gave them away to the Sailors, then said to Pantagruel, that Beds were much cheaper at that place than in Chinnonois, tho' we have there the famous Geese of Pantile ; for the old Bedlam had ask'd him but Five-pence for a Bed, which in Chinnonois had been worth above twelve Francs.

CHAPTER XVII

How we went For-wards, and how Panurge had like to
have been kill'd

WE put to Sea that very Moment, steering our Course Forwards, and gave Pantagruel a full account of our Adventures, which so deeply struck him with Compassion, that he wrote some Elegies on that Subject, to divert himself during the Voyage. When we were safe in the Port, we took some Refreshment, and took in fresh Water and Wood. The People of the place, who had the Countenance of jolly Fellows, and boon

Companions, were all of them For-ward Folks, bloated and puff'd up with Fat; and we saw some who slash'd and pink'd their Skin, to open a Passage to the Fat, that it might swell out at the slits and gashes which they made; neither more nor less than the shitbreech Fellows in our Country bepink and cut open their Breeches, that the Tafety on the inside may stand out and be puff'd up. They said that what they did was not out of Pride or Ostentation, but because otherwise their Skins would not hold them without much Pain. Having thus slash'd their Skin, they us'd to grow much bigger, like the young trees, on whose Barks the Gardeners make Incisions, that they may grow the better.

Near the Haven there was a Tavern which forwards seem'd very fine and stately; we repair'd thither, and found it fill'd with People of the forward Nation, of all Ages, Sexes, and Conditions; so that we thought some notable Feast or other was getting ready : But we were told that all that Throng were invited to the Bursting of mine Host, which caus'd all his Friends and Relations to hasten thither.

We did not understand that Jargon, and therefore thought that in that Country, by that Bursting, they meant some Merry-meeting or other, as we do in ours, by Betrothing, Wedding, Groaning, Christening, Churching (of Women), Shearing (of Sheep,) Reaping (of Corn, or Harvest home,) and many other Junketing-bouts that end in *ing*. But we soon heard that there was no such matter in hand.

The Master of the House, you must know, had been a Good-fellow in his time, lov'd heartily to wind up his Bottom, to bang the Pitcher, and lick his Dish; he us'd to be a very fair Swallower of Gravy-Soupe, a notable Accomptant in matter of Hours; and his whole Life was one continual Dinner, like mine Host at Rouillac. But now having Farted out much Fat for ten Years together, and water'd the Marigolds with much Wine of his own Burning, according to the Custom of the Country, he was drawing towards his Bursting-hour; for neither the inner thin Kell wherewith the Intrails are cover'd, nor his Skin that had been jagg'd and mangl'd so many Years, were able to hold and enclose his Guts any longer, or hinder them from forcing their way out; like a Wine-Vessel whose Sides fly out. Pray, quoth Panurge, is there no remedy, no help for the poor Man, good People? Why don't you swaddle him round with good tight Girts, or secure his natural Tub with a strong Sorbopple-tree-hoop? Nay, Why don't you

Iron-bind him, if needs be ? This would keep the Man from flying out and bursting. The word was not yet out of his mouth, when we heard something give a loud Report, as if a huge sturdy Oak had been Split in two ; then some of the Neighbours told us, that the Bursting was over, and that the Clap, or Crack, which we heard, was the last Fart : And so there was an end of mine Host.

This made me to call to mind a Saying of the venerable Abbot of Castillers, the very same who never car'd to hump his Maids but when he was *in Pontificalibus*. That pious Person, being much dunn'd, teiz'd, and importun'd by his Relations to resign his Abbey in his old Age, said and profess'd, That he would not Strip till he were ready to go to Bed ; and that the last Fart which his reverend Paternity was to utter, shou'd be the Fart of an Abbot.

CHAPTER XVIII

How our Ships were Stranded, and we were reliev'd by some People that were subject to Queen Whims (" qui tenoient de *la Quinte ")*

WE Weighed and set Sail with a merry Westerly Gale, when about seven Leagues off (twenty two Miles) some gusts or scuds of Wind suddenly arose, and the Wind veering and shifting from Point to Point, was, as they say, like an Old Woman's Breech, at no certainty ; so we first got our Starboard Tacks aboard, and haled off our Lee-Sheets. Then the Gusts increas'd, and by fits blow'd all at once from several Quarters ; yet we neither setled nor braded up close our Sails, but only let fly the Sheets, not to go against the Master of the Ship's Direction ; and thus having let go amain, lest we should spend our Topsails, or the Ship's Quick-side should lie in the Water, and she be overset, we lay by and run adrift, that is, in a Landlopers phrase, we temporis'd it. For he assur'd us, that as these Gusts and Whirlwinds would not do us much good, so they could not do us much harm, considering their Easiness and pleasant Strife, as also the Clearness of the Sky, and Calmness of the Current. So that we were to observe

HIS WHOLE LIFE WAS ONE CONTINUAL DINNER

339

the Philosopher's Rule, Bear, and Forbear; that is, Trim, or go according to the Time.

However, these Whirlwinds and Gusts lasted so long, that we perswaded the Master to let us go and lie at Trie with our Main-Course; that is, to hale the Tack aboard, our Sheet close aft, the Boling set up, and the Helm tied close aboard; so after a stormy Gale of Wind, we broke through the Whirlwind. But 'twas like falling into Scylla to avoid Caribdis, (out of the Frying-Pan into the Fire.) For we had not sail'd a League, e're our Ships were stranded upon some Sands, such as are the Flats of St. Maixant.

All our Company seem'd mightily disturb'd, except Fryar Jhon, who was not a jot daunted, and with sweet Sugar-plum Words comforted now one, and then another, giving them hopes of speedy Assistance from above, and telling them that he had seen Castor at the Main-yard-arm. Oh! that I were but now ashore, cry'd Panurge, that 's all I wish, for my self (at present) and that you who like the Sea so well, had each Man of you Two hundred thousand Crowns; I would fairly let you set up Shop on these Sands, and wou'd get a fat Calf dress'd, and a hundred of Faggots, (*i.e.*, Bottles of Wine) cool'd for you against you come ashore. I freely consent never to mount a Wife, so you but set me ashore, and mount me on a Horse that I may go home; no matter for a Servant, I 'll be contented to serve my self; I 'm never better treated, than when I 'm without a Man. Faith, Old Plautus was in the right on 't, when he said, The more Servants, the more Crosses; for such they are, even supposing they could want what they have all but too much of, a Tongue, that most buisie, dangerous and pernicious Member of Servants; accordingly 'twas for their sakes alone, that the Racks and Tortures for Confession were invented, tho' some foreign Civilians in our time have uncivilly drawn alogical and unreasonable Consquences from it.

That very moment we spy'd a Sail that made towards us: when it was close by us, we soon knew what was the Lading of the Ship, and who was aboard of her. She was full freighted with Drums: I was acquainted with many of the Passengers that came in her, who were most of 'em of good Families; among the rest, Harry Cottiral, an old Tost, who had got a swindging Ass's Touchtripe fasten'd to his Waste, as the good Women's Beads are to their Girdle. In his Left-hand he held an old overgrown greasie foul Cap, such as your Scald-pated Fellows wear, and in the right a huge Cabbage-stump.

As soon as he saw me, he was over-joy'd, and bawl'd out to me, What Cheer ho? How do'st like me now? Behold the true Algamana, (this he said, shewing me the Ass's Tickle-gizard.) This Doctor's Cap is my true Elixir; and this (continu'd he, shaking the Cabbage-stump in his Fist) is Lunaria Major, you old Noddy, I have 'em, old Boy, I have 'em; we 'll make 'em when thou 'rt come back. But pray Father, said I, whence come you? Whither are you bound? What 's your Lading? Have you smelt the Salt Deep? To these four Questions he answered, From Queen Whims; for Touraine; Alchymy; to the very Bottom.

Whom have you got o' board? said I. Said he, Astrologers, Fortune-tellers, Alchymists, Rhimers, Poets, Painters, Projectors, Mathematicians, Watchmakers, Sing-songs, Musitianers, and the Devil and all of others that are subject to Queen Whims. They have very fair legible Patents to shew for 't, as any body may see. Panurge had no sooner heard this, but he was upon the High-Rope, and began to rail at them like mad. What o' Devil d' ye mean, cry'd he, to sit idly here like a pack of loitering Sneakbies, and see us stranded, while you may help us, and tow us off into the Current! A Plague o' your Whims, you can make all things whatsoever they say, so much as good Weather, and little Children, yet won't make haste to fasten some Hawsers and Cables, and get us off. I was just coming to set you a'float, quoth Harry Quotiral; By Trismejistus I 'll clear you in a Trice. With this he caus'd 7532810 huge Drums to be unheaded on one side, and set that open side so that it fac'd the end of our Streamers and Pendants; and having fastened them to good Tacklings, and our Ship's Head to the Stern of theirs, with Cables fasten'd to the Bits abaft the Manger in the Ship's Loof, they tow'd us off ground at one pull; so easily and pleasantly, that you 'd have wonder'd at it, had you been there. For the Dub-o-dub Rattling of the Drums, with the soft Noise of the Gravel, which murmuring disputed us our Way, and the merry Cheers and Huzza's of the Sailors, made an Harmony almost as good as that of the Heavenly Bodies when they roul and are whirl'd round their Spheres; which Rattling of the Celestial Wheels, Plato said he heard some Nights in his Sleep.

We scorn'd to be behind-hand with 'em in Civility, and gratefully gave 'em store of our Saucidges and Chitterlings, with which we fill'd their Drums; and we were just a hoisting two and sixty Hogsheads of Wine out of the Hold, when two huge Whirlpools with great fury made towards their Ship, spouting more Water than is in the River Vienne (Vigenna) from Chinon to Saumur : To make short, all their Drums, all their Sails, their Concerns, and themselves were sows'd, and their very Hoze were water'd by the Collar.

Panurge was so overjoy'd seeing this, and laugh'd so heartily, that he was forc'd to hold his Sides, and it set him into a Fit of the Cholic for two hours and more. I had a mind, quoth he, to make the Dogs drink, and those honest Whirlpools e'gad have sav'd me that Labour and that Cost. There 's Sauce for them ; αριστον μὲν ὕδωρ, Water 's good, saith a Poet, let 'em Pindarise upon 't ; they never car'd for fresh Water, but to wash their Hands or their Glasses. This good Salt Water will stand 'em in good stead for want of Sal Armoniac and Nitre in Geber's Kitchen.

We could not hold any further Discourse with 'em ; for the former Whirlwind hinder'd our Ship from feeling the Helm. The Pilot advis'd us henceforwards to let her run adrift and follow the Stream, not busying our selves with any thing, but making much of our Carcasses. For, our only way to arrive safe at the Queendom of Whims, was to trust to the Whirlwind, and be led by the Current.

CHAPTER XIX

How we arriv'd at the Queendom of Whims, or Enthelechy

WE did as he directed for about twelve hours, and on the third day the Sky seem'd to us somewhat clearer, and we happily arriv'd at the Port of Mateotechny, not far distant from Queen-Whims, *alias* the Quintessence.

We met full-but on the Key a great number of Guards and other Military Men that garrison'd the Arsenal ; and we were somewhat frighted at first, because they made us all lay down our Arms, and in a haughty manner ask'd us whence we came ?

Cousin, quoth Panurge to him that ask'd the Question, we are of Touraine, and come from France, being ambitious of paying our Respects to the Lady Quintessence, and visit this famous Realm of Enthelechy.

What do you say ? cry'd they : Do you call it Enthelechy or Endelechy ? Truly, truly, sweet Cousins, quoth Panurge, we are a silly sort of grout-headed Lobcocks, an 't please you ; be so kind as to forgive us, if we chance to knock Words out of joint ; as for any thing else, we are downright honest Fellows, and true Hearts.

We have not ask'd you this Question without a Cause, said they ; for a great number of others who have pass'd this Way from your Country of Touraine, seem'd as meer joltheaded Doddipoles as ever were scor'd o'er the Coxcomb, yet spoke as correct as other Folks. But there has been here from other Countries a pack of I know not overweening, self-conceited Prigs, as moody as so many Mules, and as stout as any Scotch Lairds, and nothing would serve these, forsooth, but they must wilfully wrangle and stand out against us at their coming : And much they got by it, after all : Troth we e'en fitted them, and claw'd 'em off with a vengeance, for all they look'd so big and so grum. Pray tell me, Do's your Time lie so heavy upon you in your World, that you don't know how to bestow it better than in thus impudently talking, disputing and writing of our Sovereign Lady ? There was much need that your Tully, the Consul, should go and leave the Care of his Common-wealth, to busie himself idly about her ; and after him, your Diogenes Laertius the Biographer, and your Theodorus Gaza the Philosopher, and your Argiropilus the Emperor, and your Bessario the Cardinal, and your Politian the Pedant, and your Budeus the Judge, and your Lascaris the Ambassador, and the Devil and all of those you call Lovers of Wisdom ; whose Num-ber, it seems, was not thought great enough already, but lately your Scaliger, Brigot, Chambrier, Francis Fleury, and I can't tell how many such other junior sneaking Fly-blows must take upon 'em to encrease it.

A Squincy gripe the Cods-headed Changelings at the Swallow, and eke at the Cover-weesel ; we shall make 'em ;—But the Dewse take 'em ; (they flatter the Devil here, and smoothifie his Name, quoth Panurge, between his Teeth :) You don't come here, continu'd the Captain, to uphold 'em in their Folly, you have no Commission from them to this Effect ; well then, we 'll talk no more on 't.

Aristotle, that first of Men, and peerless Pattern of all Philosophy, was our Sovereign Lady's Godfather ; and wisely and properly gave her the Name of Entelechy. Her true Name then is Entelechy ; and may he be in Tail beshit, and entail a

Shit-a-bed Faculty, and nothing else on his Family, who dares call her by any other Name; for whoever he is, he do's her wrong, and is a very impudent Person. You are heartily welcome, Gentlemen; with this they coll'd and clipt us about the Neck, which was no small Comfort to us, I 'll assure you.

Panurge then whisper'd me; Fellow-traveller, quoth he, hast thou not been somewhat afraid this Bout? A little, said I. To tell you the truth of 't, quoth he, never were the Eph-raimites in a greater Fear and Quandary when the Gileadites kill'd and drowned them for saying Sibboleth, instead of Shib-boleth; And among Friends, let me tell you, that perhaps there is not a Man in the whole Country of Beauce, but might easily have stopt my Bunghole with a Cart-load of Hay.

The Captain afterwards took us to the Queen's Palace, leading us silently with great Formality. Pantagruel would have said something to him; but the other, not being able to come up to his heighth, wish'd for a Ladder, or a very long Pair of Stilts; then said, Patience, if it were our Sovereign Lady's Will, we 'd be as tall as you; well, we shall, when she pleases.

In the first Galleries we saw great numbers of Sick Persons, differently plac'd according to their Maladies. The Leprous were a-part; those that were Poison'd, on one side; those that had the Plague on another: Those that had the Pox, in the first Rank; and the rest accordingly.

W.H.R.

CHAPTER XX

How the Quintessence Cur'd the Sick with a Song

THE Captain show'd us the Queen, attended with her Ladies and Gentlemen, in the second Gallery. She look'd young, tho' she was at least Eighteen hundred Years old; and was handsom, slender, and as fine as a Queen, that is, as hands could make her. He then said to us, 'Tis not yet a fit time to speak to the Queen, be you but mindful of her doings in the mean while.

You have Kings in your World, that fantastically pretend to cure some certain Diseases; as for Example, Scrophube or Wens, Swell'd Throats, nicknam'd the King's Evil, and Quartan Agues, only with a Touch: Now our Queen cures all manner of Diseases, without so much as touching the Sick, but barely with a Song, according to the nature of the Distemper; he then shew'd us a Set of Organs, and said, that when it was touch'd by her, those miraculous Cures were perform'd. The Organ was indeed the strangest that ever Eyes beheld; for the Pipes were of Cassia Fistula in the Cod; the Top and Cornish of Guayacum; the Bellows of Rhubarb; the Pedals of Turbith; and the Clavier or Keys of Scammony.

While we were examining this wonderful new make of an Organ, the Leprous were brought in by her Abstractors, Spodizators, Masticators, Pregustics, Tabachins, Chachanins, Neemanins, Rabrebans, Nercins, Rozuins, Nebidins, Tearins, Sagamions, Peratons, Chasmins, Sarins, Soteins, Aboth, Enilins, Archasdarpenins, Mebins, Chabourins, and other Officers, for whom I want Names; so she plaid 'em I don't know what sort of a Tune or Song, and they were all immediately Cur'd.

Then those who were Poison'd were had in; and she had no sooner given them a Song, but they began to find a Use for their Legs, and up they got. Then came on the Deaf, the Blind, and the Dumb, and they too were restor'd to their lost Senses with the same Remedy; which did so strangely amaze us (and not without reason, I think) that down we fell on our Faces, remaining prostrate like Men ravish'd in Extasy, and were not able to utter one word, thro' the excess of our Admiration, till she came, and having touch'd Pantagruel with a fine fragrant Nosegay of White Roses which she held in her Hand,

345

thus made us recover our Senses and get up. Then she made us the following Speech in Byssin Words, such as Parisatis desir'd shou'd be spoken to her Son Cyrus, or at least of Crimson Alamode.

The Probity that scintillizes in the Superficies of your Persons, informs my ratiocinating Faculty, in a most stupendous manner, of the radiant Virtues, latent within the precious Caskets and Ventricles of your Minds. For, contemplating the mellifluous Suavity of your thrice discreet Reverences, 'tis impossible not to be perswaded with Facility, that neither your Affections nor your Intellects are vitiated with any Defect, or Privation of liberal and exalted Sciences; far from it, all must judge that in you are lodg'd a Cornucopia, an Encyclopedia, an unmeasurable Profundity of Knowledge in the most peregrine and sublime Disciples; so frequently the Admiration, and so rarely the Concomitants of the imperite Vulgar. This gently compels me, who in preceding Times indefatigably kept my private Affections absolutely subjugated, to condescend to make my Application to you in the trivial Phrase of the Plebeian World; and assure you, that you are well, most well, most heartily well, more than most heartily welcome.

I have no hand at making of Speeches, quoth Panurge to me privately; Prithee, Man, make answer to her for us if thou canst; this would not work with me, however, neither did Pantagruel return a word; so that Queen Whims, or Queen Quintessence (which you please) perceiving that we stood as mute as Fishes, said: Your Taciturnity speaks you not only Disciples of Pythagoras, from whom the venerable Antiquity of my Progenitors in successive Propagation was eman'd and derives its Original; but also discovers, that, through the Revolution of many Retrograde Moons, you have in Egypt press'd the Extremities of your Fingers with the hard Tenants of your Mouths, and scalptiz'd your Heads with frequent Applications of your Ungicules. In the School of Pythagoras, Taciturnity was the Symbol of abstracted and superlative Knowledge; and the silence of the Egyptians was agnited as an expressive manner of Divine Adoration; This caus'd the Pontiffs of Hieropolis to Sacrifice to the great Deity in silence, impercussively, without any vociferous or obstreporous Sound. My design is not to enter into a Privation of Gratitude towards you; but by a vivacious formality, tho' matter were to abstract it self from me, excentricate to you my Cogitations.

Having spoken this, she only said to her Officers, Tabachins a Panacea; and strait they desir'd us not to take it amiss, if the Queen did not invite us to dine with her; for she never eat any thing at Dinner but some Categories, Jecabots, Emnins, Dimions, Abstractions, Harborins, Chelimins, second Intentions, Carodosh, Antitheses, Metempsycoses, transcendent Prolepsies, and such other light Food.

Then they took us into a little Closet, lin'd through with Alarums, where we were treated God knows how. 'Tis said, that Jupiter writes whatever is transacted in the World, on the Diphthera or Skin of the Amalthæan Goat that suckled him in Crete, which Pelt serv'd him instead of a Shield against the Titans, whence he was Nicknam'd Egiochos. Now, as I hate to drink Water, Brother Topers, I protest, it would be impossible to make eighteen Goatskins hold the Description of all the good Meat they brought before us; tho' it were written in Characters as small as those in which were penn'd Homer's *Iliads*, which Tully tells us he saw enclos'd in a Nut-shell.

For my part, had I one hundred Mouths, as many Tongues, a Voice of Iron, a Heart of Oak, and Lungs of Leather, together with the mellifluous Abundance of Plato; yet I could never give you a full Account of a Third part of a second of the whole.

Pantagruel was telling me, that he believ'd the Queen had given the Symbolic Word us'd among her Subjects, to denote Sovereign good Cheer, when she said to her Tabachins, A Panacea; just as Lucullus us'd to say, in Apollo, when he design'd to give his Friends a singular Treat, tho' sometimes they took him unawares, as among the rest, Cicero and Hortensius sometimes us'd to do.

CHAPTER XXI

How the Queen pass'd her Time after Dinner

WHEN we had din'd, a Chachanin led us into the Queen's Hall, and there we saw how, after Dinner, with the Ladies and Princes of her Court, she used to sift, searse, boult, range, and pass away Time, with a fine large white and blue Silk Sieve.

We also perceiv'd how they reviv'd Ancient Sports, diverting themselves together at

1. Cordax.	8. Calibrismes.
2. Emmelia.	9. Molossia.
3. Sicinnis.	10. Cernophorum.
4. Iambics.	11. Monodia.
5. Persica.	12. Terminalia.
6. Phrygia.	13. Floralia.
7. Thracia.	14. Pyrrhice.

And a thousand other Dances.

Afterwards she gave Orders that they should show us the Apartments and Curiosities in her Palace; accordingly we saw there such new strange and wonderful things, that I am still ravish'd in Admiration every time I think of 't. However, nothing surpriz'd us more than what was done by the Gentlemen of her Household, Abstractors, Pazarons, Nebidins, Spodizators, and others, who freely and without the least dissembling, told us, That the Queen their Mistress did all impossible things, and cur'd Men of incurable Diseases; and they, her Officers, us'd to do the rest.

I saw there a young Parazon cure many of the new Consumption, I mean the Pox, tho' they were never so pepper'd; had it been the rankest Roan-Ague (Anglicè, the Covent-garden Gout) 'twas all one to him, touching only their Denti-form Vertebra thrice with a piece of a Wooden-shooe, he made them as wholesome as so many Sucking-Pigs.

Another did thoroughly cure Folks of Dropsies, Tympanies, Ascites, and Hyposarcidies, striking them on the Belly nine times with a Tenedian Satchel, without any Solution of the Continuum.

Another cured all manner of Fevers and Agues, on the spot, only with hanging a Fox-tail on the left-side of the Patient's Girdle.

One remov'd the Tooth-ach only with washing the Root of the aking Tooth with Elder-Vinegar, and letting it dry half an Hour in the Sun.

Another, the Gout, whether hot or cold, natural or accidental, barely making the Gouty-Person shut his Mouth, and open his Eyes.

I saw another ease nine good Gentlemen of St. Francis's Distemper, in a very short space of time, having clapt a Rope

THE OFFICER HAD HIS HANDS FULL

349

about their Necks, at the end of which hang'd a Box with ten thousand Gold Crowns in 't.

One with a wonderful Engine, throw'd the Houses out at the Windows, by which means they were purg'd of all Pestilential Air.

Another cur'd of all the three kinds of Hectics, the Tabid, Atrophes, and Emaciated, without bathing, Tabian Milk, Dropax, *alias* Depilatory, or other such Medicaments; Only turning the Consumptive for three Months into Monks; and he assur'd me, that if they did not grow fat and plump in a Monastick way of living, they never would be fatten'd in this World, either by Nature, or by Art.

I saw another surrounded with a Croud of two sorts of Women; some were young, quaint, clever, neat, pretty, juicy, tight, brisk, buxom, proper, kind-hearted, and as right as my Leg, to any Man's thinking. The rest were old, weather-beaten, over-ridden, toothless, blear-ey'd, tough, wrinkled, shrivell'd, tawny, mouldy, ptysicky, decrepit Hags, Beldams, and walking Carcasses. We were told that his Office was to cast anew those She-pieces of Antiquity; and make them such as the pretty Creatures whom we saw, who had been made young again that Day, recovering at once the Beauty, Shape, Size, and Disposition, which they enjoy'd at Sixteen, except their Heels that were now much shorter than in their former Youth.

This made them yet more apt to fall backwards when ever any Man happen'd to touch 'em, than they had been before. As for their Counterparts, the old Mother-scratch-tobies, they most devoutly waited for the blessed Hour, when the Batch that was in the Oven was to be drawn, that they might have their turns, and in a mighty haste they were pulling and hawling the Man like mad, telling him, that 'tis the most grievous and intolerable thing in Nature, for the Tail to be o' fire, and the Head to scare away those who should quench it.

The Officer had his Hands full, never wanting Patients; neither did his Place bring him in little, you may swear. Pantagruel ask'd him, whether he could also make old Men young again. He said, he could not. But the way to make them new Men, was to get 'em to cohabit with a new-cast Female; for thus they caught that fifth kind of Crinckams, which some call *Pellade*; in Greek, 'Οφίασις; that makes them cast off their old Hair and Skin, just as the Serpents do; and thus their Youth is renew'd like the Arabian Phœnix's. This is the true Fountain of Youth, for there the Old and Decrepit become Young, Active and Lusty.

Just so, as Euripides tells us, Iolaus was transmogrifi'd; and thus Phaon, for whom kind-hearted Sappho run wild, grew young again for Venus's use; so Tithon by Aurora's means; so Æson by Medea, and Jason also, who, if you'll believe Pherecides, and Simonides, was new-vamped and died by that Witch; and so were the Nurses of Jolly Bacchus, and their Husbands, as Eschinus relates.

CHAPTER XXII

How Queen Whim's Officers were employ'd; and how the said Lady retained us among her Abstractors

I THEN saw a great number of the Queen's Officers, who made Black-a-moors white, as fast as Hops, just rubbing their Bellies with the Bottom of a Pannier.

Others with three Couples of Foxes in one Yoke, plow'd a Sandy-shoar, and did not lose their Seed.

Others wash'd burnt Tiles, and made them lose their Colour.

Others extracted Water out of Pumice-Stones, braying them a good while in a Mortar, and chang'd their substance.

Others sheer'd Asses, and thus got Long-fleece-wooll.

Others gather'd Barberries and Figs off of Thistles.

Others stroak'd He-goats by the Dugs, and sav'd their Milk in a Sieve; and much they got by it.

Others taught Cows to dance, and did not lose their fidling.

Others pitch'd Nets to catch the Wind, and took Cock-lobsters in them.

I saw a young Spodizator, who very artificially got Farts out of a dead Ass, and sold 'em for five Pence an Ell.

Another did putrifie Beetles. O the dainty Food!

Poor Panurge fairly casted up his Accompts, and gave up his Half-penny, (*i.e.* vomited) seeing an Archasdarpenin, who laid a huge plenty of Chamberlee to putrifie in Horsedung, mish-mash'd with abundance of Christian Sir Reverence; pugh, fie upon him, nasty Dog. However, he told us, that with this sacred Distillation, he water'd Kings and Princes, and made their sweet Lives a Fathom or two the longer.

Others built Churches to jump over the Steeples.

Others set Carts before the Horses, and began to flay Eels at the Tail; neither did those Eels cry before they were hurt, like those of Melun.

Others out of nothing made great things, and made great things return to nothing.

Others cut Fire into Stakes with a Knife, and drew Water with a Fish-net.

Others made Chalk of Cheese, and Honey of a Dog's T—d.

We saw a knot of others, about a Bakers dozen in Number, tippling under an Arbour. They top'd out of jolly bottomless Cups, four sorts of cool, sparkling, pure delicious Vine-tree Syrup, which went down like Mother's Milk; and Healths and Bumpers flew about like Lightning. We were told, that these true Philosophers were fairly multiplying the Stars by drinking till the Seven were Fourteen, as brawny Hercules did with Atlas.

Others made a Virtue of Necessity, and the best of a bad Market, which seem'd to me a very good piece of Work.

Others made Alchymy (*i.e.*, Sir Reverence) with their Teeth, and clapping their Hind-retort to the Recipient, made scurvy Faces, and then squeez'd.

Others in a large Grass-plat, exactly measur'd how far the Fleas could go at a Hop, a Step, and Jump; and told us, that this was exceeding useful for the Ruling of Kingdoms, the Conduct of Armies, and the Administration of Commonwealths. And that Socrates, who first had got Philosophy out of Heaven, and from idle and trifling, made it profitable and of moment, us'd to spend half his Philosophizing time in measuring the leaps of Fleas, as Aristophanes, the Quintessential, affirms.

I saw two Gibroins by themselves, keeping Watch on the top of a Tower; and we were told, they guarded the Moon from the Wolves.

In a blind Corner, I met four more very hot at it, and ready to go to Loggerheads. I ask'd what was the cause of the stir and ado, the mighty coil and pother they made? And I heard that for four live-long-days, those over-wise Roisters had been at it ding-dong, disputing on three high, more than Metaphysical Propositions, promising themselves Mountains of Gold by solving them; The first was concerning a He-Asse's Shadow: The second, of the Smoke of a Lanthorn: And the third, of Goat's Hair, whether it were Wool or no? We heard that they did not think it a bit strange, that two Contradictions in Mode,

Form, Figure, and Time, should be true. Tho' I 'll warrant the Sophists of Paris had rather be unchrist'ned than own so much.

While we were admiring all those Men's wonderful doings, the Evening Star already twinkling ; the Queen (God bless her) appear'd attended with her Court, and again amaz'd and dazled us. She perceiv'd it, and said to us ;

What occasions the Aberrations of humane Cogitations through the perplexing Labyrinths and Abysses of Admiration, is not the Source of the Effects, which sagacious Mortals visibly experience to be the consequential Result of Natural Causes ; 'Tis the Novelty of the Experiment, which makes Impressions on their conceptive, cogitative Faculties, that do not previse the facility of the Operation adequately, with a subact and sedate Intellection, associated with diligent and congruous Study. Consequently, let all manner of Perturbation abdicate the Ventricles of your Brains, if any one has invaded them while you were contemplating what is transacted by my Domestick Ministers. Be Spectators and Auditors of every particular Phænomenon, and every individual Proposition, within the extent of my Mansion, satiate your selves with all that can fall here under the Consideration of your Visual or Auscultating Powers, and thus emancipate your selves from the Servitude of Crassous Ignorance. And that you may be induc'd to apprehend how sincerely I desire this, in consideration of the studious Cupidity, that so demonstratively emicates at your external Organs, from this present Particle of Time, I retain you as my Abstractors. Geber, my Principal Talachin, shall Register and Initiate you at your Departing. We humbly thank'd her Queenship, without saying a word, accepting of the Noble Office she conferr'd on us.

CHAPTER XXIII

How the Queen was serv'd at Dinner, and of her way of eating

QUEEN WHIMS after this, said to her Gentlemen, The Orifice of the Ventricule, that Ordinary Embassador for the Alimentation of all Members, whether Superior or Inferior, importunes us to restore by the Apposition of Idoneous Sustenance, what was dissipated by the internal Calidity's Action on the Radical Humidity. Therefore Spodizators, Gesinins, Memains, and Arazons, be not culpable of Dilatory Protractions in the Apposition of every re-roborating Species, but rather let 'em pullulate and super-abound on the Tables. As for you, Nobilissim Præsustators, and my Gentilissim Masticators, your frequently experimented Industry internected with perdiligent Sedulity, and sedulous Perdiligence, continually adjuvates you to perficiate all things in so expedititious a manner, that there is no necessity of exciting in you a Cupidity to consummate them. Therefore I can only suggest to you still to operate, as you are assuefacted indefatigably to operate.

Having made this fine Speech, she retir'd for a while with part of her Women, and we were told, that 'twas to bathe, as the Ancients did, more commonly than we use now-a-days to wash our Hands before we eat. The Tables were soon plac'd, the Cloth spread, and then the Queen sate down; she eat nothing but Cœlestial Ambrosia, and drank nothing but Divine Nectar: As for the Lords and Ladies that were there, they as well as we, far'd on as rare, costly, and dainty Dishes, as ever Apicius wot or dream'd of in his Life.

When we were as round as Hoops, and as full as Eggs, with stuffing the Gut, an *Olla Podrida* was before us, to force Hunger to come to terms with us, in case it had not granted us a Truce; and such a huge vast thing it was, that the Plate which Pythius Althius gave King Darius, would hardly have cover'd it. The Olla consisted of several sorts of Pottages, Salads, Fricasees, Saugrenees, Cabirotadoes, Rost and Boil'd-meat, Carbonadoes, swindging pieces of Powder'd-beef, good old Hams, dainty Somates, Cakes, Tarts, a world of Curds after the Morisk-way, fresh Cheese, Gellies, and Fruits of all sorts. All this seem'd to me good and dainty; however the sight of it made me sigh; for alas, I could not taste a bit on 't; so full I had fill'd my Puddings before, and a Belliful 's a Belliful you know. Yet I must tell you what I saw, that seem'd to me odd enough o' Conscience; 'twas some Pasties in Paste; and what should those Pasties in Paste be, d' ye think, but Pasties in Pots? At the bottom I perceiv'd store of Dice, Cards, Tarots, Luettes, Chess-men, and Chequers, besides full Bowles of Gold Crowns, for those who had a mind to have a Game or two, and try their Chance. Under this, I saw a Jolly Company of Mules in stately Trappings, with Velvet foot-cloths, and a Troop of

Ambling Nags, some for Men, and some for Women; besides, I don't know how many Litters all lin'd with Velvet, and some Coaches of Ferrara-make; all this for those who had a mind to take the Air.

This did not seem strange to me; but if anything did, 'twas certainly the Queen's way of Eating; and truly 'twas very new, and very odd, for she chew'd nothing, the good Lady; not but that she had good sound Teeth, and her Meat requir'd to be masticated; but such was her Highness's Custom. When her Præustators had tasted the Meat, her Masticators took it and chew'd it most nobly; for their dainty Chops and Gullets were lin'd through with Crimson Sattin with little Welts, and Gold Purls, and their Teeth were of delicate white Ivory; thus, when they had chew'd the Meat ready for her Highness's Maw, they pour'd it down her Throat through a Funnel of fine Gold, and so on to her Craw. For that reason, they told us, she never visited a Close-stool but by Proxy.

CHAPTER XXIV

How there was a Ball in the manner of a Tournament, at which Queen Whims was present

AFTER Supper, there was a Ball in the form of a Tilt or Tournament, not only worth seeing, but also never to be forgotten. First, the Floor of the Hall was cover'd with a large piece of Velveted white and yellow chequer'd Tapistry, each Chequer exactly square, and three full spans in breadth.

Then thirty two young Persons came into the Hall; sixteen of them array'd in Cloth of Gold; and of these, eight were young Nymphs, such as the Ancients describ'd Diana's Attendants; the other eight were, a King, a Queen, two Wardens of the Castle, two Knights, and two Archers. Those of the other Band were clad in Cloth of Silver.

They posted themselves on the Tap'stry in the following manner: The Kings on the last Line on the fourth Square, so that the Golden King was on a White Square, the Silver'd King on a Yellow Square, and each Queen by her King; the Golden Queen on a Yellow Square, and the Silver'd Queen on a

White one, and on each side stood the Archers to guard their
Kings and Queens; by the Archers the Knights, and the
Wardens by them. In the next Row before 'em stood the
eight Nymphs; and between the two Bands of Nymphs, four
Rows of Squares stood empty.

Each Band had its Musicians, eight on each side dress'd in
its Livery; the one with Orange-colour'd Damask, the other
with White, and all play'd on different Instruments most
melodiously and harmoniously, still varying in Time and
Measure as the Figure of the Dance requir'd. This seem'd
to me an admirable thing, considering the numerous diversity
of Steps, Back-steps, Bounds, Rebounds, Jerts, Paces, Leaps,
Skips, Turns, *Coupés*, Hops, Leadings, Risings, Meetings,
Flights, Embuscado's, Moves, and Removes.

I was also at a loss, when I strove to comprehend how the
Dancers could so suddenly know what every different Note
meant; for they no sooner heard this or that Sound, but they
plac'd themselves in the Place which was denoted by the
Musick, tho' their Motions were all different. For the
Nymphs that stood in the first File, as if they design'd to
begin the Fight, march'd straight forwards to their Enemies
from Square to Square, unless it were the first step, at which
they were free to move over two steps at once. They alone
never fall back, (which is not very natural to other Nymphs)
and if any one of them is so lucky as to advance to the opposite
King's Row, she is immediately crown'd Queen of her King,
and after that, moves with the same State, and in the same
manner as the Queen; but till that happens, they never
strike their Enemies but forwards, and obliquely in a diagonal
Line. However, they make it not their chief business to
take their Foes; for if they did, they would leave their
Queen expos'd to the adverse Parties, who then might take
her.

The Kings move and take their Enemies on all sides square-
ways, and only step from a white Square into a yellow one,
and *vice versa*, except at their first step the Rank should want
other Officers than the Wardens; for then they can set 'em
in their place, and retire by him.

The Queens take a greater Liberty than any of the rest,
for they move backwards and forwards all manner of ways in
a straight Line, as far as they please, provided the place be
not fill'd with one of her own Party, and diagonally also keeping
to the Colour on which she stands.

The Archers move backwards or forwards, far and near, never changing the Colour on which they stand.

The Knights move, and take in a lineal manner, stepping over one Square, tho' a Friend or a Foe stand upon it, posting themselves on the second Square to the right or left, from one Colour to another, which is very unwelcome to the adverse Party, and ought to be carefully observ'd, for they take at unawares.

The Wardens move, and take to the right or left, before or behind them, like the Kings, and can advance as far as they find Places empty; which liberty the Kings take not.

The Laws which both Sides observe, is at the end of the Fight, to besiege and enclose the King of either Party, so that he may not be able to move; and being reduc'd to that extremity, the Battle is over, and he loses the Day.

Now to avoid this, there is none of either Sex of each Party, but is willing to sacrifice his or her Life, and they begin to take one another on all sides in time, as soon as the Musick strikes up. When any one takes a Prisoner, he makes his Honours, and striking him gently in the hand, puts him out of the Field of Combat, and encamps where he stood.

If one of the Kings chance to stand where he might be taken, it is not lawful for any of his Adversaries that had discover'd him, to lay hold on him; far from it, they are strictly enjoin'd humbly to pay him their Respects, and give him notice, saying, God preserve you, Sir; that his Officers may relieve and cover him; or he may remove, if unhappily he could not be reliev'd. However, he is not to be taken, but greeted with a Good-morrow, the others bending the Knee; and thus the Tournament uses to end.

CHAPTER XXV

How the Thirty two Persons at the Ball fought

THE two Companies having taken their Stations, the Musick struck up, and with a Martial-sound, which had something of horrid in it like a Point of War, rouz'd and allarm'd both Parties, who now began to shiver, and then soon were warm'd

357

with warlike Rage; and having got in a readiness to fight desperately, impatient of delay, stood waiting for the Charge.

Then the Musick of the Silver'd Band ceas'd playing, and the Instruments of the Golden-side alone were heard, which denoted that the Golden-Party attack'd. Accordingly a new Movement was played for the Onset, and we saw the Nymph, who stood before the Queen, turn to the left towards her King, as it were to ask leave to fight; and thus saluting her Company at the same time, she mov'd two Squares forwards, and saluted the adverse Party.

Now the Musick of the Golden Brigade ceas'd playing, and their Antagonists began again. I ought to have told you, That the Nymph, who began by saluting her Company, had by that Formality also given them to understand that they were to fall on. She was saluted by them in the same manner with a full turn to the left, except the Queen, who went aside towards her King to the right; and the same manner of Salutation was observ'd on both sides during the whole Ball.

The Silver'd Nymph that stood before her Queen likewise mov'd, as soon as the Musick of her Party sounded a Charge; her Salutations, and those of her side, were to the right, and her Queen's to the left. She mov'd into the second Square forwards, and saluted her Antagonists, facing the first Golden Nymph, so that there was not any distance between them, and you would have thought they two had been going to fight, but they only strike side-ways.

Their Comrades, whether Silver'd or Golden, follow'd 'em in an intercalary Figure, and seem'd to skirmish awhile, till the Golden Nymph, who had first enter'd the List, striking a Silver'd Nymph in the hand on the right, put her out of the Field, and set her self in her place. But soon the Musick playing a new Measure, she was struck by a Silver'd Archer, who after that, was oblig'd himself to retire. A Silver'd Knight then sally'd out, and the Golden Queen posted her self before her King.

Then the Silver'd King, dreading the Golden Queen's Fury, remov'd to the right, to the Place where his Warden stood, which seem'd to him strong and well guarded.

The two Knights on the left, whether Golden or Silver'd, march'd up, and on either side took up many Nymphs, who could not retreat, principally the Golden Knight, who made this his whole business; But the Silver'd Knight had greater Designs, dissembling all along, and even sometimes not taking a Nymph when he could have done it, still moving on till he was come up to the main Body of his Enemies, in such a manner, that he saluted their King with a, God save you, Sir.

The whole Golden Brigade quak'd for fear and anger, those words giving notice of their King's danger; not but that they could soon relieve him, but because their King being thus saluted, they were to lose their Warden on the Right-wing, without any hopes of a recovery. Then the Golden King retir'd to the Left, and the Silver'd Knight took the Golden Warden, which was a mighty loss to that Party. However, they resolv'd to be reveng'd, and surrounded the Knight that he might not escape; he try'd to get off, behaving himself with a great deal of gallantry, and his Friends did what they cou'd to save him, but at last he fell into the Golden Queen's hands, and was carried off.

Her forces not yet satisfied, having lost one of their best Men, with more Fury than Conduct mov'd about, and did much mischief among their Enemies. The Silver'd Party warily dissembled, watching their opportunity to be even with them, and presented one of their Nymphs to the Golden Queen, having laid an Ambuscado; so that the Nymph being taken, a Golden Archer had like to have seiz'd the Silver'd Queen. Then the Golden Knight undertakes to take the Silver'd King and Queen, and says, Good-morrow. The Silver'd Archer salutes them, and was taken by a Golden Nymph, and she her self by a Silver'd one.

The Fight was obstinate and sharp: The Wardens left their Posts, and advanc'd to relieve their Friends. The Battle was doubtful, and Victory hover'd over both Armies. Now the Silver Host charge and break through their Enemy's Ranks, as far as the Golden King's Tent, and now they are beaten back. The Golden Queen distinguishes her self from the rest by her mighty atchievements, still more than by her Garb and Dignity; for at once she takes an Archer, and going side-ways, seizes a Silver'd Warden. Which thing the Silver'd Queen perceiving, she came forwards, and rushing on with equal Bravery, takes the last Golden Warden, and some Nymphs. The two Queens fought a long while hand to hand; now striving to take each other by Surprize, then to save themselves, and sometimes to guard their Kings. Finally, the Golden Queen took the Silver'd Queen; but presently after, she her self was taken by the Silver'd Archer.

Then the Silver'd King had only three Nymphs, an Archer

and a Warden left; and the Golden, only three Nymphs and the right Knight, which made them fight more slowly and warily than before. The two Kings seem'd to mourn for the Loss of their loving Queens, and only studied and endeavour'd to get new ones out of all their Nymphs, to be rais'd to that Dignity, and thus be married to them. This made them excite those brave Nymphs to strive to reach the farthest Rank, where stood the King of the contrary Party, promising them certainly to have them Crown'd, if they could do this. The Golden Nymphs were before-hand with the others, and out of their number was created a Queen, who was dress'd in Royal Robes, and had a Crown set on her Head. You need not doubt, the Silver'd Nymphs made also what haste they could to be Queens; one of them was within a step of the Coronation Place; but there the Golden Knight lay ready to intercept her, so that she could go no farther.

The new Golden Queen resolv'd to shew her self valiant and worthy of her Advancement to the Crown, atchiev'd great Feats of Arms. But in the mean time, the Silver'd Warden takes the Golden Knight who guarded the Camp; and thus there was a new Silver'd Queen, who, like the other, strove to excel in Heroic Deeds at the beginning of her Reign. Thus the Fight grew hotter than before. A thousand Stratagems, Charges, Rallyings, Retreats and Attacks were try'd on both sides; till at last the Silver'd Queen, having by stealth advanc'd as far as the Golden King's Tent, cry'd, God save you, Sir. Now none but his new Queen could relieve him; so she bravely came and expos'd her self to the utmost Extremity to deliver him out of it. Then the Silver'd Warden with his Queen, reduc'd the Golden King to such a stress, that to save himself, he was forc'd to lose his Queen; but the Golden King took him at last. However, the rest of the Golden Party were soon taken; and that King being left alone, the Silver'd Party made him a low Bow, crying, Good-morrow, Sir; which denoted that the Silver'd King had got the Day.

This being heard, the Musick of both Parties loudly proclaim'd the Victory. And thus the first Battle ended, to the unspeakable Joy of all the Spectators.

After this the two Brigades took their former Stations, and began to tilt a second time, much as they had done before; only the Musick play'd somewhat faster than at the first Battle, and the Motions were altogether different. I saw the Golden Queen sally out one of the first, with an Archer and a

Knight, as it were angry at the former Defeat, and she had lik'd to have fallen upon the Silver'd King in his Tent among his Officers; but having been baulk'd in her Attempt, she skirmish'd briskly, and overthrew so many Silver'd Nymphs and Officers, that it was a most amazing Sight. You wou'd have sworn she had been another Penthesilea; for she behav'd her self with as much Bravery as that Amazonian Queen did at Troy.

But this Havock did not last long; for the Silver'd Party, exasperated by their Loss, resolv'd to perish, or stop her Progress; and having posted an Archer in Ambuscado on a distant Angle, together with a Knight-Errant, her Highness fell into their hands, and was carried out of the Field. The rest were soon routed, after the taking of their Queen, who without doubt, from that time resolv'd to be more wary, and keep near her King, without venturing so far amidst her Enemies, unless with more Forces to defend her. Thus the Silver'd Brigade once more got the Victory.

This did not dishearten or deject the Golden Party; far from it, they soon appear'd again in the Field to face their Enemies; and being posted as before, both the Armies seem'd more resolute and chearful than ever. Now the martial Consort began, and the Music was above a Hemiole the quicker, according to the Warlike Phrygian Mode, such as was invented by Marsias.

Then our Combatants began to wheel about and charge with such a swiftness, that in an instant they made four moves, besides the usual Salutation. So that they were continually in Action, flying, hovering, jumping, vaulting, tumbling, curveting, with petauristical Turns and Motions, and often intermingled.

Seeing them turn about on one Foot after they had made their Honours, we compar'd them to your Tops or Gigs, such as Boys use to whip about, making them turn round so swiftly, that they Sleep, as they call it, and Motion cannot be perceiv'd, but resembles Rest its contrary: So that if you make a Point or Mark on some part of one of those Gigs, 'twill be perceiv'd not as a Point, but as a continual Line, in a most divine manner, as Cusanus has wisely observ'd.

While they were thus warmly engag'd, we heard continually the Claps and Episemasies which those of the two Bands reiterated at the taking of their Enemies; and this, join'd to the variety of their Motions and Musick, would have forc'd Smiles out of the most severe Cato, the never-laughing Crassus, the Athenian Man-hater Timon ; nay, even the whining Heraclytus, tho' he abhorr'd Laughing, the Action that's most peculiar to Man. For who could have forborn ? seeing those young Warriors, with their Nymphs and Queens, so briskly and gracefully advance, retire, jump, leap, skip, spring, fly, vault, caper, move to the Right, to the Left, every way still in Time, so swiftly, and yet so dexterously, that they never touch'd one another but methodically.

As the number of the Combatants lessen'd, the Pleasure of the Spectators encreas'd ; for the Stratagems and Motions of the remaining Forces were more singular. I shall only add, that this pleasing Entertainment charm'd us to such a degree, that our Minds were ravish'd with Admiration and Delight ; and the martial Harmony mov'd our Souls so powerfully, that we easily believed what is said of Ismenias's having excited Alexander to rise from Table and run to his Arms with such a warlike Melody. At last the Golden King remained Master of the Field : And, while we were minding those Dances, Queen Whims vanish'd, so that we saw her no more from that day to this.

Then Geber's Michelots conducted us, and we were set down among her Abstractors, as her Queenship had commanded. After that, we return'd to the Port of Mateotechny, and thence strait o' board our Ships ; For the Wind was fair, and had we not hoisted Sail out o' hand, we could hardly have got off in three quarters of a Moon in the Wain.

CHAPTER XXVI

*How we came to the Island of Odes, where the Ways go
up and down*

WE sail'd before the Wind, between a pair of Courses, and in two
days made the Island of Odes; at which place we saw a very
strange thing. The Ways there are Animals; so true is
Aristotle's Saying, that all self-moving things are Animals.
Now the Ways walk there; *Ergo*, They are then Animals;
Some of them are strange unknown Ways, like those of the
Planets; others are High-ways, Cross-ways, and Bye-ways. I
perceiv'd that the Travellers and Inhabitants of that Country
ask'd whither do's this Way go? Whither do's that Way go?
Some answer'd, Between Midy and Feurolles, to the Parish-
Church, to the City, to the River, and so forth. Being thus in
their right Way, they us'd to reach their Journeys end without
any further trouble, just like those who go by Water from
Lyons to Avignon or Arles.

Now, as you know that nothing is perfect here below, we
heard there was a sort of People whom they call'd Highway-
men, Way-beaters, and Makers of Inroads in Roads; and that
the poor Ways were sadly afraid of them, and shunn'd them as
you do Robbers. For these us'd to waylay them, as People
lay Trains for Wolves, and set Ginns for Woodcocks. I saw
one who was taken up with a Lord Chief Justice's Warrant,
for having unjustly and in spight of Pallas taken the School-
way, which is the longest. Another boasted that he had fairly
taken his shortest, and that doing so, he first compass'd his
Design. Thus Carpalin, meeting once Epistemon looking
upon a Wall with his Fiddle-diddle, or live Urinal, in his Hand,
to make a little Maid's Water, cry'd, that he did not wonder
now how the other came to be still the first at Pantagruel's
Lever, since he held his shortest, and least us'd.

I found Bourges High-way among these. It went with the
deliberation of an Abbot, but was made to scamper at the approach of some Waggoners, who threatned to have it trampled
under their Horses Feet, and made their Waggons run over it,
as Tullia's Chariot did over her Father's Body.

I also spy'd there the old Way between Peronne and St.

Quentin, which seem'd to me a very good, honest, plain way, as smooth as a Carpet, and as good as ever was trod upon by Shoe of Leather.

Among the Rocks I knew again the good old Way to la Ferrare, mounted on a huge Bear. This at a distance would have put me in mind of St. Jerome's Picture, had but the Bear been a Lyon; for the poor Way was all mortified, and wore a long hoary Beard uncomb'd and entangl'd, which look'd like the Picture of Winter, or at least like a white-frosted Bush.

On that Way were store of Beads or Rosaries, coarsely made of wild Pine-tree; and it seem'd kneeling, not standing, nor lying flat; but its sides and middle were beaten with huge Stones; insomuch, that it prov'd to us at once an Object of Fear and Pity.

While we were examining it, a Runner Batchelour of the Place took us aside, and shewing us a white smooth Way, somewhat fill'd with Straw, said, Henceforth, Gentlemen, do not reject the Opinion of Thales the Milesian, who said that Water is the beginning of all things, nor that of Homer, who tells us, that all things derive their Original from the Ocean: For, this same Way which you see here, had its beginning from Water, and is to return whence she came before two Months come to an end; now Carts are driven here where Boats us'd to be row'd.

Truly, said Pantagruel, you tell us no News, we see five hundred such Changes and more every Year in our World. Then reflecting on the different manner of going of those moving Ways; he told us, he believ'd that Philolaus and Aristarchus had Philosophis'd in this Island, and that some indeed were of Opinion, the Earth turns round about its Poles, and not the Heavens, whatever we may think to the contrary; as when we are on the River Loire, we think the Trees and the Shoar moves, tho' this is only an effect of our Boat's motion.

As we went back to our Ships, we saw three Way-Layers, who having been taken in Ambuscado, were going to be broken on the Wheel; and a huge Fornicator was burn'd with a lingring Fire, for beating a Way, and breaking one of its sides: we were told it was the Way of the Banks of the Nile in Egypt.

BURN'D WITH A LINGRING FIRE

365

CHAPTER XXVII

How we came to the Island of Sandals; and of the Order of Semiquaver Fryars

THENCE we went to the Island of Sandals, whose Inhabitants live on nothing but Ling Broth. However, we were very kindly receiv'd and entertain'd by Benius the Third, King of the Island; who, after he had made us drink, took us with him to show us a spick-and-span-new Monastery, which he had contriv'd for the Semiquaver Fryars; so he call'd the Religious Men whom he had there. For he said, that on t 'other side the Water liv'd Fryars, who stil'd themselves her sweet Ladyships most humble Servants. Item, the goodly Fryar-minors, who are Semibreves of Bulls; the smoak'd-herring Tribe of Minim Fryars; then the Crotchet Fryars. So that these Diminutives could be no more than Semiquavers. By the Statutes, Bulls, and Patents of Queen-Whims, they were all drest like so many House-Burners, except that as in Anjou, your Bricklayers use to quilt their Knees when they tile Houses, so these holy Fryars had usually quilted Bellies, and thick quilted Paunches were among them in much repute: Their Codpieces were cut Slipper fashion, and every Monk of them wore two; one sow'd before, and another behind, reporting that some certain dreadful Mysteries were duly represented by this duplicity of Codpieces.

They wore Shoes as round as Basons, in imitation of those who inhabit the sandy Sea. Their Chins were close shav'd, and their Feet Iron-shod; and to show they did not value Fortune, Benius made them shave and powl the hind part of their Poles, as bare as a Bird's Arse, from the Crown to the Shoulder-blades: But they had leave to let their Hair grow before, from the two triangular Bones in the upper part of the Skull.

Thus they did not value Fortune a Button, and cared no more for the Goods of this World, than you or I do for hanging. And to show how much they defi'd that blind Jilt, all of them wore, not in their Hands like her, but at their Waste, instead of Beads, Sharp-Razors, which they us'd to new grind twice a Day, and set thrice a Night.

366

Each of them had a round Ball on their Feet, because Fortune is said to have one under hers.

The Flap of their Cowls hang'd forwards, and not backwards, like those of others; thus none could see their Noses, and they laugh'd without fear both at Fortune and the Fortunate, neither more nor less than our Ladies laugh at barefac'd Trulls, when they have those Mufflers on, which they call Masks, and which were formerly much more properly call'd Charity, because they cover multitude of Sins.

The hind part of their Faces were always uncover'd, as are our Faces, which made them either go with their Belly, or the Arse foremost, which they pleas'd. When their hind Face went forwards, you would have sworn this had been their Natural-gate; as well on account of their round Shoes, as of the double Codpiece, and their Face behind, which was as bare as the back of my Hand, and coarsely dawb'd over with two Eyes, and a Mouth, such as you see on some Indian Nuts. Now, if they offer'd to waddle along with their Bellies forwards, you would have thought they were then playing at Blind-man's Buff. May I never be hang'd, if 'twas not a Comical sight.

Their way of Living was thus; about Owl-light they charitably began to Boot and Spur one another: This being done, the least thing they did, was to Sleep and Snoar; and thus Sleeping, they had Barnacles on the Handles of their Faces, or Spectacles at most.

You may swear, we did not a little wonder at this odd Fancy; but they satisfied us presently, telling us, That the Day of Judgment is to take Mankind napping; therefore to shew they did not refuse to make their Personal Appearance, as Fortune's Darlings use to do, they were always thus Booted and Spurr'd, ready to mount when ever the Trumpet should sound.

At Noon, as soon as the Clock struck, they us'd to awake. You must know that their Clock-bell, Church-bells, and Refectuary-bells, were all made according to the Pontial Device, that is, quilted with the finest Down, and their Clappers of Fox-tails.

Having thus made shift to get up at Noon, they pull'd off their Boots, and those that wanted to speak with a Maid, *alias* piss, piss'd; those that wanted to Scumber, scumber'd; and those that wanted to Sneeze, sneez'd. But all, whether they would or no (poor Gentlemen!) were oblig'd largely and plentifully to Yawn, and this was their first Breakfast (O rigorous

Statute !) Methought 'twas very comical to observe their Transactions; for, having laid their Boots and Spurs on a Rack, they went into the Cloysters; there they curiously wash'd their Hands and Mouths, then sat them down on a long Bench, and pick'd their Teeth till the Provost gave the Signal, whistling through his Fingers; then every He stretch'd out his Jaws as much as he could, and they gap'd and yawn'd for about half an Hour, sometimes more, sometimes less, according as the Prior judg'd the Breakfast to be suitable to the Day.

After that, they went in Procession; two Banners being carried before them, in one of which was the Picture of Virtue, and that of Fortune in the other. The last went before, carried by a Semiquavering-Fryar, at whose Heels was another with the Shadow or Image of Virtue in one Hand, and an Holy-water-sprinkle in the other; I mean of that Holy Mercurial-water, which Ovid describes in his *de fastis*. And as the pre-ceding Semiquaver rang a Hand-bell, this shak'd the Sprinkle with his Fist. With that, says Pantagruel, This Order contra-dicts the Rule which Tully and the Academics prescribed, That Virtue ought to go before, and Fortune follow. But they told us, they did as they ought, seeing their Design was to breech, lash, and bethwack Fortune.

During the Processions they trill'd and quaver'd most melodiously betwixt their Teeth I don't know what Antiphones, or Chantings by turns: For my Part, 'twas all Hebrew-Greek to me, the Devil a word I could pick out on 't; at last pricking up my Ears, and intensely listning, I perceiv'd they only sang with the Tip of theirs. O, what a rare Harmony it was! How well 'twas tun'd to the sound of their Bells! You 'll never find these to jar, that you won't. Pantagruel made a notable Observation upon the Processions; for, says he, have you seen and observ'd the Policy of these Semiquavers? To make an end of their Procession, they went out at one of the Church-doors, and came in at the other; they took a deal of care not to come in at the place whereat they went out. On my honour these are a subtle sort of People, quoth Panurge, they have as much Wit as three Folks, Two Fools and a mad Man; they are as wise as the Calf that ran nine Miles to suck a Bull, and when he came there 'twas a Steer. This Subtilty and Wisdom of theirs, cry'd Fryar Jhon, is borrow'd from the Occult Philosophy, may I be gutted like an Oyster, if I can tell what to make on 't. Then the more 'tis to be feared, said Pantagruel; for Subtilty suspected, Subtilty foreseen, Subtilty found out, loses the

Essence and very Name of Subtilty, and only gains that of Blockishness. They are not such Fools as you take them to be, they have more Tricks than are good, I doubt.

After the Procession, they went sluggingly into the Fratry Room by the way of walk and healthful Exercise, and there kneel'd under the Tables, leaning their Breasts on Lanterns. While they were in that Posture, in came a huge Sandal, with a Pitch-fork in his Hand, who us'd to baste, ribroast, swaddle, and swindge them well-favour'dly, as they said, and in truth treated them after a fashion. They began their Meal as you end yours, with Cheese, and ended it with Mustard and Lettuce, as Martial tells us the Ancients did. Afterwards a Platter full of Mustard was brought before every one of them; and thus they made good the Proverb, After Meat comes Mustard.

Their Diet was this :

O' Sundays they stuff'd their Puddings with Puddings, Chitterlings, Links, Bolonia-Saucidges, Forc'd Meats, Liverings, Hogs-Haslets, young Quails, and Teals; you must also always add Cheese for the first Course, and Mustard for the last.

O' Mondays, they were crammed with Pease and Pork, *cum commento*, and interlineary Glosses.

O' Tuesdays, they us'd to twist store of Holy-bread, Cakes, Buns, Puffs, Lenten-Loaves, Jumbals and Biscuits.

O' Wednesdays, my Gentlemen had fine Sheeps-Heads, Calves-Heads, and Brocks-Heads, of which there's no want in that Country.

O' Thursdays, they guzzled down seven sorts of Porridge, not forgetting Mustard.

O' Fridays, they munched nothing but Services or Sorb-apples; neither were these full ripe, as I guess'd by their Complexion.

O' Saturdays, they gnaw'd Bones, not that they were poor or needy, for every Mother's Son of 'em had a very good fat Belly-Benefice.

As for their Drink, 'twas an Antifortunal, thus they call'd I don't know what sort of a Liquor of the Place.

When they wanted to eat or drink, they turn'd down the Back-points or Flaps of their Cowls forwards, below their Chins, and that serv'd 'em instead of Gorgets or Slabbering-Bibs.

When they had well din'd, they pray'd rarely, all in Quavers and Shakes ; and the rest of the Day, expecting the Day of Judgment, they were taken up with acts of Charity. And particularly,

O' Sundays, Rubbers at Cuffs.

O' Mondays, lending each other Flirts and Fillups on the Nose.

O' Tuesdays, clapperclawing one another.

O' Wednesdays, sniting and fly-flapping.

O' Thursdays, worming and pumping.

O' Fridays, tickling.

O' Saturdays, jirking and firking one another.

Such was their Diet when they resided in the Convent, and if the Prior of the Monk-house sent any of them abroad, then they were strictly enjoin'd, neither to touch nor eat any manner of Fish, as long as they were on Sea or Rivers ; and to abstain from all manner of Flesh whenever they were at Land, that every one might be convinc'd that while they enjoy'd the Object, they deni'd themselves the Power, and even the Desire, and were no more mov'd with it, than the Marpesian Rock.

All this was done with proper Antiphones, still sung and chanted by Ear, as we have already observed.

When the Sun went to bed, they fairly Booted and Spurr'd each other as before, and having clapt on their Barnicles, e'en jogg'd to bed too. At Midnight the Sandal came to them, and up they got, and having well whetted and set their Razors, and been a processioning, they clapt the Tables over themselves, and like Wire-drawers under their Work, fell to it as aforesaid.

Fryar Jhon des Entoumeures, having shrewdly observ'd these jolly Semiquaver-Fryars, and had a full account of their Statutes, lost all Patience, and cry'd out aloud ; Bounce Tail, and God ha' mercy Guts ; if every Fool should wear a Babel, Fewel would be dear. A Plague rot it, we must know how many Farts go to an Ounce ; would Priapus were here as he us'd to be at the nocturnal Festivals in Crete, that I might see him play backwards and wriggle and shake to the purpose. Ay, ay, this is the World, and t' other is the Country ; may I never piss, if this be not an Antichthonian Land, and our very Antipodes. In Germany they pull down Monasteries and unfrockifie the Monks ; here they go quite Kam, and act clean contrary to others, setting new ones up, against the hair.

CHAPTER XXVIII

How Panurge ask'd a Semiquaver Fryar many Questions, and was only answer'd in Monosyllables

PANURGE, who had since been wholly taken up with staring at these Royal Semiquavers, at last pull'd one of them by the Sleeve, who was as lean as a Rake, and ask'd him,

Hark 'e me, Fryar Quaver, Semiquaver, Demisemiquavering Quaver, where 's the Punk ?

The Fryar pointing downwards, answer'd, There.

PAN. Pray have you many ?
FRY. Few.
PAN. How many Scores have you ?
FRY. One.
PAN. How many would you have ?
FRY. Five.
PAN. Where do you hide 'em ?
FRY. Here.
PAN. I suppose they are not all of one Age ? but pray how is their Shape ?
FRY. Straight.
PAN. Their Complexion ?
FRY. Clear.
PAN. Their Hair ?
FRY. Fair.
PAN. Their Eyes ?
FRY. Black.

PAN. Their Features ?
FRY. Good.
PAN. Their Brows ?
FRY. Small.
PAN. Their Graces ?
FRY. Ripe.
PAN. Their Looks ?
FRY. Free.
PAN. Their Feet ?
FRY. Flat.
PAN. Their Heels ?
FRY. Short.
PAN. Their lower Parts ?
FRY. Rare.
PAN. And their Arms ?
FRY. Long.
PAN. What do they wear on their Hands ?
FRY. Gloves.
PAN. What sorts of Rings on their Fingers ?

FRY. Gold.

PAN. What Rigging do you keep 'em in ?

FRY. Cloth.

PAN. What sort of Cloth is it ?

FRY. New.

PAN. What Colour ?

FRY. Sky.

PAN. What kind of Cloth is it ?

FRY. Fine.

PAN. What Caps do they wear ?

FRY. Blue.

PAN. What the Colour of their Stockins ?

FRY. Red.

PAN. What wear they on their Feet ?

FRY. Pumps.

PAN. How do they use to be ?

FRY. Foul.

PAN. How do they use to walk ?

FRY. Fast.

PAN. Now let's talk of the Kitchen, I mean that of the Harlots, and without going hand over head, let 's a little examine things by particulars. What is in their Kitchens?

FRY. Fire.

PAN. What Fuel feeds it ?

FRY. Wood.

PAN. What sort of Wood is 't ?

FRY. Dry.

PAN. And of what kind of Trees ?

FRY. Yews

PAN. What are the Faggots and Brushes of ?

FRY. Holme.

PAN. What Wood d' ye burn in your Chambers ?

FRY. Pine.

PAN. And of what other Trees ?

FRY. Line.

PAN. Harkee me, as for the Buttocks, I 'll go your halves : Pray, how do you feed 'em ?

FRY. Well.

PAN. First, what do they eat ?

FRY. Bread.

PAN. Of what Complexion ?

FRY. White.

PAN. And what else ?

FRY. Meat.

PAN. How do they love it dress'd ?

FRY. Roast.

PAN. What sort of Porridge ?

FRY. None.

PAN. Are they for Pyes and Tarts ?

FRY. Much.

PAN. There I'm their Man. Will Fish go down with them ?

FRY. Well.

PAN. And what else ?

FRY. Eggs.

PAN. How do they like 'em ?

FRY. Boil'd.

PAN. And how must they be done ?

FRY. Hard.

Pan. Is this all they have ?

Fry. No.

Pan. What have they besides then ?

Fry. Beef.

Pan. And what else ?

Fry. Pork.

Pan. And what more ?

Fry. Geese.

Pan. What then ?

Fry. Ducks.

Pan. And what besides ?

Fry. Cocks.

Pan. What do they season their Meat with ?

Fry. Salt.

Pan. What Sauce are the most Dainty for ?

Fry. Must.

Pan. What 's their last Course ?

Fry. Rice.

Pan. And what else ?

Fry. Milk.

Pan. What besides ?

Fry. Pease.

Pan. What sort ?

Fry. Green.

Pan. What do they boil 'em with ?

Fry. Pork.

Pan. What Fruit do they eat ?

Fry. Good.

Pan. How ?

Fry. Raw.

Pan. What do they end with ?

Fry. Nuts.

Pan. How do they drink ?

Fry. Neat.

Pan. What Liquor ?

Fry. Wine.

Pan. What sort ?

Fry. White.

Pan. In Winter ?

Fry. Strong.

Pan. In the Spring ?

Fry. Brisk.

Pan. In Summer ?

Fry. Cool.

Pan. In Autumn ?

Fry. New.

Buttock of a Monk ! cryed Fryar Jhon, how plump these plaguy Trulls, these arch Semiquavering Strumpets must be ! That damn'd Cattle are so high fed, that they must needs be high metall'd, and ready to winse, and give two up's for one go-down, when any one offers to ride 'em below the Crupper.

Prithee, Fryar Jhon, quoth Panurge, hold thy prating Tongue ; stay till I have done.

Till what time do the Doxies sit up ?

Fry. Night.

Pan. When do they get up ?

Fry. Late.

Pan. May I ride on a Horse that was foaled of an Acorn, if this be not as honest a Cod as ever the Ground went upon, and as grave as an old Gatepost into the bargain. Wou'd to the blessed St. Semiquaver. and the blessed worthy Virgin St. Semiquaverera, he were Lord Chief President (Justice) of Paris. Odsbodikins, how he 'd dispatch! with what an Expedition would he bring Disputes to an upshot! what an Abreviator and Clawer off of Law-suits, Reconciler of Differences, Examiner and Fumbler of Bags, Peruser of Bills, Scribler of Rough-drafts, and Ingrosser of Deeds, would he not make! Well, Fryar, spare your Breath to cool your Porridge: Come, let 's now talk with Deliberation, fair and softly, as Lawyers go to Heaven. Let 's know how you Victual the Venereal Camp.

How is the Snatch-blatch?

FRY. Rough.

PAN. How is the Gateway?

FRY. Free.

PAN. And how 'st within?

FRY. Deep.

PAN. I mean, What Weather is it there?

FRY. Hot.

PAN. What shadows the Brooks?

FRY. Groves.

PAN. Of what 's the Colour of the Twigs?

FRY. Red.

PAN. And that of the Old?

FRY. Gray.

PAN. How are you when you shake?

FRY. Brisk.

PAN. How is their Motion?

FRY. Quick.

PAN Would you have them Vault or Wriggle more?

FRY. Less.

PAN. What kind of Tools are yours?

FRY. Big.

PAN. And in their Helves?

FRY. Round.

PAN. Of what Colour's the Tip?

FRY. Red.

PAN. When they 've been us'd, how are they?

FRY. Shrunk.

PAN. How much weighs each bag of Tools?

FRY. Pounds.

PAN. How hang your Pouches?

FRY. Tight.

PAN. How are they when you 've done?

FRY. Lank.

PAN. Now by the Oath you have taken, tell me, when you have a mind to Cohabit, how you throw 'em?

FRY. Down.

PAN. And what do they say then?

FRY. Fye.

PAN. However, like Maids, they say Nay, and take it, and speak the less, but think the more; minding the work in hand, do they not?

FRY. True.

PAN. Do they get you Bairns ?

FRY. None.

PAN. How do you pig together ?

FRY. Bare.

PAN. Remember you 're upon your Oath, and tell me justly, and *bonâ fide*, how many times o' day you Monk it ?

FRY. Six.

PAN. How many Bouts o' Night ?

FRY. Ten.

Cat so, quoth Fryar Jhon, the poor fornicating Brother 's bashful, and sticks at Sixteen, as if that were his stint. Right, quoth Panurge, but could'st thou keep pace with him, Fryar Jhon, my dainty Cod ? May the Devil's Dam suck my Teat, if he does not look as if he had got a Blow over the Nose with a Naples Cowlstaff.

PAN. Pray, Fryar Shakewell, does your whole Fraternity quaver and shake at that rate ?

FRY. All.

PAN. Who of them is the best Cock of the Game ?

FRY. I.

PAN. Do you never commit Dry Bobs, or Flashes in the Pan ?

FRY. None.

PAN. I blush like any black Dog, and could be as testy as an old Cook, when I think on all this ; it passes my Understanding. But, pray, when you have been pumpt dry one day, what have you got the next ?

FRY. More.

PAN. By Priapus they have the Indian Herb, of which Theophrastus spoke, or I' m much out. But harkee me, thou Man of Brevity, should some Impediment honestly, or otherwise, impair your Talents, and cause your Benevolence to lessen, how would it fare with you then ?

FRY. Ill.

PAN. What would the Wenches do ?

FRY. Rail.

PAN. What if you skipt, and let 'em fast a whole Day ?

FRY. Worse.

PAN. What do you give 'em then ?

FRY. Thwacks.

PAN. What do they say to this ?

FRY. Bawl.

PAN. And what else ?

FRY. Curse.

PAN. How do you correct 'em ?

FRY. Hard.

PAN. What do you get out of 'em then ?

FRY. Blood.

PAN. How 's their Complexion then ?

FRY. Odd.

PAN. What do they mend it with ?

FRY. Paint.

PAN. Then, what do they do ?

FRY. Fawn.

PAN. By the Oath you have taken, tell me truly, what time of the Year do you do it least in ?

FRY. Now.

PAN. What Season do you do it best in ?

FRY. March.

PAN. How is your Performance the rest of the Year ?

FRY. Brisk.

Then, quoth Panurge, sneering, Of all, and of all, commend me to Ball, this is the Fryar of the World for my Money ; you 've heard how short, concise and compendious he is in his Answers ? Nothing is to be got out of him but Monosyllables ; by Jingo, I believe he wou'd make three bits of a Cherry.

Dam him, cry'd Fryar Jhon, that 's as true as I am his Uncle ; the Dog yelps at another-gat's rate when he is among his Bitches ; there he is Polisyllable enough, my Life for yours : You talk of making three bits of a Cherry ! God send Fools more Wit, and us more Money : May I be doom'd to fast a whole Day, if I don't verily believe he would not make above two Bits of a Shoulder of Mutton, and one Swoop of a whole Pottle of Wine : Zoons, do but see how down o' the mouth the Curr looks : He 's nothing but Skin and Bones ; he has piss'd his Tallow.

Truly, truly, quoth Epistemon, this Rascally Monastical Vermin, all over the World, mind nothing but their Gut, and are as ravenous as any Kites ; and then forsooth, they tell us they 've nothing but Food and Rayment in this World : 'Sdeath, what more have Kings and Princes ?

CHAPTER XXIX

How Epistemon dislik'd the Institution of Lent

PRAY did you observe, continu'd Epistemon, how this damn'd ill-favour'd Semiquaver mentioned March as the best Month for Catterwawling. True, said Pantagruel, yet Lent and March always go together ; and the first was instituted to macerate and bring down our pamper'd Flesh, to weaken and subdue its Lusts, and curb and asswage the Venereal Rage.

By this, said Epistemon, you may guess what kind of a Pope it was, who first enjoin'd it to be kept ; since this filthy Wooden-shoo'd Semiquaver owns that his Spoon is never oftener or deeper in the Porringer of Letchery than in Lent ; add to this, the evident Reasons given by all good and learned Physicians, affirming, That throughout the whole Year no Food is eaten, that can prompt Mankind to lascivious Acts, more than at that time.

As for Example ; Beans, Pease, Phasels or Long-peason, Cices, Onions, Nuts, Oysters, Herrings, Salt-meats, Garum (a kind of Anchovies,) and Salads, wholly made up of Venereous Herbs and Fruits, as,

Rocket,	Parsley,	Hop-buds,
Nose-smart	Rampions,	Figs,
Taragon,	Poppy,	Rice,
Cresses,	Sellery,	Raisins, and others.

'Twou'd not a little surprize you, said Pantagruel, should a Man tell you, that the good Pope, who first order'd the keeping of Lent, perceiving that at that time o' Year the Natural Heat (from the Centre of the Body, whither it was retired, during the Winter's Cold) diffuse it self as the Sap does in Trees, through the Circumference of the Members, did therefore in a manner prescribe that sort of Diet to forward the Propagation of Mankind. What makes me think so, is, that by the Registers of Christnings at Touars, it appears that more Children are born in October and November, than in the other ten Months of the Year ; and reckoning backwards, 'twill be found that they were all made, conceiv'd, and begotten in Lent.

I listen to you with both my Ears, quoth Fryar Jhon, and that with no small pleasure, I 'll assure you. But I must tell you, that the Vicar of Jambée ascrib'd this copious Prolification of the Women, not to that sort of Food that we chiefly eat in Lent, but to the little licens'd stooping Mumpers, your little booted Lent-Preachers, your little draggle-tail'd Father Confessors ; who, during all that time of their Reign, damn all Husbands, that run astray, three Fathom and a half below the very lowest Pit of Hell. So the silly Cods-headed Brothers of the Noose, dare not then stumble any more at the Truckle-bed, to the no small discomfort of their Maids, and are e'en forc'd, poor Souls ! to take up with their own bodily Wives. *Dixi*, I have done.

You may descant on the Institution of Lent as much as you please, cry'd Epistemon ; So many Men, so many Minds ; But certainly all the Physicians will be against its being suppress'd, tho' I think that time is at hand, I know they will, and have heard 'em say, Were it not for Lent, their Art would soon fall into contempt, and they 'd get nothing, for hardly any body wou'd be sick.

All Distempers are sow'd in Lent ; 'tis the true Seminary and native Bed of all Diseases; nor do's it only weaken and putrifie Bodies, but it also makes Souls mad and uneasie ; for then the Devils do their best, and drive a subtle Trade, and the Tribe of canting Dissemblers come out of their holes. 'Tis then Term-time with your cucullated Pieces of Formality, that have one Face to God, and another to the Devil ; and a wretched clutter they make with their Sessions, Stations, Pardons, Synteerses, Confessions, Whipping, Anathematizations, and much Prayer, with as little Devotion. However, I 'll not offer to infer from this, that the Arimaspians are better than we are in that Point ; yet I speak to the Purpose.

Well, quoth Panurge to the Semiquaver Fryar, who happen'd to be by, Dear bumbasting, shaking, trilling, quavering Cod, what think'st thou of this Fellow, is he a rank Heretic ?

FRY. Much.
PAN. Ought he not to be sindg'd ?
FRY. Well.
PAN. As soon as may be ?
FRY Right.

PAN. Should not he be scalded first ?
FRY. No.
PAN. How then should he be roasted ?
FRY. Quick.

PAN. Till at last he be ?

FRY. Dead.

PAN. What has he made you ?

FRY. Mad.

PAN. What d 'ye take him to be ?

FRY. Damn'd.

PAN. What Place is he to go to ?

FRY. Hell.

PAN. But first, how wou'd you have 'em serv'd here ?

FRY. Burnt.

PAN. Some have been serv'd so ?

FRY. Store.

PAN. That were Heretics ?

FRY. Less.

PAN. And the number of those that are to be Warm'd thus hereafter is ?

FRY. Great.

PAN. How many of 'em d' ye intend to save ?

FRY. None.

PAN. So you 'd have them burnt ?

FRY. All.

I wonder, said Epistemon to Panurge, what Pleasure you can find in talking thus with this lousie Tatterdemallion of a Monk ; I vow, did not I know you well, I might be ready to think you had no more Wit in your Head, than he has in both his Shoulders. Come, come, scatter no Words, return'd Panurge ; Every one as they like, as the Woman said when she kiss'd her Cow ; I wish I might carry him to Gargantua ; when I 'm marry'd, he might be my Wife's Fool. And make you one, cry'd Epistemon. Well said, quoth Fryar Jhon ; now, poor Panurge, take that along with thee thou 'rt e'en fitted ; 'tis a plain case, thou 'lt never 'scape wearing the Bull's Feather ; thy Wife will be as common as the Highway, that 's certain.

CHAPTER XXX

How we came to the Land of Satin

HAVING pleas'd our selves with observing that new Order of Semiquaver Fryars, we set sail, and in three Days our Skipper made the finest and most delightful Island that ever was seen ; he call'd it the Island of Frize ; for all the Ways were of Frize.

In that Island is the Land of Satin, so celebrated by our Court-Pages. Its Trees and Shrubs never lose their Leaves or Flowers, and are all Damask and Flower'd-Velvet: As for the Beasts and Birds, they are all of Tapestry-work. There we saw many Beasts, Birds and Trees of the same Colour, Bigness and Shape of those in our Country, with this difference however, that these did eat nothing, and never sung or bit like ours; and we also saw there many sorts of Creatures which we had never seen before.

Among the rest, several Elephants in various Postures, twelve of which were the six Males and six Females that were brought to Rome by their Governour in the Time of Germanicus, Tiberius's Nephew; some of them were Learned Elephants, some Musicians, others Philosophers, Dancers, and Shewers of Tricks, and all sate down at Table in good Order, silently eating and drinking like so many Fathers in a Fratry-room.

With their Snouts or Proboscis's some two Cubits long, they draw up Water for their own drinking, and take hold of Palm-Leaves, Plums, and all manner of Edibles, using them offensively or defensively, as we do our Fists; with them tossing Men high into the Air in sight, and making them burst out with laughing when they come to the ground.

They have Joints, whatever some Men, who doubtless never saw any but Painted, may have written to the contrary. Between their Teeth they have two huge Horns; this Juba call'd 'em, and Pausanias tells us, they are no Teeth, but Horns: However, Philostratus will have 'em to be Teeth, and not Horns. 'Tis all one to me, provided you will be pleas'd to own them to be true Ivory. These are some three or four Cubits long, and are fix'd in the Upper Jaw-bone, and consequently not in the lowermost. If you hearken to those who will tell you the contrary, you 'll find your selves damnably mistaken, for that 's a Lye with a Hatchet: Tho' 'twere Ælian that Long-Bow-man that told you so, never believe him, for he lyes as fast as a Dog can trot. 'Twas in this very Island that Pliny, his Brother Tell-truth, had seen some Elephants dance on the Rope with Bells, and whip over the Tables, *Presto*, Be gone, while People were at Feasts, without so much as touching the Toping Topers, or the Topers Toping.

I saw a Rhinoceros there, just such a one as Harry Clerberg had formerly shew'd me; methought it was not much unlike a certain Boar which I had formerly seen at Limoges, except the sharp Horn on its Snout, that was about a Cubit long;

by the means of which that Animal dares encounter with an Elephant, that is sometimes kill'd with its Point thrust into its Belly, which is its most tender and defenceless part.

I saw there two and thirty Unicorns; they are a curst sort of Creatures, much resembling a fine Horse, unless it be that their Heads are like a Stag's, their Feet like an Elephant's, their Tails like a wild Boar's, and out of each of their Foreheads sprouts out a short black Horn, some six or seven Foot long; commonly it dangles down like a Turkey-Cock's Comb. When an Unicorn has a mind to fight, or put it to any other use, what does it do but make it stand, and then 'tis as straight as an Arrow.

I saw one of them, which was attended with a Throng of other wild Beasts, purifie a Fountain with its Horn. With that Panurge told me, that his Prancer, *alias* his Nimble-Wimble, was like the Unicorn, not altogether in length indeed, but in Vertue and Propriety: For as the Unicorn purifi'd Pools and Fountains from Filth and Venom, so that other Animals came and drank securely there afterwards; In the like manner, others might water their Nags, and dabble after him without fear of Shankers, Carnosities, Gonorrhæa's, Buboes, Crinckums, and such other Plagues caught by those who venture to quench their Amorous Thirst in a common Puddle; for with his Nervous Horn he remov'd all the Infection that might be lurking in some blind Cranny of the Mephitic sweet-scented Hole.

Well, quoth Fryar John, when you are sped, that is, when you are married, we 'll make a Trial of this on thy Spouse, meerly for Charity-sake, since you are pleas'd to give us so beneficial an Instruction.

Ay, ay, return'd Panurge, and then immediately I 'll give you a pretty gentle Agregative Pill of God, made up of two and twenty kind Stabs with a Dagger, after the Cesarian way. Cat 'so, cry'd Fryar Jhon, I had rather take off a Bumper of good cool Wine.

I saw there the golden Fleece, formerly conquer'd by Jason, and can assure you on the Word of an honest Man, that those who have said it was not a Fleece, but a golden Pippin, because Μῆλον signifies both an Apple and a Sheep, were utterly mistaken.

I also saw a Chameleon, such as Aristotle describes it, and like that which had been formerly shew'd me by Charles Maris a famous Physician of the noble City of Lyons on the

Rosne ; and the said Chameleon liv'd on Air just as the other did.

I saw three Hydra's, like those I had formerly seen. They are a kind of Serpent, with seven different Heads.

I saw also fourteen Phœnixes. I had read in many Authors that there was but one in the whole World in every Century ; but if I may presume to speak my Mind, I declare, that those who said this, had never seen any, unless it were in the Land of Tapestry ; tho' 'twere vouch'd by Claudian or Lactantius Firmianus.

I saw the Skin of Apuleius's golden Ass.

I saw three hundred and nine Pelicans.

Item, Six thousand and sixteen Selucid Birds marching in Battalia, and picking up stragling Grashoppers in Corn-Fields.

Item, Some Cynamologi, Argatiles, Caprimulgi, Thynnunculs, Onocrotals, or Bitterns, with their wide Swallows, Stymphalides, Harpies, Panthers, Dorcas's or Bucks, Cemas's, Cynocephalis's, Satyrs, Cartasons, Tarands, Uri, Monops's, or Bonasi, Neades, Stera's, Marmosets, or Monkeys, Bugles, Musimons, Byturos's, Ophyri, Scriech Owls, Goblins, Faires, and Gryphins.

I saw Mid-lent o' Horseback, with Mid-August and Mid-March holding its Stirrups.

I saw some Mankind-Wolves, Centaurs, Tigers, Leopards, Hyena's, Camelopardals, and Orix's or huge wild Goats with sharp Horns.

I saw a Remora, a little Fish call'd Echineis by the Greeks, and near it a tall Ship, that did not get o' head an Inch, tho' she was in the Offin with Top and Top-gallants spread before the Wind ; I am somewhat inclin'd to believe, that 'twas the very numerical Ship in which Periander the Tyrant happen'd to be when it was stopp'd by such a little Fish in spight of Wind and Tide. 'Twas in this Land of Satin, and in no other, that Mutianus had seen one of them.

Fryar Jhon told us, that in the Days of Yore, two sorts of Fishes us'd to abound in our Courts of Judicature, and rotted the Bodies and tormented the Souls of those who were at Law, whether noble or of mean Descent, high or low, rich or poor : the first were your April Fish or Makerel, (Pimps, Panders and Bawds) the others your beneficial Remorae's, that is, the Eternity of Law-Suits, the needless Letts that keep 'em undecided.

I saw some Sphynges, some Raphes, some Oinces, and some

Cepphi, whose fore-feet are like Hands, and their hind-feet like Man's.

Also some Crocuta's, and some Eales as big as Sea-horses, with Elephant's Tails, Boar's Jaws and Tusks, and Horns as pliant as an Asse's Ears.

The Procuta's most fleet Animals, as big as our Asses of Mirebalais, have Necks, Tails and Breasts like a Lyon's, Legs like a Stag's, have Mouths up to the Ears, and but two Teeth, one above, and one below; they speak with human Voices, but when they do, they say nothing.

Some People say, that none e're saw an Airy or Nest of Sakers; If you 'll believe me, I saw no less than Eleven, and I 'm sure I reckon'd right.

I saw some left-handed Halberts, which were the first that I had ever seen.

I saw some Menticores, a most strange sort of Creatures, which have the Body of a Lyon, red Hair, a Face and Ears like a Man's, three Rows of Teeth which close together, as if you join'd your Hands with your Fingers between each other; they have a Sting in their Tails like a Scorpions, and a very melodious Voice.

I saw some Catablepas's, a sort of Serpents, whose Bodies are small, but their Heads large without any Proportion, so that they 've much ado to lift them up; and their Eyes are so infectious, that whoever sees 'em, dies upon the spot, as if he had seen a Basilisk.

I saw some Beasts with two Backs, and those seem'd to me the merriest Creatures in the World; they were most nimble at wriggling the Buttocks, and more diligent in Tail-wagging than any Water-wagtails, perpetually jogging and shaking their double Rumps. I saw there some milch'd Craw-fish, Creatures that I never had heard of before in my Life; and these mov'd in very good order, and 'twould have done your Heart good to have seen 'em.

CHAPTER XXXI

*How in the Land of Satin we saw Hearsay who kept a
School of Vouching*

WE went a little higher up into the Country of Tapistry, and
saw the Mediterranean Sea open'd to the right and left down
to the very bottom, just as the Red-Sea very fairly left its bed
at the Arabian Gulph, to make a Lane for the Jews, when they
left Egypt.

There I found Triton winding his silver Shell instead of a
Horn, and also Glaucus, Proteus, Nereus, and a thousand other
Godlings and Sea-monsters.

I also saw an infinite number of Fish of all kinds, dancing,
flying, vaulting, fighting, eating, breathing, billing, shoving,
milting, spawning, hunting, fishing, skirmishing, lying in Ambuscado, making Truces, cheapning, bargaining, swearing and
sporting.

In a blind corner we saw Aristotle holding a Lantern, in the
Posture in which the Hermit uses to be drawn near St. Christopher, watching, prying, thinking, and setting every thing
down.

Behind him stood a Pack of other Philosophers, like so many
Bums by a Head-Bailiff; as Appian, Heliodorus, Athenæus,
Porphyrius, Pancrates, Archadian, Numenius, Possidonius,
Ovidius, Opianus, Olympius, Selenus, Leonides, Agathocles,
Theophrastus, Demostratus, Metianus, Nymphodorus, Ælian,
and five hundred other such plodding Dons, who were full of
business yet had little to do ; like Chrysippus of Aristarchus
or Soli, who for eight and fifty Years together did nothing in the
World but examine the state and concerns of Bees.

I spy'd Peter Gilles among these, with an Urinal in his Hand,
narrowly watching the Water of those goodly Fishes.

When we had long beheld every thing in this Land of Satin,
Pantagruel said, I have sufficiently fed my Eyes, but my Belly
is empty all this while, and chimes to let me know 'tis time to
go to Dinner ; Let 's take care of the Belly, let the Soul abdicate
it ; and to this effect, let 's taste some of these Anacampserotes
that hang over our Heads. Pshaw, cry'd one, they are meer
Trash, stark naught o' my word, they 're good for nothing.

W. HEATH ROBINSON.

HEAR-SAY

I then went to pluck some Mirabolons off of a Piece of Tapistry whereon they hang'd, but the Devil a bit I could chew or swallow 'em, and had you had them betwixt your Teeth, you would have sworn they had been thrown Silk, there was no manner of savour in 'em.

One might be apt to think Heliogabalus had taken a Hint from thence, to feast those whom he had caus'd to fast a long time, promising them a sumptuous, plentiful and imperial Feast after it : For all the Treat us'd to amount to no more than several sorts of meat in Wax, Marble, Earthen-Ware, painted and figur'd Table-Cloths.

While we were looking up and down to find some more substantial Food, we heard a loud various Noise, like that of Paper-mills ; so with all speed we went to the Place whence the Noise came, where we found a diminutive, monstrous, mishapen, old Fellow, call'd Hear-say; his Mouth was slit up to his Ears, and in it were seven Tongues, each of 'em cleft into seven parts. However, he chatter'd, tattled and prated with all the seven at once, of different Matters, and in divers Languages.

He had as many Ears all-over his Head and the rest of his Body, as Argus formerly had Eyes ; and was as blind as a Beetle, and had the Palsie in his Legs.

About him stood an innumerable number of Men and Women, gaping, list'ning, and hearing very intensely ; among 'em I observ'd some who strutted like Crows in a Gutter, and principally a very handsome bodied Man in the Face, who held then a Map of the World, and with little Aphorisms compendiously explain'd every thing to 'em ; so that those Men of happy Memories grew learned in a Trice, and would most fluently talk with you of a world of prodigious Things ; the hundredth part of which would take up a Man's whole Life to be fully known.

Among the rest, they descanted with great Prolixity on the Pyramids and Hieroglyphics of Egypt, of the Nile, of Babylon, of the Troglodytes, the Hymantopodes or Crump-footed Nation, the Blæmiæ People that wear their Heads in the middle of their Breasts, the Pygmies, the Cannibals, the Hyperborei and their Mountains, the Ægypanes with their Goat's-feet, and the Devil and all of others ; every individual word of it by Hear-say.

I am much mistaken if I did not see among them Herodotus, Pliny, Solinus, Berosus, Philostratus, Pomponius Mela, Strabo, and God knows how many other Antiquaries.

Then Albert the great Jacobin Fryar, Peter Tesmoin, *alias*

Witness, Pope Pius the Second, Volaterran, Paulius Jovus the Valiant, Jemmy Cartier, Chaton the Armenian, Marco Paulo the Venetian, Ludovico Romano, Pedro Aliares, and forty Cart-loads of other modern Historians, lurking behind a piece of Tapistry where they were at it ding-dong, privately scribbling the Lord knows what, and making rare work on 't, and all by Hear-say.

Behind another piece of Tapistry on which Naboth's and Susanna's Accusers were fairly represented, I saw close by Hear-say, good store of Men of the Country of Perche and Maine, notable Students, and young enough.

I ask'd what sort of study they apply'd themselves to ? and was told, that from their youth they learn'd to be Evidences, Affidavit-men and Vouchers ; and were instructed in the Art of Swearing ; in which they soon became such Proficients, that, when they left that Country, and went back into their own, they set up for themselves, and very honestly liv'd by their Trade of Evidencing ; positively giving their Testimony of all Things whatsoever to those who feed them most roundly to do a Job of Journey-work for them ; and all this by Hear-say.

You may think what you will of it, but I can assure you, they gave some of us Corners of their Cakes, and we merrily help'd to empty their Hogs-heads. Then in a friendly manner they advis'd us to be as sparing of Truth as possibly we could, if ever we had a mind to get Court-preferment.

CHAPTER XXXII

How we came in sight of Lantern-Land

HAVING been but scurvily entertain'd in the Land of Satin, we went o' board, and having set Sail, in four Days came near the Coast of Lantern-Land. We then saw certain little hovering Fires on the Sea.

For my part I did not take them to be Lanterns, but rather thought they were Fishes, which loll'd their flaming Tongues on the surface of the Sea, or Lampyris's, which some call Cicindela's, or Glow-Worms, shining there as ripe Barley do's o' Nights in my Country.

But the Skipper satisfied us that they were the Lanterns of the Watch, or more properly Light-houses, set up in many places round the Precinct of the Place to discover the Land, and for the safe Piloting in of some outlandish Lanterns, which like good Franciscan and Jacobin Fryars, were coming to make their personal Appearance at the Provincial Chapter. However, some of us were somewhat suspicious that these Fires were the Forerunners of some Storm ; but the Skipper assur'd us again, they were not.

CHAPTER XXXIII

How we landed at the Port of the Lychnobii, and came to
Lantern-Land

Soon after we arriv'd at the Port of Lantern-Land, where Pantagruel discover'd on a high Tower, the Lantern of Rochel, that stood us in good stead, for it casted a great Light. We also saw the Lantern of Pharos, that of Nauplion, and that of Acropolis, at Athens, sacred to Pallas.

Near the Port, there 's a little Hamblet inhabited by the Lychnobii, that live by Lanterns, as the gulligutted Fryars in our Country live by Nuns : they are studious People, and as honest Men as ever shit in a Trumpet. Demosthenes had formerly lanternis'd there.

We were conducted from that place to the Palace by three Obeliscolichnys, Military-Guards of the Port, with high-crown'd Hats, whom he acquainted with the cause of our Voyage, and our Design, which was to desire the Queen of the Country to grant us a Lantern to light and conduct us, during our Voyage to the Oracle of the Holy Bottle.

They promis'd to assist us in this, and added, that we could never have come in a better time, for then the Lanterns held their Provincial Chapter.

When we came to the Royal Palace, we had Audience of her Highness, the Queen of Lantern-Land, being introduc'd by two Lanterns of Honour, that of Aristophanes, and that of Cleanthes, Mistresses of the Ceremonies. Panurge in a few words acquainted her with the Causes of our Voyage, and she received us with great Demonstrations of Friendship, desiring us to come to her at Supper-time, that we might more easily make choice of one to be our Guide, which pleas'd us extreamly. We did not fail to observe intensely every thing we could see, as the Garbs, Motions, and Deportment of the Queen's Subjects, principally the manner after which she was serv'd.

The bright Queen was dress'd in Virgin Christal of Tutia, wrought Damask-wise and beset with large Diamonds.

The Lanterns of the Royal Blood, were clad partly with Bastard-Diamonds, partly with Diaphanous Stones, the rest with Horn, Paper, and Oyl'd Cloth.

The Cresset-Lights took place according to the Antiquity and Lustre of their Families.

An Earthern-dark-lantern shap'd like a Pot, notwithstanding this, took place of some of the first Quality, at which I wondered much, till I was told, it was that of Epictetus, for which three thousand Drachmaes had been formerly refus'd.

Martial's Polymix Lantern made a very good Figure there : I took particular notice of its Dress, and more yet of the Lychnosimity, formerly consecrated by Canopa the Daughter of Tisias.

I saw the Lantern Pensile formerly taken out of the Temple of Apollo Palatinus at Thebes, by Alexander the Great.

I saw another that distinguish'd it self from the rest by a Bushy Tuft of Crimson Silk on its Head. I was told, 'twas that of Bartolus, the Lantern of the Civilians.

Two others were very remarkable for Glister-pouches that dangled at their waste. We were told, that one was the Greater Light, and the other the Lesser Light of the 'Pothecaries.

When 'twas Supper-time, the Queen's Highness first sate down, and then the Lady-lanterns according to their Rank and Dignity.

For the first Course, they were all serv'd with large Christmas-Candles, except the Queen, who was serv'd with a hugeous thick, stiff flaming Taper, of white Wax, somewhat red towards the Tip, and the Royal Family, as also the Provincial Lantern of Mirebalais, who were served with Nut-lights ; and the Provincial of Lower Poitou, with an arm'd Candle.

After that, god wot, what a glorious Light they gave with their Wicks : I do not say all, for you must except a parcel of Junior Lanterns, under the Government of a high and mighty one. These did not cast a Light like the rest, but seem'd to me dimmer than any long-snuff-farthing Candle, whose Tallow has been half melted away in a Hot-House. After Supper we withdrew to take some Rest, and the next Day the Queen made us chuse one of the most Illustrious Lanterns to guide us ; after which we took our leave.

CHAPTER XXXIV

How we arriv'd at the Oracle of the Bottle

OUR glorious Lantern lighting and directing us to Heart's content, we at last arriv'd at the desired Island, where was the Oracle of the Bottle. As soon as Friend Panurge landed, he nimbly cut a Caper with one Leg for Joy, and cry'd to Pantagruel, Now we are where we have wish'd our selves long ago. This is the Place we 've been seeking with such Toil and Labour. He then made a Complement to our Lantern, who desir'd us to be of good Cheer, and not be daunted or dismay'd whatever we might chance to see.

To come to the Temple of the Holy Bottle, we were to go through a large Vine-yard, in which were all sorts of Vines, as the Falernian, Malvesian, the Muscadine, those of Taige, Beaune, Mirevaux, Orleans, Picardent, Arbois, Coussi, Anjou, Grave, Corsica, Vierron, Nerac, and others. This Vine-yard was formerly planted by the good Bacchus, with so great a Blessing, that it yields Leaves, Flowers, and Fruit all the Year round, like the Orange-Trees at Surêne.

Our magnificent Lantern order'd every one of us to eat three Grapes, to put some Vine-leaves in his Shoes, and take a Vine-branch in his left-hand.

At the end of the Close, we went under an Arch built after the manner of those of the Ancients. The Trophies of a Toper were curiously carv'd on it.

First, on one side was to be seen a long Train of Flaggons, Leathern Bottles, Flasks, Cans, Glass-Bottles, Barrels, Nipperkins, Pint-pots, Quart-pots, Pottles, Gallons, and old fashion'd Semaises (swindging Wooden-pots, such as those out of which the Germans fill their Glasses) these hang'd on a shady Arbor.

On another side was store of Garlick, Onions, Shallots, Hams, Botargos, Caviar, Biscuits, Neat's-Tongues, Old Cheese, and such like Comfets, very artificially interwoven and pack'd together with Vine-stocks.

On another, were a hundred sorts of drinking Glasses, Cups, Cisterns, Ewers, False-Cups, Tumblers, Bowls, Mazers, Mugs, Jugs, Goblets, Talboys, and such other Bacchic Artillery.

On the Frontispiece of the Triumphal Arch, under the Zoophore, was the following Couplet :

> You, who presume to move this way,
> Get a good Lantern, lest you stray.

We took special care of that, cry'd Pantagruel, when he had read them ; for there is not a better, or a more divine Lantern than ours in all Lantern-land.

This Arch ended at a fine large round Alley, cover'd over with the interlaid Branches of Vines, loaded and adorned with Clusters of five hundred different Colours, and of as many various Shapes, not natural, but due to the skill of Agriculture, some were Golden, others Blewish, Tawny, Azure, White, Black, Green, Purple, streak'd with many Colours, Long, Round, Triangular, Cod-like, Hairy, Great-headed, and Grassy. That pleasant Alley ended at three old Ivy-trees verdant, and all loaden with Rings. Our enlightned Lantern directed us to make our selves Hats with some of their Leaves, and cover our Heads wholly with 'em, which was immediately done.

Jupiter's Priestess, said Pantagruel, in former days, would not like us, have walk'd under this Arbour. There was a Mystical Reason, answer'd our most perspicuous Lantern, that would have hinder'd her. For had she gone under it, the Wine, or the Grapes of which 'tis made, that 's the same thing, had been over her head, and then she would have seem'd overtopt and master'd by Wine. Which implies that Priests, and all Persons who devote themselves to the Contemplation of Divine Things, ought to keep their Minds sedate and calm, and avoid whatever might disturb and discompose their Tranquility ; which nothing is more apt to do than Drunkenness.

You also, continu'd our Lantern, could not come into the Holy Bottle's Presence, after you had gone through this Arch, did not the noble Priestess Bacbuc first see your Shoes full of Vine-leaves; which Action is diametrically opposite to the other, and signifies that you despise Wine, and having master'd it, as it were, tread it under foot.

I am no Scholar, quoth Fryar Jhon, for which I 'm heartily

sorry; yet I find by my Breviary, that in the Revelation, a Woman was seen with the Moon under her Feet, which was a most wonderful Sight.

Now, as Bigot explain'd it to me, this was to signifie, That she was not of the Nature of other Women, for they have all the Moon at their Heads, and consequently their Brains are always troubled with a Lunacy: This makes me willing to believe what you said, dear Madam Lantern.

CHAPTER XXXV

How we went under Ground to come to the Temple of the Holy-Bottle; and how Chinon is the oldest City in the World

WE went under Ground through a plaister'd Vault, on which was coarsely painted a Dance of Women and Satyrs, waiting on old Silenus who was grinning o' Horseback on his Ass. This made me say to Pantagruel, that this Entry put me in mind of the Painted Cellar, in the oldest City of the World, where such Paintings are to be seen, and in as cool a Place.

Which is the oldest City in the World? ask'd Pantagruel. 'Tis Chinon, Sir, or Cainon in Touraine, said I. I know, return'd Pantagruel, where Chinon lies, and the Painted Cellar also, having my self drunk there many a Glass of cool Wine;

LET'S GO BACK

neither do I doubt but that Chinon is an ancient Town :
Witness its Blazon ; I own 'tis said twice or thrice.

CHINON,

Petite Ville, grand Renom,
Assise sur pierre ancienne :
Au haut le bois, au pied la Vienne,

CHINON,

Little Town,
Great Renown,
On old Stone
Long has stood :
There 's the Vienne, if you look down ;
If you look up, there 's the Wood.

But how, continu'd he, can you make it out, that 'tis the oldest
Town in the World ? Where did you find this written ? I
have found in the Sacred Writ, said I, that Cain was the first
that built a Town ; we may then reasonably conjecture that
from his Name he gave it that of Cainon. Thus, after his
Example, most other Founders of Towns have given them their
Names ; Athena, that 's Minerva in Greek, to Athens ; Alexander to Alexandria ; Constantine to Constantinople ; Pompey
to Pompeiopolis in Cilicia ; Adrian to Adrianople ; Canaan
to the Canaanites ; Saba to the Sabæans ; Assur to the
Assyrians ; and so Ptolemais, Cæsarea, Tiberias, and Herodium
in Judea, got their Names.

While we were thus talking, there came to us the great Flask
whom our Lantern call'd the Philosopher, her Holiness the
Bottle's Governour. He was attended with a Troop of the
Temple-Guards, all French Bottles in Wicker-Armour, and
seeing us with our Javelins wrapt with Ivy, with our illustrious
Lantern, whom he knew, he desir'd us to come in with all
manner of Safety, and order'd we should be immediately
conducted to the Princess Bacbuc, the Bottle's Lady of Honour,
and Priestess of all the Mysteries ; which was done.

CHAPTER XXXVI

How we went down the Tetradic Steps, and of Panurge's Fear

WE went down one Marble-Step under Ground, where there was a Resting, or (as our Workmen call it) a Landing-place; then turning to the left, we went down two other Steps, where there was another Resting-place: After that, we came to three other Steps, turning about, and met a third; and the like at four Steps which we met afterwards. There, quoth Panurge, Is it here, how many Steps have you told? ask'd our Magnificent Lantern. One, two, three, four, answer'd Pantagruel. How much is that? ask'd she. Ten, return'd he. Multiply that, said she, according to the same Pythagorical Tetrad? That's ten, twenty, thirty, forty, cry'd Pantagruel. How much is the whole? said she. One hundred, answer'd Pantagruel. Add, continued she, the first Cube, that's eight; at the end of that fatal Number you'll find the Temple-gate; and pray observe, this is the true Psychogony of Plato, so celebrated by the Academics, yet so little understood; one moiety of which consists of the Unity of the two first Numbers full of two Square and two Cubic Numbers. We then went down those Numeral Stairs all under Ground; and I can assure you in the first place, that our Legs stood us in good stead; for had it not been for 'em, we had rowl'd just like so many Hogsheads into a Vault. Secondly, our Radiant Lantern gave us just so much Light as in St. Patrick's Hole in Ireland, or Trophonius's Pit in Bœotia: Which caus'd Panurge to say to her, after we were got down some seventy eight Steps;

Dear Madam, with a sorrowful aking heart, I most humbly beseech your Lanternship to lead us back. May I be led to Hell, if I be not half dead with Fear, my Heart's sunk down into my Hose; I'm afraid I shall make Butter'd-Eggs in my Breeches. I freely consent never to marry. You have given your self too much trouble on my account; the Lord shall reward you in his great Rewarder, neither will I be ungrateful when I come out of this Cave of Troglodytes. Let's go back, I pray you. I'm very much afraid this is Tænarus, the Low-way to Hell, and methinks I already hear Cerberus bark.

395

Hark, I hear the Curr, or my Ears tingle; I have no manner of kindness for the Dog; for there never is a greater Tooth-ake, than when Dogs bite us by the Shins : And if this be only Trophonius's Pit, the Lemures, Hob-thrushes and Goblins will certainly swallow us alive, just as they devour'd formerly one of Demetrius's Halbardeers for want of Bridles. Art thou here, Fryar Jhon? Prithee, dear, dear Cod, stay by me; I 'm almost dead with fear; has thou got thy Bilbo? Alas, poor Peelgarlick's defenceless; I 'm a naked Man, thou know'st; let 's go back. Zoons, fear nothing, cry'd Fryar Jhon, I 'm by thee, and have thee fast by the Collar; eighteen Devils shan't get thee out of my Clutches, tho' I were unarm'd. Never did a Man yet want Weapons, who had a good Arm, with as stout a Heart; Heav'n would sooner send down a shower of them; even as in Provence, in the Fields of la Crau, near Maraine, there rain'd Stones (they are there to this day) to help Hercules, who otherwise wanted wherewithal to fight Neptune's two Bastards. But whither are we bound? Are we a going to the little Childrens Limbo? By Pluto, they 'll be-pawh and conskite us all; or are we going to Hell for Orders? By Cob's Body, I 'll hamper, bethwack and belabour all the Devils, now I have some Vine-leaves in my Shooes. Thou shalt see me lay about me like mad, old Boy. Which way? where the Devil are they? I fear nothing but their damn'd Horns; but Cuckoldy Panurge's Bull's Feather will altogether secure me from 'em.

Lo! In a Prophetic Spirit, I already see him, like another Actæon, horn'd, horny, hornify'd. Prithee, quoth Panurge, take heed thy self, dear Frater, lest, till Monks have leave to marry, thou wed'st something thou dost'nt like, as some Cat o' nine Tails, or the Quartan Ague; if thou dost, may I never come safe and sound out of this Hypogeum, this Subterranean Cave, if I don't tup and ram that Disease meerly for the sake of making thee a cornuted, corniferous Property, otherwise I fancy the Quartan Ague is but an indifferent Bedfellow. I remember, Gripe-men-all threatned to wed thee to some such thing, for which thou call'st him Heretic.

Here our Splendid Lantern interrupted them, letting us know this was the Place where we were to have a taste of the Creature, and be silent; bidding us not despair of having the Word of the Bottle before we went back, since we had lind our Shooes with Vine-leaves.

Come on then, cry'd Panurge, let 's charge through and

through all the Devils of Hell ; we can but perish, and that 's
soon done : However, I thought to have reserv'd my Life for
some mighty Battle. Move, move, move forwards. I am as
stout as Hercules, my Breeches are full of Courage ; my
Heart trembles a little, I own, but that 's only an effect of the
coldness and dampness of this Vault ; 'tis neither Fear nor an
Ague : Come on, move on, piss, pish, push on ; my Name's
William Dreadnought.

CHAPTER XXXVII

How the Temple Gates, in a wonderful manner, open'd of themselves

AFTER we were got down the Steps, we came to a Portal of
fine Jaspar of Doric Order, on whose Front we read this Sentence
in the finest Gold, EN OINΩ AΛHΘEIA, that is, In Wine Truth.
The Gates were of Corynthian-like Brass, Massy, wrought with
little Vine-branches, finely inemall'd and ingraven, and were
equally join'd and clos'd together in their Mortaise, without
Padlock, Key-chain or Tie whatsover. Where they join'd,
there hang'd an Indian Loadstone as big as an Egyptian Bean,
set in Gold, having two Points, Hexagonal, in a Right Line ;
and on each side towards the Wall hang'd a handful of Scordium
(Garlick Germander.)

There our Noble Lantern desir'd us not to take it amiss
that she went no further with us, leaving us wholly to the Conduct of the Priestess Bacbuc ; for she her self was not allow'd
to go in, for certain Causes rather to be conceal'd than reveal'd
to Mortals. However, she advis'd us to be resolute and secure,
and to trust to her for the Return. She then pull'd the Loadstone that hang'd at the folding of the Gates, and throw'd
it into a Silver Box fix'd for that purpose ; which done, from
the Threshold of each Gate she drew a Twine of Crimson Silk
about nine foot long by which the Scordium hang'd, and having
fasten'd it to two Gold Buckles that hang'd at the sides, she
withdrew.

Immediately the Gates flew open without being touch'd,
not with a creaking or loud harsh noise, like that made by
heavy Brazen-Gates, but with a soft pleasing Murmur that
resounded through the Arches of the Temple.

Pantagruel soon knew the Cause of it, having discover'd a small Cylinder or Rowler that join'd the Gates over the Threshold, and, turning like them towards the Wall on a hard well-polish'd Ophits Stone, with rubbing and rowling, caus'd that harmonious Murmur.

I wonder'd how the Gates thus open'd of themselves to the right and left, and after we were all got in, I cast my Eye between the Gates and the Wall, to endeavour to know how this happen'd; for one wou'd have thought our kind Lantern had put between the Gates the Herb Æthiopis, which, they say, opens some things that are shut; but I perceiv'd that the Parts of the Gates that join'd on the inside were cover'd with Steel; and just where the said Gates touch'd when they were opened, I saw two square Indian Loadstones, of a blewish Hue, well polish'd, and half a Span broad, mortais'd in the Temple-wall. Now, by the hidden and admirable Power of the Loadstones, the Steel-Plates were put into motion, and consequently the Gates were slowly drawn. However, not always, but when the said Loadstone on the outside was remov'd, after which the Steel was freed from its Pow'r, the two Bunches of Scordium being at the same time put at some distance, because it deadens the Magnes, and robs it of its attractive Virtue.

On the Load-stone that was plac'd on the right-side, the following Iambic Verse was curiously engraven in ancient Roman Characters.

Ducunt volentem fata, nolentem trahunt.
Fate leads the Willing, and th' Unwilling draws.

The following Sentence was neatly cut in the Loadstone that was on the left:

ALL THINGS TEND TO THEIR END.

CHAPTER XXXVIII

Of the Temple's admirable Pavement

WHEN I had read those inscriptions, I admir'd the Beauty of the Temple, and particularly the Disposition of its Pavement, with which no Work that is now, or has been under the Cope of Heaven, can justly be compar'd ; not that of the Temple of Fortune at Præneste in Sylla's Time ; or the Pavement of the Greeks, call'd Alerotum, laid by Sosistratus at Pergamus. For this here was wholly in Compartments of precious Stones, all in their Natural Colours : One of Red Jasper, most charmingly spotted. Another of Ophytes. A third of Porphyry. A fourth of Lycophtalmy, a Stone of four different Colours, pouder'd with sparks of Gold as small as Atoms. A fifth of Agath, streaked here and there with small Milk-colour'd Waves. A sixth of costly Chalcedony, or Onyx Stone. And another of Green Jasper, with certain red and yellowish Veins ; and all these were dispos'd in a Diagonal Line.

At the Portico, some small Stones were inlaid, and evenly join'd on the Floor, all in their Native Colours, to imbellish the Design of the Figures, and they were order'd in such a manner, that you would have thought some Vine-leaves and Branches had been carelessly strew'd on the Pavement : For in some place they were thick, and thin in others : That Inlaying was very wonderful every-where ; here, were seen, as it were in the Shade, some Snails crawling on the Grapes ; there, little Lizards running on the Branches ; on this side, were Grapes that seem'd yet greenish ; on another, some Clusters that seem'd full ripe, so like the true, that they could as easily have deceiv'd Starlings, and other Birds, as those which Zeuxis drew.

Nay, we our selves were deceiv'd ; for where the Artist seem'd to have strow'd the Vine-branches thickest, we could not forbear walking with great Strides, lest we should intangle our Feet, just as People go over an unequal stony place. I then cast my Eyes on the Roof and Walls of the Temple, that were all pargetted with Porphyry and Mosaick Work ; which from the left-side at the coming in, most admirably

399

represented the Battel, in which the good Bacchus overthrew the Indians; as followeth.

CHAPTER XXXIX

How we saw Bacchus's Army drawn up in Battalia in Mosaic Work

At the beginning, divers Towns, Hamlets, Castles, Fortresses, and Forests were seen in Flames; and several mad and loose Women, who furiously ripp'd up, and tore live Calves, Sheep, and Lambs, Limb from Limb, and devour'd their Flesh. There we learn'd how Bacchus at his coming into India, destroy'd all things with Fire and Sword.

Notwithstanding this, he was so despis'd by the Indians, that they did not think it worth their while to stop his Progress, having been certainly inform'd by their Spies, that his Lamp was destitute of Warriors, and that he had only with him a Crew of Drunken Females, a low-built, old, effeminate, sottish, Fellow, continually raddled, and as drunk as a Wheel-barrow, with a Pack of young Clownish Doddipoles, stark naked, always skipping and frisking up and down, with Tails and Horns like those of young Kids.

For this Reason the Indians had resolv'd to let them go through their Country without the least Opposition, esteeming a Victory over such Enemies more dishonourable than glorious.

In the mean time, Bacchus march'd on burning every thing; for, as you know, Fire and Thunder are his Paternal Arms; Jupiter having saluted his Mother Semele with his Thunder; so that his Maternal House was ruin'd by Fire. Bacchus also caus'd a great deal of Blood to be spilt; which when he is rouz'd and anger'd, principally in War, is as natural to him, as to make some in time of Peace.

Thus the Plains of the Island of Samos, are call'd Paneca, which signifies Bloody, because Bacchus there overtook the Amazons, who fled from the Country of Ephesus, and there let 'em Blood, so that they all dy'd of Phlebotomy. This may give you a better insight into the meaning of an ancient Proverb, than Aristotle does in his *Problems;* viz., Why 'twas formerly said, Neither eat nor sow any Mint in time of War. The reason is, That Blows are given then without any distinction of Parts

W. HEATH ROBINSON

PAN

401

or Persons, and if a Man that's wounded, has that day handled or eaten any Mint, 'tis impossible, or at least very hard to stanch his Blood.

After this, Bacchus was seen marching in Battalia, riding in a stately Chariot, drawn by six young Leopards; he look'd as young as a Child, to shew that all good Topers never grow old; he was as red as a Cherry, or a Cherub, which you please; and had no more Hair on his Chin, than there's in the inside of my Hand; his Forehead was grac'd with pointed Horns, above which, he wore a fine Crown or Garland of Vine-leaves and Grapes, and a Mitre of Crimson Velvet; having also gilt Buskins on.

He had not one Man with him, that look'd like a Man; his Guards, and all his Forces consisted wholly of Bassarides, Evantes, Euhyades, Edonides, Trietherides, Ogygiæ, Mimallonides, Mænades, Thyiades, and Bacchæ; frantick, raving, raging, furious, mad Women, begirt with live Snakes and Serpents, instead of Girdles, dischevell'd, their Hair flowing about their Shoulders, with Garlands of Vine-branches instead of Forehead-cloths, clad with Stag's or Goat's Skins, and arm'd with Torches, Javelins, Spears, and Halberts, whose ends were like Pine-Apples; besides they had certain small light Bucklers, that gave a loud sound if you touch'd 'em never so little, and these serv'd them instead of Drums; they were just seventy nine thousand two hundred twenty seven.

Silenus, who led the Van, was one on whom Bacchus rely'd very much, having formerly had many Proofs of his Valour and Conduct; he was a diminutive, stooping, palsied, plump, gorbellied, old Fellow, with a swindging pair of stiff-standing Lugs of his own, a sharp Roman Nose, large, rough Eye-brows, mounted on a well-hung Ass; in his Fist he held a Staff to lean upon, and also bravely to fight, whenever he had occasion to alight; and he was drest in a Woman's yellow Gown. His Followers were all young, wild, clownish People, as hornified as so many Kids, and as fell as so many Tigers, naked and perpetually singing and dancing Country-dances; they were call'd Tityri and Satyrs; and were in all eighty five thousand one hundred thirty three.

Pan, who brought up the Reer, was a monstrous sort of a Thing, for his lower Parts were like a Goats, his Thighs hairy, and his Horns bolt upright, a Crimson fiery Phyz, and a Beard that was none of the shortest. He was a bold, stout, daring, desperate Fellow, very apt to take Pepper in the Nose for vea and nay. In his Left-hand he held a Pipe, and a crooked Stick in his Right. His Forces consisted also wholly of Satyrs, Ægipanes, Agripanes, Sylvans, Fauns, Lemures, Lares, Elves, and Hobgoblins, and their Number was seventy eight thousand one hundred and fourteen. The Signal or Word common to all the Army was *Euohe*.

CHAPTER XL

How the Battle, in which the Good Bacchus overthrew the Indians,
was represented in Mosaic Work

IN the next place we saw the Representation of the Good Bacchus's Engagement with the Indians. Silenus, who led the Van, was sweating, puffing and blowing, belabouring his Ass most grievously ; the Ass dreadfully open'd its wide Jaws, drove away the Flies that plagu'd it, winc'd, flounc'd, went back, and bestir'd it self in a most terrible manner, as if some damn'd Gad-bee had stung it at the Breech.

The Satyrs Captains, Serjeants, and Corporals of Companies, sounding the Orgies with Cornets, in a furious manner went round the Army, skipping, capering, bounding, jerking, farting, flying out at Heels, kicking and prancing like mad, encouraging their Companions to fight bravely ; and all the delineated Army cry'd out *Euohe*.

First the Menades charg'd the Indians with dreadful Shouts, and a horrid Din of their brazen Drums and Bucklers ; the Air rung again all-a-round, as the Mosaic Work well express'd it. And pray, for the future don't so much admire Apelles, Aristides the Theban, and others who drew Claps of Thunder, Lightnings, Winds, Words and Spirits.

We then saw the Indian Army, who had at last taken the Field, to prevent the Devastation of the rest of their Country. In the Front were the Elephants with Castles well garison'd on their Backs. But the Army and themselves were put into Disorder ; the dreadful Cries of the Bacchæ having fill'd them with Consternation, and those huge Animals turn'd Tail, and trampled on the Men of their Party.

There you might have seen Gaffer Silenus on his Ass, putting on as hard as he could, striking athwart and alongst, and laying about him lustily with his Staff, after the old fashion of Fencing. His Ass was prancing and making after the Elephants, gaping and martially braying, as it were to sound a Charge, as he did when formerly in the Bacchanalian Feasts. He wak'd the Nymph Lotis, when Priapus full of Priapism had a mind to priapise, while the pretty Creature was taking a Nap.

There you might have seen Pan frisk it with his goatish Shanks about the Mænades, and with his rustick Pipe excite them to behave themselves like Mænades.

A little further you might have blest your Eyes with the sight of a young Satyr, who led seventeen Kings his Prisoners, and a Bacchis, who, with her Snakes, hawl'd along no less than two and forty Captains; a little Faun, who carried a whole dozen of Standards taken on the Enemy; and goodman Bacchus on his Chariot, riding to and fro fearless of Danger, making much of his dear Carkass, and cheerfully toping to all his merry Friends.

Finally, we saw the Representation of his Triumph, which was thus: First, his Chariot was wholly lin'd with Ivy, gather'd on the Mountain Meros; this for its scarcity, which you know, raises the Price of every thing, and principally of those Leaves in India. In this Alexander the Great follow'd his Example at his Indian Triumph. The Chariot was draw'd by Elephants join'd together, wherein he was imitated by Pompey the Great at Rome in his African Triumph. The good Bacchus was seen, drinking out of a mighty Urn, which Action Marius ap'd after his Victory over the Cimbri near Aix in Provence. All his Army were crown'd with Ivy, their Javelins, Bucklers, and Drums were also wholly cover'd with it; there was not so much as Silenus's Ass, but was betrapp'd with it.

The Indian Kings were fasten'd with Chains of Gold close by the Wheels of the Chariot; all the Company march'd in Pomp with unspeakable Joy, loaded with an infinite number of Trophies, Pageants, and Spoils, playing and singing merry Epiniciums, Songs of Triumph, and also rural Lays and Dithyrambs.

At the farthest end was a Prospect of the Land of Egypt; the Nile with its Crocodiles, Marmosets, Ibides, Monkeys, Trochilos's or Wrens, Ichneumons or Pharo's Mice, Hippopotami or Sea-Horses, and other Creatures its Guests and Neighbours: Bacchus was moving towards that Country under the Conduct of a Couple of horn'd Beasts, on one of which was written in Gold, Apis, and Osiris on the other; because no Ox or Cow had been seen in Egypt till Bacchus came thither.

CHAPTER XLI

How the Temple was illuminated with a wonderful Lamp

BEFORE I proceed to the Description of the Bottle, I 'll give you that of an admirable Lamp, that dispens'd so large a Light over all the Temple, that tho' it lay under Ground, we could distinguish every Object as clearly as above it at Noon-day. In the middle of the Roof was fix'd a Ring of massive Gold as thick as my clench'd Fist. Three Chains somewhat less most curiously wrought, hang'd about two Foot and a half below it, and in a Triangle supported a round Plate of fine Gold, whose Diameter or Breadth did not exceed two Cubits and half a Span. There were four holes in it, in each of which an empty Ball was fasten'd, hollow within, and open o' top, like a little Lamp; it's Circumference about two Hands breadth, each Ball was of Precious Stone; one an Amethyst, another an African Carbuncle, the third an Opale, and the fourth an Anthracites: they were full of burning Water, five times distill'd in a Serpentine Lymbeck, and inconsumptible like the Oil formerly put into Pallas's Lamp at Acropolis of Athens by Callimachus. In each of them was a flaming Wick of Asbestine Flax, as of old in the Temple of Jupiter Ammon, such as those which Cleombrotus, a most studious Philosopher, and Pandelinus of Carpasium had, which were rather renew'd than consumed by the Fire.

About two Foot and a half below that gold Plate, the three Chains were fasten'd to three Handles that were fix'd to a large round Lamp of most pure Christal, whose Diameter was a Cubit and a half, and open'd about two Hands breadth o' top; by which open place a Vessel of the same Christal, shap'd somewhat like the lower part of a Gourd-like Lymbeck, or an Urinal, was put at the bottom of the great Lamp, with such a quantity of the afore-mention'd burning Water, that the Flame of the Asbestine Wick reach'd the Centre of the great Lamp. This made all its spherical Body seem to burn and be in a flame, because the Fire was just at the Centre and middle Point: so that it was not more easie to fix the Eye on it, than on the Disque of the Sun; the Matter being wonderfully bright and shining, and the Work most transparent and dazzling, by the Reflection of the various Colours of the precious Stones, whereof the four small Lamps above the main Lamp were made, and their Lustre was still variously glittering all over the Temple. Then this wandring Light being darted on the polish'd Marble and Agath, with which all the inside of the Temple was pargetted, our Eyes were entertain'd with a sight of all the admirable Colours which the Rain-bow can boast, when the Sun darts his fiery Rays on some dropping Clouds.

The Design of the Lamp was admirable in it self; but, in my Opinion, what added much to the Beauty of the whole, was that round the body of the Christal-Lamp, there was carv'd in Cataglyphick Work, a lively and pleasant Battel of naked Boys, mounted on little Hobby-horses, with little Whirligig-Lances and Shields, that seem'd made of Vine-branches with Grapes on them; their Postures generally were very different, and their childish Strife and Motions were so ingeniously exprest, that Art equall'd Nature in every Proportion and Action. Neither did this seem engrav'd, but rather hew'd out and imboss'd; in Relief; or, at least, like Grotesque, which by the Artist's Skill has the appearance of the roundness of the Object it represents; this was partly the Effect of the various and most charming Light, which flowing out of the Lamp, fill'd the carv'd Places with its glorious Rays.

CHAPTER XLII

*How the Priestess Bacbuc show'd us a Fantastic Fountain
in the Temple*

WHILE we were admiring this incomparable Lamp, and the stupendous Structure of the Temple, the Venerable Priestess Bacbuc, and her Attendants came to us with jolly, smiling Looks; and seeing us duly accoutred, without the least difficulty, took us into the middle of the Temple, where just under the aforesaid Lamp was the fine Fantastic Fountain.

CHAPTER XLIII

*How the Fountain-water had the Taste of Wine, according to the
Imagination of those who drank of it*

SHE then order'd some Cups, Goblets, and Talboys of Gold, Silver, and Christal to be brought, and kindly invited us to drink of the Liquor that sprung there, which we readily did; for to say the truth, this Fantastick Fountain was very inviting, and its Materials and Workmanship more precious, rare, and admirable than any thing Pluto ever dreamt of in Limbo.

Its Basis or Ground-Work was of most pure and limpid Alabaster, and its height somewhat more than three Spans; being a regular Heptagone on the out-side, with its Stylobates or Footsteps, Arulets, Simasults or Blunt Tops, and Doric Undulations about it. It was exactly round within. On the middle Point of each Angle and Brink stood a Pillar orbiculated, in form of Ivory or Alabaster solid Rings.

Each Pillar's length from the Basis to the Architraves, was near seven Hands, taking an exact Demension of its Diameter through the Centre of its Circumference and inward Roundness ; and it was so dispos'd, that casting our Eyes behind one of them, whatever its Cube might be, to view its Opposite, we found that the Pyramidal Cone of our Visual Line ended at the said Centre, and there, by the two Opposites, form'd an Equilateral Triangle, whose two Lines divided the Pillar into two equal Parts.

That which we had a mind to measure, going from one side to another, two Pillars over, at the first third part of the distance between them, was met by their lowermost and fundamental Line, which in a Consult Line drawn as far as the Universal Centre, equally divided, gave in a just Partition the distance of the seven opposite Pillars in a right Line ; beginning at the Obtuse Angle on the Brink ; as you know that an Angle is always found plac'd between two others in all Angular Figures odd in Number.

This tacitly gave us to understand that seven Semidiamiaters are in Geometrical Proportion, Compass and Distance, somewhat less than the Circumference of a Circle, from the Figure of which they are extracted, that is to say, three whole Parts with an eighth and a half, a little more ; or a seventh and a half, a little less, according to the Instructions given us of old by Euclid, Aristotle, Archimedes, and others.

The first Pillar, I mean that which fac'd the Temple-Gate, was of Azure, Sky-colour'd Saphir.

The second of Hiacinth, a precious Stone, exactly of the Colour of the Flower, into which Ajax's Cholerick Blood was transform'd ; the Greek letters, AI, being seen on it in many places.

The third an Anachite Diamond, as bright and glittering as Lightning.

The fourth a Masculin Ruby Ballais (Peach-colour'd) amatistising, its Flame and Lustre ending in Violet or Purple, like an Amatist.

The fifth an Emerald, above five hundred and fifty times more precious than that of Serapis in the Labyrinth of the Egyptians, and more verdant and shining than those that were fix'd instead of Eyes in the Marble Lion's Head, near King Hermias's Tomb.

The sixth of Agath, more admirable and various in the Distinctions of its Veins, Clouds and Colours, than that which Pyrrhus, King of Epirus, so mightily esteem'd.

The seventh of Sienites, transparent, of the Colour of a Beril, and the clear Hue of Hymetian Honey, and within it the Moon was seen, such as we see it in the Sky, Silent, Full, New, and in the Wain.

These Stones were assign'd to the Seven heavenly Planets by the ancient Chaldeans; and that the meanest Capacities might be inform'd of this, just at the Central Perpendicular Line, on the Chapter of the first Pillar, which was of Saphire, stood the Image of Saturn in Eliacim Lead, with his Scythe in his Hand, and at his Feet a Crane of Gold, very artfully enamal'd according to the Native Hue of the Saturnine Bird.

On the second, which was of Hiacynth, towards the left, Jupiter was seen in Jovetian Brass, and on his Breast an Eagle of Gold enamal'd to the Life.

On the third, was Phœbus of the purest Gold, and a white Cock in his Right-Hand.

On the fourth, was Mars in Corinthian-Brass, and a Lion at his Feet.

On the fifth, was Venus in Copper, the Metal of which Aristomides made Athamas's Statue, that express'd in a blushing Whiteness his Confusion at the sight of his Son Learchus, who died at his Feet of a Fall.

On the sixth, was Mercury in Hydrargyre, I would have said Quicksilver, had it not been fixed, malleable, and unmoveable : That nimble Deity had a Stork at his Feet.

On the seventh, was the Moon in Silver, with a Greyhound at her Feet.

The Size of these Statues was somewhat more than a third part of the Pillars on which they stood ; and they were so admirably wrought according to Mathematical Proportion, that Polycletus's Cannon could hardly have stood in competition with them.

The Bases of the Pillars, the Chapters, the Architraves, Zoophores and Cornishes, were Phrygian Work of Massive Gold, purer and finer than any that is found in the Rivers Leéde near Montpellier, Ganges in India, Pô in Italy, Hebrus in Thrace, Tagus in Spain, and Pactolus in Lydia.

The small Arches between the Pillars were of the same

Precious-stone of which the Pillars next to them were. Thus that Arch was of Saphir which ended at the Hiacynth Pillar, and that was of Hiacynth which went towards the Diamond, and so on.

Above the Arches and Chapters of the Pillars on the inward Front a Cupola was raised to cover the Fountain; it was surrounded by the Planetary Statues, Heptagonal at the bottom, and Spherical o'top; and of Crystal so pure, transparent, well polished, whole, and uniform in all its parts, without Veins, Clouds, Flaws or Streaks, that Xenocrates never saw such a one in his life.

Within it were seen the Twelve Signs of the Zodiac, the Twelve Months of the Year, with their Proprieties, the Two Equinoxes, the Ecliptic Line, with some of the most remarkable Fixed Stars about the Antartic Pole and elsewhere, so curiously engraven, that I fansied them to be the Workmanship of King Necepsus or Petosiris the ancient Mathematician.

On the top of the Cúpola, just over the Centre of the Fountain, were three noble long Pearls all of one size, Pear-fashion, perfectly imitating a Tear, and so joined together as to represent a Flower-de-luce or Lilly, each of the Flowers seeming above a Hand's-breadth. A Carbuncle jetted out of its Calix or Cup, as big as an Ostridge's Egg, cut Seven-square (that Number so belov'd of Nature) and so prodigiously glorious, that the Sight of it had like to have made us blind; for the fiery Sun, or the pointed Lightning, are not more dazling and unsufferably bright.

Now were some judicious Appraisers to judge of the Value of this incomparable Fountain, and the Lamp of which we spoke, they would undoubtedly affirm, it exceeds that of all the Treasures and Curiosities in Europe, Asia and Africa put together. For that Carbuncle alone would have darken'd the Pantharb of Joachas the Indian Magician, with as much ease as the Sun outshines and dimns the Stars with his Meridian Rays.

Now let Cleopatra, that Egyptian Quean, boast of her Pair of Pendants, those two Pearls, one of which she caused to be dissolved in Vinegar, in the Presence of Anthony the Triumvir, her Gallant.

Or let Pompeia Plautina be proud of her Dress cover'd all over with Emeralds and Pearls curiously intermix'd, that attracted the Eyes of all Rome, and was said to be the Pit and Magazine of the Conquering Robbers of the Universe.

The Fountain had three Tubes or Channels of right Pearl, seated in three Equilateral Angles already mention'd, extended on the Margent; and those Channels proceeded in a Snail-like Line winding equally on both sides.

We look'd on them a-while, and had cast our Eyes on another side, when Bacbuc directed us to watch the Water: We then heard a most harmonious Sound, yet somewhat stopt by starts, far distant, and subterranean, by which means it was still more pleasing than if it had been free, uninterrupted, and near us; so that our Minds were as agreeably entertain'd through our Ears with that charming Melody, as they were through the Windows of our Eyes, with those delightful Objects.

Bacbuc then said, Your Philosophers will not allow, that Motion is begot by the Power of Figures; Look here, and see the contrary. By that single Snail-like Motion, equally divided as you see, and a five-fold insoliature, moveable at every inward meeting, such as is the *Vena cava* where it enters into the right Ventricle of the Heart; just so is the Flowing of this Fountain, and by it an Harmony ascends as high as your World's Ocean.

She then ordered her Attendants to make us drink: And to tell you the truth of the matter as near as possible, we are not, Heav'n be prais'd! of the nature of a Drove of Calf-lollies, who (as your Sparrows can't feed, unless you bob 'em on the Tail) must be ribroasted with tough Crabtree, and firk'd into a stomach, or at least into an humour to eat or drink: No, we know better things, and scorn to scorn any Man's Civility, who civilly invites us to a Drinking-bout. Bacbuc ask'd us then how we liked our Tiff? We answer'd, That it seem'd to us good harmless sober Adam's Liquor, fit to keep a Man in the right way, and in a word, meer Element; more cool and clear than Argyrontes in Ætolia, Peneus in Thessaly, Axius in Migdonia, or Cydnus in Cilicia, a tempting Sight of whose cool Silver Stream caus'd Alexander to prefer the short-liv'd Pleasure of bathing himself in it, to the Inconveniences which he could not but foresee would attend so ill-tim'd an Action.

This, said Bacbuc, comes of not considering with our selves, or understanding the Motions of the Musculous Tongue, when the Drink glides on in its way to the Stomach! Tell me, Noble Strangers, Are your Throats lin'd, pav'd, or enamel'd, as formerly was that of Pythilus, nicknam'd Theuthes, that you can have miss'd the Taste, Relish and Flavour of this Divine Liquor ? Here, said she, turning towards her Gentlewomen, Bring my Scrubbing-brushes ; you know which, to scrape, rake, cleanse and clear their Palates.

They brought immediately some stately, swindging, jolly Hams, fine, substantial Neats-tongues, good Hung-beef, pure and delicate Botargos, Venison, Saucidges, and such other Gullet-sweepers. And to comply with her Invitation, we cramm'd and twisted till we own'd our selves thoroughly cured of Thirst, which before did damnably plague us.

We are told, continu'd she, that formerly a Learned and Valiant Hebrew Chief, leading his People through Desarts, where they were in hopes of being famish'd, obtain'd of God some Manna, whose Taste was to them, by Imagination, such as that of Meat was to them in Reality before : Thus, drinking of this miraculous Liquor, you 'll find it taste like any Wine that you shall fancy you drink. Come, then, fancy, and drink. We did so ; and Panurge had no sooner whipp'd off his Brimmer, but he cry'd, By Noah's Open-shop, 'tis *Vin de Beaulne*, better than ever was yet tipp'd over Tongue, or may ninety six Devils swallow me. Oh, that to keep its Taste the longer, we Gentlemen Topers had but Necks some three Cubits long, or so, as Philoxenus desir'd to have, or at least like a Crane's, as Melanthius wish'd his.

On the Faith of true Lanterners, quoth Fryar Jhon, 'tis gallant sparkling Greek Wine ; Now, for God's sake, Sweetheart, do but teach me how the devil you make it. It seems to me Mirevaux Wine, said Pantagruel ; for before I drank, I suppos'd it to be such. Nothing can be mislik'd in it, but that 'tis cold, colder, I say, than the very Ice, colder than the Nonacrian and Deræan Water, or the Conthopian Spring at Corinth, that froze up the Stomach and Nutritive Parts of those that drank of it.

Drink once, twice or thrice more, said Bacbuc, still changing your Imagination, and you shall find its Taste and Flavour to be exactly that on which you shall have pitched. Then never presume to say that any thing is impossible to God. We never offered to say any such thing, said I ; far from it, we maintain He is Omnipotent.

CHAPTER XLIV

*How the Priestess Bacbuc equipt Panurge, in order
to have the Word of the Bottle*

WHEN we had thus chatted and tippled, Bacbuc ask'd, Who
of you here wou'd have the Word of the Bottle ? I, your most
humble little Funnel, an 't please you, quoth Panurge. Friend,
saith she, I have but one thing to tell you, which is, That when
you come to the Oracle, you take care to hearken and hear the
Word only with one Ear. This, cry'd Fryar Jhon, is Wine of
one Ear, as Frenchmen call it.

She then wrapt him up in a Gaberdine, bound his Noddle
with a goodly clean Biggin, clapt over it a Felt, such as those
through which Hypocras is distill'd, at the bottom of which,
instead of a Cowle, she put three Obelisks, made him draw on a
Pair of old-fashion'd Codpieces instead of Mittens, girded him
about with three Bagpipes bound together, bath'd his Jobbernol
thrice in the Fountain ; then threw a handful of Meal on his
Phyz, fix'd three Cocks Feathers on the right-side of the
Hypocratical Felt, made him take a jant nine times round the
Fountain, caused him to take three leaps, and to bump his
A—— seven times against the Ground, repeating I don't know
what kind of Conjurations all the while in the Toscan Tongue,
and ever and anon reading in a Ritual, or Book of Ceremonies,
carry'd after her by one of her Mystagogues.

For my part, may I never stir, if I don't really believe, that
neither Numa Pompilius the Second King of the Romans, nor
the Cerites of Tuscia, and the Old Hebrew Captain, ever
instituted so many Ceremonies as I then saw performed ; nor
were ever half so many Religious Forms used by the Soothsayers of Memphis in Egypt to Apis, or by the Embrians, or at
Rhamnus to Rhamnusia, or to Jupiter Ammon, or to Feronia.

When she had thus accoutred my Gentleman, she took him
out of our Company, and led him out of the Temple through
a golden Gate on the right, into a round Chapel made of transparent speculary Stones, by which solid Clearness the Sun's
Light shined there through the Precipice of the Rock, without
any Windows or other Entrance, and so easily and fully dispersed it self through the greater Temple, that the Light
seem'd rather to spring out of it, than to flow into it.

413

The Workmanship was not less rare than that of the Sacred Temple at Ravenna, or that in the Island of Chemnis in Egypt. Nor must I forget to tell you, that the Work of that round Chapel was contriv'd with such a Symmetry, that its Diameter was just the heighth of the Vault.

In the middle of it was an Heptagonal Fountain of fine Alabaster, most artfully wrought, full of Water, which was so clear, that it might have pass'd for Element in its Purity and singleness. The Sacred Bottle was in it to the middle, clad in pure fine Crystal, of an oval shape, except its Muzzle, which was somewhat wider than is consistent with that Figure.

CHAPTER XLV

How Bacbuc the High-Priestess brought Panurge before the Holy Bottle

THERE the Noble Priestess Bacbuc made Panurge stoop and kiss the brink of the Fountain ; then bad him rise and dance three Ithymbi. Which done, she order'd him to sit down, between two Stools placed there for that purpose, his Arse upon the Ground. Then she opened her Ceremonial-Book, and whispering in his Left-Ear, made him sing an Epileny, inserted here in the Figure of the Bottle.

When Panurge had sung, Bacbuc throw'd I don't know what into the Fountain, and strait its Water began to boil in good earnest, just for the world as doth the great Monastical Pot at Bourgueil, when 'tis High-Holiday there. Friend Panurge was list'ning with one Ear, and Bacbuc kneeled by him, when such a kind of Humming was heard out of the Bottle, as is made by a Swarm of Bees bred in the Flesh of a young Bull kill'd and drest according to Aristæus's Art, or such as is made when a Bolt flies out of a Cross-bow, or when a Shower falls on a sudden in Summer. Immediately after this was heard the Word *TRINC*. By Cob's Body, cried Panurge, 'tis broken, or crack'd at least, not to tell a Lye for the matter ; for, even so do Crystal Bottles speak in our Country when they burst near the Fire.

Bacbuc arose, and gently taking Panurge under the Arms, said, Friend, Offer your Thanks to Indulgent Heaven, as

Reason requires, you have soon had the Word of the Goddess Bottle ; and the kindest, most favourable and certain Word of an Answer that I ever yet heard her give since I officiate here

Bottle ! whose Mysterious Deep
Do's ten thousand Secrets keep,
With attentive Ear I wait ;
Ease my Mind, and speak my Fate.
Soul of Joy !   Like Bacchus, we
More than India gain by thee.
Truths unborn thy Juice reveals,
Which Futurity conceals.
Antidote to Frauds and Lyes,
Wine, that mounts us to the Skies,
May thy Father Noah's Brood
Like him drown, but in thy Flood.
Speak, so may the Liquid Mine
Of Rubies, or of Diamonds, shine.
  Bottle ! whose Mysterious Deep
Do's ten thousand Secrets keep,
With attentive Ear I wait ;
Ease my Mind, and speak my Fate.

at her most Sacred Oracle : Rise, let us go to the Chapter, in whose gloss that fine Word is explain'd.   With all my Heart, quoth Panurge ; by Jingo, I am just as wise as I was last Year : Light, where 's the Book.   Turn it over, where 's that Chapter ; Let 's see this merry Gloss.

CHAPTER XLVI

How Bacbuc explain'd the Word of the Goddess Bottle

BACBUC having thrown I don't know what into the Fountain, strait the Water ceas'd to boil, and then she took Panurge into the greater Temple, where was the enlivening Fountain.

There she took out a hugeous Silver Book, in the shape of a Half-tierce, or Hog'shead of Sentences; and having fill'd it at the Fountain, said to him; the Philosophers, Preachers and Doctors of your World feed you up with fine Words and Cant at the Ears; now, here we really incorporate our Precepts at the Mouth. Therefore, I'll not say to you, read this Chapter, see this Gloss; No, I say to you, Taste me this fine Chapter, swallow me this rare Gloss. Formerly an Ancient Prophet of the Jewish Nation eat a Book, and became a Clerk to the very Teeth; now will I have you to drink one, that you may be a Clerk to your very Liver. Here open your Mandibules.

Panurge gaping as wide as his Jaws would stretch, Bacbuc took the Silver Book, at least we took it for a real Book, for it look'd just for the world like a Breviary; but, in truth, it was a Breviary or Flask of Right Phalernian Wine as it came from the Grape, which she made him swallow every drop.

By Bacchus, quoth Panurge, this was a notable Chapter, a most Authentic Gloss o' my word! Is this all that the Trismegistian Bottle's Word means? i' troth I like it extreamly, it went down like Mother's Milk. Nothing more, return'd Bacbuc, for Trinc is a Panomphean Word, that is, a Word understood, us'd and celebrated by all Nations, and signifies Drink.

Some say in your World that Sack is a Word us'd in all Tongues, and justly admitted in the same Sense among all Nations; for, as Æsop's Fable hath it, all Men are born with a Sack at the Neck, naturally needy, and begging of each other; neither can the most powerful King be without the help of other Men, or can any one that 's poor subsist without the rich, though he be never so proud and insolent; as for Example, Hippias, the Philosopher, who boasted he could do every thing. Much less can any one make shift without Drink than without a Sack. Therefore here we hold not that Laughing, but that Drinking is the distinguishing Character of Man. I don't say Drinking, taking that word singly and absolutely in the strictest Sense; No, Beasts then might put in for a share; I mean drinking cool delicious Wine. For you must know, my Beloved, that by Wine we become Divine; neither can there be a surer Argument, or a less deceitful Divination. Your Academics assert the same when they make the Etymologie of Wine, which the Greeks call ΟΙΝΟΣ, to be from *Vis*, Strength, Vertue and Power; for 'tis in its power to fill the Soul with all Truth, Learning and Philosophy.

If you observe what is written in Ionian Letters on the Temple-gate, you may have understood that Truth is in Wine. The Goddess Bottle therefore directs you to that divine Liquor, be your self the Expounder of your Undertaking.

'Tis impossible, said Pantagruel to Panurge, to speak more to the purpose than does this true Priest; you may remember I told you as much when you first spoke to me about it.

Trinc then: What says your Heart elevated by Bacchic Enthusiasm?

With this, quoth Panurge,

> Trinc, Trinc, by Bacchus, let us tope,
> And tope again; for, now I hope
> To see some brawny juicy Rump,
> And tickle 't with my Carnal Stump.
> E'er long, my Friends, I shall be wedded,
> Sure as my Trap-stick has a red Head;
> And my sweet Wife shall hold the Combat,
> Long as my Baws can on her Bum beat.
> O what a Battel of A—— fighting
> Will there be! which I much delight in.
> What pleasant Pains then shall I take
> To keep my self and Spouse awake!
> All Heart and Juice, I 'll up and ride,
> And make a Dutchess of my Bride.
> Sing Iö Pæan! loudly sing
> To Hymen, who all Joys will bring.
> Well, Fryar Jhon, I 'll take my Oath,
> This Oracle is full of Troth;
> Intelligible Truths it bears,
> More certain than the Sieve and Shears.

CHAPTER XLVII

How Panurge and the rest rim'd with Poetick Fury

WHAT a Pox ails the Fellow, quoth Fryar Jhon ? stark staring mad, or bewitch'd, o' my word ! Do but hear the chiming Dotterel gabble in Rhime. What o' Devil has he swallow'd ? His Eyes rowl in his Loggerhead, just for the world like a dying Goat's. Will the addle-pated Wight have the grace to sheer off ? Will he rid us of his damn'd Company, to go shite out his nasty rhiming Balderdash in some Bog-house ? Will no Body be so kind as to cram some Dog's-bur down the poor Cur's Gullet, or will he Monk-like run his Fist up to the Elbow into his Throat to his very Maw to scoure and clear his Flanks ? Will he take a Hair of the same Dog ?

Pantagruel chid Fryar Jhon, and said,

Bold Monk, forbear, this I 'll assure ye,
Proceeds all from Poetick Fury ;
Warm'd by the God, inspir'd with Wine,
His Human Soul is made Divine,
For without Jest,
His hallow'd Breast,
With Wine possest,
Cou'd have no rest,
Till h' had exprest
Some Thoughts at least
Of his great Guest.
Then strait he flies
Above the Skies,
And mortifies,
With Prophesies,
Our Miseries.

And since divinely he 's inspir'd,
Adore the Soul by Wine acquir'd,
And let the Toss-pot be admir'd.

How ! quoth the Fryar, the fit Rhiming is upon you too ‹ Is 't come to that ? Then we are all pepper'd, or the Devil pepper me. What would not I give to have Gargantua see us while we are in this Maggotty Crambo-vein! Now, may I be curst with living on that damn'd empty Food, if I can tell, whether I shall scape the catching Distemper. The Devil a bit do I understand which way to go about it; however, the Spirit of Fustian possesses us all, I find. Well, by St. John, I 'll Poetise, since every Body does; I find it coming. Stay, and pray pardon me, if I don't Rhime in Crimson; 'tis my first Essay.

> Thou, who canst Water turn to Wine,
> Transform my Bum by Pow'r Divine
> Into a Lantern, that may Light
> My Neighbour in the darkest Night.

Panurge then proceeds in his Rapture, and says,

> From Pythian Tripos ne'er were heard
> More Truths, nor more to be rever'd.
> I think from Delphos to this Spring,
> Some Wizard brought that conj'ring thing:
> Had honest Plutarch here been toping,
> He then so long had ne'er been groping
> To find, according to his Wishes,
> Why Oracles are mute as Fishes
> At Delphos: Now the Reason 's clear,
> No more at Delphos they 're but here.
> Here is the Tripos, out of which
> Is spoke the Doom of Poor and Rich.
> For Athæneus does relate
> This Bottle is the Womb of Fate,
> Prolific of mysterious Wine,
> And big with Prescience Divine:
> It brings the Truth with pleasure forth,
> Besides, you ha 't a Penny-worth.
> So, Fryar Jhon, I must exhort you
> To wait a Word that may import you,
> And to enquire, while here we tarry
> If it shall be your luck to Marry.

Fryar Jhon answers him in a Rage, and says,

> How Marry! by St. Bennet's Boot
> And his Gambadoes, I 'll ne'r do 't.
> No Man that knows me e'er shall judge
> I mean to make myself a Drudge,

Or that Peelgarlick e'er will doat
Upon a paultry Petticoat.
I 'll ne'er my Liberty betray
All for a little Leap-frog play,
And ever after wear a Clog
Like Monkey, or like Mastiff-Dog :
No, I 'd not have upon my Life,
Great Alexander for my Wife,
Nor Pompey, nor his Dad in Law,
Who did each other clapper-claw.
Not the best he that wears a Head,
Shall win me to his Truckle-bed.

Panurge pulling off his Gaberdine and Mystical Accoutrements, reply'd,

Wherefore thou shalt, thou filthy Beast,
Be damn'd twelve Fathoms deep at least ;
While I shall reign in Paradise,
Whence on thy Loggerhead I 'll piss.
Now when that dreadful Hour is come,
That thou in Hell receiv'st thy Doom,
Ev'n there, I know, thou 'lt play some trick,
And Proserpine shan't scrape a prick
Of the long Pin within thy Breeches.
But when thou 'rt using these Capriches,
And Catterwawling in her Cavern,
Send Pluto to the farthest Tavern,
For the best Wine that 's to be had,
Lest he should see, and run Horn-mad :
She 's kind, and ever did admire
A well-fed Monk, or well-hung Fryar.

Go to, quoth Fryar Jhon, thou old Noddy, thou doddipold Ninny, go to the Devil thou 'rt prating of ; I 've done with Rhiming, the Rhume gripes me at the Gullet. Let 's talk of paying and going ; come.

SHE'S KIND, AND EVER DID ADMIRE A WELL-FED MONK

421

CHAPTER XLVIII

*How we took our leave of Bacbuc, and left the Oracle of
the Holy Bottle*

Do not trouble your self about any thing here, said the Priestess
to the Fryar; if you be but satisfied, we are. Here below
in these Circumcentral Regions, we place the Sovereign Good
not in taking and receiving, but in bestowing and giving; so
that we esteem our selves happy, not if we take and receive
much of others, as perhaps the Sects of Teachers do in your
World, but rather if we impart and give much. All I have to
beg of you, is that you leave us here your Names in Writing
in this Ritual. She then open'd a fine large Book, and as we
gave our Names, one of her Mystagogues, with a Gold Pin,
drew some Lines on it, as if she had been Writing; but we
could not see any Characters.

This done, she filled three Glasses with fantastick Water,
and giving them into our Hands, said, Now, my Friends, you
may depart, and may that Intellectual Sphere, whose Centre
is every where, and Circumference no where, whom we call
GOD, keep you in his Almighty Protection. When you come
into your World, do not fail to affirm and witness, that the
greatest Treasures, and most admirable Things are hidden
under Ground, and not without reason.

Ceres was worshipp'd, because she taught Mankind the
Art of Husbandry, and by the use of Corn, which she invented,
abolish'd that beastly way of feeding on Acorns, and she
grievously lamented her Daughter's Banishment into our
Subterranean Regions, certainly foreseeing that Proserpine
would meet with more excellent Things, more desirable Enjoy-
ments below, than she her Mother could be blest with above.

What do you think is become of the Art of forcing the
Thunder, and Cœlestial Fire down, which the wise Prometheus
had formerly invented? 'Tis most certain you have lost it;
'tis no more on your Hemisphere; but here below we have it.
And, without a Cause, you sometimes wonder to see whole
Towns burn'd and destroy'd by Lightning, and Ethereal Fire,
and are at a loss about knowing from whom, by whom, and

to what end those dreadful Mischiefs were sent. Now they are familiar and useful to us; and your Philosophers who complain that the Antients have left them nothing to write of, or to invent, are very much mistaken. Those Phænomena which you see in the Sky, whatever the surface of the Earth affords you, and the Sea, and every River contain, is not to be compar'd with what is hid within the Bowels of the Earth.

For this reason, the Subterranean Ruler has justly gain'd, in almost every Language, the Epithete of Rich. Now when your Sages shall wholly apply their Minds to a diligent and studious Search after Truth, humbly begging the Assistance of the Sovereign God, whom formerly the Egyptians in their Language, call'd, The Hidden and the Conceal'd, and invoking him by that Name, beseech him to reveal, and make himself known to them, that Almighty Being will out of his infinite Goodness, not only make his Creatures, but even himself known to them.

Thus will they be guided by good Lanterns. For all the Ancient Philosophers and Sages have held two things necessary, safely and pleasantly to arrive at the Knowledge of God and true Wisdom; first, God's gracious Guidance, then Man's Assistance.

So among the Philosophers, Zoroaster took Arimaspes for the Companion of his Travels; Esculapius, Mercury; Orpheus, Musæus; Pythagoras, Aclophamus; and among Princes and Warriors, Hercules in his most difficult Atchievements, had his singular Friend Theseus; Ulysses, Diomedes; Æneas, Achates; you follow'd their Examples, and came under the Conduct of an Illustrious Lantern: Now in God's Name depart, and may he go along with you.

THE ◌ ◌ MOST CERTAIN, TRUE AND INFALLIBLE
PANTAGRUELIAN PROGNOSTICATION ◌ ◌ FOR
THE YEAR THAT 'S TO COME, AND ◌ ◌ EVER
AND AYE. ◌ ◌ CALCULATED FOR THE BENEFIT
AND NODDIFICA- ◌ ◌ TION OF THE GIDDY-
BRAIN'D AND WEATHER- ◌ ◌ WISE *WOULD-BE'S*.
◌ ◌ BY MASTER *ALCOFRIBAS NASIER*, ARCHI-
TRICLIN TO ◌ ◌ THE AFOREMENTION'D *PANTA-
GRUEL*

TO THE COURTEOUS READER; GREETING

HAVING consider'd the infinite Abuses arising from whole
Cart loads of Lovain Prognostications made in the Shadow of
a Pot of Drink, or so, I have here calculated one the most sure
and unerring that ever was seen in Black and White, as hereafter you 'll find. For, doubtless, considering what the Royal
Prophet says to God in the 5th Psalm, Thou shalt destroy them
that speak leasing; 'tis a heinous, foul, and crying Sin, to tell
a damn'd wilful Lye, thereby to deceive the poor gaping World,
greedy of Novelties ; such as the French, above all others, have
been, time out of mind, as Cæsar in his *Commentaries*, and
John de Gravot in his *Gallick Mythologies*, have set down.
Which is daily observable throughout all France, where the
first Questions, which you shall put to People newly arrived
are, What News ? Is there no News stirring ? What do they
say ? What 's the Discourse Abroad ? And so inquisitive
they are, that they 'll be stark staring mad at those who come
out of strange Countries, unless they bring a whole Budget-ful
of strange Stories, calling them Dolts, Blockheads, Ninny-
hammers, and silly Oufs.

Since then, they are so ready to ask after News, and consequently the more glibly swallow down every flim-flam Story
that 's told them ; Were it not expedient that some People,
on whose faith we might depend, should hold Offices of Intelligence on the Frontiers of the Kingdom, and have a competent Salary allow'd them for nothing else but to examine the
News that is brought, whether it is true or no ? Yea, verily
Friends. Even so did my good Master Pantagruel through
all the Countries of Utopia and Dipsody ; whence it comes,

that his Territories are so prosperous, that at present they can't tell how to make away with their Wine fast enough, but are fain to let it run about in waste, if plenty of good Fellows from other Parts do not come to help them off with it.

Being therefore desirous to satisfie the Curiosity of every good Companion, I have tumbled over and over all the Pant-archs of the Heavens, calculated the Quadrates of the Moon, hook'd out whatever all the Astrophyles, Hypernephelists, Anemophylaxes, Uranopetes, Ombrophores, and the Devil and all of them have thought ; and then having confer'd with Empedocles upon the whole, who, by the way, desires to be kindly remembred to you, I have here cramm'd the Pith, Marrow, and Matter of the Substance of it into a few Chapters ; assuring you that I say nothing of it, but what I think ; and that I think nothing of it, but what it is ; and there is no more to be known in those Matters, than what you are going to read. As for any thing that may hereafter be said over and above, it will come to pass, per'anture ay, per'anture no.

Take notice by the by, That if you don't believe every Syllable, Iota, and Tittle of it, you do me a great deal of wrong, for which either here or elsewhere you may chance to be claw'd off with a vengeance ; and a good Salt-eel, Crab-tree, or Bull's-pizzle, may be plentifully bestow'd on your outward Man. You may take Pepper in the Nose, and snuff and suck up the Air as you would Oysters, as much as you please ; 'tis all one for that. Well, however, come snite your Noses, my little Children ; and you old doating Father Grey-beards pull out your best Eyes, d' on your Barnacles, and in the Scale of the Sanctuary weigh me every tittle of what I 'm going to tell you.

OF THE GOLDEN NUMBER

THE Golden Number *non est inventus :* I cannot find it this year by any Calculation that I have made. Let 's go on, *Verte folium ;* turn over leaf.

CHAPTER I

Of the Governor and Lords Ascendant this Year

WHATSOEVER these Blindfolded, Blockheadly Fools, the Astro-logers of Lovain, Norimberg, Tubinge, and Lyons, may tell ye, don't you feed your selves up with Whims and Fancies, nor believe there is any Governor of the whole Universe this Year, but God the Creator, who by his Divine Word rules and governs all ; by whom all Things are in their Nature, Propriety and Conditions, and without whose Preservation and Governance all Things in a moment would be reduc'd to Nothing, as out of Nothing they were by Him created : For of Him comes, in Him is, and by Him is made perfect every Being, and all Life and Motion, as says the Evangelical Trumpet, my Lord St. Paul, Rom. the 11th.

Therefore the Ruler of this Year, and of all others, according to our Authentick Solution, will be God Almighty. And neither Saturn, nor Mars, nor Jupiter, nor any other Planet, nor the very Angels, nor Saints, nor Men, nor Devils, shall have any Virtue, Efficacy or Influence whatsoever, unless God of his good Pleasure gives it them. As Avicen says, Second Causes have not any Influence or Action whatsoever, if the First Cause did not Influence them.——Does not the good little Mannikin speak truth, think ye ?

CHAPTER II

Of the Eclipses this Year

THIS Year there will be so many Eclipses of the Sun and Moon, that I fear (not unjustly) our Pockets will suffer Inanition, be full empty, and our feeling at a loss. Saturn will be retrograde, Venus right, Mercury as unfix'd as Quicksilver. And a Pack of Planets won't go as you would have them.

For this reason, the Crabs will go side-long, and the Ropemakers backward ; the little Stools will get up on the Benches, and the Spits on the Racks, and the Bands on the Hats ; and many a one's Yard will hang down and dangle, for want of Leathern Pouches ; Fleas will be generally Black ; Bacon will run away from Peas in Lent ; the Belly will waddle before ; the A— will sit down first ; there won't be a Bean left in a Twelf-cake, nor an Ace in a Flush ; the Dice won't run to your wish tho' you cog them, and the Chance that you desire will seldom come ; Brutes shall speak in several Places, Shrovetide will have its day, one part of the World shall disguise it self to gull and chouse the other, and run about the Streets like a parcel of addle-pated Animals, and mad Devils ; such a hurly-burly was never seen since the Devil was a little Boy ; and there will be above seven and twenty irregular Verbs made this Year, if Priscian don't hold them in.   If God don't help us, we shall have our hands and hearts full.   But on the other side, if He be with us, nothing can hurt us, as says the Celestial Star-gazer, who was wrapt into the Third Heaven, Rom. the 7th ; *Si Deus pro nobis quis contra nos ?*   If God be with us, who will be against us ?   In good faith, *Nemo domine;* No body, an 't like your Worship ; for He is as Powerful as He is Good.   Here for the same, praise ye his Holy Name.

CHAPTER III

Of the Diseases this Year

THIS Year the Stone-blind shall see but very little ; the Deaf shall hear but scurvily ; the Dumb shan't speak very plain ; the Rich shall be somewhat in a better case than the Poor, and the Healthy than the Sick.   Whole Flocks, Herds, and Droves of Sheep, Swine, and Oxen ; Cocks and Hens, Ducks and Drakes, Geese and Ganders, shall go to Pot ; but the Mortality will not be altogether so great among Apes, Monkeys, Baboons, and Dromedaries.   As for old Age, 'twill be incurable this Year, because of the Years past.   Those who are sick of the Pleurisy, will feel a plaguy Stitch in their Sides ; those who are troubled with the Thoro'-go-nimble or Wild-squirt, will often prostitute their Blind-cheeks to the Bog-house.   Catarrhs this Year shall distill from the Brain on the lower Parts ; Sore Eyes will by no means help the Sight ; Ears shall be at least as scarce and short in Gascony, and among Knights of the Post, as ever : A most horrid and dreadful, virulent, malignant, catching, perverse, and odious Malady, shall be almost Epidemical, insomuch that many shall run mad upon 't, not knowing what Nail to drive to keep the Wolf from the Door, very often plotting, contriving, cudgelling, and puzling their weak, shallow Brains, and syllogiz-ing and prying up and down for the Philosopher's-Stone, tho' they only get Midas's Lugs by the bargain.   I quake for very fear when I think on 't ; for I assure you, few will escape this Disease, which Averoes calls Lack of Money : And by Conse-quence of the last Year's Comet, and Saturn's Retrogradation, a huge drivelling He-Scoundrel, all be-crinkum'd and colly-flower'd shall die in the Spittle ; at his Death will be a horrid clutter between the Cats and the Rats, Hounds and Hares, Hawks and Ducks, and eke between the Monks and Eggs.

CHAPTER IV

Of the Fruits of the Earth this Year

I FIND by the Calculations of Albumazar, in his Book of the great Conjunction, and elsewhere, That this will be a plentiful Year of all manner of good things to those that have enough ; but your Hops of Picardy will go near to fare the worse for the Cold. As for Oates, they 'll be a great help to Horses. I dare say, there won't be much more Bacon than Swine : Pisces having the Ascendant, 'twill be a mighty Year for Muscles, Cockles, and Perrywinkles. Mercury somewhat threatens our Parsly-beds, yet Parsly will be to be had for Money. Hemp will grow faster than the Children of this Age, and some will find there 's but too much on 't. There will be but a very few Bon-Christians, but Choak-pears in abundance. As for Corn, Wine, Fruit, and Herbs, there never was such Plenty as will be now, if poor Folks have their wish.

CHAPTER V

Of the Disposition of the People this Year

'TIS the oddest Whimsy in the World, to fansie there are Stars for Kings, Popes, and Great Dons, any more than for the Poor and Needy. As if, forsooth, some new Stars were made since the Flood, or since Romulus or Pharamond, at the making some body King : A thing that Triboulet or Caillette would have been asham'd to have said, and yet they were Men of no common Learning or Fame ; and, for ought you or I know, this same Triboulet may have been of the Kings of Castille's Blood in Noah's Ark, and Caillette of that of King Priam. Now, mark ye me, those odd Notions come from nothing in the World, but want of Faith : I say, the true Catholick Faith. Therefore resting fully satisfy'd, that the Stars care not a Fart more for Kings than for Beggars, not a jot more for your Rich Topping Fellows, than for the most Sorry, Mangy, Lousy, Rascal, I 'll e'en leave other addlepated Fortune-tellers to speak of Great Folks, and I will only talk of the Little Ones.

And in the first place, of those who are subject to Saturn : As for Example, such as lack the Ready, Jealous or Horn-mad, Self-tormenting Prigs, Dreaming Fops, Crabbed Eve-droppers, Raving, Doating Churls, Hatchers and Brooders of Mischief, Suspicious Distrustful Slouches, Mole-catchers, Close-fisted Griping Misers, Usurers and Pawn-brokers, Christian-Jews, Pinch-crusts, Hold-fasts, Michers, and Penny-fathers, Redeemers of dipt, mortgag'd, and bleeding Copy-holds and Messuages, Fleecers of Sheer'd-Asses, Shoe-makers and Translators, Tanners, Bricklayers, Bell-founders, Compounders of Loans, Patchers, Clowters, and Botchers of old trumpery Stuff, and all moping, melancholy Folks, shall not have this Year whatever they 'd have; and will think more than once how they may get good store of the King's Pictures into their Clutches; in the mean time, they 'll hardly throw Shoulders of Mutton out at the Windows, and will often scratch their working Noddles where they do not itch.

As for those who are under Jupiter, as Canting-vermin, Bigots, Pardon-pedlers, Voluminous Abbreviators, Scriblers of Breve's, Copists, Pope's Bull-makers, Dataries, Pettifoggers, Capuchins, Monks, Hermits, Hypocrites, Cushion-thumping Mountebanks, Spiritual Comedians, Forms of Holiness, Pater-Noster - faces, Wheadling - gabblers, Wryneck'd Scoundrels, Spoilers of Paper, Stately Gulls, Notch'd-cropt-ear'd Meacocks, Public Registers Clerks, Clergy-Taylors, Wafer-makers, Rosary-makers, Engrossers of Deeds, Notaries, Grave-bubbles, Protecoles, and Prompters to Speakers, Deceitful-makers of Promises, shall fare according as they have Money. So many Clergy-men will die, that there will not be Men enough found on whom their Benefices may be conferr'd, so that many will hold two, three, four, or more. The Tribe of Hypocrites shall lose a good deal of its ancient Fame, since the World is grown a Rake, and will not be fool'd much longer, as Avenzagel saith.

Those who are under Mars, as Hang-men, Cut-throats, Dead-doing Fellows, Free-booters, Hedge-birds, Foot-pads and Highway-men, Catchpoles, Bum-bailiffs, Beadles and

Watch-men, Reformado's, Tooth-drawers, and Corn-cutters, Pintle-smiths, Shavers and Frig-beards, Butchers, Coiners, Paultry-Quacks and Mountebanks, Renegado's, Apostates, and Marraniz'd Miscreants, Incendiaries or Boutefeu's, Chimney-sweepers, Boorish Cluster-fists, Charcoal-men, Alchymists, Merchants of Eel-skins and Egg-shells, Grid-iron and Rattle-makers, Cooks, Paultry-Pedlers, Trash-mongers and Spangle-makers, Bracelet-makers, Lantern-makers and Tinkers, this Year will do fine things ; but some of them will be somewhat subject to be Rib-roasted, and have a St. Andrew's Cross scor'd over their Jobbernols at unawares. This Year one of those Worthy Persons will go nigh to be made a Field-Bishop, and, mounted on a Horse that was foal'd of an Acorn, give the Passengers a Blessing with his Legs.

Those who belong to Sol, as Topers, Quaffers, Whipcans, Tospots, Whittled, Mellow, Cupshotten Swillers, Merry-Greeks with Crimson-snouts of their own dying; fat, pursy Gorbellies, Brewers of Wine and of Beer, Botlers of Hay, Porters, Mowers, Menders of Til'd, Slated, and Thatch'd Houses, Burthen-bearers, Packers, Shepherds, Ox-keepers, and Cow-herds, Swine-herds and Hog-drivers, Fowlers and Bird-catchers, Gardiners, Barnkeepers, Hedgers, common Mumpers and Vagabonds, Day-labourers, Scowerers of greasy Thrum-caps, Stuffers and Bumbasters of Pack-saddles, Rag-merchants, idle Lusks, sloathful Idlebies, and drowsie Loiterers, Smell-feasts and Snap-gobbets, Gentlemen generally wearing Shirts with Neckbands, or heartily desiring to wear such ; all these will be hale and sharp set, and not troubled with the Gout at the Grinders, or a stoppage at the Gullet, when at a Feast on free cost.

Those whom Venus is said to rule, as Punks, Jills, Flirts, Queans, Morts, Doxies, Strumpets, Buttocks, Blowings, Tits, Pure Ones, Concubines, Convenients, Cracks, Drabs, Trulls, Light-skirts, Wrigglers, Misses, Cats, Riggs, Try'd Virgins, Bonarobaes, Barbers Chairs, Hedge-whores, Wagtails, Cocka-trices, Whipsters, Twiggers, Harlots, Kept-wenches, Kind-hearted-things, Ladies of Pleasure, by what Titles or Names soever dignified or distinguish'd ; Bawds, Pimps, Panders, Procurers, and Mutton-broakers ; Wenchers, Leachers, Shakers, Smockers, Cousins, Cullies, Stallions and Bellibumpers ; Gany-medes, Bardachoes, Huflers, Ingles, Fricatrices, He-whores and Sodomites ; swaggering Huffsnuffs, bouncing Bullies, Braggadocio's, Tory-rory Rakes and Tantivy-boys ; pepper'd, clapt and pox'd Dabblers ; shanker'd, colliflower'd, carbuncled Martyrs and Confessors of Venus ; Rovers, Ruffian-Rogues, and Hedge-creepers ; Female Chamberlains ; *Nomina mulierum definienta in* ess *ut* Laundress, Sempstress, Hostess, etc., and *in* er *ut*, Mantua-maker, Bed-maker, Bar-keeper, Fruiterer, etc., all these will be famous this Year. But when the Sun enters Cancer and other Signs, let them beware of the Crinkums, and its Attendants ; as Shankers, Claps, Virulent Gonorrheas, Cordees, Buboes, or Running Nags, Pock-royals, Botches, Wens or Condyloms, Tetters, Scabs, Nodes, Glands, Tumours, Carnosities, etc. Nuns shall hardly conceive without Carnal Copulation ; very few Virgins shall have milk at the Breasts.

As for those who come under Mercury, as Sharpers, Rooks, Coseners, Setters, Sherks, Cheats, Pickpockets, Divers, Buttock-ing-Foiles, Thieves, Millers, Night-walkers, Masters of Arts, Decretists, Picklocks, Dear-stealers, Hedge Rimers, Com-posers of serious Doggril-metre, Merry-Andrews, Jack-puddings, Tumblers, Masters in the Art of Hocus Pocus, Legerdemain, and Powder of Prelinpinpin ; such as break Priscian's Head, Quibblers and Punsters, Stationers, Paper-makers, Card-makers and Pyrats, will strive to appear more merry than they' ll often be ; sometimes they 'll laugh without much cause, and will be pretty apt to be blown up, sh——— i' th' Plum-bag, and march off, unless they find themselves better stor'd with Chink, and stronger of the Cod than they need to be.

Those who belong to Madam Luna, as Hawkers of Al-manacks and Pamphlets, Huntsmen, Ostridge-Catchers, Fal-koners, Couriers, Salt carriers, Lunaticks, Maggotty Fools, Crackbrain'd Coxcombs, Addlepated Frantic Wights, Giddy Whimsical Foplings, Exchange-Brokers, Post-boys, Footboys, Tennis-Court-keepers-Boys, Glass-mongers, Light-horse, Water-men, Mariners, Messengers, Rakers and Gleaners, will not long stay in a place this Year. However, so many Swag-bellies and Puff-bags will hardly go to St. Hiacco, as there did in the Year 524. Great numbers of Pilgrims will come down from the Mountains of Savoy and Auvergne, but Sagittarius sorely threatens them with kib'd Heels.

CHAPTER VI

Of the Condition of some Countries

THE Noble Kingdom of France shall prosper and triumph this Year in all Pleasures and Delights, so that Foreign Nations shall willingly retire thither. Presents of Nosegays, and Feasts on Birth-days, and Saints-days, Treats, Pastimes, and a thousand Sports, shall keep up the Mirth. There will be plenty of delicious Wines; many Radishes in Lymosin; store of Chestnuts in Perigord and Dauphine; a deal of Olives in Languedoc; whole shoals of Sand in Olonè; a world of Fish in the Sea; swarms of Stars in the Firmament; abundance of Salt at Brouage; and prodigious quantities of Corn, Pulse, Kitchen Herbs, Flowers, Fruit, Butter, Cheese, Milk, and other Dairy Goods. No Plague, no War, no Vexation. A Fart for Poverty, hang Sorrow, cast away Care. Old Gold, such as your Double Ducats, Rose-Nobles, Angels, Spankers, Spur Royals, and Well-wool'd-Sheeps of Berry will once more be in fashion, with plenty of Seraphs and Crowns with a Sun upon them, however about Midsummer you are threaten'd with an Invasion by black Fleas, and Weevels of la Deviniere. *Adeo, nil est ex omni parte beatum;* Nothing is yet found that's perfectly happy; But care must be taken to curb them with store of Evening Nunchions.

Italy, Roumania, Naples and Sicily will remain where they stood last Year. People will be very thoughtful there towards the latter end of Lent, and sometimes will rave and dream at Noon-day.

Germany, Switzerland, Saxony, Strasburg, Antwerp, etc. will thrive upon 't, if they don't fail to do so. Woe be to Pardon-Pedlers if they come among them; I dare engage that there will not be many yearly Obits, Trentals and Services for the Dead founded there.

Spain, Castile, Portugal and Arragon will be subject to sudden Thirsts, and Young and Old will be wofully afraid of dying, for which reason they'll be sure to keep themselves warm when 'tis cold; and will often tell over their Money, if they have any.

England, Scotland, and the Easterlings, will be but indifferent Pantagruelists. Wine would at least prove as wholesome to them as Beer, provided it were good and delicious. When they sit at Table, their best hopes will be in the aftergame. St. Traignant of Scotland will work Miracles and sh—— Wonders like mad ; but the Devil a bit he 'll see the better for all the Candles that will be offer'd him, if Aries ascending does not fumble, and rumble, tumble, stumble, and be humble, though he grumble, and scorn'd, and unhorn'd.

The Moscovites, Indians, Persians, and Troglodytes, will often be troubled with the Bloody Flux, because they will not be ridden, tupp'd and ram'd by the Romanists, considering the Ball of Sagittarius Ascendant. The Bohemians, Jews and Egyptians will not be brought this Year to conform with the said Romanists, as they expect. Venus bitterly threatens them with Wens at the Throat ; if they do not condescend to the Will of the King of the Papillons.

Escargots (Snails) Sarabouytes, Cauquemares (Nightmares) Cannibals shall be pester'd with Ox Flies (Informers, Promooters) and will have but little heart to play on the Cymbals, and Tongue and Keys (or, to letcher) unless Guyacum be in request.

As for Austria, Hungary and Turky, by my Troth, my dainty Lads, I can't tell how they 'll do, neither does Peelgarlick trouble his Head a jot about it, considering the Sun's rare entrance into Capricornus ; and if you chance to know more of the matter than I do, pray scatter no Words, keep it to your selves, but stay for the lame Post.

OF THE FOUR SEASONS OF THE YEAR

CHAPTER VII

Of the Spring

IN all this Year's Revolution there will be but one Moon, neither will it be New. I dare warrant you are damnably down o' the Mouth about it, you who do not believe in God, and persecute his Holy and Divine Word, as also those that stand up for it. But you may e'en hang yourselves out of the way, I tell you there will never be any other Moon than that which God created in the beginning, and which was plac'd in the Sky to light and guide Mankind by Night. But in good sooth, I 'll not infer thence that it never shews to the Earth and Earthly People a decrease or increase of its Light, according as it is nearer the Sun or further from it. No, no, why should I say this ? For, wherefore, because, however, notwithstanding, that, etc., and let none of you hereafter pray that Heaven may keep her from the Wolves ; for they 'll not meddle with her these twelve Months I 'll warrant you. *A propos*, now I think on 't, you 'll see as many Flowers again this Season as in all the other Three ; neither shall that Man be thought a Fool, who 'll have Wit enough to lay by Money, and get together more of it this Quarter than he will do of Cobwebs in the whole Year. The Griffons and Marrons, Men who make the Ways passable in great Snows, and dwell on the Mountains of Savoy, and Dauphiné, and the Hyperboreans, that are perpetually furr'd with Snow, are to miss this Season and have none on 't ; for Avicenna tells us, 'tis not Spring till the Snow is melted away on the Mountains. Believe the Lyar. I have known the time when Men reckoned Ver, or the Spring, to begin when the Sun enter'd in the first Degree of Aries. If they reckon it otherwise now, I knock under, and Mum's the word.

CHAPTER VIII

Of Summer

IN the Summer I can't justly tell you what kind of Wind will blow ; but this I know, that it ought to be warm Weather then, and now and then a Sea-Breeze. However, if things should fall out otherwise, you must be sure not to curse God ; for he is wiser than we, and knows what 's fit for us far better than we our selves ; you may take my word for 't, whatever Haly and his Gang may have said. It will be a delicious Thing to be merry and drink cool Wine, though some have said there is nothing more contrary to Thirst. I believe it ; and indeed *Contraria contrariis curantur.*

CHAPTER IX

Of Autumn

IN Autumn Men will make Wine, or before or after it, 'tis all one to me, so we have but good Bub and Nippitati enough; foul Mistakes will then be in season, for many a one will think only to burst at the Broadside by the way of Fizzlecumfunk, and will foully give their Breeches a Clister with a fecal Decoction. As for those Men and Women who have vow'd to fast till the Stars be in the Heavens, they may e'en from this present Hour begin to feed like Farmers by my particular Grant and Dispensation. Neither do they begin of the soonest; for those pretty twinkling things have been fix'd there above sixteen thousand and I can't tell how many days, and stuck in to the purpose too, let me tell you. Nor would I have you for the future hope to catch Larks when the Sky falls: For on my Honour that will not happen in your time. Legions of Hypocritical Church-vermin, Cucullated Sham-Saints, Pedlers and Hawkers of Pardons, Perpetual Mumpers and Mumblers of Orisons, and other such Gangs of rascally Scoundrels will come out of their Dens. Scape as scape can, say I. Harkee me, take heed also of the Bones whenever you eat Fish, and God preserve you from a Dose of Ratsbane too.

CHAPTER X

Of Winter

IN Winter, in my silly Opinion, those Men will not be over-wise who 'll sell their Furr'd Gowns, Swans-Skins, and other warm Cloths to buy Fuel; neither did the Antients use to do so, says Avenzouart. If it chance to rain don't fret your selves, so much the less Dust you 'll have when you go abroad. Keep your selves as hot as Toasts, d' ye hear, beware of Cathars. Drink of the best, till the other sort mend; and pray henceforth sh —— no more o' bed. Oh, ho! Poultry do you build your Nests so high?

THE END OF THE
PANTAGRUELIAN PROGNOSTICATION

435

An EPISTLE by Pantagruel's Lymosin, Grand Excoriator
of the Latiale Tongue, mention'd Book ii. Chap. 6.

To his own Amicissim, residing at the Inclite and Famosissim
Urb of Lugdun.

OUR Auricles, percuss'd by Fame sonorous,
Your mirabundous Acts have brought before us.
Your placid Life, here inaudite before,
Repletes the Town of Lugdun ore and ore.
Where Nymphs convening three Times thrice Divine,
Prostrate themselves as Vot'ries at your Shrine.
Some voluntary fly into your Arms,
For your Opiparous or Aureous Charms :
Some, tender Souls ! on you themselves obtrude,
Moved by your Tongue's most melleous Dulcitude.
Your Phrase, robustly propt, with ease produces
Fractions in many weak Virgineous Cruises ;
When you 're placientated the Fort is won,
Id est, when e're y' impel the matter on.

You therefore, if your Appetite desires
New Dapes each hour, pursue what that requires.
If sated with your Urban Stale Fruitions,
Or with your half unnatural Coitions,
You to your Neighb'ring rural Fund migrate,
And there your Lassate Corps reanimate.
There ev'ry Joy to you is an Oblation
In which your Ingeny finds delectation.
The gay Merule and warbling Philomel,
To please you, strive each other to excel.
Their plaisant Notes tristitious Thoughts confound,
And wake your Soul with their letating sound

To that amæne Recess the rural Quire
Sylvanus, Satyrs, Fauns and Pan retire ;
Gods, Demigods, Nymphs, Dryads, Nayads meet,
And leave their Mansions for your Dulcior Seat ;
And, when the Turb is once accumulate,
Jucund Jucundity 's immensurate.
With sumptuous Cates Divine Ambrosia joins,
And Nectar there exuperates all your Wines.

With this each dry Esurient Guest replete is,
As at the Feast of Peleus and his Thetis.
Then All arise, the Tables are sublate ;
In Arbors some themselves refocillate,
Some in ferine Venation take delight,
For Cony-caption some have Appetite :
In fine, Ludes omniform are there invented,
And ev'ry Indoles and Sense contented.
Pleasure invades, Pain abdicates the Mind,
What more in Heav'n can its grand Tenants find !

While we alas ! must still obambulate,
Sequacious of the Court and Courtier's Fate.
O most infaust who optates there to live
An aulic Life no solid Joys can give.
We 've been cruciated, since your last Migration,
With an indefinent obequitation :
Our Boots and Legs have not been separated,
While we the Burgade Lands have conculcated.
Lute, Unds and Sands did long our March oppose
And asp'rous Rocks, the Bulwarks of our Foes.

But now I 'll not too many Verbs effund,
Nor with our Ills your Auricles obtund.
Nor all our Martial Conflicts represent,
Obsesses, Storms and Fights Sanguinolent ;
When angry Mars Burgundia cicatris'd,
And Friend with Friend in Dolors sympathis'd.
Desp'rate of Conquest, through dire Accidents,
Apert we jac'd to th' Æther without Tents.
At last the kind, tho' rigid Brume came on,
The Camp was derelict, and all are gone.
For when Hybernal Evils appropinque,
The Legions on their Hybernacles think.

So, when the Bellic Season was expir'd,
Wisely the Regal Majesty retir'd.
To Fonsbellaqueus now the Monarch's come.
The noblest Master to the noblest Dome :
No more had Nero's match'd its noble Pride,
Than with the King the Tyrant could have vy'd.
Were ev'n Diana's Temple rais'd again,
The Regal Palace would eclipse the Fane.

'Tis true, you 've ocul'd it in Times *præterit*,
But ev'ry day 't has meliorated merit,
And Those who supervis'd it noct hestern,
In Hodiern bores, will major Things discern.
Opining to revise a Structure new,
Where Art surpassed its self, and Nature too.

Now, to apply my primary Ingredient,
That you move huc I think it not expedient ;
For, shou'd you come before the Brume's abated,
Th' Opime you 'd linquish for the Macerated.
Since, thanks to Jove's Benignity you 're valid,
Choose not a frigid State, while yours is calid ;
Unless Salubrity you vilipend,
And, from your own, become your Medic's Friend.
For in veracity these Times denote
Morbs to the Sane, and Obits to th' Ægrote ;
And alterate the suavest Pulchritude
To the Complection of its native Mud.

Incluse with Sylves behind, and Lakes before us,
Our outward Man wants something that 's calorous.
Scarce one poor Fascicle we can acquire ;
In fine all Solaces from us retire.
And were we not (in this Extremity)
Juvated by the Town's proximity
To which we equitate with maturation,
And to kind Nature make Sacrification,
Soon in our Sepulchres we shou'd all hide us ;
For, sure, one Hebdomad wou'd here occide us.

By this Imparity you plainly see,
Our Life 's Distress, and yours Jucundity ;
Our State 's naufrageous and periclitating :
If then you sape, as we are cogitating,
Hither till Spring return make no Transition,
Tho' you were stimulated by Ambition.
What tho' Honorabilities it offers,
Large heaps of Numms to fill your largest Coffers,
Imperial Favour too, and what not else ?
Ample Munificence, and Office celse,
Such as you execute when here ; yet these
Have no intrinsick Valour, tho' they please.

Our Means of Life, are Pote, and Cibe, and Vest ;
Who jugulates himself for Wealth 's, a Beast.

To this Epistle *Finis* now we 'll fix,
Which to your School a Transit do's adnix ;
Where Rules to polish Loquels are prescrib'd,
And Doct Verbocination is imbib'd ;
Excoriating the Language Latiale.
To make Reply let not your calam fail ;
But atrament at large the candid Chart
With corresponding Rimes transcending Art.
Which will to him be th' altest Obligation,
Who is

   Your Serve with maxim Veneration,

     DESBRIDE GOUSIER.

An EPIGRAM

ALL strive of late to bring to Purity
Our Tongue, that once lay in Obscurity ;
And profligating all Barbarity,
With th' Attic set the French in parity :
So, to revive its old Nobility,
They shun the Phrase of our Mobility ;
But, thus disguis'd by a Fatality,
'Tis meer excoriated Latiality.

The PHILOSOPHICAL CREAM of Encyclopedic Questions, by Pantagruel

Which were Sorbonicoficabilitudinissely debated in the Schools of the Decree near St. Denys de la Chartre at Paris.

UTRUM, A Platonic Idea, hovering to the right on the Orifice of the Chaos, might drive away the Squadrons of Democratical Atoms.

Utrum, The Flickermise flying through the translucidity of the corner'd Gate, might, Spy-like, discover the Morphean Visions twirling and unwinding in a circular manner the thread of the *rete admirabile* that wraps up the Attili of ill-caulk'd brains.

Utrum, The Atoms turning about at the sound of the Hermagorical Harmony, might make a Compaction or a Dissolution of a Quintessence, by the substraction of the Pythagorical Numbers.

Utrum, The Hybernal Frigidity of the Antipodes, passing in an Orthogonal Line, through the homogeneous solidity of the Centre, might warm the superficial Connexity of our heels by a soft Antiperistasis.

Utrum, The Tassels of the Torrid Zone might so far be dipt and wetted at the Cataracts of the Nile, as to moisten the most Caustic Parts of the Empyreal Heaven.

Utrum, By reason of the long Hair that was bestowed on the Bear, at her metamorphosis, if her Breech were but shav'd the Italian way *à la Bougarone*, to make Triton a Beard, she might not be Keeper of the Artic Pole.

Utrum, An Elementary Sentence might alledge a Decennal Prescription against Amphibious Animals, and *è contra* the other respectively put in her Petition in case of Seisure and Novelty.

Utrum, An Historical Grammar, and Posteriority, by the triad of Articles, might find some Line or Character of their Chronicle on the Zenonian Palm.

Utrum, The *Genera generalissima*, by a violent Elevation over their Predicaments, might crawl and clamber up to the Stories of the Transcendents, and consequently let the special and predicable Species follow, to the unspeakable loss and damage of poor Masters of Arts.

Utrum, Proteus that transform'd himself into all manner of Shapes, turning himself into a Cigale, and musically trying his Voice in the Dog-days, might make a third Concoction with Morning-dew carefully bottled up in May, before the full revolution of a Zodiacal Girdle.

Utrum, The Black Scorpion might bear a solution of the *Continuum* in his substance, and, by the effusion of his Blood, darken and blacken the milky-way, to the great loss and grief of the Swag-bellied Jacobites.

FRANCISCUS RABELÆSUS,
Poëta Sitiens, Ponebat.

Vita, Lyææ, sitis ; liquisti, flebis, adures ;
Membra, hominem, tumulum ; morte, liquore, face.

Two EPISTLES to two Women of different Humours

To an Old Woman

OLD toothless, pox'd, mischievous Hag of Night ;
Old graceless Witch, who liv'st in Virtue's spight ;
Old treach'rous Beldam, burden to the Earth ;
Plots, Broils, and Wars from thee derive their Birth.
Old errant Bawd, by whose destructive Trade,
The Lewd are sold, the Modest are betray'd.
Honour thou never knew'st ; thou, living Tomb,
Whor'd with thy Father in thy Mother's Womb.
Thy Charity do's like the Devil's prove,
And damns the Wretches who thy Lewdness love.
Thy livid Blood with poisonous Rage is swell'd,
Thy Breast with Gall, thy Head with Mischief fill'd.
Thou ne'er of any but thy self spok'st well,
And for Detraction ev'n surpassest Hell.
Old Brimstone Bawd, with Brandy flaming Red,
That mak'st a curs'd rank Brothel of thy Bed,
Propitious to all Malice and Ill-luck,
That hast a Teat to give the Devil suck ;
Damn'd Witch, thou dost in Magic far excel
Medea, and the Blackest Fiends of Hell :
Thou mak'st thy hideous Phiz more dreadful still ;
But when thou do'st, we shou'd thy Hagship kill,
Lest thy redoubl'd Ugliness affright,
And, like Medusa's, ruin us at Sight.
Thou, Scarlet Whore, ne'er mourn'st for doing Ill ;
Thy only Tears are Rheums, and Wines distill'd ;
Thy only Sighs are vented at the Bum,
Outstink a Carrion, and outroar a Drum.
Old monstrous Hag, of matchless, dreadful Kind,
Thou the three Furies in one Body join'd.
Satan, outdone by thee, do's envious grow,
And longs to burn thee, in revenge, below.
Dissembling Witch, whose Tongue, still muttering, dares
Mock frowning Heav'n with thy unhallow'd Pray'rs.
Thou, bold bad Spright, with Satan's borrow'd Force,
Pretend'st to turn a rapid River's Course,
With Spells, to Paleness fright th' astonish'd Moon,
And darken quite the blushing Sun at Noon.

Base murth'ring Sorceress, with relentless heart,
On Innocence thou try'st thy cursed Art,
Bewitching Infants in their Mother's Arms,
And Death alone can end the painful Charms.
No God thou own'st but thy insatiate Gut ;
Thou mak'st each Trull turn up her filthy Scut.
Pity thou slight'st ; by Pity thou 'rt abhorr'd,
And more deserv'dst a Faggot than a Cord.
Thy cruel Heart with Rancour has its Load,
Natural to thee, as Poison to a Toad,
Thou worst of Mischiefs, Guide to endless Death,
Who scatt'rest Plagues with thy contagious Breath ;
Can'st thou expect unpunish'd to remain,
And for each Crime to 'scape a double Pain ?
Millions against thee will in Judgment rise,
And loudly call for Vengeance to the Skies.
Those whom thy Arts to lawless Flames decoy'd,
Shall be below to burn thy Soul employ'd.
But thou 'rt the worst of Hells for impious Deeds,
T' other perhaps in Punishments exceeds.
Prepare, prepare for its revenging Pains,
There to be rack'd in everlasting Chains.
Tremble, and loudly to the Mountains call,
That they may gape, and crush thee with their fall ;
For still thy latter Sins the first excel,
And, living on, thou 'lt grow too bad for Hell.
Damn'd Harridan, with reeking Lust more drunk
Than Messaline, that great Imperial Punk ;
Ne'er tir'd nor sated, thou outdo'st her more
Than she outdid the utmost stint of Whore.
Thy sweaty Carcass (which kind Heav'n confound !)
With noisom Steams offend us all a-round,
Old drunken Piss-pot, Sink of Filth and Sin,
Plaister without, and Rottenness within,
Curs'd Lump of Lees, thou universal Sore,
Thou putrid Product of the Common-shore,
Thou lowest, last degree of Infamy,
Thou very highest top of Villainy ;
Repent, or know I 'll double ev'ry Curse ;
But no, thou can'st not mend, nor e'er be worse.

An Epistle to another Woman of a quite different Humour

HAIL ! Rev'rend Matron, Virtuous as you 're Fair
Hail ! you, whose Autumn may with Spring compare ;
Matron, adorn'd so richly in your Mind,
That in your Looks the Treasures we may fiud.
With pious Doctrine you your Faith improve,
Shun idle Talk, and Books of idler Love ;
And setting Vice and needless Forms apart,
Your suff'ring God ingrave within your Heart.
While you on Earth a heav'nly Saint commence,
Your Charity is like the World, immense ;
Ready to ease th' Afflicted of their Load,
At awful distance y' imitate your God.
So sweet, so modest, and so void of Pride,
That ev'n God do's own you for his Bride.
You to all Folly wisely shut your Eyes,
And dare the World's alluring Joys despise.
That Sacred Writ alone is your delight,
Which saves the Soul from everlasting night.
You Temper still, yet never to a fault,
Your Wine with Water, and your Words with Thought,
And never cherish'd an Unchast Desire,
Or cou'd be warm'd, but by the Nuptial Fire ;
But, waiting for your Saviour, pass away
In Pray'rs the Night, in Pious Acts the Day.
In Faith, in Piety alone extream,
You shun Applause, yet best deserve Esteem.
The Prophets great Inspirer fills your Breast ;
Your Head, your Heart, by the Whole God possest.
While some unthinking Virgins are betray'd,
And made Proficients in Hell's thriving Trade,
Your wise Advice, your great Example, draws
The thoughtless Wretches out of Satan's Jaws.
Matron, in Wedlock faithful and sedate,
An honour to that honourable State :
Not Weakness made you wed, but Piety,
Thus to encrease the Saint's Society.
Those wanton Toys cou'd ne'er your Heart entice
Which stifle Virtue and encourage Vice.

Matron, whom All the Christian Pallas term,
Wise is your Conduct, and your Courage firm.
I prize, admire, and love your matchless Store :
Your outward Beauties much, your inward Graces more.
From Heav'n you came, and to that Heav'n are born,
Virtue adorns you, Virtue you adorn.
Oh, that I may, ev'n to my latest hours,
Advance in Knowledge, contemplating yours.
May you obtain Below what Earth can crave !
What Heav'n can grant, Above, you 're sure to have.

LETTERS written by Francis Rabelais, M.D., during his stay in Italy in the Year 1536

LETTER I

To my Lord Bishop of Maillezais

My Lord,

I writ to you at large on the 29th of November, and sent you some Naples-grain for your Sallads, of every sort that is eaten on this side, except Pimpernel, which then I could not procure. I have sent you no great quantity at present, because it had been too much for the Courier at one time ; but if you please to have more, either for your Gardens, or to dispose of otherwise, I will send it you upon Notice. I had written to you before, and sent to you the four Signatures concerning the Benefices of Fryar Dom. Philip, obtain'd in the Name of those whom you had set down in the Instructions you gave me. I have not receiv'd since any Letter from you that mentions the receipt of the aforesaid Signatures. I receiv'd only one dated from l'Ermenaud, when my Lady d'Estissac came thither, in which you let me know that you had receiv'd two Pacquets from me ; one from Ferrara, t' other from this City, with the Cypher which I writ to you : But for ought I understand, you had not yet receiv'd the Pacquet where the Signatures were enclos'd. I can now give you an Account, that my Business has been granted and dispatch'd better, and with more certainty, than I cou'd have wished ; and I have had therein the Assistance and Advice of worthy Men, particularly of the Cardinal de Genutiis, who is Judge of the Palace ; and of the

Cardinal Simonetta, who was Auditor of the Chamber, a very knowing Man, and well vers'd in such Matters. The Pope was of opinion, that I should proceed in my Bus'ness *per Cameram :* The abovemention'd Cardinals were of a mind, that it should be by the Court of Contradicts ; because, that *in foro contentioso,* it cannot be revocable in France ; and, *Quæ per contradictoria transiguntur transeunt in rem judicatam ; quæ autem per Cameram, et impugnari possunt, et in judicium veniunt :* Those things which are transacted by Contradictories, pass as determin'd ; but those things which are done by the Chamber, may be call'd into question, and try'd over again.

Upon the whole, I have nothing more to do, than to take up the Bulls *sub plumbo.*

My Lord Cardinal du Bellay, as likewise my Lord Bishop of Mascon, have assured me that the Charges shall be remitted me ; tho' the Pope, by old Custom, remits nothing except of what is dispatcht *per cameram.* There will remain to be paid only the Referendaries, Proctors, and other such-like Scriblers and Blotters of Parchment. If my Money falls short, I will recommend my self to your Lordship's Alms ; for I don't think to leave this Place till the Emperor goes.

He is at present at Naples, whence, as he has written to the Pope, he will part on the 6th of January. This Town is already full of Spaniards : And he has sent an Extraordinary Ambassador to the Pope, besides him who constantly resides at this Court, to give him notice of his coming. The Pope leaves him half the Palace, and all the Borough of St. Peter for his Retinue, and has order'd three thousand Beds to be prepar'd, according to the Roman custom, that is to say, with Quilts : For the City has been unprovided of 'em ever since it was sack'd by the Lanskenets. He has got together as much Hay, Straw, Oats, Spelt-corn and Barley as he could find, and of Wine as much as is arriv'd *in ripâ :* I fancy he 'll be at no small Charge, which can't be very easy to him in this his great Poverty, so apparent in him, more than in any Pope for these three hundred Years past. The Romans have not yet resolv'd how to behave themselves upon this Occasion, and have had many Meetings, by Order of the Senators, Conservators, and Governor ; but they can't agree in their Opinions. The Emperor has declar'd to 'em, by his said Ambassador, that he does not design his People shall be entertain'd at Free-cost, but as the Pope shall think fit to entertain 'em ; which does the more sensibly touch the Pope : For he understands well enough, that by this saying, the Emperor means to see how and with what Affection he will treat him and his People.

The Holy Father has sent two Legats to him by the choice of the Consistory, to wit, Cardinal of Siena, and Cardinal Cæsarini. Since which, the Cardinals Salviati and Rodolph are also gone to him, and with them my Lord de Saintes. I understand 'tis about the Affair of Florence, and concerning the Difference between the Duke Alexander de Medicis and Philip Strossi, whose Estate, which is considerable, the Duke had a mind to confiscate. Next to the Fourques of Ausbourg in Germany, he is counted the richest Merchant in Christendom ; and the Duke has set People here to poison or kill him, whatever came on 't. Being advertis'd of this Attempt, he obtain'd of the Pope to go arm'd. And he commonly went attended with thirty Soldiers arm'd at all Points. The said Duke of Florence having notice (I suppose) that Strossi, with the above-mention'd Cardinals, was gone to the Emperor, and that he offer'd to the Emperor Four hundred thousand Ducats, only to give Commissions to People who might inform against the Tyranny and Baseness of the said Duke, left Florence, constituted Cardinal Cibo his Governor, and came to this City the Morrow after Christmas-Day, the twenty-third Hour, entring at St. Peter's Gate, follow'd by fifty Light-Horse in white Armour, with Lances, and about a hundred Harquebusiers. The rest of his Train was but little, and in no very good order. And no Soul went to receive him, but the Emperor's Ambassadour, who met him at the same Gate. As soon as he was in Town he came to the Palace, and had a short Audience of the Pope, and had Lodgings in St. George's Palace. The next Morning he went away, attended as before.

Eight Days since, News came to this Town, and his Holiness has receiv'd Letters from divers Parts, that the Sophi, King of Persia, has defeated the Army of the Turks. Yesterday Night arriv'd here the Nephew of Monsieur de Veli, the King's Ambassador to the Emperor, who assur'd my Lord Cardinal du Bellay that the thing was really true, and that this has been the greatest Slaughter that has been heard of these Four hundred Years ; for above Forty thousand Horse were kill'd on the Turk's side.

Consider what a Number of Foot fell there ! As likewise on the Sophi's side. For, among People that do not willingly fly, *Non solet esse incruenta Victoria :* The Victory does not use to be without Blood.

The principal Defeat was near a little Town call'd Coni, not far distant from the great City of Tauris, for which the Sophi and the Turk contend; the other Action was near a Place call'd Betelis. The manner was thus: The Turks had divided their Army, and one part was sent to take Coni; of which the Sophi having Intelligence, he, with his whole Army, rush'd upon this separated part, before they could stand upon their guard.

See here the effect of ill Counsel, in dividing his Army before he had gotten the Victory. The French can give a good Account of this, when the Duke of Albani drew out the Strength and Flower of the Camp before Pavia. Upon the News of this Rout and Defeat, Barbarossa is retir'd to Constantinople, to secure the Country; and says by his good Gods, That this is nothing, considering the mighty Power of the Turk. But the Emperor is eas'd of the fear that he had of the Turks coming into Sicily, as he had threatned at the beginning of the Spring. And this may give Repose to Christendom for some considerable time; and those who would lay Tithes upon the Church, *eo pretextu*, that they would fortifie themselves against the Approach of the Turk, are but ill furnish'd with demonstrative Arguments.

LETTER II

My Lord,

I have receiv'd Letters from Monsieur de Saint Ceredos, dated from Dijon, in which he tells me of a Process that he has depending in this Court of Rome. I dare not answer him, without running the hazard of incurring a great deal of Displeasure. But I understand he has the greatest Right in the World, and that he suffers a manifest Injury; and that he ought to come hither in Person. For there is no such Affair, how equitable soever, that is not lost for want of a Man's own solliciting in it; especially when he has a strong Party, who can over-awe with Threats those that sollicit for him. The want of a Cypher, prevents my Writing to you more at large: But it troubles me to see so much as I do, particularly, being sensible of the great Kindness you have for him; and likewise because he has of a long time lov'd and favour'd me. In my Opinion Monsieur de Basilac, Conseiller (one of the Judges Assistants) in the arliament of Tholouse, came hither this Winter on a less Occasion, and is older and more infirm than he, and yet has had a quick dispatch to his Content.

LETTER III

My Lord,

The Duke of Ferrara, who went to the Emperor at Naples, return'd hither this Morning. I know not yet how he has determin'd Matters relating to the investiture and homage of his Lands. But I understand he is come back not well satisfi'd with the Emperor. I fear he will be forc'd to empty his Coffers of those Crowns his Father left him, and that the Pope and Emperor will fleece him at pleasure; considering also that it was above six Months before he refus'd to espouse the King's Interest, notwithstanding all the Emperor's Remonstrances and Threats. My Lord Bishop of Limoges, who was the King's Ambassador at Ferrara, seeing the said Duke without acquainting him with his Design was retir'd to the Emperor, is return'd to France. 'Tis fear'd that My Lady Renée will receive no little displeasure by it : The Duke having remov'd Madam de Soubise her Governess, and order'd her to be serv'd by Italians, which don't look well.

LETTER IV

My Lord,

Three days since arriv'd here a Post from Monsieur de Cressé, who brings an Account that some of the Lord Rance's Men, who went to the relief of Geneva, were defeated by a Party of the Duke of Savoy's. With him came a Courier from Savoy, who brought the News of it to the Emperor. This may unhappily prove *Seminarium futuri belli,* the cause of an ensuing War. For these little wilful Broils draw after them great Battels, which is demonstrable from Ancient History, as well Greek and Roman as French, as appears by the Battel at Vireton.

THE WORKS OF DR. FRANCIS RABELAIS

LETTER V

My Lord,

About fifteen Days since, Andrew Doria, who went with Stores to those who hold the Gouletta near Tunis for the Emperor, as likewise to supply them with Water, (for the Arabians of the Country make continual War upon them, and they dare not stir out of their Garison,) is arriv'd at Naples, where he staid not above three Days with the Emperor, since when, he is sail'd hence with nine and twenty Galleys. 'Tis said, in quest of Judeo and Cacciadiavolo, who have burnt a great deal of the Country of Sardinia and Minorca. The Grand Master of Rhodes, who was born in Piedmont, is lately dead, in whose room the Commandeur of Forton between Montauban and Tholouse is chosen.

LETTER VI

My Lord,

I here send you a Book of Prognostications, which busies this whole Town ; 'tis intitl'd, *De eversione Europæ*, of the overturning of Europe. For my part, I give no credit at all to it. But Rome was never seen so wholly given over to Vanities and Prophecies, as it is at present. I am apt to think the reason is, because *Mobile mutatur semper cum principe vulgus.* The giddy Multitude always change with the Prince. I have also sent you an Almanack for the ensuing Year 1536. I send you besides, the Copy of a Brief which his Holiness has lately decreed for the arrival of the Emperor : As likewise the Emperor's Entry into Messina and Naples, and the Funeral Oration at the Interment of the deceas'd Duke of Milan.

My Lord, I humbly recommend my self to your good Favour, praying to our Lord for your good Health and long Life.

Rome, *Dec.* 30, 1536.

LETTER VII

To the Lord de Maillezais

MY LORD,

I HAVE receiv'd the Letters you were pleas'd to write to me, dated the second of December; by which I understand that my two Pacquets are come to your Hands; one of the eighteenth, the other of the two and twentieth of October, with the four Signatures which I sent you. I writ since to you more at large, on the nine and twentieth of November, and thirtieth of December. By this time, I believe, you have receiv'd the said Pacquets. For Mr. Michael Parmentier, Bookseller, living at the Arms of Basil, writ to me the fifth of this Instant, that he had receiv'd and sent them to Poitiers. You may assure yourself, that the Pacquets which I shall send you will be safely deliver'd at Lions; for I put them into the great seal'd Pacquet, which is for the King's Affairs, and when the Courier comes to Lions, he is dispatch'd by the Governor; then his Secretary, who is much my Friend, takes the Pacquet which I superscribe on the first Sheet, to the aforesaid Michael Parmentier. Afterwards there is no difficulty, unless from Lions to Poitiers, which is the reason that obliges me to set an extraordinary Postage upon it, that the greater care may be taken of it by the Messengers at Poitiers, in hopes to get a Spill by it. For my part I constantly encourage this same Parmentier with some small Presents, which I send him of Novelties on this side, or to his Wife, that he may be the more diligent to engage Merchants or Messengers at Poitiers to deliver the Pacquets to your Lordship. And I very much approve of the Advice which you gave me in your Letter, that I should not trust them to the Hands of the Banquiers, for fear they should be pick'd and broke open. I think 'twill not be amiss, the first time you write to me, especially, if it be business of Consequence, that you write a Line to the said Parmentier, and inclose a piece of Gold to him in your Letter, in consideration of the Care he takes to send your Pacquets to me, and mine to you. A small matter sometimes highly obliges honest Men, and makes 'em more diligent for the time to come, when the Case requires speedy dispatch.

LETTER VIII

MY LORD,

I HAVE not as yet presented your Letters to my Lord Bishop de Saintes, for he is not yet return'd from Naples, whither he went with the Cardinals Salviati and Rodolph. He will return in two Days; then I will give him your Letters, and desire an Answer of 'em, which I will send you by the first Courier that goes hence. I understand their Affairs have not had that success with the Emperor which they hop'd for: And that the Emperor had positively answer'd, That at their Request and Instance, as likewise, at the late Pope Clement's, he had created Alexander de Medicis Duke of the Territories of Florence and Pisa, which he never thought to do, nor would have done: Meanwhile to depose him, would be the trick of some Stage-player, which do's and undo's the same thing. However, that they should resolve to acknowledge him as their Duke and Lord, and obey him as his Vassals and Subjects, and be sure they did so. As to the Complaints they made against the said Duke, he would take Cognizance of them when he came to Florence.

For he designs after some stay at Rome, to pass through Sienna, and thence to Florence, to Bolonia, to Milan, and Genoa. Thus the aforesaid Cardinals, together with the Bishop of Xaintes, Strossy, and some others, returned, *re infectâ*, (as wise as they went).

The thirteenth of this Month, came back hither the Cardinals of Sienna and Cæsarini, who had been elected by the Pope, and the whole College, Legates to the Emperor. They have so negotiated the Matter, that the Emperor has deferr'd his coming hither to the latter end of February. If I had as many Crowns, as the Pope would give Days of Pardon, *Proprio motu, de lenitudine potestatis;* Of his own free Will, out of the Lenity of his Power, and other such like favourable Circumstances, to any one that could defer it for five or six Years to come, I should be richer than ever was Jacques Cœur. Here are great Preparations made in this City for his Reception; and a new way is made by the Pope's Command, by which he is to make his Entry; that is, through Sebastin's Gate, towards Champ-doli, *Templum pacis*, the Temple of Peace, and the Amphitheatre, and he is to pass under the Ancient Triumphal Arches of Constantine and Titus, of Numetianus, and others,

Then on one side of St. Mark's Palace, by Campo de Fiore, and by the Palace Farnese, where the Pope us'd to reside, then by the Banks, and below St. Angelo's Castle. To make and level which Way, above two hundred Houses, and three or four Churches, are pull'd down to the Ground, which most People take for an ill Omen. On the Day of the Conversion of St. Paul, his Holiness went to St. Paul's to hear Mass, and made a Feast to all the Cardinals. After Dinner he return'd, passing through the above-mentioned Way, and lodg'd at St. George's Palace. But 'tis a sad sight to behold the Ruins of the demolish'd Houses that are not paid for, nor have the Landlords any recompense made 'em.

To day arriv'd here the Venetian Ambassadors, four brave old gray-headed Gentlemen, who are going to the Emperor at Naples. The Pope has sent all his Family before 'em; his Bed-chambermen, Chamberlains, Janisaries, Lanskenets; and the Cardinals have sent their Mules in Pontificalibus.

Likewise, the 7th of this Month, the Ambassadors of Sienna were introduced in good order, and after they had made their Speech in open Consistory, and that the Pope had answer'd 'em in fine Latin, they suddenly parted for Naples. I believe Ambassadors will be sent for all Parts of Italy to the Emperor, and he knows well enough how to play his Game, to get Money out of 'em, as it has been discover'd about ten Days since. But I am not yet fully acquainted with the Subtilty which ('tis said) he made use of at Naples; hereafter I may give you an account of it.

The Prince of Piedmont, the Duke of Savoy's eldest Son, dy'd at Naples fifteen Days ago; the Emperor order'd him a very honourable Interment, at which he assisted in Person.

The King of Portugal, six Days since, commanded his Ambassador at Rome, that immediately upon receipt of his Letter, he should return to him in Portugal, which he did the same hour, and came ready Booted and Spurr'd to take his leave of the Most Reverend the Lord Cardinal du Bellay. Two Days after, was kill'd near the Bridge of St. Angelo, in open day, a Portuguese Gentleman, who sollicited here for the whole Body of the Jews that were baptiz'd under King Emanuel, and have been since molested by the present King of Portugal, that he might succeed to their Estates when they dy'd. That King has also exacted several things of them against the Edict and Ordinance of the King Emanuel. I doubt we shall hear of some Sedition in Portugal.

LETTER IX

My Lord,

In the last Pacquet I sent you, I gave you an Account, that part of the Turk's Army was defeated by the Sophi, near Betelis. The Turk did not very long delay his Revenge, for two Months after, he fell upon the Sophi with the greatest Fury imaginable; and after having put to Fire and Sword, a great part of the Country of Mesopotamia, he has driven back the Sophi on the other side of Mount Taurus. In the mean time, he causes a great number of Galleys to be built upon the River Tanais, by which they may come to Constantinople. Barbarossa is still at Constantinople to secure the Country, and has left several Garrisons at Bona and Algiers, lest the Emperor should by chance attack him. I have sent you his Picture, drawn by the Life; as also the Map of Tunis, and of the Sea-port-towns adjacent. The Lanskenets, whom the Emperor sent into the Dutchy of Milan to keep the strong Places, are all drown'd and lost at Sea, to the number of fifteen hundred, in one of the biggest and stoutest Ships belonging to the Genoeses, and it was near to a Port belonging to the Commonwealth of Lucca, call'd Lerza. The occasion was; because they being weary of the Sea, and desirous to get ashoar, which they could not for the Tempest and Stress of Weather, imagin'd that the Pilot of the Ship would still keep them off at Sea, longer than he needed: for which cause they kill'd him, with some other of the Officers of the said Ship, after whose death the Ship remain'd without a Commander; and instead of taking in their Sails, the Lanskenets hoisted them, as being unpractic'd in Sea-affairs, and in this Confusion they perish'd within a Stone's throw of the aforesaid Port.

My Lord, I understand that my Lord Bishop de l'Avaur, who was the King's Ambassador at Venice, has had his Audience of Leave, and is returning to France. The Bishop of Rhodez goes in his place, and is now at Lyons with all his Retinue ready to go, when the King has given him his Instructions.

My Lord, I humbly recommend my self to your Favour, praying to our Lord, to give you a long Life in good Health.—Your most humble Servant,

FRANCIS RABELAIS.

Rome, *Jan.* 28, 1536

LETTER X

My Lord,

I writ to you at large all the News I could learn, the 28th of January last past, by a Gentleman, Servant to Monsieur de Montreuil, call'd Tremeliere, who return'd from Naples, where he had bought some Horses of that Kingdom for his Lord, and was returning to him with all speed. The same Day I receiv'd the Pacquet that you were pleas'd to send me from Legugé, dated the 10th of the said Month, in which you may see the Method I have taken for the delivery of your Letters, by which they are safely and suddenly brought to me here. Your said Letters and Pacquet, were deliver'd at the Arms of Basil, on the one and twentieth of the same Month, the eight and twentieth they were deliver'd to me here. And to encourage at Lyons, (for that 's the Point and principal Place) the Bookseller at the Arms of Basil to be diligent in this Affair, I repeat what I writ to you in my aforemention'd Pacquet, if you chance to write to me about any thing of Consequence : That it is my Advice, that on the first occasion of writing to me, you write a word or two to him in a Letter, in which be pleas'd to inclose some Gold-crowns, or some other piece of old Gold, as a Royal, an Angel or Salutation, in consideration of the Pains and Care he takes of them, so small a matter will more and more endear him to your Service.

Now, to answer your Letters, I have diligently search'd the Registers of the Palace, since the time that you commanded me, that is, the Year 1529, 1530, and 1531, to see if Dom Phillippe's Act of Resignation to his Nephew were to be found, and have given the Clerks of the Register two Gold-crowns, which is but a small recompence for the great and tedious Trouble in it. In short, they have found nothing of it, nor ever heard News of his Procurations ; wherefore I doubt there is some foul play in his Case, or the Instructions you writ to me were not sufficient to find 'em. And that I may be more certifi'd in it, you should tell me, *cujus Diocesis,* of what Diocess the said Fryar Dom. Phillippe was, and if you have heard nothing to give more light in the Matter, as if it was *pure et simpliciter,* or *causâ permutationis.*

LETTER XI

My Lord,

What I writ to you of my Lord Cardinal du Bellay's Answer, when I presented him your Letters, ought not to displease your Lordship. My Lord of Mascon has sent you an Account of the whole Matter, and we are not yet like to have a Legate in France. 'Tis certain, that the King has presented the Cardinal of Lorrain to the Pope. But I believe, that the Cardinal du Bellay will endeavour by all means possible to get it for himself. The old Proverb is true, which says, *Nemo sibi secundus*. And I shrewdly suspect by certain Signs that I see, that my Lord Cardinal du Bellay will engage the Pope on his behalf, and thus be made acceptable to the King. Nevertheless be not uneasie, if his Answer be a little ambiguous in your Concern.

LETTER XII

My Lord,

The Grains which I sent you, I can assure you, are the best of Naples, of the same which his Holiness has caus'd to be sow'd in his Privy-Garden of Belveder. There are no other kinds of Sallads on this side but those of Nasidord and Arroussa, but those of Legugé seem to me altogether as good, and somewhat more sweet and grateful to the Stomach, and particularly better for you ; for those of Naples, in my Opinion, are too hot and tough.

As for the Season for sowing 'em, you must caution your Gardeners not to sow 'em altogether so early as they do on this side, for it is not warm Weather so soon with you as here. They may very well sow your Sallads twice a Year, that is to say, in Lent, and in November ; and they may sow the white Cardes or Thistles in August and September ; the Melons, Pompions, and the others in March ; fencing them for some days with Mats, and a thin Layer of Horse-dung, not altogether rotten, when they fear it will freeze. Many other Grains besides are sold here, as Alexandria Gilliflowers, Matronal-Violets, and Shrubs, with which they refresh their Chambers in the Summer, call'd Belvedere, and other Physical Herbs. But this would be more for my Lady d'Estissac's turn. If you please to have of all sorts, I will send them you without fail. But I am forc'd to have recourse again to your Alms ; for the thirty Crowns which you order'd to be paid me here, are almost gone, yet I have converted none of them to any ill use, nor for eating, for I eat and drink at my Lord Cardinal du Bellay's, or at my Lord of Mascon's. But a great deal of Money goes away in these silly Postage of Letters, Chamber-rent, and wearing Apparel, tho' I am as frugal as I can be. If you will be pleased to send me a Bill of Exchange, I hope I shall make use of it wholly to your Service, and not remain ungrateful. I see in this City a thousand pretty cheap Things, which are brought from Cyprus, Candia, and Constantinople. If you think fit, I will send what I think fittest of them to you and my Lady d'Estissac. The Carriage from hence to Lyons will cost nothing.

Thanks be to God I have made an end of my Business, and it has cost me no more than the taking out of the Bulls, his Holiness having, of his own good Nature, given me the Composition. And I believe you will find the Proceedings right enough, and that I have obtain'd nothing by them, but what is just and lawful. But I have been oblig'd to advise very much with able Counsel, that every thing might be according to due form ; and I dare modestly tell you, that I have in a manner hardly made use of my Lord Cardinal du Bellay, or my Lord Embassador, tho' out of their Kindness, they not only offer'd me their own good Word and Favour, but absolutely to make use of the King's Name.

LETTER XIII

MY LORD,

I HAVE not as yet presented your first Letters to the Bishop of Saintes, for he is not yet returned from Naples, whither he went as I writ to you before. He is expected here within these three Days : Then I will give him your second, and intreat an Answer of it. I understand, that neither he, nor the Cardinals Salviati, and Rodolph, nor Phillip Strozzi, with his Money, have done any thing with the Emperor in their Affair, tho' they were willing to pay him a Million of Gold upon the Nail, in the Name of all the Foreigners and Exiles of Florence, also to finish la Rocca (the Fortress) begun at

Florence, to maintain a sufficient Garison in it for ever in the Name of the Emperor, and to pay him Yearly an Hundred thousand Ducats, provided and upon Condition he restor'd them to their former Goods, Lands, and Liberty.

On the contrary, the Duke of Florence was most honourably receiv'd by him at his arrival; the Emperor went out before him, and, *post manus oscula*, he order'd him to be attended to the Castle of Capua in the same Town, where his Natural Daughter has an Apartment; she is affianc'd to the said Duke of Florence, by the Prince of Salerne, Viceroy of Naples; the Marquis de Vast, the Duke D'Alva, and other Principal Lords of his Court. He held discourse with her as long as he stay'd, kiss'd her, and supp'd with her; afterwards the above-mentioned Cardinals, the Bishop of Xaintes and Strozzi never left solliciting. The Emperor has put them off for a finall Resolution to his coming to that Town, to the Rocca, which is a Place of prodigious Strength, that the Duke has built at Florence. Over the Portico he has caus'd an Eagle to be painted with Wings as large as the Sails of the Wind-mills of Mirebalais; thereby declaring and insinuating, that he holds of no body but the Emperor. And in fine, he has so cunningly carry'd on his Tyranny, that the Florentines have declar'd before the Emperor, *Nomine Communitatis*, (in the Name of the Commonalty) that they will have no other Lord but him. 'Tis certain, that he has severely punish'd the Foreigners and Exiles. A Pasquil has been lately set up, wherein 'tis said,

To Strozzi;

Pugna pro Patriâ. (Fight for thy Country.)

To Alexander Duke of Florence;
Datum serva. (What's given thee, keep.)

To the Emperor;
Quæ nocitura tenes quamvis sint chara relinque.
Quit what will hurt thee, tho' 'tis ne'er so dear.

To the King;
Quod potes id tenta.
Dare what thou can'st.

To the Cardinals Salviati and Rodolph;

Hos brevitas sensus fecit conjungere binos.
Pure want of Sense unites these Blocks,
As petty Tradesmen join their Stocks.

LETTER XIV

My Lord,

I writ to you, That the Duke of Ferrara is return'd from Naples, and retir'd to Ferrara. Her Highness, the Lady Renée, is Brought-to-bed of a Daughter ; she had another fine Daughter before, between Six and Seven Years of Age, and a little Son of Three Years old. He could not agree with the Pope, because he demanded an excessive Sum of Money for the Investiture of his Lands. Notwithstanding, he had abated Fifty thousand Crowns for the Love of the said Lady, and this by the Solicitations of my Lords the Cardinals du Bellay and Mascon, still to encrease the Conjugal Affection of the said Duke towards her. This was the occasion of Lyon Jamet's coming to this Town, and they only differ'd for Fifteen thousand Crowns ; but they could not agree, because the Pope would have him acknowledge, that he held and possess'd all his Lands intirely in Fee of the Apostolical See, which the other would not. For he would acknowledge no more than his deceas'd Father had acknowledg'd, and what the Emperor had adjudg'd at Bolonia, by a Decree in the time of the deceas'd Pope Clement.

Thus he departed, *re infectâ*, (without doing anything,) and went to the Emperor, who promis'd him at his coming, that he would easily make the Pope consent, and come to the Point contain'd in his said Decree ; and that he should go home, leaving an Ambassador with him, to sollicit the Affair when he came on this side, and that he should not pay the Sum already agreed upon, before he heard further from him. The Craft lies here, that the Emperor wants Money, and seeks it on all hands, and Taxes all the World he can, and borrows it from all Parts. When he comes hither, he will demand some of the Pope, 'tis a plain case. For he will represent to him, That he has made all these Wars against the Turk and Barbarossa, to secure Italy and the Pope, and that he must of necessity contribute to it. The Pope will answer, That he has no Money, and will manifestly prove his Poverty to him. Then the Emperor, without disbursing any thing, will demand the Duke of Ferrara's of him, which he knows he may command at a Word, and this is the Mystery of the Matter. Yet 'tis not certain whether things will be manag'd thus or no

LETTER XV

My Lord,

You ask whether the Lord Pietro Ludovico, is the Pope's Legitimate Son, or Bastard. Be assur'd, the Pope was never marry'd; which is as much as to say, that the aforesaid Gentleman is certainly a Bastard; The Pope had a very beautiful Sister. There is to be seen to this day, at the Palace in that Apartment where the Summists reside, built by Pope Alexander, an Image of our Lady, which ('tis said) was drawn after that Gentlewoman: She was marry'd to a Gentleman, Cousin to the Lord Rance, who being in the War, in the Expedition of Naples, the said Pope Alexander * * *: Now the Lord Rance, having certain knowledge of the thing, gave notice of it to his Cousin, telling him, That he ought not to suffer such a Wrong done to their Family by a Spanish Pope; and that if he would endure it, he himself would not. In short, her Husband kill'd her; for which Fact the present Pope griev'd: And to asswage his Sorrow, Alexander made him a Cardinal, being yet but very young, and bestow'd several other Marks of his Favour upon him.

At that time the Pope kept a Roman Lady, della Casa Ruffina, and by her had a Daughter who was marry'd to the Lord Bauge, Count of Sancta Fiore, who died in this Town since I came hither. By her he has had one of the two little Cardinals (who is call'd the Cardinal of Sancta Fiore.) The Pope likewise had a Son, who is the said Pietro Ludovico, concerning whom you enquire, who has marry'd the Daughter of the Count de Cervelle, on whom he has got a whole Houseful of Children, and among others, the little Cardinalicule Farnese, who was made Vice-Chancellor by the death of the late Cardinal de Medicis. By what is said, you may judge why the Pope did not very well love the Lord Rance, and, *vice versa*, (on the other side) the Lord Rance put no great confidence in him: Whence arises a great quarrel between my Lord John-Paul de Cere, Son to the said Lord Rance, and the above-named Pietro Ludovico, for he is resolved to revenge the Death of his Aunt.

But he is quit of it on the part of the said Lord Rance, for he dy'd the 11th Day of this Month, going a Hunting, in which he extremely delighted, old as he was. The Occasion was this : He had got some Turkish Horses from the Fairs of Racana, and as he was Hunting on one of them that was very tender-mouth'd, it fell, tumbl'd over him, and bruis'd him with the Saddle-bow so severely, that he did not live above half an hour after the fall. This was a great loss to the French, for the King in him has lost a good Servant for his Affairs in Italy. 'Tis rightly said, That the Lord John-Paul his Son will be no less hereafter. But it will be a long time e're he gets such Experience in feats of Arms, or so great a Reputation among the Commanders and Soldiers, as the late brave Man had. I wish with all my heart that my Lord d'Estissac, by his death, had the County of Pontoise ; for, 'tis said, it brings a good Revenue.

To assist at the Funeral, and to comfort the Marchioness his Wife, my Lord Cardinal has sent to Ceres, near Twenty Miles from this Town, my Lord de Rambouillet and the Abbot of St. Nicaise, who was a near Kinsman to the Deceased, (I believe you have seen him at Court) he is a little Man, all life, who was call'd the Arch-Deacon of the Ursins ; besides, he has sent some others of his Prothonotaries ; which likewise my Lord of Mascon has done.

LETTER XVI

My Lord,

I defer to my next, to give you more at large the News concerning the Emperor ; for his Design is not yet perfectly discover'd. He is still at Naples, but is expected here by the end of this Month. Great Preparations are made for his coming, and abundance of Triumphal Arches. His four Harbingers have been a good while here in Town ; two of them Spaniards, one Burgundian, and the fourth a Flemming.

'Tis great pity to see the Ruins of the Churches, Palaces and Houses which the Pope has caused to be demolished and pull'd down to make and level him a Way. For the Charges of his Reception, he has laid a Tax on the College of Cardinals, on those who have Places at Court, and the Artificers of the

Town, as much as the very Aquarols. The Town is already full of Foreigners.

On the 5th of this Month the Cardinal of Trent (*Tridentinus*) arrived, being sent here by the Emperor. His Train is very numerous, and more sumptuous than the Pope's. He had with him above a hundred Germans all dress'd alike ; their Gowns were Red, with a Yellow Galloon ; and on their right Sleeve was embroider'd a Wheat-sheave tied close, and round it was written *Unitas*.

I hear he is much for Peace, and reconciling all the Christian Princes. He eagerly desires a General Council, whatever is done in other Matters. I was present when he said to my Lord Cardinal du Bellay ; His Holiness, the Cardinals, Bishops and Prelates of the Church are against a Council, and will by no means hear any thing of it, tho' they are pressed by Secular Princes on that Subject ; but I see the Time at hand when the Prelates of the Church shall be reduced to demand a Council, and the Laity will not hearken to it. This will be, when the latter have taken from the Church all the Wealth and Patrimony which they had given ; while Ecclesiastics, by the means of frequent Councils, maintained Peace and Unity among the Laity.

Andrew Doria came to this Town on the 3rd of this Month, in no very good Equipage. No manner of particular Respect was shewn at his Arrival, save only that the Lord Pietro Ludovico conducted him as far as the Palace of the Cardinal Camerlingo, who is a Genoese, of the House of Spinola. The next day he saluted the Pope, and the day after went away for Genoa, on the Emperor's behalf, to inform himself under-hand concerning the Dispositions of the French about the War.

We have had here a positive Account of the Old Queen of England's Death ; and they add, That the Princess her Daughter lies very ill.

However, the Bull that was to be issued out against the King of England to excommunicate him, and to interdict and proscribe his Kingdom, did not pass at the Consistory, because of the Articles *De commeatibus externorum et commerciis mutuis*, Of the Passages of Foreigners and Mutual Intercourses ; which my Lord Cardinal du Bellay and the Bishop of Mascon opposed in the King's Name, on account of the Interests which he pretends to have in it. It has been put off till the Emperor's Arrival.

My Lord, I most humbly recommend my self to your kind Favour, praying God that it may please him to keep you long in Health and Prosperity.—Your Lordship's most humble Servant,

FRANCIS RABELAIS.

ROME, *Feb.* 15, 1536.

THE END OF THE LETTERS

PRINTED BY
MORRISON AND GIBB LTD
LONDON AND EDINBURGH